Empire Ascendant

- UnderVerse -

Book 6

2nd Edition

Jez Cajiao

TABLE OF CONTENTS

THANKS

Hi everybody! Okay, well, phew! That's been a hard few months I tell you, rewriting the first season of UnderVerse was both a joy, and a massive undertaking. I had the help of an amazing editing team to help me get through it all, catching the occasional bit of sanity that slipped through the net and stamping it down mercilessly!

Seriously though, I wanted to straighten out the first season before I began the next, making sure the foundation was solid to build upon, if you see what I mean. There's a lot of stories yet to be told here after all, besides Jax's, and only some of them will be mine to tell.

With that in mind, I need to do some thanks, this is both a privilege and a pain, frankly, because I can never thank everyone that deserves it, and as such I always feel like I've let people down.

First and foremost my family; Chrissy, as always, my rock that keep s me sane (more or less) fed, and makes sure I stop to rest and see daylight as well as my kids and family, rather than crashing and burning.

Max. My first born and cool little dude, you're getting so big, and every hour I don't spend with you, your brother and your mother feels like I've lost something precious. What I do though? I do for you all.

Xander, my utterly crazy garbage disposal of a child. You'd eat me out of house and home given the chance, and the laughter when we blow on the hanging light in your room is a balm to my soul.

I love you three more than I'll ever be able to express.

Mum, you raised me, kept me on the straight and narrow (more or less) and taught me to mix my drinks, as well as instilling a love of reading in me. All that I've become, is built on the solid foundation of love that you gave me.

Gillian, my second mum, Meemaw to our kids and quite possibly the person they love most in this world, thank you. Thank you so much for all you do and are. Also; we all know I'm the favorite child really.

I could go on massively, describing Paul, my step-father who took me on and taught me so much, or Alan, My recently lost father-in-law who was one of the best men I've ever known. My brothers, my sister and sister-in-law, their partners and children…the clan feels like it grows every week, and I love you all, more or less as you deserve.

Next I need to thank my editors, Michelle, Evan, Jenny, Emily & Jack, you all helped in many ways to get this to the point it is, and believe me, I know it wasn't easy. Emily, our long-suffering formatter has worked literal magic with these manuscripts, as well so thank you so much.

Next; Geneva and Kristen, my PA's, damn you girls work a lot of hours! Thank you for handling so many of the other jobs, and from keeping me from stabbing people in the face. I like not being ion prison it turns out.

My Beta readers; Scott, Spencer, Ben, Shawn, Chris, Neil, Denny and Richard.

Last but never least I need to thank you. My supporters, readers, friends and helpers, you've made all of this possible. I get to sit and hallucinate without the aid of drugs and rant about the voices in my head, and I don't get locked up! What's even better? My kids and my family have a home and a wonderful life thanks to all of you, and that's a debt I'll never be able to repay.

Thank you all, -Jez 30/10/2022

LYDIA

LUCIAN

Lucian reached up and scratched his hair, picking a bit of dried blood free. He grimaced at the reminder of how much he needed a bath. To be summoned before the Scion of the Empire in such a state…

"The Scion." Lucian shook his head as he stared down at the dried blood. He picked it out from under his nails and flicked it away over the side. It plummeted from sight as the ship lifted into the air, engines firing hard as she turned.

The acceleration pressed him into the top of the wooden barrel he sat upon and made Lucian smile somewhat subconsciously.

More than seven hundred years had passed since anyone could lay claim to the title of Scion or any true rank of the nobility. And, out of the blue, he sent an airship for a damned creature like him.

"My Lord…um…refreshments?" a sailor asked nervously, moving closer. Lucian stared at him for a few long seconds before answering.

"I'm no lord, but thank you, and thank your captain for me," he said, reaching out and accepting the cloth-covered tray from the nervous cabin boy. He waited as the boy moved away, then carefully twitched the cloth aside, finding a cup of watered wine, dried meat, a good mellow cheese, and thickly cut bread.

Lucian looked it over, swallowing hard as he tried to reconcile the last week with the last few hundred years.

Only an hour ago, he'd been trying to decide if he'd finally lost his grip on reality, if his mind had actually snapped, or if the Great God of Light Himself, Sint the Righteous, had really reached out in the silence of his soul and ordered him to wait here. The airship that had been flying south had veered slightly and come in to land, the captain of the ship coming to greet and make Lucian the Banished, Faithless of the Legion, *welcome* aboard his ship.

It had started a week before that, when he'd been deep in the forested hills above G'Norrimesh, a small, outlying gnomish town, having spent a week tracking the slavers who'd raided it. He had been sitting, close to tears, looking at the small bodies he'd found.

They'd clearly tried to flee, using typical gnomish ingenuity to free themselves, and they'd been caught. Two of the eleven children taken had been "made an example of" to ensure the others would behave.

They'd been stripped, tied to bamboo staves, and had been whipped half to death before…

Even now, he shook that memory aside, instead recalling Sint's voice coming to him as he rested, waiting the sun out, ready to make the most of his nocturnal gifts.

He'd been sitting cross-legged, too furious to sleep, meditating and waiting, old enough to know that pushing his body through the noonday heat, uphill, and deep through forests and jungles was a fool's errand.

Instead, despite all his urges, he forced himself to rest, to prepare, and that was when the God had come to him.

He shivered at the memory. The sudden feeling of divinity, the pressure, and the sure and certain knowledge that the being that appeared across from him yet inside his mind wasn't mortal had been…mind-blowing.

"I have need of you, my child," the God had said, and Lucian had found himself suddenly no longer sitting cross-legged in a blood-spattered glade. Instead he was…elsewhere.

The light-filled cathedral that surrounded them was indistinct, yet still, when he dropped from his unexpected standing position down to his knees, head bent and fist to heart, the grain of the creamy stone felt smooth and solid under his knees.

The gentle warmth of a spring day, filled with the distant, worshipful choir and the song of birds mingling with the scent of the sea, had overwhelmed his senses, confusing him.

"My child?" The voice had come again, and Lucian had panicked, realizing that the God had asked him for something, and he'd been too distracted by the damn world around him to answer!

"Lord Sint, I am at your service!" he'd barked, recognizing the figure before him from long in the past. Then he cursed himself for the volume before clearing his throat and going on in a more subdued tone. "I…I am at your eternal service, Lord Sint. If I may ask, your commands are, of course, the most important I will ever know…but…"

"But you wish to free the Gnomes that you have been tracking," Sint finished for him, gesturing for Lucian to stand. "I would not take you from freeing the wrongfully imprisoned. Instead, I will arrange transportation. I have need of you. The Realm, the Empire, and the Legion have need of you, Lucian, so I shall aid you." Sint smiled gently before going on.

"When you open your eyes, you will feel my boon. A minor Endurance boost will not aid you much, but it will ease your travel, gentling the heat and assisting your feet to find the path of least resistance." Sint had paused as Lucian stood, looking up at the imposing, armored, yet gentle-seeming being.

"Believe me, Lucian, I have spoken with Amon's heir, and he is worthy of your trust and your service. He has need of you, though he knows it not. Free the Gnomes, return them to their kind, and travel to my marker. You will be met by those I send."

With that, Lucian had simply bowed his head in assent, and when he opened his eyes again, the world was back to normal. The grim, blood-splatted glade reeked anew as his heart swelled with hope, and he saw the two new additions.

First was a marker, pulsing gently in his mind, atop a hill some few dozen miles to the north. To the west, a second marker had appeared, and a buff had lightened his steps.

He'd stood, the unnatural smoothness of his movements testimony to the hundreds of years of hard work he'd endured, and without a further thought, he'd reached out, gently touching his fingers to his lips before pressing that kiss to the cold stone of the small cairn he'd raised.

That done, he'd turned and set off, moving smoothly from a jog to a run, to a full sprint, glorying in the feeling as the world around him blurred with the oppressive heat of the summer's day. Here, in the southern reaches of the continent and far from the wind's caress, the sweltering miasma was banished and replaced by a gentle spring warmth by the buff instead.

As Lucian dug deeper, lengthening his stride and settling into a steady run that he could only maintain for a few hours under normal circumstances, the second phase of the blessing took root in him. As his muscles pumped and stretched instead of feeling the slight strain, he felt invigorated in a way he'd not experienced in long years.

He raced down the hill he was on and up the far side of the gully, jumping across the rippling stream and landing easily, feet touching down gently amongst the leaves and moss-covered boulders. Lucian barely left a print before he was off again, passing deer that had burst into startled flight.

For hours he ran, simultaneously glorying in the enhancement, yet still he examined the encounter over and over. He'd not doubted at all that it was Sint, gone these hundreds of years, mute when the world fell and billions died, cursing the silent Gods. Yet now He had returned, and He'd come to speak to Lucian of all beings.

The sun fell, and Lucian's heritage took over, enhancing his strength, his speed, and allowing him to see as well in the dark places of the realm as he had in full sunlight earlier.

More and more, he passed startled animals, leaping across the remnants of camps his quarry had left behind. The hours that came and went before the blessing finally died allowed him to make up most of the days that he had been behind.

The sprint that he managed would have been the stuff of legends, had any but the bears and denizens of the forests seen it. But, by the time the sun reached its peak again, he slowed.

He took a knee, panting, exhausted, and staring across the gentle dip in the hills to the grim sight of sixteen slavers dragging nine chained and beaten gnomish children up the far side.

Even at this distance, the filth on them wafted to greet his nostrils, and the scarcely stifled sobs from the children reached his ears, not to mention the ruckus the slavers made.

Their kind were always easy to spot, even from a distance. The unimaginative bastards appeared to believe filthy leathers, washed only in the chance crossing of a river or in an infrequent rainstorm, were the ideal garment. The stench made Lucian's instincts bare their bloody teeth.

He stayed there, forcing himself to wait while his stamina refilled, drinking lukewarm water, having refilled the canteen an hour before from a forested stream. He swallowed the water gratefully. The victims he could see would be "watered" only at dusk and dawn, treated like beasts. Every drop he drank, while needed, was a luxury they would beg for.

He watched them struggling up the far side and back into the cover of the trees before judging his recovery was enough and setting off again. He jogged steadily up the far side, maintaining his silence as best he could, and drawing his bow from the bag of holding. Shrugging his quiver into place, he tugged a simple arrow free. His experienced fingers sorted the shafts one from another, making sure that the one he selected had a head that, when laid on the bow, would rest on the horizontal, rather than the vertical axis.

It had been long years since he'd accidentally used an arrow aligned for the vertical gaps in a deer's ribs, instead of the horizontal gaps in a humanoid's ribs, but still, it'd been an experience that had stuck with him.

As he flitted through the trees, closing the distance and hearing the voices growing louder ahead, his fingers searched, confirming that all the arrows in this quiver were killers. He came to halt behind a gnarled willow, staring down at the laughing slavers as one of their number kicked a small figure's rump, making it cry out in distress.

Lucian didn't hesitate further. Drawing the bowstring back, the fletching of the arrow's vanes tickled his cheek as he selected his first target, the kicker, and aimed for the junction of his lower back and posterior.

The arrow cut the air with a solid *thrum* before embedding deep into the spine of the scruffy, dark-haired slaver, right where the ass became the back.

As the slaver let out a surprised grunt, eyes flying wide, the sudden cessation of control over his lower body made itself known a millisecond before the pain did.

"What's up, Jory? Put your hip out?" one of the other slavers called to him, seeing him tip sideways out of the corner of his eye. As he turned, he caught a flash of movement. Another of the band, a short, bearded man the group relied upon for more complex negotiations, pointed behind them before sprouting an arrow from the eye and collapsing bonelessly.

Two more of the group fell before the fact they were under attack truly registered with them all.

The slavers were no strangers to violence. Their line of work required that they be both skilled and ruthless, but the lack of a visible target and the speed of the arrows caused the group to react more slowly than was their norm.

"Balsan, Timo, Sern, grab the slaves! The rest of you, with me!" Red screamed, drawing a rusty sword and racing toward the trees uphill from their position. He let out a low growl as a single man stepped out to the right, and he adjusted his aim, racing in that direction, as the man calmly and silently killed another of his men.

Five of them were down, maimed, or dead, and as the first of them, the scout Francis, closed the distance to Lucian, he simply slid the bow into his bag and drew a huge hand-and-a-half greatsword instead.

It was old and clearly well-used, but the speed with which the dark man wielded it…Francis, the fastest of their number, attempted to dodge, stepping aside as Red had likely seen him do a dozen times. A contemptuous sneer appeared on the slaver's face before the sword shifted. Francis was spitted like a suckling pig then casually kicked off the massive blade.

Lucian roared and let loose the need for bloodshed.

He attacked, no longer content with waiting for them to come to him. He raced down at them, the blade held almost negligently in one hand as the other slapped a mace from the air.

The enormous blade beheaded Alimoth, the group's cook, then slammed into Grant's upper chest. Grant was a shit useless guard, slept more than he worked, and farted like an Imp with a bad belly. The sword parted him from left shoulder to navel before it was lifted back into the air in a clearly inhuman display of strength.

The charge faltered, the screaming Grant spraying blood everywhere as he was shucked like an oyster from the blade, then Lucian latched eyes on Red.

Red's bowels turned to water, barely managing to get his orders out. The glowing blue eyes that glared at him were terrifying, and Lucian had used them to instill fear in the heart of many a foe.

"We'll kill them," the shaking slaver managed to say, before swallowing and trying again. "Stop! Or we…we'll kill them," he tried again. "Just…we can share…Just stop…urk!" Then those eyes were right before him.

Lucian flung the sword with a blur and unerring aim to flip end over end, pinning Balsan to a tree. He didn't even need a *weapon*. Lucian slapped Red's one-handed axe aside with enough force the haft snapped. The other hand tore the shield Red had strapped to his left arm free, a crack ringing out as the twin bones in his forearm shattered.

Before Red had time to register it, Lucian drew back and stiffened the fingers of his right hand into a blade of bone. Then he rammed them into the slaver's stomach, punching through the flab that coated the once rock-hard abdominal muscles, angling upwards.

Red gasped in shock and pain, eyes going wide as Lucian drove his hand upwards, searching, until he found what he wanted, gripping the slaver's spine from the inside.

The clearing seemed to hold its breath as Lucian and Red stared into each other's eyes from a space of a few inches. "Please," was all that Red managed to get out.

Lucian ripped a fist-sized chunk of Red's spine free, dropping the slavers' leader to the floor. The victim grunted, his torn and quivering diaphragm refusing to draw a breath as he attempted to close the yawning wound or move his lower half at all.

Lucian stared at the remaining two slavers, four having fled into the woods already, and he casually threw the section of their leader's spine aside before pointing a single, gore-coated finger at the one closest to the slaves.

"Touch them, and I'll make this far, *far* more painful," he warned.

One of the men nodded frantically, holding his sword and shield wide apart and shaking as he backed away. The other, nervously licking his lips, glanced from Lucian to the slaves, to the bodies, then made the last mistake he would ever make.

He lunged forward, grabbing the nearest, a small girl child of perhaps seven years of age. He lifted her, turning to where he'd last seen the figure, raising his dagger toward her neck, planning to threaten her life to get free.

Instead, he screamed as his right arm snapped halfway down the length of his forearm, the shattered ends jutting free in the humid afternoon air as Lucian seemed to materialize before him.

He had a split second to register bright blue eyes and pointed teeth as his own blood sprayed across him. Then fingers locked around his throat, yanking him upward and in close.

The slaver dropped the weak, struggling child. A pained gurgle was the only sound that could escape the vice-like grip on his throat as he was slammed into the floor. His knees were shattered; a booted kick was all it took before a cold and distant voice told the children to cover their eyes. The slaver was rolled onto his front, his remaining whole arm stretched out behind his back and a boot braced in his armpit as his throat was released.

He drew in a deep breath and *screamed* in pain and fear as the figure tore his arm from the shoulder socket with inhuman strength.

"Call for them," Lucian said as the slaver stared in disbelief, his lifeblood spraying from the torn flesh that was once his shoulder. "Call for them!" Lucian barked again. "Let them know what's coming."

"Timoooooo!" he screamed, then the sound was cut off by his rapidly descending former favorite arm.

...

"My Lord?" The voice came again, and Lucian blinked, shaking his head free of the memories and glancing at the cabin boy again.

"What?" he asked, confused.

"Umm…the Captain…he asked for the pleasure of your company…for the evening meal?" the boy asked.

Lucian stared at him, still waiting for someone to recognize him and tear this long desperately desired civility and inclusion away from him.

"I…I would be delighted," Lucian whispered, the screams of the slavers still ringing in his ears. The forced civility that even the Gnomes had greeted him with upon returning their children made him fear this veneer of kindness would be stripped away again soon.

He swallowed hard, then forced himself to his feet. At his nod, the boy smiled and gestured to the captain's cabin, the scent of hot roast beef floating free.

PROLOGUE

Explain yourself, Paladin!" the archpriest snarled, sitting back on his iron throne and glaring down at where Edvard knelt in supplication before him. "The Dark Hunters are the best option, Archpriest, lest we let loose a thousand or more men from the city."

"Not possible." Archpriest Thaddeus Baruman waved his hand. "It's taken the Church over two hundred years of dedicated work to undermine the nobility. We finally have the fool Barabarattas handing over authority in the city, and now you think I'll remove the elites from it? To deal with one lucky upstart? Over my dead body!"

"An upstart who managed to slaughter half the Legion!" Edvard ground out through gritted teeth.

"Bah!" Thaddeus shook his head. "He slaughtered the fodder. That's what they're *for*, need I remind you?"

"He didn't just slaughter the fodder, he killed over ten percent of the elites as well, not to mention fifteen Blessed with the Dark Gifts of the temple." Edvard raised his flashing eyes. "He and his people have been both skilled and lucky, and unless you'll allow me to take a large enough force to dig them out of the tower they call home, then I need the Dark Hunters!"

"The Dark Hunters require a significant investment, both in time and in mana, not to mention custom-built armor! No, there has to be…"

"There is no other way!" Edvard snarled. "He literally turned one of our best against us; he's the champion of one of the Elder Gods, and he's gaining more and more forces every day! You know what he's doing, don't you? When we buy slaves and make them into fodder, elevating only the very fortunate few, he's freeing them all! They worship the ground he damn well walks on, according to those we captured. They'll not only die for him without hesitation, but more importantly, they'll *live* for him as well!"

"That makes little sense, Paladin," one of the priests, who stood subserviently to the side, reproached. "Surely them dying for him is far more important."

"You *would* think that, wouldn't you, Rekka?" Edvard shook his head. "Shows how little you actually understand the slaves."

"They're animals. That's all," Rekka shot back.

"They're people!" Edvard retorted. "People who lost everything. They fucked up, and it cost them their future. Now, all they have left is their lives." He shook his head, willing his hands to stop shaking. "Giving that up? It's no great hardship, even in battle. After all, how many bodies are lost to Washout Cove every week? We deliberately let the slaves throw themselves off the cliffs to weed out the weakest."

Spittle flew from Edvard's mouth. "That's how they choose death. The strongest seek life, and once they are given the chance to live, they become not only incredibly loyal, but powerful! Think about it! Those who simply exist *always* end up as fodder, but the strongest of the elites? They all have one thing in common: they were all slaves!"

"Foolishness!" Rekka snapped back. "Wasn't your own protégé one of the slaves? The one who turned his back on the God and attacked us, having led our forces into the battle and positioned them for the ambush to do the most possible damage? Explain this, Paladin! Explain how your supposed favorite was actually a spy, and you had no idea!"

"Thomas had the potential to be one of our greatest assets, priest, and he'd had the Dark Gift in its entirety within him. Regardless of what he'd wished, even if he'd *intended* to betray us, it would have been impossible. Unless, of course, you're suggesting the God wished him to do just that?"

"Of course not!" Rekka shook his head violently.

"In that case, please, Rekka, explain to the rest of us how Thomas managed to leave the citadel without being assessed, healed, or having his connection to the God replenished. After all, it was *your* job!"

"I passed the duty to an under-priest!" Rekka snarled, a glint of fear in his eyes immediately swallowed up by aggression. "As you well know, *Edvard,* no priest can deal with all the thousands of calls on our time each day. Or do you fight every battle yourself? Why would you have soldiers, in that case?"

"Exactly, Rekka. You passed the job on. And that under-priest ordered another, even lower priest, who sent one of the accursed Light God's priests to do it. He was a priest who had no authority to request the Dark Ceremony be performed, had he even bothered to do the healing or testing that YOU were ordered to carry out."

Edvard practically hissed at the now-visibly-nervous priest. "Had you done your damn job, there would have been no way for any of this to happen. Thomas would be either a pile of torn muscle rotting in the forest or still loyal, and the apostate would be dead!

"Instead, we're short on fodder, unable to devote even a fraction of the necessary resources to deal with the issue at hand, and might I remind you, IT IS NIMON'S WILL THAT WE KILL THAT FUCKER!"

The last echoes of Edvard's shout hung in the air as the priests watched each other. The archpriest glared at the paladin before Edvard finally continued.

"We are left with two choices. First, we appeal to the God for time, build up our forces, and consolidate our grip on the City of Himnel. We pull in the entire Dark Legion force from the citadel and any roaming patrols, secure the city, and purge it of any and all who oppose the God's will. Then, we round up those who serve no honorable purpose, and we begin their training." Edvard glanced around, assessing the responses to that option, then went on.

"When this succeeds, we can develop the city into an engine for the Church, turning out supplies and equipment until we have a suitable army, complete with airships and more. This shouldn't take more than three years, but certainly there's no way to have it done before a minimum of six months have passed."

"Impossible! Why…"

"No!"

"You can't be serious…"

"SILENCE!" The Archpriest roared, cutting off the priests as their muttering escalated "Go on, Edvard," he growled.

"Or, Archpriest…you permit the formation of the Dark Hunters of Nimon. I will take the survivors of his squad; they have no purpose now, bonded as they were in the ceremony to a traitor. Let them be bathed in the Blood and joined to Nimon. Let me lead them. If the God finds any falsehood in our hearts, He will destroy us all; then there is no cost incurred. Should He find us worthy, then a fraction of the army will be able to do what would take hundreds, if not thousands. We will kill Jax the Apostate and Thomas the Betrayer."

"Nimon will judge you," Archpriest Thaddeus said after several long seconds of silence. "You may take the remainder of his squads, both the old and the new, as they cannot be used otherwise. That will give you two full packs of Dark Hunters, eighteen in all, counting you and the woman. But Edvard?"

"Yes, Archpriest?" Edvard swallowed as his heart clenched at the confirmation of his request and all it meant for his future.

"Fail in this, and you will not be permitted to rot…I will request the God uses you as an example, leaving you on the Wailing Wall for all eternity."

"A risk I willingly accept."

Chapter One

I stretched, letting out a groan as my back popped and clicked, then collapsed with a contented sigh. I was in my room, *our* room, I supposed. Wincing at the bright sunlight streaming in through the uncovered windows, I let out a magnificent yawn.

When my eyes adjusted and I could see clearly, a sense of wonder filled me that appeared whenever I actually stopped to think about things. Not only was this mine, but all as far as the eye could see belonged to me as well.

I lay in the middle of a heavy oaken bed that was wide enough for a damn orgy, making my old double look pathetic by comparison.

I had no idea why I'd wanted to sort the room out last night, considering the amount we'd had to drink and the promise of absolutely amazing sex, but it'd been bugging me, so Oracle had laughed and helped me do it.

The bed was now set against the stone west wall, and the rising sun shone in through the eastern windows, allowing me to lie back in bed and watch the dawn light stretch across the marble floor.

The tops of the trees poked over the distant landscape, hundreds upon thousands of them, creating a canopy that was broken here and there by meandering rivers, small clearings, and the occasional deadfall all the way out to the ocean at the edge of the horizon.

The windows were tall and arched, looking more like something you'd find in a church or gothic castle than a bedroom. But, man, I loved looking out, seeing the depth of the walls and getting that sense of solidity, of stone and indomitable strength that the massive Tower conveyed.

The rest of the room was beautiful as well. Two small tables had been rescued from the Tower's collapsing furniture stores. They were at least seven hundred years old each, if not older, yet a carpenter had managed to get them repaired and strong enough that they were okay for use. Considering how much of the Tower's furniture had given way over that time to entropy and woodworm, it was damn impressive, as was the fact they'd managed to hold up to the abuse Oracle and I had given them so far.

They stood on either side of the bed with a rug, two more chairs, and a single wardrobe on the north wall, along with an armor stand and the door to my personal bathroom, with a real godsdamn magical shower. There was a huge fireplace on the south, on the same wall as the door out into my sitting room.

It was just that, in a room that was easily nine meters on a side and squareish. I guessed it'd seem bare if I were to see it in a magazine or something, but considering how little furniture we actually had for people, I refused to have anything else for my rooms, as I just plain didn't need it.

I'd even considered saying I didn't need this much, but I kinda did, and besides…Oracle and I had christened everything in the room by now, so it'd be kinda weird giving something to anyone else.

"Oh, High Lord Jax, uh, what's this stain?" Yeah, I could just see that. I snorted, propping myself up on the pillows, stealing Oracle's in the process, and glanced to the door an instant before she opened it.

When she strode in, Oracle paused to close the door behind her and smiled sunnily at me. One hand brushed her hair back as she stepped over, tray in hand. I just lay there and stared in wonder.

Sometimes, when I saw her, she would make the entire cast of many shows look flat-chested and boring. The next moment, she'd be slim and athletic. She was blonde, redheaded, and brunette, her hair so black it was purple, then a second later green, just because she felt like it. Today, she'd elected to go with an Irish look, with auburn hair, bright green eyes and a pale complexion, broken by a splash of freckles across the bridge of her nose.

"Morning, handsome," Oracle whispered, sitting on the side of the bed and setting the coffee down on the side table. She giggled as I reached out and pulled her to me, kissing her soft-as-silk lips and holding her tight.

"Morning," I said, when I let her go.

"I brought you coffee."

"I noticed, although I have to admit, I noticed *you* more," I whispered, glancing down at the view. The angle I was holding her at on the bed meant I had a hell of a view of the fantastic, firm slope of her cleavage. She giggled again, pulling me down for a kiss.

"Well," she whispered back to me a few seconds later, staring up into my eyes. "There're a million jobs out there to do, but maybe they could wait?" The sensation of cool silk suddenly brushed against my skin.

I cast my glance downward, finding her clothes had vanished, replaced by a lacy, black silk nightdress. As I reached down, putting one hand on her thigh, my fingers brushed the top of her stockings and the clip that led to her suspender belt.

I kissed her deeper, both of us giving out a little moan of desire as my fingers moved up and across her lower belly, pushing the nightdress fabric up, before exploring lower.

"Who needs underwear beyond this?" she whispered into my ear as she pulled my face downward to her chest, the silk whispering aside to allow me access to one firm nipple, even as her hand closed around me, making me moan again in desire.

By the time we laid back on the bed later, the coffee was cold, the sun was fully risen. As Oracle laid against my chest, the pair of us relaxing in post-coital bliss, I stared out over the forest, wondering again how the hell I was so lucky.

"Why two cups?" I asked her eventually.

She held one casually in her hand and conjured a fireball in her other hand, holding it just out of reach of the cup and waving it closer and farther away, warming the cup up before passing me the now-broiled coffee in a mug so hot it made my hand tremble in pain.

"Sorry!" Wincing and reaching for the other mug, she searched for somewhere to throw the second cold mix, likely planning to pour the broiled one into the new cup.

"It's all right." I winced as I set the coffee down and shook my hand out, letting out a sigh of relief as she healed me.

"So…the second cup?" I asked again.

"I wanted to try it," she answered with a shrug.

"But you don't need to eat or drink?"

"I know, but, um, Jax...you know when you did...what you did...at the village of Wayland's Crossing?" she said carefully.

"Which part?" I asked with a grimace. "The bit where I was taken over by the soul of the old Emperor and nearly killed everyone, reducing the entire village to dust, or when I almost killed you and Bob?"

"The part where you *saved* Bob and me." Oracle reached out and took my hands in hers, shifting around to shoot me a serious look. "Jax, what happened certainly wasn't your fault, and deep down, you know that. Stop torturing yourself over what 'might have been,' okay? You saved Bob and me, and you not only gave him the missing parts he needed to have a soul of his own, to really *live*...but you made some changes to me as well."

"I...I'm sorry, Oracle, we've not really talked about it. I was afraid, and I almost lost you."

"I know, and it's as much on me as you. I should have talked to you before now. Hell, I made up my mind to talk to you this morning, first thing, so we wouldn't get interrupted by anyone. So, I went and made you coffee...then I ended up with my mouth too full to talk..." She winked at me, making me laugh.

"Well, I couldn't exactly speak either?" I offered, winking back at her.

"I remember!" Her cheeks reddened slightly. "But anyway, my point is that we both knew we needed to talk about it, yet we keep getting distracted by anything else. We do need to talk, though, because the changes you made...you healed me, Jax, you healed me, and you changed me even further than that."

"What do you mean?" I asked carefully, a little afraid of what she'd say.

"Bob and I, we both needed your mana and your health to exist, now neither of us do. Bob absorbs the ambient mana around him easily, and while he can't cast any spells yet, it's only a matter of time, I think. And as to me..."

"Yes?" I asked, squeezing her hands gently, hoping to all the Gods and then some that I hadn't hurt her.

"Jax, I'm alive in a way I never was before," she said in a rush. "I taste things, I sense things, and I can access the mana all around us. I can't use it, not directly, not fully, but I can feel it again, and it sustains me. And, Jax?" Oracle took a deep breath before letting it out slowly. "Jax, I have a class." She looked into my eyes, searching them for a reaction.

"Okay?" I said, shrugging. "I never realized you didn't have one before, although it's obvious, I guess. What is it, and what does that mean?"

"I'm a mage, and it means I'm evolving," Oracle whispered, wide eyes watching me.

"Okay," I repeated, still not getting it as I frowned at her. "Clearly, I'm missing something, so can you, you know, give me a hint?"

"Evolving Jax, like I'm changing, *from* a wisp..."

"And you're changing into...?"

"I don't know."

I cocked my head at this. "What do wisps normally evolve into?"

"We don't," she said. "All creatures have the capacity to evolve, but it's usually a single step, like the way Bob went from, well, a minion, to a sentient creature. Once you hit sentience, that's supposed to be it for my kind. Just like we can't have children, we can't evolve."

"Wait, but if you can't have kids, where do wisps come from?" I asked, confused.

"We are magical creatures Jax, fully magical, not simply able to manipulate it, like the Djinn. We have different lifecycles from mortals. In our case, it takes dozens of wisps joining together to birth more.

"We combine our essences and our magic, reducing ourselves to birth more. As the new wisps are born, the aged often spend years recovering from the process and guiding the infant wisps until they become fully sentient.

"That's one of the reasons why wisps are so rare. Many die in the fusion, then infants are seen as powerful prey for mortal creatures. Consuming us leads to massive growth for the creature; normal beasts can become great beasts and leap toward sentience themselves. Not to mention the uses we were put to by the already sentient races and the Empire," she added.

"So, when people are always so amazed at you all, and I've never seen any with anyone else, not in the city or anything…" I said slowly, feeling my heart drop.

"We're dying out, Jax. Others recognize me, but it's mainly from legends and rare tales. People assume that we must be 'elsewhere' because we were in so many legends and stories, but that's just it, Jax. I don't think we are…I think we might be all that's left: Seneschal, Hephaestus, Tenandra, and…me."

"No, no you can't be!"

"Think about it, Jax…I might be one of the last of my kind, and I don't think the four of us who are left are strong enough for the fusion, especially not if I evolve into something else."

"No," I said firmly, leaning forward and picking Oracle up. Taking her in my arms, I sat back, her head resting lightly against my chest, her five foot-odd frame dwarfed by my nearly six and a half feet of bulk. "No, there are others out there. Think about it, Oracle: this land was wild, even before the Cataclysm. It was barely explored, and the Cataclysm made that less likely. Hell, this Tower is nearly three miles high, and no fucker knew it was here…"

"It was protected by magic…"

"And so are your other people. They'll be hiding, that's all. And don't forget about the other Towers and the Prax!" I added.

"We can't have just stumbled across the only Prax out there with a damn wisp in the vault." I shook my head. "We'll repair the Prax first. Yeah, we'll get the godsdamn continent sorted, *then* we'll repair the Prax. If we have to scour the entire realm, we will. I'm sorry, Oracle."

"What for?" she asked, confusion entering her gaze as she met mine.

"For thinking this is all about me and what I want," I said as my shoulders sagged. "I've been so focused on doing what I needed that I didn't even ask you and the others. I know you've all got quests, you've all got needs. Well, we've beaten back the Dark Wanker's forces, we've got the Tower repaired, so it's time we sorted ourselves out. We've got Tommy back, and yeah, he's even uglier than I remember." I squeezed Oracle to me. "But we're in a better place than we've been at any point before this. It's time to sort shit out, my love."

"Where do we start?" she asked, smiling up at me.

"With a shower, some fresh coffee, and a meeting, as much as I hate admitting that last bit."

She laughed at that. "Well, you've half an hour before morning exercise starts." Oracle nodded to the sun outside. "If you really want to get started, then go get in the shower. I'll remake the coffee, then we can fly down, and at least you won't have Restun mad at you to start the day…"

"I both like and hate that idea." She got up, and I shuffled to the edge of the bed, clambering up awkwardly as I admired her bare ass while she sashayed away from me. "Don't suppose I can convince you to join me in the shower?" I asked hopefully, willycoptering as she turned around, laughing as she shook her head.

"Behave yourself, you clown!" she said as she reached the door, opening it and slipping through. "You know Restun will break you if you're late for training!"

"I'd rather try to break you again!" I called after her, before walking to the shower and stepping in. Her laughter was cut off by the closing door as I stepped into the small room.

This was my favorite thing about the new quarters that Seneschal had made for me when he'd repaired the Tower. I had no idea how it all worked. I had a proper toilet, a mirror and washstand, and best of all, I had a real shower.

I was stuck, or blessed, depending on perspective, in a practically medieval, magical world. We had flying airships, the ability to shoot sodding lightning bolts from our hands and more. Hell, I was head over heels in love with a wisp who could shapeshift into anyone I wanted, should I ask her to. Still, the shower was one of the absolute best things in a Tower that reached to the heavens and a world that had real Dragons.

I smiled as I tapped the oval set into the wall, and the water cascaded out, slamming into me hard enough to stagger me slightly.

I swept my hand across the oval, edging it to the right, the water shifting from lukewarm, all the way up to the hottest I could handle. My skin tingled, and I winced as I scrubbed at my skin. The rough, caustic version of soap we had made me think longingly of the stuff my ex had bought me once, but it was still far better than nothing.

I rinsed myself off, then swiped the temperature down to a more manageable level and rested for a long minute, reveling in the feeling of the powerful jets washing me down.

By the time I stepped out of the shower, shaking myself and stripping the water away with my hands before grabbing a rough towel from the pile by the door, I felt like a new man. While I knew damn well I'd need a shower again after training, showing up reeking of sex seemed disrespectful.

I found Oracle fully dressed, sitting in one of the chairs waiting for me. The two mugs were replaced with piping hot coffee-filled ones, and I pulled my training clothes on, sitting down and smiling at her as I picked my cup up.

"Are you ready?" I asked.

She shot me a wink. "I remember you asking me that last night, and my answer's the same…"

"Yes, but be gentle?" I grinned.

"Yes, but I'll see if I like it before trying it again!" she corrected with a laugh and a naughty look in her eyes.

"Well, let's face it: you'd never really tried the shower before, now you know you like it." I shrugged. "I bet coffee's going to be the same."

"I hope so." She lifted it to her lips and tasted it before pulling back and looking down at the cup then touching her lips in wonder.

"How is it?" I asked.

"There're so many flavors…" she whispered. "…and the effect!"

"Oh, hell yes…Plus three to Intelligence and two to Wisdom for an hour is a hell of a difference, but I'll point out that it's only for *this* coffee, as it's the good shit. The normal stuff only gives a single point to Intelligence for thirty minutes."

"Still, for most people, that's a hell of a change!" Oracle said, amazed. "And the feeling as it goes down…"

"Oh, yes." I winked. "I love that feeling as well!"

"Dirty bugger!" She laughed.

I grinned at hearing the idiom slip from her. Only a few days around Tom…Thomas, and she was picking up his favorite phrase already. "Damn, Oracle," I said slowly, shaking my head. "I can't believe we actually did it…found Tommy, I mean."

"I think he feels the same way…especially after everything he went through, he'd never expected to be free again, let alone find you."

"I know." I sighed. "I'm going to have to talk to Lagoush, aren't I?"

She smiled. "I think so. She adopted him as Her Champion to save both his life and yours, and She used a hell of a lot of Her accumulated power to do it, so I think you need to do something nice for Her, and soon."

"I will." I sadly pushed myself up out of my chair. "Well…if you're not gonna get naked, then I'm going to have to go get my ass kicked."

Oracle stood with me. "You know I'd happily get naked, but you need this; we all do. You'd have died in the forest, if not for the training you had and for the Legion arriving when it did. Looking back, there're a lot of things that could have been avoided or made easier if we had the proper training. So now, we've finally got some time, while the Dark Legion licks its wounds, and we decide the next step. We need to make the most of it."

"I know. Still sucks, though."

"I know," Oracle said, standing on her tiptoes to kiss me. "But look on the bright side…"

"Oh?" I frowned.

"So do I…" She winked and sent a mental image at me, then shifted into her diminutive form and blurred from the room, even as I tried to grab her.

"Dammit, Oracle!" I shouted after her, before sighing and shaking that image and memory from my mind. Striding from the room, I stopped to grab my bags on the way out and attached them to my belt. Before long, I was heading out into the hall, nodding a greeting to the legionnaire who stood on duty today, protecting my room.

I hesitated, then sighed, feeling a presence as Tang slipped out of the sitting room behind me.

"Really, dude?"

He stood up, shrugging. "You know one of us is with you at all times, Jax. No reason to stop now."

"Any sign of him?" I asked, and he shook his head.

"He'll turn up, don't worry," was all he said, but I sensed the same concern coming from him as I set off along the corridor and out of the section of rooms set aside for us, passing a second Legion guard and nodding to her.

"Tang, I'm going to fly down. So unless you want to ride me, and I know you really, really do, you've got a long walk ahead of you." I grinned as I gestured to the nearest window I could open.

"You're a bastard, you know that?" Tang said with a frown. "You're going to training, aren't you?"

"Yeah, but why…?"

"Because it means I'll be late for it," Tang growled. "And Restun will have my head for that!"

"Oh really?" I said in mock horror. "Such a shame. I mean, if only I'd known that before…ah well, never mind, shit happens."

"I'll get you for this," Tang warned me, even as I hopped up onto the window ledge and gave him the finger before diving off into the open air.

The last I saw of him as I twisted around, grinning manically, was a blur as he sprinted off towards the nearest stairwell.

I plummeted, deliberately not activating the ability until I couldn't take it any longer, that nameless dread that this might be the time, the one time that, for some reason the magic didn't work, and I instead fell to my death.

Thankfully, the ability triggered instantly, and a few seconds later, I was hurtling through the air, my arms spread out as I alternated between doing an Ironman and a Superman impression, trying to decide which looked cooler.

The pain of my health and mana being slowly drained away by the ability was nowhere near enough to stop me from using it, and, as I hurtled towards the ground and the hundreds of people gathered there, moving into the areas Restun and the other trainers had set out, I had to admit to myself that I goddamn loved it.

CHAPTER TWO

flipped over, shoving toward the ground at the last possible second. There was a brief second in which I wondered if I'd mistimed it, before impact. I'd timed it almost perfectly, negating my downwards speed and inertia with the flip.

But, in my panic, I over-charged the flip the other way, half-jumping into the air before landing and staggering a few steps, cursing as a round of low laughter rang out around me from my team and the legionnaires who were determined to earn a place in the Praetorian Guard.

"Didn't feel like stopping there, Jax?" Augustus asked.

I glared at him before grinning. "Nearly turned my knees into paste is more like it," I admitted, shrugging. "Ah well, I'm getting there. Who've we got today?"

I recognized the legionnaires, just over two dozen of them, but the newer legionnaires, the ones from Narkolt, were being unsubtly moved back from the inner ring now, much to their irritation.

"What's going on, Augustus?" I asked carefully, nodding a greeting to Jian, Lydia, and Yen, who were close by, then flashing a smile as Grizz pushed his way through the crowd, taking up the empty space left for him, right alongside Yen.

"Narkolt was bad, Jax," Augustus said grimly. "There's a lot we need to bring you up-to-date on, stuff we didn't tell you yesterday on your name day…sorry, *birth*day. Today, well, once we've had morning fitness, then there's a lot to take care of, not least of all will be the Oath, I'm afraid."

"Why is that a problem?"

He gave me a dark smile. "Because the upper echelons of the Narkolt Legion had been killed and replaced by Drow," Augustus said flatly. "And I'm really hoping that the Oath will be sufficient to show any of the lying bastards who might be here today, hiding somewhere…"

"Shit," I muttered. "You should have told me yesterday."

"You were barely awake and in no state to make command decisions. Plus, if you remember, I *did* tell you on the ship, after we picked you up.

"Either way, you were certainly in no state to use your abilities. We greeted you for the name day, shared a cake as is your custom, and we gave gifts. Frankly, I think that was a push for you by the end, but it was worth it to see how flustered you were." Augustus smiled gently. "Now…"

"Attention!" came the booming voice of Restun as he climbed the steps to the front of the exercise area, halting at the front of a raised patch where he could watch over us.

"Talk later," Augustus said quickly.

"Good morning to all of you!" Restun boomed out. "We'll be starting with a light jog to warm up, followed by a sprint. For those who are new to our ways here, there will be three groups, and each will have separate regimes. For Improve, that warmup will be three times around the exterior of the Tower. For Maintain, that warmup is ten laps." Then he grinned at me. "For Excel, it's a single lap…to the top of the Tower and back down."

My jaw dropped as I stared up at him. He pulled a whistle out of his pocket and blew on it three times before hopping down and jogging towards the Tower.

"Is he serious?" one of the legionnaires near me whispered, shaking his head. I glanced over, seeing Denny. I reached out and gave him a fist bump as I passed, the line running right to left as we peeled after Restun in smooth rows.

"You know the Praetorian Primus," Augustus said, grinning back at Denny. "He's always serious. Anyway, Jax…I'll fill you in briefly as to the events in Narkolt again. You might not remember much, as when I told you last time; we were carving you up…"

Three hours later, as I got my leg swept out from under me for the fifth, or maybe sixth time in a row by Restun, I collapsed to the floor, panting, and tried very hard not to glare at him as he rested the blunted sword-staff he held against the center of my chest and looked down at me.

"You're getting better, Jax," he said, sounding as if the compliment caused him real physical pain. "You need to watch your footwork, though. After this, we're doing an hour's Asha'tuun, and it's going to be feet we concentrate on. No matter how strong the castle…"

"If the foundation is weak, it might as well be sand before the sea." I let my head drop back against the battered ground. "I know, Restun, I know," I ground out, more irritated at myself that I couldn't seem to get this right than anything else.

"Perhaps a break is in order, Praetoria Primus?" Cai asked innocently. I frowned at him, surprised he'd interrupt.

He smiled, lifting a jug to where I could see it.

I blinked as cool, refreshing condensation rolled down the jug's clay exterior. My mouth was drier than a box of cat litter in the Sahara as I glanced up at Restun imploringly.

"Fine, fine." Restun acquiesced, rolling his eyes and flipping the sword-staff over, then reaching down and offering his hand. I took it, and he hauled me to my feet with ease, again making me wonder at the damn man, considering that Prefect Romanus had said that Restun trained *him*. For the thousandth time I contemplated a spell, just a little one, to examine him, before again dismissing the instinct.

Knowing Restun, it'd fail, and he'd be pissed that I tried, and that pain wasn't worth it. I knew he was loyal and he appeared human. In a world of magic, I wasn't going to ask for more than that.

I groaned as I shifted and tried to get the last kink out of my back, and Restun joined Cai and me as he poured drinks, each of us letting out a little sigh of enjoyment at the cool, sweet melon juice.

"That's amazing," I whispered, glancing at the jug, then frowning as the jug glowed slightly, and what looked like frost flowed inside. "Wait…did that just…"

"Ame," Cai replied, but he smiled widely as he said it. "She took one look at my poor, worn out Isabella and her staff, and she and her apprentice started making these jugs. She's made a dozen of them now. 'Simple' she says, but each of them has a rune inbuilt. They cool anything placed inside so long as the bearer holds the jug here." He shifted the jug around to show me the flat part of the handle and the rune carved there.

"It pulls your mana?" I asked, and he nodded. "Ingenious!" Restun agreed before snorting and shaking his head. I glanced at him questioningly, and he nodded to the side. I peeked over to where Grizz was examining the jug one of the serving girls had taken to his group, where they were all training with sword and shield.

"He'll be trying to figure out if it'll work with his ale, mark my words," Restun said. I grinned, getting a faint smile in return.

It was one of the few times Restun had let his guard down around me, and it made me realize just how hard being the Praetoria Primus must be, considering he was the most elite of the elite, and the gatekeeper to the highest position a legionnaire could aspire to.

I decided to make no big thing of the gesture before jutting my chin back to the ring regretfully.

"How long do we have left, Primus?" I asked. He stiffened slightly, the mask sliding back into place.

"Fifteen minutes: that's time for three rounds, Jax. I expect you to hit me at least once, or you get to be the tail for the day…and what happens to the tail?"

"It gets beaten," I growled, determined to win at least one round.

Fifteen minutes later, I sat on the floor, shaking my head and holding a rag up to my broken nose, waiting for the bleeding to stop.

I could heal it, I knew, but it always felt weird healing yourself in the face for some reason. Since it'd stop on its own in a minute, and Oracle was nearly to me, I waited for her to do it.

"Well, you didn't manage to hit me, but I'll accept that you certainly gave it your best shot," Restun said, sounding proud. "I'd considered making you the tail still, but then I saw Grizz try to pocket the jug the serving girl put down…so I think he earned it, instead."

"Oh, hell yes, and thank you, sir!" I muttered, nodding fervently as Restun straightened up from crouching next to me and marched over to Grizz to give him the good news. As he left, the man mountain that was Augustus strode over in his place and looked down, blocking out the warm mid-morning sun and making me squint up at him.

"Augustus?" I raised one hand to shade my face. "Good man, sit," I ordered, gesturing to the grass next to me. He sat, letting out a sigh. I conjured a fountain nearby, the new healing properties of the water meaning that, once I'd filled the jug from it and taken a few swigs of the icy cold water before passing it to Augustus, my nose was entirely healed by the time Oracle arrived.

"What happened?" she asked, looking at my bloody training clothes as I rubbed dried blood off my face and washed it from my beard.

"Restun got carried away," I said.

"Well, you will spar with the one man who'll never pull his blows," she said, shaking her head. "Honestly, it's a good job I was coming down to see you, anyway."

"Is it time?" I asked, and she nodded.

"Good. Man, it feels like I give one of these welcome speeches every godsdamned day…"

Augustus snorted, shaking his head. "It seems it to you, and to be fair, I've seen you give a few Oaths out now. But you've added nearly half again to the population of the Tower between the legionnaires and ex-slaves from the river market we raided. They deserve a formal welcoming, not to mention once we know they're not infiltrated, we'll be able to make good use of them."

"Right, I'll get to that next, and…" A new shadow fell over me. Augustus stiffened, his hand reaching for his belt and the weapons concealed in the bags.

I blinked up, the sun at just the wrong angle to let me see a new figure who slowly and carefully walked through the crowd, hands held out to his sides to show he was no threat as he came to a halt next to me.

"High Lord Jax," he said, sinking to one knee and looking at the ground. "I thank you for sending your ship for me. Sint, God of Light has charged me with serving you, and should you wish it, with aiding you in bringing the rule of Law to these lands once again."

My eyes adjusted to the glare, and I forced myself upright, moving around to see the figure better without the sun directly searing my retinas.

The man who knelt before me was…strange. He looked tall, broad-shouldered, and with a narrow waist, heavily muscled, but not stupidly so, clearly used to wearing the black and silver enameled armor he wore now. As he pulled a truly massive hand and a half greatsword from his bag, about to offer it to me, Augustus and the others tightened in around me. They half-drew weapons, tensing at the possible threat.

"Welcome…I'm sorry, I don't know your name, mate," I said, looking down at him.

"Lucian, High Lord Jax. I am Lucian D'Aquitaine." He winced, as though admitting to some kind of crime.

The legionnaires around me began swearing, closing ranks and preparing to fight.

"Hold!" I snapped, looking around, and making sure my order had been accepted, before looking back at Lucian. "I'm sorry, Lucian, you say your name like it should mean something, and clearly it does to the rest of the Legion, but it doesn't to me. Get up, man, and put your sword away before they have a collective heart attack!"

"Yes, Lord," he said, straightening and sliding his sword back into his bag.

"Always gives me the willies the way that works," I muttered, shaking my head.

"Lord?" Lucian asked, confused.

"The bags…You just slid a sword that must weigh half a damn ton in steel alone and as wide as my thigh, as well as being what, five feet long? You just slid it into a tiny damn pouch…"

"Ah…it is a bag of holding?" Lucian started to explain, confused.

"I know, oh I know, just freaks me the hell out. Anyway, doesn't matter. Welcome to the Great Tower, Lucian," I said, holding my hand out.

He paused, then with an unsure half-smile, he reached out hesitantly to grip my forearm, glancing around as though expecting to be attacked at any second.

"Do you…do you mean that, Lord?" he asked after a tense moment as we both released each other's arms.

"Of course…" I started to say, when I noticed Augustus's face and the way the rest of the Legion were glaring at Lucian, not to mention the way that Restun looked like someone had pissed in his coffee, judging by the way he was striding over.

"You!" he snarled, glaring at Lucian and practically vibrating with an inner fury at the sight of the other man. "You dare to show your face here? I hoped you were dead long since!"

"Greetings, nephew." Lucian bowed his head. "Congratulations on being raised to Praetoria. It must have been hard-earned."

"Lord Jax, you have no idea what this creature has done…please, allow me to see justice done and kill him now!" Restun grated out.

"Uh, what the everliving fuck is going on here?" I asked slowly, the sight of the usually unflappable Legion Primus being so clearly apoplectic with rage making me both confused and freaked out. It was as if a cat had barked like a dog, a total non-sequitur.

"Now nephew, you know…"

"You were banished on pain of death, and don't call me that!" Restun snarled, cutting his apparent uncle off as everyone gathered around, staring.

"Right!" I snapped. "That's about enough of this. We're going to go somewhere where we're not surrounded by hundreds of onlookers, and we'll sort this out. First, though, I need to make arrangements, so Lucian, *yes*, for now, and pending whatever the *fuck* is going on, you are welcome here. Restun, no, you can't kill your own fucking *uncle*, and we're all going to sort this shit out. CAI!"

The cat-man appeared by my side a few seconds later, bowing slightly. "Yes Jax?" he asked calmly, totally ignoring the stress in the air.

"Today is a day to sort out issues, it seems. First and foremost, while I get to the bottom of this, I need you to organize the Tower. We're going to have an Oath ceremony tonight. That should be long enough to get everything ready. I want everyone, and I mean *everyone* here. Yes, I know some ships will be out on patrol. That's fine, though, because they've already sworn. Beyond that, I want the entire population here.

"That means nobody sneaking off to hide somewhere so they don't swear, understand? I don't know how you'll make sure of that, so speak to Seneschal and Heph, maybe. They can probably help, as can Oracle. Sort out a metric fuckton of food and drink, make sure everyone has plenty for afterward. Once we've had the Oath, we'll be going inside to the cathedral, and we'll all pray to our Gods. That covers all the basics and should make everyone happy."

"Oath…food…Gods," Cai confirmed, making a few notes.

"There'll also be an announcement tonight on the Tower, and its future. Oh, and a Title given out, maybe two, so make sure everyone knows there's something to look forward to." I shrugged. "Beyond that, I'm going to be busy today. I need to sort this shit out, speak to the Gods, and see the glasshouse and alchemy gardens, not to mention making plans for the next few days…and…" I steeled myself to ask the question, and Cai shook his head sorrowfully.

"I'm sorry Jax, no word on Bane yet," he said, anticipating my question.

"Dammit. Okay, thank you."

I glanced over, seeing Thomas moving through the crowd, only to be stopped at the edge of our little group by a legionnaire who was clearly unsure who he was, and on edge after Lucian's arrival.

"Looks like I need to add in a welcome speech to that shit tonight as well," I muttered, shaking my head.

"Padraig!" Augustus called, seeing the direction of my gaze and realizing what was happening. "Let him through."

The Legionnaire stepped aside, and Thomas grinned at him and said something before patting him on the shoulder and moving through the crowd with easy grace.

"Hey, bro," Thomas said, his smile changing to a frown as he felt the tension.

"Hey, Thomas, don't worry about it. Come on, you're with us." I turned back to the small group. "Right, this is going to be a fun conversation," I said to Restun and Lucian, eyeing the way the others were glaring at him as well. "So, Cai, organize refreshments, and please, for the love of the Gods, bacon sandwiches, if you can. We'll be near the cathedral, if there's a room there with both seats and a door?"

Cai winced. "There're rooms with seats…but no doors on the bottom floor yet."

"Dammit, fine, okay, we'll take a walk to the north and stay outside, then. Get a bit of sun, and we can damn well just sit and enjoy the grass." I gestured and led the small group away.

A dozen steps into the walk, I noticed the procession we were dragging with us, and I turned to Augustus.

"Augustus, mate, why is half the sodding legion coming with us?"

"Jax, he's…" Augustus nodded towards Lucian.

"He's here by both my invitation, and that of the God of Light and sodding Order, mate. He's to be named His *Champion,* for fuck's sake. I don't think Sint would send someone to join me who's a direct threat, so how about you stay, and everyone else buggers off?"

"I don't think that's wise, Jax, you see he's…"

"A guest, and you're being rude, man. Don't make me order this." I cut him off, shaking my head.

"Legionnaires, return to your duty," Augustus ordered after a few seconds. I nodded to Lucian, after exchanging a look with Thomas that was all rolling eyes and tiny visual cues, transmitting a thousand words in a second.

Thomas grinned, and I grinned back. The feeling of having my brother back was enough to make almost everything better in the world at this point.

"So, Thomas," Oracle said, smiling up at him as we walked along, hand in hand. "I bet you can tell me a lot of interesting stories about Jax?"

"Don't you dare," I warned him, glaring.

"I've hundreds of stories for you, Oracle, believe me," Thomas said to her in a whisper that carried, and he winked. "But shhhh, don't let him know I've told you."

"Prick," I muttered, shaking my head before turning my attention towards the other family dynamic in the group: Restun and Lucian.

"So, Lucian, clearly this is going to be a hell of a tale, but before we get to that fun stuff, and while people can still overhear us, how was the flight?" I asked, watching him.

"It…was glorious, High Lord Jax," Lucian said, smiling wistfully, a look of wonder filling his face. "For many years, I've watched the airships as they fly back and forth, seeing the gnomish wonders as they test their latest designs on occasion. Yet I never dared let myself dream I would be permitted to board one, certainly not as an honored guest. No matter the outcome of this meeting, I thank you for that. It is a memory I shall treasure."

"You're…very welcome, mate." I was slightly taken aback by his answer. I personally loved the sensation of flight, both in my own right and sitting on the deck of an airship, but most people seemed to view the ships as merely an expensive carriage, shrugging off the wonder each time. "I feel the same way. There's a sense of joy to flying, isn't there?" I asked, getting a genuine smile in return.

"I've only been aboard two ships myself," Thomas said, joining in the conversation and grinning over at Lucian. "But man, the view…it's fantastic, isn't it?"

"Breathtaking." Lucian agreed as Thomas rubbed his chin in thought.

"I wonder, man, do you think it would be possible to do a ship out as a restaurant? I mean, imagine it: people board, and you fly up, slowly circle the area while they eat, then drop them off and load up again, over and over. You'd make a fortune," Thomas said.

"Dude, we're at war!" I shook my head. "I'm not giving you an airship to make into a restaurant, no matter how cool it'd be."

"I imagine the Gnomes could make an amazing one," Lucian whispered, staring off into the distance. "And the food, forgive me, it has been a long time since I attended such a place."

"An airship restaurant? Someone's done one?" Thomas asked, crestfallen.

"No, a restaurant," Lucian said. "I once loved to dine in the restaurants of the cities, back when there was peace."

"There hasn't been peace for longer than you have lived," Restun snapped. "And you know why."

"I am not the architect of the world as it stands, Restun. You know this, or would, if you would give me the chance to explain!" Lucian snapped back, showing the irritation under his cool exterior.

"You were banished on pain of death," Restun snarled.

"And I was invited to the Great Tower by both the God of Order and Light and High Lord Jax himself!" Lucian snapped back, exasperated. "I would say that, if any could overturn my banishment, it would be that combination, wouldn't you?"

"Look, I don't know what the hell is going on here, but save it, we'll go over…there," I said, pointing to a stretch of grass that was clear, with nobody within a hundred meters or so. "Until then, let's all play nice and pretend to get along, all right?"

I shook my head and shot a meaningful glance down at Oracle then across at Thomas, who shrugged as we covered the short distance in silence.

Once there, the seven of us sat, Cai having joined us at my gesture when we'd started to walk away. I took one final look around, making sure we were alone, before starting.

Tang's presence hovered close by, but that was fine. I had no secrets from him. I noted the way that Thomas and Cai seemed to have no clue Tang was there, but Oracle, Augustus, Lucian, and Restun had all glanced over at him.

"Don't worry about Tang; I trust him…more or less. Right, I think there's a hell of a tale here, so why don't you start, please, Lucian?" I asked, lying back on the grass, half-propped on my elbows as the others made themselves comfortable around me.

"Well, it's a long story, yet fairly simple, High…"

"Just Jax, please, that's fine." I closed my eyes and enjoyed the feeling of the warm mid-morning sun on my shoulders.

"Thank you…Jax," Lucian said. I cracked one eyelid, peeked over at the small smile on his face, and nodded to him. "Well, I suppose the thing that needs explanation the most is my banishment. But before that, I might as well start at the beginning. Forgive me Jax, but it's a long tale."

"As long as I get a bacon sandwich and a damn drink sometime soon, that's totally fine, mate."

"Well, I was born in the days following the fall of the Empire…"

"Wait, what?" I asked, confused.

"He's a Vampyr, Lord Jax," Restun snapped, glaring at him. "He's an unclean creature who was banished when he looted the legion coffers and shamed the force that took him in. He's a Vampyr and a traitor and should be executed!"

There was silence as we all looked at each other and at Lucian. Finally, the man sighed and nodded.

"While inaccurate, there is some truth in what he says," Lucian admitted.

I sat up fully, watching the man who sat across from me. "Well, shit…" I stared at the Vampyr that was the Champion of the God of Light.

CHAPTER THREE

"Right, look," I said, rubbing the back of my neck with one hand. "There's clearly even more of a story here than I expected, and it's going to be either awesome, weird, or more likely, a mix of the two. How about you tell the whole thing, Lucian, then Restun, you can say your bit. I guess, if need be, I'll ask Sint to join us."

"You will *ask* the God of Light to 'join us'?" Lucian asked slowly, his eyes wide.

As he started to speak, I squinted, seeing it more clearly now that I was looking for it. But the air around him was slightly warped, a dulling of the bright mid-morning light. "Also, what the hell is with the air around you?"

"Well…okay…" Lucian said, clearly searching for words. "I…I'll start at the beginning, but the light, well, it is true in part that I am a Vampyr, or more accurately a half breed. Bright sunlight is uncomfortable for me, but not directly harmful, more like a severe case of sunburn if I spend too long in it.

"As such, I learned long ago to warp the air around me slightly, much as the Chameleon spell redirects light around the target. This simply filters the light slightly, so that only a fraction hits me. My enhanced regeneration takes care of the rest." He rubbed his chin.

"I was born in the days following the fall of the Empire and the Great Cataclysm. My family was a large one, holders of a minor title and some land to the north of what is now the village of Asha, directly north of Himnel.

"When the Cataclysm destroyed the realm, the tidal waves and loss of the island of Imshi off the coast meant that our fishing fleet was destroyed." He shook his head. "This sounds innocuous, considering the events that were going on. But, as our family wealth was tied up in the fleet and supplying the surrounding area with food from the sea, we essentially went from being wealthy to paupers, and quickly."

I nodded, thinking of the madness that would have come when fishing fleets that supplied hundreds were suddenly gone.

"Over the years, my father had collected many trinkets and magical baubles, and he tried his best to sell them to provide for the family and keep it afloat. From what I remember being told as a child, he was a good man. He'd work from long before dawn until exhaustion took him, trying to get a ship working again, cobbled together from the various scraps of the fleet that washed ashore, and the little he could scrape together from the markets.

"Shortly before I was born, he decided to explore a cave system at the foot of the cliffs, believing that it was likely in a location where much of the debris of various ships would have been washed ashore." Lucian sat still as he spoke, his gaze far away even as he gently stroked a worn signet ring on his little finger.

"The cave system was far greater than he believed, longer and deeper, branching off into subsidiaries and separate caverns that stretched for miles, yet still he, his few remaining staff, and his brothers searched, even going so far as to take his eldest son with them. They were gone for several days, but when he returned, finally, to gather more food, ropes, and supplies, he was both elated and frantic.

"He'd found a pocket of debris, literally the remains of dozens of ships, and sunk in the water inside this huge cavern, pushed there by the tide of centuries, he discovered what was possibly hundreds of vessels. He was elated by the possibilities, as well as the salvage. The tiny amount he'd brought out with him was enough to buy food, equipment, and more, and he pressed it upon my mother eagerly before returning there, believing all their financial troubles were over." Lucian sagged at the memory.

"In the cavern, he'd found the answer to his prayers. After hours of exploring and cataloging, they'd gathered to leave, thinking to return and get supplies, and he found his son was nowhere to be seen. They searched for hours before finally picking up his trail, leading deeper into the cavern.

"With torches running low, food almost gone, and the fresh water supplies practically used up, they made the difficult decision to leave the cavern, returning to the surface to gather more supplies and return to rescue the boy, this time knowing the direction he'd gone in, and that he'd had some food and water. They hoped he would last long enough for them to rescue him."

"A hard decision," Cai cut in. "Leaving the boy to wander alone in the dark, knowing that, if they didn't leave him, they would run out of food, water, and light, resulting in them *all* being lost? A choice I'd not want to face."

"Exactly, yet after two more days of searching, and by now many, many miles travelled deep in the ground, they found the boy, passed out, exhausted, and near death," Lucian said, idly picking up a stem of grass and stripping it between his fingers.

"They brought the boy out, and as they returned to the surface, they saw signs of an animal attack on him. He was covered in small but vicious wounds, and his pale, sweating form shook with fever. They did what they could, feeding him, cleaning his wounds, and taking the boy home."

"Weeks passed as my father used the wealth he'd found to rebuild the family fleet, returning time and time again to the cavern, stripping the ships and wreckage he could reach of valuables, and all the while my eldest brother weakened. By the time I was born, however, three things had changed in our house.

"First, our father, the head of the family, had managed to recover some of the wealth and prestige he and the family had lost. In the years following the Cataclysm, a man who could lead, turn around a family's ailing fortunes, and bring food in consistently was a man who rose fast.

"He spent more and more time in the city, growing in importance, and spending less and less time at home. Akanji, my eldest brother, finally started to recover, having been brought into my mother's bed at night. As heavily pregnant as she was, she was unable to run to him in the night, when his screams of terror woke the house, or so I was told." He sighed, shaking his head.

"Lastly, my mother started to wake more and more drained, wandering the house in a daze. The toll of the final days of her pregnancy was simply too much, combined with the need to care for my brother and three sisters. I was born, finally, one of two twins, the only one to survive childbirth, I am told, with only Akanji there to help my mother through it." He paused, his mouth working as he searched for words.

"I fear we will never know the truth of those last days, but from what my father told me, and the servant she had sent to bring my father home told him, there was an attack on our home. Some kind of monster had struck, leaving only Akanji and myself alive. The other bodies had been drained and fed upon, blood smeared across the walls in terrible sprays, and the bodies were left as dried husks." Lucian sat for long seconds looking at his feet as he spoke.

"My father took us to the city, to a new home he purchased, and he raised us, filled with guilt and fury, determined to make up for the time he'd lost and the family he'd forgotten about in his rush to be important again.

"Akanji was changed by the attack. The laughing child he'd apparently been before this, and presumably before the cavern, was never seen again. Instead, a mean-spirited child who delighted in cruel games was all I knew growing up. As the years passed, our father married again, and his new wife bore him two girls, Ester and Anna." At this, Lucian smiled, and though his eyes were suddenly full of tears, he stared back across the centuries with love written large across his face.

"They were the sunshine after the rain. Both girls had hair like gold and hearts that wished only to lift those around them. They loved everyone, and everywhere they went, they brought smiles to people," Lucian whispered. "To me, they were both wonderful, sweet baby girls. Although, as much as it pains me to admit it, Ester was my favorite. She would sit in my lap and beg for stories, and when she woke with terrors in the night, she would run to me, unlike Anna, who would run to our father and his new wife.

"Akanji would alternate between having nothing to do with the girls and watching them in a way that, even as a child, made me uncomfortable. But, as he reached the age of majority, thirteen in those days, and went to the Legion to begin his training, we saw less and less of him."

"He was a legionnaire?" Restun asked coldly, clearly not wanting to, yet needing to know more.

"No," Lucian said shortly. "He was refused, failing his training and removed in dishonor from the Roll of the Legion after some kind of incident. Father wouldn't discuss it, but it marked a changing point in the family.

"Before this, Akanji had always been…well, if not respectful, he'd been wary of our father, not wishing to cross him. After this, it changed, even as I started to change as well. For me, it was less overt than Akanji. He was given over to murderous rages and demands. I remember him screaming at my father and sending the servants running terrified. The final straw was when he beat Anna bloody for trespassing in his room."

"I had been in the garden with my father, and Ester, as she often would, was sitting and watching as I trained." He sighed and shook his head quickly. "I should have said this before, but after what happened at our home, father became obsessed with the Legion.

"He was one of the few in the city in power who spoke in favor of the Legion, and he went so far as to promise his son in service. Well, after Akanji shamed him so, he began to train me, starting far earlier than was customary. I was little more than six or seven, and even the poorest noble houses didn't expect their children to start formal training until thirteen in those days."

"We were all given basic fitness, fighting, and moral training, in addition to our schooling, you understand?" Lucian continued, not waiting for a response. "But after Akanji, Father hired a retired Legion Primus to train me.

"I'd begun to Demonstrate Abilities far earlier than I should, and while I had no class yet, obviously, I was starting to manifest greater than expected Strength, Agility, and Dexterity. As such, Senittus had asked my father to watch that day as he ran me through my training. It was intended to be a source of pride for my father, I think, a way to show me off and prove that the Gods had not abandoned us entirely, by showing the grace I had been blessed with. Instead, it ended with screams and blood."

"When we found Akanji, Senittus was the first to him. The old Primus slammed Akanji back with his shield, probably saving Anna's life, and all hell broke loose, screams and shouts, accusations. Priests were called to examine Akanji…." Lucian broke off, shaking his head in mixed disgust and sadness.

"They were powerless, but in those days, the few surviving priests from the Great Cleansing, as it was called when Nimon slaughtered his brethren's followers, were still trying to hide their loss. They told my father that Akanji was simply a troubled young man. We wouldn't find out until later that they'd been unable to properly examine him at all." Lucian snorted, shaking his head before going on.

"In the end, Akanji was sent back to our family holdings in the north. A group of servants, guards, and a dozen families were sent with him, with a plan to build a new village around the remains of our old home that had long since fallen into disrepair. He was essentially given a banishment from society, a priest to talk to about his worries and to guide him, servants, and people to live around him, all he could need, as well as guards."

"Sounds like he got a hell of a good deal out of that," Thomas said in a low voice.

"It was far better than he deserved, but our father felt that Akanji's actions were from him failing the boy, nothing more. He hoped that a position of limited responsibility and some time away would be what he needed, and that they would reconcile in time, allowing Akanji to take over for our father when he was older," Lucian admitted sadly.

"The years passed, and while Anna was hurt by the events on that day, the sudden lack of Akanji in our home was marked. The house slowly filled with joy, despite the hard times around us. Monster attacks were rising, food was short, and the realm was in upheaval. Eventually, the priests were found out, and the Gods were basically abandoned, save the God of Death.

By the time I was accepted and began my training in the Legion, the balance of the land was gone. Starvation was the norm, pestilence, wars, the fleet was smashed over and over again. Great Leviathans of the deep, things not seen near shore in millennia, were suddenly roaming the shallows, driving the fish away and sinking ships. Pirates attacked, and I spent less and less time at home as I became a full legionnaire." Lucian smiled as he described the realm collapsing. It seemed strange to hear him describe those days while we sat on the grass, in warm sunshine, and watched the serving staff hurrying over, bearing platters of hot sandwiches and cold drinks.

We all took food and drinks and waited as Lucian continued with his tale.

"Eventually, things became so bad, that we, the Legion I mean, were ambushed by a large force of bandits, and, we suspected at least, that a noble had reinforced them. Half the Legion was lost, and I was injured badly. The healing I underwent, and the discussions around the fight, resulted in a skilled healer being brought from Narkolt Enclave to examine me. The results were…unpleasant to hear."

"What happened?" I asked. "With the healer and the injuries and so on?"

"I'd lost many of my brothers and sisters that day, and, well, I'd almost lost my mind in rage and sorrow, I think. I'd snapped, determined to sell my life as dearly as possible, pushing past pain, ignoring crossbow bolts, fire, and lightning. I'd rampaged through their ranks, eventually collapsing, seemingly dead at the hands of my enemies. There were hundreds of dead on both sides, and in all the confusion, and with me covered in blood and unconscious as I was, I was assumed to be dead. My brethren took my pack and bags and buried me in a pit filled with our dead. I suppose I should be thankful they didn't just burn us all, as they did with the bandit's bodies," he said with a dark chuckle.

"You survived," I said, needlessly, considering he was sitting across from us now.

"I did," Lucian acknowledged. "I survived, but not how any man would wish to. I was buried with hundreds of my brothers and sisters, and when unconscious, I was literally bathed in their blood. I fed on them, drawing it in, and awoke to a new life as a fully blooded Dhampyr."

"A what?" Thomas asked, confused. I shrugged, turning back toward Lucian.

"A Dhampyr, a half-Vampyr," he said with an almost apologetic glance at the ground. "I'd fed, reduced to an almost animalistic state through pain, blood loss, and the darkness, crawling around in the pit, growing stronger by the second as I fed on my dead brethren.

"I drank their cooling blood and absorbed stat points from them, growing stronger and stronger, until I finally managed to dig myself up and out of the pit, dragging myself up through a sludge of churned mud and detritus in the middle of a thunderstorm. It took hours before I could think enough to look for the survivors and days before I caught up with them. I couldn't travel during the day, and I was new to the blood, with painful changes wracking my body constantly."

"When I reached the Legion, I was greeted with open arms, tears of shame at their abandonment, then fury and hatred, suspicion and ire, as I told my tale, not knowing what else to do. I was restrained, trapped in a chest, returned to the city and to the Enclave, where I was questioned repeatedly, as they tried to work out when I'd become a Vampyr. They summoned the healer, and he examined me and those around me, even as the Legion frantically kept the secret, not wanting to warn my master," he said grimly, shaking his head.

"Eventually, after more than eight months investigating, after even Senittus was called in to give evidence, they figured out what had happened. *Akanji.*" Lucian spat the name now, his fists clenched as he went on, before forcibly smoothing his hands out.

"Akanji had been turned by something in the caves, probably a beast, rather than a sentient Vampyr, and as the strain grew stronger in him, evolving him, he changed. He'd fed on our mother, we thought, and he was the beast that attacked our home.

"He'd probably either taken me, thinking to have me later, or some remnant of what he had been had kept him from feeding on both of the newborns, until my father arrived and rescued me. When he'd fed on my mother, being so new to it, he'd basically spread his essence about. We suspected it was what had killed her; weeks, if not months of him attacking her as she slept. But it'd taken time, time enough for that essence to infect me and my twin, the unborn children in her womb," Lucian whispered, balling his fists again.

"They investigated further and found that not only had I never fed before, but I was so horrified by what I'd done…even subconsciously…well. There were records of other Dhampyr, and one had ended up as a member of the Praetorian Guard. So, if one could be trusted that high, and that close to the Emperor…my life was held in the balance, with equal numbers on either side calling for me to be given a chance or to be executed.

"The final vote was to be given to the primus who'd half-raised me, as it was decided he knew me best of all. He declared that, while he trusted me and believed in me, there was one other who should be counted in making this decision, and that was my father." There was a long pause as Lucian sat there before glancing up at us all in sorrow.

"Except, in keeping the secret, they waited too long. My father had taken the entire family to visit his son, and to see what his firstborn had accomplished with the beginnings of a village. When the Legion realized what it most likely meant, I was left there, in the dark, to worry and panic. Five full combat maniples of the Legion were mustered, and they descended on the village. Needless to say, it wasn't what they hoped to find. In the end, ninety legionnaires were killed in the purging of the village, and some three hundred people were killed, having been found to be carrying the seed of the Vampyr. Their master, Akanji, was never found, but dozens of fully fledged Vampyr were…and of all my family, only little Ester survived. Thanks to the essence that had infected my mother, our father had been infected to some degree, as well. That meant, when she was examined, she too had the signs."

"My great, great, great, grandmother," Restun added.

"Aye, and as I said, Nephew, I loved her dearly. To you, she was a figure in your history. To me, she was a child I bounced on my knee and who ran to me when she was afraid of the thunder or the creaks in the night." Lucian leveled Restun with a meaningful look before turning back to me.

"I was acquitted, although it took many, many years before I was fully trusted again, and I raised her in the Enclave. Ester became a legionnaire in time and rose to the rank of Speculatorae. She served with high honor until a corrupt noble had her executed for interrupting one of his orgies, after he'd had his wife meet an 'unfortunate accident'."

"And you shamed her memory!" Restun growled.

"*I did no such thing!*" Lucian snarled, glaring at him. "I was banished! Banished from a Legion that grew corrupt. And when I stepped in, I was falsely accused! I spent the next two hundred and fifty years scouring the entire damn continent for my brother! I've had neither home nor succor for centuries, and still, the first thing I am greeted with by my kin is accusations and hatred!"

"Corruption?" I asked, holding a hand up to stop Restun, who was glaring daggers at Lucian.

"Yes!" he snapped, before realizing who he was talking to. "I…I apologize, my Lord. Yes, the accusations were baseless. I was accused of redirecting legion funds, of purchasing luxuries and the time of young girls, of bringing them in as chattel to feed upon.

"I knew nothing of what appeared to be a coordinated campaign to discredit me until I returned from nearly a year in the field, travelling to meet with other Justicars, as by then searching out such corruption had become my life. Foolish of me. I should have spent more time looking at my peers rather than aiding the island nations, it seems."

"I have seen the records, the sworn affidavits of the legionnaires who caught you in an orgy of depravity, feeding on the girls, girls you'd drugged and bought from whorehouses," Restun said grimly.

"And when did they do that?" Lucian replied coldly, clearly trying to keep his voice even. "I disembarked from my ship, expecting that the legionnaires that were waiting for me were an honor guard sent to welcome me home, only to find myself hauled away, gagged, and dragged before the Legion General and his cronies! I was never given the chance to plead my case, to see any form of justice done. The Oaths were supposed to ensure we could all trust one another, yet they only protect the upper ranks from the lower, never the other way around!"

Restun stared at his ancestor "I saw the…"

"Yen," I interrupted. "Yen told me a tale about a Legion General who took advantage of the Oaths, and he and the others essentially started living lives of luxury."

"That was nine years ago," Restun growled. "We removed him, and we…"

"Yen said that, Restun. She said that the new era of conservatism and so on began then, but you've been with the Legion for how long now?" Restun snapped his mouth shut, refusing to answer. "Restun…" I said warningly. His gaze shot daggers at me before he remembered his place and mine and forced himself to answer.

"Ninety-seven years, sir."

Startled, I took a good look at the man. He seemed maybe late forties, early fifties, the kind of guy who'd end up looking the same and running marathons until one day he dropped dead to everyone's stunned surprise.

"Holy shit," I muttered, then I glanced to Lucian and back to Restun, raising one eyebrow in question.

"It's not that!" Restun snapped before pausing and speaking slowly and carefully. "I apologize, Lord Jax, but no, it isn't that. An ancestor was elven. The bloodline is pure, despite my looks, giving all the family vastly increased lifespans."

"It's not," Lucian said with a frown. "It may be in part due to Ranviir's blood, but he fell in love with Shireen after they fought together for nearly sixty years. She was in her eighties when she had your great grandmother.

"I'm sorry, Restun. I know you hate me, and all you have heard of me, but you *know* I cannot lie. On my Oath as a legionnaire and to the Empire, I swear that I neither fell through corruption, nor desire, but instead was betrayed by the legionnaires I trusted. I swear upon my beloved sister, Ester, that you carry some of the bloodline and the gift, dark though it may be. Hiding from this does yourself and your family no honor."

"I...I..." Restun sputtered.

I held up a hand, stopping all conversation.

"And now we've reached a crossroads. If Restun believes in the Legion, then he must believe you, Lucian. But if he cannot, then he must believe there is something wrong with the Legion he's sworn and devoted his life to. He's been taught all his life, I assume, that you were corrupt."

Restun nodded, red-faced. "I was hounded, constantly punished, pushed to breaking and beyond, always while being told that I was incapable of being a true legionnaire, that corruption was in my bloodline. *Seventy years* of being the best it took to bury those rumors, then you show up..." Restun snarled, biting back the words he was about to say.

"Then, there is an easy way to deal with this," I said, smiling before clambering to my feet and taking a deep breath. Lucian and the others all rose as well, confused, until I waved them back down. I knelt, pressing my right fist to the ground and my left to my heart, as I cast the spell.

I tuned out the sounds of the world around me as I pulled in the required forms from my mind, weaving the various aspects of the spell together and selecting light as the primary thread.

It took seconds, but when it was complete, everyone nearby knew exactly what I'd done, as I spoke the words aloud. "Sint, God of Light and Lord of Order, will you speak with us?"

"Jax," The voice was solid and strong, echoing slightly as though coming from a vast distance, but at the same time, there was a sudden overwhelming sense of presence, the way there always was when one of the Gods responded. The world around us bathed in a gentle light as Sint continued to speak. *"Thank you, Jax, for summoning one of my most favored to me. I have reached to you in your dreams, Lucian. Do you know me?"*

"Sint," Lucian whispered, tears filling his eyes as he frantically dropped to one knee. "Lord of Light, I am but a humble..."

"You are the last true Justicar, one trained by survivors of the Empire, and I ask you to do as your heart demands. I charge you to be my Champion and to seek out and punish the guilty wherever they may hide."

"Lord, I am not worthy," Lucian whispered, clearly in shock.

"Lord Sint," I interrupted. "Lucian was accused..."

"I heard. I heard the accusations, and I investigated. While I slept away the ages, I was neither truly gone nor able to act, but I see the truth, Lucian. I am not omnipotent, not even the Gods are, in truth.

"I see you, however. I see your soul, and I have read the truth of your heart. For those who doubt you, I say this: Lucian is an honorable legionnaire, a Justicar above reproach, who has dedicated centuries to bringing justice to the wronged. I declare him to be as without sin in his heart as it is possible for a mortal to be."

"I'm not worthy..." Lucian said.

I snorted.

"Lucian, when the God of Light and Order says you *are* worthy, believe me, you're worthy. Sounds like you've been shit on from a great height in the past, and were probably used as a scapegoat, but either way, you are welcome here." I turned to Restun, who knelt there looking stunned.

"Restun?" I asked.

He flinched. "I…I'm sorry, Lord Jax…I…"

"You'll need time to deal with things, I'd imagine." He nodded firmly. "Good man. I'm sure you can go and take your confusion out on someone?" I suggested.

He nodded sharply, springing to his feet and bowing once jerkily in the direction that Sint's voice had come from, before pausing as he passed and hesitantly patted Lucian's shoulder. He jerked his hand back as though burned and hurried away.

Lucian reached out to him, a second too slow for Restun to see. "Restun…"

"Give him time, Lucian," I ordered. "He spent his whole life suffering in the shadow of you being a traitor and hating you for it, only to find out irrevocably that he was wrong, and that he'd been lied to by his leadership. He spent his life believing a lie, and it was one told by those he had the most faith in. He's going to have some troubles after this."

"He is a good man and will come through this trial stronger than ever," Sint's voice rumbled. ***"You have, however, brought my Champion as requested, and as such, I will grant you the rewards we agreed. The weapon he bears is a powerful one, yet it is weak compared to the greatsword Justice that you recovered from the Prax, Glorious Retribution. I would bless Justice and affirm him in his position, should you choose to grant it to him?"***

"I'll do that happily," I grunted, awkwardly pulling the massive sword free of my bag of spatial folding. Before I could offer it over to him, I paused and smiled, thinking better of it. "Actually, can I ask a favor?"

"Ask."

"Could you bless this tonight? I'd like to make a formal declaration of Lucian's position, innocence, and formal acceptance back into the Legion. It would go a long way in settling people's minds if you could bless his weapon then?"

There was a long pause before Sint responded. ***"I would be honored to do so, Jax,"*** He replied. ***"Call upon me when the time comes, and I will publicly bless this weapon."*** With that, the sense of His presence faded, and I let out a breath in relief as the heaviness subsided.

"Well, that was both awesome and terrible. Thanks for the dark tale, Lucian." I said, smiling.

"I…uh, you're welcome…Jax." He forced a smile of his own.

"Cai, arrange for Lucian to be given quarters in our section, and Augustus, spread the word, will you?" I asked, getting nods from them both.

"Thank you, now I know this isn't going to be easy, considering the ingrained reactions to Lucian we've seen so far, but people need to understand that he's here to stay, hopefully, and that he will be in charge of justice." I paused making eye contact with Augustus, Cai, and Lucian. "As such, we will introduce him formally tonight, but for now, make sure people understand the situation."

"I'll make it clear, Jax," Augustus promised.

I nodded to him, his word all I needed. "Thank you. Now, I need to go and speak to the Gods, might as well do that the right way, and do it in the cathedral, I suppose. Then I've no doubt there'll be a million things Cai needs to bully me with."

"Bully?" Cai feigned shock. "I would never do such a thing! I simply…encourage…you to make the decisions required, that's all!"

"Yeah, it's called bullying." I glanced across at Lucian, who seemed both amused by the conversation and like he felt he was intruding. "Honestly, Lucian, he threatened to 'accidentally' interrupt me every time I started getting some loving if I didn't sort out some of the issues he brought. I mean, come on, who does that?"

"It sounds terrible," Lucian said, a faint smile playing across his face.

"It really was…three hours he had me reading reports the other day. Seriously, do I look like the kinda guy who likes paperwork?"

"It is a necessary evil, Jax." Lucian said carefully, his lips still quirking upward in barely disguised humor.

"Nope!" I declared, stepping towards the Tower as the rest of the group followed along. "Amon hated paperwork, so he had his advisors, his Senate, and his Grand Vizier deal with that kind of shit, while he flattened islands and blew shit up. Clearly, it's a family trait."

"Well, at least some things never change," Thomas said to Augustus. "He used to tell the teachers to get fucked when they gave us homework. Now he's gone all the way into 'royalty doesn't have to do that' mode."

"Maybe I should set someone up to just deal with all the paperwork for me. Someone I could trust, you know, like a *brother*." I sent Thomas an unmistakable look.

"Fine by me." Thomas shrugged. "Hey, Cai, you got any requests in there for a whorehouse that needs, *ahem*, *personal* attention?"

"Three requests so far actually, formal ones, I mean. Dozens of subtle ones as well."

"That's fine, I can deal with those!" Thomas said, waving at me dismissively. "Don't you worry, bro, I've got your back…it might take me a few days…or weeks, to interview the prospective staff, but I'll do it. Night and day, I'll work…"

"Asshole."

"Wanker," he shot back, grinning as I laughed and shook my head.

"Right, Cai, I'm going to check my notifications, so give me a few minutes free of the bullshit, please. Augustus, Lucian, you're welcome to come with us if you want to. We're going to tour the glasshouse and the alchemy gardens after the cathedral.

"Or, you can bugger off, it's up to you. Tang, we're inside the Tower, I know, and therefore slightly safer than outside. But seriously, dude, doesn't it drive you mad being stealthed all the time?" I asked the seemingly empty air next to me. Tang laughed, rather than responding.

I shrugged, figuring he was going to follow no matter what I said. Instead, I pulled up my notifications, steeling myself for the mass of them I knew were waiting from the battle with the dark legion.

Congratulations!

You have killed the following:
- 58x Church of Nimon Slave-Aspirants of various levels for a total of 143,144xp

- 92x Church of Nimon Soldier-Aspirants of various levels for a total of 703,892xp

- 53x Church of Nimon Sanctified and Blessed Soldiers of various levels for a total of 482,353xp

- 17x Church of Nimon Dark Chosen of various levels for a total of 439,637xp

A party under your command killed the following:
- 112x Church of Nimon Slave-Aspirants of various levels for a total of 274,960xp

- 103x Church of Nimon Soldier-Aspirants of various levels for a total of 787,126xp

- 58x Church of Nimon Sanctified and Blessed Soldiers of various levels for a total of 519,213xp

- 37x Church of Nimon Dark Chosen of various levels for a total of 960,076xp

Total party experience earned: 2,541,375xp
As party leader, you gain 25% of all experience earned
Progress to level 28 stands at 2,615,321/910,000

*

Congratulations!

You have reached level 28 & 29!

You have 14 unspent Attribute points and 0 Meridian points available

Progress to level 30 stands at 695,321/1,120,000

I grinned. Sure, the big fights were a nightmare. Hell it was like the world devolved into spinning steel and fire, explosions, and a severe ass kicking each time, but killing hundreds of enemies was *awesome* for levelling.

I decided to save the points until I'd read the rest of the notifications, and moved onto the next in the list.

Congratulations!

**Through hard work and perseverance,
you have gained points to the following stats.**

Continue to train and learn to raise this further.

**Agility +1
Charisma +1
Constitution +3
Dexterity +1
Endurance +2
Luck +4
Strength +2**

I couldn't help but be relieved at the number of stat points I'd gained over the course of the last few days. The three points in constitution in particular were well-earned, considering I remembered how godsdamned painful having my armor cut from me had been.

I skipped through the next few notifications, ignoring details on skills that had climbed, until I finally hit one that made me grin like I'd gone insane.

Congratulations!

You have raised your spell Cleanse to level 10.

You may now choose your first evolution of this spell.

*

Congratulations!

You have raised your spell Cleanse to its first evolution.

You must now pick a path to follow.

Will you pick the path of PURITY or the path of SCOUR?

Choose carefully, as this choice cannot be undone.

Purity:
Cleanse has been so thoroughly used to strip your body of toxins, that it has taken on an entirely new form. Purity will remove anything that is not part of your target's genetic code, resulting in a truly pristine and sterile version of your target.

Scour:
You've stripped your targets of contamination time and time again, but rather than strip the entire creature of contaminants, what if instead you only focused on a tiny area?

I thought about it as I strode across the grass, my mind racing with the possibilities. Stripping away any toxins sounded awesome; I could literally eat and drink poisons to learn more about them, then boom!

I could become immune to *all* poisons…

Then my brain caught up to me, and I examined that. If Cleanse was such a basic spell, and it could do that, then why were poisons even a thing? After all, any low-level mage could get rid of them…I read the details more carefully and grunted.

Add in my basic school level of biology, and suddenly I knew that using Purity on a living creature suddenly seemed like an unbelievably bad idea. Not only would you lose things like nutrients and so on, but you'd damn well have no antibodies to anything. You'd be killed by a cold!

Scour, on the other hand, seemed like it could be useful. It was a more viable option at least, as had I had this spell when I was injured last, I might not have had to be *literally* flayed alive…I grunted to myself as I accepted Scour as my choice, knowing damn well it'd evolved in that direction because of the uses it'd been put to in healing me, and considering how infrequently I had used it…

"Oracle, did you…?"

She nodded. "Literally every other spell was Cleanse when we were keeping you going. Plus, there's a second option you didn't consider for Scour."

"Oh?"

"No need for showers." She smiled.

"Bite your tongue, woman! I thought you liked the shower?" I retorted, winking at her.

"I do, but I meant out in the field, after a fight, bang! Clean again…you have no idea how useful that could be on your clothing."

"Oh, good Gods, yes! No more dried blood in my undercrackers making my balls itch, thank you!"

"I really didn't need to hear that," Cai said, shaking his head.

"Well, now you know what we have to put up with," Augustus said. "Believe me, after a particularly messy fight, you swear you've scrubbed *everything*, and two days later, you'll find a fingertip or something."

"It's as though they hide and wiggle out when you least expect them, isn't it?" Thomas chimed in. "I mean, seriously, days later, and then 'where the hell did that ear come from'?"

"Perhaps you need to clean yourself more carefully?" Lucian asked in a low voice, a faint smile on his face.

"Dude, seriously, how old are you? If you've not found this shit happening, then you've either lived a boring life, or you're far too careful." Thomas grinned at Lucian, who smiled again and went back to being quiet, clearly uncomfortable with the topic of his age being discussed around the others.

The next few minutes passed in random chatter as I checked my last few dozen notifications, all dealing with the tremendous damage done to me and the effects on my body of using and reusing the spells over and over again.

By the time we reached the front of the Tower, I'd managed to get through all of them, barring one, and had acknowledged that once again, a Champion had been recruited, so I'd made a bit more progress in my quest.

You have made progress in a Quest!: Bring back the Old Gods
Bring back the Old Gods to displace Nimon and return balance to the realm. Aid each to find a champion that suits Their aspect, and spread knowledge of the Gods to bring about a new Golden Age.

Gods Awakened: 9/9

Champions Chosen: 6/9

Reward: Blessings of the Gods, 100,000xp, Random local notable locations identified

I checked the map, but found no more details added, thankfully, considering how far behind with my quests I was getting, but I had received 300,000 experience from Thomas, Lucian and Lydia each becoming Champions of their respective Gods. I pulled up my stat sheet and looked it over, before making a few quick changes and taking a deep breath. Leaning against the side of the Tower just inside, out of sight, I activated the changes and practically bit through my tongue in the crazy flare of nerve impulses it caused.

Of the fourteen points I had available, I decided to go for gold and put six points into Dexterity, taking that from a base of fifty-nine to sixty-five, and moving to a boost to fifty-five percent on my chances of a crafting success.

That one, I'd mainly chosen because I intended to do a lot of alchemy over the next few days and weeks. The difference was notable as I worked, I'd realized, the little slight changes, like being able to catch a vial in the air when you knocked it over, rather than trying and backhanding it across the room accidentally as I'd done on more than one occasion.

The remaining eight points, I'd put directly into Wisdom, working on the general principle that, no matter what I did these days, I always needed more magic. While the initial barrage I could let loose was fantastic in comparison to what I'd started with, I was still running damn short in the long term, often ending my battles frantically burping up the remains of mana potions or wishing I had them.

Name: Jax Amon	

Titles: Strategos: 5% boost to damage resistance, Fortifier: 5% boost to defensive structure integrity, Champion of Jenae: One search for hidden knowledge every 24 hours, Kobold Ravager: +25% damage to Kobolds, Valspar's Bane: +25% damage to Valspar	
Class: Spellsword > Justicar > Champion of Jenae > Imperial Magekiller > Imperial Justicar > Imperial Overlord	Renown: Imperial Scion, Lord of Dravith
Level: 29	Progress: 995,321/1,120,000
Patron: Jenae, Goddess of Fire and Exploration	Points to Distribute: 0 Meridian Points to Invest: 0

Stat	Current points	Description	Effect	Progress to next level
Agility	40	Governs dodge and movement.	+300% maximum movement speed and reflexes, (+10% movement in darkness, -20% movement in daylight)	4/100
Charisma	31 (26)	Governs likely success to charm, seduce, or threaten	+210% success in interactions with other beings	14/100
Constitution	55 (50)	Governs health and health regeneration	1100 health, regen 64 points per 600 seconds, (each point invested now worth 20 health)	81/100
Dexterity	65 (60)	Governs ability with weapons and crafting success	+550% to weapon proficiency, +55% to the chances of crafting success	14/100
Endurance	46 (43)	Governs stamina and stamina regeneration	1380 stamina, regen 35 points per 30 seconds, (each point invested now worth 30 stamina)	12/100
Intelligence	58	Governs base mana and number of spells able to be learned	580 mana, spell capacity: 32 (30 + 2 from items)	66/100
Luck	34	Governs overall chance of bonuses	+24% chance of a favorable outcome	69/100
Perception	43 (33)	Governs ranged damage and chance to spot traps or hidden items	+330% ranged damage, +33% chance to spot traps or hidden items	95/100
Strength	46 (43)	Governs damage with melee weapons and carrying capacity	+36 damage with melee weapons, +360% maximum carrying capacity	38/100
Wisdom	45 (35)	Governs mana regeneration and memory	+525% mana recovery, 5.5 points per minute, 350% more likely to remember things, (+50% increased mana regeneration from essence core)	41/100

When I could see again, I blinked the tears free of my eyes and took a deep breath before addressing the group.

"Okay then, people, as I said, cathedral, glasshouse, alchemy gardens, and then some actual alchemy for me, then I need to meet the new Legion officers, followed by a meeting of the council, I think. Cai, in the chambers please, right before we all come down and do the ceremony tonight. Ah…time-wise…"

Cai smiled, holding his hand up. "I have a suggestion regarding timing, but it would be better instituted from tonight, after you explain it to everyone. Simply put, a bell. Seneschal can make it ring at a low tone through the night and a higher tone during the day, and he can make it audible throughout the Tower, make it ring once for each hour, so at five in the morning, it rings five times, same for the evening. I suggest implementation *after* the ceremony, as some cities use bells to warn of attacks and people might panic, if it's not explained first."

"Fine. I like it; we'll do it, but for time tonight…"

"How about the ceremony starts an hour before sunset? At this time of year, that's around seven in the evening, so, ceremony at six, the council meeting at five, the Legion at four…that gives you, even after this morning's exercises and the meeting, nearly five hours?" Cai suggested.

"That's perfect, thanks, Cai," I said with a pleased smile, and Thomas shook his head in amazement.

"Also, Jax, you need to speak with Mal's father and Lord Hannimish; do you want me to arrange a meeting?"

"Fuck, no, bring them along tonight, I'll swear everyone in; we'll make it all impressive and shit, then I'll talk to them, I guess."

Cai blinked. "I recommend not. Make it tomorrow when you have sobered up. Speak to them tonight and invite them to the ceremony, yes, but don't have the official meeting yet…"

"Seriously, dude, you're like Siri and Alexa rolled into one, not to mention the added functions of Geneva, and all while smiling. Can you sing, too?" Thomas asked Cai, grinning at his look of confusion.

"I can sing, Thomas, but…"

"No!" Augustus said quickly. "Please, Cai, for the love of the Gods, no. Thomas…Cai is a Panthera, his voice…singing…please never ever ask for that…it's *memorable*."

"Isabella enjoys my singing," Cai said, sounding wounded.

"I'm sure she does, but unless you want the Legion to come running expecting someone being butchered, please, don't do it outside of your quarters." Augustus smiled wryly.

"Okay…" I said looking from Cai to Augustus to Thomas and back, before shrugging. "Well, I've got shit to do, who's coming this way?" I gestured to the passage that led off to the cathedral.

"I will," Thomas said, and Oracle took my hand, even as Cai and the others made their goodbyes.

"Am I permitted to roam the Tower?" Lucian asked. "I can retreat to my quarters until you introduce me, if you wish…"

"Hell no," I said. "Lucian, you can go where you want; you don't need to hide out or avoid people. In fact, Augustus, can you take him to the Legion armorers and tailors, explain his position, and make sure he's given any repairs and fresh gear he needs. And, for the love of the Gods, again, explain the *truth* of what happened. I want that to have a chance to get around before tonight. You being seen to accept Lucian will help that massively."

"Of course, Jax, and you're more than welcome to walk with me, Justicar Lucian," Augustus said.

I nodded to them as Lucian thanked us both, and we all went our separate ways.

CHAPTER FOUR

Oracle, Thomas, and I walked across the main entry area, passing the massive staircase that led upwards in the middle of the area. We headed for one of the corridors that lead off it, directly back and to the right, angling behind the stairwell.

As we walked, we spoke of little details, of daft things and memories, like the castles in our own home world.

"Man, I thought their walls were insane…you remember that time we tried to walk the whole of Hadrian's Wall in a day?" Thomas said, and I laughed, shaking my head.

"What's that?" Oracle asked.

"It's a wall, literally a big wall that runs from one coast, where we used to live, to the next. It was built by the Romans, who were a sort of equivalent of the Legion, I guess? Anyway, they built a wall from east to west across the country to stop the Scots coming south. They basically met the Scots and gave up on trying to conquer them."

"They were that fierce?"

"The Roman Empire had conquered most of the known world by then. I mean, in comparison, size-wise, imagine that the Empire had conquered all of the continent here, then they reach this section of the far north. It's cold, it's wet, and the people are just insane.

"You send Legions up to conquer the area, you know damn well there's not that many people living there, and a week later, the locals are all walking around with your missing Legion's gear on, telling you to your face they don't know what you're talking about." I shook my head, grinning.

"You send more and more. After a while, you just decide, 'you know what, we've conquered just under two million square miles, this last few hundred miles…let's just put up a wall and pretend it doesn't exist.'"

"It's like, about ninety miles long, the wall," Thomas added, smiling. "Or about that, anyway. We'd heard the record was sixteen hours to run it, and the average was five to six days to walk it, plus I'd met this girl that lived pretty much at the other end of it on a night out."

"So, he calls and tells her to make us some tea, as we were going to come see her, and me and him set off first thing in the morning thinking we can do what these professional runners do," I chimed in.

"Except it wasn't exactly first thing, either, because we decided to stop for a good breakfast, then the next two hours were us complaining about how full we were," Thomas added.

"Yeah, by the time we made it out of the city and onto the wall, we were knackered, and neither of us had prepared. We were both in jeans and a t-shirt, light jackets…man, we didn't even have a bag, a torch, nothing!

"A storm hit late in the night, we were totally lost, couldn't see anything, and ended up sleeping under a hedge and arguing over whose fault it was. Next morning, we found a little village, fully expecting it to be nearly at the end of the walk…"

"And instead we'd gotten turned around at some point, because huge sections of the wall have been lost, you know, nicked by farmers for building materials, or just collapsed and grown over so they look like small hills. We'd gone from the wall to what we thought was the next section…and had been following farmers' fields and so on for hours. We were about ten miles from Newcastle, where we'd set off. Soaked, clothes wrecked, and generally pissed at the world," I finished. "We went home, and Thomas got the train to her the next day."

"Claimed I'd walked it all, still managed to get her into bed," Thomas said wistfully, smiling. "What was her name again? Gemma?"

"Gods know." I shrugged. "She lasted, what…a week?"

"No idea, probably not even that, too much hassle."

Oracle smiled. "So, you tried to walk a distance you could have travelled easily, by this train thing, and got lost, all because you wanted to have sex, Thomas?"

Thomas nodded. "It was pretty much the driving force in my life at that point, Oracle."

"Well, we're here." I cut off the conversation as we walked in through the newly fitted main doors to the cathedral.

"You two really are twins, then; Jax is the same…" Oracle quipped.

I glared at her, getting a grin in return. "I'm not that bad," I muttered, looking away from the incredulous look she gave me.

The room was huge, round, and had a vaulted ceiling with nine alcoves spaced equidistant around the room. The entrance was at the six o'clock position in the room, and Jenae, my Goddess and the chief of the Pantheon of Flame, sat at the twelve o'clock position, with four on either side.

I gestured around the room, seeing that a few additional features had been added since I was in here last. While the magelights that climbed the walls bathed the room in light, the additional gold leaf and various donations to the Gods made it glitter even more.

There were seats, more like benches than anything else, but spread around, and even touches like rugs placed before each altar for the supplicants.

It was far from the kind of cathedral I was used to, especially in terms of the little touches and all the old wood, but what it lacked in material goods, it more than made up for in sincerity.

The huge room somehow absorbed the acoustics of my footsteps and the people in it, rather than making it echo the way it seemed like it should. I came to a halt before the Altar of Jenae.

I sank to one knee, closing my eyes and taking a deep breath before speaking softly.

"Jenae, I've had a little time to think, very little, but hey…and I wanted to thank you." My right knuckles pressed to the ground as I pushed my mana out, knowing it was going directly to Her, and that, being this close to Her altar and directing myself to Her, She would hear me, if She chose to, but didn't need to respond if She didn't want to.

"Thank you for everything, Jenae. I know we've had a few falling outs, a few arguments even, but you've saved my life, you've helped me when you can. Even when I've been, well, a bit of an arse, you still, you know, didn't smite me, I guess. Besides, you brought Thomas to me and helped me find the way through to free him. You advised me, and you told me when to pull my finger out, and when to calm the hell down. So, again, thank you."

"Thank you, Jax," Jenae whispered, Her voice echoing gently in my mind. *"That is both the sweetest and most heartfelt prayer I can remember. I have gained much from your help as well, my Champion, my ally. You have earned any aid I give you ten times over. So never fear, I am well pleased with the relationship."*

"Good." I smiled, opening my eyes and looking up at the Altar. "Because I think I should have some points to use for the Constellation by now?"

"Hah!" Jenae's voice was filled with mirth as She spoke. *"I should have known you were being too sweet! Yes, my Champion, you have enough to open either one more field in the first ring, such as Crafting or Governance or to continue in the Enhanced Construction area you have already begun to use. Or, of course, you could use the point on a complementary field then save your points and tier instead and unlock something from the Second Level of the Constellation of Secrets."*

I frowned, pulling the Constellation of Secrets up and looking at it. It was a complicated system, yet so simple as it appeared before me.

There was a single central sphere, like the sun, and glowing out in a ring around it were six stars, each pulsing gently.

"I already unlocked Mundane Construction, right?" I asked Jenae.

"You have, Jax. In all that occurred since you left the Prax, I had not thought to mention it. My apologies. I recommended you examine the Constellation several days ago, but never followed up on that. You unlocked Mundane Construction, and as such, all constructions made within your territory benefit from a five percent increase in their efficiency. While this doesn't seem like much, it is a surprisingly large difference, one that soon adds up, or will, once you construct more buildings."

"There's always a fucking catch," I muttered.

"Jax, you chose mundane. The Tower is anything but mundane, and the five percent increase in efficiency will make a huge difference. Honestly, have your people construct a logging camp or mines, and see what you gain. For others inside your territory, such gains have already become apparent."

"Really?" I asked, brow knitting in confusion.

"The Mer are already aware of the change. It may seem small, but when you are a village, food is carefully managed. To have food reserves you managed to raise increased by five percent, seemingly for nothing? They are very impressed, as are your farmers in their fields."

"Good point," I said, suddenly feeling much better about that choice. "So, I have enough to unlock any one area, or I could invest in opening up a section of the second ring,"

I groaned, looking at the details as they floated before me. I had no idea how much I had accumulated so far. I opened my mouth to ask, only to have the vision before me alter slightly. Now, in the bottom right of the map, there was a counter, and it showed some seventeen hundred and forty Marks of Favor I had available, along with thirty-four thousand mana.

"Okay, thank you, Jenae." I could clearly either save the details for the second Tier, despite having no clue what I would get there, or I could use the points on the first one. I thought carefully about the Marks and the mana.

At first, getting a single Mark for every two people I brought to Jenae had seemed like a little reward, then as I was bringing thousands to her worship, it became almost ridiculous, when the cost for the Marks of Favor to purchase the level was only five for the first tier.

But when I considered that each tier rose in cost by five times the one before. Tier six would cost me more than fifteen thousand Marks and thirty-one million plus points of mana. Looking at the fact that I couldn't keep bringing large numbers into the Empire forever. I mean, yeah, okay, if I conquered Himnel…*when* I conquered Himnel, that was tens of thousands of people. But once those Marks were used, they were gone. And to get them at all, I had to fight literal wars.

To get the mana was easier in that I simply had to have people pray to the Gods, or specifically to Jenae, but still…

I shifted around, moving to sit on the floor cross-legged, not even realizing as I did it, staring at the Constellation as I thought my way through it. I could afford to buy my way into three tier one areas…or I could save for tier two.

It'd be a few days, hell maybe a week for a tier two, but…the glasshouse was an awesome gift, and from what Jenae had said, I'd get a blueprint with each star I unlocked. The planets, or sub-specialties, not so much, but they would, in turn, come with their own bonuses.

I shook myself out of my thoughts and gazed at the stars. I had one lit, with its attending planet, and that was Enhanced Construction. Next to that was Magical Research, Crafting, Governance, Personal Enhancement, and Exploration.

No, as much as I wanted a tier two star, right now a few good improvements were better than one amazing one.

I needed better governance, I damn well knew that, especially with my plans for both the Tower and the territory from tonight, so I reached out and selected that first.

There was a long pause, then the dim red star that slowly rotated began to glimmer brighter. As the seconds passed, what started as a faint light erupted into a bright flame and grew. It changed quickly, stuttering and flickering at first, but swiftly going from red to yellow to blue and eventually to white, glowing with a bright, clean intensity, before sending a glow flaring to connect itself to the central star.

When the light reached the center of the constellation, that star brightened slightly, and it sent an answering flare of power out, one that flowed along the line connecting it to both Crafting and Personal Enhancement, giving them both a faint glimmer of life.

Once the Governance star was fully lit and stable, the first prompt popped up, filling my vision.

Empire Ascendant

Congratulations!

You have unlocked Governance from the Constellation of Secrets.

All aspects of governance for your population and lands will be improved by this selection, with bonuses and positive enhancements for your Empire being 5% more likely to come about.

You have gained access to the following specializations, which will unlock further options:

Population, Economy, and Law, and you have received a bonus rare blueprint.

Seat of Power:

The formal Seat of Power for your Government may now be constructed, granting a +5% morale boost to any of your population within ten miles, as well as a +10% to production and defense ratings.

(Note: Corruption indicator has now been introduced and will rise in direct accordance with any dips in morale.)

Construction materials required:
- 25 Steel Ingots
- 500 Copper Ingots
- 20 Glass Panels
- 10 Manastones (average or higher in size)
- 500 Units of Marble

Note: This structure is regarded as the physical Seat of your Power. Should it be captured, morale will drop by 75%, regardless of reason.

I read and re-read the description, trying to decide if this was a good thing or not. Yeah, okay there were unnamed boosts for generally everything by having a Government building, and morale was all good and everything…but…

I shook myself and moved on, hoping that the various aspects of the Governance selection would prove to be more worth it.

The star seemed to dim slightly, and three planets rose to circle the star, spaced equidistantly, and the first rose to my eye, making me frown as I watched it slowly spiraling.

The night side of the world lit up, roads and more being obvious as lines of light spread, and I realized what had thrown me about the planet.

It was covered in cities. Cities like I remembered from Earth.

I stared as the viewpoint fell farther and farther, and the differences quickly became obvious. This was a world that used every square inch. The cities were made up of skyscrapers and acropolises, huge single buildings that were tens of thousands of miles across with hundreds of billions living inside.

As I watched, the population grew and grew. At first, seeing the way it continued to expand, I was worried, expecting at any second to see the entire world spiral out of control, but…it didn't.

The people seemed happy, living in harmony, and healthy. There was no frantic rush, and all seemed to be at peace.

I waited, watching, and each time I saw the counter drop by deaths, more life entered the world to replace it. Everywhere I looked, it seemed that the population lived hand-in-hand with the world. There was no litter, no slums, as the people worked to rise as one, striving toward evolution and improvement, rather than stabbing each other in the back, as my own people would have done.

I nodded as I understood that Population, while it could be read as many different things as possible to different people, in the starscape, it equated to enabling the people of the Empire to *grow* together.

Once that realization came to me, I was drawn upward, into the sky as the world fell away beneath me.

The next world to spiral toward me was different again, yet similar. When the last world had been all about people moving up, this was about keeping things going and a degree of competition, it seemed. As I watched, Economy came into view.

This world was stunningly beautiful, dominated by a single City that sat astride the day and night as I fell inward to see it.

The streets teemed with people on both sides. People partied and danced on the night side and bartered and created on the day side, and I watched the honest love of the deal played out in a thousand little ways.

People created things…items, not for the need of survival, but for the pleasure of trade. Their culture, their world in fact, was built around the art of the deal, and people bartered, traded, and lied mercilessly about how wonderful their product was. I watched as lesser craftsmen were shamed but taken aside to be taught.

My first instinct was that, where the other worlds had been wonderful, this one was markedly less so, until I saw a failed craftsman, one whose work had been shoddy and who had been too prideful.

He was taken back into a hall, a hall filled with people who each worked, some silently, some laughing or singing softly to themselves. He was shown the wonders others were making, and he was given the chance to try again, rather than being put down. His work was gently mocked before being rebuilt with the aid of others who stepped forward.

The man was taught the value of his hard work, of pushing and reaching higher, of striving for perfection, and soon he stood tall again, holding up his little creation.

This time, when he showed it off, the people gasped and praised him. He bargained honestly, adding the failures and the successes up, and people loved him for it.

I shrugged, seeing the truth of the system, and recognizing that it was essentially a capitalist society, but one where the goal was the deal itself, not the accumulation of obscene wealth. People seemed to want each other to rise as well, as opposed to the stamping down of competition, these people welcomed it.

I nodded, learning a lesson there as well. Before I knew it, I was rising to the sky one last time, floating in the heavens, enjoying the silence of the space between worlds, as the third world spiraled toward me: Law.

I watched the World of Law rising, spiraling gently, and I waited, watching to see what a world dedicated to the rule of law would be, images of people in chains, or massive prisons springing to mind…

And I saw none of that.

I was more surprised than ever as the world resolved into view, it was clean, and pleasant, kids ran and played, people laughed and partied. I saw courts where people debated the law, but there was none of the stagnant society I remembered, with criminals laughing and escaping justice.

Instead, people seemed…content. There were fights and disagreements, but people stood up and were honest, they admitted their faults and were helped, rather than punished, in the main.

The root causes of the criminal activity were the subject of debates, but rather than politicians banging their chests, then getting campaign funding and doing sod all, decisions were agreed, then implemented with the aim of helping people.

Everyone was out to help each other, rather than stab them in the back, and I found I understood more about the nature of the law as a concept as I watched. In a perfect world, the law was to make sure everyone was safe and happy, and nobody was taken advantage of. In my own past, my experience of the law had been vastly different.

Where I'd grown up, the law wasn't really interested in helping people. The police cared, at least where I lived, despite a few bad ones that made the news and made everyone question the rest. But the law itself had been railroaded by lawyers to be a moneymaking scheme.

I knew deep down that what the law and the legal system was really interested in wasn't helping the victims or even punishing the guilty. There *should* be punishment, and if it was the guilty person, well, that was a bonus. But what the law I'd known was interested in *really*, at the bottom of it all was *fear*.

Fear stopped the innocent from becoming guilty by making sure they didn't run the risk of succumbing to temptation. Fear of losing the little they had, of having their personal freedoms taken away, of losing the little respect the others they perceived as good had for them. Fear stopped the average person from becoming the guilty one, and that kept the workload down and manageable.

The problem was when the fear lessened, then more and more people tipped the balance. The iron fist was exposed as a rusted glove when people broke the law and walked away with impunity.

That was where Tommy and I had come in. Not because we believed in the rule of law; I'd come to understand all this later in life, after losing Tommy. No, we'd come to bring balance to the force. We'd force-fed dealers their shit when they cut it with bath salts. We didn't care about them selling drugs, not our problem. We cared about them selling shit drugs that killed our friends.

We didn't care if people had fights and killed each other, as long as it was fair and the line wasn't crossed. Some guys had a fight, and it got out of hand, and someone died? Well, that's a shame and all, but shit happens.

Some scumbag breaks into a little old lady's house and beats her half to death to steal from her? Expect a visit. A very painful visit that had lifelong repercussions.

I grunted to myself as I watched the way the world worked below my feet, and came to understand more about the law, and why it was so…needed. Not everyone could deal with things, not everyone was, frankly, as much of a pair of bastards as we were. As such, they needed protection, people needed a set of rules, and it had to be more than my basic "Don't be a dick."

I nodded to myself, and the world fell away. As I spiraled upward into the air, coming to a halt back in myself again, I stared down at the glowing lights of the Constellation of Secrets.

I sighed and shifted, getting more comfortable as I checked the details I'd been given, seeing that I had two points to spend.

I could invest them both in this area. hell, I could invest them both in law, or neither, I could invest them into the Constellation of Secrets and unlock two totally separate areas, if I wanted…

That way, I'd probably get blueprints for two more things, either buildings or who knew what. I struggled with thinking about the potential benefits of each area, of investing two points in law or spreading them out, before realizing I was chasing my own godsdamn tail.

I shook myself and made a decision.

Yes, I *might* get a good bonus to the Tower if I selected Law or Magical Construction. But I *knew* I'd get a blueprint if I unlocked the star for another area, and that was more important at the minute, considering that the glasshouse we'd gotten last time was one of the most important buildings we could have gotten so far. The damn thing was going to feed us, after all.

I read over the remaining stars I could see: Magical Research, Crafting, Personal Enhancement, and Exploration. I debated asking Jenae for a clue, but shook my head. She'd not give me one, and if she did, it was the same as abdicating responsibility, anyway.

It was the same if I asked Oracle or the others their opinions with this, as well. At the end of the day, some decisions had to be made, and possibly fucked up, by the man in charge.

I looked over the four options again before smiling faintly to myself and reaching out, unlocking Personal Enhancement. It didn't mean personal as in me, but to each person.

At least, I damn well hoped so.

The telltale flare of fire leaped from the sun at the center of the map and rocketed across seemingly tens of thousands or even millions of miles of empty space, only to smash into the still, dead star rotating slowly on its axis.

There was a ripple as the fireball impacted, the dead star seeming to be liquid as the flames raced across the surface. The area behind the onrushing fire rose and fell like water after a stone was dropped into the depths. The outwards rush of flame looped all around the spinning form, vanishing from sight, then reappearing, racing back toward the impact point.

This time, it drew a line of fire with it, as the dead star ignited, glowing with life and building in intensity.

It was like watching the start of a new sun, a billion miles away, and knowing that, one day, my choices would result in a new star glimmering down from the night sky upon my Empire.

The seconds passed, the wave running around and around the world, returning to the beginning again and again, each lap making it shine brighter, until finally it stabilized, and settled into a steady red Dwarf, huge and powerful, granting life to the new worlds that flowed around it, worlds that seconds before had been dead lumps of coal, glowing with embers, yet now, suddenly were growing green and blue, red, white, and more.

The expected prompt popped up, and I let out a sigh of relief, reading it quickly.

Congratulations!

**You have unlocked Personal Enhancement
from the Constellation of Secrets.**

**Personal Enhancement is the art of improvement,
but rather than improving a crafting ability, or a community,
it is personal to the individual.**

**Through unlocking this tree, you have gained
five ranks to distribute across your skills.**

**You have gained access to the following specializations, which will unlock
further options: Mental Training, Physical Training and Skill Training.
You have also received a bonus legendary blueprint.**

The Imperial Academy:
The Imperial Academy was a singular school dedicated to the improvement of the future leaders of the Empire, be they military, magical, or skilled. All were welcomed and were taught in their way.

(Note: Because you already possess blueprints for the Training Grounds and a damaged Labyrinth, this blueprint has been altered by Jenae and Svetu working in harmony, to take both of these facilities into account, resulting in a single, mighty edifice that will require far greater construction materials.)

Construction materials required:
- 800 Steel Ingots
- 500 Orichalcum Ingots
- 280 Glass Panels
- 150 Manastones (average or higher in size)
- 1000 Units of Marble
- 250 Gold Ingots
- 15 Platinum Ingots
- 30 Golem Cores

Note: While this building is expensive, it is also extremely potent, resulting in a 15-50% decrease in training time for skills, magic and both physical and mental statistics when used correctly.

"Well fuck me with an inflatable chicken and call me Charlie."

CHAPTER FIVE

"What's up?" Thomas said.

I grunted at the interruption, having gotten up and moved out of the way, now leaning heavily against the wall. "I thought you were going to talk to Lagoush?"

He gave me a dismissive shrug. "I kinda did last night. Now I need some time to think, before…you know."

"Before you admit that you'd be dead if She hadn't helped you?"

Thomas glared at me. "I'd be fine if I hadn't helped *you*, you cocksucker. We still need to talk about that, and other things, like why the fuck you started a war with Nimon!"

"He's a dick," I said, shrugging.

Thomas' eyebrows shot up his forehead. "He's a fucking God you fucknut."

"Doesn't mean He's not a dick."

"Maybe not." He seemed to give the matter a moment of thought. "Also doesn't mean you have to pick a fight with Him."

"Go talk to Lagoush, you soft shite. I'm thinking." I aimed a dismissive wave in the direction of Her altar.

Thomas, bastard that he was, was not to be deterred so easily. "You just swore like something went wrong. What was it?"

I paused, weighing my options before deciding it didn't make any sense to hide it from him. "I got a blueprint for a training academy, one that'd make a hell of a difference in our…well, in everything we train. Physical, mental, the lot."

"And?" Thomas prompted.

"And it'll cost a fuck ton of everything. Like it even needs godsdamn golem cores. We could build…well…thirty golems for the cost of this place."

"Shit." Thomas' eyes widened in realization. "I'd rather have the thirty golems, personally."

"Then you're an idiot," came a voice from the side, and we both turned, seeing Mal standing there.

"Hey Mal." I smiled. "I knew I liked you for a good reason. Insulting my idiot brother is definitely up there."

"This academy," Mal asked. "Would it train skills as well?"

"Uh, give me a minute." I pulled up the details again. "It says it covers 'military, magical, and skilled.' Weird phrasing, that."

Mal scratched his chin. "So, you have a blueprint for a building that you could make, that's what, rare?"

"Uh…holy shit, it's *legendary*!" I said, having missed that on the first read-through.

"Fuck me." Mal shook his head. "Seriously, kid, if you don't believe anything else I tell you, believe this, that building is the most valuable thing you could make for us."

"Okay, not really a big fan of school myself, but I know we need one…"

"No, Jax," Mal said. "We don't need a 'school.' You said it's a legendary building, one that can speed up training of all kinds: magical, physical, and skills? Are you insane? Think about it! You could have the lunatics that Restun is punishing every day, the magical ones I mean, you could have them teaching the others in those classes. What kind of an increase do they get?" He asked, looking around to make sure nobody was close enough to hear.

"Ah, I saw it before," I mumbled, before stopping and staring at the notification.

"Well?" Thomas asked.

"Fifteen…" I said as Mal jerked violently around to stare at me in shock, seeming on the verge of having a heart attack, and I went on. "to fifty percent reduction in training time, when 'used correctly,' whatever that means."

"Probably that you need skilled teachers," Thomas said, watching Mal as he gaped at us both. "Are you going to be okay, dude?"

"Fifteen…at the minimum?" Mal whispered, before shaking his head and glaring at me. "Seriously, you need to stop and think! Speak to the Legion lunatics if you don't trust me; we *need* this! Fifteen percent reduction in training time for skill growth…Hell, think about your training with Restun, he's a Legion *master trainer*, right?"

"Yeah, wait, he'd count as a teacher. He'd count…"

"He'd count as the top-end trainer," Mal said. "As a master trainer, he'd be able to train you in half the time in that place. Think about it! Hours less training each day. Hell, if you're a sucker for punishment, you could fit in two or three more skill training sessions in the same amount of time, if you wanted to!"

"I wish…" I said, shaking my head.

"Why the hell not?" Mal looked like he might burst a vein. "I could have my crew trained up in half the godsdamned time! We could make the fleet into a damn lethal force, so come on, explain to me why the hell not!"

"Because we need a shit ton of supplies, Mal. Because not only do we need thirty golem cores–cores we don't have–we need two hundred and fifty ingots of solid gold and fifteen ingots of platinum, two hundred and eighty glass panels, a hundred and fifty more manastones, and…hell, we need practically everything!"

He grinned at me like an idiot. "Is that all? Tell you what, I solve this little problem for you, and I get my crew trained, for free…and as the absolute top priority, deal?" Mal smiled like a Cheshire cat. "And including them all learning magic, you know, healing and a fireball or some shit, and I'll tell you how to fix this."

"Fuck, no!" I said.

"Wait, what?" Mal's eyes flashed with ire. "Boy, we need this!"

"Aye, and you want to make sure you get everything you want out of it. You say 'we' need it, but you want me to pay for it. You know how to solve this? Fine, you want training? You'll get it. One problem though, Mal, you don't get to sit on the outside and include yourself in 'us' and 'we.' You're in or out, mate."

I met his gaze with flint in mine. "You know *me*. I'll make this happen, with or without your help. Hell, you'd make it easier, much easier, knowing how twisty your fucking brain is, but you either do it as one of us, you join up, and you take a commission or a role in the Empire, or you stay on the outside. I like you, mate, but you can't play both sides."

"I dropped everything for you!" Mal's face turned bright red. "I dropped everything, and I left Narkolt. I left my godsdamn father and everyone to bring you the Legion, to save your godsdamn life, and you say it's not enough?"

"No, Mal," I said calmly. He went even redder, his hand sliding to rest on the hilt of his magitech crossbow in its holster. "I'm saying it's not enough. I'm saying it's not enough to not be part of the Empire. I'm saying you need to stop fucking about on the outside, stop claiming to be independent and alone.

"Stop telling everyone that you're better than them because you're free to go where you want. Stop pretending to be one thing and fighting against me, trying to take my fucking eyes out of my sockets, then screwing yourself over to help me!"

"You little!" Mal snarled as he drew the crossbow, his hands shaking. "You don't know what I gave up, what I did…"

"No, I fucking don't, Mal!" I roared, rising to my full height. "I don't know because you haven't fucking told me! You don't come to the council meetings because you're a 'free man' and don't want to be burdened with that shit. Well, I've got news for you! I don't want to deal with it, either!" I stabbed him in the chest with one finger, driving him backward as I snarled out my words.

"I don't want to have to send people to their deaths. I don't want to sit on a fucking uncomfortable seat indoors hearing about plumbing problems, hearing how many tons of salt we need to preserve the meat, how many days of food we need, or the fucking complex equations that say if we can celebrate someone's life with a feast, after they died for me, when I know winter is coming and we need that food!"

"You think I don't care?" Mal whispered, his lips white with fury.

"No, Mal!" I shouted. "I know you care! I godsdamn well know you care, yet you still insist on being on the outside. I know you can help us, you can make all of this…" I gestured around at the Tower generally. "I know you can make this run better; hell, you're probably a better man for this job than I am! What boils my absolute fucking piss is that you're lying to us all, yourself included!"

"You're calling me a liar now!" The bolt of his crossbow came to rest against my groin as he stared into my eyes from a bare few centimeters away. "I'd be a mite careful about your next words, boy…might make a big difference to the rest of your life."

"You're a liar, and you're lying to yourself," I repeated. "You need to take a long fucking look in the mirror, Mal, and you need to decide what you want.

"You want to have your people trained? Fuck yes, I'll give them training, even that cock-holster, Jay. If you say he needs a fucking Demon summoning spell so he can get his own personal Succubus, then I'll get him one, because I know that you'll be asking for it for his best interest, and for your ships, and for the godsdamn Empire!

"What I don't know, Mal, is why the fuck everyone else but you knows that we can rely on you, but you keep fucking playing this game! I don't know what you gave up because you won't tell me shit. I never know if you're here or if you've fucked off already! I need you, Mal. The Empire needs you, and you damn well need us, and that scares the shit outta you!"

"I don't know why, but you need to godsdamn figure this shit out and either join me, and join me properly, let me give you the shit you need in exchange for being with us, or don't, and just fuck off, so at least I know where I stand!"

Mal and I stared daggers at each other for long seconds before he slammed his crossbow home in its holster and took a step back. I started to open my mouth, the air between us full of rage and regret. But before I could speak, he punched me in the face, then turned and walked away.

Legionnaires around the room, as well as citizens, reached for weapons before I waved them off, letting him storm from the room.

There was a long moment of pregnant silence before Oracle's healing spell hit me. I grimaced as my nose popped back into place, a wash of hot blood pouring free.

I held up one finger to Thomas. "Not a word, bro. Seriously." I wiped at my face before grunting and pulling my top off, wiping my face properly with it, scrubbing to soak up the last of the blood from my healed nose, then casting the new Scour spell on it.

The top was clean in seconds, with the blood seeming to break down into its component parts and become dust that blew away into the air. I sighed and pulled it back on before turning and facing Oracle and Thomas.

"I went too far," I admitted with a shrug.

"Uh, yeah." Thomas shook his head. "Dude, seriously, that guy dropped everything to come and get you. I spoke to him on the ship. When hardly anyone would speak to me, he did."

"I know, he's…fuck it." I lowered my head. "He's a good guy. He just boils my piss, and he's always out to fucking rip me off, you know? Any chance he can, he takes it all, then the next time I see him, he's dropped it all and came running to help."

"Sounds like a good friend," Thomas said quietly.

"Sounds like a fucking dick," I retorted, before letting out a breath. "*And* a good friend."

"What are you going to do?" Oracle asked.

"I need to finish what we came here to do then find him and speak to him."

"And if he leaves?" she pressed.

"Then he's left. If I chase him down now, as pissed as he is, he won't listen. I need to give him time to cool off." Even as I spoke, I knew it was a mistake.

"If he goes…" Thomas muttered, and I shook my head.

"I know. Fuck. Fine, I'll deal with this and fly up there, wait for him on his ship. It'll take him at least an hour to make it there, half an hour if he runs all the way, then get his crew together. I need to finish this," I said grimly, looking over my skills before doing what I'd been thinking of for a while and adding the five skill ranks into life magic, grunting as I gained a prompt.

Congratulations!

You have reached level 9 in Life Magic!

**All Life Magic spells you cast will now cost 9% less
and have 9% more effectiveness!**

I grimaced at how close I was to evolving the skill. Considering how often I got injured and how frequently I cast these spells, I really needed to level it faster, but the reality was that it took time to level an entire School of Magic. I sighed, sitting back down and pulling up the Constellation of Secrets, feeling Thomas grip my shoulder and squeeze it once in solidarity. He released me, then wandered off, presumably to speak to Lagoush.

Oracle shrank and sat on my shoulder, watching as the view shifted in the starscape, and we fell forward into the void of space.

The three planets arose again, and I plummeted in, watching as the world that represented Mental Training flew up, surrounding me.

The white fluffy clouds flew past, and I shifted, glancing to the side as something flashed past me, then another. Seconds passed until I was out of the clouds, and my jaw dropped in stunned amazement.

The flashes I'd seen were people flying, like I did with Soaring Majesty, but without the cost in health and mana. Instead, they'd simply developed to the point that gravity no longer applied to them.

Buildings of beautiful, airy design surrounded me, glass and steel reflecting the sun, gardens of green life and cool pools of water, as beautiful people flew around, alighting briefly to talk. With a gesture, they raised seats that dissolved into nothingness when no longer needed.

A rumble of thunder in the distance drew the eyes of the population, who banded together, each donating a seemingly tiny amount of mana into a mix that grew in terrible and magnificent complexity in seconds to form a hive mind, or consensus.

The needs of the natural world: water, the air pressure, all of it was assessed, and votes were tabulated, before the central mind dissolved. The people threw up personal shells, shields that stopped the rain, even as the thunderstorm grew, and everyone simply got on with their day.

I somehow knew that, had the decision gone the opposite way, the storm would have been unraveled, and the day would have remained sunny instead.

The people smiled and danced, summoned and cast, and they all seemed aware of me, nodding companionably to me, even as they left me to ponder the mysteries a world of mental development posed.

I examined the feelings and the knowledge sinking into me, and I realized that, should I choose this path, each investment of points would come with a slight increase in this area for my people.

More mages would rise, and magic would be that little bit easier for the citizens of the Empire.

I nodded in satisfaction, aware that I was barely touching on it. While there was more to be gained from this path, much more, that was the essence of it. As soon as I accepted that, I lifted into the air again, flying upward through the clouds, rising to see the next world floating serenely toward me.

Where the last world was a garden, a sprawling single metropolis filled with quiet places to think and research, the next world was vastly different.

As I neared it, thunderstorms rolled, typhoons and high pressure areas rose before me. Massive mountain ranges jutted into the dark sky, where figures struggled against the lack of oxygen, forcing themselves to put one foot before the other as they climbed on, determined to conquer the mountain.

Deep oceans lay beneath, where figures sat, regulating their breathing. The pressure of billions of gallons of water compressed them, making their bodies develop in new and interesting ways.

Huge armies raced across fields to clash into each other, weapons slamming into flesh, and explosions of power detonating underfoot. The 'dead' were dragged aside, healed, then they took time to watch and learn, training to be faster, to jump higher, and to resist the fight that tiny bit longer.

Pictures of physical perfection surrounded me: massive muscles, trim bodies, and perfect genetics. Nobody there wouldn't have won modelling contracts by the thousands on earth, and I shook myself in amazement as a thousand men and women dove into the sea naked, swimming for the love of the race and the joy of pushing themselves that tiny bit harder.

Oracle was taking lessons from the women, evaluating her forms against theirs from her spot on my shoulder. I reached up, patting her legs in reassurance, even as I deliberately ignored the men, all of whom were ridiculously well-built.

I squashed a touch of jealously and refused to compare them to me, as I accepted that a point or more here would grant my people a tiny, almost infinitesimal improvement in their physical potential.

This would unlock the facility to improve the Academy with pressure zones, somehow. Those areas would enable faster growth in stats for all those who made use of them, and I had to admit I was damn tempted.

If I invested in that, my people would be stronger, faster, and more as their physical stats grew. I was mainly tempted by the Constitution bonuses I could sense. Even a tiny bit more health could enable my people to live longer.

My feet left the ground, and I flew upward, severely tempted to do a Superman pose, stopping only when I reminded myself I was still physically sitting on a rug on the floor in the cathedral.

Once I passed through the upper atmosphere of the Physical world, I paused to watch the world of Skill approaching, intrigued by its potential.

A shining patch of the world resolved as it came closer until it passed into the night side of the planet. I stared as the lights that had covered it illuminated the world below.

I blinked as I tried to make sense of what I was seeing, until it suddenly clicked into place, and I grunted in amazement.

The shape I watched slowly moving in direct opposition to the clouds that streamed past was a floating city…hell, it had to be a floating *continent*!

It was a majestic sight, huge and imposing, yet it gave a sense of wonder as I flew in closer. Rather than being a huge edifice of rock and metal, blotting out the sky and probably being hated by those below, it seemed to bring life to the land as it passed. It generated its own water cycle, with rain falling from the underside to nourish deserts.

It brought light and life as it went, even as smaller craft left its bays, flying down and landing smoothly, disgorging golems that strode forward, eliminating creatures that arose from the dust and bringing the injured back to full health with ease.

It was a world at war, I realized, as I fell downwards, landing with a small puff of dust. As I turned, wondering at the conflict, I spotted a trio of figures in the distance, flying across the ground on wheels of bone, even as behind them, tens of thousands of bone minions arose.

I looked at them, my mouth going dry at the sheer *artistry* of the creations. They made my attempts with Bob look hideous and malformed, even as I wondered at the levels this trio of necromancers must have attained.

Their creations grew from literal dust, and I was stunned again as one was hit by a concentrated blast from the golem, blowing it into a thin film of dust that coated its fellows.

I took another look around, realizing that the entire world was being constantly reborn and destroyed by the opposing factions, the floating cities bringing new life even as the undead brought devastation.

The golems would destroy the undead to such a degree that all that was left was dust. Then, from the bone dust, new creations would arise.

I saw the potential of billions of undead, armed and armored with magic weapons, and siege engines of terrifying complexity and simplicity, magical and mundane, being countered by the creations of another group. Warriors fought in leather armor that was as flexible as silk, as breathable as cotton, and harder than adamantium. Their weapons could devastate continents, then the level of healing that was brought to save those same lands.

I saw it all in seconds before lifting away again, as I considered the changes such knowledge could bring to my people, the changes that Thorn alone could bring to the Empire's armorers, should she be gifted with the right experiences and training.

I visualized armor that was essentially a magically powered mech, striding through the battlefield and ignoring the blows sent against it. For a fraction of a second, the Pattern of Alchemy flashed before my mind's eye, and where the lesser patterns, such as poison, fit into it. Each piece brought complementary knowledge that made grandmasters look like ignorant fools.

I realized then, that while some had guessed and hinted that grandmaster was not the end of the journey, and that it was theoretically possible to climb higher, here, in this single glimpse, I understood that there were at least two more levels beyond that, the levels of Sage and Divinity, and a tiny hint that maybe even that was not all.

I blinked, finding myself sitting, watching the slow revolving of the stars again, and I shook myself wondering if I just looked like I was in a daze to the rest of the world as I did this.

With one final stretch, I focused on the final decision I would make for now. I paused, considering selecting one of the options I'd just been granted, and instead shook my head, determined to unlock each area and thereby know my true choices before accepting any of them.

I'd selected Enhanced Construction, Governance, and Personal Enhancement so far, and the mixture of Governance and Personal Enhancement had revealed a new star, one that sat dead and cold in the distance. When I focused on it, I received nothing. No hint, no name, and I grumbled under my breath as I chose between the remaining three options of Magical Research, Crafting, and Exploration.

I considered then dismissed the one that I figured I might actually see the least improvement from since Exploration would hopefully give me an exploration-themed building. I had no intention of doing any exploring in the short term beyond the local map markers.

That left me with Crafting and Magical Research. While both would be good, in theory, the Academy would provide somewhere to research, as well as teach subjects, and while it'd probably provide somewhere for the crafts, too, I figured I had a lot more crafters than I did potential magical researchers.

I selected Crafting and watched as the almost mundane fireball launched from the star and re-lit the gently glowing ball of charcoal that was Crafting.

Congratulations!

You have unlocked Crafting from the Constellation of Secrets.

**Crafting is as much art as science, and as such,
it speaks to all who wish to hear its voice.**

By awakening the Secrets of Crafting, you have granted those within your Empire that are sworn to you a 1% chance of making a breakthrough to a higher tier when they create an item using a blueprint.

**You have gained access to the following specializations,
which will unlock further options: Magical Crafting,
Non-Magical Crafting, and Consumable Crafting.
You have also received a bonus rare blueprint.**

The Crafter's Hall:
The Crafter's Hall grants a 5% increase in the chance to create an item of one level higher than the crafters current tier and reduces the chance of a failure by 5%.

Construction materials required:
- 200 Steel Ingots
- 100 Iron Ingots
- 22 Glass Panels
- 47 Units of Unformed Glass
- 100 Units of Stone/Wood

I stared at the slowly rotating worlds that spun around the Crafter's Sun, and I shook my head to clear it, allowing the Constellation of Secrets to vanish, unwilling to tempt myself any more than I already had, especially now that I could no longer afford anything.

I forced myself to my feet as Oracle lifted from my shoulder. Cracking my back and taking a deep breath, I moved stiffly toward the Altar of Lagoush, where Thomas was still kneeling, his lips moving in silent discussion.

I diverted, heading to the Altar of Tamat. Seeing it was empty of visible supplicants at least, I took the opportunity to speak to Her and Svetu before I went chasing after Mal.

I came to a halt before Tamat's Altar, trying to decide if I truly wanted to do this, before sighing and kneeling, closing my eyes and speaking to the Lady of Darkness.

"Tamat, Goddess of Darkness and Dark Deeds, are you there?" I asked.

A chuckle rumbled behind me, and someone blew in my ear, making me jump.

I spun around, seeing nobody, and growled as I knelt again, hearing the same chuckle before She spoke.

"My, my, so jumpy, Eternal. You need to learn to relax more." Tamat whispered, a tinge of humor coloring Her voice and absolutely no regret for scaring the shit out of me. ***"You might have a heart attack."***

"Only if you keep that shit up," I muttered, forcing a smile. *"I came for two reasons, Goddess. First, and most importantly, Bane. Your Champion went missing during the fight against the Dark Legion. I was badly injured and in no state to search, but is he alive?"* I asked plaintively, fearing the answer.

"He lives and he is well, although he is not close by. I sent him on a small detour for me, as it also serves your needs. Since you were protected, he agreed. I warn you, however, Eternal, I am not used to having to bargain with my Champions to get them to fulfill their Oaths. Should I need to continually do this, I may remove my grace from him, permanently."

"Oh, thank the Gods! Wait, you sent him on a mission for you?"

"Exactly! I sent him on a mission for me, and he tried to refuse! I had to convince him of the righteousness of my needs! This is unacceptable; had I more Knives ready, he may have received a demotion, the permanent kind," Tamat said sourly.

"And if you kill him or injure him in any way, Tamat, you'll have me as an enemy, remember that!" I snapped at her. *"He's my friend, and we agreed, he is first and foremost my bodyguard. For you to send him away has opened gaps in my defenses. Bob isn't ready to take over from him, not yet, and possibly not ever, despite the changes I made to his soul. You should have asked me!"*

"And you should remember your place mor—Eternal." Tamat retorted. ***"I am a Goddess, and—"***

"And you tried confrontation with me once, Tamat, how'd that work out for you?"

"You think to fight me, little one?" Tamat asked coldly. ***"You think that attacking me when I was wounded and freshly reawakened compares to when I'm ready and able? I would crush you like—"***

"I didn't attack you, Tamat. You started this, YOU! And now you've sent my bodyguard away when I damn well need him, despite the deal we made. What the hell are you playing at, and where the hell is Bane?"

"Since you ask so nicely, he's at Nimon's Citadel killing my brother's supporters," she said with a purr of amusement. ***"He's slaughtering our enemy's strongest supporters and strengthening me as he does it, so I suggest you reconsider your attitude towards me, little one. Each kill he makes in my name makes me stronger, makes our Pantheon stronger, and makes you less important to our efforts. I suggest you remember your place."***

With that, She was gone. I stood up, snarling and muttering under my breath. I stomped over to Svetu's Altar, taking a few seconds to calm myself as I knelt there. In a few minutes, I reached out to the Tinkerer God.

"Great Svetu, are you there?" I asked.

Nothing. I called out a second time, then finally got a distracted response.

"Hmm?" Svetu responded, halfheartedly.

"Svetu, Lord of Artificers and Crafters." I said, and He seemed to sigh in frustration before paying me more attention.

"What is it, lad?" He asked me bluntly. *"I be busy."*

"Ah, all right, fine. Look, mate, I've been busy, and I've not got to the site you wanted me to check out yet. Any details you can give me? And how long will it take to link the various areas once I claim that site? Also, you said you needed me to claim things from there; what am I getting? Do I just grab everything? Do I get to keep half for the Tower? I need some details," I replied, giving up and throwing careful discussions to the winds.

"Humph!" Svetu grunted. *"Gave you that quest days ago, was a time that'd have been a priority, when a God gives out a quest."*

"Yeah, yeah, like I said, I've been busy," I interrupted, all patience gone after my conversation with Tamat and how distracted Svetu was.

"Well, okay, fine," Svetu said, seemingly unoffended. *"It feels like Goblins in the outer halls. It's badly overrun, probably hundreds of the little bastards. As to the site, you may share the goods gathered, less the items I need. I am unsure as to what's still there, so I'll make the quest a general one."*

Congratulations!

You have discovered a new Quest: Rescue my Gear

The God Svetu has charged you with recovering items He and His chosen people require to construct their wonders. As these items are currently in a Goblin-infested pit, He recommends you kill the Goblins first.

Kill the Goblins: 0/?

Kill the Goblin Matriarch 0/?

Recovery of missing tools 0/?

Reward: A working Control Facility for the Great Tower and secondary links on each of your captured sites (requires further investment and construction), 100,000xp, Possible bonus facilities for the Great Tower

Accept: *Yes/No*

"Whoa, what's this 'requires further investment' bullshit?" I asked.

"I will provide the blueprints and the main facility on the Great Tower; you'll need to build the remote Towers on each facility yourself," Svetu grumbled. *"I've not got time to visit each one and build it for you. Provided the site is intact, it'll be simple. Just order the Control Center to make it as part of the site. They'll all have had one originally, so they should accept it fine."*

I started to swear, before choking my words off and hitting accept. I'd pretty much conned Ashante into making the deal that netted me this after all, rather than doing it the proper way. Frankly, drawing His attention to it was more risk than it needed to be.

I shook my head and decided to move on.

"Thank you, then, for your help, Great Svetu," I said as I accepted it. I got a grunt in return, then the sense of His presence was gone. With a harrumph of my own, I stood up and walked over to the next altar, taking a knee for what I hoped was to be the final time for now, at least. I reached out to Lagoush, kneeling side-by-side with my brother as he mumbled under his breath.

"Goddess Lagoush?" I called out, wondering if there'd be an issue with us both talking to Her at once, then shook that thought free as ridiculous. She was a bloody *Goddess* after all.

"Greetings, Jax," Lagoush answered calmly in my mind. I couldn't help but smile; there was something comforting about Lagoush's presence. **"What can I help you with?"**

"I needed to thank you," I said. *"If not for you, my brother and I would be dead. I don't know exactly what you did, but you saved him, and you gave me the time I needed when he came to my rescue. So, thank you, I guess?"*

"You're very welcome, Jax." Lagoush replied. **"In truth, I had not chosen a Champion because I had no need for one yet, and in all honesty, Thomas is not one that I would have chosen under normal circumstances. However, my choosing and raising of him enabled me to purge him of Nimon's remaining influence, not to mention, due to our enmity, making his Oath powerless to him."**

"You healed him and made him your Champion," I said, before taking a deep breath and going on. *"Sooo, I guess I owe you? Is there anything you need from me?"* I waited for the inevitable list of demands.

"Thank you Jax, but in all honesty, no. I have no needs. Perhaps, in the future, when you have grown more, and your Empire expands, I will ask a favor or two. But for now, I would simply ask that you continue to encourage Healers to come to my banner and perhaps you could take a new altar to the pod of Tia'Almer-atic you discovered in the nearby lake?" I nodded absently, already getting the feeling that this favor might end up as a thousand little "could you just do" jobs, rather than a single big one I could point to and declare "that's it, we're even."

It reminded me of getting blowjobs from my ex. Thousands of little requests and seemingly reasonable favors, all of which added up to a hundred or more times the effort she'd put in originally. Any time you tried to refuse, you were met with a look that said you were being rude and unreasonable.

Then I remembered the point of all this; this wasn't getting a blowjob. She'd literally burned through Her powers to save Thomas's life, and my own by extension, at a time when She barely knew me and needed that strength.

"Of course I will, Lagoush, and again, thank you. He's my brother, and if not for you, I'd have lost him," I admitted, suddenly feeling terrible that I'd thought of Lagoush in the same sentence as the manipulative creature I'd dated.

"Where will I get this altar?" I asked carefully, and Her power built as the altar before me began to glow.

It lit with an internal light, one that built slowly into a shimmer as condensation formed in the air before it. It started slowly as a mist, then droplets, then a rippling, roiling form of water, a twisting snake that flowed in and out, seeming to lose its shape and become stronger with each second that passed.

Less than thirty seconds later, the slithering serpent of water flowed down from the air, no longer looping around and upon itself.

Instead, it flowed downward as though poured from a jug into a mold. Splashing against the sides of an invisible form and deepening in color, growing green and blue, it took on the form of a single horn of coral patterned in greens and blues, with white striations running through it.

I reached out hesitantly and tapped it with one finger, finding it solid and cool to the touch. I nodded my appreciation, even as I recognized the same feeling emanating from it.

"Say, Lagoush?" I asked. *"One of the asshole Dark Legionnaires had a piece of your altar in his bag, right? That was how you managed to save Thomas?"*

"Yes. I, like all the Gods, am linked to my altars. I felt many such fragments spread across the Dark Legion forces, it seems they are viewed as trophies of some kind." Lagoush said grimly.

"Fine by me. After all, it means we managed to save Thomas." I paused, my mind whirling as I considered that the Dark Wankers might be carrying bits of these altars all over the place, and I tried to figure out a way to make them regret it. I couldn't see a way immediately, but a sense niggled away at me, a tiny sensation that I was missing something, and I decided to think about it when I had more time.

"Thank you again, Lagoush, for saving my brother," I said. *"I'll take the altar to the Mer on my way tomorrow."*

With that, Her presence withdrew. I stood, moving aside to give Thomas a few more minutes to speak to his new Goddess.

Oracle shifted, becoming full-sized and reached out, taking my hand in hers and smiling as I pulled her in for a hug.

We stood there for a few more minutes, talking about general details, pointing out the patterns in the walls that Seneschal was growing or repairing, enjoying each other's company for a little while before Thomas groaned, coming to his feet and looking around as he massaged his knee and back.

"Man, I'm too old for this shit," he muttered, walking over as he cracked his back, twisting it this way and that.

"Bollocks. You're just lazy," I told him, grinning.

"Listen, old man…"

"I'm literally minutes older than you!"

"Boys…perhaps you could argue later?" Oracle interrupted as we started on our standard sibling bickering. With a regal movement of one hand, she drew my attention to the figure who stood waiting, not wanting to interrupt.

"Thorn!" I greeted, the massive half-Orc smiling as I led the way over to her. "Thomas, this is Thornapple, best Legion Armorer in the business, and she runs the Tower forges."

"Thank you, Jax," Thorn said, smiling when I was done. "I heard you were headed this way, and I wanted to ask you to visit the forge when you got the chance…"

"Yeah, I need to sort some more armor. Sorry, Thorn, seriously, I'm trying. But, you know, magical weapons, fights with Gods and big fuckers, it just never lasts…"

"I know," she said. "Amongst the refugees, those you saved from the slavers, there was a master smith, I want your permission to hand the forge over to him, lord."

"What?" I asked, surprised and confused. "I thought you liked running it?"

"I do, but…look, there's a lot of bonuses from having a higher-ranked smith run a forge, rather than a lesser. I've spoken to Grenback; he's willing to do it, but…look, he's got some issues, and he doesn't know how long he's going to stay. He wants permission to run the forge to train us up. I want to make him master of the forge and take a position as his second, but he's not Legion…"

"And you need permission for that, and as it's my forge, *et cetera*. Okay," I said, nodding as I comprehended matters a little better now. "Tell him I'll talk to him about it, I…"

"If you could speak to him now, then we could get the bonuses straight away, and they'd be reflected in your armor," Thorn interrupted. "I've got the basic spares from the Narkolt Legion, and we've plenty of people. With his bonuses, we could literally double the learning speed of the trainees, which would mean much faster production of the basic armor for our forces."

"Really?" I said flatly, before shaking my head in irritation. "Fine, I'll be along soon."

Her smile was wide as she crashed her fist to chest in salute, then ran off in the direction of the forge.

I glanced at Oracle and Thomas, who shrugged before we all left the cathedral, marching outside.

"Right, bro, I need to go talk to Mal, stop him before he leaves, if that's what he's going to do. I'll probably be a few minutes. You can wait or do whatever you want; you don't have to hang out if you don't want to."

"Nah, I've nothing else to do." He flashed a bastard grin. "Besides, I like watching you get shit constantly. I'll wait."

"Asshole." I took a few steps away from him and cast my gaze upward, taking a deep breath and launching myself up. With that, I hurtled into the air as Oracle, shrunken down into her diminutive size, whooped and cheered, pressed flat against my chest as we rocketed upward.

It took almost no time at all to reach the twenty-sixth floor, the vast open arch in the side of the Tower marking the entrance and exit for the airships to dock. Thankfully, I reached it before Mal could leave, flipping over and blasting inside, landing on the deck of his ship and skidding to a halt a few feet from him as he snapped orders at people.

"What the…what the hell do you want, boy?"

I bit back my instinctive response, instead catching my breath and looking at him calmly, even as Oracle hit me with a heal to replace the lost health.

"I want to talk to you, Mal…"

"Really? Seems you said everythin' you needed to, to me b…"

"And to apologize." I finished, making him stop. He looked at me, and I held one hand up in supplication. "Seriously, Mal, can we just sit and talk, no egos, just explain this?"

He paused, his gaze flicking over to the captain's cabin, then to me, then back over the ship. "Fine," he said, gesturing to the cabin. "But it be your ego that's causing the issues. I ain't got one."

Even Soween, who was standing by his side, twisted around to look at him after that comment. He flicked a glance to her out of the corner of his eye before growling and gesturing again at the cabin.

I walked in ahead of him, and he followed me, tugging the door shut behind him to exclude Soween, who seemed surprised, and doubly so when Oracle slipped out to talk to her, leaving Mal and me alone.

"Well?" he said flatly.

"Mal…I'm sorry," I said, letting out a sigh. "Seriously, I am. Look, since we met, you've helped me out a shit ton. You really have. You've gone above and beyond, again and again…and so maybe I misread this when I thought that you wanted more than to be a mercenary captain."

"A merc…what?" His eyebrows shot up.

"Let me finish, mate." I shoved some dirty clothes off a seat and sat down.

He stomped to the cupboard and cracked it open, pouring a good dash of something into two glasses. As he passed me one, he sat down on the other side of what looked to be, under the piles of dirty clothes and random trinkets, the ship's map table.

"Go on then. I ain't stoppin' you," he said, taking a swig.

I did the same, and practically coughed a lung up, as whatever the hell was in the glass did the flavor equivalent of washing a flamethrower down my throat and punching me in the balls at the same time, combined with a feeling that suggested that Taco Bell and my ass were not simpatico.

"Wha…Jesu…hell…" I groaned, shaking my head and staring at him in shock as he calmly sipped the vile concoction.

"You got two minutes, boy," was all he said.

I growled, gritting my teeth and soldiering on.

"Right…look, you act like a mercenary, okay?" All pretense at being nice was washed away by the flames that were licking both ends right then. "You say it like all you're interested in is the money, and if that's the case of it, then that's fine. I'll pay you well for your help.

"But the things you do, the way you do them, fuck Mal, seriously, you don't act like it! You're either a great friend, an asshole, or a mercenary who's setting me up to be robbed blind, and so help me, I really don't know which it is. Just tell me, and let me know," I said, shaking my head.

Mal colored at the idea. "I dropped everything to come help you!"

"Mal, thank you, man. Seriously, I didn't ask you to, and I want to know that I can count on you. You say that you want to be an 'independent contractor,' and that you don't want to join the Empire, then you act totally different. You know damn well that Nimon…"

A rumble of thunder interrupted as I mentioned his name, and I glared at the porthole, sticking two fingers up at the clouds in the distance, then muttered a quick "fuck you, dickbag" before going on.

"You know the Dark Wanker isn't going to accept that. Hell, you literally saved my life from him and his people killing me. If you're *not* with the Empire, then you're all alone out there. Seriously, dude, join me, please! Take the Oath. Hell, take a rank; you want to be outside the chain of command? You've got it; you'll answer only to Flux and me."

"Why Flux?" Mal asked quickly. "I've met him like…once."

"He's my master of spies," I said. "He's in charge of all the sneaky underhanded shit I've got planned. Training assassins, the works."

"What do I get out of it?" Mal asked after a long minute.

"What do you want?"

"Gol…"

"And don't say fucking gold!" I snapped, cutting him off. "We both know you've probably got more gold in this ship than you have godsdamn wood!"

"Fine. What you got, then?" Mal asked grudgingly.

"Magic," I said. "Magic and gear, a cause, and a home." He said nothing, watching me for long seconds as I went on. "Mal, you want to be part of this, please tell me I'm not wrong. Every godsdamn instinct I have says I can trust you, even if I want nothing more than to punch you in the face at times."

"Might be true," Mal said grudgingly.

"Then you know, just like I do, that we're the little guys here, facing off against the world. Thing is though, Mal, there's not as many of them as it seems. If we take out the head, the body dies."

"Tell me plain; what's the plan?" Mal asked.

I shrugged, a grin spreading across my face. "Fine. I'm going to conquer the world."

"And then?"

"And then? What, conquering the world isn't enough?" I grinned. "Then we'll bring in real laws, rules like no more wankers in the nobility shitting on everyone."

"Seems a mite simple to be a good law," Mal said slowly, sipping his drink again.

I let out a good-natured snort. "Yeah, well, maybe it doesn't need to be complicated. If everyone is living for the good of the Empire and helping each other, maybe we don't need complicated laws and loopholes. Maybe we just need a simple few…"

"Like don't be a dick." Mal said, grunting. "Fine, I'll think about it."

"That's all I ask, Mal, seriously. Look…today, four o'clock, I've a meeting with the Legion. Five is with the council, then six we're having a ceremony outside to celebrate the lives of those we lost and to welcome everyone to the Tower. I'd like you to attend them all, but it's up to you. It'll be in the council chambers."

"Fine, ain't got much better to do." Mal shrugged, watching me as I stood and strode to the door.

I paused before opening it and gave Mal a hard stare. "Were you really going to leave?"

He shrugged again, saluting me with his glass. "We can talk about my pay later. I'm thinking it's time the nobility of the land was reconsidered. Maybe adding a new one into the mix would be the right idea."

I pulled the door open and spoke over my shoulder.

"Reeve Mal the Sheepshagger does have a good ring to it," I called, his growled oath cut off as the door banged shut behind me.

"So, all sorted, then?" Soween asked.

I smiled. "I think so, but you know Mal."

"I do, sir, and because I know him, I know he's listening at the door now," Soween said calmly, before Mal shouted from the other side of the door.

"No, I'm not. Dammit, Soween!" Mal snarled, his heavy footfalls stomping away and kicking something inside the room.

"So, how did he manage to make that room into such a mess in what? A week?" I asked.

"Nearly two now, sir, since we liberated the *Falcon*. But yes, it's…impressive."

"Yeah, seems like it. Anyway, if you can get Mal to the meetings on time, four for the legion, five o'clock in the council chambers, then six outside for the ceremony tonight, I'd appreciate it." She nodded as Oracle and I stepped up to the edge of the railing.

"He'll be there, sir."

I smiled at her as Oracle and I jetted up and out, spiraling into the clear air, flipping over and diving back down. We shouted in the pure joy of flight before flipping over again and slamming to a perfect three-point landing just beyond Thomas, making him swear and jump back.

"Holyshitfuckonabiscuit!" he yelped, reaching for his sword, then kicking dirt at me.

I grinned in his face. "Seriously, man, you can't fly yet? What were you doing all this time?" I shook my head in mock commiseration before pointing across to the small forge that was literally growing upwards from the ground slowly as we arrived.

"Time to go play in the forge!"

CHAPTER SIX

The forge had been a divine gift from Jenae, clearly Demonstrating that She was growing in power again. As we neared, hammers thudded; metal and leather creaked as it was twisted and shaped. The thousand and one smells, tastes in the air, and vibrations through the floor identified this as a place where people worked metal into new forms.

One peculiar smell rose in intensity as I closed the distance, part burned steel, coal, and wood, plus the multitude of sweaty, massive figures, and part sheer determination to *achieve*.

As we turned the corner, rounding the edge of the small building, we entered an open area in the middle, a massive forge already glowing with bright flames and gleaming steel, as two men steadily worked the bellows, keeping the flames steady.

I walked forward, admiring the layout of the forge, even as it slowly grew. It had a central area, clearly intended to revolve around a huge forge that could be accessed from all areas.

There were bellows getting attached in various places around the outside of the giant forge, built into it with chains that led to them, permitting someone to stand and pull on the chains, steadily raising the temperature in a particular area of the forge.

I stopped and stood there with Oracle and Thomas, watching with rapt attention as three men rushed around, two working hard to maintain a set temperature around the entire forge. The other man dripped sweat as he frantically tried to get the area he was working on hot enough for the Dwarf who stood next to him, showing him the correct way to work the bellows.

Around the ring of the forge itself were a dozen small stations and one large one, with sections clearly delineated by slowly rising walls that would eventually provide extra rooms, storehouses, and more.

I nodded as I walked, glancing over them in satisfaction before coming to a halt just inside the ring of the forge's heat.

The Dwarf turned, raising one eyebrow at me then turning back and giving instructions to the man behind him.

He pivoted back towards me. "Ah be Grenback, Master Smith, ah take it yer be Lord Jax?" he asked. I nodded, noting the lack of any deference from the Dwarf, and the lack of a string of Oath-sworn loyalty between us as well.

"I'm Jax, High Lord of Dravith," I confirmed, then cast about the forge, spotting Thorn eventually at the very back of the room, working with the apprentices.

"Good ta meet ya, lad," the Dwarf said, following my line of sight and nodding to himself. He gestured to one side, where a pot of hot water was boiling. "Perhaps we should have a drink and a wee chat, eh?"

I nodded, the three of us following him over. It didn't take long for the water to boil, and to my surprise, Grenback made the coffee himself, pulling cups and even milk from his bag and passing them around. Then, he gestured to the wide mat that covered the ground in place of chairs to one side.

"Let's sit and discuss things. Ah have a feelin' ah know why yer here."

"Really," I said carefully, mirroring his movements as I sat.

"Aye, considerin' ah told tha' Thorn lassie less than an hour ago ah'd no' be takin' over the forge wi oot yer approval, then she goes missin', comes back all smiles, then you arrive? Aye, Ah'm bettin' ah've been set up." He smiled then sipped from his cup.

I nodded slowly, taking a sip of my coffee and grimacing before putting it aside. It was Gods awful.

"Yes and no," I said. "I bumped into Thorn, and she asked me to talk to you. Plus, I needed to come and see how my order for an upgraded suit of armor was coming along, as well as to make sure that Thomas—this is my brother, Thomas and my companion, Oracle—I wanted to make sure that Thomas and my team all had suitable armor for the next mission leaving tomorrow."

"Hmm, goin' ta be a fun one, then," Grenback said, forcing a smile even as he put his coffee cup aside. "First of all, do this be an Imperial Forge or a Legion one?"

I blinked. "What do you mean?"

"Literally tha'. Ya be the new High Lord of the Continent, an' ya be tha Scion of tha Empire, right? Master of us all?"

"I try not to be a dick about it, but yes."

"Fine. So, is this forge tha property of tha Empire, tha property o' tha Legion, or somethin' in between?" He smiled patiently. "It cannae be all o' them."

"Why not?"

"Because yer have a journeyman armorer there who was running this forge when Ah arrived," Grenback said, pointing in Thorn's general direction. "Now, if this be a Legion forge, tha's fine. She be one of tha highest legionnaires here. And while tha Armorer from Narkolt, Mashin, Ah think his name is, be a wee bit more experienced than she is, it were her forge. She set it up an' was here when he arrived. So, even if they be the same Legion rank, he'd have at least had ta be polite to her. Tha issue here is that Ah'm no legionnaire, an' Ah'm a master smith."

"Go on," I said with a raised eyebrow.

"Yer have a journeyman, an' a journeyman, tha' be tha maximum they each ever reached, because they be held back by tha limitations of tha Legion," Grenback said bluntly. "They be ordered ta make tha same damn thing over an' over again. Once ye' done tha' enough, yer starts to lose the experience from it. That happens in tha apprentice ranks, so by tha time they be reachin' journeyman, that be as high as they were reasonably expectin' ta' reach. Ever."

I gave a slow nod. "And where did you come from if you're a master smith and not a legionnaire?

He flashed a genuine smile. "Ach, laddie, it be a wee tale, and one for a time when we're no drinkin' this muck, but suffice ta say ah lost ma forge. Ah lost everythin', monster attack, ye ken?"

I nodded that I understood.

His smile vanished. "It were aboot six months back. Ma village be doon south, aboot two hun'red miles south by west o' Narkolt. Wee shite place, but ah were happy. Monster did all o' that in. Lost ma wife, ma wee babies, ah were ready ta end it all, 'til ah were asked ta help tha survivors get ta somewhere safe.

Ah helped, figurin' ah'd just kill masel' when they be safe. No rush, nearly made it ta Narkolt. Took a few weeks, but six o' us were still alive, then bang. Damn slavers." He spat on the floor, then sipped the coffee and grimaced again before setting his cup aside as well.

"Ah were rescued by yer people when yer raided tha slave camp, an' ah thank ye fer tha', truly laddie, thank ye from tha bottom o' ma heart. Ah did'na want ta be a slave fer ever.

"Ah ended up on tha ship, then here, wandered in a daze for a day or two, no really sure wha' ta do. Nearly ended it all a time or two on the ship on the way here, ye ken? Just stood at the railin, thinkin' aboot ma wife and ma wee babies."

He sat still for a long minute, staring at nothing before going on.

"As ah say, found tha forge, an' tha state it were in, an' ah just started helpin', showin' a wee laddie how ta hold his hammer, that sort o' thing." He shrugged, then looked at me. "This be tha heart o' tha matter, laddie. Ye be tha lord, an' ah accept yer authority an' all, please do understand tha', because ah've no interest in tha headsman, nor tha prison, but also…ah've fuck all ta live fer, yer understan' tha'?"

I nodded. "What you're saying is that you don't particularly want to die or be locked up, but you've lost everything and don't really give a fuck beyond that?" I pulled out a small bag of coffee beans and passed them to him. He took them, sniffed the bag, and smiled cautiously before pulling out a new set of coffee grinders from his pouch.

"Aye laddie, tha' be it, but this…this be more like it!" he said, carefully examining the coffee and sorting it into a small cylinder.

"So, you found the forge, which as you can see is still growing, and you just, what…took over?" I asked gesturing for him to go on.

"Aye, laddie. Well, ah started makin' wee suggestions. Thing is, journeyman smiths, as yer have, might be amazin' lads an' lassies when it comes ta that one thing tha' they be used to, but tha overall bonuses that tha forge gets from them? It be low. A master, on tha other hand, now ah can bring real improvements. Do ye know how tha ranks work, ma Lord?"

"Not really." I said, watching him and trying to decide what was going on here.

"Reet. Simple thing ta explain, then." He pulled out a sheet of paper and a pencil, drawing quickly across one side of the paper and making small marks, then up the other side, adding quick markings up to seven. "Startin' here," he said on the bottom line. "We be havin' novice, apprentice, journeyman, expert, lord, master, and grandmaster. And on the other side, we've got five, ten, twenty-five, fifty, a hun'red, an' two hun'red." He drew a line from the bottom of the paper upwards diagonally across the sheet, showing a simple graph.

"Now, this do be for both quality and experience, dinna get me wrong. It be no exact, but it be an average. So, yer journeymen smiths, if they be in charge o' tha smithy, they be grantin' a ten percent bonus ta any quality and tha speed o' learnin' fer them that's below them. Ah, on tha other hand, give a hun'red." He looked at me from under bushy eyebrows, waiting to make sure I understood before pouring the coffee out.

I nodded and took the coffee before going back to watching him.

"What this means, ma Lord, is that because o' ma experience, ma skills, and ma love o' tha craft, ah can bring a hun'red percent improvement ta yer smithy, both in terms of learnin' speed and quality o' tha work that comes oot. It's no' exact, as there be a chance for a master smith ta make shite, and a journeyman ta make a grandmaster item. There's always tha chance, it just be, well, fuck all really. A master smith'd melt that shite down, an' a journeyman who'd made a grandmaster item, well, they'd be leapin' up tha ranks anyway."

"So, Thorn seems to want you to take over the forge, and it kinda looks like you need this project as much as they need you?" I asked, getting a little laugh from him.

"Aye, when Thorn saw what ah was, well, she's been on at me since. Look, ah'll make it simple. Ah do no want ta be here, no as in 'here' in tha forge, ah mean alive. Ah got nowt ta live fer. Only two things in ma life were ma family an' ma work. Ah neglected ma family, chasing bein' a master, an' now all ah've got is tha work. Ah stood on tha edge, watching tha ship lift into tha air an' ah waited, ah decided ta wait until there be no one doon there, no need ta hurt someone else when ah jumped, am ah right?" He stared at his hand as he scratched a scab free, flicking it aside.

"Then it were forests, an' ah did no want to end up smashin' up a tree an' surviving,' so ah decided ta wait again. Then there were sea, an' ah be afraid o' drownin'." He sighed and shook his head. "Ah be afraid o' dyin,' laddie," he mumbled. "Ah do no want ta go on, but ah do no want ta die, neither. Ah ended up hidin' on tha ship, we landed here, and ah just…ah wandered aboot, ain't nobody told me ta go nowhere or do nothin,' so when ah heard tha forge hammers singin,' ah decided ta come help." At that, he looked up from the scab on his hand and shrugged self-consciously.

"Ah could'ne just ignore tha call o' the forge, ye ken? An' seein' what they be doin'? Ah can give up a wee bit o' ma time, 'til ah build up tha courage ta be wit ma family, by helpin' ta get yer smiths trained."

"I think that Thorn and the others would like that very much," I said softly, watching the Dwarf as he stared at his coffee cup.

"Aye well…mebbie it be wha' ah need, more'n it be whut they need," Grenback said, sniffing and wiping his nose before looking at me through red-rimmed eyes, clearing his throat roughly. "But ah'm no doing shit fer free…"

"Oh?" I asked, smiling.

"Aye, now ah know yer got real coffee, Ah'm no puttin' up wit' this shite." He gestured to the pot that was sat boiling away at the edge of the coals. "Ah need real coffee, an' Thorn said somethin' aboot ye givin' 'er a challenge? A quest?"

I smiled and nodded.

"Yes, mate, I have a challenge for you. Not sure if I can make it a formal quest, though."

"Ach, just inject mana into tha words as ye speak, iffin it be heartfelt enough. It works on occasion." He smiled.

"Fine. Make me armor," I said, focusing and pushing my mana out at the same time as I said the words.

Congratulations!

You have given: Master Smith Grenback and his team a scalable Quest!

Create the next generation of Legion Equipment!
The Imperial Legion has moved on, growing in need and in its collection of enemies, yet losing more than 90% of its forces, supplies, and capabilities. Today is a new dawn for the Imperial Legions, and as such, it needs to be recognized with a more appropriate set of equipment!

Create blueprints and prototypes for:

Armor:

> **Standard Armor:** 0/1
> **Legionnaire Armor:** 0/1
> **Scout Armor:** 0/1
> **Mage Armor:** 0/1
> **Praetorian Guard Armor**: 0/1

Weapons:

> **Standard Weapons Set:** 0/1
> **Legionnaire Weapons Set:** 0/1
> **Scout Weapons Set:** 0/1
> **Mage Weapons Set:** 0/1
> **Praetorian Guard Weapons Set:** 0/1

Rewards: 100,000xp for completion of the entire quest, 10 Platinum Coins, ???

Do you accept? *Yes/No*

I looked the notification over, smiling as I somehow knew that, while the first bit was for my eyes only, the rest was what he and his new team would see.

There was a long pause as they looked it over, and I wondered at the silence, not to mention how detailed it was, when all I'd said was "make me armor."

"It's a bit complicated to explain," Oracle said. "But it's the way reality and the Gods work. It's never really been worth doing until the Tower was sorted out, as that experience has to come from somewhere and it's the mana being used from the Tower that's supplying it, and the money is from the treasury. Do you want me to explain more?"

I shook my head, even as I received notifications that the entire team were accepting my quest.

"Well, laddie, looks like ah've got ma work cut out fer me, then." His head wagged side to side in wonder. "That reward..."

"Is split between you all, with you doing the splitting," I said firmly. "I don't have enough platinum to pay you all that much individually!"

"Ha, ah was wondering!" He grinned. "No, yer said yer were comin' fer armor. Let's get that sorted, then ah'll get lookin' at what they been workin' on so far wit' this..." His voice trailed away to a mumble as Thorn stepped up and passed him some designs.

"Jax, I can help you with armor," she said as the others gathered around, grinning like fools and desperate to get us sorted and out of their way so they could get to the 'fun' jobs.

Twenty minutes later, we were being hustled out of the forge as they all fell in around Grenback, pointing out details and striking up a good-natured argument.

"Well, that was…strange," Thomas said as we walked back towards the main doors of the Tower. "I mean, I was half-expecting that you'd need to fight him or something. Instead, you gave him coffee?"

"That shit is worth more than gold, mate!" I said firmly.

"Na, still can't get away with it. All tastes the same to me, like ash and sourness." He smirked. "I mean, yeah, I'll drink it, but you know me. I'll drink anything."

"Man, I thought after all this shit, you'd have grown up."

That elicited a laugh. "Jax…weird calling you that again after all this time, but anyway…what's the next stop? Seems weird, all of this, do you just run from job to job all day?"

"Basically," I confirmed with a noncommittal gesture. "Since I got here, I've been running around like a blue-arsed fly. I've had no time to get things sorted and stable, so whenever I'm in the Tower, it's like everyone needs me for something. Then I go out, get fucked up, and well, bring back more problems. I get pestered to shit, then I go out again, and the cycle repeats."

"Sounds like a nightmare, but at least you've got a home," Thomas said wistfully.

"So do you now, you ugly bastard." I punched him in the shoulder. "What, you think you get to escape all of this?" I asked, seeing the look on his face.

"Well, no…I hadn't really thought about anything much, to be honest. After the last year, I've just kinda gotten into the habit of just surviving, and letting the brain free-wheel. After my time in the dungeon, well, you learn not to make plans, because shit happens, and they're all over before you can do anything."

"Well, what do you want to do?" I asked as we crossed the main floor and started up the stairs inside the Tower, headed for the glasshouse.

"I…I don't know," Thomas said slowly.

"Do you have any skills? I mean besides farting and wanking?"

"Sod off." He grinned back. "Well, yeah, sort of, but you're going to laugh…"

"Really? Oh, this is too good. Come on, gimmie."

Tommy looked a bit sheepish. "Tomb raider."

"What?! You took that as an actual class?"

"Nah, profession," Thomas said. "That and…well, herbalist and appraiser."

"Okay, explain this." I couldn't help but grin watching him. "Do you run around in short-shorts or what?"

"No, you asshole, see, I knew you'd go there!" Thomas grunted. "I spent a lot of time raiding tombs, and one day it offered me the profession, the realm, I mean. Probably because it was always me who was interested in the gems and the artifacts more than just hawking them for the first offer, I gained appraiser as well. It lets me evaluate the real value of something easier, while tomb raider helps me to spot things, like hidden doors and so on. Herbalist, well, because it meant I would occasionally spot shit I could sell." He shot an inscrutable look at me. "So, come on then, what did you choose?"

"Alchemist and trapmaker."

"Alchemist any good?" Tommy asked. "We both hated chemistry at school. Thought about trying it, but always thought it would be too expensive."

"Not really that expensive. I bartered for a basic set of gear before I left home. Wait, you know the gear from the Arena…what happened to the stuff you won?"

"I kept it," he said with a quick shrug. "Bag of holding on the first guy I killed, stuffed everything into it and kept it."

"From the people you killed directly, or the stuff they had?" I asked pointedly.

Tommy thought for a few seconds. "The…wait, you mean they had stuff they'd won?" Outrage knitted his brows.

"Yeah, man. Took some pointed requests in the open, but I got everything brought out before I went through the portal. Then I sold it back to the nobles. Man, that prick was pissed." I smiled as I remembered the look on the Baron's face.

"I bet…bring anything decent from home?"

"Few things. Not much that's really from home, though. I managed to find a whole chest full of paperbacks later on. Turns out there was a guy who wanted to read when he got here. I think Grizz still has them." With that, the conversation diverted into random jokes and discussions of people, places, and our histories since we'd last seen each other, making the hour-long walk to the glasshouse pass quickly.

Oracle, though she mostly left us to catch up, laughed and probably made mental notes of the things Thomas and I let slip in our efforts to wind each other up.

By the time we came out onto the glasshouse floor, a floor I'd passed through several times already, each time promising myself I'd visit later, it was almost as though we'd never been apart, and I felt more relaxed than I had in years.

The glasshouse floor was one of the last large ones before the Tower narrowed near its apex. As we walked onto the floor, it was obvious that it was a special area.

The circular staircase that wound around the outer ring of the Tower here exited onto a floor that seemed essentially a wall of glass with condensation running down it. The opposite stairwell ascended to my left, as the one I'd just exited lay to my right. But as our small group stepped forward, I stared up at the glass wall before me, feeling the warmth it gave off.

The doors were large, ten feet high easily, and at least six feet across, with a seal down the middle, letting them be opened wide or individually. As I opened the right hand one, I was met by a warm, humid breeze that made me sigh.

It was like I'd stepped out onto a tropical island.

We filed in and closed the door, feeling the pressure change as soon as the door closed, and we looked around, stunned. Row upon row of planters didn't greet me as I'd expected. Instead, it was a self-contained ecosystem.

When we walked in, we had to step up a short flight of stairs, before standing on a dirt path that led through what appeared to be a damn orchard.

We wandered aimlessly for a few minutes. Only the distant ceiling, almost obscured by an artificial sun, proved we were still inside, speaking in hushed tones as we explored.

There were dozens of rows of trees. The first were apple, or so it seemed to me. However, as we went farther in, we saw more and more different varieties.

There were cherries, rows of blackberries and grapes, then, as we finally stepped from behind the last tall row of grapevines, I came to a stop, gaping at the room beyond.

The Tower was about a third of a mile across at this level, or somewhere near that, being the sixteenth floor, but seeing the entire floor dedicated to a single, huge growing area was insane.

Sure, most farms were far bigger than a square mile, which this worked out roughly to. But seeing it was something else entirely, the hundred or more people who worked in here, and in the distance, the four towering forms of the tenders and guardians of the grove.

I pointed them out, hurrying in their direction as I explained the deal with them to Thomas, cursing as I realized that I'd not yet arranged the golem for the Arbuton yet.

It took a few minutes to reach the hundred-meter-square section that the tenders were working in, the guardians giving me distrustful looks as I approached.

"Woodite!" I called, recognizing one of the tall figures as he rose to his feet, carrying a small plant to the next row to begin planting.

"Lord Jax," he said amicably, looking up from his planting.

"How are you? You got here okay, then?" I asked, and he smiled.

"Yes, the guardians kept myself and…Hazel…safe on our travels. Once we explained our presence, we were greeted warmly." He gestured to the second grove tender, and it glided over smoothly, watching me and my small party as we looked it over. "This is Hazel, my mate," he introduced.

I smiled at her, noting the slight size differences and her greeting of a simple nod.

Where Woodite was bigger and slightly wider in the shoulder, she was slimmer in a way that spoke of steady strength and dependability. Woodite gave off an aura of excitability and curiosity about the realm and his place in it, while Hazel seemed more stable.

"Greetings, master of the Tower." Her voice was gravelly but somehow still gentle. "I am Ha'AnZel Lish'I'Ara, but you may refer to me as Hazel."

"Thank you, Hazel. I would never have managed to pronounce that without biting my tongue. So, you both made it here safe. How is the glasshouse, and the guardians…are you all settling in okay?"

"We have all we need, thank you. The soil is nutritious, and the light is pleasant. The water is full of compounds that aid growth, and our charges flourish here. I shall return to my work, if there is nothing else?" she asked.

I shook my head, a little nonplussed. "Thank you, Hazel," I said, and she gave me a single, abrupt nod before walking away again.

"Forgive my mate," Woodite said, smiling. "She is incredibly focused. We have estimated the time it will take to bring the Alchemical Grove to life, and she will not deviate from that timetable without need."

"That's fine." I pulled out the few dozen plants I had that were alive in the herbalist pouch. "I harvested these along the way; are they of use here?"

He sorted through the plants, quickly setting some aside and approving, while others he handed back before gesturing to a table at the far end of the work area.

"Your pouch is there, filled with as many alchemical ingredients as we could gather before setting off," Woodite said.

I inclined my head in thanks to him. "Is there anything you need from me?" He shook his head, making me smile as the logistics to feed everyone seemed the easiest and least trouble now. "Thank the Gods. Okay, I'll drop the golem off in the grove on my way past tomorrow, and I guess I'll leave you to it, Woodite, uh, tell me if you need anything, I guess.

"Or, better yet, tell Cai; he's in charge of the council here. Oh, and there'll be a ceremony tonight at sunset before the Tower. If you want to come, you'd be welcome." He nodded again, and the two grove guardians glared at me as I collected the alchemy supplies and walked past, leading my small group out of the glasshouse.

I explained more about Woodite and the grove to Thomas as we left, before heading up the Tower, stopping off finally with Esse and Tel, the herbalist and alchemist, respectively, three floors farther up.

The pair had apparently grown considerably closer than I'd realized, with a section of this floor being dedicated to a huge pool. Amoth, Esse's husband, I vaguely remembered was a farmer, but considering that Esse and Amoth were Mer, members of the same amphibious species as Bane, and far more at home in the water than on land, "farming" wasn't really what I'd thought of when I saw the huge pool.

It turned out the Esse primarily grew underwater herbs, and Amoth 'farmed' vast colonies of fish, while Tel had essentially set up his alchemy laboratory on this floor so that he could have ready access to both the small alchemy garden he was cultivating with Esse's help on the balcony outside, and the large number of underwater herbs she grew.

I smiled as I came to a halt on this floor, the windows removed and the central walls replaced with arches as much as possible, resulting in shadowy alcoves and bright, sunlit patches here and there.

The surface of the flowing pool rippled with currents and splashes, trees that grew up out of the water, and seemingly haphazard collections of boulders here and there, making me believe this would be a fisherman's dream to visit.

"Holy shit," Thomas muttered, gaping out over the specially constructed floor. I'd passed it before, since it'd been finished. But the hundreds of floors and the fact that, when I actually walked the Tower these days, rather than flying, I was usually not walking. In fact, I was sprinting and praying desperately for the heavens to open and the Gods to kill me to get me free of Restun's training schedules. So, while I'd seen it, briefly, I'd not really explored it.

I walked onto one of the small bridges, looking out over a scene of tranquility, ripples flowing across the surface of the pool, even as hundreds of fish flitted past underneath the glittering magelights.

The floor was divided into shallow and deeper pools, with bridges and paths crisscrossing the entire stretch, small seating areas and here and there what looked like actual fishing stops.

On the far side, there was a large space where the doors had been, opening out onto the balcony and the alchemical garden there, with Esse and Tel standing at a pair of large benches sorting through some plants. Another pair of people stood on either side of them, getting training in the basics of herbalism and alchemy.

My small party and I strolled across, coming to a halt next to the group and getting a stunned collection of bows and curtseys from them.

I waved it away and they stood. Within moments, I'd stepped in and gave the ingredients on the table a once-over.

"Is this…Moonwort?" I asked Esse, getting a pleased nod as I recognized it.

"Very good, Lord Jax! Yes, the Moonwort is growing well, and once this batch has been cleaned and the outer layers stripped, it will be ready to be worked with. Are you here for any particular crop?"

"No, in fact I'm here to go over some alchemy work and discuss a few discoveries I've made, and I wanted to introduce my brother, Thomas. He's a herbalist…"

"Novice," Thomas clarified quickly, looking over at Esse and holding his hands up defensively. "Believe me, I'm literally only at the basic stage, level nine…"

"Well, let's see if we can get you to ten today, then," Esse said with a *thrum*. Thomas looked confused, until I stepped in.

"I think Thomas has only met a few Mer before, Esse, so he might not have recognized your laughter for what it was."

Her tendrils lifted and flickered about in interest as she examined him using her sonar or worldsense, as they called it.

"I won't hold that against him," she said, the *thrum* of amusement going again. "Would you like to join us, Thomas?"

Tel was practically bouncing on his feet, ready to discuss the alchemy side of things.

"Uh, yeah, that'd be great! Jax…do you need me?"

"Tell you what, mate, we've got the meeting with the Legion at four. It's just after twelve, so how about we have three hours? Then we can head straight to that meeting. I want to introduce you to them, then the council and everyone else. So stick with me today, bro; tomorrow, your time's your own, okay?"

"Happy to have the company, to be honest, man," Thomas said before stepping over to Esse and smiling down at her. "So, what are we doing?" He gestured to the work she'd been busy with.

I turned toward where Tel and his two helpers waited patiently.

"Right, then, do you have somewhere set up for alchemy?" I asked with a smile. "If not, we need to make do for now, but I'll be dedicating a proper section of the hopefully soon-to-be-built crafter's hall to it."

"Ah, yeah, that'd be great. I've got a room set up, but a dedicated area would be good." Tel led the way to a small room off to one side. Beyond the three tables, the seats, and a tube that sucked the air out, keeping the room constantly clear of the sometimes-noxious fumes that alchemy created, it was remarkably bare.

"Right, we're going to work on this, but am I right in assuming that the other crafting disciplines are much the same as this? Bare bones, and that's it?" I asked, getting a nod from him. "Fuck, I've been so busy I've not had the chance to even see this."

Tel spoke up quickly. "Oh no, we're fine, my Lord, honestly! We don't want to be a bother…"

I ran my hand through my hair. "Yeah, of course you don't, but neither does anyone else. So everyone makes do, and we're stuck at bare-bones subsidiary level, rather than properly growing."

"Well…"

I waved a hand dismissively. "It's okay, it'll be a part of the meeting this afternoon. Anyway, these are…?" I asked, looking curiously at the pair who stood quietly listening.

"Oh!" Tel jumped, twisting and gesturing toward them both. "This is Aen." He pointed to a tall, thin man. "And Katheen." The second person was a tall elven woman who wore a sock or something over her hair, keeping it contained in a long sleeve of fabric.

"Welcome to alchemy then, I guess. Uh, gotta ask…" I gestured at her hair.

With a smile quirking at one corner of her mouth, Katheen pulled the sock-looking covering off, exposing bright red hair so vibrant it practically glowed.

"It's the best way to keep the smell out of my hair," she explained. "I soak the cloth in a mix overnight, then wear it through the day. It keeps my hair from knocking people out with the smell after a day's work!"

"Not a bad idea, to be fair." I remembered some of the noxious stenches that had escaped from my alchemy set since I got it.

"Well, thanks for explaining that, but I think we need to get comfortable, because we've got a lot to discuss, starting with the skills you're all going to need to be able to reach the next levels of alchemy. First, your book," I said to Tel, passing it over.

"Thank you!" He flipped the book open and skimmed excitedly through the pages until he saw I'd made notes of my own in there. Clearly pleased, he pocketed it to read later.

"Secondly, while I need to tell you a lot of things I've found, there's absolutely no point, if you can't use the skills I'm discussing, so…Oracle and I are going to be upgrading your skills with magic by teaching you the latest version of the Examine spell: Greater Examination as well as Organic Examination. Once you each have that, well, this is going to get complicated. I'm going to be giving you a specific mission to work on each day for me, on top of the usual things, but believe me, it'll be worth it!"

I stepped over to the doorway and looked out, seeing Oracle happily speeding around above the pools, one hand dangling down to occasionally touch the water, drawing the fish up to investigate as she zipped away, giggling. I waved her over, getting a wave in return as I turned and went back inside.

"One thing, guys…" I said, as a thought occurred to me. "It's not exactly warm in here. Hell, it's cool at best; what are you going to do come winter?" I gestured toward the huge doors that had been removed to allow a steady breeze to enter the floor.

"Well, yeah, that's going to be a problem," he agreed. "The Mer spend most of their time underwater, and the open breeze prevents stagnant water and suchlike. Esse tried to explain it to me, but it was a bit boring, so…"

"So, they need it to be open, but you're freezing your tits off in here?" I asked, getting nods all round. "Fine, as I say, I'm working on a crafting area, but for now…" I broke off as Oracle sailed in, a huge smile on her face as she landed.

"Hi everyone, sorry, I was playing with the fish." She beamed, not at all apologetic.

"No worries," I said with a grin of my own. "Okay everyone, let's sit on the floor for this. It'll be a hell of a lot easier on us all."

The connection was quicker and easier this time, or it was for me anyway, considering that I was acting as the start of the chain, and pushing my knowledge out to the others.

Oracle had grown an extra pair of arms, which thoroughly weirded me out, and she knelt between us, palm pressed to each of our heads. I could feel her presence in my mind as I focused on the spell, and pushed it out to her.

It was a peculiar sensation, especially as Oracle and I had grown closer. I could feel her rummaging around in my mind, concepts suddenly springing to the front, flashing past like I was watching a giant screen, and details flickering forward and back, some vanishing before they could amount to anything, while others were added to the mass I was sharing.

Minutes passed, then I felt Oracle's cool hand lift from my brow, and I opened my eyes, seeing hers were still closed, with a frown prominent on her face as she worked.

I looked to the others, seeing much the same expression on theirs as well, until one by one, they settled back as she lifted her hands away, blurring back into her fully humanoid form.

"You should all have access to the spells Greater Examination and Organic Examination now, is that right?" I asked and got a nod from all three. "That's great, because this is where it gets complicated, partially because I'm going to be talking about atoms, molecules, and subatomic particles, and mostly because I barely know more than you do about them." I rubbed the back of my neck, pulling out my spare bedroll from my pack and spreading it on the floor to make myself more comfortable.

"Okay, it's like this. Everything you see is made up of little parts. We call these atoms and molecules. Think of the Tower. Get it in your mind, okay?" I looked from one to another, getting a series of nods. "Okay, imagine you're on the airships, coming to the Tower for the first time, what do you know about the rooms inside?"

"Nothing?" Tel ventured.

"Exactly." I nodded enthusiastically. "You didn't know there was anything inside, and from far away you couldn't see anything, but now you know that there's thousands of rooms inside."

"Look at this apple," I said, pulling four free of my storage and passing them out. "If you look at it from a distance, it's just one thing…right? An apple?" Nods. "Now hold it up to your eye, and what can you see?"

"Uh…the skin?" Katheen said slowly.

"Okay, yeah, that works, so you have the skin. Take a bite." I ordered, doing that myself as a chorus of distinctive crunches sounded around me.

"Now, if you look at where you bit, you can see the skin, the flesh of the apple, seeds, a stalk…" I looked around, getting nods. "Now, what you've just seen is that the apple, which seemed solid and to be just one thing from a distance, is actually made up of lots of little parts, right? Well, molecules are the tiny, tiny bits that make these up. You need a powerful sight to see them, but if you look very, very closely, you can see the tiny bits that make up every part of the apple. Understand?"

There was a pause while they all stared at the apples, then glanced at each other.

"Look, just trust me on this, okay? The apple, hell, everything around us is made up of tiny parts that work to form bigger things," I said dryly. "I'm not a teacher. I can barely make myself understand it, but it's important that you understand this is the nature of reality, because, to advance as an alchemist, you need to know this shit."

"You mean the way that a potion is made up of different ingredients? But to someone who doesn't know, it's just a potion?" Tel asked.

That gave me pause. "Well, yeah. Okay, a potion would have been a far better way to describe it." I shrugged. "So…this *potion* is made up of things you can't see, but you know they're there. They form a pattern and a structure that together make the effect you want. It's a magical structure, if that helps you to visualize it. Now, when you scan this…" I said, pulling a handful of pergola tubers from my storage and passing one out to each of them. "You'll start to sense a pattern, I hope."

The next hour was spent in discussion as I tried to explain what it should feel like, what I'd seen and why. By the end of it, Tel had gotten it, and I sort of believed Katheen had seen it, but Aen was still totally confused.

"We'll work on it together," Tel promised, and I nodded my thanks to him.

"Okay, well, the pattern is Fire Resistance, and I managed to find several more plants that had pieces of that pattern hidden inside them," I explained excitedly. "The thing is, using those plants and ingredients, preparing them, treating them, meant I managed to make…this!" I said holding a small jar aloft before them.

Anti-Fire Balm		Further Description *Yes/No*		
Details:		This apprentice grade balm will grant a 7% resistance to all forms of fire for eleven minutes when spread evenly on a surface.		
Rarity:	**Magical:**	**Durability:**		**Potency:**
Rare	No	100/100		4/10

"Now, I know this doesn't look like much…" I passed the jar around, and they looked it over before passing it back. "Buuuut…this is a substance that resists *fire!*"

"Yes…?" Tel asked slowly.

"As in, if you could get more of the pattern together, you could make a stronger version, one that, in theory, could resist one hundred percent of fire for a period of time…" I smiled as they considered it.

"You mean…" Aen said, and I nodded to him to go on. "You mean you could put it on a shield, and it'd just ignore fire damage?"

"Yes! Or you could put it on your skin! You'd be immune to ALL fire damage. A mage could hurl a Fireball at you, and you'd be totally fine!"

"Shit," Tel muttered, looking at the little vial with new respect. "That's…"

"Weak!" I said cutting him off. "This is a weak, apprentice grade version. I'm exploring Healing Patterns and Poison Patterns now. I've managed to find fragments of the Healing Pattern that has raised me to eleven of one hundred, and poison to twenty-three of a hundred. We could make poisons with this that can kill Gods, or healing potions that will raise the fucking dead!" I sat forward, waving the little pot around.

"In using the Pattern, examining it as I work, I've found out so much! Like the pergola tubers! Look here, using your new spell, I mean, search for the pattern." When they all nodded to confirm they'd found it, including Aen now, I went on. "This pattern is in this section here…" I pointed to the part of the plant that contained tiny seeds, each held in place by a section of fibrous root like a leek's layers. "If you take this bit out, you know you've got the pattern, right?" My students indicated their understanding, leaning in with keen interest. "Now, boil it…" I said, quickly doing that, and as soon as it was boiling in a small beaker, I gestured them forward one at a time. "Go on…examine it."

"It's…it's stronger." Aen said eventually, hesitantly, but growing surer of himself.

"Exactly! Something in the act of boiling it changed the pattern minutely and strengthened it! Now watch when we do this instead…" I chopped and ground the same section from another untouched pergola tuber into a paste. "We've still added water, so it should be the same, right?" I offered it around, and they examined it.

"It's not, though…it's weaker…almost gone," Katheen said slowly, clearly confused.

"EXACTLY!" I shouted, thrilled with the discovery. "It's weaker! It means that we know that to make a better Fire Resistance potion from these ingredients, we need to boil them. To make a better potion using the mora telendril, we need to add a tiny amount of water and crush it, then you boil that and sieve out the bits. Then throw the water away, keeping only the sieved remains! We can do tests on all the ingredients we have, one at a time. Yes, it'll take a while, but once we know how best to prepare them, ALL OF THEM, even our weakest potions will be stronger!"

"Wait…we can use this to figure out the recipes to…to anything," Tel whispered, going white-faced with shock. "No more wasted batches, no more wasted time. We can literally figure out the patterns to things and make the strongest potions ever!"

"Yes and no," I said, holding up my hands. "It'll make your potions stronger, and you'll be able to make potions by combining the ingredients, and constantly examining the resulting mix, but you'll still need to experiment constantly to do this. If anything, you'll probably lose more, because you don't know if the recipes you know already are right or not. You need to experiment with them, but…it does mean we now have a logical way to learn!" I smiled encouragingly at each of my pupils before pulling out my alchemy set and gesturing to one of the tables.

"Right, if we move some of these across to that table, then I can set mine up on here, and we can work in two teams. We can make a set of new health potions using the methods I've just shown you and a recipe I've discovered so far. Once we've made a couple of batches, then we can all experiment with a mana potion!"

With that, the room exploded into action as we set to work, gathering up the gear spread out across the tables and consolidating them onto one before working on the new potion together.

I laid out my personal notes so that the others could work on them, and I started with the knowledge I had inscribed on my brain, losing myself in the magical bubble and motion of potion-making.

Chapter Seven

Several hours later, a very bored Oracle pulled me free of the alchemy lab. She'd played with the fish for a while before going out to do random jobs. She'd completed these and returned to find that, not only was I going to be late, but I'd managed to stink the entire room out and was scrubbing the bottom of the alembic clean, grumbling to myself about ginseng and its sticky residues.

When she told me that the legionnaires were gathering, I swore, grabbed Thomas and the three of us set off running all the way to the council chambers. We were still the last to arrive, with the group of legionnaires waiting for me outside the chambers, standing and talking quietly until they saw me approach.

Instantly, the new group, who made up the majority of the people attending, stiffened, then dropped to one knee, making my purposeful stride falter. I slowed and came to a halt before them.

"High Lord Jax, Scion of the Empire!" a legionnaire at the front intoned, drawing his sword, as did the others in a ringing salute of steel reverberating through the air. He offered his sword to me, hilt-first, holding the pommel out, even as he stared down at the floor. "I am Jon Astar Wentarin, Legion Tribune of the Narkolt Legion. The Legion stands ready to obey."

"Tribune Jon." I greeted him with a smile, reaching out and pulling him to his feet by the wrist. "Thank you, all of you, for the gesture, but please, I don't need you to kneel before me. Stand and be welcome." I gestured to the door and led them inside.

"Sorry, people," I said to everyone already inside and gave an apologetic wave. "I was working on healing potions, and it got out of hand. My fault entirely." I walked across to the chair set at the ostensible head of the table and sat, prompting everyone else to follow suit.

Rather than the usual group of legionnaires I tended to have in the meetings, mainly Romanus, the Prefect of the former Himnel Legion, Augustus, my Heir and Primus of the Second Maniple, and Restun, the new Primus Praetoria, there were a dozen or more in the room. As Thomas sat next to me, there were a lot of raised eyebrows directed at him; people clearly remembered the armor he'd worn until recently.

"First of all everyone, again, I apologize for being late. I hate it personally, so for me to be late, especially to meet you all, most of you for the first time, is doubly rude, so I'm sorry. Secondly, because most of you don't know me, we will be starting with some ground rules, as it were." I paused, evaluating the bland looks I was getting from the majority of the new people. Clearly, they were used to hiding their feelings around nobles.

"First and foremost, I'm both irreverent and rude, as has been proven, so get used to it. I expect, no I *order* you to speak up when you feel there's a need. Romanus and Restun here have given me constant advice, and I trust them with my life. Augustus here is my heir. Should something happen to me, he will take over as the new leader of the Empire." I gestured to Augustus who shifted uncomfortably but kept quiet.

"Lastly, this is Thomas, my brother. He's been cleansed of all taint from the Dark Wanker and now serves Lagoush and the Empire," I said, taking a deep breath and forcing a smile as I finished. "Now, who the hell are you all?"

A few seconds of glances passed between them before Tribune Jon started to speak.

"Ah…thank you, High Lord Jax. I am, as I said, Tribune of the Narkolt Legion. I brought those I knew I could trust with me and ordered others to bring the bulk of our forces on foot."

I nodded, watching the man. He was short and slim in build, with a cast to his skin that showed he'd been severely ill until recently, sparking a memory of being told the only surviving high-ranked legionnaire of the Narkolt forces had been poisoned by some kind of spider.

I tried not to say anything as I thought about Illoth and her little helpers and almost missed his next words.

"…is Centurion Hennen. He has taken over as my right hand, essentially picking up the tribune position, while I act as prefect and general both. Tern is Legion Primus of the Second Maniple, with Optio Fillon and Petin aiding Tern by leading the two cohorts of the maniple. Centurions Arkon and Wessex are aiding Fillon and Petin, respectively." I nodded to each of them, accepting the way they stood and clapped fist to chest each time, until he came to the last two, the first of whom looked the most nervous. "And finally, these are Smith Vestry and Intaglio. Vestry is, surprisingly enough, our primary Smith, and Intaglio, well, Intaglio is our special case."

I nodded to them in turn. Intaglio smiled slowly. She seemed battered, worn down, and haunted almost, with large circles encompassing her eyes. She was clearly thinner than she normally would have been, bones protruding from her wrists, and cheekbones you could have cut glass with, yet she also gave off a self-satisfied air and a determination that reminded me of Bane.

"Well, welcome, all of you," I said slowly, checking the threads that connected me to those who had given Oath. They reached out to everyone in the room, well, except Thomas, but our bond was greater than any Oath could show. "I can see you are all loyal to me and have accepted the Oaths, so I'm going to be quite open and honest with you all, as I find that's the best way to move forward. I am Jax, as I said, and this is my brother, Thomas. Now, as Romanus, Restun, Augustus, and most of the Legion from Himnel are by now aware…"

I was interrupted by the arrival of Tribune Alistor, who strode into the room and glared around before reaching for a chair, his teeth gritted as he spoke in a scathing tone. "My apologies for being late, I was not made aware of the time of the meeting," he snapped, glaring at me.

There was silence as we sized each other up, both waiting for the other to speak.

"You weren't invited to the meeting, Alistor," I said.

"Yet you invited the Tribune and lower officers from Narkolt's Legion? You seek to disrespect me in every way, is that it, *High Lord*?" he said through a forced smile. "Then I apologize, and I shall leave."

I cut him off with a wave of my hand.

I noted the stunned look on the faces of the newer legionnaires, and clearly furious looks on the faces of others around the room, notably Romanus and Restun. Augustus had gripped the arms of his chair so tightly they were in danger of breaking.

"No," I responded. "You won't, Alistor." I sat forward, clenching one fist in the other and looking at him over the steepled grip as I tried to control the seething anger inside. "I hadn't intended to do this, but you give me no choice. Augustus, where is Lucian?" I asked, shooting a glance to the side at the massive legionnaire.

"He…he's in the rooms Cai arranged for him. Do you want…?"

I nodded. Augustus leaped to his feet and strode out quickly, making me glad I'd ordered Cai to find him a room on this level.

"While we wait for the last member of the meeting to arrive, Alistor, you may sit in silence and consider your actions." I turned to the rest of the group.

"As I was saying, yes, I am the Scion of the Empire, and for your information, and to make what will probably be a lot of strangeness in my actions clear, neither I nor Thomas are from this world. When the Cataclysm struck, the asshole nobility that disappeared? You're all aware they left you, yes?" I asked, getting a series of nods about the time Augustus returned with the Justicar. "Good. Ah. Welcome, Lucian. Have a seat, please." I cleared my throat and went on.

"So, as I was saying, they fled this realm and travelled to my realm, Earth. They spent the next seven hundred years bemoaning the lack of mana on my world and essentially causing a lot of little wars because they were shitbags. They also had a great many children, and from time to time, they would send them here, through a portal they constructed at great expense on their side."

"That's where Thomas and I come in. He was sent to this world five years ago, and I earned the right to join him a few months back. The thing is, not all the nobility were complete assholes. Some were okay, and primarily, the Emperor was a good man.

"When he was destroyed by his children, they were unable to kill him completely, due to the levels of magic he was protected by. Nimon aided the nobles to essentially fracture Amon's soul. A fragment of it was left in us. What happened was…"

The room was utterly still as I told them our tale. When I was finished, they looked at us in shock, and I smiled reassuringly.

"Well, now you know who we are and where we came from, and you'll know why, when we ask you something that seems bloody stupid and against common knowledge, it's because it's not that way where we came from."

"The Eternal Emperor…Amon the Great, He speaks to you?" Jon asked, and I held out one hand and waved it back and forth.

"He does on occasion. He's not entirely sane. Seven hundred years of seeing your descendants slaughter each other and torture the innocent to death for shits and giggles will do that."

"This makes a great deal clear," Alistor said coldly. "You have essentially usurped control of the Legion through an insane spirit, and now you seek to lead us to our doom, well…"

"Alistor," I said, anger simmering barely beneath the surface. "Shut the fuck up. That's an order." His mouth snapped shut so quickly he nearly bit his tongue off, and he glared pure hatred at me. "Now, I've made it quite clear since I started that my aim is very simple to understand.

"I intend to bring about the complete rebirth of the Empire. I will see it rise from the ashes or the fragments burn away entirely, because sitting in the Enclave and hoping things will get better is no fucking solution at all. I've freed literally hundreds if not thousands of slaves since I arrived here. I'm at war with the God of Death Himself and His Dark Legionnaires, and you know what? I'm still fucking here."

I glanced around the room, taking the time to make eye contact with them all.

"I've reawakened the Gods of Old, and They're fighting against Nimon with us, so it's time for you all to pick a side. I called upon your Oaths, and you came. Thank you for that, truly, but you didn't know what you were getting into. Now you do. You have until tonight to make that decision. I'm sorry to rush you, but by dawn, only those who are loyal will be inside the Tower's grounds. We have too much to do to put up with possible infiltrations."

"Ah…we…that is…" Jon said, clearly unsure of where to go with what he needed to say.

"You were infiltrated already by the Drow," I said, getting a sigh from him.

"Yes, Lord…we were infiltrated, and the upper ranks were all in the process of being eliminated, with the clear intention of turning the Legion into their own personal forces. This is why we have so many in places of interim command and why I mentioned Intaglio. Normally, she would have been the kind of person introduced with far less…company around."

"Go on," I said, curiosity piqued.

"I'm a spy and assassin," she said. "I specialize in covert operations, infiltrate and eliminate, so when the Drow started, I was one of the first casualties. They took me and tried to use their abilities on me. Then, when they failed, rather than killing me like they did the rest of my team, they kept me to extract information."

"How long were you held for?" I asked.

"Nine months," she said with a wan grimace of remembered pain. "Primus Augustus found me in my cell when they tried to take him. Their original explosive attack killed the Centurion Primus and the Primus of the Second Maniple, so I don't think they were prepared for the experience of dealing with a full Combat Primus."

"I'm a little fuzzy on the whole structure here," I said, when Alistor snorted in contempt. Before I could unleash the pure, bloody fury that ratcheted through me, Romanus snapped out an order.

"Restun! Take Tribune Alistor for a full field-equipped tour of the Tower! He can consider his attitude on the way."

"Thank you, Romanus, but stop," I said, forcing myself to remain outwardly calm while inside I wanted to kick the shit out of Alistor. My knuckles itched as I forced myself to smile at him.

"Alistor, from the minute we met, you've been as rude as you felt you could reasonably get away with. Today, you've crossed that line by a wide fuckin' step. So, here's what we're going to do. I'm not going to do what *I* want to do, which is kill you by throwing you out of that window," I said with a predatory smile, gesturing to the beautifully stained-glass window in one wall.

"Or even better, nailing you to that chair with my giant murder stick. No, you've obviously got a problem with me, so we're going to sort it out in the best possible way, because I'm both your commanding officer *and* your liege. And that's for you to get a chance to prove yourself."

"First, you're no longer a Tribune. I strip you of your rank."

A look of disbelief on his face confirmed he had received the notification of his demotion.

"I assign you the rank of Legion-Aspirant. Unfortunately, due to your position, you know far too much for me to just turn you out and kick you out of the Legion, which believe me, I *really* want to do right now. Instead, I'll give you the choice. Prove yourself. Prove that you're not just the whining, complaining, rude wanker you've shown yourself to be. You'll undergo basic training again, pass, and you'll be reinstated as a legionnaire. Prove yourself there, and you'll rise in rank fast…or…"

"Or what?!" he snapped.

"Or, I'll build a prison, and you can sit there for the rest of your term of enlistment, as you'll have proven you cannot be trusted as a legionnaire nor as a free man. How long is left on your term?"

"Twelve years," Romanus said.

"Prefect!" Alistor said, shaking with shock. "You can't let him do this, surely!"

"*Let* him?" Romanus said slowly. "What the hell do you mean, *let him*? He's the Scion of the Empire! We serve at his pleasure. Hell, we *live* at his pleasure, you fool!"

"And congratulations," I said, looking around the room, seeing the shocked looks on the faces of almost everyone. "I see what you were trying to do now, Alistor, in attempting to drive a wedge between myself and the newly arrived legionnaires. It's obvious now, in hindsight."

"Ah, I mean, we…" Tribune Jon said, looking shocked and troubled.

"You weren't expecting this, and neither was I, Jon." I sighed. "I'd hoped for this to be a nice, straightforward meeting, and to fold you into the Empire in truth smoothly. Either way, now you'll have a little time to consider how you wish to proceed. I know you've all suffered greatly with the Drow's actions, and with the way things have been. Joining me in a time of war certainly isn't ideal, either, but hey, shit happens. In addition to all the other little things that are guaranteed to twist your mind right now, I'd like to introduce Lucian." I said, gesturing to Lucian, who sat ramrod straight at the end of the table.

There was a general chorus of polite greetings.

"His full name is Lucian D'Aquitaine, and he serves here and in the Empire as its Chief Justicar." There was utter silence as his name sank in, doubts rising on the faces of the new legionnaires and smug triumph painted across Alistor's features before I went on.

"I accepted him to that role after the *God of Light*, Sint Himself recommended him and assured me of the truth of his life. It turns out that Lucian was betrayed and used as a scapegoat for a shitbag of a former Legion General and his cronies."

"I swear on my Oath as a legionnaire that the God Sint informed us of this personally this morning," Restun added when I paused. The general look of suspicion morphed into one of awe as they accepted Restun's words as gospel.

I paused, then shared a look with Augustus and Romanus as they saw the same thing and were equally amused by it. The word of the future Emperor was all well and good, but the word of the Centurion Primus was something different altogether.

"I'll prove myself." Alistor glanced around with an obviously fake look of contrition. "I apologize for my attitude, Lord Jax," he said formally.

I almost snapped at him. Instead I paused, taking a deep breath, then responded formally.

"Thank you for that, Aspirant Alistor. Congratulations on remaining in the Legion, then. Restun, Aspirant Alistor here has failed as a legionnaire once already. I'd hate to see him pass his basic training then fail again, however, so I'd consider it a personal favor if you'd take charge of his training. I know I ask a lot of you, but..." I watched Alistor's face freeze, the half-hidden sneer crumbling as Restun did the thing all enlisted feared most.

He began to smile.

"I'd be happy to, Lord Jax," Restun practically purred. "The fact that a legionnaire passed his basic training and rose to such a rank without learning the realities of life in the legion reflects a personal failure in my eyes. As such, I will ensure that there is no chance of this happening again. With your permission, Lord?" he asked, nodding towards the door.

"Of course, Primus Praetoria; you're dismissed." I grinned even wider at the look of utter horror on Alistor's face. The Primus grabbed the newly minted Aspirant by the scruff of the neck and dragged him from his chair bodily and out the door.

There was silence for a long minute before chuckles rang out from Augustus, then Romanus and a few of the Legionnaires around the room. I managed to hold on for a few seconds more, shushing everyone and fighting to contain my grin as I listened hard, before a shout of "you can't do this!" echoed down the hall, and I burst out laughing.

For a few minutes, the room was filled with laughter, even Thomas joined in as he realized that the earth equivalent for Restun's rank was First Sergeant, and the level of punishment that the rude little shit Alistor was in for.

When it finally petered out, I suddenly felt much more confident about things, and I turned my attention to the new Legionnaires, wiping my eyes and grinning.

"Ah, I tell you, I damn well needed that..." I groaned, rolling my shoulders and shaking my head, barely suppressing the fit of giggles that wanted to escape. "I wouldn't force you to join me, not with everything that's going on, not now you know the truth, but..."

"We're in, Lord Jax," Jon said firmly. "First and foremost, you are the Scion of the Empire, and our Oath requires we serve. Secondly, well, we hated our position, and we had it a lot easier in Narkolt than our brothers and sisters did in Himnel. Lastly, well, we've had a few days to integrate already. While it's been strained, what with everyone knowing that there might be more infiltrators in our ranks, we'd rather be inside pissing out, than outside pissing in, basically."

There was a brief silence before I burst out laughing and held my hand out to Jon.

"Then welcome home, Jon!" I said, smiling as we clasped each other's wrists and shook once. "Welcome home, all of you, and get ready, because while there's a lot of changes to come, there'll be a lot of good to come, as well."

The mood seemed to lighten, and I took a quick break to get myself a fresh coffee from the sideboard.

"The last thing we need to discuss, Lord Jax," Romanus said, "is the Legion's structure. Since the last days of the Empire, we have been changing, and it's not necessarily been for the best.

"The original Legion was structured differently from the way it is now, frankly because they had access to things we don't, such as mages, healers, hell, we've barely got scouts, and that's a small core. Each of the Legions originally held five thousand Legionnaires, usually anyway, depending on the function of the specific Legion.

"There were also certain roles inside the Legion, such as the cavalry, the scouts, mages and supply, *et cetera some of which we no longer have*. As we shrank, losing recruits, losing skills, we lost a lot of that, and we reorganized again and again."

Romanus sighed, looking over at Jon, who nodded his agreement.

"We ended up re-forming into smaller units, and now we have two basic groupings: the Speculatores, who are our elite scouts, some having a smattering of magic as well, and the legionnaires. This is…less than ideal, especially if you're intending on teaching the Legion to use magic again. We need to restructure."

"Go on. I'm betting you've thought about this a lot already," I said, watching the faces of those around the table.

"We need to reorganize into a single Legion, but also into smaller units, squads, and cohorts," Romanus said. "I'm thinking ten Legionnaires to a squad, ten squads to a cohort, ten cohorts to a legion; for now at least, I think that's the best way. It's going to be a long time until we have a single full-strength new-sized legion, let alone a true legion of five thousand. This way, we essentially remove the maniple designation that would come between squads and cohorts in size. It can be readded later, if we ever need to."

"So, we restructure, won't that be a kick in the tits to the legionnaires?" I asked and got wry smiles around the table.

"Not really, Jax; we got used to it happening every ten or fifteen years as we shrank, leaving entire empty sections of our forces. This way, at least there's hope for the future. If we do this, I suggest we break down the squads in the following way." Romanus gestured to the table and laid out cheese blocks as a visual aid.

"Each squad is led by an Optio with a Centurion as their second. We have too few Primuses as it is, and will need a new Centurion Primus to lead them, once Restun moves on to lead the Praetorian Guard in truth. So, I suggest each Primus is responsible for two cohorts, with a single Legion Primus responsible for the five cohort Primuses. There would be ninety fighting squads, plus one command squad made up of the five Primuses, Tribune, Prefect, Legion General, Quartermaster and Legion Primus, then nine squads dedicated to supply, traps, field construction, and so on." He paused, looking at the pile of cheese he'd been moving around the table and laughing sheepishly. "Possibly a better Demonstration would have been to use paper," he muttered, shaking his head.

"No, that works…" I looked over the smushed and crumbling mess of cheese, smiling. "And the…visual aid…was helpful."

"I should have prepared better."

"I think it's a good idea, my Lord Jax, Prefect," Jon said, looking from me to Romanus. "We've lost a great many of our upper echelons, and as such would either require a complete uplift of our more experienced legionnaires, again." He paused, sighing. "Or, we would need to be folded into the existing Himnel Legion, leaving my Legionnaires feeling as though they'd abandoned their proud past. Creating an entirely new Legion and looking to the future, rather than simply stripping my people of their heritage, would be preferred, I think." As he spoke, Jon's keen gaze watched us, looking for confirmation of how his words would be taken.

"It makes sense to me," I replied. "I trust you've thought farther on the makeup of the squads, such as having a mage and a healer?"

"Yes, Jax. Two scouts, both trained in stealth and ranged combat, a dedicated healer and a mage, with six close-quarters legionnaires would be the aim, and when in larger battles, the squads would rearrange into their respective places in line, such as the standard Legion Square made up of close quarter legionnaires on the outer ring, then mages and healers, with the scouts free to move on the flanks."

"Sounds good to me. Okay, then, figure out exactly how we're going to do it, please, and soon. I want people drilling in the new formations as soon as possible. 'The more you train, the less you bleed'." I quoted.

The meeting didn't last long after that, questions flying about them having access to the Gods, if the Legion plumes were really scrapped, and the myriad of minor details about getting the rest of the legionnaires and their dependents collected and brought to the Tower over the next few days.

Once it was done, most of them left, with Jon and Intaglio being invited to stay for the council meeting with Romanus, Augustus, Thomas, and me.

The others left, and the first members of the council drifted in, and the next round of meetings got underway, thankfully without a saboteur in its midst.

Cai and Isabella were the first to enter, of course, with Isabella and her friends arranging food and drink on the table for everyone.

"I'm so sorry," she said quietly. "I didn't realize you were starting straight away, and by the time I got the food and drinks ready for your last meeting, well…it…"

"It didn't seem like a good time to interrupt," Cai clarified, and I smiled at them both.

"It's fine, don't worry about it," I said. "This is Jon and Intaglio. Jon is the leader of our new contingent of legionnaires, and Intaglio…well she's going to be joining Flux's team." I winked, and Cai immediately understood and extended a pleasant greeting to them both. Isabella took a few seconds, but then she was smiling around and offering food as the others filtered in.

It was ten minutes or more of general chat as we waited, but finally Mal strolled in with Soween at his back. I gestured for them to take a seat.

Once they were all in place, Oracle lifted from my shoulder and landed on the table, taking a space next to the other wisps in the center, and as I'd asked her while we waited, she summoned Tenandra as well.

I was suddenly glad that we had spare chairs in the room, as we were struggling to get everyone around the table. I'd gone from a very small council to a bloody multitude, and it was a bit ridiculous.

In addition to myself, Thomas and Oracle, we had the other three wisps who were all needed for various reasons. Then we had Cai, Isabella, and Hanau covering the Tower itself and the economy. We had Romanus, Augustus, Jon, and Intaglio from the Legion, with Restun already taking great pleasure in kicking Alistor's arse up and down the Tower.

Then there were Oren and Decin from the fleet, Lydia was the only one from my team, currently anyway, as Bane was missing, but then Flux and Ame, Nerin and Riana were there as well, then just for shits and giggles, I'd invited Mal along, who I just knew would derail everything. With him, of course, had come Soween.

"Okay people, sorry to be a pain about this, but this is getting insane! There's…what? Twenty-four of us now?"

I shook my head and sighed.

"Okay, what we'll do today, besides everything else, is assign formal teams. Then only one of the team needs to attend the meeting, for those of you who are working like that." I resisted the urge to tap my finger on the table in impatience. "To start with, this is Jon and Intaglio, as I've said already, but for the benefit of those who just arrived, Jon leads the new Legion contingent, and Intaglio I asked to attend, so that she could meet you all, as she will be working directly with Flux."

Flux looked over at her and nodded in greeting, getting the same reserved greeting back.

"So, teams! First off, Tower and Economy: this is the Tower itself and surprise, surprise, the economy, and will include the treasury. We have Cai in charge of dealing with people and general day-to-day management, with Isabella organizing the staff of the Tower, and Hanau doing the economy. I'd like Cai to attend all meetings where possible, but Hanau and Isabella, if you two have other things you need to take care of, you can give reports and issues to him from now on," I said, dismissing them from future meetings as nicely as possible.

"Next, Empire!" I said, unable to ignore the thrill that word sent through every fiber of my being. "This is a smaller team and will be here whenever they can't come up with an excuse to be elsewhere. That's you, Augustus, as my heir, and Thomas, as my brother." The two hulking masses acknowledged my words with slow nods.

"Legion!" I said looking over at the group. "I expect you to attend when you can, Romanus, as I rely on your advice, but from now on, bring one other member of the team, if you need to. Otherwise, just yourself, please, and that goes for my team, as well, as I damn well *know* you're here somewhere, Tang!" I called out. "Lydia will attend when she can. If not, she can nominate another to attend and keep you all up-to-date with the shit I forget to tell you about."

"That's fair; I've got a life, after all," Tang whispered right next to my ear, making me jump as he leaned past me to pick up a sliver of pear from the table.

"Goddamnit!" I snapped, knowing Tang had done that deliberately. "Fine! You're getting bells, too!" I called in the direction he'd vanished in. "Oren, Decin, one of you report for the fleet from now on, please. Same goes for my research and development team of Riana and Ame. Nerin, you're the Tower's healer. As such, I'd like you here whenever possible; but when it's not, I guess Ame would be the next best choice? I'll leave that up to you, and stay the hell out of it."

"A wise choice," Nerin said.

A hint of a smile played across my expression at her cool acknowledgement. "Yeah, well, of everyone here, you and Ame are the most likely to hurt me so, you know, valor and all that."

"Moving on, I expect you as wisps to be here when you can, Oracle, Heph, Seneschal, and Tenandra. Mal, either you or Soween are welcome to attend."

I sighed as everyone looked around. I just hoped that quick run-through was enough to settle things for the future into a smaller council, since it would end up massive if I didn't stamp on it in the short term.

"So, first things first, I want to thank Augustus and Mal, as well as Jon and everyone else who came running to my rescue after I declared to the world where we were. It might have seemed foolish to you all, but there was a reason, and it ended up meaning that we could free the slaves from the slave market. One ship got away, and the other was basically stripped and sunk, as the fight got out of hand aboard her, I'm told." I sighed with dread as I recollected the incredible pain I'd suffered that day. It had been a near miss for a lot of us.

"Thank you all. I...*we* came seriously close to death that day. For those who've not met him already, this is Thomas, my brother. Yes, I know he's ugly, but please, don't compare him to me, it's not his fault I'm magnificent," I quipped, getting a glare from Thomas that made me grin.

"Seriously though, he was sold to the Dark Church and basically forced into serving or death, so that's why he was with them. He's free now, and he's joined me, so you can trust him. Now, as part of the fight, I freed the slaves the habieen had been holding.

"Some of these people were recently captured, but a lot of them, hell the majority, were slaves they'd kept for many years and given training to. They were kept in boxes, fed, and watered once a day like animals and permitted out of the box only to exercise to maintain their muscles." I looked around, gauging the disgusted and horrified looks that news brought.

"They were kept as a last line of defense, essentially magically trapped soldiers, men and women who couldn't escape and have spent years, in some cases, being permitted out only to train and fight, then being boxed up again. This means we have a core of suddenly available people, several hundred of them in fact, who have no idea how to live their lives. We need to bring them back into the world."

"What do we do with them? I mean, if they've been conditioned all this time to simply follow orders?" Cai asked.

"Then we give them orders," Romanus said, smiling as he sat forward. "When we take new legionnaires on, they are broken of their old lives first of all. Bad habits, fear, concerns, all of it is whittled away, until all that is left is the core of themselves and their desire to be legionnaires, then we build them up. It sounds to me like you've provided me with a core of ready-made Legion-Aspirants."

He shrugged before gesturing at the legionnaires in the room. "We all went through it; when you come to the end of your training, you are physically fitter than ever before in your life, and suddenly, those you knew as civilians are...less.

"They aren't less than you and your brothers, I don't mean it like that…" he said quickly, holding one hand up in a placating gesture. "I mean that they are less in that they cannot understand what you have been through and the changes it has on you.

"We allow our aspirants a week of freedom at the end of the first phase of training, a chance to leave if they've found the Legion is too much for them. We do lose some at this stage, but it prevents the majority of those who would quit from doing so.

"When they come back after that week, then they start true Legion training, which takes another year or more, depending on their specializations. Part of the second phase of training is teaching them to interact with civilians again, and that they are now living weapons. We gradually grant them small freedoms until they are full legionnaires and free again."

"And sometimes, they're even housebroken by the end of it," Augustus said with a dry grin.

"Occasionally," Romanus replied with a laugh, getting smiles from the other legionnaires. "My point, though, is that we need to regrow the Legion, and you have a group of almost fanatically loyal men and women of all races that you saved from a life of slavery, one that they cannot find a way back from easily. Give them the chance to serve in the Legion, and I guarantee most of them will jump at it. We'll guide them and train them, as well as building our forces for the next fight."

"How many legionnaires do we have?" I asked, and the two men spoke quietly for a minute before looking back to me.

"Three hundred and forty-seven active legionnaires, with a further sixty-three that are either retired or unable to serve through injury or disablement," Romanus said.

"Where are they, and why was I not told?" Nerin snapped, getting to her feet.

"They're travelling to us now," Jon said, confusion evident on his face.

"She'll be fixing any disablement issues, Jon," I cut in. "Any and all citizens get free healthcare as part of the deal. Those who've lost limbs and so on will have them regrown."

"Truly?" he asked, before going white-faced. "I…I didn't mean to imply that you lied, High Lord Jax…"

"Don't worry about that. And please, in settings like this, just Jax is enough. Formal situations, fine, call me Lord, or High Lord, honestly I don't care which, but here, just relax.

"Now then, there's hundreds of them that are in this position, the former slaves I mean, are you sure?" I asked Romanus, who nodded firmly. "Great, that's sorted, then. When we have the ceremony tonight, I'll order them to meet you tomorrow morning first thing…do you want more, if they want to join?"

"As many as wish to join, I'll take."

"Good." I nodded to myself. "Right then, we got a lot of them here on the first few ships, along with the legionnaires who came to rescue me, but the majority are still out there, travelling from Narkolt to here with the Legion…Oren!" I said, making the Dwarf jump as I pivoted towards him and Decin.

"Uh, aye, Jax?" he asked, sitting up straighter.

"What state is the battleship in? I imagine that it could fit everyone aboard in one go?"

"Ah, she be sealed. We finished sealing tha walls, floors, an' decks yesterday. There be a lot o' fiddly bits still ta do, but give her an escort, just in case, and she'll do it. She still be slow, though, be warned, laddie, here to where we think they be an' back be a three, maybe four-day trip…"

"Fine. Do it, and get an escort together for her. And send someone for that godsdamn sand, as well!" I ordered him, remembering we needed it for everything from windows to making our own vials for potions.

"Aye laddie, consider it done," Oren said firmly, and I smiled despite the myriad of jobs before me.

"Thanks, Oren. Right, food!" I shook my head. "I know it was only a few days ago that I was asking this and we were okay, but since then…"

"Since then, you've added an estimated eight hundred more souls to the Empire," Cai said dryly. "As we stand, no. We don't have enough food. We need to purchase at a minimum another thirty tons of grain, twenty tons of feed for the animals, more domesticated animals if you want everyone to have red meat in their diet, wine…"

"I'm going to stop you there," I said. "Put a list together for Hanau and Mal. Mal, I bet you know where we can get it all at a good price, and Hanau, I bet you can do the deals. Soween, keep them both on track, okay?"

"If they are planning on purchasing these goods, there is a great deal in the way of crafting supplies we also need…not to mention finished goods," Cai said.

"Hanau, get together with Cai and Isabella, do the list, get Mal involved as well. If you think we can afford it all, get it all. If not, get what you can, use the treasury as much as you need to." With that, I neatly wrapped up our little chat on how to feed hundreds of people. A right efficient meeting I had going, if I did say so myself.

On to the next challenge.

CHAPTER EIGHT

"Now, that brings us onto the next issue. Crafting," I said, looking around. "I went to do some alchemy today with Tel, and found that besides the three benches and three chairs, he's got only a single knife and the kit I gave him to set up with. How many of our crafters are in this state?"

"All of them," Ame said bluntly. "We've all been working as hard and fast as we can, yet we cannot make the things we require from nothing. An average blacksmith will accumulate his tools over his entire life. We have a dozen smiths, from armorers to bladesmiths all sharing their tools, but they have to finish building their forge before they can even consider building tools and the elaborate setups that each craft requires."

"We estimated this yesterday, Jax," Cai said with a tap of his pen against his notebook. "Not including time to gather ingredients and the basic stock required for the various crafts, we should be up to speed and producing at the level that the crafters were at prior to coming here in just under eleven months."

"Well, that's a kick in the tits," I grumbled. "We really need that shit."

"True, but there's another option." Mal said laconically. "You know, if you're not too busy to listen…"

"You," I started, clenching my fists and speaking slowly and carefully. "No, Mal, I'm not too busy, and I'd like to hear it."

"Glad to hear it," Mal said, grinning evilly. "Well, we need people, right? For the war with Himnel, and just about everything else…Narkolt's got them."

"They've been in a war with Himnel for how long and done shit all?" I asked.

"A while, but let's face it, they used to be more or less evenly matched. It ain't that way anymore, not since you stole the airships."

"We, Mal. We stole the airships," I said pointedly, shrugging. "It's a fair point, though, except that last time you mentioned Rewn and Narkolt, he was fighting off assassination attempts?"

"True, but I'm thinking he's got to be getting low on chances and options by now, and he did send his friend to negotiate with you, remember? Hannimish?"

"Yeah," I admitted grudgingly before sighing and scratching the back of my neck. "Fine, I'll talk to him once this meeting is over, if it doesn't take too long. Anyway, if it does, we'll speak after the ceremony." I suppressed a sigh at the thought of more diplomacy and more meetings on my part. I was going to need to stab something by the time this was over.

Even if it was Oracle with the mutton dagger…as soon as I thought that, I glanced at her, and got a grin and a languid wink in response, making me smile despite myself.

"Heph, Seneschal, the next one is for you," I said dramatically, pulling the blueprints to the Academy, the Seat of Power, and the Crafter's Hall from my storage and spreading them out on the table with a flourish.

Seneschal, once again in his small form as an androgynous figure coated from head to toe in shimmering scale mail, topped with a black cloak, stepped across the center of the table from where he'd been standing and picked the first of the blueprints up, reading quickly.

He then scanned the others, before looking to Tenandra, who nodded at the unspoken communication between them. He stepped off the table, walking to one wall, even as she did the same. She created an illusion of the tower at the far right, then giant versions of the plans alongside it, even as he started to speak.

"These three buildings are both exceedingly helpful and problematic."

I forced my mouth shut, gutted that he wasn't more excited by them.

"First of all, the most important and expensive," he said, gesturing to the massive roll of plans in the center. It shimmered, and a section of the Tower, specifically floors two to five, shifted and enlarged, becoming classrooms, gyms, pools, archery ranges, and everything in between.

"This is the Imperial Academy, or the best version of it that we could make inside of the Tower. Constructing it externally, after all, would open it to attack far easier and, frankly, would be needlessly expensive, when we have all this space to work with," he said dryly. "If we were to construct this facility, we would be able to reduce our training time in all areas between fifteen and fifty percent further than would normally be possible." At his words, low murmurs rose around the room, and a look of stunned appreciation showed on every face.

"However," I said, holding one hand up to stop the rising buzz of excitement in the room. "We can't afford it."

"No," Seneschal admitted, shaking his head. "Even if we melted down every last scrap of gold and platinum in the Tower, we couldn't afford the costs of those materials alone, add to that the manastones, golem cores, orichalcum, and more? No. We truly can't afford this." He rolled it up, getting a series of groans from everyone.

"Believe me, if we could, I'd be building it already," I said as I looked around the room.

"The Seat of Power," Seneschal said next, indicating it. A section of the Tower on the eighteenth floor suddenly unrolled and shifted, the walls and interior rooms moving about, forming offices, bedrooms, jails, and quarters, as well as a courtroom and more. "This we can afford, but it's not cheap. It would essentially clear us out of a lot of our stocks of items, such as glass and copper, and while it would increase our production and overall morale slightly, it carries a huge risk should it be captured. As a formal Seat of Power for the Empire, should it be destroyed or captured, it will result in riots and desertions, not to mention widespread corruption."

"Fine, and the last one?" I asked.

He gestured, making a small section of the Tower light up. It was the seventh floor, and again, the walls and floor altered as new rooms were built and provided.

"This one is the most affordable, yet the least directly useful," he said glumly. "It essentially gives a chance for something made inside this floor to be of a higher level than it would be normally, or a failure to not fail." He tapped the wall as Tenandra made all three blueprints vanish. "We can afford to build the Crafter's Hall, although it will take several days for me to make the needed adjustments to the Tower's structure. Once this is done, however, it would provide the crafters with a central location to work from," Seneschal offered.

I looked at him for several seconds before asking the room in general.

"Okay people, anything anyone wants to say?" I asked. "Suggestions, recommendations?"

"The Academy," Romanus said, and most of the room nodded their agreement. "Whatever we need to make the Academy should be followed up on. It does need the most, and will essentially bankrupt us, from what you said, *but…*"

"But?" I asked.

"But a legionnaire who trains for five hours a day, yet receives seven to eight hours of benefits? That's a legionnaire who still has the energy to study magic. A crafter who learns that much faster will climb the ranks quickly, and the things a master alchemist could do for us…"

"They need trainers," I said, shaking my head. "Sure, the Legion will be alright, because you have Restun, but…"

"But any trainer will increase the speed someone learns by a massive amount," Romanus said firmly. "Honestly, Jax, you asked for opinions. This is it: I recommend we do whatever we need to build this."

"Any other recommendations?" I asked, looking around, and Cai stood.

"Build the Seat of Power first," he said firmly. "Not because, you know, it'll be mainly for my team." He gave a smile and a short laugh. "But mainly for the ten percent increase in production. That might not seem like much, but it's for the entire Empire, so the mining golems that are chewing their way here will enjoy it just as much as Tel in his smelly cave of alchemy." He wrinkled his nose jokingly and went on.

"Seriously, if we can gain ten percent on everything, it will level off the cost in just under a week and a half. Then, everything it produces goes towards the cost."

I looked around the room, getting some nods, some shakes of the head, and I sighed.

"Seneschal, how much are we short on the Academy?" I asked.

"The Academy requires eight hundred steel ingots, five hundred orichalcum ingots, two hundred and eighty glass panels, one hundred and fifty manastones each at least average or higher in size. One thousand units of marble, two hundred and fifty gold ingots, fifteen platinum ingots, and thirty golem cores. We have the orichalcum, although only just, and nearly the steel, though it'd clean us out. The glass, we have half of what we need, and the manastones we need for the fleet. We're nowhere near on the marble, gold, and certainly not the platinum! Last of all, the golem cores…we have three."

"Fine, we've no chance in the short-term of building the Academy, then," I said. "Seneschal, construct the Seat of Power, then the Crafter's Hall, and start working towards the Academy. Yes, I totally want to build that, but being realistic, we just can't build it, so there's no point in starting. Can we build them both?" I asked Seneschal.

"We're short on the Crafter's Hall by fifty glass panels and a hundred copper ingots. The rest we have, but we will be out once this is done."

"Do it," I commanded. "We have glassblowers and miners, don't we?"

"We do. The glass can be made in about a week, the copper…we have miners, and we have identified two mines that are likely to have good copper ore as well as more, but the mines aren't empty. They appear to be monster lairs, and as such…"

"The Legion can take care of that," Romanus offered, straightening with confidence.

"Thank you, mate," I said, nodding. "Take a ship and the miners, get the mines cleared, and take as many men as you need for now. Also…is it possible to prioritize the conduits to search for platinum and gold?"

"There is a small chance of finding either, but frankly, it's exceedingly small. Better that we continue as we have been and collect all that we can."

I sighed and nodded my assent, about to ask another question, when Lydia spoke.

"Jax, ye need te send a golem, for tha Grove, rememba?"

I smiled and nodded, impressed by the change in her since she became a Valkyrie.

Lydia had been grim, taciturn almost, and prone to bouts of depression and mistrust that made creatures from the bottom of the ocean that lived under rocks look friendly and outgoing. But, over time, she'd grown, coming out of her shell and becoming, well, a Valkyrie, dedicated to me and my new Empire.

Although I had to admit that allowing her to beat her ex-husband more than halfway to death, then healing him up so she could do it again probably helped that.

I made a mental note to ask her what actually happened to him after Saieed had him taken away, as I sure as shit didn't want him turning up here later. Partially because he was a slaver that we'd abandoned in the fight at the slave camp, but also, well, Lydia was great, and she didn't need that kind of baggage in her life.

I decided that, if he wasn't dead, I'd let Grizz and a few others go play with him, and that'd solve that problem.

"So, the buildings are sorted. Oh, shit, meant to point this out as well. Romanus, well, everyone I guess, the Academy includes a training facility that uses a spell similar to the one that surrounds Wayland's Crossing, minus the shitty soul magic, obviously.

"It'll draw mana from the Tower and use that to power the rebirth of a bunch of skeletal warriors. I managed to understand that much from the blueprints, with them being added to the remains of the old Labyrinth, that added the functionality to summon a variety of creatures on top of the undead. Don't get me wrong, they're not really alive apparently, but…for training?"

"Jax…if there was any way you could have made me more determined that we need this building, I can't imagine what it would have been," Romanus said with surprising restraint. "WE NEED IT," he insisted.

"I know mate, I know. Okay, so, the building orders are sorted, the food, people…" I paused. "So, tonight I'm going to be giving out the Oath to everyone. As part of that, I'll be introducing the Gods, and I'll also be introducing a new member of the Council, one who I probably should have asked to stay earlier, but never mind. Lucian was a legionnaire until he was stripped of his rank by a scumbag general a few centomouries back." I paused, looking around the others.

"Yes, centuries, and no, he's not elven," I added, pre-empting any confusion when they met him. "He's also a Dhampyr, which it seems is a child who was in the womb when his mother was attacked by a Vampyr. He's an honorable man, and I know that because Sint—the God of bloody Order and Light—named him as His Champion and asked me to trust him to be the Chief Justicar for the Empire. Now, I don't know about you lot, but when a God says something like that, I tend to listen."

"Or attack them," came a low comment, and the room went silent as I slowly turned to look at Flux.

"What?" I asked him, struggling to remain calm.

"You also tend to attack them. You remember, when the Goddess of Fire admitted She'd started a fight with you, and then you went out and beat up Tamat…and…"

"What the hell is it with you guys?" I snarled, thoroughly wound up. "Seriously, I know Bane isn't here, but do you need to give me grief every goddamn day?" I did my best to ignore the low chuckles and the stunned looks that Jon and several others, who'd clearly not heard *that* story yet, were giving me.

"I'll explain it later," Romanus said quietly to Jon and a few others, before coughing loudly. "Possibly time to move on, Jax? We've not got all night."

"Man, I love it here," Thomas said with a wide smile. "He has to work ten times as hard as I've ever seen, and you all give him grief constantly. It's like I've come home!"

"I will fucking stab you," I said to Thomas before glancing back around the room. "Right, Gods aside, Lucian is a good guy, all right? He basically spent the several hundred years since he was kicked out of the Legion roaming around the continent and hunting monsters. Both the humanoid kind and the literal ones."

"He'll get a good welcome from us," Decin said firmly, and I remembered him telling the tale of the village he'd been in being attacked by a monster, what seemed like forever ago.

"Oh, Thomas, you remember a few years back, a Dream where you were in a village, fighting a monster? Yes, I know that's not exactly helpful, but you were helicoptering your cock at it and singing that 'I'm too sexy' song?"

"Not really, I need more details," Thomas said after rubbing his chin. "I went through a period of doing that a lot."

"There be another song…ma pa reminded me, somethin' aboot a 'barrrbie gurrrl' Decin said quickly.

Thomas and I both laughed.

"Yeah, I think so, little village, was it the winter? Not sure. It was an Eydrakyn, six legs, all scales and teeth, looked a bit like a big Komodo Dragon banged a wolf. Damn thing took my leg off in the end, bastard. Bled out watching it choke after I'd crushed its throat. Last thing it saw was me piss on it before it died. Good times," Thomas said wistfully, staring off into the distance.

"Well, there you go," I said, shrugging at Decin. "Thomas was the one who saved you and your family."

"Huh, did I?" he asked, looking over curiously at the normally verbose Dwarf who sat with tears in his eyes, holding his husband's hand in a death grip.

"Well, Decin is a little overcome right now," Hanau said after a few seconds. "But yes, you saved his life and that of his family. They issued a quest across the clan to find you, or what had happened to you, to thank you properly. So, get ready, Thomas, because you're a hero to a Dwarf clan, and believe me, they know how to party."

"Oh, uh, well, you're welcome," Thomas said, smiling. "It wasn't a big thing, really…"

"You flew out of the ground and beat a monster to death, saving an entire village! Forgive me, while swinging your cock at it and singing that you were too sexy to wear clothes. Believe me, the tale has only grown in the telling over the years," Hanau said, smiling and squeezing Decin's hand firmly, giving it a little jiggle to pull him from his reverie. "I think Decin's father's version of it has you beating the creature, which might be a Dragon by now, to death with your member, so be ready for a lot of curious ladies…and men." Hanau winked and gave him a smile.

"Ha, well, I'm always up for a party, at least," Thomas said, though he didn't seem as keen on the idea of a lady as I'd once seen from him, despite his joking about seeing to the Tower's whorehouse shortage earlier.

I saw the change in Thomas's mood and quickly moved on.

"Well, you can sort that out later, then. No doubt, we'll all have a drink tonight, at least," I said. "I'll also be making a few announcements and addressing Lucian's rank and that he will be creating a cadre of Justicars to bring order to the land. Once tonight is done, though, it'll be time to move on. As such, tomorrow, I'll be leaving again, along with my team."

"Your team?" Thomas asked, and I nodded.

"I need to continue to level and to clear out some of the surrounding areas, scouting areas that the Gods and my map have identified as important and basically kicking ass. You've got to make a decision as well, bro. You can join me, or you can make your own team, if that's what you think you'd be better off doing?"

"I'll come with you for now, but, yeah, I'd rather have my own team, to be honest."

"Fair enough," I said. "Romanus and Restun will probably be able to recommend some people that might be interested in joining you, and Gods know I could do with another team out there."

"I'll find you some volunteers, if you tell me what you're looking for," Romanus offered, and Thomas nodded his agreement and thanks.

"Okay, my plan essentially is to make my way to the furthest point on my map…" I said, visualizing it and smiling as Tenandra linked to me and projected it on the wall again. "Thank you, Tenandra. Okay, I'm going to head *here*…" I tapped on a point on the map that was marked with a small black star, far to the south, due west of Narkolt and in the mountains. I zoomed in on the map on the wall, highlighting the relevant area.

I nodded in satisfaction. "This is a location that Svetu, the God of Invention used to hold dear. It's now filled with Goblins. We're going to clear it out, then after that, we'll start heading back, looting and killing as we go, because we're classy like that. We'll be heading northeast and stopping off at the site of the fight between ourselves and the Dark Legion.

"Then we'll move to the slave camp, see what we can loot, because let's face it, not only do we need godsdamn everything, but the slavers will have had plenty of it. Then, we'll hit waystation one, which is about thirty miles from Himnel, so we'll need to go in under cover of darkness, followed by waystation two, then back to the Tower."

"We could send a team directly to the slaver camp and battlefield, Jax," offered Romanus.

I considered this before agreeing. "Yeah, that's a better idea, actually, before anyone else loots the place. It gets the gear back faster as well, if you manage to loot anything, so do that. Anyway, we go here…"

"Why go to these sites now? That place and the slaver camp, I mean?" Thomas asked, brow knitting with curiosity. "Seems a hell of a risk going that close when we're at war."

"Golems," I answered. "Each of the waystations held a contingent of golems. There was even the remains of a manufacturing facility in Himnel. If we can find something like that? It'd make a hell of a difference, but regardless, part of the deal with Svetu for us clearing out this site…"

I tapped the bottom-most marker. "Is that he'll show us how to build relay towers and build one on the Great Tower. Once they're built, it'll give us the ability to communicate and control golems across the areas we've taken command of, including hopefully enabling us to locate the mining golems that are on their way here."

"Mining…?" Oren asked slowly. "Wha'…"

"I took control of them during the raid on Himnel. They were damaged, and were being repaired by a servitor before being dispatched to the Tower. Once they get close enough, we'll be able to reach them, but they'll be digging their way here, making a literal path that will be filled with…metals…" I mumbled, slowly trailing off.

"That be a lot of metals," Oren said, smiling. "Any chance o' makin' tha Academy wit' them?"

"Hmm?" I asked, shaking my head to clear it of the thought I'd just had. "Possibly." I cocked an eyebrow at Romanus in question. He nodded firmly, having clearly realized what I had, and I shared a smile with him. Most of the room seemed to have no idea, but a few eyes lit up with the same possibility.

"Regardless, we *need* to take that site for Svetu. Okay, it's about half an hour before everyone is due to gather down below. Is there anything else?" I asked, getting a series of negatives. I clapped my hands once.

"That's great, then. One last point. Alistor, former Tribune of the Legion, crossed a line today. As such, he is now Alistor, Legion-Aspirant. As such, he has absolutely no authority now, just in case I needed to say that," I said, looking at everyone, and getting a series of nods and several smiles. While they looked slightly worried or pissed off about the situation, depending on whether they were from Narkolt or Himnel, one and all, the Legion saluted.

With that, I nodded and stood, leading the way out of the meeting and heading to our rooms. Once Oracle and I were inside, I waited while Tang checked the room, then thanked him as he left. Finally, I collapsed on our bed and stared up at the ceiling.

"Godsdamn, that was a long and boring day," I muttered.

"Well, you basically did what rulers do," Oracle said, sitting on the edge of the bed and giving me a kiss before leaning back against my side and facing me. "Normally, we're too busy and you leave all of this up to Cai. He's *great*, he really is, but he's still learning, and you're the Scion. You need to make the decisions, after all."

"Yeah well, I'd rather kill people and chase you around the bedroom."

"And you do that a lot!" she said, grinning at me. "But seriously, we need to expand Cai's team, get him some more help, and make sure it's the right people, so we get more time for the important things." She leaned in and kissed me, long and deep. Finally, she broke it off and moved back.

"Fighting and fucking?"

"Definitely. Now, are you wearing those training clothes all day, or are you getting changed for the ceremony?" she asked. I grunted, sitting up.

My interested and semi-aroused mood vanished as I considered the real reason for the ceremony tonight, and I got off the bed, checking the ancient wardrobe that was set up on one wall.

I pulled the door open and let out a sigh of relief as I saw two new outfits in there: another training one and the smart one I'd asked the tailors to prepare a few weeks back when I was on the battleship and had first met them and Thorn.

It seemed a lifetime ago and bloody centuries since I'd last walked the streets of Newcastle. I had a few seconds while I thought about that, about the cold rain, the neon lights and the cars, the snow underfoot the last night I'd been free, and the fight that had cost me my job.

Hell, I even remembered *her*, and her fucking her friend, the fight that had led to me being arrested and being handcuffed to a hospital gurney with a rattled brain, thanks to the baseball bat *I'd* bought her, waiting to go to jail.

I remembered the Baron, meeting the evil old bastard as he hunched there in a chair in an old drawing room, drinking brandy and smoking cigars while the world had no idea he even existed.

I remembered the beatings and the torture, the training and the laughs. Then I remembered the fight in the Arena and the look on the Baron, my father's face, as I leaped through to the UnderVerse, giving him the finger as I went.

I shook my head, grimacing and quickly pulled the clothes free, checking them over before laying them out. Then I jumped in the shower and reveled in the heat and power of it.

Five minutes later, I was standing on the balcony, smiling as Tang cursed me and sprinted off, before Oracle and I leaped out into the light of the setting sun, ready for the ceremony at last.

CHAPTER NINE

The ceremony itself was simple and as respectful as I could make it. I'd ordered that everyone be ready at the foot of the Tower for sunset. As I flew down, I saw that Seneschal, or more likely, Cai and Seneschal, had thought ahead and made me what I needed before I knew I needed it.

I flipped over and landed on a large slab of marble held aloft by two golems, and they raised it smoothly from chest height to the ends of their long arms, holding me fifteen feet in the air.

Oracle hit me with a subtle heal to wash away the damage of the Soaring Majesty ability, and I silently prayed that it would eventually evolve to be rid of the health cost to its use.

I strode forward to stand at the front of the dais, and I looked out, seeing the two or so thousand people of the new Empire standing silently, and I swallowed hard.

I'd always been a reasonably confident guy, and I had, from time to time, done massive magic and speeches since coming here. But the starting of these things always made me nervous, not to mention that this was the first time addressing so many, as many of the airships' crews and those who'd been busy this morning were here now.

"Good evening." I swallowed hard, berating myself at the bland start. "Thank you all for coming," I started again.

"Tonight, we're gathered for three reasons, but the most important of these is to say thank you. Thank you to those who gave their all in fighting to defend us and the Empire."

I looked around, making eye contact with people as I spoke, seeing nods of affirmation, sad smiles, and some curious looks as I went on.

"In time, once we have finished the current rebuilds and repairs for the Tower, and we've made sure that we are secure, then we will build a memorial fitting to those who have fallen. But, for now, I want us all to remember them. These were brave men and women who died to protect us, to save us, and we loved them deeply."

I swallowed hard against the lump that seemed to grow in my throat as I thought about those that had died from my team alone, and in my mind, they began to parade past. Stephanos, Cam, An'na, Rol…the list started, and as each name ran through my mind, I saw them again, heard their quiet comments, their laughter.

"Stephanos fell in the flight back to the Tower. He died protecting me." I told them all about him, then the others, not dwelling on any one point too much, but describing how they died, and more importantly, how they lived. I spoke of Stephanos winding Jian up, and the way he'd screamed when Horkesh had been "helping" and had woken him up for his watch.

I talked about them all, and for those I didn't know as well, some of them legionnaires or others who were more recent additions, I invited a friend to step up and speak on their behalf.

It took most of the hour, but at the end, I felt better, and I hoped those around me did, too.

"Thank you all. We've spoken of our dead and how much we loved them, how we miss and valued them. But now it's time to speak of the living. Growth is often painful, and as the Empire grows, we need to work to try and make this as smooth as possible. As such, I want to make you all aware of some changes." I looked around, seeing nervous stares as people wondered if my changes would be good for them or ill.

"First, I will be granting two new Titles tonight." There was silence as people listened, the tweeting of birds echoing as they flew in the gradually darkening sky. As dozens of magelights around the crowd slowly grew in brightness, I took a deep breath and let it out slowly.

"Cai! Step up here please," I said, and the golems lowered the platform, allowing him to climb on, before lifting it back into the air.

"Cai, you're my left hand when it comes to the Great Tower. You run the day-to-day operations and manage our people as we work to expand and regain the Empire. However, it's time that your position was formally acknowledged. Kneel, Cai," I ordered, and the Panthera sank to one knee wordlessly.

"In recognition of all you do, and have done, I name Cai'Amanth a-Ull to the position of Consul," I said, doing my best not to butcher his name too badly. "Cai will continue to run the Great Tower, but as the Empire's reach extends, so too will his power. He stands only below Heir Augustus and myself in authority."

Attention Citizens of the Territory of Dravith!

**Jax, High Lord of Dravith, Scion of the Empire,
has named an Imperial Consul!**

All Hail Cai'Amanth a-Ull, Consul to the Imperial Throne!

As always, the proclamation opened in everyone's vision regardless of their choices, overriding their wishes and remained until they read it, the fancy letters formed of golden smoke on an ornate backdrop of black surrounded by scrollwork. Being the immature bugger I was, I wondered how many people I just put off their stroke with that popping up.

I couldn't help but smile as I pulled Cai to his feet and clasped his wrist, smiling at my friend.

"Lord Jax, thank you…" he said.

I shook my head, cutting him off. "No Cai, thank *you*…you earned this, and if I could have done it before, I would."

"I gained an official title, and…and *abilities*," Cai whispered, his eyes scanning his screens before he blinked them away.

"Go on then, you bugger, go be more efficient or whatever. I only did it so you'd pester me less," I joked. The dais lowered to the sound of cheers and catcalls. The traditional Legion salute of a weapon slammed against a shield to show approval echoed around the courtyard.

Once Cai jumped down, and Thomas stepped on at my gesture, the golems lifted me back into the air. I held out my hands for quiet.

"Next, I want to introduce you all to Thomas. He is my brother and will soon be accepting responsibility and a rank in the Empire. For now, he is simply acclimatizing and looking to see where he will fit in. I ask that you help him, and whenever possible, show him patience."

There was a long, awkward silence, before a hesitant round of cheers started. Thomas waved, red-faced, before swearing to get me back for that later and swiftly jumping down, catching onto one of the golems and jumping again in his haste to be off the platform and away from prying eyes. I grinned before turning back to the crowd.

"The second and last Title being granted tonight is given to a newcomer amongst us, but as he is spoken for by the God Sint personally and, well, I'll trust Him on that! I…"

I broke off as a divine presence washed out across the courtyard, a rent in the world opening as Sint Himself stepped through, huge and powerful, standing over twenty-five feet high this time. He towered over the crowd, conveniently sizing Himself so that His head was just above my own.

He stepped forward, coming to a halt alongside the dais as He started to speak. His simple, yet obviously well-made armor, weapon, and tabard made Him stand out all the more for the impression of power He always exuded.

"Good evening, citizens of the Empire." His voice rumbled in a low note that everyone could hear perfectly with no need for amplification, even as His presence made people sink to one knee in reverence. I turned and sank to one knee as well, peeking out of the corner of my eye to see Him smile and incline His head in acknowledgement of my respect.

"I have come before you to make my feelings clear and to thank High Lord Jax, Scion of the Empire, for accepting my recommendation of my Champion, Lucian D'Aquitaine, as Chief Justicar for the Empire. I have stepped in personally to ensure that the slanderous accusations that interrupted his service with the Legion stop immediately." He glared around at the few faces that still seemed offended at Lucian's inclusion, making them duck their heads in fear.

"They were started to hide the crimes of lesser men and have grown in the retelling over the long years since. Lucian has spent the last several hundred years defending the innocent and bringing justice to the wronged across both this continent and the islands to the south and east, hunting pirates and more. He has dedicated his life to the pursuit of justice and the law, and as such, has my full support. Whosoever slanders him, slanders me." Sint finished ominously.

After a long pause, Lucian vaulted up, catching a handhold on the golem closest to him and kicking off, throwing himself higher, catching the edge of the dais and flipping over to land on his feet, then sinking to his knees in reverence before Sint and myself as I stood.

"Lord Sint, thank you for your kind words and support," Lucian said, his face red with embarrassment. "I simply did what any in my place would have done…"

"No, Lucian, you did the right thing each time, no matter what it cost you," I said, my voice echoing across the courtyard through some magic I didn't even bother to wonder at. "Lord Sint was right to recommend you. An honest man, especially one as long-lived as yourself, is the right choice to lead the Justicars!"

I took a deep breath as I went on, a tingle of magic infusing my voice. I realized I'd felt the same when I named Cai as Consul.

"In recognition of all he will do and has done in the past, I name Lucian D'Aquitaine to the position of Chief Justicar for the Empire." Immediately, the popups appeared, making me squash the smile at the thought of people getting stopped again.

Attention Citizens of the Territory of Dravith!

Jax, High Lord of Dravith, Scion of the Empire, has named an Imperial Chief Justicar!

All Hail Lucian D'Aquitaine, Chief Justicar to the Imperial Throne!

"Thank you, Jax," Sint said, bowing His head once before reaching out His right hand and gently resting it atop Lucian's head. *"Receive my blessing also, Champion of the Light and Paladin of Order. Rise now, and Serve your Lord and your God."* A bright white light surged from His hand, sinking into Lucian, who stiffened, letting out a little gasp as the power infused him.

I lifted the greatsword Justice from my bag, straining slightly under the weight of the massive weapon, and I turned, offering it to Sint with my head bowed in respect.

He smiled, then lifted the sword effortlessly, closing His eyes and sending a mighty wash of power over the weapon, making it glow with a golden light, and offered it hilt-first to Lucian.

The man who'd suffered centuries with barely his armor and whatever meager goods he could scavenge from those he hunted, stood atop the dais and received a weapon blessed by the God of his forefathers, a God who reached out a hand to him in benefaction again.

When Sint removed His hand, the world seemed to dim, and the God was gone, leaving a shaken man who climbed to his feet unsteadily. I reached out and gripped Lucian's wrist and shoulder, looking into his eyes and smiling.

His usually dark brown eyes, now faintly glowed a luminous white before they dimmed to a much lighter hazel hue. I grinned at the disbelief on his face. The years he must have spent wandering, forever believing his life to be one of exile and disregard were over. He'd found a home that was declaring him to be welcome, and more important, worthy of that welcome.

"Lucian, thank you for agreeing to come to the Empire, I know we're very fortunate to have you, and as such, let me make my position clear as well," I said, turning from him as I released his shoulder and wrist. "The God of Light and Order Himself has said that Lucian is a good man, and the right man for this role, and I agree.

"Anyone I hear giving him disrespect because of the lies that were told so long ago will earn a personal discussion with me about their attitude, and it won't be one they'll enjoy, is that understood?" I received quick nods and confirmation on everyone's faces as they stood again and relaxed after Sint's disappearance.

"Good! Now then, as I've said regularly, and will be said again in a few days' time when more of our citizens arrive, in addition to the Oath that binds us all, we are united in service to the Gods, specifically the Pantheon of the Flame, against the Dark Wanker Nimon." As usual, thunder echoed when I called Nimon that, and people looked around nervously, but nothing more happened. I grinned. "As such, if you haven't declared for a God or Goddess, I ask that you choose one, and pray to Them once a day when possible. The act of praying to the Gods gifts them a portion of your mana. This strengthens Them, enabling them to perform divine feats that help us, and the actual act of praying slowly strengthens your ability and chance to learn to use magic, so there's something for everyone in this." I took a deep breath, nodding to Lucian as he bowed to me and jumped off the platform, taking up his place in the crowd again.

"As a condition of you being a Citizen of the Empire, you are required to take the Oath of the Empire. While the Legion Oath is slightly different, the Civilian Oath is now simple, and in two parts, so I ask you all to swear it again. This enables you all to know that you are safe and can trust those around you. I warn you, refusal to swear the Oath will result in your removal from the Empire, so please do as I ask." With that, the weave released. As I'd been speaking, Oracle had already begun to weave the various sections of our mana together, forming the pattern that was required, linking herself and me to the Great Tower, even as the first notification was pushed out from me to all those gathered here.

"I swear to obey Lord Jax and those he places over me; I will serve to the best of my ability, speak no lie to him when commanded otherwise, and treat all other citizens as family.

"I will work for the greater good, being a shield to those who need it, a sword for those who deserve it, and a warden to the night.

"I will stand with my family, helping one another to reach the light, until the hour of my death or my Lord releases me from my oath.

"Lastly, I will not be a dick!"

It started slowly, hesitantly, in a few cases, but I heard the deep brogue of Oren calling the oath out. In seconds, it rumbled back and forth across the courtyard as more and more people took up the call. When the last had finished taking the Oath, I spoke to them.

"I, Lord Jax, do swear to protect and lead you, to be the shield that protects you and yours from the darkness, and the sword that avenges that which cannot be saved. As the Tower grows in strength, so shall you," I called out, feeling the heady rush of the Great Tower's mana pool streaming through me to bind these people to myself. Then I pushed out the original Oath of Imperial Citizenship.

"I swear upon pain of death, to faithfully execute all that the Emperor decrees. I swear upon my soul that I shall stand for the Empire when it calls. I shall be strong when the weak need me, generous when the poor are at hand, and merciless when my fellow citizens are threatened. I shall worship the Gods of my fathers, respect my elders, and raise up my children to stand tall.

"I am an Imperial Citizen. I claim the right to call upon the Legion in my hour of need, to hold those that wrong me to justice, and to be avenged if I cannot be saved."

As this Oath was delivered and sworn, the true burn began, as I'd experienced so long ago in the caverns below Himnel and in the presence of the Spider Queen Ashrag.

This time, the tingle that had been growing in my mana channels from so much mana passing through me evolved, going straight past the developing burn and into a searing heat that continued to build inside me.

Oracle's concern and fear rose as I desperately tried to keep the pain from showing while I ground out the final words. "I am Jax, Lord of Dravith…" I swallowed the pain down like it was a bitter potion of Legionnaire's Might. "I am Amon's descendant, and I claim his Oaths as my own."

Pain ripped through me as my mana channels were scoured clean of everything, the great wash of power tearing into me, carrying my sense of self along and out into everyone around me.

With the Great Tower's mana reserves to pull on, this had seemed like both the right thing to do and a terrible idea at once. Whatever the changes that the Gods had made in me were, and I knew they were still ongoing by the constant grinding and bone-deep aching I did my best to ignore; this, at least, was better than it had been.

When it was done, I could feel the twitching of tens of thousands of connections, each reaching out from people to link them to those around them, then flowing back to me.

I stood there, stunned for long seconds, my mind overwhelmed by the massive influx of information. Each time I'd done this before, it'd been for a much smaller segment of the population, and it'd rendered me unconscious and almost killed me.

Now, I felt it.

Each of my people were bound to the others, both by the new Oaths and by other threads. They were bound by love, by need, by familial and personal bonds, friendship and lust, greed and avarice, all of it.

I looked around, trying to remain steady as I cleared my throat and spoke, trying to make sense of the world as I said the things I'd planned on saying next, desperate to gain the time to deal with this new flood of information.

"I…uh…thank you and welcome home, all of you! Next, we go to the cathedral! Please, take a few minutes and speak to the Gods, offer a prayer to them, and choose one if you haven't already. Then return here, and the feast can begin!" I called out, a sigh of relief escaping as the golems lowered me, to the resonating thunder of cheers.

As soon as I was down, my mind whirling, Augustus took one look at me and barked an order I couldn't make out. Before I could arrange my thoughts to ask him what he'd said, two dozen legionnaires surrounded me, facing outwards, standing shoulder to shoulder and blocking any sight of me from the curious citizens.

Oracle stepped up close. She and several others of my personal retinue and the council were accepted inside the ring before it closed. She knelt next to me as I slowly sank to the floor, sitting cross-legged and closing my eyes as I continued to sort through the confusing mass of strands.

I could feel differences and see the colors of the strands, as each of them reflected meanings. Yet they were invisible to the eye, as well. I *knew* who was around me, and I spoke slowly, saying the words aloud, hoping to make more sense of them as I did that.

"I can see them all," I muttered. "The Oaths, the love, the hate, the lies and the truth that binds them to me," I mumbled, frowning as a black line led from me to another, to someone close…

"It's an Imperial Ability," Lucian said nearby.

I blinked, losing the black thread amongst the literal thousands of others of every color.

"What?" I asked absently as I looked for the thread, knowing that I shouldn't have let myself lose sight of it.

"The vision, if it's what I think it is. I have a lesser version of it as Chief Justicar, I can see it, too. It's called 'Threads of Fate,' and it was said that, through this, those few who were gifted with access to it by the Emperor could eventually learn to see the future. The records were spotty and incomplete, as they obviously never discussed the Emperor's Ability, but the version that the Justicars were granted allowed us to see the links and connections between people, to enable us to trace the truth."

"How do you know what he can see?" Augustus asked calmly, crouching and offering me a drink from a flask. I muttered a thank you, only half paying attention to the conversation and the world around as I took a swig and coughed. The water I'd expected clearly elsewhere as it felt like smooth fire in my throat, and I recognized the familiar burn of high-proof rum.

I wheezed and thanked Augustus again as I searched through the threads. They blurred as people moved, the swiftly building migraine from this data overload blooming behind my skull even as I listened with half an ear to what Lucian said.

"It's what he said. It literally describes what I can see perfectly, except I see it on an individual basis." He cleared his throat and spoke slowly. "Lord Jax, how many can you see?"

"All of them," I whispered when he repeated his question, and I realized I must have missed the question the first time around. "Everyone that was here; I can see them all."

"So, what, he can see how we all connect?" Romanus asked him.

"Yes, but…from what I managed to piece together over my years of study, studying the ancient Justicars, I mean," he clarified, "it's like being a spider at the center of a web; from there, you can see a strand that connects to someone. Follow it and focus on that person, and you'll see their connections. If you follow them to another, you can see how they connect. It's not exact, but you could tell how people felt about each other." He paused, thinking and scratched his chin as he went on.

"It was a set of training manuals and information for new Justicars I found this in, so I am simply telling you what they laid down, augmented by what I can see now, the Ability having been granted along with my Title." Lucian looked around slowly before reaching out and placing one hand gently on Restun's arm, making him come as close to flinching as anyone there had ever seen.

"Praetorian Primus Restun and I have both a familial relationship and an emotional one, gained through years of lies being thrown at him. I can see echoes of mistrust, concern, hope, and fear all etched into the line between us. I cannot tell how many lines there are radiating out from Restun, but there are literally thousands, I'd bet. If what High Lord Jax is seeing is the connections from him to everyone here, and their connections in turn, then the world must be a barrage of information right now."

"It *really* is," I said, shaking my head and hoping it'd settle down, as I vaguely remembered it doing the last time. Then I realized that I'd had to think of it before to see the connections, and I focused frantically...

And relaxed, sighing in relief as the world seemed to fade into dullness by comparison.

I blinked several times before looking around, moving my head slowly, wincing. It felt like my skull was six sizes too big and stuffed full of wire wool.

"Are you okay, Jax?" Oracle asked.

I shook myself again and winced. "Yeah, just a bit shocked, feeling like everything's in slow motion, you know? Man, what a trip."

"Are you okay?" Oracle asked again carefully.

"Yeah, I will be," I said more forcefully, punctuating my words with an attempt to push myself to my feet. I made it halfway before sagging back and getting caught by both Augustus and Grizz, with Oracle grabbing onto my shoulders and pulling.

They stood me upright and helped me to stand, only letting go when I nodded that I was okay. I moved slowly, walking like I'd just spent a week training with Restun. The group stayed around me, guiding me to my place of honor on one of the long tables that had been set out for the feast.

I sat down heavily and rested my elbows on the table, holding my head, even as Oracle swept me with healing spells and frantically checked for injuries.

I heard someone grumble, then be pushed aside and a shoulder propped me up on my right. I looked up blearily, seeing Thomas and letting out a sigh of relief.

"Thanks, bro," I mumbled, letting myself lean against him a little more as he pretended I wasn't.

"Anytime, Jack," he whispered. "Although, you know I'm gonna get you for introducing me like that, right?"

"Aye aye..." I said, rubbing the bridge of my nose.

"Jax, I think I know what the problem is," Oracle whispered, sitting across from me and holding her hands out. I put my hands in hers and squeezed them gently, even as Lydia pushed Grizz aside and sat next to me, silently propping me up, making it look like we were all deep in conversation.

"Thank you," I said to Lydia, then I nodded to Oracle. "Okay, my love, what's up?"

"Your body isn't designed for the levels of magic that it's channeling."

I snorted. "Yeah, I got that the first time I nearly killed myself pulling from the Tower, seriously though..."

"No, I mean it, Jax." Oracle squeezed my hands harder, ignoring Isabella and the others as they started bringing out food and drinks. There was a pause as the legionnaires stopped them approaching, but Augustus, with a nod from Cai and Romanus, let them through, hurrying them off again as soon as they were done.

I freed one hand and picked up a chunk of bread, sighing and dipping it in a bowl of oil they had placed nearby.

"Go on, Oracle. I think I'm going to need food for this one..."

"A mortal body can only channel so much mana," she said, after a minute's thought. "I don't mean at a time, I mean over a mortal's lifespan. That's a different amount per person, but essentially mortals have evolved to use mana, you weren't made for it.

"You aren't a creature of magic, not the way I am, and so every time you use magic, it makes a small alteration in you at a very basic level. It can happen a million times and make no difference, or it can happen the second time and it can twist you, breaking you down. It…"

"Mutation," I said slowly, and Thomas nodded, having reached the same conclusion. "You're telling me that using magic is like smoking a godsdamn cigarette? There's always the chance it'll cause a gene to mutate into a cancerous one?" I asked, disbelief clear in my voice.

"Hmm." Oracle scanned my mind, before brightening and nodding. "Yes! Well, no, but that's a good way to think about it! It's not cancer, we could cure that, and you're not ill, so don't worry about that. What it is, is that your mana channels have been strained again and again, forced to accept massive amounts of mana, and it's damaged them, and your body with them."

"But compared to Amon, I've hardly…"

"You're not Amon, not yet." Oracle squeezed my hand again. "Jax, it's okay, honestly. All that's happening is that you're starting to feel something that comes in old age to most mages. The gradual straining of their mana channels often isn't noticeable, but when you were out, Jenae and I spoke about the possibilities and what was happening to you. There're several solutions, if you're ready for this conversation?"

"Well, I'm sure as shit not wanting to have it, but I guess I need to!"

"Honestly, Jax, it's all right," Oracle said with a reassuring smile. "Most people never have these issues. Most mages never know because they only start to feel it when they're close to the end of their lives, lives which are often far longer than they would have been due to access to magic, anyway. They go one of two ways. They either accept that they're aging and go out gracefully, or they go a bit…magic daft, essentially, and a lot of them become liches."

Thomas and I exchanged an incredulous look at the thought that liches were often just geriatric mages who weren't ready to let go before smiling and shaking our heads at the same time.

"You two normally don't look that alike, you know, then you do that…" Oracle said. "Okay, so like I said, most people never know about this, and most mages never speak about it. Those who do have the need to deal with it, though, have three options. Accept it and dial back on the magic, though that's not really an option for you."

I snorted and shook my head, taking a chunk of cheese from Thomas and putting it in a flatbread along with some tasty-looking toppings, before taking a bite out of it.

"Option two, we start looking into artifacts and magical items. There are others who have had these problems, after all, so there will be magical solutions," Oracle said.

Thomas gave me a push with his shoulder. "Sounds like you need the magical equivalent of viagra, bro. Sucks to be you!"

"Really?" I frowned. "Didn't you already need a God, oh no, wait, two Gods to fix your mana channels? Man, how broken were you that it took two Gods to fix you. I feel sorry for the ladies!"

"You wish."

Lydia sighed and cut him off. "Thomas, shut the 'ell up. Oracle, what's option three, please?"

I grinned at his shocked look. "Sorry mate, she's Optio of my personal guard; if you're planning on fighting in my team for a bit, you'll be under her…" I paused, then gave him a subtle shake of the head when he opened his mouth to make an "under her" comment. He caught the look and shut his mouth with a clop, raising one eyebrow to me in question, even as Lydia totally ignored the byplay.

"Option three is that we go the Eternal route, as the Gods have already inferred," Oracle said, somehow still smiling.

"Okay…" I frowned. "You'll need to explain that a bit more." After my next bite, I waved my sandwich at her with a circular motion.

"Well, no mortal can channel that much mana over and over again, but you're not entirely mortal. As you said long ago, your bloodline is 'contaminated' with the genes of various races. The thing is, though, it's also got aspects of Amon's genes in there, and the various things He did, and what the Dragons did to him. Basically Jax, we need to look for a way for you to *evolve*!

"Amon could channel the Imperial Abilities because He was the Emperor, but also because He was blessed by all the Gods, even Nimon. It took a huge amount of effort for Nimon and His children to kill Him; think about that!" Oracle said, sitting upright and looking around, making sure there was nobody too close to us.

"It took the God of Death and dozens of His own children, attacking in concert, to kill Him. And still, enough of Him lingers to scare them all shitless and to guide you. I bet Amon was close to ascension to Godhood Himself, and Jenae has said time and time again, She can't tell you secrets of the Gods yet because they're secrets that only the Gods can know.

"She didn't say, 'hey, you're a mortal, tough titty, pal.' She said She'd tell you when She could. She's as good as told you this already, and when you broke yourself last time, it took Jenae, Ashante, Lagoush, Tamat, and Sint to put you back together."

"I remember. Well, I don't, but I remember what Jenae said and I'm still feeling the effects of whatever They did," I admitted, lifting one hand and looking at it as I focused in, flexing my fingers and feeling…something…wrong. The muscles, the bones, all of it felt like it was a click out, like I'd overdone it, and when I'd stretch, it'd click, and it'd be a relief as things settled back into place properly. Only, it never did.

"We started to use that Genetic Drift Examination, if you remember? It takes a hell of a lot of mana, and I don't think we should use the mana channels of the Tower to do it, but maybe we should push it more? I started to work on your legs with it, concentrating on the joints, and I kept doing it while you were unconscious, once we knew you would be okay. Do they feel any different?"

I flexed my legs and shrugged. "I'm not sure, honestly. I'd say the right feels better than the left, but only because I'm thinking about it, so I might be making it up…"

"You're not," she said, pride beaming from her expression. "I've been concentrating on the right leg, point to where…" she said, and I put my hand on my knee, getting a nod from her. "That's it! I managed to get your right knee to thirty-two percent. It doesn't sound like much, I know, but if you think that genetic *perfection* is a hundred percent…Jenae and I suspect that if you can get your body to that level, all of it, I mean, you'll find that you start gaining extra abilities, and things like the mana channel damage will be gone forever!"

"Okay, so what you're saying is that you can cure me and get rid of the problems, but it's down to my mana? We need to not channel as much, but we need to channel as much as we can to cast the Genetic Drift Examination and heal me with it as often as possible?"

"Ah, yeah…" Oracle winced. "And that's the problem. If we didn't have this problem, I'd have suggested we tap into the Tower and use that to provide the mana and just hammer into you."

"Can I do it?" Thomas asked, quickly followed by Lydia. Before anyone else could volunteer, Oracle shook her head firmly.

"No," she said adamantly. "Definitely not. I'm sorry, but first of all, you couldn't because you're not the master or bound to the Tower. And secondly, for all but you, Thomas, it would kill them outright. And, in your case, Thomas, you would absorb a huge amount of mana, then become either mana warped and try to feed on the Tower, destroying it, or you'd be unable to let go and essentially fill yourself with magic until you detonated and destroyed anything from yourself and your chair to the continent."

"Well, fuck."

"Yeah, thanks bro, but looks like I need to do this alone," I said slowly.

Thomas glared at Oracle. "But Jax can, so maybe…"

"No, Thomas. First, you are different, even though you're twins. Secondly, you have no wisp to aid you. Thirdly, you aren't the Emperor or Scion. You'd not survive attempting to use those levels of magic, nor would you be able to join with the Tower. I'm sorry, but this is something we have to do alone."

"So, we can't use the mana of the Tower anymore?" I asked, and she shook her head.

"No, we still can, but expect it to floor you each time. We can't use the magic of the Tower to repair you, because it'd be damaging you at the same time. It'd take hours, even at that level of mana input, as the spell can only do so much so quickly. I suggest we just get used to using it whenever we get the chance, and hope to improve it as quickly as possible."

"Okay, well, that's a bit shit," I grumbled, wiping my hand down my face and blinking.

"It is, but you're alive, and we can fix it. Seriously Jax, nothing has really changed for now. You just need to be careful using the Tower's mana like a hose, and you need to continually work to improve your body, which we were doing anyway, okay?" Oracle said.

"How many didn't swear?" I asked quietly, wanting to move on, and Oracle, Seneschal and Heph slipped into my mind to continue the conversation.

"One hundred and seven," Seneschal said. *"Of which eighty-four are accounted for by the airship crews and nobility who came with Mal from Narkolt. The remainder are Mal and his crew at twenty-one and two individuals*

who are attempting to stay hidden. One is hiding at the outer edge of the courtyard and believes herself to be invisible. The other is approaching the Hall of the Eternal, and seems to believe they are undetected."

"Good work. Take them and hold them. I'll deal with them later." I said, getting a sense of agreement and approval before their collective presence vanished from my mind. I took a bite from a bowl of unidentified meat. "Gods, what I wouldn't give for a pizza," I said without thinking, getting a series of grunts, as those around me had either heard me speak about the wonders of pizza before, or in Thomas's case, missed it as much as I did.

"Jax, ye got a minute?" Lydia asked. I frowned, turning to her, confused, before seeing the way she stood off to one side and the terrified look on the face of the woman who stood with her.

"Of course, Lydia. For you, always," I said, testing my weight on my legs before getting to my feet.

"Well, High Lord Jax, Scion o' th' Empire, Lord o' the Great Tower, this is me ma."

The woman who stood with Lydia looked utterly terrified. She was in her late forties, maybe early fifties, and had lived a hard life, that much was clear. Her clothes were well-worn but clean, and her back bent. She was blatantly terrified to be near me, staring at the floor as I moved closer, reaching out and taking her hand in my own.

"I've heard a lot about you," I said softly, and she looked up hesitantly. "But I never actually got your name?"

"M…Merry…" she stammered. "My lord…"

"Well then, Merry, welcome to the Empire!" I smiled gently. "I have to thank you, because honestly, I'd be dead ten times over and more, if not for your daughter. She's one of my most trusted warriors and my closest friends. And, knowing Lydia, and how little she likes to brag, did you know that she's the Champion of Vanei?"

"W…what?" Merry asked. I gestured to one side, and a legionnaire passed a spare chair over for Merry.

"Join us, Merry! Join us, and let me tell you all about your daughter." I smiled, seeing the notification that popped up as Lydia sat down as well, blushing, but clearly pleased.

Congratulations!

You have made progress in your Quest: A Pillar of Strength.
Your bondswoman, Lydia, commander of your personal squad and close friend, has begun to evolve into a Valkyrie. To complete her evolution and to become all she could be, she requires four things:

Resolution of the Past: 1/1
Cleansing of the Last Valkyrie 1/1
Find a Class Trainer: 0/1
Discover/Create/Recover Suitable Armor: 1/1
Reward: A full Valkyrie under your command, possibly more, 50,000xp

I read it and shot Lydia a grin, getting one in return as I started to tell Merry about how awesome her daughter really was. The next hour was a wonderful one. Others stopped by, seeing what was happening, to tell their own stories about Lydia, mainly about her skills in battle, but occasionally embarrassing ones as well…for Lydia, at least.

I loved it.

Then I heard something that made me groan.

"I, too, am pleased with Optio Lydia's progress. Unlike *certain others,* I don't have to chase her down to make her work on her skills," Restun said. My asshole clenched like it was trying to make pure neutronium.

"Ah, Restun," I whispered. Then, like the evil and total bastard I am, I smiled, turning and gesturing for Restun to join us. "Restun, have you met my brother?" I asked with a purr, reaching out and pouring the man a drink.

CHAPTER TEN

I groaned as the light stabbed into my eyes, making me roll over and look away, a line about firepicks springing to mind as I remembered reading it in a book. I sighed, pulling the blanket up and over my head.

"Jax, we need to get ready for the day," Oracle called. I shook my head in negation.

"Nope. Don't want to play today," I said flatly. My voice sounded gravelly, muffled by the blanket and raspy from the hangover.

"Are you sure? Oh, that's a shame, considering this outfit," Oracle said slowly, her voice full of promise.

I almost gave myself whiplash rolling over and sitting up, blinking in the bright light as I looked over to see her sitting in the chair by the window, fully dressed and smiling mischievously at me as she sipped from her coffee cup.

"Oh, that's just low," I growled, glaring at her.

"What?" she asked innocently. "I thought you liked seeing me in this outfit?" With a smooth gesture, she showed off her long legs in black yoga pants, a simple black boob tube for a top, and lines of camo paint on her cheeks.

"Yeah, I do, usually because when you're dressed like that, I get to hurt someone," I admitted, albeit reluctantly. "But the way you said that," I grumbled as I shuffled across the bed and stood, making my way slowly to the bathroom and using the facilities.

"Well, we're due to set off in three hours…"

I poked my head out in shock. "Wait…*what*?! You woke me when we're not setting off for three godsdamn hours?!" I stalked back through as she glided to the door on the far side of the room.

"You might have forgotten about issuing the challenge to Restun as to which of you and Thomas was the best, but I promise he hasn't!" Oracle stopped in the doorway and looked back at me as I felt my blood run cold, that traitorous memory coming back to me from the drink last night.

"Oh Gods I didn't…did I?" I whispered, and Oracle let out an evil little laugh.

"Oh, you did! Coffee is by the bed, and I told Tenandra and the team when we're leaving, so they'll all be ready. Oh, and one more thing…"

"Huh?" I mumbled, my mind still screaming at me, wondering how I could have been so godsdamn stupid as to give Restun that kind of an excuse…when Oracle blurred and leaned against the doorway, smiling at me.

She'd changed her outfit, now sporting a golden tan and long, blonde hair, wearing simple white stockings and suspenders, a tiny patch of lace that barely hid anything, and stared at me with a very enthusiastic expression on her face.

"If you win, I'll make it worth your while," she purred, before laughing and stepping from view, letting the door swing shut. Every instinct I had screamed at me to rush the door and jump on her, but I knew damn well she was gone, and I growled about the capriciousness of women in general, while quickly drinking my coffee and getting dressed.

I paused once I had drained the dregs of my coffee, then finished putting my training gear on. I looked around the room, trying to remember where the hell this contest was going to take place. When I couldn't figure it out, I reached out to Seneschal.

"Hey, Seneschal, where's Restun and that ass of a brother of mine?"

"Good morning, Jax. Restun is waiting for you in the courtyard, impatiently I might add, and seems to be taking his poor mood out on his trainees. Thomas is currently on the sixth floor and hurrying downwards to meet him."

"Crap. Okay, thanks, buddy, and good morning to you, too!" I sent before striding over to the balcony and out into the morning air. I took a couple of deep breaths and couldn't help but smile as I looked out over the mountains and forests before me. Gods, I loved this world.

I drew in a last deep lungful of the clear crisp air, then I turned around, leaned back against the railing of the balcony, then let myself tip backward, falling into the sky.

I plummeted, building speed rapidly, before activating Soaring Majesty and twisting around, turning my uncontrolled fall into flight.

It took less than a minute to reach the ground, flipping over and pushing against it to kill my momentum as I closed in. That allowed me to stop gently, rather than ploughing into the ground and killing myself.

I stopped perfectly, straightening up and looking about, ready for the stunned amazement and acclaim that was my due, only to find that Restun was looking the other way and the entire cadre he was training were doing pushups and hadn't seen.

I sagged a little in disappointment before sighing and walking over to stand next to Restun, while hitting myself with a quick heal, curing myself of my hangover completely and smiling smugly as Thomas staggered out of the Tower in the distance.

"He's late," Restun said slowly, turning and glaring at me. "And you nearly were, as well."

"And good morning to you, too, you miserable bugger," I said with a nervous smile. "Look, this competition, we've got to go on a mission today, right, so…"

"Oh, don't worry. You and Thomas pointed that out enough last night. I've had time to plan for it. He pulled out two healing and stamina potions, along with a pair of potions that looked suspiciously like…

"Are those potions of Legionnaire's Might?" I asked carefully.

"They certainly are," Restun said with pure delight twinkling in his malicious eyes. He turned to Thomas as he staggered over, panting, and waved him to stand with me, before speaking to his trainees.

"All right, you worms! On your feet!" he barked, making me stifle a laugh as several jumped up and promptly fell over from the blood rushing to their heads.

"Your Lord and Master Jax and his brother Thomas have agreed to a little Demonstration today. Thomas has been trained and inducted into the fighting styles of the Dark Legion, while Lord Jax has been the recipient of my more *tender* training. As such, they will each be set a series of tests, the winner of each round receiving a single point, then they will fight, and the winner of the fight receives two points! Highest number of points wins!"

I looked at Thomas, who winced at me, looking around at the bright sunlight and sighing, shaking his head.

"Man, I *already* regret this," Thomas mumbled. I grunted my agreement before hitting him with a heal.

"Oh, thank you," Thomas whispered, straightening up and rubbing his eyes with the heels of his hands before looking around as if seeing the courtyard clearly for the first time. "I swear, I think I was still drunk."

"I should have left you that way."

"Nah, you know you want a fair fight."

"Last thing I ever want is a fair fight," I told him, but couldn't help but grin.

"Aye, as long as it's in our favor, anyway, ha! You remember…"

"Lord Jax, Thomas!" Restun called, and we both stiffened to attention instinctively, watching him as he gestured us over. We stood where he indicated as he spoke. "Now, they will be running from here, around the inner ring of the wall, two laps to warm up, then it's up the Tower, from here to the Hall of the Eternal, the highest point of the Tower.

"Once there, they will do one hundred burpees—Gods, I love those things— then they will sprint across each floor before jogging down each set of stairs. Upon arrival on each floor, they will do ten pushups and sit-ups, then sprint to the next stairwell. The first one back here gets to rest until the loser arrives, which is when we'll start the next contest."

"Wait, run up that?" Thomas asked, looking up at the towering behemoth of stone before us. It was a mountain in its own right and took hours to walk it alone.

"Uh, you remember that in like, three hours, we need to leave, right?" I asked Restun, who smiled coldly.

"I'm well aware of that, *my lord*. If you run rather than ask foolish questions, you'll make it. If not, it's your own fault."

"Fuuuuuck," I groaned, before looking at Thomas, then over at Restun. "Ready?" I stated, half-asking it as a question, as I really wasn't sure I was.

"GO!" Restun snapped, and I set off jogging, with Thomas behind me, cursing, as he wasn't ready and had to speed up to catch up.

"What the hell? Is he serious?" Thomas asked, catching up and running alongside.

"Always. He's a Drill Sergeant to his soul, bro. But it works!"

"What does?" he asked.

"His methods. He has you living in utter terror, but you look at your gains after a session with him, and boom, you'll see it's worth it…or at least it is when you recover."

"Fuuuuuck," Thomas growled, before speeding up just a little to pull ahead.

"Oh, it's like that, is it?" I called out, speeding up as well.

"It's a race, bro! See you at the finish line!" Thomas picked up his speed. I couldn't help but grin. I was used to the Tower, after all. It wasn't easy, Gods no, but I'd done it before, and I'd do it again.

Thomas, though, was about to make a serious mistake. I pushed a little harder, settling into a comfortable pace, forcing him to actually run if he wanted to stay in the lead by much, and by the second lap of the Courtyard, I was feeling confident, until we were directed to the Tower…and Thomas showed no signs of flagging.

Six floors, and he was still going, with me now pushing myself harder and harder, running full speed to catch up, having lost sight of him several minutes ago.

I constantly expected to find him on the next revolution of the stairwell, panting and groaning, but it was like…

"Shit." I groaned as I finally remembered he was forced to run for days, eight hours and more a day straight through heavy forest in full armor!

I'd been relying on the heavy armor and knowing that Thomas hated running, so he wouldn't have been training that hard in that way, especially not considering the bugger was so heavily muscled now. Where I looked like I'd make Captain America weep with envy these days, he made heavyweight wrestlers look small.

I pushed harder, digging deeper and starting to fly up the stairs as I realized I'd fallen into the trap of assuming something, and now it might cost me the race.

Ten floors passed; still no sign of him.

Twenty floors, and I was seeing people looking over their shoulders as I appeared, clearly looking after someone who'd passed recently.

Thirty, forty, fifty.

It went on and on, with me slowly reeling him in. At first, it was the sound of his feet, then the panting, then I started to catch glimpses of him.

Crossing the floor ahead of me, I got closer and closer. I was behind him on the stairways. Finally, when I drew alongside him, it was with fifteen floors to go.

I passed him, hearing him gasping like a bellows, and saw the wide-eyed look of shock on his face as I picked up speed even further. The competition with my brother gave me exactly what I needed to dig deeper.

"How…much…farther?" he asked, his voice coming out in pants.

I considered it, looking at the floor I was passing and grunting out a reply.

"Fifteen…maybe twenty…floors…" I managed to get out, before grinning and pushing harder, ignoring the burn in my legs. I was seriously tempted to use my Overdrive and tear away from him, but that wasn't what this was about, as much as I'd have loved to see his face.

"Fuck…me…sideways!" he groaned, and he let me pull ahead. The next few floors were painful, followed by the final ten that were frankly torture.

By the time I staggered up onto the final floor, the door of the Hall of the Eternal standing locked before me, I was done. I collapsed onto the floor, dry retching and panting, unable to move. A minute passed with my heart thundering in my ears.

Two minutes, and my insane stats, in comparison to a baseline human, were already at work, calming my racing heart, even as I started to be able to hear over the sound of my own panting.

I rolled over, getting into the pushup position and forcing myself to start pushing myself up, having heard a sound coming from the stairwell.

I managed three burpees before Thomas appeared, and then because he immediately collapsed on arrival, I kept going.

Seven minutes later, well, just under eight in reality, and just as Thomas was starting his own, I was finishing.

"Enjoy!" I called to him, heading for the stairwell and ignoring his curses.

The next few floors were crippling, my muscles screaming at my every step.

The ten that followed made me want to puke.

The next fifteen or so, I settled into a good rhythm, and I started to think I was all right...until I looked back as I was leaving the floor and saw Thomas starting his pushups on that floor.

I'd lost the lead I'd had.

I dug deeper, realizing that I'd been unconsciously slowing, and I picked it up again. The jogging section of the stairwells down were harder than anything else, because it made you want to go faster. But a single slip could end you, I knew from bitter experience, and I forced myself to maintain a fast jog instead.

An hour and fifty-eight minutes after I'd entered the Tower, I staggered across the finish line to collapse onto the floor by Restun's feet.

"Acceptable, Jax." That was all he said, but I thought I detected a note of respect in his voice, which was frankly weird. I considered speaking to him, but surviving the heart attack I felt like I was having was more important, so I stayed quiet.

After a minute, I forced myself to my feet and started to walk in a small circle, doing some stretches, loosening up muscles that screamed at me, before Thomas staggered out of the Tower and fell down the last few steps.

He pulled himself up and stumbled over the line then fell again, as Restun crouched next to him, muttering about him barely passing the fitness test.

I continued to walk slowly, seeing the cadre Restun was training were looking at me wide-eyed...except for Alistor, who glared at me in clear hatred.

As soon as he'd been seen, he ducked his head, and I couldn't help but wonder if I should go and say something.

I decided against it.

I'd given him every godsdamn chance I could, and the prick had done everything he could to make my life harder each time.

"Time!" Restun barked. I looked over at him as he hauled Thomas upright.

"Let...me...die..." Thomas wheezed.

"Come on man, what's wrong with you?" I said to him, deliberately forcing myself to sound better than I felt.

"Piss off...and...die," Thomas mumbled, making me feel amazing.

"Now now," I started to say to him, before Restun cut me off.

"Right, test of Strength!" he barked, and I looked over at the massive weights that were set out in pairs. They looked like kettlebells, but squared instead of rounded, with the same handle on the top. "Pick the heaviest weight you can do reps with, then you walk from this point..." He indicated a line marked on the floor. "...to that point. Each step you lift the weight, alternate lifting up to your chest, and out as far as you can to the sides. GO!"

I was still staring open-mouthed at the second line, a hundred meters away.

This time, it was Thomas who got to it first, grabbing the heaviest weight and starting lifting, before apparently thinking better of it and taking the second heaviest. I picked one that was further down the scale, maybe fourth, and followed.

We took a step, then lifted the weights, one in each hand to our chests, reaching nipple height at Restun's barked command, before lowering and stepping forward again.

The next one was out to the side. At first, I could manage to get a full arm extension, making a ninety-degree line from my side, but after only five or six, that line dipped, and as I went on, it dipped more and more.

By the time we both made it to the far side, my arms were more like wet noodles than muscles, and it was all I could do to not drop the weights on my feet.

"Thomas wins," Restun announced. I swore, looking at my brother.

The exercise had made his massive muscles swell even larger, and I shook my head, seeing him panting and glaring at his hands, and the cracked and bleeding skin, until he finally heard what Restun had said, and he grinned, waving around at the cheering recruits.

"Final test," was all Restun said, but he gestured at the squared-off dueling ring. I staggered over, barely able to lift my arms, pulled on the padded jerkin, then stepped over the line of white painted stones that marked the outer edge before grabbing up the blunt and heavily weighted gladius and waiting in the middle of my side.

The dueling ring was a simple design. It was called a ring, but was actually a square, and there was a wide space in the middle that was an area we fought in, and a small area that was separated with another line where we each started.

The result was a square with three lines inside. We both had a rest area and the fighting section. If we needed to, we could step back and catch our breath inside the rest area at any time.

I swung the gladius round and round, getting a feel for the weapon and noting the lines of charcoal ringing the blade. These training weapons were heavier than the real thing, and blunt, but they left a nasty bruise when they connected. Just to make sure that you knew you'd been hit, they also left a black streak, making it easy for the judge to call out the strike.

I looked over at Thomas, who was grinning at me as he loosened up with his own blade. I smiled, noting for the first time that there were hundreds of people gathered around now. I'd seen them filter in, in pairs and singles, small groups and gangs, and now they surrounded the ring, making me shake my head.

I'd been so single-mindedly focused on trying to beat Thomas that I'd not noticed at first. Whenever the ring was in use, there'd be spectators. It was one of the primary forms of entertainment for the Tower now, and this time, it was the High Lord versus his brother.

Instead of being intimidated, I couldn't help but smile, and I noted the same grin on Thomas's face as we faced off.

"First to three touches on the torso, no hitting the head," Restun warned, passing us a helm each. I pulled it on and nodded to Thomas as he stepped out of his rest area, swinging the sword from side to side.

We moved closer, watching each other, and I crouched, left hand held close to my chest, fist ready, and right hand holding the gladius.

He struck first, a tentative thrust, feeling me out. I slapped it aside and slashed across the belly, missing but making him jump back. He growled and stabbed forward again, thrusting toward my chest, and I batted it aside again. But, seeing the way his left hand clenched and unclenched, I knew him well enough to know he had a plan, and I didn't take the obvious opening.

We traded a few more blows before he managed to slash across my chest after a particularly fast block left me out of position.

I grunted in pain before growling and slashing down just fast enough to catch him on the wrist.

He swore, dropping the blade as his fingers spasmed, and he punched me in the face, just as my blade landed on his chest.

"Back!" Restun shouted. I took a step back, shaking my head to clear my vision.

"Bastard," Thomas grunted, shaking his wrist. I snorted and blew out a spray of blood onto the floor, then tugged on my nose and winced as it released a veritable gush of bright scarlet blood.

"You broke my damn nose," I growled back at him, before getting a grin.

"Need a healer?" Thomas asked, picking his sword up and retreating to the rest area, speaking to me across the gap as I stood inside my own.

"Nah, I've broken it plenty of times before. How's the hand?" I asked as he held his sword in his left.

"Broken wrist, I think," he answered with a shrug. "I'll give you a chance and use my left."

"Ha, I barely use a damn sword, as well. Next time, we fight with a staff," I said, before stepping up to the edge. "You ready?"

"Let's do it." He crossed over the line and crouched with his sword held ready.

I did the same, and we slowly circled each other, then I attacked. I thrust at his blade, then slid mine down it, aiming to catch his hand and bring the fight to a fast close, but he rolled his wrist, spiraling the blade around my own.

I did the same, each of us trying to get his sword under the other's and into a position to knock their blade free, or at least out of position.

We spun our blades, then broke away, backing up when we both failed. Then Thomas struck. He rushed me, his sword flashing and trying to beat my own aside, before kicking out, a move I barely dodged. I brought my knee up the next time he tried it, catching his shin on the outside of my own. He twisted my sword, ducking as his blade flashed toward me then leaned back, stabbing forward.

The tip of my blade slammed into the middle of his sternum with rib-cracking force before he could dodge. He grunted as he backed up, coughed a little blood, then spat on the floor, before growling and attacking again, all-out this time.

I blocked a slash and had my sword slammed aside, blocked his next kick, then the next, catching them on my shins and the outside of my thighs before taking the pommel of his gladius to my face and staggering back, blinded and seeing stars.

I gasped in pain as his training gladius slammed into my side, the leaden sword cracking ribs and leaving a clear slash in charcoal across my chest, before his kick finally landed true, spinning my leg out from under me. Before Restun could call a pause, Thomas's blade slammed into my stomach, propelling me to the floor at speed.

I slammed down hard, blood flying from my nose and mouth and dust rising from the force of the impact, even as I heard Restun call out the win.

"Thomas wins!" he shouted, to cheers and boos in equal measure.

CHAPTER ELEVEN

I groaned as I looked up, clutching my chest as the sun was blocked by Thomas standing over me. He paused, sword held tightly in his hand, panting hard, and I knew what he was feeling, suddenly.

He'd been alone for too long, and the fight had brought out the old instincts, making him ready to keep going, the rage that always drove us to keep fighting.

I'd managed to tame it, somewhat, mainly I suspected thanks to sharing my mind and heart with Oracle. But Thomas hadn't, and he was still struggling.

Then he shook himself and dropped the gladius before crouching next to me and reaching out to take my hand.

"You okay, bro?" he asked, and I smiled despite the pain.

"Yeah man, never been better." I damn well meant it. I had my brother back, and while he'd just kicked my ass, it just made me even more determined to get better.

I let out a gasp as Oracle healed me, followed by the popping and crackling sound of ribs and my nose being straightened and forced back into place by magic.

I groaned, and a few seconds later, Thomas did the same. I sagged back, looking up at the sky in disbelief.

"I lost," I muttered.

Thomas snorted. "What did you expect?"

I glared at him. "Well, clearly to fucking win, you knob." I sat up, and he grinned at me.

"Bro, I've been here more than five years, fighting like this time and time again. Add to that, I had weeks of dedicated training with the Dark Legion every day all day."

"*Bro,*" I growled. "I've been fighting like this most *days* since I arrived, including in the arena, underground, and against Drow and more. Hell, I've fought your guys toe-to-toe enough!"

"And I got a good shot in, and it floored you, but is that how you normally fight?" Thomas asked.

"Well, no. Usually I use my naginata and my magic…"

"Right, and I usually use a mace, or sword, and a shield."

"Fair point," I grumbled, accepting the hand he held out and getting to my feet with his help. "Next time, we both use staffs…"

"You already kicked the shit outta me with those," he said slowly, referencing the fight in the forest.

"Uh, yeah alright…come on," I said through gritted teeth, leading him across the ring to where Restun stood waiting.

"Thomas is the winner," he called out, and a fresh round of cheers and boos rang out, before Restun held his hands up and the crowd went silent. "BUT, considering how effective this was as training, I declare Thomas as TODAY'S winner. Once Lord Jax and Thomas return to the Tower, we will have round two!"

A long few seconds passed as people realized what he'd said, then a roar of approval rose all around us, even as Thomas and I glanced at each other in shared dismay.

"We got played," I read Thomas's lips as he said it, because I sure as shit couldn't hear him. We both looked at Restun, whose satisfaction peeked through as he registered that we'd realized what had happened.

"What, you thought this was the end? I know what kind of things you're capable of now, boys, so I expect better!" he said as soon as the cheers died down enough that we could hear him.

We nodded, despite our exhaustion, and moved away, heading over to Oracle and the team, who were standing off to one side. A few hundred meters back, Tenandra had moved the ship around to us, and I sighed my thanks out.

Lydia took up her usual station on my left side, with Grizz on my right. Oracle shrank down and sat on my shoulder, much to Thomas's amusement, and the rest of the team gathered around us as we walked to the ship, picking Cai, Romanus, and Oren up as we went.

"You look terrible," Cai said, then took Thomas' condition in as well. "You don't look much better."

"Yeah, well, I feel worse," I said as Oracle started with her genetic drift treatment, once again focusing on my right knee. She was determined that, every chance she got, she was going to do it, and she was going to get that knee…why that particular body part, I didn't know, but it was what she'd focused on…up to perfection.

It felt weird, basically, like she was healing me over and over again, despite the lack of any problems. But it made her happy, and would eventually help me, I guessed, so that was fine.

"So, do you need me, Cai?" I asked as he followed us up the gangplank onto Tenandra's deck, before groaning slightly as I saw the real reason he'd been waiting…a half dozen well-dressed men stood about on the deck, clearly waiting for me, including Hannimish and a man I assumed was Mal's father.

Hannimish hurried forward as soon as he saw me, smiling nervously even as he brushed at his collar and cuffs, trying to make sure he looked the part.

"Ah, High Lord Jax, so…so nice to see that you've recovered from your injuries."

I blinked, remembering the way he'd practically forced his way in to see me on Mal's ship, before running off to be sick, considering he'd found me gutted like a fresh-landed fish.

"Yes, Hannimish," I said, forcing a smile and trying to remember that his nephew Joshua's plots were not this man's fault. "I'm well, thank you. Now, I'm sorry to be rude, but who are these people with you, and what the hell do you want from me? I'm at war and need to get on with things."

"Ah." There was a long pause as he looked at me, before seeming to deflate, and nodding. "Very well. Can we sit?"

Summoning a fountain to one side of the group, I gestured to them all to sit on the deck. Then I pulled my top off and leaned into the fountain, drinking the healing waters then casting Scour to remove the blood and sweat.

"We can talk here," I said, coming back over to them and sitting topless on the deck, relaxing slightly in the warm morning sunshine. "I need to wait for the new armor arriving, anyway," I grumbled, having seen Thorn and a few of her team walking towards the ship with purpose.

"Ah, uh…well, these others with me are nobles and close friends of the court."

I held up a hand to stop him. "No offense to you all." I looked at the gaudily dressed butterflies. "But are you here for a reason?"

"Ah," Hannimish said, his gaze darting frantically before he spoke to the four nobles behind and around him quietly. They got up and stalked off, shooting him furious looks and attempting to pretend to be friends with me as they sent me smiles.

"No," he said sadly. "They were here to either support me or to try and make a deal with you, a private one, I mean. They were nearby when I saw Mal boarding his ship, and they followed me, chasing an opportunity."

"Well, thank you for the honesty and saving me from dealing with their bullshit."

"You're welcome." Hannimish shook his head. "My dismissal of them all has certainly cost me friendships, though, and made new enemies when I can least afford it." He shook himself and straightened up before gesturing at the one remaining figure, a man who'd stretched out on the deck and looked like he was only missing a piña colada and some suntan oil to complete the impression of a vacation. "This gentleman is Hannibal." He introduced the man, who sat up and grinned at me, offering his hand. A handful of others stood around behind him, talking with Mal and watching.

I took it and shook, before realizing what I was doing, then I looked down at our hands gripping each other, then up, staring into his eyes and seeing what I was looking for.

"Earth," I said flatly. "You're from Earth."

"I am, son, born in Chicago." He grinned wryly.

"And what the hell are you doing here?" I asked, feeling an urgent desire to Fireball first and ask questions later.

"I was kicked through, same as you, nearly forty years ago. Saw the shithole this place is, and after being forced to fight by my asshole relatives, I decided I wanted no part in their war. Set myself up in the city and started work. Didn't take long to find a way to survive."

"And that was?" I stepped back from him, sensing the others moving around to watch him, even as Mal scowled at the distrust.

"Smuggling," he said at the same time Hannimish spoke up.

"Trading…wait, *what*?" Hannimish gasped.

"Tell you what, Hannimish, I think this is a conversation best had with fewer people," I suggested. "But, and let's be honest here, you're the first noble I've met, so far, who's not been a complete cock. Perhaps Cai could arrange for you to meet Riana. She's involved in all the ancient technology and research that we do here, and I think that was something you were interested in? Perhaps you could help her?" I received an actual smile of genuine interest from him before he frowned at Hannibal again then moved aside at Cai's direction.

"I'm a member of the Smuggler's Guild in somewhat murky standing." Mal's father watched Hannimish being sent off into the depths of the Tower. "Seems like my son didn't tell you much about me."

"He told me bugger all about you, except that you arranged things and liked rules. Liked others following them, anyway," I said, watching Hannibal carefully.

"All true. Makes it easier to fleece them," Hannibal said with a twinkle in his eye. "Look, my son came to me with a few details about your intentions, and I wanted to meet you. Nobles around Rewn have been disappearing, so when Mal told me about you, I decided to bring my people and come along. Seems like we might be able to make a deal or two."

"You've got my attention."

"I've been in this realm for forty years, worked my way up into the lower nobility, set up a nice little merchant empire, dealing with both the honest and the dodgy. By far, the least trustworthy group I've dealt with are the nobles.

"I just fucking love smiling at them and taking their eyes out of their sockets on deals. I hear you've got an Elf doing the economy now? Well, I want to work with them, set up a new economy that will strengthen the Empire, and I'm willing to be the liaison with the nobility, the buffer between you and them."

"So, you get to be the gatekeeper, the one who takes all the bribes and backhanders to control access to my ear?" I raised one eyebrow and thought of the dodgy chancellors in all the movies and books I'd read.

"Yes and no." Hannibal shrugged. "I get to be the gatekeeper, but I'd be under...Cai? I think it is? Also, I'd basically become a member of the council. Yes, I'll take bribes, but they'll be mainly in the nature of favors. I'm rich, son. Seriously rich. I bought my way into the nobility and could buy most of those peacocks out without making a dent. By taking me on, you get access to that. I'll set up a fair taxation system, and I'll even pay the taxes myself. Well, most of them anyway, as I damn well know how much an Empire needs coin."

"What kind of favors?"

"The kind that result in leverage," Hannibal said, grinning.

"Secrets, blackmail, and backstabbing?"

He shrugged again. "It's how the nobility operate, and how they used to back in the old Empire as well, apparently. If you want to cut that out, you need to make *them* want it gone. If I know all the secrets, I can bring the important ones to your attention and ensure the good behavior of the littler guys. Then, you make the title of the nobles an earned one, not a hereditary title, so when it passes, you can make sure the wrong ones don't step into power."

"I'm...I'm actually interested." I said, surprising myself. "But let's be clear, Hannibal. I don't know you, and I'm not setting you up for power. You'll earn that kind of a role by working with Flux, Cai, and Hanau for now, but we'll discuss it later. For now, you want a chance at that kind of position, you prove I can trust you. Swear..."

"The Oaths," Hannibal said, sinking to one knee. "My people and I are ready." I blinked, those with him were sinking to their knees as well. I looked to Mal, who shrugged, now the only one who stood.

"He's been planning this since I spoke to him back in Narkolt." Mal said laconically. "He's a bastard to have as an enemy, but you can trust him, and, hell, as a sign of good faith, and after our conversation earlier..." Mal sighed as he sank to one knee as well. "I told the crew I'd be doing this, so if you can send it to them as well?"

Oracle didn't waste any time and sent it out, and seconds later, the sound of the Oaths rang out in the still air, and I felt another set of connections blooming between me and those around me, as well as Mal's crew up in the Tower.

"I swear to obey Lord Jax and those he places over me; I will serve to the best of my ability, speak no lie to him when commanded otherwise, and treat all other citizens as family.

"I will work for the greater good, being a shield to those who need it, a sword for those who deserve it, and a warden to the night.

"I will stand with my family, helping one another to reach the light, until the hour of my death or my Lord releases me from my oath.

"Lastly, I will not be a dick!"

"I, Lord Jax, do swear to protect and lead you, to be the shield that protects you and yours from the darkness, and the sword that avenges that which cannot be saved. As the Tower grows in strength, so shall you," I called out, feeling the heady rush of the Great Tower's mana pool streaming through me to bind these people to myself, then I pushed out the original Oath of Imperial Citizenship.

"I swear upon pain of death, to faithfully execute all that the Emperor decrees. I swear upon my soul that I shall stand for the Empire when it calls. I shall be strong when the weak need me, generous when the poor are at hand, and merciless when my fellow citizens are threatened. I shall worship the Gods of my fathers, respect my elders, and raise up my children to stand tall.

"I am an Imperial Citizen. I claim the right to call upon the Legion in my hour of need, to hold those that wrong me to justice, and to be avenged if I cannot be saved."

"Why?" I asked Mal.

"Because you were right about what you said earlier. And if I've got to pick a side, well, this one's got gold and ships. I still want a title, though, and it'd better be a good one."

"Sheepshag..."

"*Not* an insulting one!" Mal clarified as they all rose to their feet.

"Fine, I'll think about it. Cai, you and the others have been damn quiet. You pleased about this?"

"I am. I'm aware of the subtle movements Hannibal has been making, meeting people and asking questions, and I believe he has the entire rank and authority structure of the Tower planned out now?"

"Pretty much," Hannibal admitted, grinning.

"I can think of a dozen things I can use a man of his talents to work on," Cai said, smiling.

"Then, I guess, welcome?" I said to Hannibal, before nodding once to Mal, both of us having put our recent disagreement behind us fully.

Hannibal and his people got up and mingled with Cai and the others, starting a new round of introductions as I turned to speak to Oren, who wore a proud smile plastered across his face.

"As to tha fleet, Ah've managed ta get tha Battleship fully sealed, an' she be ready ta go pick up tha wayward lambs anytime no'. Ah'll be leavin' right after ye, and takin' three cruisers wit' me, wit' four o' the wee scouts stayin' back here on fast launch, ready ta come rescue us iffin we're followed."

"Sounds good. Make sure you're taking some of the Legion both for protection and to speak on your behalf."

Oren nodded and looked to Romanus, who smiled faintly..

"It seems I see more of you coming and going than anything else, Jax," Romanus said, sighing regretfully. "It is as it needs to be, I suppose. But please, consider taking more of the Legion with you. I've included a small squad aboard this ship as protection for her, so please make use of them. While levelling is important for you, survival is more so."

I winced and nodded my agreement.

"And please, Jax, when you return, make time for us to talk. There is a lot we need to discuss, including more of the future of the Legion itself, structure, training, all of it. For now, as you requested, I have folded the Legion of Narkolt and my own into one, and I have accepted Jon as tribune in Alistor's place. Sadly, most of the primuses for the Narkolt forces were killed. I suspect that there may be a small number of the Drow spread throughout the incoming forces as well. We need to find a way to identify them...."

"The Oath," I said. "The Oath itself is sufficient. If they cannot swear the Oath, then they've shown themselves. I've been thinking about it. You take them in small groups and give them the Oath. Get Heph or Seneschal to help you with it, then order them to tell you their true name. Sounds simple, I know, but hopefully the legionnaires with them will know the names of their friends. When one gets it wrong..."

"Then we've found an infiltrator," Romanus finished. "It's a simple method, yet combined with the ones that I have been discussing with Seneschal, it should work. Essentially, we will be testing and trying. Hopefully, we will find one, then we'll know it works. Augustus has both legion and an imperial noble rank, so he can command both citizens and legionnaires, which should cover the bases."

"Exactly. Beyond that, well, we'll just have to see what we come up with, I guess."

"Secondly, Jax with regard to the two who were apprehended for avoiding the Oath."

"Ah yeah, I'd almost forgotten about them. Man, it sounds so wrong when you put it like that. Anyway, good excuses?"

"Fantastic excuses from one, until we gave him the choice of swearing the Oath and telling us the truth anyway. He attempted to avoid it, and was given the choice of prison or the Oath..."

"We don't have a prison."

"We do now. He claims his current Oaths won't permit a second Oath, and it'll kill him. It makes me highly suspicious, but it is a known occurrence in certain criminal gangs. He claims to have escaped the gangs and is simply attempting to 'live a free life'."

"But?"

"But he had a significant amount of gold on him and was attempting to make free with stores when we caught him, so either way, he'd be facing some prison time, I suspect. You named Lucian as Imperial Justicar, and he has ruled five years of hard labor."

"Sucks to be him, then. Fuck it, I'm not overruling my Justicar on his first day." I shrugged. "What about the other one?"

"She was highly skilled in Illusion spells, so skilled it took three hours to locate her, despite knowing roughly which room she was in. Once she was caught, however, she activated a ring, one that killed her instantly. I suspect she was a planted spy for Barabarattas, hiding amongst the common people and accidentally scooped up when we left the city. Regardless, we have nothing left but her arms and armor to identify her now. I'll continue to look into it, however."

Thank you, Romanus. Seriously, thank you," I said with a smile. "Guess we just need to stay vigilant for now."

"Yes, also, and I don't say this lightly Jax, you're doing well, but we need to work on your image."

My smile dropped. "Go on…"

"You run everywhere. Not just in training, I mean. Everything you do is done at a thousand miles an hour, and the citizens see that. It creates an impression of panic and poor planning. You need to cultivate an air of patience and professionalism. It's difficult as your life is now, I know, but consider it, please," Romanus said.

I let out a grunt. "Okay, yeah I can see that, I guess."

"Jax, we're at war, so this is understandable. But while I have the legion out clearing the monsters from the local area and training the forces of the Tower, not to mention the future legionnaires, you still give the impression of doing everything yourself.

"You need to step back and let us help. You can level through other means, such as giving orders to the legion and having them achieve certain things, setting up camps, clearing caves, et cetera."

My chin dropped. "What?"

"Jax, what did you think generals and higher officers did? Did you think that once you reached this rank, you ceased all levelling?" Romanus asked, clearly having wanted to say this for a while. "I keep asking you to direct the legion; this is part of the reason! You won't receive a great deal of experience, admittedly. The lion's share goes to those who actually fight, but the legion leadership receives twenty-five percent of the experience the legionnaires earn. With dozens of teams out each day, it climbs steadily."

"Holy shit, that's got to be…"

"It's sufficient to replace your adventures easily, Jax. But because of the vagaries of the system that ties us all together, the maximum you, personally, could earn from it is either ten percent if you were in a central command post—meaning you are giving the troops direction—or at the other end of the scale, nothing if you are not involved in the actual commands."

"Dammit. So, I could sit around and do the admin and give orders and probably level faster than I am now, or I could keep doing this."

"Yes, basically," Romanus replied. "Admittedly, in certain situations, such as the capturing of the waystations, and the quests from the Gods, you needed to do them yourself until recently. But Augustus is the designated heir, so he would be able to reactivate imperial structures now, as could others in the Legion, if you authorize them to do so in your name."

"I'll think about it," I said cautiously, every instinct in me screaming no.

"That's all I ask, Jax. We can't afford to lose you." Romanus turned to Thorn and her team, who'd been waiting for me, having kitted the others out already. "I'll leave you to the armorers, and look forward to talking when you return. Good luck, Scion," Romanus said with a smile and a clash of fist to chest.

I returned the salute, and watched them leave the ship, leaving only Thorn and her team with a collection of parts.

I nodded to them, smiling, and apologized for the delay. Thankfully, this time the fitting was quick and mostly painless. Thorn had made the majority of the changes before coming to the ship, using her knowledge of my build and needs.

The last piece she handed me was my helm. The dented-in cheek guard was repaired and the visible damage buffed out, as were most of the scratches, leaving the helm back up in the early eighties in terms of durability.

"How is it in the forge?" I asked Thorn as I did stretches and exercises at her direction then stopped for her to make adjustments.

"It's different. Master Grenback has us working on ploughshares and making dozens of tools that we smelt back down each night. It's vastly slowed our production."

"What?" I growled.

Thorn shook her head. "No, wait. He's had us doing this, but they're designs we've never done, they're things we never looked at before, as our permitted list of things was so specialized previously. It means that we're actually starting to grow in our profession again!

"I gained a damn level making rings! Rings, of all things! I'd never have made them if not for him, and they're damn ugly, but if we keep this up, we'll all gain at least five levels by the end of the week. The boost in production from that alone will make up for the loss this week. Then the week after, it'll be higher. It's...it's so simple and obvious, yet we've never done it."

"So, it's working out okay?"

She nodded then pulled a strap tight on my upper thigh, making me grunt.

"Uh, is that okay?"

I shook my head, my eyes closed as I tried to maintain an even voice. "No, Thorn...no, it's really not..." I whispered.

She looked at the strap she'd just pulled tight, going grey-faced in horror as she fumbled to undo it, while also keeping her hands as far from a particularly sensitive area as she could.

"Better?" she asked a few seconds later.

"That's...better..." I agreed, adjusting myself and letting out a groan of pain.

"Sorry Jax, I...I got distracted and pulled too hard..."

I managed a terse nod. "It's fine, just remember to never, *ever* do that again, okay?" I whimpered as the blood returned to my manhood from where it'd nearly been crushed by the tightened armor.

"I won't…" she said, wincing.

After a moment's recovery, I moved again. Despite the new ache I'd gained, I could move more freely than ever before in armor.

"Good. Thanks, Thorn."

She nodded, heading for the gangplank with her team as they all winced at what had happened.

"Try and bring the armor back this time, okay?" She called back to me as she walked away.

I waved her off, moving over to Thomas and Lydia, seeing Oracle heading over from where she'd vanished to speak to Tenandra while the armor was being fitted.

"What happened there?" Thomas asked, twisting in his gear and grinning at me. "Man, this fits so well! Not like my old gear."

"Might have more of a problem in this if you rage monster though, dude, just a heads up." I indicated the armor, and he grimaced. "That was me getting a strap tightened too far, and I think I've got bruised balls from it now, and a strap mark across my pecker," I muttered, dropping my voice.

"Ah did no' need that picture in me mind," Lydia said, shaking her head. "We're off to the Goblin cave first, right?" she asked, and I nodded. "And that's what, a day's flight?"

"About that."

"Good. I need to werk on integratin' Thomas into our formations…" Lydia said. "Is 'e a permanent addition?"

"No, I think he'll probably end up leading his own team?" I said, glancing at Thomas for confirmation.

He nodded. "I'd prefer that, I think. But for now, I'd rather spend some time with you, then I can get a team set up when we return."

I smiled. "Sounds good, bro. Go work with Lydia and the team; I'll sort some things with Tenandra, then I'll make more potions."

"Wait, what? You don't train?" Thomas asked, confused.

"It's our job to fit in around Jax," Lydia said, smiling grimly. "Get used to it, Thomas. When you've got your own team, you'll be the same, I bet. But for now, he's busy, and you get to practice."

"Uh, what's the deal with the skeleton?" I heard Thomas asking as he was led aside. I grinned, having seen little of Bob the last day, but knowing he was here made me smile.

Chapter Twelve

I'd checked in with Tenandra and found out everything was good. She was particularly pleased about the ten legionnaires who had been added to her crew, especially as they had taken over a section of the hull originally intended for cargo. She'd been able to do some reconstruction, making that area into a dedicated bunkroom with a separate room for their Optio to have some privacy and a central area for them all to relax and work on their gear and so on.

The legionnaires, under my old friend Westin, who'd recently taken the rank of Optio, were loving the change. It was essentially seen as a combination of a promotion, being charged with being there in case I needed them, and a vacation, as they apparently expected to be relaxing on the deck between training and gear maintenance.

Westin was quick to offer his people up as an "enemy" for Lydia and the team to train against. I left them to it. Jian would rather be flying the ship with Sehran and Tenandra, and probably screwing them both senseless. Arrin and Ronin, a mage and bard respectively, were particularly unsuited to close combat and might prefer to not face legionnaires. But Lydia, Grizz, and Thomas would be overjoyed.

I sat in the room that was now permanently put aside for my alchemy and worked. I essentially had a day to do it, and I hated those damn Goblins, so the first thing I did was to work on my Poison Pattern. Two hours later, I sagged and rubbed my back, checking my prompts and seeing the hoped-for growth of Intelligence.

Congratulations!

For staying true to your choices and for walking the Path of the Creationist, you have gained a point of Intelligence!

*

Congratulations Journeyman!

You have taken further steps to a wider understanding of the art of the Alchemist!

Your dedication to your art has taught you that no ingredient is one-sided, poisons can heal, and healing potions can kill, depending on circumstances.

The Path to Poison Pattern Mastery has continued! 28/100

I checked over my old notifications and grunted as a pattern emerged. It seemed that, if I made a single step along the path to mastery or if I made, like in Poison, twenty-plus steps, it made no damn difference.

As long as I continued to advance, I'd earn a fresh point. But if I made a huge advance, I still only earned a single godsdamn point. I resolved to make time to work on the pattern each day in the hopes I could increase my Intelligence rapidly.

I quickly scoured through the other advances from the hours of training, before dismissing them and looking at the twenty-two tiny vials of poison I'd managed to make.

Congratulations!

**Through hard work and perseverance,
you have increased your stats by the following:**

Constitution +1
Endurance +1
Strength +1

Continue to train and learn to increase this further.

Creeping Death		Further Description *Yes/No*	
Details:		This poison is known and feared in the Amir Basin where it was first used with gleeful abandon by the necromancer Janus to increase the corpses available for his experiments. Creatures infected with this poison are slowed by 50% for 27 seconds, lose 2 points of health per second, and have their Endurance lowered by four points for 36 hours.	
Rarity:	**Magical:**	**Durability:**	**Potency:**
Rare	Yes	100/100	6/10

I had no idea who Janus had been, besides a necromancer, and I briefly considered asking Oracle about it. Then I shrugged and went on, ignoring her mutters as she worked on her spell, slowly sweeping it back and forth on my knee.

A further two hours passed while I worked on general potions, making enough for each of us to have three health, mana, and stamina potions, then another hour while I attempted to make a replacement for the Gnomes' wonderdrug, getting three variants that seemed close-ish before settling down to work on the Mana Pattern, the one I most wanted for myself.

Five hours later, Oracle interrupted me. I sat back with a groan, rubbing my back, aching from being hunched over a small desk for so long.

"I think that's enough, Jax," she said.

I blinked blearily at her. "I'm making progress…" I said, then she stopped me with a hand over my mouth.

"I know, my love, you've been muttering about nothing else for the last hour. But seriously, it's been nine hours since you started. It's time for a break, food, drink, and some actual downtime with your friends. I think you need it."

"He does," Tang called from the corner of the room. "And I either need someone else to take a shift watching over you, or you need to start teaching me alchemy so I can help. There's nothing more boring than watching you tinkering, I swear."

"Love you too, mate. You really want to learn alchemy?"

"Hell no." Tang grinned. "And besides, I'm watching over you, so I couldn't...but it distracted you, didn't it?"

"Distracted..." I looked back to see Oracle slipping more of the alchemy equipment into my bag, sneaking a sly wink at me as I caught her.

"Break time!" she declared.

I laughed, seeing that she'd left the potions that needed to cool out, but had disassembled half the gear at tremendous speed.

"Fine, fine!" I said, clambering to my feet before cracking my back as I twisted this way and that, suddenly aware of how much I was aching. "Damn, I need to make a lazyboy or something..."

"What's that?" Tang asked, curiosity playing in his voice.

"A godsdamn comfortable chair," I said, twisting again and finally making my back crack. I sighed, suddenly glad I'd taken the time to strip my armor off when I'd first come into the lab again. "Okay then, let's gather up the potions that we've got here, then go relax with the others."

I glanced at my notifications. I'd gained a few points in Mana Pattern Mastery, but not enough to be important, so I dismissed it. Since I'd already gained a point of Intelligence today from my Path of the Creationist, I unfortunately couldn't gain another. The next notifications were more interesting.

Congratulations, Journeyman!

You have reached the second branching in your path as an Alchemist!

You must now pick a new path to follow.

Will you choose to focus on the path of EXPERIMENTATION, or concentrate on RESEARCH?

Choose carefully, as this choice cannot be undone.

EXPERIMENTATION:
You've found a new love of the puzzle, adding in new and unexpected ingredients to create potions and poisons that have been long thought lost to time. Continuing down this line of advancement will grant a further 5% gain to the strength of any desired effects in any potions or poisons you produce and result in a 2% greater chance of a breakthrough that will increase your alchemical knowledge when working alone.

RESEARCH:
Through experimentation you reached the heights of a Creationist Alchemist, but you suspect that the possible potions that can be created are limited, and that possibly the ancients had the same thought, leading them to create records of these recipes. You gain knowledge of a single cache of this ancient knowledge through your close personal relationship with the Goddess of Hidden Knowledge.

I didn't really need to consider that particularly hard, mainly because a slight increase in the strength of my potions and a slight increase in the chance of a breakthrough, compared to a possible trove of ancient knowledge was a no brainer. I chose the Research path and popped open my map, grinning at the tiny

X that had appeared just off the coast to the southeast of the Tower, just north of the village of Asha.

I got a sense of a wrecked ship or ships, and I remembered what Lucian had said about a cave system that his brother had vanished in, coming back a Vampyr, and the wreckage of dozens of ships.

I resolved to send Lucian and the Legion, possibly in force, to search the area, give him a chance to clear up any old feelings about the area and salvage some gear…not to mention gaining them and hopefully me some experience.

I checked the mana potions and sighed as I saw the mana they restored.

Mana Potion		Further Description *Yes/No*	
Details:		A simple mana potion created by a Journeyman Alchemist that has made significant breakthroughs resulting in a potion that restores 210 points of mana in a single draft.	
Rarity:	**Magical:**	**Durability:**	**Potency:**
Rare	Yes	100/100	6/10

I counted them up quickly, seeing that this batch had made thirteen potions, and they glimmered faintly, indicating that they were magically active, making me dimly remember channeling into them as I worked, a minor detail I'd totally forgotten until now.

"Hmm, maybe…" I mumbled, reaching for my bag, when I felt Oracle grab my hand. Then Tang was there as well, turning me around and pushing me toward the door.

"Out!" Oracle ordered me. "Get out and RELAX!"

I shook my head as I realized just how easily I'd been distracted by the thoughts of increasing my alchemy level and making more potions.

I let the pair guide me out of the room, along the hall, then up onto the deck, joining the others as they sat with some of the crew, and the legion escort, all listening to Ronin spinning wild tales.

It was just over an hour later when we came in to land at the lake. As I suspected, as soon as I was on the sandy shore, two Mer made themselves known, striding up and out of the water.

"Well met, Lord Jax," said a vaguely familiar figure, and I struggled for a second before recognizing his patterning.

"T'mon!" I smiled, and damn well hoped I'd got his name right. He bowed his head, and I waved him to stand. "How's the pod doing?" I asked, remembering they weren't a village but a pod, for some reason, and received a pleased shrug in return.

"We do well. Our food stores grow. Life, if anything, is easier. My son still lives, and for that, you will forever have my thanks."

"It was nothing," I said, a little embarrassed. "Anyway, it's sort of why I'm here. Flux and Ame mentioned that your people used to worship the Gods, and I was given an Altar by Lagoush. She asked me to bring it to your people so that…"

He froze, staring at the bowl-sized Altar I offered so casually, before snatching it and pressing it into the hands of the second Mer.

"Get this to Ja'la, fast!" he ordered her, before turning back to me and going to one knee. "I do not doubt you, but if this is genuine, and the Gods are returning…what is the cost for this gift to our pod?"

"Uh, there's no cost. I owed Lagoush a favor, so, you know, worship her, I guess?" There was a long silence between us before he straightened.

"Should you ever need us, call!" he said. "Now, I…I must go!" With that, he dove into the water, leaving me with the others on the sandy shore, confused to buggery about the damn weird way the Mer sometimes acted. I shrugged and followed the others up the ramp, taking to the sky again, and in a few minutes, I had banished it from my mind.

We gathered again on the deck, talking, eating and relaxing, before retiring a few hours later. Tenandra watched us, amused, before turning part of her attention from guiding her ship-body to the smaller, physical flesh-body she had grown so fond of forming. She followed, smiling as Jian slipped into the Captain's cabin with Sehran, who was already stripping off…

Chapter Thirteen

I t was just before dawn when I awoke the next day, the faint lightening of the sky as the only hint that the sun would rise soon, but next door, I heard faint voices and low laughter already.

I sat up slowly, looking around the small cabin, saw I was alone, then listened carefully, recognizing the tone and timbre of the voices.

"Oracle and Thomas…great," I muttered, shaking my head as I realized that evil bastard must be telling her stories. I rolled out of the blankets and found my clothes before sighing and starting to dress more carefully, changing from the more comfortable, relaxed clothes I'd worn yesterday, and instead putting on my padded under-armor, then the actual armor itself, strapping myself in and tightening the straps where needed.

"Tenandra, how close are we to that target?" I asked the empty room, wondering just how much she watched us.

"Good morning, Jax. We are fifteen minutes from the target currently, moving in a slow circuit around it. Do you wish to head toward it now?" she asked, appearing in the room.

"No, that's fine. I'll wait until everyone is up and ready, thank you though, Tenandra." I tucked that little tidbit of information away in my mind for the next time Oracle was feeling freaky.

We're always being watched. I dismissed the thought as I walked through into the next room, finding Thomas sitting on a low fold-down bench and Oracle grinning as he told her hugely exaggerated and embarrassing stories about our past.

I clipped him across the ear as I entered, then went to sit on the bench next to him. Just as I sat down, his shoulder shoved into mine, and I nearly fell off the end of the seat, getting a grin from him as I caught myself.

"Bastard," I muttered, and he laughed. "You getting dressed, then?" I asked, seeing he was wearing casual clothes still.

"How long 'til we attack?" He reached over to his piled bags and bedroll and started to pull his gear out, the sound of the armor being placed on the floor getting the others, most of whom had been laying around the room listening to the stories as well, moving.

"As soon as everyone's ready, we'll eat, have half an hour for the food to settle, then we move in," I said, getting a series of nods and agreement from my team.

"What do we know so far?" Lydia asked.

"Not much," I said as everyone got dressed. "It was a gnomish stronghold in the past. It was especially important to Svetu, and he's pissed that the Goblins moved in and defiled it. There'll be a lot of them, I'd imagine, and the whole point of the raid is to secure the site intact, so we need to do as little damage to the structure as possible."

"Why tell us that?" Tang asked, grinning. "I mean, seriously boss, it's always you who trashes the place, tears down walls, and so on."

"Hey, Yen does, too!" I retorted defensively, before growling as Tang laughed at having gotten a rise out of me.

"Well, regardless, per'aps less area of effect spells an' more team tactics would be good," Lydia said. "The last time we fought Goblins, we were all a lot newer to this, an' we still slaughtered them, so ah can't think that this will end differently. Per'aps a slow and steady approach'll work well?"

"Clear the site room-by-room, make sure of each section before moving onto the next," Thomas agreed, nodding to me. "Like in basic?"

"Yeah," I agreed, before passing out the potions, making sure everyone had some. The main mages, Arrin, Yen, Thomas, and myself all had four more mana potions than the others, giving us each three health, three stamina, and either two or six mana, depending on the abilities of the individual.

Once the last one was handed out, I turned to Bob, who had been sitting in the corner, watching, having no need for potions. I moved across to him, examining him as I closed the distance.

Things were a bit strange between Bob and everyone else, and I had no idea how to fix it beyond pretending nothing had changed.

Bob was fully sentient now, despite having something of an identity crisis. He was created by me magically stitching fragments of dozens of other people's souls together and forcing them to play nice to grant him full life.

"Hey, Bob, how are you doing?" I asked, getting a blank stare before he finally spoke.

"I live, and am structurally sound...despite the damage," he said directly into my mind, despite him now having the capacity for speech.

"Are you okay?" I waited again seemingly for ages before he responded.

"I am intact, more or less."

"Do you need anything?"

"Weapons, equipment...I have little of it. Was it intentional to not provide me with armor? Do I not require it?" He asked slowly, as though genuinely uncertain.

"Well shit," I said, covering my face with one hand and sighing. "No, Bob, I'm sorry. I should have thought about that and had you fitted for armor. Until now, I'd always made your armor myself. Since the transformation, well, the armor I made you has been absorbed into your body, hasn't it?"

"Long since," he said flatly.

"Okay, weapons are easy, first of all. What do you want to use?"

"All of them."

"Uh…"

"Tamat instilled an understanding of all forms of killing in me. I have many memories of techniques, but only this sword I took." He said, gesturing to a rusted and clearly shitty sword hanging from a piece of leather that I realized was supposed to be a belt.

"Well, shit." I reached into my bags and searched around, pulling weapons out, then thought better of it. Having relieved that Dark Paladin of his bag during the fight, I simply shifted things around until the bag was more or less empty, then filled it with a few different weapons, having picked plenty of them up over the last few days in the various fights.

There were swords, shields, daggers, maces, and more. I handed the bag over to Bob, helping him to attach it to a spare belt that Grizz provided.

As a sailor knocked on the door, bringing our breakfast, which was thoughtfully provided by Tenandra, we all helped Bob to prepare.

"I'll sort out some bone armor as soon as we have some, well, *bones* I guess, mate." I winced, feeling terrible all over again.

"Thank you. I also have…needs," Bob said, as though unsure.

"Okay, well, what kinda needs?" I asked, wondering if I was going to have to help him come to terms with puberty for the undead or something.

"I remember things, those left behind when I…when fragments of me were alive. Some of those aspects of me left loved ones. I must see that they are safe," Bob stated uncertainly.

"Okay, well that's a relief," I muttered. "Do you remember who these people were? Or where they lived? Hell, any idea when? I don't mean to be a dick, Bob, but the village was trapping souls for hundreds of years. It's likely the people you remember are long dead…"

"I MUST know," Bob said forcefully, the twin blue stars of his eyes flaring bright in anger.

"Okay, mate, we'll see what we can do then, I guess. Have a think about where and when, okay?" I said, getting a nod before I moved across to get some food, leaving him to think about things. I mentally cursed myself and swore internally to get him some better damn gear.

I sat with my shoulders against Thomas and Lydia, the small bench making us all hunch up as we ate. I realized that, despite all the stress, even with the weight of an empire sitting on my shoulders, I felt freer than I ever had before.

When I'd worked for other people, I was always ready to pull a sick day or take a break. Now that I had a real role and aim, I felt energized every day, and there weren't enough hours to go around. I knew my team felt the same way, from the conversations we'd had around the fire, and now, with my brother by my side, I was honestly happy.

Plus, I got to go kill Goblins today, and there was something about the little bastards that just boiled my piss.

"I miss Bane," Oracle whispered as she alighted on my shoulder, and my happy mood dipped noticeably.

"I do, too," I said, a rumble of agreement filling the air as Thomas looked over at me.

"He's doing a job for the Goddess of Assassins, right?" he asked.

I grimaced. "Yeah, he's, well, you know when the Dark Wanker sent you and your lot after me? Well, turns out that kinda pissed Tamat off, especially as She's the Lady of Darkness. He's the Death God, but He's encroached on Her section of things, somehow.

"I don't really get it, so sue me, but She's pissed, and She made Bane her Champion. When we were having our fight, Bane was merrily slaughtering his way around the outside of the group. Then She told him to go forth and kill, I guess. Hopefully, he's okay."

"He's an assassin; I'd say anyone who finds him is in for a bad day, considering how skilled the rest of your team is." Thomas smiled.

"Damn…" I muttered, shaking my head. The team really had fit in together, growing in skill and strength over the last few weeks.

"What's up?" Oracle asked, and I nodded to the group who were generally getting dressed or eating and joking with each other.

"The timeline. It's literally been only what, a month, maybe a month and a half since I arrived here? We've been in heavy combat pretty much every day since then. It just seems like it should have been longer."

"Ha, you're telling me," Thomas said. "Oracle told me about some of the crazy shit you all did…did Jian really fire that ship's cannon against the camp by accident?" Thomas quirked an eyebrow.

"You've met him. That was the first time he ever flew a ship, what do you think? You've seen the damn controls on these things; simple is not in the description!"

"Shit, yes. We need to design a car control or a fighter one or something. Imagine this thing with a control stick, gears, and a clutch. Surely, that's all you need, right? Maybe a lever for the angle of the ship engines that you can change that on?" Thomas suggested, growing animated at the idea of his own jet ship.

I snorted. "Dude, I remember you learning to drive; I'm not letting you teach the Gnomes about stick-shift gears," I retorted, then raised my voice. "Okay, people, eat up and finish getting dressed. Half an hour until we land."

I walked out of the room with Oracle still on my shoulder and headed down the corridor and up onto the deck.

Gray clouds moved in from the west and there was a fuzzy edge on everything in the distance. I grunted at the mounting evidence of incoming rain.

"Joy. Looks like we're going to get wet," I muttered.

Oracle laughed, the sound like a tinkling mass of tiny chimes. "*You're* going to get wet. *I'm* going to hide in your hood out of the rain!"

"Remember when you hid in my pocket?" I whispered, getting a throaty chuckle in return.

"I think I'd have difficulty behaving myself these days, if you still had those pockets with easy access!"

I grinned and strode across the deck toward the Wheelhouse. Jian sat at the controls, and a clearly resigned captain and helmsman sat on the seats to one side, playing cards.

They leaped to their feet when I walked in, seeming embarrassed and afraid, then with relief, they hurried out at my gesture. I watched them go, seeing Sehran sitting to one side reading one of the books I'd managed to rescue from the Prax. It looked to be one of the ones that I'd asked Grizz to look after, and had been brought over from my own world by Barry the Lich when he'd arrived.

She smiled over at me then went back to reading, muttering something about a World of Chains and bards. I dismissed it and turned to Tenandra and Jian.

"Okay people, take us in. Land us a couple of miles away from the target; if possible, I'd rather we could sneak up on it."

I got an affirmative from Jian, who turned the ship smoothly, altering course and guiding us in. His gaze roamed far away as he watched the projected exterior of the ship and referenced the map. I watched him for a long minute, seeing the casual way that Tenandra rested one hand on his shoulder and the way the open door to the Captain's Cabin was clearly full of his clothing.

I glanced at Oracle, who nodded to me. I smiled, seeing we were both on the same page.

"Tenandra, what do the captain and helmsman actually do on this ship?" I asked, and she looked at me as though confused.

"They give commands, and…"

"And you totally ignore them, don't you?" I asked, getting a sheepish look from her. "Okay, look, the Gnomes like being here, but they won't stay long-term, I don't think. They'll probably all move over to the battleship soon, or onto other projects. The Legion squad, on the other hand, are here to stay for now at least, as are your crew…do the helmsman and captain serve any actual function at all?"

"None," she replied. "When Jian is aboard, I permit him to fly as he…he understands me and my ship-body. When the helmsman is in the control seat, I simply disable the controls. He damaged my ship-body too much."

"And the captain?" I asked.

"He occasionally orders the crew," she said, wincing. "I didn't intend to remove him from command. It just…happened…"

"Just like moving Jian into his cabin and kicking him out happened?" I asked. She reddened, as did Jian.

"Jax, I'm sorry, this is my fault…" Jian said.

"No mate, it's not. Yeah, you and Tenandra getting freaky, I'll admit I didn't see that coming, but it is what it is, especially with Sehran thrown into the mix. Okay, Jian, what are your intentions here, with Tenandra and the current situation?"

"Well, I really like her? I want it to continue?" he added in a low voice, by now bright red, but taking her hand as she reached down to hold his.

"Great, sorry, I should have been clearer," I said, closing my eyes and trying not to sigh as I rubbed the bridge of my nose. "I didn't mean your sex life, mate, I meant flying the ship and working with Tenandra?"

"Oh! Uh, yeah? I love flying," Jian said, this time smiling broadly.

"Okay, and being in my team? Are you wanting to leave to fly with…?"

"No!" Jian said forcefully. "No, I don't want to leave Tenandra. I'm sorry, but if I have to choose one…"

"You don't," I said, sighing. "Okay, time to bow to the inevitable. Tenandra, I think what's going to happen here is that you will become my private ship. We'll fly together from now on. You'll transport my team and me unless there's a good reason not to. That means that you won't fly as often as you might if you had another role. Are you happy with that?"

"Definitely," she said. "When in port, I can continue my upgrades. When flying, we will all be together."

I nodded at that and went on. "Good. In that case, there's no need for the captain or the helmsman. I'll sort something else for them to do. The crew will stay, unless you want to get rid of them?" I received a shake of her head.

"Good. We'll talk to Westin, see if he's happy to take over responsibility for the ship's crew, as well as his people, unless you want to assume full command of them?"

"Again, no. Please, Jax, perhaps in the future, but for now, I am happy without that responsibility."

"Fine, we can arrange for him to lead his people and the crew. We might as well do some interior rearrangement over the next few weeks as well, if that's okay? Give people their own cabins and so on. We'll need some cargo space, but with a small crew and just us aboard, it's madness to leave the layout as unused as it is.

"And yes, Jian, you, Sehran, and Tenandra can have the captain's cabin," I said, gesturing to the door at the back of the wheelhouse. "I'll take a cabin down below." A massive grin lit up his face and the way Tenandra and Sehran smiled at each other, and I couldn't help but shake my head.

"All I ask is that you leave him able to fight the next day, okay?" I said to the pair of them, getting a laugh. "Right, in all seriousness though, Jian, what about Ty'Baronn?"

"I don't trust him," Jian admitted. "He kept pushing constantly, and had been using a glamor to make himself look bigger and stronger, essentially lying to us from the start."

"Yeah, but he's also a Demon that's sworn to you, and he has a powerful attack. You're going to have to make a decision about him eventually. Don't forget he did fight for us," I said, getting a grimace from Jian, who nodded after a few seconds.

"I'll resummon him, but he's going to learn his place, or be banished permanently," Jian warned.

"Glad to hear it, mate. Might want to get dressed to kill, then, because I hear we're nearly there?" I suggested.

He coughed, embarrassed again. "Good point. I'll be quick," he said as Tenandra gestured, the controls shifting as he released them to hurry into the cabin at the back of the room.

I nodded to the girls and left, seeing Westin in conversation with the captain. I sighed, heading over to deal with that, even as we dipped down, slowly descending toward a valley in the distance between two low hills.

"Westin…Captain," I greeted them, stepping up. Westin slammed his fist to his chest in salute, while the captain straightened and mimicked him after a few seconds, having not considered a salute before now.

"Lord Jax. Good to see you again, sir," Westin said, smiling. "I was just saying to the captain here that, if he's unhappy with the current situation, he should speak to you directly. Wasn't I, Captain?" He prodded the man.

"Uh, well…yes…" the captain stammered before sagging and speaking quickly. "I…I want to request reassignment, Lord Jax. I do nothing here, I want to learn, to…"

"Granted," I said. "I should have considered this before now. You're a captain, and you have a helmsman on a ship that needs neither. Relax, and when we get back to the Tower, go see Oren. Tell him I want you to find a new ship, as I'll be maintaining Tenandra as my personal ship from now on."

"Oh, thank the Gods…" the captain said, and I saw the worry and stress rolling off him, and he stood straighter than I'd seen him stand since he first took over. "I'm sorry, Lord Jax, I should have…"

"No. This was my mistake," I said, nodding to Westin. "But I'll need a word with my legionnaire now, so…?"

"Oh! Of course, sorry, sir!" The captain almost smacked himself on the chin with his salute, he was so desperate to run away. Once he was gone, Westin smiled.

"Right, mate, first off, are you happy for you and your squad to be attached to the ship permanently? I'm thinking if I need a team aboard, it might as well be permanently, that way you can get settled."

"Hell, yes! The legionnaires love the ship life. It's a bit awkward for morning exercises, but…" Westin said, shrugging.

"Okay, well, I'm getting rid of the captain and helmsman, but keeping the crew, so I'd be looking for your men to integrate them into your command structure. I will get you to look after them, as above you, there'll only be Tenandra and my squad."

"They're led now by a young lad called Matthew; he takes care of them, as things stand. I'll watch over him, if that's what you mean?"

"Basically, yeah. Tenandra needs a crew, but not a captain or helmsman, so this is going to be a learning curve for us all." I waved my hand. "Make sure there's food and that kinda thing; we'll make it up as we go along, I guess."

"Jax, we could teach them all spells as well, healing and ranged," Oracle suggested, a sudden smile blossoming on Westin's face.

"That sound agreeable to you, Westin?" I asked.

"Gods yes, sir!" he said.

"Fine. Not today, as we're about to go into battle. But after the missions, I guess, when we're on our way back to the Tower?"

"How many of the team?" Westin asked. I looked to Oracle for confirmation, and she sent me a quick nod.

"Well, all the Legion, I think. Teach you all ranged and healing, that way you'll be more effective. We'll look at this again once we've all had a few days to settle in, and we'll see if you actually use them both. But it seems logical," I said, smiling at his enthusiasm.

"Hell yes, sir! You'll not have any complaints from my team, I promise you!"

"Glad to hear it, mate. Right, once we land, I'll lead my squad off, and Tenandra will leave, falling back a bit to patrol and watch over the area. You keep watch and keep the ship safe, okay?"

"Yes sir. Uh, what if you need us, though?" Westin asked.

"Tenandra and Oracle can communicate at a distance, so don't worry about that."

He nodded again, clapping fist to chest and moving off to deal with his own squad.

I walked down the ship to where my people were gathering on the deck, thinking about the possibilities, making a team of legionnaires into the ship's marines, but with spells, hell, they could raid and capture enemy ships…

"Jax?" Lydia said, and I jumped, having lost myself in my thoughts.

"Sorry!" I said, shaking my head. "I was miles away…"

"No problem, but we need a plan?" she said.

"Okay, from what I could see before, this valley is fairly long and low, about three miles. Tenandra is dropping us off at the edge of the valley, then we scout it and find the little bastards. From the map, it looks like the site is a hidden cave at the top end of the valley, high in the rocks above the river, but keep your eyes open. All we know is that there are Goblins here, and it used to be a Gnome stronghold, that's literally it."

"So, Yen, Tang, go find them. Grizz, Thomas, you're wi' Jax and me. Giint, Ronin, and Arrin, you're in the middle. Bob, be'ind them, watch over 'em and keep 'em safe with Jian." Lydia arranged the group before looking at Thomas. "I don't know 'ow you normally work, Thomas, but in my squad, I expect you to wait for orders, understood?"

"Yes, ma'am," Thomas said with a faint smile that earned him a glare from her. He wiped it off his face and nodded more seriously. "I won't let you down."

"See that you don't," she said sternly before allowing herself a small smile.

"Jax, I'm going to work on that shield again, see if I can make a viable one for fighting," Oracle said as she held onto my shoulder. She squinted at the weaves only she could visualize.

"Right, people, here we go!" We turned again, lining up on the entrance to the valley we were after. We'd flown to the south almost as far as Narkolt before turning west and heading toward the foot of the mountain range, staying fairly low. Watching the huge, ancient trees and sparkling rivers zip by below us, I couldn't help but grin.

The last of the trees had fallen away behind us as we climbed into the low hills, the vast forests thinning away into scrubland and bare patches of ground as the winds grew more savage. Thunder rumbled in the distance as the gray clouds we'd seen earlier darkened again, taking on a peculiar, almost purple or green light. It told of heavy rain incoming, lit on occasion from deep within by a flash of lightning.

"Picked the right day for climbing mountains while encased in metal suits," Thomas muttered, and I grunted, looking at the rapidly approaching storm and the valley ahead.

"We should have long enough," I said grimly. "Just gives us an extra incentive to get inside, and if it lands before we do, I bet the Goblins will be hiding as well."

"You hope," Grizz said.

I grinned at him as we dipped below the ridge at the eastern end of the valley, landing next to the river that ran down it. The water gushed over the edge of the valley to fall away to our left, plummeting down a small waterfall, then widening as it headed down to the sea.

"Damn right I do! Okay, people, let's go!" I called as the sailors slid out the gangplank, and Westin and his Legionnaires saluted us.

We raced down the narrow wooden gangway, jumping onto the granite and thin soil-covered ground before turning west and heading for the valley entrance. Tang and Yen vanished into the distance as they raced ahead, and the powerful pulse of the ship's engines pushed her up and away from us, tilting to one side gently as she flew to the east, heading down the hills to establish a decent distance between us.

"Gods, I miss Bane," Lydia commented as we jogged up the hill. I grunted, feeling entirely the same.

BANE

"It can't be true!" The short, effeminate man whined, clutching his robes tighter around himself and holding a dagger in one shaking fist. "It just can't!"

"It is!" the second man snapped. "I saw him myself, hung by the ankles in his quarters and gutted! I tell you, he must have been summoning Demons; it's the only thing that makes sense!"

"But…but he doesn't have the strength for that! He wouldn't risk…" The first man scoffed.

"There were all these symbols on the walls and blood everywhere…I think he summoned something, and it killed him. I read in the Summoning Hall that if you summon a Demon that is too strong, they do that."

"You've been allowed in the Summoning Hall?" The first man gasped. "I heard they'd locked it all down after Artemis was caught with that Succubus! I thought no one was allowed in anymore!"

"I'm one of the new librarians," the second priest replied smugly. "I'm allowed to catalog the books."

"Lucky," the first muttered, sidling up to the larger and clearly higher-ranking priest and smiling ingratiatingly, even as he slipped the dagger away. "So, perhaps you need an assistant?"

"I'm sure we could come to an arrangement. Well, possibly." The second priest patted his pouch and got a smile from the first. The pair moved down the hall, the dead body that had been such an important and disturbing event a few minutes ago forgotten in the rush to acquire more rank or gold.

Bane slipped out of the small alcove he'd hidden in and sent a quick burst of worldsense into the stone halls, sensing the shape and layout. He made a mental note to find the Summoning Hall and rob it blind, if he had the chance.

He'd agreed to Tamat's demand when She'd assured him that Jax had escaped and was well aboard the ship that he'd seen escaping to the north. It would have taken him days to make it back to the Tower on foot anyway, if not weeks. A small detour to slaughter a few of the Death God's followers before setting off seemed logical.

The bonus experience that Tamat was feeding him for the slaughter was having a heady effect, though. So long as he was unseen by any but his target and left no trace of who or what was carrying out the killings, he gained double experience. As high a level as some of these scumbags were, that was a lot of experience indeed.

He'd learned that his next target had rooms on the fifteenth floor of the citadel, close to the top, and had a propensity to enjoy his breakfast on a small, private balcony.

A balcony that was both poorly made and rusted through in places. Bane suspected all it would take was a little work to loosen the bolts that held it in place, and he'd be able to move on smoothly to the next target.

Bane slipped down the corridor, his leather-clad feet making no sound as he crept along in stealth, his hearts light with the enjoyment of sneaking around his enemies' stronghold while they all backstabbed one another and made his job easier.

He'd arrived once already to kill a target, only to find another priest rifling through the man's belongings while he cooled on the floor, and he'd been stunned.

Apparently, there were a number of restrictions on the lower and soldier ranks killing each other. But in the priesthood, it was the normal and accepted method of promotion, making them almost laughably uncaring about the bodies they found.

Bane knew it wouldn't last forever, but the Lady had charged him with ten deaths, all of whom were named individuals who had apparently transgressed against her in some way. Seven down, and three to go, with a plan for the next one, and a hint of the location of the ninth.

If he could have smiled, he would have grinned from ear to ear as he crept along, keeping to the shadows and enjoying the matte black and darkness motif the Church of Nimon apparently loved. It took mere moments for him to make up for the time lost when the pair of gossiping priests had rounded the corner, forcing him to pause and hide on his way to his target.

Bane crept down corridors and across the protected balconies that ringed the upper gardens then ducked inside the citadel again and slipped behind a plant on a raised plinth. The fronds hanging down enabled him to blend into the shadows it cast easily as he waited and watched.

The room he'd entered was large and circular, with a balcony that ringed the upper level, broken by doors that led off into the adjoining gardens. The private rooms and upper floors belonged to the citadel itself. Where the lower floors had been essentially a free-for-all of priests and their servants coming and going, the upper levels had guards stationed at every entrance that led higher. The huge, black steel-and-gold-armored figures watched everyone who moved near them, demanding passes and explanations before allowing them to roam higher.

Bane paused, watching them, and toyed with the idea of slipping past them once the door was opened to another supplicant, or, even more temptingly, executing them with a Backstab or a kidney strike.

He watched the guards' slightest movements, timing how long the backs of their necks were exposed as they tilted their heads to speak to supplicants, or the way one, then another would shift as they stood watch, exposing the ring mail under their cuirass.

The back of the neck would work, and if combined with the damage multiplying effect of a successful Backstab, it'd kill one outright without any doubt, but the second...

Bane shook his head, moving back to the door and waiting for a mousy little human to clear it. Then he slipped out behind her as she mumbled to herself about the disrespect of not allowing her access to the higher floors when she'd simply misplaced her pass.

Bane couldn't help but feel amused, considering he'd personally stolen it from her not an hour past, although admittedly it was out of curiosity, as he clearly couldn't use it, being a Mer rather than human. Now here he was, less than a foot behind her, with it nestled securely in his pouch.

He darted to the side as the door swung back, her annoyed attempt at slamming it almost revealing him before she strode away across the covered walkway. The alternating shadows and brightly lit patches of sunlight made her deep black robes seem like shadow walking as she passed through, before they were exposed as a grimy mess by the sun.

Bane shook himself as he moved quickly but quietly into the corner where two walls met. He glanced up at the first of the balconies above him, less than twelve feet up and to the right. They were still cloaked in shadow, thanks to the rising sun. He grimaced, wishing there was a pool nearby that he could slip into.

Humans, Elves, and Dwarves, actually most of the land-based races, all had one thing in common for the Mer: they sweated. They sweated heavily in the warmth. To a being who tasted the air rather than smelling it, as it'd been described to him that they did, it had a much less attractive effect.

The short woman he'd been so close behind had literally tasted foul, and it was all he could do at times to not stab her to teach her a lesson.

Bane glanced around the courtyard below, seeing through a gentle pulse the plants swaying in the rising breeze and the locations of the guards before stowing his blades and moving.

He gripped the stones of the citadel carefully, his claws digging slightly into the stone that had been softened by wind and rain. He swiftly climbed, enjoying the advantage any six-limbed creature had over a four-limbed one in this arena.

As he moved, constantly waiting for a shout of surprise or the first crossbow bolt to hit him, he reflected on how strange it was that the sweat of his companions in Lydia's Squad and in Jax's protection detail didn't bother him.

Sometimes days had passed with them all together, all exerting themselves heavily, being coated in sweat, blood, and various fluids, and yet he'd been fine with it. The taste of that little female though, as sedentary a lifestyle as she clearly lived, judging from the food-spotted robes and stench of old wine, turned his stomach.

He crept further up, soon reaching the first balcony and clambering over the railing before trying the door.

Locked.

Bane pulled out his lockpicks, inserting a rod oh so carefully to avoid the slightest noise before slipping the rake in alongside it and probing gently.

The lock was old and simple, more designed to prevent the door from opening on its own rather than any concentrated effort to prevent entry. It let loose a soft click after less than a minute, letting Bane slowly push the door inwards.

He slipped a weak pulse of his worldsense into the room beyond, feeling the shape of the room. There was a slumbering, massively fat male and trio of smaller, apparently dwarven females laid uncomfortably around the old Elf.

He noted the piles of clothing, the stacked gold, and the locations of the clothes he assumed to be theirs, before finally noticing the chains, thin, apparently gold, and enchanted, that bound the females to the wall near the bed.

A growl of disgust rose in his throat, but Bane swiftly stifled it before slipping in and letting a slightly stronger burst of worldsense wash over the inhabitants, creating the sonar-like overlay that his kind saw the world by, telling him far more than he wished it to at times.

The women had been trapped in these collars for many months, if not longer, and the small barrage of scratches around the base of the chains on each of them suggested they weren't here willingly.

Bane paused for long seconds, wondering what he should do. He knew what Tamat would order, given the chance: either kill them all or leave, allowing none to know he existed.

Jax, alternatively, would kill the old *creature* and set the women free, worrying about the mission and his escape later, somehow doing it all as though it had always been part of the plan.

He accepted "part of the plan" as including him being gutted or some such. The man was a magnet for injuries.

While Bane examined the room and its inhabitants, the slug of a male released a noxious gas with a groan, settling back down, even as one of the girls gagged and awoke, shifting slowly and trying to waft the foul air away from herself. She sat up slowly and glared at the male, even going so far as to slip ever so slowly off the bed and crouched by his clothing. She shifted the black robe and jeweled garments aside, uncovering a dagger and reached for it.

She gritted her teeth and let out a hiss of pain as her hands were prevented from touching it, less than an inch from its surface.

She tried again and again before a rumble of laughter came from the male.

Bane stayed crouched in the shadows, watching as the great slug of an Elf struggled upright, his bulk requiring him to pull himself up with handfuls of the bedding before he could wheeze at her in amusement.

"Now, Shereen! I warned you what would happen if you tried that again!" He groaned, obviously enjoying what was happening. Dark satisfaction filled his voice as he watched her frantic attempts to grasp the knife.

The other two girls moaned in fear and began pleading with him, even as Bane examined them with directed pulses too faint for all but the most wary to sense.

Their bonds were older, he sensed, calluses having grown where the chains rubbed again and again, while the woman trying to lift the dagger, Shereen, had none.

She hissed through gritted teeth, panic filling her eyes as the other women alternated between begging the elven priest for mercy and pleading with her to not make it worse, even as she frantically strained against the invisible force.

"It's impossible, you know," the bastard rumbled, the jowls of his cheeks quivering as he smiled at her, while his little piggy eyes gazed out of crevices in his face. "The Chains of Gilgannon are old, old magic, and they use your own strength to feed themselves. Even should you manage to touch the blade, you'd never be able to use it as a weapon. Nothing you see as a weapon will ever be within your reach again!"

"I won't live like this!" Shereen snarled, glaring at him even as she desperately reached for the blade again, shoving herself forwards by dint of sheer determination. Bane watched as her fingers moved almost a millimeter closer.

"You'll live as long as I demand, slave!" the Elf snarled, gesturing to the items that bobbed in a row, chained to the shelf and submerged in a gently gurgling mass of liquid. "You'll live for so long as you amuse me. Then, like all your foul kind, you'll join my collection…"

Bane focused on the vat and examined it before freezing in shock. There were soul gems floating in that vat!

A sudden, horrified realization came to him, that he and the rest of Jax's cadre had been underestimating the Dark Church terribly, if a middling-level priest was able to create and fill soul gems with sentient souls, a crime alluded to only in the darkest of tales.

Bane slowly drew the matched pair of Dagomar's Daggers and moved slowly. He slid around the room, taking up position directly behind the vile creature. He paused as he gathered himself to strike and watched the others in the room.

At this point, Bane suspected how they'd respond. He guessed that the local inhabitants must be used to screaming coming from these chambers, if the freshly healed scars on the females' bodies were anything to judge by, but he needed to be ready, just in case.

He gathered himself to strike silently, until the figure spoke again.

"You and all your kind exist to serve the higher races, little one. Yet, despite our largesse, you continue to defy us. Well, perhaps it's time to teach you a more permanent lesson," he said, clearly becoming aroused by the thought as he smiled, then spoke an order.

"Shereen, pick up the dagger carefully and hand it to me, hilt-first." The force preventing her from touching the blade vanished.

Her hand slammed into the hilt, and she yanked it free with a gasp, spinning to confront him, before exhaling a horrified breath as her hands shifted on the hilt, moving to grip the blade instead and presenting it to the enormous priest. The muscles on her arms and body stood out in stark relief as she strained to overcome the magic that forced her to cooperate.

"You see?" he gurgled, smiling as he watched her quivering before him, not even bothering to take the dagger. "You'll never be free of me, and when I add you to my collection, you'll beg, *beg* for the days when you simply served me in bed!" The creature reached out, laying a pudgy, dirty hand covered in rings on the hilt of the dagger before freezing in shock at the words whispered into his ear.

"Oh, I disagree," Bane hissed, his two upper hands coming down hard. He gripped the bulbous flesh of the Elf's upper right arm with his right. His claw-tipped fingers dug into and immobilized the bundle of nerves that directed that arm, preventing him from gripping the hilt properly. Bane's other hand closed over his mouth, cutting off the words before they could form.

Then, Bane's lower arms pistoned back and forth, the blades driving deep, their tanto-style chisel tip meant for punching through armor, making short work of his bare flesh.

Bane hammered them in and out, dozens of wounds sprouting across his back, each aimed for and connecting with a specific point. His kidneys, stomach, and spleen were shredded, then he drove the daggers between the Elf's ribs and punctured the lungs. Then Bane tore the daggers sideways and ripped them free in gouts of blood.

The women gasped, but beyond that, they stayed silent, until one of Bane's strikes punched through the heart, and the huge figure who'd been whimpering and gasping, unable to get out a true cry, grunted, and stiffened, sagging forward in death.

There was a moment of silence, then the golden chains slowly unraveled, freeing the women and the bobbing soul gems. A ring fell from the corpse's finger to lay glowing on the bedsheets. Bane stepped back, letting the massive figure slump, the bed creaking in protest under the corpse's weight, even as blood pooled and began to seep through the stained covers.

The four figures looked at each other before Shereen flipped the dagger around and drove it into the cooling meat, stabbing wildly.

Several long seconds passed as the other three watched her sobbing and butchering the massive figure, before silence filled the room again.

This time, it was awkward.

"So…are you all okay now?" Bane asked eventually, breaking the silence as well as his stealth as he frantically tried to figure out what to do next.

"What?" one of the women asked, confused.

Bane cleared his throat, suddenly feeling very much like the sixteen-year-old youngling he was for the first time in months.

"I, uh, look, I've got people to kill. So…are you all okay if I leave you to it now?" he said, getting confused looks from the two longer-held females while Shereen panted and wiped blood from her face with the back of an already-stained hand.

"No," Shereen said harshly after a few seconds, just as Bane started to head for the door.

"What?" he asked uncertainly.

"No, we're not fucking all right!" Shereen snapped. "We're coming with you, and we're damn well going to gut some more priests!"

"Uh…I…" Bane muttered, straightening up and scratching his head. He'd long since rid himself of the helm and shitty armor he'd hidden himself in to blend in with the other fleeing Dark Legionnaires and was dressed only in his leathers, scalemail, and chitin armor again, with much higher quality Imperial Legion sections replacing the damaged sections he'd lost along the way. He had nothing to wear that he could use to try to pass himself off as one of the locals, and he sure as hell couldn't wear the now-cooling meat sack's clothes.

All four of them could have fit in the robes at once, for a start.

"I don't think that'll work," Bane mumbled, trying not to stare at the naked females. While they weren't Mer women, certain characteristics were the same. As young as he was, it was enough to throw him completely off his game, now that he wasn't consumed with the need to kill.

"Well, we'll damn well make it work," Shereen snapped, blowing a bloody strand of her hair out of her face with an outthrust jaw, before moving to a chest in the corner of the room. One of the other women joined her, and they pulled out clothing, while the third woman reached out tentatively to the vat on the shelf.

"What is it?" Bane asked as she laid a hand against it. After a moment, she quickly yanked her hand free, grunting in pain.

"It's a soul jar," she mumbled, cradling her fingers where the skin had gone purple with frost damage from even that minor touch. "It's bound to that piece of shit."

"What's a soul jar?" Bane asked.

"He told us all we know about them…he used to brag about it." She shrugged. "It gave him access to the power of their souls, somehow. The chains bound us all together, and he'd use us until he grew bored. Then he'd kill one, bind their soul, and put the gem in the jar. He fed off the strength of the souls in there, grew stronger…"

"What do we do?"

"I don't know," she said. "The gems can't be destroyed, and they can't be left here. Someone else will feed on them."

Bane reached out, hissing in pain as he touched the vat, before getting an idea and stepping back to the corpse on the bed.

Three fast cuts later, the hand and most of the forearm were detached. He used them to knock the vat free, sending the liquid splashing across the floor, before washing up against the barrier of the corpse he'd tipped off the bed.

There was a sizzle, and the corpse made terrible sounds as it was both burned and frozen at the same time. But the faint slope of the room guided the liquid out onto the balcony, and down the outer wall.

Bane and the woman, who introduced herself as Peshka, used some of the fat bastard's robes and bedding to gather the dozen gems, dropping them into Bane's storage.

It took a few minutes, but soon, to Bane's immense relief, the women were all more or less decent; their clothing from when they'd been taken had been kept to tease them with. As such, the three women were dressed reasonably appropriately, or would be, if Bane could get one of them a black robe to act as their owner.

The three concealed weapons about themselves, while Bane stripped the room of rings, gems, and anything else of value.

There was no way this room was going to stand up to the casual scrutiny he'd been getting away with so far, not with the women gone, and the state of the room itself.

Blood was sprayed liberally across the walls from where he'd ripped the daggers out, and the things that Shereen had done to the corpse, well, it wasn't going to make for pleasant viewing for whoever found him.

Bane suspected that even he was going to have nightmares over it, so the fact that the fat bastard had been dead when she did it was probably a kindness he didn't deserve.

Shaking the thoughts off, Bane cracked the door open slightly and peered out into the corridor beyond. He sent a pulse out, weak at first, then took a deep breath and sent out a powerful one, mapping the local area then tugging the door closed and facing the women.

"The corridors are clear. There's a stairwell on the left at the end of the hall and a handful of rooms between us and there. But I can only feel one living form in between, in the second room on the right. I think we need to sneak past and…"

"I want blood," Shereen growled, her voice low and forceful.

"Well, I want to complete my quest and escape, and you're all threatening to fuck that up for me. So either you do as I tell you, or you can go your own way," Bane snapped. "Seriously, pick one. You want to go your own way? Fine, I saved your lives, so if you wait ten minutes before you go, you can consider us even."

"We're coming with you," Peshka said, looking at the other two. There was a second of hesitation from the second woman before she nodded firmly, and the three of them lined up, ready and waiting for him.

"Shit," he muttered, wondering if this was how it always was for Jax. He just did what needed to be done, and suddenly there were people following him around. "Okay, right, we're heading to the corridor at the far end. Try the doors on the way, quickly. Leave the one with the person in it; we don't know if we can kill them before they can raise an alarm."

"Wait, are we going up?" Peshka asked. Bane nodded impatiently. "Why?"

"Because I've a quest to kill three more scumbags!" Bane said. "I'll lose the element of surprise if we wait any longer, and I damn well need it, so how about you all just do as I ask, and I'll explain more later, *if* we get out of here?"

"Fine, but I want to kill some of these priests," Peshka said, a motion that was echoed by the other two. "You don't know what they did to us."

"Fine, you can help. Just do it QUIETLY, okay?" Bane said, already regretting this. They nodded, and he opened the door, checked again, then led the way out, gesturing for them to take separate doors on either side of the corridor.

They'd checked one door, finding it locked, when the second door on the right opened and a tall thin man slunk out, wiping his hand with a cloth. Before the door shut behind him, Bane saw the blood splatters on the walls, and he was in motion. The man looked up, his sunken cheeks and hollow eyes making him look almost like a vulture as he rubbed his hands, frowning at the trio of Dwarven ladies.

"What are you doing here?" he asked in a raspy voice, blinking myopically. There was silence as all three women stared at him, looking like rabbits caught under torchlight, until finally Shereen smiled and spoke up.

"We were sent up here, Lord Priest, and told to wait?" she lied, even as Bane slipped around behind the tall, skinny figure.

"Who sent you?" A sick smile appeared on his face as he patted his belt, quickly tucking the soiled cloth out of sight.

"A man in black and gold, sir," Pashka said.

"That's…wait, you look familiar." The priest frowned.

Pashka snarled and lunged forward, punching the older man in the stomach. Before he could shout for help, Bane grabbed him from behind and rammed a blade under his chin. The crunch and sudden spasm that ripped through the fresh corpse sounded horrific so close to the group. The women looked around anxiously, as if fearing they'd be caught, while Bane lowered the body against the wall, dragging open the nearest door, the one the man had left.

Inside was a scene of carnage. The walls were padded and white, although streaked with the blood of various species. Hanging from hooks that, in turn, dangled from chains in the ceiling, were body parts that looked to have been surgically removed for examination.

The cuts were clean and smooth, the skin peeled back and entirely removed in some places, with painstaking drawings and details noted in a thick, leather bound tome that sat atop a plinth.

The medical side of the room would have been gory enough, if not for the cadavers and the looks on the various faces that revealed, if the sprays of blood hadn't done so already, that these removals had been done while the subjects still lived.

"Help me with him," Bane ordered the three women, dragging the corpse into the room and pulling free its spatial bag. He quickly pulled free another set of robes, throwing it to the women to let them decide who would wear it and several bundles of rags. "One of you take that, go, and wipe the blood up," he ordered, checking his notifications.

He let out a sigh of relief as he saw that, possibly because no alarm had been sounded yet, the experience was still coming in at double the normal rate.

"Oh, fuck yes," Bane murmured, grinning and wondering just how many of the priests of the Death God he could slaughter, if this was the result.

"What do we do?" Peshka asked, making him jump, having been lost as he was in a world of slaughtering black-robed assholes.

"Ah, uh…we go kill the fuckers!" he burst out, expecting the plan, with its lack of detail, to draw scorn and derision. Instead of ridicule, Peshka's answering smile was like the sun coming up. She picked up a hammer from the rack next to the cadavers and weighed it in her hands thoughtfully.

"How many do you think we can get?" she asked softly.

"I don't know." Bane shrugged. "If we were here with a friend of mine, I'd have said all of them, and escape, too, but without him? Just the four of us, in the middle of the Death God's Church? Probably fewer than we'd like."

"But we'll go down fighting," Shereen said firmly, as the last of the three finally spoke up, her voice as deep and gravelly as any he'd heard as she agreed.

"Aye, ah want te' smash their wee faces in!" she said, picking up a tool that looked like a pick, but with a wide, long head, clearly razor-sharp, and a short head on the back that looked made for shattering bone.

"We need to be smart about this," Bane said to the other three. "One of my targets is on the next floor; we need to talk to him before we kill him. He should have information on the next two targets."

"What kind of quest is it?" Peshka asked.

Bane shrugged before answering, figuring they'd either believe him or not. "A divine one. I'm the Champion of Tamat," he said offhandedly, then paused, waiting for the inevitable laughter. When they said nothing, he looked at them surprised. "You're not going to laugh?"

"Why? Because you say you're the champion of a God who vanished centuries ago?" Peshka asked.

"You can call *yourself* Tamat, for all I care. You saved us, and you're helping me kill the bastards who kept torturing me. I don't care if you're mad or not; I just want to kill them all," she said with a firm nod of her head.

"Okay, sounds good. What's your name?" Bane asked the dwarven woman who'd been silent so far. She stared wide-eyed at him a moment before answering.

"Doris," was all she said.

"Fine, okay then, get anything you need quickly. Then one of you put the robes on, lead the other two along. I'll be in stealth. Best-case scenario, we take the room without anyone seeing us, then we can question him. If not, we'll need to keep searching."

The trio nodded. Peshka slipped the robes on while the other two hid their weapons.

The small group slid out of the room and into the hall, moving as quickly and quietly as they could, heading higher into the citadel, closing in on the next of Bane's targets.

CHAPTER FOURTEEN

"**H**ow many are there?" I asked as Tang appeared, shifting from stealth while still a few meters away to give us all time to see him.

"Lots. Okay…the valley is a bowl at the top end, with what looks to be a deep pool that feeds the river. There's an overhanging roof that looks like it used to be on a bunch of pillars, but they've mostly collapsed. Behind that, there's either a cave mouth or a building that's been buried by time. Looking around the outside, it seems like there's a lot of old metal. I have no idea what it was originally, but now it's rusted scrap full of Goblins. It looks like some of the Goblins are set up as sentries."

"Sentries?" I asked, surprised, remembering the feral little bastards we'd faced before.

"Yeah, this is an old clan. While there's some small ones roaming around, literally ankle biters, there's also some fully-grown and armored Goblins."

"Armored?"

"Looted dwarven or Gnome gear mainly, but there's also some leather that looks to be their own work. There are others, too. I couldn't get a clear look to see what they were, but they looked strange, as if their armor was part of them," Tang said. As he finished speaking, he spun and looked to the right, before sagging back and grinning. "Heard you, Yen," he said. A few seconds later, Yen stepped out of the shadows, crouching next to us, staying low and out of sight of the Goblins.

"You're getting better, Tang," she admitted, grinning.

"You try working that closely with Bane every day," Tang muttered before going silent.

"Yeah…well," Yen said, shrugging and looking around. "Okay, there are six sentry posts in a circle around the entrance. There's one high up, looks like it's been built to enable them to see around the valley. It'll make sneaking up a lot harder, and there were tracks of something else…lots of them. I'm betting on hunting hyenas or something else they've domesticated."

"Options?" I asked.

"Clear them out in a circle from stealth," Yen said. "They're set up in a ring around the entrance, watching outward, but there's only two or three in each station, and they're a good hundred meters apart. Start at the top, slaughter our way around, keep them from coming up behind us if we make a mistake." Yen sketched out their approximate positions on the ground before us all.

"Lydia?" I asked, and she looked at me. "I know your armor is designed for your kind." I said awkwardly. "Can you still hide your wings, or…?"

"I can, but it'll take time. I'll need ta strip tha joints off the armor first, then the bladed wing tips and guards, then I can retract my wings wi' magic."

"Okay, forget it. They're a weapon, in their own right, anyway. Besides, there's a high point we can start with," I said, rubbing my chin. "Thomas, you any good at stealth?"

"Absolutely shit at it," he admitted almost proudly.

I couldn't help but grin. "Some things never change, eh? Fine. Yen, take Grizz, Arrin, and Thomas and go left. Tang, you take Bob, Giint, Ronin, and Jian and go right. Both teams take these ones out," I said, indicating the posts at the ten and two positions, before tapping the one at twelve and gesturing to Lydia. "I'll take Lydia, and we'll take that one out. Once you've cleared your post, move to the next one to the south. Lydia and I will hit the most southern. If at all possible, be stealthy; but if not, well, fuck it. They'll soon know we're here, either way."

I got a round of nods from the others and we broke apart quickly, the others slipping away to either side as Lydia and I retreated down the remains of the road, making sure we were well out of sight before sitting and giving the others a little time to get into position.

"How are you doing?" I asked Lydia. She jumped, as she had been concentrating on watching for Goblins.

"Ah'm alright," she said slowly. "You?"

"Yeah, bit weird having Tommy back, but it's good as well."

"I bet. So what's wrong?"

I frowned.

"Oracle's said almost nothing since we arrived, and while she sometimes doesn't speak much, it's not normal. And you're normally either cracking jokes or wadin' in blood, not jus' sitting quietly. So, what's wrong?" Lydia asked, making me grin.

"Well, Oracle's working on a spell, and I'm…well…" I paused, not really sure how to phrase it.

"Just spill it," Lydia ordered.

I looked at my hands for a minute, the words finally bursting from the top of my throat. "I'm fuckin' terrified," I admitted eventually, surprising us both.

"The gob…"

"Nah, not the fucking Goblins," I said, cutting her off. "All of this." I gestured at the world in general. "I'm rearranging the Legion, telling people to write laws, and kicking them off the side of the Tower when they disobey. I'm trying to end slavery, yet I'm making everyone take binding magical Oaths to do exactly as I say."

"You're the emperor, or you will be. Let's face it, it's not like yer orderin' women to yer bed. Yer doin' this as part of the Empire, making sure we can all trust each other."

"I know. Believe me, I know, I'm just…I'm fucking terrified of screwing it all up, Lydia, seriously! I'm nobody special, I just…"

"You're just the leader of the reborn Empire, the man who's personally 'ad fights with two Gods, and calls a third the 'Dark Wanker' while swearin' at the sky and darin' 'im to do somethin'? The man who raided a city wi' ten people who weren't even soldiers, but left with over a thousand, including hundreds of legionnaires, dozens of airships, and most o' the city's wealth?" Lydia whispered, shaking her head in disbelief.

"You've gone one-on-one wi' Gods, Jax. You've been in the realm less than two months, I think? In that time, you've lit'rally freed thousands of slaves, declared war on cities, and 'ad the entire legion swear fealty to you…you! A man who, less than a year ago, was workin' behind a bar, you told me? Either you're really nothin' special, Jax, in which case the notion of the people from your realm who *are* special damn well terrifies me, or you were always special, and you jus' needed a push to bring it out."

"See, when you say it like that…" I mumbled, before taking a deep breath. "Lydia, honestly, I don't feel like I should be looked up to this way…that's all."

Lydia turned, staring at me for a long minute before speaking.

"Take your 'elm off," she said.

I frowned, pulling it clear of my head, before shaking my head in shock at the ringing slap she gave me, rocking me back on my heels.

I massaged my cheek. "What the hell?"

"You're the Scion of the Empire and our leader, and you damn well needed that! Look, you can say this shit to me because we both know you're goin' to go out there and piss on the Goblins, the Dark Legion, and fuckin' Nimon. But you seriously need to take some time out and think about 'ow far you've come!" Lydia's eyes flashed as she lowered her voice. "We didn't do this; we helped you. You led us, and you made the decisions, don't forget that."

"Crap, I think you loosened a tooth." I spat a little blood out onto the ground before looking at her. "I know what you mean though, but…hey, how did you hit me, with the Oath and all?"

"It was to help you, I guess. I knew you needed it, so maybe that's it? I don't know; all I know is that you're going to lead us up there, Jax. You're going to lead us to victory, then you're going to do the same thing when we go after the church. Seriously, Jax, I *know* this…and there's one other thing I know."

"Oh?"

"I'm proud o' you," Lydia said flatly, as though embarrassed. "You freed us because you wouldn't back down when you saw us bein' 'it. You attacked a gang of high-level slavers and adventurers, a group wi' airships, all alone because you saw us getting' abused. You've gone from a man alone to the Scion of the Empire, and you jus'…you jus' *do* it, so don't give me any of that shit. I'm proud o' you for the things you've done and the way you do them."

There was silence between us for a long minute, and I felt Oracle's agreement before I smiled and reached out, squeezing Lydia's shoulder.

"Thank you." I said. "I needed that."

"I know. Now, can we stop bein' all touchy-feely and go and kill somethin'? My wings are itchin'," Lydia asked plaintively, making me laugh.

"Hell, yes, you ready?" I asked.

Her smile broadened. "Born ready!"

"Okay, we head east into the sun, fly up high, then pick the target, and boom. Slaughter the little bastards. Quietly, if possible," I said, and she nodded excitedly. "Okay, I'll let you lead." If she had any problems flying with me following behind, I'd know and be able to help her.

She nodded, pulling off the cloth she'd been covering her wings with and unfurled them, the massive things shivering and flicking as she shook them out, the feathers glowing a bright white in the rapidly dimming light as the storm closed in.

"Let's go!" She grinned and took a few quick steps. Her wings caught the air before she beat them for the first time. Then she was rocketing upwards and away. Her massive wingspan was magically augmented by both her class and the armor of the Last Valkyrie she'd salvaged, giving her the gift of flight despite being encased in hundreds of pounds of metal.

I gaped after her for a second before Oracle pinched my ear and jerked her head after Lydia. I grinned and crouched, Man of Steel style, before rocketing after her, blasting up into the sky.

I caught up to her easily, having to slow to stay by her side as she glided. She had a look of wonder on her face, her wings shifting slightly to better catch the thermals, even as she stared downward and pointed.

"There!" she called. "By the little stand of trees, that's the ten position you mentioned."

I looked, then nodded, seeing what she'd seen. Thomas and Grizz were on either side of the little mass of trees sneaking inward. I couldn't see anything at first, then a figure moved, then another, and my eyes widened in shock.

"What the hell is that?!" I asked Lydia, as she stared open-mouthed as well.

"Fuck, we've got to go!" She pointed to the position we were supposed to be raiding, a small section at the top of an embankment, surrounded by steep sides. We'd deliberately picked that one as ours because it was both easily accessible by air, and it looked down over the other positions, so was more likely to raise the alarm than they were.

Attacking half the sentry posts at once was more dangerous, especially as we had no idea what the Goblins here were like, but it also meant that we had a better chance to pull off the attack stealthily than if we went to each individually.

Triggering Greater Examine on the creature, I was in for a surprise.

Critical success!

**Your opponent is unaware of being observed
and has no defense against your ability.**

Gromjakkit Steam-Goblin
Steam-Goblins are unique across the realm in that they are born twice in the eyes of their clans. First, they are born biologically, then mechanically, as each Steam-Goblin earns the right to be upgraded by the clan Steam-Forger Drazikk once they have earned their true name.

Weaknesses: Ice and Lightning spells do 15% more damage to Steam Goblins.
Resistances: Death magic used against Steam Goblins has a chance to hit a mechanical part and do no damage.
Critical Weaknesses: Neck, Eyes, Boiler.
Level: 16
Health: 260/260
Stamina: 215/270
Mana: 80/80

I stared at the details, shaking myself out of my reverie at Lydia's hiss of warning. I growled, pulling my naginata free and diving down, blasting through the air towards the covered sentry post.

As I drew closer, I saw what Yen had warned about. It was set up to look like a massive nest, perched atop a pillar that looked like it might collapse at any minute. It had a sharply sloping roof that protected it from the weather, and what looked like three of the Steam-Goblins inside.

One was clanking around the exterior on a walkway, while the other two could barely be seen inside. They were only visible thanks to my Perception being as high as it was.

I pulled my naginata free and sent a pulse of lightning into it, lighting the blade with a bright, white glow before landing right behind the little bastard who was clanking around the circumference on his own.

As I landed, I slammed downward with the naginata, the blade hitting the junction between its neck and shoulder in what should have been a clean kill, all while I stared in horror at the creature before me.

It was a Goblin, yeah, but it was both massively oversized and hideously malformed. Both of its legs had been replaced with posts and flat, rusted circular feet. The middle of its back had a small steam reservoir that was bubbling and hissing constantly, with both gleaming and ancient metal mixed in together all over the place.

Instead of my naginata slicing cleanly through the body, it hit the scruffy jerkin the Goblin wore and the blade was deflected, skittering across the metal that was hidden beneath, sending a veritable shower of sparks flying before beheading the creature.

I grunted in shock. The reverberation that slid down the handle numbed my fingers. I glanced to my right, inside the guard nest. Two Goblins stared at me in shock, and I froze.

One of them looked normal for a Goblin. It was tall and well-built, but still made of flesh. However, the other looked wrong on all levels, more mechanical than living, with pot-shaped armor that was fused to the flesh, a replacement claw instead of a hand, and a bright blue gem in place of either eye.

I hesitated for a second, and it opened its mouth, letting loose a high-pitched wail that was quickly taken up by others around the site.

I lunged forward, stabbing out with the naginata and taking it in the mouth, both to shut it up, and because the mouth, and lower head, seemed the most normal bits of the entire creature.

The blade sank in effortlessly, punching through the open lower jaw and severing the spinal cord before the body dropped lifelessly, the head still glaring at me for several seconds as Lydia arrived and smashed the third and final Goblin into paste.

Unfortunately, even though all three were dead, the alarm was still ringing out. I raced to the edge and stared out, the front of the Goblin nest below me boiling with dozens of the little bastards, even as more started moving around the sentry posts. I swore and leapt off the platform, blasting through the air for the next nearest guard post.

Jian gutted one of his Goblins, and I landed behind the other, about to stab him, when he was taken down by a manically grinning Giint, screaming "spare parts!" at the top of his lungs.

Seeing none left within reach, I blasted off again, hurtling upwards into the sky to search.

The next guard post was showing signs of movement, and I flew at it, ploughing into the lone Goblin that stepped outside.

I'd held my naginata just below the head, flipping it over, then used it as a club to strike out. I whipped it around, adding my inertia and velocity to the blow, and the Goblin…well, it just disintegrated, the mechanical legs remaining more or less intact. Only a few sections were falling off, as the upper half of the corpse detonated, spraying the rear of the sentry post in stinking, oily blood.

Inside, another Goblin was already dead and half eaten, making me grimace at the fact these little bastards were cannibals.

I turned, looking around carefully, the wailing still clear and joined by a screaming sound from the main entrance as even more mouths took up the cry.

I spotted the next post just as it was struck by Lydia. She landed on one of the Goblins and smashed the other into a fleshy bag of broken bones and meat paste with her mace.

I grinned, turning to look for the last site. Magic built behind me, a set of three Flamespears phasing into existence. The first hit the sentry post head-on, making it explode in flames. As two figures stumbled out, screaming and wreathed in flames. Yen threw a second one at them, the splash damage from this one shortening the last terrible seconds of the pair's lives.

With the third and final spear, she pivoted and hurled the weapon straight for the entrance. It disappeared inside then exploded with a *kaboom* and a wash of heat that sent dozens of the little bastards to the ground. Most were killed by the overpressure caused by the spear's explosion in the narrow confines of the tunnel, but others were set aflame or crushed when an entire section of the roof twisted then fell on them.

"See, I did nothing that time," I said to the others as we gathered, readying our weapons as the survivors saw us and started screaming again. "And that was totally Yen's fault." I pointed as another section of the roof caved in with a loud crash.

There was a blast of air, then a loud roar, followed by at first a few, then more and more Goblins racing out of the darkness. Most were the smaller, feral kind I'd seen before, but here and there mixed in amongst them were bigger, uglier ones, many with new limbs or armor that had been fused in place.

We braced ourselves before Oracle suddenly shouted from behind me, growing to full size.

"I did it!" she screamed. "I actually did it!"

"Did what?" I asked, sweeping my naginata in a wide arc as the first wave of Goblins hit us. Grizz, Lydia, and Thomas stood with me on the front line, Yen and Tang having taken up position on either side after climbing up on top of the large rusting metal structures. Giint had tried to climb up but couldn't, and had instead started rummaging around in his bag, swearing.

Arrin and Jian were standing ready, waiting for their turn to fight, while Ronin was playing a tune on his lute. Bob let loose a low growl before he stepped forward, shoving his way into the lead, swinging a massive war axe in either hand.

For several minutes, it was a blur of stabbing and thrusting, kicking Goblins in the face and basically smashing the little bastards into the ground, before Oracle managed to get my attention again and explained in a series of short gestures and shared knowledge that made my brain ache.

"What?!" I asked her again, wiping blood off the front of my armor, and looking at her in confusion. "What the hell is the use of a shield with a sodding hole in it?" I asked, not sure if I'd understood it right.

"Like *this*!" she said, casting. It took a while, as it was a complicated spell, but after nearly thirty seconds, it popped into place before the group, and we laughed as we killed the last of those near us.

The shield was six feet high and eight across with an open hole in the center. The hole was two feet wide by one foot high, with three feet of solid shield on either side. The rest of the shield was transparent, Goblins getting crushed by their enthusiastic brethren against the shield, while the press of bodies was reduced to one at a time through the low hole.

The positioning of the shield-wall between the massive sections of rubble and junk meant that they couldn't get through, not at any real speed, anyway. I joined in the laughter as Bob waited for them to climb through, then stomped on their heads.

"How long can you keep this up?"

Oracle shrugged. "About a minute…three minutes, if we 're full on our mana, but that'll drain all of it."

"So why did you build the shield like this? I mean, don't get me wrong, it's hilarious, but still, I don't get why?" I asked her as Grizz walked up and started pulling faces at the mass of Goblins pressed against the invisible barrier.

"It means you can fire through it, and it lets a few through at a time, giving you control over the battle," Oracle said, smiling proudly.

"Okay, fair enough, I guess…" My mind filled with new ways to use the spell, before I banished it and went back to watching Grizz taunting the Goblins.

Several had been killed already, and more were clearly close to death when Oracle called out to all of us.

"Ten seconds, then the shield fails."

I grinned at her then around at the others in the line. "Everyone get ready with a magic barrage."

"Fireball?" Thomas asked.

"Fireball," I agreed. I drank a low-level mana potion and started casting, even as Oracle slid back into her diminutive form and lifted into the air, casting the same spell but from higher up.

I couldn't help but grin as I aimed, holding onto the spell and counting down.

"Three…two…o—Jax! Behind us!" Oracle screamed.

I released the Fireball on instinct, even as I spun, my mind still locked into frying the fuckers.

Heat washed over me as screams burst from hundreds of Goblins that were immolated, frozen, and blown up by the spell barrage, before swearing and barking out orders.

"They're behind us!" I roared, spinning to face them, even as the rest of the group fell in around me.

Bob spun, glaring down at the dozens of heavily armed and armored Steam Goblins that had clearly used another exit while we were busy, relying on the mass of ferals to keep us distracted.

"Arrin, Ronin, move inside the group!" Lydia barked. "Yen, Tang, scout the area; I don't want any more surprises!"

"Bob, get your arse in line!" I ordered. He stepped up, staring at me and clearly wanting to race into the middle of the Goblins and start slaughtering them. "I don't care what you think you're doing; here, you obey fucking orders and stay on the line!" I dismissed him from my mind as we all fell in around Ronin, who started playing some dramatic tune.

"Hey, Ronin!" Thomas yelled as we started taking out the first of the ferals that had made it around the outer edge of the barrage and the oncoming mechanical Goblins.

"Uh, yeah?" he called back.

"Can you play 'Deliverance' on your banjo?" he asked.

I laughed hard enough that I almost missed my next strike. "It's not a fucking banjo!" I shot at Thomas.

"Lute, banjo, guitar, all the fucking same to me, bro. I still can't carry a tune in a bucket," Thomas grunted as he slammed his mace down and splattered one of the ferals.

They were all around us now, literally dozens, with more arriving by the second. The ferals were the lowest form of Goblin, short, bowlegged, and weak. Most wouldn't be a great threat to a well-armed child, but what the ferals lacked in strength, intelligence, and coordination, they made up for in sheer numbers and ferocity.

Dozens became hundreds, clambering over each other in their need to close with us, frantic to bite and kill.

I swept the naginata from left to right, killing four of them and taking a leg from the fifth before reversing my grip and sweeping it back, continually clearing the space in front of me. Yen was also casting, the pull of her magic familiar to me, and I found I could sense the pattern.

"Flamespear," I muttered, stopping the swing and switching to a thrust instead, punching the tip of the blade through the chest of one of the little bastards before yanking it back. "Three? No, five?" I guessed, before four flaming spears coalesced into existence above Yen's hand.

She pulled back and heaved. Half propelled by magic, and half through sheer ferocity, the spears flashed across the intervening distance and slammed into the front ranks of the steam-Goblins. The first spear hit one full-on, causing him to explode, sending blood and bits across the others. His steam reservoir went practically nuclear as it lost control, spraying the nearest creatures with blistering hot water.

The other three landed seconds later, killing seven and injuring dozens, setting off the reservoirs and causing the ensuing explosions to kill even more Goblins.

We watched the rolling explosions that rippled through the group. More and more of the Goblins stopped and looked at each other, seemingly unsure what to do as their companions detonated, spraying water across each other.

The disturbingly steampunk wave of Goblins that had looked like they'd be a serious threat seconds before, were exploding as they tried unsuccessfully to detach the reservoirs. The sight of Goblins spinning in circles, their almost comically oversized hands slapping at their backs and sides, screeching as they were alternatively boiled or blown up was morbidly amusing.

"Keep fightin'!" Lydia barked, and we swung back into motion, having slowed to watch. I paid for my lack of attention when a small Goblin, less than a foot high, leaped onto my right leg, scrabbling upward and trying to sink his teeth into my manhood.

I screamed in deep-rooted terror, spinning around, lashing outwards with my naginata as I rushed out of the defensive line, smacking my hand down and trying to catch the little bastard.

My frantic motion, more than any concentrated effort on his behalf, meant I missed the little swine swinging from side to side. I finally managed to grab him with my left hand behind his head, yanking hard, but he'd managed to get his teeth around a section of my codpiece. I threw my naginata aside, skewering two more of the little shits before punching down at it, screaming in fury.

I eventually managed to free him from my crotch, yanking the fucker off bodily and spinning him around by the legs to smash into a rock.

A sickening crunch was accompanied by a spray of blood, and the body went limp. I looked up, my chest heaving, my eyes practically glowing with unbridled fury at the next wave of Goblin ferals.

"That fucker tried to *geld* me," I hissed, glaring at the oncoming wave, even as poorly concealed laughter rumbled from the rest of the group.

"Oh, it is fucking ON!" I screamed, swinging the corpse at the next one in line. The shattered skull of the Goblin I swung intercepted the reasonably healthy skull of the second and tore its face open, thanks to the rows of jagged teeth on display. It screamed, clutching at its face. I screamed in return, pointing at my crotch, then I punted it.

My armored boot hit it between the legs, lifting it bodily from the floor and sending it flying backward into its compatriots.

There was a scream, a blur of movement, and the fight broke down as Ronin jumped onto a downed one, stamping on its neck and killing it. The careful grouping we'd kept to until so recently collapsed as it became clear that even Ronin could kill the Goblins one-on-one and unarmed.

"Kill them all!" I screamed, grabbing two of the little bastards and slamming them together, their heads making a sound like coconuts at the fair.

"Training time!" Thomas shouted, shucking his shield and mace into his storage before lifting his fists. He grinned inside his helm as he punched out, knocking a Goblin senseless and sending teeth flying with a right cross, followed by a spin kick, and an uppercut, sending three more Goblins flying.

The fight took longer, much longer than it would have if we had remained in formation, or even armed, but by the time the last wave was dealt with, and I was swiping the notifications aside, I felt better than I had all day.

Congratulations!

You have killed the following:
- 11x Steam-Goblins of various levels for a total of 4,150xp
- 84x Basic Goblins of various levels for a total of 5,040xp

A party under your command killed the following:
- 66x Steam-Goblins of various levels for a total of 28,458xp
- 184x Basic Goblins of various levels for a total of 11,198xp

Total party experience earned: 39,656xp
As party leader, you gain 25% of all experience earned
Progress to level 30 stands at 1,014,425/1,120,000

I drew in a deep breath and looked around, surveying the piles of bodies and the general trashing of the place, before speaking up.

"Was that, you know, insanely easy, or what?" I asked, catching my breath.

"Shit, Jax, you know you never say that!" Thomas said. Grizz nodded along emphatically, even as Oracle groaned and buried her face in her hands.

"It's true, boss," Grizz said quickly. "You never, ever say that; now it's all going to go wrong. You know that, right?"

I opened my mouth to say something when a scream from inside the structure cut me off. I turned, climbing on top of several bodies to see over the pile and into the dimly lit hole that vanished into the hillside.

"We've got movement," I said slowly, before they appeared, rushing forward like a river bursting its banks. "A LOT OF MOVEMENT!" I jumped back from the pile of corpses and searched frantically for my naginata. I found it stuck into a section of wood that had made up part of a sentry post, still complete with two bodies dripping gore. I yanked it free and kicked the corpses off, backing up as I spoke.

"They're beasts with bigger Goblins on their backs!"

"What kind of beasts?" Grizz asked, all serious now that the fight was back on.

"Looked like giant fucking testicles with teeth," I said grimly.

"Noospits," Grizz growled, getting groans from half the group, who'd clearly seen or heard of them before. "They're vicious bastards, generally poisoned bites. Watch out for their jump; they'll try to launch themselves at you, if they can. For the love of the Gods, don't leave one half-dead; make damn sure they're all the way."

"You 'eard 'im!" Lydia barked, setting herself in position even as I pulled my shield out and did the same, with the others setting themselves in the formation, too.

"Yen, Tang, you know they can jump up there, right?" Grizz shouted up to the pair who were standing on the raised pillars.

Tang cursed and leaped off, quickly dropping into stealth and vanishing as he rushed to find a new vantage point, while Yen ignored Grizz and started casting.

I set myself behind my tower shield, the naginata laid across the top and blade pointing forward, readying it to be used as a long spear instead of the precision instrument of death it really was. Then I braced as the bodies before us shook and the ground quivered.

A Goblin with bright blue gems in place of eyes and a set of gleaming metal teeth screamed as it rode on the back of the noospit. The very top of it was just in view, then it ducked down, then leaped to the top of the body pile between us.

It landed badly, the pile shifting as it roared its hunger at us, little piggy eyes glowing with the same bright blue light as its rider. Its massive teeth were almost obscured by a tongue that looked to be a foot or more in length, and the weirdest damn feet I'd ever seen.

They looked like a cross between a blue duck and a hobbit, huge, long, and hairy, bright blue and flat, with three claw-tipped toes.

They flapped around as it ran, the body a huge ball of scarcely controlled viciousness and hunger as it raced down the pile, before gathering itself and leaping again.

"Shield!" Lydia shouted to me, stepping forward and readying herself. I cursed and set my shoulder, digging my feet into the soil.

"Ready!" I called, and a split second later she activated the Sacrifice ability of our twinned shields.

I grunted, sliding back a few steps before halting and shaking the arm that held the shield to get some feeling back into it. The ability transferred all inertia and damage from one shield to the other once per day, and Lydia had made the most of it.

She'd stopped the creature and its rider dead, her shield held almost negligently. Instead of ploughing through the shield, the pair had come to an abrupt stop. She'd put all her effort into an overhead mace strike that had killed both rider and mount with a single loud crunch of bone and teeth.

The sight had been *wrong* in the way that all movement had ceased so that it actually slowed everyone else down, too. Both sides had stopped, as people and Goblins alike stared in shock. Lydia ripped her mace free, slammed her wings out to their full extension, and roared like the lioness she was, beating her wings once and launching herself into the air.

I stepped closer to Thomas and Grizz, with Jian suddenly stepping forward on the right and Bob on the left. The sound of Ronin playing an ominous tune quickly rose behind us. I felt the buildup of magic, as first Oracle, Yen, then Arrin let loose as well, followed by Tang, with a barrage of Lightning, Firebolts, Darkbolts, and a blast of Flamespears that bottomed Yen out by the way she sagged.

I set myself as the first one reached me, weaving through the barrage of magic. The noospit crouched, then leaped at me. I ducked down, slamming my shield forward with all my strength, hitting the giant evil bollock in the face.

There was a crunch of teeth meeting metal and a yowl as the blade of my naginata took it in the side, tearing through the skin. A ringing blow made the world stagger as its rider lashed down with a small hammer, hitting me in the head.

The helm took most of the damage, and as the creature bounced off the shield and staggered back, pulling itself free of the naginata, the rider, who'd over-extended in his excitement, fell off, landing between us.

I paused, but the mount didn't, lunging forward and biting down hard on the small figure, who screamed once before it vanished inside the noospit's mouth.

I pulled the naginata back, adjusted my grip on the shield, then straightened my helm so I could see better, grinning as the noospit gave every sign of being perfectly content with its current meal, totally ignoring me to crunch down on its rider.

I snorted and stabbed out once with the blade, giving it a charge of fire that slipped into the noospit with a sizzling sound. The blade passed through the skin, cracking bone and smashing through into the organs inside.

The creature seemed to freeze, then the tip of the blade smashed through another section of bone and hit something that made the creature spasm. Suddenly, it went limp, and I barely had time to yank my weapon free before it collapsed, dead on the floor.

I considered how best to pass the information on, when Lydia flashed across the battlefield, her mace swinging and missing everything as she cursed and lifted into the air for another pass.

"Looks like someone needs more practice!" Grizz called out, grinning, and received shouted imprecations about punishment burpees as she passed overhead.

I stepped to the side, deflecting another noospit that leapt at me. Jian spun into sight, his twin scythes flashing out and decapitating the rider before he twisted and relieved the mount of its feet, leaving the massive bollock to roll away, screaming.

I stepped forward, stabbing out at another of the creatures that rushed me, before a sudden sweet sound lifted over the battlefield, and everyone paused involuntarily.

I felt a change even as I turned to look, my head drawn to the left. The sound altered, seeming far less enticing. I blinked, seeing Sehran standing atop a pillar and…singing?

She seemed to waver in and out of focus, her voice high and rolling over the head of the valley, even as Ronin's music changed to match her song. The notes and her voice lifted into the air as the first splatter of rain arrived, coming in a faint scattering of droplets, while thunder grew louder, and flashing lightning illuminated the rapidly dimming area.

The noospits and their riders slowed and stopped, staring up at her with open mouths. The last of the strange compulsion dropped away, leaving our team totally unaffected. I looked up at Sehran, then down at Jian who grinned at me, before grinning back.

"Get them!" I roared, dropping my shield into my bag and gripping my naginata two-handed. I lunged forward, stabbing the nearest enemy in the side of its head.

The blade punched in one side, then with a crunch and a spray of gore, it exited the far one. The body collapsed as I yanked my weapon backward, the rider falling with a scream, only to have Jian lop its head off.

The magic was broken as soon as we attacked, but the distraction was all we needed. With the creatures' attention pulled away from us, the battle turned into a rout.

The noospits and their riders were surrounded and quickly butchered. The most enthusiastic of all of us was Giint, who ripped the mechanical parts out of the living and the dead as he went, somehow understanding at an almost instinctual level exactly where these terrible creations were weakest, all the while giggling and packing them into his bags.

There was the occasional explosion as a steam-Goblin with a reservoir detonated, but for the most part, the riders were standard Goblins and fell easily.

Less than five minutes after the fight had begun, we were gathering up our gear again, waiting as Giint cackled and giggled, pocketing parts left and right, until Grizz stepped in and bodily pulled him off the pile of corpses.

Giint snapped at the big legionnaire, who smacked him on the nose with two fingers.

"Bad!" Grizz barked at him. "Bad Giint!"

Giint snarled at him, but he calmed down, rubbing his nose and glaring at Grizz, who dropped him back on the floor, giving me a "what can you do" look to scattered grins.

We quickly checked each other over, making sure the dozens of small wounds had the teeth and claws removed from them, before Oracle hit us all with heals. Then, with the heavy, fat raindrops landing all around us and washing the gore off our armor, we moved inside.

Chapter Fifteen

As soon as we got out of the rain and under cover, the temperature climbed slightly. The breeze grew warmer, and we moved closer together, watching the path deeper into the ruin.

The first room we came to was square, more or less, and had the remains of old seating down the left side, with a long, low firepit built into the wall on the right. Scenes were carved into the lintel, making it look more like a fireplace, but the massive size and length…it filled one whole side of the room, and I grimaced as a charred leg poked out of the mess of cinders and glowing coals.

I strode on, my team walking alongside me. We went deeper, trying not to stand in the piles of literal shit that filled the corridor as we went.

We passed through small and large rooms that were filled with broken machinery, stacks of rotten gear, and a stink that I guessed would be better dealt with by melting the entire hillside with Dragonfire rather than any attempt at cleaning.

"Jax, when we get back, we need to talk," Lydia whispered to me half an hour later, as we cleared another room, finding nothing but cobwebs, dead bodies, and collapsed, long-dead machinery.

"Okay…?" I said, glancing over at her. She snapped at Ronin, who jumped and started playing again. His fingers had slowed to the point of us losing the buffs we gained from his music as he tried to seduce Sehran.

"But first, I think it's time Ronin and I had a chat," she growled through gritted teeth as Grizz and I exchanged winces. She grabbed the bard's ear and marched him back from the group a few meters to lecture about his role in the team, while I called a break.

Thomas, Grizz, and I were standing side by side, chewing the dried meat that the Legion always provided as trail rations, when Tang came back, finally, arriving just as Thomas was talking.

"I mean, seriously, bags of holding mean it's hot when you pull it out still, so why the hell not prepare a dozen good meals, hot bacon sandwiches, and so on, rather than this shit? It seems, I don't know, a bit masochistic…"

"It's because the leadership hate us for being too sexy." Tang completely deadpanned as he broke into the conversation, becoming visible a few feet away, and making us all grab our weapons.

"One of these days," I muttered.

"Yeah, yeah, bells, whistles, and all that…seriously, boss, we've got a fight on our hands," Tang said, waving my muttering aside.

"Oh?" I asked.

"The Steam Goblins. Whatever we've faced so far has been their little versions. There's a trio of Orcs up ahead, headed this way. The Goblin version of rogues are already out and scouring the corridors as well as their warriors, so we need to get ready. But no mages yet, at least."

"Rogues?" I asked, hating the stabby-stabby little bastards when they weren't on my side.

"The *Goblin* version of rogues, I said." He snorted. "They're normal Goblins painted black and have shivs. Seriously. The warriors are more of a danger; there looked to be forty or more, and they all have armor, weapons, and shields, not to mention they're at least half metal themselves. So, we need to be ready; they'll hurt if they hit our line without warning."

"Like the Gnomes?" I asked.

"Not even close. They were mental bastards, but clever with it. Goblins are sneaky, but cowards at heart. Hit them hard enough, and they'll run."

"Water and lightning," Oracle said, smiling.

"What?" I asked, then grinned as I realized what she meant.

"Am I missing something here?" Thomas asked.

Grizz muttered under his breath, shaking his head.

"Seriously, what?" Thomas asked again.

Grizz sighed. "The boss likes to use water and lightning together, makes pools then shocks anyone that's too close."

"Okay, standing water to conduct the lightning, sounds good." Thomas nodded appreciatively. "What's the problem?"

Grizz leveled him with a hard look. "You know how hard it is to not piss yourself when someone hits you with that?"

Thomas frowned, turning to look at me. "You shocked your own men?" he asked. "Why?"

"He interrupted me and Oracle," I said wryly.

"And?"

"Then knocked on the door and kept interrupting," Oracle added. "Don't think I don't know about the pool, Grizz." She glared at him.

Grizz started to whistle, conspicuously looking elsewhere.

"The pool?" I asked.

"There's a betting pool going on if…you know what, don't worry about it. I'm aware, and that's all you need to know," she said, smiling at me.

"Wait, what?" I said.

"Just leave it to me, please." She reached up and kissed my cheek. I looked at her and shrugged, dismissing it for now, figuring she'd tell me later when we weren't hip deep in Goblin shit.

"Fine." I shook my head. "Okay Tang, how far and…"

Tang spun around and yanked his bow out of his bag in one fluid motion, hauling back on it and aiming. There was a few seconds' wait, then a black figure stepped around the corner in full view of us all at the end of the corridor. Tang's arrow smacked to a halt in its eye.

The figure dropped like a bag of shit, and we rushed forward, with Tang cursing as he vanished around the corridor and out of sight, presumably chasing something.

I paused, looking down at the body. It was a Goblin, painted black. It looked like someone…yeah, there was a handprint on the back of its jerkin where someone stronger had literally held onto it and dipped the little figure into a vat of paint or something, then he'd been sent off to find us, suddenly "stealthed" as far as the Goblins understood.

"Fuck, they're dumb," Grizz said, kicking the Goblin's foot to make sure it was dead before resting one foot on its forehead and tugging the arrow out of its skull, then putting it in his bag. "Tang will want it back." He shrugged, and we all nodded as though it was the most normal thing in the world.

"Time to go," I said, before Jian asked us to give him a minute.

He started chanting. From almost the first word, a ring appeared by his side, and as he spoke, more and more symbols appeared inside the ring, splitting off to either side to form an inner and outer ring. After two minutes of constant chanting, Jian pulled a dagger free and cut the palm of his hand, flicked his blood liberally into the circle, then stamped one foot firmly on the ground, all while being careful to remain outside the circle itself.

As soon as he finished speaking, the ground inside the circle seemed to fall away, and a bright flare of light lifted upward, forming a tube that reached to the ceiling of the room. It hissed and boiled as the heat inside scoured dirt and debris away.

"Ty'Baronn, I summon you," Jian called out, his voice going impressively deep. Seconds later, a short figure hopped up from below, wizened and panting as it hung in the middle of the pillar of light, glaring at him.

"You abandoned me, stripped me of my power." It snarled at him before Jian cut it off.

"Twice you disobeyed me, you little cretin!" Jian snarled. "Twice you nearly got us all killed because you had to do things your way! This is your last chance! Will you obey, or do I break the contract?"

"You can't!" Ty'Baronn exclaimed, before turning to stare at Sehran as she stepped forward, joining in the conversation.

"Master Jian has been honest with you and with me, little one," she said, smiling widely. "But you lied. You broke the contract with your arrogance, and now he can banish you, taking your power for himself. So be very, very careful what the next words you say are. I'm here to stay; think the master will pick your advice over mine?"

"Whore!" Ty'Baronn snarled at Sehran. "Stupid succubai; not even in your wildest fantasies would a mortal choose you over me! I can bring him power. I can advise him, grant him the answers to the deepest questions of the realms! What can you do but suck on his member!"

"Master?" she asked Jian.

"Do it," he said. "I wanted to give him a chance, see if he'd learned his lesson, but clearly the little bastard hasn't."

"You ungrateful…"

"The contract is void," Sehran said. "The Oaths annulled, where one signatory has broken faith, let the other extract vengeance. An Ability taken, thus balance is restored, lest all contracts fall into chaos." Several other succubai appeared in the background of the tube, seemingly made of motes of light, insubstantial, yet their voices joined Sehran's as she spoke.

Ty'Baronn screamed.

The screaming went on and on, as the disc that floated above his head crumbled, turning to dust and motes of light, flashing down into the circle and glowing brighter. Phantom claws reached out, the insubstantial figures of the other succubai becoming solid as they yanked the wailing figure downward.

The light flashed once, then slammed into Jian, knocking him back several steps before Giint steadied him, and then it was done. The tube collapsed, and the light vanished, reducing the room to just the glow of the magelights we all wore and bioluminescent fungi that was everywhere in the cave system…presumably in case a hero without DarkVision wandered in and needed to see.

We all waited, trying to figure out what the hell had just happened, before I spoke up, wanting to interrupt before things got any more out of hand. Sehran had grabbed Jian and pinned him to the wall, seemingly intent on securing her nomination of the universe tonsil-hockey championships.

"Sehran, put him down," I ordered. "You don't know where he's been."

"Yes, I do," she purred, looking over her shoulder at me, and I shook my head, taking a deep breath.

"Not what I meant! Right, Jian, talk, what the fuck just happened, and why pick *now* of all times to do it?" I snarled.

"Sorry, Lord Jax!" Jian said quickly. Sehran opened her mouth to say something, before apparently thinking better of it and dropping to one knee in supplication.

"Explain," I ordered.

"Ty'Baronn had given an Oath to obey me, and to do nothing to harm me…on the source of his power as guarantee. But when he disobeyed again and again, I realized that he'd never actually intended to keep his Oath. The Oaths that bind a warlock and his summoned are…different from the normal Oaths and can be enforced or not. I wanted to give him a last chance to help us, and I figured now would be a good time for him to prove himself.

"With Ty'Baronn getting around the Oaths he'd sworn so far, he'd basically proven that, if he acted against me, attacked me, or something, as long as I didn't die and couldn't speak to declare the contract broken, he could do what he wanted." Jian looked embarrassed as he scratched the back of his neck, then I noted the way his hand seemed to reach out for Sehran's, all of its own violation.

"Sehran's contract with me is MUCH simpler than the one he'd forced on me, and she explained the loopholes he'd made, and pointed out her own contract and the lack of them. Basically, she helped me to punish him for breaking his contract, and when I told her I'd give him one last chance, she arranged for some of her sisters to be there if things went badly."

"So, what happened to him?" I asked.

"My sisters ate him." Sehran said, shrugging.

"Joy…now forgive me for being an untrusting bastard, Sehran, but what did you get out of that?" I asked her pointedly. "Tell me the truth, please." I ordered.

"Power, strength, and status, not to mention I got rid of a potential rival," she said, smiling. "Honestly, unless you ask me 'is this the biggest you've seen' or to rate you in bed, I'll always be honest with you, my Lord. Ty'Baronn had an impressive and rare ability, but he was a sneaky little shit. When Jian told me what he'd done, I was concerned and wanted to look at his contract. There was over a hundred conditions of general waffling designed to hide three important clauses.

"First, that any power he gained, HOWEVER he did so, was his to keep. Secondly, that he could break any terms that were laid down by the Master, if there was need. And third, that the definition of need was by his standards. So, if he needed to, he could eat Jian's heart and get away with it, basically.

"The contracts we write are reflections of our intent. Mine is five phrases, mostly dealing with my master not causing me physical damage or feeding on me. To make Jian agree to the mass of clauses, he added in two very foolish ones, though. First was one that the Master, should he state his wishes clearly to a denizen of the hells to be free of the contract, then he would be. The other was that he could strip the Ability from Ty'Baronn if he needed to. Obviously, the little bastard never expected anyone to be able to read the clauses, as they were written in Infernal."

"Holy shit!" Jian growled, holding his right hand up as a golden disc eerily reminiscent of Ty'Baronn's signature ability appeared and disappeared at his will.

"Can you use it?" I asked him, and he read the details on his status screen, before nodding.

"I can...but it'll use ALL my mana if I do, and Sehran needs it..." he said, dismissing the disc with a sigh.

"That's okay." Sehran smiled. "Mana is like air for us, in this realm. As long as you've got a little, we can survive. It's simply...unsatisfying. Use the Ability, then drink a mana potion. I can hold my breath," she finished with a bawdy wink.

"Okay...I'm not even going to go there." I shook my head, hearing what sounded like a scream in the distance. "We need to go; explain your gains, quickly," I ordered Sehran as we started hurrying along the corridor.

"I gained status in my realm for arranging such a tasty morsel for my sisters, who will have also fed on his other abilities. Power, because I share in my master's power, and strength, well, because I drew in some of his strength from the master. The potential rival was because there are two of us, or *were* two of us, bonded to our master." Sehran shrugged. I wondered for an instant if it was unintentional or if she deliberately distracted the entire room by bouncing like that.

"Ty'Baronn might have turned the master's head and convinced him to remove me at some point, as there was no domination clause in the contract. Should I be bonded to another Demon through the master, one of my clauses is that I would be higher, should their bond come after my own."

She shrugged again, making her impressive chest nearly escape from the leather outfit as we all ran towards the sound of fighting. Oracle zipped off my shoulder, landed on hers, and started whispering something in her ear that made Sehran giggle.

I shook my head, banishing the thoughts that rose unbidden and instead accepted that Sehran had acted in Jian's and my own best interests. Admittedly, her own as well, but hell, she *was* a Demon, after all.

The next hallway was clear, but after it we entered a long, low room. Tang was fighting at the far end with a pair of black figures...both significantly larger and clearly stronger opponents than any we'd faced thus far.

"Tang!" I shouted, hoping to distract them. He dove to one side, the heavy *twang* of Giint's crossbow going off before we'd covered half the length of the room.

It slammed into the wall above the twin figures, then detonated, spraying a glittering cloud of dust into the air and making both figures, as well as a crouching third that we'd not known about, visible.

Tang rolled to one side, flipped onto his back, and dove again as a pair of throwing stars slammed into the ground where he'd stood a second before.

"Water!" Oracle sent to me, as I heard her voice rising and falling as she spoke the ritual words. I grinned, my fingers flickering awkwardly around the haft of my naginata as I muttered the words, dual casting Healing Fountain at the glittering rogues.

The water burst to life a bare instant before the lightning arced out. The first fountain washed a large amount of the glitter off one figure, while the second fountain soaked the third rogue where he slunk aside, trying desperately to stealth.

The Stunning Lightning Bolt hit the first enemy in the face, blasting him backward, arms flailing as it flowed down and into the water, spreading across the ground and travelling up and into the third, who thrashed and collapsed into the water, screaming.

Before Tang could get clear, the second figure leaped at him, clearly intent on finishing the job, and stabbed out with a twin pair of copper daggers that seemed to trail a faint miasma through the air.

Tang ducked and weaved, kicking one blade free of the rogue's grip, and slashing at the other hand. He missed and swore viciously as the daggers nicked the back of his.

The rogue turned and ran, clearly believing there was no need to do more, even as Tang took two quick steps after him, then drew his arm back and threw his shortsword end over end.

It slammed into the back of the rogue's right thigh as he ran, staggering him and sending him to the floor, before a trio of Magic Missiles slammed into him, each one targeted unerringly at the rogue's head.

The first blew off his ear and a good portion of skin, the second slammed home into the same spot, cracking the skull and sending a gout of blood out, while the third punched through the weakened skull and detonated inside. The corpse's limbs thrashed one last time as the jolt of magic massively overrode the signals controlling them.

Before either of the two lightning-struck rogues could gather themselves, we were there. Thomas leaped forward to take one down as he tried to run, head-butting the figure and knocking him clean out, thanks to the thick, padded Legion helm he wore.

The second met Bob in the worst possible way.

An instant before anyone else could close the distance to the second figure, a spear, glowing a sickly black and green, slammed into him, punching through his back as he turned to flee. It erupted out of his stomach as ghostly chains sprang into being, linking the now-screaming figure to Bob.

"BONES!" Bob screamed into the minds of all close by. *"GIVE ME YOUR BONES!"* His claw-tipped hands slammed down, gripping the chain and yanking backward, hard.

The figure screeched in pain as it was dragged from its feet and across the ground towards Bob, who was practically salivating at the thought of the bones inside the meat sack who'd tried to run away.

"Uh, Bob?" I said slowly, watching as he yanked the dying rogue back closer and closer. With each beat of the rogue's heart, a pulse of red washed down the chains and into Bob, who gave a satisfied groan as that energy became his.

"I..." A hiss of horror from Oracle stopped me a second before Tang collapsed. I was at his side in seconds, as were the others, leaving Bob to his grisly feeding. We gathered around Tang, who'd started to convulse.

"What is it?" I asked Oracle, even as my mind filled with information through the link we shared as she examined him.

"Poison," she hissed. "A nasty one..." Seconds passed as she started to heal, working faster and faster as she targeted certain areas, before cursing again.

"It's breaking down his organs. It's all I can do to keep his brain clear of it. Arrin, start on his lungs," she ordered. "And his heart, Jax."

I grunted, casting immediately, our shared awareness filling me in even as her words explained more to the others.

"Keep them clear of the poison, attack and cleanse it as soon as it appears, and repair the organs. There's a limited amount in him, so as long as we can get those clear, we can save him."

Arrin and I went to work, with the others guarding us. I concentrated on the heart, scanning it and locking it firmly in my mind, then focusing on it entirely to the exclusion of everything else.

Each beat of the muscle brought in more poison, a seemingly never-ending supply, even as the damn thing ate away at the tissues like an acid, making me race to catch up.

I nearly missed the warning sign, the building pain and dullness that spread through my mind, slowing my reactions, until I felt a vial being pressed to my lips.

"Drink!" Thomas ordered. I did, not seeing him, only the heart before me.

Slowly, the steadily blackening sections reversed the direction they flowed, growing lighter, redder, and healthier, as the blood that came through with each beat grew less and less contaminated.

Minutes passed, and I heard the sound of fighting more than once, before a second vial was pressed to my mouth, and I downed that, too.

Eventually, my head began to pound for the third time, and the world began to doppler in and out of focus. I could find no more poison in the blood, and I heard Oracle asking me to meditate.

I relaxed with a sigh, closing my eyes and shutting the world out, ignoring the sound of metal striking metal, or the screams as Goblins were torn limb from limb. Instead, I activated Peace, focusing on the winds, the high places of the realm, and the cool freshness in the air.

At first, it was hard, but as the seconds became minutes, I settled into it. The structures of mana grew less and less difficult to maintain, and I slid the sides of the boxes together, fitting them in and feeling the mana twist and condense, growing tighter and tighter. The next level locked into place, the now-familiar radiance seeming to emanate from me, as I tried to fit the third level together.

I'd always ignored the light before, convinced it was an aberration or a side effect of the mana. Now, instead of ignoring it, I tried to guide it, *pulling* the light to form the panels.

It whipped around, forming tendrils that slid and slapped, and I almost lost the connection in my shock before one slid across the edge of a panel. For a split second, it aligned perfectly with it.

The sliding and thrashing tendril suddenly glowed brighter and solidified. As it did, the shock tore through me, almost costing me the entire structure.

I quickly banished all thought, settling my mind, and only once it was clear, and the structure was glowing patiently again, did I try and replicate it. This time I held two sides in place with my mind, and pressed the threads of light into the edges, finding they gripped tight, and the structure no longer shifted and leaned from side to side. Now, it was rock solid.

I tentatively added more sections, finding that I could construct them perfectly, but the final one wouldn't fit anymore.

It seemed like madness. There'd never been a problem with them fitting until now…I tried it again and again, coming at it from all angles.

I slid it from above, from below. I pulled at the threads, and I shoved at the panels with all my might. I examined them for differences, swapping the final panel with each of the other five one at a time. Regardless of appearance, the panels being comprised of light after all, they were still somehow the same *size*.

It made my head ache, and I was about to dismiss it, despite the steady draw that Oracle was using, when I had a memory.

A memory of a wooden star that my mother had bought me when I was small. It had six pieces, each identical, and like this, they fit together easily, but the final one couldn't be slid in, no matter what you did. I frowned to myself, trying to remember the secret.

Suddenly it was there, the memory clear and bright, her laughter as I grew frustrated and threw it aside. She scooped the pieces up and me as well, settling me on her knee and kissing the top of my head, before whispering in my ear as she taught me.

I couldn't hear the words, but I felt the kiss still, and I remembered her teaching about logic and patience. It was like a balm to my soul, and somehow, somewhere, I knew she was proud of me, and all I'd accomplished.

"I love you, ma," I whispered, taking the panels and rearranging them into two sets of three. I made mirror images and rotated one by forty-five degrees, then *pushed*.

They slid together seamlessly, no resistance at all, as the next set of boxes fell into being in my mind. Something changed, even as I imagined I could hear a familiar voice whisper in my ear:

"I love you, too, son."

CHAPTER SIXTEEN

blinked my eyes open, tears flowing down my cheeks and sizzling into mist at the bright white light that blazed out from me.

Congratulations!

You have practiced enough to raise your Meditation skill to its second evolution!

Through combining several different methods into one, you have shown an understanding that is beyond your years.
Continue to practice and learn, to increase this skill further.

You must now pick a path to follow.

Will you choose to widen your boost with NATURE'S WONDER,

or will you continue to specialize with OBSESSION?

Choose carefully, as this choice cannot be undone.

NATURE'S WONDER:
The natural world around you no longer distracts you, instead, by working in an open place, surrounded by nature and life, you can increase your gains significantly, gaining +2 on top of your current +5 for a total of +7 per level of compression you manage, gaining this across all Aspects, health, mana and stamina.

OBSESSION:
By focusing obsessively on this single aspect of your ability, you are beginning to see the true power of Specialization, ignoring your health and your stamina and risking the attacks that can come when you are distracted, you suspect you can increase your gains significantly. Gain +10 to your mana regeneration for each level of compression you achieve.

I didn't need to even consider this. I could gain another thirty points of mana regeneration per minute if I managed to put all three levels together. Including my already goddamn impressive mana regeneration of just under seven points per minute, I would now have thirty-six point seven five points per minute; that was my entire manapool in sixteen minutes. If I could increase that again…my mind boggled at the possibilities, even as the pain made my muscles twitch as neural pathways were realigned and improved.

I was left with the annoying knowledge, presumably from the Gods, though who knew where the damn hint came from really, that this was as far as it could be pushed at the minute. I sighed, relaxing as I accepted that it was still sodding amazing, either way.

The glow died away as I came to my feet, and I looked around, seeing the awe on the faces of my companions. They quickly worked to hide it, with Thomas asking me if I'd been snorting something fun. But before I could give him a sarcastic answer, Bob moved in front of me.

"Bones," he said, gesturing at the piles to one side.

I nodded. "I get it, mate, I'll make your armor; just give me a minute." Holding up a hand, I turned to Oracle and Tang.

I knew, thanks to our bond, that Tang was fine. But still, knowing something and seeing it with your own two eyes was very different. I sighed with relief as I observed his gray, hollow-eyed expression, at him hunching down awkwardly next to the door and watching the room.

"Are you okay?" I asked, and he forced a smile.

"Yeah, I'm fine, boss," he croaked, before clearing his throat and trying again. "I'm fine, honestly, just a bit…worn out…that's all. Thanks, Jax, Oracle. Hell, thanks everyone." He took a long, appraising glance around, receiving a chorus of "you're welcome" and "don't worry" as well as "you owe me gold" from Giint. The little bastard.

I grinned, clipped Giint across the back of the head, then turned to Bob.

"Okay Bob, the bones…"

"Magical, rebuild me." That was all he said, but I looked back at the bones and focused in, activating the ability to sense their composition and their inherent magical affinities, before grunting in shock.

The bones of the rogues were gleaming darkly in this new sight, while the bones of the Goblins were glowing with white and gray light. As I looked around the room, I saw more and more bones, most broken down long since into fragments, spread all over the floor and up the walls.

I grimaced as I realized the tiny fragments were mainly buried in the shit that coated everything from hundreds of Goblins living here for years, possibly centuries, but, well, magic was magic.

I pulled up the details and couldn't help but whistle.

Bones		Further Description *Yes/No*	
Details:		These humanoid bones have been infused heavily with darkness aligned mana, adding +1 to stealth per kilo of bone included in crafting.	
Rarity:	**Magical:**	**Durability:**	**Charge:**
Uncommon	Yes	87/100	N/A

It didn't sound like much, not for a kilo of bone, but considering there was just over twelve kilos of bones per corpse, there was enough for a plus thirty-six boost to Bob's stealth skill.

That didn't seem a great deal until you considered that, to reach just that level naturally, when you were a skeleton that was nearly seven feet tall, you would have to do some serious voodoo.

The ability to add that kind of an improvement to him was huge.

"How did the bones get infused with mana like this?" I wondered aloud, rubbing the splintered end of one of the bones curiously.

"It's not that unusual, really," Yen chipped in, looking over the pile of bones and the second, messier pile of flesh that Bob had left off to one side when he'd stripped the bones free of the bodies.

"The more magic you do that's focused inward, the more you'll change your own bones and flesh. Think about Tang and Bane, especially…I mean, I do scouting, always have, really, but I don't do the stealth thing all day every day, not the way they do." She gestured at Tang, who was crouched by the wall at the edge of the room, watching down the corridor.

"I mean, seriously, he crouches when he rests now; it's gone that far. It's become a part of him now, like Grizz's bad jokes, or Ronin trying to look down Sehran's top." Grizz looked slightly hurt at that, while Ronin went red and pretended not to have been in danger of his eyeballs falling out down Sehran's cleavage.

"So, you're saying all we need to do to level Bob up in stealth, or anyone really, is to loot the bones of stealth-based creatures and use them in crafting?" I asked, a dark plan coming to mind.

"Well…yes and no. In Bob's case, you can rebuild him over and over, adding more bones in, and that will make a massive difference. For one of us? It's what…?"

"Plus one point in stealth per kilo of bone."

"Wow, okay, so if I wanted to be completely invisible at will at stealth level one hundred, not even grandmaster, just the top of master ranking, I'd need a hundred kilos of bone attached to my clothing? When a full suit of legionnaire's armor weighs what, thirty-five to forty?" Yen winced. "I'd rather do it naturally, boss, thanks anyway."

"Ah, fair point." I rubbed my chin as I considered the implications. "Okay, then. Well, let's get you armored up for now, Bob. We can review the options for upgrades in the future. Actually, is there anything you want me to do, in particular?" I asked, suddenly realizing I'd been about to crack on with the changes without consulting him.

"Repair. These bones to repair and strengthen me. Those to form armor," he said grimly, tapping the bones from the rogues first, then gesturing towards the pile of little bones. I examined them, finding a mix of Goblin and others, and smiled at the bonus they gave.

Bones		Further Description *Yes/No*	
Details:		These humanoid bones have been infused heavily with creation aligned mana, adding random bonuses to crafted items	
Rarity:	**Magical:**	**Durability:**	**Charge:**
Rare	Yes	49/100	N/A

"Okay…tell me if this hurts," I said, activating my ability to rebuild him, and examining the image I got. He was fairly damaged again, but whereas before I'd had an exploded view of the skeleton figure in my vision that I could manipulate and alter at will, now it was different.

In the middle was a mass of black smoke with blue, glowing eyes. The smoke filled the skeleton form, and here and there, shining sections that I could only guess were fragments of souls glimmered through, before vanishing again.

When I removed sections, starting with a finger to test it, Bob showed no sign of discomfort, and the black mass of smoke that had been infusing the finger flowed out and back to the main body, leaving an impression of…of a pattern. Like it was used to flowing in a set way, but it was no big deal to change.

I nodded and removed his right arm entirely, stripping the section away and pulling in the darkness-infused bones. I molded them into the same shape, mimicking a human arm, but far denser, not having the need for marrow or ligaments and flesh after all. I made more permanent joints from half-remembered designs from medical programs and the way I'd seen them attaching a mechanical socket into an army vet once on TV.

I built it up from scratch, then added half-copied and half-created new sections to hold it in place, enabling movement and protection for the new joints.

I shifted and altered sections, moving the joint back and forth, then smoothing the surrounding area and reforming parts again. I tested them over and over until I had a final design that felt right. Inside the magic, minutes passed as I worked, possibly even hours, but thanks to the wonder of the Ability and the many practice attempts I'd had, seconds passed for the rest of the world.

Once the arm was intact, fully functional, and frankly as awesome as I could make it, I reattached it, watching the way his essence flowed out from the central core to permeate the arm. I made sure it worked for him, then realized that, in doing only his right arm, condensing and altering the bones as I had, I was down to less than four kilos of darkness-aligned bone left.

I blinked in surprise, then sighed and swept the bones into a pouch for later use. I pulled in the dozens of kilos of bone fragments from around the room, mixing them with the pile of bones that Bob had managed to collect and used them in his structure. I filled in the dozens of cracks, reluctant to use the infused bone for such a mundane usage at first, but resigning myself to the fact that at least now I had an idea about…

"Giint!" I called out suddenly, pausing as the bonemeal was being compacted and fused into Bob's frame. The little Gnome jumped, startled, and landed with his teeth bared as he clutched the small square of metal that he always played with to his chest, before realizing it was me, and smiling hopefully.

"Giint hears…Lord have…" he said, and I fumbled one of the recent attempts at making his drug out of my bag and held it up, making his eyes go wide at the sight of it.

"Giint, this is a new drug, one I've made especially for you, but you can't have it yet, not 'til this place is cleared out." His face fell, and I quickly went on. "BUT, you can have a tiny bit now, if you've got some bones in there I can use for Bob."

I nodded towards his bags, and he slid the cube from sight, rifling through them. He kept looking up to make sure I'd not put the drug away, until he found the bag he was looking for. He tugged it open and dragged out a bone as long as my leg and as thick as my thigh.

"Bone good?" Giint asked me hopefully, as my jaw dropped.

"What the hell?" I had suspected the little pack rat might have had something in there, but not *this*!

"Drug?" Giint held his hand out and smiled as patiently as he could.

"Here, but first Giint, what is this and where did you get it?"

I passed him a tiny bit of the drug. He eyed it in clear disappointment before mumbling something about a Dragon, then popped the fingernail-sized piece into his mouth and chewed frantically.

"A Dragon?" I mumbled, then hit the bone with an examination.

Bones		Further Description *Yes/No*	
Details:		These draconic bones have been infused heavily with water aligned mana, adding +3 to water damage per kilo of bone included in crafting	
Rarity:	**Magical:**	**Durability:**	**Charge:**
Rare	Yes	98/100	N/A

"The ice drake!" Grizz said. "The mad little bastard stripped as much as he could from it, I bet that's where this came from!"

"Oh, hell yes!" I said, reactivating the bone spell and pulling the huge new bone up in my view, before splitting it down the center, taking both the nubs off one end, but leaving them on the other, extending and flattening them as I went.

I shifted the bone around, spinning it and smoothing sections, re-adding the removed sections in a few strategic areas, then filling the hollow areas with bonemeal from the Goblins and compressing it, hardening it over and over again. After a few minutes for everyone else, and over three hours for me, subjectively, I was done, and Bob examined his new form as I grinned at him.

He stood at over seven feet tall now and was wide-shouldered. He appeared to be humanoid, wrapped in a cloak, but where he'd been cracked bone before, now he was smooth and polished. His right arm was a deep, matte black with gleaming white spikes at the shoulder, elbow, and across the knuckles. Each finger was tipped with a gleaming white claw.

The rest of his body was made of a mix of yellow-white and gleaming white bones, thicker and heavier than normal, but appearing more like a particularly unusual armor design, rather than a skeletal warrior. In his right hand, he held a huge two-handed warhammer made from the thigh bone of the ice drake.

I examined him, finding that he'd gained a boost of thirty-two to his stealth skill, and his unarmed punches with his right hand would do plus four damage thanks to the spikes, and his warhammer, well…

Ice Drake's Revenge	Further Description *Yes/No*
Damage:	45 + 5-35
Details:	This two-handed weapon was once the thigh bone of an immature Ice Drake and has retained several of the magical aspects its species is famed for. **Strike**: Overhead full force blows using this weapon deal triple damage when connecting. **Icewind's Devastation**: Once per day, the wielder can call upon the Spirit of Icewind and imbue their next attack with Freezing properties. **Protection**: -5 Damage taken from Water or Ice attacks.

Rarity:	**Magical:**	**Durability:**	**Charge:**
Unique	Yes	100/100	1/1

Bob studied himself and the hammer before striding to the front of the group, gesturing down the corridor before us.

"Now, go?" he asked.

I checked, then swiped aside the notifications I received, dealing with increases in my necromancy skills and the rise in the power of my Skeletal Reaminator spell. I'd reached the stage where, frankly, I didn't care any more about the little rises in skill. Once it hit ten or a multiple of it, hell yes, but until then, bugger it, it was just more crap I didn't need to deal with.

Bob started off down the corridor, and we all followed, deciding that stealth was basically out of the window by this point. The Goblins knew we were here; we'd already killed hundreds of the little bastards. And while we'd been healing Tang, I'd essentially been glowing like I had a core from a nuclear sub rammed up my arse, so why even try anymore?

Plus, Bob wanted to lead the group, and the propensity for poison shown by the rogues would result in a nasty surprise for them if they tried it on him.

He wore the cowl of his cloak up over his head, keeping his face in shadow. So apart from the glowing blue eyes, he could easily pass for a living humanoid now, if a particularly heavy and terrifying one.

"What were the rogues?" I asked Oracle as we hurried down the corridor.

"Oh, you were still meditating at that point," she said with a quirk of a smile in my direction. "They're Orcs. Looks like we know how the Goblins managed to put all the mechanical parts in now!"

"Do we?"

"Oops." Oracle facepalmed. "Okay, quick racial lesson for you, darling. There're three main groups of Orcs out there. They call themselves all sorts of things, but everyone else just refers to them as thugs, mechaniks, and loons. The thugs are the kind you remember from the games and books you used to read, heavily muscled fighters, mostly. Their culture is all 'respect me' and that crap." That last bit was said in a fake deep voice that made me chuckle.

"So, they're like the ones from your games, you remember Gromesh who you fought in the Arena? He was one. They're by far the most numerous and skillful fighters of the three clans. They live for battle, and honor is literally all they care about. The loons are crazy, like full-on mental.

"They were an offshoot of the thugs that got exiled due to a werewolf infestation. As time went on, they discovered they liked the power it gave, and well, they breed fast. The thugs and loons are in a constant state of war with each other, both groups having a rite of passage which involves raiding the other and killing them before they're counted as adults."

"Don't forget the other races," Yen interrupted calmly, and Oracle smiled at her as she added in details. "Seriously, the loons aren't just werewolves; they've got bears in there, rabbits, basically any kind of shapeshifter is welcome. It makes them a weird culture to meet, but if you're lucky enough to meet them when they're calm, a damn interesting one."

"Yen was the one telling me all about this," Oracle said. "Most of the details are still the same from the old days of the Empire, but back then, the Orcs were either more civilized, like normal people, or rarely seen. Anyway, the last group are the mechaniks; they're...well, Giint will like them." Oracle shrugged. "They make weapons and simple explosives, carts and ships, no airships as far as I know, but that's something they'll do eventually.

"They're like massive, violent, psychopathic Gnomes. Their inventions shouldn't work, but somehow they do...no idea how or why. The rogues had parts replaced by the mechaniks, so it is possible they were either part of the clan, or..." she shrugged again, and I returned her gentle smile before replying.

"So, why send the Goblins at us? If there are Orcs who know how to fight in here, and that understand stealth?"

"We think they're most likely prisoners," Yen said. "The rogues had collars on with explosives attached, and we've still not seen any more of them. If they'd attacked when we were distracted by the ferals, they'd have done real damage. Instead, it was almost like they were reluctant to fight."

"Not *that* reluctant," Tang called back, and I nodded in agreement.

"I meant reluctant for Orcs," Yen said. "Usually Orcs run at you screaming, and their idea of stealth, well, the thugs' and loons' idea of stealth is to attack when it's dark, or to cover their own eyes and shout *'You can't see me!!'* while swinging blindly with their weapons. Much like a toddler thinks if they can't see you, you can't see them.

"Mechaniks are *much* smarter, easily as smart as the average human. Many are far more intelligent, but wisdom is a lacking trait in their cultures. They view it as a stat for lesser beings, so once their mages have used their spells, they tend to fall back on axes."

"Takes them forever to regenerate their mana...got it," I said as we slowed to enter another room. This one was long and boasted high ceilings with a clearly ancient and cold forge taking up most of the left of the room. "This is going to sound terrible, but Thorn is a half-Orc..."

"She's not a true half," Yen said. "It's more a case of somewhere in her ancestry, there was an Orc. There's a lot like her, perfectly normal people who have the occasional hint of something different in their makeup. Nobody thinks less of a half-Elf or a half-Dwarf, but people will judge a half-Orc as soon as they see them because of the way the majority of their race act. Thorn has been fighting against it her whole life, but what you probably want to know is that she was most likely related to a Mechanik."

"Okay, and to be very clear, I LIKE Thorn," I said. "She's a hell of an armorer and a good person. I'm not judging her, just confused."

The ceiling had runners coated in centuries of grime and crap, but here and there hung arms that had clearly once been used for construction. As to the forge itself, residual heat radiated off it, even from here, despite the entire thing appearing black and dead.

We searched the room quickly and spotted three doors leading off. One was on the wall to the left, at the far end of the forge and half-buried in a rockfall. The door on the wall opposite the entrance we'd used was sealed shut. It was a massive stone door that had been repeatedly hammered and assaulted, yet stood firm. Despite the collection of broken hammers and various crap strewn about it, the few tiny scratches that marred its otherwise pristine surface made it clear that it was magically sealed.

The final door, set to the right at the back of the room, had a well-trodden pathway leading to it. It had obviously been kept clear from the piles of blankets, tarpaulins, random crap, and rubbish that filled the rest of the room.

I looked around as we went, suspicious of the piled crap that littered the room, well aware that anything could be hiding in it, but we barely slowed. We moved on quickly, exiting the room and entering the next corridor.

This one, like most of the others, was long and narrow, but the walls that had until now been made mostly of brick, suddenly changed into large slabs, as well as including far heavier reinforced pillars every few dozen feet.

The ceiling rose steadily until it towered over us at nearly twenty feet high, the slight arc that had characterized it now becoming a grand one, with the ceiling covered in almost entirely obscured frescoes, visible only here and there as they peeked out from under the miasma of the ages.

I slowed, staring curiously, before a grunt of protest from Thomas brought me back to myself. With a huff, I sped up again until I'd almost caught up to Bob.

At the end of the corridor was a left turn with a door set into the wall. We slowed, looking inside at heaps of scrap metal, piled sections of machinery long since dead, and rusted hulks that were entirely unidentifiable. Faint shuffles of movement scrabbled somewhere in the depths of the room, but we ignored them and continued, deciding a fast advance was more effective than a clearing action.

Moving on, we took the right turn at the end of the corridor and passed the next four rooms, all of which had open doors and were clearly used as sleeping quarters and a mess hall. We'd started to slow, letting Bob draw ahead again as we all calculated the hundreds, if not thousands of ferals these rooms could accommodate. That was not to mention the larger Goblins and the obvious lack of any of them we'd come across so far. Thought of that fled, when Bob turned the corner ahead, and a roar of fury shook the floor.

We sped up, stomachs dipping as we turned the corner and saw the room ahead.

It was huge and rectangular, with the door at the end of the corridor exiting in the center of the wall. Dozens of towering forges and what looked like construction bays lined the sides of the walls, ending in a raised dais that was clearly intended to watch over the room. Laid atop the dais was an enormously fat Goblin matriarch, surrounded by dozens of rows of Goblins, all of whom were heavily armed and mechanically augmented.

We spilled out around Bob and gathered ourselves, seeing the room in more detail as the matriarch slobbered and tore at a hunk of meat held in her hands, glaring at us with piggy eyes.

While the room must have been a workshop of tremendous capacity, clearly intended for both massive and small constructions to be developed alongside each other, the majority of it was now made over into holding cells, sleeping nests for Goblins, and areas for mechanical prosthesis to be created and surgically fused to the warriors.

Only one forge was lit and operational, and that seemed to be barely functioning. The expected, steady light it would have emitted along with the heat was instead a mottled glow as piles of floating impurities and slag mixed with the glowing light of the forge.

There were racks for weapons, but most of those placed on them were useless, with dozens of the racks buried under piles of broken equipment.

I glanced around, partly stunned by the size of the room, but also amazed by the fact it appeared to be a hoarder's pit.

The lines of Steam Goblins between us and the matriarch shuffled and spat, coughed and shoved each other, small fights breaking out amongst them. A single line of Goblins stood inside the ring on the mid-tier steps leading up to the dais around the matriarch.

"Okay, there's well over a hundred of them," Thomas said slowly. "What's the plan?"

"Quiet!" Lydia snapped. He glared at her, but did as he was told, while I watched them all carefully. Shifting my gaze from one Goblin to another. I finally spotted a cage near the dais that was occupied by people, whereas the vast majority were empty or crammed full of broken gear.

There were a dozen or so Orcs sitting in the cage, dispiritedly watching the world, with one old, white-bearded Orc staggered from the forge to an anvil, hammering on a bent piece of metal and glaring at it as though it'd done him a personal disservice by not being cast perfectly straight.

I watched him for a second, seeing the way he glared around at the Goblins, then in a seemingly deliberate action, smacked his hammer down on the end of the anvil, bending the leg he'd been working on and making it as rough as possible.

I realized he couldn't see us, as far away and dimly lit as the room was, but the Goblins could, and they were glaring at us with obvious hate.

"MORE FOOD!" the Goblin matriarch screeched into the air, pointing at us as the mass of Goblins sprang forwards. A tall, hunched figure in tattered robes cackled as it directed them and scurried back to her side.

These Goblins weren't like the ferals, unthinking creatures that moved like a wave, intent on nothing but their goal. These were soldiers, foot soldiers to be sure, the vast majority stupider by far than the lowest and thickest of those that would ever be accepted into any real fighting force, but there were still hundreds of them, and quantity had a quality all of its own.

"Water," I said grimly, as Oracle lifted into the air, beginning to cast. She started dual casting, creating first one, then three, five, and more, going on as I spoke to the others, creating fountain after fountain that bubbled up to create pools of standing water that the Goblins pattered through as they strode forward, their force screaming as they rushed forward as a single wave.

"Yen, prepare Flamespears. Thomas and Arrin, missiles. Aim for the steam reservoirs. Grizz and Lydia, be ready with shields. Ronin, work with Sehran to distract them at the best opportunity, preferably as soon as they reach the middle of the water. Jian, use that beam attack; aim for the matriarch.

"Bob, stay close. You're to protect the group and kill stragglers. Giint, I want an explosive in the middle of that fat fucker's face," I said, gesturing to the matriarch before turning to Tang. "Stealth and get around to the side; I want you ready for whatever the robed shitbag does. If they're a leader or a mage, kill them. Everyone fires AFTER Oracle and I," I said, setting my gaze where she hovered. "I'll do a Compression. Once that hits, do as powerful a lightning blast as you can."

Oracle nodded to me, switching from creating the fountains at my words and starting to cast, even as I popped the cork out of a mana potion and downed it, a sudden idle thought entering my mind about whether Oracle could use mana potions, now that she could get boosts from coffee.

I started to cast Explosive Compression, choosing not to play with it and instead simply building it as cleanly and quickly as I could. I compressed it as far as possible, taking the extra few seconds to force it down, making the weaves tighter and closer together before ramming my hands forward with a huff of air. The spell screamed away from me, its passage across the room stirring up wind as it approached the sound barrier.

Before it could truly build an insane degree of speed, it hit the first Goblin, blasting through a gray-skinned, yellow-eyed face that not even its own mother could have loved. The head detonated, one long, flappy ear flying into the air and turning end over end as it sailed free of the rest of the skull, clearly happy to be free of the fugly little bastard.

Blood had barely begun to spurt from the remains of the lucky winner's neck when the spell smashed the second Goblin's face into a gray mist and began to unfurl.

The spell rolled out, then the ritual circle slammed down and bathed the room with an evil light. The Goblins closest to the rollout staggered, many screaming in fear and confusion, insubstantial runes flashing through them. Then, it entered phase two, and the very air was sucked from their lungs as it was pulled inwards.

Then the party really started.

The Goblins nearest felt it first, as suddenly, to their minds, the floor was no longer down. Gravity shifted, pulling them sideways towards the center of the new gravitational field.

There were grunts of surprise, then screams, then crunches and howls of agony. The noises were sometimes interspersed with the whine or whistle of steam reservoirs and voices screaming in so much high-pitched terror, I had to wonder whether their testicles had been compressed as well.

Finally, just as they were starting to get crushed in tight and dragged through pools of water that were splashing across them all, their bones popping and cracking as they shattered, Oracle's supercharged Lightning Bolt arrived.

It slammed into the middle of them, the arc bending slightly from the Goblin she'd targeted, as even its power was twisted, slamming into the metallic backside of the one next to the leering face she'd aimed for. But the water coating everyone more than made up for that.

The first Goblin had time to screech for a quarter of a second before it was forcibly changed at an almost molecular level from "Grey-skinned Steam-Goblin #12" to "Extra Crispy #42 With Suspicious Meat."

Then the lightning arced out from the point of impact, racing across a handful at first, then dozens of them. It spread into hundreds of Goblins before it eventually ran out of charge, doing little more than giving an annoying zap to the last forty or so.

Had that been the end of the attack, the majority of Goblins would have lived…for a few more minutes at least. But it wasn't the end.

While the lightning spread out, and the Explosive Compression had detonated, killing a handful, then crushing dozens, the Magic Missiles were still incoming. Thomas fired three longer and considerably more powerful missiles than Arrin did, but Arrin's five were shorter and more maneuverable.

In the end, it made no difference, as all eight slammed down into their targeted steam reservoirs and detonated, causing the unstable portable bombs to reach a new level of danger.

Whereas a particularly hard glare had been known in the past to set off an explosion, now actual missiles exploding did the job. It sent a blast of destruction radiating outward and into the reservoirs of others packed side by side with the unlucky bearers.

Those who so far had survived the crushing force of the Explosive Compression and the pain and shock of the Lightning Bolt had, by and large, begun to hope that they would live. They frantically held on as weaker and lesser Goblins died around them.

Then, here and there, above the wails and crunching, the screams and the howls, came a terrifying sound they all knew too well. The building hiss of an unstable steam reservoir approaching critical mass.

More screams rang out as the building pressure forced containers to fire their nails free, cutting through those nearby and further weakening other already damaged units.

Then the Flamespears arrived.

Yen had created five of them, staggering them throughout the now crumpled and wounded formation, and they arrived with a scream of tearing air. Where they landed, they sent out shockwaves that killed anything within the first few feet, simply vaporizing any who were lucky enough to be hit point-blank, then in a radius of ten feet, they did gradually lessening damage, ranging from instant death to merely third-degree burns. Goblins were hurled from their feet into walls, spikes, rusting metal, and more.

Even with all of this, there would have been survivors, had the Flamespears not been spread out in a specific pattern, creating a concussive blast wave that Yen had refined with me over long talks around campfires, over meals, aboard ship and on marches.

Instead, the blast waves overlapped, tearing flesh and metal apart, sending bone flying and setting off more and more unstable steam engines.

Sehran and Ronin stood ready, as did Grizz, Lydia, and Bob. But when the smoke and steam, the screams and flying blood, bone, metal, flesh, and scalding water finally cleared enough to see the way, only the matriarch, her assistant in its tattered robes, and the Orcs still lived.

There was a long minute of silence, broken only when the matriarch, staring around open mouthed while clutching a gnawed bone, spoke up.

"FoOoOd?" she warbled, clearly unable to understand the turn of events.

Giint nudged Grizz and passed him something.

"What's this?" Grizz asked, shaking the strangely glowing device.

"Bomb. You throw," Giint said, crouching down and putting his arms over his head.

"FUUCK!" Grizz shouted, hurling the bomb at the matriarch.

In his shock and haste, he missed slightly, hitting the robed figure full in the face and knocking him backwards as the bomb exploded, shaking the entire room and possibly the hill it was located under.

When the air cleared again, at least a third of the back wall was missing. The entire dais where the matriarch had lounged was gone, as was the robed Goblin, the forge, and the vast majority of any possible loot from the dead Goblins. It left only Tang, stalking out of the swirling smoke and dust, teeth gritted in naked fury and fingers reaching for Giint's throat.

"Yen, get Tang. Grizz, speak to Giint. Everyone else, come with me," I said after a few seconds of stunned silence. None of us had expected the fight to be anywhere near that one-sided, and the bomb that Giint had thrown was, in fact, completely unneeded…but either way, it'd been AWESOME.

If terrifying.

CHAPTER SEVENTEEN

I wandered the remains of the battlefield with Oracle and Thomas, as we all spread out, looking for Goblins or Orcs who still lived.

The first stop was the cage that had held the Orcs we'd been able to see from the door. We opened it, finding two living Orcs on the far side…out of eleven. The others had clearly piled in around these two to protect them. Even then, with their sacrifice, the pair were badly injured.

I hesitated, knowing that I'd be blamed for the deaths of their friends, and considered just letting them die. They were close to it already, after all, waiting a minute would be all it took, but as I watched the two small figures, blatantly children, even if orcish ones, I just couldn't bring myself to do it.

I had barely started with my healing spell when Oracle hit them with hers, and Thomas started sorting through the bodies, searching for any other survivors.

He was back in a few seconds, shaking his head and holding their open wounds closed so that it was easier to heal them over. We did two rounds of healing, then used mana potions on ourselves, a healing potion on each of the kids, then cast again, quickly running out of mana before they were entirely healed. I was forced to sit and meditate while Oracle continued to work.

The next hour passed quickly, as we'd barely stabilized the pair, before the old Orc who'd been working the forge was found half-buried in a pile of debris with his clothes smoldering, as the forge began to crack next to him.

Grizz and Tang dragged him over, while Bob continued to search the area, and I stayed in my meditative fugue. Oracle, meanwhile, drained me again and again, but I was too exhausted to even make a "yeah baby, yeah" style comment about how frequently and skillfully she emptied me. The thought skittered across the outside of my meditative bubble, proving, at least to myself, that even in there, I was still me.

By the time the old Orc was stable, and the forge had been banked with enough crap piled around it to keep it in one piece for now, it was late. Even here, in the heart of the Goblin camp, we could hear the crash of thunder as water seeped down a long crack in one wall.

"Oracle, where's Tenandra?" I asked, suddenly thinking about how rough it would be on the decks of the ship.

"She tried to fly above the storm, but it got too high and too strong, so I sent her away. She'll return as soon as the storm moves on, but she thinks it'll be mid-morning at the earliest," Oracle said. "She reached out when it was getting too much, but we were fighting, so I gave her orders rather than distract you."

"That's fine. Good reasoning, but tell me next time, okay?"

"Of course."

I turned, bleary-eyed, to the two orcish children watching me. The older Orc lay between them, back inside the cage. "Why…"

"My decision, Jax," Lydia said. "Ah wanted 'em somewhere safe, where we didn't need many te watch over 'em. Ah removed the dead an' gave 'em blankets, the door is no' closed, and they know it's fer their safety."

"Okay," I muttered, slowly clambering to my feet and looking around. I pulled up the notifications and was bombarded with my experience earned for the kills.

Congratulations!

You have killed the following:
- 34x Steam-Goblins of various levels for a total of 15,117xp
- 46x Basic Goblins of various levels for a total of 5,040xp
- 6x Tamed Noospits of various levels for a total of 1,850xp

A party under your command killed the following:
- 275x Steam-Goblins of various levels for a total of 85,525xp
- 116x Basic Goblins of various levels for a total of 7,110xp
- 27x Tamed Noospits of various levels for a total of 8,350xp
- 9x Orc Mechaniks of various levels for a total of 42,150xp
- 3x Orc Rogues of various levels for a total of 14,150xp
- 11x Goblin Rogues of various levels for a total of 1,280xp
- 1x Goblin Matriarch level 67 for 58,150xp

Total party experience earned: 216,715xp
As party leader, you gain 25% of all experience earned
Progress to level 30 stands at 1,090,610/1,120,000

I glared at the damning indictment showing that we'd killed the Orcs, once again remembering the deaths of the innocent people in the streets of Himnel before pushing it aside to worry about later, searching for the quest details.

Congratulations!

You have progressed on your Quest: Rescue my Gear

The God Svetu has charged you with recovering items He and His chosen people require to construct their wonders. As these items are currently in a Goblin-infested pit, He recommends you kill the Goblins first.

Kill the Goblins: 830/830

Kill the Goblin matriarch 1/1

Recovery of missing tools 0/?

Reward: A working Control Facility for the Great Tower and secondary links on each of your captured sites (requires further investment and construction), 100,000xp, Possible bonus facilities for the Great Tower.

I looked over the details, seeing that the last requirement was to find Svetu's tools, but considering the state of the place…

"Oracle, would somewhere like this have a Command Center"? I asked, my eyes widening.

"Uh, probably, yeah!" As she turned her soft gaze on the children, her sorrowful expression melted away.

"Okay, where would it be, though?" I gestured in the general direction of the room's terrible devastation.

Oracle winced. "Probably on the dais."

"Maybe, maybe not. Heal me up quick, just in case." I took a deep breath. I'd taken almost no damage and was only a handful of points below my full health, but just in case, I wanted to be able to activate my Mana Overdrive ability if I needed it. I took a deep breath and, while mentally crossing everything that could be crossed, I reached out to my abilities and mentally toggled on the Ability that Jenae had gifted me with many weeks ago.

As soon as Seek That Which is Hidden activated, the room went from dull and dimly lit, to the inside of a star in less than a second. I winced, as I tried to process it all. I saw a barrage of things all seemingly at once, ranging from the way that Jian was trying to be subtle about holding Sehran's hand, clinging on for dear life to the ancient Succubus, and the small but obvious smile on her face with it, to the speculative looks Yen and Grizz were shooting at each other the second they thought the other wasn't looking, and finally to the way one of the orcish children had hidden a length of sharp metal and was ready to use it on anyone who tried to hurt him.

They were just the closest contenders for my attention, as the walls, floor, ceiling, and half the facility lit up before my eyes. My jaw dropped open as I realized that, what I'd thought was the entirety of the structure, with possibly one or two rooms at the most hidden, was actually the entrance and only the lowest-level workshops.

"There," I said, pointing to a crack in one wall, where water was trickling down and seeping out through another crack by the floor. "There's a false door behind there." I shook myself as the vision faded away.

"Is it tha Control Center?" Lydia asked.

"No, it's…it's a lot more than just the Control Center," I whispered, still struggling to believe what I'd seen and forcing a smile as I turned to Bob. "Bob, mate, can you open that door, please?" I blinked, trying to banish the tightness that signaled an oncoming migraine from the sudden, insane amount of information and light I'd been hit with. The massive skeletal figure stomped across the floor, swinging his warhammer in both hands like he was trying to loosen up, though what he expected to free up was anyone's guess.

He took up station before the wall, looking it over slowly, before nodding in satisfaction at what he saw. He turned slightly and stood ready, paused for two long heartbeats, then slammed the warhammer into the wall, once, twice, then a third time. With the final blow, an entire section of the wall collapsed away from us, exposing a hidden chamber. A blast of air roared out as the seal over the far side was disturbed.

Stones fell with a rumbling series of thumps in the distance. Then, crashes and booms of something collapsing echoed, followed by the thunder of dozens of feet, running toward us.

"Uh, Bob, back the fuck away from there," I said as the others retreated to stand near me. A few already-damaged sections of wall nearby shifted under the vibrations before collapsing, and dust billowed up again.

"How about we back the hell up?" Thomas muttered, crouching behind his shield and readying his mace.

"Lydia, get airborne. Oracle, do the same," I ordered, glaring at the hole in the wall. "Tang, stealth and be ready to backstab. Arrin, Giint, back it up and be ready. Ronin, buffs. Sehran, be ready. Jian, get that beam ready, and damn good job for not using it earlier…Grizz, Bob, either side of Thomas and me," I barked as I readied myself. Tugging my shield free of my bag, I hunched behind it, naginata at the ready as I stared into the shadowed passage.

It started weak, the light that was approaching, making the shadows bounce and shift. It then grew brighter and brighter, spreading out into multiple points. The stream of shadows grew and grew, along with footfalls going from a rumble to thunderous cacophony, until suddenly they were there.

The first one sprinted out of the darkness, slamming its feet down and skidding to a halt, its massive stone shield hitting the floor with a boom and scouring it clean as it stopped. A veritable pile of blood, viscera, various body parts and debris built up on the near side of it as two glowing eyes regarded us in overt warning. The creature held a massive stone spear rock-steady, pointed at us.

More followed the first one. Two, then five, then thirteen. After the first six formed a shieldwall, the spears covering the only gaps between the shields, the huge figures in the first row dropped to one knee, braced themselves, and waited.

The next to emerge took the central position, with three more bounding out and skidding to a halt on each side of it. They leveled massive siege crossbows at us, as glowing bolts of mana grew from a central gem, the insane weapons clearly loaded and ready to wipe us from existence.

"Stand down and surrender to the Empire, trespasser!" the central figure boomed, its voice deep and hollow, echoing around the chamber. I straightened in shock, recognizing the other twelve, if not the central figure.

"Fuck me…you're imperial war golems!"

"STAND DOWN, THIS IS YOUR ONLY WARNING!" The golem boomed, and I straightened up speaking quickly.

"Stand down! Lower your weapons!" I barked out, dropping my naginata and shield into my bag, even as the others moved to comply.

"War golem, what is your function here?" I called out, wincing as the words came out. Having never encountered a golem that was capable of speech before, I had no idea how to phrase things.

There was silence for a long minute. The only sound was the crackle of glowing mana-bolts on the enormous weapons as Oracle and Lydia slowly lowered themselves to the floor to stand by me.

"War golem, I am Jax, Acknowledged Scion of the Empire. I order you to stand down," I said carefully, and still received nothing in response. "Oracle, a little help here?"

She slowly grew to her full size, stepping forward to stand by my side. She reached out and took my hand. I took a deep breath, squeezed her hand in mine, and stepped forward.

The crossbows focused on me. I froze, waited, then, when nothing else happened, rising irritation blossomed into annoyance, then anger.

I'd spent the last weeks since finding out that Oracle's and my own emotions sparked each other off, learning a degree of self-control that was frankly unbelievable compared to my younger self, but when faced with blatant disrespect, I still had serious issues.

"Golem…I'm going to use magic to examine you. This is not an attack, and I order you to take no action," I said through gritted teeth, glaring at the central figure who watched me.

Advanced Imperial War Golem
Advanced Imperial War Golems are the fourth level of seven possible creations, at this level the golem has developed limited levels of sentience and can respond in set ways to events, they can give orders to their lesser brethren, report to higher and carry out simple objectives with set rules. This level of golem is also the first to be able to employ speech communication, but are limited in their capacity.

Weaknesses: Unknown
Resistances: Unknown
Level: Unknown
Health: Unknown
Stamina: Unknown
Mana: Unknown

"Well, that's fucking helpful…"

"No, look at the phrasing, Jax. 'They can respond in set ways.' You've just not triggered the correct orders…hmm," Oracle said carefully, thinking and watching the golems. "They'll attack if we do something wrong, but there must have been commands built in, in case something happened, and they've been running all this time, so they're Imperial commands."

"Golem, I am a member of the Imperial Family; identify me," I tried. It stood silently watching. "Crap."

"Golem. High Lord Jax of Dravith is here to claim control of this facility in the name of the Empire," Oracle said.

"Request for control of the facility is denied. Leave this place at once," its voice boomed out, making everyone flinch.

"Golem, state the requirements for High Lord Jax to take control of this Facility," Oracle said quickly. There was a pause, before it spoke again.

"Control of the facility can only be granted to one of Imperial blood carrying a token."

"Well fuck me gently with a long-handled spear, what the hell is a token?" I muttered, before looking at Oracle. "Jenae!" we both said at the same time and grinned at each other.

"Golem, I am going to speak to my Goddess; nothing that happens here is an attack," I said before going to one knee and closing my eyes, casting the communication spell again after a minute without a response.

"Jax?" Jenae's voice came to me, clearly strained. *"I'm a bit busy."*

"Sorry Jenae, we're in an old Imperial facility and the golems are still active, they're demanding a token, any idea?" I said quickly, getting a sigh of frustration.

"The tokens were a way that the Imperial Family could identify themselves easily. There is a way around it, but you're not going to enjoy it."

"Doesn't matter if I enjoy it; I need to do it," I said, and She snorted in my mind.

"That's what you say <u>now</u>. But fine, the only way a member of the Imperial Family can be identified if they are not bearing a token is by a bloodstone. It's a pain in the ass to make, as it's literally a stone you wear made from your compressed mana and blood. I'll teach Oracle the method, as frankly, she's easier to teach. Good luck, and don't forget to eat your greens after this." With that, the sense of Jenae's mind vanished from my own. I opened my eyes, just in time to catch Oracle as she sagged, clutching her head.

"Are you okay?" I asked frantically.

"Yeah," She whimpered. "Just…oww."

"What?"

"The way to make the bloodstone," Oracle said quietly, looking up at me and squinting, "Jenae gave me a LOT of information. You've got flesh to absorb the data; I don't…"

"Uh, okay?"

"Just…just give me a few minutes." She massaged her temples. I stood, lifting her in my arms easily, and faced the golems.

"I will provide identification using a bloodstone, but my companion is injured and my team exhausted. We're going to rest back there…nothing we do is intended as an attack," I said again, just to be as safe as possible.

There was a long pause as the golem watched me, clearly assessing its parameters, before it finally spoke. "Use no weapons. Do no damage to this facility."

I paused in the act of turning away and looked back at it. "Seriously, dude?" I asked it. "*Seriously?*" A crack sounded behind me in the distance, and a section of wall collapsed, the general devastation of the site making it almost impossible for me to see where it had happened, between the strewn corpses, the already-collapsed wall, and the piles of debris.

I gestured at the room, one hand lifted from under Oracle in a "what the fuck" gesture, before I shook my head and walked away from the golem, muttering about dumbass programmers.

It took Oracle a few minutes to recover enough to sit up and function again, or speak without clutching her head, anyway, so I used that time to clear a space on the floor and pull out my bedroll. The others did much the same, and we made ourselves comfortable, also getting some food out for the Orcs and passing them some spare blankets that Grizz had in his pack.

We ate and drank, letting Oracle recover and think, before she finally spoke.

"Okay, there's a lot of information here to process, but there's good and bad bits, starting with the fact it's going to leave you exhausted, and it's going to hurt."

I shrugged. "Pain is pain; I'll get over it."

"Yeah, well, a bloodstone is old magic, like *really* old. It's a stone made from your blood and your condensed mana. The problem is, though, it's usually made when the wielder is a newborn, and then they add to it as they age, because by the time they're an adult, and they've begun using the various kinds of essence, they've corrupted their blood."

"Right," I said, thinking about the essence cores I'd already used.

"Secondly, you're a descendant. You've been acknowledged by Amon, and that bypasses ninety percent of all the issues for the rest of the world, but for the golems trapped here, running on the original commands, they need proof. So…" Oracle paused, wincing. "Either we pretty much drain you dry of blood, then you drink potions of Legionnaire's Might and we heal you up, making fresh blood, then repeat, over and over, screening out the impurities and refining your blood until it's good enough…"

"Or?" I asked her.

"Or we go away, you claim the surrounding territories until this one is accepted as inside your borders, then we use our other golems, preferably one at the same or a higher rank, to order them to stand down, then you claim the facility and force the golems to accept you."

"That'd take days, weeks even."

"It would, but the other option is that we bleed you," Oracle whispered, watching me sadly. "It's not going to be pleasant, because the entire time the blood is coming out of you, someone with an acknowledged rank in the Empire of Duke or above has to channel mana into it."

"Well, that's a stupid rule."

She nodded. "It's designed to make it so it can't be done easily," Oracle acknowledged, "and as the only people in the realm with that authority is either Augustus, or you…"

"I'll be channeling mana the entire time I'm bleeding out. So, mana migraine as well…joy," I muttered, before shrugging. "Fine, let's get this over with."

"Couldn't you get the God of this place to override them?" Thomas asked. I glanced at Oracle, who shook her head.

"Svetu wouldn't. He'd say that the deal was to capture this place before He gave you more aid. He's supposedly a stickler for the rules, and besides, as much as this is a pain in the arse, if you need one of these in future, better to have it ready?" Oracle suggested, getting a nod from me.

"Fine. Looks like it's time to make yourselves comfy, everyone," I said, before arranging my bedroll better and getting some food and a cup of steaming hot coffee out of my bag. I blew on the surface, sending the smell of freshly roasted coffee beans across the room and making everyone look at me in shock. "Gods, I love these magic pouches," I muttered, taking a sip and relaxing, despite what I knew was coming. Then I pulled out a large steaming jug and set it down before me. "Go on then, dig in, you blasted vultures…" I winked and prompted a mad scramble for cups before it all ran out.

I watched them, blowing on the cup again to cool it, and smiled internally as they tried to portion it out fairly between them all. I wondered if I should tell them that I had two more jugs in my bag, then elected to wait a bit first.

It'd been an experiment to see if it worked the way I'd suspected, and by the Gods, it was paying off.

I shivered slightly as Oracle bathed my left arm with Scour, removing all impurities and possible infections from my skin and the blade of my dagger. She hesitated, so I glanced at Tommy, who stood next to her. He nodded somberly and took the blade.

"I'll sort it," Thomas said to Oracle and the others, glancing up at me, and getting a nod, as he placed the point of the dagger at the protruding veins on the inside of my wrist. "You ready, bro?"

I grunted. "Nope."

"Shit happens, then, eh?" he said, then cut. The sharp blade sliced deep into my skin, parting it and digging into the veins with ease.

There was a barely perceptible pause between the blade sinking in and the blood bursting out, running down into the palm of my hand as he pulled back. Arrin stepped up, looking down grimly.

Oracle cast the spell, even as Arrin prepared a heal to seal the veins as soon as he was allowed to. Everyone watched; tiny fractions of blood lifted into the air, the rest flowed out into my hand then dripped to the floor, pooling there.

The tiny fraction of pure blood, uncontaminated in any way, and containing my genetic traits, began to slowly glow, pulsing in the air in time with the beats of my heart as it pushed ever more scarlet blood out.

It slowly changed, compressing further and further as Oracle channeled into it, the pure blood and our mana mixing, forming a solid core as Arrin reacted to her gesture, sealing the wound. Grizz handed over one of the potions of Legionnaire's Might he'd taken to carrying. The stone gave a single bright pulse as it dropped from the air into Oracle's waiting hand.

"Whoo," I mumbled. My head swam, and I blinked, feeling lightheaded.

"Jax, it's blood loss. Drink this, and it'll be okay." Oracle's words traveled to me as though from a great distance. I nodded and took the vial from Grizz, lifting it to my lips and pouring it in. The substance ranged from a gritty, foul sludge to a close attempt at concrete as I tried to swallow it, practically having to chew the horrible stuff.

I tried to choke it all down, before sweeping up my coffee and drinking, regardless of the heat. It burned as it flowed, searing my throat, but mercifully cleaned away the foul concoction that had almost choked me.

Minutes passed while I waited for the world to stop spinning, before Oracle judged that I had begun to digest the sludge and let Arrin heal me again.

This time, the world made a little more sense, and I looked around, shaking my head.

"Wow, what a rush," I mumbled. "Glad that's done, so..." I paused, noting the expression on Oracle's face, then down at the tiny stone she passed to me.

I lifted it, and it let out a feeble glow, responding to my body, my mana, and all that made me into, well...me. It was beautiful, a deep, bloody red, shot through with golden veins and black strands that seemed to pulse and flare faintly, like neural pathways firing.

I lost myself for a long minute staring into the depths, and almost missed Oracle's words, before catching the very last bit.

"...times that size to work..."

"What?" I asked, looking at her.

"I said, it needs to be at least four times that size to work! Better if it was six or seven, but..." Oracle winced as she held onto my arm.

"You are *shitting* me," I said hoarsely, looking down at the huge pool of blood that was seeping closer to the edge of my bedroll. I glared at it before opening my mouth, and Oracle cut me off.

"That's waste blood," she said with a sad shake of her head. "Blood without the genetic template of the Imperial Family, or it's contaminated with the essence cores...it's useless."

I growled before using Scour to cleanse the area, grumbling under my breath and glaring at the golems, daring them to do anything.

"Four or five more times," I muttered. "Tell me we've not got that many potions," I asked Grizz hopefully.

"Since I started running with you, boss, I carry six at all times," he answered, grinning and getting a glare in response. "Sorry, man, but it's damn hilarious watching you choke it down."

"Hey, Lydia, doesn't Grizz owe you some burpees?" I asked. Grizz's eyes went wide at the betrayal.

"Oh aye, 'e does, thank yer fer that!" she said, smiling sweetly at him. "Grizz…"

I sighed and got myself ready, before nodding to Thomas. He took my arm again, settling himself and watching for Oracle's signal. As Grizz started grunting, jumping up from his first pushup, Thomas sliced into my arm again, drawing a groan and my blood in equal measure.

Chapter Eighteen

Six hours later, I stood before the golems again, still feeling woozy, and held up the bloodstone, showing it to them as it glimmered with an inner fire.

"I'm Jax, Imperial Scion and High Lord of Dravith. By this bloodstone as proof, I order you to stand down and accept me and my people as authorized to access and claim the facility," I mumbled, glaring at the advanced golem.

There was a long break while the golem examined the bloodstone held tightly in my hand, before all of them shifted at the same time. The kneeling spearmen stood and lifted their shields aside. They maneuvered their spears away into a non-threatening pose while the six archers relaxed, their bows no longer humming with lethal intent as both the magical strings and the glowing, power-wrought bolts faded away.

The advanced golem that was clearly in command straightened and clapped its fist to its heart in salute before stepping back and to the side, allowing us access to the facility.

I strode through, my triumphant entry only slightly marred by a stumble on the loose debris and the exhaustion that filled me.

Oracle was on my right, Grizz on my left, and they helped me forward, even as Thomas grabbed my shoulder from behind.

"I'm okay." I smiled weakly at them. "But thanks, guys." I leaned a little more on Grizz than I tried to let on as we moved down the corridor.

This entrance to the main facility was like most of the rest. Brickwork ran along the bottom of the walls, then transformed to slabs of marble about halfway up, with large slabs that comprised the floor and small bricks forming the arched ceiling. The main difference here, though, was that the facility behind the hidden door was apparently intact. The walls, rather than being covered in crap, instead were covered in murals.

There were Gnomes worshipping their God, Svetu, yes, but there were also other races. Humans, Orcs, Goblins, and hell, dozens of creatures I couldn't identify. There were depictions of giant Prax being constructed, of ogres wearing sodding togas as they lifted walls into place.

Naga swam through the seas, plunging deep to bring rare materials to the surface, and Dwarves that offered up glowing gems that pulsed with power. Elves coaxed their woodland homes to shape trees in ways that could be used, and Dragons breathed flames into forges.

We walked and walked, staring open-mouthed as the creatures of a thousand children's tales walked the walls, while the denizens of nightmares wore monocles and drew arcane symbols that guided the others.

It was amazing, and it was terrible, because I saw just how far the realm had fallen. I saw the creatures who were at each other's throats, who fought and slaughtered each other. I wondered how many tens of thousands had been born and had died having never achieved their potential, when in older times, in golden ages long past, they would have been integrated into the great creations by Svetu.

I wondered how many wars might have been averted, and how many times the smartest and greatest minds had been chained to a plough or forced into drudgery, simply because the opportunities no longer existed for them to be more.

I strode into the main hall of the facility, seeing it was a dozen floors high. Buildings like great pyramids and assembly lines sat side-by-side, all basking under the glow of dimly lit magelights that even now gave off warmth and light for the uncaring denizens.

"What happened here?" I wondered, looking around and seeing that it was essentially a small city in all but name, missing only the citizens to bring it back to life.

"I think they were all sent home," Oracle whispered by my side, looking around in awe as I did. "I mean, there's no sign of the rush or panic that I remember from the attack of the SporeMother, and the destruction of the Cataclysm…is it possible that this survived intact?"

"How?" Thomas asked.

"Looks like they abandoned tha 'real' facility an' made do with tha smaller one. Maybe they jus' didn't 'ave enough people ta make it werk? Who knows, but Ah bet there's plenty 'ere we can use."

"Hell yes," I said, looking over my shoulder at the advanced golem that had followed along behind us.

"Golem, where is the command center?" I asked. It pointed upward, toward the top of the pyramid in the center of the massive, hollowed-out cavern. "Typical," I muttered before thinking, unsure if it was truly sentient or not.

We set off walking, taking only a handful of minutes to reach the bottom of the pyramid, but another fifteen to walk to the top, stopping a few times, as I needed to rest after my blood donations.

By the time we finally staggered, or I did at least, to the top of the pyramid, I had to sit down, my elbows on my knees and head in my hands as I panted and shook, barely staying on the good side of shock. I waited, slowly recovering, and pulled out more coffee for everyone.

As we all ate and drank, Oracle slipped her hand into mine. I resolved to put the vambrace and gauntlet I'd removed for the bloodletting back on again soon, but for now, I just enjoyed holding the hand of the woman I loved and looking out across the cavern.

The buildings were constructed of a mixture of materials, mainly sandstone and marble, with long-dead plants in planters. Rows of urns that had probably once held flowers and marble colonnades made the entire facility look like something out of a Greek fantasy.

Patches of dead earth dotted the floor, with seats set out around them. The massive, gleaming copper arms were laid out in rows reminding me of a modern car factory and smaller stations meant for the operator to work at.

Storage facilities and cradles for vehicles lined the back wall. A half-finished object that looked vaguely familiar lay coated in dust in one, and I frowned as I looked at it.

"What the hell is that?" I wondered, before Oracle spoke up, excitedly.

"It's a mining golem!" she said. "Look at the drills on the head, the arms! It must have been nearly finished when they closed this area down."

I nodded, fascinated, and wondered about the facility, until I swallowed hard.

"Oracle, if they could make mining golems…"

"Then they must have a production facility here; a Genesis Chamber!" she finished for me.

I scrambled to my feet and looked around. Set in the middle of the flat top of the pyramid was a small building with rounded sides. I hurried over to it quickly with the others keeping watch over me as I went.

The door was stiff, but it didn't take long to force it open. Some of the frame twisted and popped as I forced my way in, and the Control Center sat unoccupied and silently waiting before me.

I strode across and sat down, reaching out and laying my hand on the manawell of the Creation Table that had been used in place of a desk. I couldn't help but smile at the barrage of prompts that burst to life for me.

Congratulations!

You have reached the control center of Dravith Production Center One and have the prerequisite authority and abilities to claim this structure and the surrounding land, adding it to your territory as a claimed location.

As this territory holds less than ten (10) percent of sentients that are actively hostile to your rule, it can be claimed.

Do you wish to annex this territory now?

Yes/No

Not really a hard decision to make there, I reflected, hitting the Yes.

Congratulations!

You have cleared Dravith Production Center One.

In clearing this location, Repairs, Production, and Restructuring options have been made available!

*

Congratulations!

You have annexed new lands into your own, providing the following benefits if the land is worked:

Production Facility:
This site contains a Pre-Cataclysm semi-intact production facility.

If this site is repaired and provided with the requisite staffing and resources, gain the following:

- **1-50 Golems** per 144 hour period, depending on class (site facilities are currently capable of producing classes 1-4)

- **Automated Logging Camp**: There is an abandoned automated logging camp in the borders of this territory, located at the foot of the hills, and long since buried by the forests. This facility requires considerable repairs to be brought up to minimum standards. When repaired, gain +100-150 Hardwood logs per day.

- **Automated Mining Facility**: This now abandoned facility was set up here primarily due to the heavy concentration of rare materials located in these mountains. Automated mining golems were dispatched into the mountains, and for many years, they provided a constant stream of resources. When the facility was shut down, the mining golems were recalled, three reached their charging cradles, but one did not.

*

Congratulations!

You have discovered a quest: Locate the missing mining golem!

Locate the missing mining golem and return it to its charging cradle:

Missing mining golem found: 0/1

Rare resources gained: 0/10

Area explored: 0/1

Reward: Fully automated mining facility returns to full production, site is secured and ready for habitation, 25,000xp

Accept: *Yes/No*

*

Attention, Citizens of the Territory of Dravith!

Lord Jax of Dravith has expanded his territory and has claimed an additional six hundred and seventeen square miles of land by defeating the previously hostile occupants!

All Titles, Deeds, and Laws in the Territory of Dravith are held for review, and can be revoked, altered, annulled, or approved.

All Hail High Lord Jax of Dravith!

I read through everything before accepting the quest and pulling up the details on the facility with a simple tap on the table and a thought. As I did so, a barrage of information flowed into me.

It felt like a fire hose being rammed into my brain as first a handful, then dozens of designs sprang to life. The layout of the facility, the dozens of additional rooms, and the three floors still hidden from casual sight sprang to life before me.

There were armories for the golems and storage areas, most long since having lost viability, as everything from plants and wood, to cloth, foodstuffs, and ingredients had perished.

The main mana gathering systems were long since dead, but the secondary ones were still partially operational, having only started to fail in the last century.

Then I sensed *HIM*.

On the lowest floor, hidden deep below the ground, was a mind that slumbered still. I felt a sense of genuine trepidation as I realized my awakening of the facility had also begun his awakening.

He was currently in the golem equivalent of REM sleep, stirring but not really conscious. However, the draw on the already weakened mana collectors to bring him back to life was significant.

I looked at him, drawn like a moth to a flame, and couldn't help but groan. He was designed for exploration, I somehow knew. He was designed to access one of the final areas that the Empire had been unable to explore, the depths of the great oceans, deeper and far, far bigger than those of Earth, were destined to be the next stage in the Empire's expansion. They needed sanitizing before any more of the islands or continents that were out there could be discovered.

I remembered discussions with Oracle where she'd pointed out that, in terms of the Empire's age, Dravith had only recently been discovered. Work on conquering and civilizing it had only begun in the last two or three hundred years of the Empire, before the Cataclysm.

That had seemed insane to me, especially considering I'd been from England and had played in ruins growing up that were a thousand years old or even older, while America, as the world commonly thought of it, was less than two hundred and fifty years old.

I'd considered the things that the continent had seen, the rapid expansion of people across it, and couldn't work out why Dravith, which was smaller, after all, hadn't been completely explored and sanitized.

Oracle had sorted through my mind and seen my confusion, then laughed, pointing out that Dravith was home to monsters that would have slaughtered the first explorers, and that the main advantages that the western settlers had in taming the world weren't found on Dravith. Guns and so on had never been invented, and if they had, they'd have been quickly countered by shield spells, making them useless.

We'd discussed again and again, through long nights and around campfires, the nature of the realm, and that, as far as they knew, there wasn't an actual limit to it. Dragons that had flown as high as they could, and as far as they could, had reported further continents, island chains, and more, or they'd simply never returned.

Ships either came back with tales of new lands, of new peoples and races, or never returned at all. The main reason for that hadn't been other civilizations, as far as could be worked out.

It was the monsters.

The deeps boasted leviathans that filled the oceans, sea Dragons, giant squid, sharks, and worse of all, the terrible karens. They were creatures misspelled in our legends to krakens, known to drag entire fleets to their doom, all the time screaming things that made the bravest sailors kill themselves rather than risk capture.

The tales of the Empire were of a small civilization that gradually grew, consolidating the area inside its borders, and fighting constantly to keep its people safe. No matter how far it reached, there were always more and worse creatures out there determined to kill them.

The massive golem that slumbered in the depths of the facility, was almost ready to be released into an underground sea, one that, through careful searching, had been found to lead out to the great ocean. This golem was a totally unique creation of the crafter king golem, in conjunction with Svetu.

He'd been left to slumber away the ages in the depths of the facility, never fully finished, mere months away from completion, and even now, he stirred, desperate to fulfill his function.

The design filled my mind, overwhelmingly complex, more than ninety percent lost on me, but I knew he was meant for war as much as exploration.

It was designed to face and kill the worst the oceans could throw at him, and to rescue ships that were damaged, to explore the deeps and recover treasures, clear out nests and more. He could recharge on his own and repair himself using the dozens of arms he had. The empty bays located throughout his mighty body were meant to be filled with the resources he needed, and I shook my head at the possibilities.

"We need to finish him," I whispered. Oracle, who'd been searching the facility with me, our minds twinned, gasped in amazement as she saw him.

"What?" Thomas asked. I swallowed hard, pulling my mind free of the deluge of information.

"There's a lot here," I told them. "Facilities that can make all the difference. Svetu…He said we would split what we found, and the things we have here. We can build our own golems up to class four: advanced. From there, they can rebuild the destroyed Genesis Chambers, and we can make war golems again, ones that can think and act, protect the Empire, while the Legion reacts to threats and grows. There are things here that change everything, leaping us forward by years…once they're up and running, anyway." I sat for a minute thinking.

"There's a golem in the basement here, a one-of-a-kind GIANT golem, and it's built for sea exploration and to fight things like the leviathans, designed to repair itself and to slaughter the Empire's enemies. For now, we don't have anything that needs to be fought in the seas, but…"

"Jax, you're wrong," Yen said firmly. "I'm sorry, but you are. The entire point of creating the airships was because the seas are so dangerous. The creatures in them are out of control. The ships that cross the oceans are crewed by madmen that know they're almost certain to die. If you could protect a fleet? At least one in three ships that sails out of Himnel's harbor never comes back."

"It's true, and it's not the pirates," Ronin added. "The ships I've sailed on, I sang songs to increase our luck and to hide us almost all day every day. A bard makes a fortune on the ocean; we risk our lives giving ships that tiny extra point or two of luck that makes all the difference."

"Well, we can get him finished off and set free then, I guess. He was almost completed, after all. But then, rather than just sending him out randomly, he's been equipped to repair…" I said slowly, as a thought struck me.

"Glorious Retribution!" Oracle whispered.

"Exactly," I said, nodding slowly as the possibilities sank in.

"What?" Thomas asked, confused, as the rest of the squad exchanged excited looks…except for Giint, who was swigging from a fresh bottle of boot polish he'd stolen from Grizz and didn't appear to have heard anything I'd said.

"The Sunken City, ever hear of it?" I asked Thomas, and he nodded. "Turns out they used to have flying cities, like literally flying cities, dedicated to exploration and war. When the Cataclysm struck, they were probably all destroyed.

"The Sunken City is one of them, and it's seriously fucked up. It was full of undead and worse when we found it, including that being we rescued Giint and his people from. Thing is, it's badly damaged, but if we were to repair some of its facilities, it had hundreds of golems aboard, of all the various classes.

"If we could get them recharged, then we could basically leave them to clear the place out and repair it; it's one of the real reasons they were there…give it a bit of time, and we can go all fire of the Gods flying above our enemies and slaughtering their armies."

"Shit, dude, that needs to be a priority," Thomas said.

I dove back into the systems, examining them.

I rolled through them, passing screen after screen, finding each time that, to do 'x', I needed to activate 'y' first and more, growing increasingly frustrated as I went.

The day turned to night, and Oracle told me that Tenandra was back and landed at the entrance. Westin and his team came and explored, before leaving again, and my own squad, or Lydia's anyway, came and went, exploring the site as they wanted.

Finally, after yet more hours of work, I pushed my chair back, stood up and walked away from the table, my mind fuzzy with lack of sleep and a desperate need to hurt someone.

"What's up?" Thomas asked from the door where he'd been sitting on watch, and I grunted at him, unwilling to talk.

"We need some unusual materials to finish the facilities off and fully reactivate them," Oracle said.

"Okay, like what?" he asked. I chewed on my knuckle in frustration as she went on.

"Cartium," she replied. "It's the equivalent of one of the nuclear materials you had on earth, so it's hard to find, as it's only made from breaking down two other rare materials, ones we don't have.

"Without it, we can't reactivate the main charging cradles, as they degraded a few centuries back. The secondary cradles are fine, that's why the golems are still here, but…"

"But we can't charge the mining golems without the cartium, and we can't *find* the minerals to make the cartium without the mining golems," I growled, glaring at my quest list.

"Shit, so we're fucked?" Thomas asked quietly. "I gotta tell you, bro, saying we can do something awesome like make all the golems and bringing hope to people like that, then going 'oh shit, sorry we can't' isn't going to go down too well. The others are all seriously excited."

"There's a way," I said, grimacing. "But it needs a lot of luck."

"Okay?" Thomas asked. "So what's the plan?"

"There's a missing mining golem. It's out there somewhere in the dark, under the mountain. We find it, and if we're damn lucky, it'll still have some inside it. If we can find it, and we give that to the refinery, it can break it down," I explained.

"We use the cartium to repair the cradles, then the mining golems in the cradles go out and get more, we finish the repairs, make some more golems, and boom, we set the explorer free. He goes and repairs the Prax while we pacify the local area, then we use the time that gives us to find the Drow. We slaughter those fuckers from the sky when it's finished." I grinned as I looked over at Thomas. "Nuke it from orbit."

"Only way to be sure," he said, grinning at me. "Wonder if they ever invented kinetic harpoons in this realm?"

"Probably not, but I bet we can make a magical version eventually." I mimed a huge explosion with my hands.

"Sounds like fun! Okay, so, what do we need to do?" Thomas asked.

"Not entirely sure. I got a quest earlier to find the missing golem and get it back to its charging cradle. That included finding ten rare resources, and it's only twenty-five thousand experience, so it probably won't be that complicated, considering finding this place and getting Svetu his tools back was a hundred thousand. Still need to find those tools, though…

"Okay, people!" I called out, getting some startled looks from some of the team who had been sleeping. "Damn, sorry guys." I winced at the way Yen and Grizz disentangled themselves from each other inside their blankets.

They'd hopefully not been boinking, judging from how close some of the others were sitting around them, but still…

"Okay, sorry for startling you all," I said, breaking off to yawn hugely, suddenly realizing just how tired I was. "Gods," I muttered, shaking myself and stopping another yawn as it tried to escape. "Right. We've got to find a missing golem. It's a mining one, so think big circular tube thingy like the ones we found under Himnel. They were all ordered back here and unloaded, but one never made it. Hopefully it won't be too far out, and we can find it, strip the materials we need off it, and get back without anyone knowing about us. But, that's not how our lives work, so be ready to gut anything that moves."

"Where are we looking?" Grizz asked, frowning. "Surely, if it was nearby, the Goblins would have stripped it for parts long since."

"It's in the tunnels. They made their own tunnels, mining as they went, so expect it to be a decent walk at least." I cut off as the old Orc mechanik raised a hand that shook violently. "You have something you want to say?" I asked, totally unsure of how to treat him. First, he was a prisoner, and we'd freed him, so yay us. But he was also an Orc, and he'd basically been building the Goblins into walking timebombs, so I wasn't feeling overly trusting.

"Old God is in the clan cave," he mumbled, fixing me with a stare from his one working eye.

"Uh, okay?" I said, frowning at him. "Anyone have a clue what that means?"

"Old God!" the Orc snapped. "It in clan cave!"

"Riiiight…"

"Old God eats stone, leaves ingots behind when we worship it! It in old clan cave!"

I watched him for a long minute.

Finally, Oracle spoke up. "You think the old God is what we're looking for, and it's in your clan cave?"

"Okay, will your clan let us see the old God?"

"Clan all dead," he retorted with a low growl. "All dead by Goblins and Amilith."

"Amilith…" I muttered. "That's familiar…"

"The Amilith killed your people?" Oracle asked, getting a quick nod. "Are they nearby?"

"Amilith friends once, then enemies, much shame brought on our clan. Goblins fight us, then fight them. We flee, Goblins catch, force serve, or be eat." At the memory, he held onto the small Orc children protectively.

"Okay, tell us where the old clan cave is, and you can go free," I said.

"No."

"What? Why 'no?'"

"Not safe. We serve you."

I shook my head. "We're at war. Believe me, you'll be safer without…"

"Stay here. Serve here, make. Learn," the old Orc said, crossing his arms across his chest.

"Listen, you mad bastard, I don't trust you…"

"Good. No trust. Trust earned. You kill Goblins, much honor. Mechaniks serve you now," the old Orc said with a grunt. The two kids looked up at him before glancing back at me and nodding alongside their elder.

"Well, shit…" I said, suddenly aware that gaining the support of the Orcs might have more problems than bonuses. As if to underscore this notion, one of the kids looked at Giint and growled, getting a similar response from him.

"Uh, Grizz?" I said, turning and smiling at him. "Got another job for you, mate…"

"Huh? Oh, wait no! No way, boss!" he protested.

I nodded. "Yup, sorry dude, but you know what they say. Curse of competence and all that. You managed to housebreak Giint, more or less. Let's see what you can do with the ankle biters."

With that, I turned back to the older Orc and tried to figure out what the hell he was talking about with his clan.

Chapter Nineteen

I t didn't take long to get there, maybe an hour or so, maybe a little less, but as we closed in on the cave that the old Orc had described to us, I couldn't help but whistle in admiration.

The amilith, or possibly the Orcs, as the amilith had apparently killed the Orcs and had taken over their village, from what we could understand, had built a palisade and a pair of wooden towers around the entrance to the clan cave.

A pair of hulking amilith stood guard in the towers, watching us as we neared on the airship, before one leaped down and vanished from sight, hurrying into the cave mouth a dozen meters behind the wall.

"So, the cave mouth is the only way in and out?" I asked Ronin, who'd spent longer speaking to the Orcs than I had.

"Yeah, on the ground at least. Turns out the Orcs and the amilith were neighbors, and the Orcs got the amilith to help them seal all the other caves that lead into the valley. Now, there's just this one, and a secret one that was known only to the chiefs, apparently."

"What happened to make a war between the amilith and the Orcs?" I asked as we continued to climb, passing the palisade and approaching the upper rim of the mountain and the hidden valley it contained.

"Not entirely sure. The old Orc was embarrassed, like seriously ashamed. Something happened with them and the Goblins, but he wouldn't speak about it, and I get the feeling he doesn't know that much, just that the tribe was up in arms about it. The Goblins made some kind of demand, and some of the Orcs went along with it, bringing shame onto the clan.

"Word got to the amilith, and I guess they decided that they weren't good friends after all, because they attacked both the Orcs and the Goblins. Then they retreated into the Orc clan cave and have been living under siege since. The Orcs were kicked out, and you know what happened from there," Ronin said, shrugging. "Sorry boss, that's all I could get from him. Give me some more time, and I'll get more, but..."

"That's fine..." I said, my words coming out slowly as we crested the rise and looked down into the valley spread out before us.

It was a caldera, my memories supplied. A volcano that had exploded then collapsed inwards, creating a crater-like ring, one that had eventually cooled and settled, before forming a lake. Then it had developed a dozen or more steaming geothermal pools at one end of the valley. There were a handful of rough huts around the pools, and a dozen larger ones down by the edge of the lake itself.

Behind the rougher huts was a large and skillfully built longhouse in the process of being constructed. At the other end of the valley, near the lowest point, Thomas gestured to a cylindrical shape and grinned.

"The old God, I bet," he said, and I nodded, looking at the cylindrical golem. It was similar in design to the ones I'd found under Himnel, but this one was laid on its side, wedged into place between three large boulders and clearly unable to move, its manipulators long since buried.

"What do you want to do?" Tenandra asked.

"Go down and talk to them, I guess. There's a few dozen of them, and I think we have a pretty good bargaining chip," I said with a shrug. "Yeah, to hell with it, land us at the farthest end from them and as close to the golem as you can, but be ready to take off if you need to."

She angled the ship around, dipping forward sharply and picking up speed before flaring her engines and bringing us in for a gentle landing.

Only a few minutes later, we were off the ship. Less than a minute after that, I was resting my hand on the side of the golem, feeling the gentle shudder of power running through it.

"Now, how the hell are you still alive?" I wondered, patting the hull gently.

"Human!" a voice boomed down the valley, and I turned, looking up at the group of creatures barreling towards us. They stopped at what they clearly thought was a safe distance and glared at us. "This our valley, human! Leave!"

"No, it's not," I called back. "The way I hear it, you attacked your neighbors, the mechaniks, and took their valley."

"They betrayed us!" he hissed, spittle flying as he strode a few steps toward us. "They swore we would be safe, then they gave some of our people to the Goblins!"

"Interesting, considering that the Orcs I've spoken to only knew that the chief brought some kind of dishonor onto the tribe. Apparently, it was enough that the tribe was fracturing down the middle. Do you want to tell me your side of the story?" I offered.

"No, human! I want you out of our home!" the creature barked, spraying a veritable fountain of spittle across the ground between us.

A new member of the species stepped up, clearly calmer than the other. "It was war," the new one explained. "Things were done that we regret, and we knew not all wished for our deaths, but they are a tribe. Had we killed half, the poison of their friends' deaths would have spread, and we would have been forced again to fight and kill. We did not wish this; it is not our way."

"I know…"

"No! You do not know, human!" bellowed the first one. "You have spoken with the Orcs; they have begged you to aid them to attack us. If this is so, then fight! If not, then leave our valley, but do not pretend to understand, for we must live with the deeds of our fathers, not you!"

"If you knew who and what my father was, you'd shit yourself in public, mate." I strode forward to stand halfway between their group and my own. "As to the Orcs: three live, that's it. The rest were killed by yourselves, the Goblins, or by me and my people when they attacked us, as I was unaware of the situation. Now, I've also killed the damn Goblins, so how about we try and be nice and talk things through, eh? I'll let you ask a question, and I'll answer it as best I can, then I get to ask you one. That sound like a good deal?"

"What kind of questions?"

I snorted. "Well, that wasn't the best question to start this off, but okay, I won't ask you about your fighters and how you defend yourselves, and so on, and you don't ask me the same kind of shit. Beyond that, if I can tell you, I will. Now, my turn. Have you ever heard of Durg Guntersson?"

He backed up two spaces and hissed at me.

I stayed still, my weapon still hidden away in my storage bag as I watched him. He made fewer of the clumsy movements Durg made, but still some similarities remained in the way they moved, the stance, and the nervous bobbing of the head.

The amilith species were just weird in my eyes, standing at between eight and eleven feet tall, heavily muscled, with three-fingered, claw-tipped hands. They were humanoid in that they had two arms and two legs, but the way they moved…their body was made of dozens of rings, it seemed, one stacked atop the other, a bit like a worm has segments. Or at least their chest was, enabling them to lean backwards or side to side at almost impossible angles, with broad, triangular upper frames.

Their heads looked like what would happen if you stood a hammerhead shark on its fins, tore the head off, and stuck it onto an ogre. Their eyes were on the outer edges of a flat, hammer-shaped head, with their mouth below and in the center.

Despite their monstrous appearance, the one other member of their species I'd seen was Durg, a massively muscled example of their race who followed the dwarven engineers around like a puppy and tried to outperform the golems in holding things steady or assisting them, generally.

When I'd examined him, I'd seen that he'd had a massive head trauma at some point, and the result of it had been that he was mentally reduced to a child-like state.

Whatever had happened to him, and the Dwarves weren't sure, he was kind-natured and desperately lonely before they took him in. He apparently rarely spoke, but was content to simply be around them, helping wherever he could.

As soon as I'd heard the Orc mention their race, I'd decided that this at least was something I might be able to help with.

"Durg Guntersson was stolen from us long ago, along with the other children the Goblins fed on! His father and elder brothers were lost, seeking revenge! How do you know that name!" The amilith snarled, pointing a massive spear at me.

"Because he's not dead. I've met him, he's…well…okay he's not exactly…okay, shit, no nice way to put this…His brain was damaged, and…"

"You *do* know him."

"What? Oh, wait, was he like that before he was taken?" I sagged in relief. "Thank fuck; I was worried you'd think it was something we'd done."

"What of Gunter? Or Yassika?"

I shook my head. "Never heard of them. I found Durg in Himnel. He stowed away on one of my ships. Now he lives with a bunch of my engineers on the ship. They feed him and keep him busy; he seems to like it."

"Why? Why would you help him?"

"Well, it's my turn for a question, but I'll let that slide. I haven't, not really, not until I heard you were up here, and I decided to come and see if you wanted to meet him. The Dwarves that are helping him…well, they like him. He's quiet and strong, and he helps them by holding things. He caught a panel that was going to hurt someone, I think, rescued them. And since then, boom. They keep him safe, like I say."

"Is he a slave? You wish to trade for him?" The big figure growled at me. "This is why you have come? We have little…"

"Fuck's sake!" I snarled, throwing my hands up. "Look, you dickbag. He's not a slave, he's not trapped, and he can leave whenever he wants. He's working on a ship of mine at the minute, because I've no idea what else to do with him, and I didn't want him to get hurt. He likes the Dwarves, and they like him. If you want him to come here, if this was his home, I'll ask him. If he wants to come, I'll make sure he's brought over by a ship."

"You lie," he said, drool running from his massive lips as he huffed and puffed, lowering himself closer to the ground, clearly getting worked up. I yanked my naginata out, slamming it into the ground base-first and sending a powerful weave of fire magic into it, making everyone back up quickly.

"Never…*ever* call me a fucking liar again!" I warned him in a low hiss. "I came here looking for one of my missing golems, the Orcs were worshipping it, the dumb fucks, and I'm going to take it out of here, regardless. Now, you want to live? You accept that and back the fuck up. You want to trade for it? Fine, name a price, and it better be reasonable, because I've had a BAD FUCKING DAY."

There were long minutes of silence while the amilith looked at each other before another stepped forward, speaking more carefully than the first one.

"You offer to return Durg to us? With no cost, beyond this old broken thing?"

"Hell, I'll give you Durg back, anyway. Like I said, he's not a damn prisoner!" I snapped. "Seriously, he stowed away on one of my ships. My only concern is if he wants to come, all right? As to what happened to him, well, he was in Himnel, that's all I can tell you. It's a city on the coast…"

"We know about the cities, human! They come to us, seeking to buy our loyalty…" He trailed off, and I nodded slowly as he put two and two together.

"So, looks like you attacked the Orcs, who gave you sanctuary, when it was the dickbags from the cities who took your kids. Hell, I've not even questioned Durg myself. Look, what's your name?"

"Xameesh," the big amilith snapped at me.

"Bless you," I responded without thinking, then winced. "Shit. Uh, look, Xameesh…" I took a deep breath and tried to get my irritation under control before going on. "I'm Jax, and I'm at war with the city. I don't know if there's any more of your people there, but if I come across them, I'll do my best to get them back to you, okay? That's the best I can do."

"Where is Durg?" Xameesh asked after a long pause.

"He's back at my home, a good day's flight from here. As I said, I'm at war, so I can't just send ships out to run errands like this," I said, racking my brain. It wasn't a valid use of a ship and the crew, asking them to fly solo was just risking their lives for no reason, as it really couldn't justify the use of the fleet. On the other hand, though, if Durg was mentally a child…I was keeping a child, a giant one, admittedly, but still a child, separated from his people.

"I will inform his family," Xameesh snapped, half-turning away.

"Xameesh!" I said, and he turned back, glaring at me. "Ah, dammit. I'll get the Dwarves to ask Durg if he wants to come back, all right? If he does, I'll make sure he's brought home by the next ship we have coming this way, it's the best I can do."

Xameesh looked at me for a few heartbeats, then grunted and walked off, saying something in passing to the rest of his small group who still held their spears pointed at us.

"Friendly sort," Thomas muttered. I snorted my agreement, turning and heading back to the golem. I reached up again, running my hands across it and noting the steady, if weak, humming and warmth that emanated from it.

"It's the mountain," Oracle said, moving into view from where she'd been circling the golem in the air. "There's so much air mana here, and the sun bathes it for hours each day, giving it a small amount of light mana as well. It has enough ambient mana that it's kept in a state of hibernation."

"Can we wake it up?" I asked.

She held a hand out, palm flat and wiggled it from side to side. "Possibly. We'd be better off if we all gave it some mana, enough to keep it going for a few hours at least, then we can send it off to dig its way back."

"And show the amilith, who've already proven to be untrustworthy neighbors with the mechaniks, exactly where the entrance to the facility is?" I asked.

"Well, yes, but there's a hell of a lot of golems in there, or there will be, right? There's a few dozen amilith, and most of them seem to be barely surviving," Oracle countered.

I frowned as I weighed her words. "That's true, actually. They look half-starved, but this valley is amazing." I looked around again more carefully.

The valley was a good size, and with the geothermal pools giving off a steady, simmering heat, the valley was considerably warmer than it had any right to be at the top of a damn mountain, even if it was slightly misty.

The slopes on one side of the valley were cultivated with dozens of rows of plants growing steadily, and I'd noted that the water was filled with fish when we flew over it. The valley was hidden, with plenty of food and water, yet the amilith looked like they were barely hanging on.

Add to that, there was the hole in the valley. While there were obvious cave entrances in the walls of the caldera, the hole was clearly different and had massive drag marks leading to it.

All around the edge, there were patches of torn earth where massive, or at least heavy things had been dragged and presumably pushed down into the hole, leaving torn earth and streaks of oil behind.

"The mechaniks' inventions," I muttered.

"Bet they threw them all out," Thomas said, rubbing his chin. "I wonder if there's anything valuable in there?"

"Who knows, man. We don't really have time to search, though."

"I know, just galls me to pass up on possible treasure, you know?" Thomas said, grinning at me.

"Yeah, but let's face it, if there's a magic sodding sword or something, they won't have chucked that away, no matter what game logic taught us."

"Maybe, but I'd still smash all the urns and boxes to be sure," Thomas responded, winking.

"Crazy mofo," I muttered, turning back to the golem. "Okay, Oracle, let's see if we can get it to accept me. Then, if it does, we can charge it up a bit, maybe see if Tenandra can give it a jumpstart or something." I paused, called up to her in question, and Tenandra agreed, twisting around to the left and landing carefully.

Her humanoid avatar joined us a few minutes later and examined the structure for a few seconds before nodding and gesturing to a fully buried section.

"We need to uncover here," she said.

I stepped forward and tried to figure out how to do it, when I felt a tap on the shoulder. I glanced back, meeting Grizz's gaze as he pulled a shovel out of his bag, winked, and moved in.

It took him less than five minutes, time that the rest of us spent practically ignoring the observing amilith and instead examining the golem or the valley. Tenandra had rigged up a line of metal links, with Giint's help, that should be able to conduct a big enough charge to reawaken it.

A handful more minutes passed as Grizz uncovered the side of the golem, occasionally stopping to pack more dirt around a specific location as he uncovered the crystal that was embedded in a panel on its back.

As soon as it was clear, Oracle slid into the gap, shrinking down and reaching out, her hands becoming insubstantial as they sank into the crystal.

She frowned, but then smiled, seemingly pleased with what she had found. Taking a few minutes more to sort through the barrage of data, she set to work making whatever changes she needed to.

"Jax, put your hand over mine on the crystal," she said. I moved in, half-crouching and reaching into the gap to lay the palm of my hand flat against the cool crystal.

Her hands shifted below mine, sinking into the seemingly solid structure. The crystal warmed beneath my palm, and a prompt appeared.

Do you wish to claim this Mining Golem?

Yes/No

I selected Yes and felt something inside it change. Then I was confronted with a barrage of screens.

They streamed past almost too fast to see, filling my mind with data, the structure of the nearby rocks, the current inventory, the strata it'd passed through and the current condition of the golem. All of it released in a burst of data that lasted less than three seconds.

I shook my head, disoriented, as Oracle released the golem and clambered out of the small gap, taking my hand and leading me back as I tried to assimilate it all.

"Did you see the inventory?" she asked.

"Yeah, I think…it was a blur."

"It's okay. If you did, then I got it as well," Oracle said, pausing and clearly consulting something. "We have fifty-seven units of the required ores to make cartium, more than we need!"

"Oh thank fuck." I shook my head to clear it. "Okay, can we fix this?" I asked, gesturing to the golem and getting a nod from her.

"Yes, the facility can have it fixed in a few hours with the golems they have there. The only issue is the angle it's at. I think we should bring the two golems on the ship here, have them roll it over, then it can probably dig its way down."

We were in the middle of directing the pair of war golems that had been loaded aboard the ship just in case, when Xameesh returned with two more of his kind.

"Human. I bring Durg's mother; she demands to be taken to her child. As does Tennak, daughter of Simoon," Xameesh announced.

"And I say no, but feel free to walk," I replied before turning back to the golems and concentrating. I reached out as I had once before in Himnel, which seemed so long ago, despite it only being a few weeks, and I felt the tell-tale emptiness of the golems.

I focused on the half-buried, upside-down mining golem and directed them to free it, to set it the right way up, and had the satisfaction of the three amilith jumping back in shock as the massive figures, hidden by tarpaulins until now, suddenly clambered to their feet. They marched to the side of the ship and simply jumped off, slamming into the ground with a reverberating impact as they strolled to their fallen brother.

The two I'd chosen were an advanced and a complex tier, meaning that all they needed was the order, and they'd find a way to complete it most of the time, rather than a basic which would have required me practically remote controlling it.

They got to work quickly, one propping it up, while the other dug the compacted soil and stone from around the base. It braced itself, and the other cleared the ground on the far side.

In less than a minute, the golem was fully uncovered, and we could see the significant damage done, making me wince as I imagined the kind of force that must have been required to do that.

"What happened to it?" I asked Oracle.

"Not entirely sure. The golems don't have eyes, so the best I can get is that it was mining the upper ridge and something made of flesh attacked it, tore its limbs off. There's a sensation of flight, so it looks like whatever it was thought it was food and tried to eat it, realized it wasn't and dumped it, leaving it trapped here."

"It works though, right?" I asked, and she nodded.

"It can travel, but it'll take a while to reach the facility. It probably can't drill, and it's too heavy for the ship."

"So it'll need to plod along on the ground. Fine, we can send the war golems with it," I said, nodding to myself before sighing as I saw several more amilith approaching. "Now, what do they want?"

"I am Danxia, daughter of Reyna. This is Tennak, daughter of Simoon. You are the human who holds my son captive?" she asked, her voice filled with a definite growl.

"Oh for fuck's sake…" I rubbed the bridge of my nose. "No, okay? No! Durg isn't a captive. He stowed away on my ship! The dwarven engineers look after him; they feed him and make sure he's busy and happy, and you'll remember that I godsdamn told YOU about him, you prick," I snapped at Xameesh before turning back to the two apparently female amilith.

"He's not a prisoner; he's free to leave whenever he wants. I'll have him dropped off the next time a ship is coming this way, which will be soon, if he wants to come. If not, well, tough titty."

"Titty?" The massive creature asked, shifting from side to side as though trying to examine me with one eye at a time. "I wish to see my son…as does Tennak, daughter of Simoon. You have demanded we give up the Orcs' old God.

We have agreed, yet now we wish something in return. We demand to go to him, to bring him home," she said slowly.

"Must be a cultural thing," I muttered, shaking my head. "Look, you want transport to him? Fine, but in return, you get one of your people to lead the golems out of the valley. They need to walk it. Deal?" I asked. She looked at me, then the golems, then turned and screamed something in a language that was all pops and clicks at the other amilith.

There was a brief barrage of back and forth before she turned back to me and nodded.

"We accept. We leave now," she said.

"Uh, no," I retorted, glaring at her. "We leave when I'm godsdamn ready, and I need to visit somewhere else first. So, if you want to come, you'll damn well be quiet and behave yourself, or you can sodding walk. It should take you about a month." I turned back to Oracle and the golems. "Can they travel now?"

She nodded, frowning as she stared at them. "I'm adjusting your orders to them and giving them a series of options just in case, but before we go anywhere," She broke off, smiling as the side of the mining golem opened up, and an arm on a series of runners lifted out and started depositing ingots on the floor by my feet.

It took several minutes for them all to be dropped off, including a trio of gleaming silvery bars that I frowned at, reaching out to touch them.

"Are these…?"

"Platinum," Oracle confirmed.

A smile spread across my face. "Okay, we need to get the mining golems out and damn well working, get us a shitload of this stuff. Hell, get us the gold and steel and all the rest, and we can build the Imperial Academy. Oracle, when we get back, get Heph and Seneschal to make it a priority to use the mining golems."

"You seek to mine our lands?" Xameesh asked me pointedly.

"I'm looking to mine the surrounding area," I said with a carefully released sigh. "How far do you claim as part of your lands?"

"This mountain."

I snorted, shaking my head. "Nope," I retorted. "I already own a facility further down in the mountain, and if you really want to get down to it, I own this godsdamn continent, so, you want to claim this valley? Fine. It's yours. You took it from the Orcs, well done you, even though it's looking like you attacked them for something they might not have done now, doesn't it?"

"Our children were stolen!" Xameesh thundered.

"Yeah, and they turned up in Himnel, a city that would have slaughtered the Goblins if they'd known about them, and probably the Orcs, too, so how about you stop and think about that?"

"This is our land," Xameesh snapped, baring his teeth.

"The valley is yours," I responded, starting to get damn tired of the conversation. "Now, I'm going to mine nearby, so how about you cut the shit and tell me what you want? You're clearly after something. Tell me what it is, and make it reasonable, and I might agree, or I might totally ignore you and mine this place anyway." My hackles were rising as I ran out of patience.

"We demand…"

I snarled, reaching for my naginata.

Thomas grabbed my wrist. "Bro, calm down."

I glared at him then took a deep breath. "Fine, you deal with this shit." I grabbed the ingots and slammed them into my bags before heading up onto the ship's deck with Oracle. Half the squad followed me while the other half stayed around Thomas, who was speaking to the amilith.

Fifteen minutes later, the giant females were sitting on the deck, unable to squeeze into any of the cabins, and we were lifting into the air. The war golems stomped across the valley, escorting the mining golem and being guided by Xameesh.

"What was that all about, man?" Thomas asked, coming to my side and leaning against the railing as I looked out, struggling to maintain control over my temper as I watched the valley below us.

"What?" I asked him sullenly.

"That temper, dude. You wouldn't normally have gone off like that, right?" Thomas asked.

I glared at him for a hot minute before sighing. "No, no I wouldn't."

"So, talk to me, man." Thomas reached into his bag and pulled out a hip flask, taking a pull on it then passing it over.

I took it, looking down at the silvery container. Oracle's presence was comforting as she laid her hand on my arm. I took a swig, feeling the burn of the harsh liquor as it went down.

"Damn…" I coughed, handing the flask back. He grinned but stayed quiet, watching me.

Taking a deep breath, I spoke. "Okay, yeah, I might be a little strung out, that's all."

To his credit, Thomas didn't even snort at me for stating the obvious. "Go on…"

I stared out over the sides of the valley as we cleared it, the blast of icy mountain air no longer blocked by the crater wall, making me pause as I blinked the cold away.

"The Orcs," I said finally. "As near as I can tell, were given an ultimatum by the Goblins to hand over their friends, the amilith, when they came asking for help. They were thinking about it, and they might have done the right thing, but the amilith got wind of it and attacked them. Then they had to flee, losing their homes, and the damn Goblins caught them, probably ate most of the tribe, then we came along and blew up what's left…seems a pretty shitty deal for them, that's all."

"It is," Thomas said, shrugging. "Nobody did well out of it. Especially as the amilith are dying."

"What?"

"The amilith are dying out. Fewer and fewer children are being born, and those who are born are messed up. They wanted food, mostly grains and seeds for planting, that's all."

"In exchange for us mining lower down the mountain?" I asked.

"Nah, they said we can mine wherever we want, if we give them the food. They seem to think the Orcs must have poisoned the land somehow, or they've been cursed. It's why they dumped all the shit the Orcs built in that hole." He took a slug from the flask before going on. "We got all the shit in the hole as well. Considering it's mainly metal, I figured we could use it somehow."

"So they'd let us mine the valley?" I asked, frowning.

"Yeah, they're considering moving on and abandoning it. That's why they're so desperate to get Durg back fast. They don't like to hang around once they make a decision."

"You think they'll really leave?"

He nodded. "I think they have to. You remember the stuff we learned in school about radiation?" I nodded assent and he went on. "I think there's something in the valley that's radioactive, or the local equivalent, anyway. Think about it. The kids are born deformed or die in the womb. The locals are growing weaker. Although they denied it, it was obvious by the way some of them shook even holding their spears."

"So what, you think they're dying from radiation poisoning?" I asked, suddenly feeling like an utter arsehole.

"Yeah, or something similar," Thomas said, and the three of us turned and looked at the pair of massive amilith who sat on the deck, frantically holding onto the nearest stanchion with white-knuckled grips.

"What are we going to do?" Oracle asked.

"The right thing, regardless of the cost," I said, shaking my head before straightening up and walking over to the pair. "Danxia, daughter of Reyna and Tennak, daughter of Simoon," I said, stumbling over their names. "I'm sorry for my lack of patience before. I will take you to Durg, but I have to check something, to make sure you're no threat to my people, and that you have no…disease?" I winced as I wondered if I was about to get my face torn off for insulting them. "May I examine you, using my magic?"

"No!" the younger and smaller snapped at me. "You seek to enslave us!"

"If he did, he would not have asked permission," Danxia said. "Swear an Oath that you mean us no harm and will release us from whatever spell you cast."

"I swear on my soul," I said, channeling mana into my words. There was a flash of golden light, and she nodded, feeling the truth of the Oath as it activated, before reaching one massive hand out to me.

"You may examine me, but not Tennak, daughter of Simoon," she said in tacit assent.

Oracle and I began to cast. It started as a simple scan, then as it went on, we built up more and more information. The minutes stretched, and soon I felt the distinctive warning of a mana migraine forming. Finally, we stopped and, nodding our thanks to her, examined the information we'd received.

"How bad?" Thomas asked as we moved away, me sitting with my back against the railing, and Oracle hopping up to sit on top of a barrel nearby.

"Bad," Oracle said simply. "This radiation is…well, it's deadly. It's killing them, and her body is riddled with growths. I can see why they're having trouble having children. Frankly, I can't see how the hell any of their children survive."

"Can you fix it?" Thomas asked. Oracle glanced at me questioningly.

"It'll take a lot of healing, and it'd just happen again," she said, watching me. "We can't be everywhere and help everyone…"

"We can," I said, answering Thomas's question first. "We can heal them, or at least I think so. You know, I asked one of the Baron's helpers when I was in the arena about cancer? Turns out it's really simple to heal."

Thomas clenched his fists before forcing himself to release them and calm down.

"We lost our ma, because the Baron and his kind didn't give a shit about anyone else," I said. "We'll never know if she had us through an injection, or from him…direct…but she loved us, and we loved her. He could have saved her, but he didn't give a shit. Now we're in the same place. We could save them, a whole tribe, and we're looking at where we win because of it."

"Then teach me the healing spell," Thomas said. "My own was fucked up, like seriously. My mana channels were practically burned out, and after swearing to Nimon…I don't even know exactly how but, well…anyway, teach me, and I'll work with them. I'm sod all use here; you've got your team, after all…"

"No, they'll just get sick again."

"We can't leave them to die, not after you pulled out the 'ma' card," Thomas ground out, glaring at me.

"And we won't." I forced a smile for him, even if it was a grim one. "We're going to the facility, we'll get things back on track, then we're heading back to the Tower. On the way, we'll examine the amilith, get the spells worked out, then we'll heal them. We use them as a go-between to persuade the others to let us heal them, and while we do that, we can figure out what the hell is going on in that valley."

"The mining golem was looking for rare ores, like those it needed to make the cartium…maybe it's that?" Oracle said.

"Could be. Either way, it's got to be a rare isotope-type ore, likely something from when it was a volcano. There mustn't be much of it, or they'd all be dead already, so we get the facility, we fix it, and we send a mining golem up to gather up whatever rare shit it can."

"Is that safe?" Thomas asked grimly. "I mean, if we disturb it, are we going to Chernobyl their asses?"

"I've no idea, mate," I replied. "But they're already dying. I don't know, maybe we can offer to relocate them?"

"They've got a hidden valley up in a mountain with a spa built in, you got anything like that in your lands?" Thomas asked, quirking an eyebrow in question.

"Dude, seriously, I've got no idea what or where half the stuff is in my lands. The Gods keep giving us quests and sending us out to reclaim shit. Each time I do one, I find I need to do three more things." I sighed and shook my head to clear the stress. "Ignore me complaining, man. Just batters my head at times that there's never any time to just explore, you know? We've got airships, that should make it so much easier."

"And instead, you're constantly running from one fire to the next." Thomas nodded. "Yeah, I'm seeing that, my man, aaaaand…"

"Yeah?" I asked, waiting.

"Well, I think I'm better off not being in your team," Thomas said carefully. "Look, I know we spoke about it, and I said I'd think about it. Well, there's a fuck ton of stuff that you need to do, and you can't. Like, there's no chance of you getting it all done. Especially not now I'm seeing what your life is like, but…" Thomas shrugged again.

"So you want out?"

Thomas frowned and shook his head. "Hell no, bro, I want in! See here, dude, you're backlogged to all hell, you can't so much as sit and stop for five minutes without something else coming along and kicking your ass out to deal with it. Well, that was before you had me back!

"Give me a team and a job to do, send me and my own squad to put out some of the fires, and let me help. You're the Scion, and the next Emperor. Okay, cool, fair enough. It sounds like it's going to be a sucky role, to be honest. But, as your far more handsome, skillful, and sexy younger brother, I think I'd be great at being an all-around troubleshooter."

"Wait, did you just try to stick me with the council and the ruling shit job, while you get to party and kill things?" I asked, raising an eyebrow at him.

"Pretty much, and don't forget 'explore'!" Thomas said, grinning. "You said we can't use the ships' cannons. Fair enough, give me access to a few mages. You said Oracle can help to share spells, awesome. Do that for me and my new squad. Give us a ship and send us out. Let me prove myself to you, man."

"You don't have anything to prove, bro." I smiled as my heart lifted a little.

"Maybe not to you, but to the rest? I'm an ex-dark legionnaire. Being with you helps, because they think you walk on damn water, but beyond that? Seriously. I need this as much as you do, I think."

I looked at Thomas for a long minute, then to Oracle, who gave an almost imperceptible nod.

"I don't like it." I said finally. "Not because I don't trust you, because you damn well know I do, Tommy, but because…well…I just got you back. I don't want to lose you again."

"And you won't," Thomas said. "Seriously man, five years I've been here, still around." He gave a little laugh before scratching the back of his head. "Well, mostly still around, you know, kinda got some scores to settle…"

"Don't we all, man," I said, nodding grimly. "Okay, when we get back to the Tower, we'll speak to Restun and put together a team for you. You should have a think about what you want, if it's going to be a standard layout or if you need something in particular…and no poaching my people!" I glared at him in mock warning.

"Hey, if they want to team up with the more handsome, successful, and better-hung brother, who am I to say no?" he quipped.

"That's the point; they already did!" I shot back with a grin, before gesturing as the ship curved around to land at the entrance of the facility. "Okay, enough shit, let's get going."

The second run through the previously Goblin-held facility was far less exciting, taking only a few minutes until we reached the hidden entrance to the second main section, and a brief pause as the golems went active, before they recognized me and settled down again.

Ten minutes more, and I was sitting in the Control Center, bringing up the facilities and scouring through them, finding an intact servitor-class golem, having it come and collect the fifty-seven ingots of rare materials, then bugger off to the refinery.

I set the instructions, ordering it to use the last of the reserve power that was set aside for the secondary charging cradles to restart the refinery, then to use the cartium that was produced to repair the main cradles and the mana-gathering facilities.

I checked down the list, finding that we should have an estimated six hours before that was complete. I queued up a series of repairs from there, starting with recharging the majority of the golems before giving them more orders.

There were forty-six war golems on site, twenty simple, or class two, which were essentially basic grunts, able to follow simple commands, but that was all. Twenty complex or class three, which basically meant that they could be given a general command like "patrol the base and kill anyone that's not one of my team" and they'd do it flawlessly, and six advanced, or class four.

Class four golems were far more useful, considering that they could be given complicated orders, like "Capture anyone wearing this, kill anyone wearing that, and secure this location. Warn people off, but kill anyone who attacks you."

Added to that, they could speak. As higher-class constructs, they could lead the lower classes of golems, essentially upgrading them by an entire class level because they could be tweaked in real time by the higher golems.

I was practically dancing as I ordered that they be reactivated. There were ten charging cradles on the upper level, with the rest stored in the main production facility. While the upper, secondary charging facility was intact, the lower ones weren't, thanks to a minor collapse and subsequent damage ages back.

The war golems were a wonderful addition to the army. I still didn't really trust them, having dated a girl for at least two weeks who'd been a programmer and seeing her scream at her programs when they did things logically, but wrong, after she'd told them to do exactly that, I wasn't going to ever trust them fully.

I did, however, trust Heph and Seneschal, so I resolved to have them command and watch over the golems back at the Tower, meaning that the legionnaires would be freed up from guard duty, leaving the golems to protect the Tower.

The war golems weren't the only ones in the facility though, and that fact was making my godsdamn day, as I had them moving the second set of golems to the charging cradles.

There were ten servitor-class golems, split into eight servant-class, four complex, and four advanced. Best of all, though, the remaining two were crafter golems, a complex, and an advanced.

The last two, the crafters, were the first of their kind we'd found, and in addition to being rare as all hell. They were clearly worth their weight in sodding platinum.

A complex crafter golem, I learned, could follow blueprints and literally make things on its own. All I needed to do was teach it to make a high-quality healing potion, for example, and it'd churn them out, so long as it had the ingredients.

This didn't seem that marvelous at first, considering that the servitors back at the Tower had been replacing the ships' hulls with new, sturdier ones for a while now, and similar tasks. But they required Heph to micro-control them all the time, guiding them.

These crafter-class golems would make better versions over time. They were fast, efficient, and damn well able to work around the clock, all while guiding others.

Then there was the advanced crafter golem. This was a golem that could literally improve the simple blueprints and designs it was given to work on. It also had a ten percent chance to discover new and greater designs once a week by dedicating the week to research.

That alone was seriously tempting. The thought of constructing nine more of these and having them all work on a cannon, for example, meant that there was a damn good chance that one or more of them would give me a new, efficient design within a week.

For now, though, there was a more important use for it and its slightly dumber brother.

They could build from blueprints, but they could also disassemble things, and this facility had both an intact higher-leveled Genesis Chamber, and a couple of low-leveled ones.

In the process of disassembly, they had a ten percent chance to develop a new blueprint for that item that would be more efficient, or a fifty percent chance to make a blueprint that could replicate the original exactly.

I ordered the crafter golems to disassemble one of the three Genesis Chambers in the facility immediately. It was the most basic of the three, one step higher than the one we had back at the Tower, but in doing so, they began to create a blueprint.

When I'd examined the instructions and the information on the golems, it was…strange. They weren't really made to interact with normal minds, or at least not as normal as my mind was, and I suspected that there was something missing. Heph had hinted before that usually he'd not be as involved in puppeting the golems as he was now.

When I examined the golems, data was dumped into my mind, and it was a case of sorting through. It was like someone had taken a manual on how to fully repair your car, and how to operate it, then had scrawled a few quick pages on the simple how-to of driving. They'd then taken the entire mass of a thousand pages, mixed them together randomly, and dropped them into my brain, unsorted.

The result was a system that seemed designed to be as confusing as possible, because when I reached out to the golems, they were seemingly blank spaces waiting for commands. I gave it a command and boom, it went, but if I looked at it the right way, twisting my mind into a pretzel and wondering how or why it did something, then bloop. A huge mass of disorganized data arrived.

This was what I found out just as I'd made the mistake of wondering what the crafter golem could do, while I was connected to it.

In addition to ordering the crafter golems to disassemble a Genesis Chamber, once they were fully charged, I'd ordered the servitors to begin a full repair of the main facility. They'd ignore the outer section, beyond repairing the hidden door and resealing it, ordering the final five golems that were on the main charging cradles to assist them when they were charged fully, as these last four complex and single advanced were construction class.

Then I queued up a few more orders and pulled my mind back, blinking through my exhaustion-induced headache.

As much as I had wanted to get back to the Tower, as this trip already had taken longer than I'd hoped, I couldn't just leave the facility as it was. I needed to give the various units their orders then load everything we needed onto the ship before we could leave.

It was galling, as I would have much preferred going to sleep on the ship and heading back to the Tower now, but that was life.

I let Oracle direct me, and the pair of us passed down the corridor and into a small room that had been cleaned and set aside, with my own bedroll set up for me. I thanked her and laid down, Oracle snuggling in under the blanket with me as I wrapped my arms around her, too tired to even pay attention to what she was wearing or to undress myself.

CHAPTER TWENTY

I awoke slowly the next morning, or what was morning to me anyway, considering I was in a hidden facility buried underground inside a mountain. Basically, I just needed a cat to stroke to qualify as a Bond villain.

I blinked; the light that had been dim when I'd gone to sleep was now considerably stronger. Stretching and blinking muzzily, I rolled onto my back, wondering where I was and where the hell Oracle had gone.

I listened, yawning, as I picked up the faint grumbling of the others outside. I smiled as I recognized Grizz's voice complaining about the light waking him up.

Something about knowing that others were suffering as well always made it easier, I reflected, as I pulled the blankets aside and got up. I gathered them up and dumped them into my bag of holding, yawning and scratching idly at my growing beard before heading to the door, taking one last look around the room.

It was small but clean and pleasant enough. The desk and table stood at one end of the room, with a pair of bookshelves behind it, all of which had long since succumbed to the ravages of time. The books looked like it'd take a professional just to make out the titles, and the wooden desk had been eaten through at some point by some burrowing insects. The chair looked intact, albeit coated in a thin layer of dust.

I shook my head as I realized I'd need to have a librarian come and catalog the books in here, and indeed in the entire facility. There could be dozens or hundreds of skillbooks here, despite the books in this room not having the tell-tale feeling of magic.

I really needed to have a library built for people to access, as the Hall of Memories was tightly locked down, so there wasn't anywhere to store more mundane books or information.

And I needed a librarian beyond Oracle.

Dammit.

I shook my head and ambled out of the room, looking out across the inside of the massive facility. The servitor hung spider-like from the ceiling, repairing a section of the wall and roof where a minor cave-in long ago had resulted in the damage that had buggered up the charging cradles.

I took a deep breath and leaned against the railing before me. The low voices of my friends rose up to me from one side. This was the first time I had actually looked out across the facility while not suffering from exhaustion and blood loss.

Since arriving, I'd been so focused on getting this sorted and moving to the next objective, that I'd not had a chance to admire this place.

I stood on the third level of the facility now, leaning against a balcony and looking out across the cavern as I frowned, trying to guess what might be a better word for it.

It was a cavern after all, an open space inside a godsdamn mountain, but…it was also a bit of an unhelpful descriptor. The walls were clad in sheets of yellow stone, like sandstone but far harder, with marble rings set between them, presumably to make them look more attractive.

The entire facility was set in an oval of this design, with a high ceiling overhead and a physical layout that might be more suited to an ancient Egyptian or Greek temple than a magical production facility, considering the enormous, fluted pillars and the walkways that ran between dried-out pools and gardens.

I tried to imagine it as it must have looked, fully powered and alive, with hundreds of Gnomes and more, the elite creators and engineers of the continent strolling back and forth inside it. The gardens green and flowering, the shallow pools alive with fish, and the benches taken up by laughing and conversing scholars and thinkers, with engineers shouting at them for doing stupid things like making systems that couldn't be easily accessed.

The building I stood atop was layered with quarters for hundreds, with a separate wing for production, another for design work and the final wing, arcing around the back of the living quarters, seemingly a storehouse, judging from the massive collection of random things.

There were thousands of ingots, piles of ores, gems, and plain rocks, as well as heaps of mulch, long since dried and crumbled to dust, where plants and foodstuffs had once been. Then there were insect-infested piles of what had once been timber that was considered valuable enough that they needed to be stored under lock and key, while gemstones and precious metals apparently didn't.

Below me, the plodding pair of golems that stomped around the corner carried a huge slab of stone easily between them, the much heavier and larger construction-class leading the smaller servitor-class that would aid them in the repairs.

I shook my head at the differences in their build. The constructors were bigger in size than even the war golems. They were massive, made of seemingly solid rock and metal, designed so that a main battle tank could plough into them and bounce off. The smaller and lighter servitor and crafter-class golems were faster, with multiple arms, legs, and heads, able to move in any direction and seemingly designed for delicate work.

I'd seen war golems helping to repair the ships, and servitors helping to build, but it was clear that, while any of them could be guided to do any job, their specialized forms would always be better at the tasks they were designed to do.

I shrugged, turning and moving down the flight of steps to the room below my own. The majority of the team were inside, eating and talking, missing only Grizz and Thomas.

I took a plate of eggs and beans, thanked Yen, whose turn it was to cook, and sat down, getting a kiss from Oracle as she sat next to me, stealing a bite of my breakfast.

She chewed it thoughtfully before refusing anymore, then sighed at the looks the others were giving her.

Considering she was a wisp who'd made a point of not needing food, drink, or rest before, the more recent changes had clearly been noticed. She poured herself a small cup of coffee from one of the flasks in my bag, then passed the flask to Lydia, who poured her own.

"Okay, yeah, there's a little something that's changed," Oracle said, blowing on her coffee to cool it.

"Clearly," was all that Tang said, a smirk climbing one side of his face.

"Since the fight at Wayland's Crossing, when Amon and Jax…well, since Jax made some alterations to Bob and me and our bond, there were some unexpected side effects, as well as some bonuses.

"One of those changes is that the ability to feed on mana, a staple of life as a wisp, was returned to me. It was taken from me when I was added to the Tower," she said darkly. "I no longer need to take that mana from Jax, or the portion of his health that I needed, either.

"It's not completely back, as I can't actually channel directly, and the mana I use for spells all comes from Jax, but I can feed on the ambient mana now, and for some reason, I can also draw sustenance from other sources, including food."

"So, you're exploring the world of food?" Yen asked.

"It's not really efficient, as it takes more effort to digest it fully. I get a limited amount of mana from it, after the entire process is done, but some things, like coffee?" Oracle held up the cup and smiled. "Are worth it for the taste, never mind the awesome bonuses!"

"Just wait 'til ye try some o' tha pastries tha bakery has been makin'," Lydia said, shaking her head. "Can wisps get fat?"

"Nope!" Oracle said, smiling.

"Lucky!" Lydia grunted.

I laughed, nudging her with an elbow. "Seriously, Lydia? You must go through a thousand calories an hour or more, what do you care about getting fat? We all eat like crazy any chance we get, fighting the way we do burns it all off, anyway!"

"Aye, but iffin ah had ma way, ah'd live on those pastries," she admitted, coloring slightly. "They're amazing, yer know? Ah never tasted anythin' like 'em."

"Just wait, there are better things to come," I assured her.

She raised one eyebrow in question.

"Believe me. Pizza, chips, and bacon cheeseburgers are going to rock your world," I said.

"Did I hear cheeseburgers mentioned?" Thomas asked. He staggered in with Grizz leading, before slumping to the floor and panting, trying to catch his breath as Grizz did the same, the pair of them exchanging a friendly fist bump.

I shook my head at the inanity of such a gesture being so prevalent here. I paused, considering that, in a world where so many were in full armor so much of the time, and where people wore gauntlets and still needed to be polite, while distrusting those across from you, a fist bump made a lot of sense.

It made me wonder if the fist bump was a greeting that might have come and gone across the centuries in our world as well.

"Well?" Thomas asked, sitting up and glaring at me. "I definitely heard cheeseburgers mentioned, bro, and if you don't have some stashed in your bag, you and me are going to have a falling out."

"Ah crap, sorry." I smiled. "I was telling Lydia about the wonders she has to come, as we need to speak to the cooks about it."

"Damn right, we do," Thomas said, slumping back and closing his eyes again.

"What were you doing?" I asked.

"Morning PT," Thomas answered, giving me a quizzical look. "Don't you?"

"Dude, some days we fight from dusk 'til dawn, then we get home and Restun beats my ass with PT. I'm not doing it when I don't need to."

"And that's why I'll kick your ass again next time we have a competition."

"You've had five years longer than me to level up, you bandit," I said, glaring. "If you hadn't won, I'd have been amazed." I decided to ignore the fact that I'd been absolutely gutted when I'd lost the fight.

"Yeah, well..." Thomas was interrupted by the sound of approaching footsteps as one of the massive advanced war golems arrived.

"Lord Scion. Dravith Production Center One is fully secured and ready to begin repowering," it said, the voice both booming and somehow hollow with a distinct lack of any emotion.

"Thank you." I nodded to it, vaguely remembering the request I'd given the facility that I be told when it was ready to extend the mana collectors. Clearly, it'd been listening.

I finished my breakfast and poured myself a mug of coffee, before heading up to the Control Center and sitting. I reached out and placed my right hand on the desk and experienced the peculiar, twinned effect of the data dump that came with accessing the facility, as well as the visual aspect of the table's use.

It was strange, and I wondered if it was because I was in a fully intact major facility now, or if I'd learned more and was simply able to access things I couldn't before.

I suspected it was a mix of both, as I vaguely noticed having information that seemed deeper than it should have been, from the simple screens the other control facilities showed.

I focused and mentally reached out, selecting the mana collectors and seeing the screens before me respond, confirming that my mind and the controls were linked. I smiled as, for the first time, I experienced the connection consciously.

On the screen, ancient boulders were pushed aside. Outside, earth long since settled and compacted by the ages was driven out of the way by the emergence of six massive obelisks that ringed the facility.

They moved slowly, but with the inevitability of glaciers, sliding up and out of long-hidden recesses in the ground. One of them even set off an accidental landslide in a section of the low mountains and hills it was buried in.

Great onyx pillars extended into the air, sliding up into the sunlight until at last, at a length of over ten meters, they finally stopped. Animals that had fled the sudden appearance began to return as the minutes passed, while tens of thousands of tiny filaments were repaired and refocused by the magic of the facility.

The repairs took some time. Admittedly, that time passed in an instant to my twinned consciousness, while to the rest of the team, it seemed like more than an hour, but they waited patiently. Eventually though, it was done, and without ceremony, the obelisks all began to draw in ambient mana.

Animals that had crept close, emboldened by the stillness and silence, turned tail and raced away as the first influx of mana across crystals and runes long since covered with dirt caused great arcs of electrically charged energy to tear free. Flames washed down them, and light glowed, drawing the eye from miles around. Soon, they were spotless again, and the entire facility seemed to awaken.

The light inside had been dim, but more than enough to see by when we first arrived. Once the basic repairs were complete, it changed from a twilight of conserving mana to a dull, overcast midday kind of light, the kind where you can see clearly enough, but inside the house you'd put a light on, despite it being daylight.

Now, the light had changed across the entire facility, blazing to a warm brightness that brought to mind noon at the height of summer. I smiled, knowing that the facility was truly alive again.

I pulled up the build queues; there were sufficient stores to make thirty class one golems, twenty-five class two, eight class three, or three class fours. The massive drop in possible production wasn't down to the simpler ingredients required for all golems, but instead was down to the combination of the more complex brains and the rarer materials required for them.

Golems, it seemed, could be made of almost anything, and it was entirely possible to make a golem out of wood and copper alone.

It would just be shit useless and would last a matter of hours before crumbling away.

Making a golem that would last for millennia, one that could think and learn, design new recipes, lead troops in battle or build a castle and more…yeah, that took much more unusual stock.

I ordered the facility to separate out what was needed for the golem giant in the basement to be finished. Once that was done, I found I had just enough to construct three of the class three crafters and two class ones with what was left, and I approved that, sending the more advanced servitors to work on it for now.

Next, I ordered the available servitors to prioritize repairing the incoming mining golem when it arrived, sensing it was less than two hours from reaching the base.

All but one of the advanced servitors were commanded to work on that, and as soon as it was done, they were to split into two groups. Half were set to return to work on producing the next generation of golems, while the rest were to go into the bowels of the facility and restart the construction of the golem giant.

The remaining advanced servitor was to board my ship, ready to head back to the Tower, along with the crafter golems as soon as they were finished disassembling the Genesis Chamber in an hour and a half.

While they were doing that, the other miner golems were beginning to power up, and they had their orders as well. There were three still in the facility, and then the damaged one that was on its way back here. Two were ordered to seek out as many of the rarer ores and minerals that were required for the higher golem constructions as possible, the remaining unit was to concentrate on standard resources.

As soon as the damaged unit was repaired, it was set to return to the hidden valley and start scouring it for the possible radioactives or whatever the hell the local equivalent was.

With those orders given, I also ordered one of the advanced war golems and two of the complex models to board the ship. The rest were to resume patrols, secure the base fully, and then once the giant golem was complete, they had orders to move out and secure the facility and begin repairs to the exterior.

I nodded to myself. We'd essentially done all we could with them, and I disengaged from the system, standing and moving out to join the others again.

"Right!" I said, getting everyone's attention. "We've got about two hours, then everything should be done here, and we can move on, *but* we still need to find Svetu's Tools, whatever the hell they are. So, considering we know the facility is secure, I suggest we split up into four teams, spread out, then…"

"Ah, Jax?" Lydia interrupted, and I broke off, looking at her questioningly. "Why don't we just ask tha golems? Ah mean, they can talk, or some can, and tha tools left behind by a God have ta be pretty important, right?"

"You mean…ask directions?" I asked after a long minute of mentally castigating myself. "I…it never occurred to me, I guess." I reached out and summoned one of the advanced war golems.

"Where are Svetu's Tools?" I asked it, and there was a long pause, before it spoke.

"Master Svetu has a secure private facility that is accessed through the main stairwell," it rumbled.

"Can you show us where it is and open it?"

"Yes."

I watched it for a long minute, before sighing. "Take us to the entrance to Svetu's private facility," I ordered, and it turned and stomped off. While we all followed it, I spent most of the time it took to get there muttering about machines and their need for exact godsdamn commands.

It only took a few minutes to reach the location we needed. It was a small landing on the main stairwell that led up the side of the facility, seemingly a little larger than needed, but absolutely nothing special.

As I climbed the stairs, I wondered at the mind that would insist on a hidden facility, inside a hidden facility, under a mountain, especially as there was no sign of a door to enter it.

The landing was perhaps a dozen meters across and maybe ten long, far larger than seemed required, but as blank an area as it was, I'd just assumed it was missing some tables and chairs as I passed it earlier.

The golem walked to a blank wall on the far side and reached out one massive hand. It tapped a series of bricks in a set pattern, then reached out with one finger, slowly dragging it across the stone, clearly following a path it could see.

At first there was nothing, then a line emerged as a hidden door began to slowly glow around the edges.

As the golem moved, tracing out the form of the door, it grew brighter and brighter, until finally there was a clear door, making us all wonder how the hell we'd missed it.

The golem stepped back and stopped, completely motionless as I stepped up and grasped the recessed handle, tugging and opening the door with a click.

As soon as the door opened, I received a notification; it pulsed in the corner of my vision, as I tried not to stare at the room that was exposed.

It was HUGE.

There was no other word for it, as I stepped through the door, the others following me inside. We all looked around in awe, magelights flickering to life across the room, and the massive constructions that filled it.

The room was split into three sections, a raised platform, where we stood, looking out in shock; the main floor below us, seemingly laid out like a hanger with half-finished constructions set about haphazardly and the door at the top of a stairwell that led off to the right.

I added the rooms to my mental version of the map of the facility. I realized that the map I'd seen had stopped at this point, and even my authority as Scion of the Empire and new master of the facility hadn't allowed me to know about this until I'd asked the right question.

I shook my head, seeing designs below that looked like smaller versions of the Prax, a sword that glowed an unearthly blue, a horse's head made entirely of copper, and a thousand things beyond.

Everywhere I looked, weird and wonderful creations stretched out before me, but the floor we all stood upon clearly held what we'd come for.

I stepped forward, moving across the floor toward the single table with its battered old chair and the three tools that sat atop it.

They glowed with visible power, commanding attention, even with a thin film of dust coating everything. I was almost to the table when Giint barreled past me and uncharacteristically grabbed my hand, yanking it back and glaring at me.

"No!" Giint snapped. "God's tools! Not for our hands!" I looked at the little bastard in shock, anger at him sparking for stopping me from picking the tools up and examining them, before grumbling to myself and backing away.

Every time I looked at the tools, they seemed to almost scream out to touch them, yet as I looked at them, I suddenly realized that I didn't know exactly what they were.

There were three of them, that much I could definitely tell. There were noticeable handles on two, with long rods forming the grips, but the ends…

One I'd have sworn a second ago was a hammer, now looked more like a screwdriver, and the other, looked… no, it was a single blade, thin and narrow edged, with a chisel point that…no.

Every time I looked away, they changed, yet I got the feeling that they were both unaltering and weirdly, constantly in flux at the same time. The longer I looked at them, the more they seemed to shift out of the corner of my eye, yet be resolutely the same as well.

My head began to hurt as two such diametrically opposed positions, them both being unchanging and also in a state of constant flux, seemed to be right.

"No look at God's tools!" Giint snarled, reaching up and pushing me back, before throwing a section of leather from his pouch across them, hiding them from view.

I sighed in relief even as I almost pulled the cover aside again, instinctually wanting to look and see what I was missing, to check if they'd changed again.

"Ah, dammit, I should have warned you all, my apologies," came a voice, and the now-familiar presence of a God pressed down upon us all.

"Svetu?" I asked, shaking my head and trying to get my brain back on track as I looked in the direction of the voice, seeing the small figure that ambled forwards out of nowhere with a smile on His face.

"Aye laddie, ah, but it's been a millennia or so since I was here, feels like that, anyway," He mumbled, reaching out and putting His hand on the leather that was laid across the top of His tools. *"Giint, you did well. Items that the Gods use this regularly, and that we pour this much power into, are never meant for the*

eyes of mortals. Please, understand that this is not a slight, simply a fact." He glanced around at us all, patting the table.

"Okay, so, are we good?" I asked, looking around the room one last time as he nodded and ushered us back.

"Yes, all is good now, the facility is reawakened, the Goblins are gone, and my tools are as they should be, back in my possession again," Svetu said firmly. *"My agreement with my sister still stands, and I will grant you both the plans for the Control Towers to be integrated with the smaller facilities, and I will construct the main Control Facility atop the Great Tower."*

"Thank you, Lord Svetu," I said, sighing in relief. "As to the facility, we agreed that I would claim it and we would share it. Obviously, this section is yours, so I assume that the rest is mine?" I said casually, hoping He would give assent.

"Aye, out there is all yours," He said distractedly, waving towards the door as He started to turn away. *"Ah'll need a few of the golems, not too many. A dozen crafter class or so should be enough to start with. Advanced and lord should do fine, and a few tons of resources."*

"Ah, we haven't got enough resources to craft more than a handful of advanced, once the current run is done, and we only have a few crafter class, Lord Svetu, we need them at the Tower to build more Genesis Chambers."

"So, what, you think I'll simply make do?" He asked, turning back to me.

"No!" I said quickly, shaking my head. "I'm asking you to be patient, to let us make enough golems to be able to build at the Tower and here, then to take your share. We have two crafter golems, that's it. We've never found any others, so we've been making do with the servitors so far. The crafters are needed by the Tower, desperately."

"Well, I need them, too, boy! Have you any idea how annoying it is to leave a project half-done, let alone hundreds of them? For hundreds of years?!"

"All I'm asking is a few more months, then, and you can use the class one crafters that are being produced here as soon as they're finished," I said, and He grunted.

"I'll take them, for now, but I'll need more. I need to make weapons for the war, boy! You face mortals; we face Gods and Demon princes. I cannot wait long, and I must work now. Hmm, have you searched the cities for their armories yet?"

"What?" I tried to not grab Svetu and shake the little bastard, reminding myself that He was a God, not just another annoying fucking Gnome.

"The Armories! The city Armories of Himnel and Narkolt. What, you thought that the Legion was all they had? Think, boy! Why would an empire that had war golems not have them set to protect their cities?!"

"I thought they had been destroyed or something. I mean, why the hell wouldn't they be there now, marching around the damn place? Surely that wanker Barabarattas would have set them on me, given the chance!"

"Bah!" Svetu snapped, shaking His head and throwing His arms up as if to ask the world why I was such an idiot. *"The current lords wouldn't be able to command them; they're not Imperial lords, just provincial! Think! You already knew that the local lords needed your approval to have their full titles granted, right?*

"They have no Imperial Authority beyond the lowest of the low noble rankings. Why would one of them have the authority to command a garrison of war golems? Imagine the destruction they could cause! No, the local lords might be aware of them, but they'd never be able to order them."

"So where are they?" I asked, my fingers clenching as I thought about the possibilities, an entire armory in the cities, one nobody else could command…maybe…?

"In the city, no idea beyond that, I wasn't particularly interested." Svetu shrugged.

"WHAT?!" I half screamed. "What do you mean you weren't interested! It's a fucking armory, you mad bastard!"

"I <u>create</u>, while that's simply a place to store the more basic inventions, so who cares?" He shrugged.

"THEN WHY…" I paused, coughing and trying to get ahold of myself as Oracle grabbed my arm and looked into my eyes warningly. "Okay! *Okay*…right. Lord Svetu, if you don't think much of the armories, and don't know where they are, why did you mention them?" I asked through gritted teeth.

"Because they'll be where the garrisons are," Svetu said with a noncommittal shrug. *"The main storage facilities that are holding the golems from the last days of the Empire, there won't be many crafter golems there, but there were, oh, maybe half a dozen in each? Ready to make whatever was needed."*

I stared at the little bastard. "So, what you're telling me," I said as I watched Him, desperately trying to keep my tone even. "Is that somewhere in the cities, there's a cache of golems, probably crafters, definitely war golems and more, probably weapons and so on, all sealed away?"

"Of course, didn't you think the Empire would have had contingency plans?" Svetu asked. *"Amon should have taught you better than that…"*

"HE'S A DEAD THING THAT'S FUCKIN' MENTAL AND SPENDS HALF HIS DAYS SCREAMING IN MY HEAD!" I shouted. "Okay, OKAY!" I said looking at Oracle, Yen, and Lydia, who were all holding onto me now, restraining the hands that were somehow reaching for Svetu's throat. "I'm fine…I'm fine…that's okay…Thomas! Don't, seriously…" I snapped at my brother who'd stepped forward and was glaring at the God, pissed off on my behalf.

"I don't see the problem; simply order the citizens to scour the city, or use the City Command Center and check for them," Svetu said.

"We don't have control of the cities," I ground out. "Nimon does."

"Oh, of course." The God gave an eager nod. *"That's a good point. Let's hope He doesn't have access to anyone with a competing Bloodline. He'd not have bothered looking before, but now you've claimed this facility, He'll try to unseat you as Scion of the Empire."*

"WHAT?" I snarled, before Jenae stepped forward, appearing out of thin air to put a restraining hand on my chest. It looked gentle, like She was simply asking me to calm down, but it felt like I was trying to push past a mountain, as She exerted Her immortal form to keep me there.

"Jax, calm down, please," Jenae said soothingly, gesturing my team out the door. *"Svetu, thank you for that information. I admit it's not something I was aware of, but this calls for a reconsideration of our priorities. Perhaps you should seclude yourself away here for a few days and work on some weapons for us?"*

"An excellent idea, Jenae!" Svetu said brightly. *"I shall require…"*

"You'll need some materials, no doubt; I'll arrange that with my Champion. Don't let us keep you," She said and pushed me back out of the door, the others having already taken Her gesture to heart.

As soon as we were outside, She waved a hand, and the door closed with a solid click, then shimmered and faded from sight.

"I…but…He…I…" I fumed.

"Svetu is absent-minded at the best of times, Jax, and utterly frustrating in at least ninety percent of the interactions we have with Him. He is, however, a crafter and inventor without compare, and we need Him. If you provoke Him to destroy you, this helps nobody, and if you actually kill Him? Then we'd have lost one of the few advantages we have, not to mention fracturing the Pantheon, so stop and think," Jenae ordered, before sighing and going on.

"Yes, there are things we should have considered, such as the city armories. We were all aware of such things; they were commonplace in the past, but along with other things that were lost to time, it simply never seemed relevant. I cannot see the armories. This could mean that they have been concealed, no longer exist, or Nimon has taken an active hand. I recommend that you make plans to regain control of them as a matter of urgency."

"Can he really unseat me as Scion of the Empire?" I asked, and She shook Her head.

"Not entirely, no. There are others with Imperial bloodlines surviving. Barabarattas, for example, has a claim to the throne; it is a very weak one, and the Emperor Himself has anointed you. Nimon cannot simply remove you as Scion, but He could raise a competing heir and grant them divine approval. He has the power to do a great many things, but He cannot alter the past nor make reality bend to His will, not entirely. I suggest you move ahead with any plans you have to take Himnel."

"Okay…okay," I muttered, rubbing my face as I tried to calm myself. "So, we've completed this quest…is Svetu going to sort the Control Facility at the Tower for me?"

"I'll ensure He does Jax."

"Thank you. Then we need to get back to the Tower, don't we?"

Her dark frown as She nodded didn't calm my nerves one bit. *"Yes, and I would suggest you do so soon. Much is changing in the land, and Nimon is clouding the aether, preventing me from sensing much of the continent."*

"Joy…okay, thank you, Jenae." I said, and She smiled before vanishing. I glanced around the small landing and pointed to the exit in the distance. "Come on, people, let's get the fuck out of here. They can get on with building things while we fuck off."

"I've ordered the crafter golems going to the ship to go via one of the storerooms, they're going to collect a couple of dozen golem cores each as well," Oracle sent to me, communicating directly with my mind so the others didn't hear her thinking of yet another thing I should have.

I squeezed the hand that had slipped into my own as we walked down the stairs, my mind whirling.

"What now?" Thomas asked, and the others, silent until now, leaned in to listen.

"Now we go back to the Tower. We get our people together, and we try to figure out how the hell we fix this. We need to plan for the next steps, and I get the feeling our time to prepare just got cut."

CHAPTER TWENTY-ONE

Time passed quickly aboard the ship. The remaining few golems arrived not long after we'd returned to the deck, their arms full of cores. Once they were aboard, and another golem, one of the advanced servitors, had arrived, carrying the last of the gold and platinum ingots that were in storage.

I ordered us aloft, instructing the golem to stay aboard as well. The last remaining advanced could keep things going for now, at least.

That gave us a handful of war golems, all advanced or complex, three advanced servitors and the two crafters. I examined them as they arrived, letting out a relieved breath in a long sigh.

It'd worked.

They had acquired the blueprint for the Genesis Chamber when they'd disassembled one, and thankfully it was high enough quality that it could produce all the way up to advanced golems.

I'd been constantly second-guessing myself, bloody praying that they'd manage it, and that I'd not made a huge cock up in ordering them to do it, but now, knowing that they could literally build a new one for the Tower? Hell yes.

As soon as they'd all been stowed away, we'd set off. Tenandra was clearly having issues with the dozens of tons of golems aboard as we climbed to the heavens. I'd left the others to their own devices, moving to lean against the railing and staring out towards the horizon and the twin cities of Himnel and Narkolt, glowering at each other across the bay.

We were just high enough, after two hours of flight, to see the cities, so it was as much luck as anything else that let me see the barrage of lights.

"What the hell?" I straightened up, my half-formed plans for storming Himnel collapsing in my mind as ships launched from Narkolt under what had to be heavy fire.

At this distance, I could see little more than dots and flashes, but as I spun and raced for the wheelhouse, a single thought raced through my mind…what the hell had happened to my people?

I didn't think I'd sent anyone else to Narkolt, but…I frantically wracked my brain, worried I'd given an order when I was exhausted or on the ragged edge with injuries. I remembered ordering Augustus…but no, that was weeks ago, and he'd returned from that…but then I'd told him to get ready to go back there with Hannimish…he was supposed to have gone already, wasn't he…or had I just told him to go soon? Fuck!

I burst into the cabin, nearly taking the door off its hinges, and raced to the center of the room, scanning the images in the projected clouds. The world around the ship was reflected here from every angle for the pilot to see easily.

There was a slight improvement on my natural vision, but that was it.

"Tenandra, what the hell is that?" I barked, jabbing a finger at the barrage of lights and sudden clouds. Instantly, it jumped closer, but not by much.

The vision resolved from darkness with occasional smudges, flashes, and moving dots to slightly larger fuzzy images. It showed that there were more ships than I originally thought there were, but that was about it.

"What…"

"I don't know," she said. "It's too far away, Jax, all I can make out is what you can see here."

"Shit! How long to get there?"

"As burdened as we are? Eight hours, maybe nine, depending on the wind. The best speed we could get would be if we dropped the golems and overcharged the engines. Maybe we could make it in six hours, but whatever is happening will be long over by that point."

Oracle entered, drawn by my concern, and Thomas and Lydia raced in behind her, with the rest of the team spreading out on the deck with their weapons close at hand, clearly readying themselves for whatever might come.

Jian fiddled with the controls on the control chair, altering our course slightly and studying the arcane symbols that glowed on the walls around the city and the Tower.

"Seven hours is the very best we could do to the city," he confirmed. "The wind is coming in from the east, so we'll be battling a head-wind all the way, while the Tower is almost due north of us, and it's nine hours to get back to it."

"Jax, what's wrong?" Oracle asked, and I shot a response back silently.

"Are those our people?"

"I don't think so, you haven't sent anyone that I'm aware of."

I allowed myself a little sigh of relief. *"I thought, that is, I was worried…"*

"You thought you'd forgotten something, and they were our people?" Oracle asked. Swallowing hard, I nodded to her.

"Jax, Himnel and Narkolt were at war long before you even entered this realm; it's probably a raiding party from Himnel."

"Except we stole most of their ships, or the mana stones they needed to fly them, and sank a load more," I countered. She let out a sigh of her own.

"You have a point," she conceded. **"But either way, they're not our people, and…"** Oracle was cut off as one of the small dots flashed into a bright miniature sun, then vanished, with the clouds being buffeted back, shredded from the detonation.

"Looks like someone's engines went up…or a ship's cannon," Jian muttered, agreement echoing around the room.

"I wonder how many they lost from that?" Yen asked Tenandra. The wisp, standing tall and formal in her beautiful blue suit and crisp white blouse, shook her head.

"Unknown…too distant to confirm at this point, but…"

"I can make out five dots. Ships, I assume," Jian interrupted.

I winced. When Tenandra had zoomed in, we'd counted at least seven dots and smudges moving around.

"What do you wish us to do, Lord Jax?" Tenandra asked me formally. I paused, thinking it through. Where we were now was almost due west of the city of Narkolt, and due south of the Tower. If we changed direction to Narkolt, it would lose us time we might need, and it would be for people I now knew weren't our own.

Hell, I might have us head for them, only to be attacked by whoever they were.

"The Tower." A pang of guilt ate at me even as I said it. "But keep an eye on them, please." With that, I stayed for a few more minutes before I returned to the railing and stood a barrel on its end to sit on.

I stared out, watching the flashes and dots moving, wondering at those who even now were losing their lives in the distance.

It seemed surreal that it was totally silent, even more so when a couple of the ship's crew nearby, not having noticed the battle, started telling each other shitty jokes, while I watched people dying.

Hours passed before the lights finally died away, and a few of the ships were left, limping across the sky.

I counted three of them then returned to the wheelhouse and asked Tenandra what she could sense.

"There are three ships, although I suspect one might not make it, judging from that," she said ominously. I frowned, seeing a faint blurring of smoke floating behind one of the tiny dots that were now faintly identifiable as airships.

"I wonder what happened?" I muttered.

Jian shrugged slightly. "I don't know boss, but you might get to find out yet."

"Oh?"

"They're making for the Tower, as near as I can figure," he said, nodding at the misty images.

"Really?" I asked, frowning. "How can you tell?"

"Distance." He gestured to a set of symbols and numbers on one section of the wall. "We're increasing our distance from Narkolt and Himnel, but our distance to the other ships isn't changing at the same speed. As near as I can tell, their distance to the Tower is decreasing by a bit less per hour than ours. I'd bet they're slower ships, but they're heading for our home, and they'll arrive an hour or so after us at this rate."

"Should make the trip more interesting," I said, leaving the room. I found the rest of the team sitting above deck at the far end of the ship, talking quietly.

I joined them, relaxing and talking, telling a few jokes, and explaining a few things about back home that made Thomas's stories a bit more understandable to the others.

"Hey boss, why don't you talk about your home much?" Grizz asked me at one point.

Thomas chuckled. "You mean, I talk about it too much, Grizz, and he doesn't speak about it at all?"

"Nah, I've mentioned it a time or two, but…"

"But it's only been a few months for you, while it's been five godsdamned years for me!" Thomas interrupted with a pained sigh. "You have no idea what it's been like, being unable to talk about home and having to bluff your way through everything, because you're worried that you'll get caught. If I'm talking too much about home, it's because I've not been able to do it for a damn long time."

"Aye, well, ah think this be enough maudlin shit fer one day, everyone," Lydia said, standing up. "Trainin' time! Pick yer poison. Magical or physical?"

I cast a glance at Oracle to confirm my decision. "We'll teach a few spells."

"Fine," Lydia said with a quick nod. "Those who be getting taught get a pass, the rest o' yer be trainin'. Yer get an hour physical then two fightin'. We got tha rest of tha day 'til we get back to tha Tower, let's make tha most of it!"

"Phew, dodged a bullet there," I muttered, winking at Thomas.

"Only if I learn some new magic!" he said, sitting down cross-legged before me as the others crowded round. "Teach me, oh big one, you're my only hope!"

"That's what she said," I said instinctively.

Thomas winced and shook his head. "Man, that came out weird." He glared at me. "Don't you say it!"

"That's what—oh," I said, stopping. "Ha, sorry old habits and all. Uh, okay then, people!" I said quickly, noting that Lydia was frowning.

"We're going to start with three volunteers, and it'll be a healing spell, as you can never have too many healers," Oracle said. "If you've already got a healing spell, then we can count you out, if not…"

"Dammit!" Arrin cursed as Lydia grabbed him by the back of his collar and pulled him away.

"I need a healing spell," Thomas said gleefully, as much for Lydia's benefit as mine. "I had an issue with the one I used to have after my mana channels were damaged, then after Nimon's bonding, I don't know, it just wouldn't work properly. Maybe learning another will help me to figure out what I'm missing?"

"Okay, that's one," I said nodding. "Yen, are you in?" She nodded quickly. "That's two. Who has the highest mana pool of you all?" I looked around, and to everyone's surprise, Sehran lifted her hand, smiling sheepishly.

"Probably me?" she said, then shrugged. "I understand if you don't want to teach a Demon, though."

"No, no, sit down," I said. It'd never occurred to me to teach her a new spell. She was a help in the team, and her skills so far were all about distraction. But, as a non-frontline fighter, she was probably one of the best to teach it to. "We'll try, Sehran. Not sure if we can or if there will be any issues with it, but we can definitely try."

"Thank you," Sehran whispered, blushing and sitting down next to Thomas, who winked at her and took the opportunity to admire her cleavage unashamedly.

"For the rest of you, this is just the first lesson. We'll spend the rest of this flight getting you all a few spells, okay?" Oracle said.

The rest of the team moved away, a few groans and a few smiles filling the air as they went, and I looked to Oracle in question.

"Well, yeah, it's painful and seriously tiring teaching people this way, but it's worth it. If we can get the entire team to have a healing spell, even if they're practically useless with it, they might be able to save each other's lives, one day. Besides, when we spoke about this with the Legion, wasn't it always the plan to teach everyone at least a healing and a ranged spell?" Oracle said with a self-conscious shrug.

"It was, and well done," I acknowledged, smiling. "I think as busy as we always are, things keep getting put aside to be dealt with later. We need to make more time."

"Besides, I got a lot of practice working with Heph to teach the volunteers with Restun, so it's not as hard as it was."

"How did that go?" I asked, suddenly aware I'd not asked this before.

"It was fine. We taught them a set of ranged spells as we discussed. As we were there anyway, I made a few changes to the plan. Instead of the original plan, where we let the first sixteen have the spells from the books and the remaining thirty-two wait, we worked through them in a day, just about, got them all trained, then I left Restun to break them in. It saved us the books in case we need them later, as well."

"I felt sorry for them," Yen said with a quirk of a smile. "I saw Restun leading them on a field march at one point. He was taking them out and having them fire in a barrage at anything that moved. They weren't getting much experience, as they were all sharing it, but when something is hit by nearly fifty fire, ice, dark, and lightning bolts all at once…well." She smiled.

"They were killing beasts they'd never have a chance against individually, and Restun was ordering their allocations. All Intelligence, Wisdom, and Perception. Physical traits, he's decided to beat into them."

"Wow." I winced as I thought about the volunteers. All were ordinary people that the Primus Praetoria was making into a squad of shipboard marines. The mental image of the surprise that they'd be for an enemy, though…

"Remind me to make sure they all get Magic Missile, as well," I said, imagining the spread of five darts, magnified by forty-eight casters blasting across the distance to take down the engines of an airship.

"Anyway!" Oracle interrupted. "We're going to teach you all the spell we use most of all, Surgeon's Scalpel. This is a highly evolved healing spell, made possible by repeated evolutions and by both Jax's and my own background knowledge. You won't end up with the same spell, so I need to be really clear about this." She looked around, making sure the others were paying attention and understood what she was saying.

"You *might* not even end up with a working spell, although that's exceedingly rare. You should end up with a basic healing spell that's adjusted slightly by both your own medical and magical knowledge and as much of Jax's and my knowledge as we can cram into it.

"Thomas will have an advantage here, in that he has a similar level of background knowledge as Jax does, plus he already had a healing spell. Yen is an experienced and highly trained legionnaire, as such your knowledge of how to break creatures might result in a slightly different version of the spell, anyway. Sehran…"

"My knowledge is rather more specialized." Sehran winked at Thomas, who'd been unsubtly admiring her chest and long legs. Thomas grinned at her, and as always, was totally unashamed of being caught, as she went on. "I was taught to bring pleasure and pain to mortals of all kinds. As such, I know a great deal about many arts that are connected to healing, so this should be interesting."

"It certainly should," Oracle agreed, smiling. "Okay then, I want you all to clear your minds, close your eyes, and sit back." Oracle shifted her form, climbing to her feet and stepping in front of me. She shrank to half her normal height, standing only slightly taller than I was sitting, and reached out one hand, laying it lovingly on my forehead.

I closed my eyes, feeling her reaching out to the others as well, as she seemed to order her mind and my own into one. I felt our knowledge being examined and focused on.

We started at the beginning, or the closest we could, seeing the birth of life as we knew it, with cells and genetics. I saw oxidation and respiration as cells developed, replicating and rebuilding, replacing damaged and discarded limbs. We spent time ordering our knowledge as best we could. I felt it mirrored in Thomas's mind, as for the first time, Oracle had a second source to draw upon, building and layering our joint medical and biological knowledge with our newly gained and hard-earned magical experience.

I felt theories being examined by the sudden joint intelligence that wasn't Oracle, Thomas, or myself, but a strange mélange of all three, with the subsidiary nodes of Yen and Sehran contributing strange touches of knowledge here and there.

It all intertwined, concepts that were examined and cross-referenced, knowledge that underpinned theories being adjusted and extraneous details being thrown aside as they were found to be incorrect or lacking.

I grabbed my head, wincing as a mana migraine I'd had virtually no warning for flared, and I felt and heard the others experiencing it as well, then it got worse.

Groans rose, then cries of pain. Once my mana bar was fully depleted, my health started to go. I opened my eyes wide, staring up at Oracle as she stood before us all, shaking and beginning to glow.

Patterns raced across her skin, clothes faded in and out, hair changed color and parts of her seemed to wink out of existence entirely, all the while she grew brighter and brighter, and our health drained…

"Hold on. Just a little longer…"

We all heard her voice, echoing as she called out in our minds. The knowledge built, reinforcing itself over and over again. Theories were created and tested, some discarded, others pruned, some were found to be better and were lifted up as proof.

Seconds turned to minutes as we all moaned and gritted our teeth, before someone pressed the rim of a glass vial to my mouth. I opened my eyes again, only just realizing I'd squeezed them shut in pain.

I looked up at Tang, who nodded to me as I swallowed. Then he replaced the vial with another, even as my mana shot upward. The second vial was health, and the others were given similar treatment. The various symbols in my vision that referenced them changed as they began to recover.

"Thank you…" I mumbled, frowning as I tried to make sense of the world.

"What happened?" Tang asked, his voice seemingly coming from a great distance, but I was gone again, swept away on the rushing tide of knowledge as more and more details built.

The experiences of the others were layered atop those of Thomas, Oracle, and me. I sensed our combined years of medical knowledge, our training, both in our private lives and elsewhere. The years of bandaging and dressing the wounds we gained in our Dreams were layered atop our basic medical training in the army, then the more advanced specialized training we were given at the Baron's citadel.

Years of watching crappy medical dramas with only a slight relationship to the truth were examined, and the last few months of our own experiences, the scanning we'd developed, the heals we'd learned to do.

Oracle and the others had needed to strip my skin from me, literally flaying me alive to separate me from my melted armor, and this time I saw it from both sides, as the victim and the healer.

The layers of knowledge wove together, building.

The scan was the first layer, a more in-depth version than we'd developed earlier, now driven with new knowledge, mostly gained from the experiences of Oracle examining my bones and joints at a genetic level to improve them, added to the needs to remove any corruption or foreign matter.

Next came the weaves that would stabilize a new patient and more, sanitizing and clearing out infected wounds, setting bones, replacing muscles and reattaching limbs. All of it was examined and worked into the new framework.

More vials were given out and drained, and the sun started to draw low in the sky by the time it was done. Oracle collapsed into my arms, and all of us sagged onto the deck, a new set of notifications blinking away merrily.

Congratulations!

You have completed a Divine Quest: Rescue my Gear

The God Svetu has charged you with recovering items He and His chosen people require to construct their wonders. As these items are currently in a Goblin-infested pit, He recommends you kill the Goblins first.

Kill the Goblins: 830/830

Kill the Goblin Matriarch 1/1

Recovery of missing tools 3/3

Reward: A working Control Facility for the Great Tower and secondary links on each of your captured sites (requires further investment and construction), 100,000xp, additional golems and resources.

I grunted and dismissed that one, and the one for finding the missing mining golem, knowing that the relevant ones were yet to come.

Congratulations!

You have reached level 10 in Life Magic!

All Life Magic spells you cast will now cost 10% less and be 10% more effective!

As you have reached your first evolution in Life Magic through constructing a new personal spell, you may choose to imbue this spell with a deeper understanding of the nature of Life Magic, granting all who learn it an additional +2 to their own Life Magic skill, or you may choose from the following two evolutions.

*

OPERATION:

All invasive magic you use to heal, not harm, will be 10% more effective than usual, as you gain a fundamental understanding of the interactions between your magic and the living bodies of those you assist. This will be characterized most notably by the ability to pause healing in certain areas as you work on deeper tissues, before rolling the healing forwards as those larger issues are resolved.

New Ability Gained:

> **Temporal Flow**
> Temporal Flow allows you to slow perceived time around a living creature by a factor of 1% per hour for every 100 mana invested.
>
> *Note: This will only work on ALLIES.*

IMPROVEMENT:

You have made great strides in improvements to your genetic code. This, however, is a highly costly affair. Improving a physical, living structure to its perfect state is something that will take many, many lifetimes. Instead of aiming for utter perfection in a single area, however, perhaps a new understanding would be better?

Ability Gained:

> **Imperfectly Perfect**
> Imperfectly Perfect allows you to see the flaws in yourself and others more accurately, thus allowing the identification of the areas most in need of work.

*

Congratulations!

You have created a new personal spell: Complex Healing!

Complex Healing:

A heavily-augmented healing spell drawing upon the linked knowledge of five beings, Complex Healing is the first in a new generation of self-guiding healing spells, and will begin to evolve on its own depending on usage.

Cost: 100 mana per minute of spell duration, with each additional minute of channeling costing a further 100 mana. This spell heals 100 health per minute while being channeled.

+2 Life Magic skill for all who learn this spell

I'd selected the first option almost before I knew what I was doing, the pain of the spell being constructed massively limiting the time I had to consider such things.

The other two options were both awesome, the final one especially making me think that I needed to get Oracle to work on the rest of me more, rather than just the knee we had agreed upon being rebuilt as a priority.

They were personally fantastic, they really were, but this spell? The one we'd just created? It could be a game-changer for the entire legion. All of this went through my mind in a split second, as I tried to focus my brain and re-engage it. It felt like I'd changed gears in my car, but had gone straight from sixth to first, and the gears were spinning wildly instead of working.

I lay there, panting and trying to get my breath back, well aware by the feeling of my skin that I'd had another godsdamned nosebleed as part of the experience. The spell I'd gained was great, it was self-guiding somehow, so in theory I could just fire and forget it, but I felt like I'd been whacked by a stick for several hours. I was much too sodding tired to be as happy as I should be, and the toll on the others, too…

I sat up and shifted Oracle around in my arms, looking down at her as she recovered. I stroked the hair back from her face, tucking it behind her ear as I spoke quietly.

"What the hell was that, Oracle? Are…are you okay?"

She winced before opening her eyes and looking up at me. They'd changed again, much as she often did, this time becoming possibly the clearest and brightest blue I'd ever seen, as she smiled up at me hesitantly.

"Sorry, my love," she whispered, forcing a smile. "I thought I could make an adjustment to the spell they'd receive on the fly. I didn't consider the consequences of trying to meld that level of knowledge into the spell before doing it."

"What happened?" I asked, confused as I looked around at the others, who were all sitting up and cleaning the blood from their faces as well.

"I took the spell we were able to teach, and I…I somehow fused the knowledge of how it worked into the spell itself, then I saw more, and more. I added this little detail, then that and more…each time finding more and more data, more skill, and more reasons that things were done this way or that. I sensed the reasons, and I found errors, I resolved them, smoothed the magic out.

"I adjusted the scanning aspect, then I tied it to a series of healing protocols, and each time I was nearly done, I found another detail, and other little reasons to keep going, feeling it building." She forced herself to sit up, then to stand, shakily, and resting one arm on my shoulders as she looked at me then around at the others.

"I'm sorry," she said. "Once I'd begun, I realized I couldn't stop, not without a massive backlash of pain for us all, and the spell would have been a failure as well. I kept going, and as a result, we've all gained a new spell, but for the pain and the experience, I'm sorry…"

"Don't be sorry, Oracle," Yen said, her eyes unfocused as she stared into the distance, reading details only she could see. "Have you seen the details of the spell?"

"Well yes, but…"

"No, no but anything, have you seen the level of healing this spell delivers?" Yen asked. "This isn't a simple or a basic spell; this is an entirely different level. It self-targets, rather than simply washing the entire spell out across the body, wasting most of the mana as most unguided spells do. This is a new spell, a totally new one; do you understand what that means?"

"Not really?" I answered.

Yen snorted, shaking her head and dismissing the screen so she could look me in the eyes. "It means it can be taught as it is. It's a unique spell. It's not going to break down to a lower level, depending on the caster's understanding of magic or medicine. It'll be passed on at this level as the baseline! Then it'll evolve from here with use…this is a spell that could save tens of thousands. It's a spell that the legion desperately needs, if we can roll this out!"

"We'll need some godsdamn rest first," I said.

"Gods, yes," Thomas said, rubbing his temples. "It feels like you just washed my brain with bleach and a scrubbing brush."

"Welcome to the joy of having your brain rewired and searched for information!" I said, grinning, before laying back down and closing my eyes. "Now, I'm going to fucking rest a bit, sorry and all, but hell no to the exercise side of things. I'm resting, and we'll deal with everything else after."

"Jax, you might want to get in here!"

I sighed, rubbing my eyes with the heels of my hands. "No, no I really don't. I want to go to sleep, and that's it, that's what I want, and maybe a fry up," I whispered, before sighing and getting to my feet. I called over to Jian who stood in the doorway to the wheelhouse. "I'm coming!" I waved to him. As he ducked back inside, I muttered to myself. "Damn well better be good, that's all I'm saying."

As I started to walk, still carrying a tired Oracle, a hand rested on my shoulder, a feeling of renewal washed through me, banishing many of my aches and the tiredness that made my brain throb.

I turned and looked at Sehran, who was walking to my right, headed to rejoin Jian with me, and she smiled.

"I'm sure you can't guess why a Succubus might be experienced with stamina recovery and boosting spells," she said, giving me a bawdy wink.

"How long do they last?" Oracle asked, sitting up slowly as Sehran reached out to touch her as well, casting the same spell again.

"Thirty minutes, usually. There can be a crash after that, though, be warned!"

"Damn, that's all I need," I muttered.

"Thirty minutes is always more than I need," Sehran purred, before laughing at the look on my face and slipping past me as we entered the wheelhouse. "Thank you for the spell, both of you, honestly. It makes a very pleasant change to be accepted as a person, rather than a belonging." She leaned in to kiss my cheek, then did the same to Oracle, before hurrying away to join Jian where he sat in the control chair.

I couldn't help but admire her ass as she went, before sighing and looking at Oracle, who had shifted back to her full size.

"She's not even using a glamor spell," Oracle said, shaking her head. "She's just naturally that sexy. I think I need classes from her."

"No. Hell, no, you don't." I kissed her before something out of the corner of my eye drew my attention, and I broke off the kiss, staring wide-eyed at the image that hung in the clouds of mist and vapor. "Holy shit…what the…"

"Storm Demon," Sehran said as she identified the creature. "We need to stay clear of it."

"I don't think we can," Jian said, gesturing to the image next to it. I moved around the room to stand behind him, staring at the multiple images that made up one wall of the cabin now.

Three ships were left from those that had fled Narkolt, and one was noticeably on fire, listing, and under attack. Three other creatures swooped in and around the ship, flashing down to land and grab the sailors. They dragged them over the side, leaving them to spiral to the ground as their arms and legs frantically kicked and thrashed.

The first Storm Demon, the one that Sehran had identified, was much like the others, only bigger and clearly not interested in the failing ship…it was chasing the other two.

Where the other three Demons were just about far enough away that they couldn't be seen clearly, they were obviously of the same overall breed as the one that flashed through the building storm, chasing the other ships.

It was large and humanoid, in that it had two arms and two legs, but it also had a massive wingspan and a large head that was dominated with horns that curved forwards, ending in wicked points. It had glowing, bright red eyes and grey, stone-like skin.

It looked to be heavily muscled, and it twisted and turned in the air, easily dodging the occasional flash of magic that was hurled at it.

"How far away are they?" I asked Tenandra.

"Just under an hour away," Jian said. "They've been pushing their ships damn hard." He gestured even as he twisted a dial on the desk, and the view adjusted slightly to show the ships better.

They were still too far out to make out a great many details, but even at this range, their engines were flaring a bright blue that seemed insane to me, considering the usual steady pulse of our own engines.

"And how long if we pushed hard?" I asked.

"Forty minutes." Tenandra confirmed, resting one hand on Jian's shoulder and smiling down at him, before Sehran spoke up.

"That's a Storm Demon, Lord Jax. I don't know what you know about them but-"

She was cut off by a massive blast of lightning that erupted from its open maw, slamming into the side of one of the ships and sending it reeling, barely missing the engines.

"Holy shit!" I gasped. The lightning bolt had been huge, easily as thick around as I was, and it'd carved a thick furrow in the side of the ship before it cut off, sparking fires to life, not to mention sending the ship reeling like a punch-drunk boxer as the helmsman lost control at least temporarily.

"That's only one reason you don't mess with the storm," Sehran said. "They literally live in the storms; some no longer even need to return to our realm, living off the ambient mana in the storm. These don't look like those, and that's a wonderful thing, because it means we might survive this, if you're serious about involving ourselves in this fight."

"Go on," I told her, examining the ships as the crews sprinted back and forth and people tried to put the fires out. A handful of mages were flinging spells upwards at the creature, only to have it slip aside on the currents of the wind. Here and there, archers loosed arrows, but they fared no better. I shook my head at the idiocy.

There was no way a bloody arrow was going to go where you wanted in the level of wind affecting the ships, let alone not be noticed by a creature that could dodge spells in flight.

"Do we know who they are yet?" I asked, getting a series of shaking heads, until Tenandra nodded slowly, gesturing to another wall and the image that slowly appeared.

It was fuzzy and out of focus, made worse by distance and by what looked like heavy rain at the time the image had been seen, but...

I strode to the door and shoved it open, leaning out and shouting to the others.

"Yen, Grizz, and Lydia, get your arses in here!" I shouted, and they sprinted over. Thomas followed after a few seconds.

"What's up, boss?" Grizz asked, and I gestured at the image.

"What's that look like to you?"

"It's...well...hmmm..." he said, rubbing his chin in thought.

"It looks like legionnaire armor," Lydia said, sounding unsure as she glanced from her own armor to the image, frowning.

"No, well, not entirely..." Yen corrected, gesturing to the shoulders. "These are too wide, and it's too reflective, but I suppose it could be the light, and the image...maybe?"

"So what you're saying is, it's similar to legion armor, and it might actually be legion...with a bunch of ships that fought their way out of Narkolt, and they're flying straight for the Tower, right?" I asked, getting a round of nods. "Well, shit."

"There's no way to be certain, not at this distance," Tenandra said. "I'm sorry, Jax, but that was the only time I saw that figure, so I can't say for certain if there are others below deck. But there were figures moving about until the latest attack began. They all hid below."

"Shit," I cursed again. "Fine, we have to assume that those ships are legion ships. For now, all we know is that they're running for the Tower, and they're under heavy attack. Tenandra, Jian, plot a course to the ships, get us in there. Lydia, get everyone ready, Oracle," I said, before breaking off uncertainly.

"I can do it, and I won't make any changes. Just the standard, this time," she said in response to my unspoken question.

"Thank fuck. Okay, Thomas, help Oracle. You're going to be the source for her to bridge the knowledge of Magic Missile to the others. I want everyone to know that damn spell, as it's the most maneuverable one I know."

"Of course," Thomas said.

"Oracle, how many..."

"Three others at a time. It's faster that way; I can use Thomas for the source, then do the others in batches of three. But are you really sure you want to teach Grizz more magic? It is Grizz after all, not to mention Giint."

"Oh, I'm sure I don't want either of them casting spells," I responded with a grin. "But, unfortunately, that's just how shit outta options we are. Teach them all as quick as you can, please, Oracle."

I turned to Sehran. "Okay, tell me about these Storm Demons."

"Yes, Lord Jax," Sehran said formally. "They are known by their full name as Oshi'unru'kai in our realm. They live for the storms, and it's considered a great act of dishonor for one of them to set foot upon the land unless it's for one of three reasons: to give birth, to claim the corpse or belongings of an enemy, or to accept the surrender of an enemy faction.

"Any other reason usually results in the offender being made a crawler. That's their term for any creature that can't fly, by the way. They say we all crawl across the ground, while they soar over it. They tear the wings off an offender if they catch them on the ground."

"No warnings?" I asked.

"That is the warning," Sehran said grimly. "A second offence, thanks to our regeneration abilities, involves their wings being torn off again, them being taken as high up as possible, and the carrier diving as fast as possible, then throwing them at the ground. With their entire family, if the offence is bad enough."

"Friendly sort," I muttered.

She quirked a smile. "Well, you know, we *are* Demons."

"Yeah, but you're a lot friendlier."

"Well, yeah, but, you know, succubai are more the exception to the rule. We like our playthings to be happy with us. And, as we are long-lived compared to most mortal races, well, we view the times where we get to interact with the other realms as a special time in our lives, worthy of the extra effort being made."

"Well, that's great, glad we're entertaining for you..." I squinted at the images again. "Okay, Tenandra, I know you've not got your weapons made yet, but you've had some time to play with the ship, so show me what you can do. We have refugees to rescue."

With that, Tenandra grinned at me and shifted, widening her stance and lifting both hands into the air theatrically, before she started to glow slightly. She pulled her hands down as though dragging an invisible bar down from above her head to her waist then shot both hands forward, and the ship responded. The engines shifted from a steady *thrum* to a powerful roar, and Jian whooped in excitement at the sudden surge of acceleration.

The chase was on.

CHAPTER TWENTY-TWO

I nodded to Tenandra and Jian, striding out and onto the deck, even as she passed the order to the crew to get below decks. The other legionnaires who'd been about the ship congregated with us, joining in as Oracle continued to teach the groups.

"Okay, people!" I called to the team before me. "Here's a quick update for you: we've got three ships…" There was a boom in the distance, faint and weak, but audible, as one of the ships, the damaged one that was trailing behind, suddenly exploded. The engines took the rest of the ship out in a sudden massive discharge of magic.

The explosion was so powerful that it stripped one of the Storm Demons from the sky, sending it plummeting uncontrollably, trailing smoke.

"Two…okay, we've got *two* ships that are under concentrated attack by Storm Demons. We don't know who's aboard, or why they're headed for the Tower, but they were under heavy attack as they fled Narkolt, and they want to get to us, so that's good enough for me. We're going to step in, shred the fuckers that are attacking them, and see who's coming for tea. Any questions?"

There were a few seconds of silence, before one of Westin's people spoke up.

"Uh…Lord Jax, the Lady Wisp…ummm…she said she was going to teach us all…spells?" the massive legionnaire asked. He was the kind of guy who looked like he should be towing trucks for kicks and bench-pressing small continents, but he asked hesitantly, lifting his hand to ask the question.

I looked at him for a long while, trying to decide if he wanted that, if he was afraid of it, or what. Meanwhile, he grew redder and redder behind his massive bushy black beard, shifting on the balls of his feet nervously.

"Yes, I'd like you all to be able to cast spells," I confirmed. He grinned, nudging a legionnaire standing by his side excitedly.

"Thank you, my Lord!" he said, ignoring the much smaller elven legionnaire he'd nearly knocked off her feet in his excitement.

"My intention is that *all* legionnaires will be able to cast at minimum, a healing spell, a ranged attack, such as the Magic Missile spell that Oracle is working on today, and a shield spell, with buffs being considered as well," I said.

"Now, unfortunately, we're not going to have time to get everyone trained up before the fight starts, buuuut…we will have some of you ready, and I want you all to wait to fire the first barrage as one, that should make it doubly shocking and effective. We also have a secret weapon, and if it comes to it, I'll need a few volunteers for that." I indicated the covered figures of the golems, laying out my plans for them all, getting nods of approval from Westin, Lydia, and many of the legionnaires.

In groups of three at a time, Oracle taught first Lydia and her squad, then the legionnaires under Westin. It took just under ten minutes per group to pass across the Magic Missile spell, and with those who knew it already, namely myself, Thomas, and Arrin, and Bane not being with us, meant that Oracle managed to teach four groups, getting four of Westin's people up to speed as well.

I'd started to flag, the stamina crash that Sehran had warned me about hitting hard, until she hit me with the spell again, sending me close to the edge of hysteria.

I strode into the middle of the groups, leaving Oracle to work with her current one to the side, even as we closed in on the ships ahead. They'd seen that we were closing on them, and after some initial hesitation, had held their course, clearly unsure of who we were.

I had a momentary thought about a flag or something, then I shrugged, dismissing the thought. They'd presumably have a spyglass aboard. As far as I knew, I was the only big bastard who went around wearing full legion armor and wielding a naginata.

"Okay people!" I called, when we were about five minutes out, and the Storm Demon had altered its course to watch us as well, closing the distance to its prey. "Get ready! I don't know why it's only attacking now and then, but…"

"Jax!" Sehran screamed, running out and waving at us all frantically. "The armor! Get rid of the armor!!!"

"What?!" I asked, before feeling a strange tingle in the air, and a thickness that felt very wrong.

I looked up. The grey clouds that had been spreading out across the sky had darkened. The Storm Demon let loose a sudden scream of joy as a deep rumble filled the air.

"Fuck!" Grizz screamed, reaching for his helm and pulling it off, dumping it into his bag. "Lightning!"

"The fucker is summoning lightning, get rid of the metal!!" There was a collective pause as we all grasped what he'd said, then everyone moved, rushing to strip off their armor and to get away from the bands of copper that ran across the ship, frantically trying to get free of any metal that could act as a conductor.

The charge continued to build, before the Storm Demon unleashed a sudden blast of lightning, one that slammed into the second ship, tearing through the wheelhouse's flimsy walls and punching clean out the far side of the ship.

There were a few seconds of silence, broken only by the wind whistling wildly, before the engines stopped and the screams started.

The Demon had not only killed the helmsman, but something in the ship that regulated the way the engines interacted had been destroyed, too.

All six engines, one-by-one, went dark, flickering out as the mighty ship soared on for several seconds, slowly dipping forwards, as it began to build up speed, the wind hitting its sails and starting an uncontrolled spin, as the massive ship plummeted towards the ground.

I'd stepped up to the railing, the distance between us all being less than a mile at this point, and I contemplated trying to reach the ship, leaping over the side and flying to it…

But I knew I was too late, even as it picked up speed.

The ship spiraled down faster and faster, with faint screams floating on the wind, fury and hatred, terror and pleading, all being ignored as the Storm Demon dove after the ship, reaching out and snatching up falling sailors, tearing them apart, taking bites, then flinging them away, and clearly reveling in the deaths.

"Why?" I asked, looking at Sehran, as I pulled the last of my armor off, standing there in my under tunic and pants. "Why did it wait until now?"

"The fear. Some Demons deserve the legends you have about them. They glory in the fear, in crushing the dreams and hopes of other sentients. Not many, but some. Some are all your legends warn you against and more."

"And the storm?"

"It will have taken time to build a true storm here, then when it saw us, it probably hoped we'd come so it could play with us, as well." Sehran glared down at the huge Demon as its massive wings beat, sending it arcing around towards us, clearly intent on a flyby. "It will have held the storm back, building it as long as it could, and now?"

The first wash of rain began to hit our decks, no longer the gentle, warm rain that had come off and on through the day. It was replaced with a cold rain that numbed the skin.

"Now, it's set the storm loose, and we'll have to weather it."

"How long?" I asked her grimly, tightening my grip on my naginata, well aware it could act as a lightning rod, but unwilling to stand here without a weapon when a Demon with a ten-meter wingspan was planning on murdering me. "How long will the storm last?"

"Not long. Not even a Demon as large and powerful as that can affect so large an area as this with weather magic for long. A single spark might have set the storm off, and it'll be powerful, but it won't last long, maybe half an hour to an hour, less probably," Sehran said. "I think, anyway, it's not really my area of expertise."

"Fine, thank you, Sehran. When I tell you to, I want you to distract that fucker." I got a dubious nod as I turned to the rest of the team, Oracle's face wan as she flew to my side. The last three who had been learning Magic Missile were now stripping off their armor with the help of the others as she landed on my shoulder, shrinking down to her smaller size.

"Legionnaires!" I called out, getting everyone's attention. "I need ranged fighters lined up on the deck, I want archers ready and waiting, with everyone holding a shield as we discussed, get ready!"

The air seemed almost torn as the Demon rocketed past, the leathery bat wings making a bone-rattling boom as it beat them. It zipped across the deck less than thirty feet above us. It was close enough that I saw its glowing red eyes and heard the feral hiss it made, baring teeth a great white would have been proud of.

It screamed its bloodlust, flipping over and curving around to maintain a watch on us as it circled the ship, and I finally got a chance to see it more clearly.

The skin was grey and leathery, with a surprisingly muscled frame, atrophied legs, and a long tail with a barbed tip. The upper arms were long and the muscles were well-defined, with six-fingered claws flexing as it stared down at us.

The head was wide with sharp horns angling back from the middle in a design that had clearly evolved for flight. It was all smooth skin, with a V-shaped jaw filled with serrated teeth. The nose was a pair of slits, and the eyes were recessed, glaring out as it watched us. The final touch, two large bone sails that looked like axe-heads swept backwards, coming out of either cheek and just combined to make the bastard ugly as all hell.

It screamed again, and the thunder rumbled overhead, so close now that the entire ship seemed to shake with it. A sudden burst of heavy rain rattled across the deck, icy cold and interspersed with hailstones that dinged and clattered off our weapons and shields.

I didn't like holding this much steel, not with the thickness of the air and the way the damn thing could hurl lightning, but without it?

The option of hurling bad language didn't seem quite as effective.

Everyone lined up, the six archers lifting their bows and tracking the Storm Demon as it spun and dipped in the winds, while the rest of us held shields to ostensibly protect the archers.

The second Demon closed the distance as well, screeching something as it came, before releasing a much weaker blast of lightning from its mouth. It tore a line across the deck and sent a half dozen legionnaires diving aside.

It broke off the attack, diving towards us, arms outstretched, clearly intent on grabbing Grizz, who was pushing himself back to his feet, when I cried out a single word.

"FIRE!" I roared, and I twisted my shield aside, exposing my right hand and the clutch of Magic Missiles that I'd summoned, hovering ready.

The others did the same, eight of us in total had been able to finish the cast, keeping our hands hidden by the shields, and the resulting forty glowing darts flashed out, the barrage slamming over and over into the oncoming Demon.

Nearly thirty darts hit, even as maneuverable as the creature was, thanks to the twin wonders of surprise and the lack of cover it had. Of those twenty-seven hits, seven tore holes in its left wing that would have caused it serious issues alone, even without any of the others hitting.

Eight more impacted across its chest and waist, blowing holes up to an inch deep in muscle and bone, sprays of blood erupting as it jerked over and over, shuddering with the force of the impacts.

Six impacted the twin sets of shoulders, both its upper arms and the enormous, muscled connectors for the wings showed exposed bone, spurting blood and glistening flesh.

Three darts hit it in the face, one taking out a bulbous eye, making the orb explode in a brief shower of vitreous fluid and gristle. A second tore its cheek open to the bone exposing the shining teeth below, and the last smashed free a section of the bone sail, the left upper most point spiraling away into the air, vanishing towards the trees below.

The final three darts were either the most vicious or lucky, depending on your point of view. They slammed into the dangling, wind-whipped manhood the Demon had been proudly displaying.

The spray of blood and the screech of utter horror and disbelief as its member spiraled away, following the section of horn towards the forest below, was ear-splitting and caused the Demon to double over.

While this was entirely understandable to any male who saw the fight, it was also a terminally bad idea when flying towards the deck of a ship, as it changed the Demon's point of aim downwards by about three meters.

There was a crunch, and the ship shuddered as the Demon ploughed into the side at full speed, and that was it. Most of us stepped up to the side and glanced down, watching as the broken form was slowly peeled off the ship by the winds to tumble away into the rain like a bug who'd just met its first windscreen on a motorway.

I turned, watching the larger Demon as it circled slowly, watching us.

Clearly, it was unconcerned by the death of its brethren, but in killing it, we'd given up the first of our surprises.

I pointed at it, then gave it the finger, knowing damn well it wouldn't get the point, but figuring it'd guess it was being insulted.

"Nice and subtle," Thomas said. I looked over at him, seeing him clambering onto the top of the wheelhouse.

"You know me. What the hell are you doing, Thomas?"

He grinned. "Well, you want him to come and play, don't you?"

I shook my head, sighing. "Do I really want to know what…"

"Remember the Jamaican lads?"

I frowned, vaguely remembering that fight. It'd started when one of them, one of the few other twins in the area, had found out that the girl who'd dumped him, had done it because she was fucking Thomas. The lad had gone round, screaming abuse, and Thomas had stood in the upstairs window, naked, and spun…

"Oh fuck. Get casting!" I shouted, lifting both hands and concentrating on dual casting the spell, even as Thomas was undoing his pants and throwing his top aside.

"Oi, you ugly fucker!" Thomas screamed into the driving rain as we searched for the Demon. The damn thing had vanished into the clouds again, and instead of reappearing on the far side, it'd clearly decided to hide. "Come on! Daddy's got something for ya!" Thomas helicoptered his cock and turned slowly on the upper deck, making sure that wherever it was, it'd see the show.

"Well, that's put me off my supper!" Yen called to Lydia above the rising winds, while Oracle just sniggered.

"Hey, it's a cold wind!" Grizz shouted, laughter clear in his voice. "Don't blame him too much; it's not his fault he's only small…"

"Watch for the fucker! Tenandra, you see him?" I asked the empty air and a second later I heard her voice in my mind.

"It must be using an ability, I can find no trace of…"

There was a flash of light from below, and an arc of lightning tore across the side of the ship, ripping an engine free of its supports.

The engine blasted away into the sky before its charge ceased, and the lightning cut off as Tenandra swung the ship to one side, avoiding the rest of the blast. I made it to the edge, staring down just in time to see the figure diving back into the cover of the clouds…clouds which were pulling in around us, enveloping the ship in a grey, wet cocoon that obscured everything.

"Motherfucker!" Thomas shouted, staggering and falling to the deck, grabbing onto it with both hands as the ship tilted.

"That'll teach you!" I shouted up to him, still holding both spells ready, a total of ten darts glowing with golden light, hovering above my palms, waiting for a target.

Distant screams and a flash of light briefly illuminated the clouds, before they grew dim again, and I swore.

"There!" shouted Lydia, thrusting her hands forward and firing her five bolts into the clouds at a swirl of movement. Others fired immediately, and I barely stopped myself joining in, as the clouds were illuminated again, this time with flashes of golden light.

A noise to my right made me whip around, glaring into the clouds, sure I'd heard the wind of its passage, but seeing nothing.

A few seconds later, another voice on the far side of the ship shouted in alarm, and a flare of light showed more firing.

The next few minutes dragged on like this, a sudden movement, and people were firing their spells off, then frantically summoning them again, even as those who waited, were forced to reabsorb the spells as they grew too unstable, having been held for too long.

One of Westin's legionnaires was the first, calling out in concern.

"I'm out of mana!" he shouted, echoed seconds later by another, then Grizz joined in. More and more were nodding and backing away from the edges of the railing, suddenly dry in their excitement over the new spells, when the Demon struck again.

This time, it flashed down from overhead, streaking across the deck and reaching out almost lazily, its flashing claws relieving one of Westin's legionnaires of her head in a single strike.

The body paused in the act of stepping back, seeming to hang there, suspended by an invisible string as blood spurted upwards in a fountain before it collapsed backward.

"Amis!" one of the legionnaires roared, sprinting forward and throwing himself to the deck, rolling and reaching out for her body, only to be grabbed by the third and final Demon, who'd clearly decided to strafe across the deck behind the first.

It grabbed onto the back of the big man's jerkin and yanked him upright, lifting him from the deck then releasing him with a roar of amusement, sending the massive man plummeting into the clouds, screaming in terror.

"Fuck!" I shouted, turning and looking as Lydia sprinted to the edge of the railing and hurled herself off, diving after him.

I hesitated for a pair of heartbeats, then saw a shadow in the clouds diving past again.

They'd seen her wings and had to have drawn her out deliberately.

I looked to Yen desperately, and she nodded, knowing what I wanted. I ran and jumped, even as she started to bark orders to the rest of our people, clearing the railing and slamming my shield back into my bag, yanking out the naginata in its place.

I activated Soaring Majesty, hurling myself down through the thick grey clouds, unable to see anything as I fell, the whistle of the wind cutting off any sound. I frantically looked around, trying to see anything, squinting against the rush of air as it tore tears from my eyes.

Seconds passed before suddenly I was out of the clouds, plummeting toward the ground, the tops of the trees only a few hundred meters below me. Ahead and to the left, Lydia beat her wings, diving hard after the falling man, apparently unaware of the larger Demon closing in on her from behind.

I twisted toward her, pushing hard on my Ability and feeling my health and mana drop. Heartbeats thundered in my ears as I pushed harder and harder, closing the distance and angling myself to come up on the creature from behind, not daring to cast a spell, as I needed the mana so badly.

Lydia reached out. Her fingers fumbled, strained, and closed the last inches before she managed to grab the man's boot. She pulled him toward her frantically, and the big man grabbed onto her with panic clear in his eyes as she flared her wings, pulling up and trying to adjust her flight from ploughing into the ground at full speed.

As soon as she flared her wings, catching as much air as possible and slowing, the Demon closed the distance, reaching out, its claws flexing in anticipation of rending her flesh.

Before it could reach her though, I reached it, my blade slamming into the first joint of its right wing and shearing it off, sending the leathery appendage flapping away on the wind. Its former owner screamed in pain and fear, flipping over as its one good wing beat instinctively, sending the creature plummeting to its doom.

I flashed toward Lydia, grinning at the legionnaire who clung to her like a child seeking reassurance from its mother. I slid my weapon into my bag, seeing how hard Lydia was beating the air, still struggling to clear the trees, as I reached out.

I drew alongside her, her left hand grabbing my right, and I pulled up, even as I spun myself around, facing her and grabbing her other arm at the elbow where it was wrapped around the legionnaire.

The clouds roiled overhead. My health and mana hit half, and I gritted my teeth, hauling upward and pushing down with equal ferocity.

Our path slowly changed from aiming at the ground, to arcing upward again. Seconds later, we were ascending, climbing through thick clouds and heavy rain, frantically searching for the ship as we went. I clung to Lydia's arms, and she shifted her grip to cling to me, slamming her mighty wings down, lifting us faster and harder with each beat.

"There!" shouted the legionnaire, pointing to a shadow in the clouds. We looked, ready to dodge, only to see it grow and grow, becoming the underside of a ship's hull.

"Go!" I screamed to Lydia.

Using her wings for power, letting me do the majority of the directing, we climbed past the side of the ship, reaching up and out. Lydia twisted us around, flaring her wings and giving a final almighty beat, blasting back a trio of unfamiliar men holding halberds with the sheer force of her wings.

Then we landed, and I cut off the flow to my Ability. Lydia shook out her wings and let them droop in exhaustion, while the legionnaire grabbed the deck, seemingly intent on holding onto it for dear life.

"Halt!" a voice said. I looked up wearily, feeling physically and mentally drained, only to see another half dozen men running out from an ornate wheelhouse, all brandishing weapons, while a fop in gold and silver inlaid armor peered around the corner of the door at us, apparently terrified.

"Who be you! What…" One of the men, a wild-eyed and sweat-drenched brute of a man who looked to have been interrupted mid-shave yelled at me. I grabbed the head of his halberd, swiping his weapon aside, shaking my head and standing up.

"Fuck's sake!" I swore. "Wrong godsdamned ship!"

CHAPTER TWENTY-THREE

I staggered slightly and grabbed Lydia's hand when she started to stand as well, helping her, as she tiredly folded her wings and glared around.

"Well fuck," Lydia muttered, as the guards encircled us, pointing their weapons and waiting for the order to be given.

"Where is it? Actually, where are they?" I mumbled, turning in a slow circle, staring out into the clouds, and squinting. I couldn't see anything, not with my eyes, but with my soul, and my heart. I felt it, as I shifted my mind and perception slightly, making the world come alive in a new and fantastic overlay of strings and threads.

Gossamer spider's webs and chains seemingly forged of iron and gold, appeared in my vision, leading from me outward, and from the void beyond the clouds leading back to me. "There!" I said after a few seconds, picking a small number of threads out, and a single ruby red and gold rope, thick as my leg, that led me straight to Oracle. "There's the ship."

"What do we do?" Lydia asked, ignoring the guards as if they were beneath her. "Do we fly?"

"You...you, stay where you are!" the same half-shaved man barked at her, jabbing his halberd forward in warning.

The legionnaire on the floor finally seemed to take notice of the voices and looked up. There was an almost animal growl, then he was moving. He reached up and grabbed the haft of the weapon, using it to pull himself to his feet, sweeping the other weapons aside, and he leaped into their midst.

The first man, the unshaven one who'd spoken up, went down with a single punch, unconscious before he hit the ground. The next one over, who was standing close enough to the first that their shoulders had practically been touching, was grabbed by the front of his ornate breastplate, yanked across in front of his companions, and thrown at them, taking down two more.

Then the legionnaire really got to work as he leaped across the group. He landed inside the reach of another man's weapon, beating it aside with the outside of his wrist, then swept his leg from under him.

In less than ten seconds, he'd taken down more than half of the guards, and he looked to be getting a load of stress out, so I shrugged and left him to it. I took a swig of both a healing and a mana potion, my health and mana replenishing before I looked around the ship and squinted.

"Can't see the flying cocksucker anywhere," I muttered. Lydia grunted, reaching down and picking up one of the halberds.

"This might be all right some places, but on a ship?" she said, hefting it and looking at my bag. "Is this 'ow 'heavy your murderstick is?"

"My naginata?" I shrugged and pulled it free of my bag as the legionnaire grabbed the last guard who was trying to back away.

He was screaming and punching, shouting incoherently and clearly on the ragged edge, as I turned to him and passed the naginata to Lydia to weigh in her hands.

"Legionnaire, ATTENTION!" I barked out.

He dropped the mumbling, semi-conscious men he held in both hands. Slamming his fist to his chest in salute, back ram-rod straight, he stared at a position a few inches above and to the right of my ear. I looked at him, at his red-rimmed eyes, the tear slowly trickling down one cheek, and the generally broken condition of the men around him and nodded.

"Legionnaire, I'm sorry to have to do this to you, but for now, I need an escort, a bodyguard, someone I can entrust my life to…can I trust you?" I asked him bluntly, remembering the way he'd rushed to the dead woman's side. If I left him alone now, I might be short another legionnaire soon.

"Yes, Lord Jax!" he barked, his teeth clenched, as he shook with suppressed emotion.

"Good man! What's your name, legionnaire?"

"Alistair, sir!" the massive man barked, making me wince at the similarity between his name, and the dickhead of a tribune back at the tower.

"Well, you need some gear, Alistair. What weapon do you usually use?" I asked, reaching into my bag and searching.

"Uh…" He said before being cut off by a voice from behind.

"I say…just who the hell are you?!" The man in the stupid shiny armor asked, stepping out. He lifted his sword toward me, the tip of the blade shaking as he pointed it in my general direction. I glanced at the glorified knitting needle with clear derision.

"I'm High Lord Jax of Dravith, Scion of the Empire. This is Lydia, Lady Valkyrie, Optio of my personal guard, and this is Alistair, a legionnaire who single handedly beat the living snot out of all your guards while unarmed," I said. "Now, who the fuck are *you*, why are you headed for my Tower, and what the hell happened?"

"I…well…" he said, clearly not sure where to start, before a voice from behind him interrupted, and he turned his head glaring at someone who was hiding behind the door. "Yes, YES! I know, thank you! Now be quiet…let me talk!" He scowled, before pausing and starting again. "Well, I will if you stop interrupting! No…I…oh." He dropped the conversation we could only hear one side of, and coughed, red-faced, before stepping forward.

"I am Lord Rewn, Lord of Narkolt, and well, uh…" He gestured with his right hand, seeming to forget he was holding a sword in it.

As soon as the blade moved, Alistair was there, slapping the flat of the blade with the back of his right hand knocking it aside, then slipped forward, gripping Rewn's wrist with one hand and jabbing his thumb into a cluster of nerves in the city lord's elbow, making the short foppish man cry out as he dropped the sword.

Alistair moved to the side, then back a second later, the slim, rapier-like blade now gripped in one hand as he searched Rewn roughly, finding a dagger and that was all.

"Storage devices?" Alistair growled at Rewn, who flinched and carefully tapped the belt he wore and the three small pouches that were spaced across it. "This it?" Alistair asked. As he pulled it free, Rewn nodded shakily.

"That's fine, Alistair," I said, smiling. "What do you want, Rewn?" I asked, and he flinched before swallowing hard and rubbing his elbow.

"I…uh…well…" He was clearly rattled and trying to gather his thoughts.

"Out with it, man! We've still got a fucking Demon to kill!" I snapped my fingers, making him jump.

"I…I was attacked!" he blurted out frantically, his words falling over themselves in their haste to escape his mouth. "Drow, it was the bastard Drow! They attacked me, over and over again, killing my guards, killing my friends…then they came back! My friends were alive again, but it wasn't them! And they tried to kill me!"

"And what the hell are you doing here, Rewn?" I snapped. "Where the hell did the Demons come from!"

"I don't know!" he wailed. "There was nowhere else to turn! Hannimish said that you were a good man, that the legion served you. I went to them, I needed them, and they weren't there!"

"Well, maybe you should have thought about what happens when you need us and we're gone BEFORE all this shit," Alistair muttered in a low voice that carried.

"Well, he's not wrong." I rubbed the back of my neck. "Right, fine, so you came running to me for help, is that it?" I asked, and he nodded frantically. "Lydia, Alistair, keep watching for that fucker," I said to the pair, noting they were doing it anyway, but it felt better to make sure while I looked around, thinking.

"What do you bring to me?" I asked him after a few seconds, before flashes lit up the clouds again, coming from the direction of the other ship as my little surprise clearly joined in the fun. "Dammit, I need to get back out there…" I stepped up to the railing and looked out.

"We both do," Lydia said quickly.

"I need to stay the hell on solid ground," Alistair muttered.

I grinned, seeing the way he swallowed and avoided looking down. "There's an argument for that, mate, but we need to catch a Demon first."

"Wait, you can't go!" Rewn cried, stepping forward and reaching out to me. Before he could touch my arm, Alistair was there, slapping his hand aside and glaring down at the little man.

"Ah! You struck me…again!" Rewn clutched at his hand. "Legionnaire…how dare you!" he whined. I shook my head in disgust.

"Fuck's sake, I asked you a question, Rewn!" I snapped. "I'm wasting time on you, when you've already caused the death of one of my legionnaires. Now tell me what you offer, or we're leaving this shithole of a ship!"

"What do you want?" he whimpered, tears streaming down his face and ruining what was clearly carefully applied makeup. "I thought you were different! Hannimish said you helped people!"

I was torn between feeling terrible for this man and wanting to backhand the fucker into the middle of next week to try and make him aware of the realities of life.

"I…oh, for fuck's sake. Okay," I growled.

"There!" Lydia shouted, casting her Magic Missile as a shadow blurred past, dragging a wake of disturbed air with it. I caught sight of a cruel face, jaws cracked open in hatred with blackened holes in its flesh and a forked tongue flickering over bloody teeth, before the wings beat and it was gone again, a triumphant cry echoing in the air behind it.

"Motherfucker!" I cast while frantically looking around, but it was gone long before the spell was ready. I spun and glared at the quaking city lord, seeing his weakness as the reason for the deaths of more of my people. "Rewn…" I growled, before getting ahold of my temper, even as the spell finished, flickering and dancing in my hand.

I hadn't cast Magic Missile, despite planning to use it for this fight, knowing it was more versatile and partially self-guided, which I sure as shit knew was better. Instead, I'd reacted instinctively and cast a spell that was a lot more go-to for me. Fireball slowly spun above my outstretched palm, bringing a flickering and almost ominous light to my face as it reflected off my skin.

"Rewn, what the hell do you want from me?" I said, my temper going colder and tamping down, building past the stage of throwing my arms around and shouting, and instead entering a colder, more destructive phase.

"I want help! I want the Drow to pay, and I want my city back!" Rewn whimpered, fear in his eyes.

"Fine. I'll kill the fucking Drow, and I'll take your city. But, from now on, you work for me. You'll swear the Imperial Oath, and an Oath of Fealty, you and all your people. Do this, and I'll save you."

A look of stunned horror twisted his face, the beginnings of a backbone forming through the shock as he opened his mouth to refuse.

"If you don't," I snarled, "then I hope the storm has mercy, because you're either with me or against me, and I have none." I turned away from him. I jumped onto the railing, balancing on the edge precariously, and waited, watching the clouds.

There was silence from behind me, broken only by sniffling, as I stared out. I knew the damn thing was there still. Every few seconds, there would be a sudden swirl in the mist and a sound like tearing cloth as the bastard flashed past.

I waited, the hairs on the back of my neck prickling as I stood on the edge and offered myself as bait.

"Get ready," I said quietly.

"Boss, it should be me," Alistair said.

I snapped my head to the right, a movement out of the corner of my eye alerting me at the last possible second.

The Demon was there, mere meters away and closing at a horrific speed, arms outstretched. I twisted around, shoving the spell out toward it, and I had the split-second vision of sudden alarm filling the Demon's face, before it rolled to the side, letting my Fireball flash past it.

I cursed as the Fireball passed within inches of the Demon's scaled chest. It passed close enough that I saw actual wisps of burnt skin, flash-cooked by its proximity, in that weird bullet-time effect of high-stress encounters, before it flew past it. The Fireball disappeared into the clouds behind. The Demon shifted its glare from the fireball and locked eyes on me, arms reaching out.

Then it was there, the last thing I'd expected, a halberd with a length of chain wrapped around it, flashing out to spear into the Demon's side.

My eyes opened wide at the perfect cast Lydia had managed. When my Fireball had caused the Demon to twist to one side, it'd flown directly into the path of the rising weapon and the length of chain it was attached to.

The chain snapped taut, whipping the Demon around and allowing its own inertia to piledrive its face into the deck just before it could reach me. The hatred and bloodlust turned to pain, shock, and horror as its graceful, soaring flight turned into a cartwheel of destruction.

It slammed into the deck. Bones crunched and screams flew from the guards as well as a terrified, high-pitched squeal from Rewn. The Demon rolled over and over, the impact shaking the ship and throwing me outwards from my perch on the railing.

Shock registered on Alistair's face, and stunned disbelief lit on Lydia's that her hit had landed and that I was still falling. Then a millisecond later, I remembered I could damn well fly, and rose back up, chasing the ship.

In the three seconds or so it took me to get back into the air and close with the railing, Alistair had spun, ignoring the blades he'd taken from Rewn as viable weapons. Instead, he flung them at the Demon, the sword glancing off and leaving a shallow cut in one leg, the dagger sinking into the Demon's upper right arm with a meaty *thunk.*

As soon as his hands were free, he ripped a halberd from one of the cowering guards and flipped it over, swinging the head around and burying it in the Demon's thigh.

It screamed and opened its mouth wide, a bright glow seeming to build from nowhere as it aimed for Alistair. The lightning roared out in a powerful burst, one that Lydia caught on her shield, grunting as she stepped between the Demon and legionnaire.

The pair were shoved backwards by the force of the blast, both screaming in pain, but otherwise okay. Skin was singed, and nerves were overloaded. I rocketed over the railing to the right of the blast and flew forward. I had no time to do anything else, so I punched the damn thing in the face.

It reeled back, stunned, and the lightning arced away into the sky before dying out. I grunted in pain, feeling my knuckles break.

Its jaw hung loose, dangling out of its joint. I followed that blow with an uppercut, my left fist slamming into the underside of its jaw and smashing it closed, sending teeth flying.

I grimaced in pain. It was like punching stone. The joints were weaker, allowing me to damage them and dislocate things, but the actual bones? My own were breaking from the force I was using, and I had a split second to wish I was still wearing my gauntlets.

It struck back then. The slashing attack came from the left, raking across my chest and driving me back a few steps. My padded underclothes were shredded, and my chest leaked blood as its claws came away glistening.

I roared in pain, and before it could bring its arm back. I spun, kicking high and slamming my foot into the back of the halberd that was still embedded in the thickest part of its thigh.

It screeched in pain, and a sudden wash of healing magic flowed through me, making me grin as Lydia used her new spell for the first time.

My bones popped back into place and magic wrapped around them, holding them straight as they were flash-regrown. They itched as they settled back into place, and I grinned at the massive creature as it shifted, using one wing to brace its wounded leg as it struggled to stand upright, the other wing flapping brokenly as it tried to pull it in.

It screamed in rage and pain, before turning furious eyes on me, glaring, even as Oracle closed in.

I couldn't help it.

I grinned at the Demon, a creature that, even wounded, shaking with atrophied legs that could barely hold it upright between their inherent weakness and their injuries, still overtopped me by at least a meter, now it was upright.

I called out to the deck at large. "None of you fuckers interfere; this is between me and Princess here."

"Pwin…thesss…?" it growled, the sound coming out as a lisp due to its dislocated jaw. Even with the low rumble of its voice, it was fucking hilarious.

"Aye! You'll be remembered as Princess from now on, and I'll tell everyone that was your name, when they ask how I got my new Demon-skin rug!" I said, as Lydia's spell finished mending me, and my health reached full.

"Pew-uny morthal! Aye am…" the Demon said, before I cut him off.

"Princess!" I roared, activating my Mana Overdrive. I flashed forward, covering the few meters between us faster than the Demon could follow, punching out with all the force I could muster and striking it in the stomach.

Anger and disbelief turned to shock and pain as the blow landed, doubling it up and bringing its head down to where I could reach it.

I grabbed it, my left hand holding tight to the damaged remains of one of the bone sails, while I half-hooked my right around the back of the other, my fingers broken and knuckles smashed again. I brought my knee up with all the force I could muster, slamming it into the Demon's nose slits to the twin crunch of my kneecap and the front of the Demon's face shattering.

I staggered, trying desperately to maintain my balance and to stay upright, even as Lydia continued to channel into the spell, her face strained as she emptied her entire manapool.

It was enough, though; my knee repaired itself, fixing the kneecap and reattaching most of the ligaments before the spell cut off.

I straightened, watching the Demon as it collapsed backward, landing atop its damaged wing, and filling the air with the snap of more broken bones.

The Demon mewled piteously, its face half-crushed, the head of the halberd still in its leg, its shoulder pierced with a dagger, and it had been made my bitch in public.

I leaped into the air, powering my jump with Soaring Majesty and was shocked as I raced upwards at three times the speed, flipping over and plummeting with a spinning axe kick.

It connected with the middle of the Demon's sternum. The bones in my leg gave way with a sickening snap, my knee dislocated, and I barely kept from screaming.

Its chest, the Demon equivalent of its sternum, fractured, and it coughed a fountain of blood into the air.

I released Mana Overdrive and floated back, landing on my undamaged left leg, and I looked at Alistair.

"Go, he's all yours," I said. He nodded, yanking a short, wicked-looking dagger from his belt and striding forward, as Lydia passed me a healing potion.

"Thanks." I downed it, then used a healing spell. I'd barely begun casting when Oracle hit me with her own spell, her blend of magic and the drain on our shared pool making it clear who had cast it, even before I looked.

I could barely make out her form on the shadowy ship that pulled in close by, but my heart knew her as well as it could know anyone.

I bit down on the inside of my cheek, staring out across the gap between us, tasting blood as the bones in my leg popped and crunched, shifting around and realigning.

I shook slightly, close to screaming with the pain, before the pain began to retreat. I dared to relax my jaw slightly, and the gush of blood that filled my mouth as soon as I did was unexpected, as I hadn't realized how deeply I'd bitten.

The magic worked to fix it, a tiny thread of a spell, compared to the river of magic that was reconstructing my leg, even as I swallowed, feeling shaky.

"I…uh…" came the voice from behind me. I stiffened, twisting around and feeling the pain roar up my leg, as I glanced at Rewn.

The foppish city lord had come out with a dozen others from the captain's cabin, mostly young women who were barely kept within the confines of their dresses as they curtsied. The single older woman who was either his wife or favorite among the girls, was half-dragging him forward.

"I…I…" Rewn babbled, looking from me, to Lydia, to Alistair, who was butchering the Demon while it screamed in pain, flopping around on the deck, already missing its arms and more.

I stared at Rewn, before looking to the woman, who paled then dipped into a low curtsy.

My brain froze for a second in an instinctual male reaction as she almost fell out of her dress, and I wondered inanely if that was why the greeting was preferred by the nobility, just for the chance of an idle eyeful.

"My Lord…uh…High Lord Jax, Scion of the Empire…ah…" Rewn babbled again, before the woman straightened up.

"I am Carmen, High Lord Jax," she said simply. "City Lord Rewn agrees to your conditions, and we stand ready to swear fealty."

Her voice was hoarse, and her eyes were red. She'd clearly been crying and was having a bad day, but she was easily the most in control of the group, and the ladies behind her all deferred to her.

I glanced around the group, most of whom kept their heads bowed, and examined the way they were dressed. They looked ready for a ball, or a party at the least, but their clothes were battered, some torn, others with spatters of blood or other fluids here and there.

Their hair was mussed and their makeup more so. The two men who stayed conspicuously at the back were both unarmed and wore what could only be described as an entire boudoir's supply of silk and lace. Yet they were here, and clearly desperate for my protection.

"I'll make this very clear," I said, raising my voice over the sounds the Demon was making. They had changed from screams and roars to mewling and whimpers as Alistair, with tears streaming down his face, extracted vengeance for his lost companion.

"In the Empire, we follow the old laws. Slavery is an offence punishable by death, as is murder or torture…"

At that point, I was cut off by a bubbling screech from the Demon as Alistair sawed through its cock, before stuffing it into its own mouth, clearly intent on making it choke on its own member. We all paused for a second, the conversation derailed about as thoroughly as possible.

"Where was I? Oh, yeah, no torture," I said, then closed my eyes as the Demon began to choke and convulse. "Okay…right, well, obviously this is an *exception*, you know, no torture beyond this kind of thing."

Alistair kicked the dying Demon.

"You know what? Perhaps we should take this inside?" I suggested brightly, feeling Oracle closing quickly. She had either left the ship and was flying over under her own power, or we were all going to die in the next few seconds as we crashed.

Relief crossed the faces of those gathered before me, and I smiled and held up a hand before they could rush away.

"That is, we'll go inside and talk, *after* the Oaths," I clarified, even as Oracle landed next to me, and I felt the subsequent dip in my mana as she used it to send out the Oaths to the overdressed group and their guards.

CHAPTER TWENTY-FOUR

Ten minutes later, the mood had changed completely. Tenandra had taken up station alongside the *Phoenix Rising*, Rewn's personal ship. After a handful of legionnaires had jumped across, the ship was now getting back into some semblance of order.

I'd taken one look around the inside of the captain's cabin, or in this case, the city lord's, and been appalled at the state of it.

It looked like an interior designer from the late seventies had an LSD-inspired fit while holding a never-ending bag of gemstones and glitter.

There was a leopard print mural on one wall, a sex swing in the corner, and the entire ceiling was a bunch of mirrors. The room reeked of incense, and I shuddered at the sight of the only two chairs in the room. They were clearly designed to be accessed from all angles, and blacklight would likely make the room look like a Jackson Pollock painting.

"There is no fucking way I'm sitting…hell, touching anything in this room," I stated, shaking my head and looking over at Rewn.

His cheeks were bright red, and looked like he'd been caught by his grandmother with his pants around his ankles, beating the bald-headed bishop, and the rest of the group didn't look much better. Only Carmen would meet my gaze, and she looked like she felt much the same as I did.

"Everybody back outside," I said. "Looks like we get to have this conversation on the deck in the fresh air, because to get you to my ship, and to a REAL cabin, one that's clean…I'd have to touch you, and that's not happening."

I shooed them all out of the room, before following and exchanging a look with Oracle.

"Is this all for sex?" She asked me through our link.

"Yeah, don't touch the toys," I recommended, looking over at the dozens of sex toys that sat in special custom-built holders on the wall. Most were wooden, but several with inlaid faceted gems on them that I had to assume would be uncomfortable at the least…not to mention a pain in the…*awkward. They would be awkward to clean*, I mentally amended.

"But why do they need so many? And all of them, in this one room?"

"They're a harem, I guess," I said. *"A group that's built around one primary member for, well, fucking, basically. Sometimes it's relationships and so on as well, but mainly it's just for fun."*

"Okay, you're going to have to explain this one later, I think. I can understand it with a few of them, but, well, there's only so many ways you can do it, and so many people that can get into you at one time, surely? What do the rest do while you're busy?"

"No idea."

"I'm serious. If, say, the three guys are all playing with Carmen, that's great, and I'm sure they'll all be having fun and whatever, but what about the other ten girls? Do they play with each other? Do they do their nails and watch, or talk?

"I mean, surely that'd ruin the mood, if you're doing that and you look over to see them discussing it and judging your performance? I love you, Jax, but there's times when you pull the funniest faces."

"Aaaaand let's stop this conversation right there. You want answers to the questions? Ask Carmen; I think she'll be the best to explain it to you, honestly. Right now, I can't help but wonder what faces I pull and when, and I'm going to be wondering that when we're having sex next, so it's going to totally ruin my rhythm. Plus, they're all looking at us, and it's pissing down," I said, shaking my head at the group as they huddled in the rain, looking thoroughly embarrassed.

"Rewn, Carmen, you can stay. The rest of you, you've sworn the Oath so, I guess, go and behave yourselves elsewhere." I gestured vaguely and stepped aside. Only a few piled back into the cabin. The rest separated out into small groups and wandered off across the deck or disappeared into the ship.

"Right, Rewn, what the hell happened?" I looked to Carmen when Rewn started flapping his lips, but no words came out. "Is he always this articulate?" I asked, getting an amused smile from her.

"Only when he's terrified," she said, before going pale. "Lord…I mean, Sorry, my lord, I should…"

"Doesn't matter." I glanced back at Rewn. "Okay, let's find somewhere to sit that's mostly out of the rain and you can tell me what the hell is going on."

I got a nod from Rewn and a smile from Carmen, who appeared to have pulled her dress lower. I hid a grin as Oracle shifted slightly, her own top straining as she cheated and expanded beneath it.

I led the way to a section of the ship's deck, where there were a few barrels overturned. I sat on one, gesturing for the others to do the same. I thanked Alistair as he came over and rigged a simple shelter over us with a tarpaulin.

"Come on then, Rewn, Carmen…explain," I ordered, looking from one to the other. Several seconds passed as Rewn tried to get his words together, before Carmen gave up on him.

"It started several weeks ago, maybe as long as two months," she explained. "People started disappearing, then they'd turn up a few days later and act strange. They'd look and speak the same, but things they should have known were often slightly off.

"You'd ask them questions about important things, and they knew straight away, but simple, personal details, like asking Chineka about her cousin, she had no idea what I was talking about. Then, the next day, they knew everything about whatever you'd asked."

"They'd been coached?" I asked. She nodded. "A bit obvious, surely?"

"Yes and no. These are people we didn't interact with daily, and often we talked when we'd been using our herbs for relaxation or drinking heavily at feasts. At first, I just thought I'd remembered things wrong or mixed someone up, as it was people on the outside of the group, you understand? The nobodies.

"Then it happened more and more, and I got really worried that it was me…that the smoke and the drink were messing with my mind, so I cut it back, I pretended to still do it, so I wasn't left out." She sat carefully on the edge of the barrel, and as she spoke, she watched both Rewn and me. From his expression, this was as new to him as it was to me.

"Without the smoke and the drink, I started to see more and more. I noticed the smoke was stronger, each time I'd have just a little, and it would have an effect like I couldn't believe, so I examined it, in ways I hadn't in, well, forever." She seemed to deflate from the perfectly poised position to sagging and speaking from her heart.

"Okay, look, I'll explain how it is, all right? I've been with Rewn for about two years now; I've been one of his favorites for a while, but I always knew it wouldn't last. While fooling around with him and the others was fun, eventually they'd get bored of me, and I'd be gone, never to enjoy things like that again."

"No! I would never abandon you!" Rewn said, shocked as she quirked an eyebrow at him.

"Really? What about Lisbeth? Taren? Melissa? Rewn, honey, I could go on, but let's face it, you think with your dick. As soon as there's another pretty girl who catches your eye, you'll be after them."

"No! No, I want you to be with me always," he said, but even I could read the lie in the way he said it. Carmen and I shared a look, both of us recognizing that he was lying to himself more than us.

"That's sweet, my lord, thank you," Carmen said eventually, taking his hand and squeezing it before looking back to me. "So, as I was saying, I knew eventually I'd be set aside, so I spent most of the last two years gathering skillbooks and training. I learned alchemy and specifically the various drugs that the court was enamored with…I was preparing myself to be put aside and to keep a semblance of my nice life by supplying what they wanted.

"I tell you this so you know that I know my drugs and how strong they should be. I made up special variants that would give me a buzz, but not leave me with a crash like the others. When I examined the drugs we were using, though, it was different. Someone was changing the drugs that were delivered to new stuff. I spent days experimenting, trying to figure out what it was, until the day of the Holy Dawn Festival."

"Go on." I said.

"A few weeks back," Oracle whispered in the silence of our minds, and I squeezed her hand tighter in thanks.

"I tested the herbs for the party. It was early in the morning, and it'd just been put in place, ready for the party that evening. I'd seen it delivered, so I knew what it was, or what it was supposed to be, at least. As soon as I opened the burners, I recognized it, seeing herbs I did know, but not what had been delivered and not what was supposed to be there. The drugs would have left anyone who breathed in the smoke catatonic. I didn't know what to do, so I told Rewn."

"When she woke me," Rewn said, "I summoned the captain of my guard, and had him investigate. He brought the three who were responsible for the herbs and preparing my chambers to us, and he questioned them. They all denied knowing anything, but when I ordered them to breathe the herbs, putting them in a small room with a glass wall and filling it with the smoke, two of them were confused. They were worried, but that was it.

"The third, Hildairn, a man who'd cleaned my chambers since I ascended to the lordship, went insane and attacked the others, trying to escape." Rewn spoke haltingly at first, but was getting a hold of himself as he went on. He, at last, was showing some of the backbone that Hannimish had described, if not much of the sense.

"I watched him attack the others, frantic to escape the herbs," Carmen said. "Before he could do more than beat them, the smoke started to affect him. He was staggering, missing as he attacked, yet he still managed to drag one of the others to the glass wall and threaten to kill her if he wasn't set free. He held her up from the floor with one hand, choking her."

"He was in his eighties, and while not entirely frail, he wasn't that strong, either. I know I couldn't have held her up like that," Rewn said with a haunted look in his eyes.

"What did you do?" I asked.

"We refused, and he broke her neck," Carmen said sadly. "Peter, the Captain of the Guard, advised us not to open the door, said we'd be caught by the smoke if we did, so we did as he suggested."

"Once she was dead, he tried to reach the man on the far side of the room. But before he could, he collapsed. It took a few minutes for all the herbs to burn, and the smoke was thick in the room but eventually the smoke cleared, Hildairn was gone, and a Drow lay in his place," Rewn said slowly, shaking his head.

"Peter went in and checked on him, made sure he was alive, then the guards chained him up. They took him to the dungeons where they planned to question him. While they waited for him to wake up, someone killed the guards, and they vanished," Carmen added.

"A few hours later, they tried to kill me. Four of them, all Drow, attacked when I finished holding court. They cut through my guards like…like…"

"Like a scythe through wheat," Carmen said grimly. "Luckily, Peter had been paranoid after the Drow escaped, and he brought in some mages. They slowed them down, and the guards managed to kill them all, but most of the guard were wiped out."

She straightened before going on. "Lord Rewn hired more guards, and we all tried to get back to normal, but over the next few days, more and more of the people around us vanished. The last was Peter, and that was when we realized what it meant. We gathered those we knew we could trust, and we ran for the Legion Enclave, thinking that if anyone could protect us, it'd be them."

"They'd abandoned their post! They weren't there!" Rewn said, shaking his head.

"No, they weren't," Carmen agreed. "And when we realized they weren't there, we ran for the shipyards, taking Lord Rewn's personal ship and the handful of others that were available, fleeing the city. We tried to keep it secret, silent…but…"

"Truly we did; I barely told anyone about it. Just my counselors, the guard, and my servants," Rewn whispered, shaking his head sadly, oblivious to the annoyed look that Carmen shot him.

"We were barely in the air when new guards arrived. They attacked without warning, and mages sent Fireballs after us. The ships dodged as best we could, but one was taken down before we even got into the air. We fled, spells following us, and finally the Demons came. We headed to the Tower, guessing that was where the Legion must have gone."

"Where they'd fled when they abandoned us!" Rewn cursed. "They'd abandoned their post!"

"What?" I asked, confused.

"The Legion! It's their job to be there always, to battle the monsters and to protect me and the nobility…"

I cut him off with an upraised, blood-covered hand. "Whoa, no it fucking isn't!" I said. "First and foremost, the Legion exists to protect the Empire. They left the city because they came to aid *me*, as the Scion of the fucking Empire. Their entire job is literally to serve me first, and to protect the innocent citizens of the Empire always.

"The Nobility? Fuck no, most of the time you all shit on their Oaths and expected them to thank you for it. Let's start this off the way it's going to continue: as a lord of the Empire, you're supposed to be someone those lower in rank can look up to."

"My citizens look up to me all the time!" Rewn interrupted, looking shocked. "I provide them with daily examples of what they could achieve, if only they worked hard!"

"Really? They could be a noble, could they?"

"Well, no, but they could become a concubine or a servant. Those roles are open to all," he retorted, flustered.

"Provided you're pretty," Carmen said dryly.

I looked at her. She was quite possibly one of the most beautiful women I'd seen here: full lips, light green eyes, long black hair, and a figure to die for, all shown off to perfection in a red dress with gold patterning that ran up the sides and across the bust, clearly and deliberately drawing the eye.

"You seem to have done well out of it?" I suggested.

"Well, yes." She blushed. "I saw the chance, and I took it. Why not make the most of what the Gods gave me?"

"True," I said, shrugging. "Okay, look, Rewn, Carmen, I'm going to make this very clear. In the Empire, we are examples to the citizens; that means you get to grow up." I looked at the pair of them, seeing a lack of understanding on one of their faces. "This means that you actually work to look after the city and its people," I clarified to Rewn.

"I already do that!" Rewn said with relief, relaxing as if he thought it was over.

"Really? Okay, I admit I'm not familiar with your city beyond the basics, so how many schools are there?"

He frowned. "How would I know?"

"Okay, hospitals? Places that people can go to be healed? No? Okay…"

I spent the next ten minutes asking him for details about the city, stopping Carmen when she tried to answer for him, and seeing him get more and more worked up as he couldn't answer the questions.

"But why would I know all that?" he wailed, throwing his hands up. "That's why I have advisors and servants!"

I paused, trying to reconcile the man before me with the man Hannimish had described.

"Rewn," I said slowly, after a long pause. "Who makes the decisions in the city?"

"I do!" he said promptly.

"But you don't know any of the details. You don't know what your basic crops are, you don't even know how many guards you have. What about ships, Rewn? I was attacked recently by a bunch of ships crewed by the Drow and some normal soldiers; they had SporeMothers aboard."

I paused as confusion crossed his face, and I closed my eyes, slowly shaking my head as it all came together. "You're a figurehead, and you don't even know it," I whispered, seeing the sad confirmation on Carmen's face.

"No, I'm not!" he blustered.

I shook my head. The irritation that had been building drained away from me, replaced with tired sadness.

"When you make the decisions, who brings them to you? Who advises you?" I asked.

He smiled, relieved at a question he could answer. "Well, Senanth does!" he said, relaxing. "He served my father and his father before him. He advises me on what should be done and how to look after the city."

"And where is Senanth now?"

Carmen shook her head.

"Was he one of those who disappeared?"

"Yes," she said, her voice a low whisper as Rewn looked stunned.

"Okay, Rewn, that's fine, that's all I needed to know; you can relax now." He stood and bowed to me, before pausing and swallowing hard. "Lord Jax, I…I know I'm not the man my father was. I'm no warrior, and I'm not as smart as some, despite all that everyone says. But I won't let you down! Help me retake my city, and I'll defeat Himnel for you, don't you fear!"

I smiled at him, feeling sad inside, but nodded, putting my hand on his shoulder and forcing myself to speak calmly.

"I know, Rewn, thank you. I'm going to have to think on things, and I'll probably pick some new advisors for you soon, but for now, why don't you go to your cabin and relax? I need to speak to Carmen for a few minutes, then I'll be going back to my ship. Why don't you consider the city and how best we could take it back?"

He nodded and smiled, before clumsily clapping his fist to his chest and bowing his head again. "I won't let you down!" he repeated, then strode off into the cabin.

The door had barely shut before I turned to Carmen and raised an eyebrow in question.

"He's a fucking idiot, isn't he?" I asked her bluntly.

"He's…not as intelligent as I'd like," she hedged after floundering for a response for several seconds and apparently deciding honesty was the best policy. She shifted on her makeshift seat and relaxed. The poised, ladylike way she'd gone back to displaying vanished as soon as Rewn was gone, and she rubbed the bridge of her nose, clearly lost for words.

"What's really going on in Narkolt?"

"I told you the truth," she said, but when I jerked my head in the direction of his cabin, she sighed, and nodded. "Okay, yes there's more to say there, I guess. His father wasn't much brighter, truth be told, but Senanth kept the city going well.

"He's elven, long-lived, so he's served the city for well over a hundred years now. He held the city to the old ways as much as any, no slavery and so on. He tried to interest Rewn and his father in running the city, but neither had the brains for it. So, well, he does it, or did it. They trot Rewn out and tell him what to say, give him choices, but make sure he knows which is the right one to make, that kind of thing."

"Why doesn't Senanth just run the city? Remove Rewn entirely?" I asked.

"He's loyal to the city and the old Lord, or he was. He limits the others as much as possible as well, keeping the corruption at a reasonable level…more or less."

"So basically, what's happened here, and stop me if I get this wrong, is that I've just rescued an idiot who only knows how to party and who thought he was in charge of the city, while the chief advisor and the Captain of the Guard were replaced by fucking Drow. And, since everyone in charge knows Rewn is a fucking idiot, they've no reason to wonder where he is. They'll probably think that Senanth decided to make the decisions himself?" I asked slowly, and she glared at me.

"He's not an idiot!" Carmen snapped, before taking a deep breath and going on. "High Lord Jax…he's a good man, but he's always had his hand held by Senanth and the council. Yes, he could be brighter, he could be a better man, and he really only has two things going for him, that he's amazing in bed and he's kind, but he tries! When we were fleeing, he kept trying to take the servants with him. He wanted them all to be safe as well as us, and I had to practically gag him to stop him warning more people and starting a panic."

"And the rest of them?" I asked, gesturing to the cabin.

"The others?" She shrugged. "Mostly regular members of his harem or minor nobles who'd stayed for a party and were nearby when it happened."

"And you?"

"As I said, I'm a member of the harem, but not for much longer, I guess. Most of them are younger than me, and frankly, dumber. So, I used my time with him to learn, to set myself up for when it was over. The various herbs and drugs that the nobility use cost a fortune, so I spent most of my time figuring out how to make them. Frankly, it's been a fun way to spend the last two years."

"Great. So…wait a minute, you're basically a pharmacist, but for drugs?" I asked, for the first time thinking that the entire event might not have been a bust.

"I don't know the term, but I can make drugs, yes."

"Fantastic. When we get to the Tower, you're going to have a few jobs ahead of you, mainly for the fucking Gnomes. You ever come across their wonderdrug?" I asked. She shook her head. I searched my bags, finding the tiny amount I'd set aside to compare against my efforts, and I snapped a bit off, passing it to her.

She examined it, sniffed it, and eventually bit off a tiny amount, checking it and frowning, before shrugging.

"It seems simple enough, though I'd need an alchemy set to examine it properly, it appears to be mostly…valerian?"

I nodded. "Yeah, catnip," I said. She frowned, opening her mouth. "Ah don't worry, that's the name I knew it by. Yeah, it's weird stuff, and no, I don't think it'll do much for you, but if you can make this up, as it is, I'll be pleased. The Gnomes love it. I have a Gnome in my crew who'll happily test it, but, and I can't stress this enough, you don't give this to anyone, ANYONE without my permission, okay?"

"Of course, High Lord," she said, bowing her head.

"Good. Also, the drugs you do know? If they were illegal in the Empire, then they're illegal now in mine, at least until I know what they are and that they can be regulated. I really don't give a shit what people do in their normal off-time, but I need to know what you do is safe, and that when I call you, you're going to be able to answer, not be stoned to fuck and passed out in a gutter. Once we have some time, you can make up a batch of whatever you normally use, and once it's proven to be safe, and we're not at war, we'll look at making it legal. Until then, you get to make healing concoctions and so on, sound good?"

She nodded. "That's fine, High Lord. I know several different potion recipes, and…"

"Fine, I'll get you introduced to Tel; he's one of our alchemists, and you can talk over the recipes and so on. For now, though, you seem to be the most sensible one out of the lot here, so keep Rewn under control and make sure the others behave themselves."

"What about the harem?" she asked.

I shrugged, not really understanding the question. "Uh…have fun?" I suggested. "Or don't, you know, you do you and all that."

"I mean, is it permitted?" she asked.

I blinked. "Yeah, as long as everyone is doing it by choice, have fun. If anyone is being forced into it, though…" I said, a glower coming to my face.

"Oh, no, nobody is forced to participate; I simply wanted to be sure of the rules."

"Look, who you fuck, I really don't care about," I said. "You can all have a gangbang, or small groups, relationships, whatever, don't judge and don't care, as long as everyone's having fun."

"And you, High Lord? Would you care to join us?"

Oracle, who'd been conspicuously quiet all this time, cut her off with a glare.

"Uh, or not?" she finished lamely.

"See, I knew you were smart. This is Oracle," I said, gesturing to her as she smiled at Carmen. "I should have introduced her earlier, so my apologies, but that cabin kind of threw me off track. So, Oracle is my Lady, my lover, and a wisp. Specifically, she's in charge of knowledge for the Tower and the Empire, I guess. She can alter her size and shape, and be basically anything I need or want, and I love her, so, you know, not really interested. Thanks for the offer, though."

"Lady…wisp?" She inclined her head slightly, then moved to a full curtsy as neither Oracle nor I said anything.

I reminded myself to do something about Oracle's official status, as this was bound to come up again at some point.

I mentally ran through options, lover, partner, girlfriend, lady, wife…

At that thought, my brain kind of locked up, and I froze, having never thought of myself as the marrying type before. But Oracle was bonded to me for all our lives, so maybe that was the closest comparison?

I shook myself, dismissing the thought for now, realizing I'd basically gone silent, and the other two were watching me.

"Okay! Thank you, I think I need to get on with things now, so follow along, and we'll take you to the Tower, I guess," I said, straightening up and waving over Lydia and Alistair, even as I gestured for Carmen to leave us.

She curtsied and left, and I waited until she was out of earshot before relaying the situation to Lydia and Alistair.

"So I want you to stay here, Alistair, keep an eye on them, and make sure they stay alongside us and come to the Tower. I'll get a few more of your squad to join you, but Lydia and I need to return to our ship."

"Of course, my Lord." Alistair said, slamming a fist to his chest.

"Thank you. I'm sorry for your loss, Alistair," I said softly.

"Thank you, sir," he whispered.

I turned to Lydia. "You ready for this?" I asked.

She nodded, grinning as she flexed her wings. "Hell yes!" was all she said before jumping over the railing and opening her wings wide, catching the breeze and being lifted into the sky with a loud whoop of joy.

I couldn't help but smile, especially as Oracle reached out to me. I took her hand, and together we rocketed into the sky, feeling the wind rushing past.

We spiraled upward, hands gripped tight together, the joy of freedom and of flight reflected in her face. Wind rushed past us, making it hard to hear anything as we flew straight up, vanishing into the low grey clouds.

I pulled her in close, staring into her eyes as she looked up into mine. We shared a long, deep kiss, and I felt her arms around me as she moved in closer, clinging tight to me, as I enfolded her in mine.

We lifted through the last of the clouds, emerging into the dying light, seeing the sunset miles to the west as we paused, my power holding us aloft for a handful of seconds in perfect peace and privacy.

"I love you," I whispered, and she smiled up at me, turning from the sunset to kiss me again and reply.

"I love you too, Jax."

With that, we enjoyed a final long kiss before I leaned backwards, and we fell back into the clouds. The world vanished as we picked up speed, passing through the damp, dark grey world. The only sound I could hear was her delighted laughter as we flew back to our ship and headed for home.

CHAPTER TWENTY-FIVE

It was late when we arrived back at the Tower. The lights radiating from the windows and doors were strange to see, especially from a distance. But as we drew closer, the welcoming light that emanated from the flight deck guided us in, with Rewn's ship following along behind.

Fortunately, the deck had been expanded recently, and where there had been berths for two or three ships before, now five could fit, even if snugly.

Tenandra had barely finished landing, when the terrifying sight of both Mistress Nerin and Restun storming up the gangplank, made me seriously consider jumping off the back of the ship and running the fuck away from here.

Before I could make that most brave of decisions though, Oracle had a hold on my hand and was standing firm. Truth be told, I still considered abandoning her, but it was a childish impulse, and I sighed as I dismissed it, watching the rest of my team gathering up their gear and heading off.

"Mistress Nerin, Restun. Good to see you both," I said, forcing a smile as they came to a halt. Restun saluted and Nerin eyed me with clear annoyance.

"Welcome home, Lord Jax," Restun said. "I was discussing the new training regime with Mistress Nerin, and we were fortunate enough to see your ship arriving."

"The new training regime!" I clutched that straw with frantic need. "Yes! How's it going?"

"We agreed that we need to increase the number of healers for the Legion. As highly skilled as Mistress Nerin is, she cannot be everywhere, and it's inappropriate to expect her to be on the front lines, where she would be needed the most," Restun said. "As such…"

"Way ahead of you." I said, holding up a hand. "We had a breakthrough on the ship on the way back here. Oracle managed to develop a new spell, as in an entirely new healing spell. The baseline version she can teach is both highly efficient and self-guiding. It took a hell of a lot out of her, but believe me, it's worth it."

"Self-guiding spells are rarely as good as they are expected to be." Nerin said.

"That's true, but this one seems to work, add to that the fact she can teach it to three people at a time. I discussed the need with Tenandra on the way back; she will work with Oracle to help teach the Legion. That gives us six people an hour to learn Complex Healing, along with Magic Missile and another spell to be determined.

"While it's admittedly tiring, both Oracle and Tenandra believe they can keep it up for several hours. They'll be working through the night tonight and all day tomorrow, as they don't need sleep. Six people an hour, with an hour to rest for every three hours teaching, that gives us one hundred and eight people in twenty-four hours." I paused my babbling and forced myself to stop.

"One hundred and eight," Restun said slowly. "To have one hundred and eight healers of any grade in the Legion is beyond belief."

"Damn right, Restun. It should make a hell of a difference. Westin has had all of his people trained as well. Each of them and all of my squad now have Magic Missile and Complex Healing as a minimum. But, I'm sorry to say this, Restun, we lost three of the Westin's squad. Storm Demons were attacking a convoy of ships. We managed to save one of seven, well, eight, one never made it out of the city," I reported with a tired sigh.

"Hello!" called Rewn from the far side of the ship, and I winced, putting my hand over my eyes.

"And that's something else we have to address. Rewn, City Lord of Narkolt was on the surviving ship and has sworn to me. He's also, *and I didn't say this*, a complete fucking idiot. We need to train him to make him competent, at least, and probably power level him so that he can invest heavily in his Intelligence and Wisdom."

"Why do I have the sudden feeling I know who's going to be training him?" Restun asked with a quirked eyebrow.

"Now, that's just evil," I said, smiling. "I was considering just sending him out with any of the Legion, maybe discussing it with Romanus and seeing who he'd like to volunteer. If you're offering, though, thanks for that. I'll sleep a lot better knowing he's under the best the Legion has to offer."

"I didn't offer," Restun said, before pausing, taking a deep breath, and nodding. "Of course, Lord Jax. My apologies, is it just City Lord Rewn or…"

"You know Alistair?" I asked. He frowned, nodding. "Well, he was knocked over the side of the ship in the fight, unarmed and due to the lightning, unarmored. Lydia and I caught him, and we ended up on the wrong ship…long story…" I said, holding my hand up as Nerin frowned and opened her mouth.

"Anyway, Rewn's guards surrounded us, six of them, with halberds. They threatened me, and Alistair beat the shit out of them, all before they knew what was happening. He didn't get a single scratch, I don't think."

"Alistair is good, but if they were armed and armored, they should have had some luck, even against him. How many…?"

"No idea, honestly. I left them to it while I beat the Demon like a red-headed stepchild…" At the look on their faces, I sighed. "It's a saying from my home. It doesn't mean anything…"

"Unless, you know, you're a red-headed stepchild," Thomas said as he walked by, grinning.

"Thanks for that, Thomas." I growled, shooting him the finger. "Okay, look, there're a few on the ship who will need serious help, and most of his friends are…"

I trailed off as we all turned to watch them trooping down from the ship, the gaggle of harem members gawking around at the Tower in amazement, while being barely decent.

"…that." I finished, sighing heavily. "His friends are that."

"That's a harem," Nerin stated. "I don't heal sexual diseases."

"And I don't blame you for not wanting to, but you do heal them," I responded grimly. "You're the Tower's healer, like it or not, and if they're riddled, you need to at least make sure they don't pass it on to any of our boys and girls."

"Fine. Whatever…but that's not why I'm here."

I appraised her cautiously. "Go on…"

"Dinner," she stated. "You agreed we would discuss things. We agreed that, at least once a week, you and I would meet. You would tell me about your home, your world, what you had for breakfast, I don't care. We agreed that you needed to talk, and it's been more than a week since we last spoke."

"We're kind of at war, Nerin."

"And you breaking down will help the war effort?" she asked with a challenging glare.

"I'm not going to break down! I…"

Oracle grabbed my arm, and I glared at her, realizing as the echoes came back to me that my volume had been steadily rising.

"Jax, please, she's got a point," Oracle said.

I instantly felt betrayed, but forced myself to calm down, telling myself she wasn't doing this to piss me off.

She was doing it because she loved me.

"Okay," I whispered, patting Oracle's hand, feeling her love for me radiating through the bond. "Okay, Nerin, I'm sorry for snapping at you. Dinner, you said?"

"Humph," Nerin grumbled, gesturing vaguely in the direction of the floors below, where the kitchens were. "Knowing you, you've probably not eaten properly, therefore we can get some food and talk now."

"I have a better idea," I said. "We can go to one of the balcony gardens and talk, we'll grab some food from the kitchens and take it there, if that's all right?"

"Fine. But we'll go to the balcony two floors up, and you can send someone for the food; I'm not going up and down." She reluctantly agreed. Surprisingly, I found I actually felt relieved.

"Thank you," Oracle said, standing on her tiptoes to kiss my cheek. "I'm going to arrange things with Tenandra, then go see Romanus, get him to send us volunteers to start learning healing spells. The next few days are going to be busy."

"They are," I agreed, kissing her again. "But we can't afford to relax. First thing tomorrow morning, there'll be a Council of War so we can plan the next step. I know it'll cost you time that you could be teaching, but at first light, I want you there."

She nodded, then shrank down to her smaller size and took off up the Tower, clearly aware of where Romanus was already.

"Lord Jax, I…" a pompous voice rang out.

I held up a hand as Rewn strode over already talking, and I spoke to Seneschal instead.

"Hey buddy, I'm back, and I've got good news…" That was as far as I got before my head was almost split by the triumphant shout of Heph, who'd clearly spotted the golems aboard the ship.

"Advanced!" he crowed. ***"They be advanced class, ah can start a wee upgrade program, hell ah can…"***

"Hello to you, too, Heph," I said. *"Yes, there's advanced golems. There's two crafters, as well as war golems. The crafters have the blueprints to make more Genesis Chambers, and we have a load of cores, as well as control of a facility that can make more. That's the great news."* I couldn't help but smile as I passed on the good news, standing there aboard my airship and wishing that the armored undergarments, or hell, my regular armor had goddamn jeans pockets. I missed the comfort of putting my hands in them!

"Okay, the good news is that it was reasonably intact, and it even had mining golems. They're out looking for the rare materials needed to make more cores now. The bad news is that, once the current batch of golems are done, we need to share with Svetu, as he led us to it, and he used to have a part of the facility anyway."

"Ah do no care aboot tha'! Ah've got golems again! Ah can make proper wee creatures!" Heph sounded far too excited to be reasonable, so I just nodded.

"Fine, well, you get to control them and get them started on the various projects now please. Get the second Genesis Chamber underway, and we need to build the control towers on each of the waystations. When that's done, we should be able to locate the mining golems I set to head here from Himnel." I paused, reorienting myself and deliberately ignoring Rewn, who kept trying to speak to me.

"Once we locate the mining golems, take control of them and the regular golems that are following. When we have that sorted, we can really up the ante. We've got a shit load to do, and no real time to do any of it, so I need you to hit the ground running with this. The advanced war golem can take over the war golems we have, get them organized and patrolling or whatever."

"Ach, laddie, ah canna wait!" Heph crowed.

I couldn't help but smile as I directed my thoughts to Seneschal, ignoring Hephaestus' excited babble.

"Seneschal, this should let you get control over some of the servitors now and direct them to do their usual roles. You can get them helping with the kitchens and so on, whatever you need. On a side note, and totally not the main reason I started this conversation, can you get in touch with someone in the kitchens and get some food sent up to the balcony garden a few floors up? Enough for both Nerin and me?"

I received a sense of amusement from Seneschal.

"Of course, I'll take care of that now. Thank you, Jax. I have many positions the servitors can make themselves useful in. Shall I pass the word to the council that there is a mandatory meeting at sunrise tomorrow?"

"Yeah, thanks buddy," I said, pulling out of the connection. As Cai and Isabella approached, I let out a relieved breath.

I waved back Rewn and the group gathered around him as I strode across the floor toward Cai, smiling my greeting as they arrived.

"Cai, Isabella," I greeted them warmly. "Thank the Gods you're here!"

"Always, Lord Jax," Cai replied as Isabella echoed him. "How may I serve?" He watched the nobles out of the corner of his eye.

"I need this gaggle of…nobility settled somewhere, unfortunately; they're basically refugees, and they need somewhere to be. I'll be having a council meeting at first light, and we'll sort things out then. For now, quarters and some food for them, please," I said to the pair, getting nods and smiles before I turned to Rewn and his people. "Okay, can I have your attention, please?"

Several of the minor nobles ignored me and continued their conversation.

"Oi! Shut the fuck up!" I barked, getting shocked looks. "Okay, let's make a few things nice and clear here. If I speak, I expect you to listen. That's not complicated now, is it? Okay. This is Cai and Isabella. They're in charge of people here in the Tower; they will arrange food and quarters for you.

"However, if you have bedding and so on in the ship, I suggest you take it now, as our facilities are still quite bare. If you have questions, direct it to them. I'll sort something more permanent for you all in the morning, but for now…"

"I'll require a suite for my companions, and rooms appropriate to my status."

I held up one hand, getting a glare from Rewn as I interrupted him interrupting me.

"Rewn, your fucking status at the minute is 'refugee;' you get a slight bit of an allowance because you're a city lord, and you're sworn to me. Your people bring nothing to the table, and by refugee, what I mean is that you have come here with fuck all to add to my war effort beyond more troubles, so how about you shut the fuck up?" I took a deep breath and forced a quasi-patient smile onto my face.

"Let's be very clear! Cai runs the Tower and holds the rank of Imperial Consul. As such, he is so far above the majority of you in rank that you can barely see his feet. As the Empire grows, he will continue to grow in power and rank, being responsible for all the people in the Empire. Again, he is my First Counsellor.

"In comparison, Rewn, if, and I really do mean *if*, you are given authority as the city lord of Narkolt, you will be in charge of a minor city in the Empire. Dravith will one day have an Imperial Governor. That Governor will answer to Cai, who will answer to me, so please, for your sake and mine, don't piss him off."

Rewn tore his gaze free from the interested look he had been giving Isabella, so I hastily moved on to the next point.

"Isabella is his assistant and his love, so behave yourselves. If it helps you to grasp shit, consider yourselves as the most junior nobility in a city, and he is the city lord. Now, I have things to do, so congratulations, you are safe from the Drow and most of the assholes out there. Don't make me throw you off the Tower." With that, I gestured to the balcony leading out into the open air, before turning back to Cai and Isabella.

"Sorry to leave you both with this shit, but I need some rest, and I have a dinner date with Nerin."

There was a chorus of gasps from behind me. I looked over my shoulder in the direction people were pointing. Behind me, the pair of hulking Amilith stomped across the floor. Yet another frustration to be dealt with. "I also need you to get these two to the engineers on the battleship. They have an Amilith called Durg with them; this is his mother…" I ignored the winces from Cai and Isabella as I turned to Restun. "Walk with me, Restun; we can talk on the way."

He clapped his fist to his chest as I set off, ignoring Rewn, his people, and the huge Amilith pair as Cai stepped forward and tried to establish some order.

I strode across the floor, the engineers' singing as they worked on one of the ships making me feel at home already. I let out a long-held breath, then drew another to begin speaking to Restun.

"That was childish, wasn't it?" I asked eventually.

"Dressing down a refugee city lord who's surrendered to you in front of his people, then walking off as if they're not worthy of your time? Of course, not, my Lord Jax," Restun deadpanned.

I winced. "Shit. Yeah, that was a piss-poor way of dealing with things. But fuck man I'm tired, stressed enough, and I still have to sit and talk about my feelings with Nerin." I clenched and unclenched my fists at my side. "I wanted to make sure Cai didn't get any grief from them, that's all."

"And that's a good aim, Jax," Restun said, gaze flicking back and forth across the sky as if searching for the right words. "Legion Prefect Romanus is better suited to advising you in this arena. But as you asked, well, cutting him down in front of his people wasn't the best move.

"You could have explained Cai's rank to him and asked him to deal with his people instead. Think of him as a junior officer, new to his rank. You just treated him like a fresh aspirant, equal to those around him, not their leader."

"Shit. Okay, thank you, Restun. I'll deal with that tomorrow, make a point of it, somehow. Was there anything else?" A wry smile crept onto my face. "Besides, you're no doubt intending on torturing me?"

"I wouldn't say torture, but yes. I intend to assist you in gaining higher skills and physical fitness, if that's what you mean." Restun didn't seem apologetic in the slightest. "I wanted to bring you up to date on the marines you asked me to create."

"Thank you, Restun. I'll make sure they get healing training soon as well."

He nodded once. "That would be helpful. The few who hadn't already have now reached level ten across the board, and they've begun specializing in shipboard combat. They're using every available point they gain to build their mental characteristics, while I develop them physically.

"For most, it's been a very humbling experience, but I have found five that have risen above and beyond the rest. They will be ideal as the new unit's leadership. As things stand, they are a unique group, and are outside of the Legion. I have trained them as equals so far, but I feel it's time we decided their future. Will they have ranks? How many will form a team? Are they auxiliaries to the Legion? Will they strive for full legionnaire status?"

"Right," I muttered, rubbing the back of my neck. "I've given some thought to this, but I need your advice and probably Romanus' as well. I'm thinking that teams of ten will be the best way, as that gives them the best chance when fighting other ships.

"If they fire ten Fireballs all at once, or ten mages cast Magic Missile, getting five each and firing a full barrage of fifty missiles at an enemy crew? Hell, let's face it, if they fired off fifty missiles at the engines on one side of a ship, that's it, the ship is down, no matter what they try to do. Ten is probably the best number."

"We have forty-eight," Restun reminded me.

I snorted. "I know, don't worry, I haven't forgotten." I reassured him. "Do you think you could find another three among them who you'd feel comfortable leading a team? If we can put together eight teams, each team made up of six mages, as well as four melee fighters, with the melee members trained for healing as well?"

"Melee fighters are generally not best-suited to healing; it usually requires a larger mana pool," Restun replied.

"True, but I've had time to consider things while I was on the last mission. Ideally, the squads would be groups of ten, but that would restrict us to only five teams, and would require two more members to join them.

"Originally, I chose the numbers at forty-eight because we had sixteen low-level spellbooks we could afford to use. The time it took Oracle to teach the others at that point was the main bottleneck. But, from her experiences, we now know that the fastest and most efficient way to train people is with her sharing the spells in groups of three."

"Okay…" Restun enunciated slowly.

"So, what I'm thinking is that we can train the remaining four people for each of the teams in eleven hours, and that would be to give them healing spells. We fill these four positions from the Legion, with the leadership of the squad going to a legionnaire, and the second position will be the leader you identified from the teams you've trained. So, that way we have a legionnaire in charge of close in-fights and shipboard duties, including physical training and behavior.

"That should bring the Marine teams into line with the Legion, while still being their own group, as we'll need specialized teams for airship combat in the future either way, I think."

"And the trainee in the secondary leadership, or centurion role, will be highly ranked enough that they can legitimately raise concerns and issue orders in case of magical combat," Restun said. "While the legionnaires can carry out close-range support and healing when they can't engage the enemy. Okay, that makes sense. But, ideally, the legionnaires would also be able to use ranged offensive magic." Restun glanced at me out of the corner of his eye. "I know that many legionnaires are immature at times, but granting them…"

"Restun, it's fine," I interrupted. "I fully intend to give them all magic, regardless. In the long term, I want everyone in the Empire, citizens and legionnaires alike, to be able to heal and defend themselves. The Legion will have basic healing, offensive spells, shields, and a buff, at a minimum. The reality of our situation is that I can either focus on a small group and have them trained to do all those spells, or we can train the majority in just one or two spells. Truthfully, what would be more useful, a few dozen legionnaires like that, or a hundred with only one or two spells?"

"The majority," Restun said with a grimace. "I don't mean to second-guess you, Jax, but frankly, you spend a lot of time running around, and your plans are often…"

"Half-baked and shit?" I asked with a grin.

"I was going to say 'unfinished'," Restun responded with a rare half-smile.

"Well, thanks for blowing sunshine up my arse, but I know what you mean, Restun. Seriously I do, and I'm sorry for this. I know that I've been running from issue to issue and trying to factor it in around everything else." I glanced at him, smiling wryly. "Unfortunately, there's only so much time to do it all, and the result is this, where I have to keep changing the plans. Believe me, I know it's not ideal, but as I say, better to learn and adjust on the fly than make a plan and hold to it when we learn a better way."

"I'll consider the options and come back to you with my recommendations in the morning, Lord Jax. I assume that you'll be joining the noon training session?" The glare I got when I opened my mouth made it clear there was only one correct answer, and as such, I said it, nodding ruefully.

"I'll be there," I said, getting a twisted smile of approval.

"Then I'll bid you goodnight and leave you to your discussion," Restun said, saluting before turning away and returning to the stairwell behind us.

I'd been lost in our conversation and hadn't realized that I'd closed the distance to the garden until I was there, standing at the entrance, with a towering golem standing guard before me.

It stepped aside when I approached, and I stepped out onto the verdant grassy area just outside the Tower.

Somehow, in the space of my short chat with Restun and the others below, someone had managed to find time to get a blanket set out on the grass by the edge of the small pool. They had also cleared out the balcony garden as well as stationing a golem ready to prevent anyone from wandering in and ruining my little therapy session. Surprisingly, as I took a deep breath, I felt both trepidation and relief.

Nerin was there already, watching the play of tiny fireflies as they flew across the surface of the water, occasionally vanishing with a clop as a fish lunged up from the depths.

I walked over and sat down next to her, reaching into the basket and finding a wedge of cheese and taking a bite as I looked around, marveling again at the beauty that nature had created here.

The balcony gardens were wonders of wild beauty mixed with the Tower's structure, and they had been so even when I arrived. But now, with the majority of the Tower repaired, it had only grown more stunning.

The old planters, once the only home of plants on these levels, were now long gone, shattered by hundreds of years of weather beating down. The death of a thousand plants and the buildup of around seven centuries of plant debris, dirt, and the various droppings of tens of thousands of birds were gone, too.

Instead of the foot or so of dirt that the plants had scrabbled to survive upon as they slowly spread out, colonizing the balcony, there was now a few feet of solid dirt, and the plants had been shifted slightly, leaving the entire area a mix of manicured gardens, overgrown orchards, and secret glades.

It was sodding beautiful.

"Well, this is nice," I whispered, feeling myself unwind slightly. Nerin turned to face me, her eyes patient, the seemingly bad-tempered persona nowhere in evidence as she spoke softly.

"It is, and you need to remember more often that these places exist, Jax…all the power in the realm does you no good if you lose interest in wielding it, or more importantly, why you wield it."

"What do you mean?" I asked cautiously, half-expecting her to snap at me.

"The boy who was brought to me in the city, half-gutted by his own hand, with Gods interfering to save his life, no less, would have moved heaven and earth to help a single legionnaire out. I watched you in those first days, and despite everything, I gave up my life to follow you." Nerin turned and looked back out over the water, idly taking a piece of cheese for herself and looking it over as she spoke.

"My shop was ruined, yes, but I had my reputation still, and everyone needs a healer eventually. I could have made it known that my shop was raided and called in outstanding debts. My possessions would have been returned, probably bloodstained, but I would have gotten them back." She looked me dead in the eyes.

"In the last few weeks, you've been forced again and again to send your people out to fight, and many of them have died for you. Not for the Empire, *for you*," Nerin said softly.

Her words carried the weight of the world, threatening to crush me, as another spoke the words I'd been saying to myself over and over.

"I know; they're dead because of me," I said quietly.

"No." She shook her head. "No, they're not. I said that to test you, boy, to be sure of what I suspected, and now I am." She paused, waiting until I looked her in the eye, before going on.

"You carry the guilt of their deaths, and that's not right. Yes, it's entirely correct that you carry their deaths in memory, and a *share* of the guilt, because it was your orders that they were ultimately following when they died, but not *all* of it," she said sadly, but her voice was firm as she made her point.

"They made their choice to follow you, and you denying them the honor of that choice so that you can wallow in self-recrimination dishonors their sacrifice."

"What?"

She shook her head. "No. Listen, boy, this is important," she warned, fixing me with a steely glare. "You've been growing hard, developing callouses on the soul, as it were. That's fine, it has to happen, or no leader would ever get anything done, but you have to decide if the man you're becoming is the one you want to be. For example…"

The next two hours were both unpleasant and cathartic, with me feeling everything from hating Nerin with a passion to being humbly grateful to her as we talked. We discussed my past, Amon, the influence his voice had on me, the Dreams, the deaths of those close to me, and the hundreds I'd killed.

By the end, as I helped her to her feet and we scattered the last crumbs of the bread and cheese out for the birds, I felt lighter in my soul. I didn't even flinch when Nerin told me we'd be talking like this again next week.

Or at least, I didn't flinch *much*.

CHAPTER TWENTY-SIX

The next morning, I was awoken by the vision of loveliness that was Tang as the bastard kicked my foot then retreated. Unexpected pain radiating up my leg, I woke at full speed, adrenaline flooding my veins. I leaped to my feet and reached for a weapon before my brain caught up.

"What the hell?" I growled.

Tang snickered, already heading toward the door.

"Oracle asked me to wake you up, boss, but let's face it. You always try to hump her when she wakes you up. It's not a risk I was going to run."

"Asshole," I snapped, shaking my head and looking around the room, the memories of the last hours before bed coming back to me slowly.

I'd gone to my rooms after talking to Nerin, finding it weird that Oracle wasn't with me. I'd brought a chair out onto the balcony and relaxed, sitting there and listening to the world for hours.

The sounds of others gently floated up to me, everything from laughter to a child's sobs after a nightmare to arguments and the call of a hunting cat somewhere out in the darkness.

Voices drifted from above, squabbling. Occasionally, feathers from a terminally unlucky pigeon floated past, as the imps I'd adopted hunted the Tower's externals.

They'd rarely been seen since arrival, but the wild bird population seemed to be steadily declining.

Dozens of species called the Tower home, and I'd been rushing around and basically neglecting them. Now that I had taken the time to think about them, I realized I had been missing so much.

Yes, I'd been doing my best. I'd been consumed with the war effort and saving everyone, but when I'd gotten people back here, I'd only been half-helping them and leaving the details to my advisors to fix.

I'd spent hours thinking about it, and while I knew I couldn't fix it all, I'd at least have to try.

With that in mind, I dressed quickly, Tang throwing good-natured insults at me as I did. I returned them in kind, enjoying the banter even as we both missed Bane terribly.

As soon as I was ready, I headed to the council chambers. For the first time in ages, I arrived before the others were there. I took my seat and waited, even as I reached out to Oracle.

"Good morning, beautiful," I called to her, and I got a sense of a warm hug, a kiss, but no more. I withdrew, knowing she was in the middle of training the others still.

I opened my eyes with a sigh, and Tang spoke up, surprising me, as he and the others usually left me alone, beyond watching over me at times like this.

"Hey, Boss?" Tang asked.

I turned to where he stood to my left, smiling as I regarded my bodyguard and friend. "What's up?"

"Ah, have you given any more thought to Alistair?" he asked.

"What do you mean?" I asked.

"Were you serious about having him as a bodyguard?"

"Well, I don't know, to be honest. I was thinking more of while we were on the ship at that time, not further than that. He'd just lost someone and…"

"Amis," Tang confirmed. "His friend and lover, and yeah, you were right to give him something to do. Since then, he's been waiting for more orders from you. You asked him to guard you, but didn't tell him anything else, so he turned up at your room last night to take a shift on watch."

"Crap," I muttered. "He seemed like a good guy, certainly skilled in a fight, but is he any use in stealth?"

"Gods, no," Tang replied with a grin. "Alistair's about as straightforward as possible. He couldn't lie to save his life and snapped the first three bows he was being taught with. He barely passed the Legion courses because it's a requirement to be able to use all weapons. But give him a sword and a shield? A line to defend or a target to take? He's a hell of a fighter."

"Okay, maybe not a good idea for bodyguard and basic spy training, but he sounds like he might be good for Thomas's team."

"Definitely. I think he needs something to focus on right now, and he's picked you; most of us have. He's raw after Amis's death, so possibly push him in that direction sooner rather than later?" Tang suggested.

"Will do. Anything else?"

"Just the usual. We're getting asked a lot from the other legionnaires what the plan is, if the Legion will be continuing or changing, if there's going to be a war after sorting out the local area, if Nimon really hates you. You know, the usual."

"And what did you tell them?"

"That you're the boss, and we kill who you say. If that's as legionnaires or something else, that doesn't matter. If you want some local monster or the God of Death himself nailed to the door by His fucking ears, then that's what we'll do."

"And what did they say?"

"Mostly just nodded and accepted it." Tang got a faraway look in his eye then smiled. "A few asked to be in on the fight with Nimon directly, if there was a chance. After all, it's not every day you get to pick a fight with a God."

"Fair enough. Tell them I'll see what I can do." I smiled. I was relieved that the Legion were still so prosaic and battle-crazed at the same time.

Tang and I sat talking quietly as the others filed in over the next half an hour. Just as the sunrise was touching the Tower, bathing it in beautiful light, the food arrived with Isabella and Cai. The entire room went silent as my special request was laid out on a long table against one wall like I'd asked.

I saw them all looking at each other in confusion, all that is, barring Thomas who already had a plate in hand and was gesturing for me to move the fuck along before he stabbed me with his fork.

"Okay, people, this is called a 'full English breakfast, buffet-style.' You get your plate from the end, and you just damn well load up with whatever you want. You keep going back until you're done, or it's all eaten.

"We've got bacon, sausages, hash browns, roasted tomatoes, and fried mushrooms, fried, scrambled and poached eggs, fried or toasted bread, hell, we've even got a passable attempt at baked beans and black pudding, so you're all in for a treat!" I declared, before starting in the line, piling my plate high and taking it back to the council table. Thomas was in right behind me, but there was momentary hesitation as people clearly tried to reconcile "important council meeting" and "huge fuck-off fry-up" into a single event.

"Seriously, people. You can eat or not, but I've got a fuck load to do today, and I'm intending on eating while we deal with this shit, so get stuck in or go hungry, your choice!" I stated, already dipping a slice of toasted bread, slathered in butter, into a perfectly fried egg yolk. A little moan of satisfaction may have escaped my mouth when I bit down, but if so, nobody dared to comment.

Romanus and Restun stepped straight up, followed by Mal and Soween, then Oren. At that point, the floodgates broke open, and everyone was reaching for food.

Ten minutes later, most of the room had been fed, and there were only three of us still eating. Unsurprisingly, it was Thomas and me, but the other was strangely Isabella, who seemed intent on eating her own body weight in fried bread dipped in beans. The atmosphere was now much more relaxed, and we started the council meeting properly.

"Okay people," I said, pushing my plate aside and groaning as I sat back. "We've a lot to do and not much time to do it. Romanus, I know you and Jon were getting things sorted with the restructuring of the Legion, and I saw the battleship below, so I take it we've got the rest of them are here now?"

"Yes, Jax. Athena and Oren took Jon to collect them and arrived back several hours before you. As of now, we have a total of four hundred and three legionnaires who are combat-ready, with another hundred and fifty or so involved in various roles in the supply chain that could be called up as auxiliaries. Beyond that, we have two hundred and ninety-seven volunteers in training as aspirants, not including the forty-eight designated as marines."

"That's fantastic," I said, smiling. "We also have several dozen war golems, and they'll be available for general patrolling duties, so hopefully that will free up some of the teams. Have you sorted out the new squads yet?"

Romanus shook his head. "Not yet, Lord Jax. We've laid the groundwork, including selecting people for the various teams, but we have made no announcement yet, as we wanted to get the new arrivals settled in first."

"Fine, have you folded Jon into the new structure?"

"I have." He gave a faint, lopsided smile. "As I said the other day, I simply accepted him as Tribune, replacing Alistor directly. I assumed you'd have no issue with that?"

"Gods, no," I muttered to a round of smiles. "Sorry Romanus, but that man was an utter wanker. Jon, congratulations, I guess, and commiserations. I'd forgotten that you told me already, so sorry for that. Right, we'll have a welcome ceremony tonight, food and all that, and make sure the new arrivals feel welcome. We'll get them all sworn in and start moving them into their respective positions. Heph, Seneschal?"

The two figures that had been standing silent at the center of the table straightened, listening.

"I need to ask you to assist Oracle and Tenandra in training the legionnaires. I had hoped not to have to ask you to do this, mainly because I know you're both incredibly busy looking after all the golems and the Tower, respectively.

"But, if you took turns, working around the clock, and using your ability as wisps to form a knowledge bridge, that would be another seventy-two legionnaires trained in a damn day. By the time we include all the aspirants and existing legionnaires, regardless of status, the number of people we need to train jumps to nearly nine hundred.

"If Oracle and Tenandra are working together around the clock, only taking breaks now and then, while you two alternate an hour at a time, that brings us up to one hundred and eighty people a day, or just under five days to get everyone up to speed with at least a healing spell and a ranged spell."

"Of course, Jax, we have already begun preparations and will assist as required," Seneschal replied.

"Thank you both." I said, relieved at their willingness to assume some of this burden. "I didn't want to draw you away from your normal roles, considering how busy you both are, but it's necessary."

Satisfied, I turned to Romanus. "There you go, Romanus, your Legion will have healing magic soon. We'll get the full hundred and eighty done today, with, I think, more than sixty done overnight. Tomorrow, it'll drop to just Heph and Seneschal trading off, as I'll be taking Oracle and Tenandra with me. They can work on legionnaires while we travel to the next location and clear it."

"Ah! I was unaware the meeting had begun!" called a voice from the corridor, as Rewn tried to push past the two legionnaires on duty outside. "Excuse me, Legionnaire! Step aside!"

My productive meeting thoroughly derailed by yet another uninvited noble, I couldn't help but sigh in frustration, resting my head in my hands.

"City Lord Rewn..." Cai said.

I held up my hand to stop him, before rubbing my face and sitting upright.

"Okay, it's okay," I reassured Cai and the others. "Let him in," I called, and Rewn flounced in, pausing as he scanned the room, noting those in attendance and the food before bowing to me.

"I apologize for missing the beginning of the meeting, Lord Jax, but nobody came to wake me! And...uh, I don't see a chair set aside for me?" Rewn said, his voice sliding from pointed to hopefully questioning by the end of the speech.

"That's because you weren't invited, Rewn," I said with a twitch in my jaw. "This is a meeting of my council. You don't have a seat on it."

"But as a city lord?" he interrupted, smiling ingratiatingly.

"As a city lord, I'd imagine you have plenty to do normally, but as you're here, fine. Someone get him a chair, please," I said. To everyone's surprise, Mal stood up.

"I'll get another chair. He can have mine next to my father..." he said, smiling faintly as he glanced at Hannibal.

Rewn spoke up again, distracting me from worrying over whatever sneaky shit Mal and his father were planning.

"And my advisors?" Rewn asked, gesturing to what looked like half his harem out in the corridor looking in hopefully.

"Can go and stay out of the way somewhere," I stated, staring at him.

Rewn swallowed hard and nodded, gesturing them away, before I lifted one hand, stopping him. "Is Carmen out there?" I asked. When he nodded, I sighed. "Fine, she can come in as well, as she's the most sensible of your people."

There was a general grumbling at that point, and a few small arguments started up, stopping abruptly when I ordered the legionnaires to clear the corridor, and they pointedly drew weapons at the sound of complaints.

"Do you need me, Lord Jax?" Restun asked, and I shook my head. "In that case, I'll oversee the training regime and begin the integration of the newly arrived remainder of the Narkolt legionnaires into this morning's exercises, as well as the aspirants."

With that, he stood, offering his seat to Carmen, and left, as Isabella summoned several of her team to clear away the food.

Once Mal was back, squeezing in between Hannibal and Rewn, and everyone was seated again, I re-started the meeting up.

"As I was saying, Oracle and Tenandra will continue training people onboard the ship, as we head to the next notable location," I said, before Hannibal sat forward and indicated he wanted to speak.

To Rewn's surprise, I indicated for Hannibal to continue.

"I spent some time in discussion with my lord Rewn last night, Lord Jax, and he made me aware of the situation in Narkolt."

"And?" I asked.

"And I was wondering if you'd consider a change of direction?" he asked with enough caution in his phrasing to give me pause.

"I'm not going to like this, am I?" I asked, eyes narrowing.

He grinned. "There's a good reason for it; will you listen?"

I waved for him to get the fuck on with it.

"Okay, so City Lord Rewn has been deposed, probably with an imposter in the city pretending to be him, if the conversation I had with him and Primus Augustus is any judge of the situation."

"Right?" I said grimly.

"So, all I'm saying is that, if the Drow were numerous enough to simply take over the city, they would have done so. Nobody likes them, but most people would ignore them if they took over, because nothing would change for the majority. One set of nobles for another; it's all the same for the lower ranks, right?"

"Go on."

"Well, they won't want to hide if they can avoid it. They're arrogant fuckers; they want everyone to know who they are and that they're in charge. Augustus killed over a dozen of them, though; if they'd had the numbers on their side, they'd not have been sneaking around. They resorted to hiding and infiltration, which, yeah, is a Drow specialty, but you know what the fuckers are like.

"They want everyone to worship them and their kinky spider Goddess. They wouldn't be hiding if they had the numbers to run the city properly. So, what if we stormed it? A surgical strike, take out the palace and anyone in it? Yeah, a few hundred will die, mainly servants, which is shitty, but once the city is taken, and Rewn comes out of hiding, he can order the guard and the army to stand down and to follow you.

"It lets us sidestep the need for you to level by clearing monster nests, because you damn well know there'll be a fuck load of fighting in this. Add to it that one of your biggest issues has always been numbers and resources. If you take Narkolt, you solve this. An entire outfitted city can supply you with the resources to build the Academy and outfit the Legion and its Aspirants.

"It also stops the Dark Wankers cold: if they march on the Tower, the Narkolt army can take their citadel. If they march on Narkolt, the Legion can hit them from behind and grind them up against the walls of Narkolt, while the army and the guards hammer them from above." He shrugged, sitting back with a faint smile.

"I…hmm." I paused. I'd been about to tell him no, that we needed to do other things first, but the way he'd described the situation, it did make tactical sense, especially since the damn Drow couldn't have had time to get more established yet. It'd been a few days at most, and getting back there, slaughtering the limp-dicked assholes made both serious martial sense, as well as a leveling one.

"Romanus?" I asked. "What do you think?"

"I think we know too little," he said firmly. "It makes sense that this is the case, but we have no way of knowing what the Drow intend. There could be a thousand of them in the city as easily as ten, simply spread out."

"But if that was the case, they'd have been blatant about taking charge, Romanus, you know the Drow," Hannibal said quickly, before being cut off by Lucian, who had sat silently thus far, content to watch, waiting his turn to speak.

"The Drow are a highly-insular race with a small population. Traditionally, should they feel the need to take something, they would do it in a raid, appear by stealth, kill and maim, then return to the caverns under the world you all know. I have spent years at a time tracking them, killing their kind in retribution for these raids. For them to give that up and attempt to take a city?" Lucian shivered. "This makes little sense; in fact, it's a direct reversal of their standard method of accruing territory, meaning that they must have been ordered to do it…most likely by either their Queen Bellatrix or by Illoth herself." He furrowed his brow, considering his words as he went on.

"These kinds of changes are rare because the Drow are more arrogant than any human noble ever dreamed of being. They wholeheartedly believe that the way they have done things for millennia, raiding and returning to the darkness of the Underworld, is the best way. They hate the sun and the races that live under it with a passion. Forcing a Drow to walk above ground takes tremendous authority, and for Bellatrix to send seemingly dozens to hundreds to infiltrate the city means they're after something important…or…"

"There were Drow below Himnel," I said slowly, thinking about the bastards we killed below the city. "More than thirty of them, raiding the smugglers and watching the city, with a Drider leading them…"

"Driders are also rare. For one to have been sent out with only thirty is unlikely; it's more likely that there were others and that was only a small force that you encountered," Lucian replied. "If there are more than a hundred Driders alive on the continent today, I'd be very surprised. I've encountered four in my life, and I've killed well over a thousand Drow through my centuries of existence."

"Okay," I asked, glad to have someone with experience to talk to about this. "What do you think about the numbers in the city?"

Lucian hesitated as if weighing options in his head. "Most likely less than a hundred. Hannibal is correct that the Drow are arrogant and, I would add, are easily prone to histrionics. The loss of City Lord Rewn, for example, would normally be cause for the deaths of those ordered to capture him.

"For them to be attempting to take the city by replacing the highest in authority speaks to their probable low numbers. If there were more than a hundred, I would expect them to have simply stormed the palace, killing all inside, probably after setting their more poisonous pets loose in the army and guard barracks."

I turned to my resident smuggler. "Mal, you've been quiet in all this, and that's frankly fucking unusual in itself; what's your take on it?"

"I don't like the Drow," he said with bored simplicity.

"Yeah, well, shit happens. I hate black licorice myself, doesn't answer the question though, does it?"

He shot me the finger, getting a shocked gasp from Rewn and Carmen. "Well, shut it and let me finish, you prick..."

Hannibal clipped him across the back of the head. "Show some respect son, he's the Scion!"

Mal glared back at his father then turned back to me and stood up, bowing with a flourish before speaking. "I apologize, oh great lord and master, for speaking so to my betters..." he said, words fairly dripping with sarcasm.

Before I could say anything else, Thomas leaned toward Cai, "See, I fucking knew I liked Mal," he whispered, loud enough for his words to carry across the room.

"Shut it, you wanker," I shot at him, glaring, before turning back to Mal. "Right, you've managed to derail shit, which is kinda the norm for you, so what now? Are you going to make the standard insightful comment that surprises everyone and proves you've been paying attention, or the idiotic aside you usually have waiting? Come on, Mal, I've not got all day."

"I...fine," he said, properly grinning now. "You got me. I'm thinking a small strike force would be better than a full attack by the Legion. You take a few dozen legionnaires, drop them into the city from our airships, hell, no need to bother fighting through the streets.

"The lord's palace has these big, ornamental gardens at the back. We take a few ships, come in hard and fast, land, drop troops off, and the ships are away again, up into the sky, well out of range of the dicks. The Legion storm the palace, kill everyone inside to be sure, then Lord Rewn here takes his throne back."

"No, I want to keep innocent casualties to a minimum," I said, chewing my knuckle as I thought. "Rewn, is there a Command Center for the city? Where is it?"

"Such things aren't customarily discussed before..." he gestured at the others, and I snorted.

"They're all higher in Imperial rank than you are, Rewn. Seriously, speak up," I said with a "get on with it" wave of one hand.

He swallowed hard, looking around. "Very well." His voice had gone cold, my cue that I'd crossed a line. "There is a Command Center, and it's in the original keep, although it's rarely used anymore, beyond ceremonial purposes."

"Thank you, City Lord, and I apologize for snapping at you," I forced myself to say, inclining my head and feeling bloody stupid as I did it. Even then, I couldn't help but marvel at the idiotic mentality that would use the massively useful Command Center for only ceremonial events.

"Okay, if I take command of the city, we'll be able to find out exactly how many Drow are inside the city walls," I said. "Then we join the city to my territory, and I can take command of any Imperial Facilities inside it. Hopefully there will be something useful."

"Like the armory?" Rewn asked.

I stopped dead, turning to face him. "What exactly do you know about that?"

"The armory? It's buried in the city, some old facility. I made some drawings of it once," he answered, making me slightly unkindly think of a crayon scrawl done by a toddler.

"And what do you know about it, Rewn?" I repeated, carefully keeping my tone even. I deserved a fucking Bafta.

"The armory…it's some kind of storage place, buried in the city," Rewn said dismissively, before stopping. "What, didn't you know?" A smile threatened to break out as he cast an excited glance around the room, and I tried not to throttle him.

"Darling City Lord, not everyone is as versed in Narkolt's history as you are," Carmen said quickly, trying to distract people from Rewn's gloating. She smiled at him and reached for his hand. "It's an old Imperial facility. Both Narkolt and Himnel have one.

"Narkolt's is shown on some of the oldest maps using a sword symbol, with Himnel's marked on the same maps as a shield, drawing some researchers to wonder if there are similarities to the locations or if they're intended for a separate use."

"Interesting," I said slowly, looking at the others. "What do you think, Lydia?"

She smiled, coldly. "Ah'd like another chance ta meet tha Drow."

"So would I," Augustus spoke up.

"Sorry, mate, I have a job for you already." I said, shaking my head with regret. "It's not glamourous, but it's important, very damn important."

"Of course, my Lord, whatever you need."

I winced at his formality. From a friend, that tone felt like a cold shoulder.

"I need you to go to each of the waystations, activate the Command Center, and order the facility to construct the remote towers. Once you've done that, Seneschal and Heph can add them into the territory and command any golems inside the boundaries from here. Then I need you to go to the facility to the south.

"Take a ship with plenty of cargo space, and as soon as you get there, activate the remote facility, then load up on cores and golems and bring them back here."

Augustus' eyes narrowed almost imperceptibly at my command.

"Honestly, Augustus, I'd damn well prefer you with me. I promise I would; but as my heir, you're the only one that can do this."

"It's okay Jax, I understand," he said, a sad smile showing. "I'd rather be by your side in the fight, but…" He shrugged.

I nodded once. "And I'd rather that, as well."

"Can I not help?" Thomas asked.

I shook my head. "I need you with me, and you need a team. Romanus?"

"I can arrange a team, although Restun might be better to ask?"

"Good point. Okay, Thomas, go to Restun after the meeting, tell him you need a team, and what you want. He'll give you some recommendations, as I need you back up to speed. Once you've had some time to integrate with the Legion, we can send you out doing this kind of thing.

"But for now, no offence, bro, but they don't know you beyond being an ex-dark legionnaire, so it'd cause a fuckton of problems. Take command of a squad, fight with them, and let them see the real you, not just the wanker I know," I said with a wink. "Then they'll spread the word confirming you as one of their own."

"Makes sense, just blows for you, Augustus," Thomas said.

"It's okay, Jax. Thomas. I serve as needed, always," the big man said.

"Well, I note that Hellenica didn't come with you, but I have another job for the pair of you, if you don't mind?" I asked, getting a more genuine smile from him. "I know her children have been without her for a long time, and she was working to break some of their less-appreciated skills, but I could do with an aerial team." I paused as he nodded, clearly jumping ahead and probably realizing what I needed better than I did.

"I'd like twenty of them," I said, "along with ten of the Alkyon to be a part of the raid. I know you'll have more than ten of the Alkyon you can speak for, but I've no idea who would be the better choices from the Djinn." I closed my eyes, damn well knowing I was going to regret the words I was about to say. "Plus, I think a small, and I damn well mean SMALL group of the imps would help, as between them, they can probably infiltrate any group of fliers out there, just in case. So, if you could pick them out, and arrange for them to start working together?"

"Of course, Lord Jax." He clapped his fist to his heart and inclined his head once.

"Thank you, my friend." I grabbed the thick edge of the table. "Right. If I'm going to do this, I need a competent team behind me, large enough to cause some serious trouble, but small enough that we can slip in and out without sending the entire city into a panic. I'll take my squad, plus the thirty or so fliers, and a hundred of the Legion. Will that cause issues, Romanus?"

"Define issues." Romanus raised an eyebrow. "I'll have every single legionnaire trying to beg, borrow, or steal a way into the raid, but beyond that, no. That's a large enough group to keep you safe and achieve the objective, provided there's not too large a force waiting for you. And, if there is, the airships will be able to get you out. I assume you'll be taking Tenandra?"

"I will. Think of her as my ship from now on," I said, before shooting a comment to Oren. "Oh, and Oren? The captain and helmsman on her need a new role. They're just wasting a berth onboard her; she doesn't need either of them."

"Ach, Ah can always do wi' more o' both!" Oren replied with an enthusiastic grin.

"That's fine," Romanus responded to my earlier comment. "So, with your ship's capacity at around forty, at a push, and the total around a hundred and forty, you'll need three more ships the same size, or a pair of cruisers."

"Best to make it a pair of cruisers and me," Mal said. "You'll need backup, and if you just take the cruisers, you don't have that. Besides, I can set off early, come in from the sea, pretend to be a normal ship, land and have a scout about, maybe take some of your spies with me. Then, when you arrive, I'll have a little advice ready."

"Good point; thank you, Mal," Romanus said.

I snorted, waiting for the other shoe to drop. In three, two, one…

"Although, for my people to be really effective, a few spells for them, just in case, wouldn't hurt," Mal suggested innocently, as most of the people round the table started to laugh. "What?"

"There it is!" I said, shaking my head.

"Oh, so you're saying that it wouldn't be useful to have my people ready with spells? Or as a mobile platform for the fliers to use as a jumping-off point?"

I smiled as I replied. "No, you're right on all counts; I just knew as soon as you spoke up, it was going to damn well cost me. Fine, Flux?" I asked, looking over at the older Mer where he and Ame sat close together, silently watching the conversation.

"I will arrange a team to go with Mal, to act as your eyes and ears," Flux said, and as soon as I nodded, he went on. "And as you are currently without Bane, I will accompany you personally, both to watch over my teams and to protect you."

"I don't think…" I held up my hand as both Nerin and Ame opened their mouths. "On second thought, that's fine. Great, even. Glad to have you with us, Flux," I said quickly, not needing even more of a tongue-lashing than I was already going to get from Ame for breathing wrong or something.

"Thank you," Flux said. I noted the way that both Nerin and Ame turned to him, as though daring him to say another word. I had to wonder if I was saving myself from the grief or giving him an excuse to escape their clutches for some peace.

"And Cheena will go with you, of course." Ame turned to me. "You have no objections, I trust, Lord Jax?" she half-asked, half-ordered.

"Nope, no problem there. Cheena is always welcome with me," I said, almost too quickly. "Okay, so we're raiding Narkolt and taking control of it for the Empire. We'll have a second meeting with the Legion leadership and a small cadre of others who will be involved in the fighting after this. But for now, let's finish up with the outstanding issues. Cai?"

"I have two outstanding issues. One crosses over with Lucian, so I'll let him raise that one. The other is the influx of people and is a much larger issue. We essentially have a large population for a fledgling town, which I'm finding is the best way to look at this, but we have no trade for the people to be working in."

"We're on a war footing, meaning we have no trade caravans to send out, therefore the goods that are created are for our own consumption only. While this is fine in the short term, and for now the population is happily working together to improve their own and their fellow citizens' lives, there will come a time when that's not enough. People are built to want to better themselves, to want to gain items they can't make. Without an actual economy, including so many new influxes of people, that will cause issues soon."

"Hanau, you and Hannibal are working on the economy, right?" I asked and got nods from them both.

"Yes, but we have both a problem and a solution there," Hannibal said, grinning. "We were looking to establish trade with the smaller villages and towns, and of course the Gnomes far to the south. Narkolt could fix the trade issue for us.

"It'll take some time, as essentially we were considering the city as a possible neutral party and a target for conquering later, but now, if you can take it in short order, we'd clear out a lot of issues. We'd also have a massive manufacturing base to use, customers by the thousands, a market for all our goods, as well as somewhere to buy from."

He gave a bastardly grin. "Essentially, we take the city, set up a marketplace for the Tower there, and undercut the rich cocksuckers who have been fixing the prices for years. I'll sort a tax system out that'll be fair, reasonable for all to pay, and have as few loopholes as possible. The money from that can help us to pay our people. Once they're being paid, they can buy items. The items they buy generate profit. We tax the profit to provide the wages, and your various projects all get paid for."

"Okay, I like it. What about the Smuggler's Guild?" I asked.

"I'll pull their teeth, make most things legal, just control the situation, cut the profit out of smuggling. Plus, I know all the routes." He underscored his words with a little wink in my direction.

"If it was illegal…" I said.

He held up a hand. "Most of the things that were illegal are because it makes them more profitable. House Sarat, for example, is the primary house that pushed through the law that made Dreamweed illegal, along with Moondust. Moondust is used in a hell of a lot of higher-end cooking. It prevents the food spoiling and is mildly relaxing, a bit like when our own chefs used booze in cooking, that level of effect. Dreamweed is a narcotic, yes, but again a minor one. We're talking weed, not heroin."

"Okay…" I said, frowning. "Sarat, why's that familiar?"

"Joshua was one of the leading members of the house. I believe you killed him," Rewn said sadly.

"Oh yeah, that little prick," I muttered. "Anyway, they kept them banned?"

Hannibal nodded. "Yeah, they did, and they made damn sure they were the only sellers of them through the Smuggler's Guild, going so far as to make some very messy lessons of anyone else who tried. It kept the price at nearly three times what it had been when they took over the market, netting them a nice profit.

"I intend, with your approval, of course," he said quickly, glancing at me in question. "to remove all the monopolies for houses like that and make an Imperial trading house. The house will have the backing of the Legion, selling items from the Tower and so on, meaning we can undercut those fuckers and make a nice profit still, stimulating the economy and costing the noble houses directly, weakening them economically.

"As the Imperial trading house will be protected by the Legion and the Empire as well, it means when one of them gets out of line and tries to make an object lesson, it'll be a high crime, and the Legion can deal with it. Nice and simple."

"Do a review of the illegal shit for me," I said after a few seconds of thought. "Cai, go over it with him, and then take it to Lucian. Once all three of you have agreed on it, bring it to me, and I'll make it law that they're legal or illegal, respectively. Frankly I don't give a shit if people are high as fuck, as long as they do it safely and don't do it when they're working.

"Make up something to that effect, and I'm fine with it. Legionnaires and essential workers are to be drug-free when we're at war, however, and when they're working. If they take time off, have fun."

"Sounds good. Ah, what about prostitutes and brothels?" Mal asked.

"Never took you for the sort, Mal," I retorted with a glance in his direction. "Thought you'd have your pick."

"Go to hell," he snapped. "I mean they're illegal in Himnel and legal in Narkolt."

"Make them legal, provided the workers *want* to be there. It's their bodies; I don't give a shit about what they do with them but make it law that they have to be clean and healthy. Get the healers to take care of that side of things." I turned and glanced at Nerin, who'd straightened up.

"I know how you feel about treating sexual diseases, so to be clear, this is an order, so let's not have any confusion in it. If they're a bum on the streets, or a whore, or a baker, or whatever, they all have the right to health. You and your healers WILL help them, am I understood?"

"Of course," Nerin said, nodding in understanding. "I jest with the legionnaires about not treating infections they gain from seeing whores, but I would never turn them away, and they know that."

"I thought that was the case, but I wanted to be sure. Thank you, Nerin. Right, what was the other issue, Cai, Lucian?" I asked.

"Ah, one point," Hannibal interrupted. "The healers, are they free to the nobility as well as the people?"

"Yes, they're free to everyone in the Empire. But, include a small tax on the wealthy toward it. Not a stupid one, literally a small one, but enough that it'll pay the costs toward maintaining their facilities and so on," I said, getting a nod of satisfaction from him before Lucian spoke up.

"Thank you, Jax. Yes there've been several issues, small matters that have been easily dealt with under the law, mainly fights and a few arguments. The Oath prevents a great many of the usual issues, thankfully. The one that I need your assistance with is a child."

"Caron," I interrupted, putting my face in my hands. "It's fucking Caron, isn't it?"

"I'm afraid so. He's too young, under your rules, to swear the Oath. As such, he's becoming quite the accomplished thief. When he was caught, he managed to use an ability to escape the first time. Unfortunately, for him at least, he was recognized, and when we raided his rooms…well." Lucian pulled out a handful of golden necklaces, rings and more, most of which had a subtle glow to it.

"He had that in his room?" I asked.

He snorted. "This is less than a quarter of what he had in the room, and I suspect he has several more stashes around the Tower. Seneschal and Hephaestus have admitted they cannot track him, and he's begun to linger around the entrances to locations I don't feel comfortable about, such as the treasury and the Genesis Chambers."

"Where we have a large number of gems for construction. Right, after the meeting, I want to see the little shit. Being allowed to not swear until now is me being nice in case they want to leave the Empire later. In his case, he can ask to be released from the Oath if he wants to leave, but the little sod gets the option of swear or fuck off today," I told them bluntly.

"Very well." Lucian said with a faint smile. "To be fair to him, I have discussed it with him and, while he insists on lying to my face, I can detect no ill-will in him. He simply refuses to believe he is incapable of getting himself out of any trouble. As such, he believes he is above petty things like laws. As he stated once, if the items weren't claimed, why shouldn't he take them if he finds them?"

"Because they belong to me, and the little fucker was already told to stop this shit. Fine though, I'll give him a chance. And bring Kayt from the herb gardens along at the same time. He's fixated on her, or he was, at least. Let's see if she can rein him in, rather than a parent."

"Very well," Lucian said again, nodding.

"Fine. We've done the economy, the Legion, and legal. Crafting, fleet, and research teams, anything for me?" I asked Ame, Oren, and Riana, respectively.

"Crafters are happy, for the most part, and are settling into groups, especially knowing that a dedicated crafting area that will grant bonuses is coming. Our harvesting teams are going out and returning with the local items we can locate. However, some items, such as sand for glass, clay, various kinds of wood, the various thousands of ingredients the crafters need, are limited. We'd like a ship to be allocated to the crafting teams…permanently, if possible."

"A ship!" Oren grunted. "Ah've already told ye, ah need all ma ships!"

"Yes, Oren, you have said this. I've told you, however, if you want to do the ingredient runs, then that will be fine. But you don't, and every time we run out of an ingredient, it takes days to get more! That's days that a particular crafter is sitting, useless. As such, I have done that which I warned you I would, and have raised it here," Ame said shortly.

"Okay, clearly, this is an argument that's been going on for a while. Oren, we need the ingredients. Explain, please," I ordered.

"Aye, ma apologies, Jax, Ah know we need tha shit, but she damn well knows Ah need all ma ships. Keepin' up patrols, training schedules, runs, all take time. Yer need ships noo fer that trip ta Narkolt, two cruisers ye say," Oren complained.

"Yeah, I'm taking two of MY ships, mate," I said, crossing my arms. "Deal with it."

"Ah, well aye, Ah know they be yer ships, sorry, Jax. Ah didn't mean…" Oren broke off and sighed. "Tha problem be one of timin,' that's all. Ame and tha others all come at me an' demand a ship reet noo. Never any notice ta sort things oot, so ah tell them they'll be waitin', otherwise ah get nowt done but write trainin' schedules that be changed an hour later."

"Fair enough." I scratched my chin, looking for the middle ground here. "If you're constantly badgered, then I agree with Ame. Simple solution is that the crafters get a single ship dedicated to their needs. They can sort it out from there and make sure it's made into as efficient a ship as possible, that way they stop pestering you."

"Aye, iffin that were all they wanted, Ah'd have agreed by noo, Jax. But then yer have the woodworkers wantin' entire trunks. Yer have fishermen demandin' ships they can fish off tha side of. Yer got people wantin' ten ton o' clay, or thirty o' sand. A single ship be nowhere near enough, Ah warn ye…" Oren said, shaking his head with the overwhelming nature of the need.

"And that's fine, Oren, but that's all Ame is getting." I turned to Ame and smiled, knowing she'd sense the meaning in it. "Ame, you wanted a ship, and that's understandable. But, to be clear, you getting one is one ship. You don't get to swap it out for others more suited. Oren will assign one of the merchant ships, with a crew and so on to you, and you'll get a golem, one that can be commanded directly by you or a member of the crew you designate. It'll be a war golem, so that if you get into shit, it'll be able to deal with it, that way you won't need a Legion team." I mused, nodding to myself.

"Yeah, you manage it, Ame. That way, the ship will get used to your needs, send them out as much as you need, plan on regular supply runs, and take the crafters with you. If you think you need a Legion team, the option is there, but I think anything that might attack you, meeting a fully armed war golem instead?"

"Sounds good ta me…any chance of a few more? Do they be capable o' ranged attacks?" Oren asked hopefully.

"Yeah, the war golems are capable, and we brought spare bows for them from the storage in Himnel," I said. "They fire some kind of manabolts. Not really seen them in action myself yet. There was one of them on the ship when the Storm Demon attacked, but I ordered it to hold back until it was certain of a hit. The damn thing crashed into the other ship before the golem got a chance to do more than poke a few holes in it."

"We could definitely do with some of those; any chance we can have one to study?" Riana asked hopefully, fingers curling possessively already.

I snorted. "Have you fixed the cannon issues yet?"

She grimaced, holding her hand out, palm flat to the ground and shaking it back and forth. "Yes and no. We've got a design that's safe enough to use that I'd be happy to fire it myself, but it's weaker. Much weaker."

"How big is it?" Thomas asked before I could.

"About a quarter of the size of the originals, and before you ask, no we can't simply scale it up, there are issues with integrity," Riana said, slumping in her chair. "We tried that, and it exploded." She reached up absently to pat the side of her face, and I noted much shorter hair on that side of her head, probably from it all being regrown.

"Okay, but the smaller cannons, are they as mana-intensive as the normal ones?" I asked.

"No, they're actually cheaper to fire than the size alone would suggest. They're much more efficient, but…"

"What about other cannons being close to them? Any issues with that?" Thomas asked. I grinned at him as we both had the same mental image.

"No, you could have a dozen or more close by, but they'd still be smaller, and need to be aimed, we'd need a huge number of gunners," Riana said slowly, looking from Thomas to me.

"No, we wouldn't…you thinking what I'm thinking?" I asked Thomas, who pulled some parchment out of his bag along with a quill and ink bottle. "Oh, look at Mister-Fancy-Pants with his quill," I taunted, and he shot me the finger before going back to the sketch he was working on.

"Okay, Riana, what if you set them like this? You could make them smaller, if that helps, and make say, five on a side?" he said, drawing a square, then filling it with a grid that was five by five. "You put this on a mount you can swivel, with a little targeting sight on the top, and let your gunner fire all twenty-five at once. A broadside like that would seriously fuck up anything it hits."

"Hmm." Riana plucked the drawing from his grasp, and she and Ame began arguing over the best way to produce it.

"Okay, sounds good to me," I said over their bickering. "Test it please, see if it's a dream or realistic. Hell, you could fire them in relays, or on a single second delay between cannons, lets you adjust your aim for the next one. You ladies figure that shit out, and I'll see what I can do to get you an enemy to fuck up with it." Leaving them to their already-absorbing interest, I turned to Oren. "Okay, bud, last chance for fleet time. Any news?" I asked.

"No' really, ta be honest. We be getting there, most o' tha smaller ships have had tha armor improved, makin' 'em lighter and stronger. Tha battleship, well, she's sealed up noo, thanks te tha golems an' tha engineers. But beyond that, she's gonna be weeks away from bein' safe ta fly in a fight. Too big, too slow." He shrugged.

"Beyond that, all good. Crews are trainin', getting better, the marine team that went out on *Ragnarök* yesterday tried oot firin' from tha ship, found some wee harpies, real ones Ah mean, up in tha mountains. It had a Legion team on board, too, worked well. Beyond that, we just be working on tha battleship an' tha wee ships, hopin' that Riana gets me a set o' cannons soon."

"Fair enough. That works; well done, mate. Okay, I guess research is done as well, so that'll do me. Anyone else have anything to raise?" I asked, getting a series of shakes and negatives. "Good, thank you all. Flux, Lydia, Thomas, Mal, Hannibal, and the Legion, stay behind, please," I said, nodding toward the door for everyone else.

CHAPTER TWENTY-SEVEN

The room cleared quickly, including Cai and the others, but while Carmen stood with the others, Rewn simply settled in and reached into his bag of holding for a glass of wine.

"Rewn?"

He nodded, smiling, before going red. "Oh! Of course, my apologies, Lord Jax." He fished around in his bag and produced a second, much more battered cup for me.

"Thank you, but no." I didn't even want to even think about where that cup had been or what could be growing in it. "Is there something you want to talk about?"

"Well, it's *my* city," he said, frowning in confusion. The expression made him look a bit like a prune wearing too much make-up. "You'll need me!"

"Are you a seasoned fighter?" I asked, struggling to maintain a semblance of calm. "Have you led troops? Do you know where the Drow are, and how many? Who they've captured? Where their base is?"

"I, well, I know some of them! Peter…" Rewn said.

"Was killed," Carmen said from where she lingered near the door. "We don't know exactly who was taken. We know that some of them will be Drow, but not which ones. Some will have simply been drunk or have taken time out. We only know those who attacked us directly at that point were Drow; they might have taken new disguises."

"But this is *my* city!" Rewn whined. "I deserve to be in charge of the assault. They're going to take my city back, so I should be leading them!"

"You should be leading?" I said in wonder. "Rewn, you have no experience with troops; why should you be leading them?"

"Because I'm a noble!" He gestured as if this was the only explanation anyone would ever need to do any batshit thing he asked of them. "We're better than the common folk! My father, he taught me…"

"Wow, well fuck me sideways, this clears up a lot." I rubbed the bridge of my nose. "Okay Rewn, you've sworn allegiance to me. Do you understand what that entails?" I asked, my eyes closed as I tried to make sense of the world.

"That I have to do what you say, but…"

"That's right, Rewn." Realizing we'd been over this before, I switched up my tactics. "Look, what level are you?"

"Seven!" he stated proudly.

"Level seven!" My entire train of thought derailed and wrecked in a glorious fireball of this man's stupidity. "Why the hell are you so low a level?"

"Because, as a *noble*, we don't need to level!" He smiled contentedly. "We're the chosen ones; we've got the *right* to…"

"Stop," I ordered him, holding up one hand so I wouldn't slap him with it. "Stop right the fuck there. Fuck's sake, so much about the leadership of this realm has become so clear."

"Lord Jax, should we leave?" Romanus asked.

"No." I shook my head. "No, Romanus you shouldn't because, and I'm damn sorry to do this, as I know how busy you are, but I'm going to need your help with this. Thomas, you, too."

"Butterbar?" Thomas asked.

"Yeah, definite butterbar," I replied with a grunt. "Okay, Romanus, Thomas, fuck's sake, all of you, and that includes you, Carmen, we all have a new role, and that's to teach Rewn." I straightened and stared him down, taking a deep breath.

"Rewn, since we met, I've been more than a bit confused with you. The simple reason is this: you hold to the old ways as you see them. You seem to be, as near as possible for a noble, a nice guy, and you genuinely seem to care about your city."

"I do!" he said, still smiling as he sipped his wine.

"And yet, not only do you *constantly fucking interrupt me*, your new liege-lord and master, but you have absolutely no idea about how the real world works." I masterfully resisted the urge to yank my hair out by its roots. "You've been taught that levelling is beneath you. Tell me, Rewn, when did you take over as city lord?"

"When I was four," he said sadly. "My father died in a hunting accident, and his advisors helped me to rule since then."

"And these advisors, they told you things, like that levelling was beneath you?"

He nodded. "The upper nobility don't need to do such things. Levelling puts points into your body and mind, making you stronger, but I don't need that, as I have servants and guards to carry out my wishes. And my Intelligence is already the highest in the land," he said proudly.

I couldn't help but to shake my head.

"It's not, Rewn," I said as compassionately as I could muster. "I'm sorry that you've been in this position, sorry that you've been lied to all this time. Hannimish said you were old friends and that you grew up together." I took a long, hard look at the man before me. "How old are you?"

"Fifty-three," he said slowly, shaking his head. "No, there's something you don't understand, here! Clearly, there's something wrong!"

"You look like you're in your early twenties, Rewn." I leaned in. "How is that possible? Elven blood?"

"I...some of us, the nobility, that is..." He glanced nervously around the room. "There's a way for us to use...*things* to change ourselves. If you don't know about it, I'm not supposed to say, but..."

"You mean the monster cores?" I guessed. "You absorbed one, probably as a child, at someone else's direction, didn't you? An advisor?"

"Hannimish's father, the *Old* Lord Hannimish. He was my personal advisor when I first took the throne. When he died, Hannimish's eldest brother took over in his place, and Hannimish was exiled to the Sunken City, although he didn't know it. He's...not very bright." Rewn trailed off.

I nodded, seeing that he was starting to understand. "And Senanth?" I asked, curious where he fit into everything.

"Pfff, an old fool. I allowed him to deal with the simpler details. But from time to time, I made my wishes known, and I gave such orders out personally, or through Hannimish's brother, Wentworth."

"Holy shit," I muttered, rubbing my eyes as I realized they'd used Senanth to do the day-to-day running of the city, so that he didn't suspect them, and they'd maneuvered Rewn into a position where he was even less use than I'd thought he was.

"They controlled you, Rewn. They used you as a puppet, and the one person who was actually your friend, Hannimish the younger, was kept from you as much as possible, so that he wouldn't guess what was happening and ruin it for them." I looked at the make-up-covered fop, and couldn't help but feel sorry for him.

"They kept you docile with your pretty harem, drink, and drugs, and when the Drow killed them and took their place, they probably just didn't understand any of it, or they'd have simply continued with it and not risked anything.

"I'm sorry, Rewn. Sorry that I've dismissed you as much as I have, because I don't actually think any of this is your fault. You've been set up to be a puppet, and until now, you had no idea, did you?" Shock and stunned horror was written all over his face as the noble's world came tumbling down.

I turned to Carmen. "Did you know?"

"No," she said softly. "I mean, I'd started to suspect that something was wrong, but not like this, not so much."

She wiped at her eyes and took Rewn's hand, holding it tight as he stared at her, at me, and shook his head. The individual sections were finally lining up enough that even for someone as dense as him, or as indoctrinated as those on the inside were, it was plain to see.

"No," he whispered. "No, it…it can't be true."

"It is, Rewn, I'm sorry," I said.

He stared at me, searching in vain for the joke, for the trick, before his shoulders heaved and he started to cry, tears making tracks down his powdered cheeks with all the pathetic misery of a small, bereaved child.

"I'll take him," Carmen said quietly, standing up and tugging on his hand, drawing him up next to her.

"I'm sorry that it came to this, Rewn. I wish I could have helped." I said again, feeling terrible for the man.

"Why?" he asked, voice hollow. "Why would you help me, when those I trusted all my life did this?"

"Because not everyone is a piece of shit," I said, a hint of grit in my voice. "Rewn, if you want to improve, if you want me to help you to become what you could be, and to become the city lord in truth, I will. Take some time, but if you want to, and you want a distraction from all of this, come to the base of the Tower at noon and find me. You can train with me and my team."

"Thank you," Carmen whispered sadly. With a grateful nod in my direction, she drew Rewn away. Once the door closed behind him, I sighed and shook my head, looking around the room.

"Wow," I said eventually. "That was unexpected."

The others nodded, Jon especially looking shocked. "I take it you had no idea?" I asked him, then looked to Hannibal.

"None," Jon said, shaking his head.

"Not entirely, although a lot of things make sense now. Things he'd say in meetings, or times he'd declare something, then go back on it later. Clearly, his keepers changed their minds or had to step in and issue new orders. Damn," Hannibal said, shaking his head.

"What did you mean by butterbar?" Augustus asked.

I laughed, the thought shaking me out of my pity for Rewn and making me think again of an old friend.

"A butterbar is a newly trained officer in the army, one with no experience whatsoever, and the most dangerous person of the lot. It's said the most terrifying comment anyone can ever hear, scarier than Restun even, is when a butterbar says, 'I've been thinking'."

"Interesting, and your comment in reference to Rewn?" Augustus asked.

I gave a small, wry smile. "A butterbar is where all officers start. It doesn't mean they're all idiots, just that they have no real-world experience. I'm thinking that Rewn, well, he's had a shitty hand dealt to him, but it doesn't have to define him. With a little help, and a lot of levels, he could make something of himself. Let's face it, his advisors kept him as a child; all we have to do is teach him."

"In a war," Augustus said, his mouth set in a grim line.

"Never said it'd be easy." I spread my palms on the table before me. "The other option is, we basically leave him as he is: a city lord, but a complete idiot. You want to leave him in charge of Narkolt once we've conquered it?"

"Hell, no," Augustus said, his sentiment echoed around the table.

"In that case, then, we train him, treat him like he's a brand-new officer straight out of training…or I guess I could set him up in a nice house and just let him smoke and fuck himself into oblivion, then set someone else up as city lord." I shrugged, thinking it was an either-or situation now.

"You mean give him a squad?" Augustus said, shocked.

"I do. One of the most experienced and reasonably levelled, a team we can use to keep him out of trouble. I'd imagine there's a legionnaire or two who are good teachers? Both of general history as well as military matters?"

"There're a few that have a passing interest in it, specifically the Empire's history…" Romanus said dubiously.

"Centurion Hennen," Jon recommended. "He's a good man, interested in the world as much as any, and patient beyond almost any others I know. Plus, no offence, he's from Narkolt, so he can talk about events in Narkolt from a local perspective. He's been serving as an interim primus, but with the recent shift of the legion structure, he claimed an Optio's slot instead."

"Then let's make Hennen his minder. See what Hennen wants as a reward, and if we can make it happen. If he keeps Rewn alive and makes something useful of him, then he can have it. We'll see if Rewn wants to learn, see if he can learn to be a basic officer first, then we upgrade him to an actual person later on," I said, rubbing my eyes.

"Now, as much as it's Rewn's entire life we've just totally derailed, let's move on; we need to get this sorted. Tenandra, can you show a map of the city for me, please?" I asked the wisp. She bowed her head in acquiescence, reaching out and placing her hand on the table, somehow restructuring her form to include a 3D map that we could interact with.

"Right, my plan is this." Mal spun the map around and gestured out to sea. "I'll come in from the sea, low enough that they're not sure if I'm sea or air. Once I'm docked with the spies, we'll go exploring and see what we can find. While this happens," he said, gesturing for the map to turn. "The other ships come in from the north a day or so later, make it late at night and as hard to see as possible."

The planning session took just under three hours, but by the end of it, not only did we have a solid plan, but we also felt we had a reasonable chance of success. That was two things I was used to not having at the start of my fights.

Once the meeting broke up, Lucian left the room for a few minutes, before bringing Caron, Kayt, and Ronin in, gesturing for them to stand before me.

"Ah, hi Jax. Is there a problem?" Ronin asked worriedly.

I nodded, watching Caron, who ducked his head and refused to meet my gaze, while glancing at the totally bewildered and wide-eyed Kayt.

"Yes, and you're here because you damn well caused it, Ronin," I said. "Caron, you've been told to stop thieving, breaking into rooms, and basically to stop being a shitbag brat. What do you have to say for yourself?" I asked as Lucian emptied handfuls of gold, jewels, and valuables onto the table by my side with a loud clatter.

"I didn't do it," Caron said straight away.

"Yes, you did," I said. "I'll make this as simple as possible, Caron. We know. We know you've been taking these things from the sealed rooms, from the storerooms if they've been left unguarded, hell, you've been giving them to Kayt, a girl who's totally confused by all the attention, as she's what, eleven?" I asked her.

"Nine, Lord," she corrected, fidgeting with the hem of her dress' sleeve.

"Fuck's sake, Caron, how old are you?"

"I'm ten!" Caron said, eyes flashing with childlike offense. "I just didn't know no better, but I do now! I'll be good, okay? Can we go now?"

"No," I said, clenching my fists at my side. "No, you damn well can't." I sighed and rubbed at my mouth, watching Caron, before going on. "Look, Caron, I'll be honest with you. I don't like having to use the Oaths, as it reeks of forcing people to do my bidding, close to slavery in some ways, but…it lets us all know we're safe from each other.

"People know they can leave their doors open and their stuff is safe, and they know they can ask to be released from the Oaths, and I'll let them go. The thing is, all of this is built on trust, trust that the Oaths are applied to everyone equally. You've just fucked that up. Not just for yourself, but for the entire godsdamned Tower and the Empire!"

"I didn't mean to," Caron whispered, now back to staring at his shoes.

"And I believe that. Otherwise, you'd already be on a ship heading to a village as far from here as possible, to be dumped there," I warned him. "The thing is, I don't want to do that, not to anyone, let alone a kid who's been with me through all of this. Ronin thought you'd have learned your lesson with the experience with Restun the other week, but clearly not, so…"

"Don't send me away, please!" Caron pleaded.

I grimaced, shaking my head. "As I said, lad, I don't want to, but you've fucked up a lot of things for us here. You've left me with only two choices: send you to a village or…"

"Please, Lord Jax, don't send him away," Kayt whispered, so terrified she was barely able to look up at me through her hair.

"Or?" he begged frantically.

"Or I let you swear the Oaths early, with the proviso that when you reach sixteen, you can choose to stay or go, and I'll remove it if you want to leave. *IF I let you stay, you're clearly getting into a lot of trouble without a job, so you'll have one."*

"I've got a job!" Caron said quickly. "I help with the skinning!"

"Does he?" I asked Lucian, who shook his head.

"No. He was supposed to be help them, but after two days, he stopped turning up. As he's a child, they assumed he'd been given a different job, and nobody thought to ask in the confusion of daily life here," Lucian clarified calmly.

"See, this is how it is, Caron. It's time to choose. You either swear the Oath, and you do the job I give you, or you get dumped in a village at the edge of nowhere. I'm trying to plan a war here, and finding out that you've broken into my rooms and stolen from me isn't helping," I warned him bluntly.

"I didn't!" he cried. "Okay, yeah, I took some stuff, but it wasn't anyone's! It was left in the rooms that the dead locked hundreds of years ago! It was all free!"

"And there's the problem," I said. "First of all, it's not 'free stuff', this is MY land, these are *my* rooms, and anything inside them is mine. Secondly, some of these are powerful magical artifacts. We left them where they were until we could examine them and find out about the people whose rooms they were.

"Some items would have been sold and others given away, but first, we needed to understand who these people were. They gave their *lives* in defense of the Tower, and now we'll never know because you stole it all from them!" I knew I was laying it on a bit thick, but I needed to get through to him.

"Some of these magical artifacts are powerful, things like the necklace and rings that let nobles on the other side of the world communicate with Kayt, except they could be different. I've found vampiric items already, Caron, do you know what they are?" I asked, seeing the way Kayt had flinched when I mentioned the noble that she'd accidentally talked to in her sleep.

"No," he mumbled, red-faced.

"They're items that steal your life away, feeding it to someone else. Items that will kill the wearer, like a ring that could have drained Kayt of her life!" I snapped at him, seeing him shrug.

"But it didn't, and I'd not have given her one of those!"

"But you wouldn't know!" I snarled.

"I do! I dumped them in the trash!" he retorted, tears starting down his face. I bit back my deep, abiding need to shout, as I processed his words.

"You…wait, what?" I asked him.

"I put the evil stuff, the rings like that, the chains, and the knife…I put them all in the trash," he said. "Are you going to send me away now?"

"Where?" I asked, glancing over at Lucian, who nodded his understanding and strode toward the door. "Where did you put them?"

"The trash pile, where the bits that the hunters can't use go. It's a pit; they burn it all at the end of the week," he said, wringing his hands.

"WHERE?" I roared at him.

"The north side! By the old tree stump. It wouldn't burn, so I buried it there!" he cried, and Lucian was out of the door in a second, racing for the steps.

"Right, come with me, Caron. Kayt, I'm sorry, I thought I needed you here, to make sure that Caron understood the severity of this, but it seems he understands more than I hoped. Go back to whatever you'd normally be doing now, and thank you for your time," I ordered, standing and leading the boy down the hall and into the stairwell as she curtsied and sprinted off.

It took us half an hour to reach the ground floor, and when we did, we arrived in time to meet Lucian coming the other way, a small sack in one hand.

"What is it?" I asked, and he hefted it suggestively while inclining his head to one side where nobody would accidentally overhear us.

"It's what young Caron advised we would find. Some cursed items, some vampiric, and a few transmission devices."

"Really?" I looked into the sack as he opened it. A few of the items looked a bit wrong, but nothing stood out. "How do you know?" I asked Lucian.

"I have a particularly evolved Identify spell. The real question is how Caron knows, considering several of these items are indeed cursed, and appeared benign at first glance." Lucian gestured to where Caron was attempting to back up into the crowd. "I think it's time for the Oath, Jax, before he can get himself into any more trouble."

Ronin had spotted Caron's motions and grabbed him, yanking him back next to him, and he held the boy's arm as we approached.

"Okay, Caron, how did you know?" I asked.

"Didn't know nothing," Caron muttered. Ronin clipped him across the back of the head.

"Not the time for that, Caron; tell him what he wants to know," Ronin growled.

"You said to never admit anything!" Caron wailed.

Ronin covered his eyes, exasperation written all over his features. "Yeah, when they don't know for sure. But when you're caught red-handed, you tell the truth, and you make the best of it! Come on, Caron, for the love of the Gods, tell him what he wants to know, dammit!"

The boy winced, then gave the matter a few seconds of thought. "I felt it," Caron admitted, finally.

"What? What do you mean…" I asked, confused and half-expecting he was lying to me again.

Lucian grabbed my arm, silencing me. His fingers dug in tightly, his expression solemn.

"Go on, Caron, explain what you felt," he encouraged the boy.

"It just…it felt wrong, most of them, anyway. The others felt like the one I gave Kayt before. You said they weren't safe, so I didn't give her them, either." He shrugged, pulling out a thick metal band that had been hanging on the inside of his pant-leg, tied to a string on his belt, and held it out. "The others are in here."

I reached out and examined it, finding to my shock that it was a *Ring* of Holding. I concentrated, getting a small inventory notice, and finding it stuffed full of gold, platinum, and three spell scrolls, not to mention a dozen books, including supplies to make more.

"This is a scribe's training manual," I said, pulling out a book and examining it carefully, feeling the magic that radiated off it. "This is a way for a scribe to learn to make magical skillbooks and spellbooks, and you had it in your fucking pants?"

I glared at the boy, who seemed on the verge of wetting himself. In that moment, I honestly didn't know if I should praise him or scream blue murder. Lucian saved me from either choice by pulling me far enough aside that we couldn't be overheard..

"He's a sensitive," Lucian said.

I frowned. "So what, he'll cry if I shout at him?"

"No! Well, yes, probably, but no. I mean that he's sensitive to *magic*. He can feel things about the items. Without any form of training, he picked out the items that would harm him or another and tried to dispose of them. It's an exceedingly rare gift, less than three on the continent that I've ever heard of, and they were all highly respected mages. He's a child with no training and no clue what he could be."

"So, what do we do?" I asked.

"Ame."

"Ame," I repeated, smiling evilly. "Now, that's a solution!"

"A good one for everyone. She gains an apprentice with tremendous potential. He gets someone who'll keep him on task and make sure of where he is at all times."

"True, but if he's got that kind of potential…let's not waste it." I took a deep breath, then nodded as I made the decision.

"Seneschal, can you arrange for Hellenica, Ame, and Flux to meet me at the foot of the Tower as soon as they can, please?" I sent to him, getting a sense of agreement and acknowledgement before he vanished from my mind again.

"Come on, let's get ready for training. We'll wait for the others there," I ordered and glared at Caron. "You want to stay, Caron?" He nodded frantically. "Good. This is your last chance, though, and you've crossed the line now. As such, I'm going to arrange training for you, and make you into the best version of yourself you can be." I frowned at him for a long second to underscore my point.

"Take the Oath, and you'll have two options. Either be the very best you can be or suffer through every day of the lessons and training, and I'll release you on your sixteenth birthday and let you go wherever you choose."

"What training?" he asked, tilting his sweaty head.

"Doesn't work like that, boy. You'll find out once you've sworn, but believe me when I say that, if you can do this, you'll have a life like no other, and you'll be respected and valuable to the Empire." Then I quirked a smile, remembering what it'd been like to be a child. "You'll love and hate it with equal measure, but I bet Kayt and the other girls will be impressed."

"I'll do it," he said quickly, getting a snort of laughter from me.

"I thought you might. All right, let's go," I said, leading the way out to the second scheduled training session of the day.

It took nearly an hour before the others arrived, and by the time they did, we were already into full swing, sprinting around the outside of the Tower in groups. Caron was desperately trying to keep up, so Ronin ran with him, enjoying the excuse to take it easier for once.

As soon as the others gathered, I cut out of training and jogged to them, slowing from a full sprint and letting my racing heart calm down.

"Lord Jax," Flux said in greeting.

"Thanks for coming," I managed with a pained grin. "I'm sorry to summon you again so soon, especially after seeing you at the meeting. Flux and Ame…" I took another deep breath. "It's good to see you, Hellenica." I smiled at the Clan Mother as I mopped sweat from my forehead.

Hellenica was a Djinn Clan Mother, one of the insanely rare females of her species. While she seemed to be composed entirely of mist one second, the next she could be surprisingly real and solid, not to mention sodding terrifying, especially when she thought I was going to try to absorb the souls of some of her children.

"It's good to see you again, Jax," she said.

"Are you happy with things? The kids all right?" I asked, the automatic reaction of meeting a friend you'd not seen in a few days outside of a formal setting meant I defaulted to polite conversation, before blinking and remembering what and where I was now.

"Very good, thank you, Jax,"

"Good. First of all, you're all aware of Caron?" I asked, and got a round of nods and agreement.

"That makes it easier, so I'll cut straight to the chase. Ronin, the little fucker, had basically begun training him in rogue skills when he was hiding in the Tower. The result of which, seeing as he's not given any Oath to behave, is that Caron's been robbing me blind." I looked around at the collection of frowns.

"You wish us to punish him?" Hellenica guessed, her voice making it clear how uncomfortable she was with the prospect.

"Yes and no. As part of the investigation, we found this," I said as I handed the bag of magical shit that Caron had tried to destroy to Ame.

"This is…these…" she muttered, flicking the items apart with a claw-tipped finger before using her examine ability and grunting. "As I suspected, these are evil items. I recommend we dispose…"

"We will," I assured her, cutting her off. "You're a highly skilled runesmith, and you needed to use your abilities to be sure of what they were. He just felt they were wrong, so he tried to destroy them. Lucian thinks he's magically sensitive."

The three looked from one to another, before Ame and Hellenica both offered to teach him at almost the same time.

"I don't really understand why I'm here, Jax," Flux admitted after a minute.

"Because, if he's this good with magic, I don't intend on wasting him." I said and grinned broadly. "He will be taking the Oath as soon as one of the wisps is free, then he'll begin training with Hellenica *and* Ame. Hellenica, you get to teach him magic.

"Ame, you teach runecrafting and the twisty way you look at the world. No, not worldsense, I mean logical thought and planning, and Flux? You're going to train him to be a spy."

All three looked at me, before, to my surprise, they all agreed, seeming to think it was a great idea, whereas I'd expected comments about his age.

I was going to ask them why, then shut up, remembering that, not so long ago in my own world, children would have been taught their parents' trades from a much earlier age.

I waved Ronin and Caron over, and I broke the good news to the boy, before having Seneschal help me with the Oath, rather than interrupting Oracle.

Once that was done, I sent Caron off with his new teachers to get acquainted, feeling slightly evil about how happy he was and the sure knowledge that he'd be hating life soon enough. Then, I returned to my training, justifying my practical enslavement of the boy by telling myself the oldest lies in the world.

The end justified the means, we were at war, and I had no choice.

Fortunately, I stopped short of the three most popular ones, and didn't tell anyone I loved them, the check was in the mail, or that I wouldn't cum in their mouth. Honest.

The following few hours were horrific as Restun tried to make up for every single second I'd missed in training. He pushed me to train harder and faster until I collapsed from sheer overload and laid there in the mud, as the heavens opened, drenching us all.

According to Restun, of the three hundred and seven who'd joined training today, only seventy-three had survived to the end of the session, the others falling by the wayside or taking breaks then slinking away rather than rejoining the pack.

I lay there, in the muddy grass, and I panted, my heart thundering in my ears as I tried to make sense of why the hell I did this shit to myself. According to Romanus, I could have just sat back and given quests out to my people to level up, then allocated the points to reach the same level.

I knew it wasn't the same, and that doing so would shortchange myself in the long run, but damn, it was tempting…especially as Thomas splashed over and prodded me in the side with a boot.

"Get up, you lazy turd," he wheezed, too tired to risk bending over to help me up.

"No," I whispered. "I'm dead, go away."

"Restun's coming," Thomas said.

"Don't care. I'm dead," I repeated.

"He's smiling…"

"Fuck." I muttered, straining and rolling over to my knees, then getting back to my feet, before looking around. "Where…oh, you bastard," I said, shaking my head.

"It got you moving, bro, and I'm not carrying you up to the quarters," He said, a half-grin stretching across his weary face.

"Oh Gods, no," I whispered, shaking my head. "Seriously, fuck that, think we can get a ride on a golem or something…or get a ship to take us up?" I asked, only half-joking.

"You're the boss, and there's a ship right there," Thomas suggested hopefully, pointing at a merchantman that was sitting in a cradle a few hundred meters to the left of the tower.

"No, that would be too lazy," I muttered after a minute's thought.

"Looks like we do it old school, then."

We set off together, stumbling toward the tower as I checked my notifications for my stat gains, reading, then dismissing the experience from the fight with the Storm Demons, and ignoring the rest for now.

Congratulations!

**Through hard work and perseverance,
you have increased your stats by the following:**

**Agility +1
Dexterity +2
Endurance +3
Strength +2**

Continue to train and learn to increase this further.

I grunted in satisfaction, seeing I'd managed to gain another eight points in a single day, but damn the effort was insane.

"Uh, did you see Rewn?" Thomas asked me. I frowned, remembering I'd offered to let him train with us, and shook my head.

"No, did you?"

He shrugged. "I might have, not sure really. There was a guy I almost stood on in the second lap of the warmup. He'd collapsed. We just went round him, didn't think about it a second time to be honest, just remembered."

"Fuck. I'll go look for him," I muttered, vaguely remembering, but I hadn't paid any attention beyond making sure I didn't step on him. I groaned, stretching until my back cracked as I turned and searched the training area.

"I'll help." Thomas grunted, shaking his head. "But you owe me, brother. Seriously, I need a shower…got swamp balls like you wouldn't believe right now."

"Really didn't need to know that." I groaned, shaking my head. As much as I didn't need to know that, I told him to stand still anyway and hit him with Scour, which made all the sweat and dirt that coated him turn to dust and dissolve into nothing after a second, then hit myself as well.

We checked the local area before jogging towards the outer wall. It took us ten minutes to find him and, when we did, I honestly didn't know what to do at first.

He was wearing his expensive clothes, and was tucked into a corner of the wall, his legs pulled up, arms wrapped around his knees, and was shaking as he cried.

"Rewn?"

He pulled his legs in tighter rather than respond.

"Shit," Thomas muttered. "He's practically catatonic. Do we leave him? Send his girls to take him back up?"

"No." I said, sighing. "You go, bro, I'll sort this."

"You sure? I can help," he offered.

"No, but thanks, though, mate, go on." I gestured toward the Tower, and Thomas nodded and headed off.

I sat next to Rewn, the mud squelching as I groaned and settled next to him, my ass getting soaked and even more filthy as the rain pooled by the base of the walls.

A couple of minutes passed while I waited, but eventually Rewn seemed to cry himself out, and he stuck his head up, showing that not only had he been totally inappropriately dressed, but he'd still been wearing makeup when he started.

He looked like a fucked-up clown with a crack habit.

"You…you started without me," Rewn mumbled.

"Yeah, training starts at noon and sunrise. If you're late, you get to make up the time, usually with a particularly evil legionnaire screaming at you to go faster. It's best not to give them the excuse to pick on you."

"But you're the Scion!" he mumbled. "They wouldn't dare!"

"They damn well better, or I'm wasting my time," I said. "Would I rather they went easy on me? Of course I would, but it'd be pointless."

"Why?" he sniffled, wiping his face with one terminally stained lacy sleeve.

"Because if they don't push you, you'll never get anywhere. Look, how many points did you get today?" I asked. He shrugged, before looking and gasping.

"Four!" he whispered. "I got four points in Strength, three in Agility!"

"And Endurance?" I asked, getting a frown.

"Well, none, of course."

"Why 'of course'?"

"Well, you know..." he said in a way that sounded embarrassed.

"Clearly, I don't, or I'd not have asked. Just say it."

"Endurance is my highest stat."

"Why?" I asked. "You do nothing all day apparently but fu...oh."

I broke off, frowning as I realized what that meant on two levels. First of all, his only exercise was screwing his harem, and if the only stats he gained from that were Endurance, that was some serious dedication to the deed.

Secondly, I'd *never* gained any stats from banging the hell out of Oracle, so either I was already well past the point that could count as exercise, or I wasn't putting as much effort into the deed as he was.

I looked him over, paying particular attention to the muscle tone of his upper body, visible through his soaked clothes as less than that of an overstretched rubber band, and I refused to accept that.

"What level is your Endurance?" I asked.

"Sixty-eight," he admitted, and I couldn't help but stare at him.

That was just under half again of my own, and Restun had said you couldn't physically get past fifty by exercising, hadn't he? Or was it a hundred? Fuck it.

"That's it," I muttered to myself. "Oracle's getting broken over the table tonight."

"What?"

I shook myself, dismissing the stray thought. "Nothing important. Okay, what happened? Why are you sitting here like this?" He shook his head, refusing to answer. "Fine, let's be logical, then. You were late to the party, and you tried to catch up, right?"

He nodded sullenly.

"Okay, so if you were late, you probably didn't do any stretches, and you just ran straight into the group?" He nodded again. "Did you injure yourself?"

"No," he said, ducking his head back down. I tried not to get annoyed, feeling like I was dealing with a recalcitrant toddler.

"You collapsed, though...wait, you didn't have an injury and you've got insane stamina, so why the hell did you collapse?"

He muttered something, and I leaned in closer, eventually getting it the third time he said it.

"...fell over..."

"You fell over?" I asked. He nodded, glaring at me from red-rimmed eyes. "Why didn't you just get back up?"

"Nobody came to help me," he said sullenly.

"Why the hell would they?"

"I'm the Lord of…"

"No. No, you're not, Rewn. Fuck's sake, this is the problem, you entitled little shit," I snapped at him in disbelief. "You fell over, and you fucking lay there in everyone's way, expecting someone else to make it better for you.

"All you had to do was get back up! Hell, people moved around you, giving you plenty of room, and all you had to do was try. You didn't even try, though, did you?" I said, shaking my head in disbelief.

"Fuck." I muttered, finally seeing the enormity of the problem. Once again, it was sodding worse than I'd first believed. "Right, Rewn, you've got a decision to make. You've sworn loyalty to me, and I accepted you as a noble, if only the lowest rank.

"So, I'll tell you what I'm going to do. I'll leave this in your hands, and you can either grow or stay as you are. You're going to be getting a visit from a centurion later on." I looked him over, seeing the way he peeked over filthy knees at me, reddened eyes glaring over the injustice of it all.

"He's going to teach you the basics of the world around you. You probably know most of it, but he's going to help you. If you want to grow and to one day be a real noble, then listen to him and learn. He'll take charge of your training, as well as taking you out to patrol the area with a squad. He'll teach you to lead them, and they'll teach you to fight. You'll get levels, and you'll damn well only split them between Intelligence and Wisdom for the next ten levels, and we'll see how you do then." I broke off, watching him as he glared at me, tears tracking down his cheeks.

"And if I don't?" he asked spitefully.

"Then you don't," I responded. "I accepted you, so I bear some responsibility for you. As such, I've no doubt there will be some nice palaces around the city that will be left without owners in the upcoming fights. I'll put you in one of them with a generous amount of wealth, a minder to watch over you, your harem if they want to stay, and I'll put someone else in charge of the city."

"It's MY…"

"It's not your city anymore, Rewn," I told him for what felt like the zillionth time. "It never really was. You've been controlled forever, and the only thing you ever had was a pretend title. You surrendered to me, but you brought nothing, having already been deposed.

"The only way you get your city back is if I give it to you. So damn well prove you deserve it. When Hennen comes to you, be polite and do as he says, or don't. It's your choice." I pushed myself upright and looked down at the little man, sitting in a puddle of mud with makeup streaming down his face and his clothes ruined.

I shook my head. "Seriously, Rewn, you've got a long way to go, but every journey starts the same, mate, you have to get up and start walking," I said, before looking about and nodding to myself. I had spotted a legionnaire off to one side pretending not to watch us.

Clearly, Hennen hadn't wasted any time and was here already. That, or one of us was being stalked by a particularly fugly groupie.

I activated Soaring Majesty and left Rewn to make his decision. As I flew upward, the rain splattered into me harder as I rose. It didn't take long to get to my apartments. I floated inside and landed with a sigh as I cut off my Ability and healed myself, barely noticing the pain now.

I stripped off, dumping the clothes on the floor, and ducked into the shower, where I spent the next half an hour relaxing.

When I left, I felt recovered. I was hungry and achy, but I was ready for the next job. I squared my shoulders, knowing that it had the potential to either be fantastically helpful or a nightmare, and I honestly had no clue which it would be yet.

I flew up the outside of the Tower, coming to rest on the level that she'd chosen for this, when I'd given her the choice and asked her to do it.

"Lydia…are you ready?" I asked, landing and striding forward to join her.

"Aye, Jax…Ah am," she said, looking down at the shrunken figure laid on the marble bier in the middle of the room.

I had no clue what the room had been used for originally, but I agreed with Lydia that it was perfect for her needs.

This floor was small and high up in the tower, just under two miles from the ground. It had three rooms arranged in a half-circle around the central one, the stairwells rising around the outside. The rooms all led into one another and had clearly been intended for an aerial species to inhabit, considering the doors were intact and had seemingly been ignored by even Caron, which was saying something.

The central room held multiple beds, all laid in a circle around a central point which Lydia had filled with a small, handmade shrine to Vanei, the Goddess of Air. The two rooms on either side were to be used as an armory and a private space for reflection, should she ever find herself some sisters to join her. The middle room was their barracks and a place to commune with the Lady of the Sky. Where I'd arrived was a long, narrow ledge that led out into the open air.

It was a perfect place for a Valkyrie to make her home, despite the fact that she refused to be more than a few rooms away from me at any time.

For now, we'd settled on the compromise that this would be the eventual chambers for her and her sisters and the resting place for the last Valkyrie.

I stopped when I saw the figure that lay on the bier, and I bowed my head in respect, feeling, as I had back at the village of Wayland's Crossing, the spirit of one who'd not moved on.

I took a deep breath, exchanged a long look with Lydia, then reached out with my ability and searched for her soul.

To my surprise, she was there, but stayed silent.

"Hello?" I said. In return, I received the sense of being looked at, examined, then dismissed. "I'm Jax, Scion of…"

I felt her cut off the communication entirely. "Cheeky fucking bitch," I muttered darkly, before trying again. "I am Jax," I used my ability again, trying not to swear as she cut off the contact for the second time.

"Right, you mardy cow!" I snapped as I made contact the third time. "What the fuck is going on here! You want to talk, I can fucking feel it!"

An enormous shift in the room brought her spirit face-to-face with me.

She looked different from the desiccated corpse, but not a great deal. The skin was sunken and lined, the hair white-blonde and fly-away fine. Unlike her corpse, her spirit still wore the armor that she'd gifted to Lydia. The real kicker, though, was the glowing bright white light that shone from the depths of her eyes, and the hiss that escaped her as she stopped millimeters from my face.

"I care not for your whining, boy!" The animated spirit spat at me in a voice that sounded like it needed a seriously good drink. "I am here to judge her…now be silent, or I shall leave for good!"

I opened my mouth to respond, but she glared at me, and I shut it again, scowling at her as I stepped back. I still channeled the magic to her but gave her some room.

"Little sister," she whispered eventually, stepping closer to Lydia as light rippled across her form. Lydia swallowed hard, clearly seeing her now.

"Ah'm here…" Lydia whispered, staring at the spirit in awe.

"Why did you come to me?" the spirit asked.

"Ah…Ah need a trainer. Ah need a guide," Lydia said. "Ah don' know what Ah'm doin'."

"You're a Valkyrie, the first in hundreds of years, and the first to forge her own path in tens of thousands. You don't need me, little sister, you need only listen to your heart."

"Na, Ah need more, Ah need help."

"What do you need?" the spirit asked, clearly evaluating Lydia as she struggled with the words.

"Ah need te know how it happened and why Ah'm different. Loads o' wee girls wanted te be Valkyries when Ah grew up. We'd all play at it. Why me, an' no' them?"

"You're broken," the spirit answered.

I growled in anger, taking a step forward, but halted as compassion lit her glowing eyes. The spirit shook her head and gestured for me to wait. "Those who are broken are those who can grow. Think of your muscles: you train, you work, you tear them, hurt them, break them, and they grow back stronger, yes?"

Lydia nodded, unshed tears pooling in her eyes.

"The spirit is the same as the body. Work hard, test your limits, then break them. There have been tens of thousands of girls born in the centuries since I passed who had the potential to join our ranks. I know this, somehow, but only one was strong enough, only one found her own way, despite all we know declaring it to be almost impossible. Still, you managed it." She smiled, shaking her head as she looked down into Lydia's wide eyes.

"Now you come looking for guidance? Lydia, child, you don't need me to tell you how to be a Valkyrie, no more than a fish needs to be taught to swim! I can guide you, help you to bring others to our ranks. I can show you to our Ancestral Halls and the armories.

"I can teach you of the Sunken Shrine and the treasures that lie there, awaiting the strongest of us, or I could guide you to where others of our sisters lie resting, waiting for their successor, but as to your path? Your powers? Only you can choose that."

The approval of this mythical woman, creature, whatever, hit Lydia like a ton of bricks. The changes that had begun with her claiming the role of Optio and that had solidified with her kicking twelve shades of shit out of her father and ex-husband, had now been completed with the benediction of the last Valkyrie.

Lydia had been reborn, and the spirit reached out, touching the Tower gently and looking to me, the Tower's master, for permission. I granted her the right to draw on the mana, only a tiny amount, as I wasn't that fucking trusting, but it was enough to sustain her without me, and the spirit gently dismissed me from her presence.

I reached out, gripping one of Lydia's pauldrons and giving her a little shake to let her know I was there. Then I turned and left, leaving the pair to talk. With a sigh, I headed off to my next job: alchemy until sunset, when I'd give the latest batch of arrivals a welcome speech. We'd all eat and drink, and I could finally climb into bed before going to war tomorrow.

I couldn't wait to leave, but as I went, I pulled up a notification I'd been hoping to see sooner or later. I couldn't help but nod in satisfaction, feeling that this, at least, was somewhere that I'd made the realm a slightly better place.

Congratulations!

You have completed your Quest: A Pillar of Strength.
Your bondswoman, Lydia, commander of your personal squad and close friend, has completed her evolution into a Valkyrie. To complete her evolution, and to become all she could be, she required four things:

Resolution of the Past: 1/1

Cleansing of the Last Valkyrie 1/1

Find a Class Trainer: 1/1

Discover/Create/Recover Suitable Armor: 1/1

Reward: A full Valkyrie under your command, possibly more, 50,000xp

I now knew what the last section meant. Lydia, aided by the spirit of the last Valkyrie, could begin recruiting the next generation, and eventually, the realm would have Valkyries flying again, kicking ass and saving people.

I sighed, smiling, and headed off, determined to make the alchemy time count.

BANE

"**F**uck's sake, Doris!" Bane snarled, pulling her away and yanking the hammer from her hands, trying to hold her back from the white-faced upper priest who shook with terror, even as Bane shoved his gag back in. It had blocked most of his screams for help from escaping, until she'd lost patience and started to really go for gold.

"Ye said Ah could kill 'im!" she said with a wild-eyed glance at Bane, who shoved her backward again.

"Yeah, I did. I also told you to be quiet, and that you had to wait until I got the information I needed out of him. Smashing his legs in six places and braiding them together is NOT the way to avoid attention!" Bane snapped back.

"But 'e deserves it!" she growled.

With frustration rolling off him in steady waves, Bane pulsed his worldsense hard at her, shocking her for a second.

"Do you think I care?" he asked through gritted teeth when she'd recovered. "You can kill them all, for all I care! The deal was you help me get my targets, *then* you can kill whoever you want, and his screams just fucked that up!"

"They're coming," Shereen called from the balcony where she'd hidden, watching over the edge as the guards responded to the screams from on high.

"Fuck," Bane muttered, scanning the room, stunned by the sheer wealth on display, even if it was all splattered with blood from the upper priest and the three scribes who'd been diligently working when Bane and his small party arrived to play.

"What do we do?" Shereen asked, encircling herself with her arms in panic.

Bane hesitated for a second, asking himself what Jax would do, before snorting in grim amusement. The insane bastard would shout something about being hung like a horse and leap out of the window, somehow landing perfectly, and would attack them all before getting his ass handed to him, just as the rest of the team arrived in time to save his life.

"We run," Bane said. "Grab the books, all of them."

"There're hundreds!" Peshka said, backing away from the door as the pounding of running feet echoed up the corridor.

"Then start grabbing!" Bane was strode to the door and braced himself against a bookcase. He heaved it over, letting it slam into the door, wedging it shut before moving to the next and repeating the process, tipping the shelves over and keeping the door closed.

"That should keep them back for now," Bane muttered, opening his bag and tipping entire shelves of books into it.

"Thirty seconds!" Bane called to the Dwarves. "You've got thirty seconds!"

"Ach, tha' no be enough time!" Doris snarled. She had to jump to reach the higher shelves, grunting as she knocked more books down for Shereen to sweep up.

Peshka, showing slightly more sense than the others, steeled herself against the wall and rocked the bookshelves nearest her forward. When one fell, she used her species' surprising strength to flip it over, leaving a pile of books that she simply shoveled into her bag.

"Ten seconds…" Bane called, sprinting to a new shelf and starting again, before calling to Doris. "Kill him. We've no time for questions now, and he knows we'll kill him, anyway."

Doris swept up her mattock and grinned at the priest, who frantically shook his head at her pleadingly, while the blood-soaked gag sopped up the tears rolling down his cheeks.

"Ye remember me, laddie?" she asked him, one eyebrow arched high as she tapped the mattock against one palm. "Ye remember whut ye did te ma friend, Mikael? 'Cos Ah do…Ah'll remember it fer the rest o' ma life.."

The priest mumbled something, and he frantically shook his head, then she brought the mattock around and smashed it into his face, caving his skull in and killing him instantly.

"Ah've bin waitin' fer tha' one!" Doris muttered, planting her booted foot on his groin and bracing herself, levering the overlarge hammer out of the corpse's face.

"How do you know it was him?" Peshka asked her.

"Recognized 'im," Doris said, as though it was obvious.

"No, there's twins, isn't there?" Peshka asked. Doris swore, marching forward to examine his right hand, cursing louder as she found three fingers, with the last knuckle of each removed as punishment for thieving, long-since healed.

"Ah fuck it be tha wrong one!"

Bane pulled up his notifications, swearing as he, too, realized the error. His ninth target was still alive, as was the tenth…and he'd not gained the double experience for a stealth kill, either.

"Doris," he said in a low, cold voice. "I'm going to kill you for this."

"Get in line," Shereen called, pulling out a key from the dead priest's robes.

"What?" Bane snarled.

"I said, 'get in line'!" Shereen shouted back. "We all just lost a chance at our own targets, thanks to that!" She stomped over to the chest set against the wall and slammed the key in, turning it with a satisfying *clunk* of releasing locks.

Shereen tried to open the chest, but found it was still solidly locked, and frowned, shoving harder on the lid before kicking it.

Instead of bouncing off or opening, the entire chest tilted slightly, rocking to one side on hidden hinges.

"Bane…!" she called, stunned, as she dropped down and examined the base of the chest.

"What is it?" Bane asked, appearing next to her and dropping to one knee as well. Shereen gave the base a low push, and the entire chest tilted sideways, exposing hidden stairs into the floor below.

Bane sent a pulse into the inky black. "Go!" he ordered after seeing that it was both clear and heavily fuzzed, probably full of cobwebs.

Shereen wasted no time, rolling to her feet and trotting down the stairs as Bane held the chest up and out of the way. Peshka followed, and finally, Doris paused by him, opening her mouth as if to say something.

"No time!" Bane snarled, shoving her into the darkness before diving in himself, tugging the chest down and twisting the lock on the inside to re-engage it again.

He barely made it inside before the door, the bookcase blocking it, and the furniture he'd piled next to it was destroyed in an explosion of flame and shadow magic, waves of blackness rolling out to obscure the room, searching for living targets to punish.

The spell roiled back and forth for several seconds before winking out as it found no victims. Bane and his friends were already two floors below and hurrying away.

When the inquisitor finally stepped inside the devastated room, eyeing the bloody messes that had once been Upper Priest Vertoon and the remains of the three scribe acolytes, he screamed in rage.

Not only had one of his closest confidants been killed, no doubt by some middling-level priest wanting a bigger apartment or more slaves, but they'd killed everyone and stolen years of work to hide their tracks!

This was intolerable.

"Find them!" he snarled to the dark paladin who stood behind him. "There must have been at least half a dozen involved in this, to take so much, so quickly. They'll be trying to hide the books and Vertoon's possessions. Scour the citadel. Anyone you find involved in this, kill them and bring their possessions to me. I must recover certain items for the God's work!"

"Lord Inquisitor," the dark paladin rumbled. "How will we know? Many books are taken from the Halls, many items are bloody."

"Then kill any you suspect!" the inquisitor snapped. "There's too many under-priests as it is, and they'll soon learn their place when a few more are sent to meet the God personally!"

"Yes inquisitor!" the paladin acquiesced, slamming one mailed fist against his heart in salute before striding out of the room and summoning his guards.

"I told you your trusting nature would be the death of you, 'old friend'," the inquisitor sneered at the corpse of Vertoon, before stepping forward and searching the corpse, helping himself to the few things the thieves hadn't found. "It was time for a cleansing, anyway."

The inquisitor shrugged, turning and strolling back out of the room, not even bothering to ask how the assassins had managed to escape, since there was a window, so it must have been their point of egress.

"The world is full of opportunities," Bane whispered to Shereen as they reached the bottom of the stairwell. They stared out through the thin slits in the wall, cut in a way that minimized notice, while permitting them to see out, showing the kitchen storeroom before them.

"What opportunity?" Shereen muttered. "All I see is a fat cook getting a handjob."

"Which means they're both distracted," Bane whispered, drawing the other two in close and showing them what he could sense beyond the wall.

"Urgh, so not what I needed to see," Peshka muttered, shaking her head.

"Pay attention!" Bane hissed. "Watch them and tell me what you see."

"Do we have to?" Shereen asked in a disgusted whisper, shaking her head. "Fine, the head cook and one of the others are giving each other a hand, literally."

"Idiot!" Bane hissed. "What *else* do you see?"

"Th' rest o' tha kitchen be empty," Doris muttered, having taken a single glance through.

"Exactly. What else?" Bane asked them.

"There're boxes stacked inside, lots of them, but they are in the way. They've just got a delivery," Shereen added, eyes widening in realization.

"Exactly! There's a recent delivery, people will have been in and out, the cooks are distracted, but won't be for much longer," he said, reaching out and smearing a little oil on the rusty hinges.

"Where'd you get that?" Peshka asked

Bane shook his head. "Always think of what you might need." With that, he pulled on the hidden door. It slid open without a sound, and he led the way into the storeroom. Appearing behind a case of dried fruit, he tipped a few handfuls into his bag of holding as he waited for the cooks to look the other way, having both paused to look out into the kitchen at some slight sound.

As soon as they were distracted again, he moved, sliding closer under stealth, daggers at the ready, even as the Dwarves slipped out of the room.

He crouched, ignoring the grunts coming from the pair, utterly uninterested in their antics beyond making sure his companions weren't seen. As soon as the three were out of the room, he followed.

The kitchen beyond the storeroom was massive. The long, low ceiling leading to a massive row of steel-doored ovens. Behind them, the smell of freshly-baking bread nearly drove all four into drooling desperation, before Doris pointed to a stack of cooling loaves off to one side, dumping them by the dozen into her bag.

Shereen and Peshka quickly followed suit, grabbing ripe cheeses and hanging meat. Bane, ever vigilant, slid across to the massive cauldron of meat that blipped and bubbled away, the minced mystery meat filling the air with an appetizing aroma. He *thrummed* in satisfaction, pulling out a small container of potent poison and added it into the stew, stirring it and backing away at the groans from the storeroom.

"Now, quickly!" Bane hissed, hurrying over to the trio who waited by the door, gnawing on a bun each.

"We're waiting on you!" Shereen whispered harshly, but in seconds the four had passed through the door into the drab, utilitarian corridors beyond. They vanished toward the loading dock where wagons were being loaded, and harnesses creaked as animals prepared to haul them away, returning to Himnel and beyond.

CHAPTER TWENTY-EIGHT

I leaned on the railing as Tenandra lifted us into the air, her ship-body sailing gracefully. The gathered members of the Council below, along with a great many friends and family of the crew, waved us off.

"Are you ready for this?" I asked Lydia.

Her grim exterior cracked for a moment as she winked at me. "Aye, we'll not let yer down, Lord Jax!" she barked out, saluting me with a laugh.

"You're too cheerful by half," I grumbled, then let a grin slip onto my own face. "I know the feeling. Gods, I'm ready to be free of that shit." I gestured back at the council as I straightened up, looking out into the distance. I could just make out Mal's ship far to the east, flying close to the treetops with his engines set to full power.

He'd set off late last night, less than an hour after the swearing in of the remaining Legion and the rest of the refugees, his ship filled with Flux's small band of spies and assassins.

Tenandra, and the two ships that were taking off right behind her, had the majority of the legionnaires aboard, including a single marine squad on either of the two that followed us. Oracle and Tenandra would be working for the rest of the next two days teaching Magic Missile, Explosive Compression, and Complex Healing to as many as possible.

"Three an hour each. They're pushing for as long as they can, up to five hours now before a short break. That's thirty people for one, or ten for all three spells per five hours," I mused, getting a grunt from Lydia.

"Ah can add it up masel', ya know," she whispered. "And Ah was there when we came up wi' this plan."

"I know." I frowned. "I wasn't talking to you, well not really…just…"

"Just nerves…Ah know," Lydia said.

"Hell yes." I ran a hand through my hair. "This whole thing feels weird, me leading troops into battle."

"You're tha Imperial Scion," Lydia pointed out.

I shot her another hard look. "And you know why that's bullshit." We'd discussed my past enough times since we teamed up; she knew better by now.

Her snort confirmed that she was thinking along the same lines. "Aye, Ah know yer…ma Lord Jax. How many have yer killed in combat now? Who killed a SporeMother, oh wait…be it two or three now? Yer fought tha Drow, made a spider almos' tha size o' this ship swear loyalty ta yer, became arena champion, an' kicked tha Skyking to a greasy stain on tha floor, conquered tha Sunken City…have Ah left anything out? Oh yeah, yer faced tha ENTIRE FUCKING DARK LEGION on yer own."

"No, I didn't!" I retorted.

"Well, it was'ne far off. Ah saw tha state o' tha fuckin' forest afterwards. Ah saw tha storm, an entire *storm* yer summoned. Yer call tha God of Death tha 'Dark Wanker' and shout shit at Him whenever yer annoyed, and yer even kicked tha crap out o' tha' Gods who be allied ta yer when they pissed yer off.

"Let's let tha' sink in fer a minute Jax…tha *Gods* who are ALLIED ta yer. Not tha Empire, t' YER…and yer wonderin' iffin yer can lead a hundred or so legionnaires te sack a city and kill some Drow? Ah'm starting te wonder if we should all just hit tha first bar an' leave yer te deal with it all yerself," Lydia said, scratching the base of her neck, just above her wings. "Gods, these damn things itch at times."

"Here," I said, reaching over and scratching the base of her neck and the spot between her wings.

"Oh Gods…if yer could cook, Ah'd marry yer right now," Lydia muttered, before blushing at what she'd said without thinking. I laughed, glad to hear that she was starting to joke about marriage and relationships at last.

"Ha!" I laughed, continuing to scratch her wings as she arched her back slightly. "Seriously though, you're one to talk, *VALKYRIE*," I said, pausing for effect.

"Let's consider you. A simple housewife who was enslaved. A slave who rose to lead a squad. You became a soldier who then claimed the rank of Optio in the Legion. Who leads the elite team that protects the Scion of the Empire. Arena Champion, and I seem to remember you beating the shit out of more than one of the Anubai, creatures that the Legion fears to go one-on-one with.

"Dark legionnaires, mad Gnomes, the undead, a lich…literally hundreds of Goblins, hell you slaughtered sporelings and SporeMothers, DarkSpore, the Drow, giant spiders. You even went one-on-one with Bane when we first met him and kicked his ass.

"Plus, you fought and killed slavers, the Dark Legion *again*, specters, weird ass drach and their riders. Fuck, you even brought an extinct class back from the great beyond, changing your own species from human to Valkyrie, all because you were too stubborn to accept it couldn't be done." I grinned at her, seeing the rising redness in her cheeks as I went on.

"So, don't give me any of that shit; everything I've done, you've been by my side. You're going to have generations of little girls growing up dreaming they could be half the woman you are, and don't you ever dare forget that."

I took her by her shoulders and turned her around, holding onto her and looking into her eyes as I spoke.

"I'm proud of you, Lydia. You're one of the best friends I could ever imagine having, never mind that you're also an amazing example to people. Never let anyone tell you different."

"Thank yer," she whispered, red-faced. "But seriously, that's just shit that 'appened. Ah was terrified half tha time, and tha way yer say *that*…it's no' me, Ah'm just…*me*."

"And that's exactly how I feel," I said, my voice low. "Seriously! I mean, the only differences are that it's more than half the time that I'm terrified and that I also get to shit myself that I'm fucking it all up with my plans and changing shit."

I shook my head and looked out, leaning on the railing. "All I can do is hope, I guess." I thought of how many people lives could be fucked up if I didn't get this sorted out.

"Well, we'll be there wit' yer, an' if all else fails, we'll just keep stabbing them 'til they give up."

"Thank you." I smiled back. "Right then, I guess it's time to get on with things," I muttered, straightening up.

I'd had Tel and his little team in the alchemy department working through the night creating mana, stamina, and health potions, making sure the entire team going with me had three of each, more than most of the legionnaires had carried at a single point at any time in their careers.

The potions that were given out were pretty much the standard ones now, each doing between one hundred and fifty and two hundred and seventy points of healing, depending on who's batch they'd gotten. Either way, they were far better than none, so we made sure everyone had as many as we could produce.

I hid myself away in my lab. I was desperate to experiment and knew that, if I could discover just one refinement, it might make a hell of a difference, but I couldn't afford the time. So instead, I worked on mana potions first. I knew damn well how badly they were needed, especially for those who were new to magic, as they could use their entire mana pool in a few spells, leaving them suffering from mana migraines while they tried to fight.

I made another seventy over the next five hours, before stopping to train with Flux and the others, sick of the sight of the alchemy set, yet desperately wanting to continue.

I opened my door, stepping out into the corridor, and had a blade at my throat instantly, drawing a grunt from Tang as he shook his head, becoming visible again.

"I could have slit your throat, you know that, boss? You really need to consider paying more attention."

I grinned at him, then pushed the blade aside, shaking my head.

"Tang, I know you're trying to make up for Bane being missing, but seriously man, relax. I do pay some attention, you know?"

"Really?" Tang asked, narrowing his eyes.

"Seriously, like, I know that Intaglio and Flux are to the left of me as well, and that Cheena is on the other side of you, hidden."

"You're getting better, Jax," Flux said from beside me.

I turned my bastard grin from Tang to Flux. "Thank you, my friend," I said with a nod in his direction. "You offered to continue my training earlier?"

Flux nodded as he and Intaglio stepped forth and dropped their stealth, shimmering into existence.

"I did, and I think it's a perfect time for it, and to introduce you formally to Intaglio."

"We've met already, but it's good to see you again." I said, smiling at her. "Surely, you'd have been better sent with the others though, rather than here with me?" I glanced from her to Flux.

"I had considered it, but Romanus and I agreed it would be better for your own guard to be as strong as possible, especially considering how gifted most Drow are with stealth," Flux said firmly enough to invite zero contradiction on the subject.

"Fair enough, so…training?" I suggested, for once not giving my stealth team sass about their desire to protect me.

Flux nodded, gesturing to a door further down the hall.

"As overfull as the ship is, most people are on the deck, so we will train in here," he said, leading the way.

I followed him down the corridor, with Intaglio behind me, as well as Cheena and Tang. The last two took up post outside, while Flux, Intaglio, and I went inside and closed the door.

The room was small and well-kept, with a table that folded down from one wall, two chairs that were folded and attached to the wall currently, and four bunks, two on either side of the room, their beds made and a single small porthole looking out over the ocean of clouds.

Flux opened it, a fresh breeze sweeping through the room.

I nodded as I looked around, seeing it was sparse but well-kept, and guessed that it must be a crew quarters. But, as Flux lowered himself into a fighting stance, I realized what the sneaky bastard had in mind.

"What, no warm-up?" I asked him.

"Do you get to warm up before assassins come for you normally, Jax?" Flux asked, but before I could reply, I felt the prick of a blade at my throat, and I froze.

"And you're dead…my Lord Jax," Intaglio whispered in my ear.

"Distraction," Flux said. "You need to learn to clear your mind and see what is there, not that which you expect to see. You know I'm your friend, but for the purposes of this session, I am an assassin, one of two that has managed to reach you when you are alone and vulnerable in this small room."

"Great," I muttered, shifting position until I had them both in sight, looking from one to the other as they waited.

"So…you guys want to talk about this?" I asked them after a few seconds of silent appraisal, but as soon as I opened my mouth, they attacked.

Flux lunged forward, his upper hands curled into fists, the lower ones extended and flat to form blades as he chopped at my arms. While he went high, Intaglio went low, sending a spinning kick at my legs.

I stepped back, thinking I'd dodged her, concentrating on all four of Flux's arms as he struck out, only to have Intaglio flip herself around onto her palms, flat against the ground, and lash out at my head with her feet. I was already too close to Flux, and the next thing I saw was her boot as it connected with my jaw, staggering me.

I hit the folded table, spat out some blood from a split lip, then blocked Flux's next punch, jabbing at his ribs.

Both his lower hands grabbed my wrists, encircling them while he brought both palms down hard against my ears, cupped for maximum effect, bursting my eardrums.

I cried out, and he twisted and kicked, his right leg hooking behind my knee and yanking me even further off-balance. His lower right elbow took me in the stomach, doubling me over. His upper right arm closed around my neck, leaving me doubled over and securely held under his arms.

I used a quick heal, my hearing popping back in with a startling amount of pain, even as Intaglio knelt before me, looking up into my eyes and shaking her head amusedly.

"I see we've got a lot of work to do, then," she said, a faint smile on her face.

"Why…you…so happy?" I forced out as Flux half-choked me, while I tried to break his grip.

"Well, usually I can only fantasize over beating a noble to shit," she admitted. "Today's gonna be fun!"

"You're still holding back, Jax. Remember, in here we are not your bondsmen, but your enemies. Now, fight!"

I coughed, glowered, then grinned, gripping Flux around the waist and triggering Mana Overdrive. I straightened explosively, twisting around and lashing out with my right foot, even as I gripped Flux tighter and squeezed as hard as I could with my left arm, ripping his other arm free with my right.

My boot connected with Intaglio's face, sending her sprawling with a crunch of breaking cartilage. I tore Flux from me and threw him across the cabin to slam into the wall.

"Like…that…you mean?" I gasped, getting my breath back as I cut off the ability, then healed myself.

Flux grunted as he stood, arching his back and gasping as something clicked, before he straightened and nodded, letting a *thrum* of amusement free.

"Yes, Jax, exactly like that!" he said happily. "I'm pleased to see you can still surprise me. However, Intaglio appears to be in a bad way…" He trailed off, as he noticed her lying still on the floor.

"Oh shit," I grunted, throwing myself down to her, and reaching for the pulse in her neck. The next thing I knew, I was restrained on the floor, her legs pinning my arms, and a knife-hand levelled over my throat.

She smiled down from where she straddled me, even as my brain whirled, trying to figure out what the hell had happened.

"Rule one," she said sweetly. "I, and any other you face, are not your friends. Distrust everything."

"Fight with all you have every time, Jax. Trust that we are strong enough to handle it," Flux confirmed.

I turned my head in Intaglio's surprisingly tenacious grip to regard him, my brow furrowed in question.

"But then all it takes is a little slip, a single fuck-up, and you'll be dead," I said as Intaglio rolled off me.

"Uh, look, Lord Jax, sweet as it is that you're concerned for my wellbeing, but no offence, I've killed a hell of a lot of people over the last five years. I think I'll survive."

"No," Oracle said, flitting in through the open porthole and making everyone jump. "No, Intaglio, you wouldn't. If you all go all-out, at least one of you won't leave this room alive, not to mention the chances of the ship itself being destroyed."

"Thanks for the vote of confidence!" I said to Oracle, smiling as she landed on a bunk and shifted, becoming full-sized and letting out a little groan as she massaged her temples.

"Honestly, I just need a break from magic for half an hour, and seeing you getting all sweaty seemed to fill a need," she quipped, moving herself around to get more comfortable. "Don't let me stop you."

"Very well." Flux said, nodding. "I suggest we do a light warm up normally, but if we are to train, we must start as we mean to go on. Jax, would you heal Intaglio, please?" He gestured towards her obviously broken nose.

"Ah, no there's no need," Intaglio said frantically, but it was already too late as I'd started casting a healing spell on her. I used our usual mix of healing, scanning, and examining as I went, straightening a few minor issues that I sensed as I did it, making her groan as she straightened up.

"Gods, that's better." She rubbed the small of her back, where I'd found malignant growths in her kidneys, the spell having cleared them away in seconds. "Thank you, my Lord."

"Intaglio, seriously, we're fighting each other, and you're teaching me. When it's not a formal situation, just call me, Jax, okay?"

"Then call me Lio," she said, smiling faintly before rubbing her back again. "Seriously, though, I don't know what you just did, but Gods, I feel better."

"I'm surprised Nerin didn't catch this when you joined us at the Tower," I said, frowning as redness rose in her cheeks.

"Ah, well, that's the issue," Lio dropped into a fighting stance and balled her fists.

"Explain," I ordered.

She grimaced. "I don't like magic," she said, then attacked.

She was fast, her hands slipping between knife-hands and fists, then slapping aside my counterstrikes with a cupped hand.

"Yeah, you're gonna need to explain that," I said, counterattacking and chasing her across the floor. I sprang into the air as she spun around, dropped low, and kicked out.

As her feet passed under me, I pulled my knees up to my chin, then dropped, unfurling my legs as she spun again, this time going for a high kick that was seemingly aimed to remove my head.

Instead, I triggered Soaring Majesty for a split second and flashed across the distance between us, grabbing her and twisting, throwing myself onto my back, and flipped her across the room.

I landed hard, scrambling back to my feet.

She rolled upright and nodded to me. As she stepped back, Flux took her place.

"A lot of the Legion are like me, Jax," she explained, sitting back on the bunk and folding her legs to sit cross-legged as Flux and I circled each other. "Magic is rare and expensive to learn, not to mention often devastating when used against a non-magical foe. So, as I say, a lot of the Legion don't like it. I simply told Nerin I didn't want to be healed and stayed away from her. It wasn't hard."

"Well, you were dying," I said, still watching Flux. "You had a problem with your kidneys. I bet you've been pissing blood for a while now. Few more months, and you'd have died from that. Now, for a few minutes' effort on my part, and a little patience on yours, you're fine. See how easy that was?" I asked, blocking the first of Flux's strikes, then deflecting the next and letting loose with a Sparta kick aimed at his stomach.

Flux dodged easily and grabbed my ankle, yanking my leg straight and making me hop awkwardly.

"Really, Jax?" He shook his head in disgust. "You should know better," he warned, dragging me along in circles around the room.

"So…anyway, thank you." Lio said, shrugging uncomfortably. "I feel kind of stupid about avoiding magic now."

"Well, you should," I said, twisting and jumping into the air, lashing out to kick Flux in the head. He ducked, then grabbed my other ankle as I hit the floor, before stepping forward and resting one foot on my ass.

"So, I think we'll agree this is a bad position for you to be in?" he said, pulling on my legs and pushing with his foot. "All you have to do is surrender."

"Get bent!" I snapped, as I flexed my arms and tried to flip him.

I twisted and turned. I tried to reach things to give me leverage, but he kept dragging me about, until I finally realized the one thing I hadn't tried. I planted my palms flat and shoved as hard as I could, driving Flux backward. When his back hit the outer hull, I twisted again, pulling with my right and pushing with my left, bringing my body around to grab his legs and yanked him from his feet.

We both crashed down, then rolled apart, before coming to our feet, and squaring off again. This time, I didn't wait, and rushed forward, relying on my greater size and weight, determined to get in close. I took two quick strikes on my shoulders, then a kick on my right thigh, before I managed to catch his right upper arm with my left hand.

Using the grip I had on him, I yanked him forward and slammed my fist into his upper left arm, numbing the muscle. I ignored the pain of his lower arm's claws as they opened my right cheek, and I brought up my knee, slamming it into his stomach.

He folded around the blow with a grunt, and a bone or two gave way with a snap as he coughed blood onto the floor. I released him and backed away quickly.

He forced himself to his feet, but I held up my hands, making him pause, even as Oracle groaned, then hit him with a heal.

"Sorry about that," I offered sheepishly as he rubbed his lower chest. He shook his head.

"Don't be," he said, straightening in either relief or pride. "I told you to fight to your full ability so that I could assess you."

"And?"

"And you've improved, but I expect nothing less from Bane watching over you. Very well, I think we'll move on to some forms, starting with a series of strikes and kicks."

It took a few minutes of Demonstration until I could carry them out consistently, then both Flux and Lio watched me, pointing out changes and making me do each series over and over again.

"So, you were saying about magic?" I asked Lio, getting a grunt as I pressed on a sensitive subject.

"There's a few of the Legion who distrust magic, that's all," she said, shrugging. "We tend to avoid it whenever we can, and when we can't, well, we put up with it."

"But you know you're going to learn magic, right?" I asked.

"I might. Chances are, I won't have to." She shrugged. "I've always managed to avoid it 'til now."

"Nope," I said, shaking my head and twisting, screwing up my kick and getting a grunt of irritation from Flux. "All legionnaires are going to learn at a minimum two spells, one offensive and one healing. So, like it or not, it's happening," I said. "You should have been told by your commanding officer when your turn is?"

"Nope!" she said, grinning.

I thought about it, before getting a clip from Flux.

"Pay attention!" he said, before Demonstrating again. "Your form has wavered, you keep doing this…not *this*!" He showed off a kick that looked like he was waking up with a bad cramp, then a sudden smart kick for emphasis.

"Asshole," I muttered, before frowning. "Wait a fucking minute, Flux, *you're* Lio's commander!" He hesitated as soon as I said it. I shook my head as the realization dawned on me. "You fucker. You've been distracting me so I don't include you as well!"

"I have no need of magic," he said with as much finality as he could muster beneath my withering gaze. "I have my own natural abilities and need no more. Better that a legionnaire have the opportunity…"

"Yeah, no," I said, straightening up and abandoning the stance. "Oracle, who've you got next?"

"No idea, Jax," she replied. "I've been letting the legionnaires sort it out."

"Okay, we need these buggers included. After all, they'll be with us, so we need to rely on their abilities."

"Fine, come here, the lot of you," Oracle said with a tired wave of her hand that contrasted the firmness of her tone.

I smiled, stepping across to sit next to her on the bed as she reached out both hands toward both Flux and Lio's foreheads, while a third hand rested on mine.

"I don't…" Lio said.

"This is an order, legionnaire. Get your ass over here." I turned my glare toward Flux next.

"Jax…" he said, and I held up a hand.

"I don't want to hear any shit about how 'the Mer aren't meant to have magic' and so on. I had enough of that bullshit with Bane, and he's getting damn good with his Firebolt spell, last I saw."

"We rarely have any aptitude to learn them, Jax. The effort should be saved for…"

I interrupted him, gesturing to Oracle's outstretched hands. "Kneel, now, the pair of you." I ordered, then added, "Oracle, wait a second."

"Cheena! Get in here!" I called to the guard. The door burst open a second later as she and Tang searched for threats, finding only Flux and Lio kneeling. They hesitated, standing around uncertainly.

"Tang, I know you're sorted spell-wise for now, but Cheena isn't, so she's joining these two in getting a healing and ranged offensive spell." I waved for Cheena to join the nervous little band.

"Really?" Cheena asked, taking an unconscious step forward.

"Hell yes!" I said, cracking a smile at finally having a willing participant in the room. "Unless you're going to tell me some bullshit about why you shouldn't get trained?"

"Hell no," she said, crossing the room at near top speed. "What are you waiting for?" she asked the other two.

"They're afraid of magic." I said, deliberately goading them. The glare I got from Lio before she and Flux shuffled to where Oracle could reach them, told me I'd hit the nail on the head, but their pride wouldn't allow any other response.

I felt the sensation of Oracle searching my mind, gathering the knowledge to form the bridge between myself and the others. Whereas before, the longest part had been gathering the spell and including the various additional knowledge, this time it felt far smoother, as she was clearly growing more skilled with practice.

It still took just under an hour, mainly because the concept of channeling mana and casting spells was fresh to all three. Sharing spells between Arrin, Nerin, and myself was much faster for more spells, but that was down to us already being skilled mages by that point.

Eventually we were done, and I sat back, waiting for the weird ache of Oracle's rummaging in my mind to fade, while the others wore similarly shocked expressions as they explored the magic that had suddenly been unlocked for them.

"This is," Flux muttered, looking down at his hand as he summoned the beginning of the Complex Healing spell again. He'd spun it up three times now and absorbed it each time.

"Not what I thought it would be," Lio finished for him, looking at the glow of the same spell as it built in her hands.

"It's fantastic! Thank you, Jax," Cheena said, bowing her head once, before striding back out of the room and resuming her position on guard. She had a gleeful almost-skip to her step as she rounded the corner.

I'd been very clear with all three of them as soon as Oracle was done, ordering them not to try casting the Magic Missile inside the ship, but explained about spinning up and then reabsorbing the healing spell.

It gave no experience for using it, but it did make it more familiar for the future.

"You know what this means, Jax?" Flux said slowly.

"What's that, mate?" I asked, holding Oracle's hand as she relaxed, getting ready to return and start again with the legionnaires on the upper deck.

"Now, not only do we no longer have any real concern about harming you in training, but we will actively be able to improve our skills by doing so and healing you afterward!"

"Fuck," I muttered, closing my eyes. "I'm not going to get any rest today, am I?" I asked.

"Not yet," Flux said, a wicked smile stretching across his face. "We've got five hours left before it gets dark, and we change direction for Narkolt...time to get practicing."

CHAPTER TWENTY-NINE

The rest of the day passed in a blur of pain, mainly mine, as I found that, despite saying otherwise, Flux and Lio had in fact been pulling their punches and deliberately not inflicting the kind of damage they were capable of.

The new level of training was both far more efficient and far messier, with a corresponding level of damage to the room by the time we were done.

"Remind me to apologize to whoever owns this room later," I whispered, laying across the remains of one of the beds. It had broken my fall after Flux flipped me over his back into the air, and Lio intercepted me and spin-kicked me across the room.

I heard multiple bones break when I landed, as well as the bed's frame, and I lay there while they argued over whose action had put me down.

That had become the decider for who got to level up their healing. The three of us had gone at each other, the only rule being that the fight stopped when one of us couldn't continue, and the one who was responsible for inflicting that state got to do the healing.

I was getting no experience healing the pair, and the score was now tied at fifteen points each…for them.

I coughed, warm blood trickling down my chin, then shifted, wincing in pain as they continued to argue. I pulled up my notifications, dismissing most of them, but appreciating the levels of improvement across my skills.

In particular, unarmed combat was coming along nicely, sitting at level sixteen, while my staffs skill, which affected my naginata, was all the way up to eighteen, making me hope a new breakthrough was on the way. With a good spread of skills close to a threshold now, I hoped some would evolve in the next few days.

I dismissed my level up and left the points unallocated, since I wanted to wait until I had a few days to think them over. It was stupid to not do it before we went into battle, I knew, but it wasn't like it was the stupidest thing I'd done since coming here, or hell, even this week.

Basically it came down to the choice between long term, and short term gains. Short term gains would be adjusting my build for this battle, making it easier, but also undermining my long term build. If instead I took a few days, thinking about it when I had some time? It could massively help.

Besides, if I really got in the shit, I could take a little time–I hoped–and do it then.

I'd also managed to increase several stats, so I pulled up my status screen, examining it, and forced myself to read the details while I waited for the pair to decide who got to heal me.

Empire Ascendant

Congratulations!

Through hard work and perseverance, you have increased your stats by the following:

Intelligence +1
Luck +1
Perception +1

Continue to train and learn to increase this further.

Name: Jax Amon				
Titles: Strategos: 5% boost to damage resistance, Fortifier: 5% boost to defensive structure integrity, Champion of Jenae: One search for hidden knowledge every 24 hours, Kobold Ravager: +25% damage to Kobolds, Valspar's Bane: +25% damage to Valspar				
Class: Spellsword > Justicar > Champion of Jenae > Imperial Magekiller > Imperial Justicar > Imperial Overlord		**Renown**: Imperial Scion, Lord of Dravith		
Level: 30		**Progress:** 229,826/1,245,000		
Patron: Jenae, Goddess of Fire and Exploration		**Points to Distribute**: 30 **Meridian Points to Invest**: 0		

Stat	Current points	Description	Effect	Progress to next level
Agility	41	Governs dodge and movement.	+310% maximum movement speed and reflexes, (+10% movement in darkness, -20% movement in daylight)	58/100
Charisma	31 (26)	Governs likely success to charm, seduce, or threaten	+210% success in interactions with other beings	71/100
Constitution	56 (51)	Governs health and health regeneration	1120 health, regen 69 points per 600 seconds, (each point invested now worth 20 health)	61/100
Dexterity	67 (62)	Governs ability with weapons and crafting success	+570% to weapon proficiency, +57% to the chances of crafting success	77/100
Endurance	50 (47)	Governs stamina and stamina regeneration	1500 stamina, regen 40 points per 30 seconds, (each point invested now worth 30 stamina)	65/100
Intelligence	59	Governs base mana and number of spells able to be learned	590 mana, spell capacity: 31 (29 + 2 from items)	3/100
Luck	35	Governs overall chance of bonuses	+25% chance of a favorable outcome	17/100
Perception	44 (34)	Governs ranged damage and chance to spot traps or hidden items	+340% ranged damage, +34% chance to spot traps or hidden items	23/100
Strength	49 (46)	Governs damage with melee weapons and carrying capacity	+39 damage with melee weapons, +390% maximum carrying capacity	35/100
Wisdom	45 (35)	Governs mana regeneration and memory	+525% mana recovery, 5.5 points per minute, 350% more likely to remember things, (+50% increased mana regeneration from essence core)	67/100

"Nice," I whispered before grunting as Lio hit me with her Complex Healing. I shook uncontrollably as the healing passed through me, ribs popping back into place, the jagged edges grating against each other, before they clicked. I let out a sigh of relief.

"Come on then, no time for lying about!" Lio called cheerfully as she strode over and reached down, grabbing my hand and hauling me upright. It was a hell of a feat, considering she barely came up to my shoulders.

"You know what, guys? I think I need some sleep," I said before they could lay into me again, holding my hands up and getting a round of complaints from the pair of them.

"Jax, training is important, how else do you believe you can…"

"Come on, Jax! You're better than this! You'll win one soon!" Lio assured me, speaking over Flux.

"Hell no," I said.

"You can't just leave us like this; it's a tie!" Lio said, shaking her head. "Tell you what, the winner of this fight is the overall winner!"

I paused, my hand reaching for the doorknob, and looked back at her, an eyebrow raised in question.

"Seriously, we're both at fifteen; whoever wins this next round…" she said, wheedling me to go through another round of ass-kicking. I wanted to say no, but the knowledge that I'd lost thirty godsdamned fights in a row…

"One last fight," I grumbled, rolling my shoulders as the other two moved into position. Lio grinned, and Flux let loose a *thrum* of pleasure.

It didn't last long. As soon as Lio went for me, Flux went for her, sweeping her legs out from under her. She fell and rolled, barely avoiding my snap kick to the face. I brought both arms up, crossed in an x as Flux leaped at me. I caught him and took the force of the dive, knowing he'd try to grab me, as he had done several times. Instead of trying to shake him off, I rolled my wrists, grabbed onto him and yanked him forward into a head-butt.

The actual shape of his skull was similar in shape to my own, but when I struck, I managed to get a lucky angle, stunning him for a brief second. I swept his legs, sending him crashing down as two of his arms came up to defend his head. Another one had been about to punch, leaving only one to hold on to.

As he fell, and I started to think I might actually have a chance, I cast about the room, looking for any sign of Lio.

The little fucker had vanished!

I slammed both elbows back and up. My left hit only air, but my right glanced off a stealthed form, and I dove forward, hitting the ground on the far side of Flux and rolling to my feet.

I stood, just in time to catch a flying kick, blocking with a twist of my waist and my forearms pressed together. She shoved off, jumping backwards, landing on one leg. She grinned as I spun into a low, sweeping kick. But she hopped over it, leaping into the air and lashing out with a snap kick to my face.

It rocked me backward, but having felt it several times now, I kept going. I straightened, launching into an uppercut even as I saw stars, my fist catching her mid-thigh as she landed on the leg she'd just kicked out with, and kicked again.

She grunted as I staggered backward, her leg numbed and my nose bloody for about the twentieth time today.

I lifted my fists, grinning at her, before I spread my fingers, shaking them and shouting "Jazz Hands!" at her.

Flux took advantage of her second of confusion and swept her legs from under her, rabbit punching the side of her head and flipping her end over end from his strike.

She hit the floor with a crunch and a groan, rolling onto her back and bringing her hands up to shield her head, even as I stepped up to face him.

Flux and I traded strikes, his four arms giving him an advantage that was only partially offset by my greater height and higher strength. The next few seconds passed in a blur of flashing hands and claws.

I eventually put too much force into a block, my left arm sweeping his aside and travelling a fraction of an inch too far before I could correct it.

That was all it took. His right upper hand grabbed that wrist, twisting it, and pulled my arm further aside as his lower one grabbed the elbow, pushing upward and twisting my arm before I could stop him.

Once my arm was extended and fully locked, I knew I'd lost.

I still tried to win, a combination of punching out at him and hooking his leg with my own, taking us both to the floor, but even there, he rolled before I could, using my arm for leverage. The bugger ended up on top of me. His feet were planted solidly against me and he heaved hard, dislocating my shoulder with a pop.

I shouted, and then groaned, slamming my fist down on the deck beneath me, as Flux released my arm. I heaved myself to my feet, before grunting and shaking my head as my arm swung loosely, pain radiating through me.

"Fine!" I groaned. "You win!"

"Oh, I know…" Flux said, laughing, before casting his healing on me, followed by bottoming his mana out by healing Lio.

I shook my arm out, standing up and twisting, feeling my back pop and click before waving to them both.

"I hate you both and thank you. Now I'm going to get some sleep. Well done, Flux," I muttered, heading out of the door.

Behind me, Lio called to Tang as I passed. "Hey Tang, fancy a quick session?"

"Depends, sparring or sex?" he called back nonchalantly.

"Definitely sparring," she replied.

"Then I'm on duty, so fuck no."

"You'd have said yes if it was the sex though, right?" I asked as we headed down the corridor, the door swinging shut and cutting off Lio's grumbling.

"Hell yes. I'd have gotten Flux to take my place for a bit. A man has needs, after all," Tang said.

"She'd eat you alive," Cheena said, shaking her head.

"I can only hope!" he agreed with a wink.

I laughed, but despite the constant healing, I was too sore and exhausted to really care. I stumbled into my alchemy room, collapsing on the bed I'd set up earlier and passing out within moments.

It felt like only minutes, but, in reality, a few hours passed before Oracle shook me awake.

I blinked muzzily up at her as she smiled at me. Exhaustion rimmed her eyes with dark circles.

"Are you okay?" I asked, sitting up and taking her in my arms. She let out a little groan of relief as she cuddled in tight.

"I am now," she mumbled. "I've never been so tired!"

"You should have stopped earlier, then!" I told her, worried, but she shook her head.

"No. I needed to get as many taught as possible. Every single legionnaire who can heal is one more chance for this to go smoothly. A hundred or more of them being able to heal means you've got no excuse for getting hurt again."

"I wish it was that easy," I whispered, holding her. She nodded, her face pressed against my chest.

"I know," she sighed. "I thought you might like a cuddle for ten minutes before it's time to get ready."

"Definitely," I whispered, before falling silent, enjoying the next few minutes as we lay close together, relaxing as I held her tight. In the cabins around us, as well as on the deck above, stomping footsteps vibrated the floor. Armor clanked as it settled into place, and good-natured, nervous pre-fight ribbing that military forces across time and space had engaged in since the dawn of time added a soft murmur.

All too soon, it was over. Someone knocked on the door, followed by Lydia calling out that it was getting close.

"I'm awake," I called back, even as Oracle let loose a sigh of regret before sitting up and climbing off the bed. The door opened, and Lydia stepped in, having to half-turn sideways to avoid banging her wings.

"Hey Lydia," I said, rubbing my face and stretching.

"Jax, Oracle," she said with a distracted air, adjusting her armor and tugging the laces on the inside of the wrists tighter, making sure the bracers were right.

"Okay, time to get dressed," I muttered, standing up and stripping down to my boxers. Lydia was totally unconcerned as I did so, having seen it all before with the number of times we'd all changed in front of each other.

I quickly pulled a fresh set of the padded under clothes out of my storage and started dressing, wishing again that one of the magical inventions they had was super deodorant. Yeah, Cleanse worked wonders, as did Scour, since it evolved, but damn, I missed decent deodorant and aftershave.

As I set my armor in place, Lydia checked it over with me, helping to make sure it was ready to protect me, and filled me in on the events while I'd slept.

Mainly, it was small things. Most of the team had managed to level with their primary weapons through their training, the legionnaires were excited by their spells, and the teams were ready. They had drilled over and over again on the targets they were to take. It was still good to hear, reassuring me for the hundredth time that Lydia was the best person for the role of optio of my personal squad.

"How are you doing?" I asked her, stopping to look her in the eyes.

She frowned. "Ah'm fine, why?"

"Well, we've not really talked about it since Cornut, but your dad..."

"Be a scumbag who made tha realm a better place by dyin'," she said, jaw tightening.

"True, the man was a fucking arsehole. Doesn't change that he was your dad, though, and you beat the shit out of him before we let him die," I pointed out.

"Best thing 'e could do fer tha entire realm was becomin' fertilizer," Lydia said.

"True, but despite it all, he also gave the realm you," I retorted. "Look, Lydia, you don't want to talk about this? Fine, no stress, but if you ever do want to talk about it, just tell me. Remember, my father was a shitbiscuit, too, and if I ever see him, it'll be a fight to see who lives, so I understand."

"Thanks, but Ah'm fine." She nodded as she stepped back. "Armor is good, yer ready fer this?"

"Probably not, you?" I asked.

She snorted. "Hell no. Ah tend te just beat tha shit out o' people 'til there's no more o' them. When that 'appens, it's generally all over."

"Yeah, that works for me," I agreed with a laugh, turning to Oracle. "You ready?"

With a little shiver, she shrank from her full-size body to what I'd started to think of as her treat-sized form. She had returned to the foot-high version of herself and was clad in her fighting outfit of a black boob tube and yoga pants, complete with two stripes of camo paint on her cheeks, and was tying her hair up in a ponytail.

The gesture of tying it up struck me as a little weird, considering her hair shifted in length, style and color at a thought from her, as it was, like the rest of her body, a mix of mana and magically-constructed flesh.

That didn't mean that she was any less a woman, though, and as such, she did shit all the time I didn't understand. I shrugged and dismissed it, gesturing to the door.

"Let's go kill some Drow then, I guess," I said, striding forward. The others, Flux, Lio, Cheena, and Tang, my apparent new bodyguard team, were arrayed around the door. As soon as we stepped out, they split, Cheena and Tang leading the way, while Flux and Lio took up the rear as we clattered down the corridor, Lydia muttering as her wings constantly brushed against things.

Once on deck, it became clear that the rain that had been threatening earlier was settling in to stay now. I was probably the last to be ready, as the legionnaires were everywhere, mostly warming up and cracking jokes. I nodded to people, smiling as I passed through them, moving to the joint wheelhouse and captain's cabin, while Lydia split off to check on the team.

I ducked inside, unable to help myself as I shook my head over the way that Jian sat at the helm, his hands moving steadily as he adjusted and improved our course. Comparing his actions and his skill to the ham-fisted fucker who started the war with Nimon earlier was like night and day. I damn well knew it was in part, at least, due to Tenandra, who stood by his side, speaking quietly and guiding him.

"Jax," Jian said as I entered.

"Hey, guys, how's it looking? Are we close?"

"Fifteen minutes from the city walls," he acknowledged. "They'll be watching us by now, but they don't know who we are, so they'll be expecting to talk to us when we land." A grin threatened to overtake his face.

"You're enjoying this, aren't you?" I asked.

"Hell yes!" Jian was beaming openly now. "We're about to make the city guard shit themselves and change how cities are attacked, permanently!"

"How about the other ships?" I asked. Tenandra gestured to the cloudy images projected on the walls of the cabin, showing the other two ships in on the assault as we closed the distance to the city.

I glanced back in the direction of the Tower, remembering the argument with Rewn just before I left. He'd declared he would ignore my orders and join the assault, before finding himself gripped by the strands of the Oath's enforcement.

It had begun as a warning pain, then quickly escalated until he'd squealed and swore to remain behind and to obey.

I hated allowing the Oath to go that far, I really did, as it rang too much of slavery for me. But to permit him to come along would not only jeopardize the assault, it would potentially cost hundreds of lives if he tried to interfere with the chain of command. Then, on top of that, his current condition as an incompetent puppet had been made clear in the meetings. Without someone to guide him, I couldn't leave him in command of Narkolt, as much as I wanted to. As such, until I made a decision regarding him, he was practically a prisoner in my Tower.

There were a lot of people back home who would have a field day with the Oath, but there was nothing I could do about that. Being stuck where I was, I had to get on with things as best I could.

I looked from one ship to the next, seeing the legionnaires on the deck getting ready, to my relief. On the second ship, *Ragnarök*, I could just make out Thomas and his team preparing for the assault. They all stood or sat awkwardly around Thomas, clearly bonding, but not yet fully trusting the ex-dark legionnaire in their midst. Nigret was a member of his team, as was Alistair, who'd performed well against both the Storm Demon and Rewn's guard.

"Well, war has a way of fixing that," I muttered, silently wishing him good luck before turning back to the images of the front of Narkolt.

We were arriving in the middle of the night, just over an hour past midnight, when most of the city was slumbering. I took the time to look it over, admiring the differences between this city and the shithole that was Himnel.

Where Himnel belched flames from factory chimneys and lit the night with a mixture of mana engines and constant construction in the massive shipyard, Narkolt seemed almost sedate, with the streets lit by flaming lamps that popped and danced in the constant downpour.

As far as I could see, even with the enhanced, magically brightened screens showing us far more than any unaided eye could, there were only a few people hurrying here and there avoiding the rain, while guards on the walls and in the towers simply watched us, bored.

That'd change soon, considering that the other two ships were behind us, tucked in close, with only a single light on their fore and aft decks glimmering to show the three of us where each other were.

As soon as the city saw that there wasn't a single ship, and there were instead three keeping close together, we'd go from curiosity straight to possible attack from Himnel. So, this was likely to be the most peaceful part of the night for us, and no matter how hard my people tried, tonight was going to result in the deaths of innocents.

If we were lucky, it'd be guards and soldiers, trying to protect those they believed to be their leaders, having no clue about the Drow. But, if we were unlucky, it could be dozens or hundreds of others.

Jenae's comments about making a wall fall and crushing an orphanage echoed in my mind, and I buried it down deep, forcing myself to accept the truth of what she and Amon had been trying to teach me all along.

Sometimes, I needed to accept that the innocent would be put in harm's way in the course of my actions, as much as it warred with my personal beliefs to permit it.

I checked on a few more details, comparing the streets ahead to those marked on my map, before I nodded to Tenandra and Jian then gave them a few minutes of privacy to say goodbye. As I left the room, I froze at the sight of Sehran strolling out of the bedroom at the back, completely naked and unconcerned. She waved happily and winked as she grabbed her clothes from around the room.

I shook my head and left, moving out and speaking to a few of the legionnaires I knew as I went, knowing damn well when Sehran had left the cabin by the way Westin's voice trailed off mid-sentence as he stared over my shoulder.

I turned and sighed. She carried her boots in one hand and tucked herself into her corset-like top as she wandered after me, smiling at everyone around her.

"Sehran," I said with the tired voice a parent with a perpetually streaking toddler would use. "Please put your damn top on BEFORE you leave the cabin in future, okay?"

"You have to admit, though…she's got a great figure!" Oracle said, her voice carrying clearly. Sounds of agreement rose around us as she smiled at Sehran.

"Thanks!" Sehran said, grinning up at Oracle as the Demon reached us. "So do you! Oh, and I will, sorry Jax." She tried to look all serious while making no effort to put her impressive chest away. Her corset was mostly buttoned up now, but the, uh, focus of all the legion remained nestled happily atop the fabric.

"Fine, have it your way." I shrugged. "But if Jian gets worked up over these buggers drooling over you, it's your fault," I said, washing my hands of it. For a split second, I caught a glimpse of the ancient Demoness underneath the carefree sex-kitten persona. She deflated slightly, regarding me with irritation as she covered her tits, tucking them down and out of sight.

As much as they could be in a damn corset.

I moved back through the crowd, eventually rejoining Lydia on the foredeck as Oracle whispered into my mind.

"You know she was testing you, right?" she asked.

I nodded. *"What else was I supposed to do?"*

Oracle snorted in my mind. *"She just wants to know that her charms work on everyone, that's all. She's a little paranoid about it. She spent most of the last couple of hours before everyone went to sleep trying to get a rise out of Lydia as well. Let her catch you staring at her, and she'll stop it."*

"Jian won't be very happy if he's the one who catches me," I pointed out with a frustrated sigh.

"Then don't let him catch you," she said, snuggling in closer to my neck and speaking aloud. "Why haven't you got your cloak on yet?"

I grinned, pulling it out of the bag and settling it across my shoulders. I was amazed again at how, now that Oracle knew I was hers and not wanting to screw around, she was totally fine with me admiring other women.

That probably had to do with the fact that she could assume other forms, though. A split-second memory of her flipping through the forms of porn stars I'd had in my mind a while back appeared, and with it the knowledge that she'd improved on every single one as she did so.

I shook my head again, resettling the cloak and making room in my hood. Oracle shrank even further and slipped in, now standing on the inside and leaning against the side of my head as she theatrically stripped water off herself and flicked it onto the ground.

"Are we ready?" I asked Lydia, hearing the subtle tune of "Luck's My Mistress" being played again by Ronin.

It was a weird song, seemingly different every time I heard it, yet always somehow identifiable. Ronin's song gave anyone who heard it and was in opposition to me a minus five modifier to their luck, which was amazing in any situation. Now that he'd managed to level it up again, we received an additional three points to our own luck for however long he played.

It wasn't much, but in a fight, how lucky you were could be the difference between life and death.

"We're ready. 'Ow long 'til we drop?" Lydia asked, and I gestured forward with my chin in the direction of the tower we were going to pass over in a few minutes.

Our altitude was dropping quickly, and our objective came into view. About a dozen buildings stood behind the tower. The long, large, and flat roof of the guard house was marked as one of three targets for tonight, and Thomas and his ship angled in slightly, aiming for it.

I couldn't see the second target, the shipyard and barracks for Narkolt's small army, not yet, anyway. But it was somewhere up ahead.

Their army numbered nearly a thousand, so in combat, the team of thirty legionnaires would be swiftly overrun. The convenient thing about the barracks was that it doubled as a storeroom for the manastones as well. After all, who would want to rob the place the army called home?

That made perfect sense, I reflected, as Mal had explained when he pointed out that the building was also heavily reinforced, with almost the entire army's weapons and armor stored inside.

The standard complement of guards was fifty at all times, but they were basic soldiers, not legionnaires. It'd be the middle of the night, and hopefully we'd have the element of surprise.

All the third ship had to do was land, take the building, and seal it, preventing the army from joining in the fun. They'd also have a small contingent of our fliers to keep any mages suppressed, just like Thomas would.

My Legion contingent's target was the palace. We'd land in its sculpted gardens inside the fortified wall. The majority of the Alkyon were with us, while the Djinn and imps were going with Thomas and Denny in teams of two and three respectively.

Between taking down the army, locking away the manastones, and capturing the guard and the palace, we would claim a significant portion of the city. At that point, from all we could find out at least, I could then claim the city through the Command Center, due to the previous ruler having declared himself to be my vassal.

In theory, it should be straightforward. But, in reality, I just knew it was going to be a right clusterfuck.

I took a deep breath, looking out over the night, and waited. My stomach dipped as Tenandra took over, angling the ship sharply forward and descending, while Jian hurried out of the wheelhouse and cabin and across the deck to join us.

Gravity pressed us into place as the engines fired. I exchanged a smile with Amaat, being damn well overjoyed to find out he was still leading the Alkyon.

He'd claimed the rank of Optio on his own merit, leading all the ex-harpies he'd captured to join the Legion under him, forming a wing of considerable strength. While it seemed like forever since I'd seen him, in reality, it was only a few weeks. While I'd been busy, he'd been close to insane.

He'd beaten, battered, bribed, and cajoled his fellow Alkyon, including those already in the Legion, into accepting him as their leader. Then he'd trained them around the clock, day after day, until he could take them before Romanus and Restun and declare he was the Optio of the new Alkyon Legionnaire Wing.

There were eighty-seven of them in total, from ex-thugs and gangsters to legionnaires and three carpenters, of all things. They had come together, and between the small crossbows they'd looted, the recurve bows, and now that ten of them had gone through Oracle's magical lessons, they were a force to be reckoned with.

Those ten Alkyon were lined up on either side of the railing as we passed over the tower, and as soon as we were out of sight of it, directly above, they jumped.

BELLADONNA

She awoke slowly, the world a confusing mix of red and grey, shadows that roiled, and pain, making her arch her back and grit her teeth, forcing it down. She stamped the pain away under a trap door in her mind, before she finally forced her eyes open again, not having realized that she'd closed them.

The room she was in was circular, and she hung from chains embedded in the wall. The manacles on her wrists and ankles left her hanging there, naked for all the world to see. Her confusion and tiredness burned away on the rising tide of fury's fire.

She didn't know where she was or how she'd gotten here, but whoever had stripped her was going to suffer for this indignity. Groaning echoed from her right as someone else stirred, an enormous, hairy, and deformed figure hanging suspended from the wall the same as she was, a few feet away.

She stared, instinctually assessing him as either a threat or prey. He had massive muscles and thickened skin, but his neck looked poorly protected. She flashed a feral smile, her teeth lengthening as she focused on the thick, pulsing vein in his neck.

She jerked back, suddenly realizing what she was doing. His neck? Why the hell was she concentrating on his neck? She mentally stamped down the hunger that sent aching pangs through her stomach, hammering it into the trapdoor along with her pain, and glanced around the room, able to make out more details now than she had upon first awakening.

The room was circular, with a single brazier that dangled from the ceiling on a trio of thick chains, its contents smoldering. Below that was an altar of black and grey marble, shot through with gold, and in the middle of it…

She froze at the sight of the two creatures that had been eviscerated and drained of blood, gagged and chained to the table, their eyes dull and dead.

"No…no!" she whispered in mixed fury and terror. "Not that! I wasn't even in command of the assault! Why would they?" She groaned, panic flaring as she realized why she'd been so focused on the other figure's throat and why he was so monstrous.

There was only one rite that she knew of that was done like this, and it had not been done in years. It was only carried out for the most heinous of targets, and carried out on those who had failed the God utterly.

"Dark hunters," she whispered, her throat raw and painful, her body already changing and in desperate need of the sustenance that legends said it would be unable to accept.

"Yes, Belladonna, you are quite correct," said a voice.

She snapped her head around. A figure stepping forward, appearing as if by magic from the shadows on the far side of the room.

She glared at him, recognizing him instantly. He would have been there for some time, watching her.

"Tentos!" she snapped, her lip curling in disgust. "I expect this is your doing, then? Got sick of trying to watch me bathe and decided to make sure you got to see it all? Well, come on then, you pathetic worm, look all you want, because when I get free of here…"

"You'll do nothing, huntress." Tentos smiled. "Yes, I wanted you, and I'll make no bones about that, but you made the mistake here, Bella, and…"

"Don't call me that! You've lost all right to call me that name!"

"Fine," he sneered. "Sergeant Belladonna, second in command of the dark hunters, you have failed in your first life and have been given the gift of a second. Fail this time, and the centuries will seem endless for you as you rot, nailed to the walls of the Wailing Wall." Tentos turned to look at the massive figure that groaned again.

"Edvard, accursed and blind failure of a dark paladin that you were, wake now! Wake and explain to your sergeant the decision you made for her!" Tentos smiled cruelly, staring up at the pair of them, ignoring the others that slowly mumbled and twitched their way toward wakefulness around the room.

"What?" Belladonna whispered, looking at the massive mutation that shared a wall with her, chained and bound. The monstrosity was far from human, but Tentos had called it…"Edvard?" she said hesitantly, hoping that it wasn't true.

"Bella…donna…sor…sorry…" the creature mumbled, its tongue hanging limp from its lips, swollen and dry, making it hard for the creature to talk.

"You were…dying…only…way to…save…"

"You were dying, dearest Bella," Tentos said. "You were dying, and due to the influx of the Dark Lord's blood, you couldn't be healed. The only choice was to open you to Him and allow you to receive his blessing in truth, which you could never deserve, after your failure, or to gut you and drain you of every last drop of His gift. Oh, how we argued over it, the priesthood, I mean. For days, we deliberated!" He smiled, shaking his head in fond memory.

"Should we let you die? The Blood of the God needed to be returned to Him, but after your failures, it would be sacrilege to permit it. But, should you live, you must be executed. No, we went round and round in circles, before Edvard provided us with the most wonderful solution."

"Sor…ry…" Edvard mumbled again, stirring in his chains and groaning as a ripple of pain tore through him.

"Yes, terribly sorry to see you come to this end, Bella—my apologies, Sergeant Belladonna, I mean!" Tentos' voice was oily and nonchalant. "But, it's your own fault. Had you been more respectful in the past, then perhaps I would have reached out my hand and sheltered you from this end."

"Lies," she hissed. "You're a pathetic little worm with delusions of grandeur. It'd take a miracle for you to ever have a chance at real power, let alone the chance to help me!"

"A miracle, you say?" Tentos wondered, rubbing his lips nervously with two fingers, licking them and stroking his mouth, in a habit that had stayed with him from childhood. "Yes, perhaps, but recent events? Well, one could almost say the God lent a hand in my promotion. After all, so many of the upper priests dying so suddenly, and so violently." He shivered in ecstasy, rubbing his lips faster.

"Oh, you should have seen it, Bella…the deaths, so many deaths, all feeding our Dark Master. They were killed so wonderfully, so…so passionately!"

"An attack…on the…church…dozens…dead…" Edvard mumbled, shaking himself. "Water…please…"

"Water? Oh, but certainly…" Tentos whispered, an excited smile crossing his dry lips. He pulled a flask of crystal-clear water from a bag, condensation frosting the sides of the glass as he raised it, then slowly poured it into Edvard's mouth. Bella's mouth grew even drier at the sight, and she swallowed hard, biting the inside of her cheek to stop herself from begging that weasel for a drink.

"Yes, that's it…enjoy!" Tentos whispered, pocketing the vial and rubbing his lips again, stepping back quickly as Edvard started to convulse and choke.

"Spit it out!" Bella cried to Edvard. "Spit it out, you idiot! You can't drink it!"

"Hush, Bella, let him make his own discoveries," Tentos whispered, clearly enjoying Edvard's panicked choking and her own naked body thrashing around nearly as much, his eyes passing over her again and again.

She hissed in anger and grabbed the manacles, twisting and pulling, yanking on the embedded restraints, glaring at the perverted little priest who reached for himself as he watched her.

She howled in rage and twisted around, managing to lock one foot against the wall and used it as a point to brace from. She grabbed the chains in both hands and leaned out, gritting her teeth and flexing muscles that had been hard-earned in both training and battle, and she heaved.

Nothing happened at first, beyond the heavy breathing of the priest who sidled even closer to enjoy the view afforded from her arched back, but then a single crack split the air.

A section of stone around the manacle, weakened from centuries of supplicants and victims straining against it, came loose, and the manacle shifted. Three bolts held the manacle in place, but as the rock fractured, the anchor points became points of failure. The force grew, and more cracks radiated between them.

There were half a dozen heartbeats where the world seemed to hesitate, held in the balance, then the chain tore free, and Belladonna closed her grip around Tentos' throat.

She didn't hesitate, her teeth lengthening in anticipation, and the flesh at the edges of her mouth tore in an orgy of pain and pleasure. Her jaw lengthened, making room for the new serrated teeth that erupted from her abused gums as her change manifested.

The pathetic excuse for a priest screamed once as her jaws closed around his face. The scream ended abruptly as she bit down, the bones shattering as her evolved form took hold, replacing the pathetic musculature of the Elf maiden with that of two species that were never meant to mix, further enhanced by the blood of the Dark God that Thomas had gifted her in an attempt to save her life.

She tore the skull apart, feeding on the disgusting priest, barely noticing as she ripped her legs and remaining arm free of the restraints. She landed heavily and rose to a new, considerably greater height as she threw back her head and roared in triumph.

The door to the ritual chamber slammed open as guards rushed in. Overjoyed at the sudden appearance of so much fresh meat, she roared a challenge at them, tossing the headless body of their previous master aside before bounding into their midst.

She laid about her with claw-tipped hands, the chisel-like blades tearing through flesh and bone, tossing the merely human guards about like the pathetic toys they were.

The entire squad was dead in seconds. She paused, glaring around, huffing as she tried to make sense of the world. Her newly enhanced vision was overlaid with senses she'd never known. Heat patterns painted the world red and blue. Scents filled her nostrils of the voided bowels and naked terror of the last seconds of her victims' lives, along with the infrequent bathing habits of the priesthood, all combined to make her want to claw her own nose off.

"Be…lla…" came a voice from nearby. She spun around, glaring at the misshapen figure chained to the wall. She sniffed the air, growling deep in her throat at the wrongness of him. It was hard to think, hard to remember, but he had…he was…

"Edvaaaaard," she rumbled, the sound coming from deep in her chest. She stomped over, her motion both peculiar and strangely right. Her newly bent-backward knees granted her an awkward gait. She reached up, tapping one long claw-tipped finger against his chest. "You…Edvaaaaard."

"Yes…you Bella…donna…friend…" he hissed. She cocked her head to the side, baring her teeth in challenge. He struggled against the restraints then sagged, lifting his head in supplication, exposing his neck.

Bella stood taller, glaring down at him before turning around, meeting each member of the Dark Hunter pack in turn and locking eyes on them.

Some hesitated, but most bared their throats immediately, accepting her as the alpha. Those few who didn't strained against their restraints briefly before accepting that she was stronger, and they were helpless.

By the time she'd turned back to Edvard, he had recovered from his coughing and was watching her, seemingly considering something.

"Edvaaaaard…whyyy?" she asked, her anger and curiosity raging against one another.

"Thomasss!" came a hiss from her left, and she spun to face the figure that hung on the far side of Edvard. "Thomasss betrayed usss!" it hissed. Her anger built. She remembered Thomas, remembered watching him, thinking about him…a feeling…a hunger for him…a desire.

Now she felt a new hunger, a need for him, but it was to taste his blood, to feed on him, to tear him limb from limb. The feeling ebbed and grew, warring with her previous desires, and her memories of him carrying her through the forest, him saving her from spells, and beating back the Legion for her.

"Whyyyy?" she growled. "Whyyyy!"

"He betrayed…the God…turned…his back…on us all," Edvard forced out, coughing up phlegm and shuddering.

"Yessss!!! Betraysss usss!" the second figure agreed, glaring at her and at Edvard. "Huntssss him, we mussssst, killsss him, eatsss him…God sssavesss us!"

Bella watched the figure, seeing something familiar in the way it shifted its head, the breathing. The scent was wrong, though, too musky, but…

"Corrrran…" she whispered as things clicked together for her.

"Betraysss usss, leavesss usss behind…." Coran hissed.

She growled at that thought. That Thomas had betrayed the God was one thing, but to make her feel, then to leave? To save her life, then abandon her?

"Noooo…we huntssss him…" she growled, reaching out and grabbing the manacle that held Edvard's right wrist against the wall. She tensed, readied herself, then heaved with Edvard helping. A second later, it gave way, snapping off with a crack and a groan of tearing metal.

The rest of his restraints went the same way, then between the pair of them, they freed Coran, then moved to the others until the entire pack was free. Some tried to feed on the corpses, managing to choke down blood and hunks of flesh. It filled their bodies, but the others weren't so far gone and rebelled against the idea of eating their fellow soldiers.

Bella didn't care. She ordered them to eat quickly, before she picked up the nearest weapon, a longsword, and looked down the length of it. She'd always been strong, unusually so, even for an Elf maiden that trained as a warrior, but this…this new body, these new instincts…they screamed power at her in a new way.

"Sssshouldn't be able to eatsss…" Coran muttered, and she turned to him.

"Explain," she rumbled.

"Hunterssss…we sssstarvessss until we findssss him…water and meat isss poisssson," he hissed, confused.

She growled as she remembered it as well. Edvard had choked on the water the priest had given him. Belladonna frowned, finding it hard to think, to remember, but forcing her brain to work through sheer determination alone.

She remembered the same tales, and she turned, sniffing as something caught her nose, following the scent to a bowl that sat on the floor under where Edvard had been shackled.

She sniffed it, wrinkling her long nose and backing up, before kicking it away, sending the liquid spraying. She turned to Edvard, moving close and sniffing him. The scent was weaker, but it was there. She snuffled, following the scent down, across his chest, and lower, finding it on his left hip. There was a small design carved into his flesh with a thin dagger, the liquid filling it, causing raised welts.

She growled and grabbed him, drawing her talons across it, tearing the skin and setting the liquid running down his side.

He snarled in pain, but he took one look at her, and it died away. Obediently, Edvard followed her as she dragged him to a corpse, tearing some cloth free and scrubbing it across his bloody flesh roughly, rubbing the skin raw.

In seconds, he vomited, shaking uncontrollably, as something changed in him. He collapsed to the floor, twitching and shuddering, coughing and vomiting up a thin bile.

Cries came from farther down the corridor, questions for the guards that were supposed to be outside the ritual hall. Bella grabbed the belt from the priest with all its bags and pouches and held tight to it. Rising to her full height, she gave orders to the others. Two were to carry Edvard, the only one among them who had been maimed with the sigils so far, another one to carry the bags from all the soldiers, and the others were to surround the group.

She didn't know what was happening, not truly, not yet, but both sides of her called out for Thomas, so she'd go to him and deal with whatever happened, when it happened.

CHAPTER THIRTY

The ten Alkyon swarmed the tower below us in seconds, before splitting into two teams of four and heading straight back out into the rain, with the remaining two taking up watch in the tower, along with their unconscious victim.

They would stay there until the other two towers had been neutralized, then the entire ten-man squad would set off and fly directly to the palace, staying high, ready to help defend my team from any fliers as we gained entry. Once we were inside, they were to head to the secondary objective of the army barracks and aid the Imps that would be stationed there.

This was partially because no bugger actually trusted the imps as far as they could throw them, while the Djinn who were going with Thomas had stated that they'd protect that section of the Legion from air attacks.

It almost made me irritated about the casual dismissal the imps received, until I spent five minutes with them, explaining their orders. By the end of it, I was ready to skewer all seven, so I decided not to be so judgmental about attitudes to them in the future.

As soon as the Alkyon were away, we dipped below the level of some of the higher buildings, cruising along the main street at high speed, headed straight for the palace. I stood up, grabbing a support and standing on the railing, where I could turn and look back over the gathered legionnaires.

"Legion!" I called, no longer caring about subtlety, as the damn thrum of the engines was making windows on either side of the street vibrate and occasionally shatter as we went past.

"Today we take the fight to the enemy! The Drow have captured Narkolt, using their stealth and magical skills to appear as innocent citizens, as well as dickbag nobles. We're here to slaughter the fuckers and capture the city for the Empire! No longer will it be us against the world, as the next few hours decide our future in the greater war against Nimon and his forces. Should we take this city, we will go from an annoyance to an equal with Himnel and the Dark Legion. No longer will they dare send teams against the Tower, as we'll be too close and too ready to strike, should they try it." I took a deep breath and looked around, trying to think of what else I needed to say to them.

"In taking this city, we start to retake the Empire, forcing the nobility who have fed on the wounded remnants to back off. We will bring the law to this city, and in return, we will have all the support it can give! Troops, ships, and weapons, food, and magic. But we're not just doing it for that; we're doing it to grow our home, to make sure that our friends and our families are safe.

"This won't be easy, but in taking this city, we also get to burn the Dark Wanker's churches, loot them, and piss on His altar. I don't know about you, but knowing that fucking cocksucker was responsible for the death of the Eternal

Emperor Amon, I'm planning on shitting on His holiest relics just to make sure He remembers my fucking name!"

Thunder rolled and rumbled, and I grinned, staring upward into the rain, blinking as it hit my face, and I called out to him.

"You heard me! I'm going to find your priests and nail their fucking balls to their ears, then I'll kick you out of Himnel, and one day? One day, I'll chase you down personally, bitch slap you until you scream, and bury you in a barrel of shit headfirst! I'm fucking coming for you, dickbag!" I yelled into the air, hearing the rising laughter of the Legion.

It'd started as nervous chuckles, but as I railed and shouted at the God of Death, they cheered, loving the feeling of standing on the edge of the world and pissing off it.

"Get ready!" Lydia called up to me, and I grinned at them before turning my attention behind and to the left of our ship. The engines of the *Ragnarök* flared as she slowed as far as possible. A blur of multicolored lights erupted as the Djinn summoned some air magic that acted as a cushion. That allowed the legionnaires that leaped over the side, falling some twenty meters, to land with a gentle bump before running for the doors leading down from the roof and into the main building.

The other half of that team of legionnaires, led by Thomas and his new squad, leaped over the far side of the ship, plummeting sixty plus meters before landing in a cloud of magical air. Their fall was arrested by it, and they barely grunted, their armor and weapons clattering, before they rushed forward, kicking the doors in and storming the guardhouse.

I grinned. The Djinn had almost collapsed from the strain of their spells, but the little guys had done an amazing job with it. I'd make damn sure to tell Hellenica about it when I got back.

I leaned out to the other side of the ship, hanging over the edge and holding on with one hand on the support, catching a glimpse of the ship that was angling toward the army buildings. I grinned as I turned and stared straight ahead.

"Lord Jax!" came a voice.

Sehran frowned with concern as she looked to the left. "Someone just opened a portal to my realm, a big one!"

I reached down to her and held my hand out. When she took it, I pulled her up and held onto her.

"Where?" I asked.

She pointed at a tall building with a long, low balcony that led out from the topmost level.

"There! It's…. it's another Storm Demon!" she cried, pointing to the light that was growing on the top of the building.

"How long until it's here?" I asked.

She paused, clearly examining it with a sense I didn't have. "A few minutes; it's building fast…and it's BIG!"

I looked back, glancing toward the Tower, not seeing any of the Alkyon available yet, before Lydia stepped up, grabbing the same support and called out loudly for the Legion to hear.

"This un's mine! If any o' yer let Lord Jax get so much as a bent nail, ye'll answer te me!" she shouted, getting a round of "Yes, Optio!" from the legionnaires as she snapped her wings wide as the speed of our passage caught them and lifted her from the deck into the air.

"Be careful!" she yelled at me, even as she beat her wings hard, rocketing upward and twisting around, ready to go one-on-one with a Storm Demon.

"You first!" I turned to Sehran, who held onto me tightly, grinning. "So, you want to go down?" I asked her, approximately half a second before realizing what that sounded like.

She licked her lips before jumping down with a laugh. She walked over to Jian and grabbed his hand, grinning at him.

"She thinks she got to you there," Oracle whispered. I shook my head, subtly adjusting myself.

"She almost did with that damn dirty smile, then I remembered your ability to suck a golf ball through a hosepipe. Once this is sorted, we're finding a bedroom, a clean one," I corrected myself, shaking my head as I remembered Rewn and his harem. "And I'm going to break you over something."

"Not if I break you first!" Oracle winked, and I let my gaze linger over her.

She'd strolled to the outer edge of my shoulder inside the hood. I could see her, but nobody else could, and she showed me her new form, a variant on Sehran, but simply more beautiful.

"Behave!" I told her, grinning.

She blurred back to normal with a little laugh, before leaning in and planting a gentle kiss on my cheek.

"Okay, time to concentrate," I said, banishing carnal thoughts as I looked over in the direction that Lydia had gone. Her wings beat occasionally as she closed the distance.

Hoping she'd be okay, I turned and looked forward. Westin clambered up onto the railing by my side, looking back over at the legionnaires and called out in a clear voice that carried across the ship.

"Optios, Centurions, legionnaires! Get ready! We land in a few minutes!" Then, he turned to me and raised one eyebrow. "The Legion Prefect and the Primus Praetoria ordered me to protect you. We're not going to have to have a falling out over who I listen to first, now are we?"

"Hell no, they'd kick my arse as well," I said, forcing a smile before nodding forward. The high inner wall of the Palace District loomed into view. "Looks like we're getting close."

"The wall is in sight!" he shouted to the legionnaires, who started final checks on their armor. Ronin started to sing, playing "Luck's My Mistress" again from the beginning, this time getting a few legionnaires singing along.

He stopped dead, reading a notification nobody else could see before grinning and shouting to everyone.

"Your singing is boosting it! Sing, you fuckers!" he shouted, before taking a deep breath and starting again. "Oh, the ladies of the sea are sweet on me, the ladies of the land all ask for my hand, but…"

I glanced at the notification, and paused, stunned.

Buff: Lucky Bastard!

Effect: Boosts the luck of all allied forces who hear this song, further boosted by the faith of those who join in singing along. +8 Luck to all allied forces, -12 Luck to all enemy or undeclared forces. Lasts 15 minutes.

"Sing!" I barked at them all, before raising my voice and joining in, despite my godsdamn awful singing voice.

"The ladies of the mountains might love my pick, while the ladies of the lake keep a man awake, but…"

The song echoed out, with more and more people singing, uncertainly at first, but with ever-growing fervor as they saw the bonuses climbing. The effect stopped at minus twenty Luck for our enemies when the entire complement of the ship singing with full enthusiasm.

"There!" Sehran shouted in glee, pointing to the building that Lydia had flown to, as the light was cut off in a burst of red and yellow fire, the top of the building detonating in a shower of stone.

"Lydia!" I shouted, letting out a relieved breath as her shadowy figure blocked out the flames for a few brief seconds, having dived over the side at some point. "What happened?" I asked Sehran, who grinned.

"The summoner stopped channeling. I'm betting Lydia got them! The spell backlash did that!" She pointed to the spiraling stone blocks that fell from sight as smoke and flames rushed up into the darkness.

"Well, she officially kicked this fight off!" I called to the others, grabbing onto the support and holding tighter as Tenandra angled upwards, arcing over the wall. There was a startled cry from below as a guardsman finally saw us. Seconds later, a bell clanged an iron warning across the palace grounds, even as we dipped again, the ship angling around and heading straight across a gleaming white stone carriageway towards the front of the palace.

Rewn had drawn me a map when he thought he still might have a chance of accompanying us. After I had looked at it, I asked Carmen to redo it, getting a version that didn't look like a ham-fisted toddler had drawn it.

Tenandra slowed, the engines angling forward and firing hard, arresting our motion sharply, even as more and more bells rang out in warning.

"Go, go, go!" I shouted, gesturing to the side of the ship as the crew ran out the boarding ramp. It was narrow and barely held as we all boarded, bouncing if more than a handful of us were on it at the same time. Thankfully, most of the Legion were well within the realms that most on Earth would call superhuman.

The majority simply jumped from the side of the ship, plummeting to the ground and landing with a grunt before racing forwards. The weaker members of the team, basically just Ronin, took the ramp, while the rest were already sprinting forward with the archers firing arrows up at the towers, making the occupants duck out of sight.

Neither Mal nor any of his team were anywhere to be seen. They should have been waiting with information for us. With a growl, I resolved to kick his fucking arse into the next time zone after this fight, though I had no time to be distracted by it now.

Two out of each squad paused, casting Magic Missile. Everyone in the team could cast it, as the four squads with me had all learned the spell. But there was no need for overkill, as eight sets of five darts were launched at the three towers, the barrage blasting bits of the stonework free, making the small contingents of mainly lazy soldiers throw themselves down in panic.

I had given the Legion very specific orders. Where possible, they were to minimize casualties, as these people would hopefully have been simply conned by the Drow, but, when it came to a real risk to the Legion, they were to use excessive force and resolve it as fast as possible.

Where my squad had sprinted to the side and either jumped down or clambered, I'd instead taken to the air, blasting upward and straight across at the target that Lydia and I had chosen for ourselves in the planning stages, the small tower over the entrance to the palace that we were intending to use.

It held up to four guardsmen and had a container of magically heated lead permanently on the boil, ready to be used. In times of need it would be poured into a channel that would rain it on any who approached through the tunnel under the tower, permanently ruining their day.

The window that led into their small guard post was only half a meter wide, small enough that they could avoid incoming fire, while being large enough that they could use a variety of weapons through it and still have ornate gilding and such crap around it.

It was also the perfect size for me to smash though in one go, when I did like Superman and flew straight at the glass with my naginata extended.

The glass shattered, sending a wash of shards across the room. The three guards inside flinched back, covering their eyes.

I'd planned to be as gentle as a raider could be, but one of the men moved at just the wrong time, as I had closed my eyes to avoid the spray of glass, I skewered his arm, punching clean through the shoulder and out the back. I lifted him screaming, pinning him to the wall as the blade dug in, leaving him suspended half a meter off the floor by the force of my arrival.

I spun, the other two already reacting. One was slow and uncertain, and the other a young boy, barely old enough to grow a beard, judging from the pathetic scruff trimmed into a goatee.

I spun to face him, sweeping his legs from under him with a spin kick. Then I continued the spin to bring myself around again, straightening to catch him with an explosive uppercut as he fell. It sent him flipping over with the crunch of a broken jaw.

I came to my feet, shaking my hand. The second guard, clearly a professional, had his sword out and was lunging for me. I sidestepped, backing away as soon as I'd avoided his sword, trying to get back far enough to use magic, but his blade swung again and again in short, controlled stabs, driving me back farther and farther as I tried to circle the room.

"Should have been watching the stairwell..." came a voice from behind me as a dagger was pressed to the gap between my cuirass and the chainmail that covered the joints.

I froze, lifting my hands out to the sides, and the man before me straightened, letting out a sigh of relief.

"Why is that?" I asked the man behind me, as the other guard turned back to check on the one pinned to the wall.

"Because then I'd not have gotten the drop on you," he said smugly. "Now, face the wall, hands apart and braced!"

"Or," I said, as though just thinking of it, "Perhaps I saw you coming out of the stairwell and used the opportunity to let my companion get behind you…just a thought."

"If your companion was in here and behind me, I'd be dead already. Now, who the hell are you, and what's going on!" he snapped.

"First off, I'm Lord Jax, rightful Lord of the City, as well as the Continent. Secondly, I'm here because the Drow have overtaken the city…oh and third? Oracle," I said with all the cool certainty of a man who'd won.

There was a brief scream as the Lightning Bolt slammed into him, the stun effect clearly coming into play as he almost bit through his tongue, shaking and juddering before collapsing to the floor.

The other guard, halfway back to his friend, turned at the sound and was hit in the face by my Lightning Bolt, sending him flying back and into his friend, the human butterfly pinned to the wall, who moaned piteously.

With three of the four down, I stepped forward, grabbed my naginata and yanked, letting him drop to the floor with a scream. He was hit with a heal from Oracle, thoroughly confusing him. I shrugged and apologized before punching him as hard as I could in the temple, sending him sprawling and unconscious.

"Well, that was fun," Oracle said, smiling at me.

"Wasn't it just!" I grinned over how straightforward fighting regular human guards was compared to the assholes I usually dealt with. "Come on, then!" I said cheerfully, striding across the room and yanking the lever that opened the doors below me, allowing the Legion entrance to the next level of the palace.

The others streamed through the tunnel, the sudden deep twang of crossbows going off. Steel-tipped bolts slammed into armor. Cries of pain rang out, discordant against the ringing of metal on metal. I sprinted to the stairwell, finding stairs up and down.

I figured downward would lead to where the others already were, so I headed upward, Oracle flying alongside me as we ran. The next floor was sealed with a massive wooden door studded with iron spikes.

I reached out tentatively, grabbing the handle and twisting, more than a little surprised when it opened smoothly, revealing a covered walkway that led left and right, surrounding the courtyard that the Legion were in now.

I glanced from side to side. Three men stood on the left, with one on the right before the walkway vanished from sight, turning the corner.

The men I could see crouched, frantically reloading, then jumped up and took a shot before ducking back down. I grinned as Oracle started casting, aiming at the man on his own. I focused on the other direction, pointing my naginata down the corridor. I triggered Soaring Majesty, blasting across the distance that separated us and lancing straight into the side of the nearest man, along with a wash of fire mana flooding my weapon.

The blade punched clean through his jacket, encountering no resistance as it passed out the far side in a shower of blood and hissing, white-hot metal.

They were firing on my people from a position of strength. In an instant, my intention went from subdue to kill, with the mana I was still only starting to understand responding to my will.

As soon as the weapon was free, I twisted it around, deflecting a crossbow bolt fired at me in a panic, and blasted forward. The blade dipped and lifted again, slicing through the second guard's wrist, sending his hand flying free in a welter of blood.

I released the haft of my naginata with my left hand, reaching out and grabbing the man by his collar. I turned, spinning and yanked him from his feet, bringing him around and hurtling toward the third man.

He fired his freshly reloaded crossbow.

The bolt slammed into the back of the man I held, drawing a horrified grunt and a simultaneous crunch of bone. I threw him forward, slamming him into his friend and striking out as fast as an adder's bite, the bladed tip whistling through the air to dip once, twice, and a final third time.

I opened the artery in the shooter's thigh, his wrist on the next strike, then sliced the other's neck before he could complain about his friend giving him what was probably a fatal injury anyway.

Just like that, all three were dead or bleeding out. I cut off my ability, my feet landing on the floor and skidding as I twisted, sliding around the corner.

There was a twang, and a bolt flew past me. Before I had a chance to react, the shooter screamed in pain, a barrage of five, then five more Magic Missiles slamming home.

Each missile detonated, doing little damage individually. But even a slight cut, little more than a papercut, could kill, if it was over an artery.

Six of the missiles hit the crossbowman's throat and neck, and his head was barely connected by the final detonation.

I winced as the corpse collapsed, the eyes still blinking in shock, as Oracle turned the far corner, pausing as she looked at the four bodies in the section, all taken down by the Legion and the spells she'd taught them.

"Shit." I muttered, wincing as I remembered the no-lethal rules I'd asked the Legion to abide by where possible. Right now, that seemed pretty fucking stupid, considering I'd killed three so far myself and left four unconscious.

"Jax, you crazy motherfucker!" Grizz shouted up from below and I moved to look down at him.

"Yeah? Whadda ya want, ya bandit!" I called back, a sudden feeling of déjà vu springing to mind.

"You're gonna get us murdered by Lydia if she finds out you went off on your own again!" he warned.

"Well fucking try to keep up, then!" I said, unable to help myself, and grinned as Giint gave me the finger.

"We're on our way!" Grizz said, pointing to the stairwell in the corner of the side I was on. "Meet us at the bottom of that, boss," he half-requested, half-ordered.

I nodded, jogging into the dimly lit stairwell and running down the stairs. I passed a serving boy wearing his nightclothes who ducked down, covering his head as he wailed in fear.

I trotted down two more revolutions of the stairwell before finding a door and yanking it open. There were half a dozen fully-armored guardsmen rushing towards the door, and I shook my head, yanking it closed again. With fumbling hands, I slammed the latch back into place, leaning on it to hold it shut.

These weren't the same guards we'd faced so far. Their armor was much higher quality, and rather than simple uniforms, they wore full plate. Their weapons had a subtle glow about them that screamed, enchanted, and the way they ran at me?

Nope.

I'd found their elite troops in an area that was about as badly suited to my fighting style as it was possible to get, given that it was the bottom of a narrow stairwell, and my weapon of choice was essentially a staff with a sword blade on the end.

They rattled the door, then banged on it, and in a fit of insanity, I called out to them. "Who is it?"

"The guard, open up!" a voice shouted back after a few seconds, sounding angry and confused.

"Uh, no thanks!" I shrugged as Oracle floated down beside me and locked eyes with me, grinning. She had to feel the slight battle hysteria that the situation was engendering, snickering silently as she fought to maintain control.

"Open this door!" the voice boomed again.

"Uh, no! Told you already, I don't want any!"

"Any what?"

"Any guards!" I clarified.

"Uh, we're not guards?" the voice called back after a hurried bout of whispering, and I stifled a giggle.

"Are you sure? You said you were before, you know," I replied, even as Oracle started casting Healing Waters in front of the door. I took a drink, then listened.

"Well, we're not! Now open this door!"

"Who are you, if you're not guards?"

Oracle summoned another fountain. I continued leaning on the latch, stopping them from opening the door.

"Uh..."

"Are you door-to-door salesmen?" I asked, prompting a brief conversation, before the first voice was replaced with a new one.

"Yes! We're door-to-door salesmen, now open this door in the name of the guard!" the new voice boomed, and I shouted back at him straight away.

"You just said you were salesmen! I'm not letting you in; you're liars!"

"This is your last chance!" The voice screamed, the latch shuddering as they tried to force it, even as Oracle finished a further two fountains, nodding to me as she backed away.

"Have you got any ID? If you have, I'll let you in..."

"Fine! Yes, we've got ID!"

I let go of the latch, backing up the stairs as I started casting.

The door was practically yanked off its hinges as they tried it again and unexpectedly found no resistance. Instead, they found four fountains spraying water directly at them, and a sudden wash of water that had been building up on my side of the door, held in place by the age of the door and its irregular usage.

"What the…!" the owner of the second voice cried, shaking himself as water sprayed across his armor, soaking him. I shook my head as I looked down at him.

"I don't really care if you've got ID," I said. "I fucking hate door-to-door salesmen." With that, I let loose with the Lightning Bolt I'd been charging, as did Oracle.

Mine slammed straight into the groin of the armored figure before me, who screamed and started shaking, even as the charge passed from him. It flowed into the others in the small group, all conveniently gathered close to the door and standing in the wash of water.

Oracle's spells lashed out, hitting the two on the outer edges. Since it was dual-cast, she'd managed to split it into two bolts, and the overlapping shocks took all six to the floor screaming.

I felt bad about it for a second, considering I'd totally confused them all first. But, as Grizz and the others appeared at the far end of the corridor, I couldn't help but grin. They raced over and gave a damn good kicking to the few who were trying to get back up.

"About time you buggers showed up!" I shouted to them. "Lydia's going to be pissed!"

"What am Ah goin' te be pissed about?" Lydia asked from right behind me.

"Uh, that you missed all the fun?"

"Not tha' yer went off on yer own again, then?"

"Not exactly alone," I replied with a nonchalant shrug, hoping it'd disarm her. "It was always a part of our plan that we would storm the higher levels. You were busy, so I did it without you. What happened with the Storm Demon, then?"

She glared at me before a grin cracked through the façade. "There was a Drow in tha middle o' summonin' it when Ah arrived, two dead elven guards by 'is feet anyway, so ah was fairly confident o' who an' what 'e was. 'E didn't so much as turn around, so Ah smashed 'is skull in from behind 'fore tha Demon could fully pass through tha portal. It snapped shut, killing tha Demon, then tha spell tore out o' control, so I got tha 'ell out of there!"

"And?" I asked, knowing that there was something she wasn't saying.

"An' Ah got tha experience fer killin' tha Demon, three Drow, an' a dozen guards…no sure what side they were on, but fer that experience drop? Ah'll accept it."

"Fair enough. Better that you killed the Demon before it could do anything, anyway."

"Ah thought that, too. Right, Ah saw that tha upper floor is cleared, an' yeh've clearly been playin' down 'ere…are yer ready te move on?"

"Did you see the Legion when you arrived?" I asked, getting a brief nod.

"They were taking turns te heal tha few that got injured, an' there was an argument goin' on about if it was worth injurin' each other deliberately ta get more healing experience when Ah landed above." Lydia shook her head in amazement. "Honestly, sometimes Ah'm in shock they survived this long."

"Which ones?"

She gave a derisive snort. "All o' them! It's tha entire damn Legion! Romanus is tha only sensible one in tha entire force, an' don't get me started on Restun; 'e's just evil!"

"I thought you liked him?" I asked her, confused, as I looted one of the twitching, groaning forms on the floor, slipping his faintly glowing sword into my bag first. "Oh, that's nice. Mine! Okay, people, you've got thirty seconds, then we're moving on!"

"Ah do, 'e's just damn scary an' never stops. Ah saw 'im runnin' laps up an' down tha Tower tha other night, literally just doing sprints again an' again," Lydia said, and I nodded in agreement. I searched the figure roughly, pulling his bags of holding free, then stepping on his wrist when he fumbled for a dagger at his waist.

"Stay the fuck down," I warned in a low voice. "I kicked your ass easily, and you're now unarmed. Take this as a loss and stay down, because if you don't, I'll have to kill you." I pulled his dagger free of its sheath and pressed it to the underside of his throat, looking into the scared eyes that peered out through the slit in his helmet.

"O…okay…" he whispered, still shaking. I nodded, straightening up and taking the dagger away from his throat.

"Good man. Lie there for a bit, maybe have a nice nap. This will all be over before you know it," I said, turning away and looking to Lydia. "So, the plan of the palace we had wasn't that good, but I'm thinking back up the stairs, then take a left?"

"That's tha entrance ta tha upper hallways, should lead us into tha palace proper without too much fuss, especially as they'll still be scramblin' an' tryin' te figure out what's 'appenin'."

I was about to answer when there was a sudden commotion from one side and a brief scream. It ended in a wet gurgle and the rapid clattering of metal on stone as one of the elite guards was stabbed, his hands frantically trying to staunch the wound in his throat as Grizz pulled a dagger free.

"What happened?" I asked grimly.

"He tried to cast a spell. Sorry, Jax," he replied, shaking his head in disgust. "Damn fool, he had to know he didn't have a…shit!"

Grizz took a step back involuntarily, as a figure beside him stabbed out with a stiletto that punched easily through the gaps in the plates of his leg armor. He cursed, then, being the double-hard bastard he was, grabbed the hilt of the weapon and punched the wielder in the face, before reaching down and yanking the helm free.

He exposed a narrow, grey-skinned face; short-cropped, bone-white hair; and dark red eyes. The Drow lifted his right hand, twisting his fingers in a complicated pattern, then clicked them. Before Grizz could think to stop him, there was a flash of bright white light that momentarily blinded us all.

When my eyes had recovered enough that I could see and hear beyond the cursing and staggering mixture of both forces in the hallway, I saw the empty space where the bastard had been and caught a single glimpse of movement at the far end of the hall as a hidden door slid back into place.

"Shitfuck!" I snarled, shaking my head as Oracle hit me with a healing spell, then started healing those around me.

"What…who was that?!" A voice said from my left, and I looked down, seeing one of the elite guards had propped himself up on his elbows and was staring wide-eyed after the vanishing figure.

"A Drow," I snapped, glaring at the rest of them suspiciously. Nothing but stunned amazement, horror, and fear returned to me from their expressions.

"What did you do to Fenn!" the guard asked in a horrified whisper, staring at me.

"We didn't do shit," I assured him, eloquently. "We're here to kill the fucking Drow." I looked around quickly before grunting as Lydia opened a door nearby, glanced inside and turned back to me.

"It's empty; want te toss them in 'ere?"

I nodded.

"Wait, who the hell are you, and what Drow? Where did he come from?" the guard asked, clearly panicked.

Lydia slid her fingers into the top of his armor, between the rim of the cuirass and his chest, and yanked him upright, sending him staggering toward the doorway.

"No time, pretty boy," she answered with a shove. "Get in there an' shut tha 'ell up. We'll let yer loose when tha Drow are all dead."

"But…"

Lydia ended the conversation by booting him in the armored ass, sending him staggering through the door to fall over, his limbs still weak and shocked from the overcharged Stunning Lightning Bolts.

The rest were shoved inside as well, or dragged, depending on their condition. The door closed while Grizz and Tang dragged a statue over and propped it against the door, preventing those inside from escaping.

"Hope that holds them," I muttered. "I'd hate to have to kill them all."

"Me too," Lydia admitted, even as Flux called out in triumph from the other end of the corridor.

"Jax!" He gestured to a doorway that slid open in the wall. It was the same one that the Drow had escaped through moments before.

"Fuck," I muttered, well aware that we needed to assist the Legion raiding party. That required catching up and taking out anyone attacking them from above, but we also couldn't afford to let the Drow escape. "Flux, take Grizz, Cheena, and Lio. Hunt those fuckers down and kill them all!" I ordered, waving at Flux as he tried to disagree.

"We can't go that way; the Legion needs us to clear the upper halls. This fight stopped being stealthy as soon as those assholes triggered the alarms. Grizz will give you all the muscle you need, now go!" I turned back to the stairwell that led up to the next objective.

"Everyone else, with me!" I snapped, matching actions to words as I started running up the stairs.

There was a second's hesitation as people moved around, and the team split up. Then the clatter of running, armored fighters filled the stairwell behind me, interspersed by the occasional note that floated through as Ronin kept up his steady song.

We erupted onto the upper floor again seconds later, pausing briefly as over a dozen heavily armored figures on the far side spun, readying weapons before they relaxed and sprinted to the same door we were aiming for, waving a salute as we recognized each other. Clearly, Westin had sent them up to help watch over me, despite me being in ostensible command of the assault.

"Hold please, sir!" one of them said in a way that was definitely not a request. She held her arm out to keep me back as two of the biggest legionnaires I'd ever seen braced themselves, then sprinted to the door.

The woman who'd spoken kicked the door open then spun out of the way as a trio of crossbow bolts sailed past her, embedding themselves in the shields the charging pair of legionnaires held.

The vast majority of the Legion carried what I'd come to think of as the standard Legion shield. It was a tower shield with twin points on the base that could be driven into the ground for added stability, and a pair of runes that were inexpertly engraved on the rear of the shield, enabling them to link together with other shields pressed against them, magnifying their strength and spreading out damage.

It was an old Imperial design, and it was great, although I had serious plans to improve it, especially after seeing Ame's sneers of derision at the poor rune smithing shown by the Legion armorers. They simply copied the ancient designs, but didn't understand them, resulting in slight weaknesses and variants over the millennia.

These two carried different gear, though, marking them out as two of the Narkolt elite legionnaires.

I'd been told where Himnel had focused on creating a maniple of legionnaires who were better than the standard legionnaires at everything, namely Augustus's Second Maniple, producing legionnaires like Grizz. The Narkolt force had gone the other way, creating a smaller special forces maniple. Rather than dozens of elite legionnaires, they'd created fifteen.

Most of them were dead, but Lio was one of them, and these two were members of the same team: Jacko and Scotty Ramm, or the Battering Rams, as I'd heard them referred to, were fucking big bastards. Half-ogres, they had heavily invested in their Intelligence, raising it to a level slightly above the average legionnaire, as ogres and even half-ogres were naturally thick as pig shit. However, where they might only be average in mind, despite their hard-won efforts, they were well, well above average in body.

They stood over eight feet in height at the shoulder, wearing armor that had to be custom-built for them, carrying a pair of shields that, while based on the standard, were anything but normal.

The shields were six inches thick, made with solid metal, and most legionnaires couldn't even lift them. The three crossbow bolts that slammed into them barely scratched the paint, and the pair had to duck and advance in single file to pass through the door before angling out and picking up speed on the far side. They roared a pair of taunts that made my blood boil, and I wasn't facing them or even their enemy.

"The Battering Rams are in, boys and girls!" the legionnaire who'd stopped me screamed to the rest of her team. "Get your arses in before we miss out on all the fun!" Then she turned to me and nodded.

"Sorry sir, Primus Praetoria's orders!" she said, before following her people into the room, forcing us to follow her.

The next section was a short corridor, ending at a T-junction that led left and right, with a pair of broken metal barricades bent to one side at the end of the hall.

As I passed them, having seen the Battering Rams splitting to go left and right as we entered, I shook my head in amazement, slowing to look.

The barricades were designed to be slid out of the walls to provide cover in case of assault, and the three crossbowmen had clearly been hiding behind them at one point.

Now all three were piled against the wall, groaning, with their crossbows snapped in half and their armor dented where a fist or foot had seemingly elaborated on the wielder's suggestion that the defenders surrender.

One of the barricades was bent at almost a ninety-degree angle, while the other was laid flat on the ground, torn out of the wall entirely.

"What the hell?" I muttered, looking them over, and shaking my head in amazement.

"Impressive, aren't they?" Yen called to me, following as I chose to take the left passage. "I met them once in a tavern brawl. Scary, scary bastards armored up, but real gentle giants, you know?" She grinned, shaking her head as we passed two more groaning defenders.

"I'm thinking we should have just sent the pair of them!" I said.

"Don't say that, it'll make Grizz try and prove that he's better than them!" she called back. Lydia grunted, shaking her head, even as Tang passed me, racing forward.

The corridor turned again, this time splitting into multiple passages that ran off the main one to the left and right, often interspersed with doors. The handful of legionnaires who had preceded us were over twenty meters ahead at this point, having sprinted to catch up to their Ram.

They hadn't noticed a group of five guards that had just come out of one of the connecting corridors behind them, the four guards holding shields in place between the Legion ahead and the fifth member of their team, who began to cast something that looked a hell of a lot like Fireball as we closed in on them from behind.

"Get him!" I snarled, running full tilt. My naginata glowed as I channeled mana into it, even as the others picked up speed as well.

I was perhaps two meters from them when the first barrage struck, swiftly followed by a second and third. Three sets of Magic Missiles, fifteen projectiles in all, slammed into the back of the mage, just as they seemed to become aware of us charging up from behind.

The Fireball, if that was what it actually was, detonated, the spell backlash finishing off the mage before I could reach him. It flash-fried his front, even as his back and head vanished in a ripple of exploding darts, flesh flying free to cover the corridor and us. Flames poured out of the failed casting, searing across the back of his guards, licking down into crevices and gaps in their armor, eliciting screams as the formation came apart.

I lifted my point of aim from the back of the figure before me as he collapsed, shedding his weapons and frantically rolling as the fire spell revealed itself to have been filled with a magical version of napalm.

I leaped over the liquid fire that had splattered across them, avoiding most of it. Some small splatters hit my armor and ran down it, but thankfully none found a way in, even as I landed on the far side of the group and barreled on.

I ignored the screams from behind us as we sprinted, well aware that, if we stopped, we'd either have to heal them and try to capture them or kill them outright.

For now, the kindest option was to let them burn, and that was a damning indictment all on its own.

The legionnaires ahead looked back at us and the rolling, burning forms of their attempted ambushers behind, and received a few brisk nods in respect, before the Ram slammed into a closed door at the end of the corridor.

The door held for a brief second before bursting open, prompting screams on the far side as Scotty staggered and collapsed, planting his shield and hunching down behind it, panting hard. His abilities and strength had apparently reached the end of their run and started their cooldown.

The other legionnaires locked their shields to his and crouched, forming a low wall. We ran forward, skidding in behind them, lifting our shields, my own Legion shield tugged free of my bag just in time.

I slammed it into place, having never formed a turtle or shieldwall before. But as soon as the shields connected, I felt something similar to a magnetic pull, twisting the shield slightly, moving it into the correct alignment as it stopped with a solid *clunk*.

Do you wish to join Legion Shieldwall?

Yes/No

I tagged Yes mentally and felt a sudden drain on my mana as the twin runes on the back of the shield flared to life.

The shield vibrated slightly, growing in pitch until it matched those surrounding it. A weird rightness radiated from the shield, even as I ducked slightly to look through a small gap.

The Ram had started it, forming the center of the shieldwall, with the rest of his escort forming the lower level, kneeling in place and holding their shields steady. My team had slid in at the rear and slotted our shields atop theirs, creating a semi-solid wall that virtually filled our end of the room.

Which was bloody lucky, really, as my eyes widened involuntarily as I beheld the forces arrayed against us.

Whereas the rest of the palace so far had been filled with a combination of sleepy guards just waking up and the night shift, bored and probably the lowest on the totem pole, here we faced fully armed, wide awake, and aware elite troops, guarding a prepared position.

We'd left the main palace and had come out on the outer wall that surrounded the original keep, the new palace being constructed around the old, integrating the ancient walls into the structure.

I swore as I looked out of the small gap. We'd finally reached the place we were looking for, rather than the palace proper, as Carmen had described it. This was a much older building, dating back to before the beginning of the Imperial City.

Where we'd exited the structure behind us, we now stood atop a narrow, sloping floor leading down from a balcony that ringed the killing ground, surrounding an ancient keep that squatted in the center.

It was old, seriously old apparently, dating back to before the Empire. It was made of solid black onyx slabs that resisted any attempts to beautify it, resulting in Rewn, and his father before him, living in a much more luxurious palace built off to one side in the gardens, using this older, original keep for emergencies and for the most ceremonial events. However, in days long past, their ancestors had used it to make changes to the Control Center of the City.

It was our target now, and judging from the dozens of elite soldiers and guards hunched down behind barricades surrounding the building, the Drow had made it theirs already.

CHAPTER THIRTY-ONE

I checked to the left and right, eyeing the balcony that ran around the inner wall, designed as a safe place to rain fire down on anyone who tried to cross the killing ground below us toward the keep. While our shieldwall protected us from the front and sides, when we tried to get down to the floor below to join the assault, we would be easy targets thanks to the narrow walkways.

There were dozens of guards, soldiers, and mages on the wall around us, ringing a second turtle of the Legion below, and it was getting hammered with everything from crossbow bolts to fire, lightning, and ice. Summoning circles that were growing around them suggested that the Legion might soon be wishing for good old Fireballs again.

There was a commotion to the right, as Jacko and his half of the team burst through a door farther 'round the balcony. He skidded to a halt before he could fall off the side or accidentally run down the ramp. Then he slammed his shield down, bracing it into the ground, as he hunched down behind it. His shield was rocked repeatedly by crossbow bolts and spells, until the others slid in and started connecting themselves into place.

They were nearly ready, having required mere seconds to take their places, when an enterprising mage decided to change her target from the group on the main floor, to the one that wasn't nearly as well-protected yet.

The first spell couldn't have been worse, all things considered, and proved that we were dealing with much stronger mages than we normally did. It was a lance of ice and looked like the top section of an iceberg had been picked up and thrown by an angry giant. When it hit, the shieldwall was still being established, so the magical ability to spread the impact out hadn't yet reached a high enough level.

The result was catastrophic. Three legionnaires died instantly, their bodies slammed backward into the wall, crushed by multiple tons of ice. Then, the second phase activated, and the Iceshard detonated into a screaming, whirling blizzard of sharpened, jagged projectiles.

The entire group, their shieldwall included, vanished behind a swirling blizzard, and I gaped in horror.

A maniacal laugh rang out across the field. I turned, glaring across at the figure who stood behind two tall defenders, swirling her hands and clearly controlling the icy whirlwind while she laughed and giggled. Cries of pain echoed out from the collapsing shieldwall as more and more of the legionnaires were consumed by the spell.

"Jacko, no!" Scotty screamed, staring over at the devastation, shaking. He barely had the stamina to hold onto his own shield as it was hit over and over again by spells and crossbow bolts.

"Lydia! Take charge!" I ordered, locking eyes with Oracle, who nodded to me. As I turned from the shieldwall, Tang leaned over and grunted as he took my shield as well, clinging onto them both and gritting his teeth as he fed double the mana into it.

"Ronin! Louder!" Lydia barked, hammering out orders to the others. "Arrin, Yen, target tha fuckers between us an' tha second team, Magic Missiles only. Giint, Ah know yeh've got somethin' yer can use against those bastards ahead: get it ready. Ah'll make sure they get it. Jian, get ready with healin' magic; if we see a single legionnaire in there fer even a second, Ah expect 'em healin'! Sehran, distraction. Ah know yer good, now's tha time te show everyone just how good yer are, an' that yer deserve yer place with us on yer own merit!"

Oracle and I stared into each other's eyes, our minds joined together as we started to build a spell. This was our single shot to have a counter argument to the spell the mage had used, as I damn well knew that it was them or us now.

We couldn't risk using anything less than our most devastating attacks now, so I needed to make this count.

We started simple, a single orb designed to travel from here to the target with no deviation. The outside would be solid rather than popping like a soap bubble, as many of our spells did; there were too many projectiles flying about to risk it going off too early.

Next, we started on the seed: gravity. I tore Explosive Compression apart in my mind, rebuilding it at a speed that would have horrified any master of destruction, mentally tearing sections of the spell apart, using them like children's building bricks to construct the structure I wanted.

Once I had the section I needed, thinking of it as the attract/repel part of the spell, I mimicked it over and over, setting a ten-meter limit containing ten of the seeds inside. I made them capable of flipping polarity, going from pulling to pushing and covering a five-meter radius each, making sure that they'd overlap like crazy.

Then I added in a randomizer, making a ritual circle that would store all the mana, while the seeds would have a set amount each. The ritual circle would send mana out to recharge the seeds, but each time a seed touched anything, it would change the mana's direction of travel. With everything that I intended to have flying around on the inside of the spell, that would happen a lot. I gave some seeds a lot of mana, some almost none, and flipped them again and again.

While I was doing this, Oracle was adding in additional bits, the flaming napalm spell that we'd seen before, lightning, and a random invisible mass of solid air.

We didn't have time to make the spell pretty, or even efficient, and without a wisp, there'd be no way of making something like this as quickly as we had without killing ourselves in the process, but in less than a minute, it was done, and we broke the gaze.

I turned back to stare at the keep as I started to cast. Oracle was suddenly standing behind me, her arms lengthening and doubling as two pairs of additional hands reached around and guided the formation as I worked. My fingers wove patterns, sliding streams of mana into the center of a growing ball.

"Arrin, left side! Yen, Flamespears te tha far right! Ronin, mana regeneration! Giint, hurry tha FUCK up!" Lydia barked, even as the Legionnaires with us and Tang continued to hold the shieldwall. "Bob!" she barked as something blurred to the left. She pointed, snapping her fingers.

Bob reacted as I continued to weave, adding more and more layers. The design existed in my mind now, but in reality, it needed far more work as it tried repeatedly to come apart under my clumsy hands.

Bob stepped to the side of the shieldwall, grinning at the blur of a stealthed Drow that was attempting to sneak up on us. He lifted both hands to chest height, and cupped his palms, his shield and sword clattering to the floor as he released them, and he pressed inward.

Reality warped between Bob's hands, threads of black, yellow and neon green swirling into existence, compressing further and further as the Drow gave up on stealth and started sprinting forwards. The Drow appeared less than a dozen meters away, the daggers in both of his hands glimmering evilly. His black silk clothes flowed in an unnatural breeze that propelled him faster than a mortal should be capable of.

He covered half the distance to our group at a speed Usain Bolt would have sold his mother to achieve but still, it wasn't enough.

The light that Bob had conjured ripped forwards suddenly, solid and barbed. It formed a long harpoon, that, by its size, looked like it could be used for whaling and probably torture, too, judging by how jagged and barbed it looked. It covered the distance to the Drow in less than a second, tearing through his stomach and hurling him from his feet, screaming.

As soon as the harpoon slammed into him, a thick glowing chain appeared in Bob's left hand, leading to the Drow. He hauled on it, dragging the screaming Elf across the floor, even as pulses of red and black flowed down the chain, visibly feeding Bob. He ignored the occasional crossbow bolt that bounced off him, as they barely had time to crack his bone armor before the Drow's life energy repaired it.

I saw the fighting in my peripheral vision, but ignored it as I gritted my teeth, frantically twisting and spinning my fingers. Words fell from my lips as I rushed to add the somatic components of the spell, even while my hindbrain added more. There was knowledge that Amon had shared, teachings that hinted that mana was as much a living thing as I was, and I was merely guiding it, cajoling it to take the required form.

I had to convince it that not only was this form correct, but it had ALWAYS been correct, and it was required to form it perfectly. Amon nudged the weaves subtly, adding in a hint here and there, and I let him do it, on the grounds that, if he fucked me over now, we were all dead anyway, and any hidden plans he had would be fucked, too.

The final section flowed up and over the spell, seeping from another realm into this one, sealing the entire spell away behind a single orb the size of a baseball. Despite my upbringing as a man insisting only six distinct colors existed in the universe, this orb was filled with dozens, maybe hundreds of them.

Oracle frantically suppressed their desire to be free. She flicked her hand to Lydia in a gesture so fast I barely saw it, but Lydia had been watching and waiting, so she barked at Tang.

"Now!" she screamed.

Tang yanked his arms apart, breaking the seal of the shieldwall, opening it, and dropping out of the way as I threw my hands forward.

The ball left our control in a split second and hurtled across the distance to slam into the wall right behind the fuckin'-cold-o-mancer, who leapt aside at the last second.

She landed a few feet further from the impact site, looking down her nose at me triumphantly before the world shifted around her as gravity realigned itself.

It was weak, but it was enough to draw her attention, making her spin to stare at the spell in horrified fascination. The second phase went active, and she backed away, frantically speaking, trying to finish the last segments of her own spell before it could fail and tear into her.

She broke into a run, the two guards she'd had on either side looking after her in shock, then back at the orb embedded in the wall behind them, shivering, sending miniature cascades of dust falling around them.

One of them, a massive bear of a man with a red beard sticking out of his helm as though it was looking for someone to fight on its own, reached out and tapped the surface of the orb with one gauntleted finger. He proved that, even at the other end of reality, there's always that one asshole who has to push the button.

The orb shattered, weaves of compacted magic unravelling like an octopus with severe limb-numbering issues. Lines flashed out in a rush, slamming into place to form a hemisphere around the orb. Blue-black symbols and lines sprang into being, pulsing weirdly as the ten seeds rocketed outwards, slamming into place at designated distances from each other. One side of the ritual circle lay flat on the ground, while the other climbed the wall, sitting at a ninety-degree angle that was going to make things even worse for the thirty or so people inside its radius.

They looked around, their fire trailing off as they tried to make sense of the ritual circle, wondering if one of their own had done it to add to the defense.

Then one of them spotted the mage running, her fingers frantically flashing as she tripped over her words, conjuring another massive spear of ice into being.

She'd almost made it out of the circle when the third phase activated, and the slight pull of additional gravity changed entirely. The central seed, and all ten around the exterior, flared with a powerful black light that flashed out then pulled in, creating their own miniature black holes.

People screamed as they were yanked from their feet and tugged in different directions. Some flew upward, heading toward a seed on the wall above and behind them. Others dropped to their knees, tugged downward with force sufficient to break bones and tear muscles.

Screams echoed and cut off abruptly as people died, yanked onto each other's weapons, crushed together, or torn apart as the fourth phase went active. The pulsing mana oscillated wildly, flipping the polarity of the seeds, forcing people who'd been lifted into the air to plummet with horrific speed, only to be yanked sideways when they smashed into the floor as another seed exerted its own force on them.

The mage was nearly finished with her spell when she was yanked from her feet and hurled across the circle, slamming into a barrier on the far side with a crunch of broken bone.

She screamed as her Iceshard spell tore loose, hurtling off in the wrong direction to take out a totally uninvolved section of the keep's wall. She yanked a necklace free and snapped a charm from it, barely breaking the seal as a shield popped into being, deflecting a guard in full plate that was tumbling towards her. The fifth and final phase went active as I collapsed to my knees, panting frantically. Blood ran from my nose and ears as health was taken in place of mana to activate the last stage.

Oracle's special additions now joined in, roiling waves of liquid fire, ice sheets that froze sections solid, and worse.

The spell lasted another two seconds before cutting off. It'd only lasted eight seconds in all, but for the majority of those inside, it'd lasted the rest of their lives.

I knelt there, hunched over, as the silence spread, having just killed dozens with a single, horrific spell. I pulled the details up, notifications pulsing, and wearily acknowledged them.

Congratulations!

You have killed the following:
- 13x Elite City Guards of various levels for a total of 142,405xp
- 9x City Guards of various levels for a total of 19,465xp
- 2x City Mages of various levels for a total of 34,117xp
- 1x Drow Sorcerer, level 47 for 34,921xp

A party under your command killed the following:
- 17x Elite City Guards of various levels for a total of 204,067xp
- 59x City Guards of various levels for a total of 131,410xp
- 1x Drow Rogue, level 27 for 13,501

Total party experience earned: 348,978xp
As party leader you gain 25% of all experience earned
Progress to level 31 stands at 547,978/1,245,000

*

Congratulations!

You have created a new personal spell: Gravitational Vortex!

Gravitational Vortex:
Creates a wildly fluctuating Gravitational Vortex laid in a hemisphere that triggers increasing and reducing gravitational effects based on the mana charge of the nearest Gravity Seed.

Additional Status effects of Flaming Napalm, Ice, Lightning, and Bludgeoning will be randomly enacted within the area of effect (AOE).

This spell, while cobbled together from the parts of other spells, has been refined enough to be acknowledged as a fully-formed spell, and as such will begin to level and evolve as your understanding of its properties grows.

Cost: 500-800 mana, depending on AOE.

I grunted, shaking my head in numb amazement as I read the details, then dismissed them. That spell was insanely powerful, but the cost…Draining my mana pool for a single spell was a lot, even with the damage it had done.

I forced myself to my feet, pulling a mana potion from my bag and chugging it before chucking the vial aside. I glared out of the gap between the shields, examining the devastation our spell had left behind.

A full quarter of the defenders were dead, and not just dead. There were…bits…of the defenders strewn about liberally. As I watched, an entire section of the wall where the spell had gone off sagged forward and collapsed, exposing the interior of the keep.

I grinned, thinking we had an easy way in, until a wave of darkness flowed out, and the screaming began.

CHAPTER THIRTY-TWO

The first to scream were the defenders closest to the makeshift entrance, as they saw the flood that rolled out for what it was: hundreds upon thousands of small spiders. They were little more than the size of an average man's palm, but in such quantities that they made a living, crawling carpet that flowed across the ground, racing towards the defenders.

Those closest to the breach never stood a chance. They were swarmed and subsumed, falling screaming and thrashing to the floor as they died from a combination of thousands of vicious bites and hundreds of times more venom than their bodies could ever survive.

The next closest tried to run, but most of them fell in seconds, the hesitation that made them pause as they tried to understand their new reality cost them their lives.

The only survivors of that ring of defenders were those who were most traumatized by the sight of Spiderkin, reacting instantly by running, many trapping themselves as they raced away in directions that led to places they couldn't escape from.

Even the survivors, those lucky or sensible enough to head straight for the ramps up and out of the kill zone, would spend the rest of their lives reliving that experience, waking screaming from the soundest sleep as memories of that sight returned.

The Legion defensive positions collapsed as they turned tail and ran, dragging their friends with them. They raced for the ramps, rushing upward, even as I stared, open-mouthed at the mass approaching us.

"Oracle! Wrath!" I shouted, still woozy from the massive drain on my mana as I started to cast Flames of Wrath, the evolution of my beloved Cleansing Flames spell, even as Lydia barked out orders, knowing damn well what our best chances of surviving this were.

"Yen! Flamespear that opening! Arrin, Fireball or whatever yeh've got, Ah want a line o' clear ground behind tha Legion! Giint, yer better have that…"

Giint held up a weirdly pulsing metal ball. What looked like dry ice smoke cascaded out of small holes dotting its surface, running down the sides. It made the Gnome cough, even as he grinned.

"Press. Throw, run away!" he said, indicating a small button on the top.

"Is it powerful?" she asked.

He glared at her as if offended. "Run. Away," he repeated, then he set off at a sprightly gallop, heading back through the doors behind us, suiting action to words.

"Fuck," Lydia muttered. "Scotty!"

The massive legionnaire who'd stampeded our way through the last section of the palace, was sitting, staring at the dissipating Icestorm to our right, waiting for sight of his brother. As she said his name, he looked at her in question, and she passed him the bomb. "Press tha top, then throw it at 'em, get it as far in there as possible…" she said, gesturing forward before twisting around and shouting as loud as she could for all the Legion to hear to fall back on us.

Scotty nodded, winding up and pitching the smoking thing as hard as he could. It flew through the air like a rocket, hitting one of the larger spiders in the face and killing it instantly, before it exploded with a sound that was barely audible above the cacophony of the battle.

The sound was like nails on a chalkboard. A ripple appeared, like a tear in space, but it'd barely begun to open before it slammed shut again, killing a bare handful of the enemy.

"Fuck's sake, Giint!" Lydia screamed as his amazing bomb failed miserably. "Legion! Fall back on me, that's an order!"

The Legionnaires around us moved immediately. Even as those below us, already heading for the ramps up to our level, dug deeper and picked up speed, outdistancing the flowing wave of spiders, and the panicking, screaming defenders.

I slammed my Wrath spell down, right behind the Legionnaires, well aware I was condemning some of the palace defenders to death. The spell activated between them and safety, so they were forced to either run through it, receiving horrific damage, or to slow, skirting the edge, but frankly, the Legion was my only concern now.

I grunted as it activated. Oracle sent her own cast of Wrath down in the center of the swarm, with hundreds screaming as they burst into flames.

I checked my mana, seeing I had just over a hundred left. With it, I summoned a pair of fountains just in front of the oncoming horde, before summoning two more. I chugged a mana potion as Oracle charged her most powerful Lightning Bolt spell.

A court mage in red and gold called down a fiery column from the sky directly upon himself, pulling lava from the ground to kill hundreds of spiders at once, even as he screamed, his body consumed by the liquid magma.

Fighters stood their ground, swinging swords and spears, weapons totally unsuited to the enemy. They died bravely, determined to gain their charges more time to flee.

A young boy, barely more than ten years old, yet clearly a magical prodigy, spun in a tiny circle. His arms windmilled furiously as he summoned blasts of wind that blew the racing spiders back from his group.

He lasted a handful of seconds before a tall, stick-thin man swept him up and ran straight for the side of the wall closest to him. He threw the boy upward, and the child's little fingers barely reached the upper level. The man below turned and fired weak blasts of air out at the onrushing spiders. Two other guards formed a human pyramid, bracing themselves, and called to the older man to climb.

He patted the lower man's shoulders in thanks, then clambered up him, before a new force entered the fray.

Behind the swarm of spiders came their kin, five misshapen Drow males, each with spider legs protruding from their back. They drew back on huge bows, sending arrows as long as my forearm hurtling out.

The old man was pierced through from behind, the arrow pinning him to the guard who'd been trying to help him escape. The pair of them fell atop the lower man, who tumbled down as well, trying to save his friend and charges.

The uninjured one rolled free, yanking the injured mage off his friend and throwing the mage over his shoulder as he tried to run for a ramp.

Behind the Drow spiderkin came a Drider that had to shoulder sections of the wall apart to clamber out, clearly the queen of the hive. As she straightened up, she arched her back and screamed in pleasure at being free of the constraining walls of the keep.

The Drider was half-woman, half-spider. Her lower body subsumed into a massive arachnid, with her humanoid torso growing up and out of the cephalothorax. The spider's massive fangs erupted from the front of her body, and I winced at the mouth that twitched and gibbered and long, flexible pedipalps twitching on either side.

The legs were long and wickedly barbed. The sound of each landing was like a steel-tipped spear slamming into stone. The massive abdomen behind her lifted and fell as she walked free. A single death's-head mark gleamed in bright red on her back in what must be nature's most insanely un-fuckin'-necessary warning ever.

The humanoid upper half of the Drider ran from the stomach upwards, with mottled grey and white flesh. A pattern that looked something akin to a zebra's stripes extended from behind her back to her sides, the tips of the stripes pointing inward to her bulging belly.

She had no tits to speak of, and I was glad for that, as I was already thoroughly weirded out by her. When it came to her face, she had a split jaw that swung outward as well as down, opening to reveal rows of teeth and glistening flesh that vibrated as she threw her head back and howled in bestial bloodlust. Her bone-white hair settled across her shoulders as she leaned forward.

Then, after the briefest hesitation, her legs drove her towards us with terrifying speed.

"FUCK ME!" Ronin screamed, his song faltering as he beheld the monstrosity racing in our direction.

I backed away, a Fireball held pulsing in my hands. It looked insignificant next to the horrifying creature that was chasing us.

I threw the Fireball at the ground before her, deliberately spreading the effect across her and the swarm at the same time. It did, as I had suspected, little damage to her, beyond a slight sooty staining of her flesh and a singeing of the hairs on her lower body, but at least I had killed a few dozen spiders.

"Get back here!" I roared at the wounded legionnaires who were only just emerging from the icestorm. They stumbled forward, dazed and bleeding as they tried to figure out what had happened.

Jacko was the first to respond, seeing how close the drider and the tens of thousands of spiders were. He lifted his shield, blood dripping from dozens of wounds, even as ice fell from him, and he screamed.

The sound echoed, pulling at everyone in hearing range, a bestial challenge that rang out, even as he drew a sword that must have weighed more than I did fully armored.

"For the Legion and Lord Jax!" he screamed, and he sprinted forward.

How he was even moving, I couldn't guess, seeing the state of the legionnaires that were backing away behind him. But somehow he ran forward, lumbering up to the edge of the balcony, and slammed straight through it.

The thin stonework, mostly ornate and ornamental after centuries of mismanagement and ill-fated improvements, shattered, pieces of stone tumbling free as he leaped out into the air, plummeting to the ground with a boom.

"Brother!" Scotty howled, turning to me. "Lord, PLEASE," he begged. I nodded to him once, knowing exactly what he was asking.

Relief crossed his face as he stopped backing away. He inhaled deeply, then he was off as well, racing forward, screaming.

The cry was echoed by his injured twin, even with blood leaking from dozens of wounds. He raced forward, massive shield held high and sword pulled back. The Drow spiderkin opened fire, their bone arrows slamming into his shield and shattering, leaving noxious clouds behind, poisons, powders, and tiny burrowing mites that streamed into the gaps in his armor and attacked him. Even as he raced forward, I grunted, feeling my mana dip drastically as Oracle started to heal him.

"Healing!" I screamed, realizing what I'd missed. "You can all heal; get up here!" I ordered. The retreating forces skidded to a halt and turned, racing forward to support me.

"This is a helluva risk!" Lydia snapped at me before starting to cast. I pulled mana potions free and started downing them, seeing the survivors of the squad to my right healing each other and drinking their own potions, racing toward me.

"She's right; we should be using their sacrifice to make it to a defensible location," Yen said, shaking her head at me before hitting Jacko with a heal.

"No, they're giving us the best chance we could hope for," I said, as Scotty slammed to the ground and raced to join his twin. A joyous scream of challenge rang from him, one that carried all the magic of the Taunt, forcing the wave of spiders that had closed on Jacko to lose interest and turn to Scotty.

Even the Drider queen turned to regard Scotty, before swiveling her head back to Jacko, just in time to see the massive legionnaire swinging his greatsword in a wide arc.

The blade cut deeply into the tree-trunk-sized leg closest to him with a crunching sound quickly overwhelmed by her screech of rage and pain.

"Magic Missiles!" I ordered. "Aim for where her legs join her body!"

I started casting along with the others, a grouping of five darts appearing in the air above my hand, soaring upward and arcing down, all five aimed at the joint of her back leg.

My five missiles were joined by more than fifty others, rising in a wave to slam down again and again, deflected by a shield that flared bright with magic, even as the drider cackled in satisfaction.

"That shield is too strong!" came a voice from the side. I turned, seeing a burned, soot-covered, and battered mage glaring at me, the one who'd hit us with the ice. "Give me mana potions; I'm our only chance!"

I paused, glaring at her, fighting my instinctual desire to spit her with my naginata. "Now, dammit!" she snarled. I tugged one free, throwing it at her before checking my mana and downing my last mana potion.

"Ronin, for fuck's sake, mana regen!" I snapped, before looking at Lydia and grinning.

"Don't yer fuckin' dare!" she snarled.

"Tell me who else can break that shield!" I called to her over the cacophony of the battle. Legionnaires around me cast barrage after barrage of missiles, while those with larger mana pools concentrated on healing.

"Give it te someone else!" she demanded.

I shook my head. "I can fly, and I can channel."

She slammed her previously folded wings out to their full extension and glared at me as though daring me to go on.

"You're going to be too busy," I told her, pointing upward. She looked where I was pointing, then closed her eyes and nodded once.

"Distraction," she acquiesced.

I nodded. "I can't get close without her distracted, and the Rams won't last much longer."

"An' ah can draw their attention." She nodded once. "Fine, but yer get in an' get out, break tha shield an' get free. Yen will make sure tha next wave hits."

"Of course!" I agreed, well aware that none of them were fooled by a word I said.

Yen swore, then took command and started barking out orders.

I took a couple of steps to the right and took a deep breath before grinning my thanks to a legionnaire who passed me a healing and mana potion from his pouch.

"They're high-end, make them count, my Lord!" he said.

I nodded, settling my helm and cinching it tight before grabbing my naginata. I leaned forward, letting myself topple over, even as I activated Soaring Majesty and rocketed off, the sudden g-forces making me grit my teeth.

I'd pushed hard, maybe too hard, as I blurred past several bodies, angling myself to stay in the center of the circular walkway, arcing around the outside of the keep. The opening I wanted appeared at the last possible second. I jerked to the left and shot out, lining up to come at the drider from behind.

As I did, Lydia burst through the gap that Scotty had left, her wings slamming down hard and blasting her up into the air, drawing the attention of the drider and her escort, while the mindless hundreds of drones raced onward. They reached a freshly cast Wrath that covered the only way to the others, making spider after spider burst into flames as they crossed the line of the ritual circle.

Dozens died, then hundreds, their tiny health pools vanishing in an instant before the spell was exhausted. The roiling wave of glistening bodies rolled forward as the spell vanished, only to have a second one slam down in its place.

Oracle desperately began casting a third time, while Lydia flew upwards, roaring her own, far weaker version of Taunt at the enemies gathered below.

I leaned backward, angling around ever tighter, as I held my naginata out ahead of me, streamlining my body as far as I could. I channeled my mana into the naginata, flames bursting to life. They grew as I forced more and more mana in, until I felt them flowing down my body and coating me, forming a protective shield as I became a living plasma-lance.

I covered the distance between me and the drider queen in a heartbeat, slamming into the shield that protected her and tearing through it like a spear encountering a soap bubble. The spell detonated, three small charms around her neck exploding in white fire as they attempted to activate, only to be destroyed one after the other as I screamed through.

The drider spun, her right and left forelegs chopped almost through. Jacko had already collapsed, kneeling in death with a living blanket of spiders rolling over him, biting and chewing into his still warm flesh, while Scotty screamed and howled, spinning around and killing spiders in their dozens.

As the drider turned to face me, recognition flared, overriding the habitual hatred of everything and anything that wasn't her. She slammed her hands forward, cruel claw tips punching through the shield and tearing the containment of the plasma-lance, setting free a blast of contained power that felt like I'd been hit by a truck head-on.

I flew sideways, smashing into the wall of the keep, my armor ringing like a bell and bones breaking as I tumbled senseless to the floor

The drider mewled. The entire left side of her chest was missing, her dangling flesh and pulsing organs on display, as she staggered drunkenly, at least half her body broken, the two closest spiderkin shattered and smoking.

The drider collapsed to her knees, her mighty spider limbs unable to hold her weight as her body went into shock, even as one of the spiderkin leaped to her, landing lightly on her abdomen.

It leaned around, the motion eerily spiderlike, and it paused, examining the wounds, before lifting its head and letting loose a screech that went through the Legion like nails on a chalkboard. The sound echoed unnaturally, building on itself as the others took up the call, streaming inward.

The spiders abandoned their swarm, turning and racing back to their queen, carpeting her in a living, disgusting blanket, as the queen stirred, shifting her head, before lunging at the spiderkin that crouched atop her, sinking her teeth into its neck to feed.

Seconds passed as heals landed on me. What felt like an age later, I managed to stumble upright, groaning in pain, and looked over at the horrific blanket. More and more of the spiders collapsed to dust, their lifeforce and bodies drained in ribbons of crimson light that streamed back to the queen, even as she finished her ghastly meal and dropped a desiccated husk that was less than a quarter of the size of the original spiderkin that'd inhabited it.

"She's healing herself!" Yen screamed. Legionnaires, now out of mana, formed up, ready to charge and either kill her or die in the attempt.

Lydia hovered above, staring down with a powerful ache inscribed on every line of her face, every clench of corded muscles as she grasped the air between us. She reached out to me, her injured master, as much with her heart and soul as with her hands and arms, lips fumbling to activate powers she probably didn't fully understand yet.

My Valkyrie shook, head thrown back in agony as blood dripped from her outstretched gauntleted fingertips. She arched her back, her wings beating erratically, wildly as she drew in a deep breath and screamed to the heavens.

The clouds above the keep parted, and the starlight sky shone through, growing brighter as the stars themselves seemed to rejoice in a Valkyrie summoning the Power of Starlight to aid her.

It was an ability long since lost to the mists of memory, referenced in few surviving sources, mainly carvings on the filth-strewn walls of the Sunken Temple, and Oracle, who'd whispered bits of it to me as we'd held each other.

It had been once known as the Temple of the Winds, but it had long since been lost to the ocean, when the island it was on sank beneath the waves.

Here and there, aquatic residents caught glimpses of hints, and snippets had been retold in the Tower wisp's hearing. But now...the full glory unfurled like white wings.

As Lydia pulled the power down in the far distance, bathing her essence in it, a set of armor, long since buried in silt, shuddered and shimmered as it responded to the unconscious call of its rightful inheritor.

The stars flared, bathing the city in multiplying, growing pinpricks of light that spread to outshine a full noonday sun before narrowing, focusing into a single beam of solar radiation channeled by the winds.

The air spun, growing from a faint breeze into a twister in seconds, picking up speed as it tightened the beam.

Finally, it released the power in a single, smooth blast that centered atop the drider.

A spotlight like the searchlight of a warship back home slammed into the drider, covering a diameter of at least five meters before shrinking again.

The drider screamed, sucking in more life from its minions as the area around her flash-boiled. Steam erupted from everything inside the beam's radius, scalding anything that didn't die instantly.

Even as it raised its voice in pain and outrage, it choked off, steam hissing from its mouth and the horrific wounds it had only just begun to heal. The beam narrowed even farther, growing in power exponentially as it shrank in radius.

By the time it reached the width of a coffee cup, it had punched clean through the drider queen, jerking back and forth, chopping her upper body into sections that fell and bounced across the floor.

Lydia's scream faltered, and the beam cut off as she plummeted from the air, wings limp. I grunted in desperation. Slamming my power into the ground, I covered the dozen meters to catch her as she fell in record time.

I grabbed her from the air and pulled her in close as my mana bottomed out. We flew sideways, crashing through another section of the balcony barrier and rolling across the floor, with me now as exhausted and as broken as she was.

I came to a halt on my back with Lydia draped across me. Frantically, I reached down, checked her pulse, and sighed with relief, letting my head sag against the stone with a clang as my helm hit the floor.

Within seconds, the others sprinted to me, gathering around and rolling Lydia off me, checking on her as I caught my breath.

"Are they dead?" I asked in a tired voice, even as I lifted the mana potion that the legionnaire had given me to my lips and downed it, keeping my eyes closed against the mana-migraine.

"All dead," Yen confirmed.

"And the locals surrendered?" I asked, before a voice I recognized as the mage spoke up, then choked off in surprise.

"We certainly have not! You started...urk!" I forced one eye open and looked over, seeing Flux standing behind the mage, holding a dagger at her throat, another pressed to her chest, its tip resting just above her sternum, with two more angled toward her eyes with less than an inch in clearance.

"My apologies for our lateness, Lord Jax," Flux said. "We encountered a nest of Drow, and it took time to subdue them. Now, I believe the Lord was asking if you'd surrendered. *Don't nod*," Flux said with considerable exasperation to the mage in his arms who'd nearly killed herself. "Just answer yes while my friend removes your bags, and we'll see about you swearing an Oath to the Lord here, or…" He moved the blades slightly, drawing a single, ruby-red drop of blood on the tip of the dagger nestled above her cleavage.

The mage closed her eyes, taking a shallow breath. "I take it you're the Lord of Dravith?" she said.

I grunted tiredly from the floor as Oracle reached out, sending the Oath to those nearby who hadn't sworn, then healing me.

I grunted again as grinding noises, clicks, and crunches erupted from my body. That unsavory business dealt with, I sagged back in relief, even more tired, but at last able to breathe without the feeling of a rib sticking into my lung.

"I swear to obey Lord Jax and those he places over me; I will serve to the best of my ability, speak no lie to him when commanded otherwise, and treat all other citizens as family.

I will work for the greater good, being a shield to those who need it, a sword for those who deserve it, and a warden to the night.

I will stand with my family, helping one another to reach the light, until the hour of my death or my Lord releases me from my oath.

Lastly, I will not be a dick!"

It started slowly, even hesitantly, in a few cases, but it didn't take long for those present to swear, and when the last had finished taking the Oath, I replied to them.

"I, Lord Jax, do swear to protect and lead you, to be the shield that protects you and yours from the darkness, and the sword that avenges that which cannot be saved. As the Tower grows in strength, so shall you." I whispered, my voice still somehow carrying, even as my mana bottomed out again to bind these people to myself. I then pushed out the original Oath of Imperial Citizenship, as Grizz passed me two mana potions, including a greater potion from another nearby dead mage's bag.

"I swear upon pain of death to faithfully execute all that the Emperor decrees. I swear upon my soul that I shall stand for the Empire when it calls. I shall be strong when the weak need me, generous when the poor are at hand, and merciless when my fellow citizens are threatened. I shall worship the Gods of my fathers, respect my elders, and raise up my children to stand tall.

I am an Imperial Citizen. I claim the right to call upon the Legion in my hour of need, to hold those that wrong me to justice, and to be avenged if I cannot be saved."

"Well, that's all done now. Yeah, people, good job. Take the rest of the day off." I mumbled, staring up at the stars that were slowly being eclipsed by the clouds that rolled in, and the rain that started, quickly growing from a patter to a stream, then a steady deluge.

CHAPTER THIRTY-THREE

Eventually, I gathered the strength to roll onto my side, reaching out and accepting Grizz's hand. He pulled me to my feet as I looked over at Lydia. She lay unconscious, surrounded by an escort of grim-faced legionnaires who glared at anyone who made the slightest noise.

I couldn't help but smile as Oracle left her side, moving to mine. She blurred, becoming full-sized and stepped into my embrace as she let out a sigh of relief, mixed with a sob of mourning for all those we'd lost.

I had no way of knowing what was happening elsewhere in the city, not yet, but we'd lost almost half our force, I'd been told. As I looked over at the hulking form of Scotty, I shook my head in regret.

Somehow, he'd come to signify all the losses we'd suffered today as he stood over the corpse of his brother. The massive legionnaire was still kneeling upright, held in place even in death by the sheer size and solidity of his armor.

I walked through the mass of legionnaires and waiting locals, all of whom parted for me as I strode down the ramp toward Scotty and Jacko, with Oracle walking beside me.

When I reached him, even though he was standing with his head bent, I still had to reach up to put my hand on his shoulder. I looked him in the eye for a few seconds, getting a sad but proud nod from him as I spoke.

"I didn't know him long, Scotty, but he was a good man, a hell of a legionnaire, and I'm proud of him. I hope you are, too." I didn't know what to say, especially not to this mountain of a half ogre who'd just met me. He'd survived hundreds of fights in his life, only to lose his brother the first time he was fighting by my side.

My honesty seemed to touch him. Picking up his shield, he clapped his massive sword to his armored back, where some magic locked it firmly in place.

"I am, Lord," he said simply. "Is it over?"

"Not yet," I said. "I need to claim the Command Center for the city first, then I can order the various forces to stand down."

"Then I'll grieve later," he said, patting his kneeling brother's corpse before taking up station behind me. Silently, the others joined him, all save the group who surrounded Lydia.

"Is she okay?" I asked Oracle.

"She will be; she's exhausted, but sleep is all she needs right now, besides a week to relax and a good bath."

"We could all do with that." I agreed, wishing, not for the first time, that there was some way to take all my people to a Greek island for a week of drinking and relaxing. I sighed, accepting that it wasn't to be, and squared my shoulders.

I took Oracle's hand, leading her across the courtyard. The ornamental grass crumbled to dust beneath my boots as I went. A gentle breeze sprang up around us to sweep the dust away as I strode forward.

I frowned, feeling…*something*…as the breeze carried the dust away, and I glanced at Oracle for confirmation.

"It's the young boy. He drove the dust away; I think he's a little in awe of you," she said, using our mind-bond.

I smiled. *"I'm glad he survived…I thought I felt something, though?"*

"It's the touch of magic, his mana guiding the wind to blow the dust aside. Congratulations, my love, you're growing more sensitive to mana and taking another step into a wider world."

I didn't answer as I stepped across the broken slabs of onyx, helping Oracle to cross them. But as I glanced back, I spotted the young boy. His tear-streaked face regarded me with wide-eyes. I couldn't help but smile slightly as I inclined my head to him. Awe brightened his dark eyes as I acknowledged him before I turned back to Oracle, following her deeper into the keep.

The floor was covered in shattered stone, dust, fallen wall hangings, and more as we entered. The deeper we went, the darker it became. The dust and debris had been replaced with spiderwebs and shattered glass.

An occasional golden candelabra lay fallen across the path, while the red carpets and gold inlaid tapestries looked like they'd been buried in a tomb for millennia, the dirt and cobwebs were so thick.

Here and there, watching eyes sent a tingle up my spine. Regardless of the death of her drider, Illoth still had her eyes on me.

"We need the original Cleansing Fire spell back," I grumbled to Oracle, and she sent a pulse of agreement before beginning work. I smiled as she started to reconstruct it from the scattered memories we shared.

"I'll work on a better version," she promised. I marched onward, guided by a faint tingling pull that seemed to want to show me something.

I turned left as we exited a short corridor, a downdraft of musty air informing me that a stairwell awaited. I climbed, still holding Oracle's hand. We climbed two more revolutions of the central tower, ignoring the floors that came and went. Doors led off and windows seemed to have been abandoned for at least a century, until we came to a single wide room at the top of the stairs.

It was circular with a raised dais in the center that held a throne and a table before it, coated in dust and loose fragments of stone. As soon as I saw it, I knew it was the Command Center of the City of Narkolt.

It had been abandoned here, who knew how long ago, as the various lords used their puppets to rule, reluctant to allow them access to the Command Center and therefore unable to use it themselves, in turn.

I snorted in amazement at their unwillingness to make full use of such a powerful tool and slid into the seat, wiping my hand across the table and sending dirt, dust, and debris showering to the floor before putting my hand on it.

Congratulations!

You have reached the control center of Narkolt City and have the prerequisite authority and abilities to claim this city and the surrounding land (1,114 square miles), adding it to your territory as a claimed location.

Despite the currently hostile inhabitants exceeding the prerequisite ten (10) percent, it can still be claimed, due to its previous master, City Lord Rewn, having surrendered to you.

BEWARE!

Until the city and surrounding territory have been purged of dissidents and enemies, and the general morale has been raised from -25 (Distrustful) to a minimum of 0 (Neutral), this territory will suffer a penalty of 35% to all production, including lifeforms.

(Time since morale was last at 0 (Neutral): 35,411 days, 17 hours, 47 minutes, 12 seconds)

Do you wish to annex this territory now?

Yes/No

There wasn't really a hard decision to make there, I reflected, although I was amazed at how long the entire population of the city had apparently been pissed off for. I hit the Yes option and grinned as I wondered how many people's horizontal jogging I'd just interrupted.

Attention, Citizens of the Territory of Dravith!

The City of Narkolt has been claimed by a worthy aspirant of ancient bloodlines!

All Titles, Deeds, and Laws in the Territory of Dravith are held for review and can be revoked, altered, annulled, or approved.

All Hail High Lord Jax of Dravith, Scion of the Empire and Master of Narkolt!

*

Congratulations!

You have claimed Narkolt City.

In claiming this location, Repairs, Production, and Restructuring options have now been made available!

*

Congratulations!

**You have led your forces to victory in a formal War for the first time, overcoming a more numerous and entrenched opposing force.
As such, you have earned a Title!**

Blitzkrieg: Level 1
You may now choose a bonus for your forces. This bonus will stack with others and will grow as you grow in experience.

Sapper level 1: All troops led by a Blitzkrieg Sapper gain +5 damage to offensive skills for the duration of hostilities. This boost extends to all troops within a 20ft radius of the Sapper.

Commando level 1: All troops led by a Blitzkrieg Commando gain +5 to the stealth skill while within 100ft of the Commando for the duration of hostilities.

I selected Commando and moved on. A bonus to stealth was going to be insanely useful to my troops when the time came to attack Himnel.

Congratulations!

You have annexed new lands into your own, providing the following benefits if the land is worked:

City Facilities: See addendum:

<u>Imperial Facilities:</u>

Imperial Armory: (12%)
The Imperial Armory was once a secure facility to produce arms, armor, and Imperial armaments to aid the Empire. The facility is currently at twelve percent (12%) and must be repaired to a minimum of 68% before any production can begin.

Imperial Docks: (1%)
The Imperial Docks at Narkolt were once one of the wonders of the continent of Dravith, now only a sliver of their glory remains. To make use of the Imperial Docks, they must be repaired to a minimum of 46% capacity.

Imperial Manastone Mine (14%)
The Imperial Manastone mine is one of four such mines on the Continent of Dravith and is currently producing at 14% capacity. To increase production, repairs must be made to the following sub-systems:

> **Mana Collectors**: 0/11 currently active.
> **Mana Purification substrates**: 0/4 currently active.
> **Bio-Mana Converter**: 1/4 currently active.

I cursed as I searched, eventually finding that the location Svetu told us would hold more golems was the City Armory rather than the Imperial Armory. The City Armory was long since destroyed. The entire facility had been lost and built over hundreds of years ago, and I was left hoping that the Himnel one was either destroyed or buried so deep they couldn't reach it.

I dismissed the city facilities section as soon as it opened, as I saw a massive list of every single business, illicit or legal, in the city with the production percentages next to each, including the taxation options and much more. I just shook my head and resolved to set Hannibal and Hanau loose on the entire thing.

Do you wish to name access rights for additional personnel?

Yes/No

I froze, then decided that it was probably best to get on with this. I set four people to have the prerequisite authority to access the system and grinned when it asked if it was permitted to link to the Great Tower to allow remote access to the designated people.

"Fuck yes, you can," I muttered, approving Augustus, Cai, Hanau, and Hannibal for remote access. Then I frowned as I noticed where my hand had been resting since I'd started exploring the systems.

It was a dead manawell, empty and not even attempting to draw from me, making me look at Oracle in question.

She sensed my gaze and frowned, clearly deep in thought, then noticed the well and shook her head sadly before going back to work.

This city, or this keep, at least, had once been a wisp's home. Now it was its tomb.

I flicked through several more screens, mainly seeing a deluge of control options, ranging from the silly to the sublime, including restructuring options for the entire city. I approved the repairs to the keep, restricting it to that for now. Meanwhile, I kept searching, gritting my teeth at the time this was taking before finally coming to the section I needed.

<u>City Forces</u>:

Guards: 1,294

Elite Guards: 104

Narkolt Armed Forces: 4,154

<u>Facilities…</u>

I dismissed the facilities, concentrating on the forces, and sure enough, a popup appeared.

Greetings Scion of the Empire, High Lord of Dravith and Master of Narkolt.

Do you wish to set new orders for the forces of Narkolt?

Yes/No

I spammed Yes repeatedly until it accepted it, and suddenly the world was different, as for the first time I experienced the City Defense Overlay. I saw the entire city before me, even as I watched the various forces contesting it. The city guards that fought my troops were now marked as hostile to the city, while other pockets of them were marked in yellow as they'd stopped fighting but hadn't yet declared for me.

I concentrated and, feeling bloody stupid, I reached out and spoke, somehow knowing that all those in the city would hear me.

"I am Jax, Scion of the Empire, High Lord of Dravith and Master of Narkolt. City Lord Rewn has surrendered the city to me and pledged loyalty after Drow infiltrators drove him from the palace. I hereby claim Narkolt as a province of the Empire. As it was of old, so shall it be again," I said, remembering the ritualistic phrase the Legionnaires had used when I took command of the Prax.

"As it was of old, so shall it be again!" echoed from all around. I went on, a slight smile making its way onto my face.

"I hereby order all forces of the City of Narkolt to stand down. All armed forces inside the Empire are subordinate to the Imperial Legion or will be declared as an enemy of Narkolt and the Empire. Those forces holding the guardhouse and army barracks are Imperial Legionnaires, tasked with securing the city to enable the Drow to be eliminated. I say again, stand down. This is your only warning."

With that I leaned back, watching as more and more forces changed. The red and yellow of enemy and undeclared troops changed to the grey of neutral or green of loyal, depending on the commander's personal position. Only two groups had stayed red, and I had a good guess why that was. One appeared to be an airship, while the other…

I frowned, watching them, trying to make sense of their location, guessing it to be a fallback position or a nest of the fuckers. I gritted my teeth and straightened, leaning into the system again.

"All forces of the Empire be aware, the airship currently attempting to escape the city is an enemy vessel. It is to be grounded and all inside arrested. If they do not surrender, then kill them all. No airship is to attack it; let it get out beyond the city walls before beginning pursuit, as we can't risk it using its ship-mounted cannons on the city."

I leaned back out of the system, glancing to the side as a voice called out to me. It was the female mage who'd killed half of Jacko's squad, standing with a handful of others under close watch by several legionnaires.

"What's the reward should we capture them?" she asked, nonchalantly.

I glared at her, my feelings of loss still too raw to happily move on. "Capture them and find out." I turned back to the system, the green friendly and loyal ships moving from the shipyards in pursuit of the enemy ship.

That's when the world suddenly went terribly wrong.

"Jax…" Oracle asked me suddenly, wide-eyed as she realized something I'd missed in the frantic fight for the palace. "Where's Mal?"

"Fuck," I muttered, my eyes equally wide. "He was supposed to meet us, him and his spies." I turned to Flux, and he gestured to Lio and Cheena. They all darted from the room, even as the legionnaires closed ranks, holding the line between the local mages and guards who'd come along to the upper tower, and me.

MAL

"Come on, man. The whores hit harder…than that. Put some effort into it…" Mal mumbled, forcing his head back up and trying to focus on the figure before him.

He hung from a pair of posts, kept vertical with his wrists and ankles shackled to them, chains linking them together and running up to the ceiling and down to the ground.

"I usually…prefer the rooms…upstairs, more wine, an'…better company…" Blood dripped from Mal's mouth to join the puddle below him. He blinked, trying to straighten out his vision, before a pop-up appeared.

Attention, Citizens of the Territory of Dravith!

The City of Narkolt has been claimed by a worthy aspirant of ancient bloodlines!

All Titles, Deeds, and Laws in the Territory of Dravith are held for review and can be revoked, altered, annulled, or approved.

All Hail High Lord Jax of Dravith, Scion of the Empire and Master of Narkolt!

"Heh…looks like you're…fucked then, fellas," Mal whispered, grinning through bloody lips, his teeth gleaming even where they had broken three with an iron bar.

"I think not. We might not have gotten you to talk before it was too late, but you clearly know more than even I suspected. We'll be very sure to get every last scrap of knowledge out of you."

"They'll come for me. They're going to free me, then you an' me are gonna dance a little…" Mal mumbled.

"No, smuggler…the Lady will reward me greatly for taking you to her," the Drow said as it stepped closer. "Kill the rest, make it painful," he ordered to someone Mal couldn't see before grabbing his hair and lifting his head with it, making sure Mal could see the two figures lying inside the cage in the corner of the room.

Alyssa looked out at Mal, her daughter, Becca, clutched to her bare chest as the Drow sneered over at her.

"You and your whore will make a pleasant gift for her, and her brood is always hungry. The ship's core will suck the soul from the little one yet." The Drow smiled coldly, even as cries for help and screams of agony lifted from the rooms on either side of the one Mal hung in.

Mal closed his eyes as he recognized the voices lifted in agony. He knew them all, having transported them on his ship over the last few days.

More Drow came in quickly, spattered with blood and grinning as they unchained him, ignoring his weak attempts at freeing himself as they dragged him to a chest. They forced him into a fetal position and shackled his wrists and ankles together before dumping him inside, slamming the lid closed.

Mal whimpered in pain before the sound shocked him out of it. He bit down on the inside of his cheek, flooding his mouth with blood and bringing desperately needed clarity to his mind.

He'd been held for the entire day. Somehow, the Drow had known when he landed that he wasn't a merchantman. They had waited until he left, heading to see Alyssa. He had acted as if he was some paladin of Sint, here to make sure she and her girls were safe and to make them stay inside for the next day, just until everything blew over.

He'd walked in the door, only to find three Drow waiting. Their freakishly fast reactions had let them dodge the two crossbow bolts he'd managed to get off, before a spell took him down. He'd awoken a short time later in the brothel's basement, hearing the Drow playing with others, with Alyssa and Becca weeping in the cage in the corner.

"I do like these rooms," the Drow said happily, looking around the dungeon, then picking up a handful of the tools and slipping them into his bag with a contented little sigh, looking forward to playing with them later.

"Athos!" the Drow squad leader barked. Seconds later, another figure stepped out of the room to the right and glared at him, his lip lifted in the beginnings of a contemptuous sneer.

"What is it, Porta? You said we had time to break these creatures!"

His comment earned an irritated look from Porta, who shook his head despairingly. "Athos, you're an idiot. That accursed apostate has claimed the city, which means the Clan Queen is dead, and he can now sense us, should he think to claim the city command node. There's no time for a leisurely breaking, no time for days of fun. Kill them; make it slow and painful, but we're leaving."

"You don't make any sense, Porta! You want me to be quick, but kill them painfully and slowly?" Athos hissed in irritation. "You already gave us our orders…"

"I'm telling you this again because I know what an idiot you are. Despite it being common sense that we need to flee, now. You're too dense to understand, so listen well…*I'm* leaving. Stay and play for as long as you like, and maybe you can play with the apostate personally."

With that, Porta turned, holding up a small crystal, and moved across the room. He sat atop the chest that held the chained human and giggled at how uncomfortable the creature must be, bent over into such a small space.

He pulled a long, narrow crystal rod from his bag of holding and twisted and pulled on the symbols that ringed the wand, changing its configuration to allow tracking by the conjoined wand on the ship's control deck.

The captain was loyal, as much as any could be, and would be bringing the emergency measures into play now, feeding power into the ship and bringing her to them, ready to spirit them free of this city.

Once they were aboard, though, perhaps it would be time for one of the slaves to be released and left to play? It would cover their retreat nicely, after all…

"Tell me, human...have you ever seen a SporeMother?" the Drow asked Alyssa, who still cowered, holding little Becca. They'd both been stripped naked and whipped, more for the fun of it than any sexual desire on the Drow's part. While they normally would have taken their time to have fun with the various whores and inhabitants of the Kneeling Lady, they hadn't had the time nor the prerequisite stiffening potions. "Well, if not, you will soon!"

Porta smiled as a thought came to his mind. "Stop!" he shouted, his voice echoing through the chambers. "Change of plans. Don't kill them. Keep them alive and bring them. The SporeMother can start with these."

"We're setting it free?" came an excited voice as a lanky Drow with mottled skin rushed through, ignoring Athos, who'd stepped out to make another complaint at the changing orders.

"Most definitely," Porta said with a wide smile, liking the thought more and more as he walked over to the cage and peered down at the shivering, bleeding forms within. "We'll set her free, give her the meat we've captured here to start her off, then we'll leave the city to be taken."

"They'll not be able to chase after us, not with her running loose, making a nest in the city somewhere." The Drow giggled and rubbed his hands together. Grey and black diseased skin fell free as he did so. The others were used to such sights and paid it no mind. "Oh, how I wish I could remain to watch her work!"

"Then stay, Tesha. Stay and be added to her slaves," Athos growled, stomping back out of sight. His reappearance in the cell he'd just left was greeted by screams of pain again.

"Athos!" Porta snarled. "Don't..."

"Don't kill them, I know!" Athos replied with a sneer. "I barely touched her, despite the fact that the entire reason we took this place was for us to have a little fun! Goddess, this is pathetic."

"Plans change, Athos," Porta retorted, thin lips puckered like he'd sucked a lemon dry. "If we'd not found out about the apostate's ally, we'd never have known to keep watch for him, and the city would have been riddled with his spies."

"And, if you'd taken the time to properly break him, then we'd have known it wasn't a scouting expedition but an attack!" Athos snapped.

"And who was it that declared it was a scouting expedition, Athos? Who shouted it loud enough that all our little birds could hear, changing their songs to match? This failure was your fault, and the Lady knows it!" Porta snarled as Athos stepped into the room, fingering the hilt of the long, wide-bladed dagger that dangled from his hip.

"Oh, please, Athos...please compound your failures by attacking me when we need to leave the city. Make it even easier for the priests to decide who to blame when the time comes."

Athos glared at his supposed leader before turning on his heel and returning to the corridor, barking orders to the others to bring their slaves out of the private chambers set aside for torture and beatings, as these whores understood them.

Athos and his kind had inflicted a new level of understanding on the previous inhabitants as to how their roles should be carried out in truth. While two of the females had been broken, one had so impressed the Drow who captured her that he was allowing her to break one of the spies in turn, instructing her as she went on making the wounds as painful, yet as non-lethal as possible.

The rooms emptied as the Drow stumbled out, several half-naked, all blood-spattered and experiencing a wild mix of euphoria and gnawing frustration from having their fun interrupted while their prey was still alive.

Complaints arose from them all, but Porta quickly silenced them by hitting the most vocal, and drunkenly stumbling, member of the cabal with a Bolastrike.

The spell, one of several taught only to the upper leaders of infiltration squads, was both painful and impressive. A single, glittering core of ridged steel appeared in Porta's hand before being imbued with the requisite mana and thrown at his target.

The ball was small, perhaps the size of a child's clenched fist, but while the core was solid chromium, the chains that were wrapped around the outside were tantalum alloy, a metal that reacted to mana input by shifting its state over and over.

When the ball impacted the loudly complaining Drow's stomach, it didn't bounce off. Instead, the chains unfurled, flipping out and wrapping around their unlucky victim.

The figure struggled for a quarter of a second before realizing what had happened, and sobered with horrific speed, begging for forgiveness.

Porta sneered and yanked on the mana thread that connected him to the device, sending the chains shifting. The smooth links flexed into different patterns. Sharp, multi-pointed stars, cruel hooks, and barbed spikes all appeared, still joined by the chains that drew tighter and tighter, gouging into the Drow's flesh and making him squeal in pain as those around him laughed.

"Do any others wish to complain?" Porta questioned, glaring around at the others. They scowled, but bowed their heads one-by-one in subservience. "I thought not." He flicked his hair back and checked the silver rings that held it in place were secure.

"Master…" a hissing voice sounded from the end of the hall, and the Drow stepped back, curious and thankful for the diversion. "Others come…wish to enter house…"

Porta spat on the floor. "Fine. Assume the form of this one, then take them upstairs, draw them away from each other, and kill them."

The creature slinked forward, its claws clicking on the artfully designed dungeon stones.

Alyssa hissed in recognition and shrank back from the creature that pressed itself against the bars, staring in at her. It was short, mainly grey, with the occasional black stripe or twist that deepened its coloration. It had a long, smooth head of scaled flesh running back to a low crest similar to that of a lizard where it joined the shoulders, before growing out to form twin sails that ran down its back.

The beasts were descended from a species of lizards that spent their time high in the great trees of the central forests. They could leap gracefully from tree to tree and use their spine and leather sails to glide from one to another, using their ability to alter their appearance to blend in when they encountered a threat.

They'd been of simple intelligence, believing their lives were perfect, until the Drow encountered them. Hundreds of years of selective breeding had resulted in the alteration from the simple little creatures to the changeling that stood before the cage, examining Alyssa carefully.

Its flesh changed slowly, shifting color and lightening to an almost porcelain white, as limbs elongated, hair began to lengthen, and its body began to grow. After less than thirty seconds, the changeling paused, panting, the change half-completed. It looked at its master pleadingly, receiving a glare of disappointment, before additional mana was slammed into it, making it scream and writhe, even as it clung to the bars.

A little more than a minute later, the Alyssa-Changeling rose to her feet, shaking her body out, testing the muscles and hair for comparison between it and the original.

While it had been in motion, the Drow had finished gathering up their playthings and prisoners, convening at the end of the hallway, with two of the lowest caste members being used as mules to carry the chest and drag Alyssa and Becca.

The changeling shook for several seconds before hurrying across the floor and sweeping up a gown on its way past, then taking the main stairs back to the upper brothel.

"Beast!" Porta snapped at it. It froze in pained anticipation, waiting for direction. "Once the interlopers are dead, convince any others who come that this house is closed, and do whatever you must to make them leave. You are to remain here, preventing any entry to the house for as long as possible, before triggering the gem."

"Yes master," it whispered, bowing low on legs that shook in mingled fear and desire, its claws stroking the gem that hung around its neck, the warning tingle that came from the Devastation enchantment making it gasp with hope.

Soon, it would all be over…

CHAPTER THIRTY-FOUR

"Yen, secure the area. You're in charge here and have all our forces at your command." I turned to the others. "Westin, support her." I opened my mouth to bark an order to Lydia. "Lydia…"

"No." Lydia shook her head emphatically. "No, yer are no' goin' off on some harebrained assault on no damn ship! We need yer ta lead us all, not get shot down by…"

"Lydia, shut the hell up," I ordered, not having time to listen to what was probably a very reasonable point of view that would result in me being a good boy and staying here.

Lydia's mouth snapped shut, and she glared at me.

I held up a hand. "I don't want to do this, but think about it. Think of the damage Jian did with a single shot from the ship on an unsuspecting camp. Now think about who is likely to be in charge of that ship, and what they'll do for fun, now that they have nothing left to lose."

"Tha Drow." Lydia swore, and I nodded at her. "Fuck, Ah hate it when yer right."

"So do I." I turned back to the system and leaned into it. I selected all the aerial forces we had in the city. Unfortunately, it was less than we'd had when we arrived, but three imps, nineteen Djinn, and six Alkyon were easily identified from the system. I reached out to them mentally and directed them to gather at a point halfway between the ship and the palace where Lydia and I would join them. Once that was done, I leaned out of the interface and stood, looking to the remains of my squad. With Yen in command here, Tang, Arrin, Grizz, Giint, Bob, Jian, Sehran, and Ronin were all I had left, and I gathered them round with a gesture.

"Arrin, Giint, we need to chase down a Drow ship and take it out. No offense, but you're both too slow to keep up, you as well Ronin, so all three of you stay here. Protect Yen," I ordered, even as I pressed Yen into the Control Chair, ordering the city to permit her full access in my place.

"I could…"

"Giint fast!"

"But…"

"No!" I snapped. "There's no time for this shit. I'm sorry, you know I'd rather have you with me, but I need to know Yen is safe as well." Their desire to come with me, and their loyalty, competed with their knowledge that, realistically, they'd only slow us down. "Jian, Grizz, Bob, I know you can't fly, but we'll sort something the fuck out, because I need you three. Tang…"

He appeared a few inches from me, glaring into my eyes. "You leave me behind, and Bane will murder me, boss, and you know it. I'll make my own way onto the ship, if I have to."

I hesitated a split second before nodding.

"Fine, the six of us, then." I looked over at Sehran. "Actually, seven." I grinned suddenly. "If you can keep up?"

She spread out her wings, beaming.

"Great! Yen, organize the others, make sure their locations are secure, then, *and only fucking then*, they are to move on the Drow fallback position marked in red. Reach out to our ships and make sure they stay well back from it. They're only allowed to use their cannons and any forces they have if the ship opens fire on the city. My team and the fliers will storm the ship first."

With that, and after making damn sure Yen understood her orders, we turned and set off at a run. The thundering echo of our boots in the hallways grew by the second as I looked back. Not only were my small squad of six racing at top speed, but behind us came Scotty. The massive, heavily armored legionnaire was running at full tilt. Arrayed behind him were dozens of the elite guards from the palace and the remaining three mages from the defense.

It took only a few minutes to sprint through the hallways, as they were now clear of obstruction and fighting, leaving the old keep then passing through the new palace. The bodies that were piled here and there, all too often including those of my own legionnaires, served as a grim reminder of the terrible cost of this war.

I gritted my teeth in grief, and the minutes passed quickly. As we sprinted down the last corridor and out into the courtyard, the sound of running boots moved from the thunderous clatter of steel on stone and the occasional carpet, to the splash and clatter of steel slamming home in puddles and across cobblestones.

The drawbridge lowered as someone saw or heard us coming. It was the first line of defense, one that we'd conveniently bypassed by using our ship, and it was weird to exit though an imposing entrance I'd never entered by.

The cobbles outside the palace were, if anything, even slicker as we ran. They were coated in a combination of muck, rainwater, and the metaphorical and literal crap of thousands of people who lived in close proximity to animals and vermin every day.

As we ran, several slipped and fell, usually as we took a corner. The standard level of the street's cleanliness was clear by whether the reaction was a grunt of irritation from the faller or the horrified spitting and declarations of eternal enmity against some species, depending on the type of mess they'd fallen into.

It took us three streets before Tenandra was there, swooping low, her engines flaring and netting thrown over the side, hanging within easy reach. We all diverted course, sprinting and leaping for the ropes.

There was a notable difference between the instant trust of my own team and the other legionnaires of the ship. A much longer pause transpired before the city forces started grabbing at anything they could as well.

By the time the three mages boarded, I gave up on the guards who were apparently less than elite, judging from the huffing and ill-fitting armor as they fell farther and farther behind, so I called up to Tenandra, knowing she'd hear me.

"Leave them; we need to go!" I ordered, feeling a surge of acceleration from the ship's engines as the nets we clung to swayed, and we clambered over the railing and jumped to the deck. Next to me, a pair of bright eyes looked up as the little air mage from earlier held on tight.

"You," I stared at the young prodigy, judging from the power I could damn well feel in him. Despite his gifting, battle was no place for a ten-year-old. "You stay on the ship and help where you can," I finished lamely.

"Tenandra, I need a map of the city," I ordered, turning from him as the rising sun fought against the torrential downpour to brighten the sky.

"Yes, my Lord," Tenandra responded, her kitsune flesh body striding forward from thin air to stand next to me, her right hand offered palm-up as a magical map of the city appeared. The enemy ship and our own were marked clearly on it, even as Jian took off straight for the cabin at her smile and nod.

I frowned, reaching out and turning the map this way and that, tapping a location that was as near as I could make it.

"Here, this is where the last holdout of those assholes is. I'm betting that's a Drow hideaway, and that means this is a Drow ship," I said in disdain, gesturing toward the ship. I glared at it as others crowded in around us. Oracle shifted, becoming full-sized and staring down the ice mage who'd leaned in, seemingly expecting her to move as she was "only small."

When the mage finally sniffed and backed down, walking around and forcing an elite guardsman to step aside so that she could look at the map, Oracle had already lost patience with her, turning to Lydia and nodding to the mage in warning as she clearly jockeyed for position.

"Right. We've got our fliers incoming." I gestured to the collection of dots flying on an intercept course for us. "When they arrive, we're going high. I want a fast, hard boarding. Lydia, Oracle, and I will distract the ship, while the close-range fighters board her. The Djinn will cushion your landing," I assured the elite guards and my own legionnaires. "Mages, I want that ship taken down as quickly as possible, so use your heaviest attacks on the helmsman. Kill them by whatever means are necessary, but leave the controls intact! Jian will take control of the ship." I looked to him for confirmation, realizing suddenly that he was gone, but Tenandra nodded in his place.

"He can hear you, my Lord, and understands," she said.

"Thank you. If need be, he can fly it to wherever we want it. Or, if they've landed by the time we arrive, then all the better. It'll be harder for them to get away. If they have, the mages are to concentrate fire on the helmsman, then anyone who's firing at us, in that fucking order."

"I can get Jian down there and protect him," Sehran said, before the ice mage cut her off.

"You? Ugh. *Please* tell me you didn't bring your…*entertainment* along for a fight?" She glared first at Sehran, then smiled at me.

Lydia, always the soul of subtlety, slammed her wings out to their full extension and leveled her mace at the suddenly grey-faced mage.

"Speak te a member o' ma team like that again, an' Ah'll smash yer teeth so far down yer throat yer'll be shittin' 'em."

"I…uh…how, how DARE you!" the mage gasped, recovering and straightening up. "I am Arch-Magus Fyre! One word from me, and you'll spend the rest of your natural life in the dungeons!"

"One more word like that from you, and you'll be eating the rest of your meals through a straw," I snapped, glaring at Fyre. "Let's make this clear, because we've had no time yet to do this. Chain of command in this situation goes directly from me, as Scion of the Empire and High Lord of the fucking *Continent*, to the Optio of my Personal Guard, who, by the way, is the Valkyrie you're about to get curb-stomped by.

"Then it goes to Grizz, Oracle, and Tenandra. They're the wisps and that massive bastard over there." I gestured to Grizz, and Tang appeared. "Then Tang, Sehran, and Jian, who's currently flying this airship. Then, and only then, do I give a single shit about your ranks. Believe me, until you impress me OR DON'T in this fight and from here on, your ranks are held pending approval. You want to stay arch-magus? Wind your fucking neck in and stop acting like a prat."

"Wha…how?" she sputtered.

I cocked my head at her, before asking in a low voice. "Are you one of the arseholes who's been manipulating Rewn?" The split-second look of wide-eyed guilt was all I needed, and I had to stifle my urge to throw her over the side. Instead, I had to content myself with thinking over the stupidity of her name being Fyre with a y, yet she studied sodding ice magic.

"Lord Jax, we're in sight," Tenandra warned. In the distance, more than two dozen figures swooped over a building up ahead, then angled toward us.

"Good timing!" I shouted, grinning, as Amaat and his people flared their wings and landed around us. The six Alkyon dropped to their knees, heads raised to expose their throats in ritual surrender. As they did that, the Djinn arced in, their magic flaring as the small figures came to a halt. Their leader, Xerix, smiled as he held his hands to the sides and bowed his head low, the wiry, muscled upper body of a quarter-sized teenager tailing away into mist that floated free from his waist.

"My Lord Jax, the Djinn stand ready," Xerix said proudly, as Amaat stood at my gesture and stepped in close. I grabbed his shoulders and headbutted him, hard, sending him staggering. He caught himself and lifted both arms into the air, shrieking his approval. The other Alkyon did the same, as Xerix shrugged and smiled. I gave him a slight bow of the head in turn.

"The imps are…ah. Here they are," Xerix said, gesturing to a group of three imps who fluttered over, landing on the deck panting as the ship nearly passed them.

"Friend imps," I said in greeting, before shaking my head as I recognized one of them. "Tats, is that you?" The little grey-skinned, heavily-tattooed figure was panting as he tried to catch his breath.

"Yesses," Tats mumbled, his mouth open as he panted like a dog. His short, potbellied frame looked as if it was barely capable of being kept aloft by his small wings.

"Okay, thanks for coming." I forced myself to smile at him as I turned and looked at the projected map. I felt myself being pressed to the deck by gravity as the ship picked up speed, engines flaring as we lifted higher, until the other ship became clear on the other side of a section of tall buildings.

"What are they doing?" I asked Tenandra, waiting as she examined the ship in the distance before responding.

"They're cutting their speed and coming in for a landing. They appear to be intent on collecting those at the hideout, as you suspected."

"How maneuverable are they?" I asked cautiously, getting a snort from her.

"It looks like a barge they attached engines to, and it flies like a brick." She shook her head. "The only issue that Jian will have when he's flying it is keeping himself from giving up and crashing it in disgust."

"Well, it'll make him appreciate you more," I offered unthinkingly, getting a throaty chuckle in response.

"So, I should let you have someone else for a night so that you appreciate me more afterwards?" Oracle asked.

I closed my eyes, counting to three. "No, totally different situation, Oracle."

"But Jian and Tenandra are…"

I'd already opened my mouth to cut her off when I saw the evil grin on her face.

"Okay, yeah you got me," I conceded with an amused snort, going back to staring ahead at the ship that was lining up to land in the courtyard at the end of a road.

"You've been pretty short-tempered lately; I thought you needed it," Oracle offered, no longer teasing, now simply concerned.

"We lost a lot of people…A lot of good people, on both sides, thanks to the fucking Drow. Now Mal and the advance team are all missing…scares the hell outta me," I admitted without taking my eyes off the ship.

Tenandra was right about the ship's design. It was huge and boxy, its lack of grace reminding me of military troop carriers I'd been aboard in my time in service. It had five engines to a side providing the lift, with three of them pointing vertically and two horizontally. The pushing engines had dimmed until they were merely cycling, while the lift engines gradually reduced the thrust, lowering the ship toward the cobbled ground below.

The ship was listing to one side, clearly either unbalanced, or the helmsman was shit at their job. But the design, while bulky and graceless, had two things going for it.

The first was a massive cargo capacity, while the second was that, while it seemed about as agile as a gang of elephant seals having an orgy, it was armed to the teeth.

The ship was split down the middle. It had a lower deck running the length of the ship, with a single massive cannon protruding from the front, and two scorpion ballistae on raised platforms to either side. The helmsman stood atop a raised deck at the back of the ship, and a bunker was constructed around him to protect him while he flew.

I frowned, seeing something familiar in the design, something that brought me back to the fight with the Drow as we fled the Prax.

"Why does that thing make my butt pucker," I whispered, frowning, before Oracle hissed in hatred. She stared at the massive doors that were slowly pulling open below the cannon's muzzle as the ship landed and extended a ramp toward a gaggle of figures who were leaving the storm cellar of a building on one side of the courtyard. She growled a single word as they dumped a handful of battered figures onto the floor in front of the ship.

"SporeMother!"

"Motherfucker!"

The long, spidery limbs of the SporeMother unfurled and started forward. It dragged its bulk out into the hated light, even as a blurring effect shimmered above and around it, protecting it from the ravaging sun.

The creature was almost fully grown, standing at maybe twenty feet tall and twelve across. The blunt, triangular prow of its head was covered with dozens of eyes, set in a V-shaped row across the front with a bone frill rising from the back of the skull.

Its jaw, as it opened its mouth wide to scream its loathing of all life, was filled with row upon row of jagged teeth, making me think of a great white shark. We closed the distance, and Tenandra twisted around to face the ship below us, even as the SporeMother reared up and howled a challenge at us.

"Free the slaves; kill the Drow!" I barked at the rest of the ship, before taking three quick steps to the railing and vaulting off the side. The solid *whump* of Lydia's wings launching her into the air followed, even as Grizz leaped free as well. Jian ran to the side of the ship. Sehran grabbed him, unfurling her wings and flipped the pair over the side to hurtle the eighty feet or so to the ground.

I flipped myself over in midair, determined to kill that fucking creature before it could do anything to the city. I pushed out and *up* with Soaring Majesty, slowing my fall and landing in a perfect three-point stance. I clenched my naginata in one hand, its metal already glowing as the SporeMother reached the bottom of the ramp. The heavy downpour added to the fuzzing of the air and obscured the rising early morning sun that would have normally killed her by now.

Lydia slammed down next to me, and a handful of seconds later, so did Jian, carried by Sehran. Bob simply slammed into the cobbles then stood back up, while Grizz leaped from the slanted roof of a building he'd landed on to break his fall, then slid down a second, using the interlocking roofs as a ski slope of destruction, sending misshapen tiles rocketing free.

"Fleshling...prey...food..." an all-too-familiar mental voice rumbled in my mind. I paused, assessing it.

The first SporeMother I'd faced had exuded a sense of horrific pressure, a feeling of ancient evil that carried the weight of centuries of unrestrained malice against every single form of life that wasn't itself.

But this one was...childish.

It was simple in intelligence, and while truly evil, as it hated all other sentient creatures and wanted to make them suffer, it was also a victim. From the psychic scream of hatred, I got the sense of its mind being driven, beaten, and forced into compliance carrying over with the wave of pressure it exuded.

When I'd first faced the ancient SporeMother, Oracle and I had only recently bonded, and were both as immature as this creature before us now. But after the months we'd spent partially inhabiting each other's minds, creating spells by fusing our joint knowledge and falling deeper in love with each other every day, we were now one.

We were one being that, while I formed our physical offensive and defensive capabilities far more strongly than she did, she held sway in equal measure over our mental ones.

The SporeMother had reached out, fully expecting to force us to obey. Expecting us to stumble forwards unwittingly, all self-control lost to her desires, enabling her to feed on us or impregnate us with the DarkSpore she even now summoned with half her mind, leaving herself even weaker in terms of a mental struggle.

She'd dominated the first few whores and staff of the Kneeling Lady who were thrown before her so easily that, when she reached out to us, she simply demanded and expected compliance. She did the same to those who the Drow shoved forward from the ship's hold to fall on their knees, bleeding and exhausted before the creature.

She was badly mistaken.

CHAPTER THIRTY-FIVE

The insidious fingers of compulsion slipped into my mind, demanding that I obey her, that I march forward and surrender my will to her.

It was like resisting a toddler holding up a plastic phone and pretending to call you. Yeah, there was a desire to obey, to play along, but fuck that.

I shrugged it off, glaring at the creature, amazed by the difference between Amon's attempts in the past to take me over and this pathetic attempt, even as Oracle snorted.

She'd locked our minds down hard, allowing only a single path inside, to assess our enemy. Now she abandoned that as overkill, and instead began to counterattack, slipping her mind between the cracks in the SporeMother's defenses, assessing, even as I took a step and my naginata at the foul thing.

"Obey me, fleshling," it demanded in my mind. I paused, tilted my head to one side and looked at it, expecting far worse than this juvenile, "I told you to do it, so you'd better do what I said or else" shit.

"Get fucked," I retorted.

Where the original SporeMother had been decrepit, yet horrifying, both in presence and potential, this one was…less so. It was far more physically potent, despite muscles that were clearly stunted from however it'd been kept. It was neither half blind, nor a geriatric grandmother of the species, but the mind that had so horrified me in my first encounter with this species was nowhere in evidence.

I looked up at the creature that had filled my nightmares since I'd first encountered it, and I smiled grimly, knowing much had changed since those heady first days.

For a start, I was now such a powerful mage that a certain headmaster would have cracked open the rum and waved me on to bitch-slap his opponent back into the grave with a happy hand. Secondly, I was in possession of a body that would have made Olympic competitors weep with envy.

Plus, I had a magic fucking murderstick and could fly.

While I was grinning up at the creature, Grizz lunged forward to engage the nearest Drow, blocking a low stab with a contemptuous ease before smashing his shield into its face, sending the figure reeling. He lopped off another Drow's arm at the elbow before taking its head and freeing the naked woman and child it had been dragging toward the ship.

Bob was terrifying to the Drow, attacking them without the slightest thought to his defense. He ploughed into the group trying to escape the building and board the ship, taking two down with conspicuous pleasure, snapping the arm free of the first when he tried to stand again.

The second pulled out a small carved idol and snapped it in half, screeching out a series of syllables and casting it at the floor, where, seconds later, a much simpler bone golem began to rise…until Bob attacked it, falling upon his prey like a wolf on a rabbit, tearing it limb from limb.

Jian and Sehran formed a matched pair, her whip flashing out to slash across one dark Elf's face, flensing it to the bone, before she sang at another, her full-on Glamour ability used around me for the first time.

The world seemed to grow dimmer as she sang, her voice lifting into the air with an irresistible quality that made you want to join in, until a split second later, it ended, and the two Drow who had been her targets stood open-mouthed in shock.

"Protect me," she whispered, her voice filled with weird harmonics. One of the pair released the grip they'd had on their slave. Then the Drow spun, stabbing out with a dagger that sank deep into the unwary side of her gaping and stunned companion, digging around as it was angled upward, searching for their heart, even as the victim screamed and returned the favor with fervor.

Jian was a blur, his dual wielded Drow-made scythes, the points he'd invested and the training by Restun combining to make him easily the equal of any of the sallow-skinned fucks that tried to take him down.

Lydia beat her wings as she glared down at the creature from above, while Tenandra arced her ship-body around the grounded ship, bringing the mages into position. As she did, someone on the enemy ship screamed out the order to attack.

The enemy ship sprouted dozens of Drow, all armed to the teeth. I yanked my shield from storage and rolled to the side as the first barrage screamed out. A single Drow mage who stepped into view on the upper deck directed the archers in two groups, half aiming at Tenandra, the other half aiming for Lydia, Oracle, and me.

Arrows flashed out, dozens of the deadly missiles that my own squad had claimed and used so sparingly in our fights, in fear of running out. Unfortunately, they were turned against us, slamming into the ground where I'd stood a second before.

The majority that hit Tenandra's hull struck home without doing damage as she slid from side to side, maneuvering with a grace no helmsman could achieve with a creation of wood and magic. The rare few that hit their target, striking one of the engines, caused flares of magic to escape, weakening the control runes and chipping the regulators, making Tenandra shift her hull around to spread the damage out.

Others flashed past Oracle as she slipped into her small form, laughing as the arrows passed through the air where she'd stood seconds earlier. Ringing and cracking sounded as arrows shattered against Lydia's shield and armor, a bare handful making it past to nick her skin, until a lucky shot lodged into a wing bone.

Lydia screamed in fury, having to discard her shield before reaching out and yanking the arrow free, but the damage was done. She fell, unable to maintain her flight, but even as she fell, and I looked up, judging the angle I needed to be able to catch her, Tenandra counterattacked.

The Legion were first, as always, running forward and leaping over the side of the ship. They had total confidence in the Djinn who had attached themselves to the legionnaires, slowing them to land perfectly with a blast of air at just the right time, before turning to the elite guards who followed the Legion, catching them and releasing them into the fight.

They had timed their leap perfectly, falling between two barrages of arrows, shields angled to deflect the next wave. But as they hit the deck of the enemy ship, the Drow threw their bows aside and drew swords, rushing to engage. As they did that, a handful of Drow mages stepped to the edge and released spells, showing we weren't going to have this fight all our own way, as they'd been preparing as well.

The signature spell of Arch-Magus Fyre was in evidence, as a massive shard of ice, reminiscent of an iceberg, appeared and flew with deceptive slowness at the bunker that protected the helmsman, while the two mages who joined her let loose with a pair of spells that assisted her.

The young boy added a ferocious wind that twisted around the Iceshard, tugging it into a spin that built with wondrous speed, looking like a twister that was yanking the shard down, rather than lifting it up. The other mage, a man with a pot belly and robes of black and green who had barely made it aboard the ship in time, had added a choking miasma that flowed after the shard, drawn in its wake.

The spell hit as I launched myself into the air, barreling across the intervening distance to catch Lydia. I flipped over as I crossed the courtyard, grabbing her and pulling her close before landing with my boots against the wall of the building on the far side.

Naked fury twisted Lydia's face. She leveled her mace at the SporeMother that even now flooded the area before it with DarkSpore.

The DarkSpore were flashing gleefully to burrow into the slaves the Drow had shoved towards the creature in offering.

"Get me there, *now!*" Lydia ordered, and I kicked off, pushing with all the force I could muster, both magically and physically. The wall that had been our perch for bare seconds shattered with the force of it.

I crossed the distance in a blink, Lydia throwing herself free of my embrace to twist and land at the back of the slaves with a crash of falling armor and a scream of blind rage. I continued on, landing in the middle of the slaves.

I spun my naginata in a wild arc, channeling pure light mana through it, making it burst to life, radiating a bright white flare, even as the DarkSpore, forming a terrible cloud, poured forth.

Lydia stepped forward, grabbing the nearest slave and hurling them backward, free of the cloud's furiously outstretching tentacles, even as she blocked a strike by the Drow slave handler that leaped at her.

"Surrender, filth!" the Drow sneered at Lydia, grabbing at her throat with his left hand as his right brought a dagger towards the eye slit on her helm.

"Fuck ya!" Lydia snarled, whipping her mace across her chest and smashing the outstretched gauntlet into a mangled ruin, then grabbed his other arm by the wrist.

The Drow's eyes widened, the speed of Lydia's reactions testament to how carefully she'd been allocating her points and to the bonuses her new species brought her.

"Did'na expect tha' did yer, ya prick?" Lydia snapped, yanking him forward into a head-butt that caved the front of his face in on the reinforced crest of her helm.

While Lydia fought the Drow, and I spun and danced, trying to kill the DarkSpore before they could reach more of the slaves, the majority of the Drow sprinted down the side of the fight, bypassing the SporeMother with scarcely a glance.

Until, that is, the Iceshard fell.

It hit the grounded ship directly above the bunker that the helmsman hid inside, a shield springing to life as it impacted, shimmering through a thousand glowing tones before it went dead black, shattering into iridescent fragments that faded from reality as they fell away.

More than half the shard had been destroyed by the impact against the shield, but the remainder was more than enough to crack the bunker like an eggshell, slamming into the three Drow inside.

Their personal shields sprung to life, even as one of them began a counter spell of some sort. Then the final fragment arrived. The base of the Iceshard slammed into the shields, bringing them close to overload before the entire shattered mass of ice, now laid around and atop the bunker in fractured chunks, detonated.

Hundreds of shards flew in every direction, the razor-sharp fragments slicing through clothing and shields. They punched deep into wood and eviscerated flesh.

The barrage came on fast. It swept most of the upper deck clean. Like a claymore mine, it shredded those before it, with the green and black poisonous cloud leeching into the bodies of the dead and dying.

I swore viciously.

I had a split second in which to act. I could either dodge the barrage and leave the chained, kneeling, and already-wounded slaves behind me to die, or I could risk it all on a single toss of the dice.

I choose to risk it. I let go of my naginata with my left hand and held that hand out, fingers splayed as I focused. The mana surged in me, power rushing through my veins and my soul.

I took it all, all the power I could contain, feeling it gathering inside my weak, fleshy form. I slammed it into the shield rune tattooed on my left palm, the form flickering before bursting to life.

Mana washed out in a sudden blast, my mind influencing the shield rune to form a shape that was larger than any I'd configured before, making a semicircular shield form before me for less than a second.

It was enough. The ice hit it and shattered, filling the far side of the shield with a terrible hell of a thousand icy flechettes flying back into the already devastated area.

The SporeMother took the spray to the face, screeching and backing up as the rift that she'd been dragging DarkSpore through snapped shut. She roared as dozens of small gashes spread across the flesh that lay exposed between the joints of her carapace, hissing as a handful of her eyes were slashed into jellified mush by the final fragments.

I fell to the floor, gasping even as the SporeMother reeled backward. The world spun around me as I tried to make my fingers obey. I reached for the bag on my hip, fumbling for a mana potion I remembered being there.

The world reoriented as my frantically spinning inner ear told me that left was really down. I tilted, collapsing onto the floor on my left side, fumbling with fingers that seemed to have been replaced with sausage balloons and were flapping like crazy.

A pair of hands appeared suddenly, brushing my own out of the way, and grabbing the blue bottle I'd only just managed to find. They popped the cork and the entire potion, a grand one I'd stolen from the arch-magus's pouch before handing it back on the flight and poured it into my mouth, almost drowning me.

I'd drained almost every single drop of mana from myself with my mad instinctual activation of the rune. That lack of mana had permeated my very cells, sending me into shock. However, the sudden introduction of more mana than I'd ever held, apart from when I'd been drawing on the Tower or the Storm, sent my mind the other way, stunning me into insensibility as it crackled through me, arcing between my very cells.

A screaming, dripping wet and naked woman grabbed my chin, yanking my face to look at her as she yelled something at me, before leaning back and slapping me, nearly separating me from teeth, she hit so hard.

"Why…are you…naked?" I mumbled, unable to get my brain into gear.

"Fucking men!" Alyssa screeched to the uncaring sky above, before glaring at me. "Mal needs you, you fucking idiot! You hear me? My Mal needs you! Save him! I'll do anything, just SAVE HIM!"

"Mal?" I mumbled, my brain restarting slowly, even as Oracle, buoyed by the insane level of mana, landed on my far side, striding forwards to place herself between me and the SporeMother, flaring to her normal full size as she did so.

Oracle didn't stop, striding forward as she glowed with a light so bright it hurt to look at. Mana unconstrained by any form, law, spell, or rune made her glow like a small sun going nova. The SporeMother screeched in pain, the light causing its flesh to bubble, searing deep into its foul form.

"GET AWAY FROM HIM!" Oracle screamed at the towering creature, shaking with unbridled fury, until one of its huge front legs, a massive thing closer in form to a lobster's claw than a leg, lashed out with blinding speed, slamming into her before she had time to make herself incorporeal.

The light vanished as Oracle was sent hurtling to one side, bouncing across the rain-soaked courtyard to roll to a halt in a puddle, stunned and wounded beyond anything she'd ever encountered.

Her pain tore through me, the backlash of our conjoined minds and souls making me scream in sympathetic agony. Mind and body reeling, I rolled to my feet.

The world around me went dark as everything changed in an instant.

Everything ceased to have meaning. The buildings, the floor, the sky, other people. None of them existed in my mind as important anymore.

There was only Oracle, wounded and weeping in pain, and the creature that had done it to her.

I screamed in rage. My body was already at full health, and my mana the same, until I activated Mana Overdrive and burst forward.

I pushed off with enough force to snap a weaker being's leg in half. The muscles that supported and guided the leg shredded then healed in a terrible flash. A second foot touched the cobbles, pushing harder still.

Somewhere in the back of my mind, the grating of breaking cobbles was identified, and the knowledge of it happening was set aside for later examination.

I crossed the twenty feet between the SporeMother and my previous position with a blur of movement. The creature's reaction registered in slow motion, lifting one leg and lashing out. The narrow middle legs were longer, spiked, and chitinous, like a spider's, yet as it came for me, I sneered in unconscious contempt, jumping and landing on the leg as it stabbed out, taking two more steps along it, then leaping into the air.

I landed on the SporeMother's front elbow, just before the spot where the thorax flowed into the main body, and I barely paused before leaping again, climbing higher. This time, I landed on her shoulder and flooded the Shock and Add runes on my right hand with raw mana.

My fist glowed with a sudden, terrible light, and I lashed out with all the force I could muster, punching the huge creature in the side of the neck, right where a massive vein pulsed.

The force of my fist striking it, driven by the massive quantity of mana I'd poured into myself, and combined with the Shock rune sent a powerful electrical charge directly into its brain, even as the sudden cessation of blood flow from the equivalent of a vagus nerve strike sent the SporeMother reeling to the ground with terrible force.

The massive creature shook and spasmed, giving me the opening I needed.

I leaped into the air, lifting my legs and tucking them under me then landed on the side of its shoulder. Grabbing the flesh at the edge of its mouth for purchase, I plunged my hand into my Bag of Spatial Folding.

The handle of the weapon I wanted slammed into my palm as the bag responded to the will of its owner. Before I'd even fully pulled it free, my thumb flicked the 'on' lever, making the terrible, wonderful sound of the kill-stick echo around the courtyard.

I pulled back, then slammed it hard into the underside of the SporeMother's massive skull, pressing it forward as the circular teeth tore into the flesh and under the protective chitin. It skittered off bones, sliding over them and into a gap. It dug deeper and deeper, sending the massive form into a paroxysm of convulsions, the entire body shaking and shuddering as the vicious weapon dug its way inside, chewing into nerves and more.

The head thrashed, the foul creature clearly starting to recover. But before it could regain control, I found what I wanted, and the entire left side of the SporeMother shook violently, before collapsing to lie still, the nerve stem that controlled that side of the body severed.

I yanked the kill-stick free.

With madly rolling eyes, the SporeMother mewled like a sick kitten. I brought it around, ramming it into a row of eyes, feeling the shuddering as it bounced across the ridged bone between them, making the eyes pop, then a juddering as it hit bone, then another pop as it went along the line blinding the huge thing.

The head thrashed weakly, snapping its mighty jaws close to my leg. I sneered, pulling my leg back then shoving the kill stick in my bag as I whaled on its face.

The Mana Overdrive was draining me with terrible speed, far faster than normal, as I'd somehow flooded every ounce of excess mana into the ability. But while it lasted, it was also much more powerful, making me feel like a God amongst men. I screamed in rage at what this bitch had done to my love, pounding my fists into her skull over and over.

At first it was like hammering the bonnet of a car. The ring of my metal gauntlets echoed around the courtyard as they slammed into bone, leaving tears and cracks. As the seconds passed, and the SporeMother frantically tried to force her failing body to respond, cracks radiated outwards as I literally beat her skull in.

The rest of the battle had paused, shocked into a brief lull at the sheer bloody insanity of me leaping up and beating one of the most feared creatures in the realm to death with only my gauntleted fists.

"Please!" Alyssa begged Grizz as he yanked his blade free of the second last Drow's chest. "Please, Mal's in there!" she cried, pointing to a small chest off to one side. It was bare inches from one of the SporeMother's flailing legs, yanked backwards by the single remaining Drow.

"Crap!" Grizz snarled, kicking the dying Drow that he'd been fighting backwards in a spray of blood, before twisting around and throwing his blade at the one dragging the chest. It sailed end over end, flying straight and true, until the Drow saw it coming and spat a curse, releasing the chest and diving aside.

By the time it came to its feet, and raised its right hand, sneering as it cast a spell. Grizz was halfway to it.

A pulsing, blood-red ball the size of a marble formed above its hand, and the Drow lifted it, as though to show Grizz what he held, before taking a deep breath to blow the ball at him theatrically.

The Drow and Grizz both had a shared awareness of the spell's lethality, but Grizz, the warrior at heart he was, continued to run, teeth gritted. The fury that had filled him coalesced into the determination to do his duty, to take down the Drow and save his prisoner, regardless of what it cost him personally.

Then Tang was there, flashing past the Drow, his twin swords blurring, and sending the dark Elf's right hand and foot spiraling free. He spun and decapitated him, sending the head spinning into the air, borne aloft on a crimson fountain of blood.

The spell disintegrated with a crack that shook the few windows that had survived the violence so far. The mana backlash turned the hand that the spell had rested against into a spreading cloud of blood and bone fragments. Tang blurred back into stealth, and cold sweat covered Grizz at how close he'd come to death.

He skidded to a halt by the chest, grabbed it by one handle and yanked it a handful of feet farther from the SporeMother, before grabbing the latch and tearing it free. He pulled the lid back to expose a bare back covered in weals and whip marks, held down by iron chains.

Grizz grabbed the chains, yanking the hog-tied Mal out of the box and into the open air with a grunt of effort, before sprinting back from the SporeMother.

He skidded to a halt next to Oracle, dumping Mal, who cried out in pain and shock as his bare skin tore on the wet cobbles.

Grizz rolled Oracle onto her back and grimaced, not understanding her form enough to be able to assess her for injuries, but reacted as he'd been taught, and cast his new healing spell.

He almost stopped. Oracle was a wisp, and those generally couldn't be healed the way that flesh and blood members of the team could, until the spell latched onto her and began to work.

His eyes shot open. "I need more mana! Oracle needs help!" Grizz bellowed.

That got through to me. I paused my frenzied beating of the SporeMother's face, even as Lydia quickly finished off the last of the DarkSpore.

Oracle was virtually immortal, but the fear in Grizz's voice gripped me hard, making me turn and leap free of the insensate creature.

I landed hard, skidding on the wet ground, then sprinted forward, the last dregs of my mana ran out as I crossed the final feet and dropped to my knees, reaching out to Oracle, even as I almost went blind from the mana migraine.

Her body was cold and wet as I dragged her into my arms. Grizz released her, but continued to channel the spell into her, even as he yanked healing and mana potions out, opening them and pressing them to my lips.

I didn't so much as look, opening my mouth and swallowing, trusting him with my entire being as I focused on Oracle. The naked woman who'd spoken to me before appeared, lunging for a chained and tightly bound, equally unclothed Mal.

As soon as my health hit full and the debuff was banished, my body came back to life. I examined Oracle, my mana climbing, but too slowly to be able to do anything yet.

"I need healers!" I roared, seeing what must have alarmed Grizz so badly. The extent of her injuries was heart-stoppingly alarming.

The legionnaires, who by now had almost cleared the ship's upper deck through a combination of their extreme skill in melee, and unexpected Magic Missile barrages, dropped everything, turning and sprinting to me, leaping over the side of the ship to fall to the ground.

Unaided by the Djinn's magic, some of the legionnaires landed badly, some clearly breaking bones, but they ignored their injuries to rush to my side. Any Djinn without healing magic continued the fight alongside the imps, but as my mana regenerated at an agonizingly slow rate, first one, then three, then seven, then another dozen healing spells slammed into Oracle.

She hissed in pain as the magic that her physical form was interwoven with finally began to recover, in turn healing the flesh-form she had been tied to when I'd bound my soul to her back at the village of Wayland's Crossing.

Long seconds became minutes, with constant healing spells hitting her as the Legion ignored their own pain and their countless wounds, disregarding themselves to heal my love, my Lady Wisp, my Empress in Waiting.

CHAPTER THIRTY-SIX

Eventually, it was done, and she sank into a peaceful slumber. I raised my right hand, palm out. The Legion stopped. Silence suddenly filled the air as I opened my mouth to speak. My voice was hoarse and filled with unshed tears, but thankful.

"She lives. You saved her," I called out.

The thunder of cheers that rang out was nigh on deafening.

"Boss, what about the Drow and the SporeMother?" Grizz asked.

I lifted my head from where I cradled Oracle against me, black fury filling my heart. "Bring me the heads of the Drow!" I snarled. "Make them suffer!"

All around me, the Legion growled as the fliers took to the air again, rejoining a battle that had stalled at the hatches of the ship.

"And the SporeMother?" Grizz asked, flexing his fist.

"Sehran!" I called. A few seconds later, she was by my side, crouching on one knee and looking at me in question.

"You want me to look after her while you kill it?" she asked, proud that I had called for her, until I shook my head.

"No, for now, she stays with me," I said. "You told me before that you gain strength and abilities by consuming the souls of sentients, the more powerful, the better?"

"Yes, my Lord," she said, her voice trailing off in confusion, before her eyes opened wide, realization dawning. "You mean…you'd permit me to…?"

"Fuck, yes." I nodded towards the SporeMother. "Kill her, feed on her, and make sure she feels every second of it, but before you finish, let everyone hurt her, a cut, a kick, whatever…that'll be enough to count, right? To get you all the experience?"

Their grins spread in anticipation.

"Then kill on," I ordered, already turning back to Oracle.

The legionnaires roared in approval, rushing the terrible enemy that lay insensate and paralyzed, its only chance at life being the mercy of the Legion.

It found none.

Sehran clambered up its side, her form subtly shifting as she relaxed. Her teeth grew sharper, muscles larger, and her eyes became catlike as she hissed in pleasure, watching the SporeMother that eyed her as she strolled up its side, aiming for its throat.

The huge creature shuddered, almost managing to lurch to its feet, before collapsing again, snarling in a combination of pain, fear and hatred.

Sehran leaped into the air, beating her wings and hovering over the SporeMother. She landed deftly on its massive upper arm and squatted down next to its head.

She lay a pointed talon on the SporeMother's face and slowly drew it down the skin, cutting the tough membrane and allowing blood to run free. Then she lifted the talon to her lips and licked it clean with a suddenly forked tongue.

Her eyes slitted in pleasure, pointed tail flicking from side to side as she pulled her talon free, smiling down at the terrified monster.

"I suggest you hurt her," she called to the legionnaires who surrounded the creature, at least half of whom stood mesmerized by Sehran's ass as she bent over in the tight short-shorts.

The group moved quickly, each of them taking a few seconds to stab, kick, or punch the massive form, pausing as soon as they confirmed they'd done damage. Those who punched or kicked the creature clearly developed a new level of respect for me as they seemed to realize how hard it was to injure something as thoroughly armored as this, let alone crack its skull or take it down with a single blow to the neck.

"Tenandra!" I bellowed. The ship pivoted, returning to me as I pushed off the floor and lifted into the air, Oracle held protectively in my arms. I flew across to the deck and landed gently then strode forwards to the captain's cabin. While I knew Tenandra could manifest anywhere, she didn't need the extra strain from me demanding that she had to appear before me.

As I entered the cabin, three Djinn and four Alkyon, who had apparently dedicated themselves to watch over me, landed and prevented anyone from following me, much to Fyre's irritation.

"Tenandra," I said.

She appeared in her kitsune form and bowed to me before stepping forward and taking her sister-wisp from my arms.

I hesitated, not wanting to let go, but that was why I was here. "Protect her," I ordered, my voice rough. "Do whatever you have to do. Burn the continent to the ground if need be. I trust you."

"She will never have been safer than she will be until you come for her, my Lord," Tenandra said.

I could scarcely tear my eyes from Oracle. "Thank you, Tenandra."

"What will you do now?" she asked.

"Now?" My lips curled back in an animalistic snarl, savoring the words. "Now I'm going to slaughter the fucking Drow!"

With that, I turned and left the cabin, pausing before the dozens of mages, ranged elite guards, ship's crew, and fliers who crowded the upper deck.

"Do some damage to the SporeMother and do it quick. She'll be dead in a few minutes. It's best to get a share of that experience if you can." With that, I strode to the edge of the ship and peered over the side.

"Lord Jax, I feel we should discuss," Fyre started to say, her voice oily and wheedling. She broke off as I stepped over the side of the ship. Ignoring her completely, I floated down to land on the cobbled street.

I picked up my naginata and lifted into the air again. I floated over the convulsing, whimpering body of the SporeMother, making eye contact with Sehran briefly as I passed and exchanged a nod. I landed on the far side and marched toward the closed and reinforced doorway that led into the hull. As I did, Sehran opened her mouth wide and lunged, biting into the throbbing vein I'd so thoroughly traumatized earlier and sucked the very lifeforce from the huge creature.

Grizz appeared on my right and Jian on my left, with Tang bringing up the rear. The small group of legionnaires and elite guards gathered around the door, trying to break it open, drew back respectfully as I approached.

I lifted my right hand, a terrible, cold fury boiling inside me, my sense of calm incredibly fragile. I scarcely maintained a tenuous grip on emotions that threatened to burst free at any second.

Fury warred within me, terror and fear, mainly at the thought of how close I'd come to losing Oracle. I didn't know which emotion would overwhelm the others should they break free.

So, I buried all emotion, all thought, and focused on doing instead of thinking.

In my hand, I placed all my fear, my anger, and all the little feelings that were threatening to break free. Instead of weaving a spell the normal way, I created a cup with my mind, pouring all the emotions I felt into it, trapping them and tamping them down, before twisting the weave around the outside.

I inspected the *thing* that floated above my hand. When it was done, the knowledge of how I'd formed the cup was gone from my mind, having operated on pure instinct. But the result was this: a ball of my festering hatred for the Drow. It was an orb that contained all my guilt at Oracle's pain and injury, the fear of losing her, and the shame that I wasn't strong enough, even now, to protect her, to protect *all* of them.

I saw it in my mind's eye as much as with my physical sight, a small shape that slowly twisted upon itself, forming circles and stars, spines and ridges. It was black, shot through with a thousand colors I had no names for, and, as my calm stabilized, I looked up from the thing I held.

I stared at the door that had been built to open only from one side, the ridged iron that surrounded it, and the bands of metal that reinforced it. I sneered in contempt, setting the spell free.

It hovered over my palm for a brief second before it tore forward, the air itself ripping as it broke the sound barrier. It covered a dozen feet before impacting the center of the door.

The door shattered down the center, blasting backward as if kicked by an angry God. The spell detonated inside the ship, turning solid wood and blackened iron into fragments that tore through the defenders, transforming them into bloody chunks.

I strode forward, ignoring the danger, knowing that there was none, at least not to me. I was starting to understand that the mana was as alive as I was, and it made my knowledge and my adamant belief into reality, as the fragments ricocheted off the surrounding bulkheads but missed me and my people.

I stepped over the fresh, headless corpse of a Drow as a mewling, eyeless figure lay curled into a ball on the floor. It received no more attention than the others from me, but Grizz stabbed down with his sword as he passed. The sharp tip of the blade dipped between its ribs and sliced deep into the heart, Grizz twisting his sword as he moved on. The Drow exhaled its last breath with a gasp.

We ducked around arches and support beams, seeing that while they were structurally required, they were also devoid of any redeeming features. As I strode through the ship, not even a single part of it suggested any form of artistry, of a love of shipbuilding craft, or of any pride in its creation. I silently decided that I would dedicate years of my life, if need be, to either freeing the Drow of the corrupting presence of Illoth, or to exterminating the entire fucking lot of them.

I ducked under another arch, hearing the screams from up ahead, and, as the corridor took a ninety-degree right turn, I finally found the stairs to the next level.

As we'd been moving, Grizz had been detailing others from the group that followed me to search the rooms that branched off to the left, the right of the ship clearly being the holding cell for the SporeMother.

Silence came from each of the rooms we passed, but as I started up the stairs, flying, rather than walking, I found the first living Drow. There were five of them gathered around an altar to Illoth, praying for guidance.

They knelt with their backs to me, facing a midnight-black shard of onyx that looked to have been rammed into an older, more ornate altar. On the shard sat a single spider, carved entirely of the reflective, blemish-free volcanic glass, squatting there, seeming to watch me as I strode forwards.

One of the Drow snarled, lifting his head to the side to stare at me "Bow, you fool! The Lady…" He cut off, having clearly expected one of his fellow Drow.

I drove my naginata through his side. It entered one side of his chest and exited the other in a single smooth motion. Bones cracked, and a sudden gasp escaped his throat. His flimsy shirt offered no protection as his lungs were torn open.

The others turned to see what had happened to their companion, when my people stepped forward and joined in. Lydia, Jian, Bob and Grizz were like swinging metronomes, grim-faced and taking little pleasure in their task. Their arms rose and fell, taking off limbs or heads and killing three of the Drow in seconds.

The only female in the group was at the front, and she drew a deep breath and opened her mouth wide, summoning one of the weird spider-in-the-throat tricks. Its long limbs dragged it into view as she gagged while staring at us in triumph.

Her expression was still triumphant as Tang appeared behind her, driving a sword lengthways through her throat from back to front, skewering the spider and severing her nerve column at the same time. The body collapsed as he yanked the blade free. He kicked her twitching body away before spinning back into stealth.

I reached into my bag and examined it, searching, before I shrugged and pulled my hand free. I was a bit annoyed that I didn't have a warhammer in there, and instead had to make do with a mace I tore from the dead hands of one of Illoth's own supporters.

I stepped up to the altar and knew damn well that Illoth was watching me through the eyes of Her spider. I stared back at Her for a few moments before speaking.

"I'm going to find every single one of your altars, and I'm going to destroy them," I said, pressure building in the air around me as I spoke the words aloud. Illoth was evidently trying to interfere, but the restraints the Gods labored under were clear again, even if the reasons weren't. "I'm going to collect every single piece of every single altar You've ever had, and I'm going to bury them in the latrines.

"I'm going to have my army shit on your holiest things every fucking day. I'm going to tell them why they have to do it, and they're going to laugh and call You the turd-spider. In a decade, that'll be the name that everyone will remember. Not Illoth, not the spider queen, or whatever fucking crap you want them to use. It'll be Lolly, the Turd-Spider," I promised Her before slamming the mace into the head of the carved spider, shattering it into hundreds of pieces that cascaded to the floor. The altar that the shard had been buried in seemed to shudder in relief, as if it was freed of an infestation.

I reached out one hand and touched the green stone, feeling a familiar sensation as Ashante, Lady of Nature, spoke to me.

"Eternal, you have discovered an old and powerful altar of mine, one that Illoth will deeply regret losing. Will you consecrate it to me again?"

Congratulations!

You have been offered a Quest: Cleanse that which was defiled.

Ashante's Altar of the Western Woods was taken hundreds of years ago and defiled. Illoth sank Her fangs into the Lady of Green Places' heart, and feeds on it. Will you reconsecrate the altar to Her? To do this, take the altar to a place of natural splendor and have three priests of Ashante and their familiars praise Her name to the realm.

Accept? *Yes/No*

I chose yes, of course, but I decided that, for now, the altar could stay there. I felt Ashante's acceptance and thanks as the sense of the Goddess vanished. I turned away and strode back through the piled corpses and out into the corridor. From the floor above, screams and bellows rang out, spells exploded with cracks and pops, and the injured howled. A low moan grew in volume, so I led my team in that direction.

We passed three more empty rooms before we found the final stairwell. I flew up it, twisting around to ensure I wasn't ambushed at the top.

Then I paused, huffing out a laugh as I called Bob forward.

The green and black miasma that had followed the Iceshard down was suddenly clear in its nature. Shambling, wide-eyed corpses, I guessed they'd be zombies really, fell upon the now-panicked Drow. The legionnaires watched with grim expressions, letting the undead Drow finish off their former allies.

I grunted, shaking my head, then turned to Bob, who stood stoically, staring at the undead that flowed over the Drow, tearing them apart and feeding on them. The last of the dark Elves had fled, running toward us and calling out for mercy. It received a swift kick in the face from Grizz and was thrown back into reach of the zombies.

"Why did you summon me to watch this?" Bob asked me after long seconds of silence.

"Because you've said before that you're not alive, or that you're not as real as any of the rest of the team." I tried to force the appearance of emotion through my cold state to help my friend. "Look at them. They're undead; they're empty inside, animated husks. But you, my friend? You're *ALIVE*, and you're better than any of them, the Drow included. Remember that."

Bob stared for a long minute before nodding once. I turned, marching towards the rear of the deck. I passed several nicer lanterns hanging outside more ornate doors before coming at last to a large door at the end of the corridor.

I gestured to the door as I approached, and Grizz took a few strides ahead, then leaned back and hammered his boot above the latch twice. On the third and final kick, the latch broke, and the door swung open. As it did, three crossbow bolts slammed into the shield he held aloft, filling the small space with the ring of metal on metal.

Grizz stepped forwards, clearing the doorway and moved to the right. He hunched behind his shield, glaring out at the last four figures of the Drow infestation that remained alive, three of them frantically reloading their crossbows while the fourth stared daggers at us.

"Surrender!" the fourth figure demanded, her voice melodious even when filled with wretched loathing.

"Don't be so fucking stupid," I retorted, glaring at them. "Surrender, and I'll make your deaths quick."

"Your arrogance is offensive, human," the Drow snapped. Something blurred nearby as a fifth Drow moved, stealth slipping away as he lunged, a pair of daggers extended.

Then he screamed, as a blade swept out of the darkness, taking both hands off at the wrists and sending them pirouetting through the air to bounce on the wooden deck. Tang appeared for a brief second, flashed a devilish grin, then beheaded the screaming Drow.

"Last time offered," I stated coldly, sneering at the shock on her face.

Lydia stepped forward and threw her mace end over end.

It slammed into the cold, beautiful face of the Drow captain with a crunch of breaking bones and a spray of blood and teeth. She fell backwards with a scream.

The crossbowmen gawked for a split second before Grizz, Jian, and Bob fell on them. Lydia stood by my side as we watched the three slaughter the Drow, then we dragged the ship's captain to her feet.

"I surrender," the captain declared through bloody lips and broken teeth.

"Too slow," I said grimly. "The offer of a quick death is rescinded. Grizz, chain and gag her. The city can see her die on a fucking spike tomorrow."

Shock registered on her face, the last drops of color draining away as she tried to struggle. Grizz punched her in the side of the head with one massive, meaty fist, knocking her into unconsciousness.

"Let's get out of here." I turned and stomped out of the cabin and through the ship, stepping over the bodies of the dead and dying Drow. I passed the undead that stood, slowly swaying as a breeze hit them, and I walked down into the courtyard.

The battle for the City of Narkolt was done, and the first city of the continent had fallen to the Empire Ascendant.

CHAPTER THIRTY-SEVEN

The trip back to the palace aboard Tenandra was far calmer than the trip down had been, as only my squad was with me this time. The elite guards had stayed behind to take control of the local area and issue orders to the regular guardsmen, who arrived shortly after the battle was done. There had been several hundred of them, led by Thomas, who'd apparently been heading for the fight with his own team when he'd found the group on their way and had assumed command.

Thomas had waved me off when I asked him if he was coming back to the palace, choosing instead to stay with the guards and get an idea about the local situation before coming back.

I sat with Oracle, who was still unconscious, as we flew back. We landed in the narrow inner courtyard we'd previously avoided for fear of being hit from all sides by the defenders.

Now we landed smoothly, the defenders no longer fighting against us. The several hundred who had been waiting for our return instead fell to one knee and saluted, fist to heart. The gangway lowered, and I stepped down, carrying Oracle.

I strode down the flexing ramp and out onto the well-maintained grass, ignoring the churned and bloody areas that marked the deaths of men and women from both sides.

The massive body of the drider queen still lay before the entrance to the keep, the corpse already stinking as it lay in parts where it had fallen.

"I am Eberhardt, Captain of the Guard, my Lord Jax, and I stand ready to formally swear loyalty to the Empire, as do my forces," a mustachioed, blond-haired man in gleaming silver and green armor at their head proclaimed in a voice that carried across the grass.

He was clearly proud of his rank and position, but considering how friendly I'd been to local forces, I stifled my sigh and gestured for him to stand.

The ten minutes of flight time across the city, holding Oracle as she apparently slumbered, had been a balm to my soul. My concern for her had finally simmered down to a more manageable level, rather than the all-consuming terror and fury that had filled me before.

"Well met, Captain Eberhardt," I called in a loud voice, intended to carry for the troops that knelt behind him. "Thank you for your pledge. We will carry out a formal Oath later today, once I have had time to prepare. I'll rest easier knowing you and your men are on guard."

He stood straighter at that simple lie. I stifled a smile, knowing damn well that, until things massively changed, I'd be sleeping well because I was guarded by the damn Legion, not these shiny troops who'd just lost their city to a fast attack by my team.

"Thank you, Lord Jax!" Eberhardt declared, stroking his mustache and nodding to me informally. "We'll be on watch and will keep you safe."

"Thank you," I replied. "The Legion will remain on guard as well, of course. But they will be moving to a shift system so that they can get some rest as well. After all, we had a busy night."

"Ah, uh…yes, Lord Jax," he agreed with a grimace.

"How many troops are normally on guard around the city?"

He shrugged. "Around the city? Perhaps five hundred. The wall is watched over by the guard, and that takes almost a hundred men. There are also several sites where the guard is gathered, ready in case of riots. At any time, some are on patrol, or at the prison," Eberhardt said dismissively. "The elite guard are restricted to the palace and guard the city lord and highest nobles. I have personally selected those who will form your personal guard, and…"

"Lord Jax," Flux said, stepping forward and slipping from stealth, along with Cheena. "I have examined the local area and stand ready to advise on the guard."

"How dare you!" Eberhardt snapped, glaring at Flux, even as he and the guards rested hands on their weapons. "I was speaking and you…"

"They appear to be loyal to the city and not too corrupt. Those who manipulated Rewn appear to not have a particularly strong foothold in the guard," Flux carried on, ignoring the guard captain.

"Good to hear, thank you, Flux," I said, nodding to him. "I'll meet you inside. For now, protect Oracle. I know I can trust you to make sure that nothing gets close to her."

With that, Flux and Cheena made a point of bowing before they vanished into stealth. The captain of the guard was still clearly furious as he looked toward the entrance to the keep, obviously planning a heated discussion later with Flux, even as Grizz carried Oracle inside. My people were on either side of him, protecting her for me.

"Flux there is the head of a section of my government," I said to the captain and the guards. "As such, he investigates a great many things at my direct order, and that includes those who liked to run the city without City Lord Rewn's advice and orders. The way the city has been run until now is over, and new, or should I say *old* laws will be reintroduced.

"Make no mistake, as of now, the city is moving to a war-footing. All production will be geared towards the war effort. We will conquer Himnel and drive out the Dark Legion before bringing about a new golden age!

"Those who do well will rise in rank, just as those who fail me will fall. The next few days will be full ones, I can assure you of that. For now, I need you to send out patrols, make sure the populace understands that they are at least as safe today as they were yesterday, if not more so." I glanced from one face to another, seeing the uncertainty in their eyes.

"They can go to work, and they can raise their children without fear. Send out the patrols to reassure them, secure the palace and the city walls, and welcome to the Empire!" I finished with a roar, my voice having climbed as I spoke, going from tired but firm to a declaration of intent.

The guards all slammed a fist to their chest in salute, and I returned it before marching for the keep. Jian and Sehran were half a step behind on either side of me, and Tang watched over us all from stealth.

As soon as I entered, moving through the damaged outer area and into the keep proper, the door behind me clicked shut. I relaxed as I moved through the building.

Once I reached the throne room with the interface, I found a series of cots had been set up, with Oracle already laid on one, weakly protesting that she was fine.

I went to her first, kneeling and taking her in my arms, crushing her to me as her arms reached out to encircle me as well.

"Thank the Gods," I muttered, kissing the top of her head, before drawing back to look into her eyes. "Are you okay?"

"I'm fine," Oracle whispered, smiling up at me. "I got hit, but I'm alright. It just knocked me out, that's all."

"How, Oracle? How the hell did that happen?" The fact that she was practically immortal and incorporeal, not to mention impossible to injure without specialized cages or spells and so on, until now had been one of the things I'd come to rely on most of all. "You're a fucking wisp, how the hell did that thing cold-cock you?"

"I'm not," she whispered, shaking her head. "Not anymore, anyway. I'm not a wisp anymore, Jax, at least not entirely. Not since Wayland's Crossing."

"What the hell are you, then?"

"Something else. Something unique," she replied. "I have all the gifts from my life as a wisp, but now, I can feel and do so much more, including getting hurt."

I gritted my teeth, breathing through my nose and trying to calm the sudden rising terror that declaration had brought with it.

"Jax, it's okay," Oracle said softly, reaching up and caressing my cheek. "I should have told you, but the more…biological I become, the stronger my connection to my magic grows. It makes no sense. I was a wisp; I was literally a being born of magic. Yet, with the changes you made to me, I retain so many of the gifts I was born with, including shapeshifting and incorporeality when I wish it. But where that was my natural state before, and it required mana to solidify myself, now it's the other way around. While it seems insane, my connection with our magic grows stronger by the day!"

"You're damn right, you should have told me!" I snapped, before sighing and pulling her close to me again. "Seriously, I nearly shit myself!"

"Yer not tha only one." Lydia said from one side.

I straightened, lifting Oracle and shifting around to sit on the cot she'd been laid on, now with her sitting across me, leaning back into my chest and facing the room again. "Seriously, Oracle, yer scared tha shit out o' us all. We're used te yer being practically indestructible, an' yer getting hurt sent Jax off tha deep end."

"I know, and I'm sorry…"

"No, Oracle, yer don't," Lydia said. "Jax attacked tha damn SporeMother head-on, an' 'e beat tha shit outta it unarmed. An' ah mean *beat tha shit outta it*. 'E took it down wit' a single blow, stunned an' reelin', then 'e tore half its throat out, before cracking its skull open with 'is bare fists!"

"I had these on!" I held up the gauntlets I'd been wearing, grimacing as I looked them over. "Thorn is going to kill me," I said.

Not a single part was intact, most having bent, cracked, or lost the connecting sections on at least one side. Three fingertips were gone on the right hand, and the left was held together only by the support struts, the actual overlying steel missing entirely.

"You beat the SporeMother to death with your hands?" Oracle asked in a dangerous voice. "What the hell were you thinking? Your naginata could have absorbed its soul!"

"Nah, I told Sehran to feed on it," I said. "I guessed she'd get more out of it than we would."

"You fed a SporeMother to a Succubus?" Oracle asked, incredulous.

"Yup."

"Yup?" Oracle snapped. "YUP? You fed a descendant of the Valspar, a creature that could have enslaved the entire city in only a few days, to your pet Succubus? And I bet you did it without even considering the power differential!"

Power differential? "Uh…"

"Jax, Sehran is a Succubus. She grows more powerful depending on the souls she harvests, and you fed her a creature that could conquer continents, given enough time. Thank the Gods we've got an Oath from her," Oracle whispered, covering her eyes and shaking her head in horrified wonder.

"Well, it seemed a good idea at the time. Besides, I trust Sehran; she's earned the chance I gave her."

"Okay, okay!" Oracle said, clearly forcing herself to calm, before smiling brittlely at me and the others. "Anything else I need to know? And just to be clear, I trust Sehran as well, I just…it was unexpected, that's all."

"We rescued Mal," Grizz said. Flux nodded, looking relieved.

"I searched the prison records, the guard reports, and questioned several of the upper echelon. They answered my questions truthfully for the most part. Any dissembling seems related to their own bribes and familial connections more than anything else, but I found no trace of Mal anywhere.

"I left the higher members alone, believing that the ideal person to question them would be Inquisitor Lucian, rather than myself. But before I could make any headway in locating him, you'd found him yourself." Flux reported, sagging with exhaustion.

"Fair point. We'll need to get Mal here, along with a lot of the council, but the only way Rewn comes back, for now, is if he's under tight control. He needs to learn to govern and to trust those who can do it better than him." I grinned and turned to Jian, who sat to one side. "Fancy a trip back to the Tower?"

He nodded. "Of course, boss. Who am I going to get?"

"Probably half the Tower, at this rate. I think there's a way Rewn can learn to rule here again, and for now, it's by my side and under Romanus."

"You think that's a good idea?" Grizz asked dubiously. "I don't know, boss. Don't take this the wrong way, but he's an idiot who thinks with his cock, and this is me saying it."

That got a low round of laughter from around the throne room, and I couldn't help but grin as Yen laid her face in her hands and groaned.

"Very true, mate…" I said. "But he deserves at least the chance to be better. He wants to grow, and he's sworn the Oath, so what we'll do is put him and Romanus in charge of something together. Romanus will guide Rewn, as will

Lucian. Between the pair of them, they'll get a good idea about what he's capable of." I rubbed my chin with one hand as I thought.

"Hannibal will take control of the treasury, along with Hanau. They'll sort out the taxes and get the economy going properly, not to mention quickly gutting the illegal markets, especially with access to the control center.

"This city presents an opportunity for us to massively level up the Empire, everything from construction and food production to recruitment for the Legion. I can't make this any clearer; we need to make this work, and as such, I need some of the council here."

I thought for a few moments before speaking slowly. "Go back to the Tower, get Cai…and Isabella, I guess. Get Romanus and Hannibal, as well as Nerin, Riana, and Lucian. Augustus is to assume overall command of the Great Tower, and Ame the Tower's healers, Hanau the economy, and so on. Tell them to take a day to get things sorted out as best they can, then get them back here." I saw nods from those around me as I continued.

"Bring a couple of fast attack scouts, and the remaining cruisers. Leave the battleship there with as many of the Gnomes, golems, and engineers working on it as are needed. We need it as ready for war as it can be, and as quickly as possible.

"The only way that Himnel can stand against both the Tower and Narkolt combined is if they can take one side down fast. Bringing our ships here to bolster Narkolt's fleet should ensure air superiority, at least as soon as we have cannons that work. For now, we'll work on more marines."

"And the land forces?" Grizz asked hopefully.

"They'll be folded into the Legion command structure, under Romanus. The guard will be responsible for protecting Narkolt, but the army will be stepping up seriously, both in terms of training and in terms of responsibility. I'm assuming they don't have the same standards in training and ability as the Legion does?"

"They wish…" Grizz snorted. "The army is where those who wash out of the Legion go, if they want a nice, easy life. The Himnel one, at least, is full of those too lazy or cowardly to join the Legion, and too dumb to get a craft, but who still want to eat."

"Great," I grumbled. "I was kinda hoping that wasn't the case."

"Well, better I disappoint you now boss, than when you rely on them and they fail in battle," Grizz said grimly. "Sorry, Jax, but it's true. In the field against Himnel's army, it'd be even odds. If we spend a few months training them and beating them into shape, we can temper them from iron to steel, no doubt, and they'll wipe the floor with Himnel's forces. But against the Dark Legion? As they are now, they'll be slaughtered."

"Fuck," I muttered. "And the Dark Legion outnumbers us by four or five times as many."

"True, but that's in numbers alone. Remember, numbers don't mean as much when you've got terrain or situational modifiers in play," Grizz said, ticking off on his fingers. "First of all, battlefield! A well-prepared defensive position can turn a five times negative modifier into the opposite. A secure, well-armored position can destroy an offensive force ten times its number with the right support."

"Secondly, support! Magic is a force multiplier, a highly trained mage can be the equal of a hundred lesser mages, or a thousand poorly trained infantry. Third, and most vital of all, morale! The force that goes into battle believing it has already lost, has. No battle plan survives contact with the enemy. The more aware, skillful, and fluid a commander, the better the chance of their force."

"You forgot communication," I said, eyeing Grizz as he clearly parroted someone he'd listened to.

"What?" Grizz asked, confused.

"Communication. What happens if the orders can't get to a specific unit?" I clarified, before pausing as Grizz stared at me blankly. "Okay, what am I not getting here?"

"Battle or war leaders," Grizz pointed out, grinning. "Looks like that's one of the advantages we have over your realm. The designated leader of one side's forces, as accepted by those forces, directs them all through an Ability that they get as a battle or war leader. Basically, like everything else, they can level it up. As it grows, and they direct more and more troops, they are able to take more under their direct control. You've got it, right? I mean, you should have?"

I frowned and held up a finger in the universal "wait one…" gesture, pulling my notifications up.

Congratulations!

You have killed the following:
- 21,843x Spiders of various levels for a total of 26,912xp
- 1x Drow Priest, level 29 for 15,050xp
- 78x DarkSpore of various levels for a total of 3,400xp

A party under your command has killed the following:
- 47,096x Spiders of various levels for a total of 58,327xp
- 3x Drow Spiderkin of various levels for a total of 79,216xp
- 1x Drider Queen, level 46 for a total of 51,062xp
- 1x SporeMother, level 11 for 89,000xp
- 21x Drow Soldiers of various levels for a total of 401,050xp
- 3x Drow Priests of various levels for a total of 69,180xp
- 123x DarkSpore of various levels for a total of 5,150xp

Total party experience earned: 752,985xp
As party leader you gain 25% of all experience earned
Progress to level 31 stands at 781,586/1,245,000

I dismissed the kill notifications, grunting as I realized how little I had actually seemed to contribute to the last two fights, if I just went off the numbers, and I pulled the next notification up.

Congratulations!

You have proven a deeper understanding of the secrets of magic!

+10 to Light Magic
+10 to Dark Magic
+10 to Life Magic
+10 to Death Magic
+10 to Fire Magic
+10 to Water Magic
+10 to Earth Magic
+10 to Air Magic

*

Congratulations, Eternal!

You have reached a new plateau in your understanding of magic, and as such, instead of only receiving a minor evolution in your abilities, due to your patronage by the Lady of Hidden Knowledge, you have unlocked a deeper secret!

Mana is only ONE side of magic!

**Spellforms, Potions, Incantations, Runes, and Prayers
are each aspects, not the entirety.**

True magic, like all things, has not one side, but two.

*

Congratulations!

You have discovered a new Quest: The Deeper Secret

Your unexpected ascension to a new understanding of magic has unlocked access to the great quest that has been followed by thousands of mages through the eons, but will you succeed where they have failed? Magic has many faces, yet has two sides. Of the ten aspects that exist, you have discovered five so far, and each of those includes mana. Now know, however, there is more to magic than this singular side.

Discover Mana's Antithesis and the five opposites to those magical aspects you are familiar with in order to stand a chance of gaining access to abilities and powers, long since lost to the realm.

Forms of Magic Discovered: 5/10

Reward: New forms of magic, 10,000,000xp, Unknown

Accept: *Yes/No*

I paused as I read the notification over and over again, then frantically pulled up my magical skills and confirmed it. It was real.

First of all, the five aspects of magic I knew about included mana, but if there really were another five out there, a way of using magic that didn't require the complex spellcasting or demands for the formula of potions, or carving runes, that would be massive, not to mention insanely powerful!

If I could access magic without those limitations, my powers would be tremendous. I'd been skirting around the edge of an understanding for a while now. What had started in Himnel so many weeks ago, when my rage had allowed me to use Imperial Abilities to free the slaves, and those imprisoned…

I could feel it, the edge of a shape of an idea. It was like saying I had twelve percent of a plan. It wasn't a plan, it was a fucking outline, a hunch, but…I was touching the edge of it, I just needed to explore it…

I nodded to myself. I'd figure this shit out, but for now, I needed to check the rest of these details and move on. I hadn't gained ten individual skill evolutions, which sucked a bit, but this was way more important, so fuck it. I pulled up the details and checked on the prompt again.

The difference of plus ten in each school of magic didn't sound like a huge amount, not at first, but considering if I'd worked to get that by say, leveling my original Firebolt spell, I would have needed to have hit a cool hundred in the Firebolt subsidiary school.

Every spell of these schools just took a significant jump in power and drop in cost. Each fire spell now did ten percent more base damage and cost ten percent less mana to cast, add to that the individual levels I'd already achieved, and hell…I was at level twelve in fire magic, meaning that each hit from a fire spell did a minimum of twelve percent more damage. If I made a spell that dealt fire damage for each shard when it detonated, the way that Fyre's Iceshard had, it would have shredded most enemies regardless of their armor.

My healing spells now did twenty percent more healing for twenty percent less cost. I stared at the details, my mind racing as I tried to work my way through the discoveries I'd made subconsciously, hoping to make another breakthrough, until Grizz cleared his throat, bringing me back to reality.

"Shit," I muttered, before remembering what I'd been looking for. I kept scanning, seeing the last prompts and acknowledging them before dismissing them again.

Congratulations!

You have made progress in a quest: My God is Better Than Your God (3)

For each altar or sanctified place of worship dedicated to Nimon, Ardat, Asmodeus, Baphomet, or Illoth that you destroy, you will receive a Mark of Favor and a random blueprint for your crafters from the Goddess Jenae.

*

Beware!

You have reached a new low.

You are now HATED by the Lady of Spiders, Illoth.

**She will now encourage all those who worship Her
to seek your death ever more fervently!**

Beware the tiny eyes that crawl unseen!

I shrugged at that. It wasn't like the spider bitch was going to be able to kill me twice, and the real queen of the spiders, as far as I was concerned was Ashrag, who by now had to be damn close to reaching the Tower. I grinned evilly as a thought occurred to me.

"I think I've found it, Grizz," I muttered, scanning through the various skills I'd ignored as they didn't grant me an immediate bonus. "But before I forget, Jian, I want the *Star's Glory* brought here as well, with as many of the soldier spiders aboard as it can hold. Ask Horkesh how far away her mother is, and if she's close, talk to her. If not, then deal with Horkesh. I want as many as possible of the biggest, meanest spiders they have that are ready and willing to fight against the Dark Wanker's forces. The Legion's getting some fucking cavalry." I grinned as I imagined just how godsdamn terrifying that would be for the assholes on the other side.

Congratulations!

Your skill War-Leader has reached level eight.

Continue to level this skill to gain further bonuses.

(Level eight War-Leader includes bonuses gained from sub-skills Strategos: Level 1, Fortifier: Level 1, and Sapper: Level 2, level up these skills to gain additional bonuses.)

"Okay, yeah I'm level eight in it," I confirmed to Grizz, getting a grin from him in return. "Okay, come on then, give me the bad news."

"Prefect Romanus is level thirty-nine and can control up to fifteen thousand in a battle, I think. The Legion hasn't had the numbers for that for a long time, but you know, leading small-scale battles and raids on camps and so on for half his life helps!"

"Damn, looks like I know who'll be in overall command in the fight for Himnel, then," I muttered, shaking my head. It felt wrong even considering someone else being in command in the fight to come, but if I was realistic, the simple fact I'd never even known about this before told me it shouldn't be me.

That the city command facility showed the incursion of the Drow had been really helpful, especially the way that it'd highlighted their locations, but unless this was something unique to Narkolt, which I seriously doubted, we were going to be at a massive disadvantage in the upcoming war.

It would be exponentially worse if my side was running on the orders I gave at the beginning of the fight and that was it, rather than having a system that I could...that *Romanus* could give up-to-date orders through, reacting to changes as they happened.

"Okay. godsdamnit." I shook my head. "I need Romanus here as soon as possible." I dismissed all the notifications, including the one that reminded me that I still had thirty stat points and a meridian node available.

I wanted to slam those points in right now. But if I did that, and just used them on the spur of the moment, it would be insane. I desperately needed those points and more to have a chance in the upcoming fight. Wasting them now would be too fucking stupid.

"Lastly," I said, taking a deep breath and looking at Jian. "And I damn well know this is going to piss Heph off…I want the crafter golems, some construction golems, and ten of the war golems, including the highest leveled one as their commander. We have to secure the city. We know there are seriously damaged Imperial facilities here, and we have to get them in order as fast as possible."

"Ah, yes boss, Heph is going to be upset," Jian agreed, wincing.

"I know, but shit happens. Sorry to dump this on you, mate, but I need those reinforcements here now."

"I can do it," Jian said. "So, Cai and Isabella, Romanus, Hannibal, Nerin, Riana, Oren, and Lucian, along with whoever they need. Rewn and his harem, the golems, and the spiders, anything else?"

"Tell Romanus to bring as many of the Legion as he feels are needed," I said after a few minutes thought. "He's to sort with Heph and Seneschal to leave as many as are needed to ensure the Tower is well-defended, but I want the rest here.

"The Tower has golems, and they'll be making more, while here we'll be getting ready for war. If Himnel set off to attack the Tower, we can either take them in the ass in the field, attack their ships in the air from both sides using the Narkolt fleet, or let them lay siege to the Tower and assault the city behind them. I don't think they'll dare to attack. I think we might have earned enough time to turn things around." I muttered the last part, unsure, but hopeful.

"I'll get Sehran, and we'll leave immediately," Jian said, before grinning. "You know she can barely walk right now?"

"Ten points to you then, mate. You've done it right when she's like *that* afterwards," I quipped, grunting as Oracle elbowed me in the chest. My armor rang softly, and she grumbled about my metal dress sense while rubbing her elbow.

"Ha! Ah no, Jax. I mean after feeding on the SporeMother. It was like she was drunk; she staggered into the lower hold on Tenandra and locked herself away to sleep it off!"

"Ah, well, it just means there's less chance of you hitting a mountain or something on your way back…less distractions!" I offered, grinning tiredly.

"That's true, unfortunately!" Jian agreed before climbing to his feet. "I'll be back as soon as I can. Keep him alive," Jian said to Lydia, who nodded firmly. With that, he left.

I sagged back a little, relaxing on the cot until the sound of feet climbing the stairs roused me. Only then did I realize that the conversation in the room had died away some time ago as more and more of us fell asleep.

I straightened. At some point, Oracle had slipped from my arms and moved to the throne. She had begun examining the interface, but as the echoing footsteps climbed the stairs, she stood, ready, even as the others around the room stirred.

"You bunch of lazy shitbags." Thomas flashed a tired grin as he stepped out of the stairwell, getting a round of grumbling and offensive hand gestures before people started to settle back down. "Seriously, there I am, working with the guard, finding out what they do and where, and you buggers are all having a nap!" he grumbled, before spotting a spare cot nearby and sighing.

"So, what did you find out?" I asked as he edged around people and over to the cot next to mine. He reached up for the latches on his armor and disassembled it with an ease I had to admit, if only to myself, was annoying. I was still searching for the clasps half the time, while he was stripping his armor off in seconds.

"They're not as bad as I was afraid of." He groaned as he peeled the cuirass off and set it on the floor next to his feet, before sitting on the cot and tugging the rest off. "Don't get me wrong, the majority of them are lazy as all hell and only have pretty basic training, but they're not as corrupt as Himnel's guard. Beyond a few bribes and shit I think you'll get anywhere, that is. Most of them are just average people, need a good kick up the arse, but I can work with that."

"You're happy to work with them?" I asked.

"I'll do whatever you need, bro, but at least I understand them." He shrugged. "After my time in Himnel's prison and with their guards and jailors, I know the little tricks they were pulling, so I can stamp them out."

"What about training?"

"Depends what you want from them, really. Do you want them to be city guards, or what?" He inclined his head. "The army needs to be as good as possible, and yeah, they're definitely going to need a lot of work. But, if you can give me a good few Legionnaires to help, I can beat a lot of the guards into shape; there's not that many of them, after all."

"Just under fourteen hundred, with nearly two hundred elites," I said.

"Fuck," Thomas grumbled, before shrugging as he pulled his boots off and laid back. "Okay, give me a dozen or so legionnaires who can kick their arses. I'm gonna break them into a few smaller groups and work them one-by-one. I'll change their shifts around so that they get more days off, then I'll use those days to train them."

"That'll make you popular." I grinned.

He snorted. "They don't have to love me; they just have to do as I say. Mix our old army basic training in with the beatings that Restun likes to give, and I'll make useful members of society out of them in short order," he promised, closing his eyes. "Now, if you don't mind, I was working while you were all up here napping, so shush."

"Cheeky fucker," I muttered, and he lifted one finger to his lips.

"Shhhh!" He mimed locking his lips and throwing the key away, before settling back and letting out a contented sigh.

I gave him the finger, to a handful of tired chuckles around the room.

CHAPTER THIRTY-EIGHT

I slept for nearly three hours before being awoken by an argument downstairs. By the time I'd dragged myself from the cot and made my way downstairs, the argument was in full swing. I was almost ready to gut both sides, until I stumbled out and saw Mal and the naked woman from earlier, thankfully both dressed now, arguing with the captain of the guard.

Mal had drawn his crossbow, as had Soween. Jay had one of the guards by the throat and another on the floor, skidding across the stone to come to a stop by my feet, unconscious. Josh was lifting both hands and gathering his magic with a manic grin.

"What the hell is going on!" I snapped. "Josh, stop that. Mal, Soween, stand down. And Jay, I swear, if you've fucking killed anyone, I'll bury you in a latrine up to your eyebrows!"

After I said that, silence reigned for a handful of seconds until the captain of the guard spoke up.

"High Lord Jax, this ruffian bribed and threatened his way through the forces securing the palace somehow. He was demanding admittance to you, despite…"

"Eberhardt, he's a member of my *council* and, despite his dickish ways, a friend." I sighed and rubbed the bridge of my nose. "So, stand down, please."

The guards backed off slowly, looking unsure.

"Yeah, that's right!" Jay sneered, looking around at the guards. "We're all his friends, so you'd better watch yourselves."

"Actually Mal, Soween, and Josh are," I corrected him, pointing a finger at his chest. "I still think you're a prick." The look of shock, followed by total outrage was entirely worth it, as I turned back to Mal. He was grinning, but clearly exhausted as he stood by the woman who'd practically slapped me senseless a few hours earlier.

"Hey, Jax." Mal said, before gesturing to the keep. "Think we need to step inside and have a conversation away from other ears."

"Come on, then," I said, nodding, before turning back to the Captain of the Guard. "Eberhardt, I know he's a prick. I have no doubt that Mal made the meeting between you far worse than it needed to be. But, for now, if someone comes claiming to be a member of my council or one of my companions, please ask a member of the Legion.

"I'll discuss this with him now and find out what's happened, then I'll start with the meetings I need to have. Please summon any of the city leaders that survived the Drow infestation and get them ready. We'll only have a small gathering today, as it's already past noon, and I fought through the night. Tomorrow, I will hold court and do all the formal stuff. For now, please gather a handful of the upper leadership that are close by and get them ready for a quick meeting in, say, two hours."

"Of course, Lord!" Eberhardt said, smiling. He saluted quickly before hurrying off.

"You just gave him a hell of a lot of power, you realize that, don't you?" Soween said. "He's going to be able to arrange who gets access to you for the meeting. Regardless of anything else, you can believe that those he doesn't like will be ignored when it comes to invites."

"I guessed as much," I agreed with a sigh, turning to one of the guards who was standing nearby. "What's your name, guardsman?"

He stood to attention with a creak of metal before responding. "Johansson, High Lord!" he barked out. I withheld a frustrated sigh, accepting that the lack of formality I'd been enjoying of late was probably over.

"Thank you, Johansson. I'd like you to go and find Arch-Magus Fyre. Tell her that I want her to gather the local powerful and important people, just a few of those who are nearby, for an informal meeting in two hours. Also tell her that there will be an official, formal meeting tomorrow."

"Of course, sir!" he barked. "Is this in addition to the group that Captain Eberhardt is gathering?"

"The two groups should ensure that those left off the list are kept to a minimum," I said. "Gather them all in the throne room, I guess. I assume there is a throne room nearby, an official one, besides the keep one, right?"

He nodded, gesturing to one of the buildings to the side. "On the other side of that building is the formal throne room, High Lord!"

"Good man, thank you."

I led Mal and the others inside. Not only had Oracle followed me down and been standing behind me, but so had Lydia, Grizz, and most of the team. "Guys, it's okay. I'm going to talk to Mal; you can rest," I said tiredly, getting a general shaking of heads and muttering of support from all of them.

"Okay then, what's so important?" I asked Mal, sitting down in the first room we could find that was neither filthy nor open to the elements. The dozen chairs inside were all stiff and formal, but at this point, I really didn't give a shit.

"Couple of things…but first, any chance of a heal?" Mal asked. I blinked, straightening, my fatigue forgotten as I realized how gingerly he was walking. Before I could cast it myself, Oracle had started, swiftly followed by Lydia and Grizz. Mal shivered and, before he could ask, a second barrage hit his companion, making her sigh as their injuries were washed away in a flood of magic. "Damn, thanks, kid, everyone." Mal nodded as he looked around at the others.

"Anytime, Mal. I'm sorry for making you wait; I should have thought about it earlier. Actually, why the hell were you outside? You were on the ship when we got back here."

"We had Tenandra and Jian drop us off at the shipyard when they left," Mal said with a sheepish look. "Turns out Soween and the crew had been turning the city upside down searching for me."

"Next time you go to a whorehouse, tell us the right one; it would have saved us a lot of trouble," Soween grumbled. I shot a look at her, then back at Mal and the lady who sat by his side, visibly avoiding so much as touching his hand, despite her distress when he was locked in the box.

"Okay, let's be clear. The last thing I remember, you were supposed to set the spies free to search the city and get things ready for the assault, but instead you went to a fucking whorehouse?" I growled in a low voice. "You were getting your sodding dick sucked when you were supposed to be helping the spies get set up!? Where the hell were they? Were they getting their rocks off as well?" I snapped, my anger rising.

"Our spies were captured by the Drow as soon as they left the ship," Flux reported from near the door. I glared at him for interrupting, and he raised a hand in apology. "I'm sorry, Lord Jax. I found out what happened from the survivors when you returned from the fight.

"They were captured by Drow who were leading the city guard, then they were smuggled out of the palace and taken to the same whorehouse that Mal was captured in. They were tortured, and more than half were killed, either by the Drow or the DarkSpore. The survivors will need some time to recover, but all have expressed a desire to continue, if you'll still have them."

"It was my fault," the woman sitting next to Mal said, drawing my attention from Flux. She stood, before curtsying low and almost falling out of her dress, clearly waiting for me to look. I managed to avoid it with a truly herculean effort and nodded for her to sit back down.

"And who are you?" I asked, trying to keep hold of my temper.

"Alyssa, High Lord Jax. My name is Alyssa Marintensian, and I'm the proprietor of the Kneeling Lady…I…ah…" She paused, clearly trying to decide how to put it, before looking at Mal and shrugging, her refined accent evaporating as she sighed and leaned back. "I run a whorehouse. Mal's been a customer of mine, a private customer, for a lot of years. When he arrived here, he came looking for me. He said he wanted to make sure me and my girls were safe."

"Sounds like Mal," I agreed, leaving them to wonder which part I was referring to.

"Yeah well, the problem is, when he was here last, he left in a hurry to go meet you. I sent a couple of my girls to follow him and see if he was really going to you, or if he was bullshitting me about being your friend." She glanced at Mal's shocked expression and snorted, patting his cheek in commiseration.

"Mal, honey, you're too pretty to be this innocent," she chided before going on. "Anyway, I didn't realize that one of my girls sold that information on the side. It got to the Drow, then apparently so did she. I didn't see her again.

"Then, two days ago, a bunch of Drow showed up at my door. They closed the house down and started questioning me and my people, torturing some of us, killing others, and generally playing whatever sick games they wanted. I guess we're lucky they couldn't get it up, or there'd have been rape thrown in as well."

She grimaced before shaking her head. "Sorry, I know most people don't consider rape against people in my trade as a particular issue, but despite what you might think…"

"It's worse," I finished for her. "I had a friend who was in your line of work a few years back. She was attacked like that and, a few weeks later, she took her own life. Believe me, of all the crimes out there, that is one of the worst, in my eyes. I'll happily teach those who commit it a lesson, using this." I pulled my naginata out of my bag.

There was a long silence as everyone considered what I'd said, before she nodded to me in thanks.

"Well, that's a refreshing outlook from a member of the nobility, thank you. Anyway, they told me they'd been waiting for him, and when Mal arrived, he wandered into their trap." She tried to make her shrug come off casual. "They used me to hurt him, and the other way around, as well as other methods, such as truth potions."

"They'd used up their store of them on her and the staff before they took me, but it means that they learned a lot about the Smuggler's Guild. Most of that information is tightly held, and they sent it out of the city with a handful of Drow."

"And this is important because…" I closed my eyes and sighed. "Because the smugglers have other ways into the city, and now the Drow know them all." I groaned.

"Exactly, but," Mal said, holding up one hand and smiling. "We know those ways, too; all we have to do is lay a few traps, and…"

"And we get to slaughter them on their way back to the city, while closing up all the smuggler's routes as well." I said, nodding in understanding. "Won't the guild come looking for you if we close the routes they use?"

He nodded. "Bloody hope so. I was already marked as a target for the deal we did last time, since, by the laws of the guild, I should have reported you to the Council of Smugglers. However, with a little hedging, and the rights to the entrance to Himnel that you claimed, I managed to get the price taken off my head. Fair enough, I say," Mal snarled, before taking a deep breath and glaring at me.

"But now they've gone and banned me from all the good drinking houses, and while I'm no longer under a death-mark, I'm still very much unwelcome. Me! Unwelcome in bars that allow *fucking guardsmen* in!"

"So, you're willing to go to war with the Smuggler's Guild because they banned you from your favorite bars?"

Mal glared daggers at me. "Look, you clearly don't get this…but…"

"Oh no, no, I do, actually," I replied. "I'll happily go to war with the Smuggler's Guild for just about any reason, because, let's face it, they'll be ripping me and my fucking treasury off, now that I'm in charge. They're also likely to have both the best magical artifacts and the drugs we need to keep the Gnomes in line."

"So…you're okay with this?"

"Totally fine with it. Do you still want to make out it's because they banned you from the bars, though?" I asked. There was a brief pause before Mal nodded, looking sheepish.

"They need to be taught some respect for a man, you understand," Mal muttered.

I nodded as though agreeing. "So, we'll be taking the Smuggler's Guild down. Alyssa, you own a whorehouse, and you and Mal are…?"

Alyssa shrugged self-consciously, while appearing uncertain. "Truthfully, I don't know. Mal was a client for a lot of years, but we were considering dinner at one point?" she said tentatively, turning and looking at Mal.

Mal froze, clearly not ready for their situation to be discussed, and the entire room paused with bated breath.

*Come on, Mal…*I thought. *You're not that fucking dumb, are you?*

"I uh…" He fumbled for words for the first time since I'd known him. Soween coughed, and he looked to her, getting a glare that clearly told him he was being an idiot.

"I understand, of course," Alyssa said as she stood, a brittle smile on her face as she curtsied to me. "With your permission, Lord Jax, I'll leave. This is obviously no place for the likes of me."

"Says who!" Mal said, straightening up as his brain finally kicked into gear. "You've earned the right to be anywhere you damn well want, Alyssa, and not just because you know enough about the nobles to bury them all!

"You're a damn successful businesswoman, and you'd be respected for it if people knew it was your business! As to you and me, hell yes, we damn well ARE!" Mal grabbed her hand and pulled her back into her seat. He held her hand firmly and glared around, as though expecting an attack at any minute.

"Ah, stop your glaring, Mal!" I said, grinning. "You might not know this, but she slapped the shit out of me when I didn't move fast enough to save 'her Mal'!"

"Is…is that true?" Mal asked, getting a firm nod.

"It is, but also because he was looking at my tits without paying," Alyssa said, prompting a cough from me as everyone turned to look in my direction.

"Hey, I was low on mana, and she appeared out of nowhere, stark naked, and nearly knocked me out with them! I mean, come on, have you seen the *size* of them? I was in shock!" I babbled in my defense, pointing at her chest before closing my eyes and taking a deep breath.

"Aaaand let's just move on, okay?" I suggested when I'd got control of my tongue again.

"Hmmm, you and me are gonna have a talk later," Mal declared with another of his hard stares.

I sighed and nodded. "Fine, fine…" I muttered with another released breath, realizing all this sighing wasn't tamping down my rising frustration. "Look, you're both from here, I'm going to go have a meeting with the local leadership soon. I'd like you both there, and you too, Soween. You might spot something I don't."

"I'm not interested in those idiots who think they're important," Mal started, but Alyssa put her hand over his mouth, cutting him off as he narrowed his eyes.

"We'll be there, High Lord," she said. Soween agreed. Josh shrugged, while Jay just glared at me. Daggers for eyes must be catching.

"While we've got a bit of time, though," I said, taking a deep breath and turning to Oracle with the question clear in my mind. She nodded and smiled, then stood up and reached out, placing one hand on my head, gesturing for Josh to sit in front of her.

"Uh…What?" Mal started to say.

"You waited until you got here to ask for healing, when you damn well should have used a potion or got someone else to heal you, so now Josh gets a few new spells. We can teach three at a time, so Josh and two others. Who else wants magic?" I asked the group. There was a long pause before Soween stepped forward, dragging a chair up to sit next to her husband, who took her hand with a wide smile as I turned to Mal and Alyssa.

Jay stepped forward. "Uh, yeah I'll…"

"Sit down and shut up, Jay!" Soween, Mal, Lydia, and I all snapped at more or less the same time, making the huge man snarl in anger before throwing himself into a seat in a sulk.

"So, Mal, Alyssa, who wants it?" I asked as Alyssa looked at me wide-eyed.

"You'd teach me magic?" she asked slowly. "You know what I am."

"You're Mal's lady," I said firmly. "And despite the shitbag that he is, he's one of the smartest, sneakiest fuckers I know. If he says you're trustworthy, then you are, as far as I'm concerned. If Mal doesn't want to learn magic, then you can." Mal watched me for a few seconds before turning to her and gestured her forward.

"You learn this time. I'll do a deal with him next time for me," Mal said, smiling at the excitement that shone in her eyes as she turned and nodded to me, pulling her chair forward.

I closed my eyes and felt Oracle reaching into my mind, as we joined and spoke in a blur. We examined the spells that we thought would be best for this small group, before agreeing on Magic Missile, Complex Healing, and for shits and giggles, Explosive Compression. The hour it took seemed to drag on longer than normal as the blur of symbols and knowledge had to be reconstructed again and again, layered repeatedly in Soween, of all people, as she had the least natural magical talent of anyone I'd ever met.

By the end, I was aching as I shifted, cracking my back, while the other three grinned and compared mental notes, discussing concepts that were new to them.

"Josh," Oracle said, and he broke off in mid-discussion, turning to her with a massive smile.

"Yes, Oracle?" he asked, boyishly cheerful as always.

"We've got about half an hour before we're due in the throne room. Would you mind if we learned Blizzard from you?" Oracle asked, making Josh frown.

"Of course not, I mean, yeah go ahead…you don't have it?" he asked, sitting back down and looking from Oracle to me in confusion.

"No, we don't," I said. "I was going to learn it with the spellbooks, but…" I shrugged as I avoided stating the obvious.

"But I chose it!" Josh said. I nodded. "I'm sorry…"

I shook my head. "Don't worry about it. I offered you a choice, and you made it, nothing wrong with that!" I smiled. "We're short on time but, as it's only one spell, we might be able to get this done and get to the throne room without being too late, if, you know…" I gestured to him.

"What? Oh…OH!" Josh exclaimed, shaking his head and leaning forward, smiling suddenly in embarrassment. "Sorry I…I just…"

"It's fine, dear," Soween said. "Now shut the hell up and let them do their thing." She watched us carefully. "This won't hurt him…?" She relaxed when I smiled and shook my head. I stopped moving as Oracle put her hand on my forehead and created the connection between us.

It didn't take long, less than twenty minutes in the end, probably closer to fifteen, but when I opened my eyes, I knew all I needed to about forming a blizzard. I knew about the movement of freezing air, the way the heat that formed most convection currents could be drawn away, and far more.

"Wow," I muttered, my mind filled with a wealth of new knowledge and a thousand ideas to make my spells more lethal.

"Wow indeed," Oracle whispered, staring into the distance. "I think we could use this with the old cleansing flame base. I mean, I know it's evolved now, but we could try it. If we use the wind and the ice, we could slow your enemies, while it heals you, maybe even buffs you?"

"Hell yes…wait, for buffs, could we buff Ronin?" I asked suddenly, my eyes widening. "What if we could make a spell that magnified his buffs?"

"We could do that…maybe?" she replied, frowning. "Wait, we could learn from the mages here, too!"

"Hells, yes!" I grinned. "If we could learn a few of their super spells?"

"Oh, Gods yes…No! Wait, no Jax, no we can't."

"Why not?" I asked with some surprise. "It was your idea, and it's a brilliant one!"

"No, it's not, because a mage that's as powerful as they are would be able to attack you directly, mind to mind, and there's nothing I could do about it. They could kill me and wipe your mind or make you into a mindless slave if they had the slightest desire to do so.

"Worst of all, the only thing the Oaths would do is punish them after they did it. Would you trust Fyre in your mind?"

"Huh, yeah, okay…good point." I muttered, grunting and standing up, looking around the room. "Okay, thank you for that, Josh. It's always good to learn a new spell."

"I have a few others, all spells that I learned from the memory you gave me," Josh offered.

"I'll learn them soon, if you don't mind; but for now, I have a meeting I need to attend." I smiled to him, Soween, and Alyssa.

Where Soween had simply stepped back and returned to watching the room, Alyssa had sat next to Mal, but was now staring wide-eyed into the distance.

"Are you okay?" Mal asked her eventually, having sat quietly watching her while I was learning the spell from Josh.

"I…I am…yes, it's just…it changes everything," Alyssa whispered.

"Like what?"

"Like…oh Mal, you have no idea…magic, it's everywhere! Learning to channel it…I have to learn more, it's like seeing a tiny part of a stained-glass window, all the colors, the beauty, after all my life without color. Before, it was like I was seeing through bare windows, but now I see the world for what it can be!"

"What the hell did you teach them?" Mal asked, glaring at me, as I gestured to the door.

"Let's walk and talk, mate," I said, heading out, smiling as the others, Thomas included, fell in around me. "You can all get some sleep, you know, if you need to?"

"No' 'til they've sworn tha Oaths," Lydia said grimly. "'Til then, we canna trust none o' them." I started to open my mouth, then shut it firmly. I honestly agreed with her, and as I heard similar sentiments voiced by the others, I realized just how stupid I'd been by not binding the rest of the guards to me already.

"I asked you a question," Mal growled, but I cut him off.

"Yeah, I know, Mal. I taught them all three spells. Complex Healing is basically what it sounds like. It's a complicated but damn powerful healing spell. It will level up and grow as they use it more and more, so I seriously recommend you make them practice it.

"The second is Magic Missile. It creates five darts that can be targeted independently. They don't do a great deal of damage at the base level, but they explode when they hit, and I've lost track of how many we've killed by landing a hit at just the right point. All five darts impacting a sensitive location will kill most creatures."

"A sensitive location, oh my lord, you don't know how badly some people are going to suffer now," Alyssa said, grinning at me.

"Well, as long as they deserve it, and it's not just settling old scores. Remember, this city is under Imperial Law now."

"The scores I'll be settling will be with rapists and murderers," Alyssa informed me coldly.

"Fine, but if you leave witnesses, make sure they understand that, and if you end up before Lucian, I'll abide by his decision, so remember the line and where it lies. I'd prefer you bring this kind of thing to the Legion and the Justicars, but when immediate responses are needed, well…have fun."

"And the last spell?" Mal asked, making me grin.

"Yeah, that's one of my personal spells. It's a little bit more powerful and evil, I suppose. It forms a ball that can be fired at a target. When it hits something, it sends out a gravitational distortion, making everything fall towards the center of the ball, before it explodes outwards, hurling everything away.

"It's a spell that could take out a ship if used right, never mind the individuals I imagine you'll be using it against most of the time. Be careful, but…use it when you need to, I guess." We left the keep and started walking across the grass. We picked up a Legion escort when we walked past, the legionnaires that were spread across the city last night having fallen in on the keep as we rested.

It didn't take long to reach the throne room, as it wasn't exactly hard to find. We walked down the main corridor of the building we'd been shown earlier, following the deep plush carpets and expensive carved steps inlaid with gold. But as I drew closer, I felt myself growing more and more annoyed.

The sounds that grew louder and louder as we approached, made it clear that my idea of the local few people in charge and the interpretation of Fyre and Eberhardt was completely different.

I strode into the hall at the head of almost a hundred legionnaires, with my squad and close friends drawn up around me and Thomas's growing squad behind my own, yet we were still well outnumbered by the hundreds of minor power brokers in the city.

I strode down a narrow walkway of golden carpeting. The interweaving red and black patterns that ran its length were almost hypnotic, and I looked away deliberately as I realized yet another thing.

First off, nobody would ever have a carpet like this by choice. Secondly, Fyre, who was standing where an advisor would on one side of the throne, and Eberhardt, who stood across from her staring daggers, had not only ignored the clear intention of my orders, but had blatantly done what Soween had said they would and had sold access to this informal meeting.

My temper rose as I marched down the aisle. I was going to set this fucking carpet on fire, and I was going to teach the locals that my orders weren't fucking requests. And, if I was lucky, I'd do it in one fell action.

I strode up the five steps to the throne before turning and facing the room, watching the hundreds of people that were gathered before me, as silence fell…mostly.

Several knots of people continued their conversations, and judging by the way the others around them deferred to them, and the metric fuckton of gold and enchanted crap they were wearing, they were clearly people who thought themselves to be the most important here. I turned to Fyre and Eberhardt and spoke quietly.

"Get down." I said, gesturing from the raised dais, the controlled fury in my voice clear to all who heard it. The pair of them swallowed hard and moved, scuttling down the steps to the bottom one before turning back to regard me, as though to ask if that was far enough.

The glare I gave them sent them running, even as two of the three groups that had continued to speak started to snicker…loudly.

"We took the SporeMother's head as a trophy," Grizz whispered, just loud enough to be clear to me. I grunted in response. "Want it?"

I nodded, gesturing to the floor before the throne.

Grizz turned and barked a quick command to three legionnaires, who sprinted from the room even as I pulled my naginata out of my bag and glared around at the gathered idiots.

"Legionnaires," I called out. "Seal the hall. Nobody who isn't part of the Legion enters or leaves until I'm finished," I ordered. The legionnaires saluted before they peeled off and moved to the various doors and balconies around the room, taking up station as the conversations died out.

I noted the huge quantity of glittery fucks at the front of the room, and that the amount of gold and crappy jewelry reduced each foot farther to the rear.

I couldn't help it, and I sneered in disgust, shaking my head as I waited.

Several minutes passed in silence, with the crowd shuffling and muttering uncomfortably, until each group had fallen silent, quieted either by my glare or by those around them.

All except one group, and they had gathered around a grossly fat man who looked to be having a lot of difficulty standing, having started to visibly sweat. He wore multiple rings on each finger, red and gold robes that looked to be woven gold thread, and square, gem-encrusted chains that clearly weighed more than he thought when he put them on.

He also wore a hat that basically looked like a pork pie that had been dipped in gold and put on while still hot, judging from the trickling sweat that had left lines in his makeup.

The fuck glared at me as though I was the one out of order here, but as the huge double doors were opened and shut again, and the three legionnaires Grizz had sent marched down the middle of the corridor carrying the head of the SporeMother, the atmosphere changed notably.

The legionnaires dumped the head to one side of the throne, facing the crowd, and it started leaking blood, spinal, and brain fluids onto the carpet, staining it beyond repair.

With that, I nodded in satisfaction and tapped my fist to my chest in thanks to the three legionnaires.

"Thank you all for coming," I said, my voice carrying clearly for all to hear. "As you're all aware, City Lord Rewn has surrendered Narkolt to the Empire and to me personally. This began due to a combination of events, namely the infiltration of the Drow and their attempted assassination and usurpation of his position, along with the corruption that has been running unchecked for years.

"This has resulted in your pathetic performance recently in your war with Himnel, and the ease with which the Drow stole warships from you and used them to attack ME." My naginata flared with light as I slammed its base down hard and continued to speak.

"Until I judge the city is suitably under control, I will rule here personally. When and *if* the city is judged to be loyal and at a level I decide is acceptable, then I will pass control of the city back to Rewn."

I made a mental note at the relieved smiles and the faces of those who were obviously plotting, before going on.

"Or possibly someone else! Before this can happen, however, the city needs to be brought into line and the war with Himnel won. I intend to do these in short order, and as such will be changing the entire city to a war-footing immediately.

"This means all prices will be held from today, and all required items and resources that are judged vital to the war effort are now the property of the Empire. I will not permit those who have, for example, a large stockpile of iron, to triple their prices and weaken the war effort. Those of you who hold such resources currently will be paid a fair market value for them. I will not steal from you, but those who support the Empire wholeheartedly will be thanked and raised up."

I noted the change in the mood, and the number of them that looked furious or pleased.

"As a city under the Empire, there are two options open to you. First and foremost, you can swear allegiance to the Empire and to me. Being a citizen of the Empire comes with a great many benefits, including training, free healthcare, and a path to personal power, should you prove yourself to be worthy of wielding it. This path will also include, should you earn that honor, the restoration of titles and possibly the accumulation of more."

"Restoration?" the fat man gasped. "We are *already* nobles of the realm!"

"No," I said, regarding him coldly. "You *were* a noble, and a self-proclaimed one, at that. Upon my ascension to the role of Imperial Scion and High Lord of Dravith, all titles were revoked or held, pending approval. I already stripped that arse Barabarattas of Himnel of his titles, and I frankly enjoyed it immensely, so don't test my patience."

Whispers and muttering rose around the room, growing in volume to become a roar, until Grizz slammed his sword against his shield with a crash that rang out across the hall. The other legionnaires swiftly followed suit until the room rang with the sound of steel on steel. I let it continue for almost a full minute before raising my hand. They fell silent, the last echoes ringing in the air as I spoke again.

"The second option, should you decide that you don't want to be a Citizen of the Empire," I paused, looking around the room. "…is exile.

"You can leave the city. I'll permit you to take as much of your property with you as you can carry in your own two hands, but no more. All else you own will be taken by the Empire as back taxes owed for your protection."

"What protection!" the fat man sputtered. "We've never even seen you before!"

"You've seen the Legion, though," I snapped. "You've watched them leave day after day, returning bloodied and with empty places in their formation as more and more fell, so that you could sit safe and warm, feeding on the remnants of the Empire." I shook my head in disgust.

"Let me be clear to all of you. Today marks an end to the way things were and a new beginning. Your choices are to take the opportunities that are offered and gain massively, to fight me on this and die, like *she* did," I said, gesturing toward the slab of cold flesh that was already attracting flies. "Or to leave." I shot them all a cold smile as I looked around.

"I would prefer you all stayed. You have an opportunity here, one that, should you make the most of it, could see you rising into the realms of true nobility, claiming ranks in the ruling senate that advises me and becoming a member of my council, or a war leader.

"You could become a merchant prince, cornering the market on certain goods, or an engineer creating the next generation of weapons and ships, based on the secrets waiting even now in the soon to be salvaged wrecks of the Sunken City and her sisters. You could be selected to rule other cities in my name.

"Or you can try to rip me off." I stared daggers at the three groups who had continued to talk when I'd arrived. Some looked embarrassed and ashamed, while others looked defiant.

"Some of you have already crossed the line in many ways, as far as I'm concerned. You were corrupt and bartered favors in Rewn's court, including making decisions for him that he knew nothing about!"

A few of those who were the most richly dressed flinched and stared at me, as though trying to make sure of what I knew.

"Others decided to sell invites, including others in meetings that they *had no business being in!*" I stated coldly, glaring at both Fyre and Eberhardt before going on.

"That is a detail for another time, however. As of now, there is one decision for all of you to make. You can thank those who invited you here today for the opportunity to make your position clear immediately, rather than having too much time to think about it. You can choose to swear the Oaths to me and the Empire now, or you can choose to be exiled."

With that, I turned and sat on the throne as the Legion around me separated, no longer standing in an arrow formation at the base of the dais. Instead, they spread out to form a line, weapons drawn, and making it very clear they were ready to attack, should the need arise.

"The first ten of you may step forward, and I will administer the Oath..." Oracle called out, her voice ringing and clear. I looked at her, really looked at her, for the first time since leaving the keep, realizing that I'd been so consumed with the meeting and discussing magic with Mal, that I'd missed her changing.

She stood tall and beautiful, wearing a long, silver dress that looked appropriately regal. Her hair was as dark as a raven's wing, her skin a healthy golden tan, and her green eyes and red lips made me smile as she shot me a wink.

Where I still wore my gore-covered armor, she looked like a queen of legend, and I couldn't help but wonder if I would be better off sticking to hitting people and leaving her to deal with the diplomacy.

The fat fool stepped forwards, holding up one hand and ordering the others nearby to step back as he opened his mouth, glaring at me.

"I don't know what right you think you have to request these changes, but I *assure* you…"

"Conquest." I snapped. "I make these *demands*, not requests, by the right of conquest."

"Well, I have hundreds of soldiers, and unless you wish to face them in battle, you'll…"

"Where?" I asked flatly.

"What?" He snarled, indignant at being cut off again.

"Where are your troops?" I asked. "Your soldiers? I saw none of them this morning when I fought that thing in the streets of the city."

"So you say, but for all we know, you found it dead and cut off its head years ago, storing it in a holding container, ready for just this opportunity, and now…"

"Fyre!" I called. "You were there this morning, hurling magic at the Drow. Tell them what you saw."

There was a pause as Fyre watched me, before she curtsied, then stepped forward and turned to face the room.

"The High Lord beat the SporeMother, a creature of nightmares, to the ground with a rod the length of my forearm and his bare hands. The cracked skull you see there is from his gauntlets. I swear upon my life and my magic that this is the truth as I saw it," she said formally, before curtsying to me again and stepping back to her place in the crowd.

Once she was done, I pulled the gauntlets out of my bag of holding where I'd dropped them earlier and tossed them onto the floor with a clatter where everyone could see the broken and bent metal.

"This is your one chance, fat man," I said to the chubby noble before me who was now drenched in sweat, makeup irrevocably ruined. "Support me or be exiled, and decide quickly."

He eyed me for long seconds before straightening and shaking his head in negation.

"I refuse! I shall be no slave to you!" he declared.

I shrugged, gesturing to Grizz, who stepped forward, grabbing him by the scruff of the neck and dragging him to one side.

"That's fine by me. As rich as you were, I'd imagine you'll probably be able to fund a lot of the war effort alone," I said uncaring, dismissing him. "Next!" I bellowed, and Fyre stepped forward, Eberhardt stepping up as well. They strode toward the dais, eight others following, several of whom were from the fat man's own group, which made him stare before he attempted to order them back into their places. Fyre and Eberhardt had already sworn, but I understood the ceremonial gesture and appreciated it.

"Thank you for your willingness to serve the Empire," I said to them formally, and Oracle pushed the Oath to them.

"I swear to obey High Lord Jax and those he places over me; I will serve to the best of my ability, speak no lie to him when commanded otherwise, and treat all other citizens as family.

I will work for the greater good, being a shield to those who need it, a sword for those who deserve it, and a warden to the night.

I will stand with my family, helping one another to reach the light, until the hour of my death or my Lord releases me from my oath."

"Lastly, I will not be a dick!"

"I, High Lord Jax, do swear to protect and lead you, to be the shield that protects you and yours from the darkness, and the sword that avenges that which cannot be saved. As the Tower grows in strength, so shall you," I replied, feeling the drain of my mana pool streaming through me, to bind these people to myself, swiftly followed by Oracle pushing out the original Oath of Imperial Citizenship.

"I swear upon pain of death, to faithfully execute all that the Emperor decrees. I swear upon my soul that I shall stand for the Empire when it calls. I shall be strong when the weak need me, generous when the poor are at hand, and merciless when my fellow citizens are threatened. I shall worship the Gods of my fathers, respect my elders, and raise up my children to stand tall.

I am an Imperial Citizen. I claim the right to call upon the Legion in my hour of need, to hold those that wrong me to justice, and to be avenged if I cannot be saved."

I gestured to the right, where they waited, watching as others stepped up to take their place.

The ceremony took another hour. As each group was led forward, and they swore the Oath, I would thank them and direct them aside, then wait for my mana to recover. The drain on my mana wasn't excessive, now that I was used to this, but a few minutes here and there meant that I was merely tired by the end of the line, rather than being utterly buggered, as I would have been before.

All but eleven of those gathered had sworn, and eleven out of three hundred and forty-four was fine by me. I suspected that, had I taken the next step immediately upon the fat man refusing to take the Oath, I would have lost only him, but I had used the opportunity to clear out the other arseholes in the crowd. Unsurprisingly, all eleven were decked out in gold and jewels and were watching the events unfolding before them, looking amused.

"Well, High Lord?" the fat man demanded, smirking. "You must know that between us we represent more than half of the power of the city!"

"Well, fat man, that just means that there's a fuck load of space for others to fill, doesn't it?" I retorted, smiling coldly.

I used my ability and brought up his name and those of the men and women around him, reflecting that the one good thing I could say about Narkolt was, unlike Himnel, speciesism wasn't a thing. Out of the eleven, only four were human. There were also three Elves, three cat people of various races, and a single Minotaur.

"How dare you cast a spell at me!" the fucker gasped as one of his rings glowed a bright blue. I grinned at him.

"It was Examination, as you damn well know. I needed to know your true name. After all, calling you fat man wouldn't work for this, now would it, Bescarina Enanimon?" I said, carefully enunciating his name before taking a deep breath and doing what I'd been looking forward to since I'd met the fuck.

Attention, Citizens of the Territory of Dravith!

Lord Jax, Imperial Scion, High Lord of Dravith, Master of the Great Tower and Narkolt, today and effective immediately, revokes the title of Lord Bescarina Enanimon, stripping him of all titles and possessions and declares him exiled.

Let no citizen offer the criminal Enanimon succor, lest their titles be stripped from them and their lives declared forfeit.

All Hail High Lord Jax of Dravith!

There was a long moment of silence before the bastard wailed in denial, shaking his head in horror, his face turning grey and hands shaking.

"Grizz, take a detachment of the Legion and a hundred of the elite guards under Captain Eberhardt to the exile's property after this. His staff, guards, and family are to be taken into custody. They will be released once they swear loyalty. Otherwise, they join him as an exile, with only the possessions they can carry with their own two hands…And no, they can't carry bags of holding."

"Turn them out of the city gates at sunset?" Grizz asked, clearly enjoying how brutal I was with this. I nodded firmly, ignoring the sudden clamoring by the others in the group to change their minds.

One-by-one, I exiled them, and for each I gave orders for the guard, led by a legionnaire I trusted, to take their staff, employees, family, and soldiers under their control, holding them under armed guard, before bringing them to me.

I finished the audience with the crowd by thanking them for accepting me so graciously, which was complete bullshit, but seemed like the kind of thing I should say. I gave some vague hints about redistributing the wealth of the assholes I'd just stripped of power, then I sent them all on their way before gathering up my escort and following Grizz and his team.

I met with the family of the now former lord Enanimon and his staff, soldiers, and employees, beginning all over again with a new speech and a simple offer for his heir to assume his place with a fifty percent tax to the Empire, or to be exiled with him.

All in all, by the end of the day, I was beat and desperate for a shower, sleep, and a little sexy time, not necessarily in that order.

The hour that Oracle spent working on my left knee, bringing it, oh so slowly up to the same level as my right seemed like an insane waste of time, as I considered all we could be doing in that hour. But as she worked, I listened to details about the city and studied.

When Oracle finally agreed that she had done all she could for the day, I swept her up in my arms and carried her off to bed, too damn tired to even bang her brains out.

CHAPTER THIRTY-NINE

The next two days followed the same pattern, as Oracle spent every hour that she wasn't teaching our people magic working on me, and not in the way either of us wanted.

We agreed that rebuilding and perfecting my body was the best use for the time, though, especially considering the possibilities that the fight with the SporeMother had made clear. My side of those hours was spent in various meetings, most of which were far less explosive than the first one. And the groups were much more polite than the first, at least to my face.

I swore in the remaining minor nobility, assuring them that if they behaved and essentially played nice with the other kids, sharing their crayons and eating all their dinner, then they'd be allowed to play still. I even made a gesture of goodwill to two who showed respect, and that Flux's spies had already identified as being both honorable and useful, making them official emissaries of the Imperial Court, sending them out to the surrounding towns and villages to summon their leadership to the city to take the Oaths.

In Amon's day, he'd had specialists who could administer the Oath in his name. He had, through the magic of the Great Towers and all the various rights and abilities he had as Emperor, carried out annual Oath swearings across the entire Empire.

Millions, if not billions of people all swore simultaneously. Through local Imperial forces, the Great Towers, and the various magical facilities of the Empire, he could manage to do it all at the same time. I was struggling with doing more than a few thousand a day, and Narkolt had a population of close to ninety thousand.

In the process of meeting and evaluating the locals, as well as having them swear to me, I took command of the majority of the private garrisons around the city, many of which accepted it with good grace. The fact that we were officially in a war likely helped with that. The few dozen in each force who were willing to swear to me but not serve in the army were marked down and set free to seek other employment.

That list was kept just in case, as I damn well knew there were ways around the Oaths by now.

The city guard was ordered to start recruiting, as was the army, with the guard expected to grow from less than two thousand to nearly four, as additional responsibilities were being added to their roster, while the army needed to expand dramatically.

The army had sat at just over four thousand members for well over a century. With the war, there'd been an attempt to grow it, but beyond another fifty or so joining, that was it.

As part of the new rules I instituted, a member of the army was not only paid a respectable wage, starting at three silvers, a massive difference from the previous wage they had been earning of a few coppers a week, but they also received regular meals as part of the deal.

It seemed obvious to me, but one of the biggest issues that people had, considering most of the army was usually made up of the very poor, was that here they couldn't afford to join.

The food had been abysmal, the pay was worse. They had expected those who joined up to maintain and provide their own weapons and gear and to be thankful for the opportunity to die for their betters.

I had almost summarily beheaded the dozen highest-ranking officers when I attended a meeting and found them feasting on roast boar stuffed with quail, while their soldiers were on the edge of starvation. I also discovered that the wages the city paid to these twelve men was the equivalent of a third of the army's total costs, with another half of the entire budget going to the elites, meaning that only a tiny portion actually went to the majority.

The entire group was given the choice between the army, with their rank reduced to sergeant, or exile.

Most of those who chose the army lasted less than a day, with one of them turning up a mere twenty minutes after the beginning of training nailed to the underside of a cart that was on its way out of the city…apparently by his own troops.

I'd been about to order them to be dealt with harshly, needing to maintain discipline, until I found out what he had demanded of the troops. After hearing what he had done, I had him healed instead and thrown out of the city, much to the cheering of the soldiers.

Those who had been exiled, and many of the increasingly discontented elite left at the first chance. Most were headed for Himnel to join the war against me, apart from a small group who were attempting to gather a resistance to my rule and were planning on going to one of their former country mansions.

I was informed of this by a grinning Mal, so, entirely for shits and giggles, I named him Earl of Sarat, in place of the fat fuck, Enanimon. As it turned out, the former Lord of Sarat only had one son, a little bastard named Joshua, who I'd met on the Prax.

Once Mal had been declared Earl of Sarat, he'd taken his ship and flown straight for the county home of the former lord, beating him and his bedraggled followers there by less than an hour.

He then dragged the former noble, who was by now much thinner, to the edge of his lands and literally kicked him off into the river, where he promptly drowned. The rest of the group was either arrested or given a warning and pointed to the nearest neutral territory, depending on how rabid they were. Mal took some personal time and introduced Alyssa to the new reality of being his woman, as well as a member of the nobility, with all the perks that came with it.

She had apparently given him a beating with the first thing that came to hand and told him that she was her own woman. If he ever wanted to play the kind of games he'd enjoyed with her before, it'd take some serious effort on his part in public. I stayed out of it, laughing my arse off, and deliberately kept doing things like sending her flowers from an anonymous admirer, knowing it'd make Mal furious.

The prison was full when I arrived and took control of the city. But after Thomas went through it with an insane level of dedication to duty, with Oracle teaching him how to get the prisoners to swear an Oath to speak only the truth, the prison was almost emptied in three days, giving me another bloody prompt.

Quest: Return the Rule of Law, Bring Freedom to the Enslaved, and Peace to the Unquiet Dead IV

Punish Breakers of Imperial Law: 1042/500

Free Unjustly Imprisoned Citizens: 362/500

Grant Uneasy Revenants their Eternal Rest: 1,037/500

Reward: 2,500,000xp, Access to Fifth Tier of Evolving Quest

Over a hundred inmates were offered the option of service instead of incarceration and were folded into the new army when they agreed. Of the eight hundred or so that remained, two hundred and seventeen were there for murder and rape or other capital offenses. They were decapitated and essentially harvested for experience, while all the others were found to either be innocent or to have been arrested for such minor offences that Thomas ordered them released.

One boy aged seven, the son of a stableman, had been caught sitting on a noble's horse and was sentenced to life in prison as an example.

That boy, now a young man of fifteen, was freed, and Thomas walked him home personally, delivering him to his sobbing mother at her door. He'd left enough gold as an official apology that they'd never have to work again.

Camps were set up, ready to begin training both the new and old troops. The preexisting army contained just over four thousand soldiers, and with the new recruits, who numbered almost seven thousand when I capped it, that brought the army up to around eleven thousand troops.

They were split into eleven maniples, with the veterans spread out from the original four thousand to help the others, as they all began again from scratch.

All ranks were declared provisional, and the chance to rise quickly was made obvious, along with examples of those who tried to bribe their way into such slots.

The camps were exceedingly basic and badly cramped, having been set up in less than a day, with the army applicants being made to swear the Oaths, then accepted, provided they weren't wanted criminals.

One of the first jobs for the fresh recruits was to make their new homes and set up the camp, including digging a full perimeter trench and using the freed earth to make a raised rampart and wall.

Plans were made over meals, using information from both Thomas and my own memories of our history lessons, and from the Legion's current field fortifications.

The few legionnaires with specialized magical abilities, such as our resident elven Stone Singer, aided the army, as did half a dozen people from the city, each of whom were seemingly stunned when the promised pay for their help was actually given out.

The majority of the nobles' vaults were raided, occasionally with their permission, but more often without. Any and all magical artifacts, spellbooks, skillbooks , and memory crystals were claimed for the Empire and basic compensation was promised, although any shops that had books and magical gear were paid a fair market price upfront for them.

It took less time than I thought it would for the first attack to come from Himnel. It arrived on the morning of the third day, as a trio of airships were spotted flying from the city, headed out to sea.

Four hours later, they were back, high in the sky and clearly thinking they were stealthy…somehow.

I had ordered the launch of the five Narkolt fast attack cruisers as soon as the three Himnel ships had set off. In addition, I added my own two cruisers to the group, with a total of forty legionnaires spread out aboard the ships, all capable of Magic Missile.

I stood with a few of the others on the battlements of the keep, watching out to sea, before snorting in disgust and going inside, utterly unimpressed.

They intercepted the incoming ships a mile or so out to sea to ensure the city was safe, then basically waited for them. The Himnel ships dove towards my own, flying as fast as they could, and fired their main cannons again and again until the charges were depleted…missing repeatedly.

At that point, my seven ships, who'd had strict orders to fire the cannons as a last resort only, surrounded them, and the legionnaires bombarded the three ships with a barrage of a hundred Magic Missiles each.

By the third barrage, both surviving ships were smoking, the decks were covered with the dead and wounded, and they couldn't surrender fast enough. Before being guided down to the shipyard, the Alkyon boarded them and made damn sure that the ships landed nicely, and nobody tried to fire the cannons again. Amaat proudly declared his wing had pacified the ships crews, while they were at it.

The surviving ones, anyway.

By the time our ships arrived from the Tower, I was both exhausted and frazzled, having expected them at least a full day earlier. As a result, when they landed with six ships stuffed to bursting with all but the skeleton force of the Legion, who'd stayed at the Tower to protect it, I met them with an immense feeling of relief.

The ships took turns landing in the killzone around the original keep, offloading their passengers then moving to the shipyard or out to land near the army camp once the shipyard was full. One of the first people to disembark was Romanus himself, swiftly followed by Restun and the rest of the training cadre.

"My Lord Jax, High Lord of the Continent of Dravith and Master of Narkolt!" Romanus said respectfully, coming to attention and slamming his fist to his chest.

"Romanus, good to see you, man!" I grinned at him and the others. "I see you emptied the Tower?" I asked, only half-joking, as I gestured to the ships landing and lifting off. The air was filled with a mix of shouts as legionnaires disembarked and Optios barked orders, many of them turning the air blue as one legionnaire or another ran with their gear.

"When we got your message, it seemed prudent. Between the golems and the overall capabilities of the Great Tower, not to mention the distance between the Tower and Himnel, I judged the risk to be worth it. Any ships that depart Himnel to assault the Tower will be both obvious to us and liable to interception, plus they would leave the city in a weakened state which will make their defeat easier," Romanus said. "Cai and the others are taking a tour of the city from the air, trying to be as prepared as possible, and have made plans on the way over."

"Well, that's going to be seriously useful," I smiled at him. "Where's Rewn, though?" I asked, slightly confused by the city lord's absence. "I thought he'd have been one of the first off the ships."

"He would have been, but unfortunately, he and several of his harem appear to have eaten some bad shellfish. Coincidentally, this occurred right after Carmen asked if it would be best if he was delayed by a day or two. Nerin healed them the morning we set off but recommended that he wait a few days to clean the cabin out fully, as the flight would have been…unpleasant…otherwise."

"I *like* Carmen," I declared, grinning at Romanus.

"Yes, so do I. She's always helpful in little ways."

"No Oren?" I asked, and Romanus laughed.

"He's at the shipyard. He made us drop him off there. Between us, I think he's searching for a bigger warship to be his flagship."

I snorted and shook my head, believing that theory completely. "Okay then, it's great to see you all. Let's take this inside, and we can have this conversation in the keep. It's become my interim home away from home, now that the spiders are gone."

"Spiders?" Jon asked, and I grinned at the look on his face.

"Yeah, the Drow had a Drider nest set up inside the keep. It was breeding them by the thousands, I think. It's okay though, turns out there's now an easy way to remove both spiders and spies from any location we decide to use."

"Oh?" Jon asked with a hopeful expression.

"I have a spell that creates a circle around me which burns the shit out of anything that's not allied to me. Oracle spent nearly two days working on it, so we now have a new and seriously nasty version of it, thanks to the knowledge she has access to, and the fact that the keep has begun its repairs. Using the mana collectors that power the keep's systems instead of just my own mana, we cast Frostfire Circle of Cleansing twice a day at random times. When we cast it, it creates a circle around the keep, and anyone who isn't sworn to me inside the circle gets burned to shit. The first time I used it, we found seventeen spies. All but one worked for the various noble houses and rich merchants in the city, and that last one was a spy from Himnel."

"And what did you do with the spies?" Restun asked, getting a chuckle from Flux.

"We turned them," Flux replied dryly. "We gave them the option of joining us and feeding back what we wanted to their employer, or being outed as spies to the city at large then locked up in the prison. The combination of losing their anonymity, the advantage that Jax broke all their Oaths as he became the Lord of Narkolt, and the minor detail that they were burned and frozen to hell all at once really helped to focus their minds."

"So wait, you turned ALL of the spies?" Restun asked. "Are you sure they actually turned?"

"Are they playing games, you mean?" Flux asked. "That was a concern at first. That's the reason why, when we did this yesterday, we not only had the spies swear a more specific Oath, one that was very carefully worded, and ask them for the truth of their intentions, but we also explained our own plans for them moving forward.

"We turned all but two, one of whom refused any Oath and is in the jail now. Most of them were both underpaid and shunned outside of their own small circles, but as Covert Imperial Agents, they not only get paid well, but they'll be getting some very specific training, and a lot of it will be magical."

"The offered magical training on top of being valued and respected convinced the majority, I take it?" Lucian asked.

"It did, as Flux said. Two chose not to join us. The one who isn't in prison, well…it turns out that taking the new Oath when you're secretly plotting to kill the person you swear to, is a very, VERY bad idea," I said with a wince.

"How messy?" Romanus asked, grinning.

"Fairly. I know the cleaning staff aren't happy with me and we had to relocate Flux's office, put it that way." I shrugged and continued to lead the way up to the throne room.

It had been converted into a full-on command center filled with desks, chairs, and cots spread out around the room for those who needed to get some sleep but didn't want to take the time to travel to a room in one of the surrounding palace buildings. The five rooms inside the keep had all been claimed by my team and, although most were shared, Oracle had put her foot down and insisted that our room was to be private before showing me exactly why.

"How many spies in total have you caught?" Restun asked Flux as we climbed the spiral staircase.

"Twenty-eight," Flux said with his species' version of a chuckle, the low *thrum* echoing up the stairwell.

"Twenty-eight, and only two of them failed to join you? That's very impressive…or lucky," Romanus said dubiously.

"That's what I thought," I said. "Honestly, I'm fully expecting that there's still some way around it, but I'm going to leave this one with Flux. We've done all we can with the stick, now it's time for a little honey."

"Honey?" Flux called up, as I exited the stairwell, but before I could respond, Thomas did it for me.

"Yes, dear?" he called, grinning at me.

"What?" Flux asked, highly confused, as Thomas and I laughed.

"Sorry, Flux," I apologized. "Old joke."

"I see. Perhaps you'll save the explanation, as there have been so many already that I can't keep track." Flux sighed.

"Sure thing," I said, leading the way to a group of chairs set against a wall. I sat in one, smiling around as Lydia, Thomas, and Oracle joined us.

"Oh, it's good to see you all!" Oracle said, smiling as she flew over, landing on a seat I pulled out for her and shifting to full size as she did so.

"It's good to see you too, Lady Wisp," Romanus replied. "Jax was telling us about your new anti-spider and spy spell?"

"It worked better than I hoped," she said, turning to Lydia and sighing heavily. "It was as we thought; Lindon was in the wall between our quarters."

"Ah'll deal with tha' arsehole personally," Lydia growled, before sitting back and folding her arms, her face even grimmer than usual.

"What's this?" I asked, confused.

"One of the spies, Lindon, was hiding behind a false wall between our room, Lydia and Yen's, and…"

"An' tha Bathin' Room," Lydia growled. "'E was there fer a full day, an' appears te 'ave been watchin' us bathin', as well as other things."

"Okay, wasn't Lindon the one who…"

"T' one who refused te take tha Oath at all and be in jail," Lydia confirmed. "Aye, tha's tha one."

"Well, he won't take the Oath, and he's not one of our people, so, since he refuses to tell us anything, have fun. If he's not with us, and he won't answer any questions, then he's against us, and there's no Geneva Convention here. If the fucker was watching you ladies bathing, then I say you get to question him all you like. If he decides not to answer the questions before he dies, that's his problem," I stated, my cold indifference to assholes clear to those around me.

"What are your plans for the war?" Romanus asked into the silence, and I nodded my thanks to him.

"The Army of Narkolt is apparently on about the same level as the Army of Himnel in that there's a couple of dozen elites, all level forty and higher, who are paid a horrific amount to do fuck all except intimidate others, and the other ninety percent are both under-leveled and under-trained."

"Don't forget under-equipped, under-paid, and under-fed," Thomas interjected.

"That, too," I agreed with a grunt. "Against the Himnel army, they'd probably do fine, and against the fodder class of the Dark Legion, they'd win, provided they outnumbered them a bit."

"By about fifty percent," Thomas said. "The Dark Legion fodder squads are still wearing better armor and have more training. Need a decent numerical advantage to offset that."

"Yeah, but one-on-one, they're not far off equals. The problem comes from the Dark Legion elites, or the 'true' Dark Legion," I said, looking around. "Thomas, how many elites are there?"

"There's about eight hundred of the Dark Legion that I'd class as true legionnaires," Thomas said, sitting upright. "The elites I'll come to in a minute, but for the average dark legionnaire, you're looking at somewhere between level fifteen and thirty-five, with the true elites beyond that. Those eight hundred are all well-equipped, well-trained, and there's at least one magic user in each squad, sometimes two or three, but usually with very limited spells. The elites, though, are a separate breed entirely. They are officially referred to as the Blessed, Chosen, or as 'those fucking nutters' by most of us, until I joined their ranks anyway."

Thomas paused, getting to his feet and shifting uncomfortably, as he thought through what he was trying to say.

"I had damage to my mana channels, damage the dark priests couldn't or wouldn't fix. I was told that the only way I could regain my mana-based abilities and spells that I'd spent five damn years acquiring, was to take the next step and become one of the Blessed."

Thomas rubbed the back of his neck and stared into the past, clearly thinking about the day he'd opened himself to the Death God. "The Blessed aren't just absolute animals, although, yeah, some really are. The process of becoming one of them involves your closest friends lowering you into a pool of some sort of black blood under the citadel.

"As part of the process, you have your arms slit from the elbow to the wrist, lengthways, and deep." He lifted his arms, showing the faint, puckered scars that were still visible, despite the healing spells he'd had cast at him since joining us.

"You bleed out into the pool, and the black blood of Nimon pours back into you. It joins with you, and it changes you. I had no idea I was a berserker, not until about a week later. I just knew that I'd been healed.

"Most of those who go through the process are just healed of their injuries, that's literally it, but you're somehow viewed by the priests as more trustworthy afterwards, and everyone else around you sees you as a fucking ticking timebomb. Those who *do* change do it in a variety of ways. Some are like me, or like I was, anyway." Thomas grunted, flexing his fist as he spoke.

"I became a dark berserker, insanely strong, but unhinged. It's a mix of three classes, as far as I could make out. The massive muscle growth of the juggernaut, the insanity and lack of empathy or fear of the berserker, and the sheer desire to hurt the enemy from the punisher. That seems to be the combination, as near as I could work out, and I know that the other variants are a mix of three as well.

"The majority seem to be either melee like me or assassination mixes, heavy on the stealth and murder. There's only one that I've heard of that was a magic-based hybrid, and it was literally only a rumor that there'd been one. The thing is, while all those who are Blessed have the capacity to develop these powers, or some mix of them. Most don't, and we were all thankful for that. There's something…wrong…with you after the blessing." Thomas shook his head as a few of the group started to ask him questions.

"No, you don't get it, and I don't really understand it completely, but people who've accepted the blessing go…bad, I guess is the best way to describe it. That little voice that tells you that you shouldn't do something, well that voice just goes away.

"Those who use the gifts often, well, they grow stronger at an insane rate, but they also tend to go fucking mental. At that point, the priesthood hunts them down and kills them, all the while praising what they were. Seriously, Nimon's Chosen are fucking insane," Thomas said with a wince.

"How many of the elites can change?" I asked.

"There's maybe two hundred elites all told, that's those who have the gift and can change, and those who don't have the gift, as far as I know, but are strong enough or skilled enough that I'd still rate them as a hell of a threat."

"So, even if we count the armies on both sides as canceling each other out, then there's still the issue of the Legion being outnumbered five to one or so…these numbers are after the fight in the forest, right?" I asked.

"Yeah, there were closer to two thousand before."

"Well, that's just fucking peachy," I muttered, sitting back and looking around the room. The only two involved in the conversation who didn't appear to be downhearted or even mildly concerned, were Restun and Lucian.

"You two seem remarkably confident," I commented, looking between the two of them.

"We'll win," Restun stated, much in the same way that another man might say "fire's hot" or "water's wet."

"And you have a plan for that?" I asked, getting a slight shake of his head, but I could not escape the faint smile and the way he watched me…like the bastard was waiting to hear the plan he knew I had.

"There were several Imperial facilities here, facilities that could aid our war effort," Lucian said slowly. "I'm not sure if they survived."

"They did, but not in any particularly usable state," I replied, smiling slightly. "If we can maintain the current situation and hold Himnel and the Dark Dickhead there, we could possibly repair the Imperial docks to a point that they're usable, or there might be a way to repair the armory."

"Armory?" Romanus asked, and Jon sat bolt upright, staring at me in shock.

"Yes, the city had three Imperial facilities, all of which are still there, even if they are severely damaged: the Imperial docks, the armory, and the Imperial manastone mine. The problem is one of logistics. First of all, the docks…" I said, getting up and moving across to the Control Center for the keep.

I pulled up the city map, which was a brilliant addition, and interfaced it with my own, showing the current layout, then a rough wire drawing that slowly grew brighter, as though lifting from beneath the surface.

"Okay people, as you can see, Narkolt is a weird ass shape at the best of times, but what you might not know, is that some of these areas aren't what they seem." I turned the map slightly to make it more visible for everyone.

Narkolt was a peculiar shape for a city, or at least it was when you looked at the way it was laid out *now*.

The city itself was roughly the shape of an iconic starship, squared off at the rear with a pair of legs on the right, a narrow river running through the middle and out into the bay, with the bay being where it started to get weird fast.

Where most things here, especially when it was to do with the land, were rugged and flowed naturally, the rocky outcroppings that led out into the bay were anything but natural.

There were two sections, similar to the cutting blades of a pair of scissors extending out into the bay, with the lower leg being squared off, shorter, and fatter, and the upper leg being longer and thinner.

The two legs extended out into the water and were clearly, from both the map and knowing that such a thing had once existed, part of the Imperial docks. They had once been massive, but now a tiny section of the original stonework was all that remained, and the entire mass had been overrun by housing, shops, and warehouses that, when I looked the map over, could never have been intended as part of the original design.

There were sections of towers, clearly intended as ancient defenses, but houses and shops had been built around them, obscuring the sightlines from the archer's slits and more.

I gestured to the map, drawing my finger along the glowing lines that led down the first leg to the center where a collection of nobles' mansions were clear, and up the other, before shaking my head in amazement.

"This is the original outline of the Imperial docks. Unlike the Great Tower, these docks were built rock by rock and weren't entirely magical, so we can't simply provide them with a fuck ton of mana and let them take care of themselves. Some sections of the original structure remain, so they can be rebuilt by the golems, and the docks themselves can be selectively repaired. That's a job for the future, though, as, while it'd be great to have massive shiny fucking docks ready for trade and all that, we've got nobody to trade with, really, and there's a war on."

I smiled and gestured to a peculiarly shaped area of some ornamental gardens that were hidden away in a section of the city filled with large mansions and expansive parks. As I did, I slowly drew an outline on the map, including the roads that led up to and away from the site, marking a huge section of land.

"No, the section we really need to be looking at is this…the ancient Imperial armory." As soon as I said those words, the focus on the map went from curious and attentive to laser-like, and I couldn't help it as I started to grin.

"The Imperial armory is damaged, hell, most of it's been built over, so the lower sections are all that's left, as near as we can tell, and they're buried deep. That's why I wanted the golems here, and why I'm going to need to send at least two ships to the production facility to strip it of all the resources we need, as well as every damn golem that isn't essential, because…"

I paused for dramatic effect before tapping my finger in the middle of the ruined structure.

"Some of these facilities still exist. To be exact, twelve percent of the original facilities still exist, according to the keep interface. Considering that the original facilities will be where things like the airship cannons we're struggling to make will have come from originally, we need to uncover them, repair the facilities, and start production as fast as possible!"

"What kind of facilities are down there?" Lucian asked. "I don't mean to rain on your parade, but…"

"Piss in my cereal," I replied with a nod. "I know what you mean, Lucian, where I come from, it's 'piss in my cereal,' but I understand. The truth is, we have no idea what's down there.

"For all I know, the twelve percent of the original facility that still exists could be the foundations, or it could the most powerful weapons facilities they ever produced. We have no way of knowing, but I damn well know that the risk is worth it." I sighed and sat back in the control chair.

"We're at war," I said after a long minute. "We're outnumbered in terms of skilled warriors, and we're facing a God who can bless His troops to make them far harder to kill than we are, while our own divine help is…not as strong. Their city was already being geared up for war, rather than this one, which seems to have been paying lip service to the war effort, as far as I can tell.

"That's fine, though, because we've got some massive advantages as well. We just need to ensure we've got the time to make them work for us." I swiped the control center map aside. I had spent many hours using it recently, and, as a result, I'd found a few useful facilities.

I pulled up a more detailed map of the city, populated by thousands upon thousands of random dots of every color, from a handful of tiny reds to tens of thousands of grey, a few thousand of both green and blue and with more mixed in all over.

"This is the city," I said. "The grey dots are people who haven't sworn to the Empire; they're basically just rocking on with their lives. The green ones are now Imperial citizens, they were just those who were loyal before, but it changed when we started giving out the Oath, and the blue are the Legion or allied forces, such as the guard and the army. As to the other colors, well, I think I'm the purple, and the rest, I have no fucking idea yet, beyond the red, which are enemies."

"Enemies?" Romanus asked quickly, leaning forward to look closer.

"Minor ones I think, judging from the severity. When we first took the city, there were two groups of reds, both turned out to be Drow, and they were such a bright red that it practically burned my damn eyes out. These are minor blips in comparison, so I'm guessing they're criminals, but either way, the guard are on their way to each of these locations already, having been given their orders this morning."

"I can see this being very useful," Lucian said.

I grinned at him.

"Oh hell yes, especially since this is an Imperial Control Center, so it has certain safeguards built in that I didn't know about at first. Basically, the map and several other low-level facilities are available to whoever claims it, but to have access to the entire thing, specifically this map of individuals and the greater map which I'll show you next, you need to be a member of the Imperial nobility."

"Interesting," Lucian said, looking it over.

"It is, isn't it! It means that, where I was panicking and thinking that when we assault Himnel, they'll be able to see us coming and easily command their forces through it, they won't. It took me wondering about when we raided Himnel to find the rules for access, as I should have been glowing a sodding red, bright enough for anyone to see from orbit, since I was in a state of declared war with Himnel. Instead, nobody even knew we were there."

"It's another Imperial site," Romanus said with twisted smile.

"Damn right it is. I don't know what's in Himnel, beyond the single facility that we already claimed, but that's fine, because we're damn well going to take the city, and we'll find out then!"

I scrolled the view out and brought the entire city into view, then continued zooming out, showing the whole continent.

The majority of it was in greyscale, with fuzzy details showing little beyond outlines that had clearly been transposed from my own map, but the areas we'd claimed showed in a variety of subtle colors. In various locations on the map were yellow dots, dots that made me smile as I tapped on them.

"These are the golems we have control over," I said, gesturing to the main clusters. "This is the production facility in the mountains, and this…" I shifted the map to show the Tower. "This is the Great Tower, and yeah, this is where we have the majority of the golems, but they're mainly servitors and construction class. Between those, we've gotten up and running, thanks to looting the various sites, and those from the production center, we've got thirty golems I think we can free up, but they're going to have to be collected from a few places."

I tapped on a set of glowing dots near to the Tower. "These are the first set of freshly produced golems from the Himnel facility. They're simple class. Hell, I'd forgotten about ordering that they be built, as I've been busy, but they're right behind a pair of mining golems. The first looks to have been drilling its way across for days before the second caught up, and I'd guess that a week or so after that, the squad caught up to them. The control towers mean that Heph will be able to command them once they get a little closer, since they're just outside his range now."

"Why the difference in colors, if I might ask?" Lucian said, making me smile at his formality.

"Seriously Lucian, you're one of my advisors now. I don't really do well with formality, so just ask whenever you have a question," I told him. "As to why, well, the various sections are in colors that represent the control we have over them. This one…" I tapped the Tower and its surrounding territory flashed in response to my gesture. "…has green because we have full control over it. This next section is blue, because the Arbuton has control over it, but he's allied to us. The other sections here…" I indicated a few of the waystations and their connected territories.

"…these are green, but lighter in color because, while we've claimed them, the control towers in some aren't fully operational yet. Augustus is clearly still moving from one to another, or they haven't finished the alterations. Once that's done, Heph will be able to assume control over all the golems and start gathering them. For now, though, the airships will have to make some trips."

"What are your intentions for the golems?" Romanus asked.

"Frankly, Romanus, I'm going to do what I didn't want to do, and I'm going to use them in war," I said, looking around the group. "The Legion are the best fighting force in the realm, and I've confidence in them going toe-to-toe with anyone else, including the Dark Legion.

"Hell, even if we were outnumbered by double, I'd still believe we could do it. But they outnumber the Legion by closer to ten times, and that's not including their magical abilities and defenses. Remember, we're going to be assaulting the damn city of Himnel, their walls alone will take a heavy toll, and while we could make a lightning assault with the airships, they also have them. As far as I can tell, we're left with three choices.

"First, we sue for peace and use that time to get our forces up to scratch before attacking them. That sucks because they'll be doing the exact same, and it'd give the Dark Wanker time to make more of his elites, so that's a fuck no from me," I declared, getting a chorus of agreement.

"Second, we assault them unprepared, relying on sheer fucking balls, luck, and throwing everything at them, including airships bombarding from the air. Then we send the golems to take the walls down and get us inside. We fight from house to house and street to street through the city to the palace, take that, and claim control of the command center.

"At that point, we can use its facilities to mop up the survivors of the Dark Legion and that arse Barabarattas's forces." I paused and looked around, seeing the carefully neutral expressions on their faces, before I snorted and shook my head.

"Fuck's sake people, I'm not that stupid. If we did that, we'd be lucky to win at all, let alone with acceptable losses. We'd have nobody to keep things together, and I'd give us a week before we'd be murdered in our fucking sleep." I grunted as relief and agreement washed over every face.

"That leaves us with option three, as far as I can tell, but if any of you have a better plan, speak up. Option three is that we contain them as best we can, for as long as we can, hopefully for at least a few months. We use our greater number of airships to keep theirs close to the city, and attack and harry them when they leave the walls.

"If we stop their ships getting in, besiege them, and starve the city, we can weaken them as much as possible, while we train our armies and build more golems. When the time is right, we use our new airship weapons and attack, taking their ships down first.

"Once they're gone, we split the airships, sending half to attack the Dark Arsehole's citadel, with the golems forming a perimeter around it. While they contain the Dark Legion, and our army holds the Himnel troops off, the Legion can fly in on the other half of the airships and assault the palace directly. Once the city falls, we mop up any resistance and use the airship weapons to reduce the citadel to fucking rubble, burying the Dark Legion inside."

"They won't just stay inside and let you bombard them," Thomas pointed out.

I grinned. "I didn't think they would, but if we can get another fifty or so golems built, they can attack us all they like, and the golems will slaughter them in their hundreds before falling. At that point, the Legion gets to mop up the rest, with the army backing us up," I suggested, my grin widening.

"It sounds good," Romanus said. "but..."

"But no plan survives contact with the enemy," I replied. "I know it won't go this easy, but our choices are crap, mate. Yes, there's the Smuggler's Path and probably another somewhere, but..."

"Perhaps a few small alterations to the plan, then, to make the most of our new capabilities?" Romanus suggested.

"Feel free, mate." I said, dearly hoping he had some wonderful plan up his sleeve.

"Well, you've mentioned the mining golems, but I've not seen them before. I assume they're large and mobile?" Romanus asked.

"Oh, yeah sorry, they're cylindrical. Great big drill on one end, and a multitude of arms around it. It basically drills into the rock and chews it all up, smelting the ore as it goes. It stores the ingots inside the inbuilt storage bin until it's full, at which point it just leaves the finished ingots behind itself like a trail of shit."

"Perfect, how tall are they?"

"Ummm, about two and a half meters, I think?"

"So more than tall enough for our forces to follow along in the tunnels then."

"Oh yeah, easily...shit," I said, seeing what he was getting at.

"Exactly," he said. "We use the army to keep their attention, marching out openly and the airships to contain them and force theirs to land. At this point, the Dark Legion will most likely bolster the Himnel army on the city walls and protect their citadel, splitting their forces.

"While they do this, the Legion will follow the mining golems underground. We drill through the ground underneath and bypass most of the walls and city. We come up in the palace, kill the criminal Barabarattas, and claim the city. You can then order the forces of the city to stand down.

"Not all will obey, but most will. When the city is lost, the Dark Legion will most likely retreat to their citadel, and we'll let them. We will then close the city to the Dark Legion and besiege the citadel.

"The Dark Legion will have the choice of either assaulting one of the cities or attacking us in the open field, where they'd be outnumbered, instead of us," Romanus suggested, smiling gently as he Demonstrated an experienced commander's skills compared to my own.

"What do we do with the Dark Legion?" I asked.

"They'll have been bloodied as they flee the walls. After all, we'll have the army out there. We'll give them orders to use ranged weapons and spells only, while the airships bombard them. That should thin their numbers and make sure they don't linger. Then, once they're in the citadel, we besiege them properly.

"We let no supplies in or out, starving them and weakening them by the day, while we continue to train and prepare, build more golems, and use the airships to bombard the citadel while the construction golems build us defenses around the perimeter of the siege.

"We force them to assault our walls, turning the advantage the defenders have against them, all the while giving our forces more practice with their magic."

"And the magic will be the force multiplier we need," I agreed.

"The traditional way to learn spells is by hundreds of hours of painstaking study, or by the very limited number of spellbooks that are produced by mages and scribes working in concert. The fact that you can teach so many spells to your forces, in such a short time, is a massive advantage, as are the golems. I know you don't trust them to fight alongside the Legion or army, and frankly, none of us really trust them either, but better that they take the losses than us." Romanus said, smiling.

"Definitely," I said, mutters of agreement rising from all around the group.

"Excellent. So, with that in mind, I suggest we dispatch spies to see what they can find out, while we train our forces. We need to see what the armory contains or can be made to produce. From what I remember, the army here was always underequipped, and the Legion could sorely do with spare gear," Romanus said, getting a smile and a nod from me.

"That's the plan, then, unless someone else has any ideas?" I offered and got a few shakes of heads, until Flux spoke up.

"I think assassins could be extremely useful as well, but that raises another set of issues. We have seven spies and assassins currently in training who I believe are far enough along that they could be trusted to do this, but…"

"But if we send assassins out, what's to stop them doing the same?" I muttered.

"Definitely. With us only having seven, and that includes Tang and Lio, we can't defend you and attack them at the same time. It's one or the other."

"Keep Tang close; he'll be enough to watch my back, but send a team and tell them to slaughter the Dark Legion and the priesthood at any opportunity, as well as any of the army leadership they can," I ordered after a few minutes thought. "This raises the question though…where the fuck is Bane?"

"I expected him back by now, from what you told us the Goddess Tamat said." Flux tilted his head. "But unless you wish to ask Her, we will have to wait."

"Well, I'll be speaking to Her soon regardless, but first things first. We've a plan for battle, and we need to get the city and our people in order as well. Romanus, Restun, Jon, I'm leaving the training and control of the army in your hands. Make them stronger, skilled, and deadly, and do anything and everything you can to improve them. I'll get the armory uncovered and will get you more equipment as quickly as I can."

Romanus stood and touched his fist to his chest in salute, the others following along a second later.

"Thank you all," I said. "Thomas, you're in charge of the guard. I know you've basically kicked their arse over the last few days, clearing out the prisons, and refilling them with the various parasites that you've found feeding on the city, so now you and Lucian are to take control of them and the judicial system.

"Get the laws reviewed, scrap any that are fucking ridiculous, and get the guard under control. I need them ready to deal with any civil shit and to defend the city as much as needed."

"You think they're going to be needed?" he asked.

I laughed. "Well, I doubt the nobility that I'm about to strip of their lands are going to be happy, put it that way," I said, grinning.

"Fuck man, are you just declaring war on the nobles, or what?" he asked, shaking his head.

"No, but they've been feeding on the Empire forever, claiming to uphold its laws, and maintaining things for the Imperial Throne, since that's the source of their right to tax the locals. They just haven't had to hand over the difference to the Empire for a while.

"Now, those debts have come due, and besides…the site that they built over was the Imperial armory, so it wasn't theirs to start with." I shrugged. "I'm just taking it back. On the upside, I'm planning on pulling them all in and letting them remember they declared their allegiance already. Then, I'll point out the back taxes due, and the fact that some of those taxes are to maintain forces in readiness for the Empire to call upon.

"It turns out, it's part of the Oath they take when they are accepted as the heads of their houses." I couldn't help but grin, thinking about when I had found out the Oaths that the head of each noble house swore were still the same as they had been in the days of the Empire.

Himnel had abandoned that side of things, but, as part of the more traditional way that Narkolt operated, they still swore allegiance to the Empire. All I needed to do was to make the point that they had already sworn to follow these rules, and, as they'd sworn to me as the Imperial Scion, I could order them to hand over anything I needed.

I'd already raided their strongrooms for magical artifacts, although I'd paid for some of them. While they weren't happy about it, if I was to actually pay what they were still expecting to be handed over, I'd bankrupt the treasury in one fell swoop. No, it was time to get that back in spades.

"You think that'll work?" Thomas asked, dubiously.

"I'm hoping so, but that's why I need the guard to be loyal and ready. They're the priority today. Get them gathered, and we'll get the new members sworn in."

"Well, the Legion are here now as well," Romanus said, shaking his head ruefully. "What are we going to do with regard to guarding you, though?"

"The city has elite guards who normally had the job of this kind of work, bodyguards and so on. As much as I would rather only have the Legion around me, we can't afford to show that level of distrust to people who have sworn to me. The elite guards will watch over the palace's secure areas, such as the keep, and I'll entrust Flux to select a small group to watch over me. The rest of you are going to be too busy, as we need the Legion everywhere as trainers, recruiting the next generation of the Legion and getting ready for the war," I said reluctantly.

"I don't like the idea of you being watched over by people other than the Legion," Romanus said, and I nodded in agreement.

"I feel the same, but they have sworn the Oaths, and I'll always have some of the Legion nearby, it just can't only be the Legion, that's all."

"I understand," Romanus acquiesced. "We'll get straight to it, then. If you need me, I'll be in the Legion Enclave. We'll reclaim it and begin renovations."

"Good plan, and Romanus? Requisition anything you need for that, to be clear, the Legion's days of being the poor cousin are fucking over. Go on, I'll see you later, no doubt." I waved them off as I turned to Thomas. "Right, mate, I need the guard sorted out. Elites are going to be in demand, so I suggest you split them into two shifts and four teams, that way one can be on guard and one can be out hitting the criminals, while the other shift sleeps."

"Yeah, I'll sort it, bro. Leave me to it. Man, how weird is it that we're the ones giving the cops orders, though?"

"Fuck, man, tell me about it," I grumbled, shrugging. "Well, I guess this is how empires start." I broke off as Cai walked in. Thomas and Lucian took the opportunity to disappear, claiming they had a lot to do, after one look at the massive sheaf of paperwork Cai had for me already.

CHAPTER FORTY

The rest of the day passed in a blur of meetings, each somehow more mind-numbingly boring than the one before it, until finally the complaints and demands from the nobles, many of whom had their lands stripped from them unceremoniously by my golems, led by a handful of legionnaires, grew too loud and strident to ignore.

"Fine!" I roared, the fifth time I was interrupted by a terrified palace servant telling me that the nobles were getting out of hand. "They're out of hand? I'll show them out of fucking hand!" I snarled, turning and storming away from Cai, the latest maps and plans lying blessedly forgotten across the table behind me.

I strode down the corridor, passing knots of legionnaires and elite guards, many of whom fell in around me as we went.

I subconsciously triggered Mana Overdrive just as I reached the doors to the main audience chamber, where raised voices argued.

I didn't bother checking if the doors were locked, I just planted both hands flat and shoved as hard as I could. The resulting sounds suggested that they *had* been locked, or at least latched. But the doors burst open regardless, the screech of tortured metal announcing my presence, right before both doors slammed flat against the wall on either side of the doorway with a resounding boom.

"Ah, High Lord Jax," snapped one man, stepping forward and not bothering to bow. "I have had my land *stolen* by your Legion ruffians, and I demand…"

"SILENCE!" I bellowed, charging past him, ignoring the look of outrage on his face, just as I ignored the attempt he made to grab my arm. I also ignored the scream he made when Grizz grabbed his outstretched arm, bending it back sharply, before kicking his legs out from under him and slamming him face-first into the floor.

I climbed the dais to my throne and spun to face the dozen or so nobles before sitting down and glaring at them. More than one opened their mouth to speak, before shutting it quickly as he caught the ire in my gaze. I held the silence for a long minute, Demonstrating my point before speaking.

"Clearly, there's been some mistakes made here," I said.

"Yes!" another noble said, interrupting me. "Yes, mistakes! My land…"

"The land is my land until I decide otherwise!" I roared. "The next one of you overdressed butterflies that interrupts *me*, I'll interrupt permanently!" I yanked my naginata out and let it flare to life with a burst of flames that filled the room with a severe wash of heat, driving most of the nobility back several feet. I was protected from the effects by dint of it being my magic, and the Legion and elites were just strong enough to ignore it.

"Right." I snapped, gathering myself. "Let's start this audience again. You are here because you've some kind of issue with how I am pursuing the war...*tough*! I know some of you built mansions over the Imperial armory grounds..." I glanced around, seeing maybe half of those gathered avoiding looking at me.

"You built on reserved Imperial land. I don't care when you did it, and if it was your ancestor, or you personally, that's tough. The armory is buried under that land, and it will be cleared and rebuilt. If you built over the top, regardless of whether you believed you had permission or not, *you didn't.*

"Secondly, I've been told that others in this group are here because you object to my 'Legion ruffians' giving you orders or taking command of your personal forces. Again, that's tough. Part of the Oath you take when you ascend to the nobility covers the raising of forces for the Empire.

"Specifically, that all those you command are Imperial troops, and when I have need of them, they are mine to call on and conscript! What the hell did you think was happening here? We're at WAR!"

"B...but Lord Jax..." one of the nobles blurted, clearly terrified and expecting me to strike them or something. "You've already stripped our treasuries, exiled our family members, now you claim our homes. We'll have nothing left!"

"I promised to pay you a fair price for the items I had removed from your treasuries, and I only exiled those who refused to accept my authority. I've been interrupted again and again by complaints coming from the nobility. Do you know how many nobles there are in this city?" I asked, getting a few shaken heads.

"Less than two hundred, in a city of over ninety thousand, yet I've not had a single hour since I took the city that at least one of you hasn't caused a disturbance. I've been here four days, and I've only had ONE other person give me grief. ONE!"

I paused, aware I was starting to shout, and that, as much as I disliked these fuckwits, I damn well needed their support, and I forced myself to speak slowly and calmly.

"I will be forming a noble council, a council that Rewn will probably be a part of, so spread the word. I will permit you to put forward ten members for the council. I will *consider* members for that council from the candidates you put forward. I will choose those who I think will be the most useful in resolving the issues you've brought before me.

"Each city in the Empire will have such a council, and the leader of the council, along with the city lord, will have a place in the senate, able to stand and debate your grievances with me, and those I have placed in the senate to deal with such issues.

"I will not have time to rule everywhere, considering how consumed with war the realm is. As such, when I am busy, the senate will rule in my place," I declared, dangling the carrot of possible power before them all. "Go, spread the word, and in three days, I will meet your recommended representatives and decide who will be on the council." I gestured toward the door.

There was a pause, before the nobles left *en masse*, streaming from the room and making me sigh as I released my Mana Overdrive, sagging as the debuff took hold.

"I suspect that what they think they heard and what you intend don't match up," Cai said in a low, amused voice while looking at me askance. I winked at him.

"I don't know what you mean." I grinned, despite myself, hitting myself with a heal and sighing as the debuff vanished.

"Hmm, let's see. You said you would create a council with a council leader that would have the ear of the emperor, as a member of the senate, and you invited them to nominate people to join that council."

"True, and the council leader will be able to talk to me, through the senate."

"The senate you haven't set up yet?"

"Details, details," I said, lazily waving my hand and winking.

"Hmmm, and the leader of the council, you never mentioned how that leader would be chosen. And you never actually said you'd listen to their recommendations. You just said you'd let them put forward members for it."

"I didn't, did I?" I grinned. "They also missed the purpose of that council."

"It's your shit job team, isn't it?" Cai asked, smiling toothily.

"It certainly is." The shit job team, or council, as I'd publicly named it, was going to be a position that the most assholish and vocal members of the nobility strove for. But that was fine, because, in exchange for the modicum of personal power they'd get, I would be directing issues like these nobles kicking off about their properties being seized to the council.

Essentially, I'd just created an unpaid position that the most sneaky and underhanded nobles were going to fight over, and I intended for them to deal with the problems I didn't want to.

We left the audience hall and headed out into the killing ground, meeting up with a few more of my personal squad on the way. I tramped across to the two thousand or so new recruits that had gathered on my order and were waiting to swear the Oath.

I spent the next two hours using potion after potion and swearing all of them in, accepting salutes and cheers as they went. I had to force myself to smile and cheer with them, when in reality, I was bored, exhausted, and had a splitting mana migraine by the end.

By the time I stumbled into my bed, finding Oracle already laid there, exhausted from having spent the entire day with Yen and Tenandra teaching the legionnaires magic, I was utterly fucked, and I fell asleep in seconds, holding her.

The next two days were filled with meetings, arguments, and trying to keep my godsdamned temper as people asked me the same questions again and again or tried to drop hints about how X was the only reasonable choice for the position of leader of the council.

By the time Rewn landed in the kill-zone and marched heroically down the ramp, flanked by his harem and friends, I was relieved beyond all measure.

"Finally! Welcome home, City Lord Rewn!" I declared, clasping his wrist and smiling a little more than I expected to in response to the wide smile he gave me, as his friends and companions all bowed or curtsied.

"It's good to be home, High Lord Jax!" he said. "I am ready to retake control of my city!" I paused at that and raised an eyebrow. I considered reminding him that we'd agreed he would do some training before we assessed his suitability to rule again, but I let it pass, telling him to dismiss his friends and to accompany me into the keep, bringing only Carmen.

He seemed surprised, then leaned forward, coughing and blushing. "Uh, Carmen isn't a part of my inner circle anymore," he said, speaking in a whisper that practically echoed off the walls.

I took a deep breath before I responded. "And why is that, Rewn?" I asked, somehow managing a whisper.

"She was responsible for the poisoning we all went through."

"Oh?" I asked, knowing damn well it was true.

"Yes, you see, she decided to cook for us all, and well, after several days of struggle, we managed to pull through, but, well…I clearly can't trust her now!" he told me in a whisper that was likely audible from Himnel.

"Did anyone die?"

"Well, no."

"Yet, despite poisoning you all, you all pulled through?"

He frowned. "Well, yes, we were extremely fortunate."

"So did Carmen say she tried to poison you?"

He shook his head. "Well, no, but she's not going to admit that, now is she?"

"Did she eat the same meal?"

"Well…yes."

"So she cooked the meal and fell ill as well, despite her supposedly intentional poisoning of you, and she tried to what…kill herself to allay suspicion?"

"Carmen is an alchemist, after all, she…" He paused, looking at me for a few long seconds.

"Yeah, she's an alchemist; that's a fair point. She's someone who could, if she wanted, kill you *easily* with poisons you'd never catch," I pointed out, making Rewn look uncertain. "Listen, Rewn, I'll be honest. I think you've made a mistake here. If Carmen wanted to poison you, she'd have killed you, and if she did it, she wouldn't have eaten the food. It sounds more like you all just caught some form of illness."

"But I already dismissed Carmen," Rewn said slowly. "I can't forgive her now; I'd look like a fool."

"Tell you what, Rewn, I think she's got a great deal of potential, and she's very intelligent. Why don't you bring her to me. I'll find her a job that's more suited for her abilities."

"Excellent. Captain? Release Carmen and have her brought to the keep, please," He called to the captain of his ship, who nodded and moved off, climbing back aboard the ship. The various nobles of Rewn's harem spread out, heading to meet family and friends, or hung around, awkwardly trying to listen in.

"You had her locked up?" I asked Rewn, not sure if I'd understood that right, and he nodded.

"She tried to poison me, you see…oh, oh dear…" he said, clearly having issues mentally changing direction quickly.

"Okay!" I said, forcing a smile. "Come on then, Rewn, let's go have a chat. Lydia, would you go and get Carmen, take her aside, and give her the chance to get a change of clothes or something before she comes to the keep, maybe discuss some of the situation with her?"

Lydia sighed, then nodded as she changed direction and headed back to the ship.

I led Rewn to the throne room, coughing loudly and raising one eyebrow when he moved to sit on the throne, before grabbing his arm as he stared at me, confused, and still went to sit down. I hauled him out of the way and shoved him towardsa normal seat, before sitting in the one next to him and waving Romanus to another as he entered the room.

When I looked at Rewn, I felt like I was kicking a puppy. He meant well, but the man was a complete imbecile.

"Rewn, I'm glad you're back, but we discussed this. We agreed that you cannot rule here, not yet. You know you're not capable. With that in mind, I do intend for you to rule here, at least officially, but first you need to learn how to do it, mate."

"But…you mean you'll teach me?" he asked, eyeing me dubiously.

"No." I snorted. "Well, I will help, and give you some advice from time to time, but the majority of your training will be by Romanus, Restun, Hennen, Cai, and another advisor I'll be naming soon.

"I want you to be part of the City Council, Rewn. It'll be hard work, and there will be difficult decisions to make, but it'll only be an hour or two a day. The rest of the time you'll split between training with Centurion Hennen and…" I paused. "Where the hell is Hennen?"

"Oh, I ordered him to remain behind at the Tower," Rewn admitted with a wince.

"Are you fucking kidding me?" I glared at him and realized that the Oaths he'd sworn to me, and his official position as a city lord did give him the authority to order Hennen to remain there, despite the chain of command being what it was.

"He was constantly harassing me, and…" Rewn mumbled, picking at his fingernails.

"Rewn, he was there to help you," I hissed, trying to keep my temper under control.

"He kept insisting on speaking to me, every single day! And not even about anything interesting, just the past and boring things," Rewn tried to explain, waving his hands aimlessly.

"HE'S YOUR FUCKIN' TEACHER!" I roared at him, before taking a deep breath and pacing back and forth as I tried to calm down. Everyone else was keeping very quiet.

"Okay Rewn, this is how it's going to go…" I stated in an icy voice. "You're going back to the Tower aboard your ship right the fuck now. You're going to spend the entire trip exercising until you drop from exhaustion, and I'm going to send a legionnaire with you to make sure you do." I glanced at Romanus, who nodded that he understood.

"When you get to the Tower, you will apologize to Hennen and ask him to take his place as your teacher. You won't be taking command of a squad, as I'd originally intended, because you're clearly not capable of that. If, and I mean this, Rewn, *IF* Hennen CHOOSES to forgive you and to teach you, you will learn all you can from him, and only then might I permit you to take a role on the council.

"I'd been intending for you to lead it, but that's clearly beyond you…fuck's sake, Rewn!" I burst out, glaring at him. "What the hell did you think was going to happen when you got here! Did you think I was going to forget I'd assigned you a teacher?"

"Well, I…I just," Rewn spluttered. I leaned in close and stared at him for long seconds, waiting, before he fell silent.

"Rewn," I said slowly, forcing my voice to stay steady. "Think about your answer before you give it. Do you want to be the lord of this city, or do you want to be a minor noble? I'll set you up with a significant amount of wealth and one of the nicest palaces in the city, so you'll be rich and still a noble, but you won't have any of the responsibilities that you'll have as lord of Narkolt…"

"Well of course," Rewn straightened up, glaring back.

"…Because, Rewn, if you want to be the lord of this city in truth, you'll be learning every fucking day. You'll be exercising and learning to fight with the men, studying diplomacy and numbers, trade, and all that shit every minute that you're not physically training.

"You. Will. Not. Rest," I snapped. "I mean this, Rewn. Consider what you want, if you want to relax with your harem, drink, party, and all that shit, then just say the word, and you can. Otherwise, you'll be growing up right fucking now, and you don't get to make this choice later. No, in fact…yes you do. Romanus!"

I turned to him and straightened up in response to his salute. "Get me someone that will kick his arse into gear for the entire trip to the Tower. He's to go there immediately and beg Hennen's forgiveness, then Hennen is to train him all the way back. On arrival here, he gets to choose his future. Now, get him out of my sight."

"Yes, Lord Jax," Romanus said, hiding his smile as he yanked Rewn out of his seat and set him on his feet. "Come along, lordling…"

"No…wait, I…" Rewn complained, even as I overrode him, injecting my mana into the declaration I had made on the spot.

Attention Citizens of the Empire!

Effective immediately, the Legion of Dravith is declared outside of all traditional chains of command by the Scion of the Empire. No more will the Legion be forced by Oathbindings to obey any but the Emperor, the Imperial Scion, the Heir, and its own chain of command.

While the Legion will continue to follow the relevant authorities, where they believe those orders conflict with the Emperor, Imperial Scion, or Heir's intentions or communicated orders, they will be free to act against local authority to carry out their orders.

Hear this and bear witness, the age of untouchable nobility is over, and the Empire rises again!

"There, that should deal with that issue," I growled, glaring at Rewn as he was dragged from the room. I shook my head in stunned amazement as I thought about the little sod's blatant belief that he'd get away with it. Then sat back down, chewing on my knuckle as I thought about everything else I had to do, while I waited.

It was a little over half an hour before a flustered and harried Carmen was led into the room. Her makeup was freshly applied, and she was dressed in clean clothes, but was visibly worn out from several days in the ship's brig at Rewn's order.

She curtsied.

"Found 'er in tha brig," Lydia said. "Single room, bucket fer a toilet. Apparently, she's been on dry bread an' water as a lesson since leaving tha Tower."

"Fuck's sake, Rewn." I rubbed the bridge of my nose and gesturing to a seat as Carmen waited for me to acknowledge her genuflection. "Yes, yes, welcome and all that. Shit, Carmen, are you all right?" I asked, getting a wan smile from her as she stood and staggered to the seat.

I raised my eyebrows at Lydia, and she shook her head in disgust.

"Chained te a bench fer tha entire trip; tha chains were too short fer her te stand properly or lie down."

"Fuck's sake! Legionnaire!" I bellowed, and a legionnaire I didn't know the name of popped his head into the room. "Run and tell Romanus that I said Rewn is to be run absolutely ragged. He is officially on my shit list, and as far as his trainer for the flight goes, I want them to view him as a fresh boot who was caught pissing in my coffee!"

"Yessir!" The legionnaire barked before vanishing again.

"Right, Carmen, let's get this over with. Until I say otherwise, you are to answer any and all of my questions with as much honesty as you can, do you understand?"

She stiffened, the Oath forcing her to obey.

"Yes my Lord!" she grunted in dismay.

"I'm sorry, Carmen, but I need truthful answers here. Right, did you cause the illness that put Rewn and the others down for several days with the shits and vomiting?"

"Yes."

"Why?"

"To give you time at this end to get the city in order without Rewn and the others interfering, and to prove myself as someone you could trust," she whispered, closing her eyes.

"And what are your intentions regarding me and your future?" I asked grimly.

"I want to rise to a position where I don't have to put up with the shit that characterized my life until now. I don't want to be valued exclusively for my tits or how good I am in bed. I want to be valued for my mind, not just my looks, and I want to be powerful enough that nobody can shit on me ever again.

"I believe you're the best path to that, so I'll do anything I have to, to make you see my value. I intended to seduce you if I had to, offering myself to your wisp first, if need be, and…"

"That's enough." I said, smiling slightly. "Finally, do you bear me or mine any ill-will, and do you intend to work to strengthen the Empire? Should I give you the authority to do so, will you be loyal to me, regardless of the ease of the task which I set you?"

"Yes!" she said quickly. "I am loyal, and I will be. I bear you and your people no ill will. I want to grow, to be all I can be, and you've already given me more chances to do that than any other, asking for less in return."

"Excellent!" I grinned. "You can relax now, and you're no longer required to tell me the absolute truth and so on," I declared, waving my hand vaguely. "I'm sorry I had to do that Carmen, I really am, but I had to know what kind of a person you are before this next bit."

Lydia smiled. "Wish Ah could see their faces when yer do this," she said. I grinned, closing my mouth and pausing, rather than making the proclamation as I'd intended.

"That's a good point, why shouldn't we enjoy this, after all?" I said, before turning to Carmen. "Carmen, you've got an hour, get yourself as sorted as you want, to take part in an Imperial proclamation before the nobility. You might want to make an effort, because they're going to be paying a lot of attention to you from now on."

CHAPTER FORTY-ONE

"Thank you all for joining me," I said, leaning back on the throne in the main audience chamber, looking out over the sea of figures before me. Where I'd normally met the various nobles, notables, and rich or otherwise influential people of the city in one of the lesser audience chambers, with Rewn crossing the line, I'd decided it was time to stop fucking about.

Due to the shitty speed of his ship, Rewn was expected back from the Great Tower in six days' time. When he arrived, I'd decide if he was to be given further training to one day ascend to the rank of city lord, and eventually earl or some such, or if he was to be set up as a minor noble, given a wedge of gold, and told to bugger off and spend the rest of his life banging his harem.

I expected the vast majority of his harem would leave him quickly in that situation, and, as he had caused Carmen to sever all emotional ties to him with his behavior, well…I mentally shrugged and dismissed it as his problem.

I looked out at the crowd, seeing the hundreds gathered before me, some of which had already sworn, although the majority hadn't. I smiled faintly as Thomas stepped into the room at the back and gave me a nod, signaling that he and his men were ready.

"I've summoned all of you here to discuss the future of the city and the Empire, as well as the war and your role in it. Just under half of you here have already sworn the Oath of Allegiance to me personally, and to the Empire, so before we continue, I'll ask that all others here do so.

"If you feel you cannot swear the Oath for whatever reason, then I suggest you leave the room now." I paused, waiting for a full minute as people shifted nervously. When nobody left, I stood. I took a deep breath, before exhaling in relief, half afraid that some of them would take the opportunity.

Oracle stepped forward from where she'd stood to the right of the throne, while Tenandra stepped out from the back of the hall. The pair of them lifted their arms and let the subtle weave they'd been developing take form in the air between them.

The crowd grew restless, watching as lines of color and washes of light appeared, floating and coalescing before each wisp or woman, as they appeared to the crowd. The two sides of the spell slowly grew outward, both reaching for the other and filling the hall.

Strands of magic touched each and every person in the room, passing into and through them before moving on. The spell connected every one of them with a gently glowing thread of light that flowed back to the ball in Oracle's hand, before I stepped forward and placed my own hand atop it.

"This spell is an interesting one," I said, smiling at the nervous crowd before me. "It does nothing at all, save from registering the answer to a question…is the person connected to the orb sworn to the one who holds it." I smiled as more and more people seemed to guess the significance of the various colors of the threads now.

"As you can see, the thread glows red if you're not sworn, white if you are, and green for those bound to me more deeply, such as the Legionnaires. It can also be gold, for those who are bound to me by love. You've probably noticed that, at the other end of the threads, leading away from the orb I hold, the colors are different. This Demonstrates my connection to you…" I informed them, noticing the happiness on Oracle's face as she saw the solid gold line flowing between us.

It was one of over a dozen golden threads, although the others were all lesser in brightness, reflecting a different kind of love, as it reached out to my friends, and now, my family.

I exchanged a smile with my squad, seeing them gathered around, unshed tears glistening in the eyes of Lydia and others, as they saw, for the first time, complete proof that my feelings matched their own.

Then, with my closest and dearest acknowledged, I looked out across the room and took a deep breath before going on.

"This means that those of you who intend to pay lip service and not actually take the Oath will now be very clear to all of us, so I ask again, do any of you wish to leave?"

There were far more shuffling feet this time, as over two dozen people pushed free of the crowd, moving swiftly toward the exit. As she walked, one woman complained loudly that it was a disgrace to treat people this way, and that it was due to my distrust that she would not be taking my stupid Oath.

I let them all go, smiling as they went. There were two less than the predicted group. The group that had left was made up of members of the Smuggler's Guild, the Veloturr Gang leadership, and one of the two Himnel spies we'd identified, as well as several nobles who were members of various smaller criminal gangs and a merchant we were investigating for slavery or "indentured servant contracts," as he was calling them.

As they left the room, they were met out of sight by Thomas and a group of elite guards, who bound and gagged them. The guards stripped the group of all their possessions, making sure they couldn't use any mundane or magical means to alert their friends, who were currently being raided by members of the guard who had sworn to me.

All over the city, the few hundred red dots that represented criminals were being rounded up, their possessions confiscated, and their businesses closed for investigation, but nobody in the room knew this…*yet*.

"Thank you all for your confidence, and those who left for their honesty," I said, pulling a pair of greater mana potions out of my bag, popping the tops and getting ready as Oracle reached out, sharing the first Oath with all present.

"I swear to obey High Lord Jax and those he places over me; I will serve to the best of my ability, speak no lie to him when commanded otherwise, and treat all other citizens as family.

I will work for the greater good, being a shield to those who need it, a sword for those who deserve it, and a warden to the night.

I will stand with my family, helping one another to reach the light, until the hour of my death or my Lord releases me from my oath.

"Lastly, I will not be a dick!"

The first few voices to rise in the crowd were hesitant, but as more and more took up the chant, they grew stronger, some proclaiming proudly their decision to join me, while others mumbled, uncertainty clear in their voices.

It only took a few minutes, but by the end, I'd popped the first vial, and I prepared to take the second as I spoke.

"I, Lord Jax, do swear to protect and lead you, to be the shield that protects you and yours from the darkness, and the sword that avenges that which cannot be saved. As the Tower and the Empire grows in strength, so shall you," I said, feeling the heady rush of my mana being pulled from me to bind these people to myself, before Oracle pushed out the original Oath of Imperial Citizenship.

"I swear upon pain of death, to faithfully execute all that the Emperor decrees. I swear upon my soul that I shall stand for the Empire when it calls. I shall be strong when the weak need me, generous when the poor are at hand, and merciless when my fellow citizens are threatened. I shall worship the Gods of my fathers, respect my elders, and raise up my children to stand tall.

I am an Imperial Citizen. I claim the right to call upon the Legion in my hour of need, to hold those that wrong me to justice, and to be avenged if I cannot be saved."

By the time this Oath was finished, I'd taken the other potion, and was seriously considering grabbing a third, before the drain finally stopped. I let out a sigh of relief, the burgeoning mana migraine making its presence known for a few seconds, before dying away.

"Thank you all!" I said, pausing as a hum of voices lifted into the air, as people whispered about taking the Oath. The murmuring died away as more and more people noticed the three threads that had stayed resolutely red.

Two of them twined through the room to reach people in the crowd. One vanished into the far corner, where a figure slowly appeared, slipping from stealth as people stared their way.

The Legion grabbed the hooded spy, leading them and the other two who'd attempted to bluff their way through the spell, from the room. That only left those who were actually loyal, or at least willing to take the chance and support me, if only because they saw me as the best path to personal power.

"Well, now that all those who are untrustworthy have been removed, we can get on with business!" I said, smiling and sitting back down.

"First of all, let me assure you of my intentions. I know that many of you have fallen afoul of the changes I've brought. Some of you have lost land, for others it was wealth in the form of spellbooks or skillbooks. Some lost artifacts of the Empire or physical wealth in the form of coinage invested in properties or businesses that have suffered from my actions. For this, I apologize, but these were necessary actions.

"In a few hours, the surviving floors of the Imperial armory will be uncovered, and the next phase can begin, as we start rebuilding and reconstruction. Fortunately, all these changes, as far as I know, will be finished by the end of the day." I paused, letting that sink in, seeing the relief on the faces of those who'd feared losing more.

"Secondly, it's time to be clear about the future of the city," I said, leaning back and resting my hands on the arms of the throne. "This city was ruled by a city lord, both in recent days and in the days of the Empire, and it's only right that this tradition is continued. I have no interest in sitting on this throne for the long term. I will honestly be too damn busy, so, going forward, another will sit here and rule in my place.

"I'll be honest, the best person for that job will be the one I choose to sit here, and if that's the previous city lord remains to be seen. He was, unfortunately, given poor advice for a long time.

"However, that means that there is a chance that the next occupant of this throne…" I tapped the arm, looking around slowly, while making eye contact with as many of the people in the room as possible. "…could be one of you."

The buzz of conversation lifted, and I had to wait for it to die back down before I could continue.

"There is also a greater issue to be made clear as well: as you all know, I have conquered this city. I have also conquered the Great Tower, and the vast majority of the territory in between. I am currently at war with Himnel, much as you were, meaning that the war with them will continue. It will now, however, be pursued with considerably greater effort, rather than the pathetic raiding of each other's trade convoys and random airship fights, where both ships retreated after minimal damage.

"I intend to conquer the city of Himnel in short order, remove the criminal leadership it suffers under, and frankly slaughter the entirety of that shit biscuit priesthood of Nimon while I'm at it. The Dark Legion are worshippers of the God of Death, a God who directly caused the cataclysm, and the deaths of millions, if not billions, as well as the banishment of the rest of the major Gods, leaving only the divine equivalent of toilet scrubbers like Illoth to rise to power."

I paused as thunder rumbled overhead, and a feeling of oppressive doom filled the air. I stood, pulling my naginata from my pouch and setting it alight, before slamming the base on the floor, just as the Pantheon of Flame banished Nimon and Illoth from the area.

"Go on, you Dark Wanker! Run! I'll catch you soon enough!" I shouted at the vaulted ceiling, prompting nervous titters from some of the crowd, and stares of outright terror from others.

"Right," I said, sitting back down and still holding my glowing weapon. "I don't like having to say this, or at least in theory I'm against it, as I've always believed in the right for people to choose their God or Gods based on their own preferences. But as of now, all across the Empire, the worship of Nimon is declared illegal.

"The Empire worships the Goddess of Fire, Jenae, first and foremost, and the Pantheon of the Flame and its individual members secondly. I will ask that the Gods consecrate altars for us in the city, and any and all altars to Nimon and His sycophantic cocksuckers will be destroyed."

Attention Citizens of the Empire!

The Imperial Scion Jax, has decreed that the worship of Nimon, God of Death and the Pantheon of the Dark is now illegal. Any Citizen found to be worshipping a member of the Pantheon of the Dark is to be stripped of their Imperial Authority, Rank, and Rights as a Citizen.

Take heed, one and all, for the Gods surely have.

I cursed at the prompt that appeared, and my mana tanked, causing my head to feel like it was exploding. I almost went blind, barely able to force my eyes open as I fumbled with my pouches, pulling two mana potions free and downing them one after the other.

My mana refilled before tearing itself down again. Five more potions went down the hatch, all greater or higher, before I got control again. I blinked and looked around, finding the Legion in a ring surrounding me, facing outward with weapons drawn, ready to slaughter any threat, even as Oracle stroked my brow, holding another mana potion ready.

As soon as I stabilized, she almost collapsed in relief, before hitting me with a heal then kissing me so hard she nearly broke my face.

"You idiot!" she whispered, glaring at me from less than an inch away. "You just made a declaration to every single legionnaire that still lives, and every individual citizen like Lucian from the end of days, all of them long-lived, like the Elves that retreated into solitude after the cataclysm, all of them. Hundreds of thousands saw that message, and now they know about you."

"Is that really that bad?" I asked, scrubbing the blood away from my chin, then looking at my hand, grimacing at the visceral reminder that, when my mana was gone, spells would use my blood instead.

"I have no idea, but it means that the Baron and the others back on Earth probably know about us now, and your rank," she said, clearly worried.

"Fuck them if they can't take a joke," I grunted before wiping the rest of the blood free. I straightened up, letting everyone know I was all right, and to return to their places.

"Okay, after that…phew," I muttered, before continuing, in a louder and stronger voice. "Moving forward, the Empire will be ruled as once it was, with the Emperor at its head. Next in rank will be the heir to the throne and the Imperial council, as they are the people who I have selected to advise me.

"Below the Imperial council, which will be small in number, is the senate, made up of senators chosen for their skill and knowledge. Each city in the Empire will have two representatives in the senate, one will be the city lord, and the other will be the city council leader. Under the city lord are the various nobles: dukes, marquesses, earls, viscounts, barons, imperial knights, and finally those who are declared noble, yet hold no Imperial rank.

"The current nobility of the land, frankly, are all on the bottom rung, because without an Imperial throne to confirm your ranks, the highest noble rank that could be claimed is that of noble and lord, which is the same damn thing, in this case." I paused again for effect, looking around at the people.

"Now, what many of you have forgotten, is that the Oaths sworn upon ascension to the head of a noble line are directly to *me*, as the Imperial Scion, since there is no higher living authority in the Empire. One of those many Oaths is that you have sworn to raise fighters for the Empire, should you, for whatever reason, not have held aside the taxes required to aid in the maintenance of the Imperial forces."

Utter silence filled the room as people considered the Oaths they'd sworn, and what those Oaths meant.

"Now, fortunately for all of you, I'm well aware that the Imperial navy, for example, which had a responsibility for protecting your shores from raiders and so on, no longer exists. As such, we'll dispense with that tax entirely for now."

A noticeable sigh rippled through the room.

"Secondly, you've received little in the way of the Imperial education programs, so let's scrap those taxes as well. To be clear, I'll be starting up schools of magic very soon, but we're currently at war, so they'll have to wait. So, that's those two taxes gone, with no debts owed between you and the Empire," I offered, getting a lot of relieved sighs and nodding of heads.

"Fantastic, I can see this is going well, then. So, let's get on with the last three sections that we need to cover, before we can get to the important details of your new city council, and so on." I paused, watching many of the wolfish scumbags nodding around to their friends and preening, clearly expecting to be nominated to the council and probably the council's leadership before long.

"So, the Imperial Legion. You've all had the benefits of them fighting for you every day. They faced the creatures that are in most of your nightmares and gave up their lives, all without a second thought. But, strangely enough, I can't find any trace of some of the taxes they are due," I stated, my voice still friendly and light as I looked around. The only hint of my deep-seated anger was the teeth I bared in a grim smile.

"From what I can see, the Legion received less than three percent of the taxes, while the official tax of ten percent FOR the Legion, was collected from the city's people." I let that hang in the air for a minute, then I waved my hand in negation. "But, as the tax was collected by the city, I'm going to assume the city has that difference still to pay, and not you honest citizens." Again, there was a buzz of conversation as people relaxed.

"So, number four on my list is the support that the Empire is supposed to receive from the noble houses. This is required in terms of magical artifacts, should the house produce any, or in terms of soldiers, ready to defend the local state and be levied to assist the Empire, should they be needed.

"This, as I said before, is an Oath that each and every one of the noble houses took upon ascension to ruling their families, so I know that you know about it. Yet still, there's been no record of those forces being made available to assist the Legion or to patrol the area in times of need." I paused, and, for the first time, they felt the anger I'd directed at Nimon still simmering away.

"As those forces were never handed over, I've had to send out my own people to take command of them, wasting both my time and my resources, which is frankly…annoying," I said in a low growl.

"My people have taken command of your forces, leaving you a small guard contingent, and, as I stated already, we've examined your vaults. Since these items weren't offered up willingly, they were taken, catalogued, and you were assured compensation would be discussed.

"This, ladies and gentlemen, is that discussion. You owe the Empire this and ten times more. Be VERY thankful I'm willing to leave it at the relevant contents of your vaults and your soldiers," I informed them grimly, sitting back and glaring around at the now silent hall.

"Lastly, before we move on to the more fun side of things with the council, we have the laws of the city and the Empire to discuss, along with their enforcement. First of all, allow me to introduce you to Lucian D'Aquitaine, duly anointed Champion of Sint, Chief Justicar to the Imperial Throne." I gestured, and Lucian stepped forward from my right, a few steps down. He turned and bowed to me before turning back to smile thinly at the crowd.

"Lucian will be the highest point of law in the Empire. He commands the Imperial Justicars, a team of impartial judges and investigators who will see justice done throughout my lands. The Imperial Justicars are an old tradition, one that many of you may not be familiar with, so let me say this as simply as I can.

"They investigate crimes against the Empire and its citizens. Interfering with a Justicar in the pursuit of justice is a capital offence, and it will be met with death." I stopped speaking, watching them all, before going on. "Assault on a Justicar will bring the entire Legion down upon your head, so please understand, should you be guilty of a crime, and they come looking, your best chance is to admit your guilt and take your punishment.

"That way, the offence will be dealt with as honorably as possible. Assault or hinder them, and they, along with the rest of the Legion, will make it their personal business to examine each and every facet of your life. I believe that would be a serious mistake on your part."

"The laws of the Empire are clear and simple and will be posted throughout the city by the end of the day. For now, though, these basic tenets will guide you," Lucian said, his cultured voice carrying easily across the hall. "Harm no Citizen outside of formal combat. The enslaving of sentients is forbidden on pain of death, as is murder, treason, attempted bribery of an official of the Empire, or impersonating an official of the Empire. For most other crimes, the existing laws are kept.

"Riots, inciting riots, piracy, theft, robbery, and so on, are all declared illegal under Imperial Law and are recognized as harming your fellow citizens, or, as Lord Jax puts it, 'being a dick.' As such, these will be enforced by your Oaths, making them both extremely difficult to carry out and exceedingly painful, should you manage it.

"One addendum to the realm of capital punishment, and therefore punishable by death, is rape. Imperial Law makes no difference between the lowest servant and the highest noble in this regard, and so neither will you." There was a long pause while he let people get their head around the basics of the law, and the buzz of conversations started up again, with people noticeably shifting away from certain individuals in the crowd.

"Now, there's an argument to be made for these laws being new, even though they're not, and as such, they, and their punishments, will start from midnight tonight," I clarified, still maintaining a formal smile. "From that point forth, any who break the laws will be dealt with under Imperial Law."

I watched the relieved looks that crossed many faces before broadening my smile into a toothy grin. "But those who broke the law as it stands will be dealt with under the current laws." I held up one finger as the legionnaires, who were placed along the walls on either side of the hall stepped forward. Each of their targets had already been identified to them, as they strode through the crowd, grabbing people and dragging them out.

"Some laws were broken in little ways. Lord Bremond of House Ornithine, for example, liked to run a series of whorehouses. Nothing wrong with that. Brothels are a part of life, and personally I have no issue with them, as long as the people working there are there by choice.

"Lord Bremond used his influence over poorer families to force them into giving up people for his brothels, while never actually forcing them physically. As such, I cannot prosecute him for that under the current laws, but from tonight, that would be covered by the simple 'being a dick' law," I said with a frown, looking at Lucian.

"Unfortunately for Lord Bremond, he recently took the lives of several of his staff in a perverted party, one that he and three others took part in. That's murder." Lucian said grimly.

"Why, yes, it is." I agreed. "Hang the fuckers." I ordered, turning back to the room at large. "I'll be clear about this as well. No children in the brothels, minimum age of consent to work there is eighteen, and I really don't give a fuck about your opinions on that.

"To make this entirely clear and fair, I hereby order those arrested, if you are innocent of the crimes you are accused of, state it, and your case will be reviewed. Otherwise, until you are given leave by an official of the Empire to speak, I order you to be silent." Silence filled the hall as all those who'd begun protesting stopped abruptly.

The others in the crowd shifted their feet nervously as out of the several hundred in the room, thirty-seven were separated and dragged to the front, before being escorted past the throne and out the far door, while Lucian read their crimes.

"Rhenian Tossalov, murder. Annabeth Shinanme, poisoning of her husband. Senna Hemanth, assisting Annabeth. Thamthon, the Thadduthee Thtrangler, murder, unsurprisingly. Ute Tessalet, rape of a minor."

Lucian made a point of glaring at that one, who opened his mouth, but no sound escaped. "Ute, I order you by the Oath you have given to the Empire to respond with a yes or no, are you guilty of the murder and rape of a child?"

"Yes," Ute cried, after several seconds of attempting to remain silent.

"More than one?" I asked.

"Yes," he admitted, sagging between the two legionnaires who held him by the arms.

"Make it painful," I ordered with a grim set to my jaw, before turning back to the crowd. "As you can see, these people are being dealt with for their capital crimes. However, there are some in the crowd who are guilty of less serious crimes, such as smuggling.

"I invite any of you who have committed such a crime to step forward. Your crimes will be reviewed, and you will be given the chance to assist the Empire. If you make us hunt for you, you lose the chance of being regarded as an honorable person, and your crimes will no longer be dealt with leniently."

There was a long pause before a single man stepped forward. He was tall, heavily muscled, and broad-shouldered, with several long scars running down his face on one side, costing him that eye.

"Good man," I said, nodding to him in respect. "Who are you, and what is your crime?"

"I am Bol. Smuggler," Bol declared, standing tall and unashamed.

"Thank you, Bol. Does anyone else have this man's honesty and bravery?" I nodded as a second person stepped forward, a woman this time, who reached out and took Bol's hand, sighing.

"I am Hesta, wife of Bol, and I assisted him," she said, shaking her head as she looked up at him, and avoided looking in my direction.

"Thank you, Hesta. The two of you have earned leniency, and we will discuss how you can aid the Empire after this," I declared, after waiting a few minutes to make sure nobody else was going to step forward.

"Certain others will be taken aside at the end of this audience, and remember, you had your chance." As I said that, several others hesitated before they stepped forward, with another half-dozen speaking up and declaring their names and crimes. Once they were done, I nodded in thanks, then went on.

"Thank you again. Now that the less-pleasant side of things is dealt with, we can move on. Many of you have been wondering about the former council and its fate, as they haven't been seen since I arrived. Simply put, they were killed some time ago.

"Many of them died weeks and months before I got here and were replaced by Drow infiltrators. Those you met, many of those you drank and attended parties with, were, in fact, Drow. My people and I killed a great many of the bastards, and while more of you have seen the remains of the Drider queen, rather than the Drow, that's what happened to them.

"As such, this city now needs an entire council as well as a city lord. With that in mind, I have decided on a council leader who has shown integrity in all aspects I could see. They were highly recommended by their peers and appear to be amongst the most intelligent people of those I've met in the city." I gazed around as many of those in attendance puffed themselves up, smiling and nodding around at their sycophants.

"So, I am pleased to declare Carmen Al'Issiat as Leader of the Council of Narkolt, and declare her to also have the rank of senator in the Empire," I said, my voice echoing slightly as a door at the back of the room opened. Carmen walked in, striding confidently down the center of the red carpet.

Attention Citizens of the Territory of Dravith!

Jax, High Lord of Dravith, and Scion of the Empire, has granted an Imperial Title to a member of the court of Narkolt!

All Hail Carmen Al'Issiat, Council Leader of Narkolt City and Member of the Imperial Senate!

A stunned silence met her arrival and the prompt that confirmed her position, quickly followed by whispers and glares directed her way. She ignored them all, a slight smile on her lips as she strode the length of the hall, coming to a halt before me and dipping into a low curtsy. She wore a full-length dress that was far more elegant and demure than the ones I'd seen her wearing previously.

I stood from the throne and made a point of bowing to her slightly before gesturing to the left of the throne and sitting again.

"Thank you, High Lord Jax." Carmen said, her voice clear and carrying easily as she moved to stand on my left. She took her place slightly farther out than my squad and personal advisors, but close enough to make it clear she stood in a position of power. "As you have ordered, after the conclusion of this audience, I shall immediately begin the creation of a new city council to assist the ruler of Narkolt, whoever that may be."

The remaining whispers and glares cut off abruptly as people realized that their only remaining path to power, should they decide to steer well clear of the unstable madman on the throne, was the calm, smiling former member of the city lord's harem.

I watched the calculation in the eyes that tracked her and the hint of self-assurance building, and I silently wished them luck.

"Now, as that has been dealt with, and the criminals in our midst have been addressed, with those who wish to take my offered chance at leniency having already stepped up," I paused, waiting, and when no one else asked to take the chance, I smiled evilly and went on.

"In that case, I have some wonderful news that I doubt any but historians would be aware of. As part of the abilities that any duly appointed Imperial ruler has in the city, there are two that will make a huge difference to your day-to-day lives. The first is security, as anyone declared to be an enemy of the Empire will be readily identifiable to the Imperial Forces.

"Therefore, any member of Himnel's army, their spies, assassins, and so on, can all be recognized both on sight and on the city interface maps. Bounties will be offered for their capture; we'll start at one hundred gold, and additional payments will be made for higher-ranked individuals." I nodded as more and more seemed to realize what that meant.

"Therefore, no more spies and shitbag Drow can get into the city without us being aware, so you're all a hell of a lot safer than you were. That's one side of the coin, though. The other is that it also shows criminal activity, including the locations that said criminals frequent. Now, to make it clear for the hard of thinking in the crowd, this means that, yes, I knew all along who was a criminal in the room, as did my legionnaires and guards…"

A few people blanched when they saw the legionnaires and guards around the room staring at them individually and nodding.

"While you were here, my guard were moving into position, and right about now," I said, making a point of looking at the back of the room where Thomas held up one hand in a thumbs-up gesture. "There we go. The guard just stormed those locations with orders to arrest everyone and secure everything found there." I looked around and held up my hands, grinning.

"This means that every criminal enterprise that you thought was secure and hidden just got raided. The criminals found there will be given the choice of the hangman's rope or the Oath and time in the army, or another branch of Imperial Service, should they be more appropriate elsewhere.

"After taking the Oath, they'll be ordered to identify their fellow criminals. Expect the next twenty-four hours or so to be very, very busy for those of you with ties to the criminal underworld. This means that, in turn, the city has just become crime-free…organized crime, anyway," I informed them, seeing the horror in the eyes of many in the crowd, and the wonder in the eyes of others.

"You're all fucking welcome," I finished in a flat voice.

It was a harsh way of dealing with crime, one that Thomas and I had argued over incessantly. The problem was mainly down to the individual freedoms that using the Oaths in this way trampled on, but where we agreed on it, despite our own personal misgivings, was the innocent.

Doing this meant that the innocent people, those who didn't break the laws, and those who were always at the bottom of the pile, being robbed, beaten, and taken advantage of…the people that the Empire was created to protect, were now as safe as I could reasonably make them.

It was a horrible idea, to a human from Earth at least, to use such an Oath to essentially force compliance in many ways, and I hated that part of it, but…

It meant that people were safe.

I'd agonized over it again and again, until I'd spoken to Lydia, Romanus, and Lucian, who had all looked at me like I was crazy, with Romanus stating it the best.

"Jax, the only people who will suffer with this are the criminals. The people who don't attempt to rob, steal, or murder, have no issues with such a law. The only ones who will have an issue with it are either those who are criminals or those who intended to have the option.

"I don't know about the freedoms of your world, but here, knowing that your fellow citizens cannot rob, cheat, or murder you, when there has been that fear your entire life? The common people, and many higher, will worship your name for this."

It had seemed wrong to me, at first at least, but when I actually stopped and thought about it? It wasn't just another form of slavery, but as Romanus and the others said, compared to *actual* slavery, or having people kick your door in and murder your family, having to make a magically enforced Oath that you'd be a good person and not rape, murder, and steal, wasn't really something you'd even consider being a choice.

The end of the audience was a pain in the ass, as I'd let myself be convinced by Carmen and Romanus that some things had to be done a certain way. One of them was that, after an audience like this, even one that had been as filled with scarcely concealed threats and trickery as today, there should be an opportunity to mingle and do the small deals that seemed to make society run.

The next two hours were filled with small talk, political maneuvering, attempts to justify criminal acts as mistakes, and attempts to convince me that declaring this lord as innocent, or that lord as corrupt would help me in the long run. I directed those with a criminal issue to Lucian and moved on. One old fool even took the time to inform me, in as patronizing a way as possible, that various laws shouldn't apply to the nobility, as 'we're just not like the rest of them.'

I fucking hated it and survived by fantasizing about slaughtering ninety-nine percent of the shit biscuits in the room, until one utter arsehole tried to manhandle Oracle away to discuss something in private, apparently not understanding that, just because she wore a low-cut dress, she was neither stupid nor a whore.

The crackle of lightning discharging, and the screech he made as she slammed the aforementioned bolt into his crotch, ended all conversation in the room abruptly.

I stepped out of the corner that a gaudily dressed courtesan was trying to corral me into and strode across to where the idiot lay twitching against a nearby wall. I took one look at Oracle, who was crackling power and fury, then glared down at the man who spoke in a shaky, high-pitched voice, while cupping his balls.

"That bitch attacked me! I want her fucking head! I…" He squealed, breaking off as my boot lowered across his throat, cutting off his air.

"You're speaking about the woman I love," I said into the silence. "Not only that, but we're soul-bonded. As such, I know where you tried to put your fucking hand, and what you told her she was going to do for you *'if she knew her place and knew what was good for her…'.*" I finished in a low hiss.

"High Lord Jax," Lucian said from nearby, interrupting me as I began to pull my naginata free. "Perhaps I or one of the others in a position of neutral legal authority should step in here, before more blood is shed. After all, I believe the correct response for such a slight against a member of the Imperial household is a slow death by flogging, rather than a quick one. It lasts over several days, if I remember correctly?"

"A slow and painful death, you say?" I queried, rubbing my chin and looking back down at the fool. "Now that does sound better."

"Perhaps I should discuss this with him, High Lord, and we should let this end with a warning?" Romanus interjected. "After all, Lady Oracle was unknown, prior to today, by many of the court?"

I glanced at Oracle and saw the desire to kill in her face, as well as feeling it through the bond, but I sighed, reining in my anger, and tamping our shared fury down.

"So, it's okay because he didn't know that she could defend herself? Or that she's the one I love? No. I'll accept that the new laws kick in from tonight though, so as a compromise, I'll let you deal with this as a lesson. Make it a *very* clear lesson though, and let a few legionnaires explain it to him personally." I said, straightening up and removing my foot from his throat, before taking Oracle's hand and leading her from the audience chamber.

By the time we were back in the keep, we'd started to laugh about it, but at first, both Oracle and I had been intending to gut the idiot, right there on the floor of the throne room. The fact he clearly deserved to be punished wasn't in question, but my sheer willingness to kill someone outside of battle continued to prey upon my mind.

CHAPTER FORTY-TWO

The next morning was a long time coming, consumed, as most of my time was, by mind-numbing details and issues, culminating in meeting the Council of Mages.

The Council of Mages, led by Arch-Magus Fyre, was something I had originally been looking forward to attending. I realized unfortunately, after an hour of over-the-top, flowery introductions, and speeches, that it was essentially a gathering place for mages who'd spent their entire magical career trying to develop their own personal gravity field through sheer fucking overeating.

They had also clearly been attempting to break their own backs through enthusiastic self-patting, if their self-proclaimed "achievements" were anything to go by.

The council was made up of the nine elders and Fyre, and of the nine mages I hadn't met before, only one could fit through what I would term a standard doorway. Three apparently hadn't been able to walk for years and were attempting to match a giant slug-like alien from one of my favorite movies by the looks of them.

The others fell somewhere in between, with only Fyre herself being in any kind of good shape. Halfway through the indeterminable speeches, I turned and asked her directly about it.

"It's actually easier to move around if you're fit," she replied with almost a wink. "I'm just smarter about being lazy than the rest of the room is."

I ignored the glares I got from the speaker, but when Fyre leaned back out of range of an unsubtle whisper, I took the hint and pretended to listen to the rest of the speech, while really just fantasizing about breaking Oracle over something back at the keep.

As she sat serenely by my side, I mentally broadcast my intentions to her, getting a few equally suggestive images in return. The exchange of thoughts felt like a weird mix of foreplay and sexting that left me desperate to end the meeting as soon as possible.

An hour later, after Oracle had deliberately asked several questions that guaranteed long, exhaustive answers, just to wind me up further, we escaped. I left the meeting with the knowledge that, unless we wanted to concentrate on weather magic or building luxury items for the nobility, the Council of Mages were bugger all use to us.

I ordered them to send their apprentices, trainees, and aspirants along with all their magical learning tools to assist the Legion the next morning. Once that was done, I chased Oracle out of the Tower of Magical Excellence and all the way back to the keep as fast as I could.

By the time I strode out of my room the next morning, the sun was already up, and I was both still exhausted and feeling measurably lighter on my feet.

Oracle had left me several hours before to return to the seemingly infinite job of training the Legion, the elite guards, and the elite of the army in the three spells we had decided were to be the standard set.

They were each taught Magic Missile, Explosive Compression, and Complex Healing. Once all the elites had the spells down to pat, we would be moving on to one in ten of the army, which was still well over a thousand people.

By the time I made it down to the main hall and took a seat next to Grizz, who coincidentally looked awful, I was almost fully awake, and more than ready for breakfast. I reached out for the small golden bell that the serving staff had placed here for summoning them at mealtimes, then gaped in shock as Grizz blocked my hand.

"I wouldn't," Grizz mumbled, yawning and rubbing the side of his head with one hand. "Seriously, boss, you don't want anything in your stomach today of all days."

"Why the hell not?" I asked, confused and hungry, reaching once more for the bell.

"Your funeral," he muttered, starting to count down. "Four, three, two…"

"Good morning, victims!" bellowed a voice that bypassed my conscious brain and kicked my hindbrain into action.

"Good morning, sir!" the entire room bellowed in response, leaping to our feet before anyone had the time to think about it.

Restun strode into view, marching into the middle of the room and turning in a slow circle, eyeing us all one at a time, making sure he had our full and undivided attention before he went on.

"As you'll all remember, it is my distinct honor to be Praetoria Primus, yet I'm without a Praetorian Guard to command. So, as of today, the tryouts will begin. For those who are unlucky enough to have already been selected for a role that will require they be a member of the guard…" He eyed me and my squad slowly. "…you get to begin your training again today. I've been informed that the plan is to siege that shithole of a city Himnel. As such, we're going to be here for months! Is that correct, trainee Jax? Yes or no answer, please!" Restun demanded.

"Y…*cough*…yes, Primus!" I forced out, my voice breaking in a decidedly unmanly way.

"Excellent!" Restun slapped his hands together and made a noise that was remarkably close to the sound I imagined would herald the end of days. "In that case, as the next few months will be more regimented in maintaining and building our forces and sorting out this city, there will be no excuse for any of you not being here EVERY MORNING an hour before sunrise to begin the day. We'll be alternating between full PT and half-and-half, with the halves split into two hours of PT followed by two hours of combat practice."

I closed my eyes slowly, cursing myself for not seeing this coming. I desperately needed to increase my skills and physical abilities, but fuck me, four hours a day? Every day? While this would be seriously counterproductive back home on Earth, here in the UnderVerse, the ability to heal yourself at the end of the session meant that the body still got the gains but was essentially fixed even better than if you'd taken a week or more between sessions.

The only relief I had was that, as the Legion were still getting used to having magic on call, they hadn't realized that you could do it over and over again. In theory, you could work out for three hours, take an hour to eat and heal, then go again. I suspected that you could do it all day every day, and I'd been careful to not so much as *think* about it around Restun, just in case.

"Now, I know that silence is because each and every one of you is just overjoyed at the chance you've been given, but don't you worry, there's more!" Restun promised, a slight, evil smile tugging at the corners of his lips. "While those of the Legion, and other forces will all be given the chance to try out for the praetorian guard, those of you who need to prove that you deserve to be considered in this company don't just get the training that everyone else is getting, you'll get an extra hour each evening! With me leading that training session personally, just me and that small cadre!"

"Fuck," I muttered.

Restun glared at me. I became hyper-aware of the way Grizz shuffled ever so slightly aside to distance himself from me.

"You've all got five minutes to get outside in your training gear, starting a minute ago! Go, go, go, go, go!" he screamed at us.

We all ran for it, stumbling over each other in our rush to get through the doors and up to our rooms to get changed.

As I staggered and bounced off the outer wall of the stairwell on my way up, I realized that Grizz was ahead of me, already fully dressed in his PT gear, making my jaw drop in shock.

He had escaped the stairwell ahead of me and vanished before I could ask him how or why, but by the time I was back outside, redressed in my training gear, I found him standing at attention.

"You fucking knew, didn't you!" I whispered, skidding to a halt and standing at attention next to Grizz, watching while Restun talked to the other trainers, Flux and Cheena included, as they discussed the plans for the day.

"He arrived three days ago. There was no way he was going to pass up the chance to make us all pay for escaping training again." Grizz replied out of the corner of his mouth. "I passed him in the hall yesterday, and that damn glint in his eye…I knew the hammer was ready to fall."

"We've been fighting and working around the clock; it's not like we were fucking partying," I muttered, then I shot Grizz another look, seeing the slight sheen of sweat and the bloodshot eyes. I sniffed, getting a wash of stale beer. "Wait…you *were* partying!?"

I glared at Thomas as he arrived, straightening to a position of attention and bringing his own cloud of stale beer with him.

"You utter bastards." I shook my head. "You didn't even invite me!"

"Tried to," Thomas grunted, staring straight ahead, even as the others fell in around us. The handful that had been here when I arrived had grown to dozens before petering out at just over a hundred as we talked. "You breezed past us, dragging Oracle into your room for some sexy time. Not our fault you chose arse over beer!"

"With that arse, it was the right choice to make."

"To be fair, you're not wrong," Thomas agreed. "She doesn't have a sister, does she?"

"I don't know, man. I keep thinking that we should try and find more wisps, and recruit them to help, but then I think about it, and realize I'd die from exhaustion."

"But what a way to go," Grizz replied, and we all looked to one another, our minds going overdrive at the thought of a village full of wisps like Oracle.

"Attention!" barked Restun, and we all jerked upright, glaring ahead as he set off among us, separating us into small groups with the other trainers taking command of the various teams. I heard them naming their groups, as Restun himself stood before our team. I knew from the movements in the corner of my eye that there were new people in the group, but I didn't dare look. Restun began to speak, his voice booming out across the grassy kill-zone.

"You have now been sorted into your new training teams! Each team has been given a name, the name of their personal trainer! You will be pitted against the other teams in everything, from PT to combat training, and each failure will be the failure of your trainer! Each time you fall in the mud, your trainer has fallen, and their name is smeared!" Restun ended each sentence with a roar that only a drill sergeant could manage.

"Each and every day, at the end of the day, your performance as a team will be evaluated, and the trainer of the lowest-performing team will have a forfeit," Flux called out, stepping forward. "Believe me when I say, I can't wait to see my fellow trainers carrying out these forfeits, and if I have to carry so much as a single one out myself, I will make my team's life a living hell!"

To my shock, Centurion Westin stepped up and let out a bellow of his own. "So, now you know what you're all competing for. And to add to the glory, those of you who want a place in the Praetorian Guard, be aware that I'll be taking twenty of you, the top twenty only! There are one hundred and twenty of you here. That's one hundred failures surrounding you, so I suggest you fight harder than you've ever fought!"

I hadn't realized he had a training position, but as I looked around, I realized that there just weren't enough primuses, not if there were six teams and some of the ranking legionnaires like Augustus were off on other jobs or back at the Tower.

"Now, for the warm-up, a nice gentle jog around the palace grounds…five times!" Restun bellowed, slapping his hands together, as Westin blew sharply on a whistle three times. "Go!"

I hesitated for a split second and was almost trampled to death by Grizz, barely keeping my feet and staggering in the direction Restun had indicated.

The "jog" was led by another legionnaire, who was blatantly setting the pace as hard as possible. Before we'd finished the third lap, two of those who had wanted to join had fallen out and been informed they'd failed.

While I wasn't surprised that they were guardsmen rather than legionnaires, they were elites, which was slightly unexpected.

The rest of the training session was brutal, with each and every one of us focusing on simply surviving it without embarrassing ourselves or causing our personal squad leader to be the loser.

For a few seconds, I considered fucking up badly enough to make Restun the failure, but then I thought about how he'd make me pay, and I redoubled my efforts in sheer terror.

The next four hours were hell, and more than once, I lamented not assigning my thirty points yet. At various times of the day, I decided that I'd put them into Strength, then Endurance, then Agility, all thirty each time, as I staggered and collapsed, groaning as I tried to keep up with people who'd done this all their lives.

By the end of the session, when the halt was called and we were permitted to collapse into sweaty, broken heaps, I had several notifications flashing for attention and no energy to deal with them. I was also receiving a splitting headache from Oracle, who was throwing herself into training our forces with a determination that was downright scary.

After a few minutes of trying to remember how to breathe, I let Grizz haul me to my feet and staggered back to the keep with the others, heading for the large, sunken baths below it.

Until now, I'd made do with the bath in my room, having it filled by the serving staff. But after that session, I joined the others in gathering up clean clothing and a fresh towel, then trooping down into the lower halls toward the bathing pools.

There were three pools down here, buried under the keep, and they'd been cleaned out the day before yesterday. Apparently during the Driders' occupation of the keep, they had been a snack-holding area for the Drow and spiderkin, filled with rows of webbed corpses and worse.

Now they were back to their proper layout; the water had been cleansed and the hot springs fixed. The braziers were lit, and fragrant herbs had been added so that the entire section was filled with a warm, comforting haze of scented mist.

I followed Jian, who was in the lead. We entered a room with a fork in the path where the ladies took the left path and we took the right, entering small cubicles where we stripped off, leaving our belongings with trustworthy staff.

From there, we trooped out to the first bath, a large, slightly ragged pool that simmered with heat as bubbles rose continually in its center. I hesitated for a few moments, until Jian simply stepped off the edge and sank like a rock.

He bobbed up a few seconds later, kicking off from the edge and moving closer to the middle, scrubbing himself furiously before taking a deep breath and sinking again.

"It gets hotter the closer you go to the middle," Thomas said, stepping off and sinking with a loud splash.

I shrugged and stepped forward, then jumped up and tucked my legs under me, shouting "Cannonball!" as I dove in. I was grinning ear to ear as I managed to time my landing just as Thomas came back to the surface, splashing him.

"Arsehole!" he snapped, then laughed and splashed me in return when I came back up.

"Holy hell, it's hot!" I groaned, backing up to the edge and giving my skin the chance to adjust, before floating closer to the center.

"It's amazing, isn't it," Grizz groaned, massaging some aching muscles.

"It feels a fuck load better than a normal bath," I admitted, before holding a hand up to block the sight of Jian clambering out of the pool. "Fuck's sake, Jian, little warning next time!" I laughed.

"Bah! Time for the second pool, boss. You use the first one to clean the sweat off, the second to wake up. Then you relax in the third, come on!" He laughed, and I swam to the side again, clambering out with the others. As we strode across the small gap to the side of the second pool, I was thinking that all we needed was a cameraman right now, and we'd sell millions of posters.

The group varied greatly in size, both height and width, but the one thing all of us had in common, was that we'd make Olympic athletes weep in envy at our bodies. That wasn't even including the man mountain that was Grizz, who could probably steal a certain heavyweight wrestler's lunch and have the man shake in fear and apologize if it wasn't tasty enough.

"Come on, boss, you can go first," Jian offered evilly, gesturing to the narrow pool before us. It was a deep blue, and where the other had been bubbling and letting off steam, this one was placid, and looked to have little bits of ice floating on the top. It was perhaps two meters wide and six meters long, the far end of the pool disappearing into fog, where I could just make out steps leading further into the room.

"Nut up or shut up!" Thomas grunted and, being the loving brother that he was, pushed me before I could get ready.

I tumbled head-first into the icy water. The cold was horrific, practically sending my body into shock as I thrashed and shook, before managing to force myself up and into the air again.

"C…c…c…c…cold!" I managed to gasp out, hearing them all laughing at me, the utter bastards. I frantically stroked to the other end of the pool and staggered up the steps and out of the water, seeing the third and final bath a few meters further away, with seats, small loungers, and so on scattered around the area next to it.

I stumbled ahead as splashing and gasps came from behind me, and strangely echoed from somewhere up ahead as well, before I made it out of the water on numbed feet, hurrying across the slippery stone floor and into the final pool.

Where the others were a sharp drop-off, going vertically down from the edge at least ten meters, this was a more gradual slope. The second my feet hit the water, I nearly bit through my tongue.

The hot water on skin that had virtually frozen was a horrible shock, but after several seconds of wincing and wading, I felt my body recovering, and by the Gods, it was good.

I continued toward the center of the pool hearing the others stumbling into the water behind me, and I turned around to give Thomas the finger. Seeing the grins on their faces and the none-too-subtle staring into the fog, I spun back around, continuing on.

There was nothing at first, but then, as I went deeper, the blurry outlines of others further away coalesced in the distance. One of the outlines was unmistakable, thanks to the wings.

I groaned, the water having finally reached high enough to return some feeling to my balls, and I lowered myself into the water, turning back and seeing the others doing the same. They relaxed in the water, watching me and grinning as I half-swam, half-crawled back to them.

"It's a mixed pool, isn't it?" I asked Thomas, who continued to grin at me.

"Yeah, the middle is nice and deep, but unless you're trying to catch the girls naked, you should, you know, stay on this side," he warned me, shaking his head in mock disapproval.

"You dick." I rolled over and got comfortable in the water.

"Well, it would have been hilarious," Grizz admitted, sighing as he stretched out. "Don't get me wrong, boss, it's fine to swim around both sides, but you walking through the middle, swinging it around for them to see until you realized…it would have been something we could wind you up about for years to come."

"Bastard." I grinned in spite of myself.

"This is ridiculous," Giint gurgled, splashing towards us. He was barely able to keep his head above the water due to the depth of the pool, so we moved back into a shallower area, letting him catch his breath.

The girls joined us after a bit as we all moved closer to the indefinable middle of the pool, while navigating to the north end where it was shallower.

It was a little weird at first, with all of us lying there in the water together, as it was less than waist deep, but if we moved any further in, Giint would probably drown.

We'd been around each other for weeks, constantly getting changed, bathing in streams, scrubbing ourselves free of…bits…of our enemies and worse, and it meant that there was virtually no modesty left between our small group, especially with the number of times they'd all walked in on *me* naked.

Yet, for some reason, it seemed totally different when we were all stark naked in a shared pool, especially for poor Lydia, who kept accidentally submerging Giint with her wings when she twitched in the wrong way.

We were close to getting out, when splashing and squealing nearby alerted us to others arriving. I couldn't help but grin when I saw Oracle, flanked by Tenandra and Sehran.

The three of them had absolutely no issues with body modesty, which meant that the view was fantastic for all of us, as even Yen and Lydia took the time to admire them. Thomas reached over, giving me a fist bump and a sad shake of his head.

"Seriously bro, if you ever get a hint that she's got a sister out there, I'm going looking." He grinned.

But as I looked over, barely able to tear my eyes away from the incoming trio, I saw it in the last second, the look of sadness and regret on his face.

"What…?" I asked, before dropping it when he shook his head and turned back to the rest of the group, striking up a conversation with Jian.

"Hey, my love," Oracle whispered, flowing into my arms and kissing me, getting an instant reaction that I did my damn best to hide and stop. I shifted around under the water and got a sense of amusement through our bond as she damn well knew what her wet, silky-smooth skin did to me.

"I'm worried about Thomas," I sent to her through the bond.

"I know. We need to try and keep him busy, let him get over things in his own time," Oracle replied before splashing Thomas and jokingly asking him if he was happy to see the girls, considering the way he was watching Sehran and Tenandra.

He coughed and looked away, getting a knowing grin from Jian.

"I know. I'm lucky," Jian said, floating back into the Succubus's arms. Tenandra shook her head and struck up a conversation with Thomas, asking him questions about our lives before here, while he frantically tried to keep his eyes focused on her face.

After a few minutes of relaxing and occasional joking with the others, I sighed and gave Oracle one last kiss.

"Okay then, you lazy buggers. Unlike you, I've got a lot to do today, and I didn't expect to lose the morning. See you all soon," I said, moving away. After a few comments from Thomas and Grizz, asking if I was going to crawl the entire way, I sighed and stood. I shook my ass at the girls, then laughed and strode away through the shallower areas, heading for the changing rooms.

It took less than three minutes after leaving the baths, fully dressed and ravenous, before Cai caught me. He and Hannibal proceeded to hammer me with questions and recommendations, even as we headed to the main hall, and I got my much-delayed breakfast.

The rest of the afternoon passed slowly. I met representatives of the Merchants' Guild, the Captains' Cabal, as the captains of the sea ships called themselves, the engineers from the shipyards, and dozens of others, including a fun meeting with Mal's partner, Alyssa. She had been named as the head of the Seamstresses' Guild, and was simply there to make sure I understood that she and her guild wouldn't be, and I quote, "taking it lying down" if anyone was bad-mouthing the Empire.

Apparently, my insistence that she and several of her immediate staff be given healing magic to help their people, and the hanging of a noble who'd been both a frequent visitor to their establishments, and too powerful to hold to account for his actions, had encouraged an almost rabid following amongst their sector. There were also promises of freebies should I wish to visit and discounts on their services for any legionnaires.

That last part had apparently been declared last night and had resulted in a sharp upswing in the number of tired legionnaires this morning, as well as a rush to the recruiting station.

The next issue involved the massive cathedral at the center of the city. While it had originally been dedicated to all the Gods, Nimon had converted it to a place to worship only Him and His Dark Pantheon, with the dozens of smaller temples and churches around the city being split between Him and one other member of His Pantheon at each site.

I'd taken the time to speak to the Gods, primarily Jenae, and They'd assured me that the next day They would appear when I called, and would lead my people in consecrating the cathedral, followed by appearing at each site, cleansing them and claiming them for the entire Pantheon.

The cleansing of the churches would be a massive undertaking, but considering that there were over ninety thousand people in the city, it was well worth it, even if only a small percentage of them turned into worshippers.

The last duty of the day, at nearly seven at night, was to attend the armory site. The golems had finally cleared the upper levels to the point that the sealed chambers were now exposed, although anybody who didn't have Imperial blood or a certain level of Imperial authority still could not open them.

I was fairly sure that Romanus, at the very least, and probably the upper leadership of the Legion, could have opened the sealed doors, but I was still thankful for the excuse to attend and be the first inside.

CHAPTER FORTY-THREE

I was told that it would take at least an hour to reach the armory site by carriage. So, being the Scion and having access to my own ships, I told the idiot offering to arrange carriages at "a reasonable cost" to get fucked, and I used Tenandra instead. I was almost impressed that someone had just tried to shake me down, before Carmen informed me that the palace actually paid for every carriage ride they required. A noble had talked Rewn into selling him the carriages a few years back for a seemingly insane price.

They had then rented the same carriages back to Rewn at an even more ridiculous rate and made the cost of buying them back in under a year, earning horrific profits since then.

When I heard that, I told Hannibal to buy the palace some carriages, then tell the Gnomes to get them as fantastic as possible. We'd use them in place of the noble's scam. Hannibal, of course, loved that idea, and asked to be the one to tell the noble about it. I shrugged and told him to have his fun.

I marched down the gangplank as soon as we had landed, having to dodge around a small party of Gnomes who were desperately trying to get to Tenandra.

The city, as it turned out, had a large contingent of regular Gnomes living in a few heavily guarded buildings. They'd gone absolutely apeshit when they found out that not only had their God returned, but that Wisps from the last days of the Empire were suddenly available to share its knowledge.

As I'd been busy, I had foolishly sent Giint to meet them, and now they seemed to be in a mix of religious fervor and drug-fueled shock. I kept my distance, deciding that, once the Gnomes arrived from the Tower, I'd let the more sensible members of the group deal with them instead.

The section of the city we were passing above had been more attractive at night. The parks we flew over had small paths winding here and there, with soft lights shining to keep the place bright enough that citizens could walk the streets at night.

Still, I had noticed that this was a series of parks and richer homes in the nobles' section of the city, as opposed to the slums on the far side. I made a mental note to look into getting the slums cleared.

I didn't want them flattened and the people killed or moved, as so many politicians seemed to want back home. No, this was where the majority of the manual laborers, unskilled workers, cleaning staff, and servants lived. They were the cheapest homes and the least safe.

I'd been there. I'd had enough times in my life where I had fuck all and could either pay my rent and my other bills, or I could eat, and never more than one of them. So, I knew what the richer, more upstanding citizens did not.

These people they looked down on, the cleaners, the janitors, the food service staff and warehouse workers, everyone that the politicians viewed as disposable were utterly indispensable.

They formed the bedrock that society lived on, the solid, dependable base for people to build their lives. Without them, bugger all got done.

I made a mental note to check out the slums. If I could fix them up, making the homes better, safer, and more affordable, hell, even make the beer better and cheaper, I'd have a level of support that would exponentially grow.

I'd have people who would reach out, quietly, to the guards when they saw wrongdoing, assuming they didn't just deal with it themselves on the spot. I grinned at that thought, before striding across the torn grass and clasping the wrist of an Elf I recognized.

"Finbar, is that you?" I asked, and he grinned in pleasure at being recognized.

"Lord Jax! Welcome to the Imperial Armory," he said, waving his arm to encompass the dig site.

It was huge, easily a mile square, if not more. A mile didn't seem that big to anyone who hadn't tried to dig a garden over, but the thought of the massive amount of effort that had been devoted to the clearing of this site made my nuts shrivel. I looked out at the pits, the sloping paths that led down to exposed stonework and the piles upon piles of dying trees, bushes, and more.

There were carefully trimmed topiary bushes, half-buried by dirt and debris, the remains of expensive pathways, and an ornamental pond all in a mound on one side, as a pair of massive golems dug with a speed that was frightening.

They had uncovered the stonework that had lain forgotten beneath the gardens with a speed that would have astounded a modern construction crew, and they just didn't stop.

"Holy hell," I muttered, stunned.

"Tell me they take coffee breaks?" Thomas said from beside me, and I shook my head. "All I need is a pair of these and a ticket back to Earth. Builders that don't require coffee breaks would be magical on their own, but the way they work? I'll be a billionaire in a month!"

"Except you need magic for them to work, so they would stop working after a week," I pointed out.

"Still better than most builders."

I snorted, remembering the mess we'd found when a friend had bought a new kitchen and hired a company to get it fitted. They'd asked for the money upfront. She'd paid it, foolishly.

They had come and taken the old one out without checking if the parts were right for the new one, leaving her without a kitchen. Needless to say, half of it was missing, and while it only took a few days to get the bits replaced, they'd said they were too busy when the correct parts had arrived.

They kept promising to come back in a week or so and never did, until we met her one night in the pub and heard all about it. We'd ended up butchering the kitchen when we installed it for her, as we weren't experienced or trained, but after six frigging months without a kitchen?

Once we'd fitted it for her, we visited the builders personally, and "explained" the situation to them. They turned up on Monday the following week, refunded her, and, as an apology, they redecorated her house at their expense.

Thomas breaking the fingers of the owner one at a time with his own hammer had made our lack of sympathy for his personal problems clear.

"Yeah, builders are always an experience…remember Tony and Peter?" I asked.

He grunted, nodding. They had been the opposite end of that spectrum, honest, hardworking, and damn good at their jobs. It was kind of weird the way we always seemed to meet people that were one or the other, never just the average Joe. I shrugged and moved on, stepping across one of the numerous wooden plank bridges, and looking down into the deep trenches that had been dug seemingly at random.

"So, Finbar…"

"The trenches were to locate the buildings. While there's probably more structures that are still hidden, at least we now know these were the main facilities."

"So, what happened here?" I asked, looking about. "They just buried the buildings?"

"As far as we can tell, most of the buildings were destroyed in the Great Cataclysm, and the locals foraged the debris for spare stone to help in the rebuilding. The lower floors were secure areas, so they were sealed by magic, and they somehow stayed like that until now."

"There're active mana collectors, then." I exchanged a pleased look with Oracle. "If we can repair them…"

"We can speed up the Oaths!" She nodded. "That would be amazing. I hate how long this is taking with the current groups."

"I could dump all my points into Intelligence," I offered, starting up a conversation we'd had a dozen times already.

"No, not until we know more of how this is going to work out. You know you'll just regret it. A mass of points like that makes a huge difference, and dumping them in somewhere to make a tiny improvement would be a waste," Oracle said tiredly.

"It would." Thomas opined. "I spread my points out when I hit thirty, evened up a load of areas, but you wonder what it would have been like, you know? If you'd put them all in one place? I'm going to put all my points when I hit forty into one area, just to see what happens."

"What level are you now, dude?" I asked.

"Thirty-seven, but just so you know? That's like asking a woman her bra size, personal info that a lot won't share."

"You're my brother."

"And that's why I don't give a shit, but still, I got slapped a few times for asking the same question, so be warned, dude!"

"Fair enough, thanks for the heads up," I said, stepping off a plank that bowed and bounced as we clambered along it, landing on a loose patch of muddy ground and skidding slightly as some of it shifted under me.

I adjusted my balance, only noticing the movement because I'd skidded a few inches down the long ramp that led into the hole. I realized that I'd been doing it constantly, as the loose earth adjusted. But with my superhuman levels of Agility, I hadn't consciously registered it.

I was about to continue moving, heading across the narrow strip of grass to the next plank bridge, when something exposed on a rock farther down in the ditch caught my eye, a pattern I recognized.

I shrugged, and rather than fighting to walk down the slope, I kicked off and slid, skidding down the four meters to the muddy bottom, and landed with a grunt. I planted my foot firmly on a pile of rock before crouching to look at the pattern. I had only seen it from above because of the contrast between the wall and the dirt filling the deeper sections.

"You know there's a better way to the doors from up here, right?" Thomas called down, gesturing to the wooden bridges that crisscrossed the entire site.

"You know I can fly…right?" I grinned and received a finger in response as Thomas headed for the door his own way. I turned back and looked at the symbol.

It was a starburst, set inside a spiral that ran round and round, expanding out to over a meter in diameter. Without thinking, I touched it, sweeping the dirt free and fully exposing the pattern, digging with my fingers in places to work the dirt loose.

As soon as it was complete, and I could see the symbol clearly, I knew.

Recognition rose from somewhere deep inside, and my lip curled in a mix of remembered pride and disgust for what the team that bore this symbol had done.

"Hey bro, want me to open this door then, or what?" Thomas called down, grinning, his fingertips already reaching for the handle.

My blood ran cold.

"No!" I shouted. "Fuck no, get back!" Kicking off hard, I slammed power into Soaring Majesty and flashed through the air, flipping over to land between Thomas and the nearest door, now knowing what was most likely behind at least one of them.

"Everyone fall back from the site!" I roared, my voice echoing louder than it should, as the golems responded to my subconscious will, stopping all excavation and moving everyone back from the uncovered buildings.

A shudder wracked the place as something inside the building reacted to its prey backing away, giving up on pretending to be innocent.

"Fuck!" I shouted. "Romanus, get the Legion here! Thomas, Lydia, get everyone back! Jian, get on Tenandra and get people out of here! Sehran, you're with me!" I bellowed, snapping the orders out rapid-fire.

"What is…oh," Oracle whispered, breaking off mid-question as she felt the wash of concern and fury coming off Amon. She barked orders to the others, telling them to get ready, even as I yanked my naginata out and stood before the crystal door, which rippled as something moved behind it, only dimly visible.

"What's going on, boss?" Grizz asked, stepping up to my shoulder and eyeing the door.

"Valspar," I replied. "This is one of the first that came through. It was trapped in here for study, then the Cataclysm came, and I guess it escaped confinement."

"What do we do?" Grizz asked.

"We fuck it up. It's awake now, since it's probably sensed us all, and the site isn't as secure or strong as it used to be. If we bury it again, it'll just burrow its way out eventually. Besides, the area it's in will have been the heart of the facility. If it's not totally trashed it, then that's exactly where we'll find everything we've been looking for." I rolled my shoulders and wished I'd worn armor, rather than the pseudo-uniform that the tailors had provided for meetings.

I slammed the base of my naginata into the soil and tugged the dress jacket off, tossing it over my shoulder into a ditch before grabbing the buttons of my shirt and tearing it off Hulk Hogan style.

"Well, that was impressive, but the tailor is going to kill you," Yen said, grinning. I couldn't help but smile back.

"Yeah, but at least now I can move again. If I thought I had the time, I'd get rid of these pants and boots as well," I said, shaking my arms out with much-improved freedom of movement.

"Promises, promises!" Sehran sang before shooting a guilty look at Oracle, who winked at her.

"All right, people," I said, looking around at the small team who stood with me. "This is gonna be a clusterfuck of a fight, but we need to kill it and fast. This thing is an ancestor to the SporeMother, one of the original Valspar hosts, and nobody knows where the hell it comes from.

"All we know is that it was in the realm between the stars, feeding on something else when the Imperial mages found it while scrying for other life. It forced its way through the portal, slaughtered every fucker nearby, and started breeding. That kicked off a massive war between the Empire and its kind, and the only reason we won is because a fuck ton of greater Dragons sacrificed everything.

"This thing CANNOT get to the city. If it does, and it's able to feed, it'll start breeding, then the entire realm is fucked. No matter what, it dies, understand?"

In addition to my squad, five of the Legion stood with us, as well as three of the city's elite guards who were close by.

Thomas and Lydia pushed people back. Lydia helped Finbar across a wide ditch by the expedient method of physically picking him up and flying, while Thomas, being easily recognized as my brother and the de facto leader of the guards, commanded an automatic obedience from most of the locals.

They were clearly itching to get back to my side, but they did as I asked. I stared back at the crystal doorway before me, taking a deep breath.

"Get ready, people…" I called, even as Grizz pointed to some of the blocks that made up the wall nearby, which were slowly bulging outward.

"Boss," he said in a warning tone. "I think it's getting close to breaking out."

"Then let's make sure it's here rather than there." I grunted, reaching out with my mind the way I did with the crystal doors at the Great Tower.

"Open," I ordered. There was a split second of hesitation before the magic recognized me as its rightful master and released the field that was holding it together.

The crystal shimmered and parted, the nearby torches and magelights shining into a scene from hell. A roiling black cloud of eyes and teeth shifted, bunching up, then striking. A tentacle-like limb nearly the size of the doorway scythed across where I was standing mere seconds before.

I leaped aside, the rest of the team scattering as it slammed into the ground. I had a split second to register oily flesh, a mass of what looked like teeth and spines, and an insanely rolling eyeball the size of my fist that glared its hatred before I slashed at it. The blade barely sliced the upper layer of its skin, but as I slammed mana into the naginata, it shone with a bright, white light.

A tremendous scream burst from inside the doorway as the flesh closest to the radiant weapon bubbled and smoked. The last few inches of flesh the tip had cut blackened and separated like powdered sherbet. The nearby flesh crumbled to dust and fell, even as it yanked the limb back.

I grinned, peering into the doorway, and got a split second of satisfaction as the blackened flesh pulled away, before the edge of a massive face appeared, the mouth opening, pointed in my direction.

It looked weird, like a cross between an octopus and a Dragon, with a bulbous head and pulsating flesh, complete with enormous eyes, dozens of them. But the mouth…

It was triangular, filled with serrated teeth, and, as I watched, an unhealthy green tongue slid into view, splitting along the middle and peeling apart, exposing a hollow core that sprayed viscous gunk at us.

I saw it coming far too late, and the stance I was in wouldn't allow me to dodge. I barely had time to close my eyes before Grizz was there, and the world dissolved into bloodcurdling screams and howls.

He had slammed his shield between the liquid the creature was vomiting and me, holding it high to cover my upper body, while he took the brunt of the fluid on his side and lower legs.

It seared into his flesh, dissolving it, turning metal black with corrosion and causing the leather of his under armor to char and flake free. Through it all, Grizz held his shield over me, protecting me with his body, as much as the metal slab that he held.

Arrows and Flamespears roared past us, as I stared into Grizz's eyes, seeing them roll up as he fought to stay alive long enough to protect me. I screamed my refusal of it, my disbelief that I could lose my friend so quickly and so completely, as his flesh began to rot away.

Pride and satisfaction crossed his face as the stream stopped, then he collapsed, hitting the floor in a boneless clatter of armor and flesh.

I screamed again, a barrage of light rocketing past me as a handful, then dozens of Magic Missiles soared into the darkness, punching holes in the creature and detonating, before I spun and kicked off.

I flew across the distance between me and the Valspar, landing inside the doorway, and skidding. I slashed the naginata sideways, slicing open its chin and cheek. It yanked its head back, already reeling from the barrage.

"Heal him!" I bellowed, the command ringing in the air as the Legion closed in, with Romanus leading. They diverted squads to hammer Grizz with spell after spell, unable to prevent the entropy that was consuming him from continuing, but the massive influx of healing magic rebuilt flesh, bones, and muscles over and over again, waging a war against the entropic sludge he was coated in.

Oracle was by my side as I flashed to the right, a tentacle landing where I'd been seconds earlier, leaving shattered stonework in its wake as it slithered back. The room was lit by the dim glow of my weapon, exposing the sloping floor and the stairs that led down to the next level, where the primary mass of the Valspar waited some twenty meters below.

The creature was huge, but mainly made up of oily smoke and glowing eyes. Its bulk shifted continually, and it lay sprawled over several massive Genesis Chambers of a design I didn't recognize.

Its head pulled back, and a limb shot forward in its place. The clicking and popping of bones made it clear that it was taking them from somewhere else to lengthen this one, somehow able to internally rearrange itself on the fly. As it lashed out, Lydia raised her shield, taking the blow and being hurled backwards through the air.

I grunted and dove aside, swooping around and twisting into a barrel roll in midair, slashing out with my glowing blade and digging deep into its limb, drawing another screech.

Before the long spear of flesh and bone could be yanked back, I twisted my naginata and ripped it upward. The weapon dug deeper and sliced into the bone, doing serious damage to the limb before it retreated, yanked back with tremendous speed and force.

I clung to my naginata, being pulled along with it before seeing the oily wall of flesh ahead of me at the last second. It towered in front of me, flowing away from the limb like a cliff, as segment after segment of the limb slid back inside. The flesh shifted around as the bones were redistributed to form a ring that grew as I flew towards it.

I slammed into the creature's chest, hanging onto my weapon for dear life, as I planted my feet flat against the ridged bone, using the flesh wall as my floor. I braced myself and ripped the weapon free, even as Amon raged and gibbered in my mind, screaming to be set free.

As soon as I'd realized what was here, I had also been fighting a second battle, between Amon and myself, both of us fighting for ascendancy, as I sensed the line of his thoughts.

If this thing had survived, along with the Valspar we'd found at Wayland's Crossing, and the one that I'd torn from my chest in Himnel, then this land needed to be cleansed.

The deal we'd struck, where Amon's fragmented, insane remnant would help, sitting back and guiding me as I grew to take his place, was forgotten in the desperate need to protect the realm against the Valspar, and I couldn't risk what he'd do.

I yanked my weapon free of the Valspar's flesh, kicking off. But rather than soaring as I intended, my leg bones grated together. The sections that made up the spear-like limb, tens of dozens of what looked like giant fingerbones, had been laid end on end, and rearranged themselves around a central point.

Exactly where my feet had come to rest against its flesh.

The bones shot forward, acting like a jaw as it closed around my legs. The massive nubs that had made up the end of each fingerbone were encased in flesh and pressed hard against my thighs, squeezing them with enough pressure that they threatened to break, even as the new mouth inverted, slowly carrying me downward. Searing pain enveloped me as hollow fangs punctured the flesh of my legs in multiple places and started to suck.

Oracle glowed like a miniature sun as she built a Lightning Bolt of insane scale. Crossbow bolts and arrows flashed through the air, slamming into the creature, even as a golden light flared outside, washing inward and making the creature shudder.

The Valspar pulled back from the entrance, everything else forgotten as the massive wave of healing magic that had been constantly pouring into Grizz, frantically fighting against the entropy of the realm between the stars, passed some mysterious level and drew divine attention.

The world seemed to shift as I thrust my naginata into the flesh at the base of one of the fingers and yanked it sideways, carving through the oily skin and releasing a noxious wave of reeking yellow fluids as Oracle let loose with her spell.

The supercharged Lightning Bolt roared across the distance separating her and the Valspar with a sound like the world ending, impacting with a boom that shook the walls and made my ears bleed. Sound dropped to a weird, pressure-filled sensation, like being underwater.

The Valspar took the blow to its face like a champ, staggering and screaming its defiance. It slashed at her with a pair of tentacles that she dodged with a sneer of disgust before hurling an Explosive Compression spell at the junction between the tentacles and where they met the creature's body, high on its back.

I grunted in pain as more teeth sank into me, the sucking pressure climbing as it literally sucked my blood out, like a drunken tart on my neck in a nightclub.

I drove the naginata deeper, flooding it with magic, grimly aware of all the potions that I'd grabbed when I had seen them in the treasury. I'd used most of my mana potions in that stupid display of Imperial Right yesterday afternoon, and at the rate this battle was going, we were fucked if we couldn't find a way to end it quickly.

The Valspar shifted with an audible and palpable scream, flowing over the top of the nearest Genesis Chamber and bunching up, leaping to the wall and hauling itself up into the doorway.

It had felt the touch of our spells, and, even now, Explosive Compression was breaking bones and shattering sections of its back, rendering limbs useless. But the divine presence outside was busy, and it had to take the chance to flee or to strike the God down if it was ever to be free again.

I screamed as I was slammed into the wall again and again, most of my ribs and my left femur shattering, even as my naginata burned its way deeper, causing several of the creature's fingers to be cut loose, making me sag to the side.

"Jax!" Lydia screamed, landing in front of the Valspar, holding her shield up proudly and daring it to strike her.

She was the only thing between it and freedom, and we could all sense the divine attention that had come to bear on the smoldering, screaming figure of Grizz.

"Jax, shield!" she screamed, waving the shield overhead before flaring her wings out to their full span, making herself as tempting a target as possible.

I frowned, my adrenaline-filled mind trying to make sense of her comment, until my eyes opened wide in realization. I yanked my own identical shield free of my bag and imbued it with an Ability that we'd only used once before.

"Do it!" I screamed, setting the shield on the middle of my back and bracing the naginata against the underside of my armpit. I clung on to it for dear life, even as Oracle hit me with a heal.

Sacrifice was a weird Ability. It allowed all the force, damage, and inertia of an impact to transfer from one shield to the other. If one of the wielders was about to be killed, but the other could take the hit and survive? They could swap the impact. They would be taking a hell of a hit, yet not suffering any of the force, displacement, or damage, so they'd be left in a perfect position to counterattack.

That was, if the aim was to save one of the bearer's lives.

Here, it just might provide the push I needed. It was horrifically risky and would be painful beyond measure, as Lydia damn well knew, but she'd taken my warning to heart: either we killed this thing, or we *all* died.

The Valspar snarled as it squeezed its way through the gap, rearing up to stand over its prison of centuries, if not millennia. As it reached its full height, it swungone of its mighty forelimbs down toward Lydia with terrifying force, as she hunched under her shield, triggering its ability.

I curled under my own shield, or at least as far as I could. My right leg was still being tugged down by the thin tentacle that gripped it, the teeth digging in deeper and scraping bone as I gritted my teeth.

Then the Valspar hit Lydia, and all hell broke loose.

CHAPTER FORTY-FOUR

The inertia hit me like nothing I could imagine. The impact of hundreds of tons of weight alone should have been terrible enough, but the combined muscles producing the force that slammed into the shield I had pressed to my back made it so much worse.

I blasted through the already weakened fingers or whatever it was that held me like a truck through cardboard. The next impact was the creature's skin and the flexible layer of bone that coated the inside, and I barely managed to hold my breath as I entered that terrible monstrosity.

I cut a ring that was almost the size of my body loose with my naginata, so that layer wasn't too much of a hinderance, either. It was the weird layer I hit next that was the real problem.

It was like rubber.

It was only a few inches thick, but fuck it was strong, and while the sudden acceleration from zero to about three hundred miles an hour would have killed me if I was fully human, the resulting deceleration of hitting that layer still almost managed to do it.

Bones fractured.

Dozens, possibly hundreds of spiderweb cracks raced across my bones in insane fractal patterns, even as the naginata sliced through that layer with ease. The tear in the Valspar grew as my body was forced through the path my naginata had cut, quickly widening it, before I entered the inside of the original beast.

As I passed through the layers of the Valspar's body, my magic faded fast. I entered the innermost layer, and a mana migraine flared, making the light that shone from my weapon, which was arguably the most damaging part of my attack, fade. To my shock, the Valspar was not entirely biological, but a hybrid creature.

It shook and shuddered as its core, a massive spherical orb that pulsed with green and black, felt the touch of light. Where the outside was merely being badly burned by the nearby magelights, flames, starlight, and more, the inside was being horrifically mauled by the dying light I bore.

I fumbled for my pouch, screaming internally at my fingers to obey, to move or just to godsdamn WORK, but it was useless. They were a mass of shredded bones, having taken some of the worst of the damage, forcing the wounds open around the slim shape of my weapon and guiding the path of destruction as my arms went through next. Meanwhile, the impact of the shield had been primarily against my shoulders and upper legs.

My torso screamed in pain, too, but given time, that would have healed even without magic.

The rest of me, though? Fuck, that needed magic.

I twitched and shook, trying desperately to reach my pouch as the last of my air dwindled away. I squeezed my eyes shut as they burned. The noxious interior of the Valspar was clearly incompatible with most life, not surprising for a creature that had developed far beyond any planetary atmosphere.

With a grunt, I forced myself to keep holding onto my weapon, slashing it wildly, desperate to do enough damage to kill the fucking Valspar before I died in turn. Oracle was out there somewhere, desperately trying to get to me, but a flailing tentacle sent her flying.

A sudden flash of light burst across my retinas, visible even through my closed eyelids, as something insanely bright went off. A wracking scream tore through the Valspar, reverberating against me, the walls of its insides acting like a giant fucking drum, before it hit me.

A heal.

My bones mended, as heals by the dozen slammed into me, bringing me back from the brink like I was a phoenix rising from the ashes.

I opened my eyes as the sweet kiss of air wafted across one sodden cheek, and they appeared then: the Legion.

Dozens of my people formed a circle on the side of the creature, staring down at me. More filed in behind them, physically straining to hold back the edge of the wound, heaving at it, pulling it harder and harder, tearing it wider through sheer fucking determination, as I was exposed.

I looked up at them, drew in a deep breath, and shouted up to them all. "LEGION! FUCK THIS THING UP!"

The answering scream was insane.

It rose from hundreds of throats, made up of the roar of trigaras, the deep-throated bellow of half Orcs, the bloodcurdling scream of insane fucking Gnomes and the deep bass of Dwarves, the higher piccolo of the Elves and the middle-of-the-road sound of humanity.

Dozens more were in there: imps flashed past overhead. Djinn came screaming down out of the darkened sky, their spells pushing back the flesh from me, even as the Valspar warbled and shrieked. Through it all, the divine presences grew, and through it all…there was Oracle.

Sweet Oracle, *baying* for the Valspar's heart on a fucking platter. I looked up to the legionnaires, and I called out, grim and furious over everything that had happened.

"If you want to kill this thing before the Gods do, you'd better be fuckin' quick!" I roared, and an answering bellow rose as they attacked with renewed ferocity, stabbing and bashing with abandon.

I turned and yanked a potion from my bag, my freshly fixed fingers working perfectly. I downed the liquid, then followed up with another, mana, stamina, mana. Then I attacked, the naginata flaring to life as I carved my way into the Valspar, my people hauling back against the thing's frantic attempts to heal the wounds.

It was on its side now. I had no clue how that had happened or why, but it was, its thrashing tentacles falling dead, one after another. I saw it again, the gem that had pulsed and screamed at me to take it: the core, something that in a normal creature would be the size of a thumbnail, here was the size of my torso, and it screamed with power.

I slashed up and down, the flesh peeling back easily, the darkening spread of the light burn crumbling the flesh and muscle to dust, radiating outwards from the sliced segments. I grunted, dipping low with my left hand, stabbing the blade into the newly revealed surrounding tissue.

The core was embedded into a mass that looked like cooling lava, a faint green glow emitting from the cracks. As I stabbed out, the blade crunched into it, sending a keening scream through the creature, reverberating against the walls and making my head throb like a drum.

I pushed deeper, cutting into it. More lights shone inside, the outer crust flaking away as more and more of the gleaming essence cores were exposed, and I grinned as I realized what they were. This wasn't the Valspar's core, or at least not only; these were the cores of creatures the Valspar had consumed!

There were dozens, hundreds possibly, and I gritted my teeth and yanked, freeing the blade and twisting it around, peeling the flesh back from the mass like a butcher stripping tendons and ropey fat from a sweet fillet.

The more I cut, the louder the screams and the wider the wounds became, until a single voice echoed through all of our minds at once.

"Stop…stop…I beseech you!" it implored, weakness clear, before a second voice echoed over the top of its begging.

"Stop," a second voice said. I growled in anger, determined to claim my kill, and the prize I saw before me, before the same voice echoed in my mind alone. ***"Please, Jax, you do not know what will be lost if you kill this creature,"*** Jenae whispered.

"It killed Grizz!" I snarled, and I felt the truth as she responded to me.

"No. It tried, but it failed, thanks to the concerted efforts of his brothers and sisters, not to mention Lagoush. Their determination to save him, combined with his sheer refusal to give in and to go quietly into the night kept him going long enough for my sister to lend a hand. It was through her examination of the nature of the wounds that we learned the truth. You cannot kill the Valspar mother, Jax."

"Watch me!" I snapped, drawing back my naginata, but even as I did, I saw more and more of the glowing cores, as thousands of cracks radiated outwards, spreading like wildfire, exposing more of the creature's essence core.

"Jax, please!" Jenae begged.

I hesitated, Oracle nudging me gently in my mind to listen, knowing damn well how close I was to striking.

"The Valspar isn't what we thought it was; it's not what Amon thought it was. Please wait!"

"Fuck's sake, Jenae!" I snapped. "It and its kind killed millions! They killed Shustic!"

"Yes, Jax, and it needed to."

"WHAT?!" I roared, fury rising.

"Jax, for life to exist, so must death! Without death, trillions of beings would exist in unending pain and hunger; death is the opposite side of the coin to life. We cannot kill an Avatar of Death itself, not fully. But trust me, and there is much we can gain!"

"I will…serve you…teach you…" a voice whispered insidiously.

I snarled, lifting the naginata high again, aiming for the center of the mass of essence cores as the voice fell silent in pain and terror.

"Jax, if you kill it, you will gain experience, true, but that's it. Satisfaction and experience. If you give it to us, we can strip its memories of the worlds it visited, knowledge of the truths of every aspect of reality, power beyond anything we have ever experienced. It would enable us to stand firm against Nimon again!"

I heard the hunger in Jenae's voice, and I held myself in check, not letting the thoughts finish forming in my mind, deliberately wiping my mind as clean as I could, even as my skin grew cold with worry.

"Think of it, Jax. Rather than setting the Valspar mother free, we could interrogate it, draw out its power. Yes, it's dark, but we can find a way to cleanse that."

"You want to use its power?"

"Yes!" Jenae replied quickly. *"For good! Think of all we could accomplish, Jax!"*

I felt it then, the need, the hunger that my fury had buffered me from. Her voice mumbled on, but I stopped listening to her, hearing a new voice instead.

"I could serve you, only you." The voice rumbled through me, even though I knew it was in my mind alone. *"The others are too weak, too pathetically concerned with their own needs. You, I could serve. I could raise you up, teach you, and stand by your side. We could teach them all!"*

As the voice whispered, images formed in my mind, images of Jenae and the others squabbling over the power and bringing about a new cataclysm. I saw myself beating Them back, snarling at Them in fury, and the Gods falling to Their knees, admitting they were wrong.

They were lesser creatures. They might be Gods, but wasn't that because they'd been gifted the power somehow? They hadn't earned it, not the way I had…no. Power like this needed more.

It needed a master who could wield it for the good of the Empire! Not the squabbling people that backstabbed and fought, stealing and murdering their fellows, not those sycophantic fools who tried to serve but secretly plotted to take what was mine.

As for the innocent, what were they, but fools who'd been too scared, too weak to take the chances that life offered to the strong? They were the sheep, and they were meant to be ruled by a wolf! They…

"I love you." I heard her voice as if from far away, weak and small, and felt a small hand caress my cheek and tiny lips kiss my brow.

I opened my eyes, seeing Oracle hovering before me as the world grew darker, the outer skin that we'd labored so hard to slice open, sliding inexorably closer together, the legionnaires releasing it as they grew distracted, listening to voices and seeing possibilities that only they could see.

Oracle was all I could see, and I ignored the voice whispering into my mind in favor of staring into her eyes.

She floated there, her wings blurring, her hands resting on my cheeks, barely six inches high. She stared into my eyes, and the warm glow of her love filled my heart, even as I sensed the Gods, the Legion, and more all around me.

I flicked my eyes to the sides, keeping my mind as blank as possible, yet filled to bursting with her love, in place of the contempt for all life that had been there seconds before.

The Djinn that had followed me into the literal belly of the beast were slowly slid down to the ground, ground that was reaching up for them, opening with teeth sliding slowly out, ready to…

"NOW!" I roared to Oracle, not even knowing why I spoke aloud, whipping the naginata up from where it had drooped, magic flaring to life as I stabbed forwards, punching the blade in deep and activating Mana Overdrive.

Oracle slammed mana into herself, flaring with a golden white light as she screamed at everyone, making them flinch back to awareness.

Screams and roars of fury rang out, then a high-pitched screech of pain as my naginata bit deep, digging through layers and layers of essence cores. They crunched as they fractured apart, their millennia of being compressed and fitted tight breaking open as I rammed it deeper and deeper.

Even as teeth sank into my legs, my arms, a fleshy maw stretched out of the flesh wall next to me, aiming for my head. I closed my eyes, pushing deeper, refusing to pull back, though the walls of the body closed in.

I could yank the weapon free. I could slice and dice and remove the immediate threat. But that was what IT wanted, anything that stopped me from cutting deeper and reaching its heart was losing this fight.

In the few seconds that we'd stopped attacking it, as we all fell slowly under its spell, listening to its promises to serve, even as it started to twist who and what we'd do, the wounds had begun to heal, to close with amazing and terrifying speed, as if they'd never been.

Now the Legion were attacking again, the Gods awoke from their stunned state. A furious roar ripped from one of them as the entire body shook with an impact.

"My heart is PURE!" a voice bellowed in outrage.

I grinned, even as I shoved harder, the blade slipping deeper and deeper, inches at a time, the maw stretching open wider as it reached out.

"Oh, you went and pissed Sint off," I grunted, glaring at an eye I'd not noticed before, smirking at the way it glared back at me. "And even if you kill me, He's gonna rip you a new arsehole!"

The skin around me was constantly blackening and crisping away, burned by the light that Oracle gave off, but it wasn't enough.

A sudden blur of movement nearby caught my attention, and the maw was sliced apart in a blur of blades moving so fast I could barely register them.

Oracle's light grew brighter.

The blur moved faster, now that the maw was gone, literally shreds of flesh where it'd been, flesh that poured with the creature's version of blood, the wounds unhealing. The other appendages that held me in place lay shredded.

"Bane!" I gasped, my mouth speaking before my brain had finished processing it. For a split second, he spun nearby, his blades flashing out in an intricate dance of death that carved the flesh back, giving me room. He became visible, and his resonant chuckle reverberated around the pocket we all stood in.

"I can't leave you alone for five minutes," he called. I couldn't help but grin as I pushed harder and harder before yanking sharply downward.

The naginata was deeply embedded by now, and with its magical properties, it was practically impervious to damage. The amalgamation of essence cores packed in around the Valspar's equivalent of a meridian wasn't, though, and it cracked. The huge mass of essence cores fractured and opened outward to reveal a glowing, pulsing core in the center that was the size of my damn head.

I paused, dumbfounded at its size, before growing and striking out again. Where the other cores glowed and shimmered with every spectrum of color imaginable, the Valspar's core was black as midnight, radiating a shimmering, pulsing wave of darkness that seemed almost solid.

I slammed my naginata into it again and again, shattering chunks off it, sending them falling away like embers from a firepit, glowing with darkness, pulses of red, purple, and green dying as the shattered sections hit the ground.

Bane whirled around me again and again, carving the reaching flesh back, even though I moved continually, my feet dancing across ground that constantly tried to swallow me. Oracle burned it to ash, yet it continually regenerated.

I stabbed over and over, the body around me quaking wildly as the Valspar frantically tried to kill me, while outside, hundreds attacked the massive form.

Bane flashed around me again, his blades glinting in Oracle's light to carve paths through the flesh, before diverting suddenly and hammering out a strong blast of his worldsense.

It caused the walls and floors that were the flesh and bones of the creature to vibrate painfully. It wailed, even as I gritted my teeth and cursed him internally, before stabbing out again and again. Finally, the blade punched through to erupt into freedom on the far side, and the core that sat at the center of the hundreds of lesser essence cores crumbled like unbaked clay.

The flesh all around us went into a frenzy, thrashing and reshaping, shuddering constantly, before sagging loose, the frantic attacks suddenly stopping.

"This way!" Bane spoke up. "The next one's this way!"

"Next…one?" I gasped, panting and wiping blood and burning acidic fluids from me, even as Oracle hit me with another heal. "You're fucking kidding me! There's more?!" I groaned, then I shook my head and gestured to Bane to lead the way.

This was going to be a long fucking night.

Four hours later, I sat on a low chunk of stonework, my head in my hands as I listened to the death toll.

"Twenty-seven legionnaires, one hundred and fourteen city guards, eleven imps, and three Djinn," Cai told me sadly, sitting on a low wall across from me, as Isabella held his hand, her eyes red from weeping and their clothes both torn and filthy.

"There was nothing we could do, Jax," Romanus said. "We're damn lucky we survived that as well as we did, and we wouldn't have done so, had the Gods themselves not joined in the fight."

"Yeah, wish they fucking did it earlier, though," I muttered, the memory resurfacing of the moment it had become clear that we'd been the carnival sideshow, not the main event.

Bane had carved us a path through flesh, Oracle wearing herself thin hammering both of us over and over with healing spells, even as I downed potion after potion, going so far as to chew on sodding ingredients as I went, just for the tiny uptick in my mana regeneration that provided.

Just as we'd been closing on the next meridian, a sword the size of King Kong's fucking shlong had slammed through the body just ahead of us, and Sint had waded in.

The God of Light had been glowing enough that we backed the hell off. It was that or have my eyes burned out of their sockets, and Sint had casually ripped the ball of essence cores apart, tossing them sideways in the air to vanish into a pocket dimension.

It'd all been over but the screaming after that, yeah, there was a lot of cleaning up to do. Turns out, a creature the size of a fucking skyscraper that could compress itself down to the size of a room has some *weird* parasites, but it'd become a mopping up operation after that, one that could have been far worse, if not for the arrival of Tenandra and Oren.

She'd essentially grabbed every mage who wanted to remain on my good side and every single healer in the city, bringing them to play. Once she'd dropped them off, she'd acted as a mobile platform for the Legion's magically trained to both barrage the creature and heal from. Oren did the same with a shitty scow he'd commandeered, seemingly keeping it in the air by furious willpower alone.

Most of those who had died had taken a solid hit, one that couldn't be avoided or dodged, while anyone else who'd been merely badly injured was back up on their feet in minutes.

Lydia had ended up flying around the big bastard in circles, giving it a moving target, glowing like the Valkyrie she was and rallying our side. Tang had essentially been supercharging himself over and over with his twin swords leeching the life and mana from the Valspar, vanishing and healing or hitting it with magic, then doing it again and again.

Yen had gone a bit mental during the fight, seeing Grizz sacrifice himself for me. She had gone all out, channeling enough mana into a single Flamespear that she'd ended up draining more than half her health into it as well. It'd blasted one of the Valspar's eyes into a mass of gristle and jelly that had showered dozens before she passed out from the shock.

Grizz was, as Jenae had said, alive. While not exactly well, he'd recover.

More than seventy percent of his body was eaten away, and it'd taken the direct intervention of Lagoush to save him, followed by three of the other Gods taking a hand to help rebuild him.

He was currently burning up and alternating screaming in pain and practically shouting the city walls down in ecstasy as his body changed. The Gods performed other minor adjustments to him as they worked, rewarding him for his bravery and sacrifice.

He was still going through the changes, and probably would for several days yet, Lagoush had informed us, as they'd all gotten a bit carried away.

Jenae and the others had spoken little since then, attacking with a ferocity that was unnerving for all that witnessed it. But it, and Their presence here tonight, made damn sure that, at the consecration of the Cathedral in a few short hours, there'd be a lot of new followers for all the Gods today.

All the Gods save Nimon, anyway. More than one conversation I'd heard the guards having, or the people who'd turned up to help the wounded, revolved around how Nimon would have left them to die, gaining His power that way instead of helping them all.

"The Gods joined when they chose to, and despite our involvement in their affairs of late, They are the Gods, Jax, and you must remember this!" Romanus chastised me in a low voice. "Had They decided to watch and leave us to our fate, I would have been less surprised than having them join in and save us all. Their motives are Their own. They. Are. Gods."

"Quite so," Cai said sadly. "Even with that firmly in mind, however, I wish they had taken a hand earlier, and been less…pleased with themselves."

I grunted, glaring at the ground as I thought about the way they'd torn the massive collections of essence cores free and had cheered before leaving through portals they summoned immediately.

Dozens were left crying for help that Lagoush could have given, or lay trapped beneath sections of the corpse that one of the other Gods could have lifted free easily.

People had fucking died because the Gods were too busy patting Themselves on the back, and I was seriously pissed about it.

"They be assholes," Oren had growled grimly, seeing things much the same way I did, after he'd practically crashed the ship he'd been on to land it, then stomping out to help as best he could.

"They did what they did, and it's time for us to move on," Isabella stated. "Lord Jax, have you looked at the armory yet?" She knew damn well I hadn't. I straightened, looking at her for a few seconds, before sighing and shaking my head. "Then perhaps it's time to find out if the cost was worth it?"

I grunted, straightening up and taking a deep breath. *Time to put your big boy pants on, Jax.*

I forced a smile. "You're right, Isabella, thank you," I said, hopping down from the section of stone I'd been sitting on and gesturing to the remains of the crystal doorway it had torn its way free of.

The Valspar's corpse was massive, but after the Gods had stripped it for the essence cores, which were apparently as useful for them as they were for us, most of its internal structures were utterly demolished, leaving mainly rubbery skin and a deflating body.

What had been physically huge had turned out to be shifting segments of itself under the skin to make it seem like it was this massive, indomitable creature, while in fact, its millennia of isolation had resulted in it being more than half-starved and probably entirely insane.

It was still huge, but it was also weirdly deflated, covering a good third of a mile, but shrinking in on itself as more and more of the flesh and the mess beneath was burned away by the starlight.

Whatever this creature was really, and where it'd come from, even the darkness between stars must be alien to it, and that sent my mind round bends and twists I couldn't handle right now.

"Bane?" I asked the air at random, and a cough came from my right. I whirled toward the figure that stood there.

He'd changed in his time away from us, growing physically, but also in terms of presence and self-assurance. Now he was dangerously cocky, and I just knew I'd never live down him finding me literally in the belly of the beast when he returned.

"Yes, oh Lord and Master, High Lord of the Continent?" he asked mockingly.

"Just checking you'd not wandered off. You know, getting lost in the forest and taking weeks to return," I retorted.

"Seriously, that was a weak attempt," he said with a bastardly grin.

"Yeah, it was, to be fair. I'll get you, though. Anyway, who the hell are the Dwarves?"

"Peshka, Doris, and Shereen," Bane said slowly. "They're…well, they're kind of my assistants, for now. I'll be handing them over to Flux for some more advanced training as soon as we get back to whatever hole you're calling home these days."

"Oh?" I asked, both curious and sensing a string to pull in the careful way he was talking and the way the trio kept him in sight at all times, despite being asked by the legionnaires to stay back. An uneasy compromise had been reached where the Dwarves were hanging around about five meters away, but they were clearly listening to every word we said and were waiting for something.

"I found them in the citadel. They were being tortured, and I helped them. In turn, they helped me," Bane said, enunciating slowly.

"Really? Helped you *how*?" I asked, glancing at Thomas, who waggled his eyebrows suggestively, making me grin a little.

"Not like that, you idiots," Bane snapped. Having met Thomas all of four hours ago, he'd clearly decided to show him the same respect he did me, which was to say, none. "They helped me question the dark priests."

"Dark priests! So, it *was* you that's been killing them?" I grinned as I pulled up one of the notifications I'd been looking at off and on, trying to figure out what the hell was happening.

> **You have progressed on your Divine Quest: My God is Better than your God (4)**
> Jenae and the Pantheon of the Flame have offered you a Quest. Travel to the Fallen City of Himnel, storm its walls, and throw down its defenders. Conquer the Citadel of the Dark Church, and destroy Nimon's altar, as well as those of the Pantheon of the Dark.
>
> **Bonus:** Free the City of Narkolt or bend it to your will: 1/1
> **Destroy the Dravith Dark Citadel**: 0/1
> **Kill the Dravith Arch-Priest of Nimon**: 0/1
> **Kill enemy Priests, Clerics, and Paladins**: 37/100
> **Capture the City of Himnel**: 0/1
> **Capture/Liberate the City of Narkolt**: 1/1
>
> *Bonuses will be given for exceeding these numbers.*
>
> **Reward:** Territorial Claim increased, 100,000+ Citizens, Access to City treasuries and capabilities, 5,000,000xp

"Yeah, that was pretty much me and the girls," Bane replied, his *thrum* of amusement filling the air. "Tamat gave me a quest to kill as many priests by stealth as I could. Certain ones in particular had offended her, apparently. I was assured that you were safe on the ship and that I couldn't catch up to you at the time. Which, according to Tang, wasn't entirely true."

Bane hung his head in shame. "I'm sorry, Jax. I never suspected Tamat would lie about that. I honestly believed you were safe. I'll take whatever punishment you decree."

"Oh, don't worry, I'll think of something, probably including a fucking bell," I assured him, grinning, before reaching out and pulling him close into a hug. "It's good to see you man."

We released each other, and I turned, feeling a hell of a lot better about Bane being back with me than I could believe, and started clambering across the stonework. I kept one eye on the path and one on the dozens of other prompts. Most of them had been shit, but a few stood out.

Congratulations!

You have assisted in the killing of a Valspar Elder God

Despite losses of 155 of your people, the killing of an Elder God is no small feat, all those who aided in this achievement will receive the following:

- 3,000,000xp, 1 Lesser Boon from the Gods and +10 points to Luck attribute

You personally, as leader of a faction which took significant losses, and did recognizable damage will gain the following in addition to the general rewards:

- 1x Greater Boon and an additional 5,000,000xp

Progress to level 31 stands at 8,781,586/1,245,000

*

Congratulations!

You have reached levels 31 to 35

Progress to level 36 stands at 946,586/2,135,000

**You have 65 unspent Attribute points and
two unspent Meridian points available**

*

Congratulations!

**Your Evolving Weapon has reached an important milestone
in claiming the souls of its victims.**

You can now choose a new Bonus Ability!

Increased Capacity:

You choose to convert the essence of the souls most recently captured into increasing the weapon's ability to absorb and feed on the souls of its victims, rising from 150 to 300. This will lower the current capacity from 75/150 to 1/300, reducing its current damage done from 24-40+75 to 24-40+1

God-killer:

Your weapon has tasted the Blood of the Gods, and it hungers for more! Attacks against tier six and above creatures will do triple damage, attacks to all tiers below six will do 0.5x damage

Anti-shield:

This weapon has pierced the shields of dozens of casters, gain 50% increased damage to shields along with the ability to entirely pierce magical shields, should the relevant element be matched.

Choose carefully, as once made, this choice cannot be undone.

Naginata			**Further Description** *Yes/No*
Damage:			24-40 + 75
Details:			This two-handed weapon was built from a combination of modern Earth techniques and traditional Japanese skills, creating a weapon that is truly deadly in the hands of a skilled user.
			Enhanced; This weapon has been enhanced through silverbright and has absorbed some of the souls of its victims. Current capacity: 75/150
			Bonus ability: Magical infusion: Casting your spells through this weapon will infuse it with that ability for the duration of channeling and cause X damage where X is equal to the damage done by the cast spell.
Rarity:	**Magical:**	**Durability:**	**Charge:**
Unique	Yes	85/100	N/A

I'd pulled up the details on my naginata four times now, staring at them as I tried to make sense of it. From what I could tell, the option to evolve came when its capacity was half filled, so if I went with the increase in soul capacity, the next one would come at one hundred and fifty souls…souls which I couldn't even confirm I could get.

I thought I'd get the souls each time I killed an enemy with it flooded with mana, but that didn't work out, and I was up to a minimum damage of ninety-nine points per strike at the minute. That was insane!

I could kill someone with a thousand health by stabbing them in the foot eleven times!

It didn't really work that way, not really, and damage was a case of the most possible damage calculated against the actual injury, with the force, the angle, the situation, and all of it combined. If it was a million points and I nicked someone's finger, they wouldn't just die on the spot; it was more of an assurance that it would do the maximum damage it *could* in the appropriate situation.

I didn't really understand it all, despite Lydia talking me through it at a rate that a small child would understand, so I'd given up on it thanked her for the explanation, despite the little voice in the back of my mind that recommended I go stab someone I didn't like over and over in the foot to double check the details.

I'd considered the second option for the upgrade, liking it, then dismissing it, simply because doing half damage from now on against EVERYTHING else was insane. I'd never even heard of tiers of beings and had no clue where I stood in relation to others. For all I knew, I was a tier one and, except for the Gods, there were no other tiers. Plus, hopefully while I'd get a few stabs in, it'd be the pantheons against each other, not me literally stabbing the Gods. Although, 'Godslayer' did have a nice ring to it, I conceded inwardly, and I would like to kill the Dark Dick myself.

Anyway, it came down to two choices for the naginata: upgrade the capacity or the effect. Using it against shields was already useful, as it slammed straight through them up to a point; the more powerful, the greater force that was needed.

That was common sense, and my ability to channel through it meant that taking that ability I could imbue the weapon with, as an example, fire, then if someone had a fire-based shield, I'd not need to worry. The naginata would pass through it easily!

I'd probably get my face burned off when I got too close, but the weapon would pass through.

I sighed and selected the one I knew I had to, increasing the capacity. As much as I liked the other, bumping it up to three hundred capacity meant literally that, regardless of anything else. If I got further options to update or not, then I could still, provided I harvested enough souls, grow my weapon to do at least three hundred and forty-two damage at a maximum.

I hated doing it, as I just knew the shield choice was going to come back to bite me in the ass, but this way, I'd hopefully get another upgrade choice at a hundred and fifty.

I also glanced at the points I had to allocate and closed that screen down instantly. Putting that many points into myself in one go was a surefire way to knock myself out, and the three million points the others had gotten in experience had really shown those who thought about their actions as well.

Ninety-seven guards had flat passed out around us, most after they suddenly bulked the fuck up. One guy now drew EVERYONE'S eyes, as he'd been a level nine nobody, and had hit level twenty-three. He'd gained a grand total of sixty-six points in one go, gaining three points per level, and the standard ten and twenty at hitting level ten and twenty respectively. He appeared to have put everything into Charisma in one go, however, and now even the most insanely straight legionnaires were eyeing him consideringly.

I banned him from any job requiring intelligent choices on the spot, considering he'd just proven he didn't make those, and moved on.

The legionnaires, many of whom gained multiple levels, had taken it all in their stride, of course, and so had most of the elite guards.

There was also one small child, who'd been happily watching the golems for days and had apparently seen the Valspar smash one of them, so she'd pulled out a dagger and stabbed its nearest tentacle at *just* the right time.

She was four years old, an orphan, level twenty-two, and totally confused by the screens that had popped up. She was being looked after by Sehran, who apparently loved kids and had promised faithfully that she probably wouldn't eat her.

Sehran had tried to use her distraction abilities on the Valspar, but had been totally ignored in the fight. Then she had latched onto the Valspar in the end, trying frantically to feed on an Elder God. She'd been tugged off it in the end by Tamat and slapped hard enough on the nose that she'd needed Lagoush to fix it.

All in all, it'd been a highly fucked-up evening, when all I'd expected was a tour of an old facility and to hopefully find some systems that could be resurrected.

In the end, half an hour later, and seven levels below ground, I finally sat in the Command Center of the facility and brought up the screens, sighing in relief as I saw three operational systems out of ninety.

I'd half expected to find nothing.

CHAPTER FORTY-FIVE

The system that hovered before me was insanely complex. Dozens of levels interconnected with what I could only think of as tables and trees. Lines slid between them, showing that each section was dependent on another, that thing required this other thing.

I stopped, and while I desperately wanted to see what we'd gotten, I needed to actually understand this, if we were to have any hope of using the systems. Searching for a root, I traveled to the uppermost levels and selected the first option.

It was dark, the tile barely responding, just a single flash of acknowledgement, and that was it. But when it flashed, I got…not information, but a sense of something. It was like someone had walked past me with perfume on, and I'd picked up an individual thread of a scent that sparked a memory. It was gone a second later, leaving me with just the impression.

This was like that, only the impression was…rock? I shifted through the other top-level symbols, listening to my instincts, and found water, something to do with animals, and the last two made no sense at all, leaving me with impressions of wonder and of reaching for the sky.

I looked at the next one, finding that many of the first level joined together after this, combining to form…things. A few moments passed before I smiled, shifting in my chair as a sense of satisfaction filled me. "It's a supply chain!"

The system had once been able to take things that were literally only water and unrefined metals, and probably manastones and leather or something like it, and each level refined it, made simple things, or refined the parts for use in the next level.

Moving down, I had the sense of simple, but well-made components, things like shafts for arrows…reaching for the sky! It was wood! Trees reaching for the sky! I grinned, moving on.

Dozens of tiles made no sense to me, but some did, weaving metal into chainmail, or tighter into something else, something that gave an impression of silk, soft and pliable, yet turning blades with ease.

Eventually, I came to the three that were intact. One was an end point, and it needed a huge number of things to produce the end product, which was some kind of panel made of thirty-seven different metals, layered with crystal and diamond, with a top that flowed like water, forming symbols…no RUNES when it was given the right input. It was like a liquid crystal display, forming the relevant runes as they were needed to do different things, such as shields for the Prax.

It'd have been horrifically expensive to run, even in the days of the Empire, considering it'd hardly ever been used. But it was intact, and it even had some of the hoppers filled. Although, most of the organic materials, like a spongy white leather, were well buggered by now.

The other two intact machines were much smaller, yet so much more valuable to us.

One created arrows. That was all, just arrows, one at a time. But rather than boring regular arrows, these fuckers were enchanted, each and every one. And the system had ten different versions it could produce in its memory. I pulled the list up, finding they ranged from freezing to fire to lightning, some kind of entrapment arrow that fired a sticky net out, two different versions of tracking arrows, depending on the size and environment of the creature being tracked…

That made sense, I supposed. If you were hunting a leviathan from a ship, it'd need a different arrow than you'd use for a deer. But that was about as far as my interest went in that way, as the last four arrested my attention.

Firestorm. An arrow that when it hit exploded into an honest to Gods firestorm! It covered a ten METER radius and lasted thirty seconds, burning the living shit out of everything inside it.

Mage-killers. An entire arrow that was covered in runes was named a mage-killer. It pierced shields, it poisoned the target, *and* it hit them with a confusion, a bleeding, *and* a silence debuff, all at once! I checked the hoppers and found there were enough for forty of them, and I was having them as soon as bloody possible, I decided.

The ninth arrow was marked "spectral assassin," and essentially, it killed anything that was incorporeal. I had no idea how that was even possible, but clearly the Empire had decided that just because we couldn't touch it, didn't mean we shouldn't be able to fuck it up.

The tenth, though…the tenth arrow was an arrow that was just called "slayer" and basically translated as "for someone you really, really don't like." It was a tubular device that, once it was fired, opened up into a spread of six arrows, all imbued with a hunter-seeker enchantment.

The first to hit was an anti-shield arrow, the second a silence and stun, third was a chainfire, which apparently held the target in place and wrapped them in burning chains. Fourth was a firestorm, with the fifth looking evil as all hell: a set of six hollow, glass teeth that were enchanted to dig deeper and deeper into the body before tiny needles deployed, locking them in place and bleeding the victim until they were cut out.

The final arrow was basically overkill, as near as I could tell, in that it was a disorientation device called "Banshee's wail," which deafened and damaged the victim, bursting their eardrums with a horrific sonic attack that left them reeling while the others continued to work.

There was enough in the hopper for three of those. Yes, please.

I decided that Tang had been a good boy of late and waved him over, telling him to look at the system, mentally sliding the details over to the edge where he could reach them, as I turned to the last machine.

It was a general-purpose runic engraver. That wasn't its name; the people who'd built it had called it "general purpose seven," but fuck that. The runic engraver was an assembly point that could make any of a dozen basic designs and engrave them with the needed runes at any angle needed.

It was damaged, it was empty, and it required a hell of a lot of things doing to get it working, being at four percent when I looked it over, but it was fantastic for our needs.

Yes, a storage shed of a million magical weapons and armor in every size would have been more appreciated, but this? This could make anything magical. This was the production version of Ame, and it had dozens of runes in its memory. We needed her to figure them out and to decide on the layout and placing, but this was exactly what we needed.

"Flux!" I called, barely able to keep from grinning. "We need Ame, and we need her here fast!"

"She's at the Tower, Jax," Flux reminded me, making me curse. "But Riana is here; she's examining the corpse outside."

"Great, send someone to get her, will you?" A spark of hope shot through me as I closed the main screen of production facilities, blinking as I caught the look on Tang's face. "You all right, man?"

He stared at me in shock. "The arrows," he said eventually. "I NEED those arrows."

"Yeah, when we get things up and running, I'll get you some, don't worry. Which ones?"

"Yes," he said, nodding his head.

"No, I mean, which arrows did you want?"

"Yes!" he replied again, nodding more emphatically.

"You want them all, don't you?"

He grinned maniacally, nodding like he was trying to get his head to come off.

"Okay, well, we'll see what we can do. Remember though, dude, these are enchanted arrows, one-use things, because they're magical. Half of them have powdered manastone as an ingredient; you know how much a miss is going to cost me?"

One eyebrow raised. "You ever seen me miss?"

"Point," I conceded. "Okay, I'll sort you some arrows when we get things up and running, but for now? Back away a little, you're kinda freaking me out."

He was grinning at me like a maniac from about a foot away from my face. When the screens were all active, hanging in the air between us, it was fine, but now, I wasn't sure if he was going crazy or what.

He nodded, then tore off to tell Giint. I dreaded him explaining to the most unstable member of the team that, not only was I the source of free drugs, as Carmen had conveniently uncovered a recipe for them, then made me a dozen batches of his shit, but I now had access to magical arrows.

He had a crossbow, not a bow, but he didn't give a damn, and was pestering me within a minute.

I ended up snapping off a stick of his catnip and throwing it as far away as I could, nearly braining Riana as she and Hannibal wandered into the section.

She jumped back, cursing, until she saw I'd been the one who'd thrown it, and she snapped her mouth shut. She plastered a patient smile on her face before nearly screaming as Giint ploughed into her leg again and bounced off, knocking her over.

"Fuck's sake, Giint!" Lydia snapped as he vanished from view. "Ah swear Ah'll get 'im 'ousebroken

"That was totally not my fault." I lied, turning to Riana. "Hey Riana, I've got good news and bad, which do you want first?"

"Um, the bad?"

"Okay, bad news is that the system is currently buggered, and we need a lot of base parts, mainly various refined metals, crystal, and powdered manastone," I said, looking at the details as best I could, while reaching out and summoning the crafter golems down from the upper level with Oracle's help.

"*Powdered* manastone?" She winced. "That's insane! Manastones are horrifically expensive, and…"

"This machine can engrave your cannons for you in a few hours," I interrupted. She froze. "That's the good news. It can literally put runes on anything. I'm going to get Ame here, and we're going to figure out a few basic runes, like a shield, a way to charge it, then we're going to replace the Legion shields with enchanted ones, all of them. Probably in a matter of days. And swords. Fuck, axes, maces, all of them. This is going to level the playing field for the Legion." My eyes unfocused as I stared into the distance.

"I don't care how much it costs, it'll be worth it," Riana whispered, staring at me wide-eyed.

"That's my feeling, too. Okay, we need Ame here, and we need her fast. Jian, how long?"

"A day and a half. We can use a lot more mana in the engines, hammer it through, and get higher speeds, but it'll mean we need time to recharge afterward. High storms or manastones, one or the other…" he warned.

"Fine, man," I said, clapping his shoulder. "We need Ame as fast as you can, so go, and yeah, I know you'll only pester and distract Tenandra otherwise, so take Sehran with you as well. The three of you can have fun, no doubt."

"Well, yeah, we will, but don't forget, I'll have Ame aboard for the trip back."

I winced, then coughed and pretended I hadn't, glancing at Flux.

"You have an issue with my mate?" he asked Jian sternly.

The pilot went pale as he tried to stammer out an answer.

"No, no, we will discuss this the only way we can," Flux replied, voice booming. "When you return, we will face each other in the sparring ring, and you may explain your rudeness!"

Jian looked at me, opening his mouth as if pleading for intervention. Instead, I waved him to the door.

"Go, Jian, we can get a carriage back through the city. Get out of here," I said, sighing at the realization that, for the next few days, my time of easy travel around the city had come to an end.

"That was cruel," I said to Flux once Jian and Sehran were out of the room. He laughed, Bane and Cheena joining in from around the room, hidden in stealth.

"I know, but I couldn't help it. I love Ame, I do, but she can be…formidable at times. I suspect Jian's ardor may be dampened knowing that Ame can sense everything they do aboard ship." Flux let out a low, rumbling chuckle, clearly amused by the entire situation.

"Doubt he'll think that far," I countered, shaking my head. "He'll close the door, and as soon as Sehran and Tenandra are naked, that'll be it. He won't be thinking with his big head."

"Big…head?" Flux asked slowly, and Thomas gestured to his crotch.

"Little head, big head," Thomas whispered, pointing at each in turn.

"Ah!" Flux grunted, shaking his head. "An understandable phrase at last! Thank you, Thomas."

"Yeah, don't worry. Jax is still learning. He thinks with the little head a lot, too."

I opened my mouth to make a comment, then shut it again. The others would all join in, and I'd lose regardless. Better to suffer in silence. Instead, I shot him the finger and went back to studying the details. After a moment or two, I swiped the main system free of the panels that showed the trees and tables of interconnecting systems.

The Imperial Armory was still huge. Most of it was underground, with a few small sections still entirely buried, but the most important features, besides the actual production chambers, as far as I was concerned at least, were the mana collectors.

There were eight of them, small onyx pillars that ringed the facility. All but one lay buried still, five of those buried were damaged or disconnected, and the other two were barely pulling in anything, thanks to their position.

The entire facility shield had been maintained by the single working collector that was standing smack bang in the middle of a noble's garden just outside the line that had been considered the outer edge before.

That meant that all the others would most likely be outside as well, and I'd told the nobles only a few hours ago that they were safe from more damage for a bit. Dammit.

The crafter golems stomped into the room and turned to watch me, ready for their orders.

They'd brought the resources necessary to build an entire Genesis Chamber from scratch, but so far, they'd been working on clearing the rubble along with the rest of their brethren.

It'd felt like a waste, not using them to their full potential, but wherever they would have built the Genesis Chamber would have been a pain. It needed mana, and that was only going to be freely available in the quantities it needed inside the armory. So, building it anywhere else just seemed pointless. Yes, it could be moved, but that wasn't a good option. I'd only done that back at the Tower out of fear it might be crushed by falling rocks.

Then there were the damaged Genesis Chambers. They were huge. Yes, I wanted them working, oh so badly. But they required more resources to repair than a brand-new standard one cost to build. They were on the list, though. For now, it made better sense to have the crafters work alongside the others and just put up and shut up.

"I need you to fix this runic engraver," I told them, gesturing to the massive construction in the corner of the room. Both the golems turned to look, before stomping off and examining the system. "Tell me what you need to fix it, and to repair the mana collectors for the site, as well as to set…say two of them up at the keep."

There were long minutes while they examined the systems and the construction, before they paused, seeming to communicate with the site systems then turning back to me.

"The Imperial Armory requires the following systems to be brought online to fully operate this unit," one said, before listing an absolute shit ton of things. After a minute, I held up a hand and told it to stop.

"I don't intend to run the full facility. Just the units that can be repaired. Tell me what you need to fix them," I ordered, before being barraged with data again.

Two hours later, and I was at the end of my tether, frustrated by the number of questions I'd had to ask before they finally gave me the data I wanted, having learned in the process that I had to ask them insanely specific questions to get the answers I needed.

It came down, fortunately, to several tons of gold, various stones, marble, base metals, and chromium, along with a dozen diamonds, three manastones, and an absolute butt-load of copper wire…as well as a wheel of cheese, a single live mouse, and some lube.

I chose not to ask about that.

Once we'd got them figured out, I gave them their orders, got the various resources ordered and arranged, and led my people out into the early morning sunshine. The golems began work, pestered constantly by Riana.

"Somebody get us a carriage or whatever," I ordered one of the guards who had turned up and was now standing ready around the outer edge of the perimeter.

It took a few minutes, but two massive, elaborately gilded, and annoyingly uncomfortable carriages were summoned. We all stood around talking while we waited, before being bounced and jostled across the city to the palace.

When we finally clambered out, I felt worse from the carriage ride than I had from the fight. I grumbled my way through the keep, headed for the baths again.

Restun found me there, along with the rest of the squad, half an hour later, squatting next to the edge of the pool in blissful silence. So much silence, in fact, that when I finally noticed the lack of conversation and opened my eyes, he was inches away, thanks to a ridge that ran around this section of the bathing pool.

Normally the sight of him, this close and clearly waiting, would have induced bowel-numbing terror in any legionnaire, and me as well, but after the night I'd had?

"Restun, good," I said, letting my exhaustion show. "Last night was a shitshow that ended with the death of an Elder God, so I'm sorry we missed training. We won't be doing it today, either, as frankly, I almost got digested last night. I need some fucking sleep. So do my people, so…you can accept that shit happens and join us in here, or you can be in a huff. But as High Lord, I'm declaring this a day off for my team, so deal with it."

"You realize that I faced a forfeit last night for you?" he said slowly.

I snorted. "No, but more fool you for accepting it while we were battling a thing from between the stars," I said, still unable to summon a fuck. "Seriously, Restun. Relax, you can murder us all tomorrow in retaliation. More than half the team nearly died last night. Hell, the entire realm nearly died, so…"

"You think I ended up this filthy by falling on my way to breakfast?" he asked.

I cracked open an eye again and regarded him with more attention. He was grimy, and his legion armor was dented, torn, and damaged. Dried blood covered one side of his cloak, and black burn marks covered most of the rest.

"Fuck. I didn't even see you there," I muttered, getting a snort from him.

"Perhaps not, but I saw you. I saw all of your team, and while you're uncoordinated, sloppy, and willful, you survived. So, from tomorrow, training is changing," he declared, straightening up as he came to his feet, striding to the side of the baths and stripping off. Then, he vanished into the pools that led up to where we lay.

We could hear him going through the plunge pools, the hot and the cold. He washed himself before returning to us a few minutes later, squeaky clean and looking more human than ever before.

He swam over to where the rest of us relaxed in the water, Giint occasionally sinking when he lost his footing, and we all made room for him in the middle of the group.

"As I was saying," he continued calmly. "Training will be changing from tomorrow. No longer will you fight as individuals; instead you get to fight as a team. Unarmed for the first few days, then we'll introduce weapons.

"Be warned: now that the training cadre have seen how much punishment you can take, we'll be increasing our expectations. Fights will be to unconsciousness or tap-out, with the losing team facing an extra day of training when all other teams get one day off a week."

"Fuuuuuck." I groaned, similar mutterings rising around me.

"Flux and Lio also shared an interesting fact with me…your training sessions with them aboard ship," he said evilly.

I frowned, then my eyes flared open in shock and fear. "They didn't!"

"They did," he confirmed, then raised his voice to make sure all could hear him clearly.

"Scion Jax fought Intaglio and Flux at the same time aboard ship, and they fought without mercy. All blows, save instant kills permitted, with the victor getting to practice their healing magic on the loser."

Silence reigned as he paused, smiling beatifically around like a tiger who'd just turned up unexpectedly for tea. "I think this is a wonderful method and will allow you to train far more efficiently."

"Flux, you're going to pay for this." I said, wincing as I sat up and rubbed the water from my face. "Well, you managed to well and truly bugger any relaxation I was enjoying, you bastard. I know it was effective, though, so fair enough, tomorrow it is. I'll see you all soon."

There was a moment of silence as I strode from the water, Oracle shifting from her full-sized figure that had been floating comfortably in the water nearby, into the smaller version and shimmering slightly as she spun clothing out of the air.

I strode through the water, reaching the shore and out into the humid fog, momentarily regretting that I'd not thought to bring clothes. A few seconds later, I praised the name of Isabella, who really did think of everything. I recognized her handwriting in the scratchy letters spelling out my name on one bundle of clothes near the door.

I pulled the clothes on quickly and left the room, walking through the halls with Oracle flashing to my shoulder and riding me that way.

I passed Cai and Isabella, thanked them for the clothes, and invited them to join us next time, barely registering the massive blush that rose in Isabella's cheeks. I moved on, climbing the stairs to my room and lay down on the bed, barely taking the time to get undressed.

Oracle grew to full size and kissed me, telling me to get some rest. She backed off before I could get my hands on her properly, and I growled in irritation, annoyed I'd been too slow. She spent an hour working on evolving me before slipping away.

I'd desperately wanted her to join me in bed, even if it was just to cuddle her. But it was time she could spend teaching our forces life-saving magic, so I relented with a sigh, keeping the mental image I'd been conjuring to myself, for now.

I laid back and slept. The last thing I heard was the legionnaires confirming to her that the only way anyone would disturb my sleep was over their dead bodies.

CHAPTER FORTY-SIX

When I woke with a groan a few hours later, it was to find that the afternoon had the shine worn off it, and there was both a steaming cup of coffee and a veritable mountain of bacon sandwiches sitting by the side of the bed.

I'd been awakened by the combination of those scents and the click as the door to my quarters closed. I sat bolt upright as my brain, still wondering who'd brought the food in, was completely bypassed by my stomach.

I bit down before I'd even consciously addressed the food being there and let out a moan of happiness. Besides sexual antics, this was the best damn way to start my day, before mentally amending it to restart my day, seeing as it was technically halfway through by now.

"Bane?" I asked the room at large, pausing in my meal. A second later he was there, lounging in the corner.

"Yes, Jax?" he asked.

I swallowed a mouthful, then sighed. "Damn, I'm glad you're back, man," I managed, then downed a generous gulp of coffee. "Don't get me wrong, you're ugly as sin and creepy as fuck the way you sneak around my bedroom."

"Believe me, the things I've seen will forever haunt my nightmares," Bane quipped, then sighed. "But, I'm glad to be back. I spent most of the time there terrified I'd get a notification at any second saying you'd died."

"Me too, man. We were all worried about you. The constantly climbing dark priest death counter gave me hope, and Tamat said you were alive, but still…"

"I know. I'm…I'm sorry, Jax. If I'd known…"

"No, Bane, you were lied to by a Goddess, one I introduced you to and encouraged you to serve as a champion. I know you need to serve Her from time to time as well, and I'm fine with that. Hell, I know there's a few sites that we need to hit to get you some gear, don't we?"

"Tamat did try to convince me to go to one of the sites upon leaving the citadel," Bane recalled. "It'd have taken over a month on foot, but…"

"You came here instead," I said, nodding.

"Of course. Although, I admit, I wasn't expecting to find you fighting an Elder God. We hid amongst a group of servants leaving the citadel, then when they headed back to the city we just peeled off, took three days of hard running and hiding, then boom, here we were. We joined the refugees trying to enter the city. By the way, that's a mess."

"The refugees?" I asked, and he nodded. "Okay, I'll add that to the list of jobs to look at. Want a bacon sandwich?"

"Got one when Isabella brought them in," he replied, a low *thrum* of amusement clear.

"Ah, so it was Isabella!" I crowed. "I wondered who the hell the legionnaires would let in so easily."

"Yeah, I think you might want to consider something else in future, though."

"Oh?"

"Bedclothes," Bane said, the amusement resonating even stronger. "You'd kicked the blanket off, and she appeared to be shocked by the view."

"Fuck," I muttered, facepalming. "I flashed Isabella, didn't I?"

"Oh yes." Bane was clearly loving the fact I'd given him something to wind me up with already.

I sighed and polished off the food before dressing quickly and carrying my steaming coffee with me. I smiled at the legionnaires by the door as I passed, noting the small table near their post and the empty coffee cups and plates.

I set off down to the throne room of the keep, idly remembering the conversation with Romanus that had led to that minor addition and his shock that I believed legionnaires on guard duty should be allowed to partake.

It'd seemed like common sense to me, as well as common courtesy that if I was getting coffee and bacon, or something short of a proper meal, that the people who had to stand there for the entire damn day be given the same. While he'd been against it at first, for sensible reasons like distraction and possible drugging, I'd eventually overruled him.

It didn't seem like much, but the nods and smiles from those on guard duty made a massive difference to my day. I was willing to take it for that minor risk, despite Bane berating me for allowing the guards to be so easily distracted.

I strode into the throne room, greeting the team who were there already. Even Giint was present, despite the fact he'd just blatantly never gone to his room, judging from the drool on his face and the snores that reverberated around the room.

"Morning, all," I said, sending a tired smile around before sitting in the command chair and bringing up the system.

"Afternoon's more like it, bro," Thomas corrected with a grin.

I shot him the finger, pulling up the details on the golems' work. I was pleased to discover that they were only a few hours away from finishing the repairs to the mana collectors. After that, they'd be installing the two they'd taken at the keep, and the mana storage that the keep could provide would begin to fill.

It wasn't massive storage, not like the Tower was. With every section of it being mana-impregnable, it could hold significantly more mana than a living body could store. But this was still a small keep, and the Tower was more than two miles high and over half a mile across at the base, so yeah, there was a significant difference in load capacity between the two.

The keep, however, wasn't battling against the winds miles up and having to reinforce itself constantly, or providing mana to the golems or a million other things. It naturally pulled in a small amount of mana from the environment, and that alone was enough to run the keep's facilities, like the command center.

That meant that once the main collectors were up and running, they'd provide me with a hell of a lot of mana directly, with Oracle's help to handle it.

It was dangerous, and I didn't dare use it in a battle. Not after Oracle, Heph, and Seneschal had explained in excruciating detail just how easy it would be for me to lose myself in the mana and essentially have my soul washed away, becoming some kind of mana vampire lich thing that would drink it in over and over until I exploded, destroying the realm for miles around.

No, I'd use it in careful and specific circumstances, with Oracle or another of the wisps acting as a buffer and guide, allowing me to bind the people of the city to me in massive numbers.

I smiled at the thought of not having to do it over and over again, and I checked the various screens, finding the golems were working well. The mining golems closest to the Tower had closed the distance. They were at most a few hours away from completing the tunnel there, along with the golems trooping along behind them.

The golems that were following were strung out strangely, so I focused on them. I found a small amount of information attached by Heph, telling me that once he'd taken control, a few hours earlier, he'd directed half the golems to run full pelt back along the tunnel, collecting all the refined ingots the miners had left, and drop the unneeded stuff.

The end result was that some of the golems wouldn't reach the Tower until the day after tomorrow, possibly later, due to their being burdened down with heavy metals. But the majority would get there today at some point. The mining golems would be unloaded then sent back out to work, hunting down specific veins of resources, with one of the new crafter golems that was in production in the new Genesis Chamber at the Tower finishing in just under an hour as well.

That crafter would begin production on a third Genesis Chamber, this one entirely from scratch. While it would take several weeks, it would eventually be capable of class four, or advanced golems.

The build time for this was weeks, even with the secondary Genesis Chamber producing advanced golems now, but I had a million jobs to do, and nowhere near the time I needed to do them. Therefore, the second Genesis Chamber was going to alternate building crafters with advanced war golems and a handful of construction ones as well.

As soon as one was finished, they were off to help here or there…the piecemeal approach frustrating me no end. In a game, I'd risk it all by building up my infrastructure massively, then produce hundreds of one kind, such as the war golems, and roll over my enemy with them. In reality, it was too much of a risk.

I needed everything, so that's what I had to build. One of these, one of those, and be patient, basically.

I sighed and moved on, checking that the more basic, dumbass golems had taken up their new station at the manastone mine. It was long buried as well, but in a much more unpleasant way. Part of the facility had apparently been dedicated to processing biological waste.

That, of course, was the surviving part of the mine. Its mana collectors were long dead, and the only intact section was literally purifying the city's sewage.

The upside was that the mine had kept going, buried and forgotten for centuries, so there had to be a decent supply in there. The bad side was that it was not only going to reek, but the facility would have to be uncovered and repaired, so the entire city would end up stinking for weeks.

Five more crafters would arrive today from Production Facility One, three advanced and two simple. They were, in turn, to begin working with the two I already had here.

As soon as the crafter golems finished the mana collectors for the keep and repaired the production facilities, they were starting on assembling the new Genesis Chamber in place of one of the utterly destroyed units in the Imperial armory. As soon as that was done, they would begin production of a second and a third.

With seven of them working on the assembly of the Genesis Chamber, as they had all the needed resources, the project would take two days. By that time, the resources for the second would be ready, and they'd be able to move straight over.

I'd had a second look at the details for the larger Genesis Chambers as well now, and decided they were a project for another time. Yes, they'd be brilliant if I wanted new designs produced, but they'd need to be created, as the original systems were fucked to hell. What we had, essentially, were larger and more complex Genesis Chambers, but their control modules were utterly buggered. That meant they could be used to produce only the stuff we already had access to until we learned or created more. They were also going to cost a fortune to fix, so it just wasn't worth it right now.

The newly built facility would produce more crafters, and they'd make weapons and basic armor, ready for the army and the expanded guard force, while the Legion armorers were working on making as much for the Legion as possible. Hopefully, Ame would arrive soon with some plans in place for the use of the runic engraver, and we could make better armor and weapons.

Until then, we were continuing with the current plans for the city, and that meant…

"Jax, are you ready?" Cai asked me from the door. "I put off the meetings as long as possible after last night, but…"

I sighed, leaning back and letting the various screens fall away. "Hey, Cai. Yeah, I'm about as ready as I ever will be." Reluctantly, I climbed to my feet. "Thomas, how's the guard coming along?" I asked him as I passed.

"We're getting there," he said. "I'll fill you in later, but for now, we're getting there. Training camps are in place, and the first batch of trainees are out digging trenches and sprinting laps. They complain that it's got nothing to do with being a guard, but I tell them it's physical fitness.

"They can join me in doing that, or they can join the Legion trainees." He shook his head in amusement as he went on. "Their trainers run them past us once a day at my request now. Shuts my guys right up when they see that." He grinned.

"Damn, I bet!" I laughed, thinking about the looks of shock and horror on the faces of the brand-new Legion recruits whenever they saw the absolute beating those of us fortunate enough to train under Restun suffered daily. "Maybe pick a few of the more vocal ones and have them join us for training with Restun one day? Then let them spread the word?" I suggested, getting an evil grin from Thomas as my answer.

I left the room, falling in beside Cai and tried not to imagine the hell that was waiting for the guard recruits when they joined us tomorrow.

"So, where are we with things?" I asked Cai. He sighed, shuffling through reams of paperwork.

"Most areas are starting to fall into line. The shock and awe tactics you ordered to round up the criminal gangs and the swift culling of their leadership helped, as did Bol and his wife Hesta. placing them in a well-paid position with the guard was a stroke of genius," Cai pointed out, grinning.

"Yeah, I liked that one. But it was Thomas's idea, not mine," I said. "So, with the criminal gangs basically gutted—I mean, I know we didn't get them all, you can't—but with the leadership and all their safe houses gone and their loot taken, there's got to be a little hope on the streets, at least?"

"There is," Cai said. "Isabella's street kitchens are helping as well. The first day, there was a lot of attempts at theft and intimidation of the staff. That ended when the off-duty legionnaires helping out made their presence known.

"People now seem more willing to believe the tales and that there might be a chance for them. The workhouses have been scoured and cleansed, and they're no longer virtual slave camps. Families have been reunited, where they wanted to be, at least.

"While they all work, the children are organized into teams and watched over in set areas. Schools will be constructed as soon as possible. But for now, those who can teach a skill, especially one that we need, are doing so to those who can be useful, essentially the adults." Cai shook his head in bemusement.

"What?" I asked, having been looking at just the right time to catch the movement.

"I was a slave here. Well, I was sold to a merchant from here five years ago as an 'indentured servant,' before trying to escape one time too many. I was sold again to my last master, who sold me at auction in Himnel to feed the SporeMother." His catlike eyes stared blankly into the distance, as if his gaze scanned the past.

"Now, here I am, five years later, organizing the city and deciding who gets to learn crafts that will define their lives. I could destroy lives with a single mistake, and I'd never know it. I could reunite a family, broken apart by the workhouses, having no hope for the future.

"I can give them trades, food, a new home. It is truly beyond belief, my friend. I live in terror of failing you and of failing them, but I can't wait to start the day, and I feel freer than I could have ever imagined."

"I.. I don't know what to say, my friend," I said after a few seconds. "I count myself damn lucky that I found you. After all, you made all this possible. If not for you, I'd probably have cleared out the Tower and started it repairing itself, then have left for the nearest city and tried to find Thomas. It was you asking for a home that sparked all this off."

"Oh, I think this would have happened anyway." Cai smiled. "The realm was ready for it, and you'd have done it in the city instead of the Tower, if you'd had to."

"Well, either way, I couldn't do it without you," I told him, a smile tugging at my lips as well. "Although, it does raise another point. Refugees," I continued as we left the keep and strode across the manicured grass of the kill-zone, headed towards whichever of the palace buildings the first meeting of the day was due to be in.

"Isabella has already begun sorting the camps out. The refugees camping outside the gates have been moved off the road and to one side, to allow for easier entry and exit. Kitchens have been set up in each camp to make sure nobody goes hungry. As to allowing them access, that was on the agenda for today.

"Simply put, we know there will be spies and worse among them, but they don't know about the Oaths or the tracking magic that we have access to, so I suggest that we deal with them all in one go.

"Ask them to swear the Oath, and those who refuse can be safely turned away. Those who pretend will show up as red if they're enemies. If they're not, well, as long as they take no action against us, as refugees, they pose little threat."

"True," I agreed. "Okay, the collectors should be up and running in a few hours. How about first thing in the morning, you bring them all to the palace. That way, I can draw on it, and we'll do them all at once?"

"Better if we do it outside of the walls, but if you need the mana to do it, then that's the way it'll have to be," Cai said, making a note. "Okay, the cathedral, are we still going ahead with that tonight?"

"Yeah." I sighed. "Honestly, I'd love to put it off, mainly because I can't be bothered. Every job needs doing, and once we start with the cathedral, there's literally hundreds of smaller churches and shrines that need to be done, but…"

"But you agreed to do this with the Gods, and they don't like to be asked to hold off on gaining worshippers?" Cai asked.

"Well, yeah, there is that. But there's also the fact that we gain as much as they do, with access to the Constellation of Secrets, so yeah, tonight."

"Very well." Cai made another note, then as a guard held the door for us, we strode into a new building and down the hall, nodding our thanks as we passed. "Next, sanitation…" Cai started.

I rubbed the bridge of my nose. "That's a much bigger issue than I thought it was going to be, isn't it?"

"Much bigger," he said. "The plans for the mine make out that it used bio-converters to break down the city's bodily wastes and convert it into mana. The city was much larger in the days of the Empire, but it also had all four working and didn't have centuries of backed-up waste to deal with."

"Keep working to get us access to the actual mine. Make sure anyone who's involved in the process gets healed daily. We don't need a disease outbreak. As soon as we can get into the facility, I'll have the golems repair any of the systems that can be. Either way, we'll deal with it, even if we do it by digging a big pit outside the city and burning it all with Fireballs," I ordered, shaking my head. "Not looking forward to claiming *that* site, I can tell you."

"No, I think I might sit that one out…just in case." Cai smiled again.

"In case there's another trapped Elder God inside, or because there's a Gods-awful stench?" I asked, grinning.

"Definitely the latter, but I don't want to be there for the former, either," Cai said, leading me into a mind-blowingly garishly decorated room.

"What the hell?" I winced as I glanced around. Bright green walls, so vibrant as to be almost neon, clashed with purple stripes and a mustard yellow carpet. The seats were all red velvet, and the table that the others stood patiently awaiting me around was coated in so much gold I couldn't believe it hadn't collapsed under its own weight.

"Seriously, who the hell decorated this room?" I asked the world in general, shaking my head in disgust and noting a few scarcely hidden smiles as well as one offended frown.

The noble who was frowning at me straightened even further, before declaring, as if speaking to an idiot, "My daughter, a famed artist, decorated the room, *my Lord,* and it is considered one of the most memorable…"

"Well, your daughter is colorblind or on seriously good fucking drugs. Just because something is memorable, doesn't mean it's good. I mean seriously, if I had a hangover, I'd have been sick by now. It's damn memorable, all right!" I muttered, before waving them all to sit as I took my seat. "Right then, people. This meeting is for the new forges and smelters, right?" I half-asked Cai, getting a shake of the head just as I remembered that we had that meeting already. Damn, the days were blending into each other with all the meetings.

"This meeting is to discuss the appointment of a harlot to the Council!" Lord fancy-pants retorted.

I shot him a glare, raising one finger. "Cai, what is the purpose of the meeting?"

He sighed, shoulders slumping a little. "It was requested, and confirmed to me, as regarding the docks, including the required expansion of homes nearby and the future rebuilding of the Imperial dock. The only reason it was a meeting with you, High Lord Jax, was because it was the Imperial dock, rather than just a city issue, which Lady Carmen would have dealt with," Cai stated coldly, glaring at the Lord. The prick had lied to get a meeting with me.

"So, you lied to Cai, then?" I asked him coldly, catching the subtle way the others leaned back or shuffled their chairs away from the old fool.

"It was necessary! You must be made to see reason! No whore should wield power, let alone a position on the council that should rightfully belong to…"

I stood, activated Mana Overdrive, and grabbed the edge of the table, flipping it aside with a heave. I casually Sparta-kicked him in the chest. He flew backwards, his chair tipping over, and he screamed, clutching his chest in pain.

"Heal him," I snapped at one of the legionnaires who'd followed me into the room. He smiled and cast the spell, glad for any excuse to use his new magic. I stomped over to the panting noble and looked down at him as he froze in fear.

"You know what pisses me off?" I asked him and the rest of the room almost conversationally. "You all act like I'm a fucking idiot. Again and again, I've tried to be nice, yet still, you think your petty shit matters to me. Believe me, it fucking doesn't." I pulled my naginata out and held it with an iron grip.

"You complain because a woman who had the sense to see an opportunity for power and take it, regardless of how or what it was, should be snubbed. And you think to tell ME who should be on MY fucking council?" Flames ignited and licked along the length of the weapon as I glared down at the man.

"This is my council, my city, and MY FUCKING EMPIRE! So, get used to it! You don't like that? Fuck off to Himnel or face me like a man and spread the word. The next one of you overdressed butterflies who fucking wastes my time with shit like this, I'll gut, and then I'll disband their entire noble house!" I roared at him before taking a deep breath and stepping back.

"Now," I asked, struggling for calm. "Are any of you here with a real reason?"

"Ummm, my home is on the edge of the dock," one of the men said, pale-faced. I looked him over, noting the threadbare suit, the carefully cleaned shoes, and the trimmed hair. I recognized an ordinary man who was terrified yet trying to do his best.

"Okay, what's your name?" I asked him.

"Silas…uh High Lord Jax…my name's Si…" he stammered.

"Good to meet you, Silas. That's fine, because this is what I'm here to address." I sighed. "Come on, let's get the table back into place, and we'll sort this shit out." I took a deep breath and idly flicked a finger at the noble on the floor, who by the smell had redecorated his trousers at some point in the conversation. "And someone get rid of *that*!"

Three hours later, I was sitting in the same Gods-awful meeting room, the last supplicants having just left, and I let my forehead rest on the gilded tabletop, groaning.

"Fuck's sake…I thought that Carmen leading the council was going to mean less of these time-wasting wankers!" I complained.

"I think that your first meeting might have cut down on them on its own," Bane quipped from a corner. I snorted, sitting back up and looking over to him, then to Cai.

"Was I really that bad?"

"You broke half his ribs, threatened to kill him and remove his entire family from the ranks of the nobility…so yes," Cai replied. "But, to be fair, this is about the fifth time you've had to do something like this with them. Each time, the list of idiots who believe you can be manipulated or made to see things their way gets shorter." He grinned, and I saw just how much he enjoyed that, despite trying to be professional about it.

"I suspect this will be an end to it, or at least I hope so. Besides, you did resolve a great many issues today. Consider Silas and his family. We never would have known about the Pit-Rat infestation had you not asked him so many questions. Now we know that there are tunnels under the Imperial Docks, and that they're infested with the little bastards."

"How dangerous are they?"

"To you? Not at all. To a laborer with small children? Deadly." Cai said. "We'll need to address that as a matter of urgency. Pit-Rats usually live deep underground. Them being this close to the surface suggests something has displaced them."

"Give the job to the guard or the army. Let them send as many teams as they think they need to in, take healers and a spread of veterans and new recruits. They can all grow, get experience with their weapons and so on, with minimum risk," I ordered unthinkingly, such situations and solutions growing commonplace to me now.

"Very well, I'll speak to Romanus and Thomas tonight. The tunnels will be clear by this time tomorrow, I've no doubt," Cai stated confidently, making another note. "Now, we've just over an hour to go before the appointed time at the cathedral."

"I can take a hint." I stood up and cracked my back. "You get those clothes I asked you about sorted out?" I asked him hopefully.

"Isabella had some of her people deal with it. They should be in your room now, and I'll organize a carriage and suitable escort to be waiting when you leave your room," Cai said with a deferential incline of his head.

"Thank you, dude!" I said, smiling genuinely as I climbed to my feet. I led the way through the building and back across the grass, chatting idly with Cai, Bane, and my two Legion guards. They all wore their species' equivalent of a smile, infected by my sudden good cheer.

The reason was obvious as I entered my room, finding Oracle laid on the bed. She was relaxing, waiting for me, having sensed the plan as soon as Cai gave me the good news.

Bane did a quick circuit, then excused himself, leaving me to wash my face and dress, luxuriating in the Drow-made gloom spidersilk clothes.

The shirt, trousers, hell even the underwear was looted from the Drow, and it'd been scrubbed to within an inch of its life. I hated the thought of wearing another man's pants, especially considering the Drow men were characterized by two traits that could easily be summed up in one phrase: perverted whisky dicks.

That being said though, the feeling of gloom spidersilk undercrackers made it worth it.

The only thing I missed from home, besides Five Guys' burgers, was the godsdamned clothes. I seemed to spend my life now in scratchy, uncomfortable, and insanely hot under armor padding or fairly rough leather.

I'd taken the time a few days ago to let a master tailor take measurements and had given him direction, but even the Legion tailors, who'd managed to make me smart-looking and reasonably comfortable clothes, were light years behind the pants I'd bought from Step-One and similar places over the years.

I finished dressing in the looted clothes and looked in a mirror, shaking my head in disbelief.

"How?" I asked Oracle, catching the appreciative smile on her face. "How is it that the scummiest, most perverted godsdamn creatures we've come across can make a pair of pants and shirt made for someone half my size still feel like the softest silk and look like I should be on the cover of a fucking fashion magazine? I mean, seriously, if they just opened a clothing line, people would do anything they damn said!" I adjusted the pants.

"It's a point, but now I don't want to go out. Say, do those pants have the easy access pocket in them?" she asked, her voice a low purr as she got up and moved over, kissing me and slipping a hand into my pocket, her fingers navigating the silk easily before wrapping around me and stroking slowly. "Oh, yes, they do," she whispered, smiling and kissing me again.

"Oracle!" I groaned, pushing her back. "Gods dammit!" I half laughed at her, gesturing to the tent pole in my pants. "Now look at me!"

She laughed and made her clothing blur away, licking her lips and winking at me. "Time for a little fun before we go?" she asked, bouncing her eyebrows as well as her chest.

"Gods, I wish!" I groaned, shaking my head and moving back to the wash basin, dunking my head into the cold water and pouring the fresh jug that stood nearby over the back of my head.

"Damn, that's cold!" I shivered, straightening up and shaking my head, spraying water everywhere.

"Hey!" Oracle complained, shaking herself and letting the water fall though as she became partially insubstantial. "What was that for?"

"That's for teasing me!" I grabbed her hand and pulled her close for a deep kiss, before releasing her slowly, our tongues still tasting each other. "And that's to keep you going until later," I promised, getting a smile and a sigh from her.

"That's cruel," she told me, shaking her head sadly.

"And literally stroking my cock isn't?" I asked, laughing.

She shrugged, grinning. "I could always sit in your pocket, go all small and just play until you can't take any more?" she suggested, getting a groan and a twitch from me.

"No!" I said quickly, before I could agree. "No, we've got to be good!" I turned and headed to the door.

"Spoilsport," she complained, but a second later, she was there with me, full size and dressed in a simple silver dress, split up one side to her hip, with elegant gold bangles, earrings, and a necklace, despite the fact she could draw every eye in the room while dressed in a potato sack.

We left the room and gathered up the others as we headed through the keep, finding that the tailoring staff had done a fantastic job of cleaning the Drow clothing and mixing it with more appropriate clothes for everyone, making us all at least look impressive.

Even Giint was clean and tidy, dressed in a brand-new set of black silk overalls. He also had about a thousand bags attached everywhere, and he was still wearing his scruffy, battered cap with the cracked goggles. I'd never actually seen him without it. He'd even worn it in the bathing pools, so it was possible that it couldn't be removed.

It was clean, though, and that had to be enough, despite the mental image of him wearing it while spinning around the inside of a washing machine that kept going in my head whenever I looked at him.

CHAPTER FORTY-SEVEN

The carriage ride across to the cathedral was just ridiculous. The Gnomes were still trying to decide if the carriage they were building should have an alchemy station, an engine one of their number had stolen from an airship, or if they should remove the wheels and give it legs.

I quietly asked Cai to look into getting a normal carriage as well, just in case.

The three that carried us across to the cathedral were enormous, gilded to the point that the six horses strained like mad to pull them, and had a rider above each wheel to pull the brakes. They were still insanely uncomfortable. The seats were like sitting on a marble plinth, and between the potholes and the normal bouncing and jostling of the road, I was close to getting down and walking by the time we arrived. I winced as I climbed down, noting the faint sneer on the face of one of the locals who bowed a little slower than the rest.

I mentally marked him and waited until we were all past them, before speaking quietly to Cai.

"I take it that prick in the red and brown is the arsehole who has the contracts for the carriages?"

Cai looked around carefully, as though just checking the area out, then leaning in closer. "Yes, did you notice the seats?"

I frowned. "My arse feels like I've spent the night in a prison cell with a male porn star trying to do dental work from the inside, so yes. I noticed the seats."

"Ah…okay." Cai pulled a disgusted expression and shook his head. "What I meant was, did you notice that they were new? The leather was worn, but they'd been refitted recently, probably in the last day or two, considering the smell of glue and sawdust. The incense burner couldn't quite hide it."

"I take it he's heard that we're not going ahead with his fucking insane demands for a monthly fee for the carriages, and he's making it clear he's not happy, then?"

"I suspect as much, at least," Cai said with a nod.

I gestured to one of the legionnaires I saw nearby. He stepped in close, and I spoke quietly to him, getting a sharp nod and a salute before he pushed back through the crowds, vanishing in the direction of the carriage.

"What was that?" Thomas asked, one eyebrow raised as he jerked his head to the departing legionnaire.

"I sent him to check out the carriage and to look at the one that the prick back there came in after, see if he's playing silly buggers. If he isn't, and they just can't make a comfy seat for some reason, I'll apologize."

"What, they can make cushions and beds but not seats for a carriage?" Thomas grunted.

I nodded. "Yeah, that's my thought as well. If he is playing silly buggers, then someone's going to have a bad day." I tried not to rub my ass.

"Should be fun," Arrin quipped.

"Not seen you around much of late, mate," I said, sending him a wink.

We walked into the massive nave of the cathedral. The sudden hush that came from literally hundreds of people trying to be quiet and respectful made the room feel strange on its own.

"I've been trying to get fitter," Arrin announced. "You know, working hard, all day, all night, working up a hell of a sweat, and…"

"He got himself a girlfriend," Yen cut in.

"He's been nowhere near the training grounds," Grizz confirmed. I snorted with laughter.

"Guys!" Arrin complained, scandalized. "I was going to tell him!"

"Rubbish! Yer were gonna claim yer were workin' out constantly an' try te avoid tha sessions with Restun," Lydia said before bumping him with her shoulder and nearly knocking him over. "See? Yer need te build up some muscle!"

"Hey, not everyone needs to be covered in great slabs of muscle. Not everyone wants to look like a bull!" Arrin complained, and I stepped away quickly as Lydia turned to face him slowly, Grizz and the others splitting around her as she stepped in closer to him.

"So what, because Ah'm fit an' strong, Ah'm ugly, is that it? Ah'm a bull?" she asked in a low growl.

I cringed and sped up, leaving Arrin to dig himself out of that hole on his own. I passed groups of people who were filing into the seats that had been laid out, with the Altar of Nimon in the middle of the room and nine lesser altars around the outer wall, spaced out equally, with the massive dome of the cathedral high overhead, shining down glittering sunshine.

A team of a dozen people, mainly Alkyon fliers, but some of the other races as well, had spent the last day up there, uncovering the massive stained-glass windows that had been sealed over many centuries ago, and now the faces of the Gods beamed down at us. The nine Gods of the Pantheon of Flame did at least, as Nimon's had been uncovered, examined, and had slabs of metal put into place on either side.

I'd have broken it, personally, but the workers weren't quite so brazen and had balked at that, so we'd settled on the compromise.

I strolled out into the middle of the room, my group falling back and giving me the floor, as Oracle squeezed my hand once and stepped back as well.

I turned in a circle slowly, seeing the hundreds upon hundreds that were gathered in the cathedral. It was close to maximum capacity at just under two thousand people, and the building was set out as a vast dome.

Ten rows of benches led forward to the center of the room, where I stood on a raised dais within inches of Nimon's High Altar of Narkolt. The rows between the seats were kept clear. Nine long, marble pathways terminated in an altar to a God, and the tenth spot led out to the main doors.

Hundreds of muttering voices fell silent, as thousands of people filed in, my clear Demonstration of poor impulse control making all the difference where they were used to getting away with disrespect to others.

"Welcome to the Great Cathedral of Narkolt," I called out, my voice echoing for a few seconds. "You've all been here before, I assume, or at least most of you have. However, you were here when the cathedral was contaminated by the Dark Walker," I declared, reaching into my bag. Smiling, I withdrew the right tool for the job this time, having made arrangements for this earlier.

The crowd drew back slightly, gasps sounding in a low susurration around the room as I rested the head of the massive warhammer on the floor. Thunder rumbled overhead.

The gathering storm clouds were the peculiar greenish grey of an intense downpour, and the pressure started to build warningly in the cathedral as Nimon turned His full attention on us.

I smiled at the barely visible clouds above the city. The light that filtered through the stained glass made it hard to see clearly, but I knew three things:

Nimon could see me clearly, He knew what I was going to do, and He was PISSED.

"See ya, cockface!" I called up at Him, before spinning around and raising the warhammer high. A powerful crash of thunder and a bolt of lightning lashed out from the clouds overhead, slamming into the shield that Jenae and Her Pantheon of the Flame maintained over the city.

I grinned as I imagined the shock on Nimon's face, as those He'd believed were much weaker held Him off, the power they'd harvested from the Valspar enough to make a hell of a difference in their recovery, or so Jenae had told me.

I slammed the warhammer down with all my might, the black onyx slab practically exploding into shards as the hammer hit it. Sections flew everywhere, and my legionnaires moved in, gathering them up and storing them in a pouch I'd been given by Jenae especially for the task, as she apparently had plans for the fragments of the altar. Besides, possession of even the smallest fragment could open a path for someone to speak to Him, if they and He so desired.

As soon as the altar was destroyed, notifications started to rain in.

Congratulations!

You have made progress in a quest: My God is Better Than Your God (3)

For each altar or sanctified place of worship dedicated to Nimon, Ardat, Asmodeus, Baphomet, or Illoth that you destroy, you will receive a Mark of Favor and a random blueprint for your crafters from the Goddess Jenae.

As you have destroyed an altar to her most hated brother, you will receive a bonus item.

*

Beware!

You have reached a new low.

You are now declared a BLOOD ENEMY of the God of Death, Nimon.

**He will encourage all those who worship Him
to seek your death beyond all others.**

Beware the Knives in the Dark!

*

Nimon has personally intervened to declare any follower of the Pantheon of the Flame, any citizen of the Empire, or any citizen of Narkolt who does not rise up and seek the death of the Apostate Jax, as an Enemy of the Church.

All sanctified soldiers of the Church will receive +3 to Strength, Agility, and Endurance when facing the forces of the Apostate and his hated Gods. Killing any member of those forces will make this buff permanent. Furthermore, this buff will increase by +1 for every additional kill those soldiers make.

Kill on, Holy Warriors!

"Well, that was fun!" I called out into the stunned silence as thousands of people read that they'd been declared an enemy of a God. "Time to move onto the main event, I think," I declared, before waving to the members of my squad positioned around the room. The Altars of Illoth, Ardat, Asmodeus, and Baphomet, the four pillars of Nimon's rule, were all smashed, one after the other, and the fragments collected. Arrin stood with Grizz, waiting ready as he smashed the Altar to Illoth. The tiny spider that escaped it met a barrage of Magic Missiles that terminally ruined its day.

As each was destroyed, I got the same notification from Jenae, telling me I'd earned a random blueprint and a mark of Her favor, making it five more blueprints and a bonus item that I'd receive soon, hopefully.

"Now that the Death God, Nimon, is thoroughly pissed and has been held off with blatant ease by the Pantheon of the Flame, I'll take this chance to speak to the other Gods, the five Lesser Gods of the Pantheon of the Dark," I called out, turning slowly, noting the way the other altars, the ones of the more fervent supporters of Nimon, had been stationed between each of the Lesser Gods, separating them out.

"You saw a chance for power, to rise in stature, and you took it, despite knowing that you'd end up serving the utter wanker that brought about the Cataclysm. I can understand that. Perhaps you were scared. Perhaps you saw it as your only choice. I don't know. What I do know is that you have a choice now.

"You can stay as members of His Pantheon. You can be walked over, ignored Minor Gods, or you can leave Him, join us, and stand on your own. You'll get to keep your altars, even those people who worship you, but whatever deal you have with the deathly wanker will be done. When I wipe the fucker from the realm, you'll still be alive to tell the tale, to grow in power and respect."

I paused, looking around, noting the heavy silence that filled the air and the way that everyone hung on my words, whether interested in what I had to say or simply waiting for Nimon to snuff me from existence, I didn't know.

"You all know that Nimon hates me. Hell, the fucker's declared me an apostate and sent His little army of pissants after me. Illoth sent the Drow and Her pissy little spiders. As for the others, Ardat, Asmodeus, and Baphomet, well, I don't even know if they've tried yet. I might have missed it; they've been that fucking unimpressive so far. But I do know that I've killed every godsdamn one of them that's stood against us." I drew a deep breath before going on.

"Last night, we faced an Elder God, one of the original Valspar, a creature of fucking nightmare from between the stars, and we helped the Pantheon of the Flame fuck it up! So, bring it, you Dark Shit-Stain!" I roared, turning from the crowd and the listening Gods to staring up into the thunderous sky above.

Clouds rent as more and more thunder crashed. Lightning roared down, slamming into the shield over and over, the flashes momentarily blinding everyone. A strange screech of fury seemed to fill the world.

When I could see again, I watched dark liquid falling from the sky, pooling over the shield and collecting, sizzling and eating into it, before it was washed away in a sudden deluge of water.

Where Death tried to take hold, to batter down our defenses, Life and Nature through Ashante grew and reached back. All over the city, orchards bloomed, fruiting plants bulged with a bounty that they'd never known. Vegetables grew larger, and the living felt their bodies cleansed as Vanei purified the air.

The earth rumbled, then the walls shook a little as dust cascaded off them. Minor cracks and imperfections were fixed as Cruit made His presence and His control over the earth felt. In hundreds of thousands of ways, the Gods made Their presence clear across the city.

Forges flared and developed minor enchantments, roads were fixed, waters were purified, and the air just made you feel *good* when you breathed it. People who had been stuck, working at problems with no sign of a breakthrough, were suddenly struck by inspiration.

Minutes passed in silent war, even though neither side attacked the other directly. Nimon and His four pillars attacked the shield and the city and the others protecting it. It was obvious they were testing the waters, evaluating the other side. When it all finished and the skies grew calm again, the people in the cathedral turned to me, and I made a show of stretching nonchalantly, straightening up from where I'd been leaning on the naginata.

"Well?" I called up into the air above the city. "You saw He couldn't stand against us, even weakened as we are. Day by day, we grow in strength and He wanes. It's your choice..."

There were a few minutes of silence, then, just as I was about to speak, there came an almighty roar of thunder. The sky split again, darkness flowing over the land from horizon to horizon, as Nimon raged over the betrayal of one of His servants.

Issa, God of the Light in Dark Places, has forsworn the Pantheon of the Dark and has declared His allegiance to Sint, Lord of Light and the Pantheon of the Flame!

Let all see and bear witness!

The Pantheon of the Flame has grown in power, adding the Minor God Issa, bringing the Battlefield Healers of Issa into the fold, and denying their strength to the Enemy!

*

Darakin, God of Battle, has forsworn the Pantheon of the Dark, and has declared His Allegiance to Cruit, God of the Earth and the Pantheon of the Flame!

Let all see and bear witness!

The Pantheon of the Flame has grown in power, adding the Minor God Darakin, bringing the Warriors Three into the fold, and denying their strength to the Enemy!

Long seconds passed, then the darkness dissipated. I smiled broadly. While my speech had been shitty and rough, mainly aimed at goading Nimon and showing that I didn't give two shits, it'd achieved its goal in giving the Pantheon of the Flame the opportunity to defend a fixed point, one that they'd taken time to stealthily reinforce against Him. They had made Him look weak and foolish.

For two of His Gods, Minor though They were, to abandon Him and join Jenae's Pantheon was huge, though, especially as They brought information as much as They brought strength. I gestured to my people, and they moved swiftly, smashing the altars that belonged to the remaining three Gods who stayed with Nimon, and I took a deep breath.

"Welcome, Lord Darakin, Lord Issa!" I called out. A rumble from the crowd echoed me, even as the air shimmered before me. The first of the giant figures of the Gods arrived.

Jenae shimmered into being as though stepping from a hot sidewalk. In the same way that a mountain could be made to float by a mirage of heat, She stepped from Her realm, the Realm of the Gods, into ours. She was tall, ten meters or more tall, clad in burnished armor of bronze, copper, and steel. Flames ran up and down Her figure. The panels of Her armor were a deep red, glossy and perfect, reminding me of blood. But as She strode out, coming to a stop before me, and I went to one knee, She smiled kindly and spoke.

"Arise, My champion, My ally, and My friend. You have proven yourself to Me a thousand times, so know that I am proud of you."

I smiled to Her as I straightened. Then I strode down from the dais, calling out to those that were gathered, all practically forced to their knees by the overwhelming pressure of the presence of a living Goddess.

"All Hail Jenae, Mistress of the Flame, Goddess of Fire, Knowledge, and Exploration!" I called out, and thousands echoed my call.

She inclined Her head, stepping up onto the dais and turning slowly, before smiling and reaching out a hand in welcome, as another presence stepped forward through the shimmer of heat.

"Next, we have Ashante! The Goddess of Nature and Life, a Goddess of Growers and those who love the lush bounty of life all around us."

The air shimmered, and Ashante stepped into view, clad in a suit of green plate, adorned here and there with hints of flowers and vines adorning the metal. A long cloak of ivy hung from Her shoulders, Her black hair gently caressing the leaves. Ashante smiled around at the people gathered, regarding Her with awe, before She nodded and stepped up to stand next to Her sister, Jenae, and the two of them waited, watching the next shimmer that appeared.

"Cruit!" I cried out. "God of the Earth and Stability, Lord of Stone and Strength!" The figure that appeared wore armor of plain black and grey. It was battered and dusty, covered in minor imperfections, but somehow more solid than the mountains, and He wielded a massive warhammer in one fist.

He looked around, grunted, and stepped up to join the others, shooting me a wink as He passed. His shoulders alone looked as though He could lift a main battle tank without noticing. As He took his place, He watched the crowd, seeming placated by the interruption to His day as He noticed the Dwarves and stonemasons staring at him in open adoration.

"Sint!" I called out. "Lord of Light, and God of Order." With my words, He appeared, the flare of bright white light making everyone gasp. He stepped from the shimmer as if simply from another room, and He paused, smiling gently as He looked around at those gathered, a massive figure in full silver-plate armor.

Sint looked resplendent in a blue tabard, and I noted that He'd gained a new sigil on His pauldrons, a symbolic representation of a starburst surrounded by darkness. This was the symbol that Issa had chosen. Sint wore it to show both that Issa served Him, and that He accepted Him as part of the Pantheon.

I bowed again to Sint. Despite His formal and sensible outlook, He was probably the one I got on with the best, besides Jenae. I remembered His kind words when I'd gone to fight the Dark Legion, fully expecting to die.

I moved on, slowly circling the dais, and started to speak again as the air shimmered anew.

"Tamat, Lady of Darkness, Goddess of Assassination and Larceny," I called, smiling again when She appeared.

Her hair was long and black, curls bouncing with every step. Her lush figure was dressed, as always, in leather and blackened steel. She wore daggers everywhere, even for this, and a crossbow hung from Her back. It was Her servants that I really had to fear, since She was the Goddess of Assassination.

I bowed my head, getting a wink from Her as She turned and stepped up to join Her brethren, and I tried not to stare at Her ass too much. Considering She wore leather pants that appeared to have been painted onto Her skin, it was hard.

"Vanei, the Goddess of Air, Lady of Change," I intoned as a Valkyrie of huge proportions appeared. She smiled gracefully at the room, shuffling Her gleaming wings and stepping up to the dais. I paused for a brief second as glances turned from the Goddess of the Air and focused in on Lydia. She'd have been mortified by the attention a few short weeks ago. Now, She took it as Her due and dismissed it, having eyes only for Her Goddess.

"Lagoush, Goddess of Water, of the Depths, and of Healing and Alteration, Lady of Peaceful Passages." This Goddess was clad in greens and blues, an iridescent mix of scalemail and plate. She sent reflections across the room, making me think of the scales of a fish as She moved, sliding along so gracefully. She turned back to the room and smiled down at me.

I returned Her smile before turning to announce the next God.

"Svetu, God of Invention, and Lord of Crafters and Creators!" I called out, the air shimmering as a new figure appeared. Rather than the cranky Gnome I'd met before, Svetu manifested as a figure somewhere between human-sized and the Gods, short by comparison to them, but massive to us. He smiled benevolently.

He retained the characteristic yellowish tinge to His skin, but He was no longer clad in the hundreds of bags and random gizmos I'd seen before. Instead, He was dressed in clean leather trousers, a bag on each hip, and a bandolier of small pouches across His chest over a vest of plain white silk. He had long, pointed ears and inquisitive eyes, but one thing that hadn't changed was His cap, covered in dozens of different lenses and battered to all hell.

I stifled a grin as I realized He'd probably been told off by the rest of the Gods for His last appearance to us mortals in a ceremony, showing up as a normal Gnome and ignoring us all a lot of the time, preferring instead to work on one of His inventions.

"Thank you for joining us, Lord Svetu…and for your recent assistance." I bowed lower. He nodded, absently waving one hand to me as I moved on, turning to the last member of the original Pantheon.

"Tyosh, God of Time and Reflection, Lord of the Everlasting Chime," I introduced the figure that stepped forward. He wore a simple orange robe. His head was shaved, and His beard ran to His stomach, knotted and braided in intricate ways. He was smooth-skinned, but each movement conveyed a sense of peace and of power. He had a simple smile as He nodded His head and stepped up to stand with His brethren. A sense of peace came with Him.

I turned as the air shimmered again, and I paused, having no fucking clue who would step out, after the shock joining of the two new Gods. I bowed, then spoke up smoothly as I straightened.

The new arrival was slighter built than the rest of the Gods, and seemed tired, drained almost, compared with the others who were flushed with power and hope. Still, He towered over the rest of us, the same height as the other Gods, simply thinner and appearing old before His time. He smiled down at me, then around at the rest of the room, nervous. But I also saw relief in His golden eyes and the way He held Himself.

"Welcome, Lord Issa, God of the Light in Dark Places, to Narkolt and to the Pantheon of Flame," I greeted Him, guessing who He was by the long robes and the prominent emblem of a starburst surrounded by black.

"Thank you, High Lord Jax, Scion of the Empire. It is my honor to meet you and to join my new brothers and sisters today," He said, His voice echoing strangely, but bringing a sense of steady determination with it.

The final shimmer was clear to all, and I bowed my head again to Issa in respect and thanks for His gracious greeting before I moved to address the final God.

"Darakin! The Lord of War, Lover of Battle and Contests, please, be welcome here. I suspect you'll have many who wish to worship you in the days to come!"

The God that stepped forward this time made many stare in surprise. Where the Gods prior to Him had worn stunning armor or simple, yet elegant robes, He was clad in a mismatching array of light, medium, and heavy armor, with the dual hilts of a pair of short swords on His hips, a longsword on His back, and a trio of throwing daggers across His chest in a bandolier.

He had light hazel eyes and weathered blue-black skin that suggested He'd spent a lot of his time in the field. He wore a short-cropped black beard and had tightly curled black hair, but it was His physique that drew a lot of the attendants' attention.

He was clearly well-muscled and moved like a stalking panther, all graceful motions and pauses, and the way He smiled around at the crowd said he damn well knew how attractive a great many people found Him.

"Thank you, Jax," He said, inclining His head slightly. ***"I've watched your arrival with interest and look forward to sparring with you."***

"Uh, I look forward to that, too, Lord Darakin," I said, surprised, then I shook myself and took a deep breath before calling out to the people in attendance, all the while banishing the thought of a one-on-one fight with a God...*I bet Restun would still kick His ass.*

"These are the Gods, the Pantheon of the Flame, and They are ready, should you wish to meet them, worship them, and learn their ways," I finished formally, stepping back and rejoining my squad and friends as the individual Gods separated out, spreading out to claim a section of the cathedral, even as Jenae remained atop the dais.

The first few moments were tense, but then people began to step forward, taking the chance to speak to the Gods. They formed snaking lines of supplicants, kneeling in wonder before the titanic beings that, with a simple wave of their hands, could alter the lives of these mere mortals.

The next few hours passed reasonably quickly. As was expected, the Gods gave out certain boons to people, blessings, and They declared their intentions. Jenae called for those who wished to be priests in Her service to focus on the gathering of knowledge. Sint ordered His priests to aid the guard and bring order. Tamat, well, Tamat just grinned and spoke quietly to figures that slipped from the crowd, fuzzy and indistinct, to see Her.

The Gods and Goddesses spoke to people. As They finished, those people left, being replaced by more and more, until I gave in and asked a legionnaire how many were outside waiting their turn.

"Thousands, Lord Jax," he replied. "The streets are packed from wall to wall."

"Fuck," I muttered, turning and looking around the room. I located the legionnaire I'd sent to check the carriages and decided I might as well get some jobs done.

I gestured him over and asked in a low voice what he'd found.

"Oaken planks," he responded. "The cushioned seating inside was replaced with oaken planks and a thin layer of leather wrapped across the top. His own seats are made of some form of silken material I've never seen. I tried sitting on it."

"And?"

"And my arse will never think anything is comfortable again in comparison, sir. I'd sell my firstborn for a pillow of that stuff," he declared, smiling slightly. "Or I would, you know, if I had any kids," he finished with a wink.

"Hah, okay. That's all I needed to know. Do me a favor and take three of your friends, go get that prick of a lord, who it seems is just two away from meeting Sint. Go get him and take him to the carriage.

"Explain the situation and that I'm not fucking amused. Then, put him in the carriage I rode here and make sure he rides around the entire city for the next day straight. The only time he gets to stop is to use the toilet and to change horses and drivers.

"Make sure you swap them out as regularly as seems reasonable and tell them they are earning triple wages for the next day as they do it, all paid for by that prick. Make sure he pays it, as well. Then, at the end of the little ride, take him aside and explain that this is the only friendly warning he gets. Next time something like this happens, it'll be a spear up his arse, and he'll be hoisted over the main gate."

"Yessir, I'll make sure of it personally," he said stoically.

"Well, considering I'll need someone to make sure he actually sits for the entire trip and gets the full experience, that means you're gonna have a shitty trip, so rip the seat out of his carriage and have that for yourself. Keep it afterward, if you want," I said, shrugging.

"Seriously?" His smile nearly split his face. "Lord Jax, something like that would cost…"

"Nothing." I interrupted. "It cost me nothing, mate, as it's been kindly donated by that prick over there. Now, go and have a good trip, and take more for any other legionnaires who are joining you." I grinned as he saluted, grabbed three others, and walked over, bowing in respect to Lord Sint as they stepped before him. Then grabbed the suddenly protesting noble under his arms and dragged him off.

Sint looked over at me quizzically, and I mouthed *'I'll explain later'* to him. This elicited a snort of amusement from Him as He turned to meet the person who was next in line instead.

I met with stonemasons as they left Cruit, and I commissioned them, one and all, considering the hundreds I needed, to make new altars for the Gods, and to bring them to the cathedral in batches of twenty for each God, enabling them to be consecrated easily before being moved out and set into place in the hundreds of small churches and shrines around the city.

Hours passed. The sun set fully, and darkness fell, but there seemed to be no end of the supplicants. As it'd be pretty disrespectful of us to just walk off, I continued to do jobs, have meetings, and discuss issues with my people until deep into the night.

Eventually, Jenae stood and smiled at the throngs of people, holding one hand up. ***"Please, while we wish we could stay, we must attend to other matters. We shall return. As each altar is placed in a church or shrine, you will be able to reach out to us. When you come here, or should you possess a ceremonial relic from our faithful, you will know that we listen when you pray by our presence in your heart and by the draw upon your mana, showing your devotion to us.***

"We ask that you pray for a small amount of time each day. You will know your limits, and as you begin to feel weaker, please, please do stop. We, in turn, will bless this city. We will aid you in your fights and help you to raise your children to be strong and safe. High Lord Jax, Scion of the Empire, is both our ally and our much-beloved first servant, so we ask that you venerate him and act as he desires to aid him in all things. Thank you."

With that, Jenae and the others turned, and the air shimmered before them as they stepped from our realm and into Their own. Silence reigned when They left, and while some people were disappointed, the newly chosen priests stepped up and spoke to those who chose their God above others.

"Jax. a minor point. While I appreciate the deals we made earlier regarding blueprints and so on were made in good faith, I hope you're not expecting a blueprint for every single one of the literal hundreds of minor altars out there? I have to admit, I expected it to take a long time for you to destroy any of Nimon's altars. Frankly, I'm not strong enough to hold to that deal, not immediately," Jenae's voice whispered nervously in my ears. I snorted, shaking my head. I'd already guessed this was coming and had a response ready.

"No, no I can understand that. But, as that was our deal, and you're the Lady of Hidden Knowledge… " I said, getting an amused snort as She waited. *"I'm sure there's a hint of knowledge that you could give me instead? Spellbooks, skillbooks, that sort of thing?"*

"I'll honor the ones already owed, and I'll search you out a place that's appropriate. But, after that, you get Marks of Favor only!"

"Deal."

With that, the sense of Her presence faded, and I sighed. Hundreds and later thousands of blueprints would have been cool, but seriously, how many ways were there to make a sword? Spellbooks and skillbooks could make a massive difference now, rather than in ten years when we had time to actually use some of these blueprints.

We went outside, finding another set of carriages had been arranged for us. Unsurprisingly, they were much more comfortable, and we set off back to the palace and the keep, falling into our beds exhausted and ready for the day to end as soon as we got there.

Or at least I *was*, until we reached our room, kicked Bane out, and Oracle reminded me of her earlier offer. She shifted and blurred into a simple set of black stockings and suspenders, grinning at me as I woke up from my tired state with amazing speed.

Part of my anatomy literally stood to attention.

I took a deep breath, admiring her tanned and perfect figure, the sexy smile, and the bouncing curls, before she leaned in and straddled me, kissing me deeply.

The next few hours passed in a blur, and I loved every second of it.

CHAPTER FORTY-EIGHT

The next morning, things were back to normal. Which is to say that I was awoken by Bane trying to scare the shit out of me, as he told me we had five minutes to get into position for training with Restun.

I bolted upright, dressing with a speed that was frankly insane, and was out of the room while still half asleep, diving off the balcony and making it to the grass outside just in time, even with giving Bane a lift. Restun strode over, looking at those of us under his personal banner, a tall pennant that flapped and popped in the early morning breeze, and nodded in satisfaction.

"Good morning all!" he boomed, before going on, clearly determined to kill us all by lunchtime. "Today, we'll be training unarmed, but the person who puts in the least effort with their blows gets an extra hour of training with me, personally! This should ensure that you know to put in maximum effort. If not, I'll get to find out why and make sure that there are plenty of injuries to be healed!

"As all those who attend my sessions now have access to healing magic, this means that you all get a chance to level up your skills. The winners get to heal the losers and each other. The losers simply get the pain!

"You will be fighting first as individuals for an hour, followed by two hours of squad-versus-squad combat, finishing with a nice, gentle five-mile, fully armored *sprint*. Now, before you fall over yourselves at my benevolence in breaking you in gently to this new section of training, you get to warm up…a one-mile jog, followed by a two-mile run, then one hundred burpees, followed by a nice, friendly unarmed combat free-for-all."

Silence reigned for all of three seconds before he smiled again and finished with a threat, as we'd all expected. "And, as to the cool down at the end, whatever squad whose member is last to finish gets to spend the two hours between ten bells and midnight searching the grass here for the exact leaf I saw fly past this morning on my way here. You'll know it's my leaf when you see it, and woe befall you should you bring me the wrong one!"

That set the pattern for the day and the next several that followed, early morning abuse, horrific exercise, and fighting training. It was individual and in our squads, gaining us all a fuck ton of new injuries, which were all healed again and again. Hours of training followed by me drawing on the mana collectors and the stored mana we'd managed to accumulate to swear in a few thousand citizens at a time. That was followed by hours of meetings then I'd had to make time to visit the larger churches.

As I was a champion of Jenae, I'd occasionally even have to lead a service talking about Her and the other Gods.

I felt ridiculous doing it, but Cai said it was important. I believed him, just like I believed Denny when he thanked me and introduced me to more people daily who joined the ranks of the priesthood, as well as the few who joined his more specialized and utterly mental core.

Ame arrived and practically cursed me until my ears bled about not permitting her to come to the Imperial armory until now. Then she vanished with a small team of assistants as soon as I gave her formal authority over the armory. I shook my head at the sight of Caron being dragged along by her, one of his ears firmly grasped as she snapped orders out. Beyond an occasional demand for materials, I saw nothing else of her for days afterward.

I also grinned in relief as Renna stared awkwardly at her surroundings.

"Umm, Heir Augustus ordered me to come along with the others, Lord," she said, hesitantly, clearly expecting to be told off for coming without me personally requesting her.

"And he was totally right to do so!" I said, grinning. "Renna, you are so godsdamn welcome here. I've been so busy!" I broke off, taking a deep breath, before waving Restun over from where he was watching me. "Restun, this is Renna, she's…"

"The Imperial Arcane Tattooist," Restun responded, nodding a greeting to her.

"Exactly. Look, I know it requires people to permanently mark their bodies, but…"

"I have over a hundred legionnaires who have begged for the chance to gain this class, Lord Jax. How many are you willing to permit to be brought into the fold?"

"Oh…well, as many want to, really. Start with ten, maybe? Then, once we know it works okay, expand that to as many as you want." I suggested, getting a smile from him as he bowed his head slightly to Renna.

"Then, I'll have them ready for Miss Renna in half an hour?" he suggested as he led her off, already deep in discussion with her over the possibilities.

Tenandra, Jian, and Sehran, unsurprisingly, were worn out from the flight. It had been done at top speed, after all, so I thanked them heartily and let them rest for a few days, providing a handful of large manastones to recharge Tenandra's ship-body form.

I wasn't quite sure why Sehran and Jian were so tired, but the way they held hands a lot made me not want to speculate. I suspected his exhaustion was located more around his lower back and groin area than anywhere else.

Horkesh arrived with a hundred of the biggest, nastiest fucking spiders I'd ever seen and scared the utter shit out of the entire city as the *Star's Glory* floated over it, massive spiders dangling like the freakiest fruit ever seen.

I met with her and thanked her for coming and for bringing her warriors. In the process, I heard that her mother, Ashrag, was apparently holed up in a valley to the north of the Tower after her scouts had found a tribe of trolls living there. She was using them as a combination workforce and self-replenishing snack, thanks to their insane regeneration.

I felt bad about them for about a second, then I was just glad it wasn't me and dismissed it, sending the spiders to hunt the forest on the Himnel side of the river with orders to be ready for what was to come, along with the insane bastards that had volunteered to work with her in creating the first Spider Cavalry. It turned out to be mainly the slaves who had been freed from the cages that had been aboard the *Star's Glory* in the first place, and a bunch of others they'd talked into it.

Restun had arranged basic training in mounted tactics for them, and I arranged the wisps to take turns in teaching them magic, so we had a hundred of the scariest fucking cavalry in the known UnderVerse now, considering the sight of only one of the crazy bastards made my butthole pucker.

As the days passed, more and more of the manastone mine was uncovered, until finally on the sixth day, the entrance through the main sewer was uncovered, and I greeted the news with a mixture of elation and trepidation.

Trepidation because I damn well knew I was going to be wading through shit at least up to my knees, and elation, because after a week of meetings and arguments, I hoped that I was finally going to get to kill something.

I gathered my team, now back up to full strength, with the addition of Thomas and his squad moving along with us. We had five mana potions, five healing and three stamina each. Besides that, everyone, worryingly including Giint, was now able to use magic. We also had replaced or repaired armor for those who needed it.

I, of course, had needed practically a fresh full suit each time until now, bar my helm and bracers, so Thorn had checked all my equipment repeatedly, clearly not trusting me when I said it was good to go.

We set off into the sewers at daybreak, a small breakfast having started the day off, wearing nearly half a pot each of some insanely thick unguent that reeked of musk smeared across our upper lips and round our nostrils.

Tenandra took off, leaving us at the entrance to the main sewer, taking up a position overhead with the limited crew she needed. Ame and Nerin were aboard the ship, ready as well in case we found runes or equipment or caught some filthy disease, although they held their noses and shuddered at the thought of where we were going.

"I'm totally going to need to burn this armor after this, you know that, right?" Thomas said, looking at the massive gates that lead down into the darkness.

"Why do you think I'm not wearing my Drow spider-silk clothes?" I asked. "As far as I'm concerned, after this, everything that isn't steel gets burned."

"I think the steel should be included," he muttered, making his way over to his squad. They were a mad lot, cherry picked from the Legion, the elite city guards, and the more unstable of the Tower's people. I couldn't help but grin at the sight of Nigret, the Trigara who'd sworn to follow me.

He'd volunteered to join Thomas before the city assault and had loved the advanced training he'd been getting as a member of our squads…right up until he found out where we were going.

As a Trigara, essentially a massive upright tiger-man, he was heavily furred and shared an instinctive hatred of dirt from the cat side of his DNA. The fact we were going to be wading through literal shit had nearly made him scream in horror.

It'd been hilarious to see, and everyone had been making themselves feel a lot better about the whole thing by winding him up about it.

A small hill rose before me. The gates were set into a recessed section cut into it and led down at a gentle slope into the darkness, making it seem much more manageable than this was going to be.

One of the reports I'd had recently was on sanitation, and those who worked in the sewers were well respected in fighting circles because the things that lived in the filth were horrific.

I looked up to Oracle, who I'd just bounced on my shoulder unthinkingly, and I grinned up at her, admiring the length of pale leg that she was showing, before she winked at me and gestured to the doors.

"Shall we?" she asked.

"I think we should." I turned to the others. "Okay, people, this is going to be, sorry, a shitty job…but it needs to be done. We've got a guide, Karl, and he's going to lead us through the sewers as quickly as possible to the sections the golems have uncovered. Remember, we lost two golems down here…GOLEMS. So there's something in there that's got both shitty taste in prey, and is powerful enough to pull it off, yet knows to hide from the war golems that have been searching for it. Keep your eyes open and your nose closed," I said, smiling slightly before I turned to the little rat-featured man who was our guide.

Karl was five feet tall, potbellied, with the muscle tone of an over-stretched elastic band. He had protruding front teeth that seemed abnormally large and a scraggly beard that was practically an offense to humanity. I hadn't dared to use my Examine spell on him yet, mainly because I thought if I found out he was half Kobold, as I suspected I would, the mental images of his conception would never leave me.

I gestured him forward, and he smiled ingratiatingly, rubbing his hands together and bowing before rushing to the gates and squeezing through the small gap he'd managed to open them by.

I shook my head, following after him and thanking Grizz as he grabbed the gates, one in each hand, and easily opened them wide enough for us all to pass through.

I let the others move ahead of me for a minute as I checked on Grizz, getting a grin and a wink from him, as he assured me he "was totally fine, honest." That alone made me watch him more carefully for the rest of the day.

The gates were customarily kept locked, and even now as we filed in, a small team from the guard were waiting with two members of the sewerman's guild to chain them shut again. Their duty was to stand there and wait, killing anything that tried to escape from the subterranean shit-pit.

Once we were all inside, moving swiftly along into the encroaching darkness, the gates closed behind us with a creak and the rattle of the chain being drawn through the lock and the clank of the lock being sealed, a single flare of magic momentarily brightening the filth around us as the enchanted lock activated. The warning bell next to it let loose a single subdued chime to make all aware that a team had entered.

We followed Karl for some time, the first ten minutes or so being unpleasant, but nothing more. As we moved down the slope, it slowly grew dirtier and dirtier, the ancient stonework all around us becoming stained with what appeared to be tide marks, some higher than our heads, which made me feel sick.

"Karl," I called, seeing him freeze, then scuttle back to us, cocking his head to one side. "What's happened with this?" I gestured to the tide marks.

"What do you mean, master?" he asked, twitching his head from side to side.

"I…fine, whatever." I didn't care to have the argument everyday about what they should call me, so I just went on. "The level of the stains, why are they so high on the walls, but just a thin smear on the floor?"

"Ah...ah, the stone men, the *golems*...yes...they come, they clear it away, break through channels long sealed. It drains away, fills lower tunnels again. Means lots more work to come. Oh, yes, lots more work for poor Karl, but for now, it's quiet," he said, shifting from foot to foot and dry washing his hands as he spoke.

"More work?" I asked.

"If we do nothing now, it will build up. Oh yes, and that attracts the creatures...Slimes, Pit-Rats, Crawlers, Naga...all down here, yes they are, all down here making poor Karl's day harder," he said mournfully.

"Okay, well, why do nothing now?" I asked, gesturing for him to lead the way again.

"Because of the line. We work to keep it under the line," he said, pointing to a deeply etched chalk line on the wall, nodding to himself as he pointed it out. "It's below the line, you see."

"So?" I asked.

"So, we don't need to do anything!" he clarified, bobbing again and scuttling sideways, as though wanting to keep us all in view.

"But it'll get worse if you leave it, right?" I asked.

He nodded, looking sad.

"So why not just work on it anyway, clear it out more, or make a new line, lower down?" I suggested. He switched from a frown to a glare, straightening up.

"We don't have to!" he said emphatically. "We don't have to work if it's under the line!"

"Wait, you're telling me that you're deliberately going to let it get worse, let the creatures grow, making it more dangerous for yourselves down here, because you don't have to do anything for now if you don't want to?" I asked him incredulously.

He smiled at me before scurrying away.

I turned to look at Arrin, who was nearby. "He's fucking crazy," I muttered.

He laughed, the sound carrying, as Ronin started to play a merry tune, one he'd referred to before as "the Madman Dances.'"

The notes danced about, climbing high and tinkling low, filling the air around us. I felt my heart lift, a little of the stress I tried not to think about slipping away with the music's caress.

Ronin winked in the bouncing light of the magelights everyone wore, and I silently thanked him again. The man was a pain in the arse in many ways, not least because he was still insisting on trying to live up to his reputation as a bard with every pretty girl or boy he could find.

Hell, the maids in the keep were keeping such a regular pattern in and out of his room that Thomas had jokingly suggested a revolving door be installed for them. Despite all of that, though, he constantly provided details that made our lives easier, music that calmed, gossip that people let slip around him because he was "just a bard," and more. He gave us information on creatures, lore, and tales of the past. Hell, he even got bribed, constantly. He took it all, then told Flux what was happening. Flux used his small team of spies or passed the details to Lucian and his Justicars.

The bard, who everyone admitted they wanted to stab at least once a week, was on his way to being one of the most indispensable members of the team, much to my constant surprise.

I was broken from my musings by a cry followed by a splat. I winced, looking back at Giint. The short, muscular Gnome had stepped off the side of the path by accident and had fallen headfirst into the narrow channel that wound its way down the center of the sewer. Now, he was frantically pulling himself out, retching and coughing as we all cringed.

He got to the side, then froze, his eyes opening wide in horror. The little Gnome cried out and dove headfirst into the stream of literal shit that flowed sluggishly down the middle of the passage.

He vanished from sight, came up, and took a deep breath, then back down, then up, then down as we all looked on in horror. Even Karl came back to watch.

After more than a minute, Giint finally surfaced with a filth-encrusted block in his hand, and he dragged himself out, shaking like a dog and sending shit flying.

I summoned a fountain for him. The tiny Gnome practically vanished into it as he scrubbed and scrubbed at himself and the object he held. Oracle, who still sat on my shoulder, summoned a second one for Bane.

Bane took a few quick lungfuls in before stepping back and letting others move in, taking the opportunity to wash their hands and boots as best as they could.

It might have been pointless, I admitted to myself, considering we still had a way to go in here, but damn it felt better to do it.

When he was finally done, I asked him what the hell he'd been doing.

He held up the small cube in answer.

"Seriously, you went in after that?"

"Gift from God," he replied, putting it away carefully.

"You said that before." I remembered. "Is it? A gift from Svetu, I mean?"

"Gift. From. God," Giint repeated, glaring at me, and making it clear he was done with the discussion before pulling a crossbow out of his bag and looking around.

He'd made numerous changes to the small device he'd been carrying. The sudden change from desperately rebuilding things from damaged and utter crap into getting access to all the resources he could really use had been good for him, and the crossbow he carried now was a thing of wonder.

It was short and stubby—a bit like him really—and it fairly glowed with power. Its blazing blue light reminded me of the mana-engines, built to a subsonic whine that could set your teeth on edge when he cranked it all the way up.

The bolts were likewise short, but wide, with a triangular fin arrangement on the back and wicked points on the front. Unlike traditional bolts for a crossbow, these were made of some kind of metal and were filled with a variety of different substances.

Some were poisoned, some had flammable liquids with a sulfur compound in the head. Hell, one kind was hollow and shattered into a dozen sharpened glass fragments, designed to make sure that no one could recover from the bleed effect they'd trigger.

At first, Mal had laughed at him. Then he'd started paying more attention, and now he was paying the crazy bastard in catnip and getting his own bolts remade to do different jobs.

Now Giint had pulled it out and stood ready, making us all fall in on him, facing outward as the crazy little bastard had sensed something before we had.

I looked around, cursing as I saw that Karl had vanished.

"The guide is gone. Fall in on Giint and get ready. Fireballs and Magic Missiles first, followed by bolts, then melee, ready?" I said, getting a series of grunts in response.

"Move!" I ordered. Both squads fell in, with everyone lifting a hand that rapidly filled with magic.

The tunnel, which had been poorly lit with magelights strapped to our armor or belts, was suddenly clearly lit as more than twenty people started to cast Fireball or Magic Missile, and the creature Giint had sensed froze in the act of sneaking up on us.

It was fat and long, its bloated back clearly visible above the sludge that floated down the channel. It stared at us malevolently, the light of our magic reflecting from five large, glossy black orbs that barely peeked above the floating turds.

It was over ten meters long, just over a meter wide, and made me think of a crocodile in the way it was moving in the sewers. But instead of a long maw filled with teeth, this thing reared up slightly, lifting a narrow proboscis out of the water and waving it about, as if unsure which to attack first.

"It's a salan!" Ronin shouted. "Watch the walls as well!"

I glanced to the wall, seeing nothing, then turned back again as something caught my eye. Where before, there'd only been stone blocks and smeared shit, a faint trail led up to three creatures with backs that were patterned to match the stone they clambered across. "Every second man target the walls. Everyone else, kill that fucker!" I ordered, letting loose with my Fireball, slamming it home into the middle of the three and sending flames washing over the wall.

The smell of flash-fried turds overcame even the musk I'd virtually stuffed up my nose, and I winced as the tunnel filled with the sound of screeching, cooking creatures.

The fight was over practically before it began: almost a hundred Magic Missiles hammering into any creature, even one half-hidden in a river of sewage, tends to end things quickly. The spray that filled the passage from the detonating missiles was awful.

We hunkered down for a few minutes while everyone caught their breath, and I fired Fireballs into the piles of corpses and shit.

"Stop!" squealed a voice.

I froze, looking over, my night vision ruined by the close proximity of lights and magic.

"What?" I called.

"Identify yourself!" Grizz snapped, the goofy, laughing legionnaire gone in an instant, and one of the scariest bastards I'd ever seen in his place.

The light on Grizz's shoulder lit his face from beneath, and with his short, wide-bladed gladius in his right hand and the glow of magic wreathing his left as he summoned a new round of Magic Missiles gave him a Demonic, or at least terrifying appearance.

I glanced at Sehran unconsciously at the thought of Demonic, seeing her knee-length boots, leather corset, and tiny hotpants, shaking my head as I redefined Demonic for at least the fifth time before glancing back into the darkness.

"It…it's just…me…" came the voice, and Karl stepped back out of the darkness, wringing his hands and looking around nervously.

"Where the fuck were you?!" Grizz growled at him.

"I hid!" Karl said, gesturing over his shoulder into the darkness.

"Bane, Tang?" I asked the air, and a few seconds later, Tang appeared by my side, leaning in close to me.

"Bane's hiding near the little shit. Looks like he's better at stealth than we thought. He was hidden in plain sight, some kind of invisibility ability or spell we've not seen before," Tang whispered.

"You scout. Bane stays near him," I whispered, and Tang nodded, darting away.

"It's fine," I said loudly. Grizz paused in mid-questioning of the little man, glancing at me in confusion. "Grizz, he's not a fighter; of course he hid. But next time, Karl, you warn us all first, understood?"

I forced myself to smile. Everyone could see and feel the wrongness in the conversation. Everyone, that is, but Karl, who smiled nervously and bobbed his head. He turned and darted off into the dark again, staying conspicuously at the outer edge of the light and saying as little as possible.

He responded when asked a direct question, but the most he'd say was a few words. I'd started to get a bad feeling about him, assuaged only slightly by the knowledge that Bane was nearby.

We traveled on for another half an hour, going down side passages that were clearly normally under the water in the sewers. That was judging from the encrustation, and I tried not to consider the things that crunched and squished underfoot, pausing irregularly to summon fountains to hose down anyone who fell.

The only respite from the constant darkness and the rapidly switching trails we used was the constant low level of horror-filled sounds Nigret made.

He was near the rear of the group, and the little whines of disgust, the sharply indrawn breaths, and the hisses and panting, all conspired to make the journey so much easier for the rest of us by comparison.

I snorted and coughed, spitting out a foul taste in my mouth as I waited for my turn. A long-forgotten stairwell narrow enough that only one person at a time could use it safely had led me down to a gate. We were filtering through it when Bane shouted a warning, and something in the darkness beyond us moved.

I stared, trying to see anything, but between the shifting light given off by the magelights and the filth-encrusted walls, the narrow confines, and the rusted ancient gates, I could barely see anything.

Bane had passed through at some point, along with Karl. Tang had led the way, with Karl giving him directions. Grizz and Lydia had been ahead of me. I gripped the gate, pushing it back into place. It was the Imperial equivalent of an old English kissing gate, making everything just that little bit more fucking complicated and disgusting, considering the detritus that hung from the sides of the cage.

As soon as it was locked against the far wall, I stepped in, just making out Lydia hurrying away from me into the dark as I shuffled to the left. She made enough room that I could swing the gate back to the right to open the exit. Flashes of magic went off ahead. The light of the magelights and that given off by the spells in flight seemed far smaller than it should be, when I hurried after the others.

I'd barely gone a dozen feet before I slowed and looked around, the world seemingly having gone silent and dark. Even the floor beneath me seemed dark. I crouched, getting closer to the ground and seeing that it never changed.

Where it should have been lit by the magelight, at least allowing me to see the flattened meadow muffins. Instead, there was a dark expanse of…blankness under my feet.

I shifted my boots, listening, hearing nothing at all, including from my own armor. While I could feel things being pushed along by my boots, I saw and heard nothing. I swallowed hard, checking my HUD and seeing no markers for debuffs, and started to swear.

"If you can hear me, then be careful!" I shouted, hearing nothing, even from myself. "I can't see or hear…there's nothing!"

I paused a few seconds, listening, but heard nothing, so I drew in a deep breath, evaluating what I could tell was going on. All I could smell was the musk I'd rammed up my nose earlier, and even blowing that out of each nostril, there was nothing I could smell. I couldn't see anything, nothing real, anyway, as I could feel the mess on the floor, just like before, but my eyes told me there was nothing there.

Given the fact I could feel what *should* be there, I decided to trust the feeling rather than the vision. I couldn't hear anything, and when I cast a Fireball, again I could feel it, but couldn't see anything, literally.

I could feel the mana flowing through me, but I couldn't see the magic. To my eyes, at least, I was just holding my left hand up randomly in the air, with nothing happening.

The distinct drain on my mana was still present, though, as was the sensation of pulling from my core and the twisting, turning feeling that I associated with the building of the spell, so I went on with it.

I crouched there, building the spell quickly, seeing nothing and hearing less. I closed my eyes, and as far as possible ignored the ears, using my other senses. I reached out to Oracle first. It was instinctive by now, and I felt her relief as I did so.

"Jax!" She whispered. *"Oh thank the Gods! I was starting to panic when you didn't answer!"*

"I didn't hear you," I replied, worried that our mental conversations were failing as well, and she responded with a mental shake of her head.

"It wasn't like this, not mind to mind. I was speaking, and you just stared through me. So did the others,"

"What's going on?" I asked her quickly. *"Can you see anything?"*

"You're all just standing still, or wandering around," she said, the concern clear in her voice.

"What about Bane?" I asked, and there was a long pause before she hissed in concern.

"He's slumped against a wall. He's breathing, but I think he's out cold. The others are wandering around aimlessly. It's when they step inside the room, those outside are rushing to get in."

"Stop them, quick!" I said, getting a sense of agreement from the bond, then a few seconds later, she was back.

"Okay, Bob's come in. He sees things like I do, and he's not affected, so he's checking on the others, seeing if he can lead them back out. Your Fireball, what were you doing?" she asked.

"I didn't know what was happening, and I wanted to see if I could cast still."
I felt amusement from her, as well as a more serious undercurrent.

"Well, don't dismiss it. Turn left, a bit more, little more, there! Now, aim up a bit, aim about thirty degrees up? I think? Then throw it." I did as she asked, and she hissed, clearly seeing something. *"We've found another entrance to the mine, an old one,"* she said slowly. *"The spells are still active, still protecting it, and the room is full of corpses, creatures everywhere. There must be…right, turn to the left and walk forward, more to the right, now left, keep going."* She walked me forward like that slowly, constantly correcting me until I felt like I must be in a maze, following some insanely twisty, turning path. But eventually, she bade me stop and reached out.

The stone of the wall was slimy under my fingers, and with her directions, I dug my fingers in, feeling the filth of ages cracking and crumbling away, dropping from the wall to the floor, until I felt a symbol under my hand.

I gripped it firmly and twisted, again as she directed, a quarter turn to the left, then a half turn to the right, then back to the beginning, trying not to imagine what the hell was getting ground into my fingers and squishing through the gaps in my gauntlets.

As the latch returned to the beginning, there was an audible clunk that reverberated through the room, and it was like the world came back all in one go.

I gasped as the overwhelming stench flooded my nostrils, and the shift from the dull, omnipresent, featureless light I'd been seeing before shifted, the wall appearing and my light letting me see around me again.

The others stumbled about, suddenly aware again as their senses returned. Cries arose from all around the room, and I stared in shock.

Before, as we'd passed through the sewers, there had been the occasional decomposing corpse that we'd passed, mainly fed upon by things like the salan. Here, there were hundreds, if not thousands.

It was a large dome, and I stood on the far side of it from the gate where we'd entered, with a massive door in the wall next to me. Beyond that, the room was circular, made of ancient, muck-encrusted stones, with four pipes that led in from elsewhere near the apex.

Where the pipes fed in, there were massive piles of creatures, many half-eaten, and here and there, rats and small six-legged creatures clambered, squealing as the sudden influx of light revealed them.

I stared in shock, especially at the corpse that must have been fifteen meters long, and I heard the others entering the room, gasping as they saw it as well.

I moved over to Bane, helping him to his feet, as Oracle hit him with a heal. Then, the pair of us went to look at the beast, getting a stunned shout from Ronin as he moved up next to us.

"It's a felihim!" he gasped.

We looked at him questioningly, even as Oracle slowly flew around the room, searching for something.

"What the fuck is that?" I asked Ronin.

"It's rare, is what it is!" He pointed to the beast. "You see the way there are tiny wings there?"

I nodded, having missed the atrophied nubs.

"The felihim are an offshoot of Dragons, like wyverns are, but instead of flying, they adapted to the underground rivers and streams. Look at the long neck, the head…"

I did. Yeah, the long neck and the bulbous body did look vaguely Dragon-like. The long tail that vanished into the filth to the left was curled around the wall, but the head…

"Where's it's eyes?" I asked.

"They don't see the way we do, more like the way Bane feels the world around him. But that's not it either, from what I remember. That band muscle across its face is like a shield, and the eye should be under it. You'll be able to guess at the thing's age by how long it is," he said, using a dagger to cut the skin back and reveal a multifaceted band of gems sunken into the putrefying flesh.

The creature was clearly dead, long since, considering more than half of its flesh was gone and the remainder was chewed, but considering the size of the thing…

"How the hell did it get here?" I asked wonderingly.

"Probably got washed down when it was exploring at some point, then couldn't get back out." Ronin said, gesturing. "Look at its shoulders, there." A ring of muscles and worn-down scales suggested it'd tried over and over to push its way back through the pipes.

"I'll bet it got washed down here when it was a low tide, probably in the winter, spent the whole year eating everything else that got washed down and growing, then couldn't get back out through the pipes when the room filled up fully again."

"Well, it's certainly weird-looking," I muttered.

"Look who's talking about weird-looking," Bane said quietly, sending a subdued burst of amusement at me.

I shot him the finger in return.

"I knew I liked you for a good reason, Bane," Thomas said, coming to a halt next to us and looking the creature over. "I mean, that thing's been dead for possibly a year or more, and still I can't tell which is better-looking."

"All this time, he's been trying to tell me that different species have different tastes, and that's why I view him as so ugly. But clearly, that was a lie to salvage his confidence. Thank you, Thomas," Bane replied, and the fuckers fist-bumped.

I took a deep breath, ignoring them, then coughed over the foul odors, and I gestured to the remains of the felihim.

"So…" I coughed conspicuously. "Are they…valuable?"

"Alive? Very," Ronin said seriously. "They're massively magical creatures, like their ancestors. Everything from their bones to their organs are ingredients. Hell, the meat is supposed to taste fantastic. But in the state it's in…"

"Yeah, I'm not eating that," I replied flatly.

"Neither would I, but…" Ronin gestured to the beast's skull. "The eye is a single band of gemstones, and it can be used in a lot of ways. Plus, the bigger they are, and the more evolved, the more often creatures have essence cores. This one at least should be rare, so some noble will pay pretty copper for it."

"Ha, no," I said flatly. "Essence cores go to the Treasury from now on. Never for sale."

"Really?" Ronin asked, frowning. "The college knows that the nobles have a use for them, but they don't know what it is. They just insist that any rare ones are handed into the Bardic College."

"Then they vanish, I'm betting? Not kept anywhere anyone can see?" Thomas asked.

"They're sold or given to the nobles, or at least that's what I'm told. They're used to buy the nobles off when a particularly promising candidate is arrested."

"Ever seen that?" I asked. I was about to try and strip the corpse, searching for it, then I remembered we had someone with the skills I needed. "Giint! Get your arse over here, mate."

"What need?" Giint asked me, eyeing the corpse in interest.

"I need the essence core and the eyes out of that thing. Anything else you find is all yours."

He grinned, virtually diving head-first into the chest cavity.

"That might have been a mistake," Ronin said slowly. "They're like Dragons, remember?"

"You said that; what am I missing?" I asked.

"Dragons hoard gold and gems, platinum and so on. It's not because they like shiny shit, well, not just because of that. It's like a form of medicine for them. Scales fall out? They regrow them using various metals they digest. Same for gems; that's why everyone who hunts Dragonkin are either rich or dead. You can find all sorts in a nest."

"So, I just told Giint to strip a corpse that might be full of platinum?" I asked.

He shrugged. "Unlikely down here, but it might have some valuables. After all, it's been eating things that washed down here."

"Giint!" I called into the side of the corpse, and the feet I could just see inside stilled as he shouted something back that sounded vaguely like a question. "If you find platinum or magical shit, I need to see it first. Gold and gems you can keep." I got a grunt and a muffled agreement.

"That's pretty generous," Ronin said.

I fixed him with a hard look, one eyebrow raised in question. "You want to burrow inside of the thing?"

He couldn't shake his head fast enough. "Fuck, no. I'm fine with being on this side of the scales. It still stinks."

"Exactly," I said, stepping over to the massive doors and noting the several inches, if not feet of literal shit that lay at the bottom of them. "Looks like it's time to break out the shovels," I muttered.

"Where's the rat?" Grizz suddenly asked. I frowned, looking at him, before grunting and calling out.

"Karl!" I shouted, the sound echoing around the room.

Seconds passed, then minutes, and we all joined in the search. Even Bane took the time to let us gather at one end of the room so he could let loose a concentrated blast of his worldsense but nothing. No corpse, no response, and just as I was about to give up, thinking that something had managed to kill him, maybe a bigger version of the rats or whatever, Tang called us over to the far side of the room.

"Here," he said. There were rungs carved into the wall, rungs that were strangely free of any filth, as though they'd been used recently. Above them, high above, was one of the pipes that led in and seemingly out of the room.

"It was a trap," Nigret rumbled, his displeasure clear. "This one wondered why we saw no signs of golems and why the guide smelled so strange…"

"What do you mean?" I asked.

He bared his teeth. "Nigret hates the smell of musk as much as that of unclean places, so he leaves it alone. When Karl is close, Nigret smells him. He smells like death, like old death. Nigret thinks this is peculiar, but he is surrounded by legionnaires. Nigret decides that one small guide smelling strange is the least of this day's concerns. Now, Nigret wishes he mentioned it earlier. Nigret is sorry."

"Don't worry about it." I said. "I'd have dismissed it as well, but…"

"But 'e led us into a place tha' must've been under tha level o' tha filth fer centuries, or at least tha entrance must've been. And 'ow th' hell did 'e get out?" Lydia growled.

"I don't know, but I want to find out," I said. "Bane?"

"I'll find him," he said, nodding to me and sending a directed pulse up into the pipe overhead. He paused for several seconds, then grunted. "I've got him, right at the edge of my range, though. With all this crap about, it's muffling the return. He's headed away in a hurry, though, and he's moving fast, far faster than he should be, and he's on all fours."

"Get him. Bring him back, if you can. If not, fucking kill him." I said. Bane headed up the rungs, then vanished into the pipe, as I turned to the rest of the party. "Okay then, people, time to get to work," I ordered, gesturing toward the doors.

"Shovels if yeh've got them," Lydia said, picking up the role of command. "Ah want two teams, one gets tha corpses back, tha other gets te dig!"

The room was full of activity as everyone, myself included, mucked in, clearing it as fast as we could.

CHAPTER FORTY-NINE

t took a little less than an hour in the end. By that time, we'd dragged several tons of bone and detritus aside each, and we'd waded in, literally in some cases, to the pits we had dug to clear the doors. Eventually, it was done, and I put my hand to the small crystal in the center that Oracle directed me to.

Rather than the larger, fully crystalline door that secured the Imperial Armory and the much smaller crystal doorways that protected certain sensitive areas of the Great Tower, these were simpler, entirely stone doors.

That wasn't to say they were any weaker, however. When I pressed my hand to it, the doorway protruded a tiny needle, slamming it into my hand and withdrawing it with vicious speed, making me curse as I yanked it back, glaring at the door.

There were a few nervous seconds as the mine evaluated the blood before it finally accepted it, and the door creaked open.

The change in the room we were in was insane, literally, as we all desperately shielded our darkness adjusted eyes. The magelights inside the mine were blazing at a level that was nigh-on crippling, and we cursed roundly as we blinked, trying to adjust.

"There is no threat," Bob said to our minds, and I sighed. Being unable to see, my first thought was that we'd be attacked. But, as the minutes passed and we all recovered, we found that the facility had escaped the majority of the ravages of time, internally at least.

We stepped inside, pausing as four war golems stood ready, two either side of the door, in dedicated charging cradles. Checking them out, Oracle confirmed that not only were they active, charged by the massively abundant mana in the air, but they were each complex or level three golems. This was a massive relief, considering how easily they could have been dead or dumb.

I noted the simple design of this section. Where other facilities had been dressed in polished marble or carved granite with fanciful designs, here, it was all bare, craggy stone walls, clearly the original cave walls.

The doors that we'd passed through stood in carved niches in the wall. But beyond that, the entire facility seemed to have been left as natural as possible. As we walked deeper, that only became clearer.

Channels ran across the floor, leading to the door and the charging cradles, with what looked to be crystallized amber filling them. As we moved out from under a low cave roof, the main site came into view.

There were three doors that I could see, facing north, east, and southeast. The door we'd entered through was roughly to the south, and the entire west of the cavern was taken up by the only building in sight.

What caught my eyes, and everyone else's, was the bright glow that came from the open doors leading to the north as a pair of golems strode into view, dragging a cart along a rail track.

They brought it up to the end of the track, a circular hole carved into the ground with a massive hatch over it. Before we could say anything, they opened the hatch and began to steadily pour the manastones in.

They poured in over a thousand gemstones filled with internal light, and the hatch blazed even stronger with life and light. We raced over, arriving just as the golems shut the hatch, and I ordered them to reopen it, to no avail.

"You need to claim the Mine!" Oracle told me.

I cursed, turning and running for the building, hoping that the golems hadn't just done the magical equivalent of pouring diamonds down the toilet.

The building itself was small and simply appointed. Three rooms on the ground floor provided a barracks, a decent-sized bathroom complete with a pool, and a Genesis Chamber. Beyond it being one, I could see nothing else. I jogged up the stairs to the next floor, finding a single large room that ran the length of the floor, albeit a much smaller floor than the one below.

This room had a series of maps on one wall, two desks that were covered in dust, papers that crumbled as soon as I looked at them, and a Command Center with the attendant table.

When I sat in the chair, it recognized me instantly, pulling up the relevant screens and offering itself to "One of Imperial Right." I claimed it, sighing in relief as it brought up a collection of screens to paw through. As I pulled up the first, a report on the facility came to my attention. It matched the one I'd seen originally from the city command center.

Imperial Manastone Mine (14%)
The Imperial Manastone mine is one of four on the Continent of Dravith, and is currently producing at 14% capacity. To increase production, repairs must be made to the following sub-systems:

Mana Collectors: 0/11 currently active.
Mana Purification Substrates 0/4 currently active
Bio-Mana Converter 1/4 currently active.

Scrolling down the option, I highlighted the mana collectors first of all. Of the original eleven, only one was still on site. The rest, as they'd been above ground, had been destroyed one way or another. That final one was buried, judging from the wire diagram I got of its location. It appeared to be inside the basement of a nearby building, so I pulled up the next screen, checking the golems on site.

<u>Inventory of Assets:</u>

War Golems:
>Class 1 :0
>Class 2: 0
>Class 3: 8
>Class 4: 2
>Class 5: 0
>Class 6: 0
>Class 7: 0

Crafting Golems:
>Class 1 :0
>Class 2: 4
>Class 3: 0
>Class 4: 0
>Class 5: 0
>Class 6: 0
>Class 7: 0

Mining Golems:
>Class 1: 0
>Class 2: 0
>Class 3: 1
>Class 4: 0
>Class 5: 0
>Class 6: 0
>Class 7: 0

Servitor Golems:
>Class 1: 0
>Class 2: 0
>Class 3: 0
>Class 4: 4
>Class 5: 0
>Class 6: 0
>Class 7: 0

I tapped on the first of the servitor golems and sent it to the buried mana collector, along with a class four war golem as an escort, judging that if anyone gave it grief, at least it'd be smart enough to refer to a local authority for orders.

Moving back to the first screen, I moved from the mana collectors to the mana purification substrates.

All four were inactive. While two gave no response when I tapped on them, the other two did, they just responded…wrong. I got a sense of damage and of growths, so I dispatched a second servitor golem to it along with another war golem, class three this time, figuring that as it was inside the facility, the risk would be minimal.

Searching through the menu, I couldn't get a good description of what the hell the substrate was, but the impression I was left with was that it kept the naturally occurring manastones from becoming polluted or damaged, resulting in a higher grade of stone.

Moving onto the bio-mana converters, I found that of the three that were damaged only one still existed enough that the servitors would be able to repair it. The others were utterly buggered.

I swiped through screens, reading reports from people long dead, references to expanding the mine, and uses for the mining golem to be put to, including plans for the expansion. But the most interesting thing by far was the Genesis Chamber.

It was marked "Manastone Facility 2 Genesis Chamber," and I immediately renamed it to "Mine Genesis Chamber" for ease before running through its data. It had four designs stored, that was it, but hell to the yes.

First of all, there was a mana collector, one of the actual towers, so I set ten of those to be produced, since it was fully stocked with the requisite materials. Secondly was bio-mana converters. Yes, please. I picked four of those, figuring six in total would be enough to clear the backlog of shit, or at least I hoped so.

Third was a small, oblong drone, or at least that was what I renamed it, seeing some great long bureaucratic name and promptly wiping it. It was designed to search and map out underground caverns. I ordered four, figuring that it was better to get the maps checked and make sure there wasn't anything else living down here, especially as whatever that cocksucker Karl was hadn't shown up on the map for the city above, or at least I didn't think he had.

Lastly, there were plans for golem cores. Honest to Gods golem cores. I had enough in the hopper to make six of those at the end, and that would empty the facility, but that was fine. I'd arrange for more materials to be sent down. I spun the selection to the mining golem and ordered it out, heading deep under the city to retrieve as many resources as were needed. Then, I turned to the bit I was both worried and hopeful for…

The manastones.

The stores sat at ninety-three percent.

There were a *lot* of low-grade stones, according to the system, because the purifiers hadn't been working, and there wasn't an option to replace them, either, but the sheer quantity made up for that. There were literally thousands. The golems were involved in steadily grinding down the excess that couldn't be stored, meaning that there were literal tons of powdered crystal in the corners of the room as well.

Looking the details over, I smiled, knowing that we now had the potential to grow the Tower like never before.

I found the controls for the main doors, finding that whatever Karl had been, it'd brought us to the side doors instead. I opened the correct doors with a single tap, locating the golems outside and ordering them on to their next jobs before sitting back and sighing as I closed the screens down. I'd managed to link them into the city systems, which meant they could be controlled from the keep instead of down here.

"Okay, one last job, then we can all go back to the surface." I smiled at the relieved sighs that greeted my comment.

"Okay then, you bastard, what is it?" Thomas asked with a groan.

"Well, I don't know about you, but I think we need to find that little bastard." Growls rose around the room. "But, as Bane is on the job, and we all trust him, how about we get washed down and jump in the pool instead?"

There was a rush for the door that made me laugh tiredly, before Lydia's voice rang out, stopping everyone in their tracks.

"Hold it! First of all, there be about twenty people 'ere, an' tha' pool will hold six, maybe eight, an' only if we all get *VERY* friendly. Secondly..."

"I'm fine with that!" called an elite guard from Thomas's team.

Thomas closed his eyes slowly, putting his head in his hand, as Grizz growled and pushed people out of the way. The nearby legionnaires, both on my squad and Thomas', turned in to close around the loudmouth.

There was the sound of a low, violent discussion, centering around the fact that Lydia was an Optio in the Legion, not to mention the only living Valkyrie, and respect being due...barely audible over the sounds of fists striking flesh and armor, and Lydia resumed speaking.

"Secondly, Ah see no reason ta be naked around most of yer fuckers, not when tha actual pools at tha keep are big enough fer everyone te relax. We get a rinse off here, those like Giint who fell in, get a go in tha pool. Tha rest of us wait, unless yer think that bathing in tha funk that'll be coming off 'im floats your boat?" she asked, gesturing to Giiint.

Everyone looked at him, seeing the literal encrusted shit that was smeared across his face and covering every inch of flesh. As one, they all shivered.

"Right," I said slowly. "Good points there, Lydia. Looks like the pool is off-limits. Let's go find Bane."

There was a general rumble of agreement, until I took in the state of Nigret, who was on the verge of a breakdown. The elite guardsman who'd basically just had his teeth kicked in by his teammates wasn't faring well, either.

"Thomas, you want to secure the area here or head back?" I asked, nodding to the pair. "I don't think there's any need for us all to go."

He looked at the pair, then nodded. "Okay, people, let's wrap it up. No need for two teams down here, not with the golems, so we're heading back to the barracks!" Thomas called. His squad turned and headed for the exit happily. Nigret shot me a thankful glance on the way out that made me smile.

"Don't think you fooled me with that, you bastard." Thomas whispered to me. "We both know you're hitting the pool as soon as we're gone."

"I resent the implication I'm a sneaky bastard like that!" I said, pretending to be shocked.

"You don't say that's not what you're going to do though, I notice."

"Oh, fuck no, I'm totally doing it. I just mean I resent that you spotted it. Fuck you, bro," I said, winking at him.

"I'm gonna go back to the keep and shit in your shoes *so* hard."

"Don't make me murder you, bro," I warned him.

"Bring it to the ring!" he called back, grinning and waving a finger at me as he joined his team, walking out of the door.

"Fucker," I grunted.

Jian, who'd been close when I was talking to Thomas, sidled in. "So, boss, we...uh...going looking for Bane?" "Fuck no. Let them get outta sight, then it's fountain and pool," I said. "Lydia, how many of us can fit in the pool?" I asked, remembering what she said.

"Plenty o' space," she said, then winked at me.

"I love you!" Sehran yelled, grabbing Lydia and hugging her exuberantly. "You're just so sneaky!" Her hoarse whisper carried across the room before she hugged her again, then ran for the pool.

"Shower first!" I shouted after her.

Oracle took off, flying after her. "I'll sort the ladies. We don't need you all watching!" "Oh yeah, leave me with the sausage-fest," I muttered, gesturing to the guys. "Come on, then." I summoned two fountains: one for the rest of us and one for Giint.

Being the evil bastard that I am, I summoned it under him. He grunted, his eyes opening wide as freezing-cold fresh water blasted his nether regions.

While Giint screamed, we all took turns, getting absolutely as much of the filth off as possible, packing our armor and gear away to be cleaned later, stripping down and gritting our teeth as we went, scrubbing and sodding scrubbing.

Fifteen minutes later, I led the way to the pool, finding the ladies already inside and Bob standing watch by the door to the building, his bones gleaming and freshly scrubbed.

The pool was clean and surprisingly warm, literally bubbling constantly, like a jacuzzi. We all hurried along as we saw the girls relaxing in it, diving in with no sense of modesty, just damn desperate to be clean again.

Despite the determination to make sure we were all clean, and the girls having felt the same way, after ten minutes, we all clambered out, the growing scum line that floated across the surface being enough to end any enjoyment for us all.

We dressed quickly, sitting around and waiting, beginning to actually worry. Finally, after nearly another hour of waiting, Bane turned up dragging a spindly little creature that was all arms and legs, with a tiny body, a narrow, flexible neck, and massive eyes, a small mouth, nose, and ears, and two long twin leathery sails that ran down its back, battered and emaciated as it was.

"What the hell is that?" I asked when he dumped the unconscious body on the floor before me. He shrugged before growling out a question in response.

"You utter bastards got clean? You sent me off to crawl through the godsdamn city's toilet, and you…you…" He practically shook in disbelief, before Oracle and I summoned a fountain each for him, both acting at the same time.

"Sorry, mate," I said, unable to keep from grinning at how furious he was.

"No, you're not, you bastard," Bane snapped before dunking his head into the water and hissing at how cold it was.

I winced. I hadn't had the capacity to summon a fireball to heat the water at the same time as summoning two fountains earlier, but seeing how annoyed he was, I nearly did it. Then I remembered that he'd won the last round of our eternal fight by waking me with less than five minutes before I was due at training.

Yes, there was an argument to be made that he wasn't responsible for waking me up, but there was also an argument to be made for fuck everybody, so I dismissed the thoughts.

"So, seriously though, what is this thing?" I asked again, slowly looking it over.

"Changeling," Ronin said.

"Really?" I asked, sending him a curious look. "I mean, I've never seen one before."

He snorted. "You might think you haven't, but chances are, you have. They're slaves of the Drow, or they usually are, anyway. Nobody knows where they come from originally, but the Drow use them for a lot of things. Servants mostly, occasionally feasts as well, I hear. Basically, they're not very bright, but they're good at surviving."

"You think it works for the Drow?" I asked.

"Noooo…" It whispered, its voice flaky and weak, and we all paused to look at it.

"You don't work for the Drow?"

It shook itself, a full-body shudder. When it was done, the form was recognizably Karl, if a thinner, dirtier, and slightly less humanoid one.

"Well, fuck me," I muttered, looking him over again. "You've got some explaining to do, my son."

"Need to feed the young," it whispered. "Mate is dead, taken by the spiderkin."

"So, you thought you'd lead us into a trap and what? Nobody would come looking for us?" I asked, confused.

"Nobody ever does," it said, before trying to get free. Grizz punched it once, knocking it out, then had to check to make sure he'd not accidentally killed it.

"Give it to Lio and Flux? Or hell, the city will have torturers, have them find out what it knows," Ronin suggested. I grimaced, not liking the idea, until Bane pulled his head out of the fountain and shook it, spraying water and bits of shit everywhere.

"It attacked me when it realized I'd followed it to its nest. There was a fuck ton of random loot, a few spellbooks and magical artifacts…and these…" he said, gesturing to the bundle of rags he'd put down next to the barely conscious changeling.

I frowned as Bane shifted the cloth aside, exposing three tiny, emaciated figures that looked up in response to the light and started mewling.

"What the hell?" I asked.

"Baby changelings," Yen said, before shaking her head. "There were rumors of them living in the cities, but wow."

"What's so special about them being in the city?"

"The rumors were that the criminal gangs had some, in Himnel at least, they used them for special heists. I always thought it was bullshit, but if they're here, living in the sewers, maybe they're there, too?"

"Fuck's sake," I muttered. "Okay, we take them with us. We can decide what to do later. I don't like it, but it looks like the little bastard was actually just trying to protect its kids, so we need to take that into account."

Grizz stepped in, lifting the unconscious parent over his shoulder, while Yen took the bundle of little ones and carried it. Lydia and Sehran crowded in close to see as Oracle shifted to her tiny form and landed on Lydia's shoulder to see better.

It took less than half an hour to make it to the surface, but it took a little longer to get Tenandra to let us aboard. That was only after I promised faithfully that I'd make sure her decks were scrubbed again after we left, and I still had to give her five manastones as a sweetener.

Ten minutes after that, we were landing by the keep. Fifteen more, and I was sighing in relief, scrubbed clean and collapsing into the pool beneath the keep, the others joining me shortly after.

Flux took charge of the questioning, finding out that, yeah, it was more of a "feed my kids" thing, rather than an "attack the future emperor" one. I bade him make the most of the little bastards' skills, but keep him well away from me from now on.

He ended up leaving us happily, and we had a few hours of relaxation and a little food before Restun found us and chivvied us out of the pool with a mixture of dire threats and blatant enjoyment of how much he was going to hurt us.

Two hours later, I was crawling into bed, exhausted and bloody.

The following morning, the routine was back in place. Up early, exercise and train, then eat, then meetings. Get some jobs done, such as planning the earthworks with Romanus and Denny, who spent most of his time coming up with truly terrifying traps. Then back to training, food, and bed. It was halfway through the second day of this when it all came to a head.

The morning had started the same as always, a set of exercises to warm our bodies up, before Restun announced the run.

A few scattered moans rose, and he glared around, before barking the command to get started. We were off, jogging, then sprinting, racing around the inner wall of the killzone, while I thought about my points and wondered where to allocate them.

I'd thought about it time and time again, and as I passed one of the legionnaires, I spotted Denny up ahead, driving his squad with a mixture of laughs, curses, and good-natured grisly threats. I grinned and sped up, falling in beside him as the legionnaires and elite guards made room for me, the familiar sense of camaraderie in the face of pain in the form of PT making us all grin and joke sympathetically.

"Hey, Denny," I started.

"Jax, how's it going?" he asked, nodding to me, the Legion custom of no ranks in the training cadres allowing everyone to relax a lot.

"Not bad. Look, a while ago Grizz mentioned that there were some legionnaires you could speak to about your point allocation, maybe get some advice?" I asked, noting the way the others pulled away from us, giving us some privacy, as a bubble of legionnaires formed around us.

While the Legion were playing nice with the elites from the army and the guard who wanted a chance at the praetorian guard slots, or just to train at this level, they also didn't let any of them close enough to overhear a private conversation I was having.

"Ah," Denny smiled. "Yeah, it's a role most of the primuses take over when they claim the slot, but for you…I mean, I assume it *is* for you?" he asked, waiting for me to acknowledge before continuing. "Then honestly, I'd wait until the end of the session and speak to Praetorian Primus Restun. He's been watching you like a hawk, and if anyone can give you advice, it's that man."

"Crap," I muttered.

"I know, man. I'd not want him to be examining me at that level either, but…if I wanted the absolute best for my potential, he's the man I'd see. Well, him or Augustus, but given that there's a good reason that it's Restun and not Augustus that's the top dog? I know which one you should talk to."

"Yeah, so do I," I grumbled. "Bugger it, thanks, Denny." I got a smile from him as I fell back. I took a deep breath before mentally deciding fuck it and ducking out of the formation, heading straight to Restun. He ran a hundred meters away with the rest of the training cadre, watching us all.

Catching my desire to talk, he dropped back to a slower walk, waiting.

I fell in beside him and blew out a long breath, wondering where to start.

"You need something, Jax?" he prompted. I scrubbed my hands through my hair, feeling the loose curls that were starting to form and the beard that was getting out of control.

"Yeah, a barber," I muttered, closing my eyes and cursing my idle tongue. "Sorry, Restun, that's not why I'm here, honestly." I shook my head and winced as I looked over at him. I was surprised to see a smile on his face, and he turned, gesturing me over to a small table with refreshments set up on one side.

"Come on, lad. I think we need to talk, don't we?" he asked, seemingly much more friendly than I'd ever seen before. I had a split second to wonder if a Drow infiltrator had got to him, then I snorted, banishing the thought.

Not only would a Drow never have gotten the better of *RESTUN,* for fuck's sake, but they would have shown on the system as soon as they entered the city.

I followed him and took a mug of water, before setting it back down and pulling out a flask of coffee and two cups from my bag. He frowned but took a cup and let me pour us both a coffee, sitting and waiting for me to speak.

I took a sip of the coffee and sighed. It was one of the first batches from the small village of Sarat, now wholly owned by Hannibal in his capacity as the Imperial tax collector and smuggler. He was getting money from it. I was getting, as the Empire, a serious amount of coin and coffee, and the nobles were all fighting to buy the stuff. Yet, in some way I couldn't quite make sense of, Hannibal and Mal were ripping me off in a massive way. I just knew it.

I sipped the coffee again and decided, as long as I got all of the coffee I wanted, I really didn't give a shit.

"Okay, look, Grizz told me a few weeks back about a Legion…method? Option? I don't know, he told me that some legionnaires study the allocation of points. They can give you advice on how to allocate yours, and where, depending on what you're doing and which direction you're going…is this making any sense?" I asked Restun.

He nodded, silently sipping his coffee.

"Okay, well, I need that advice, and I don't know who else I could ask, honestly. You see me fight and train. You know what I am, and where I'm useless, so please, Restun, help?" I asked, laying it all out before him. "I've got six-five points to allocate, as well as two meridian points to use. Do you…do you know about meridians?"

He frowned. "I have studied manuscripts that mention them, but never have I met anyone that could access them."

I sighed. "Well, I can. They're something to do with a Pearl. I was gifted it by my asshole of a father. It was a shitty experience, believe me, but I guess back on Earth, it was needed."

"Explain, please, from the beginning," Restun said.

"Okay…" I took a long breath and blew it out, thinking about the experience. "So, back on Earth, there's almost no magic. The mana levels there, so far from here, are tiny. It takes days to recover even a little mana. The Pearl apparently helps with that; it somehow sorta jumpstarts the whole internal system, lets you see your stats, and so on…until I had a Pearl, I never knew about my stats, and I couldn't allocate points. I started as a level one as soon as it joined with me."

"Hmm, I've heard of something similar," he muttered.

I stopped, watching him as he thought about it.

"An accident at birth left a boy scarred, internally I mean, unable to sense the mana around him. He never leveled, died in his early teens, weak as a kitten."

"You think it could be that it's a device to allow those of us that are broken to use the system?"

"Honestly, Jax, I don't know. The comments I read about the meridians were that they were a system that were used by a race of beings from elsewhere, another realm. Through some kind of magic, the Gods made it possible for Their chosen, the noble houses, to make use of these systems as well. It was supposed to make a significant enough difference that lower-leveled individuals had a chance against those who were many levels higher. Those that had access to both the levels and training, and the meridians…well…"

"Well, what?"

"Well they don't tend to stay here," he replied. "The higher-leveled individuals, usually level fifty and higher, who also have access to their meridians, tend to move to the eastern continents. I've been told, long ago, that there's a quest that you receive on your ascension, but what that might be, I don't know."

"Ascension?" I asked, confused. "What?"

"You are classed as a tier two being," Restun said. "A tier one is a beast or monster, one without the intelligence to better itself. A tier two can level themselves, consciously making decisions that make the most of their Abilities."

I nodded when he paused, showing that I was listening.

"A tier three existence is classed as an evolved existence. Upon reaching that point, they find that not only is it merely the next stage, but this is the start of a much larger journey. By using the meridians, you unlock them, gaining access to a new set of inherent talents and Abilities. Once you've unlocked all ten, you can start to cultivate. But what that is, and what that means, I don't know.

"All I do know is that everyone that I have ever known that reached those heights, level fifty and gaining access to their meridians, I mean, received a quest that draws them to the mother continent and the remains of the Empire.

"I've never known anyone to return from the east once they've gone, so I can tell you no more. I believe there is something in the quest that actively prevents this being discussed more than the vague hints we have been left with. It seems too well hidden to be mere happenstance."

"Well, that's just fucking peachy…You mean I'm supposed to unlock all the meridians?"

Restun frowned. "Jax, if you have access to the meridians, what the hell have you been doing if you've not been unlocking them?"

"Well, I've been using the essence cores…" I said, noting the way his eyes widened in shock. "You didn't know, did you?

"Okay, this is going to be fun, then." I sat up straighter and took a deep breath. "So, the meridians aren't just a single-use thing. You can unlock, say, a single point in a meridian every five levels, or I can anyway, not sure if that's the same for everyone. Each meridian has ten levels, and each time you unlock one, there's a bonus that comes with it.

"For example, one of the first I unlocked was for my eyes. Now and then, I see a glow around something that will be useful or important. When I harvested the first sporeling, I saw all the parts in it I could use in alchemy." I paused as Restun tugged out a notebook from a small bag and started writing.

"Uh…okay, so I can see things glow slightly," I repeated, trying to get my train of thought back on track. "But, because I kinda never really trained the skill or the Ability, it doesn't really trigger very often. If I concentrate on it, I can activate it, and it'll pick up things. I could see all the herbs I could use when we landed to change over to the cruisers on the way back from the Prax. The fields were full of them, but until I started looking, I had no clue."

"And the essence cores, explain that," Restun demanded. "This could be more important than you know, Jax."

"Okay, you can slot an essence core, or you can open a meridian slot. If I open a meridian, I get one bonus. If I instead slot an essence core to a location that's a meridian slot, then I get a totally different one, such as for my brain, using the air elemental core gained me a boost to my mana regen by fifty percent, which is huge. But, I got a five percent decrease in my self control. I've not noticed anything with that yet, possibly because it's only five percent, but…" I shrugged. "If I'd used a normal meridian point instead, unlocking, say, a new slot in my brain, I'd have gotten another five percent reduction in spell cost instead, bringing me up to fifteen percent."

"Go through the other options you get for unlocking your meridians, please," Restun ordered, making notes quickly before pausing and holding up one finger to stop me, then gesturing to Flux as he ran past. He diverted and jogged over, coming to a huffing halt a few feet away. I unthinkingly summoned a fountain for him to breathe in.

He nodded to Restun, then me, ducked his head in for a few quick breaths then straightened and indicated to Restun to go ahead.

"Flux, Jax is capable of unlocking his meridians and massively boosting his physical and mental traits. Please send a request to Prefect Romanus to join us, as well as Thomas and Mistress Nerin, then take over morning training. We will not be returning today."

Flux froze, clearly stunned, then nodded and tore off, calling for others to shift around.

Restun turned back to me. "Jax, this was clearly something you have never considered before, but to make sure that I'm not missing anything else, we're going to go through your meridians, your essence cores, and more. We're going to examine everything you take for granted, because this one detail could change the war massively, not to mention the realm. Now, explain your meridians, what you get for unlocking them, and why you have chosen each," he ordered, and seeing how serious he was, I did.

I pulled up the meridian options, reading them out to him one-by-one, while he made notes, before waving Thomas to sit once he reached us, and having him confirm the options he had, the essence cores he'd taken and why.

<u>PRIMARY</u>

Brain: 1/10 Spell Cost Reduction: -10% (Primary Bonus: 1 spell slot per point)
Head: Primary Node: Additional points invested will reduce mana cost by 5% (Note: Air Elemental Core results in increased mana regeneration by 50%, self-control decrease of 5%).

<u>SECONDARY</u>

Eyes: 1/10 Vision Improvement (Secondary Bonus: +10% chance to notice important visual details)
Eyes: Important details will glow to your vision. This will level with the relevant skill.

Ears: 0/10 Hearing Improvement
Ears: Important sounds will become clearer with concentration. High levels will aid in translation.

Mouth: 0/10 Vocal Improvement
Mouth: Your voice will become 10% more likely to have a desired effect on a target, soothing, seducing, persuading as required.

Nose: 0/10 Tracking and Detection Improvement
Nose: Scents will be stronger, aiding in tracking.

Heart: 1/10 Health Increase
Heart: You will gain an additional ten points of health for each point invested in your Constitution.

Lungs: 2/10 Stamina Increase
Lungs: You will gain an additional ten points of stamina for each point invested in your Endurance.

Stomach: 0/10 Sustenance Improvement
Stomach: You will gain the abilities to resist poisons by 5% and to gain sustenance from more sources.

Legs: 0/10 Speed Increase
Legs: You will gain a boost of 10% to your speed, as well as better stability over various terrain.
(Note: SporeMother Core results in an increase of 10% to your speed in darkness. Speed in daylight will be decreased by 20%).

Arms: 0/10 Strength Increase
Arms: You will receive a boost of 25% to your carrying capacity and your damage output with melee weapons.

Hands: 0/10 Dexterity Increase
Hands: You will develop crafting abilities at a 10% increased rate, along with a greater chance to succeed in crafting complicated items.

Thomas had the same details, save the few times he'd used other essence cores, giving him new Abilities. We went through the various Abilities that were granted to us from the essence cores we'd used as Nerin and Romanus joined us. Restun's request was all they needed to know that something serious was happening.

We sat in silence while Restun explained it, and we answered several questions for them, basically going over the same details I'd already covered for Restun, just phrased slightly differently.

"So…through using the essence cores, you can absorb these Abilities? Abilities you power through your own mana or flesh?" Romanus said slowly, sharing a look with Restun.

"Well, yeah? Nerin, you were there when I told the legionnaires about this, when we were in the Arena. Why didn't you say anything then?"

Restun and Romanus turned to her, stunned.

"I was aware of the meridians and their usages from older texts, but you never explained that this was what you wanted the cores for. You simply said that, due to your bloodline, you could make use of them. I intended to speak with you about it later, but it was more in line with idle curiosity, not finding out that you have a secret inside you that the Gods themselves gifted to Their chosen!" Nerin snapped, shaking her head.

"The Gods?" I asked.

"The ability to absorb the souls of fallen enemies was spoken about in hushed whispers as something the Gods granted to the most noble of bloodlines. I shouldn't be surprised that it's something else the nobles appropriated for themselves, as it sounds in this case."

"Hold that fucking thought," I said, shifting around and going down on one knee, reaching out to Jenae.

"Jenae, are you there? Have you got a few minutes?" I asked Her in the silence of my mind, pushing the words out to Her. A handful of seconds later, I felt Her agreement, and a sudden presence that made me take a deep breath. Rather than simply speaking to me, She appeared by my side.

"Jax, for my Champion, I will always make time. If I can, anyway," She said with a faint smile. She looked smart but dusty, as though She'd been in the middle of doing something when I called, towering over me and wearing a mixture of leather and cloth. ***"We have a lot to discuss, in fact, so your timing was good."***

She shifted around and sat, a long staff resting across Her knees as She smiled at the stunned faces before looking up at the sun and closing Her eyes, basking in its warmth.

"Well, thanks for coming!" I grinned as I sat back down. The others hastily scrambled to kneel, even as She waved them to stop and to just sit down.

"Honestly, it's fine, we needed to speak anyway. Please, sit, all of you; I've not much time. So, first of all, what do you need?" She asked, fixing me with a curious gaze.

"Truthfully, the Pearls. I was given one in my world, as was Thomas, but here nobody, bar the nobles, seem to get them. I need to know what they are, why, and how to get more, enough for the entire Legion, preferably," I said.

"I'm sure you do want that! Hmm, okay. Simply put, the Pearls were an invention of Svetu. They were made for the son of a noble house who was born with issues that the healers couldn't address. He was unable to sense mana or interact with it in a meaningful manner. His father petitioned Svetu, and he created the Pearl to allow him access to it, rebuilding his mana channels and essentially making artificial means for the child to live a normal life.

"In the process, the meridians that were until then restricted to the most careful of cultivators were made achievable as well, resulting in the child growing in power significantly each time he reached a new plateau," She said, staring into the past as She remembered.

"Svetu was so proud of his creations that he couldn't wait to show them off. He taught the father to make more. In those days, we were less involved in the realm than we are now, or would become. Svetu simply handed the knowledge over, receiving some materials that interested him, and he secluded himself away again for a few years.

"When Sint had a temple sacked by a group of bandits that were steadily reducing a continent to barbarism a few years later, the entire sorry tale was brought into the light. Essentially, the father had taught his son to make the Pearls, then his son gathered friends and started to explore. He and his friends were captured by a bandit chief, and he offered up the secrets in exchange for his life.

He was ransomed back for the materials required, then killed anyway. The bandits killed the entire branch of the family, set up in the mansion, and began production and training, eventually growing into a small army that terrorized the Empire, going so far as to require Amon himself to intervene with Shustic. Over a hundred thousand lives were lost, and the Emperor killed all those who knew the secret of the construction of the Pearls, restricting it to those he could watch over personally, namely the noble houses."

"Fuck," I said, shaking my head. "There's never a nice tale, is there? I mean, this guy's son was made whole, and that couldn't just be the end of the tale," I muttered.

"Life moves on and is never simple. The law of unintended consequences extends even to the Gods," Jenae said.

"Well, now we know that shit happened, even then…what are the chances of Svetu teaching us how to make the Pearls, do you think?" I asked.

"None at all. As I said, Sint's temple was sacked, his priests and priestesses assaulted. He intervened directly, killing several hundred before demanding that the Pearls be destroyed and Amon deal with the issue. Svetu felt he was made a fool of by the nobles, and is still angry over it. It was one of the reasons he turned from most of the other races and focused on the Gnomes as his chosen people. He won't teach you, but for the local nobles to be aware of it, someone here must know the secrets?"

"Good point, thank you," I said, smiling at Her. "Now, you said we needed to talk?"

"Yes, both to discuss your boons and to look to the future. You have a great many points adding up in the Constellation of Secrets now, and soon you'll be ready to spend them again, but for now, we need to discuss the problems that are coming." She shifted, clearly getting more comfortable.

"When Svetu informed you, and reminded us, of the city armories, I attempted to find the one here and in Himnel," she said. *"I tried and failed on both counts. Here appeared to be destroyed, as you confirmed, though I was unsure until then, while Himnel. It has been found, Jax,"* She said seriously.

"Found by who?" I asked.

"The arch-priest of Nimon, who I suspect was guided straight to it. As yet, he doesn't have the required authority to open or activate it, and those in the city who have been brought to it haven't either, their blood being too weak and their right too low to access it. But, if they can find someone with a strong enough bloodline, Nimon can grant them a divine mandate to overthrow you, calling them the rightful heir.

"While such a thing will not strip you of your own authority, it would be sufficient to permit Imperial golems to respond, and simple orders would then lock them into servitude to Nimon and the priesthood instead. In addition to this, there are three more events that you must be aware of."

"Fuck, hit me with it." I shook my head, pissed off.

"First, the golem production facility under Himnel has been located, and the arch-priest has had the golem servitor that was operating the facility destroyed. It cost many lives, and the Genesis Chamber is damaged, but it is now returned to a state of waiting. Should they manage to raise a pretender, then they can produce their own golems, although the mining golem that was undergoing repairs was used by the servitor to destroy the entrance to the tunnels that lead to the tower, so that at least is secure, even though the Golem was lost." She paused and smiled sadly at me.

"It brings me no joy to tell you these things, my Champion. I am sorry," She said gently. *"Secondly, there are creatures of darkness and pain holed up somewhere in the south of the city of Himnel, underground.*

"I can find out no more, as when Nimon sensed me searching, he shielded Himnel, much as we have here. I know not what they are, but I have my suspicions, and I believe you must terminate them with speed. Such large and clearly evil creatures inside the city limits will prevent you from claiming the city as your own once you have killed Barabarattas and taken the keep, regardless."

"So, we need to kill everything there, great. Okay, and what's the worst one? I know you Jenae, You're saving the worst for last here," I said, not caring if I was too familiar for my own good with the massive Goddess.

Hell, until She dropped all the bad news, I'd been having a struggle to not check out Her tits, and I suspected being caught trying to ogle a Goddess's cleavage would result in a swift thunder-bolting, no matter how subtle I was.

"Third and final is that four Wisps were captured from a site to the far north and taken to Himnel. I believe that they are even now being broken, their abilities to channel burned out, forcing them to bond with creatures they would otherwise despise."

I sat there in shock for long seconds, staring at Her as I felt Oracle freeze. I'd unthinkingly reached out to her, sharing the news. She stopped what she was doing mid-way through teaching several elite guards basic spells. She picked it up again, thankfully before the spells could be lost, but still.

"My love, we have to help them," she whispered into my mind.

"We need to know what and where," I said, agreeing immediately. "Tell us all you know, please."

"Jax, they are lost to you, even if you assaulted the city tomorrow, leading your army through the night. It would be too late now for them. I say this not to taunt you with those you cannot save, but to make it clear: they have been lost, but the enemy will never be satisfied with those alone." She shook Her head sadly and stroked the weapon resting in Her lap.

"A Wisp nursery was found, and Wisps—one of the most innocent creatures in the realm—were captured. They didn't capture them all, though. Dozens escaped, according to Ashante, and they are scattered across the area, hiding even now. She has reached out to nearby groves, who have dispatched grove guardians to find them and save the surviving Wisps.

"Ashante was reluctant to involve you in this, partially because of your own use of enslaved Wisps. Yes, she knows you have done all you can to free them, so far," She said, interrupting Herself as She saw my outraged face.

"Jax, the Grove Guardians will be searching for humans and other trespassers. They will attack you if they find you there, hence Her other reluctance to involve you. She only made me aware when you reached out to me just now. You will be at great risk should you involve yourself, so please, consider carefully before you take any actions." With that, She sighed and climbed to Her feet, reaching into a bag and pulling free seven scrolls and a small box, holding them out to me as I scrambled to my feet, the others joining me.

"These are your blueprints Jax. Seven of them were outstanding, all in place of altars you destroyed. You have both a greater and a lesser boon remaining, and I recommend you save that for when you really need it. These will aid you for now. Last of all, I have included the two items you earned. Seeing the use that you put your tattoos to, I had Svetu make you a special pot and needle set. I think they'll help you more than anything else." With that, She inclined Her head, accepting my thanks before turning and walking away in a shimmer of heat.

Silence reigned for several seconds before I started cursing.

"What's wrong?" Romanus asked.

"What's wrong?" I asked him in return. "Not only did we get fuck all that's helpful in the way of answers, now we know that we need to move up the timescales and that I can either risk us all for a group I've never met, who might attack me on sight, or I can sit back and let innocents die, knowing I could have helped them! Fuck!" I shouted, grabbing my head. "Fuck, fuck, Fuuuuuck!"

I turned away from them, staring out at the people staggering around the inside of the wall, drenched in sweat, and I watched them for a few seconds, hands still on my head.

Thomas stepped up and stood next to me, silently letting me know he was there for me.

"Fine," I said, turning back to the others. "Romanus, emergency meeting in the keep. You've got half an hour to get everyone we need in there. Make sure we have Carmen, Ame, Flux, and Cai, as well as the head of the army. Thomas, get the official leader of the guards, Hannibal, and Mal, as well as anyone else you think we need. The war just got closer. Restun, this conversation will have to be finished later; you know the basics now, at least."

With that, I turned, striding off towards the keep, anger filling me over how royally we'd just been fucked. Not only was Nimon getting access to the golems, but we'd gained a new group of people that desperately needed our help.

And just when things were starting to run smoothly.

CHAPTER FIFTY

I strode into the keep, grim-faced, as I jogged through the lower halls and up to the Command Center. Sitting in the main seat, I brought up the screens and glared at them. I pulled the map up, a huge number of gray and amber dots displaying as Undeclared and Not Actively Hostile in my mind. While the green of those sworn to me was steadily growing, it wasn't fast enough, or at least it didn't feel like it.

I toyed with the idea of using some of the immense stockpile of manastones to tie the entire city to me but shook that thought free. I'd started the process already, using the mana converters to swear in a few thousand at a time, but the side effects…I'd been reduced to a shivering wreck for hours afterwards. I needed to look into how Amon had done it, or better yet, tell someone else to. Until then, though, I'd stick to just doing it the old-fashioned way.

Oracle had mentioned how open I was to interference when I was casting a spell. Knowing the risks I'd run of becoming a mana-wight or whatever, then exploding from the sheer influx of mana?

I dismissed it as not feasible, unfortunately.

By the time the others had arrived, I was gnawing on my knuckle and staring at the map unseeing, plans whirling around my mind as I considered possibilities.

The mining golem that was even now following a seam of copper under the northern end of the city was finishing up the current session, then returning. I'd send him back out again, this time closer to the city, so it would be ready for the next phase.

I blinked when Romanus cleared his throat, and I sat up, dismissing the screen.

"Sorry," I muttered, glancing around and seeing the room was fairly full. Cai sat by the wall on the left, with Isabella next to him, getting a notepad and quill out, just as he had. Next to them sat Carmen—Lady Carmen, I supposed I should address her as now—and Mistress Nerin sitting with Ame and Riana. Beside the ladies sat Hannibal and his son, Mal, then Romanus, Denny, and Restun with Flux, Lucian, Oren, Lydia and Thomas, as well as Oracle sitting with me and Tenandra standing at attention to my left.

Sitting next to Thomas and the others were two men I vaguely recognized: Ashen Al'Torrin and Bravos Tiedeman, the heads of the Narkolt army and guard force, respectively. They'd both stepped up when the previous heads had crossed me or had fallen afoul of our investigations, exposed as being in the pockets of the various criminal or criminally noble enterprises that had been so prevalent in the city. Or, in the case of Eberhardt, had his fingers in so many pies he made an octopus look like an amateur.

"Thank you for coming," I said as I stood. "As some of you know, I spoke to Goddess Jenae a little earlier. Some information has come to light, and we have some decisions to make.

"First and foremost, time is no longer our ally. Nimon, or one of His priests, has discovered the golem production facility under Himnel. With their forces already trained, and the city running as they desire, they can afford to throw everything into golem production as soon as they find a suitable candidate they can raise up.

"While my position as Scion is clear, and they can't affect that, the divine mandate of Nimon would raise someone with the correct bloodline to a level that they could order the golems to obey them and defend the city or face our own golems. Add to that, one of our greatest advantages has always been Oracle and her brethren."

I paused, looking around at them, seeing the agreement on some faces and the confusion on that of the army and guard commanders.

"Oracle and her brothers and sisters are wisps." I clarified for them. "Bonded to me and my seat of power, the Great Tower, or in Tenandra's case, her ship. They grant us a lot of additional options, not least the ability to manipulate mana far better than any of us could manage unaided, and the capacity to forcibly wipe orders from golems."

Understanding crossed both men's faces, along with a troubling look of contempt and avarice across the army commander's face as he glanced at Oracle. I stared hard at him for several seconds.

He looked up at me and jerked, carefully wiping his face of any expression, and I mentally marked him to be watched.

"Moving on," I said slowly, still watching him. "Himnel discovered a small wisp nursery far to the north. Four were captured and are even now being forced to bond with some of Nimon and Himnel's chosen. The others fled into the wilds. These are innocent creatures, creatures that we as an Empire already failed once, and that will not fucking happen again," I declared.

"The biggest issues we have regarding the wisps are threefold: first of all, they have no reason to trust us," I said, counting off on my fingers to Demonstrate. "Secondly, Himnel will be, if they haven't already, sending more assholes to look for those who escaped. Third and finally, grove guardians have been summoned to defend and protect the wisps.

"These are massive and exceedingly deadly living wooden golems in service to the groves, sites of ancient power in the forest." I shook my head as I lowered my hand to the table. "We are neither welcome nor safe there."

"What about the war with Himnel? Surely this takes priority?" the army commander asked, confused.

"The war will be dealt with next. Sit back and wait," I snapped impatiently. "Essentially, the war with Himnel is leaping forward, as we can no longer afford to wait. For now, this has to be sorted first. I need a squad I can trust to go to the site to the north and deal with this."

I turned to my brother. "Thomas, that's you and your team, so I hope you've got any little issues sorted out. You'll be leaving tonight, stopping off at our allied grove first. Make the Arbuton of the grove aware that we are seeking not to recruit the wisps or capture them, but to protect them.

"I need you to take the altar we found and dedicate it to Ashante, as well. Ask him to send any guardians he wishes with you, and that you will help them to reach the wisps faster. If they don't send any with you, then go to the Tower, grab Woodite and one of his protectors, take them with you to the nursery. At least they should be able to keep you safe from the damn Guardians."

"What do I do once I've found the wisps, and how do I convince them that we're there to help?" Thomas asked.

"Take Tenandra with you. She'll be able to communicate with them from a distance and guide you. They're also more likely to trust you with her. As to what you do? That's up to you, bro. We need to stop Nimon and his lot getting them, that's the real deal here. Ideally, yeah, I'd love them to join us, but realistically, that's insanely unlikely. I'd be happy if you were to take them to a grove and leave them where they'll be safe, though."

"And if Himnel has sent a ship?" Thomas asked.

I turned to Ame and Riana. "Give me good news with the cannons, ladies."

"If there was news to give, we would give it, regardless of it being good or bad," Ame retorted, before pausing as Riana nudged her. She sighed. "We have some news, but as of yet…the device you recommended, the lashing together of the smaller cannons into a single much larger device, we have managed to do this, but it is only partially stable.

"It will not detonate, not like the older cannons do. But after several shots, the cannons often start to melt, and the runes needed to dissipate the heat are complicated. Essentially, we have two of these devices working, more or less, and each can fire perhaps three times, then they require several hours of cooling, or they will fail."

"How many are lashed together?" I asked.

Riana grinned at me. "Five rows of five."

"Twenty-five?" I asked, grinning. "You've made a broadside of twenty-five magical cannons, and you think that's a failure?"

"It IS a failure, as they cannot be relied upon fully," Ame said with a dismissive wave. "The weapons should be stable enough to reproduce and use a hundred times. That is the limit we have set ourselves for testing."

"When they fire, are they all at once or ripple-fire?" Thomas asked. "And what do they do?"

"They fire a larger, more powerful version of Magic Missile on the first five, then they alternate between Lightning and Fireballs, as we found that was more efficient to spread the heat. Lastly, they fire in sequence, one after another, or as a ripple to enable targeting. This is what you requested, is it not?" Ame asked.

"Ame, you're wonderful…you too, Riana!" I said, grinning. "Have them mounted onboard Tenandra and tied in as best you can to her systems. On a side note, the Imperial manastone mine is under our control fully now, and production is beginning to pick up as repairs are carried out.

"The city's sewage problem will become a strength as it's stripped of all resources, and there will be more mana collectors being deployed around the City and tied into it over the next few weeks. I'd hoped to get a mana-store up and running to store all the excess, but that's low on the list of issues right now.

"Oh, while I remember," I said, reaching into the pouch on my belt and pulling out the scrolls and items that Jenae had given me. "What do we have here?"

| Gladius Schematics | Further Description *Yes/No* |

Details:		This scroll includes weapon schematics for a rare gladius.	
Rarity:	**Magical:**	**Durability:**	**Charge:**
Rare	Yes	100/100	10/10

Crossbow Schematics		Further Description *Yes*/*No*	
Details:		This scroll includes weapon schematics for a rare crossbow design.	
Rarity:	**Magical:**	**Durability:**	**Charge:**
Rare	Yes	100/100	10/10

Dagger Schematics		Further Description *Yes*/*No*	
Details:		This scroll includes weapon schematics for a rare dagger.	
Rarity:	**Magical:**	**Durability:**	**Charge:**
Rare	Yes	100/100	10/10

Mace Schematics		Further Description *Yes*/*No*	
Details:		This scroll includes weapon schematics for a rare mace.	
Rarity:	**Magical:**	**Durability:**	**Charge:**
Rare	Yes	100/100	10/10

Pauldrons Schematics		Further Description *Yes*/*No*	
Details:		This scroll includes armor schematics for rare pauldrons.	
Rarity:	**Magical:**	**Durability:**	**Charge:**
Rare	Yes	100/100	10/10

Gauntlets Schematics		Further Description *Yes*/*No*	
Details:		This scroll includes armor schematics for rare gauntlets.	
Rarity:	**Magical:**	**Durability:**	**Charge:**
Rare	Yes	100/100	10/10

Helm Schematics		Further Description *Yes*/*No*	
Details:		This scroll includes armor schematics for a rare Helm.	
Rarity:	**Magical:**	**Durability:**	**Charge:**
Rare	Yes	100/100	10/10

Tattooist Needles		Further Description *Yes*/*No*	
Details:		This set of needles mimics a design used by the O'migochi used to enhance the variable patterning of their fins. As such, it grants an	

	immediate and lasting strength to all markings tattooed with this set, due to the O'migochi's hostile home environment. Tattoos created using these needles and the accompanying needle set will no longer need to be reworked, maintaining their color and clarity for so long as the flesh remains intact.

Rarity:	**Magical:**	**Durability:**	**Charge:**
Legendary	Yes	100/100	100/100

Tattooist Inkpot		**Further Description** *Yes*/*No*
Details:		This set of multicolored inkpots mimics a design used by the O'migochi used to enhance the variable patterning of their fins. As such, it grants an immediate and lasting strength to all markings tattooed with this set, due to the O'migochi's hostile home environment. Tattoos created using these inks and the accompanying needle set will no longer need to be reworked, maintaining their color and clarity for so long as the flesh remains intact.

Rarity:	**Magical:**	**Durability:**	**Charge:**
Legendary	Yes	100/100	100/100

"Coolio…wish I'd had these needles and ink when I was getting mine done. Mind you, 'flesh remains intact' is a whole different issue," I muttered, automatically glancing at my own inkwork before passing them along with the blueprints to Romanus. "Hand those out to the tattooists, armorers, and weaponsmiths, please. Let's get as much of our people's gear upgraded as possible. I assume the 'ten of ten' is how many times the scroll can be used to teach someone, not just that it can make ten weapons, right?"

"That is correct," Romanus said, looking over the details on the scroll for the gladius with a faraway look in his eyes. "These scrolls can be used up to ten times to teach someone to create a weapon of this caliber. However, they would need to be highly skilled already."

"We have exceptional weaponsmiths in the army," Ashen said quickly.

"Are they exceptional?" I asked. "What level?"

"Umm, well, we have a master weaponsmith and three expert. They would be able to do much with this."

I shrugged, not really holding out hope for anything higher.

"Jax," Romanus said slowly, examining some details on the scroll. "There are spaces here for runes to be added, as well as a selection of recommended…"

Ame snatched the scroll from him, cursing as she examined it minutely.

"It's rude to snatch," I said without thinking, ignoring Thomas as he facepalmed.

"How can you people use this to write!" Ame snarled, clearly trying to make out the markings with her worldsense. "A carved slab is much easier, and…"

"And it's single use," I finished for her before sighing. "Okay, Ame, is it offering you the chance to use the scroll and learn from it?" She nodded, and I waved at her. "Then use it, it costs us one use of the scroll, but…"

"My lord!" Ashen objected. "I understand you wish your advisors to know things, but I must protest! The loss of a trained weaponsmith's production, now, when we need it the most…!"

"First, Ame is our *runesmith,* and it includes weapon runes, so I think magical weapons would help more than standard. Second, you're welcome to object and to speak your mind. Third, I don't give a shit. Ame, use the scroll." I said, before going on. "Right, while Ame uses that. Riana, what's happening with the runic engraver?"

"We've used it to produce the ripple-fire cannons so far, and it's been a fantastic addition, massively speeding up production. But long-term, we need to produce the cannons themselves, and we can only do that so quickly," Riana said.

"Well, there are four crafter golems we found in the mine, those are now available to your team. I need you to make the most of them and get me enough of these cannon systems for each ship."

"Uh…" Mal said, sitting up straighter and swallowing. "I think that maybe I could do with some of those as well, just you know, three or four stacks?" He flashed a winning smile.

"You'll get one as soon as we get to your ship, Mal. You're damn fast, I know, but are you expecting to fight toe-to-toe with the cruisers?" I raised an eyebrow in challenge. "That's what they'll be doing."

He sat back, glaring at me.

"Thought not," I said, grinning. "You'll get your turn."

"What about fixed emplacements?" Hannibal suggested, looking up from the notes he was taking. "Or on the back of wagons? That's how the Chinese made the first cannons, wasn't it?"

"Not a clue," I said, shrugging. "I hated history."

"Boy, you have no idea how much you're missing out on, then. What about gatling guns?" Hannibal asked.

I shrugged again. "I'll be honest, I don't like the idea. We start an arms race, and it'll never end well."

"We're already in one, boy. You took their shitty cannons and made a bank of missile launchers. Either we innovate with them and stay on top, or they will. I'll look into it with Ame," Hannibal said.

I waved my permission. "Fine, fine. Okay, Ame, Riana, I need those two sets you have done on Tenandra this afternoon. As soon as they're in place, Thomas is leaving, understand?"

They nodded, Ame looking a bit dazed.

"Good. Moving on. While Thomas is sorting that out, we're going to be preparing as well. Mal, I've a mission for you."

He sat up straight and paid attention.

"I know you're a sneaky bastard, so I'm giving you two sites that Tamat gave to me to check out. They hold weapons and gear for the assassins and rogues we're going to need. You're to go get them all and bring them back. But, as I know you work best with an incentive, here it is: you bring me EVERYTHING you find of value there, and you get to pick either a set of weapons or a full suit of armor from the stuff we find. If it's schematics, though, you'll have to join the queue, okay?"

He smiled, opening his mouth.

"Good." I said, cutting him off in my rush to keep this moving. "Tenandra, show him on the map where those sites are, please."

She moved to the control center, a popup jumping into my vision that I approved quickly, allowing him access. Tenandra's voice was a low murmur as she directed Mal to examine the details she pulled up that only he could see.

"While Mal and Thomas are busy, the rest of us will be preparing. I'd hoped for more time, but we just don't have it. Oren, the ships are to be outfitted with as many of the cannons as we can make, and those who don't have any will instead have Restun's marine contingent or the magically trained guardsmen aboard. Spread them out, but I want them powerful enough that they terminally ruin anyone's day on any ship Himnel launches. Three days, that's all you have for that, as that's when the army leaves Narkolt," I ordered, before looking from Oren to Ashen, who straightened and nodded.

"Good man," I said. "The army is to lay siege to Himnel." I paused as Tenandra moved to the wall, having finished with Mal, and projected a map across it. I nodded my thanks to her as I stood and marched over to it. "The first stage will be to take out any of Himnel's airships or to contain them. Once they're trapped inside the city or destroyed, our airships will be cut down to a smaller force to maintain that, and the majority of the ships will return to Narkolt and start ferrying the army over to the Himnel side of the bay. Once there, Romanus…?"

He climbed to his feet and moved to the wall, taking over the orders to make clear the next stage of the plan.

"Himnel is a port city. That can be a massive strength, but with our numerical advantage in the airships, it is instead simply one less area we need to attack. The containment force of airships will ensure no ships get in or out through the bay and along the cliffs to the south of the city.

"As you all know, a little over five miles from the city walls to the south-east stands the Dark Citadel, home to the Dark Legion and Nimon's priesthood. The space between the citadel and the city provides us with an opportunity, so we won't be moving in between these two points.

"The Dark Legion will expect us to do so to cut them off from the citadel, but that would require far more men than we have. Instead, we will surround the city to the north and the west, bottling them in and preventing them from leaving." He flashed a reassuring smile at the expressions on Ashen and Bravos' faces.

"Don't be concerned, gentlemen. I'm not that bad at strategy. Yes, I am aware we don't have the forces to take a city this size using just the army, or even the army backed by the elite guards. As it will be, the Legion will be tunneling from below while your forces maintain a simple siege.

"While you hold in place, Denny, you are to begin construction of fortified camps. These are to start on the western bluffs beyond the citadel and extend eastwards. Once the Legion takes the Command Center in the city, we will flush out the Dark Legion from both sides.

"When that happens, the logical act for the dark scumbags will be to fall back to the citadel. Our combined forces are then to harry them as they go, kill as many as possible, but not to engage in pitched battle. They are superior warriors to the standard army and guard forces, and frankly, they will kill you. They will only be faced head on by higher numbers of Legion or elite forces, and that is an order, am I understood?"

Both Ashen and Bravos nodded quickly, clearly relieved, even as Denny grinned at the thought of the traps he'd be able to make.

"Once they fall back to the citadel," I said, taking up the narrative, "we can encircle it fully, closing it off from any support. That's when the siege really starts. They will have some supplies inside, no doubt, but there won't be enough for the thousands of troops they have for long.

"Add to that once they're contained, and the golem production facilities are ours again? We will grow in strength day by day as they decline. At some point, they will attempt to break out. That's when the war golems come in fully. They will attack them head-on, acting as magnets for any spells and abilities. Once they exhaust the Dark Legion, we move in and mop up."

There was a long pause before Romanus spoke again.

"No battle plan survives contact with the enemy. We all know this; however, these are the broad strokes of the plan. Further details will be given when the time is right."

"Such is life," Ashen said, standing and saluting me, the others hastily rising as well. "I hear and obey, Imperial Scion, High Lord of Dravith, Master of Narkolt. Do I have permission to start preparations? There is much to do."

"Thank you, and yes," I said, nodding to him, as Bravos said much the same and left with him. Ame and Riana hurried from the room as well, deep in conversation about the best ways to mount the weapons for Thomas to use.

"I'd rather be with you for the fight," Thomas said to me quietly, as the group rearranged, becoming less formal.

"I'd rather have you there too, bro, but it is what it is…who else can I trust with that kinda temptation?" I said, jerking my head towards Oracle and Tenandra, who were in conversation on the other side of the desk. "After all, imagine three or four like Oracle?"

"I'd die," Thomas said. "If they're anything like Oracle, I would die a happy man, but I'd still die. Death by snu-snu."

"What a way to go," I agreed, grinning at him as we both remembered one of our favorite shows. "On a separate note, if you go to the Tower, then speak to Seneschal yourself. If not, then get Tenandra to relay the message as you pass. But I want the Tower to stop reaching for Malthus's manawell. I know he promised us unfettered access, and it's a hell of a source of power, but…"

"But there's a rabbit away somewhere with him, and it's too good to be true?" Thomas replied.

I nodded. "Exactly. Tell them to retract any links they'd extended or whatever. It just makes no sense to risk it, now that we have the manastone mines."

"What do you wish me to do, Lord Jax?" Carmen said, moving over to stand nearby. "I'm afraid I don't know much about war."

"You'll be running the city in my absence. Rewn is due back soon, hell he was supposed to be here days ago, I forget when, and he'll be a handful. He's not to be allowed power in the city, not at this point. I'll evaluate him when he arrives, based on his behavior and the report of his handler, then I'll decide what his future will hold. Until I take control back in the city, or I name a new city lord, you are the Mistress of Narkolt," I declared, and she curtsied low.

Attention, Citizens of the Territory of Dravith!

High Lord Jax has declared a new Mistress of the City of Narkolt!

All Hail Carmen Al'Issiat, Mistress of Narkolt City, Council Leader and Member of the Imperial Senate!

I grinned at the shocked look on her face as I dismissed the prompt, the formal phrasing and gilding making it clear it was a continent-wide declaration.

For the first time, I didn't consider those who I'd put off their stroke by the announcement. Partially because I was wondering what Rewn was saying right now, but mainly because the way that Carmen had frozen in shock, halfway through a formal curtsy, was showing a tremendous amount of breast.

Thomas sighed regretfully as she straightened up, and I elbowed him, making him grunt.

"My Lord, High Lord, I mean," she stammered.

I held my hand up, shaking my head. "It's fine, call me Jax, remember? In private like this, when you're in your role supporting me as an advisor as well as the Mistress of the City, just call me Jax. In public, Lord Jax is fine," I reminded her, before smiling as others stepped in to congratulate her.

"What now?" Romanus asked, stepping to the side after he'd offered his congratulations.

"Now, we get those schematics to the weaponsmiths. We get our gear ready, then we gather the fleet. I'd much prefer the battleship be involved in this, after all, she's massive and could carry a fuck ton of cannons. Until she's finished, she's just too bulky and slow. She'd get taken down easily." I paused, then cursed.

"Flux!" I called and he hurried over to my side. "Go to Ame, remind her of the shield rune I gave her and the manastones we have spare to power it now. Ask her if her time would be better spent making more cannons or shields for the ships and connections for them to pull power from manastones."

"Of course," he said, then raced from the room.

"You think it's possible?" Romanus asked.

"In Amon's memories, I saw a Prax in battle once. Thousands of lightning bolts slammed into the shields of the battle-city, and it did nothing. We can't do that. I wish, but we're a long way from that, but a simple shield? One that would even take a few hits would literally save ships, and imagine the effect on the Himnel ship's commanders?"

"They're taken down by our ripple-fire cannons, and when they return fire, the shields stop it…oh hell, yes. They'd surrender in droves," Thomas mumbled, his gaze far away. "Imagine the horror if we could get an F-22."

"Steady," I said to Thomas, shaking my head. "Some dreams are not meant to be, man."

"I know, but seriously…there's got to be a way, bro; we have literal GODS on our side! I mean, can you imagine how quick this fight would be over with one of those? Everyone else could just take the day off. I'll take care of it…."

"Dude, seriously, you can't fly a paper plane, let alone an F-22, just, no," I said sadly, childhood dreams of kicking Topgun's ass raising their head again.

"Party pooper," Thomas mumbled.

"Wanker," I said, grinning at him.

He shrugged, then took a deep breath and spoke in a voice too low for even Carmen to hear, as close as she was. "Seriously, bro, be careful," he said. I nodded, telling him the same and hugging him. It felt a bit weird still, like the five years had been longer, but also when he hugged me back, it felt like no time at all.

We broke apart, and he left to go give his squad the good news and get loaded up.

"Carmen," I said, taking a deep breath and turning away from Thomas as he left. "I know you've kept an interest in alchemy up. What have you been doing with it since you took over as Head of the Council?"

"With alchemy?" she asked, surprised. "Well, nothing. I've had no time, I'm afraid."

"Then that needs to change. Yes, there's a fuck ton of things to do. But if I can make time for everything, so can you. Or have I picked the wrong person for the job?" I asked, seeing the way she straightened and fixed me with a steely gaze.

"No my lord, you have not!" she declared.

"Glad to hear it. Okay then, your second job is that I need you to get the city's alchemists together, and quickly, pay them what you need to, and get them making mana, health, and stamina potions by the hundreds.

"We'll need at least five of each for the magically trained, and five health and stamina for those who aren't. That's roughly four hundred mage-trained fighters, plus whatever the actual mages come in as, say eight hundred, just in case."

"That's…that's four *thousand* potions," she said quietly.

"Four thousand of each," I corrected. "Four thousand each of health, mana, and stamina, and that's just for the Legion, elites, and the mages. The army itself is around another eleven thousand…hell, we don't even have weapons for some of them yet. They're training with sticks to replace spears."

I mumbled to a halt, before shaking my head. "There's just so much to do."

"I…I don't think I'll be able to get that many made up."

I snorted, shaking my head. "I don't expect you will, but try. Try very hard, because any others you make after the army leaves will have to be transported out to them, and that's another draw on our resources."

"What about the containers?" she asked.

I swore. "Nobody is going to have over a hundred thousand spare potion bottles, are they? Damn it. Okay, factor in that we need people to keep and reuse their potion bottles. Get the potions made up in big batches, transport them on the backs of wagons if you have to, then have a quartermaster in charge of replenishment," I said, sighing. "Carmen, seriously, the feeling you have now, that you're out of your depth and you're just trying to decide if you should tell me that I made a mistake, after all, or if you should bluff your way through and just try your best? That's my fucking life these days. Just do your best, okay?"

"Of course, umm, and the first job?"

"What?" I asked, confused.

"You said that was my second job. What was the first?"

"Damn it," I said, rubbing the back of my head. "Gods, I need a haircut." I frowned as I tried to remember the job I'd been planning on giving her.

"Right, that's it," Isabella said, getting up and walking from the room.

I watched her go, frowning, then shrugged and turned back to Carmen. "Okay, anyway…ah crap, that was it! I need you to get any and all essence cores you can, gather them up, and bring them to the Imperial Treasury. Most importantly of all, there will be a noble somewhere who was involved in the production of *Pearls*. Rewn will know who, I assume. Find them and get them put to work. They're to make as many as possible, and they are to be under the direct authority of Romanus. Any and all Pearls are to be considered the property of the Imperial Legion, and that is priority one, okay?

"Also, I need you to work with Hannibal, get the supply lines sorted out for me. We're going to need everything from tents to arrows to…Arrows! Shit, right, I need you to work with Ame as well; there's an arrow producer in the Imperial armory…it makes magical arrows, like seriously powerful ones.

"I set all Imperial Facilities to permit Hannibal, Cai, Augustus, and Romanus to make any needed changes. I'll get you added to it as well, then I want you to get the damn machine making as many arrows as possible.

"There was a problem with the powdered manastone as an ingredient, but the manastone mine sorted that right out," I said, moving to the Command Center chair and adding Carmen onto the list of those with access to the mine and armory, then upped her access to include most of the city systems.

I frowned as Isabella strode back into the room with a box in one hand and a very confused-looking legionnaire following her with a bowl of steaming water.

We all paused as she got it set up on a table, with a comfy chair before it, then she pointed to me, stony-faced.

"You, oh great and mighty lord of the continent, sit!" she ordered, gesturing to the seat. I frowned, glancing at Cai, who was covering his eyes, before shrugging and moving over to do as she'd ordered.

"You've been complaining about your hair and beard for as long as I've known you, but you never stop still long enough for me to deal with it," she said, opening the box and setting out a half dozen small implements, including a gleaming strop-razor.

Romanus and Restun went on point instantly, hands resting on weapons. Even Lucian and Lydia moved closer before everyone realized what they were doing and who it was.

"Now, do you have a request, or just tidy it up?" she asked with a bright smile.

"Uh, short on top, tidy up the beard?" I asked. She nodded, and I leaned back at her urging, grunting as she brushed my hair out, tugging a brush through the snarls in my hair and beard, then telling me to close my eyes as she started washing it.

There was silence in the room for a few minutes, until Isabella started to hum to herself, and I couldn't help but smile.

Of all the things I'd done since coming to this crazy slice of reality, lying back in a chair in the center of the Command Center for a city, getting my hair cut and beard trimmed and styled while giving the orders for besieging another city just made my day.

"So," I mumbled, eyes closed and just loving the feeling of Isabella massaging the soap into my hair and beard. "Anything I forgot?"

"Aye laddie!" Oren spoke up. "Tha fleet!"

"What about it?"

"Yer took ma cannons away, then ye jus' all casual like drop in tha' yer got bigger, better cannons? Yer got hundreds o' legionnaires an' marines, an elite mages ready ta ride ma fleet ta war, all magic-like an shit?" he growled.

"Uh, yes?"

He was silent for a few seconds before finally speaking. "Umm, thank ye?" he mumbled, to a round of laughter.

"We have another point to raise," Bane added, making me squint one eye open to glance at him. With one of his four arms, he placed a bag of holding on the table. "We, that is Doris, the others, and I…well, we looted the Dark Church's repository of Demon-summoning and general magical crap."

He gestured to the bag. "There's about sixty books in there, some items, some cursed objects." Laughter broke out around the table as everyone realized that Bane had not only gutted most of the priests, he'd also robbed their most holy place blind on the way out.

"Bane, man, I think you need to sit down with Sehran and possibly Ame and Nerin. Hell, any of our people like Jian as well who have an interest in the Demon side of things. See what you can make of it all. Figure out a breakdown, when you get the chance, see what we can use and what's crap." I huffed out something between a laugh and a sigh, wishing I could see the priesthood's reactions to finding it was all gone.

"We have one last thing to deal with, Jax," Restun said calmly. "But perhaps this is best dealt with in private?"

"My points?"

"Your points," he agreed.

Chapter Fifty-One

checked over my notifications to get them out of the way so Restun and I could crack on as soon as everyone else left.

I'd been deliberately avoiding those I'd earned from training for several days now, wanting to see all the changes in one go, rather than being hit every time I managed to increase one stat. Now, beard and hair sorted, I relaxed the mental barrier, letting them through.

Congratulations!

**Through hard work and perseverance,
you have increased your stats by the following:**

**Agility +3
Dexterity +3
Endurance +3
Strength +5**

Continue to train and learn to increase this further.

"Our training has been for two reasons," Restun said, as we looked at my details, displayed by my will on the Command Center display.

"First, it was to improve your body and fighting capabilities, but secondly, it was so that I could assess and observe your natural reactions and capabilities. Frankly, Jax, you're a brawler at heart. As much as you fight with grace and skill using the naginata, or even blades, you revert to fists and your body at the first opportunity.

"We have three days before we attack, so I suggest we make the most of that time. While, in most situations, I would suggest that increasing your physical capabilities, Strength, Endurance, and so on would be a waste, affecting your current at the expense of your future, it is something at least to consider seriously. Beyond all else, you must survive the coming weeks, despite my personal dislike of using points in this way."

"Yeah, I've given some thought to going all in with the points," I admitted. "You know, investing all of them into my Constitution to hit a hundred or something."

"First of all, Jax, while the circumstances mean we must consider that, it would normally be a waste. We do still need to consider your future. Secondly, achieving the century, as it's called when you hit a hundred in a single stat, is a plateau point. When you reach that level, changes are made in your body at a base level, and you become more than mortal. Several of the Legion have achieved it. I, for example, did this in Endurance, and you may have seen the difference this had made to my own exertions."

"You never seem more than slightly winded," I whispered, looking at him. "Even when we're all on our knees, exhausted and throwing up, it's like you've been for a casual jog."

"Exactly. I know Lucian…" The thought of Lucian gave him a moment's pause, but he pushed through with a breath and continued. "…I know that Lucian, being alone for so long, living on the fringes of the civilized lands, has reached the century in several areas, including Agility, Dexterity, and Wisdom."

"Wow, seriously? Fuck, he must be scary to fight," I mused. "Maybe I should take him along for the assault."

"You should definitely include Lucian in any and all assaults like this. While he and I had our differences, and things are still…strained between us, he is a warrior beyond compare. He has spent literally hundreds of years fighting in the dark places of the land. His victories are too numerous to mention," Restun said, clearly still uncomfortable.

"Okay, I will. So, you think that investing everything into one area is the way to go?"

He shook his head quickly. "No, I agree that reaching one hundred in a stat would help you in the fight to come. But, when you reach that point, you must use points to climb higher thereafter. No longer will exercise, for example, increase your strength. You need to carefully consider where and how you wish to grow, as soon it will be a case of only through point allocation will you grow. I can advise you, but that's all, this is a decision that will affect the rest of your life, and you must make it alone."

"Yeah, but it's not that big a decision, right?" I asked. He stared at me. "I mean, I know it's sixty-five points, but it's not a waste, regardless."

"Investing those points now in, for example, Constitution, would see you jump from one thousand, one hundred and twenty health points to well over two thousand points. That is the standard linear growth. But when you achieve the century, your health regeneration will jump as well. It would be in the sixty points per ten-minute range for a normal person. I say this roughly because these calculations are not exact, sometimes they vary between people slightly, sometimes even between twins.

"It is not known exactly why, but that's not the point here. A normal person would regenerate their entire health pool in a little under three hours. Because of the century effect, you could gain one or even several other effects. Lucian developed a massively increased recovery rate. For him, it's closer to a single hour. Another legionnaire I know of became immune to any and all poisons. I've found evidence in the records of people who stopped needing to sleep or eat…everyone is different. These points will boost you massively, but they will stop your attribute growing naturally. You must carefully consider your choices, Jax."

"Okay, so far you've told me a lot of 'maybe' and 'possibly'," I said, glaring at him. "I came to you for advice, man. All you've done is confused me to buggery. What should I do?"

"What do you want to do?" Restun asked.

"Dude," I said warningly. "You're starting to piss me off."

"Jax," Restun said. "Think. I am not responding as I am to annoy you, but to help you consider your position. What do you *want* out of this?"

"I want to know what I need to do to win!" I snapped. "To beat those fuckers and to keep my people safe!"

"You fight constantly with fists and feet. You are a spellsword as your base class, yes?"

"Yeah?"

"Do you WANT to be a spellsword, to fight with weapons and magic?"

"Well, yeah. I love kicking ass and being able to use my spells."

"Then, this is a start." Restun sighed. "Jax, you need to decide what and where to direct your growth. If you wish to continue to be a spellsword, that is fine, but…"

"But?"

"But you are more than this. Consider your future! Emperor Amon rode the Silver Maiden of the North, Shustic into battle. As such, he built his attributes around long-range magic, or so it is believed. You will be Emperor one day; is this the time to consider the path you must take?"

I sat for a few minutes, then shrugged. "No, no it isn't," I said finally. "I need to live long enough to get there. The only way to do that is to slaughter every fucker who stands before me. I fight best when I use everything: magic, my fists, my fucking forehead, all of it, so I need to be more skilled, faster, and have more range magically, so I don't keep running out of mana."

"Then I can advise you at last, Jax," Restun said, clearly relieved. "When legionnaires come to me, it is simple. They are stealth-based, melee, or more. I have the records to search to advise them on their best path, but for you? No. You needed to decide what you wanted first, and where you wanted to aim…so…" Restun tapped my stats on the screen and spoke quickly.

"You have two meridian points to assign, first of all. I recommend assigning these to unlock nodes. This should give you both a significant increase in the corresponding attribute and help you for the future. Bring up the nodes that you haven't invested in yet, please." I did, and he read through them quickly.

"Hmm, Ears, Mouth, Nose, Stomach, Legs, Arms, and Hands. Considering the fight to come, I'd recommend Arms and Legs. These will give you a ten percent boost in speed overall and a twenty-five percent boost in damage in melee attacks as well," Restun said.

I nodded and assigned them both. We'd managed to get a fuck ton of essence cores, and some were already in the Treasury. Others were being collected now, and there were literally going to be hundreds that could make a massive difference, such as the nephilim core that Nerin had, but…I trusted Restun, and yeah, speed and damage output were massive assists in fighting.

I didn't wait, knowing what Restun was watching me for, and I activated the changes, gritting my teeth and stiffening as pain ripped through me, my arms and legs feeling like they were on fire as billions of tiny changes were made.

At one point, I felt Restun forcing my tightly clenched jaws apart and wedging something in, but I was in too much pain to tell what. By the time it was over, and I recovered enough to see what was happening, I was laid on the floor, on my side in the recovery position. Restun had apparently wedged a knotted piece of leather into my mouth, I discovered as I spat it out, and had been keeping me still.

"Are you okay?" he asked, watching me as I regained control.

"Yeah…sucks to do two at once," I mumbled.

He sighed, clearly relieved. "Just wait until the legionnaires get to unlock theirs. Bet Grizz tries for all six," he said with a small smile.

"Probably," I groaned, straightening out and struggling back up to sit in the chair, sending Oracle a condensed explanation of what had happened and that I'd be putting more points in soon. "You know that mad bastard."

"Okay, now that you've gained those, let's see your stats again…"

Name: Jax Amon				
Titles: Strategos: 5% boost to damage resistance, Fortifier: 5% boost to defensive structure integrity, Champion of Jenae: One search for hidden knowledge every 24 hours, Kobold Ravager: +25% damage to Kobolds, Valspar's Bane: +25% damage to Valspar				
Class: Spellsword > Justicar > Champion of Jenae > Imperial Magekiller > Imperial Justicar > Imperial Overlord		**Renown:** Imperial Scion, Lord of Dravith		
Level: 35		**Progress:** 946,586/2,135,000		
Patron: Jenae, Goddess of Fire and Exploration		**Points to Distribute:** 65 **Meridian Points to Invest:** 0		

Stat	Current points	Description	Effect	Progress to next level
Agility	44	Governs dodge and movement.	+374% maximum movement speed and reflexes, (+10% movement in darkness, -20% movement in daylight, +10% overall)	68/100
Charisma	31 (26)	Governs likely success to charm, seduce, or threaten	+210% success in interactions with other beings	98/100
Constitution	56 (51)	Governs health and health regeneration	1120 health, regen 69 points per 600 seconds, (each point invested now worth 20 health)	88/100
Dexterity	70 (65)	Governs ability with weapons and crafting success	+600% to weapon proficiency, +60% to the chances of crafting success	12/100
Endurance	53 (50)	Governs stamina and stamina regeneration	1590 stamina, regen 42 points per 30 seconds, (each point invested now worth 30 stamina)	12/100
Intelligence	59	Governs base mana and number of spells able to be learned	590 mana, spell capacity: 31 (29 + 2 from items)	17/100
Luck	45	Governs overall chance of bonuses	+35% chance of a favorable outcome	43/100
Perception	44 (34)	Governs ranged damage and chance to spot traps or hidden items	+340% ranged damage, +34% chance to spot traps or hidden items	54/100
Strength	54 (51)	Governs damage with melee weapons and carrying capacity	+44 damage with melee weapons, +440% maximum carrying capacity	28/100
Wisdom	45 (35)	Governs mana regeneration and memory	+525% mana recovery, 5.5 points per minute, 350% more likely to remember things, (+50% increased mana regeneration from essence core)	88/100

We worked through the details over and over, discussing the various effects of putting all the points in one or spreading them out. After all, I could actually invest five in every stat then another five in three more if I wanted. I had that many, but eventually we agreed on the best allocation through a process of elimination. First of all, I needed to survive the coming weeks. To do that, I needed to survive the fights. That, in turn, meant that Charisma was fuck all use for the short term.

Perception was great for spotting traps and for finding things, such as harvestable components, but I had Bane, Tang, and Giint for that, so Perception was out. Dexterity was all about crafting and holding onto your weapon, making sure that when you swung it, you hit what you aimed for. That was great, but it was already my highest stat so far, so I dismissed that as well.

Constitution made me pause. Extra health was awesome after all, but…you could have a million points in it, and if you were hit just right, you were probably still dead. I kept that on the back burner, thinking maybe a few points, but that was it.

Luck was important, seriously so, and I could hit my century if I invested it all in there. But it was something that you were never really sure was working. So, I dismissed it for now, promising myself I'd work on it properly later, and just maybe add a little now.

Strength was a contender. After all, I'd leap to an extra one hundred and nine on top of the standard damage if I did that, plus another twenty-five percent. So, with my naginata doing twenty-four points at a minimum, that was one hundred and sixty, plus another twenty-five percent, that was a flat two hundred points each hit.

I *knew* it wasn't linear damage; the context made it totally different. Stabbing someone in the foot versus the throat did massively different things, after all. But still, I considered it for a few seconds, but with Restun's advice, I dismissed it.

As he pointed out, even for a standard, front-line melee fighter, that much of a jump in Strength wasn't recommended, not if their other stats weren't in line with it. Or, in my case, if I wasn't using a weapon that was geared for that style, such as an insanely large axe.

Moving on, we were left with four stats: Agility, Endurance, Intelligence, and Wisdom.

Endurance would help me last longer in the fight, but I didn't really have any issues there. Yeah, I got out of breath, but at least half of this fight would be in stages, such as being aboard ship, so that was out.

Wisdom was important, no denying that. Mana regen was a massive part of any fight, but I dismissed it. A higher Intelligence would make a massively increased manapool, and I normally ended up hammering the potions trying to get more spells, as massive time seemed to pass between my need for it, so plenty of time for the manapool to refill between fights, I hoped.

It was down to Agility or Intelligence. I had enough to hit the century on Agility, but, despite the massive difference that would make, this fight wasn't going to be all about me. I wanted to put the points there, I'd be able to dodge like a Demon, after all, and bullet time was a serious possibility when I had that kind of Agility but I needed to think about the bigger picture.

This was going to be a battle with thousands on each side, and when a single extra spell could make all the difference?

I looked at Restun and said the words he'd been waiting to hear.

"Forty-one points to Intelligence, and the last six to Luck."

"Before you finalize your choice, you may have noticed that you didn't receive your class upgrade when you hit level thirty. That's because, until you assign those points, you've not 'reached' the level."

"Fuck," I muttered, blinking. "I totally missed that."

"Well, once you assign those points, you'll be offered the choice of your next class. This is where I can advise you better, as at level thirty you gain class Abilities. In the Legion, this is the point of adulthood, and is usually celebrated with close friends, parties, and…well, ladies who enjoy the benefits of gold."

"Well, first, Oracle would kill me. Secondly, we're at war. And third, we're throwing a big godsdamn party when this is all over, mate," I said, taking a deep breath. "Okay, I've put the points in place and warned Oracle." I sent her a quick update. "Let's get it over with." I accepted the changes and felt my brain explode.

The next few minutes were filled with excruciating agony as neural synapses were rebuilt over and over again, and when it was over, and I opened my eyes, the world was changed forever.

I sat there for a while, barely able to focus, as I tried to relearn how to interact with my body and the world around me. Details seemed to fill everything I looked at. As I examined Restun, I saw a thousand things I'd never noticed before, having just accepted him as he appeared.

Restun was tired, *dog tired*, I realized, despite his hitting the century. He was the heart of the Legion, but he was pushing himself past the point he should, relying on his insane Endurance to see him through the hundreds of jobs I kept giving him. I knew instantly that this wasn't physical exhaustion as much as mental and spiritual.

"Restun," I whispered, then coughed and sat up, blinking, and speaking before I could think better of it. "You need to take some time off."

"When the war is won, I intend to. Now Jax, you will have gained an Ability or had a change made, when you achieved your personal century. What was it?" he asked. I frowned, pulling up the notifications.

Congratulations!

**You have achieved your first century in your attributes,
and as such you have gained a new Ability!**

Hyper-Cognition: Hyper-Cognition allows you to speed up the processing power of your mind, subjectively slowing time. In moments of extreme stress, actions others take will appear to take longer. While you will be unable to physically move faster, the use of this ability can appear to improve reaction speed as the user gains more time to react consciously.

Cost: 5 mana per second active

"Shit, that could be useful," I mumbled, sitting up straighter and explaining the gain to him.

"Hmm, if you increase your Agility next, you may see a boost to your ability to move as well." He nodded to himself. "Right, do you have more notifications?"

I pulled up the remaining one, seeing, as he'd suggested, a Class Evolution decision was to be made.

Congratulations, Eternal!

You have reached level thirty-six, and have a Class Choice waiting.

<u>Class Evolution Recommendations</u>

Common:

Exploratory Alchemist: You've found that the secrets of life may very well lie at the bottom of a bottle, after all. Choosing this as your latest evolution will grant you a one-off bonus of ten points to Perception, a randomly chosen recipe, and a chance to automatically discover a recipe by drinking a sample of it in potion form.

Streetfighter: You've found your place in life, and it's between those guys and whoever else you can find! As a Streetfighter, you're known for your lack of patience, your love of fighting, and your ability to take a punch and keep on coming. Choose this, and your latest evolution will grant you a one-off bonus of ten points to Constitution and five points to Strength, along with the Ability, once per day, to fly into a Berserker Rage, doubling the damage you deal and halving the damage you take for 300 seconds.

Paladin: You're on first-name terms with a variety of Gods, as well as being a Champion for one. Perhaps it's time to take the plunge? Choosing this as your latest evolution will grant you a one-off bonus of ten points to Endurance and five points to Strength, along with a boon from your chosen God.

Rare:

Fleshweaver: The Fleshweaver has been injured and healed themselves, or been healed by others so frequently, that they've learned to get by with horrific injuries, simply by pulling together the most pressing wounds and keeping on going. Choosing this as your latest evolution will grant you a one-off bonus of fifteen points to Dexterity, along with the Ability Pain? What Pain? When all seems lost, your pain will suddenly vanish, and through the hidden art of Blood Magic, your injuries will reverse, condensing into a single cast spell that will transfer all of your injuries to your target, stealing their health in turn. This Ability may be used once per 144 hours.

Arcane Knight: The Arcane Knight class is based around heavily armed, heavily armored warriors with a high understanding of magic. Choosing this as your latest evolution will grant you a one-off bonus of five points to Endurance, five points to Strength, and five points to Wisdom, as well as the Ability Stand Fast. Once per 24 hours the Ability Stand Fast can be used, granting all allies within hearing range a boost to their Endurance of 10 points for one hour.

Sorcerer: Magic is in your blood, your soul, and you wield it as one born to it. With the aid of your bonded companion you can create a secondary manapool, no longer must your companion and you share a single pool. Choosing this as your latest evolution will grant you a one-off bonus of Fifteen points to Intelligence, creating a second manapool in your companion's body that will hold three hundred mana in addition to your own, along with gaining one extra choice in future evolutions of spells.

Unique:

Imperial Overlord II: You have claimed dominance of the continent, but as yet, your claim is still contested. Perhaps a boost is just what you need? Choosing this as your latest evolution will grant you three additional Titles of your choice to award to your followers.

Please see the Examples below:

Arch-Priest: You are currently the highest ranking member of the Pantheon of Flame. Laying claim to the position of Arch-Priest formally will create the ability to induct others into the upper Priesthood, granting them bonuses, depending on their deity of choice.

High Inquisitor: People lie, even the best of them. Perhaps it's time to bring the burning light of truth into the darkest places of the soul? Using heat, pain, and sheer brutality, you shall scour the land of their filth! Granting this Title will give access to the repeatable quest Renounce thy Sins.

Whereas some of the options were repeats of the last level, notably the second level of Imperial Overlord, which granted three titles, instead of two, others were awesome, but the sorcerer class, clearly intended for summoners and those with a bonded companion, was insanely perfect for me.

I barely paused long enough to check with Oracle, seeing as it would involve changes to her body after all, and she practically screamed down my brain with her demand that I take it and do it now.

I accepted it, telling Restun. While all of this had started with me wanting his advice, there was no way I was passing up both a further increase in my Intelligence of fifteen points, which would have been the equivalent of a hundred and fifty mana normally, and the chance for Oracle to have her own manapool again.

Restun, fortunately, agreed with my choice, viewing it as a much better idea to permit Oracle her own manapool, considering her capabilities. And at the end of the day, we could both still pull on the other's pool, should we need it.

I still felt a bit ridiculous, considering all we'd done was basically talk about how I liked to kick people's teeth in and play with magic at the end of the day, then I'd made my final decisions without his input.

The next three days seemed to pass in the blink of an eye, with me on my feet running back and forth in training both insanely early in the morning and late at night, and while I started to be able to hold my own in fights against either Lio or Flux, I got my ass handed to me whenever I faced them both, or Restun.

Restun had decided that, with my predilections for fighting being as they were, and the limited time we had for him to beat them out of me, he had two choices: train me to lead the battles, overcoming my instincts. This one meant I'd need to gain a much larger overall view of the war and probably make a lot of mistakes that got people killed.

Or, he could teach me more Asha'tuun.

I'd learned some of the basics already, having given Flux a primer manual for it. He'd structured the basic self-defense and fitness training that all citizens had the chance to do from that. This was a decision that had probably helped in the recruitment of the next generation of legionnaires as well, as even Restun had been forced to admit that the new applicants from the Great Tower were preternaturally gifted and determined.

But Restun didn't want to teach me the basics.

Restun took over my training with a zeal that scared the shit out of me. He began teaching me to fight again from scratch, and as time passed, with six hours each day dedicated to it, I learned with a speed that astonished me.

The base of the art was a form of meditation, similar to the Peace ability I'd gained. But, rather than sharing a feeling of general wellness and that all was right with the world, or increasing my mana regeneration, it was all about removing the sense of self in a fight. It taught that the thought of me, of injury, of friends and danger, all of it, the thought of anything at all, was a distraction from the pure killing intent that was required.

Asha'tuun was all about a mixture of über-violence and utter lack of a sense of self. When you expected nothing, you never had to get over being surprised. It was bloody stupid, or at least it seemed like that to me.

Then, after four hours of getting beaten constantly, I finally managed to stop the thoughts coming in response to the event. I simply responded and reacted, counter-attacking and taking Flux down like I'd seen every single move he was about to make in advance, and it all became so much more real.

From that point, the training took on a new urgency, as I fought to remove any and all barriers between me and that perfectly lethal response.

Then Rewn arrived.

He'd taken a hell of a lot longer to get here than I'd expected. He took time to "recuperate" at the Tower for several days after his flight. And, as it was his personal ship, the Captain had refused to set off until he was ready. By the time he arrived back here, both the trainer we'd sent on the flight and Centurion Hennen had washed their hands of him.

Rewn had apparently done everything from break down in tears constantly, claiming injuries with every single form of exercise, even demanding Hennen be put off the ship at each and every clearing they passed. The Captain of his ship was fortunately not *that* stupid, but it'd been a close thing.

The little bit of potential I'd seen in Rewn and had hoped to be able to spark to life was well and truly snuffed out by the time I was interrupted in the middle of a meeting with, of all people, Carmen and her new council. He stormed in, demanding they all leave, as he would be taking over command of his city and the war by my authority.

I'd been in the next room, coming back from a toilet break, when I'd heard his voice. I'd paused, listening, wanting to see what he would say when he thought I wasn't there, and had facepalmed when I heard him telling the Council that they would gather on his pleasure again, and that Carmen would be relearning her place.

I'd entered then, and the room had fallen silent, or most of it had.

Rewn had been standing with his back to me, and as I entered, he was making a comment about her earning his approval if she wanted to even stay in the city, and how she'd be far too busy serving her betters to have a place on his council, let alone usurping her master's place.

The others had seen my face and had abandoned everything and fled the room, while Carmen, who'd been getting steadily more and more stressed, finally seemed to relax, permitted herself a slight smile as she suggested Rewn turn around.

"Oh!" he said, seeing me there. "I've just been dealing with a little issue here...Lord...Jax? I've been studying, you see...remembering things I was taught! After all, it is MY city?" He trailed off, and I had to stifle the urge to stab the little shit.

"Lady Carmen," I paused, taking a deep breath. "Lady Carmen is the head of the city council and a senator in her own right. She stands on MY council, Rewn," I growled.

"Well, I know she's good at what she does, but I think you've let her body distract you, eh?" Rewn said, trying to make a joke of all of it.

"Her body...Oracle is my partner, you stupid fuck. I have no interest in Carmen–sorry Carmen–" I broke off to say to her, and she smiled. "...beyond her most impressive skill, *which is fucking organization, you useless shit*!"

"But...but..." he tried to interrupt. "She's just a wh..."

"Finish that sentence, and I'll gut you." I pulled the Dagger of Ripping from the sheath I'd started to wear on my hip. "Please, Rewn, I dare you," I said in a low, furious voice, gesturing to his stomach. He fell silent, and after a long glare, I shouted toward the legionnaires on guard. "Get Hennen in here!"

I stormed past Rewn to sit in the seat I'd had earlier, the one reserved for the city lord.

Rewn frowned, opening his mouth to speak, until I leveled him with the kind of hard look that could boil ostrich eggs.

"You stand right there!" I snapped at him, gesturing to a space in the middle of the floor with the tip of the dagger. "Carmen, I'm sorry about all of this." I tried to maintain an even temper and failed miserably. "Once this is dealt with, please, find the rest of the council and get back to work. For now, though, as you've had the pain, you might as well have the satisfaction, as well."

"Scion Jax!" Hennen boomed, coming to a halt a few feet away from Rewn and saluting with a loud crash of metal as he slammed his gauntleted fist to his cuirass.

"At ease, Centurion," I ordered, nodding to him. "I gave you a job with regard to this one. What happened?"

"I was ordered to try and make him into something that could lead a squad, Scion. I failed miserably. I apologize and stand ready for your judgment," Hennen said, standing straight.

"Tell me what happened."

"Former City Lord Rewn refused to participate in anything that required any form of effort on his side. He claimed injury at every point, declared sickness, and attempted to have the captain remove me from the ship on no less than six occasions, intending that I make my own way back from the deep forest. Rewn refused to listen or participate in any form of discussion on the history of Narkolt, her political, physical, or trade ties and needs, or anything beyond the most inane gossip.

"Three of his harem stowed away on the ship and proceeded to make sure I knew that the claims of injury were faked by enjoying themselves with him as loudly as they could. Then, he proceeded to lie to my face. On one occasion, I resorted to forcing him to participate in the mandated exercise and..."

"You hear that! He admits it! He laid hands on me!" Rewn cried.

"And I was then threatened with violence by the entire ship's crew, and the captain landed the ship, giving me the option of walking back or apologizing. I believed you would be more displeased if I slaughtered the crew and needed to have the ship recovered than if I permitted Rewn to carry on as he wished." He sighed and shook his head. "Lord, I have failed you, and I stand ready for your punishment."

There was silence for a long minute, broken only by Rewn, who started to say something about Hennen being taught his place when I finally gave up entirely.

"Fine. You win, Rewn," I said, standing and looking down at the useless fop.

"Good! I like winning, I...wait..." Rewn trailed off, looking at me in consternation as he saw the look of pity on Carmen's face.

"I'm sorry, Hennen," I said with regret. "I believed there was something here to be saved and that there was both the potential to make a real city lord of Rewn and to make a man of him. I was wrong on both counts, and that's my fault.

"You were right to make sure you could return to the war, rather than wasting weeks walking through the forests. You can rejoin the Legion with my thanks, and I'll see about a suitable reward when this is over. Please give my thanks to his other trainer and my apologies for wasting his time, as well. I'm afraid I can't remember who Romanus detailed for the outbound flight."

"Legionnaire Joachim, Lord Jax, was responsible for the flight outward and stood with me on the return. I'll pass it on happily. Thank you for your understanding, Scion," Hennen said, clearly relieved.

"Then, he has my thanks as well. I'll speak to Romanus about this and see you're both given an appropriate reward. For now, please return to whatever you were doing before I interrupted you." I gestured to the door, and he saluted and left.

"What? You're not going to punish him?" Rewn said.

"Shut the fuck up, you useless shit!" I whispered. "I gave you chance after chance. I wanted to believe you had the potential to rule here, Rewn, I really did.

I gave you *one last chance* to decide your future, despite your fucking actions. Well, now you've blown it!" I pulled up the proclamation I'd prepared as I considered the worst-case scenario for him, then I slammed mana into it.

Attention Citizens of the Territory of Dravith!

Jax, High Lord of Dravith, Scion of the Empire, has granted an Imperial Title to a noble of the City of Narkolt!

All Hail Rewn, Imperial Noble of Narkolt City!

"Oh...oh well, thank you, Lord, but I was expecting at least a duke's rank...and..."

Attention Citizens of the Territory of Dravith!

Jax, High Lord of Dravith, Scion of the Empire has declared former City Lord Rewn to be removed from any and all positions in the rite of succession in the Empire, his rank as Noble of the Empire is dependent on the Mistress of Narkolt's approval and will be reviewed in one year's time.

Noble Rewn is removed from all positions of authority beyond that of his personal house.

"There," I snapped. "I think that makes it fucking clear enough. Carmen, give Rewn a modest annual payment to keep him going and a minor palace or house or whatever in the city in recognition for him bending the knee. That's it. Now, someone get that useless gobshite out of here." I gestured to Rewn, and the two city guards standing at attention outside the room hurried in and grabbed Rewn by either elbow, dragging him out as he collapsed in floods of tears.

I turned to Carmen as the sounds of an apparent toddler's temper tantrum echoed in from the hall outside.

"Sorry about that, Carmen," I shook my head. "Some fuckers always have to take it too far."

"You're sorry?" she asked. "You've raised me to one of the highest authorities in the land, given me a seat on your senate, and slapped down the only man who could have caused me real problems, while making my position very clear in the city. No, Jax, thank you!" She had a massive grin on her face, and that was that.

Another surprising meeting was the one I had with Danxia, daughter of Reyna, and Tennak, daughter of Simoon, as well as Durg Guntersson. The trio had apparently hitched their way to the city on my airships, simply boarding them and staring at any who looked like they were going to question them. Once they'd arrived in the city, they'd gotten lost and spent the next few days trying to talk their way past the guards to get in to see me.

They'd finally been seen by Thomas on his way out of the city when they'd caused enough trouble to get that far up the "food chain" with the guard. He'd recognized them, getting them on my schedule for a few days hence.

When I finally sat down with them, Durg had been ordered to accept healing, his mother simply giving him no choice. And, like the good boy he was, he'd done it. Nerin had spent five hours working on him, and in the end, while his brain would never be normal in the terms society knew them, he was at least a bit more capable of surviving without being taken advantage of.

They'd offered to swear service to me, in exchange for the healing. I'd just shrugged, basically not interested. They'd made the points of "honor requires," and "the Gods demand," and "karma will get them," that kind of thing, and I'd essentially made them promise to consider what we told them about the valley being deadly. Then I'd found them a valley near the Great Tower and showed them how much better it was for them, not testicle-shrinking cold for a fucking start, and the abundant local foods, land to expand into, and so on.

They liked it, but were afraid of being booted out, so I offered to trade the new valley for the old one, in perpetuity, provided they follow the laws of the Empire.

They promised to speak to the clan about it, and the trust that we'd built up meant that Durg's mother, Danxia, daughter of Reyna, allowed Nerin to heal her. Half an hour after she was healed, she'd talked her companion around, and half an hour after that, they were demanding transport to their old home, fully intending on dragging the rest of the tribe out of there, if need be, as they experienced good health for the first time in seemingly forever.

I told Cai to sort out transport once the war was won and dismissed it from my mind.

Denny reported in with new designs for the fortifications, as that was entirely under his command.

I took one look and called him an evil bastard.

He'd taken the half-formed plans Romanus and I had come up with, and he'd made a thing of terrible, efficient beauty.

The fortifications were set out in diamonds, as that gave us a larger killing surface, he said, and they could be easily made up and broken down. Several golems and over a hundred craftsmen being detailed to work for him helped immensely.

Each diamond was made of flexible, thin layers of wood that were laid over each other in alternating directions. As soon as I saw them, I couldn't help but think of plywood, for both the pattern and the lightness, and it was surprisingly strong. Once it was constructed into long sheets, then it was topped with a thin layer of iron, as that was both readily available and cheap.

These sections were set atop a small rise, with a ditch being dug around it, the earth being used to construct the rise. Once this was made, a small team of ten to several hundred men moved inside, depending on the size, and they used small slits in the long shield to stab out.

Once they were set in place and reinforced, the diamonds funneled people into the gap between them. This slowed the enemy and allowed the soldiers inside to stab with impunity.

These small fortifications took up almost as much space and resources as a wall would have but ensured a highly defensible and nigh-unflankable position.

But worst of all were the traps.

Denny had been rubbing his hands with glee when he told me about them. They had buried spike traps between the diamonds, razor wire, and of course, that new favorite of his, the heliomage mana crystals.

They were manastones that had been fully drained, shattered into fractured lumps of crystal, then invested with the power of the sun. Since Denny's insane slaughtering of virtually the entirety of the Dark Legion advance, six more legionnaires had joined the ranks of the heliomages, and they were all utterly fucking nuts.

Where Jenae was overjoyed at the rebirth of her specialist priest class, the rest of us lived in a state of constant terror. Denny and his little team had been experimenting for several weeks now. The city had echoed with random explosions and sudden bright sunlight at all hours. They'd also been giving the various carpenters and blacksmiths of the city little projects as they went.

The result was the Heliogift.

It was a small container, tube-like, with a fully infused crystal at the bottom and a hundred metal balls atop and around it. The original creation had nails, but Thomas and I had seen it being tested and had taken one look then turned to each other and named it as we knew it.

"Claymore!" we declared and had recommended the metal balls instead.

There were two versions, one that was to be carefully buried in a line between the nearest gate of Himnel and the Dark Citadel at random intervals and another that fired in one direction only. It covered an arc of around ninety degrees, and that was to be buried as a weapon of last resort in the gap between the diamonds, behind the spike pit.

Once that went off, it'd hopefully give the defenders the chance to fall back if they were being overwhelmed.

All of these creations were to hopefully force massive casualties in the Dark Legion, but it all depended on the luck of the draw, as anything could happen between now and them being used. Regardless, seeing the utter love he lavished on his creations, I decided that if I ever had a location that absolutely, utterly must be defended and preferably with no concern for collateral damage? Denny would be the man I'd pick for the job.

With that done, and after hundreds of meetings, dealing with advice, requests, and trying not to scream "just fuck off!" when people stuck their head in and asked if I had a minute, finally, it was done, as the notification we'd been waiting for appeared, and I knew we could spare no more time for preparation.

Attention, Citizens of the Territory of Dravith!

**The City of Himnel has been claimed by a
worthy aspirant of ancient bloodlines!**

Raised with a divine mandate from the Great God of Death Nimon to cast down the False Scion Jax, Tirana Sertino has been elevated to the position of Chosen of Nimon, and Imperial High Lady of Himnel.

All Hail Lady Sertino of Dravith!

With that proclamation, the war entered the final phase. I stood, drawing in a deep breath, and let it escape with a sigh. It had begun, and it was over.

All the preparation, all the shitty arranging, thinking, playing the what-if games, attempting to make sure that everyone in the army had a minimum of one meal choice, making sure that the latrines were dug to a depth that was appropriate, as the Legion said this depth, and the army said that...*all* of it was over now.

At last, I could go and fucking kill someone, and Gods, it was a massive relief.

CHAPTER FIFTY-TWO

I stood back, leaning against the railing and enjoying the wind ruffling my shorter hair and neatly trimmed beard, and I stared out at the sky before us as the surrounding buildings fell away below us.

The heavy cruiser *Ragnarök* soared with over a dozen ships around us as we lifted higher, leaving the ground and the thousand petty worries of ruling behind me. The deck resembled a kicked anthill as both my own squad and the Marine Squad for the ship tried to get their things stowed and ready.

The *Ragnarök* was acting as lead ship for her group, a wing of five. The rest of the fleet split up into three more groups of five and a single support and heavy platform of ten that would form the anvil, with each wing acting as a hammer that would pound Himnel's fleet.

In addition to the ships that we'd brought to the city, Narkolt had her own fleet that was holding off the threat of Himnel, even if only barely, until we'd stolen the best of Himnel's ships that day in the dock.

The heavy cruisers *Ragnarök*, *Sigmar's Fist*, and *Atlantessa* each commanded a wing with three fast scouts and a heavy scout making up the rest of it. The fourth wing was made up entirely of fast attack scouts, with the anvil made up of cruisers, heavy scouts, and four of the Narkolt frigates which were longer and narrower than the cruisers, but had fewer engines, making them both slower and shittier in a fight.

We'd made sure to put twenty magic-capable marines and elite guards on each ship of the anvil, with the other twenty ships each having as many as could fit comfortably aboard, usually ranging between five and twenty-five, in the case of the scouts to the heavy cruisers.

We barely had enough people, and that was only because Oracle had been working at an insane rate, but, thanks to the round-the-clock efforts of Ame and Riana, as well as two golems, we also managed to get one ripple-fire cannon on each of the anvil ships, and fifty-two gladii made and run through the runic engraver.

The swords now had a simple fire enchantment that pulled its power from the manastone set into the hilt of the weapon. They were good for several hundred uses before they'd start to pull mana from the user.

Carmen had come through for us on the investigation into the Pearls, finding the noble who could make them and his requirements to make more. Sadly, he had none available, but was now working on a stockpile of resources I'd ordered be handed over to him and expected the first Pearl to be ready in four days.

She'd solved the problems with the arrow machine as well, resulting in a highly ecstatic Tang, who paid dearly for the first several dozen arrows by spending a night in her chambers.

I looked over at him where he sat on the railing, staring behind us at the keep as it grew smaller, and I couldn't help but grin at him.

"She got you good, eh?" I asked. He jumped, glaring at me.

"I don't know what you mean," he said, looking away.

"Bullshit." I snorted. "She dragged you into her room and fucked your brains out. Hell, half the palace compound heard it, so what's the problem?"

"There's no problem," he snapped, but, as I watched him, he slowly shifted around and looked back to the keep.

"Seriously?" I asked, grinning openly.

"Get fucked!" He walked away.

"That's 'Get fucked, Mr. Scion, sir' to you, motherfucker!" I called after his retreating back before settling back and sighing. I just hoped I'd not have to get involved there as well. Bugger it though, Tang was a big boy, and he could boink whoever he wanted.

I couldn't help but smile at the memory of Lydia sloping off with a particularly handsome elite guardsman after dinner last night as well. Then, my mood darkened at the memory of Rewn attempting to retake the city by sneaking into the keep to access the Command Center.

He was actually worse at sneaking than the Goblins had been, and they'd thought they were rendered invisible by being dunked bodily into a vat of black paint.

He'd literally dressed all in black and had tried to sneak in, but refused to take off his jewelry, so he'd been glittering and clattering as he went.

Grizz had been at the main gate at the time, playing cards in the guard room, of course, and had recognized Rewn. So, being Grizz, he pretended not to have seen him and ordered the guards to do the same, just to try and figure out what the hell was going on.

Apparently, it'd been the adult equivalent of staring in the wrong direction and saying things like "Oh, that's a nice sunset. Come on, everyone, look at the sunset! There's definitely nobody trying to sneak in behind us," much like people would with a toddler who was convinced he was a stealth genius. Grizz sent word to me and to the guards along the route he looked to be taking to make sure he got past.

Then he had to actually find Rewn, who'd gotten lost twice. He'd commented loudly about going to different places until Rewn started following him.

I'd left a meeting at the message from Grizz and had been stuck between laughing my arse off and utter relief that I'd not let Rewn get even a modicum of power.

He managed to get himself wedged in a tiny window trying to climb in and had started to cry in the end. I'd had him removed and taken home. At first, I'd taken it with a laugh, then he tried to stab a legionnaire in a fit of bad temper.

Admittedly, it was with a knife that was barely suitable for warm butter, and the legionnaire was armored, but it was a clear and serious attempt, so I had him moved to the dungeons instead and left him there, resolving to do something with him later.

I shook my head, amazed at the idiocy, and tried to recapture the sense of relief that we were on our way at last. It'd been a manic few days, but the sight of the thirty ships of the fleet rising into the air all at once was majestic as all hell. As we lifted, gathering above the city, in the distance, across the bay, Himnel responded, scrambling the first of their ships to face us.

I'd sat through discussions from the Narkolt equivalent of a spymaster, a small, unassuming elven man called Nathaniel. He'd apparently been waiting until the situation with Rewn was resolved before making himself known, and

Flux had been over the moon with the massively expanded capabilities he brought with him when he bent the knee.

I'd seen him around the palace several times before then and had assumed that he was another one of the servants, dismissing him as such.

It had taken him walking into a meeting between Flux, Lio, Carmen, Cai, and myself to admit who he was before we had any clue, the conversation being around the total lack of any apparent Narkolt spy network up to that point. He'd walked in, carrying a tray with drinks on it, as though he'd been summoned, and had put the tray down, bowing at the waist and telling us who he was.

Three hours later, he'd produced everything from rough schematics for the entire Himnel fleet and copies of the original plans for the battleship, to a recent report, only two days old, on the integration of the Dark Legion into the running of Himnel and its defenses.

The next few hours had been strained, as we figured out changes to our plans, mainly to make use of the new information after he'd sworn the Oath and promised faithful service.

Now, as the fleet turned to head out over the bay, giving Himnel time to gather, we waited to see just how accurate the information we held would be.

The Himnel fast-response teams were the first into the air, one heavy cruiser, two repurposed merchantmen, and a single fast scout, but over the next hour, as we moved slowly closer, giving them time to gather, another dozen smaller fast scout ships lifted behind that. Half an hour later, clearly hoping that they'd not have to take part, the flagship of the Himnel fleet, a massive ship called *Destroyer* lifted into the air behind another dozen merchantmen.

Where the scouts generally had one to three cannons, and the merchantmen had one usually, the heavy cruisers had eight, two on either side and four at the front.

The plan for Destroyer said it was one of three such vessels, one having been destroyed in a battle between Himnel and Narkolt a few weeks back and the other having set off recently to the north.

I watched it rising behind the merchantman, it clearly intended to use it as a shield, and I silently wished Tommy well. The damn thing looked like it'd be a bastard to fight.

It had three levels and a dozen cannons on either side, according to the plans we'd seen, not to mention over forty crew and up to two hundred soldiers aboard.

They marked a change from the usual designs for both cities where the cannons were mounted on the front. She only had three cannons on the front, but a dozen on either side, meaning that the fucker carried twenty-eight cannons, including the massive maw that glowed an ominous blue even now, low in the bow.

The largest cannon was clearly charging now, even at the distance of over a hundred miles, which was either fucking insane or really dangerous, and I couldn't decide which.

Until one of the merchantmen turned to the side and headed away from the fleet at speed.

I looked at the Captain of the *Ragnarök*, an Alkyon by the name of Feirin. He squinted slightly, but the distance was too much for even his eyes, and he reluctantly used a charge on his Ring of Farseeing, a little bonus that we'd found several dozen of in the treasury.

"They're running!" he declared. "Others are too, they…"

The bright flash that lit up the early morning made me cover my eyes, looking away after being so focused on it. A massive lightning bolt slammed into the rear of the merchantman that had tried to run.

The entire rear half of the ship detonated in a shower of flames and fragments of wood. A scream rose from Feirin as he covered his eyes. A few seconds later, a distant rumble of thunder reached us, even here.

The other ships that had been starting to shift apart suddenly pulled in closer to each other. I swore, shaking my head in amazement.

"They're killing their own side rather than let them flee?" I wondered.

"They are cowards," Feirin growled, shaking his head and rubbing at his streaming eyes. "Cowards that I shall enjoy killing."

I nodded to him, understanding the impulse completely, even as I hit him with a quick heal, just in case.

We spread out slowly, each wing gathering into a loose formation and moving out to the side of the anvil.

Our place was the left high slot, with the others being left low, right high, and low respectively. I couldn't help but grin at the way we were laid out, the three heavy cruisers each leading our groups, and one of the scouts leading the fourth group, and each with the shield rune charged and ready.

It'd do little in the fight. Hell, in the two tests we'd run, the shields had worked perfectly once and had failed totally the second time, but even the chance of the shields' success was worth it.

"Flag!" Feirin's mate Eryn called.

A green flag was held aloft, and Feirin increased speed to the halfway mark in response, sending the entire fleet surging ahead as we went.

"How long 'til we reach them?" I asked.

"Depends if they are cowards or not," the captain spat. "Sorry, my lord, but if they speed up or slow down, it is very different." He arched his back and flapped his wings as he watched them, clawed feet flexing, before going on, "If they head for us at the same speed? Four, maybe five hours. If they choose to run? Ten or twelve, or anything in between."

"Well, that's helpful," I muttered, before sighing and thanking him, moving off down the deck to the others. Lydia had everyone keeping busy as they worked in teams, the twenty magic-capable on our ship being split into four groups of five, with Oracle and me left to our own devices.

Lydia barked out orders, the four units responding one at a time, summoning their magic, then relaxing and letting it dissipate rather than fire it as the two sides closed.

"'Ow long?" she asked me quietly when I stopped next to her.

"At least a few hours, apparently, probably four, but could be anything. Just wait and see, I guess," I muttered. "Where do you want me?"

She gestured to the team made up of Grizz, Tang, Giint, Jian, and Sehran.

"We'll be a hell of a surprise," I said with a smile, thinking that, in addition to the maneuverable Magic Missile which the entire Legion had now, we also had Explosive Compression as well, and that alone would take a serious chunk out of the side of a ship, even one the size of *Destroyer*.

The ripple-fire cannons, though, that I was looking forward to. The next hour passed with us all practicing, before relaxing and watching the ships slowly closing on one another.

There were a few early attempts on firing at us, *Destroyer*'s cannons firing a barrage. But the giant Fireballs and Lightning Bolts dissipated before they got close, and in the end, the time that it took to cross most of the bay was both boring and terrifying.

By the time we closed in, most of our forces had made their peace with it. But still, here and there, there was the occasional shout or curse as the stress built.

At ten miles, the first real shot was fired, and a massive Fireball passed through the outer edge of the anvil, two ships adjusting course slightly to avoid it.

Five minutes later, and several miles closer, the enemy opened up in a full barrage from all their main guns. The heavy cruiser and two of the scout ships, three merchantmen and Destroyer all launched massive Fireballs or Lightning, all aimed at the center of the anvil. Again, they shifted, spreading out, but this time the shots were much closer to connecting, the ships moved back into position.

I wondered who'd break first.

Several minutes passed before the yellow flag was raised, and we all got ready, the final warning that we were within the maximum range now.

Both sides closed in silently, getting ready, the fear and stress in the air palpable as everyone waited in silence.

They fired the first shot, a Fireball that crossed the distance in a matter of seconds, starting off the actual battle as both sides let out a sigh of relief before screaming orders.

Each wing moved as ordered, staying with the lead ship and heading outward, arcing out around the lead, who tilted slightly to expose the side of the ship, even as they carried on twisting around to aim for the next rank.

In any other situation, this would have been stupid. The biggest and most powerful ships literally angled around to offer their largest area for attack, but as the first Fireball to target us hurtled in, the team hunched down, ready for it.

The Fireball impacted halfway down the deck, slamming into the shield and making it visible, before two more followed it, then five.

The ninth shot slammed into it as we closed the distance, the entire magically inclined force standing steady behind the crew, who held a series of sails up before us, obscuring us from the other ship's view.

The shield was close to failing. The manastone that powered it almost totally drained, but it'd had the desired effect. Not only had it protected us, but the effect on the other side, seeing their fire breaking up and our ships sailing on undamaged, was fantastic.

The enemy fire stuttered to a halt as they stared in clear confusion, less than a mile to go, and that was when the crew dropped the sails, exposing us.

The distance was extreme still, but now that we could see, with the enemy drawing closer by the second, we targeted the ship's engines, held…and…

"Wait for it!" Lydia called. "Wait…for…"

We held our spells, the glow of nearly a dozen spells surely visible from the deck now and the other ship turned sideways, moving to the right and heading for open air.

It was a fatal mistake, because as soon as they did that, they exposed the three engines on the same side, rather than the one on either we'd been able to see head-on, and we fired at Lydia's command.

"Team One, Front Engine…fire! Team Two, second Engine, Fire! Team three…" We let loose all at once, three sets of twenty-five Magic Missiles, all hurtling across the distance between us. The final group, Lydia's own, targeted the helmsman, and he vanished with a scream into a staggering explosion of blood and flesh.

The missiles that hit the engines had a far more deadly effect than that. At first, puffs of blue glowing smoke blew free along with ceramics and fragments of steel, then more and more, until the engines failed.

The first exploded, the ship jerking to one side as if struck by a giant's hammer, while the other two simply went dark and inert.

Then the real effect took hold, as the engines on the far side of the ship continued to fire, pushing upward, even as the lack of thrust on the closer side became clear.

The ship flipped over, going from a graceful shark of the skies to a spinning, diving mess with the aerodynamic potential of a brick.

People fell from it, screaming, as we shifted our target and started to cast again, even as more Magic Missiles lifted from the ships around us.

While the wings began to fold in around Himnel's ships, they closed on the anvil. Where they'd been ready to hammer us then pull away before, now they clearly believed their only chance was to pound their way through the middle and out the far side. They opened up again and again, the main forward cannons sending terrific blasts out that destroyed our now unshielded ships.

The first minutes of the battle were horrific as the smaller ships on both sides vanished into clouds of flame and fragments of metal and wood. Screaming sailors and soldiers plunged to their doom, then our numerical and magical superiority became clear. First in ones and twos, then threes and fours, the Himnel ships fell or surrendered.

The Imperial heavy cruisers closed in on *Destroyer*, taking the blasts from their cannons at close range. We cut across its deck, slowing it down and boxing it in, firing barrage after barrage of spells at the crew and cannons. Her engines were too heavily shielded for our smaller magic missiles, and, thanks to the wild jinking she was doing, only one Explosive Compression landed close enough to damage them.

That was, until the ripple-fire cannons opened up.

Three frigates and a heavy cruiser stayed strong, remaining in her path, and as all four cannons opened up, *Destroyer* fell silent.

Forty sets of Magic Missiles, each of five, and each far larger and heavier than those cast by mere mortal spellcasters leaped out, covering the distance. Those aided in targeting as the second row went active, hurling Fireballs and Lightning Bolts across the distance and scouring the upper decks clean of life.

Of the six engines on either side, as the anvil split, barely avoiding *Destroyer* crashing into it, two on the left and three on the right were left as it exited the far side of the formation. The sails that were there to assist were all either gone or ablaze. The main mast slowly tilted to one side before crashing over, taking a screaming survivor with it. I turned to the captain, shouting up as I pointed at the ship.

"Get us above her!" I roared, before turning to the others. "We're boarding that fucker!"

The two squads grinned as they grabbed weapons.

Feirin turned us around quickly, while Eryn sounded a horn over and over to get the other ship's attention. I gestured to Destroyer, and Oren waved that he understood as I circled my naginata in the air. He directed the pursuit and destruction of the three remaining ships on their side.

I shook my head as I looked down at the sea below. A few hardy survivors remained from the ships that had been smashed from the sky. They splashed and thrashed frantically before sinking by the weight of their armor or being taken by the creatures that called the sea their home.

I checked over the ships that remained, seeing we'd lost seven, three of which had Legion crews. It was wrong to think of them in terms of Legion and other, I knew that, but the Legion were *my* people. They'd been the first to declare for me, and knowing that thirty of them had lost their lives in a handful of minutes was terrible to behold.

We curved around the outside of the fleet, and I saluted the fallen, fist to heart as the sea below became a churning mass of tentacles and white water, before I turned to the team behind me.

"Explosive Compression," I ordered, stepping up to the edge of the railing and starting to cast. It was the spell that was dropped, when need be, out of those taught to everyone by Oracle, but it'd been taught to my squad, and they stepped up alongside and fired as quickly as they could, the spells hurtling down to slam into the massive sea monster in a scattered wave.

The spells detonated, the first phase doing minor damage before the second wave, the gravity weapon, crushed and pulverized flesh and bone, dragging it all inwards towards the center of each impact point, before finally exploding outward again, ripping the wounds even wider.

The thing that had been feasting on the survivors died in seconds, entire chunks of it somersaulting free before other creatures closed in and began to feed on it, in turn.

Destroyer was listing slightly, but clearly still under power, as it tried frantically to get away, and Feirin brought us in behind it, in its blind spot.

Tang and Giint stood with Yen and two of the other team, bows ready, aiming and waiting as we closed, while the others got ready.

I grabbed Grizz, and Lydia grabbed Bob. We kicked off, launching ourselves into the air and flying down, not even bothering to land as we released. Then, I swooped back around, reaching out for Bane. Sehran grinned as she launched herself into the air next.

As Lydia, Sehran, and I played air-taxi, Grizz and Bob charged across the deck, headed for the wheelhouse.

Whereas in most of the ships, the helmsman stood clear and exposed, either on a raised platform or on the deck, in this ship, they were protected, held inside a special room with walls coated with enchanted glass.

Grizz listened to the shouts coming from inside, the barked orders to barricade the door, and he grinned, picking up speed and using an Ability he'd gained long ago, as he swung his shield around in a single, heavily practiced motion.

"Shield Bash!" he roared. For a few precious seconds, the world blurred around him as the Ability consumed a third of his stamina to triple both his speed and his impact.

In this case, the simple wooden door exploded inward in a shower of splinters and the ship's boy who was rushing for the door was sent flying, knocking the nearest two soldiers over.

"Oops!" Grizz grunted, even as his new gladius flicked out. The fire rune caused it to sizzle as it sliced through the leather jerkin and into flesh before exiting the far side and taking the second soldier in the throat.

Even as Grizz danced, his blade flashing in and out with deadly grace, Bob was an unstoppable machine, laying about him with the massive thighbone of the ice drake. Bob's warhammer needed none of the finesse and grace required for swordsmanship; he simply needed inertia. He spun it and swung over and over, and not one of those he hit came back for a second round.

By the time Lydia, Sehran, and I had ferried the others over, the wheelhouse was ours, the helmsman utterly terrified as Grizz wiped his sword clean on the headless body of the former captain before asking the helmsman nicely to set a course for Narkolt.

I glanced inside and nodded, sending Yen to keep an eye on things with Grizz, while Bob joined us, and we began our systematic sweep of the ship.

The first living member of the crew we found was the ship's cook, hiding behind the ladder down to the first level. As soon as Bob jumped down, staring at him, eye-socket to eyeball, the poor guy pissed himself and passed out.

The next meeting was a short, black-bearded Dwarf who raced out of the room at the end of the hall, a dagger in each hand, saw Giint leveling his crossbow, and tried to turn around, skidding on the floor, before the *thunk* of the bolt slamming into his chest took him off his feet and backward into another doorway.

I was scouring the other end of the hallway, Jian and Sehran behind me, while Lydia flew circles around the ship, on the opposite side to *Ragnarök*, making sure there was no chance of a friendly fire incident.

I tried one door, finding the latch wouldn't move. I leaned back, slamming my boot into the door next to the latch once, twice, then on the third time, the latch snapped free, and the door swung in, making me stagger.

Three fully armored heavy infantry faced me, shields held in place. Three others leveled crossbows at my heart.

A terrible cold ripped through me as I guessed I'd made my final mistake. Then, I was staggering against the doorway, and in my place stood Jian.

The first bolt slammed into the upper right of his chest. The second buried itself deep in his stomach. The third scored a glancing blow off his hip.

I grabbed him, yanking him free of the doorway, as Sehran screamed in fury and fear.

My eyes were drawn to the sound in the same way it would have been hardwired into primitive ancestors to flee the roar of hunting beasts.

Sehran changed, her stunning face growing gaunt, her eyes bloodshot and her skin gray. She grew taller, more heavily muscled. Her skin developed a spotting that suggested scales rather than the soft, creamy flesh she normally portrayed. Her impressive chest seemed to deflate as her legs lengthened, and fangs and claws slid out.

She flashed forward into the room, even as I turned to Jian, examining the wounds, and I looked up into his widening eyes. He looked stunned, fearful, but also *relieved* for some reason, before he tried to take a breath and coughed blood up and over his lips.

"Oracle!" I screamed, grabbing the first of the bolts and grunting as I pulled. It clung tight to the inside of my friend. Brow furrowing, I glanced at the bolt that had left the shallow wound.

It was barbed. Five backward-jutting spines made it clear that, if I ripped it free, I'd take half his chest with it.

I paused, looking him over as my mind revved up to run at a thousand miles an hour, Hyper-Cognition flaring into place as time seemed to stand still for long seconds.

I saw the next breath he tried to take, the blood that glistened as he coughed and sprayed it out, a deep, glossy red that spiked my own fear for him. Determination flared inside me, and I turned him on his side, slipping him into the recovery position. I readied him for what I was about to do, and got a better grip.

I flipped the latches on his armor, both side clasps-first, then the ones under the upper folds on each shoulder. The armor released with a sound like a bell being gently rung, even as shrieks and screams echoed out from the room Sehran was in. Oracle flashed down the corridor, headed toward me.

I called out to Oracle, even as I grabbed the bolt, my words seeming to take forever to make sense.

"Bolt to the chest. I need to push it through. Be ready to heal him." I ordered her, my words short and clipped as I focused on the wound. Oracle nodded her agreement, and I moved.

I triggered Mana Overdrive, feeling terrific strain for the first time since I first used it, it further sped up my mind and strengthened my body, making it easy to ram the barbed bolt clear through Jian's chest to erupt clean from his back. The grating of bone and tearing feeling of flesh made me swallow hard. I grabbed the head with my other hand and ripped it free, making sure it was still intact as I threw it aside.

I did the same for the bolt in his stomach, ignoring his screams and the way he tried to stop me, pushing my hand backward for all of a second, the smell of stomach acid mixing with the cloying, coppery scent of blood. I tossed that one free as well, even as Oracle's spell started its work.

I didn't use the same spell. While she used Surgeon's Scalpel, I hit him with a Scour, stripping away any contaminants and guiding it as much as I could, before switching to Complex Healing and holding off the shock building in him. He coughed froth and blood up, before he whispered a single word to me.

"Sehran?"

"She's inside," I grunted, twisting him onto his side as he tried to roll backward. Then, I slapped him on the back, hard. He coughed, triggering the body's natural response, bringing up the more of the copious amount of blood filling his damaged lung.

Before he could speak again, I felt her, the room behind me having gone deathly silent. I glanced to the right, seeing Sehran hovering in the doorway before drawing back as she heard others coming.

I ordered them past us, sending them to the next floor and to search other rooms, even as I hit him again and again with my spell, while Oracle guided hers more carefully.

Long minutes passed, punctuated by the occasional sound of screams or battle from below, before Oracle spoke in the silence of my mind. Hyper-Cognition and Mana Overdrive both slipped free of my control, shutting down. I growled at the burgeoning migraine as I tugged a potion free and downed it.

"Go to Sehran," she said.

I pulled the bottle from my lips, dropping it back into storage as I pushed myself to my feet and staggered into the darkened room, then closed the door behind me.

It was dark inside, the magelight broken and the porthole in the wall covered in blood, giving the room an ominous light.

The armored bodies, or what was left of them, were seemingly shredded by an angry giant. Sections of flesh hung from the walls and slowly slid down, dragged by gravity, slipping from the ceiling even as the room filled with the slow drip, drip of blood.

The crossbowmen were the worst. Not one of them was even vaguely intact. If I hadn't known there were six men inside the room before, I'd not have guessed it now. The three heavies were dead, very dead, but more or less intact, throats torn out, faces shredded, and the bones exposed, but recognizably human.

The crossbowmen were reduced to gobbets of flesh, spread around the room, and stamped into the floor. As I stood there, wide-eyed, sobs carried from the far corner.

Moving deeper into the room, I looked around a stack of crates, finding a small space that was as far from the door and as far from the light as possible. The glint of eyes reflected the little light back at me as I looked inside.

"Sehran?" I asked, my voice coming out rough. I swallowed, coughed, then tried again. "Sehran, are you okay?"

There was a long minute of silence before she responded, pain and fear in her voice.

"Did he see?" she asked, and I nodded. I wanted to lie, but that was pointless.

"I think so. What happened?"

"Demon blood," she said, as though that explained everything.

"Ah," I said and waited. When she said nothing else, I said the first thing that came into my mind, as I wiped a section of an arm that still had a sleeve on it across the floor, clearing a patch to sit on. "Cheese sandwich."

"What?" she asked after a minute.

"I can say random shit like it's an explanation as well," I said. "How about you explain what Demon blood is and what that has to do with you losing your tits."

There were a few long seconds of silence before she finally whispered a response.

"You saw me change into *that*, and all you're concerned about is where my tits went?" she asked.

"Well, it's a question I've had to ask a few times," I admitted with a shrug. "Back home, there's an invention like a tiny corset, it's called a bra. I've seen it worn a few places here in seduction, but they don't seem to have made it big in the realm yet. Oracle wears one now and then and…anyway, that's not important. There's one type called Wonderous Bra, and women say it's because it makes their tits look fantastic. Pushes them up and together, makes a little look like a lot." I broke off remembering the damn times I'd pulled one off, and the internal cry of "false advertising."

"Right?" Sehran prompted me, sniffling a little.

"Well, that's what the women say. We men say it's because you take the fucker off, and you wonder where the bastards went. And believe me, things like that, in Thailand, can make things very confusing very fast." I said, reaching into my bag and pulling out a flask, then taking a deep swig before holding it out in her direction.

There was a little hesitation, then a clawed hand reached out and snagged the flask, vanishing back into the darkness with it. I was tempted to use my DarkVision, but I didn't, and I waited, taking the silence as a chance to hit myself with a healing spell and wash away the debuffs.

A few seconds later, the hand emerged again and passed the flask back before she shuffled away from me again.

"Good stuff, isn't it?" I asked, taking another nip on the flask and waiting again.

"Very," she said eventually. I sat there with her in companionable silence for another few minutes before she started to speak. "It was the SporeMother. We've all got various strains of Demon blood in us. We're Demons, it goes with the territory, but we've *evolved*. We've come a long way since the original Stalkers of the Night, but that massive influx of power…it awakened a bloodline, and I don't know what to do."

"Okay, what does the bloodline do?"

"It changes us. The stronger we get, the stronger the bloodline gets, and the more it calls to us. The change is something we can't control, or I can't, at least. I know the older ones can, but I never heard of an evolved bloodline in a Succubus before."

She sat in the darkness and described the structure of the Demon realm, the hierarchy, and how each creature has its place, its rightful section, all to maintain peace in their world.

I asked her about peace in the Demon realm. She snorted, explaining that peace there is a lot like war here, with their version of war being the utter annihilation of all species in a blood-fueled rage.

She explained how the Old Ones kept them all in their places, and that the only way to move up in the hierarchy was, as she'd done, to come to our realm and grow in power.

That was the accepted way, and when she returned, she'd be respected, accepted, and those lesser than her would step aside easily, or be eaten…it being "the way things were" in the Demon realms.

I asked a few questions, gathering that this was just accepted, and I moved on.

"So, what's the problem?" I asked her.

"I'm too strong!" she snarled.

I frowned. "Okay, that's a strange thing to hear from a Demon from a society that's all about strength…"

"When I go back now, I'll be too strong! They'll make sure I can never come back!" she snapped.

"Okay, so don't go back," I suggested with a frown.

"After that? After my Jian saw me? Saw the thing that I could become…" I noted the use of "my Jian" but said nothing. "He's going to hate me forever," she whispered.

"He's alive, you know?" I said tentatively. Her eyes flashed in the darkness as she lifted her head.

"Of course, I know! I felt everything you did to him! You think I'd still be here if he'd died? My contract would have torn me back to hell already!"

"So?" I said, thoroughly confused.

"So, I'm trying to prepare myself for when he tears up our contract and banishes me!" she snapped, then sniffled. "I won't get to explain, I just know it."

I sat there for a minute, trying to twist my mind around what was happening before shaking my head in disgust, then standing up and taking a deep breath.

"Sehran, are you bonded to obey me?" I asked her, knowing the answer.

"I am," she whispered in a small voice.

"Come here," I ordered. She hesitated before letting out a sob, climbing to her feet, and shuffling out to face me.

"Please, don't make me." She looked down at her feet.

I shook my head, not knowing what she thought I was going to make her do, but sure it wasn't anything any man of honor would consider.

"Come here," I ordered again, and I took her in my arms, holding her to me. At first, she stiffened. She'd resumed her usual form, and I had to admit she filled my arms nicely. Hell, even covered in the blood of her enemies, she still somehow smelled of gingerbread and strawberries, and I spoke softly as I held her to me.

"You earned your place on my squad a dozen times over, and I'd never force you to do anything that wasn't for your own good. You really love Jian, don't you?" I asked.

She snuffled against my chest before nodding. "I do…"

"Then, before you give up on your life here, how about we ask Jian what he wants? You know he asked for you. He wanted to make sure you were okay?"

"He wanted to make sure I was gone…"

I shook my head, feeling her relax and accept the hug, rather than fearing I was going to take advantage of her.

"You couldn't see his face," I told her gently, before sending to Oracle, *"Are you okay out there? Is Jian?"*

"He is, but he's going to need to rest and recover, he keeps asking for Sehran."

"Then it's time they saw each other, and whatever happens can happen," I said, feeling her agreement. I lifted Sehran in my arms, then turned and walked to the door, trying to ignore the things I felt squishing and breaking underfoot.

Sehran tried to convince me to stop, but she didn't try very hard. As I reached the door, Oracle, who'd sensed me coming, opened it, letting me duck sideways out of the doorway with Sehran in my arms still. I crouched next to Jian and lay her on the floor, where she stared at him like a frightened rabbit.

"I…love you," Jian whispered breathlessly.

She threw herself into his arms, sobbing and holding him to her. I swallowed a lump in my throat before squeezing Oracle's hand that little bit tighter and leading her away, way down the corridor, leaving the pair to talk.

THOMAS

"So, what do you think?" Thomas asked the massive figure standing silently by his side.

"I think you and your people are going to get slaughtered." Woodite said. "There are more than thirty guardians down there. They're all looking for some of your kind aboard an airship to kill in retaliation…you fit the bill perfectly."

"Well thanks so much!" Thomas snarled, before sighing and trying again. "Look, you're one of their kind, can't you just go down there and speak to them? Convince them that we mean no harm?"

"How?" Woodite asked, frowning. "I mean, seriously, Thomas, how? The trees here are over a hundred meters high. There's nowhere to land, and as to you meaning no harm…Well, it's a bit like a flea meaning no harm to a mammoth. They're not going to care what you think."

"Well, I don't know, can't you jump or something?" Thomas asked in annoyance. Woodite laughed, his hollow frame making the sound echo peculiarly.

"Oh, of course. I jump, the guardians find my cracked and broken remains and boom, they shoot you down and kill you all. Just let me climb over the side…oh wait, perhaps that doesn't solve the problem?" he said, shaking his head in mock surprise.

"You're an arsehole, you know that?"

"I don't have one, actually," Woodite said, smiling beatifically. "Unlike you filthy apes, I was created perfectly, and have no need for waste elimination facilities. I simply absorb the sunlight, fresh rainwater, and the ambient mana of the realm…"

"Arsehole," Thomas said again, before snorting. He'd spent the last hour talking to Woodite, and found he liked him. During this last twenty minutes, though, the stress had ratcheted up a level as they grew closer to the site, watching the Himnel ship as it slowly mirrored them.

The original plan had been to attack the ship on sight, destroy or capture it, and then move on to rescue the wisps…that plan had failed miserably for two reasons.

The first reason was that the warship they faced was easily three times their size and had twelve cannons to a side, as well as four on the front counting the massive one. If Tenandra resembled a beautiful sailing ship crossed with the *Nautilus*, the ship across from them was more of a Spanish war galleon, huge, heavily armed, and with at least a hundred soldiers aboard.

The second reason was the real kicker, though. They were the reason the grove guardians below were so pissed off and willing to attack anyone.

The ship was commanded by a dark legionnaire paladin. A paladin who had a wisp hovering close to her head, slowly circling her helm.

The knowledge that one of their missing charges was so close, and yet had been corrupted and forcibly bonded already had driven the guardians to screaming rage, and every so often, they stumbled across something that didn't run away fast enough. The brief scream as a monster was beaten into paste made it clear why you didn't fuck with the guardians.

"What are our options?" Thomas asked Tenandra and Woodite, glancing over to Alistair to make sure he knew he was included in the question.

The four looked at each other, before Alistair spoke up. He had laid claim to the Optio's rank after the fight with the Storm Demons aboard Rewn's ship and was Thomas' second in command. Alistair and was a grizzled Legionnaire in his early thirties. A career military man, he'd joined the Legion ten years earlier and had risen to authority quickly. He'd grown up on his family's small fishing fleet, until a Leviathan attack robbed him of everything he held dear.

He'd survived on the land through a combination of sheer fury and stubbornness, refusing to back down from anything, meaning that a few weeks later, when a Legion scout found him bleeding to death in a gutter, she'd sighed, then done as her conscience dictated and she'd brought him to the Enclave to die among those who would care. She'd helped the healers for the next month to look after him as he healed, then backed him up as he went into the Slums again, finding the men who'd attacked him and challenging them, one-by-one.

He'd killed them all, then turned their possessions, including their homes, over to their victims. Then, he had joined the Legion, ostensibly to pay his debt to her and the healers, but also because he didn't know what else to do.

Ten years later, he was respected as a Legionnaire of few words, but devoted to the Legion with all he had. When Restun had come looking for someone to shadow the young Lord and to lay down their life, if need be, he'd come straight to Alistair.

"Three options, as I see it, Lord Thomas," Alistair said. "First, we use a rope to lower one of us into the trees, then climb down or jump, depending on how close we can get, and attempt discussions with the guardians. Second, as we can't find a clearing, we make one, using either the ships cannons or our magic, then drop a group down to clear more space. Then, we land the ship and attempt to deal with guardians one way or the other."

"Not liking either of those options so far, I'll be honest. And, for fuck's sake, man, call me Thomas, all right?" he asked for the fifth time.

"Well then, Thomas…option three is that we lower the grove tender here down on a rope, let him discuss things with the guardians, and we go and deal with *that*," Alistair suggested, pointing towards the massive ship that was slowly shadowing theirs.

"I would prefer not to be dropped into the forest," Woodite said. "I do not bend, nor do I bounce. I am, in fact, rather fragile, despite my appearance. It will take me many years to regrow damaged sections."

"We wouldn't drop you," Thomas muttered, looking over the side, and squinting at the trees below. "Probably."

"We have nearly forty meters of rope on board that could be repurposed," Tenandra said. "This would be the absolute maximum I can provide, and the remaining sixty meters would be terminal to most creatures. I suggest we take a different approach and try to draw them away. I will try to reach out to those who hide below and will encourage them to flee to the guardians. Then, we attack the enemy ship, using only your own magic. Then run and get them to chase us."

"Then we use the ripple-fire," Thomas agreed, nodding his head. "Okay, that works. But won't the guardians attack us, if we attack her?"

"At this point, the guardians are likely to attack you anyway, regardless," Tenandra offered, shrugging.

"Then I suggest we continue as we are," Woodite said. "We are both waiting for the other to make a move. We lose nothing by continuing to be patient. Should Tenandra make contact with the wisps below, she can direct them to the guardians. That will, in turn, calm them and encourage them to give us a chance at least. Should the ship attack us, we defend ourselves and use the cannons. We lose nothing but time and possibly gain the guardians as allies."

"We haven't got the time to waste!" said Thomas, gritting his teeth. "Jax will be fighting by now. Hell, he could be killed at any moment, and we're here, sodding days away from…"

"We were ordered here because this mission is important, Thomas," Alistair said. "We cannot pick and choose our responsibilities. The Scion ordered that we attempt to save the wisps and contact the guardians, not to mention destroying any Himnel ships that come. Our best chance for success is to show patience, therefore that is what we will do."

Thomas glared at him for long seconds before muttering his agreement and striding off, the others letting him go as he moved to the prow of the ship and glared out across the misty rain at the massive ship that floated across from them.

He pulled a Ring of Farseeing from his pocket and slipped it on, using a charge to look at the ship again.

It was clearly a warship, and built in a different way from most of the ships they'd seen so far, the layered and thick beams that crisscrossed the hull, and the way the engines were attached were far heavier. The cannons rested inside their own firing chambers, rather than set atop the deck. Here and there, he could make out the gleam of armor inside the ship as people moved about, watching him as he watched them.

Slowly, he crept his magical vision up to the main deck and roamed left and right until he found their captain, standing there, one hand resting on the railing, and watching him in turn.

She waited until she was sure he was watching her, then she lifted one gauntleted hand and pointed to him, as if to make it clear she was coming for him.

He shifted, undoing his belt, and flicked the clasps free on his trousers. Freeing the codpiece, he dropped it aside, before getting his cock out and clambering up onto the railing. Then, he helicoptered it around.

"You want some of this?" he shouted into the still air between the ships. "Come on, then!" he cried, before pissing over the side, fresh roars and bellows starting up as he did so.

When he was done, he clambered down, shooting her the finger and stormed off. Thomas marched below decks to sit sulking in his room, bored of the standoff.

"He's brave," Alistair said to the other two, while Woodite winced. "What's wrong?"

A fresh bellow of fury lifted from below, unclear words ringing out.

"That's a guardian…and he seems displeased that the rain he was enjoying was contaminated," Woodite said as Alistair shook his head and sighed.

"I will continue to reach out to those below," Tenandra told the others, bidding them to go inside before sighing as she looked out across the gleaming treetops, the reds and yellows of the approaching autumn blending with the evergreens to create a beautiful tableau.

Thomas was nice enough, she admitted to herself, but she missed her usual crew, especially Jian and Sehran. The Succubus was keeping some of herself back from Jian and from her, but it made sense. After hundreds of years alone, and before that, hundreds of years as little more than an assistant: un-named, unloved, and unaware of all her life could be, Tenandra was loving all the fun that she got to have with the pair. She resolved to find an excuse for a long flight soon, preferably with just the two of them aboard her.

CHAPTER FIFTY-THREE

The battle for the skies over Himnel had been impressively one-sided, the combination of the hundreds of magic users, and the ripple-fire cannons, against the poorly armed, and undermanned ships of Himnel had ended quickly. Despite almost a hundred losses on our side, the capture of Himnel's *Destroyer* and a few others, and the literal destruction of the rest of their fleet meant we now ruled the skies.

We landed back at Narkolt, the entire fleet taking turns to come in, load up, and take off again, even as we changed from the badly listing and seriously damaged *Destroyer* over to the *Ragnarök*, pausing only long enough to confirm to Oren as he came sprinting across the shipyard to us, that yes, he could have *Destroyer* as his flagship.

He paused, huffing and puffing and nodded, clutching at his chest as he tried to catch his breath, before waving it off as not worth the wait and staggered back to his ship, pausing only to wheeze to Elise and a few other engineers that *Destroyer* was to be given special treatment.

I snorted and continued on my way, the ship being boarded quickly by several dozen more legionnaires before we lifted back up, heading out into the early afternoon sun. The light shining through the slowly thickening clouds made patterns out on the bay as the ships turned, flying back out over the water, heading for the river closest to Himnel.

This was the most dangerous time, I'd been warned. If Himnel and the Dark Legion decided to roll the dice, instead of sitting in the city, waiting for us to come to them, they could toss their advantage there aside, and instead attack us as we deployed.

The fleet couldn't carry the entire army, Hell, it could barely carry a thousand of them at a time, along with their supplies and equipment, and the thousand would be on their own as the ships returned to Narkolt for more.

That meant the Dark Legion and the Himnel Army could swarm us and slaughter us before we could get reinforced. We were landing some three hours' march from the enemy city, but still, the eight-hour round trip to get the next group meant that we had to pray that they were the chickenshits we thought they were.

Denny, his engineers, and his heliomages were with us, as were the entire surviving Legion, the elite guards, and the elite soldiers of the army, but still…

The tension grew as we drew closer to Himnel, passing close by the site of the slave camp we'd raided. Then, we turned to the east, passing over the river that split the land here, the reason for the fast deployment in this area.

While the risk was high with this plan, nine hundred and seventy of us could be dropped in place to hold this bank of the river. That was better than the army marching all this way, giving the enemy time to deploy and fight back as we tried to cross the small bridges.

The airships could provide backup, now that the skies were decisively ours, but to do that they needed to be here, not back getting more troops. So, after hours of arguments, of us all changing our position again and again as we were convinced one way then the other, I finally lost my patience and declared this plan as the one we'd follow.

Now, as we dropped lower and lower, the fear that I'd fucked this up rose in equal measure. I swallowed it with a growl, leading my forces off the ship and onto the green grass of the bank. The Legion behind me formed up into their respective ranks as Denny shouted orders to his engineers.

There were a hundred of them now, and they co-opted hundreds more of the Legion and the army, giving them orders and driving them to dig, to carry, and to work, as they raced around like a kicked anthill.

I met up with Romanus, Lucian, Jon, and Restun, as well as the rest of my squad, grinning over at Augustus as he hurried up the bank to join us from his ship, the remainder of the Legion having been pulled in from the Tower to join in as well.

The Djinn were with him, all of them having accepted him as their clan father now, and the eighty that he directed to Denny filled the sky in a kaleidoscope of colors.

Above them flew the Alkyon that weren't involved with the ships, almost a hundred of them in total, ranging from battle hardened legionnaires to ex-gang members and thieves.

They'd been trained with short bows and crossbows, and now used them like they'd been born in their hands, with the tiny battle group of imps that we had flying in their midst.

The imps numbered just over two dozen, many of which were recruited from Narkolt on the promise of regular food as much as money, and the small force brought a mastery of Fire Magic that would be useful.

"Scion, Prefect Romanus, Primus Praetoria, Tribune Jon, Chief Justicar," Augustus said, greeting us one at a time, nodding his head respectfully and saluting all of us, fist to chest.

"Hail, oh high and mighty Heir to the Empire!" I called to him, spreading my arms wide and dropping to my knees. "We're not worthy! We're not worthy!" I fell forward and bowed to him.

"Ass," he accused me.

I laughed, clambering to my feet and hugging him, getting a hug in return, as well as a laugh. "Well, fuck it. None of that formal shit with me, you hear, or we'll all be formal with you." I countered, grinning at Augustus. "It's good to have you back by my side, my friend."

"I still wish you'd let me bow out and name Thomas as your heir, rather than me," he said seriously.

I shook my head. "Thomas is like me. A brawler, not a leader. If I die, I need to know that the next in line can pull the Empire together and keep our people safe. He'd lead well, but he'd do it with his gut, making the decisions that felt right. You'll listen more than he would. Hell, more than I will, and you'll do the best of all of us."

There was something about the man I just liked. He was straightforward, honorable, and damn if he wasn't just too godsdamn good-looking for his own good. I'd missed having him at my back, but as he was the heir to the throne, I'd made the decision that we couldn't fight alongside each other anymore. If one of us were lost, then the other needed to survive.

That had changed with Thomas's arrival, as I now knew that if the worst happened, he could take up the mantle. Then, it'd all changed again with the prick Nimon and His new pet.

I'd considered it and come to the conclusion that if either of us, out of Augustus and me, were to die, it would blatantly be me. I'd taken the time to discuss the situation with Jenae and Thomas, before he'd left for the North.

If anything happened to us both, Thomas was to head to the Great Tower and claim the Empire. Augustus had named him as his heir, which gave him at least as much right to lead as Nimon's pet had, and Jenae had agreed to declare him her divine choice to lead, should we die.

"I'd still rather be a legionnaire," he admitted ruefully.

I grinned. "What, you think I *want* to rule?" I asked. "Fuck no. I want what that arse Rewn is cursing me for giving him…I want a nice house and no stress, a decent allowance so I can eat all the food and drink all the booze I want, and then I'd spend the rest of my time banging the hell out of Oracle and topping up my tan. Fuck ruling the Empire."

"Well, for a man that hates to lead, you're growing into it well, Jax," Romanus said, smiling faintly. "But regardless, we need to get started. The war won't win itself!"

"True. Okay then, the first diamonds are under construction," I said, gesturing to the massive earthen works that Denny and his team were directing. "As soon as they realize what's happening, I expect the Dark Wankers to try an assault at least, so let's get ready. Romanus, you lead us overall. I have no experience in this, and as much as I know I need it, I need people to live through the fight more."

"Thank you, Jax," Romanus replied with a slight smile. "Augustus will lead the left flank, Restun the right, and I will command the overall army. Lucian, you will lead the reserve, while Jon will lead the center. Jax, you will fight in the center under Jon's direction. Your squad and three others will form his magical support. Should we be attacked before the rest of the army arrive, then we will hold as best we can, using magic at the last second to break up a charge when they least expect it." With that, the others saluted. I followed along a second behind the rest as Romanus spoke loudly, his voice rolling over the entire force as the last of the ships lifted, turning back to Narkolt.

"Forces of Imperial Scion Jax," Romanus called, his voice echoing as everyone paused to listen. "Today, the Empire takes to the field again, after long ages of slumber. The Imperial Legion is bolstered by her allies: the Army of Narkolt and the Narkolt City Guard. But you are the elite. You are all that stands between your Scion, your home, and the snarling, barbarous hordes of the Dark God.

"Today will be a day that will long be remembered in song and legend. *How* it is remembered, however, is up to you…As the steppingstone that launched the Empire and the City of Narkolt on the first steps to freedom and bringing the light of justice, honor, and knowledge out of the darkness to the lost…or as the day the Empire truly fell.

"Before us are the duped, the weak, and the foolish, persuaded to fight for the God of Death. We march for the truth, for the Gods of the Pantheon of the Flame and for the future. I ask that you do not hate them, but pity them, as you strike them down."

I listened as he spoke. Romanus was a man who'd risen to the top of the Legion on sheer merit, as a commander, as a man, and as a legionnaire. But the Legion hadn't fought any real battles against a sentient enemy in centuries. It had fought skirmishes and raids. It'd slaughtered monsters and defended the weak, but never had it engaged in full-scale wars like this, and I could feel that something was missing as he built the mood.

When he paused, I stepped forward, and he fell silent, letting me take over.

"You all know me!" I shouted, feeling Oracle doing something to help my words carry to them all, even as the gates opened in the far distance and the first rank of mounted cavalry rode out…and just kept going, dozens turning into hundreds as the seconds passed. "You know who I am, and how shit I am at making speeches." I stared across the miles that separated us from the walls.

"Well, today's going to be no different! I'm not eloquent. I'm not patient or fucking nice, and I'm sure as shit not going to tell you all to do it for the Empire. Except for the Legion, the Empire was something most of you heard about in tales of the past. What I'm going to tell you about is a useless cockwomble called Barabarattas, the former Lord of Himnel."

"He started all of this by sending slaves to the Great Tower. He sent them, not to claim it, or to work in it. He sent them because he'd found that a SporeMother, a fucking evil greater than anything that should exist, was still alive there, even after nearly a thousand years." I turned and looked around the ranked soldiers and legionnaires behind me, as they all worked, slowing to listen, but still working.

"That creature of nightmares was dying, dying of starvation. It was weak, barely able to survive from the lack of fresh meat it could get, thanks to animals learning to stay clear, and all but the craziest of sentients doing the same. The Himnel scouts had found it, though, found that it was still there, and they returned to Barabarattas, looking for backup, for help to kill that bitch." I paused again, this time looking at Lydia and the others and watching their faces as I went on.

"That useless cockgoblin sent back some of his elite troops, not to kill it, but to trade with it. He sent those slaves, and he would send others for months and even years to come, as a trade. He let the bitch feast on them and implant her spawn, and in return, he took most of them, planning to raise a slave army of SporeMothers. We know that because we found the godsdamn HeartStones he sent to it to communicate, as the fucking coward wouldn't risk himself. We know it because we've faced the Drow aboard airships from both Himnel and Narkolt, Drow who held the collars of enslaved SporeMothers."

They sent shudders and glares toward the city in the distance.

"We don't know why the Drow are working with Barabarattas. Fuck, I don't really give a shit. They're assholes, and I'm making it my personal mission to fucking wipe them out, and then I'm going to bitch slap their shitstain of a Goddess to death. All this started for me with a single life. That of a little girl, a child, that Barabarattas fed to a monster of nightmares.

"That little girl could have been the child, the sister, or the friend of any one of us, and he fed her to that thing. She was about two years old, and I know absolutely nothing else about her, save that she wore a yellow dress that had flowers stitched into the hem. We're doing this for that child, for your children, for your families and for your friends," I called out, anger bleeding into my voice as I took several steps toward the city and I took a deep breath.

"DO YOU HEAR ME BARABARATTAS? I'M COMING FOR YOU, YOU FUCKING PRICK! FOR THE SAKE OF THAT CHILD, I'M GOING TO NAIL YOUR BALLS TO THE FLOOR AND PUNT YOU INTO THE NEXT WORLD! YOU AND THAT SHITE EXCUSE FOR A GOD!"

There was a rumble of thunder as Nimon acknowledged my words, and I flicked Him the finger, knowing that the Pantheon of the Flame had my back.

I turned my back on the city and called out one last time to our forces.

"Better get to work, lads and lasses, because they're sending us someone to play with!" I snapped, walking forward and taking a shovel from a protesting man's hands, then digging in with a will.

The next hour passed quickly as Denny and his people shouted and cajoled us, at times laughing at how slow we were or praising us for our speed over the others, while all the time the earthworks grew.

We didn't have the time to create proper defenses, so we'd gone with the plan for the diamonds, but rather than building the five we'd intended, we built three bigger ones, with just over three hundred men in each.

The diamonds were thirty meters to a side, giving a rough space of nine hundred square meters inside. They were cramped, but we didn't have the time to make larger spaces, and with the ditches we'd dug before them, we just had to hope it'd be enough.

The last of us moved inside the fortifications before the riders got close enough to do more than fire a few pot shots from crossbows, all of which missed.

"Seems a bit fucking stupid," I muttered, watching the oncoming tide of riders as they slowed to a canter, then to a walk, then stopped, watching us. After a minute, one of the riders broke away from the others and rode forward, waving a blue and green flag.

"What the hell does that mean?" I asked Tribune Jon, who was standing next to me on the raised earthworks on the inside.

"Truce," he said simply. "They want to talk."

"Really? Fucking stupid flag for that, the French one works better," I muttered, turning and getting ready to push my way through the crowd, when Jon grabbed my arm and shook his head.

"Prefect Romanus will speak to them," he said. I grimaced, realizing I'd been about to undermine him as the leader of the siege. I nodded and stepped back up to his side as Romanus strode forward, leaving the protection of the fortification and stopping a dozen meters out, with perhaps twenty meters between the two of them.

"Who are you?" the Himnel emissary asked.

"I am Prefect Romanus, commander of the Legion of Dravith. Who are you?" Romanus called back, and the horse took a single step forward.

"I am Lord Barabarattas' man, that's all you need to know," he responded grimly. "You have assaulted the ships of Himnel and trespassed on her lands. Surrender, and Lord Barabarattas may show you mercy. Refuse and…"

"We refuse." Romanus called back. "The criminal Barabarattas is at war with the Scion of the Empire, and as such, all Imperial forces are at war with any who hide him. Send him out, send him to face justice. Stand down your forces, and remove the stain that is the Dark Priesthood from the City of Himnel."

"The Lord Barabarattas has accepted alliance with the Dark Legion, fool! You have one hour to stand down, to surrender your weapons, and to march out of your pretty little houses, or you'll be killed. Consider this your last warning." He snapped, before turning his horse sideways and glaring down at Romanus. "You have no idea what a true fighting force, backed by a God, is capable of, you fool."

"Oh, I think I do," Romanus purred. "Send your best, and watch as they're ground to mince."

With that, Romanus turned and marched back to us, covering barely a few meters before the emissary reached down and yanked his cloak aside, raising a fully loaded and ready crossbow into sight.

He aimed quickly, then fired as we shouted a warning, the bolt slamming into Romanus' shoulder and spinning him to the ground with a cry.

"That's it, he dies!" I snapped, hands blurring as I cast Explosive Compression, while all around me others cast as well.

The emissary twisted his reins to the side and dug his heels in, sending his horse leaping away, dirt flying up in great clods as he dropped the crossbow on a line to clatter against the side of the horse, pulling out a short stick and whipping the horse's flanks.

He made it less than ten meters before over a hundred arrows, bolts, and magical attacks landed. By the time the smoke cleared, there was nothing left but churned earth, blood splatters, and drifting smoke.

Even the horse was reduced to shreds of flesh, which I felt a little bad about, but it was war, after all.

The horsemen split apart, having clearly been waiting for this, and four ranks of ten men, all in red robes, rode forward. The air around them shimmered as an illusion spell broke, exposing the mages as they released, the emissary clearly there only to keep us in place and distracted as they unleashed hell.

The first twenty unleashed Flamespears. Three each spread out across the wide front, hammering my grouped-up and disbelieving troops hard. Explosions of earth and flame rose into the air, screams echoing and earthworks collapsing as sixty Flamespears caused horrific damage.

Hundreds of legionnaires died, aspirants fell in droves, and the only reason it wasn't worse were the four members of the newly created Imperial magekillers that managed to trigger their tattoos in time to shield themselves and their companions.

Still, of the ten who were trained, six were caught as flat-footed as the rest of us and died. The others managed to variously drain, channel, or shield their locations just in time, and they prevented the opening salvo from being our last.

Their remaining twenty mages rode forward slowly, chanting as one, their voices overlapping and thundering as they built to a crescendo, a glowing circle of red opening between us and them as the fingers of a massive creature reached up and gripped the ground at the edge of the circle, hauling itself upward from what was clearly a portal to another realm. Judging from the sulfurous stench, the glowing red light, and the screams that followed it, it was some aspect of one of the hell-realms.

"Belamananth!" Sehran screamed from my left. "He's a prince of hell, and if he gets fully into the plane…" I glanced at her then back at the line of mages who were chanting and slowly riding forward, even as hundreds of horsemen raced for the gaps in the damaged diamond's walls.

"Motherfuckers!" I roared. "LEGION! MISSILE THOSE FUCKS!"

My voice echoed, booming across the grassy river banks, as Oracle did something to make sure it did. There was a pause before lights appeared all around me, as at first dozens then hundreds of soldiers, both the Legion survivors and the elites of the guard and the army that Oracle had taught, started to cast.

The lights grew in our hands, first a glow, then a light, one that brightened into five distinct glowing golden darts, hovering above my palm.

Most of the mages were too busy concentrating on the Demon prince, but the few who had seen what was happening blanched as they realized that they'd made a terrible mistake.

Grizz was the first to release, punching his right hand forwards even as he ran for Romanus, who sprawled in the mud with the bolt jutting from his shoulder.

The first flight of five missiles was joined in under a second by *hundreds* more. The spells blasted across the distance between us all, most of them slamming into the summoning circle.

A handful of spells wouldn't make any difference to the circle, hell even a hundred would have done little damage, but over a thousand ripped through the circle like it was made of paper, making the Demon prince howl as the structure of the spell tore at him, and the portal began to close.

The massive creature was still mostly on the other side, only its head, arms, and upper chest through, and it'd been struggling to free its wings. The portal, which had slowly been growing, suddenly slammed into reverse, closing down as he screamed in terror, then pain.

The circle sliced into him, a burning smell like that of white-hot steel meeting wet flesh filled the air and made me growl in satisfaction. The creature twisted, shoving itself back down and through, frantically trying to escape the closing portal.

It paused when its left wing collapsed, sliced clean through, and there was a second's hesitation where it clearly thought about clambering upward instead of down, and that second's hesitation cost it its final chance.

The Demon twisted and writhed as the edges cut into its skin, sizzling and sliding deep into its lower chest, before bones shattered and the massive creature sagged suddenly, collapsing atop the dirt as the life went out of it.

The spell had been shattered, and the backlash had sent the twenty mages tumbling from their horses, screaming in pain. Then before they could hit the ground, the missiles that hadn't been expended on the circle hit them.

There were still hundreds of missiles, and one in the right place was more than enough to kill. The second set of twenty mages joined the first in death as they were shredded. Flesh and bones, cloth and hair flew in all directions as the horsemen charging past on either side blanched, seeing their secret weapon wiped so thoroughly from the face of the realm.

"KILL THEM!" I roared, and the second wave of magic began. The charging horsemen who were headed for the gap into the diamond tried to turn, frantically yanking at reins that were already pulled taut, and all they managed to do was make their horses crash into each other.

Hundreds fell as the charging horses collided. No longer charging full-bore, those who'd managed to keep their feet and had stayed the course arrived at the ditch, most of them having lost the momentum needed to bridge it in a single bound.

Of the roughly a thousand mounted soldiers they'd started with, less than a hundred made it across the ditch and into the gaps in the diamond.

Most simply fell, tumbling across each other or diverted to the sides, looping around and fleeing as the air was filled with the screams and whinnies of terrified horses, the pops of breaking bones and legs torn free, and the crash and clatter of armored bodies crushed under literal tons of horseflesh.

The ringing, screaming, and clattering filled the air before it was blanketed out by the whoosh and roar of another barrage of a thousand plus Magic Missiles.

They rocketed through the sky, twisting and turning, diving and flipping around as the targets their caster had mentally selected tried to dodge.

Grizz threw himself down, skidding in the dirt as he came to a halt alongside the wounded Romanus, who looked up from the dirt and locked eyes with Grizz, before muttering one word.

"Poison," he got out, his face pale and sweating.

Grizz blanched, before determination overrode his expression. He grabbed the bolt, looked at the man he'd looked up to for years, and grinned. "On three, Prefect."

Romanus nodded, unable to speak, and gritted his teeth as his breathing grew labored.

"One," Grizz said, then yanked it free, making Romanus hiss in pain as a good chunk of flesh came with it. Grizz tried to hide it, but the smell as he grabbed Romanus made him gag. The thick, sickly sweet smell of flesh putrefying rose from the wound, and as he hauled Romanus up, tossing him over one broad shoulder, the tell-tale black lines of infection climbed the older man's neck.

"Oracle!" I shouted, pointing to Romanus. "Get ready!"

Grizz raced for us, unconcerned by the hundreds of missiles streaking overhead, bringing a golden light to the dimming day.

He scrambled down the ditch, then raced up the other side. Legionnaires hauled the sides of the diamond apart to let him in, even as more Complex Healing spells hit him. Legionnaires tried to help, taking turns between their missile barrages to heal their friend and leader.

Grizz slammed down into the dirt on the inside of the diamond, skidded, and took the dozen steps to the space Oracle had cleared, swinging the by now unconscious man around and lowering him gently, even as Oracle started to cast our Surgeon's Scalpel.

I used Scour, banishing the stench that had been rising from him and making the air seem clearer. As I started to search, targeting sections of his body, Oracle snarled, finding the poison multiplying inside him.

"I need help!" she snapped at me.

"Legion! I want ten of you to heal Romanus!" I shouted, thirty men crowding in, until I ordered that the ten with the biggest mana pools stay while the rest fell back.

I turned to Jon after ordering them to work in teams of two casting the healing spell, then twenty seconds later, the next pair would start, then the next, creating an ongoing ripple of healing.

"What's happening?" I asked the Legion Tribune, and he finished giving his last order before answering.

"A handful of the riders managed to get out of range. The rest are dead, or soon will be. I've sent a hundred out to kill the injured, saving their mana. The other two diamonds are doing the same."

"How many legionnaires do we have?" I asked grimly.

"In total? Full legionnaires?" he asked, and I nodded. "Eighty-six, combat capable once you take off your squad and Denny's nutcases. Another forty or so that are past their best, but can fight. I've got them leading the green squads and providing backbone. The rest…we lost thirty in the airship battle and nearly a hundred and twenty died to that single Flamespear run…and some in the assault on Narkolt."

I'd seen the strike, and I'd seen Yen use it before to devastating effect, knowing how packed people were inside the diamond. There'd been nowhere to run, nowhere to escape it, and where she'd used it before alone, there'd been ten mages all at once using it there.

"Those mages better have died," I snarled.

"Apart from that fucker who attacked Prefect Romanus, I don't think any other group got more attention than the mages. They'll be finding bits of those cocksuckers hanging from trees ten miles away in years to come."

"Fine. Get ready to change out the healing team. As soon as they get to a third of their mana, I want them aside to recover, and more in their place…we are NOT losing him!" I ordered.

Jon gave the orders before continuing his report. "The riders ran for it, but most were cut down before they could get far. The city looks to be closing the doors and settling in for a siege. They've got to know that we haven't the men for a full siege, surely?" he asked.

"They don't know how far we'll go. After all, we could have emptied the city and made everyone that could stand up hear thunder and see lightning. Wankers like Barabarattas would have…" I shook my head and turned back to Romanus. "I need to concentrate. Jon, you have overall command," I said formally.

"Yes, Scion." Jon's gauntleted fist crashed to his chest as he straightened. "I'll not fail you!"

"Good man," I muttered, lost in Romanus' wound again.

As the sound of Jon shouting orders rose behind me, I focused on Romanus' heart. Scour went to work on it, damaging it with each casting, but the repeated heals were capable of fixing that. My cleaning meant that, instead of infected blood multiplying through the body, clean, healthy blood was suddenly being pumped around.

"Thank the Gods!" Oracle said as she saw what I was doing. "Brilliant, keep doing that!" She grabbed his temples and focused on his brain. "You clean the blood, I'll clean the brain. The rest we can fix later. Just keep them going, and we can outlast the poison, if nothing else!"

I focused in as she directed. His heart was beating erratically, the healthy, flushed red of the muscle darkening as lines of gray and putrefying green crept out, trying to spread. I picked them off one by one, barely keeping ahead of the spread. As the minutes turned to hours, sweat drenched me. I'd lost track of the potions I'd had fed to me. Eventually, Nerin pushed me aside.

Oracle was barely responsive, and it took me shouting at her to get her to stop searching for traces of the poison.

"It's done!" I shouted, holding her to me as she stared in stupefaction.

"Wha...?" she mumbled.

I wrapped her in my arms, stopping her as she reached for Romanus again.

"We did it, you did it! Nerin's here!" I told her, seeing Nerin focusing on him, nodding to herself as she searched for any traces that were left.

"You both did well," Nerin declared in a flat tone. "I've never seen anyone survive Life's Bane before, but I guess thousands of points of healing can do anything. Even if you both need to learn a hell of a lot more before I let you loose like this again!"

"We saved him!" I complained tiredly, waving away an offered mana potion as I felt bile rising in my throat.

"By practically poisoning yourself with mana potions," she said, sighing. "Don't get me wrong, I applaud the act, but the damage you all took to carry it out?"

"How is he?" Oracle mumbled, pressing herself against my chest.

"He'll live, but he'll not be taking part in the war nor any battles for weeks to come. The healing you all did saved his life, but healing magic alone is no substitute for the body's natural processes. He needs weeks of good food and rest to recover from the amount of damage done and the strain his body was put under with the constant healing." She grimaced. "He'll be unconscious for days at least."

"Fuck," I groaned, then immediately felt terrible. I was annoyed because I couldn't palm the logistics and leadership duties off on him, rather than being relieved he was still alive. "Fine, Jon!" I looked around, jerking as he appeared next to me. "Fuck man, that was fast."

"Apologies, Scion, I was..."

I waved him down and spoke over him. "I know, you were nearby. Sorry, mate. Okay, Romanus is out of action for at least a few days, but he's alive, thank the Gods. I need you to take his place out here. You'll have the army and the guard to help you, but as soon as the mining golem arrives, we're leaving," I stated flatly, and his expression dropped.

"Of course, Scion, but perhaps..."

"I need you to lead the joint forces, Jon," I said in a low voice, turning to face him fully and resting my hands on his shoulders as I looked into his eyes, Oracle stepping up to stand by my side. "I trust you, and the overall leader of our forces should always be a legionnaire."

I left unsaid that, while the guard and army commanders had sworn to me, neither had yet earned my trust in the way that the Legion had. "You'll have Denny and his mad bastards, the airships, the trainees, as well as the more seasoned elites to keep everything together. I doubt they'll stick their heads out of the city until we force them out. But if they do, retreat into the diamonds and use the airships to bombard them. The aim of this is to bleed these cocksuckers dry, while keeping our forces as safe as possible."

"I understand, Scion. I won't let you down," he declared firmly, clapping his fist to his chest.

"I keep telling you, Jon, call me Jax, dammit! All my friends do. Remember to send in the airships to hit the walls, then the golems before Horkesh goes. Make it look like a full-scale assault to draw their attention, but keep our people as safe as possible, within reason." I gave him a wink, before turning to the others. "Lydia, how are we looking?"

She stepped up, her armor gleaming and spotless, in fierce comparison to Giint, who looked like he'd been in a mud bath.

"We're good as we can be," she said. "We've lost some o' tha Legion, an' that'll make things a wee bit tighter, but we were always going te lose some, unfortunately."

"Where are we with the plan?"

She gestured out to sea. "They're on their way back te tha city, eight hours or so an' they'll be back with another five 'undred troops an' tha first set o' tha golems."

"Horkesh?"

"In place, along with tha mad bastards that volunteered fer this, they've been roamin' tha forest an' getting practice in since yer took tha city. Tha next wave o' soldiers will be 'ere soon, along with most o' tha magic arrows we had tha time an' resources te make."

"Is the tunnel ready?"

"As ready as it can be, considering it's no' started yet. Tha earthworks are in place, an' should hide it from anyone lookin', as soon as tha miner arrives, we're ready ta go."

"Fantastic," I said, smiling. "I guess it's time to get a move on, then."

I turned to Jon. He was giving the needed orders out already, the legionnaires streaming in from the other diamonds, even as people moved out of this one to make room. The camp was assembled and fires lit as we prepared for the next phase.

Getting a good meal inside us, we rested as much as we could, while the newly arrived fresh troops started repairing the fortifications, digging the ditches deeper and generally getting ready, while across the wide expanse of the grasslands, the City of Himnel waited, brooding.

BARABARATTAS

"Explain that one more time," the figure whispered, shrouded in shadows in his favorite chair, as the grimy, sweat-stained rider stood to attention before him. "The…the mages…they…you have to understand…"

"Understand?" whispered Barabarattas, watching the shaking rider. "Of course, I understand. I understand that you turned and fled the battle when they unleashed magic, when your friends and fellow soldiers died in droves and cost me my riders! All because the *mages* failed. It was nothing to do with your cowardice!"

"But, but m- my Lord," the man stuttered, his armor jingling as he shook, the scalemail shivering constantly and irritating Barabarattas even more.

"Silence!" he roared, leaping to his feet and striding across the small office, the thick gold and brown carpets muffing the sound of his footsteps. The drawn drapes and lit fire made the room oppressive and sweltering as he closed on the man, made bow-legged by a lifetime in his saddle.

"Please, have m- mercy," whispered the man, staring at Barabarattas in terror as he grabbed him by the throat, staring into his eyes from inches away.

"Mercy?" the ex-city lord repeated, as though unsure of the word. "You ask for mercy?" He stared into his eyes, watching the sweat running down the soldier's cheek, the flaring nostrils as he tried to get enough oxygen down, the way his hands twitched, instinctively reaching for the hilt of a dagger that was no longer there, frantically moving his hands away from the sheath as he realized what he'd done, and the rank stench of terror as he knew Barabarattas had seen it all.

"I have a wife! Children!" The man closed his eyes against the fires that burned in his master's gaze, shivering in fear as Barabarattas savored his fear with a quickly indrawn breath.

"And they will share your fate, traitor!" Barabarattas snapped.

The rider's eyes opened wide in horrified pleading, and Barabarattas let the change come.

Barabarattas was no longer a weak human, not now. The dark gift he'd received from Cletus, and that Cletus had received from his master all those centuries ago, was a gift of evolution for those who were worthy, and all those who weren't?

Well, there was always a need for cattle and for *fodder*.

Barabarattas' face split at the edges of the mouth, the skin straining then tearing as his jaws extended, and the true horror of his new existence became clear. As his face split apart, blood sprayed.

Veins ripped by the mass of teeth that unfolded, embedded in bands of muscle that lashed forward, dozens of them sank into the frantically screaming man's face as the bands of muscle wrapped around his head, compressing, biting down, pulling him closer. The screams grew muffled, the body thrashing as the creature that had been Barabarattas held onto it.

There was a final jerk as he tightened the muscles again, squeezing. He was rewarded with the sickening crunch of bone splintering as the skull was torn apart, fragments being discarded as his pointed tongue drove in deeper into the gray and white mass, tearing it apart with a slobbering hunger.

Minutes passed as the remains of the rider were consumed, the tastiest sections torn free and eaten in an orgy of wanton feasting, before Barabarattas paused, his senses tingling. He pulled back, dropping the bleeding, quivering remains onto the floor as the muscles retracted, pulling the sides of his face back into position as he searched the room for the presence that had disturbed his meal.

"Come out, come out…" he said, before straightening with a grimace as Cletus stepped out, frowning around the room.

"What, you call for me, then you regret it? Not very hospitable, Barabarattas, even for you," Cletus drawled, dragging a finger across the edge of the table, wiping a smear of blood off the table and sniffing it. "You need more iron in your diet." He wiped his finger clean on a silken handkerchief. "You cannot survive on the weak alone; even we do need to balance our meals."

"I eat what I choose!" Barabarattas snapped, wiping his face and glancing at the bloody mess on his hand. He snarled, stalking to the curtains and wiped his face on it, scrubbing most of the blood clear, adding to the encrusted stains that marred the once-pristine office.

"Clearly, and yet as you feed exclusively on the living, you start to decline, becoming more feral than conscious. I have warned you of this on several occasions, fledgling," Cletus snapped at him.

"And you forget your place, *hireling*!" Barabarattas snapped back. His eyes glowed with an unholy light as he straightened, glowering at the creature that had inducted him into the new world.

"I was once a hireling, that's true," Cletus admitted, strolling nonchalantly around the desk, coming to a halt before the seething Barabarattas. "But that time came and went long ago. When you accepted my blood and became part of my flock, you accepted the change in our dynamic. As I recall, you were quite passionate about the advantages I bequeathed to you. Yet, here I find you embracing the most feral of your gifts. Have you forgotten the need to conceal your predilections? Have you forgotten the consequences should we be found out?"

"You forget your place," Barabarattas repeated with a snarl.

A lilting laugh filled the room.

"Does he?" a new voice questioned as the door closed behind her with barely a whisper, the figure striding into the middle of the room and stepping over the shredded remains of the rider without giving it a second thought, beyond lifting the trailing black silk of her barely decent gown, ensuring it wasn't ruined by the patches of blood that marred the once-rich carpet. "He does rather overstep himself on occasion, that one, husband, dear."

Barabarattas scowled at the woman, who seated herself comfortably in the chair before him. Her long, black silk dress, ivory skin, and hair as black as a raven's wing ensured that every eye was drawn to her.

"I didn't summon you, Persephone!" Barabarattas snarled, yanking his eyes from her lush curves and forcing himself to remember the humiliation she'd inflicted on him when he'd thought to avail himself of his new "wife."

Scars ran up his body, starting just below the belt and rising to a point barely below the neck. She'd flensed him wide open with her fingers alone, after mocking his manhood and promising that the next time he so much as glanced at her with that in mind, she'd remove that capacity forevermore.

The wonders of his new form had closed the wounds quickly, but the ease with which she'd beaten him, shrugging off his attempts to pin her and laughing in derision, had ensured that he'd taken care to research the ways to kill their kind most carefully.

He fingered the leather-clad hilt of the dagger on his hip and stared a challenge at her. His fury rose as she laughed, another light, tinkling affair that would draw any man to admire her.

"Ah, but your pet does have spirit, Cletus, I'll give you that!" she said, smiling at him before gesturing around the room. "I came to make you aware of the latest changes, oh husband dearest! That pathetic excuse for an arch-priest demanded an explanation for the losses the riders encountered. It seems he'd given you very strict instructions to allow the apostate to land unmolested?"

"He has no authority to order me! Nor my City!" Barabarattas snarled to snorts of amusement from both Cletus and Persephone.

"*Darling,*" she drawled, examining her nails.

"Don't call me that!" he snapped at her.

She let out a heavy sigh. "Very well, Barabarattas, oh *former* Lord of Himnel, and Fledgling of the Coven. You signed the accords. You agreed to the terms, and now you have to deal with the consequences." She examined her nails theatrically. "And one of those consequences is that you are to take no further punitive action against the apostate. The arch-priest is confident in the city walls and the advantage they grant and is thankfully totally oblivious to their actual plan. He's playing right into our hands, and we'll not have you ruin things."

"We? Since when are you and the priesthood 'we'?" Barabarattas snarled. "I bet they'd not be so welcoming to you if they knew what you were!"

"No, they probably wouldn't." She smiled. "But then, I'm strong enough to live with that. I could tear most of their pretty little paladins apart with my bare hands, after all, but you? You were turned specifically so that, should we need to move on, you can be handed over to the mob, lynched, and exposed to the sun. So do remember your place, husband dear."

"She has a point, fledgling," Cletus said, drawing one nail across the desk again, this time curling up a layer of lacquer with the sharp tip. "Should we need to leave, you'll be the one sacrificed to hide the coven, and there goes your chance to grow in power. If you wish to survive, to enjoy the eternal life you were gifted with, then you need to be more patient and more careful. Using the ganglion means the body is desiccated, but recognizable as killed by magic. Feed on them, though, and you leave people wondering what did the feeding."

"Remember, child. The master put me here to support you, but I can just as easily replace you. Easier, in fact, so do be a good boy and stop playing with your food. Oh, and I ordered the rider's family released, so you don't make a scene there, either," Persephone said, standing in one elegant motion before sniffing as she looked around the room. "Now, have this place cleansed. Deal with that." She gestured to the still-leaking remains on the floor. "And get your house in order.

You want people to treat you like the lord of Himnel again? Start acting like it, and less like a spoiled child who doesn't want to leave his room."

With that, she turned and strode to the door, her seductive walk making her ass sway in ways that drew Barabarattas' eyes, even as he snarled in impotent rage at her words.

"She's right, and you know it," Cletus said, absently tapping the site of the only wound that Barabarattas had ever seen on the creature's form, one that had appeared weeks ago and that Cletus had refused to discuss with him. It had made him curious enough to dig deeper, finding the coven and the glory of the night. "Behave yourself, clean up this pigsty, and act the part of the lord you were. Most of all, leave the master to take care of the apostate. After all, he's heading right for our nest."

Barabarattas glared at Cletus then back toward the door as it closed behind Persephone, and he silently swore vengeance against the pair of them. Cletus for daring to speak down to him, Persephone for…for *everything*. He was going to use these freaks to kill off the apostate, to weaken the Dark Church, and then he would strike, he would kill them all, save *her*. She would be his to use, then to feed on.

"Fine," he said eventually. "I'll play my part, but what about when the priest finds out about the SporeMothers?"

"Then he'll assume anything that he sees is a result of them and a play for power on your part that got out of hand. He'll declare you to be a fool, but he'll weaken his forces taking them down, which in turn, will allow us to take the city back. I imagine he'll be secretly impressed with your sheer balls for daring to enslave them!" Cletus left out that it had been his plan all along and the careful days and weeks of manipulation to ensure that the correct paths were taken thus far.

"Fine," Barabarattas repeated, wiping his chin again, then scratching at the dried blood that covered it. "Send me a servant with some fresh water, and see that…"

"You'll need to dispose of the body yourself before servants attend. It'll be a valuable lesson for you, having to deal with the consequences of your actions! Oh, and fledgling? When you've cleaned it away and summoned more servants, remember that you need them. No more feeding on them, eh?"

"Don't call me that!" Barabarattas snapped, but the hint of mocking laughter fading from the air was his only response.

CHAPTER FIFTY-FOUR

The mining golem threw a great gout of dirt back at us as it paused, some ancient fault line having driven dirt down deep here, in place of the stone it had been shifting for the last six hours, and we paused in the indeterminable marching.

"How much longer?" Arrin asked for the fifteenth time.

I snorted, shaking my head as the golem shifted. It burrowed a few feet, then paused as it did whatever magic it did to change the much softer dirt into a hard-packed tunnel wall.

"How the hell would I know?" I asked. "I guess we're under the city by now, or at least we damn well should be."

"Fuck's sake, we could have crawled to the walls by now," Grizz muttered, eyeing the tunnel roof with some trepidation.

"What's up with you?" I asked, frowning.

"Nothing boss!" He said quickly, forcing a smile and enthusiasm into his voice.

"He hates being underground," Augustus said from nearby, grinning at the glare Grizz gave him. "He always did, so we made a point of sending him to anything with a cave system."

"Evil," I muttered, seeing the look of shock on Grizz's face.

"You did it on purpose?" he asked.

"Of course I did. What kind of a primus would I be if I didn't try and break you of your fears?"

"You didn't break me of them! I shit myself every night for a week after, nightmares that made me…" Grizz choked off his accusation and swallowed hard as Augustus reached out, laying one large hand on his shoulder and squeezing for a second, maintaining eye contact.

"And you still went in. You never paused, never hesitated. You were afraid, and you used that fear to drive yourself forward, never giving in to it," Augustus said quietly. For a handful of seconds, all that could be heard was the shuffling of feet and the low murmur of other conversations, with the omnipresent hum of the mining golem. "Plus, it was funny as hell." Augustus winked.

"You utter bastard." Grizz cursed his primus and the heir to the Empire in one, before giving a rueful grin and nodding at him.

"How much have you been underground since then?" Augustus asked.

He shrugged. "A few times. Mainly, it's been ruins, though, not caves."

"Is there a difference?" I asked, getting a look from them both. "I mean, the ruins are underground. So, if anything, they'd be more unstable than a cave that's been like that for millions of years?"

"Oh, thank you very much for that!" Grizz snarled, and Augustus guffawed.

"What?" I asked as Grizz shifted position to walk on the far side of the group. We all made a point of not commenting on the way that Yen reached out, intertwining her fingers with his and squeezing for a few seconds before they both resumed their masks as hard-nosed legionnaires.

"Giint doesn't like dark places either," Giint said amiably, wandering alongside us and absently playing with the cube he always held. "Bad things happen in the dark."

"You spent your entire life until I met you living in a collapsed Prax. It was as dark as the inside of my soul there most of the time," I pointed out.

His agreeable nod was almost chipper. "Yup. Bad things happened." He lowered his voice to a whisper, clearly thinking he was saying it to just us, but the hoarse sound carried better than his normal voice. "Marriage ceremony held in dark…baaaaad night."

"For you or for her?" I asked unthinkingly, before wincing.

"Both. She used to try to kill me when I slept," he said, smiling sadly. "Miss her. You'd have liked her. She gave no shits."

"Why the hell did she try to kill you?" I asked, unable to help myself.

"Was bored. Sometimes hungry." He shrugged. "It happens. Why, Oracle no try to kill you?"

I shook my head slowly, so he looked over at Augustus. "Or you lady? She no try kill you?"

"No…or at least, not yet," Augustus replied with a slight smile.

"They will. Sign you meant for each other," Giint said in a conspiratorial whisper before winking and strolling off.

"That little fucker's mad," I muttered, shaking my head.

"Totally insane," Augustus agreed, sighing. "So how are you doing then, Jax?"

I shrugged, looking forward as the golem started up again.

"I'm all right, mate, sick of always being on the run, of the short breaks, and in need of a holiday. Gods, what I wouldn't give for a portal to a Greek beach right now."

"Oh?" Augustus asked, smiling as he looked over at me.

"Gods, yes…there's an inland sea, where I come from, well, a good ways south and east actually, called the Mediterranean. One of the nations there is called Greece, and its people are the Greeks…you'd like them." I said, sighing as I thought to it. "Back in times long past, they were some of the greatest warriors in the world…you remember me telling you about Sparta?" I asked. He nodded.

"See, Greeks," I reminisced. "But when the world changed, and technology became the way forward. The Greek islands were left behind. It's rocky land, with not a great deal of resources, so they fell back on their second greatest gift…tourism.

"They welcomed people to their islands to relax, to spend their money, and to basically have parties and celebrate their lives. We called them our holidays, as in holidays away from our normal lives, not like a birthday or a religious holiday from work. We'd travel there for a week or two, and spend our time drinking, eating, and basically fucking like rabbits."

"Why a week or two only? Sounds like a good place to be for a lot longer?"

"It was," I said. "Hell, if I could have afforded to live like that, I'd have spent longer there. But it was expensive. You'd save your money all year for your holidays."

"I'd like to have seen it," Augustus said.

"Man, what I wouldn't give to take you all there!" I laughed. "The sights we'd see! And hell, the photographers would go nuts. Most of you look like Greek Gods already. Nearly a hundred of us turning up there to take over a beach? Man, I'd make a fortune just in us posing for calendar shots," I idly mused, before attempting to explain the difference between a calendar as he knew it and the kind that would net us a lot of money.

Three more hours passed with the group growing increasingly concerned and edgy, conversations drying up, and the food we forced ourselves to eat tasting like ash in our mouths as we waited and waited for the miner to break through the final area and out into the lower buildings of the City.

"You're sure there were caves under the south of the City?" I asked Augustus for at least the fifth time, and he nodded.

"They were under both the slums and the enclave, as well as some of the greater city. They were known as the warren, as those who couldn't afford to live in the slums dug into the ground there, uncovering and growing the caves.

"There were rumors of deeper, much larger areas, mainly ruins from the original city, simply built atop of, but the monster excursions there were handled by the city guard, not the Legion. It was clear we weren't welcome, so we let them take care of it."

"Why'd they do that? I mean, it's literally all they wanted you for, fighting the monsters?"

"I always assumed that it was because they could point to the guard as doing 'our job,' then divert more of the taxes their way rather than to the Empire, but who knows."

At that moment, the miner paused then sagged forward as a section of the tunnel gave way beneath it.

"Back it up!" I shouted, echoing others as they pushed back from the miner. Cracks appeared in the tunnel around it as more and more earth sagged, and cracking sounds echoed.

The miner tried to back up, the tentacle-like grasping appendages that had been laid flat against its sides slamming out. They punched into the walls, halting its slow slide, but they weren't strong enough to lift it back up. It teetered for long seconds before its situation matched a set series of commands. Finally, it adjusted course, releasing the tentacles in a pattern that swung it downward, angling to the left, before the final three released and it drove through the hole and out of sight, surrounded by the echoing of falling stone. The cracks of the tunnel mouth gave way, and in the distance, a roar of challenge echoed through the clouds of dust.

One that was quickly taken up by others.

I surged forward, heading toward the edge and staring out at the suddenly revealed cavern. My jaw dropped in stunned amazement, even as Augustus barked his first orders. Legionnaires rushed up to slam their shields together, forming the famed Legion shieldwall; the freshly revealed cavern crawled with enemies.

It was at least a mile across, and perhaps half a mile high, the ceiling dipping and climbing here and there making it impossible to be sure. But the piled masonry, sagging doorways, and unmistakable roads below us made it clear that Augustus had been right.

Seemingly, what Himnel was built atop of, besides compacted dirt and the thick stone we'd been burrowing through, was more and more of bloody Himnel!

The buildings were clearly ancient in design. Some of them appeared to be covered in designs like hieroglyphics as near as I could tell, considering the coating of bioluminescent algae, shit, and the dust and debris of millennia.

The real problem, as near as I could see it though, was that we appeared to have found Barabarattas' hidden SporeMother breeding program location. Six of the fucking creatures were clustered around a central point, a single, massive building squatting there. Unlike the others, it wasn't ruined. Instead, it was encased by a shield that shimmered a dark gray, signifying it was slowly moving to failure.

The SporeMothers turned, their collars clear even at this distance, as they gave up on their rhythmical pounding on the shield. Around them, in their hundreds, the DarkSpore-infested undead roiled forwards.

Here and there around the cavern, the occasional DarkSpore hovered or flew, but as the wave raced forward, it was clear that the vast majority were in use puppeting a corpse. I stared down at the bodies, grimacing as I guessed where they'd come from.

To a man, they were emaciated, filthy, and barely decent. Their clothes had deteriorated long past anything any moderately fastidious housewife would consider using to plug a rat's hole. Yet, almost all of them were armed. The gleam of clean, freshly finished, and sharpened steel reflected the little light that penetrated the cavern from the magelights we wore.

I blinked, realizing I'd activated DarkVision without thinking about it, and my position had mostly shielded me from the overwhelming light that was rushing up from behind me, attached to the Legion.

I almost ordered them to put them out, enabling me to see the SporeMothers and the oncoming wave more clearly, until I remembered how much these things hated ANY form of light, and I relayed what I was seeing as Oracle began her casting.

"Six SporeMothers and at least three hundred undead, probably closer to four hundred," I said to Augustus, who paused in the shouting of orders to listen. "The cavern is huge, plenty of room for others to hide, but unlikely. They've been whaling on a shielded building in the middle of the cavern, and we're apparently interrupting them."

"Six, eh?" Augustus snorted, shaking his head. "Ah well, looks like you've finally found me a fight with enough to go around. Legion! I need two rows!" He barked the orders out, the legionnaires falling into position around me as I stared out, the hole made by the mining golem quickly semi-blocked by the shieldwall. Ten legionnaires kneeled at the front, entirely blocking the bottom of the hole, with the second rank standing over them, leaning forward and locking their shields in place, creating an interlocked wall of steel eight feet tall.

The hole itself was considerably higher than that, but between the solidity of the shieldwall and the height of the tunnel, how it'd broken through the wall of the cavern, and the bottom of it being at least twenty feet above the floor of the cavern…I grinned as I realized what spell Oracle was working on.

Where she could fly indefinitely, letting her see over the shields, I had to settle for a boost. Grizz and Westin held me aloft on a shield they held at shoulder height.

I got my balance amazingly easily, grinning at the little shifts they made beneath me and the way I reacted. I had a split second to wonder if I could have been an Olympic gymnast if I'd tried.

I dismissed that thought as worthless and cast Flames of Wrath, slamming it down in the space before the wall, after Oracle had positioned hers right in front of the onrushing horde.

The shambling, frantically hurrying undead stumbled into the circle just as it went active, and flames leaped up, searing into them, rooting into the decaying flesh bags and hunting down the corruption of the DarkSpore.

Dozens fell in seconds, fifty or more before Oracle's first circle ran out of mana and collapsed. But, by that time, Oracle had the second ready to go and replaced it in seconds.

I cursed as my own barely managed to take out a dozen before dissipating. Oracle's had been so much better aimed than mine, the damn undead being slower than I'd first thought. The main body still had not arrived by the time the spell expired. So, while Oracle concentrated on the Wrath, I started with Explosive Compression, ignoring the undead and focusing on the SporeMothers that scuttled forward.

I fired it, the seemingly tiny orb flashing across the cavern to impact the lead creature's right foreleg with a crack that echoed.

Then the air warped, and it exploded.

The massive creature screamed in pain and fury as the gravity differential caused the massive limb to bend, then creak, then snap with a horrific scream.

"Oh yeah, motherfucker!" I shouted at it. "Come get some!" I cast a second one as Oracle slammed down two more circles, each taking out entire sections of the horde. I took careful aim, wanting to hit the injured SporeMother full in the face, thinking that'd kill it off. Then, there'd only be five left to deal with. A bit of luck, and hell, maybe they'd all be dead before they could reach the shieldwall…

That, of course, was when Murphy struck.

The second Explosive Compression hurtled across the space between us, the distance seeming to stretch out longer and longer, like someone was messing with a camera visual, making the objects in the background grow more distant. Then it was gone, my spell vanishing entirely…for less than a second, before it came hurtling straight at me.

I had a split second in which to see it, realizing that someone with a greater grasp of magic than I did by far had decided to play. I leaped aside, the orb slamming into the tunnel wall thirty or so meters behind me.

There were a handful of screams as the legionnaires who'd been performing rear guard were either killed by the spell or by the collapsing tunnel. Then the blast of dust and debris hit us, making it all but impossible to see for several seconds.

I blinked the dust out of my streaming eyes and clambered atop the shield on Westin and Grizz's shoulders again, and this time I searched the cavern far more carefully.

It took me a full minute or more, but on the third pass I saw it, a large, uncomfortable-looking high-backed chair, sitting against the entrance to one of the buildings on the far side. The figure in it waved at me, smiling.

I'd never have seen it otherwise. The darkness of the cavern alone had shielded it well, and the basics of DarkVision's range acted against me, barely off put by the massive increases in my Perception over the last few months that rendered the range limitation into far less of an issue.

The figure was tall and broad-shouldered, slim-waisted, and olive-skinned, with long, dark hair. Standing casually beside him, as though enjoying a chat at a party, were two others. One pale-skinned, and recognizably Drow, the other dwarven, with skin like wet coal, seeming to suck the light into himself.

The pair that stood were drinking from goblets, appearing to chat idly, while next to them…I frowned, focusing in harder, before grimacing as I remembered I had a Ring of Farseeing, popping it on my finger and activating it.

I blinked in shock, having zoomed in far more than I wanted to on the Dwarf. The little bastard was wearing tight leather pants that basically outlined his meat 'n two veg like it'd been shrink-wrapped.

I gagged as I shifted my focus, seeing the figure sitting in the chair watching me in clear amusement.

He waited until I made eye contact, lowered his goblet, and smiled. His teeth gleamed in perfect rows as he saluted me with the cup.

I snarled, pulling back and glancing at the creatures incoming, hearing Oracle cursing. The undead were closer. As she laid down another circle, with the SporeMothers closing steadily, I glared at him.

He watched the spell activate with an amused acceptance. As soon as I started to cast, he sat forward, waving a finger at me in admonishment.

I was about to shoot him the finger, when I realized that, if he could redirect my spell as easily as he had, he could have just as easily targeted it on the legionnaires as using it to close off my avenue of retreat.

My massively boosted Intelligence finally made itself known. I evaluated possibilities with blinding speed, coming up with a single clear answer.

Whoever, or whatever they were on the far side, they were clearly in control of the SporeMothers or totally unafraid of them, which meant, considering only one of them was a Drow, or appeared to be anyway, that the players I'd been wondering about in the background were finally making themselves known.

There'd been hints for some time that there was more going on. The Drow, hiding under Himnel, securing the Smugglers' Path in and out of the city. There had also been someone in command of the airships that had attacked us after we left the Prax. Those airships were filled with SporeMothers, not to mention the ship that had held one back in Narkolt. They were doing more than simply raiding.

Watching the shadowy fuckers chilling and drinking while we had the massive creatures bum-rushing us made my blood boil.

These fuckers were my real enemy.

I toyed for several seconds with using my Imperial Ability to free the SporeMothers, just to see if the bastards would be as sanguine with them free…before I dismissed it as fantasy.

I couldn't claim the SporeMothers as citizens, so I doubted it would work, but it would free the slaves in the city overhead.

Normally I'd be good with that, except that I lost points and essentially broke myself each time I used the Ability. If I was wiped out by it, then there was a good chance that the Legion wouldn't be far behind me.

No, these fucks were here for a reason, and the SporeMothers were an entrée, a little entertainment before the main event, so I had to keep that in mind.

I straightened, dismissing the zoomed-in view, and looked around the forces surrounding me. I couldn't take them all, as we'd get swarmed. The undead would be dealt with easily without the SporeMothers, but with them…the fight would be close.

That meant I needed to take the SporeMothers on.

As much as I wanted to, and every instinct in me shouted for me to protect my people by doing this alone, that was fucking stupid. I'd end up as a smear on the cavern floor if I made a mistake that way.

No, these fuckers were essentially treating this fight as a little cabaret, so I needed to maintain that impression for them.

"Augustus!" I called, still staring at the figure in the distance.

"Yes, Scion?" Augustus called up formally, clearly recognizing that this wasn't a Jax and Augustus moment, but the ultimate commander of the Legion telling his subordinate what WOULD happen.

"I'll be taking my people and fucking those things up. You're to clean out the undead first, then you can back us up. DO NOT use ranged magic against the SporeMothers or those dickbags at the back until I've distracted them. They manipulated my own godsdamn spell and fired it back at me."

"Yes, Scion," Augustus agreed, before pausing. "Lucian?"

The ancient Dhampyr stepped forward, glancing up at me. He'd been near the rear of the formation, but the legionnaires around him parted to allow him to advance.

"Yes, Heir?" Lucian asked.

Augustus stared at me in question.

"I need you," I said, smiling grimly. "It's time to see just what you're capable of, and if that shiny sword of yours is any good, after all."

"Thank you, Jax. I've been looking forward to using it, I'll admit," Lucian said, smiling wolfishly as he held the massive greatsword seemingly effortlessly in his right hand. The scabbard still hid the glowing blade. "But I think I'll leave it concealed for now, make it a nice surprise for them when I draw it."

"Damn," I said, smiling as I thought about the dislike the SporeMothers and their ilk had for the light. A weapon sanctified by the God of literal LIGHT was going to come as a nasty surprise for them, I had no doubt. "Glad to have you with us, mate." I nodded to Lucian, before turning to my usual team.

"Most of you won't be able to get straight in. That's you, Giint, Grizz, Jian, Yen, Ronin, and Sehran. Not because I don't think you can handle it, but because you'd draw the undead away from the shieldwall.

"Stay here and slaughter these fucks, then once they're down, come to us. Bane and Tang, you're stealthy mofos who can keep from drawing the undead and DarkSpore's attention, so you're with me. Lydia, because you can fly, so fuck those undead, and Oracle because, well, you know, but…hold back and use Wrath a bit first. Pare down the undead and DarkSpore as much as possible, because we're going to need the Legion and the rest of the team pretty damn fast," I took a deep breath. "Did I forget anything?" I asked, and Lio called up from the side.

"You forgot me," she said as Flux and Cheena slid out of stealth right next to her, echoing her sentiments, then blurred away again.

"Fuck. Okay, you three are with us as well," I grinned. "Looks like it's stabby stabby bastard day!" I said, shrugging. "At least it should mean I don't have to worry about any of those fuckers getting me."

With that, I held out a hand and yanked Lio up onto the shield. She caught her balance, then leaped out over the wall, vanishing from sight. The only hint she was still about was the sudden trail of undead left very, very dead in her wake.

Lydia took my hand, and I pulled her up next, jumping across the gap. She unfurled her wings as she went, swooping up and out of sight as I pulled the others up and threw them over.

The second to last of them was, to my surprise, Sehran, who'd grabbed my hand as I reached back unthinkingly.

"You can't…"

"I can do more than you think!" She glared at me, slapping her wings to their full length.

I started, shocked at the power radiating from her. Sure, she'd always had her wings, but she almost always fought on the ground and used her abilities almost exclusively as distractions. But there was no dismissing her now, no holding back. She was here, all of her power, all of her confidence and abilities—and I'd do well to remember her many skills, rather than her more…visible assets.

She dove off the far side of the shield, her bat-like wings snapping out and lifting her into the air, tail flicking. I tried to wipe the sight of that fantastic ass from my mind as she vanished upwards.

"I'm totally going to have to assume her shape one night," Oracle whispered into my ear, winking. "Or maybe I'll let her pretend she's me, then take a night off and get some rest."

I jerked my head around to stare at her, and she laughed, before kissing me and flying up out of sight, the first syllables for Flames of Wrath echoing in the air after she vanished.

"Hey boss, you're not getting any lighter, you know?" Grizz called up to me.

I jumped up and down twice. "You sure?" I called down, as the occasional grunt of a legionnaire stabbing out through a gap in the shieldwall became more frequent, the undead arriving in force.

"Sure, you're a dick!" Grizz said, grinning. I shot him the finger before taking Lucian's hand and pulling the heavily armed and armored Imperial Chief Justicar up onto the shield with me.

Grizz and Westin grunted in discomfort, and the shield sagged slightly. He leaped over the side, landing in the middle of the undead and performing a single clean sweep of his blade, one that lit the area before he slammed it back into its sheath. Nearly twenty undead collapsed at once, the controlling DarkSpore vanquished at the same time.

"Fuck me sideways!" I shook my head and launched from the shield, suddenly far more confident about the undead facing the Legion. "I should have just let Lucian take them out." Kicking off and flying straight for the SporeMothers, I yanked my naginata out of my bag and pointing it straight at the lead one, as the one with the broken leg slowly fell behind.

The blade glowed brighter and brighter. I grinned and channeled light into it, gripping the length tight, readying myself.

I cut sideways, rolling to the left and slashing out with the naginata as the massive lead monster lunged forwards, its jaws snapping closed barely a foot to my right. It pulled its head back, screaming.

My spin had let me carve a rolling line through the side of the SporeMother's face. The great bones, thick as a warship's armor plating, prevented the blade from sinking too deep. It still managed to take out half a dozen eyes and blister the entire side of its face with the proximity to the light.

I straightened out, heading for the next one, grinning as the one I'd just hit altered course, clearly incensed by the gnat that had stung it. This time I dipped down, swooping under an outstretched swipe of claws. I rolled again, slicing this one across the underside and setting a wash of noxious internals free to fall to the ground with a scream.

I twisted around, pulling up and feeling the g-forces for the first time in seemingly forever. The speed and sharpness of the angle made me grit my teeth as I rocketed upwards, pulling my weapon in close as Lydia flashed past me, going in the other direction.

Where I'd been carving furrows in them, going for grabbing their attention, Lydia was in full-on Valkyrie mode, seeing evil and determined to vanquish it.

She slammed down into the SporeMother I'd just gutted, leading with her mace. A sound like a tree trunk breaking echoed around the cavern.

The SporeMother collapsed, its limbs falling out below it as her mace shattered the skull, then buried itself deep in the SporeMother's brain, sending the creature into uncoordinated death throes.

I'd flipped over and was building speed. My lips drew back into a proud grin as Lydia slaughtered a creature that had figured prominently in her nightmares for months.

And she'd done it with a single blow.

I altered my aim, swinging around to line up on one of the charging nightmares that was about to plow into Lydia from the side. She braced her boot on the SporeMother's head and yanked, again and again, trying to free her mace.

Sehran shivered on the floor between two of the SporeMothers, appearing all "lost little girl," and my hackles rose on the back of my neck at just how wrong the image of Sehran being soft and vulnerable like that was…

For about four seconds. She drew in a deep breath and *screamed*, and the shockwave staggered both SporeMothers.

I pushed harder, picking up more speed, and focused in on it, aiming carefully. I tried to remember the bones we'd ripped free of the SporeMother in the Tower, the organs and more, and I remembered the neck. The great, sail-like frill at the back of the head had covered it, but the neck, while armor-plated from below, was bare above. I turned slightly, aiming for it.

If I built up my speed and plowed enough mana into the naginata, I could most likely get a kill in one. But, as Lydia was Demonstrating, that did you fuck all good if you lost your weapon in the process.

Instead, I pulled up, aiming not at the creature, but at the area just past it, swinging the naginata down as I directed myself past it, pulling up frantically. The blade hit, flesh tugging at it. A screech of outrage and pain, shock, and fear erupted from the SporeMother as she staggered.

I brought the blade up, glancing ahead as I turned to the right. My heart ran cold.

They all stood silent and ready, a roar of victory rising from behind me as the legionnaires broke the shieldwall apart. The last of the undead fell as the Legion streamed forward.

"Fuck no," I whispered, twisting around, drawing in a deep breath, ready to shout a warning, as "down" changed direction, and I was suddenly yanked sideways and up.

I twisted frantically, trying to reorient, but it was too late. I'd been too close to the lowering roof. I slammed into it at full speed, bouncing, before the gravity, altered by another, released and the world flipped again. I fell a second time, my naginata spinning away into the darkness as I tumbled towards the ground, a mess of broken bones and with a face that probably looked like a cheese grater had attacked me.

"Jax!" Oracle screamed, and I tried to make sense of the world, managing to send only two words through the link that bound us, before I slammed into the ground at horrific speeds, the snapping of bones filling my ears like dry twigs being stepped on.

"Trap! Legion..."

THOMAS

"Return fire!" Thomas screamed into the driving rain as Tenandra swung them around, frantically trying to avoid the incoming barrage.

The night had been dull, boring even, as the hours passed from yesterday into today. The long climb to the light of morning began.

Then, less than an hour before sunrise, while the mortals of her crew, weak and flawed creatures that they were, nodded at their posts and slumbered in their beds.

That was when the massive enemy ship slowly changed direction.

Tenandra was unsure at first, thinking it was another slight course change, a correction to keep them shadowing the Empire ship, until she'd seen the faint glow emanate from the cannons as they charged.

Even that was behind closed hatches, but to a creature of mana, any change on the environment was blatant. She shouted a warning that echoed from one end of her ship-body to the other.

"ATTACK!" she screamed. "WE'RE UNDER ATTACK!"

Thomas was one of the first to respond. Even seemingly deep asleep as he was, the ingrained habits of the prison, then the constant threats from his supposed peers and his trainers, made sure that the slightest disturbance was enough for him to go to full speed. Tenandra was amazed at how fast he went from deep asleep and drooling to firing on all cores.

He rolled out of the blanket and the bed, hitting the floor and bounding to his feet, leaping to his armor, which stood ready on the stand, and snapping sections into place with an ease that spoke of frequent practice.

In less than a minute, he headed for the door, latching the final sections as he went. The ship's motion as she altered course, rising and dipping, barely affected him, he was so in tune with her movements.

By the time Thomas made it to the deck and stared out, he was in time to catch sight of the bright, glowing cannons as they opened fire. He was fully into the mindset of war, staring across the distance that separated the two ships.

People raced here and there on the decks, the crew trying to get below. Their preparation jobs were complete, and there was little more that they could do until something changed. The legionnaires gathered, looking to him and Alistair for direction.

The heavens opened roughly at the same time that the first barrage left the enemy ship, streaking across the space between them. Tenandra fired her engines, hard.

The ship lifted up and to the left, curving around to present as small a section as possible to the cannons, but still, three shots landed square.

Two of them were Lightning Bolts, powerful and effective, especially against a wisp-ship. The cracking, discharging energy sent pain screaming along the nerves that formed her ship-body, even as sections of her reinforced hull were cracked and blasted free in showers of splinters and cascading thickened plating.

The Fireball had landed between the two Lightning Bolts, bursting apart on the lower left of the stern. The flames spread with an unnatural speed, the mana forcing the flames to multiply until it ran out.

By the time it did, though, the bottom third of the stern was entirely ablaze. The crew were sprinting to the Captain's Quarters, leaping onto Jian's bed and throwing the broad windows open, two of them holding onto the shirt and pants of a third, who leaned out and frantically threw bucket after bucket over the fire.

While that was going on, Tenandra still hissed in pain, glaring across the distance at the wisp who danced and shrieked with pleasure, echoing her mistresses' emotions.

Thomas barked orders.

The two squads assembled on either side of the starboard ripple-fire cannon. They crouched, hands held carefully below the level of the railing, hiding what they were doing.

"And…stand!" Thomas shouted, matching words to action, glaring at the soldiers that filled the deck of the enemy ship as it turned to face them. The slowly building glow of the main cannon came into view.

The Legion stood with him as Tenandra turned the ship sideways, crossing the T with her body, even as it screamed in pain.

The legionnaires held their hands up, all twenty of them glowing with Magic Missiles. Thomas grinned evilly as the paladin paused, shock clear on her from her stance alone, and the way her bonded wisp froze mid-spiral.

"Return fire!" Thomas screamed, thrusting his hand forward, releasing the missiles to hurtle towards their target, even as he started casting again, the experienced voice of Alistair rising beside him.

"Legion! Recast spell, hold to release!" he barked, his voice dropping away into a low susurration as he spoke the words needed for the spell himself.

The hundred Magic Missiles flashed across the gap in a wave of golden light, the first forty landing practically as one on the foremost port engine, the heavy shielding erupting in a cloud of splinters and bright blue gas. Then the engine, accustomed to the strain of lifting the hundreds of tons of airship, ripped free of its housing and vanished into the rain, a bright blue detonation somewhere overhead in the cloud cover, the only explanation needed.

The next forty magical projectiles slammed into the soldiers who had been drawing up in ranks, ready to assault the ship they'd assumed to be easy meat. Dozens died in seconds.

The final twenty missiles, though, were cast by Thomas and the three men standing near him. At his order, they'd staggered them, arriving in two lots of ten, turning the paladin's shield black with overload.

Then it darkened further, cutting off the paladin's vision. The helmsman, who she stood next to, protecting, wore an ostentatious sneer of contempt for their spells as they vanished into the darkness of the shield.

Tenandra snarled back.

"My turn!" she hissed as the ripple-fire cannon went off.

The barrage flashed across the rapidly shortening distance between the two ships. As the shield flickered back into invisibility, the paladin and helmsman realized they'd been tricked, their chance to dodge taken by the shield-induced blindness.

The more powerful Magic Missiles streaked across the space first, Tenandra having made slight alterations to the cannons' input. She'd fed them far more mana than was needed in her excitement, and the missiles resembled harpoons more than darts or bolts. The first five fired one after another, a second apart, and landed in the middle of the still-reeling soldiers who marched across the deck, headed for the helmsman.

As each hit, it buried deep before expending the mana they held in a single explosion. The inertia alone was sufficient to kill any the missiles impacted.

Screams rose as the soldiers realized what the peculiar collection of cylinders on either side of the deck were, then the second set of cannons began to fire.

The Magic Missiles had been as much for range-finding and to create bedlam as they were for the damage they did. Lightning Bolts, the equal of the two that had hit Tenandra, lashed out interspersed with Fireballs.

Electrical flares leaped through puddles of standing water and from the touch of armor on armor. The close confines of the upper deck made the electrical aspect of the Lightning Bolts far more horrific, even as it slightly reduced the effectiveness of the Fireballs.

Slightly.

A Fireball over a foot across that slammed into a ship made of wood, or a person of flesh, regardless of the armor they wore, was never going to be entirely ineffective, especially when the spells impacted. They surrounded the impact point in a wash of flaming liquid that was the magical equivalent of napalm—mere water couldn't extinguish the flames until the mana powering it was used up.

The cramped conditions of the ship's deck conspired against the Himnel and Dark Legion soldiers, and many of them were caught in the splash-zones of multiple Fireballs while being electrocuted. Thomas grinned at the cacophony of screams and booms that filled the air.

The pleasure was short-lived as a group of six mages took their places around the helm, two taking over the strain of the shield from the dark paladin. The remaining four started to cast, their hands glowing with DarkLight. Thomas hissed in recognition and at the memory of Jax being literally peeled out of his armor.

"Target the mages!" he shouted, suiting action to his words, and casting as fast as he could. "Fire at will!"

The main cannon on the Vanquisher continued to charge as both sides released their spells, and the smaller, more standard cannons on the ship's bow all fired, the world vanishing in the whoosh of light, spells, and the booms of detonations.

Flames spread across the side of Tenandra's ship-body, making her scream in pain as lightning raked her decks. Legionnaires fell cursing, screaming or dead, bodies juddering or cooking, respectively. She twisted herself around, gritting her teeth as she accepted the damage she knew would come. She closed the distance to the enemy, avoiding the main cannon's horrific Lighting Bolt by inches.

As it carved a great furrow in the forest below, trees detonated in showers of splinters and flames ripped to life. She offered her starboard side to the enemies' own.

Tenandra prayed the gamble would pay off, even as the first of the cannons on that side tore into her, and her crew began to die in earnest.

CHAPTER FIFTY-FIVE

I grunted, coughing as I twisted my fingers around, unable to form the words, even sub-vocally to cast healing. Instead, I fumbled with the pouch at my waist, tugging free a healing potion and raising it shakily to my lips.

I tried to bite down on the cork and winced as my jaw refused to close fully, a grating feeling of bone-on-bone warning me against trying that again. I twisted my other arm around, trapping the bottle between my arm and side, pressing it into place and fumbling the cork out, before downing the shining red potion in one go.

I sighed, then gasped. The liquid spell poured down my throat, repairing it as it flowed over damaged flesh and cartilage.

My bones realigned, pops and clicks sounding like an arthritis-riddled silent rave filled the cavern where I lay. Mere seconds after I'd downed the potion, I pulled a second one out and pushed myself upright. The wave was rolling closer.

Somehow the SporeMothers, or whoever had been controlling them, had known we were coming. The pitiful three or four hundred undead who had been around the shield, who had then left it and raced to fight us, weren't there to defeat the Legion.

They were there to trick us into a false sense of confidence.

When I'd moved far enough into the cavern, and as I'd glanced up from the SporeMothers that were sacrificial lambs, I saw the others.

Three more SporeMothers lurked, two on the right and one to the left side of the cavern, and they had *thousands* of undead waiting with them.

Even that we might have been able to take, especially in the narrow confines of the tunnel where numbers meant nothing, but the Legion had slaughtered the undead and had raced forward, giving up their defensive position in coming to my aid.

Now they were strung out in a racing line covering a good third of the cavern, if not half.

The wounded SporeMothers attacked my force, and the rest of their brethren fell in from either side.

I struggled to my feet and stared around grimly, searching quickly, before spotting the reflection off the blade of my naginata, only a dozen meters to my left. I glanced at it, then the onrushing wave of undead, and I couldn't help but shake my head in disappointment.

They were just rolling forward, no defensive measures at all. Hell, they clearly had no thought beyond "get him," and I could do serious damage, if I didn't have to get back to the others.

I set off running, stumbling at first, as my left kneecap popped and clicked, but after a handful of strides, it was secure again. I picked up speed, skidding to a halt by my weapon and bending down…only to be sent flying sideways by what felt like a truck hitting me.

I half spun over, the world blurring past before I slammed into a pile of fallen masonry, bouncing and clattering until I came to a stop. I shook my head, the word seeming to turn, and forced myself upright, blinking and trying to get my eyes to stop spinning.

I stumbled, looking around in shock, seeing the wave of undead were getting close, but it hadn't been them. As I turned around and around, there was nobody close by, but…

"You're a bit slower than I expected. Shame that," a voice said to my right.

I spun, coming face to face with the man who'd been sitting in the chair on the far side of the cavern. He smiled then bowed slightly at the waist, sweeping his hand aside like a gentleman in some old bloody period drama.

"Cletus Bartholomew Thane, at your service," he said, straightening and waiting politely.

"Jax…Jax Amon. Did you just fucking kick me?" I asked, my brain still rattled.

"Ah, yes! Yes, I did. No sense in letting you get your weapon after all, is there? Makes what is to come much more difficult."

"And that is?"

"Why, killing you of course. Shame, really. Given the choice, I'd much rather have inducted you into our little club. But you had to choose a side before we were acquainted, didn't you?" He shook his head and lifted one finger, wagging it in remonstration. "That, and the things you said about my Lady and benefactor…naughty, naughty, naughty!"

"And your Lady is?" I asked, half-suspecting that Tamat had been playing some deep game all along, since I kicked Her arse last time.

"Illoth, Lady of the Shadows and Dark Deeds, mistress of the Drow and the spiderkin," he said formally.

"Oh, that cock holster," I said, letting out a sigh of relief. "Thank fuck. I thought…well you know what, doesn't matter. So, who are you again? I swear you look familiar." I raised one eyebrow.

"Oh!" Cletus said, smiling broadly. "Yes, my apologies. Last time, we didn't really have time to introduce ourselves properly, and I wasn't wearing my mask. One second, if you please…" He tossed the last of his wine back and dropped the goblet into his bag.

"Honestly, it's a crime to just toss it off like that, but needs must. That's from the last bottle I have of the thirteenth vintage of Sennamore, lovely stuff. I'd offer you a drop, but, you know, it'd be wasted." He shrugged apologetically, then shook his head and blurred.

His entire body shifted slightly, but when he stopped, not only was he still wearing the same clothes, but he'd kept his overall shape, even his features. His skin had simply changed its tone, going to a dead bone white. His ears had lengthened, eyebrows too, of all things. But now I recognized him.

"You!" I snarled, fury filling me as I remembered the last time I'd seen him, lying there on the deck, practically broken as he fed on me, then beat Giint bloody and killed Stephanos aboard Tenandra.

He was the Drow commander of the fleet that had come for us as we fled the Prax!

"Me," he agreed, smiling widely. "You have no idea the boons my lady will grant me for this. She's been wary of me since I met my master, but this? This will gain me Her favor again, and that of Her patron, Nimon."

"You think?" I cracked my knuckles and rolled my shoulders. "I'm gonna rip you a fucking new arsehole, pal, then I'm going to find every one of that bitch's altars, exactly what I promised Her, and repeat what I did with the one in the Cathedral of Narkolt."

"Oh?" he asked, clearly curious.

"I had it smashed into pieces and used as gravel in the army latrines. My people get to shit on your Goddess day in and day out, and you know what they call Her? The turd-spider. That's all She's known as in my lands. And, guess what, shit biscuit? I'm taking back the Empire. This is my land now. Beep fucking beep, motherfucker!" I lifted my left hand and gestured for him to bring it, as I settled into my Asha'tuun stance.

He smiled, gesturing. The undead split around us, flowing like they were passing around a boulder. The SporeMothers did the same. Meanwhile, drain after drain hit my mana as Oracle fought on elsewhere in the cavern.

"Well, you'll need to suffer for that. But frankly, I'd have made your passing hard either way, just for the sheer fun of it. My lady will only be more pleased with me for what I do." He looked at me curiously before attacking, gliding across the space between us with an inhuman grace that made me grit my teeth.

I godsdamn knew I should have hammered my Agility instead of Intelligence.

He was in range of me before I knew what I was doing, and he swung a punch, making me back up. It was fast, and obviously powerful, but I managed to dodge it and the follow-up kick, then the second punch and the back heel strike, the roundhouse blow and the spin kick.

Each was faster than the last, until I was fighting at speeds that were beyond all conscious thought. I was reacting, my hours upon hours of training with Restun and Thomas kept me unscathed. But then he went even faster, and the blows started to land, a punch, then a kick, then a derisive slap that made my helm ring…I did the only thing I could and activated Hyper-Cognition.

The world seemed to slow around me instantly. A slow grin split my lips, lips that had been drawn and tight with concern. I began to see the patterns as he moved, the flow of the strikes and kicks. Each attack would have killed a normal human, and as soon as I saw them, and the pattern that lay behind them, I adjusted my own.

I stopped the wild blocks, conserving my strength, even as I heard Restun's advice in my mind, echoing back to me from days ago. "A miss by an inch or a mile is still a miss." As soon as I was sure of the direction of the blow, I simply swayed to one side slightly.

The knuckles of his right fist passed close enough to my cheek that I could feel the breeze of their passage before using an adder-strike. My left hand stiffened into a bar of bone, fingers locked in place as I slammed them into the tiny space under his right arm.

The blow was true, and the shock rippled through him, his eyes widening as he registered the strike. The damage was minimal, but the blow to his confidence and the surge in my own was telling.

I grinned then, the echoes of Restun pointing out the weight behind the blow that made his gouging thumb travel that little bit too far. As I twisted my face, I let him slam his hand into my helm instead of his thumb passing through the slit and puncturing the jelly of my eye.

The pain reflected in the slight tightening of his eyes was nothing compared to the pain that bloomed after I blocked his knee strike.

I'd shifted so his right knee grazed the outside of my left hip, bringing my left hand in at just the angle to grab the inside of that ankle. My right hand slammed down hard on the top of his right thigh as I triggered Mana Overdrive, granting myself the additional massive overpower that I needed. I dropped to one knee, twisting to the left, my left knee bent at a forty-five-degree angle and my right pressed tight to the floor, yanking him down *hard*.

As his leg landed atop my own, his right hand trying for an adder-strike of his own against my throat, I yanked his lower leg out with my left hand and his upper down with my right.

There was a sickening crack as I shattered the knee, the ligaments of his leg giving way like overstretched rubber bands as I rose again, left hand still ripping upward, right hand pressing down. The gout of blood that shot out showed how successful the move had been.

I tore the lower limb entirely free, highly pressurized blood fountaining out as I blocked the adder-strike and twisted around him as he tumbled sideways, the sallow-skinned motherfucker going into shock.

He collapsed onto the cavern floor on his left side, hands instinctively going to the fountaining bloody wound. I flipped the severed half-limb over, clutching it by the boot, and slammed it down hard on his skull.

His head bounced off the stone below him with a wet smack, the dazed look in his eyes hinting at a concussion forming, before the remains of his tibia smashed into his nose, spreading it across the front of his skull.

"That's for Stephanos!" I snarled, slamming it down again, getting a satisfying crunch of bone from the wound. "That's for my friend!" I hit him again. "That's for being fucking ugly!" I smacked it down again, snarling as the tibia snapped halfway down, the upper half flying off into the darkness.

"And this…" I growled, discarding the remnants of his leg and dropping onto his chest and punching him. "…is for me…" *Punch.* "…because…" *Punch.* "…I…" *Punch.* "…want…" *Punch.* "…a…." *Punch.* "…vacation…!" I paused, looking down at the shattered skull, hammered into a mess of bloody bone, muscle, and teeth, and I paused, realizing I wasn't making much sense.

Then it moved.

I was bucked off its body, sent rolling across the floor, and I came to my feet, staring open-mouthed as it shifted. One bloody eye on a stalk that slithered up from the mess, regarding me in fury and fear, before the creature that had been pretending to be a Drow staggered, its one good leg holding it upright while a ropey mess of sinew unfolded from the torn off limb, reaching down towards the floor.

I shook my head, stunned, but still coldly furious as whatever this *thing* was as it clearly prepared to flee.

"No," I said, the word slipping out. I lunged forward. I reached out as it tried to dodge, summoning a Fireball in my right hand. My finger curled through the somatic components as I snarled, my left hand clutching and squeezing the creature's throat, holding it down as its hands flailed at my armor, the arms slowly growing longer, chisel-like points protruding through the ends of the fingers. A sound like a steel knife being dragged down a chalkboard rose as it gouged thin lines down my cuirass.

I slammed the growing Fireball into the remains of its face, and it squealed, a high-pitched and unearthly sound before trying to retreat into its own chest.

"Fine by me," I hissed, shoving my hand into the cavity left by the retreating flesh-beast-thing. It quivered as flames poured out at all angles.

The beast held on for three more seconds before the death's head bloomed into existence, and the body changed. Where before he'd appeared human, or like a dark Elf anyway, he'd changed. The leech-like thing that was clearly inside him showed itself before it collapsed into ash, the apparently normal flesh crumbling like sand, seemingly all at once as the lifeforce was destroyed.

I collapsed, panting over the remains, and growled, the Fireball in my hands still shivering as though pleading to be released.

I straightened, looking around. The coordination of the waves of undead had broken up, and the creatures suddenly seemed intent on battling each other as their controlling SporeMothers were freed. I lifted the bottom of my helm and spat a gobbet of blood on the floor as my gaze fell on the pair that had stood near the doorway that led out of the cavern.

They were watching me in shock.

I hurled the Fireball aside, slamming it into a SporeMother to my left, and making it scream as I pointed one finger at them.

Then I flipped my naginata up into the air, catching it with my other hand and I spoke in a whisper, somehow knowing they'd hear me. "You, my son...you're fucking next," I told the Dwarf, sighting down my finger.

They looked at each other before sprinting for the door. I wanted to give chase. Hell, I wanted to slaughter everything in this fucking room, but I made myself pause.

I checked my mana and grunted, thankful for the massively increased manapool that was only now reaching the halfway point, and I crouched, sifting through the piled ash and random crap that littered the floor.

The creature I'd fought had been horrific, but...I wished I'd examined it before I faced it, him, whatever. A thought occurred to me, and I pulled up the kill list, grinning to myself in satisfaction as I saw the description.

Congratulations!

You have killed the following:
- 124x DarkSpore-Infected Slum Dwellers of various levels for a total of 121,455xp
- 136x DarkSpore of various levels for a total of 9,220xp
- 1x Elder Vampyr, level 68 for 308,483xp

A party under your command killed the following:
- 2x SporeMother of various levels for a total of 195,000xp
- 591x DarkSpore of various levels for a total of 38,100xp
- 562x DarkSpore-Infected Slum Dwellers of various levels for a total of 550,465xp

Total party experience earned: 783,565xp
As party leader you gain 25% of all experience earned
Progress to level 36 stands at 1,581,635/2,135,000

The fact I'd earned over four hundred thousand experience from this one fight so far was awesome, and a secondary pop-up opened, letting me know I had more experience waiting from the fight above ground as well. I checked it quickly before dismissing it, not needing to see the damn horses and people I'd killed to get to here. I paused only as I saw the description of the Demon prince Al'ser'neshaan and that my people had killed him. I guessed that was the big bastard who we cut in half with the portal, and he'd given me a shitload of experience, even with it being reduced so that was great. I dismissed the other details as well and simply nodded as I looked at the bottom line.

Progress to level 36 stands at 3,188,702/2,135,000

*

Congratulations!

You have reached level 36!

You have 7 unspent Attribute points and 0 Meridian points available.

Progress to level 37 stands at 983,702/2,360,000xp

Hitting level thirty-six was obviously great, but we were in the middle of storming a damn city, and I didn't have time to allocate my new points now. They'd have to wait for later. I knew I should be excited about leveling up, but since a large chunk of the experience was from killing deluded fools who most likely thought they were protecting their family, it wasn't something I was particularly happy about.

More importantly though, was the detail I'd been looking for. The fucknugget I'd just fought, Cletus, had been an Elder Vampyr, this world's equivalent of a vampire, despite apparently being at least half fucking leech as well, judging from his last seconds of life.

I spared three seconds to use the knowledge that Amon had crammed into my mind ages ago, and recreated a simple wind spell named Zephyr. Just a strong breeze, but it blasted the dust and ash that was all that was left of him away, and I swept up his possessions, grinning to myself as I spotted two rings that were of similar design to those I'd seen before.

I popped two rings off—one which gave +3 to my Endurance and Strength, and my old Ring of Pain that'd I'd gotten off the rogue I fought in the Tower back when I first claimed it—and slid them on in their place, swallowing hard as the cavern seemed to zoom out, rolling away from me, before slamming back into focus, compete with a new sense of thousands of lifeforms.

Every one of those lifeforms screamed as one as I applied a little mental gymnastics to make them stop in their tracks.

I straightened up, looking around and seeing that, in my distraction, there were a dozen DarkSpore infected undead close by, clearly headed for me…until I used the slave collars on their mistresses to stop them.

Across the entire cavern, every single SporeMother, DarkSpore, and undead had come to an abrupt halt, while the Legion who had been frantically battling them, closing their ranks to form a new, far less secure shieldwall, known as a turtle for some fucking reason.

I saw the scene through a million eyes. The world spun around me as I sagged to sit on my ass on the floor with a thump.

"Alright, you cockbags, let's get this sorted," I muttered, smiling. "Yeah, that'll do."

The SporeMothers moved to stand side by side, forced by the magic of the collar to obey, and conditioned from wearing them from nigh on birth, to simply respond as they were ordered rather than fight it.

Four SporeMothers still lived of the original six and the three that had been hidden. Lucian yanked his sword out of the skull of the fifth while I watched, and a shocked silence filled the cavern. Before the legionnaires' very eyes, all four SporeMothers, along with over a thousand undead, began to shuffle and dance along to "I'm a Little Teapot."

They did the routine twice before Bane appeared next to me, crouching and shaking his head.

"I knew that was you," he said, reaching out and helping me to my feet as I grinned at him. "What possessed you to make…*them*…do that dance?"

"Thought it'd be funny, to be honest." I shrugged as he guided me along, the strain of the multiple viewpoints making it difficult to control them all and walk at the same time.

I concentrated, determined that it couldn't be like this for slavers normally, surely. The sensory input dialed back, letting me see out of my own eyes only, and I sighed with relief.

"Well, that was fucking weird." I straightened and stopped the cavorting undead and the creatures of nightmares.

"*You* think it was weird?" Bane asked. "One moment, I'm slitting a SporeMother's throat. The next, they all stop then start dancing. Imagine how weird it was for all of us!"

"You thought you'd broken them, didn't you?"

He shrugged. "It happened literally right after I slit one's throat…I did wonder if I'd done something."

"Well, there's good news and bad," I said as I looked at the rings on my fingers, thankful I'd had the presence of mind to slide the rest of his gear into a bag.

"Oh Gods…tell me you're keeping your clothes on, at least."

"For now, yeah, so fuck you." I grinned. We picked up speed, jogging over to rejoin the Legion. As we went, rather than dodging in and out of the hundreds of undead, I mentally ordered them to step aside. They did, shuffling to one side or the other and leaving us a wide corridor to run through. The staring eyes and gnashing teeth of the undead made it a weird trip.

By the time I'd reached the others, I'd been able to feel Oracle's mixture of amusement and irritation for a few minutes. The first thing that I did when the turtle split apart to admit us was take her in my arms and kiss her soundly as she tugged my helm up and out of the way.

She cuddled in for a few seconds, then straightened and glared at me, fingering the deep scratches in my armor and the still-damp bloody marks on the cloth here and there.

"Explain," was all she said, but I smiled and nodded, gesturing for Augustus and the others to crowd in closer. Lucian stood at the back of my squad, politely at first. Then he pushed his way through urgently as I spoke.

"I saw the trap, but before I could do more than signal it to Oracle, the world flipped. I was smashed into the ceiling, then it turned over again, and I was slammed into the floor. Turns out the fuckers at the back were advanced magic users. They had control of the SporeMothers and the undead, and…" I paused, looking at Lucian. "The one I fought was an elder Vampyr."

"What was his name?" Lucian asked.

I frowned, remembering. "Cletus something…"

"Thane?" he demanded. "Cletus *Thane*?"

"Uh, yeah," I said. "You know him?"

"He was one of the guards sent to serve my brother, Akanji," Lucian whispered, stunned. "I believed the chance to face any of them was long lost to me…yet here…" His words broke off as he looked at me. "What happened? Where did he go?"

"Oh, that fucker's dead. Seriously, don't worry about him. But when I killed him, he didn't go easily. Like, there was some kind of creature inside him, all rubbery tentacles, and…"

"The true Vampyr is a form of void-leech," Lucian explained. "It can subsume its form into that of a regular flesh and blood mortal, tearing its way free only in times of extreme risk, as it kills its host in doing so. The Vampyr itself isn't sentient, but the changes it makes to the host are permanent, a shifting in their willingness to kill, a hunger for battle that grows into a hunger for flesh and blood.

"The more that hunger grows and is assuaged, the more the Vampyr affects its host's mind. I am a half-Vampyr, a Dhampyr. The true variant is much, much more powerful than I am, and my refusal to feed has reduced my own Vampyr in capacity."

He laid it all out, clear as day for those listening, obviously used to having to explain such things and totally unwilling to hide anything.

"And Akanji?" I asked, before shuddering as I released the Mana Overdrive, and Oracle healed me free of the debuffs that flared in existence.

"He embraced the life as a Vampyr, while not a true one, not being the offspring of a pair of true-blooded such creatures, he will be powerful beyond any other. When I first began hunting him, before he learned to hide himself, I found traces, evidence that he was hunting his own kind, feeding on them and using that to grow more powerful. I...I don't know if I am hopeful he is here in truth, so that we might face him, or terrified of what that would mean."

"Well, that Cletus fucker had the rings on that control these fuckers," I said gesturing to the SporeMothers. "And there were two others with him, a Dwarf and a Drow woman."

"The Dwarf, a regular Dwarf or...?"

"Black-skinned. Hey, is that like a racist thing here? I mean, I've seen Dwarves with light or tanned skin, but never a black one," I asked, interrupting myself with a thought.

"The Ebony Dwarves are rarer in these lands, their home being the islands on the far side of the Empire, but there were two in the guard...and the female Drow." He closed his eyes, shaking his head slowly. "That will be Meirin, Former First Lady of Moonhold, one of his other followers." He looked at me then, straightening up and taking a deep breath.

"Lord Scion," Lucian declared formally. "I charge you, as the highest authority in the land, to cleanse the corruption of the Vampyr from these lands.

"I will submit to any punishment by association you desire, but please, a nest of this kind has not been seen in centuries. Here, a nest is found before it can grow to encompass the land, and so, too, are found those who can oppose it. It is for this the Empire was founded. To protect the innocent, to punish the guilty, only one such force is capable of doing what must be done, and that is the Legion."

You have been offered a Quest!

Cleanse the land of the scourge of the Vampyr!
You have been offered a quest by your follower Lucian D'Aquitaine, to find his brother Akanji and all those the renegade has infected. For each Vampyr killed you will gain bonus experience.

*

DIVINE QUEST ISSUED!

Sint, God of Light and Order declares the Vampyr infection to be against all that He exists for and has upgraded your quest from a personal quest to a Divine Quest!

*

You have been offered a Divine Quest!

Cleanse the land of the scourge of the Vampyr!

You have been offered a quest by the God Sint to find and kill Akanji and all those he has infected, save the Chosen of Sint. For each Vampyr killed, you will gain additional bonus experience and Stat Points!

Accept? *Yes/No*

I accepted it. Hell yes, I'd fucking accept it, Stat points?! I was on that like a Kardlassian on media coverage, a Scotsman on free whisky, or hell, a Frenchman on a white flag.

I took a deep breath and called out so that the entire group could hear it clearly.

"Did you all get that quest?" I asked, and a barrage of nods and smiling faces shone back at me. "Then let's go kill some Vampyr!" I shouted, seeing the excitement, hope, and pain on Lucian's face before he could hide it.

"Right, no sense in us losing any of the Legion, not when we've got some disposable shock troops as well," I declared, concentrating. I gestured to the SporeMothers. They turned as one, the mass of undead sprinting away, all headed for the doorway the buggers ran out of.

"Hell, that's going to be a nasty surprise for them," Grizz muttered.

"Especially as the only Dhampyr that can use the kind of weapons that are most effective against them is Lucian," I said, resting my hand on his shoulder as we all started to break up in readiness to run. "Seriously, Lucian, you can't control your birth, and you've nothing to fear from the Empire or her people. Never again, brother," I said firmly.

After a pause, the tension left his shoulders. I smiled, gesturing to the mass racing ahead of us.

"This is your life-long quest, my friend, want to lead the way?" I asked.

Lucian grinned in earnest, setting off with a shout. "Legion…ADVANCE!"

CHAPTER FIFTY-SIX

We raced behind Lucian, feet practically flying over the uneven floor of the cavern, quickly catching up to the undead, even as those who had been farthest from the group reached the entrance. I focused on them, seeing the world through their senses, as the eyes didn't really convey the same function in a DarkSpore-controlled creature.

I frowned, slowing unconsciously as a sense of solidity filled my mind, the DarkSpore following a gap in the solid matter, my brain parsing that into the doorway. It followed a trail, one that only a creature such as it would see…a miasma of sweat particles, gently floating skin and scents, but over all of that, a glorious warmth that signified life emerged, even as twisted and feral as a Vampyr one.

The DarkSpore stumbled along. I frowned, ordering it to go faster and feeling the resistance. The creature wanted to hold onto its flesh puppet, but it discarded it at the command relayed from the SporeMother. Suddenly, it raced ahead as the corpse collapsed along with hundreds of others.

I stopped it when it reached the halfway mark, the conversion of DarkSpore in the undead discarding their flesh, keeping half to fight physically. But the DarkSpore clouds flashed forward with terrifying speed now they were free, blurring over occasional fissures that sent heated steam and glowing vapor into the cavern from below.

Almost five hundred of them sank into the doorway and dashed along the corridors, hunting the Vampyr.

I slowed even further, stumbling along now, guided by Oracle on one side and Grizz on the other. The Legion slowed to huddle in around me, protecting me as I stared through the senses of my new hunting spirits.

The corridor beyond split off into two more, then three. At each intersection, I sent the others searching, DarkSpore silently flying down them, as the rest of the Legion and I followed the primary source of life.

It took a dozen turns in the corridor, then smaller rooms, buildings, and out into another cavern. They were small but still far larger than I'd have suspected existed under Himnel, before exiting the ruins and entering well-repaired buildings.

The DarkSpore entered a doorway then vanished, a sense of pain flaring, then that was it, gone. I snarled, sending more and more.

As the handful became dozens, became a hundred, I finally saw what was killing them. A figure in black and red leather, wearing a mask that entirely covered its face, only the thinnest slits for eyes. It blazed with suppressed lifeforce, to my spirit-riding vision, magical weapons spinning and killing as the DarkSpore tried to pass it.

I changed their order instantly, sending them to possess it, and the result was spectacular.

It took another hundred, but in less than a minute, the figure stood again, shifting its body as multiple DarkSpore merged together inside the body, an evolution fighting to occur, but restricted by my orders. I sent more of the DarkSpore down the corridor, followed by the stealthy fucker, knowing somehow that we were closing in on the fleeing pair and forcing myself to hurry.

Behind us, the first few undead were filing in, but the SporeMothers were too large, making me split a section of my attention aside. As for the fuckers to have been used on the airships, there had to be a way out, so I sent all but a hundred of the undead to follow the SporeMothers and wait by the exit when they found it.

The other hundred or so I let follow us, figuring they'd be a way to tell if we were being sneaked up on, if nothing else.

Fifteen minutes passed in a blur, and I sensed we were passing away from the city we'd put so much effort into getting under, but these fuckers were just ahead now, and I had a greyhound-like focus on chasing them…

Greyhound.

Chasing a rabbit.

A rabbit that always just kept ahead of the pack…

"Fuck, it's a trap!" I snapped out, ordering them back and opening my eyes fully, looking around in horror at the room we were passing through.

At my cry, the advancing legionnaires came to a skidding halt, shields swinging up and locking into place. We all rushed into formation, shields slamming together with a crash of steel and the *whoomph* of triggering magic.

The sense I had of the DarkSpore started winking out in groups. I frantically ordered the stealth assassin to hide itself and to return to the cavern, even as I felt something through the bond. First one, then more of the SporeMothers shivered in my mind, their imprinted senses and the feeling of hatred for all life that characterized them growing fuzzy.

I ignored all the undead with them, focusing in on the SporeMothers themselves, wrapping them tightly in my mind and holding on tight, even as a sinister laugh echoed down from overhead somewhere, the room we were in the middle of slowly brightening as more and more magelights were fed power.

"Well done, little Scion," came a deep voice, along with the "slap, slap, slap" of idly clapping hands. *"You sensed the trap just in time. Still, don't feel too superior. After all, you still led your people into the middle of it,"* The voice sighed as if amused but regretful. *"After all, despite all the wonderful meat that will be wasted, you still managed to lead them into an ambush."*

We glared out through the small gaps in the turtle meant for this, waiting…and saw nothing.

Nothing at all.

Muttering started up, then irritable shifting as people tried to make out the threat without weakening the overall shield. While they grumbled, I held on tight to the SporeMothers, feeling the tingling, feather-like touches of another mind trying to pry them loose of my control.

The rings conferred control of them, I knew. They were a central point for the magic to draw back to. For a brief second, I considered using the abilities of the slave collar to simply kill the SporeMothers, reducing the risk to us and the realm. After all, I couldn't lose control of something that was fucking dead.

"Your armor is loose. Hold still," came a familiar voice from behind me, and I did as I was bid, not even thinking about it.

I glanced over at Bob, standing in the middle of the turtle, the only one of us that appeared unbothered by the wait. I wondered at that, hearing the normally phlegmatic legionnaires starting to snap at one another…

Pain!

Horrific pain tore through my lower back as something cut through my kidneys, ripping sideways and through bowel and more, before lodging between bones in my spine, and I tumbled forward, eyes flaring wide in shock and pain. A hand yanked at the dagger that was stuck in my spine.

The world moved in slow motion, the pain fighting with the Hyper-Cognition that triggered automatically under the strain.

The temporal effect of the Hyper-Cognition meant that the horrific sawing sensation seemed to simply slow and drag out. Blood pulsed with every beat of my heart, the spray hitting the inside of my armor and rebounding against flesh. The armor that had been "adjusted" had been the scalemail that covered the sections where the solid metal couldn't, lest I be restricted in a duck-like waddle.

Someone had separated it out to allow them access to my lower back, and I'd fucking LET them!

The Legion went absolutely fucking nuts. Amidst the uproar, the blur that was Augustus moved from my right, sword swinging. Lydia's wings snapped out, and her mace crashed against something metallic.

A scream of fury rang out, and Restun was there above me like he'd fucking teleported, his gladius extended over me. Oracle caught me and tried to support me as light suddenly bathed the inside of the turtle, announcing Lucian's greatsword, Justice, making its appearance.

There were a few seconds of grunts as more and more clearly acted. Then, a head hit the floor next to me, bouncing up and rolling over in slow motion.

I frowned, the sight not making any sense, especially as I recognized the Legion helm that covered most of his head. Then the world slammed back into normal speed as healing magic flared to life in my back, making me hiss in pain, as I was lowered the rest of the way to the ground.

"What? Did you think that those foolish Oaths were keeping you safe?" the voice gloated.

"The Oaths can be forsworn, boy. All that was needed was for the correct Oaths to be sworn in their place, for the heart to be dedicated and true, and a boring Imperial legionnaire becomes a Dark Legionnaire of Nimon! The Chosen of the God of Death!"

I hissed in pain as a voice told me to hold on and that the blade was stuck. I felt the first exploratory tug, then the hand being pressed to my back, the other hands angling me this way and that. I tried to keep from pissing myself, the pain was that bad, tingling running down my legs in waves as the spinal column slowly rubbed against the sharpened edge. The tell-tale warning of the skull and crossbones for poison appeared in my HUD.

"Motherfucker!" I snarled, gritting my teeth and hissing out my pain as I was held still and the dagger was slowly extracted.

There were long seconds where I felt terror filling me. A legionnaire had done this, a legionnaire whose voice I'd recognized. It could have been anyone…what if others were out to get me, too?

What if the one holding the knife now was readying themselves to drive it deeper?

I managed to look up, forcing myself as doubt filled me, and pain tore through me. Oracle stared into my eyes, and her love smothered my doubt. Her trust filled me, washing away what could have become an issue as she pushed memories into the front of my mind.

Grizz looking embarrassed as he slipped Yen a sorry-looking, bedraggled flower when he thought nobody could see. The pride on Augustus' face as Hellenica sat holding his hand at the dining table, the way he watched the Djinn, and the half-hopeful, half-mirthful way he responded to their requests as Clan Father.

I remembered Denny chasing me out of danger so that he could face the Dark Legion alone, to protect *ME.* Blowing himself up, the mad fucker, literally half-*cooking* himself in the process.

I saw the looks on the faces of Augustus and his squad, backed by the Narkolt legionnaires as they spread out around me, coming to my rescue when I found Thomas.

I watched these and a thousand more things. Romanus, Restun, Yen, Tang, Westin, Holt…they streamed past in a split second and were gone. The fear and paranoia being pushed at me broke on a tide of hope.

I didn't fear my legionnaires. That would be fearing my fingers, or Thomas. They were my brothers and sisters, sons and daughters. Hell, I looked up to some of them like the father and uncles I'd never had, Restun and Romanus especially, with Augustus more like the cool older brother.

I loved them all, and if Nimon had turned someone, well, He was a shitbiscuit all right, but He was a God as well. He'd have His ways.

Oracle smiled at me, knowing what was going through my mind. I took a deep breath as she moved around, examining my wound and taking over from whoever was healing me at the minute. Restun slid in before me, crouching down, and reaching out, taking my hand as I hissed in pain.

"Jax…I…this is my fault," he whispered, almost too low for me to hear.

"Bullshit," I hissed, before the horrible feeling of Scour tore through me, even as a blade opened me again. Oracle's mind melded to mine, showing me that it was her, opening the wounds again to make sure that she could purge the poisons.

I shook, quivering as she glanced at Augustus, who shifted the blade for her, gracefully cutting the healed skin, but with purpose and smoothly, rather than the hacking that had been done originally.

When the creeping, burning sensation of Scour died away this time, I felt new healing being done, guided by Oracle. The poisoned symbol winked out as my health started to climb.

"No, this is my failure…" Restun whispered, rolling the head over so that I could see it.

"Alistor," I muttered, then I laughed as I canceled the Hyper-Cognition.

"You cannot trust them, for…why are you laughing!" the voice snarled. I realized it'd been going on for ages; I'd just been ignoring it.

"Oh, shut your cock holster!" I shouted, wincing as I shifted, itching and burning as my people applied more healing. "You want me to distrust my *legionnaires*? Really? You expect me to distrust them on the back of Nimon managing to turn fucking *Alistor* to his side? Hell, it's like assuming I'd be upset because the sea was wet! He was a useless turd!"

I struggled, and the others helped me up, Restun loosening his grip on my hand. But I clung on, looking into his eyes.

"Don't you dare doubt yourself," I ordered him. "I trust you." I took a deep breath, then grinned as I realized that I had a great way to prove this and to show the asshole out there that I didn't fear him.

"Help me get out of this," I said to Restun. He frowned until I tapped the cuirass again and locked eyes. "Restun, I need to do this."

He nodded after a slight pause.

The next two minutes passed in a blur as I tried to catch my breath, ignoring the voice as he wombled on about being powerful and terrible, and I downed a potion of Legionnaire's Might.

"Gods, that tastes like ass," I muttered. Oracle was watching me carefully, aware from her place in my mind what I was going to do. "Remember our first night in each other's arms?" I asked her.

"I do. I gave you the choice of rest and recovery or downing one of those and fucking my brains out."

"Couldn't get the top off the bottle fast enough," I admitted to the round of unsure laughter that rose around me.

"Right then, you lot!" I called out, standing there stripped to the waist, the only armor on me covering my legs and my helm. "I know that wanker out there is trying to get me to distrust you, and to get all of you to distrust each other. I can feel his shitty little attempts to fuck with my mind. Kinda feels like my ex-girlfriend, but that's a story for another day," I joked, grinning around.

"Now, I don't care what Fuckface Von-Shitstick says, because I do trust you. Each and every one of you. That..." I tapped Alistor's side with a boot. "...was the only legionnaire I've ever met that I was unsure of. I had no clue why he was a legionnaire, because it seemed like all he wanted was to complain about everything. That's fine, though. There are times when we all want shit to be different. I'm viewing it that the God of Death, the wanker that He is, messed with his mind and got him to forswear the Oaths. That's the kinda shit He does, and I don't care to look any closer. The truth is, you're all my brothers and sisters.

"Back home, there's a saying: 'Put your money where your mouth is.' It means, basically, that all the mouthing off in the world is fucking worthless unless you back it up by actually following through.

"So here I am. I've taken my armor off and made it easier to reach my heart. Here's your chance. If anyone else wants to make a play for me, you'll never have a better chance to do it," I said, the close quarters of the turtle meaning that they were practically all in striking distance, and they were all heavily armed.

A full minute passed, then I laughed and shouted out to the voice that kept on muttering bollocks that I'd entirely stopped listening to, which was clearly frustrating it to no end.

"Right then! Now that my Legion know I trust them with my life, despite your little trick, and that you're full of shit, perhaps you can step out, and I'll ram a little something up your arse, eh?" I offered the cavern, shaking my naginata in the air as Restun and Augustus split the turtle sidewall, letting me step out, the pair of them flanking me and Lucien and Lydia following. "Come on, don't be shy, I promise to not be gentle!"

Grizz made to follow, as did many of the others, but Oracle stopped them, shaking her head.

The five of us strode into the middle of the room and paused.

"Well, come on then," I said, as though bored. "I mean, fuck's sake, Akanji, I know you're a coward, but do you really…" I broke off as a figure dropped from the ceiling where it'd been disguised, flipping over, landing on its feet, and glowered at me.

"Where did you hear that name?" it whispered, clearly curious.

"And there we go!" I said, resting my naginata against my shoulder and chest and doing a long, slow golf clap. "Ladies and gentlemen, the shittiest bad-guy arrival in the history of the realm." I cocked my head to one side as I stopped clapping.

"Wait, you thought we didn't know? You thought that you were this great stealthy motherfucker that had hidden forever? Nah, mate. You just weren't worth the trip before," I said, bullshitting for all I was worth. "We're here to sort the city, Barabarattas, AND the Dark Legion out, as well as kick a God off the continent. That's the only reason we're going to kill you, as well."

"Don't worry, though, we think of you as not so much an afterthought, but as an appetizer. You're the shitty little lemony-sorbet course in a good meal. You're all right, but not something you'd bother with unless it was included in the deal."

"You *dare*…" he hissed, eyes glowing in fury.

"Oh, I dare all right. I'd love to beat you like a red-headed stepchild."

He lunged forward, blurring past speeds that even I could see, a black blade that seemed to suck in the light suddenly extended and aimed for my heart…

…only to be smashed aside as Lucian matched his speed, lunging between us and deflecting the strike, his own greatsword suddenly unsheathed and bringing a bright white light to the room.

"Unfortunately, your arse is spoken for," I said, grinning and trying to hide the utter relief that Lucian was as fast as I had hoped. "Chief Justicar Lucian, Pride of the Legion, Champion of Sint, the God of Light, and all-round top fucking banana, would you like to do the honors?"

"Thank you, Lord." Lucian said through gritted teeth, glaring into the hate-filled eyes of his opponent. "This has been a long time coming, Akanji." He cursed as it threw back its hood, exposing its face. "It's not him!"

"Little Lucian," the Vampyr murmured, straightening up and looking down at him. "My, how you've grown." He smiled then, a predatory, unpleasant smile that made it clear the kind of creature he was. "It's been a long time, hasn't it? Tell me, did the Legion tell you about your father? About the way they found him and how he amused us in his final hours?"

"They told me enough. They told me you all killed him," Lucian said in a low, fierce tone.

"Oh, we didn't kill him. No, we had a little fun, and he was just too soft to survive the party, that was all. But then, he always was a weakling."

"He was a good man who tried his best to help people. He even tried to raise your master, hate-filled creature that he was, and I recognize you now…Nikolai."

"He was a coward and a failure!" Nikolai snarled. "A weakling who begged to be allowed to die! A coward who wept when we roasted little Anna, too weak even to end her life when she begged her daddy to save her. He was given the choice, you know?

"All he had to do was embrace the Dark Gift and feed on his wife, and we'd have spared the brat. He refused, so I changed her personally, let the blood take hold, then we spitted and roasted her alive, feeding my master's followers choice bits, while her body tried to regenerate! We killed her and her father's pathetic group over *days,* Lucian. You thought the Legion arrived in time to help? We'd already grown bored and left! Your precious Legion did what it always did, too little and too late!"

Lucian stared at him for several long heartbeats, then he sighed. "There is truly nothing left of the child that Akanji corrupted left in there, and that is a relief," he said finally. "I care not what lies you come up with. I am here to remove a stain from the family honor, a blight on the name of all those who came before me and those who lived after. You are a disgrace to the name of your father, and I strip the name of Nikolai Vanetti from you. You are not worthy of the name of that child."

I felt the mana being drawn in around us, and I smiled as the realm itself accepted the right of the Chief Justicar of the Empire to strip the name from this figure. The effect on Nikolai was immediate as he hesitated a brief second before hissing in fury.

"You think I care? You think it matters to me that I no longer bear the name that a weakling bestowed on a small boy? I have spent centuries as…"

"Shitstick," I declared, interrupting them.

"What?" the former Nikolai hissed.

"If the Chief Justicar of the Empire can strip your name from you, then you must have been a citizen of the Empire when you were named. As such, I can give you a new one. Forevermore, I formally declare your name to be Shitstick." I dismissed the notification that popped up without reading it. Since it wasn't a global or continental one, I could do that. I grinned as Shitstick's eyes widened in abject fury.

"Now, even if you somehow escape, everyone's gonna know your name, bitch." I winked at him.

"You *DARE*…" he snarled.

Lucian, on the other hand, grinned. "Let's finish this, Shitstick," he said, whipping the sword around and going for his opponent's face.

Shitstick blocked it, the dead black blade creating a cascade of sparks as the bright, gleaming blade of Justice ran down it, before punching out, one handed and aiming for Lucian's face.

Lucian leaned aside, then whipped the blade around in a flat arc, lifting from low, almost touching the ground, to flashing past Shitstick's head. The light the blade emitted was clearly unpleasant for the Elder Vampyr, but far less effective than it had been against the SporeMothers.

I looked up, a motion catching my eye, four more shadows crawling from crevices in the rocky ceiling.

"Above us!" I called, taking a two-handed grip on my naginata and grinning as the others readied themselves. "Oi!" I shouted up at the creeping figures. "You're shit at stealth!" I told them, knowing damn well that Bane and Tang were hiding here somewhere.

The figures froze before dropping down, flipping over as they fell and landing on their feet, staring at us with a mixture of disdain and hunger.

"It's been many centuries since such a rich meal wandered in and offered itself so freely," the pale-skinned Drow woman said, her voice rich and refined.

"You're…wait, give me a minute," I said, frowning, pointing a finger at her and closing one eye.

"Meirin!" Oracle called.

"Ah crap, yeah, forgot the name, sorry. So, want to have your name changed?" I asked her. "Little Miss Useless. Oh, no, what about Trixiebell?"

She screamed in rage, lunging forward, hands outstretched and fingers lengthening as broad, sharp nails extended from them.

I frowned and whipped the blade of my naginata in a circle, slamming light magic into it and bringing daylight to the cavern to twin with the steady, comforting, to us at least, light of Justice.

She flinched back, clearly discomforted by the light, then dropped, spinning and kicking my legs out from under me as the naginata whistled over her head.

I had a split second to trigger Hyper-Cognition again, the world slowing slightly as my mind sped up, and I triggered Mana Overdrive immediately afterward. My reactions sped up to almost the right speed as I released my weapon with my right hand, gripping it tightly in my left, punching out and slamming the palm of my right hand down flat against the ground, then pushing off, flipping myself over her.

She lashed out again, her fingers sliding through the air close enough to my face that I could have kissed them as they slid past.

I somersaulted over her, landed on my feet, and spun to face her. Whipping the bladed end of my naginata around low, I aimed for a few inches off the ground.

She straightened like a graceful Olympic gymnast and stepped over the blade, literally moving for all the world as though I was mired in treacle, even with my blended skills making me fast enough that I blurred to the rest of the world.

"Good try, meat!" she snarled, her mouth opening wide, then wider and wider as the sides of her jaw split apart, a line tearing down the front of her skull. A mass of teeth slid forward, aimed for my face.

I brought my left hand up, the Hyper-Cognition enough that, while I couldn't cast a spell at this speed, I could do something else.

My left palm flared to life as I slammed it out, bitch-slapping the hideous creature and sending her reeling. Instead of tearing my face off, she was hit by my activated Shield tattoo.

"Weren't expecting that, were you!" I asked, grinning as my other tattoos flared to life. My chest and sides looked like I'd gone for a full-on Nordic design now. When I'd had to have them redone, after they'd literally peeled my skin off, I'd gone all out.

Both knuckles were covered with swirling patterns now, my right fist having Lightning and the left having Fire. The back of my hands had three identical lines of runic script following the gaps between the bones: Add, Speed, and Force. Basically, they added power and speed in the form of inertia to each blow. I hadn't dared to use them before now, not in training against Restun even, in fear that if they truly worked as I hoped, then I might do real damage to a partner.

But now?

"Let's fucking do this," I muttered, grinning evilly.

I dropped the naginata, the ringing clang of it hitting the stone floor and echoing through the room as I closed my right fist and delivered an uppercut that would have torn Tyson's head off.

My body was still lagging slightly behind my mind, but that was fine. The stunning effect of the Shock rune on my right knuckles had slowed her as well, and that meant I had just enough time to trigger separate tattoos then suck the power away from those I'd been using before, creating a rolling, flowing river of power flaring through my body.

Tattoos flared to life then died split seconds later, the power never quite reaching full, but that was fine. I was still experimenting, and I didn't want this to be over too fast.

She reeled backward, feet stumbling as my uppercut connected, the split-apart nature of her face robbing it of the ability to literally behead her, had the bone been intact. Instead, I pulled back my right hand, opening it wide, and triggered the symbols in it.

As they came to life, the Fire on my left fist flared, and I slammed it into her stomach, the Mana Overdrive combining with the Add, Speed, and Force runes to deliver a flaming punch that would have made Megatron apologize for spilling my pint.

She doubled over, the air leaving her in a great *whoosh* as her diaphragm folded around my fist. The snap of bones breaking echoed in the air.

I slapped my open right palm over her face, holding the split-toothed monstrosity closed as I powered three more symbols to full life.

Life, Drain, and Slow all took effect, slowing her down, weakening her as I started ripping the lifeforce out of her as I squeezed her head in my hand.

Her eyes opened wide as pain ripped through her. Her life ebbed away, while I felt stronger by the second. The lingering worn-out feeling that was always left over after a powerful healing vanished like fog burned away by the midday sun.

She reached up, her hands seeming to move at a quarter speed, and I contemptuously slapped them aside with my left, one at a time. She thrashed and quivered, trying to get free, even as she grew weaker and weaker.

I took the time to look over at the others, seeing Lucian and Shitstick still battling back and forth, while Lydia was working to get the mace out of the head of her opponent.

I grinned as she released it, then started to systematically smash the body as the leech-thing within tried to take over.

Oracle stepped forward, creating a powerful flare of flames and washing them over the writhing body, while Restun simply sliced the arms and legs off his opponent and kicked the screaming corpse into the fire as well.

Augustus was just insane. His Commander's Blade flashed as it parried and deflected the Dwarf with two blades, each attempt by the shorter figure resulting in blood flying as Augustus, almost contemptuously, flicked the blade across his face, the tops of his arms, the inside of his wrists.

The Dwarf was staggering around in a veritable pool of his own blood, while Augustus hadn't so much as moved his feet since the fight began. His sword literally just seemed to blur then stop, magically in exactly the place it needed to be, like Neo and the agent fighting. Once he'd learned his ability, it was just…parry, parry, cut, parry, parry, kill.

I turned back to the weakly struggling figure in my hands, and I sneered before drawing a dagger and cutting through her upper arms on either side, the limbs each sagging uselessly as she flailed.

Thirty seconds later, the corpse collapsed to dust. I shuddered, the last of the lifeforce sliding into me, making me feel fucking amazing.

I turned back to the others, seeing that there was only Shitstick left. As I watched, the bright white light of Justice drove him back again.

I grinned as I picked up my naginata and channeled mana into it, attuning it to Light and bathing the entire cavern in it.

Shitstick flinched and looked back instinctively, even as Augustus fed mana into his sword. A burgeoning sense of fear began to build in the Vampyr.

Lydia concentrated, and a divine presence radiated out from her. Others stepped up as more and more of the Legion summoned Magic Missiles to their hands. The golden light from them flooded the room, and while the light didn't seem to injure the Vampyr, it certainly wasn't welcome.

Neither was the thought of hundreds of missiles, either, as he started to look about for a way out.

Seconds later, he clearly thought he'd found it, as he deflected Lucian's thrust, then did a spin kick that staggered the legionnaire. While Lucian tried to recover, Shitstick yanked something from his belt and smashed it into the floor. The tinkle of glass shattered before a sudden blackness filled the room, as all mana was suppressed.

I grunted. The sudden, massive headache from the loss of my mana combined with the darkness, the silence, and a miasma that roiled out of the middle of the room. I fell to my knees before I could think twice, even as something flashed overhead, the ripping of the air my only hint.

There was a faint scream, then nothing as the world seemed to slowly slide away from me.

It only took seconds for the world to come back, but the majority of the Legion had never experienced the wonders of a mana loss migraine and were stumbling around as if drunk. I forced my eyes to focus, searching the room and seeing both Oracle and Bob were okay. Well, Bob was clutching his head, and Oracle was swearing like a sailor with his dick trapped in his zipper, so I figured that meant they were all right.

With that most pressing of fears assuaged, I turned back to the room, searching, seeing that the others were okay. Hell, even Lucian was, although he was clutching a bloody gash in his cheek as he looked around.

I scanned the room, looking from side to side, and finally I spotted the movement I was looking for. Bane strolled over from the far side of the cavern, dragging a mewling figure.

"I think this is yours," he said laconically as he released the ankle he'd been gripping, dropping the quivering lump of flesh on the floor before Lucian. Shitstick had clearly tried to rush past Bane in the darkness, not realizing that A: he was there, and that B: Bane was a crazy motherfucker with a knife.

Or four, in this case.

He'd driven a dagger into the base of Shitstick's neck, one into either arm at the shoulder, and one into his crotch. The Vampyr was shaking and quivering, clearly unable to make a sound for the dagger driven into the neck.

I couldn't help but laugh.

"Fuck, that ended poorly for you, didn't it?" I grinned, wandering over to stand over him as the others recovered. Oracle wormed her way in under my arm to stand with me, looking down at the badly wounded creature.

"Lucian, do you mind if you don't get to kill this one?" Oracle asked.

He smiled at her, his pained grimace abating as she guided a heal into his cheek, stitching the torn-open sides of his face back together with grace and magic.

"Of course, my Lady Wisp. Be my guest," he said.

"Thank you, Lucian…Sehran!" she called.

Sehran stepped out of the group, moving forward and looking between the pinned and disabled Elder Vampyr and Oracle, clearly excited and hopeful.

"Enjoy your meal, dear," Oracle said, gesturing Sehran to the quivering creature on the floor.

"Yes!" she cried, before lunging forwards and sweeping Oracle up in a hug and kissing her soundly. "Thank you, oh thank you so, so much!" she squealed before setting Oracle down and jumping up and down, hugging herself as she looked hungrily down at the figure that gagged in pain and outrage as it recognized what was happening.

"Go on, you enjoy yourself, Sehran," Oracle said with a smile, before turning back to the rest of the room. "Well? What are you waiting for?"

"Well, I think most of them are hoping she'll bend over in that outfit," I said, grinning around and noting how many legionnaires of both sexes pretended to have no clue what I was talking about, as I redressed. Although a few, Grizz of course being one of them, nodded and openly admired the view as Sehran winked saucily. "But regardless of that, and her fantastic arse, we need to move on, people. We've not got long before Horkesh attacks the north, so let's go."

"You heard Lord Jax!" Augustus boomed, gesturing at the turtle. "Break it up, check your gear. We move out in one minute!"

"Thanks, man," I turned to Lucian. "How you doing?" I asked him, pausing, then repeating myself.

"What?" Lucian asked, jerking as I touched his arm. "Oh, I apologize, Jax…I…" He shook his head and took a deep breath. "I apologize, what did you say?"

"I was asking if you were all right, mate."

He nodded, fingering the hilt of his sword. "I am, I just…it's been centuries since I last found a verifiable trace of Akanji."

"And now it looks like either he's here, or his servants are," I finished for him.

"It's him. Akanji never lets his people stray too far, never. He's a coward who keeps his strongest closest: Cletus, Nikolai, Meirin, all of them were his inner circle. I know of two others that I suspect were part of it as well, but that's it, the others." He shrugged. "There won't be many, but those who are left will be powerful and most likely flee now, rather than risk being exposed."

"Then we need to be quick."

"Which way?" Augustus asked.

I took a deep breath, projecting my voice so that they could all hear.

"Let's move it, people!" I called, gesturing back the way we came. "We need to get back up under the city; the caves can be explored another day!"

Lucian opened his mouth to object then closed it with a quiet clop, nodding his agreement.

We quickly fell in before pausing as I remembered the damn stealth assassin. I'd planned to use them earlier, but…the damn DarkSpore were writhing like crazy inside it, desperately trying to evolve or something, and I just couldn't be fucked with the hassle.

Then, because I'm an evil asshole, I puppeted the creature across to one of the glowing fissures in the room, made it wrap its arms and legs in tight, then jump in. Might kill it, might not, but either way, not my fuckin' problem for now.

Then, slightly amused, I turned, following the line of legionnaires as they headed back out of the room, Jian holding back with the rear guard to watch over Sehran as she fed, Grizz moving over close to me as he held out a bag.

"What's this?" I asked.

He shook his head in disgust.

"I know you're the boss and all, but still, you need to check your loot now and then. Remember, they were old as hell Vampyr, they'll have some amazing shit."

I smiled and nodded my thanks, reaching out and taking it, glancing at the inventory that popped up.

"Hmm, gold, platinum, some gems," I muttered, reading aloud as I scanned them. "Some old wine. Hell, this shit is six hundred years old!" I looked at it and shook my head. "Bet it's corked." I dismissed it, moving to a collection of blades, armor, and various rings and jewelry.

I hit three of the rings with my examination spell, each time getting back that they were too high a level for me to identify. I gave in and passed it to Lucian.

"Can you Identify these?" I asked, getting a nod as he started casting. It took him ten minutes, as we returned to the main cavern and started to search it before he was done, but eventually, he came to me.

"Most of it is cursed for any other than a Vampyr to use. That which isn't is either simple wealth or gems and personal items. The others, though? There are five weapons that are both powerful and valuable, and a single ring that could be useful."

Ring of Ghost Light		Further Description *Yes/No*	
Details:		This ring can be commanded to glow and will emit a gentle light, visible only to the wearer, that extends up to fifteen feet for one hour. Any invisible, stealthed or ethereal creatures inside of that radius will be exposed to the wearer's senses, appearing outlined in a gentle light that only the wearer can see.	
Rarity:	**Magical:**	**Durability:**	**Charge:**
Highly Rare	Yes	55/100	10/10

"Oh, hell fucking yes." I said, putting that ring on. "Thank you," I said fervently, even as I triggered it, seeing the outlines of Bane, Tang, Flux, Cheena, and someone who I assumed must be Lio, and…and someone else. Someone who was clambering across the ceiling slowly, limbs spread out and spidery, in the way they managed to cling to the seemingly solid stone of this low section of the cavern.

I froze, then made a point of looking around and sighing loudly.

"Damn, I thought I'd have been able to see you with this, Bane!" I called out. "It must only work against low-level stealth."

The figure on the roof had frozen, then slowly began to move again, inching along a few feet to the side and pausing, making me think they were testing to see if they'd been spotted.

I turned, looking off to the side of them, and ostensibly looking at something else, while I gestured randomly for Bane with my other hand, hidden behind my back.

He paused, and I gestured again, moving in closer as I slowed to a walk.

"What's wrong?" Bane whispered in a voice so low I could barely hear him, staying in stealth.

"Here. Middle of the roof," I mumbled, tugging the ring off and slipping it to him before pretending to pocket it.

The light vanished for me, but a second later, I heard a low growl from Bane and knew he'd seen the figure.

"Cover your ears," I said to the others around me, grinning as Bane appeared next to me, facing the ceiling.

He took a deep breath, then let rip with a hell of a powerful blast of worldsense. It was strong enough that even standing next to him and having pressed my helm hard to one side to cover that ear, the other hand pushed up inside my helm to cover the other ear, I could still hear and feel it.

The target of the blast, though, was totally unprepared and clutched at its ears reflexively before falling off the ceiling. It plummeted the twenty feet or so that this lower section reached and slammed into the floor with a grunt.

Instantly, the others were there, weapons leveled, as the figure emerged from stealth, the skin itself changing color from the gritty stone it'd been pressed against to a more normal flesh color. It groaned, cursing, looking up at us, its eyes rolling and adjusting independently.

"What the fuck are you?" Grizz muttered, looking down at the humanoid, who rolled over, growling and reaching for a scabbard strapped to its leg in one smooth motion.

"Not what…who!" it hissed, its voice distorted by a thick tongue. "Mine! You arrrre mineeee…but…Where issss he?" it snarled, starting to drag a blade free, before Lio kicked the hand free of the hilt, yanking it away and backing up, even as Cheena did the same on the other side.

"Who?" I asked, looking down at the figure.

"HIM!" it snapped, opening its mouth wide and making me take a step back, seeing twin rows of needle-like teeth. It snapped its head around, staring at Augustus. Taking advantage of the opportunity, I looked closer at its wildly twisting eyes, the pebble-dashed skin, the way it kept bobbing slightly, and the short, broad talons that tipped each finger, the weird suction cup ridges that filled the inside of each finger.

"You have him here, or ssssomewhere close by…we sssensssed him, sssensssed his clossseness, now he hidesss! Hidesss again!" it whispered, the voice clearly unstable. "You cannot keep ussss from him…better you give him up, yesss, give him up to usssss."

"I don't know who the fuck…"

"YOU!" It snapped its head around, locking eyes on me, and tilting its head to one side. "You are target assss well, you are…him…not him? Hunt you and HIM, like you! Sssmellsss like him…feelsss like him…. but, mussst tassste…" It took a bite out of the air before lunging, scuttling across the floor. It aimed for me with its mouth open, jagged, pointed teeth ready to bite.

It managed less than a meter, despite its speed and the surprise, before the Legion reacted. Lio slashed her short sword across the back of one leg, expecting to cut deep. But the blade met something like thick leather, rather than the expected soft flesh.

She snarled, whipping it back and plunging it into the back of the thigh, point-first, even as the others attacked, stabbing down and using the blade as an anchor to tow the figure backward.

Bane drove a dagger into the side of its throat, yanking down hard and opening the windpipe. Flux drove a spear into the side of its chest. The wide, leaf-bladed spear was razor sharp, and having seen Lio's effort with the slash, he added all his strength.

Still, it was barely enough. As the blade sank between the ribs, neatly bisecting the heart, Augustus lashed out with the Commander's Sword, slamming it down into the joint of the left upper arm and shoulder.

By the time I'd stepped back two paces and started to pull my naginata free of the bag, the fight was almost over.

"Just die, you fucker!" Grizz snapped, slamming his sword into the opposite shoulder. Lydia took two steps, then leaped, using all her force to slam her mace down into the small of its back, the clear *crack* echoing around the cavern.

The figure sagged, its eyes going wide, but still struggled, trying to reach me, dragging itself along with hands alone and trying to bite at me.

Then it collapsed, and I shook my head, looking down at the corpse.

"I think I'll keep the ring…if that's all right?" Bane whispered next to me.

"Yeah, man, keep it with my blessing," I said slowly, looking at Lucian, who'd crouched next to the creature and was examining a small design carved into the left hip, a raised collection of symbols that looked vaguely familiar.

"What was it?" I asked. "I didn't get the chance to examine him."

"An Elf," he said slowly. "A dark legionnaire Elf. And this…" He tapped the symbols. "…means we've got problems." Lucian straightened up and turned to me, looking around the room more carefully. "The SporeMothers, you've still got control of them, right?"

I nodded, mentally jabbing them to make sure of it, and signing in relief as they started to dance to "I'm a Little Teapot."

"Why?" I asked.

"Because if one of them has been made, there'll be others. I'll bet Justice that they're after Thomas and you," Lucian said, sighing, before he looked over at Augustus.

"The Dark Hunters roam again."

THOMAS

Thomas stumbled, righting himself as the ship lurched to one side. He growled, hurrying forward, holding to the railing with one hand as the ship lurched again and a fresh round of cannon-fire slammed into it.

"Fuck's sake, Tenandra!" he shouted. "Leave off!" Glancing around, Thomas made certain the other two who had boarded with him—well, the two who'd *managed* the jump—were right behind. Bas, a mountain of a man, had tried to make the jump as well, but he'd totally misjudged it. Rather than landing on the deck, he launched himself just as the warship had started to rise.

Bas had slammed into the railing and had fallen backwards, stunned. A despairing scream ended in the far-away sound of breaking branches. That was all that marked his passing.

Thomas grimaced at that thought, then looked to Nigret. The Trigara had pulled his boots off before they'd left Tenandra's deck, and his claws were keeping him safe as he sprinted across the deck, aiming for the wheelhouse.

"Go!" Thomas barked to Alistair, yanking hard on the railing and dragging himself after the cat-man, the pair of them slow by comparison.

The deck tilted wildly again, smoke billowing up from the hatches below decks as flames continued to spread. The Fireballs and Lightning, not to mention the giant-sized Magic Missiles of the second barrage of the ripple-fire cannons, had done a number on the enemy ship, even as it'd torn horrific wounds in the side of Tenandra's ship-body.

Of the two of them, Tenandra was the clear winner. She remained in the air under her own power, flames put out. Most of the legionnaires and crew were still alive, even if they were wounded, but three engines had been destroyed. Engines, not to mention bulkheads and more, were few and far between on the slowly burning Himnel craft.

All they had to do was land it in the river as gently as they could. Tenandra had assured Thomas that she could strip and integrate the parts she needed. Less than a day, she promised, and she'd be faster and stronger than ever before, or…possibly a week to limp back to the Tower and another to the city.

So, Thomas had led the wild attack onto the enemy ship, knowing damn well that not only were there still enemy crew aboard, but there were a fuck ton of them.

The plan therefore was simple. Direct the ship to the river, make sure the helmsman and the paladin were dead, land, and give the survivors the choice, fuck off and live, or stay and die.

Or at least it'd seemed simple and obvious on Tenandra's deck.

The deck tilted again, slowly rolling, and Thomas grabbed onto a stanchion, shouting to Alistair to do the same. The engines on the right side flared with power, something triggering it. The left pulsed and burned steadily, resulting in a slow barrel roll.

They hung on grimly as Nigret dove into the wheelhouse, a semi-circular half shell design that protected the helmsman from the elements. It usually let them either see out or have the sights around the ship projected in the room.

Just as the door slid shut behind Nigret, Thomas swore, having seen a flash of metal and a flash of light. A scream of pain echoed from his companion.

"Fuck!" Thomas cursed. The ship was entirely on its side now, and it paused in its roll, slowly heading towards the ground, picking up speed by the second. He swung himself forward. The posts that held the railing up were spaced that little bit too far apart to be able to use like school monkey bars, and instead he was forced to swing back and forth a few times, then leap, heart in his mouth, and grab the next.

After three such jumps, the momentum was enough. Thomas managed to jump one to another, then another, all the way across, before snarling to himself and letting go, falling the five feet or so to the wheelhouse.

He landed with a clatter of metal, his armor ringing and jingling, his new sword falling free to tumble away, heading down to the forest below.

"Shit…I literally just got that one," Thomas groaned, watching the metal glint as it fell end over end before vanishing into the trees below.

Above him, Alistair made his way across steadily, having clambered through the railing, and was now climbing above it. He made the much safer route across to the wheelhouse. Thomas cursed himself for being a fool, then decided that, if he was in for a penny, he might as well be in for a pound.

Reaching down around the edge of the room and just managing to flick the latch, he let gravity do the rest as the door fell open with a crash. Thomas took a good grip on the wooden edge of the wheelhouse, taking three quick breaths, before swinging himself around and in, seeing the greatsword flashing towards him at the last second and letting go to tumble into the room, landing hard atop a bleeding and unconscious Nigret.

"Die, rebel scum!" a voice shouted, and Thomas stared up, stunned. The paladin hung from a harness in the middle of the room, swinging her greatsword and trying to reach him, but trapped in place.

The wisp was nowhere to be seen. The helmsman and several others were laid in a heap, dead on the floor in the corner, and the paladin…well, the paladin was going fucking batshit.

She was screaming, making little sense, and whipping her sword around, her helm over one eye. Blood dripped steadily from the bottom of it. Her left arm hung useless, and the right was barely strong enough to swing a sword that looked like it should have been used in an anime, possibly one with giant robots, rather than real life.

Thomas checked Nigret, finding him unconscious, but with no obvious reason why, and quickly went to heal him.

Pain ripped through him, leaving him screaming.

The world seemed to explode around him, a kaleidoscope of colors and sounds, explosions and flowers, music playing, dinner with Sara a few weeks before he'd been recruited to come to the UnderVerse, and then pain.

Pain as he was beaten to within an inch of his life. That sadistic fuck Boris, the jailer, standing over him leering as he let others pay for the privilege of training their unarmed combat skills, literally pounding him until bones broke, then pounding him some more.

All of it flared through his mind, and it took a second to realize that it wasn't actually happening right now, that they were memories, that…

"Mana!" A voice echoed in his mind, a hunger filling him. *"Mine…mine…MINE!"* It screamed in his head, the voice so loud it seemed to echo, causing a migraine to flare, the pulsing pain growing with each and every heartbeat.

"Give…it…to…ME!" the voice demanded.

His mana was torn from him, pulled out of his body. The long-damaged, then healed mana channels felt like someone had a pump attached to them, a pump that was draining the mana from him, followed quickly by the health that pulsed through him in its place.

He'd been warned about pushing too hard on his magic, about the damage it could do, the effects it would have. But right now, he wasn't in control of it. Thomas glared down, sensing the pull throughout his body was concentrated on one place…the inside of his right wrist.

He tore at the gauntlet that covered that area, locking into the vambrace and the rest of the armor. It took several seconds, but eventually, with the world spinning around him, he managed to free his hand, then the wrist, and there, fastened to the inside of his wrist, like a bloody tick drawing his life force out, was the wisp.

With every pull, every suck on his wrist, the pain grew. The incorporeal teeth that seemed to be all the fucking thing was made of became more and more solid, chewing their way in. Yet, as his hand slapped down on it, all he felt was smooth, unbroken skin.

He scrabbled at it, fingers searching, and finding a lip, an edge, and he dug his fingers in, before cursing as the pain ratcheted up to an entirely new level.

He kept going, trying to pull it free, before the damn thing bit down harder, fusing with his flesh more fully and burrowing into him. The edge he'd held onto became malleable and slipped through his fingers, then sealed more fully to his skin, gone entirely.

"What the hell is that?" Alistair asked, from right beside him, and Thomas nearly leaped out of his skin. The paladin still screamed and frantically swung her sword overhead, apparently getting weaker by the second.

"A wisp." He growled, digging at it again with his fingers. "I can't get ahold of it…"

"Can you cut it?" Alistair asked, all business.

"The wisp?" Thomas asked.

"No, your arm, of course the fucking wisp!" Alistair snapped, the legionnaire clearly agitated as he yanked a dagger free and pressed it to the back of the small figure. "You ready?"

"Do it." Thomas snapped, and Alistair stabbed, the blade puncturing cleanly and sending a gout of blood spraying out. "Fuck's sake!" Thomas groaned, gritting his teeth. "That's ME, you idiot!"

"Then the wisp is eating you," he said grimly. "It needs to die. To do that, we need to make it solid, any ideas?"

"I just let you stab me, do you think I'd have done that if I had a better plan?" Thomas snapped back.

"Okay, potions," Alistair said, pulling out two, a health first, then a mana, and pouring them down Thomas's throat, before looking up at the paladin who hung drunkenly by the restraints now, the sword dangling. "Hold on, Thomas." He pulled out his mace and smacked the sword as it moved within reach.

It fell free of the paladin's grasping fingers. Alistair shoved it aside as it fell so that it landed atop the dead helmsman, rather than Nigret or Thomas. He grunted, looking up at the slowly swaying and barely conscious, mumbling figure overhead.

The wheelhouse had a pair of low couches on either side of the room, a window in the middle of the back, and three sets of harnesses that hung from posts driven into the deck in the middle of the room. The central-most stood before a wide table arranged to be accessible standing, the wheel itself built over the desk, and an impressive collection of buttons and levers covering the surface.

The space on the left, when looking at the room from the door, had a second, smaller collection of buttons and levers. The space on the right had the remains of an attachment for a seat.

A seat that was in pieces on the floor now.

The paladin started to rotate, hanging from the retaining straps on the right-hand side, and Alistair grinned.

"Give me a boost," he said to Thomas, who grunted, before bracing himself and letting Alistair clamber onto his back, crouching then leaping up, fingers outstretched to grab the dangling closest straps.

"Arsehole!" Thomas snarled. "You need a diet."

"You need to man up." Alistair grunted, hauling himself up hand over hand. "Use the potions, but keep yourself under half." He grunted again, pulling himself up hand over hand, before reaching out and clambering up to the helm of the ship. "You ready down there?"

"Wha? Fuck no, you crazy bastard!" shouted Thomas, as Alistair reached out with his knife. "Wait!" he shouted, downing another health potion, then grabbing Nigret and dragging him aside, before looking up and giving Alistair the nod.

"Here we go, then!" Alistair called, then he cut the straps holding the barely conscious paladin, letting her fall in a huge crash of metal.

"Now what?" Thomas called up, shaking his head at the low moan that came from the pile of metal.

"Make sure she's got higher mana and health than you, and hopefully the little bastard will leave you for her!"

"And if not?"

"Then we go for the backup plan."

"And that is?" Thomas asked through gritted teeth.

"We cut your arm off. Want to try and pass it off to the paladin, or want me to come back down and cut your arm off?" Alistair asked.

"Get fucked, I'm not cutting my godsdamn arm off!" Thomas snarled.

"Your brother did."

"Well Jax is fucking crazy; I'm not!" Thomas snapped before clambering across the unconscious paladin's body. He grabbed her helm and levered it off, looking at the grim face beneath it and remembering her from the night back in the camp before he'd fought Jax, when Edvard had introduced him to the other paladins in the hope that it'd be the first step to him joining their ranks.

Now she looked far less intimidating, her face relaxed in unconsciousness, a thin stream of blood dribbling from both nostrils. Then he remembered the stories she'd told that night, of the revenge she'd gotten on the men who'd slighted her growing up.

At first, Thomas had been fine with it, having assumed it'd been abuse, but then she'd spoken of the man who'd refused her attention. He'd been happily married, and she'd tried to seduce him. When he'd turned her down, politely at first, then more firmly, she'd taken it as a slight and had his wife sold on the block as a slave to teach him respect.

He'd forced himself to laugh along with the others, but when Edvard caught his eyes and had nodded that he could leave, he'd gotten out of there at speed.

She was a fucking lunatic and saw nothing wrong with taking whatever she wanted because she was stronger than her victims. The Church of the Dark taught that might equals right. They also said that, if a priest wanted something, anything, and they were high enough ranked, it was a literal duty of the paladins to make it happen.

To torture and abuse "lesser" people, for example, was frowned upon, but only frowned. The higher the priest, the lewder and more fucked-up the action, the less it was an issue.

This mental cow had basically admitted to everything from kidnapping to murder and more and had thought it was hilarious. He'd forced himself to laugh along, but the things she'd viewed as assault against her were utterly minor, and the things she'd done in retribution…she'd have been thrown in the deepest hole in the prison system on Earth, any day of the week.

Thomas sighed, tugging her bag free and looking inside, finding dozens of both mana and healing potions inside, and grinning. No sense in wasting his own, after all.

He pulled out a mana potion first, and while his own was dropping like a stone again, and he desperately wanted to drink it, he pressed it to her lips instead, forcing it down her throat.

She coughed at first, and gagged. Then reflex took over and she drank it, an unconscious sigh escaping her lips as her mana was topped off, and he lifted his wrist to the paladin's throat, waiting.

After thirty seconds, and still no movement, he began to panic, seriously considering if he was going to have to cut his arm off.

Forty-five seconds, and he'd readied his dagger, going so far as to try and pry the wisp off again, before swearing and sheathing the dagger again, and bracing his arm in readiness.

Ninety seconds, and he'd given Alistair the nod, prepared the potions, and was heating the knife to cauterize the wound, all the while telling himself that he must be mad, and that he could do it. If Jax had, he could.

"You know what?" Thomas said, pulling his arm away and taking a deep breath. "I could just keep taking the potions, you know. We probably have enough, you could all heal me, we fly back to the city. I bet Oracle can fix it, we could just…"

"Thomas," Alistair said calmly.

"Yeah?"

"Shut the fuck up and put your arm out," Alistair said firmly.

"But…"

"Now."

Thomas took a deep breath and did as he was told, closing his eyes.

"You'll tell them all I did this, no stress, all right? That's the deal. You tell them I took it better than Jax," Thomas said slowly, eyes screwed tight shut.

"Jax did it himself, in the middle of a fight to stop a poisoned weapon, then kicked the shit out of everyone else. He led the escape from the Prax, fought SporeMothers and airships, Thomas, while missing that arm. Believe me, you're not going to win this one."

"Fuck's sake, man, at least lie to me before you cut my arm off! I bet you don't even try and seduce your girl, do you? What do you say to her? 'Bite the pillow, pet, I'm going in?' I bet that's your idea of foreplay!"

"You want foreplay? Fine. It's the biggest I've ever seen," Alistair said, then snorted. "Biggest idiot anyway, you noticed your health and mana yet?"

Thomas opened his eyes and looked at them, frowning as he saw the steady climb, before frantically looking down at his arm.

The wisp was gone.

It was attached to the paladin's throat, and she was twitching as it fed. Thomas groaned and backed away, shaking his wrist and looking down at it before downing a mana and health potion straight off.

"Thank fuck…wait, when did?"

"You literally closed your eyes as it let go," Alistair said as he pulled his way back up the straps, grabbing onto the post that acted as a back rest for the helmsman and using it, and massive upper body strength to flip himself around, slotting his feet into the braces and wrapping the restraints around himself.

Once that was done, he slowly tilted the ship, moving gradually, to get it angled the right way around first, using only his inner ear to tell him when it was done, as the various surfaces that were designed to show the outside world were dead.

"Okay, there we go." Alistair grunted, shifting the wheel and flicking a few levers. "That should do it, I think. How about you make yourself fucking useful and get out there? Give a man some directions."

Thomas moved to the door, pushing it open and bracing himself in the doorway, looking around.

"Okay, left a bit, bit more, little bit more…okay right a bit…that's it, on course for the river…try to get the arse up a bit. We want to land like skimming a stone, just drift to the riverbank, not fucking plough into it."

"You know I had one fucking lesson on flying a ship, don't you?" Alistair growled at Thomas, but he adjusted course, slowly.

"We're listing to the right…" Thomas called.

Swearing, Alistair fixed it.

"Now the left. Come on, man!"

"Do you want to do this?"

Thomas laughed. "And lose the opportunity to take the piss? Hell no! You deserve this, you shit biscuit, for making me believe you were going to cut my arm off."

"I *was* going to cut your arm off. Next time, I won't damn well hesitate," Alistair muttered as he shifted the angle of the bow up slightly, relieved that the control he'd decided on *was* the plane, not the remarkably similar-looking main cannon.

"Now that's a stupid design," he muttered to himself, glaring at the lever that controlled the power to the main cannon. It was even set right alongside the plane, so in a rush, it'd be easy to mistake the two. "Damn, if that's not proof I'm a lucky man." He shook his head as the trees on either side of the river began to rise past the ship, the leafy canopies seeming to grow upward with distressing speed.

"How we doing?" he called to Thomas, who shrugged.

"Fucked if I know. There's no more shouts coming from below decks, and Tenandra is following us, so could be good, or it might mean that we're about to get swarmed…in which case, I'm going to go with bad."

"You're a real ray of sunshine, you know that?"

"Meh, adversity builds character," Thomas called back, squinting ahead of the ship at the grassy bank and the long, narrow forms that were slipping into the river from it, dipping under the surface and vanishing.

"Adversity, eh? Let's hope that we've had all were going to get."

"Yeah, about that…you know those long things that live on grassy banks next to rivers, six legs, lots of teeth, pair of stubby tails?"

"Bartonk?" Alistair called back in question.

Thomas shrugged. "Whatever, man, stupid fucking name, though. So are they, oh I don't know, territorial or dangerous?"

"Extremely on both counts. The only thing worse is their nesting sites. Very thin-shelled, camouflaged eggs. Stand on one, and it releases a batch of pheromones that mark you to the clan. They'll chase you for miles, and I mean MILES…why?"

"Well, looks like our character just got built, because not only are there at least twenty of the fuckers, but they don't seem happy that we're in their forest."

"Fuck."

"Well, yeah, that's one way to describe it." Thomas straightened up. "Looks like we're almost there; might want to slow down a bit."

"How? Half the shit on here doesn't respond!" Alistair snapped.

Thomas shrugged. "Guess we're crashing, then. Might want to hold on." With that, Thomas broke away from the doorway and ran to the hatches, shouting a warning down each before running to the next.

He made it to the third hatch, three quarters of the way down the deck, before the keel kissed the water the first time.

The engines, failing as they were, and with Alistair frantically adjusting them on the fly, were firing in relays. The keel touched down lightly, it slowed the massive ship considerably before it lifted off again, a loud creaking lifting from the hull as it climbed again.

The second touch was far harder, as Alistair had miscalculated slightly, and the keel dug in deeper, hitting submerged rock as it landed. The rock impacted the ragged edge of a hole left during the fight. The graceful skipping of a stone across the water that he'd hoped for instead became a sharp pitch forward, the bow slamming down hard as the ship twisted to one side. The rock ripped a section of the keel clean off.

The rest of the ship floundered, jerked around, and bounced in the water, cascades flying up around the impact site as dozens of Bartonk, waiting patiently in the water for their chance to attack the flying prey, died instantly.

The ship bounced again, the engines flaring as Alistair tried to adjust. Great gouts of steam blasted around the ship as they fired, the power far more than was appropriate, and the entire ship lifted into the air again, the uneven distribution of the engines making it tip sideways.

"Fuck, fuck, fuck, fuck!" he screamed, adjusting the plane, cutting power to the engines entirely and yanking the helm around. The final flare of power, barely enough for the ship to line up with the bank, burst forwards to plow into a collection of cypress trees with an echoing boom that set great clouds of birds rising in a thunder of wings.

Thomas shook himself, the world still ringing as he rubbed at the back of his head, laid against one side of the railing. He slumped, covered in gently falling feathers. With a grunt, he pushed himself upright and looked around the ship. Despite the last bit of the landing, they'd actually made it to the bank. As the ship settled, a brief flare of blue-white light going up on one side, it seemed to be down for good.

"Well, you fucked the pooch with that one!" Thomas called to Alistair as he stumbled out of the wheelhouse, dragging the unconscious Nigret out by the legs.

He took the time to narrow his eyes at Thomas. "I don't know how fucked up your home is, but assuming that's an actual saying, then there's some people with a lot of questions to answer. Now come on, let's get him back on his feet and get ready, because this sure as shit smells like a Bartonk nest."

Thomas lifted his head, sniffing the air and getting a stench like rotten eggs mixed with vindaloo that made his eyes water.

"Holy crap, how the hell did I miss that?" he asked, covering his mouth.

"Because you're an idiot who was more interested in complaining, now move!" Alistair barked at him, letting go of Nigret and waving at Tenandra, who'd come in behind the ship and was angling around to get as close as possible.

"She's never going to get her ass in here," Thomas mused, looking up at the massive airship. "With that smell, what the hell else can go wrong now?" As soon as the words were out of his mouth, he clapped his hand over it, eyes wide as he realized what he'd said.

The woods behind them creaked, and the deck shuddered as a massive figure landed on it, mere feet behind Thomas. He spun, eyes going wide as they fell on a grove guardian. The figure was huge, easily three meters tall. It was humanoid with a left hand that was a mass of sharpened stakes, and a right that appeared to be a massive hammer, the tip a blunt wedge of obsidian wrapped all about with roots.

The figure straightened, the bright green glow that flared up from inside it, outlining the edges of the plates that made up its form. The menacing glow emanating from the eyes and mouth just served to make it more unsettling to look at. As Thomas froze, the creature leaned in, its face close to his.

There was a flare of light as it looked at him, and more of the guardians exited the trees on either side of the riverbank. Three huge crossbows leveled at the ship that floated above, and a chorus of growls rose.

"Well, fucking thank you so much, Thomas," Alistair said in an exasperated voice. "You just *had* to say it, didn't you?"

CHAPTER FIFTY-SEVEN

We crossed into the center of the cavern again, spreading out and searching while the SporeMothers crouched, still under my control. "What the hell is a Dark Hunter?" I asked Lucian.

He grimaced, glancing to Augustus and Restun before answering.

"The Dark Hunters are the creations of the Dark Church, elite soldiers that failed spectacularly or that had a specific mission were…mutated, I guess is the right word. They were exposed to Xenefier's blood, then further mutated by exposure to Nimon's blood, then constrained by enslavement circles, like the forerunners to the collars that are more commonplace these days.

"The victims of these changes became horrifically powerful, yet single-minded and, frankly, stupid. Amongst the other changes is a massive need to do whatever they were told as they were first awoken. From what a survivor told me, he'd been forced to hunt a particular criminal and had been unable to drink water or eat anything but the flesh of that enemy until he was killed.

"When he'd made his way back to the citadel with proof he'd managed his quest, the enslavement circle was cut away. There's a compulsion to hide the circle and to never speak of it. Once his was destroyed, he said that it was like his mind returned in one go. I found him some three months after that, half-frozen in the mountains, trying to find a small village I'd attended a few weeks earlier."

Lucian shook his head sadly. "The village was destroyed, every living thing in it slaughtered by a monster attack, or so I'd thought. It'd been him. A distant cousin of his target had lived there, and he'd tracked her there before finding that, as is common in a small village, they were all related to some degree. In a frenzy, he'd killed everything, feeding on them, then choking, then trying again. It was only blind luck that he'd found the criminal days later and killed him, surviving through that boost of food. When I found him, he was a broken man, desperate to make amends, and he told me everything when I gave him the chance."

"What's the blood part of it?" Augustus asked. "We've never known about that. In the records, the Dark Hunters were simply creatures that the Church loosed every so often."

"It was known in the past," Lucian said, frowning. "It was well-known, and that it has been forgotten is strange. The blood of Nimon is a magical creation, something He did to imitate the blood of the Xenefier. Although, what that is, is less clear."

"I'm interested, believe me I am, but I think we've found the door," I interrupted, as two legionnaires on the south side of the cavern moved into sight and were waving their arms to get everyone's attention.

We advanced in that direction quickly, finding a pair of great doors sealed tight and locked just around the edge of a bend in the cavern. Once we made it around, it was obvious what it was, both by the size and the shape of the doors.

"It's a hangar…a hangar for an airship," I muttered, amazed as I stepped through the smaller side door and out into the next room. The dark void led up the stairwells carved into the rock. "Right, get those doors open!" I gestured to the massive, sealed doors. "No sense in leaving the SporeMothers here, not when they can fuck up the Dark Legion for us! Lucian, go on mate." Legionnaires hurried to obey.

"Well, that was most of what we know about the Dark Hunters, to be clear, or what I did," Lucian said. "The blood of the Xenefier is a substance that was being examined in the last years of the Empire. It was believed to be both a source of great power and of change, but personally, I believe that the change aspect could be replaced by corruption and be more accurate.

"The Xenefier were a race of humanoids from before the days of the Empire, from long, long ago, hidden from the majority of citizens. They were, from the little I've gathered, the progenitors to the Prometheans. They had the ability to sculpt their flesh into a form that pleased them, those who chose to live above the ground. Those Prometheans developed wings and more, and those who chose to live beneath it grew their forms to be more fitting to those places. They built great cities, but most were destroyed in a war. The few sites that remained were claimed by Baron Sanguis. He was researching them."

"Fuck's sake, that bastard gets everywhere," I muttered as a pair of legionnaires managed to get the locks to release, the huge doors starting to slowly open in the cavern.

"You know of Baron Sanguis?" Lucian asked, and I spat on the floor.

"Yeah, that old fucker and I met."

"Wait, you met him?" Lucian's tone took on an urgent note. "He still lives?"

"Yeah, he's mine and Tommy's father. Fucking dick that he is."

Lucian stared at me. "Your father…"

"Yeah, what's with that look?"

"Your father is Baron Sanguis?"

I nodded. "Yeah. Again, why's that important?" I asked, starting to get annoyed as he prodded and prodded at a sore spot.

"It's important because I suspect that it was exposure to the Xenefier that led to his fall and to the fall of the Empire."

"Nah, he's just a dick, a complete dick, trust me," I said.

"Not according to the histories, and to those who lived through the Cataclysm," Lucian said just as firmly. "I've read the notes. I've visited the high Elves in their city, as much as one such as I was permitted to. I was able to study their records, those pertaining to the fall of the Empire anyway. They all reference a century of great upheaval as Sanguis and his brethren changed, moving from the servants of the Empire they were raised to be to instead being disillusioned with the lack of personal power. The nobility were corrupted over time. Something changed them, Jax, something that twisted them until they happily murdered their own father and helped the God of Death to destroy the world."

"So, he wasn't always a shit biscuit?" I asked, frowning, then shook my head as I joined the others in moving to the stairwell that led upward out of the cavern towards the city.

"No. Once he was a highly respected member of the noble houses, obsessed with uncovering the past, trusted beyond all others. He set up research centers to examine the various remnants of Xenefier society, both under his own banner and occasionally recruiting others to assist."

"Malthus," I whispered under my breath, my eyes going wide as I looked at Oracle. "You think…?"

"Oh Gods!" Her eyes widened. "Jenae and the others didn't know much about the city, just that it was ancient. But when we asked Her, She didn't seem interested."

"The Goddess of Hidden Knowledge wasn't interested?" Lucian frowned. "What is this Malthus? I've heard you mention it before."

"It's a sentient spirit or something like that. It controls a city under the forest not far from the Great Tower."

"A city with a well filled with power that it offered to let us attach to the Great Tower to siphon off a little to help us," Oracle said faintly, as though saying the words aloud was making it worse by the second.

"This sounds like a particularly bad idea, Lord Jax," Lucian said formally. "Why would this sentient city-being offer you free power? What did it ask for in return?"

"It wanted magic, artifacts that it claimed researchers from the Empire stole, but it was really vague about it, when I asked, and didn't seem that upset. And the Great Tower's wisps had no clue the city was there."

"We thought we'd figured out that the Tower was placed where it was to protect the pass through the mountains from the Night King's armies, but…" Oracle said, trailing off.

"These research posts, what were they?" I asked Lucian.

"They were the Towers. The remaining Tower Seeds that were no longer needed, as they had been in the past, due to the Prax being constructed," he confirmed.

I swore. "But surely the staff at the Tower wouldn't have hidden it from the wisps, right? I mean, they thought of them as just dumb magical helpers…sorry Oracle. They'd have no reason to hide that they were there for research."

"The custodians of the Tower wouldn't have known," Lucian said grimly. "They were responsible for growing and maintaining the Tower, and it was only finished a short while before the SporeMother took it. The research team probably never made it, considering the Cataclysm and everything." Lucian took a deep breath. "In my opinion, Lord Jax, we must deal with the creature you know as Malthus VERY carefully."

"I sent a dozen people to explore the city and to look for artifacts," I whispered, facepalming.

"Then we need to contact them and remove them as quickly as possible, preferably without alarming the spirit, and quarantine them until we can be sure they are not contaminated," Lucian said. "If we weren't where we are, I would recommend dropping everything else to carry this out."

"Then that's what we need to do. Augustus, pick a runner, someone you trust. Give them stamina potions and get them moving. They're to go back down the tunnel, take a fast ship, and get to the Tower. Tell Seneschal to reach out, send a golem with a message, if need be. Get them out, then keep them quarantined until

Nerin can examine them fully. I'd rather we did it so Malthus doesn't know, but given the choice, our people come first."

"The tunnel collapsed, remember? I'll sort it, though." Augustus's jaw set. "Berin!" he shouted. "Get here now." A young man in gleaming armor appeared in seconds. He was tall, good looking, if a touch rangy, but dark-haired and serious. The legionnaire looked to be barely out of his teens, but the well-developed musculature and the scar that trailed down one cheek made it clear he was no child.

"Yes, Heir?" he asked, saluting, then he saw me and saluted again, coughing an apology. "My Lord Jax, I'm sorry, I…"

"Don't sweat it," I said, cutting him off. "Augustus has a job for you, and it's seriously important. He'll explain, but believe me when I say this is MASSIVELY important. You are to take the fastest ship available and use my authority to get anything you need."

With that, I clapped him on the shoulder and moved on, the narrow stairwell that led up the chamber toward the city above shaking as the SporeMothers clambered up the rocky outcroppings.

"I wonder," I muttered, then I grinned. "What's the point of being the boss if you never get to have any fun?"

Lydia and the others were slogging alongside me, as always, so when I ordered the largest SporeMother to stop nearby, Lydia eyed me suspiciously.

"What are yer doin', Jax?" she asked.

"I'm making an entrance!" I told her, winking…and jumped over the side of the stairwell, landing on an outstretched limb and running across to stand on the SporeMother's shoulder.

Utter hatred and desire to kill me darkened those dozens of eyes as the SporeMother stared balefully at me.

I patted her cheek consolingly. "Never mind, bitch. It was me or you. This way, you get to kill more people, so that's a win for you, right?" I asked her, seeing no understanding in her eyes. I went on. "The asshole that enslaved you is up there, the one who forced you into this life. Do as I say. Climb up there, and you'll get a chance to kill him, OR let go, and we can fall now, and we'll die. What do you say?"

There was a long minute where we stared at each other, then she started climbing again, reluctantly, but clearly wanting to kill someone else before she tried her luck at resisting the collar.

"Clever girl," I muttered, wishing I had a hat on and held a shotgun. Now that I thought about it, I could probably survive that shotgun now at close range and be merely annoyed, and I had a cool helm with a row of face-ripping razorblade-spines on the top.

Eh, I was good.

"Onwards, to victory!" I proclaimed, standing on the SporeMother and striking a pose, riding her up the side of the cavern exit all the way until the sides of the chamber changed from hewn rock to the inside of a building with an apparently retractable roof.

I ordered her to clamber out to the side, and I climbed down, grunting as I looked out of a crack in one grimy, barred-over window.

We were in a warehouse, and judging from the faint haze of smog on the far side of the city and the buildings between, I had to guess we were on the edge of the slums.

I waited until the others arrived, getting a sour look from Arrin, one that instantly disappeared when I promised him he could ride the SporeMother next.

The fucking lunatic.

We gathered everyone together, had a short rest, ate, and drank, getting ready for the next stage of the plan.

"What time do you make it?" I asked Augustus.

"Around midnight, I think. An hour to Horkesh's assault," he said, rubbing his chin. "I'd suggest we wait and rest, but…"

"But it's the middle of the night, and why wait for her to start things up, when we might be able to take some of the area out?" I said, getting a grin from him.

"Yes, but there's a point that we need to consider."

"Oh?"

"We're maybe half a mile from the Emporium, at the minute. Think the golems will accept you as their master again?" he asked with a suppressed smirk.

"You evil, evil bastard." I shook my head, taking a pull on the flask of coffee I'd just pulled out of my bag. "That devious of a plan gets you a coffee, mate." With a grin, I reached into my bag for another, even as I considered that it probably wouldn't work. After all, I'd have to claim them one by one, but…

The wall of the warehouse to our left exploded inward, sending people flying as debris filled the air. A brick sailed past my head as I ducked.

"We're under attack!" screamed Augustus. "Legion, assemble on me!"

I moved in closer to him as he yanked his shield around, holding it between me and the direction of the blast, even as I pulled mine out and slammed it into place next to his, accepting the *"Join shieldwall?"* prompt.

"Get out there and kill those fuckers!" I ordered one of the SporeMothers and all the undead we had left, before turning to Augustus.

We both spoke at the same time, the same grim acceptance filling our voices.

"Ambush."

"Bane!" I snapped at the same time that Augustus called for Lio and her team, Flux and Cheena joining us.

"We need to know what the fuck is going on."

Flux nodded. "Tell your people to cover their ears, crouch down, and keep their mouths open. This will make what we do less painful," he promised, getting my nod of approval.

"Thirty seconds." I told him, turning to spread the word with the others, as a rail of crossbow bolts slammed into the building, and another section of wall vanished with a loud *boom*.

Those thirty seconds passed with agonizing slowness as what felt and sounded like an airship's cannon fired on the warehouse. Hundreds of crossbow bolts slammed into the building over and over again. The few that made it through the growing breaks and gaps in the wall bounced off our shields without any impact beyond the occasional *plink*.

Bane nodded, then stood up, with Cheena and Flux on opposite sides of the turtle we'd all fallen into. The legionnaires slid a shield aside for them, and they let loose with their worldsense.

The feeling as it first washed out, even here behind the vast majority of the blast, was uncomfortable. It came somewhere between a sonic attack capable of rupturing your eardrums and boiling your brain, to that terrible warning you got seconds before you repainted the toilet when you had norovirus.

"Fuck me." I shook my head as it finally died away, opening and closing my mouth and trying to pop my ears. "Hope they wore the brown pants today," I quipped, visualizing my favorite red-suited superhero saying the line.

"Good news or bad?" Bane asked, hunkering down again, with Flux, Cheena, Restun, and Augustus crouching next to me as the turtle sealed up again.

"Bad news first, brother," I said, shaking my head. "Always the bad news first."

"There's a few hundred waiting in defensible positions on all sides of the roads that lead away from us. They've got makeshift barriers in place on the roads, and they go from one side to the other. Lots of crossbowmen, not so many others, but a strong core of dark legionnaires on the main road there." Bane gestured to the first exit.

"Okay, now the good news."

"Well, the SporeMother and the undead are really fucking the Dark Legion and the crossbowmen up, as you sent them right at the strongest section."

"Blind luck there," I said.

"Well, it was still well done. Beyond the barricade, though, there doesn't seem to be anything waiting. They clearly didn't realize what we were doing too long ago, or they don't have the forces to respond quickly enough."

"Okay." I glanced out of a gap at the buildings around us, before grinning. "Augustus, are all the buildings here so shittily made?"

He nodded. "It's the slums, Jax, they barely remain upright through storms."

"Fantastic. Okay, Lydia, get the team together, we're going to start with…"

CHAPTER FIFTY-EIGHT

The Dark Legionnaires cheered. The paladin that was leading them pulled his greatsword out of the abomination's throat as it died, the last of the undead collapsing as their mistress did.

The barricade had been broken, and most of the crossbow-wielding city guard had died, but only half of the Dark Legion had fallen. In the fights that they'd been in of late, that wasn't bad. They'd been dispatched here with orders that the Apostate was trying to send troops in through some hidden tunnel, and they'd expected a few dozen legionnaires or Narkolt Soldiers, not a fucking SporeMother, but they'd won!

Dozens of the Dark Legion stepped up, daggers ready, waiting for the nod from the paladin to begin the harvest. They were glad the battle was over and knew damn well that the alchemists would pay a pretty copper for the remains of something like this.

Then the wall of the building behind them exploded outwards, a deluge of bricks, wood, and flaming shrapnel flying everywhere. Screams began to rise from the first of those to see what was coming.

I rode on the back of one of the SporeMothers, with Arrin, the crazy fucker, on the back of the other. Four legionnaires gathered around each of us with their shields ready. Arrin and I cast Explosive Compression. Similar shouts rose from the other side of the building as the Legion did the same there, just on foot.

The main cannon for the airship glowed dangerously. I grinned to myself, a mixed feeling of terror and exaltation filling me as I literally rode one of the most feared creatures in the UnderVerse into fucking battle, figuring I could only get more cool points for this if I were wearing a leather jacket, drinking a beer, and waving a pirate flag as I went.

I finished my spell a split second after the roar of spells launched from behind us. I hurled mine forward, aiming not at the barricade or the fleeing dark legionnaires, but at the corner of the building the barricade had been built against, the point of impact just over head height.

"Surprise, motherfuckers!" I shouted as the spells launched from behind us weren't aimed at the barricades, either. Instead, four Explosive Compression balls slammed into the main cannon on the airship overhead, followed by almost a hundred Magic Missiles taking the first two engines on the port side of the ship out in an orgy of magical energy releasing.

The Explosive Compression spells went off inside or just around the cannon, buckling the delicately inlaid runes and setting off a cascade reaction as it detonated, followed by the lines that carried the mana rupturing, and dozens of explosions tearing the ship from the sky in a horrific series of fireballs and detonating shrapnel.

On the ground, Arrin's and my blasts detonated on opposite sides of the barricade, just where it met the walls of the poorly constructed buildings. The gravity fields slammed out, shattering everything within their range, then yanking inward, compressing them down to a fraction of their previous size.

Dozens died outright from the blasts, the city guard and the injured dark legionnaires having nowhere near robust enough bodies to survive the peripheral effects. Then the buildings shifted as well.

With the entire supporting corner of the buildings missing, and a new, powerful tug from an artificial source of gravity, the buildings, which were never well-constructed anyway, sagged then collapsed, tons of bricks, support beams, and general household detritus tumbling out and landing atop dark legionnaires and guards who were fleeing the sudden appearance of the SporeMothers and their insane riders.

A bare handful stood, ready to fight. Mainly, they were the true elites of the Dark Legion. But behind the SporeMothers came the Imperial Legion, others of my team having cast Explosive Compression at the walls of the buildings on the other roads leading away. Then the legionnaires fired Magic Missiles into the exposed guardsmen before falling back as the guards ran or died.

They fell in and raced after us, and the few dark legionnaires bravely standing ready to face us on behalf of their asshole God…met Bane and his team.

Six of the elites stood side-by-side, ready to sell their lives dearly. They crouched behind their shields, trying to form an impromptu shieldwall. They were utterly focused on the threat ahead, and so missed the one behind, as Bane, Flux, Cheena, Lio, and Tang struck, daggers and dirks punching through gaps in armor, through chainmail, and through flesh.

Five died in the first strike, their spines cut through at the base of their necks as Flux had directed, the sixth having rolled her shoulders at exactly the right, or wrong time, and deflected the blow slightly, making it skitter across the edge of the upper cuirass. The dagger was rolled sideways and yanked back, hard, almost decapitating the unfortunate woman.

With that, the five turned and raced away, all but Tang ignoring the bodies as they fell. Grinning, Tang pocketed three sets of bags of holding from the elites, having to push himself to catch up again, but judging the weight of the bags as being worth the effort.

I couldn't help but point into the distance as I rode the back of my SporeMother, shouting aloud, the wind ruffling my hair and beard.

"Onward, Buttercup!"

"Buttercup?" one of the legionnaires who'd climbed aboard asked, choking down a laugh.

"Of course!" I called back, grinning widely. "I wanted a name that just oozed power and threat!"

"Fucking nutcase," the legionnaire said, shaking his head in bemused acceptance.

"That's your Scion!" one of the others grunted at him. "It's High Lord Jax, Scion of the Empire, Mr. *Imperial* Fuckin' Nutcase to the likes of you!"

"Point made. Sorry, Scion," the legionnaire said, coloring slightly.

I let out a wild laugh. "Guys, we're riding the back of a monster from legend to conquer a city, don't worry about that shit!" I called to them, leaning back and looking over the edge at the running legionnaires behind me and at Lydia, Sehran, and Oracle, who flew overhead.

"How we looking, my love?" I sent up to her.

Oracle smiled in my mind, the feeling of her love and pride filling me to bursting.

"All good from up here. Two crossroads ahead and take a left. That'll get us on track for the noble quarter. Ignore the side streets, it'll lead us all the way to the south side of Barabarattas' keep. The entrance is a block to the right of there, but the SporeMothers should be able to climb the wall, and nobody will be expecting that."

"I like it. Any sign of Horkesh or the airships yet?" I asked, a little fear worming its way into my heart. That airship shouldn't have been available to wait there for us; it should have been far too busy with the…

A flash of light flared off to the north, then another, slightly farther to the northwest, followed by a third.

"Looks like they're right on time," I said before sending her a mental kiss and pulling back from the contact, my heart awash with her agreement.

"The airships are bombarding the walls, stripping them of as many of the Dark Legion as possible. They should make sure that any that survive are more interested in hunkering down than fighting us, so hopefully, all we'll have to face will be the palace elites."

"Hopefully," one of the legionnaires muttered.

I nodded. The Vampyr had been a surprise, as had the SporeMothers and the undead army. I turned and looked at Bob standing just behind and to my left. I couldn't help but smile at the way he watched the world pass by, his shield carefully angled to cover me should anyone attack from the left.

The skeletal minion had been a hell of a good choice back when I'd been picking spells. Having him beside me, even now, gave me a sense of relief.

The next twenty minutes passed quickly for those of us flying or riding, not so much for the others, who sprinted in full armor. But as we closed in on the palace, I felt the tension rising.

The city had been shuttered against the heavy rain and the darkness, not to mention the siege that was beginning, so even the slums had been quiet. The few who ventured out ran in terror at the horrific sight of the oncoming SporeMothers, horrified enough that they simply registered the monsters and ignored the Legion riding them. Then the legionnaires rushed past in hot pursuit. Here and there cheers rose, uncertainly, as people were unsure, but the Legion pursued monsters through the city. This fact, even after all they'd been told the legionnaires did, made some sag in relief.

The streets of the slums gave way to the outer wall of the Enclave on the left and the slightly better maintained houses that filled the area between the slums proper and the edge of the noble district. The thatch, wood, and cracked stone gave way to solid stone, to brick or to tile. Here and there, a sad little garden filled with wilted vegetables broke the monotony of the blur of buildings.

Over it all, the hill rose to our right with the mansions of the right and powerful. Behind it and rolling along to end at the end of the road we raced down, was the city wall where it joined the keep.

The keep was constructed of black basalt, the huge building seeming to tower over the city, brooding as it watched the people below scurrying here and there. My lips pulled back in a snarl as it came into view.

Where the Palace of Narkolt was part of a compound, the keep being a smaller, older building in the center, Himnel had gone for the attitude that bigger was better, and the keep towered into the night. Magelights shone light from hundreds of windows on more than a dozen floors that were visible over the top of the wall. It had clearly been designed for defense. I just had to hope that our lightning assault would be enough to get us past the outer ring before they could kill us all.

We took the final bend in the road, the SporeMothers picking up speed as the road evened out. I swallowed hard, seeing familiar massive forms racing to intercept us from the street that led to the gates of the keep.

There were a dozen war golems, and at the speed they moved, weapons raised, I knew that they weren't mine.

"Fuck!" I shouted, seeing the glow of four manabolts on massive crossbows. "Jump!" I ordered, matching action to words as I moved to the edge of the SporeMother's carapace, leaping for the floor that flashed past a half dozen meters below.

I landed hard, the crash of a fully armored legionnaire impacting seconds after me, followed by two more. A screech of fury rose from the SporeMother as the first bolts slammed into her and detonated.

I forced myself to my feet, staggering and limping, and moved into cover by the side of the building. The other legionnaires and Bob followed me as Arrin and his people hid on the far side of the street.

"Jax, they're locked down," Oracle said, appearing by my side and reaching out. She poured healing into my leg, making me hiss in pain. Just as quickly, I let out a sigh of relief, as whatever I'd hurt popped back into place.

"I might be able to free them to us. Your authority is higher after all, but I can only do one at a time, and I need to touch the crystal."

"Then we'll get you close enough to do it," I said. "Those golems can help us out by taking point inside the keep."

"Jax, the bloodstone!" Oracle interrupted as I had started to move on. "You still have it, and they will be forced to examine it. Do it one at a time, and you can force them to acknowledge you!"

"Why not hit them all?" I asked.

"Forcing them to accept you now, like this, is a battle of wills. Too many at once will diffuse the effectiveness."

"Fine. I'll do them one at a time, then," I agreed.

The others took the bend, then a barrage of bolts flashed and flew past. Most missed, the lightning-fast reactions of the Legion proving their place as the best of the best.

Before she could get into cover one of the legionnaires stumbled, and a bolt took her in the head, her skull and helm detonating in a spray of bits. The body fell, slamming into the cobbled street with a clatter.

"Motherfucker!" I shouted, furious, before hefting my shield, switching the Legion shield out for the one that Lydia and I shared copies of. I swore again, then took a deep breath.

There were eleven golems: three ranged, eight melee, and I glared down the road toward them, before shouting out the orders.

"Lydia, Sehran, distract the ranged. Oracle, take them as quickly as possible. Arrin, Yen, ranged magic on the melee, concentrate on the same one. Legionnaires, Magic Missile the golems, concentrate fire on them one at a time and take the fucking things down, start on the left and walk it in!" I ordered the rest, before diving around the corner and sprinting forward, knowing damn well the stealth fuckers would be advancing already.

"Bane, you and yours peel off. If the golems are here, others will be coming; intercept them and kill them all," I called, not looking to see if there was any acknowledgement as my feet clattered across the cobblestones.

"Come on, you mother," I snarled as three glowing bolts released.

As soon as the bolts loosed, I twisted aside, triggering Soaring Majesty and flying upward, spiraling to throw off any other ranged fire.

Nothing came, save the booms of the three bolts slamming into the ground not far behind where I'd been. I flipped over, diving towards the melee golem to the right of the group, the first flashes of magic incoming. Dozens of Magic Missiles slammed home into the lumbering figures.

At first, there was little change, the impacts blowing tiny divots in the foremost one. But dozens upon dozens of impacts took their toll, and it staggered. A lucky hit landed on a weakened spot near the base of the neck, and the head came loose.

As soon as the head fell, the rest of the golem returned to the inanimate carving it resembled, crashing to the floor, only for another two dozen missiles to hit it before the casters could adjust.

I landed hard, feet extended before me, flipped over at the last second and shoved downward with all my force, already casting healing as I impacted. I was still screaming as both my ankles broke under the force, but the golem I'd been targeting fell backward. I flew up again, hissing in pain, finishing the spell and groaning as the broken bones snapped back together.

The golem I'd targeted rolled to its knees, then up. It started lumbering forwards again, but that was fine. I couldn't kill one of them, not like this. My aim had been to separate them out, and I flipped over again, changing direction and landing with a skid that made me hiss in pain once more as I faced the golem that had been forced to stop.

It raised a wicked-looking axe overhead.

"Stop!" I ordered it, holding the bloodstone up in my right hand. "I am Jax Amon, Scion of the Empire, and I order you to obey me and only me!"

The bloodstone flared with ruby light, and the crystal embedded in the chest of the golem flared in response, the swinging axe slowing as though moving through molasses. A massive pressure weighed on my mind.

The world around me vanished for a split second, and I saw only the golem before me. It was transparent, filled with blue and black smoke, but a ruby glow in its chest pushed the smoke back, growing stronger by the second.

I sensed another presence then, a young woman, sitting up in shock. I felt her eyes widening as I stared through the golem at her. I recognized the one Nimon must have raised up, giving her the right to command *my* golems.

"Tirana Sertino, order the golems to stand down, or I swear I'll rip your leg off and beat you to death with it!" I snarled, my words carrying through the golem she was linked to. A third presence forcibly interposed itself between her and me.

It was male, or it had aspects of it, at least, and it was fiercely protective. A sense of shoving, of forcing me backwards came from it, and the light in the golem's chest dimmed slightly as I mentally gave ground before growling and shoving back.

Hyper-Cognition triggered, and I used the added boost to my mind it bestowed, feeling the shape of the presence that was trying to push me out.

I felt my own force, a mixture of my Intelligence, my right to rule, and the bloodstone all combining with my link to Oracle and the insane amount of baseline knowledge that Amon had crammed into my mind so long ago. I felt the force of the sentience before me.

It was a wisp, I recognized. There were similarities to Oracle and the others, but it was young, frightened, and injured. It was filled with a hollow void where its family used to reside. The ability to sense and make use of mana outside of the bond it was now forced to share with Tirana had brought more than just magic. It'd been a way that the wisps had interacted as well, the way they shared their love and emotions, part of the way they interacted on an instinctual level.

I'd never sensed that loss from Oracle, merely the lack of mana from the ability being burned out of her, and I suspected it was because the Imperial mages who'd done it long ago had known what they were doing, leaving wisps that were fully sentient still after the process.

Now I felt the lack of that stabilizing influence and the yawning chasm of madness that filled the wisp instead.

The force it exuded was strong, but paper-thin, and with that knowledge came the automatic reaction.

I stopped pushing back against it, spreading my own ability out like a sheet, and wrapped it around the other, compressing it.

Just like that, the wisp seemed to vanish, shrinking down as I cut it off from the world again, the bond with Tirana reducing to almost nothing as the golem before me was flooded with the ruby light of my bloodstone.

A scream of terror came from the wisp, and a similar one from Tirana as she vanished. I blinked, and the golem before me was solid again, the world back where it had been with barely a second having passed.

The axe was diverted, swinging aside and slowing, coming to rest by my side. I grinned, still mentally holding the wisp constrained, somehow.

I looked around and took a deep breath before holding the Bloodstone up in the air and crying out in a voice that echoed around the street.

"I AM JAX! SCION OF THE EMPIRE! I ORDER YOU TO STOP AND STAND DOWN!" The bloodstone flared bright, and the gems embedded in the chest of the golems flared in response as the world flashed away again.

This time a multitude stood between us, the golems that raced toward my people, the four that were in combat with the SporeMothers, and the two who still fired their manabolts after Sehran and Lydia. All of them froze, transparent, hanging in the world between Tirana and me, and this time the wisp was constrained in my mental grasp.

The mental battle between us was over in seconds. The only real issue was her pleading for me to release the wisp. I frowned. I could feel her…it wasn't so much sight as a form of awareness, one that let me know she'd fallen from a comfy chair. A rough rug lay beneath her, the fibers rubbing harshly against her bare lower legs as she pleaded with me to release the wisp, to free her friend. For the first time, I considered that maybe, just maybe, not all of the keep were my enemy.

Oracle reached out to me, and I felt her advice. I agreed, forcing my heart to stone against the weeping of the woman before me and the panicked cries of the wisp I held constrained by my mind.

It had less than an hour of mana left, I knew, somehow. If I didn't release it before then to let it draw on Tirana, it'd die.

"I'm coming for you. Stand down and hold on. Surrender the city to me, and I'll protect you both," I offered, getting a furious laugh in response.

"You think I control the city? I don't control *anything!*" she wailed. There was a mental image of a small room, shutters barring the windows, a fire that blazed hot enough that she was drenched in sweat, a rough, worn rug, and a small bed shoved in the corner. The door was locked and guarded by the men who'd taken her from her family, killing her father when he didn't release her in time.

She was a child, I realized, or close enough to that anyway, very early teens at most. The image I'd had of a woman morphed to one that I knew was closer to the truth, a scared child held prisoner.

"Fuck." I didn't dare release the wisp. If I did, and I'd been fooled…"Order the golems, all of them, to obey me and only me, and I'll let the wisp go," I said, gambling for all I was worth.

I felt her hesitate, then a wash of power flooded through the golems. A dozen pinpricks of sensation appeared around me, not just the ten I had yet to claim, but two more that stood on either side of the main gates to the keep compound.

I opened my eyes again, not realizing I'd closed them to better sense the golems, and I spoke one word.

"Stop."

All the golems around me, many of them mid-fight with the SporeMothers or the legionnaires, all paused. I sent orders to the SporeMothers to halt as well, while the missiles in flight slammed into the golems and detonated, finishing off another.

The remaining six melee simple war golems, including one that had been mildly charred by being too close when Yen bombarded its brother into oblivion, turned and moved into place at the front of the line. The three ranged war golems, all complex, took up station next in line, with the SporeMothers next, then the Legion and my team.

Another legionnaire had died from a ranged Manabolt. The sheer concussive and inertial force of the impact killed him outright. The armor was practically destroyed by the full-on hit. I ground my teeth over yet another senseless death, one that was added to the tally I planned to lay squarely at the feet of Nimon and Barabarattas.

I took a deep breath, and feeling the threads of control severing fully from Tirana, I released the wisp, feeling it frantically reaching to the girl, who just as desperately grabbed at it.

We set off again, the front gate now being a far better option than the SporeMothers ferrying us over the wall. With a simple mental command, the golems standing on either side of the main gate attacked the dark legionnaires who stood by their sides, the guard dismissed by their "betters" days ago.

By the time we arrived, the dark legionnaires were all dead, the golems were basically repainted in red, and they were working on forcing the massive gates open.

The arrival of the remaining nine golems changed that drastically. With a scream of tortured metal, the gates swung open, the bar and lock failing miserably in the face of multiple tons of golem.

As soon as the door opened, a barrage of magic flashed across the courtyard. Ten huge fireballs slammed into the golems that were clustered together. Five more fell, their bodies broken into scrap.

The three ranged lifted their massive crossbows and returned fire, the explosions that rocked the air in all directions a testament to the effectiveness of their weapons, as they fired again and again.

"Get in there!" I ordered the SporeMothers and the remaining golems, and I grinned as screams reverberated from inside as people saw their worst nightmare arriving at speed.

"Let's give them a minute," I suggested to Augustus, while Lydia snorted and took off, flying up toward the tower over the gate.

"You better not even consider going up there!" Bane said, appearing suddenly about an inch away.

"GAH! Fuck's sake, Bane!" I shouted, jumping back. "I swear, a godsdamn bell!" I shouted after him as he vanished, much to the low laughter of the legionnaires and the rest of the team around me.

"Nice place," Giint said.

I glanced to the side, seeing him standing calmly in the middle of the rubble of five destroyed golems, even as more of them fell, setting something up while crossbow bolts flashed past him.

"Giint, you crazy fucker!" I shouted, until he pulled out a new shield and slammed it down with insane force. It opened out, forming a wide curve that he stood behind, and extended about a foot over his head, with a small section cut out of the front and a single slot in the back.

He fumbled around in his bag as bolts slammed into the suddenly fresh target, until after a few seconds, he grinned, holding up a manastone for us all to see. He slotted it into the repository at the back, and the entire thing flashed bright white, making us shy away, covering our eyes.

When I could see again, the crazy little bastard had his piddly little crossbow out and was firing through the small slit at targets we couldn't see. He was also cackling madly, a manic laugh that only got louder when a Fireball slammed into the shield and exploded, leaving no damage behind.

My jaw dropped as I looked at the crazy little bastard.

"Did you make a portable fucking magic shield?"

He grinned at me, before putting a finger to his lips. "Shhhh, Giint concentrating," he said, lining up a shot and laughing after he fired. "Giint kill more than Bane!" He pulled his crossbow back and cranked a handle on the side, winching the string back in seconds.

"Fuck you, Giint!" Bane shouted from somewhere, and I snorted in disbelief.

"I'll take care of this!" Sehran growled, taking a deep breath and seeming to radiate a new power as she strode out from the wall and closed her eyes, drawing in deep breaths as her impressive chest rose and fell.

"Anyway," I muttered after a few seconds of distracted silence, turning back to Augustus. "We spent forever getting shitty fucking ones working for the ships, and that little bastard…" I cursed, pointing at Giint as Augustus shook his head.

"Never try to make a Gnome understand what they did wrong, Jax," he said seriously, leaning against the wall and crossing his arms. "They don't see the world the way we do. I'm always relieved he's not killed anyone on our side yet."

"Probably not, anyway," I muttered, considering the fact he'd strapped Jay to the underside of Mal's ship once.

"Probably," Augustus agreed. "So, shall we go kill them all, or are we waiting here for a reason?"

We both glanced up, distracted by an unearthly singing.

It was Sehran, in full-on stunning Succubus form. She was hovering overhead, wings beating slowly as she sang, the words just slightly blurred to the point I couldn't quite make them out. But the notes…I felt all the stress flowing out of me, as I looked up at her, amazed at her unearthly beauty, and that song…

"Stop!" Jian shouted, slapping his hands together as loud as he could. "She says not to listen. She's holding their attention for as long as she can."

I blinked, the desire to look up one more time, the tiny outfit she wore barely covering her, and from this angle…

"STOP!" Jian shouted again, and this time Augustus joined him, slapping his drawn blade against his shield and creating a ringing disharmony. I shook my head, forcing my eyes to open wider and looked around at the others, seeing them forcing their eyes away, too, as Augustus and Restun stepped up.

"Right!" Augustus shouted, nearly bursting my eardrums. "The next legionnaire that looks up gets to spend a WEEK in private training with Primus Praetoria Restun!" he shouted.

That was that; it was like having my nut sack dropped into an ice bath.

Not even vaguely interested in what the flying woman had to say, I turned and coughed, trying to hide the moment of existential terror I'd been filled with as I focused on the fight on the other side of the wall, inching my head around the corner to see.

The SporeMothers were both dead. One looked to have been hit by a barrage of Flamespears the size of exocet missiles, and the other was pinned to the floor by a massive mountain of ice, along with two more golems.

I recognized a similar spell to Archmage Fyre's Iceshard, but where hers detonated afterward, this one clearly remained intact.

"Six on the left, two on the right!" I said, turning back to the others. "They're small groups. Three of them have cannons; they're on the left in the middle. The others are spread out and look to be mainly crossbowmen or mages. I'll take the three cannons and those around them. Everyone else, get ready to barrage the living fuck outta whatever is left."

I started to cast, knowing one spell that would do exactly what I wanted. Not only did I now have the mana I needed and so wouldn't have my health stripped, but the roof that was set above them, the walls not being open to the skies above, presumably to protect from flying enemies. It was perfect.

Building the spell took what seemed like forever, twisting the components and details until it was right. Oracle did most of the magical equivalent of the heavy lifting, while I did the more basic sections. The pair of us worked together to make the spell, as I cast Gravitational Vortex.

IVANSSON

Hector Ivansson stretched his fingers out slowly, forcing himself to release the thick hairs he'd been unconsciously tugging on.

It was only when his mount gave a hiss of pain that he'd realized what he'd been doing, and he gently smoothed the hairs back across the carapace before him, murmuring apologies to Vorn.

Others had said not to name his mount, simple creatures as they were. The soldiers apparently felt no fear, no hesitation, and no attachment to anything. But as Vorn's hiss gave way to a low rumble, he decided he didn't believe that.

"Are you ready?" A hoarse whisper came from his right. He sighed, leaning to his left and freeing his boot from the makeshift stirrup of webbing Lady Horkesh and her sisters had arranged for them all.

With his boot free, he could twist around and kneel up on his mount's back to glare down at Dinna.

"For the last time, you son of an ill-begotten goat! Calling like that travels farther than you'd believe in the dark. Shut your mouth, or I'll shut it for you!" Ivansson snapped, his voice low and filled with exasperation.

"You've got no right to tell me what to do, Ivansson!" Dinna snapped back at him, the stress making him reply far louder than he should as his mount skittered nervously under him.

"What the hell are you talking about!" Ivansson retorted. "I'm in charge of the left flank, and…"

"You're only in charge because you brown-nosed your way right up," Dinna snarled, before getting cut off by the sudden movement of all of their mounts. They spun as one, dipping low and backing away as a small, at least in comparison to the others, red and black spider appeared out of the gloom. Her markings were bright enough they practically glowed, even in the dim light. She flashed forward, coming to a dead halt in the center of the group.

"What is this? Why do you speak?" Horkesh hissed, her fangs clacking ominously as she glared around at the group before her.

Most of the riders had been silent anyway and ducked their heads in reverence at the appearance of their mistress. Only two did not.

Dinna had been leaning forward on his mount's back, playing nervously with a dagger when it had moved under him. He'd fallen forwards, tumbling to the floor and landing with a solid grunt of pain.

The fall from the back of a spider that was almost three meters high wasn't trivial, and landing on his face stunned him. It also left him with a mouthful of sodden dirt and a broken nose, and in his confused state, he saw the dagger that had fallen with him.

He crawled forward quickly, grabbing the dagger and flicking it, muzzily trying to figure out what liquid was coating the tip.

Ivansson was clinging desperately to his makeshift saddle, trying to get his other leg back into place, when he saw Dinna's mistake.

In most other sentient species, it would have been overlooked, ignored, or at the least, queried and a warning given.

What Dinna failed to understand, however, was that spiders, especially ancient cave spiders, weren't like most other sentient species. Their responses were far closer to that which their instincts dictated and were almost entirely untampered with introspection.

Or the responses of the soldier caste, at least.

Dinna had accidentally driven his blade into his mount's face as he fell, slicing and wounding it, and driving it to the edge of its instinctual frenzied attack response to any pain.

Then he'd lunged toward Princess Horkesh with a bared weapon.

Dinna's own mount was the first to attack, lunging forward from behind him, slamming down a single spiked leg into the back of Dinna's calf and yanking him backward, removing the threat from her presence.

The majority of the mounts were like Dinna's and Ivansson's. They were large, strong, driven entirely by instinct, and vicious as a lover scorned.

Horkesh, however, was also guarded wherever she went, now that she'd proven herself. The guards that she had were a breed that Ashrag had rarely used in the millennia since she'd retreated into the dark places of the realm.

These royal guardians were closer to four meters tall, with a thicker carapace, the joints guarded by imposing spikes, and a green warning cross imprinted on their abdomen. They also had, as a perfect example that sometimes nature just goes too godsdamn far, a flexible stinger that lifted from their abdomen to dance and stab from above, curled over their bodies in readiness.

Dinna's mount had attacked in response to the injury it had received, and because it perceived a threat to its princess.

The four massive royal guardians, however, saw both the action of the mount and the rider as a possible threat. They leaped into action, stingers stabbing out, slamming into the unfortunate pair, punching clean through the scruffy ex-slave and deep into the mount before darting in and biting down, tearing entire sections of carapace and legs free.

In less than a minute, the clearing was silent again, the only sound was the drip of fluids, the terrified pant of the riders, and finally…

"This was unexpected," Horkesh said. "Have I broken the agreement?"

"The…agreement?" Ivansson asked after several seconds.

"We agreed not to kill Imperial citizens," she replied, staring at the mess of torn flesh and hair coated chitin.

"Well, I guess technically he broke the Oath first?" Ivansson said. "I mean, he cut his mount."

"Then I have not broken Oath. Excellent. What was the noise from this location?" Horkesh asked bluntly, dismissing the issue as settled.

"Umm, he didn't want to do as I told him?"

"Then it was your place to kill him, anyway. My guardians should not have interfered. Next time, we will leave you to kill those who do not obey." With that, she spun around and barreled off at speed, leaving Ivansson straddling Vorn and staring open-mouthed at the remaining members of his team.

"I…uh…okay…umm, everyone ready?" he asked the others, getting quick nods that he could barely make out in the dark, the terror of the blurring movements and additional shadows that at any point could turn out to be a pissed off guardian adding to his determination.

After tonight, he was going to ask for a nice, safe job. Breeding krakens or something.

Then a signal was apparently picked up by his mount. It, like the others around them, set off at a full sprint, dashing frantically as fast as its legs could carry it through the trees and out. To his dark-adjusted eyes, the two hundred meters from the tree line to the black mass of the wall burned brighter than the sun at noonday.

He held on grimly, terror rising in him as he looked left and right, seeing the massed blur of a hundred of Princess Horkesh's soldiers racing, his fellow escaped slaves riding their backs.

At first, there was only the rush of the wind, and the occasional *clack* of a chitinous leg hitting a stone as they crossed the wheat fields. Then the first shout echoed from above, thirty meters from the outer city wall.

It was answered by a second and a third before a massive blast of flame bloomed in the distance to the right as the assault on the gates began, huge war golems sprinting forward. Mages launched barrages of Fireballs, Flamespears, and more to draw the defenders' attention.

Still, a dozen fires sparked to life above them along the wall, as defenders lit the braziers, warning of their approach.

In response, along the scattered line of former slaves, Magic Missiles flashed into existence. The glow of the casting quickly changed, lengthening and shimmering out into a spread of five deadly golden darts.

The first release was uncoordinated, lifting in a great wave with some areas hammered again and again and others being merely scratched, but the other section leaders barked their orders. Ivansson grunted, joining in and giving direction.

The second and third releases were more targeted, more effective, and far more deadly, sweeping the wall above them clear of life.

The spiders reached the wall, leaping upward and gripping tight before racing on. The world reoriented in Ivansson's vision as he clung to Vorn's back, preparing a fresh spell.

By the time the pair made it to the parapet, scrambling over the edge to pause, gathering their wits, nearly a dozen of their number had fallen. But the lightning-fast assault had achieved its objective. The wall had fallen to the spider cavalry.

They split then, breaking down into the four assault elements, two to scour the walls for any defenders that tried to regroup and two to head to the gate, slaughtering any soldiers they found.

Ivansson let his voice rise with the others, a great whoop of exhilaration as he returned to the city that had demanded his life as a slave, a city that had claimed him in supposed back-payment of taxes his village had no knowledge of.

He clung to Vorn's cephalothorax with his legs, leaning back as it raced forward, magic flaring to life between his hands. He found unexpectedly that he was grinning like a fool.

Maybe he wouldn't sacrifice himself to the krakens, at least not yet…

CHAPTER FIFTY-NINE

I stepped out into the clear area between the gently swinging doors and grinned up as Sehran's hold began to falter. The strength she was Demonstrating to hold such numbers and so many highly skilled and leveled individuals showed as her voice became hoarse with effort.

People blinked, straightening then glancing back to her before struggling to look away again. I lined up the spell, focusing on exactly where I wanted it to hit. The keep in the middle of the compound towered over where we stood. The passageway that the cannons were mounted in lay destroyed on the right in most areas. The left, however, was more or less intact, as the ranged golems had fallen before they could take those out.

The building was huge and imposing. A pair of great doors at the top of a flight of stone steps were echoed on either side by immense windows of magical glass. Multiple smaller windows stood out on different floors as the keep climbed into the air.

Two-thirds of the way up the front of the keep, there was a covered walkway, a passage that led left to right, clearly encircling the building. There, the mages, the cannons, and the crossbowmen had reached out and provided such devastating cover fire.

The right side was mostly destroyed. Great sections of the wall or roof sagged and showed evidence of the cannons on that side having detonated, creating huge craters in the surrounding floors. The left was more intact, only two of the cannons on that side having been destroyed. The stonework mainly survived, even if it was heavily cracked, with blood seeping through.

I sighted my spell on the center of the line on the left, directly above one of the cannons and close to the group of men and women who wore multicolored robes.

The spell blurred as it shot across the intervening space before smashing into the wall a few inches from where I'd intended it to land. I nodded in satisfaction as the first phase went active, rippling out, locking gravity into place and beginning to unwind.

Ten lines flashed out as the shell of the spell detonated, flinging them loose. Each of the lines held a single seed at the end.

The enclosed space meant that some of the seeds ended up directly opposite each other. Others were on the roof, while still more were on the floor, and one embedded itself in the back of a mage's head while he'd been trying to tear his eyes away from the display.

His eyes rolled up and he collapsed, the seed's entry terminally ending his interest in even Sehran's fantastic ass. The lines each rolled out further lines that moved in turn, reaching for one another and creating a ritual circle that filled the small space, while the weakening pull of Sehran's song meant that more and more of those inside the radius suddenly looked around in shock.

Only one man had the foresight to flee, and he did it in spectacular fashion, leaping from the cover of the balcony towards the ground. His hands flashed in a pattern as he spoke quickly, his plummet ending abruptly as he teleported elsewhere.

The others inside the area of effect weren't so lucky, with the space as restricted as it was. Then, the next phase went active, and a burst of black light flashed outward, then tore inward as the gravity seeds powered up.

Some of the luckiest inside that AOE were those who were merely crushed flat or were killed instantly by the gravitational anomalies, or too close to the cannons as their runes were warped and damaged, the stored mana discharging with horrific results.

The truly unfortunate were those who were caught in a nexus of forces, gravity pulling this way and that, hurling them in different directions. Some were caught between only two or three nexuses, their bodies being torn and flipped, crushed and hurled from side to side.

One unfortunate individual managed through some lucky twist of fate to be in exactly the sweet spot between four seeds, and where they interacted, he floated, blessedly free of pain, as all around him, dozens were smashed into paste, crushed, and torn.

Until the final phase went active, that is.

The oscillating mana curve flipping the power from positive to negative and back again randomly changed that. The man who thought he was surely the luckiest man alive was ripped free of his gentle floating bubble and hurled into the wall with enough force that his skull was crushed to less than an inch thick…and three feet across.

I nodded in satisfaction as the spell tore the very side of the keep apart, huge blocks of basalt reducing themselves to dust over a handful of seconds.

"That's just nasty," Arrin muttered, standing next to me as he shook his head, arms folded as he contemplated the destruction. His barrage of Magic Missiles launched with the others' and had swept the far wall clean of all life. "I mean seriously, boss, creating *that* shows you have issues." He shook his head in dismay.

"So, you don't want to learn that one?" I asked him.

"Oh, hell yes, I do. I just wanted you to know, that's all. Oracle, can we…?"

"Not now," she replied, shaking her head. "Seriously Arrin, we're in the middle of the enemy city, and you want to take half an hour out to learn a new spell?"

"Arrin, back it up an' calm down," Lydia ordered, getting a long-suffering look in response from him.

"Hell yes. Better chance I'll get to use it soon," he said to Oracle, grinning.

"Another time, Arrin." Restun stepped up to stand by my side. Arrin backed away quickly. "So Jax, there's one golem semi-functional. It has only one leg, but is a ranged version, so…"

"So, I'll tell it to set up over there and cover the main gate," I finished for him while gesturing to the corner of the wall. He nodded as I gave the orders to the golem, watching as the massive creation slapped its crossbow to its back, some magic making it stick there. It started off on both hands and one leg like a tripod.

"Looks like it's down to the Legion," Augustus said, stepping up on my other side as we headed toward the keep. I nodded, looking over to Sehran, who was still recovering from her excessive use of magic.

"Is she all right?" I asked Oracle.

"She will be. It was a serious drain on her, but if you ever wondered if letting her feed on the elder Vampyr and the SporeMother were worth it, I think she just proved herself."

"Definitely," I agreed, the others voicing low agreement. "Lydia?" I looked around and found her a few steps behind me, smiling. "There you are…what?" I frowned.

"Ye keep forgettin' we're yer team, Jax. It's all right, yer don't have ta find us all tha time. We're here," she said.

I paused, realizing that I had been doing exactly that, and I nodded my thanks.

"Okay. Augustus, Restun, open that fucking door, please," I ordered, pointing to the large door of the keep.

"Yes sir, Scion of the Empire, Sir!" Augustus responded, saluting.

"Ah, sod off, oh 'Heir of the Empire'," I said, shooting him a grin.

"I sometimes feel like I'm surrounded by children," Lucian said in his cultured, urbane voice, to Restun, who cleared his throat.

"I know the feeling…Uncle. I often feel the same." A faint smile creased his face.

"Scotty!" Augustus called, and I smiled despite all that had happened, having seen the massive half-ogre legionnaire earlier, but I hadn't had time to talk to him yet.

"Yes Primus?" Scotty responded, jogging over and coming to a halt. He started to salute before Augustus shook his head and gestured toward the doors.

"The boss wants the doors open."

"Well, I'll go open them, then," he replied, lifting his massive shield from his back and turning, lining up on the door.

"Wait one," Augustus said, frowning as he looked at the door, his experienced eyes catching something my less-experienced ones had missed.

Bane appeared a few seconds later, stepping away from the huge lock in the middle of the door. Ronin started to play a new song, something stirring and uplifting, and I recognized it instantly.

It was the theme to a boxing movie I'd loved growing up, and I'd done my best to teach it to him, despite having far less musical talent than creatures that lived at the bottom of the ocean.

The music built, and as it climbed into the air, the effects took hold. Checking the prompt, I found I'd gained ten percent Strength for the next minute, and while that was impressive for anyone, for Scotty, it was a game-changer.

The massive half-ogre powered his Ability and became the Battering Ram again. He pushed off with one massive foot, cracks appearing where he started out. As he lumbered forward, sparks showered free of his huge feet. The metal-clad boots glanced off cobblestones, but with each step, he picked up speed, running faster and faster.

We set off running after him, but the speed the massive figure built up to was astonishing, quickly outdistancing all but the fastest. They fell back as he reached the bottom of the steps and triggered the ultimate evolution of the Shield-bash and Lunge Ability trees.

It was a fantastically expensive variant of Stampede, apparently, expensive in terms of health, stamina, and mana, and only capable of being used for a few seconds at a time. As he closed on the door, he literally blurred, locking his arms and legs and bracing himself as if setting himself on solid ground. The Ability took over and physically hurled him through the air to punch the doors where they met in the middle.

Unlike the golems earlier, Scotty was still mortal and one man alone, no matter the magical advantages, could not smash doors that large open when they were locked. But equally unlike earlier, Bane had slipped in and picked the lock.

Scotty slammed the doors open hard enough that they bounced off the walls behind, one set of hinges shearing off entirely, while the other hung drunkenly on two of the four hinges that it had used originally.

The twenty Dark Legionnaires behind the door were sent flying.

Scotty collapsed to one knee, breathing like a bellows, his skin bright red, and a heat haze lifting from him. Several dark legionnaires, who had been at the very back and had been merely shoved backward, stepped up, ready to sacrifice him to their Dark God.

Before they could, Bane was there, dancing through their midst, daggers flashing and driving them back as Lio, Flux, Tang, and Cheena joined him.

The battle was brief and bloody. The stealth warriors, despite being skilled and determined, were being driven back step-by-step as we arrived, their determination being matched by that of the Dark Legion, who had numbers on their side.

I raced across the final few feet, yanking my naginata out, leaping forward and triggering Lunge. It was one that I barely ever used, but in this situation, it was worth its weight in gold. I slammed my right foot into the chest of the nearest dark legionnaire, sending him staggering back.

I flashed the bladed tip of my weapon sideways through the air, the slight scrape of the blade against the underside of the next man's helm barely registering as I sliced his throat.

A fountain of blood sprayed out and washed down his cuirass as I landed. With my other hand, I brought the shield around to block another strike aimed at Scotty's side, then twisted to the right. Stepping up to put my back to him, I faced outward at the Dark Legion.

"You want him, you get to go through ME!" I roared, triggering Taunt. It wasn't enough to get their attention fully, not as underdeveloped as it was and with the little practice I had in using it. Hell, next to the version that Scotty and his brother had used a couple of weeks before, it was downright pitiful…but then, Scotty and the others weren't the apostate.

The sight of my weapon, my different shield, and hell, the spikes running down the middle from the crown of my helm in place of a plume got their attention straight away.

The thought of the rewards the God of Death and His priests promised filled their minds. They attacked; two of those in the middle shoved the others back, making room as they drew in huge breaths. They began to grow, their armor revealing itself to be built with sections that could expand outward, accommodating the Ability.

"Fuck, berserkers!" Lydia shouted from the other side of Scotty as he huffed and tried to get to his feet to face them. But the toll the Ability had taken on him to take the doors out was clearly not something he could shrug off so simply.

"We're here!" Grizz roared, covering the last few feet to skid to a halt inside the room next to Scotty. He spun his shield around and caught a descending warhammer blow on it, grunting as he was shoved backward, even as a missile flashed past him, followed by four more.

They detonated on the outstretched right arm that held the warhammer, the first exploding on the armored forearm and making the wide-shouldered dark legionnaire flinch. The second, a few inches up from that, cracked the vambrace and made him hiss in pain. But the third, landing as it did in the crook of the elbow and detonating, sent bloody segments of flesh raining down.

The arm hinged open, the weight of the warhammer and the loss of the connecting muscles from the elbow up and down, meant that the arm bent outward and just kept going until the joint hinged apart. It popped free, much to the white-faced horror of the man.

The fourth missile impacted his cuirass, the force shoving him back with a grunt. But after the opening of his arm, all he could do was stare in horror until his head was taken from him by Grizz's backhand swing. The sparks flying from the blade's meeting with the cuirass illuminated the room slightly.

Yen and Arrin rushed forward, more spells filling their hands, but between them and the battle raced the rest of the Legion. Restun and Augustus held the center of the line, arriving seconds after me and spinning into place between Scotty and the enemy. Dozens of legionnaires pushed into the room, and I grinned as I stabbed down at the man I'd kicked backward.

He'd fallen, the shock of the unexpected kick at just the wrong time enough to overbalance him, sending him face first to the floor with a crash. Then, as I'd taken out his friend, I stamped down hard on the small of his back, stopping him from getting back up.

I stabbed out, the blade crunching into the back of his thigh, where the armor was mere chainmail. With a vicious yank and a twist, I pulled it back out, blocked a sword thrust with my shield from a third enemy, then shifted to the right and drew back my foot.

I punted the guy on the floor in the side of the head as hard as I could, his head snapping back, stunned. I stabbed down again, this time dipping into the back of his neck, twisting the blade, then yanking it back out, the fresh corpse sagging.

"Cinta!" the figure before me bellowed, seeing her friend die. Her voice echoed strangely before she kicked my shield, the force enough to stagger me.

As I moved back, trying to catch my balance, she stayed where she was. Other dark legionnaires moved around her, desperate to reach me, as she threw back her head and screamed.

The sound was…wrong…utterly wrong. It echoed in ways that made the hair on the back of my neck stand on end. Restun shouted something, pointing to her as he deflected an axe blow, then stabbed the offending attacker in the groin.

I shook my head as the figure lowered hers. Then she reached up and yanked the helm off, unlatched her shield and threw it clear of her arm, reaching down and picking up her fallen friend's sword.

I caught my balance and blocked a strike with my shield from one dark legionnaire, then I slashed sideways with my naginata, driving back another before shucking the shield off my forearm and throwing it into the man on the left's face.

With two hands to wield my naginata, I grinned, spinning the blade in a complicated figure-eight pattern that got the attention of both men before me. Then, I whipped the weighted base around and smashed it into the man on the right's unarmored knee. The loud crack that rose was echoed milliseconds later by a scream as he fell sideways, dropping his weapon and clutching at himself.

As soon as the weighted end had slammed into his knee, I'd begun the spin, the Asha'tuun training that I'd received making it instinctive to use the momentum gained from the rebound in the most efficient way possible. In this case, that was to turn my back to the pair of them, turning the naginata sideways and tucking it in close to avoid accidentally skewering Scotty. I executed a spinning heel kick, connecting my right heel with the chin of the man on the left, snapping his head sideways.

He staggered as I came around, his sword and shield well out of position. I planted my foot back on the ground firmly and stabbed out, the blade sinking into the slot of his helm's visor before he could dodge or even really see properly again.

He went limp, hanging from the end of the blade. I yanked it backward, hard, his body reluctantly letting go of the weapon.

Before I could recover, though, the woman who had screamed was there, a sword in either hand flashing at me.

I twisted my body sideways, facing to the right as a blade stabbed past my face, literally inches from my nose. I jerked the naginata left, deflecting her other sword. Then, I released my weapon with my right hand, bringing that arm up barely in time to deflect the sawing cut she tried on my throat on the way back. I slapped the palm of my hand down hard on the back of the blade, the serpentine single-edged weapon registering as unusual as I did so.

She whipped the blades around too fast for me to see properly, and I grunted as her right sent my naginata spinning from my grasp. Her left lunged forward, the tip barely being deflected by a lucky combination of my lower abdomen armor and the movement I'd made. I dropped low, unarmed, to sweep her legs from under her, the blades glancing off each other with a metallic *snick* as she scissored them inward, barely missing my head as I dodged.

I kicked out, sweeping right to left. She leaped, her face a mask of hatred and tears. Her dirty blonde hair streamed wildly as she leaped up, then fell, both blades twisting around to aim unerringly for my chest.

I felt a millisecond of panic seeing those blades closing on me, until she was sent catapulting backward by a massive fist, and Scotty leaned over me protectively as I fell onto my back.

He winced as his broad back, armored with enough steel to make a small tank, or so it seemed at times, rang with the impact of a hammer.

I caught his eye and grinned my thanks before rolling to my right and yanking a dagger out of its sheath. The legs of the figure who'd just hammered him filled my vision, then the hammer rose again. I stabbed the dagger into the side of the attacker's knee and ripped it out sideways, tearing the entire back of the joint apart and sending him screaming.

As he fell, I looked up, searching frantically for the woman who'd come so close to terminally finishing my adventure, only to find her screaming in fury as she danced with Tang.

I grinned and dragged myself out from under Scotty, grabbing the flailing arm of the man I'd just crippled and stabbing the dagger into his shoulder joint, making him screech before punching me in the face with a gauntleted fist.

My head snapped back, and I saw stars for a second. The punch was well-aimed and strong, but the helm meant I was rocked back rather than knocked out.

I drove the dagger deeper into his shoulder, then blocked his next flailing punch. Clambering up to straddle him, I blocked another punch, trapping his arm between my hip and hand. I ripped the dagger free, slamming it into the slit in his visor. The dagger lodged deep and locked into place as he spasmed in death.

"Booyah, motherfucker!" I hissed, glancing up at Tang and the woman still fighting.

The pair of them circled each other, blades flashing showers of sparks as they slammed metal on metal and carved shallow grooves in each other's armor.

She lunged for Tang after a brief exchange of blows, clearly intent on getting him out of her way to come after me. He leaned back like a world champion limbo dancer, slapping the flat of his right blade on the floor and using that impact to bounce himself back up. He came up between her extended blades with his left blade leading.

He whipped the razor-sharp edge of Hunger, the devouring blade, around slicing deep into her wrist, before slashing across her upper body, the thin line that he carved across the metal doing little damage but driving her back.

She dropped the left-handed blade with a curse.

Tang chased her back, blocking and slicing. His twin swords blurred as he dodged and danced, and my view was obscured by a hulking figure in straining plate mail as he roared, stepping between us.

"Well fuck," I muttered, suddenly aware that I'd basically laid there watching Tang and the crazy woman fighting instead of getting up when Scotty had moved back.

I grinned up at the big bugger and blew him a kiss. He snarled, whipping a hammer around with a head bigger than mine, aimed squarely at my face. I triggered both Hyper-Cognition and Mana Overdrive, allowing me to not only accurately predict the path the hammer would take, but as I twisted my enhanced body, I rolled free of the impact, pushed myself up onto my hands, and flexed again, flipping over to land on both feet.

I tucked my right booted toe under the naginata and kicked it up into the air, catching it with my left hand and stepping onto the haft of the hammer. I used it as a springboard to flip myself over as he swung the second hammer sideways. It passed under me by inches, the leather wrapped steel haft catching slightly on the spines of my helm. I landed on the far side of his right arm, even as it completed the swing, leaving that side dangerously exposed.

I slammed fire mana into the naginata and rammed it into the side of his cuirass. The Dark Legion design had straps on the sides that held the front and back together, and the gap left for the arm wasn't just under the armpit. It extended a few crucial inches lower as well.

The glowing, white-hot tip of my blade slammed into the gap, plunging deep and carving its way through his lung.

He coughed, a wet, tearing sound, before dropping his hammers and grabbing the naginata as I tried to pull it free. Sizzling erupted from his right hand where it trapped my weapon. But as he twisted, his massive strength, the solid sides of the armor, and his grip meant I could either let go of the weapon or be dragged with it toward the fresh reinforcements racing in from deeper in the keep.

I let go, dropping to the floor and letting the naginata's shaft pass over my head, before slamming more of my mana into Mana Overdrive, a vague memory resurfacing of doing this when Oracle was injured in the fight with the SporeMother back in Narkolt. My muscles swelled with unspeakable power.

In the corner of my eye, I saw my mana bar dropping faster, and I grinned. I bunched my legs under me and kicked off with all the power I could muster, driving my right fist up with everything I had.

It connected with the underside of a chin that could have been used as an anvil, and it tore clear through it.

Teeth erupted outward as his face was basically hit with a sledgehammer from below, sending him catapulting backward in a spray of blood to twitch his last on the floor.

I had seconds to use this ability, the cost was just too high, but as I moved, I knew I had a chance. Most of those entering the room weren't dark legionnaires. They were the city and palace guard, and they looked terrified.

I roared in bloodlust and triggered Lunge. It was supposed to be used with a blade in one hand, granting double damage to any injury done on impact. Hell, it was supposed to be used once per fight, the description said, but whether the short rest I'd had when Scotty hammered her backward had been enough, or the description meant per person, or hell, maybe because it was a day with a y in it, it activated when I triggered it. The five meters between me and a particularly well-polished wanker in engraved silvery plate mail vanished in an instant.

I blurred to a halt before him, his elaborately curled mustachios quivering in disbelief as I appeared. I shot my right hand up to grab his chin, palm flat across his mouth, thumb under the jaw, fingers digging in, even as I slapped his sword aside contemptuously with my left armored forearm.

I paused long enough to see the widening of his eyes, then I ripped my right hand across to my right as far and fast as I could, snapping his neck and half-tearing his head off.

I caught the sword as it started to fall from nerveless fingers, and flipped it over, throwing it full-strength into the oncoming figures, the blade slamming hard into the third man in line, making him scream as his shitty leather armor utterly failed to stop it.

I spun, bringing the heel of my right foot around and crushed another charging man's face, grabbed the halberd he'd been leveling at me and that I'd swayed aside to dodge. I yanked it free, whipping it around behind me to build momentum.

I brought it around low, literally cutting three legs apart before the aged wood of the handle broke on the fourth, the blade still sinking deep as three more fighters were taken out in less than a second.

I lunged, sweeping up a hand axe and hurling it across the room to split the head of a man wearing a shitty helm that looked like a steel mullet. It pinned him to the wall he'd been sidling along, and I turned to face the remaining twenty or so that had raced into the room.

I'd killed a fifth of their number in less time than it took for them to realize that it was all the work of one man. I opened my mouth to shout at them to surrender, when I was blindsided.

I'd seen the figure coming, but given that someone else had just disarmed him, I'd basically dismissed him as a threat. He'd seen me pause, and decided, clearly after seeing me kill or terminally injure what felt like half the room, that he would punch me in the face.

The *ding* of his chainmail-enclosed fist hitting the side of my helm rang out in a sudden moment of perfect silence.

I slowly turned my head to fix him with a glare.

A strong scent of piss filled the air, and true terror crossed the pimply face of a boy barely out of his teens. He registered that not only had the punch been a bad idea, but a tiny part of his mind was registering that he might have also broken at least one finger, while the only reaction on my part had been to turn and stare at him.

"Oh...oh Gods..." he managed, before I grabbed his collar and yanked him in close, headbutting him.

I'd seen that he was a kid, and clearly terrified, so I both pulled the blow and used the front of the helm, not the spike-encrusted crown, but I still managed to dent his helm and knock him out.

I turned my head, holding him dangling limp and unconscious from my right fist to look at the growing puddle under him, and I snorted in laughter.

It tore out of me. The sudden amusement at how pathetic the attack had been filled me.

Others picked the sound up. Legionnaires who were covered in gore, who'd just fought their way across the city. They'd been facing and taming creatures that could make nightmares call for their mummies and suck their thumbs in the corner. Yet, here we were, two dark legionnaires left alive, one elite palace guard, and thirty or so regular guards, as the last few filed in, clutching their weapons in nervously shaking hands.

"Fuck's sake, lads," I called out. "You could have at least had a piss *first*..."

"You fucking assaulted us in the middle of the night!" a voice complained from the back. "I barely had time to find my pants!"

"What, you expected me to bang a drum and book an appointment?" I asked the crowd in general. "Damn, this is pathetic. Drop your weapons and file out the door behind me. Go to the right and sit there 'til this is dealt with...unless you *want* to keep fighting?"

There was a long pause, then the woman Tang had been fighting screamed and lunged at him. She barely covered a foot before three lots of Magic Missiles slammed into her. Several legionnaires used the break to Demonstrate that not only were they hard as nails, but they had magic as well.

The woman staggered backward, arms flailing, and Tang followed her, blocking the next strike and stabbing her in the upper leg. The blade punched through the chainmail. She gasped, then grunted as his second blade slammed into her gut, angled upward. She dropped her remaining sword, grabbing onto him and staring into his eyes, her own wide as he grimly twisted the blade around, carving her insides as he searched, before slicing her heart in two.

With that, the fight was over. He stepped back, lowering the sword and letting her slide off it, the clatter of her armor hitting the floor echoing around the room.

"Anyone else?" Augustus asked grimly, and the clatter of weapons being thrown down was nigh on deafening.

CHAPTER SIXTY

Once the weapons were accounted for, we took their bags as well, prompting some grumbles. Considering they knew they were lucky to be alive, they weren't particularly fervent mutters.

I knocked back two potions I found in the first bag. Health and mana, of course, and I cut the flow to Mana Overdrive and Hyper-Cognition at the same time, feeling the world stutter into a lower gear. I pulled out two more, popping the tops off the vials and downing them, grimacing and blowing my lips out in irritation.

"Gods, the taste of these potions gets to you after a while," I muttered, as Oracle landed next to me, blurring into full size.

"Are you okay?" she asked.

I nodded, taking her into my arms and sharing a quick kiss as the last of the prisoners was kicked out of the room and ordered to stay to the far right of the courtyard. The golem stood in the left corner and was ready to kill anything it saw that wasn't us.

"Yeah, just tired," I admitted, rolling my shoulders slightly before kissing her again. "Are you okay?"

She nodded, her face resting against my scratched cuirass.

"I am now. I spent most of the fight healing our people. We lost two more."

"Godsdamn it," I whispered, closing my eyes and resting my face on the top of her head. "How many more? How many more have to die for me?"

"They died for the Empire," Lucian said, appearing next to me.

"I know," I said, and he shook his head.

"No Jax, you don't," he said, quietly but firmly. "I know you feel responsible for them, for *us* all, but the simple truth is, through your actions, hundreds of thousands of people in Narkolt, in the Tower, and soon in Himnel, will all live longer, happier, and safer lives.

"*They* are the Empire. People, not edifices or borders. The true wealth of the Empire is its people, and you must allow some of them to die to save the rest. It is hard, I know, but even now they die for you and for the Empire, as they assault the walls…"

"Oh, well thank you so fucking much for that!" I snarled, shaking my head. "Fuck!" I cursed, before calling out to the room in general, where people were gathering their gear and adjusting straps that had come loose, eating a quick snack to boost their regeneration or drinking and getting ready for the rest of the assault.

"Right, people, no time to waste. Our brothers and sisters are dying out there. Let's get a move on," I said, Oracle shrinking down and landing on my shoulder, sighing as we moved on.

"What did I say?" Lucian asked, confused.

Restun stepped up to his shoulder and, after carefully looking the older man over, smacked him across the back of the head. "You might be hundreds of years older than the rest of us, but damn you are shit with people. From now on, leave the inspirational speeches to Augustus."

Scotty led the way again, or at least as far as anyone watching would have known. Bane, Tang, Flux, Lio, and Cheena actually led the way, but where they blended in perfectly, he almost shook the hallway with each step.

We moved down empty halls, passing small rooms and great ballrooms. The only signs of life were the occasional servants who attempted to hide. They were roughly searched, then dispatched to the courtyard each time. We climbed the stairs to the second, then third floors.

As we moved from the staircase, the central mass led upward before splitting to either side to reach the next floor. Then it flowed together on the next one, the floors each patterned in alternating gold and silver colors and thick rugs. Finally, firelight shined out through the open doors of the throne room.

The doors had clearly been left open as someone had fled, and thanks to a gentle early morning breeze, they swung lazily now, the room beyond the doors half-filled with people who nervously shuffled their feet and glared at the figure on the throne, then back to us. Scotty stepped aside, recognizing that this wasn't somewhere he should be leading the Empire.

I smiled my thanks to him, stepping into the lead as Oracle flashed to her full height, landing gently and striding alongside me, clad in a long, flowing gown of silver.

"You!" The figure sitting atop the throne snarled as he looked down at me.

"Me," I agreed, looking up at where Barabarattas sat on the throne, with two more thrones ostensibly behind him.

He sat on a formal throne, one carved and gilded and obviously old that stood at the front of a large dais. Behind it loomed a second, much larger throne, clearly made for no human figure to sit in. It was recently built, judging from the perfect shine of the black material.

I mentally assigned that throne to the Great God Cockwomble and flicked my gaze to the right of the thrones, seeing a second, smaller one that an obvious priest sat in.

He was dripping gold, and had a huge paladin standing by his side, glaring down at me with hatred screaming in every ounce of his being as he gently held a staff carved with so many runes it was practically glowing.

"So," I said, pausing and cocking my head to one side. "Looks a bit crowded up there. Guess I better step up and empty some thrones, eh?" My naginata flared with a pure white light.

Barabarattas flinched away from the light, as did another figure, one who stood back in the crowd. I turned to look at him, mentally dismissing the others.

"Lucian?" I asked, the crowd parting as Lucian stepped to the side, staring at the figure that reached up and slowly pushed his hood back.

He wore an ornate mask of carved, bone-white ivory and gold, with feathers sticking out of the edges. He laughed as he pulled the mask free, bowing fluidly and smiling at Lucian.

"Well met, little brother," Akanji said, and Lucian smiled tightly in response.

"Akanji, it's been too long," Lucian said, drawing his blade and watching his brother.

"Ah, so I take it you've not come to surrender, then?" Akanji asked in mock sadness when Lucian shook his head slightly with a curled lip.

"Wait, I recognize that voice! You're the one that was talking all that shit earlier in the caverns, right?" I said.

He smiled, offered a mocking half-bow.

"Yeah, I thought so. Lucian, fuck him up when all this gets started," I ordered.

"As my Lord Scion commands," Lucian murmured, inclining his head to me with a gleam in his eye.

"Hold!" barked Barabarattas, to absolutely no effect. "I am Lord of Himnel, and I order you to hold!"

I snorted. "I've got news for you, pal. You're lord of two fucking things right this minute, Jack and shit, and Jack just packed his bags and left town." I grinned at Barabarattas, then glanced around before growling to myself. "Fuck's sake. Perfect line, perfect delivery, and fucking Tommy ain't here to hear it. He's never gonna believe I managed to work that in."

"Yes," the priest said, standing slowly. "You're the brother of the traitor, Thomas. Where are you, boy? Step forward, and face your God..." he called. I snorted again, shaking my head.

"Yeah, sorry to disappoint you. Well, not really, but you know, fuck it, Thomas is busy. I'd say he sent his regards, but he didn't. I think the exact words he used about you lot were along the lines of, 'if you see one of those fucktards, tell them they owe an apology to all the trees for wasting their fucking oxygen'."

"I..." He stood there for a few long seconds, clearly confused.

"Seriously, I have neither the time nor the crayons to explain this to you. So shut the fuck up, step down, renounce your God, and I'll let you walk your happy arse outta here. Otherwise, I'm gonna have to kill you," I said, shaking my head and gesturing toward the door.

"I see, so it was a poor attempt at an insult. Very well. I will give you a choice as well, apostate. We shall see just how strong you really are." With that, he gestured to the side of the room where a large container stood, covered with tarpaulins and surrounded by soldiers. "Tell me, apostate, did your brother tell you of the true faith? Of how those who fail the God are dealt with?"

"Not really, but I'm guessing because He's the God of Death, they're not given a puppy and a blowjob," I shot back, eyeing the box.

"No. If they merely fail the God, they are killed. But if they are convicted of a greater crime, then occasionally they will be given to a cause." He smiled, a sickly, sweet thing that made my stomach curl. "Tell me, have you met any of my dark hunters yet? Several escaped and started to hunt on their own."

"Yeah, we met one already. Wasn't particularly impressed, to be honest," I said, feigning nonchalance.

"Well, perhaps you simply met the wrong one!" the priest suggested, smiling. "Tell me, apostate, did the traitor mention what would happen to those he abandoned? Those who trusted him with their lives?"

"Nope," I said, reaching into my bag and pulling out a flask of coffee and taking a hit. "Oh, that's good. Augustus?" I offered, passing the flask to him. He nodded his thanks, taking a long draw.

"Ah, that's the good stuff," he said, handing the flask to Restun when I gestured to him. I turned back around, as though having forgotten about the others and waved at them to continue.

"Yeah, best thing we've done in ages getting that coffee sorted out, I tell you. Oh, I'm sorry, I got a bit bored, you know. Standard villain monologuing and all that. Did you get to the part where you say we'll never defeat you yet?" I asked the priest, pretending to notice him again.

"You'll…what?" the priest asked, thoroughly confused, before losing his patience and grabbing the staff that the paladin held for him. "Fine! You wish to die without the knowledge you could have gained, then I grant that wish!"

He slammed the staff down on the ground, and it flared with a terrible black light, seeming to suck in the light from the fire and the magelights from around the room as the runes lit.

The priest chanted. The paladin gestured to the soldiers standing by the sides of the covered container, even as he drew a massive two-handed greatsword from his back, stepping up and clearly ready to protect the priest.

The soldiers yanked the covering away, and the room filled with gasps and shouts of horror as the misshapen creatures inside were revealed.

There were a dozen of them, all shapes and sizes, but the one detail they all had in common was the overdeveloped muscles, the slavering teeth, and the hunger that flared in their eyes.

The figures pressed against the bars of their cage, sniffing and growling as the priest continued to chant, until one pushed forward, shoving the others aside, snarling at them.

They ducked down, deference and the fear emanating from them as it snarled. Then it reached out and grasped the bars in two enormous hands.

It stood around nine feet tall, broad-shouldered and probably female, judging from the lack of clothing that Demonstrated the obvious masculinity of several others nearby.

She was also narrow-waisted, covered in coarse black and gray hair, and looked like the wendigos I'd heard of, heavily muscled, horns that looked like those of a stag, jagged and sharp. Her hands ended in great claws and her feet were tipped with talons. Despite all of that, the most horrifying part was the intelligence in her eyes.

"Priessst!" She hissed, shoving another of her pack back as she moved closer to where he stood. "Releasssse me! Releasssse me now or die!"

Her eyes glowed, and I shook my head, amazed by the creature. There were several in the container like her, seeming to be more or less mentally intact, standing close together, ready to make a move. Judging from the looks on their faces, the way they glared at the priesthood, it wasn't us they were interested in.

The others, though…

"Therrrrre!" one of them screamed suddenly, pushing its face as far through a small gap as possible, its canine-like snout bunching as it sniffed and slavered. "Therrre! Itssss himmmmm!" It screamed, pulling and scratching at the bars in desperation as others sniffed and howled, joining him.

"Looks like they've got your scent, boss," Grizz muttered nearby as several of the Legion repositioned themselves to stand between the cage and me.

"Tang, Bane, I've had enough of this shit," I said. "Fuck that priest up." I gestured roughly to the priest, and Bane appeared a few feet behind him on the dais. Before he could close with him, though, a second form blurred into visibility, slashing at him. Five more dropped from the ceiling where they'd been concealed, blades blurring as they faced my stealth team.

Bane looked like he knew they were there, appearing as far back as he did. He flashed his two lower hands forward. Glittering, triangular throwing blades flashed through the air to sink deep into his opponent's chest.

The assassin opposite him took three steps, bringing up his blades to attack, then collapsed face-first onto the floor as Bane threw two more, both of which bounced off a shield that the priest had apparently been maintaining all this time.

As soon as the attack began, the paladin had stepped between the priest and Bane, readying his massive sword and giving Tang the opening he'd apparently been waiting for. He ignored the assassin racing for him to haul back on his beautiful Drow bow. The silver and black ash weapon creaked under the strain as an arrow appeared on the string, one of several special slayer arrows that Tang had claimed for his personal use. He grinned down the length of it as he aimed at the bouncing Adam's apple in the priest's throat.

"Surprise, bitch," he whispered and released, the horrifically expensive arrow blurring in a streak of gold and green as it flashed forward. A second arrow, one far more mundane in comparison, despite its magical nature, appeared on the bowstring next as Tang drew it back and aimed at his assassin, winking before firing it into his face.

The slayer was well-named. The sneering, contemptuous look the priest gave Tang as he saw the arrow changed as the projectile blurred, unfurling into six more that separated out, the first lunging ahead of the rest. The others spread out, even in the small distance between Tang and the target. The shield popped like a soap-bubble, the first arrow being the anti-shield variant, then came the silence and stun. The paladin twisted around as the priest leaned back, his spell completing barely in time as the arrow sliced across the side of his throat. The paladin threw himself into its path to protect his master.

A thick spray of blood leaped out as the priest staggered. Then the arrow slammed home into the paladin's shoulder. His mouth opened and he slumped, clearly trying to shout something. But the silence and stun sent him reeling until the chainfire hit.

The priest was running now, one hand clutched to the side of his neck as the bars on the sides of the container fell. Screams broke out across the room.

The chainfire arrow was thicker than most, covered in runes carved into the shape of interlinked chains. When it hit, it seemed to shatter, the sections flowing forward in a ripple of tiny, interlinked fragments.

When they hit the armor, though, instead of bouncing off, they spread out like an octopus finding a bag of cocaine. The chains flared out and slammed back in, gripping with all their might as they flared into bright white flames, eating into the armor, never mind the flesh beneath.

The fourth arrow detonated a handful of inches from the target, bringing a veritable hail of flames with it as lighting and burning oil sprayed out to envelope the silently screaming paladin, the oil spreading across the armor and seeping under it, burning.

The fifth arrow was less impressive, most of the tiny hollow glass teeth shattering as they hit the armor, all but one wasted. The one that made it into a crack flared to life, though, and dug its way in deeper. The wound it left in the flesh poured with blood as it followed the path to an artery, before tiny needles flashed out to anchor it in place.

The final arrow hit and sent the dying paladin flying. Banshee's wail ruptured his eardrums, sending the inner ear into paroxysms of wildly spinning fluid, making him believe that any direction was up or down, making it impossible for the figure to make sense of the world around him as he died.

The priest ran from the room, a half dozen of the dark legionnaires rushing after him, as all hell broke loose. The dozen or so creatures in the container split into two groups. Four of them immediately turned on each other, trying to claw at the symbols that burst into black and green glowing life on their flesh, howling as they scratched and tore, while the others rushed the Legion line.

Lucian and Akanji flew at each other, the Vampyr lord slashing the courtiers out of his path with a wild laugh as five more of his companions appeared from concealed places around the room. Oracle started casting, frantically trying to hold them off with lightning and fountains.

I rushed Barabarattas, who snarled and threw himself from the throne at me, mouth splitting wide and head opening to reveal a split-toothed monstrosity. His own guards screamed and threw themselves aside, clearly in shock and wanting nothing to do with him.

Tang's second arrow, another magical one, but a lightning one this time, slammed into the assassin who had been rushing him. The totally unneeded magical effect rippled out and shocked the fresh corpse as it fell backward, the vanes of the arrow protruding from the middle of his forehead, proving that once again, while you could have all the health in the world, some wounds didn't give a shit.

I flipped my naginata around, bringing the weighted end around and smashing it into Barabarattas's face. It was split open already, but the hearty smack of the weighted end smashing into him sent him rolling to the side.

I lunged after him, whipping the bladed end around and slicing it across his upraised right forearm. He threw his left arm forward, palm up, and a spray of redness flared out.

It hit me in the helm, most of it catching on the metal. Some made it through the slit visor and hit my flesh, and I screamed!

Pain!

My world dissolved into horrific pain as I grew weaker. I grabbed at my face, the naginata falling away and my hands finding something sticky there, and I panicked.

I was blind. I could feel my health, mana, stamina…hell my *life* being torn from me. Even as it happened, I could hear Barabarattas laughing. That sneering little bastard was laughing at me!

The world went red, not just from the thing that he was doing to me. But, as I let myself go, letting the rage flow through me all in one go, I lost my grasp on reality.

I acted entirely on instinct, unable to see as I triggered Lunge, my left hand tearing free to aim in the direction of the pull on my life. I formed it into as strong a blade as possible, fingers straight, clenched together.

I felt the ability trigger, and a split second later, I slammed into something, cutting off the laughter in a gurgle of air. I'd tried shaking my gauntlet free, but I let the fury flow as it wouldn't come away, grabbing at the back of my right hand with my left and digging my fingers in. The metal buckled as Mana Overdrive triggered and was hammered over and over again, doubling then redoubling the drain and the power surge until the gauntlet ripped free easily. I slapped my right hand onto the rippling flesh I felt under me.

Something bit down on my left arm, pressure growing as teeth embedded in flexible bands of muscle. They skittered across the surface before finding cracks to sink into, then cracked and tore at the armor between the back of the gauntlet on the vambrace.

"Jax!" Oracle wailed, feeling the pain ripping through me and seeing the enemies that were multiplying around the room, pouring inward, desperate to kill us all.

I didn't care. I gripped the flesh harder in my left hand and powered my tattoo, tearing the lifeforce out of the creature that had been Barabarattas.

It bucked wildly, pulling harder on the connection it had to my face and tearing more out of me, even as I did the same to it. We rolled back and forth, it chewing on my arm and leeching my life-force. I crushed it, ripping that life back, and kneeing it over and over again.

The pull on Mana Overdrive climbed as I dug my fingers in and squeezed harder. But the bands of muscle between them simply compressed and flexed, and the pain grew. Panic was gone now, my mind filled with seething hatred, hatred that Amon fed upon as He surged up, and I felt His ascendance coming.

We faced each other in the silence of my mind for long minutes, time outside of time as we watched the other, before He nodded to me and inclined his head.

Over the last few weeks and months, ever since the fight against the Valspar at Wayland's Crossing, and then again when we faced the true Elder God and helped the Pantheon of the Flame to defeat it, I'd felt the changes in Him, the faint senses of withdrawal, of introspection.

He'd healed himself massively, not through magical means, but through simply coming to terms with the past. Through accepting that He couldn't have changed things and that constantly punishing Himself wasn't helping anyone.

The mental flaying He'd subjected this tiny fragment of his soul to had served no purpose other than flogging Himself as He felt He should suffer.

It had helped none of those who had died or been injured through the events that had come about since the fall of the Empire.

If anything, His lack of sanity, of being able to assist me and Tommy, had compounded those mistakes. Now, after the tens of thousands of hours He'd examined himself in this altered flow of internal time, He'd come to a conclusion that had acted as balm upon his soul.

He was dead.

He was a mere remnant of a soul that had long since passed through the veil, and the only thing He could do, the only good thing He could offer to those He felt He had failed, was to help me ascend to take His place.

I wasn't Him. I'd make different choices, hell, I forgave some of those who crossed me, and I'd set the wheels in motion for another Djinn war by permitting Hellenica to breed unfettered. I hated the steps He'd taken in allowing the Wisps, a valued tool, to be enslaved.

But the line that was drawn in the sand, the point we would not cross, was entirely different for Amon and me, yet much was also the same. We both saw the Empire as the people first, and the single overriding duty of the Empire was to protect the innocent. It was to enable the simple farmer to raise the next generation in circumstances that were, at the very least, no worse than those they had lived through. We aimed at the same target to make things *better* for all our people. But the line that was drawn was more in the acceptable level of failure in accomplishing that task.

I would brook no harm to an innocent if I could prevent it, while Amon would burn an orphanage Himself, filled to the rafters with the innocents, if doing so would save a single innocent more on the other side of the scales of balance.

Amon nodded again and reached out.

I reached out to Him, knowing that this would most likely be the end. The final time that we faced each other, as His knowledge poured into my mind.

I mentally stepped aside, feeling Him slide up, like a bubble in the water, to the surface to take over our body, kneeling atop the creature that attempted to feed on us.

I parsed the knowledge out as best I could, knowing and accepting that a huge amount of it would be lost. But some of it was immediately useful. I reached out, pouring specific information into the bond with Oracle.

She dipped, her magic fluctuating and making her almost fall from the air as she integrated it, before grinning wildly as she realized what was happening.

Her spell was discarded, the mana absorbed and redirected, as she pulled new fragments out of Amon's memories, redirecting them, fixing them.

The forms I'd used as I stepped into the Realm of the Gods. The armor I'd worn, and the draconic abilities bequeathed to me through not only Shustic from our long-term bonding with her, but through the use of the silverbright and the assistance of Tuthic, weren't restricted to that realm I suddenly knew.

They were aspects of me.

They were a part of me that was tied as deeply as having legs or eyes.

I'd simply never known how to activate them before, doing it entirely on instinct.

With Oracle working on the outside, me on the inside, and Amon gaining us the time to do it, I began the change for the first time fully consciously.

I reached into myself, into the cells and more, finding the ancient magic and *pulling*.

It responded joyfully, leaping up to the surface and flowing outward, a bubbling wash of liquid metal that left scales in its place as it rippled out. Pain burst out all over my body, but as it passed, a cooling breath flowed across my flesh. My eyes blinked as Amon stood.

The red substance, sticky as it had been, drawing my life force away, crumbled into dust as Amon did something, and I felt my body like never before.

We stood in a far more fluid motion than anything I'd ever achieved before, and I felt the sudden inrush of mana as it leaped joyously to obey its true master.

The doubled and tripled Mana Overdrive Ability that I'd been using simply…stopped. It was no longer needed as mana sank into every aspect of my body, flexing and smoothing, healing and rebuilding. I felt its movement around my right knee and the relatively tiny amount that sank inside, a thimbleful compared to the bucket that was absorbed elsewhere. A tiny fraction of me nodded in satisfaction, knowing that the road I had to travel yet to reach this point without Amon was a step shorter because of the spells and improvements that Oracle had been using on me.

We looked down at Barabarattas as he thrashed and gnawed at our arm, and we felt our lip curl in disgust.

We let go of the shoulder where we'd been holding it and grabbed the back of the head instead, ripping it free of our left arm without any noticeable effort.

Then, we grabbed the creature by its left shoulder and opened our mouth. Pointed teeth separated as our jaw extended and we took a deep breath, before roaring out a gout of Dragonfire into the creature's thrashing, flapping face.

The silvery white flames washed over our arms and hands, tickling like a summer breeze. But where they comforted us, they turned the creature that had been Barabarattas into wisps of sooty smoke.

I leaned forward, breathing flames across the floor and making sure that no aspect of him survived, before turning and surveying the room.

Lucian was in heated battle with Akanji, the pair of them equals: Akanji from having absorbed the life and stats of so many over his centuries of life, and Lucian from having pushed his body to almost the same level and his skills to higher.

Augustus was ripping his sword from a dark hunter in a spray of blood, his sword flashing around to lop off the arm of another as it raced forward, trying to pass him.

Restun was holding his own against two of the lesser Vampyr, the pair of them clearly considering whether they could escape, not whether they could win.

Lydia had her hands full with a lithe dark hunter that appeared to be all scales and flashing teeth. Grizz was battling another that towered over him. Scotty was trading blows with an elite dark legionnaire who'd burst into full dark berserker mode, and Yen was tending a wound in her side, another assassin lying headless next to her.

Bane and Tang were fighting, with Flux and Cheena close by, surrounded by more assassins, clearly some kind of priest by the long robes. But these figures looked like they did anything but help people, considering the long daggers held in each hand.

Giint was busily kicking twelve shades of shit out of a fat man who'd been wielding an axe, clearly one of Barabarattas' supporters. Through it all, Ronin's music flowed and danced, adding to our Luck, Strength, Perception, and Dexterity.

Blood dripped from his fingers and smeared across his lute, yet the pure rapture on his face and the joy in his voice as he sang let me know that he was truly living his best life right now.

Sehran used her whip and her claws to devastating effect, fighting side by side with her love, Jian, who danced and spun. His dual wielding skills were clearly growing. I knew, somehow, that he would soon be offered the Bladesinger rare class. On the far side of the pair, Bob spun in a blurring dance of death.

He was neither graceful nor fast in the way that the others were, but he wielded the huge ice-drake's revenge, and between the fact that the only way to get close enough to do him any damage was to come within the range of that terrible mass of bone, and the fact that as the evolved undead that he technically was, he didn't suffer from stamina issues…well. He certainly didn't need any help.

We calmly watched as four of the remaining figures from the cage rushed us, legionnaires taking one down and slowing another, but their bounding leaps made it far harder for even the virtual supermen of the Legion to slow them.

That was fine, though.

The first one to reach us was a mix of a troll and a frog, or that's the impression we got. His long legs bunched up and sent him soaring over wide distances, and his gray, mottled skin boasted the consistency of pebbles. It landed before us, its face wide and squat, and it opened wide, the top of its head practically seeming to hinge backward as row upon row of gleaming, needle-like teeth were exposed. Then it leaped forward again, straight into a kick that sent it flying across the room to slam into the far wall.

It hit with a crunch, then slid bonelessly down the wall, a dark green, bloody streak marking its passing as a pair of werewolves bounded in.

We backhanded one, shattering its jaw and half tearing it from its face, before grabbing the other by the top of its snout and yanking it downward, then shoving it back and snapping out a single word in a voice of utter command.

"SIT!" we roared at it, and the werewolf's traitorous hind quarters hit the floor with a thump. The combination of a soldier's obedience to authority, the utter command we'd instilled in the word, along with whatever racial memory the hound fragment of its DNA had come with meant that, when that ass hit the floor, it was going to take a level of balls the creature would never have to move again without our permission.

The werewolf seemed stunned at its own actions, but it also stayed there, even as its friend got back up, staggered, then jumped toward us.

We reached out right-handed and caught it by the throat in midair, snapping its neck with a quick jerk and tossing the corpse aside, even as we walked forward.

The figures between me and the container, both guards and dark legionnaires, city elites and army soldiers, they all backed up as I strode forward, a mage in their midst shaking as he tried to conjure a spell with mana that simply unraveled each time, becoming nothing.

He focused with ferocious intent and finally managed to spark a flame to life. He grinned, looking up from the tiny ember it practically was, and Amon sneered.

"You do it like *this,* mageling," he said, lifting our hand and clicking our fingers. There was no spell. No careful weaving of the elements, no fire mixed with air, earth, and water to create the flames. The mage simply vanished inside a circular pillar of flame that rendered the marble he stood upon molten.

Yet the soldiers who were mere inches away felt nothing, save the sudden inrushing of air once the spell barrier was dropped.

A dark legionnaire roared in denial and fear, lunging forward with a hammer and swinging for our face. Amon reached up, calmly catching the hammer by the head and watching the stunned and terrified look on the dark legionnaire's face…before he crushed the head of the hammer with one fast motion.

"Leave the city. Now," we said in a voice that brooked no argument, then we dropped the remains of the hammer onto the floor. The dark legionnaire went pale with terror.

"All those who will not bend the knee to the Empire, flee. You have one minute. If I see you past that, your souls are forfeit," we said clearly, our voice echoing with timbres that made it clear we weren't to be disobeyed, before turning our back on the soldiers, making it clear that we viewed them as utterly no threat.

We strode across the room, ascending the dais and sitting on the throne, dismissing the prompts that flared to life as soon as we hit the seat. We watched with a neutral expression as a handful of them fled and more fell to one knee.

The courtiers, mages, elite members of society, and more who had made up the crowd had backed away, pressed against the wall now, as far as they could get from the fights. As we glanced at them, they fell to their knees as well. In seconds, there were only our people standing. The ring they formed around Akanji and Lucian made it clear that only one of them would be leaving the room today.

Alive, at least.

Lucian and Akanji were both covered in a dozen small gashes, cuts that had barely touched their flesh, but each suffered more than could be expected by such a light caress.

Lucian's wounds radiated thin black lines of infection and rot, Akanji's twin black shortswords seeming to devour the light as they flickered and flashed in and out. Lucian's greatsword, Justice, glowed with the light of Sint. For every tiny scratch he managed to inflict upon Akanji, the light burned into the creature that was the antithesis of everything Sint held dear.

Lucian swung the sword with everything he had, the tip blurring as he made it dance, carving a circuit around the Elder Vampyr who leaned back, sneering, then leaped forward. He slid under his opponent's guard and struck with both blades.

Lucian yanked his sword back, holding the hilt in the left hand and barely deflecting the strike on that side. He slapped the palm of his right hand to the blade aimed for his stomach and managed to deflect it down and outward. The tip of the blade punched through his upper thigh. The armor he wore, even lovingly crafted by the Legion, was no match for the tremendous strength of the Vampyr lord.

The strike wasn't deep, but it was long, cutting through the upper muscles on the right thigh, carving across and exiting the far side, tearing an entire section of the cuisses free in a spray of black blood.

"Do you feel it, little brother?" Akanji snarled. "Your death? She grows close. Time to join our worthless father and the rest of your pathetic…"

Lucian dropped his sword and lunged, hands grabbing Akanji's where they gripped his hilts, yanking the Vampyr forward and headbutting him.

The Vampyr reeled back before hissing and lunging for his brother as his swords clattered to the ground. His hands went for Lucian's throat. Long, sharp nails slid out of his fingers as he dove.

The pair of them fell, Lucian's injured leg unable to hold their weight. They wrestled back and forth, it quickly becoming clear that Akanji had obviously been trained in the sword. He had clearly kept up some form of practice through the long centuries. But he'd never been taught wrestling, or at least not like Lucian had, especially not now that he'd been refining those skills with Restun.

Lucian twisted the pair of them over, turned the Vampyr's arms outward and locked them, the bones holding them in place until he managed to lift his knee, ramming it into his opponent's sternum and arching his back, giving himself greater leverage as he twisted, then forced himself to straighten the leg.

Akanji hissed in pain and fury and tried to twist his wrists, aiming the ganglion on the inside of his wrists at Lucian, who jerked his face back a millisecond before they ejected a spray of red fluid.

On contact with the air, the red fluid became sticky as hell, similar to a spider web. It fell, coating the ground on either side of the creature, making us grunt in recognition.

Clearly this shit was what Barabarattas had tried to use on us, and we were not amused. Lucian straightened with a cry and yanked backward in one smooth motion, dislocating both of Akanji's arms and making the Vampyr lord scream in pain.

Lucian released the arms, rolling to the side and away from Akanji, before popping a potion from his belt, a glistening red that glowed with faint glitter. He poured the potion down his throat before sweeping his sword up and glaring down at Akanji, who was hissing in pain, writhing on the floor, and trying to alter his body in whatever way they did. He managed to get one arm back into place…right before Lucian hacked it off.

Akanji screamed then, loud and long, writhing to the side as Lucian lopped off the other arm, then took both of his legs. Lucian systematically butchered his brother, tears streaming down his face as he limped around the writhing remains.

We kept our silent vigil until the body was all that was left, a wriggling torso with a head, great gouges running up and down the remains. The arms and legs were cut into short sections that wriggled and twisted with an unnatural life all their own long seconds after life should have left the tattered form.

Then, Lucian finally stopped, turning to look up at us sitting on the throne, and he stumbled forward, sinking to one knee and crying out in a great voice.

"It is done, Scion. The taint is defeated, and the City of Himnel is yours. ALL HAIL LORD JAX!"

CHAPTER SIXTY-ONE

The echoes of his proclamation came back to us as we sat back, the screens that had tried to fill our vision before popping up again, and we looked them over. Standard Imperial systems, heavily degraded by time and missing most of the functionality that was common at the height of our Empire, but there were still some system functions that could be made to serve our needs. First of all, though…

Congratulations!

You have reached the control center of Himnel City and have the prerequisite authority and abilities to claim this city and the surrounding land (782 square miles), adding it to your territory as a claimed location.

Full functionality cannot be bestowed until Previous Claimant: Tirana Sertino, relinquishes access rights.

BEWARE!

Until the city and surrounding territory has been purged of dissidents and enemies, and the general morale has been raised from -25 (Distrustful) to a minimum of 0 (Neutral), this territory will suffer a penalty of 35% to all production, including lifeforms.

(Time since morale was at 0 (Neutral), 37,482 days, 4 hours, 12 minutes 5 seconds.)

Do you wish to annex this territory now?

Yes/No

We selected yes and looked aside to where Lydia waited with the others.

"Lydia," I said, forcing my way into primacy. "I need you to get Tirana and bring her here." She bowed her head, clapping a fist to her chest, while the rest of the room waited in silence.

Attention, Citizens of the Territory of Dravith!

The City of Himnel has been claimed by a worthy aspirant of ancient bloodlines!

All Titles, Deeds, and Laws in the Territory of Dravith are held for review, and can be revoked, altered, annulled, or approved.

All Hail High Lord Jax of Dravith, Scion of the Empire and Master of Himnel!

Jez Cajiao

Congratulations!

You have claimed Himnel City.

In claiming this location, Repairs, Production and Restructuring options have been made available!

*

Congratulations!

You have led your forces to formal war for the second time, overcoming a more numerous, entrenched opposing force. As such, you have earned a Title!

Blitzkrieg: level 2
You may now choose a bonus for your forces. This bonus will stack with others and will grow as you grow in experience.

Sapper: level 1: All troops led by a Blitzkrieg Sapper gain +5 damage to offensive skills for the duration of hostilities. This boost extends to all troops within a 20ft radius of the Sapper.

Commando: level 2: All troops lead by a level 2 Blitzkrieg Commando gain an additional +5 to the stealth skill while within 150ft of the Commando for the duration of hostilities.

I selected the second level of commando and moved on. They were basically the same godsdamn options I had before, so better to double down on it. It was an extra plus five to the skill, giving even Bob a reasonable chance to stealth now.

Congratulations!

You have annexed new lands into your own, providing the following benefits if the land is worked:

<u>**City Facilities: See addendum:**</u>

<u>**Imperial Facilities…**</u>

We grunted in irritation, dismissing the unimportant details as something to be reviewed once there wasn't a godsdamn fight to finish.

We quickly searched through the screens, pulling some up and tossing others aside before finding the one we wanted. Some asshole had altered the layout from the standard, and it frankly pissed us both off when we saw just how many of the details had been dismissed.

City Forces:
Guards: 5,611
Elite Guards: 47
Himnel Armed Forces: 8,422

Facilities...

I dismissed the facilities, concentrating on the forces, and took a deep breath as the next screen appeared.

Greetings, Scion of the Empire, High Lord of Dravith, and Master of Himnel

Do you wish to set new orders for the forces of Himnel?

Yes/No

I mentally clicked yes, of course, then focused, the map of the city overlaying the screen as I spoke. My voice echoed across the city, as magic formerly thought long lost activated at my demand.

"Citizens of Himnel, I, High Lord Jax, Lord of Dravith, Scion of the Empire and new Master of Himnel declare the war between the Empire and Himnel to be finished. All forces are to stand down. My forces have taken control of the city and the golems. Himnel and Narkolt are no longer at war! Instead, you shall both prosper under my banner."

I paused, the last echoes of shock hanging in the air as people all over the city were roused from sleep or from hiding under their beds.

"The Death God Nimon is now banned from all worship inside the city. All of His churches are to be closed, and the Minor Gods of His Pantheon are outlawed along with Him. To all members of the Dark Church, legionnaires and priests alike, I say this: surrender or be sent to meet your God. All City of Himnel forces, the Dark Church is your enemy. If they don't surrender, then kill them all." With that, the formerly red markers across the city changed to gray, then green, as the city forces acknowledged my orders. Not all of them obeyed. Hell, a lot simply stepped back, tides of dark legionnaires and their supporters fleeing unimpeded for the gates out of the city, but a good number did attack.

I dismissed the screen and sat forward, my body settling again, the utter power that had flooded me receding as Amon retreated.

"I am Jax Amon!" I called out in a voice that boomed. "And I declare the City of Himnel as under Imperial law!"

"All hail Lord Jax, Scion of the Empire!" The legionnaires roared, a little more than sixty of them with me were almost all that were left of the nearly three hundred that had started this fight with me. I knew all of them by face, at least, most of them by name.

I stood. "Augustus, send word to Jon. The city forces are no longer our enemy, but are also not yet sworn. They are to be watched, but permitted to fight the Dark Church. After all, I imagine they have cause to want to fight the bastards, after weeks under their control."

The throne room was packed with the nobility of the city still, but judging from the terror on their faces, I might as well take advantage of the opportunity.

"Congratulations!" I called out to them, dryly. "You get to be the first to swear allegiance!"

There were enough in the throne room that we ended up doing it in three batches, the final echoes of the Oath dying away as Lydia led a young girl through the crowd to curtsy at the foot of the dais.

"Tirana Sertino," I greeted her in recognition, looking down at her and noting the tear-streaked lines in her cheeks, before glancing to Lydia. Before she could say anything, though, Oracle was there, striding down the steps from my side and reaching out. She took Tirana in her arms and held her tight, whispering something.

Tirana had stiffened at first, then she melted into Oracle's arms, devolving into a bundle of sobbing, howling tears.

I paused, the rest of the room with me, before I shook myself clear of it, turning back to the people gathered there.

"You who've sworn loyalty may leave with my blessing. Stay out of trouble, and we'll have a formal gathering in a few days. Until then, I suggest you study the Imperial Laws and your souls. I have no doubt that some of you here will be criminals, just as some were in Narkolt. You will be dealt with. Until then, leave, unless you can assist with the war effort," I ordered. The vast majority practically ran for the door, causing a hell of a blockage as people tried to get out.

"Lucian, your brother?" I asked, glancing down at the still wriggling bits. He snorted, shaking his head.

"He died a long time ago, Lord Jax. The creature that possessed his corpse will be attached to pikes and lifted to meet the rising sun. See how long it lasts," Lucian said firmly.

I nodded. "Well, sunrise should be soon. Get that sorted, please."

"One point, Lord Scion. I haven't seen the last of his entourage yet. Persephone still remains at large, so we will need to be on the lookout for her," Lucian warned. I growled under my breath, not happy at the idea of one or more of those shit stains still being on the loose.

"Fine, rewards will be given for her head, people, very fucking generous ones. So, if you think you might have broken some Imperial Laws, or generally be in deep shit now, start looking for her. It's your best chance of getting me to listen when you explain your actions, rather than ramming a spear up your arse and leaving you on the balcony next to *that*," I called to the gaggle of figures that hadn't managed to leave yet.

I grunted, catching Lucian's eye as he nodded to them as well, before turning to the most conspicuously silent group in the room, one that had shown neither signs of aggression since the fight was finished nor any inclination to leave. I hadn't offered them the chance to swear loyalty, yet apart from one of their number, they'd also shown no interest in fighting me or mine.

"Come on out," I ordered the large female and her party of dark hunters in the container, surrounded by my legionnaires.

As soon as I'd ascended the throne, the still-living guards in the room had surrendered, and the Legion and my personal squad had shifted around, forming a protective half-circle around me and between the dark hunters and the rest of the room.

Now, with everyone else out of the room, I sat back and watched the female as she strode out, looking around warily.

"Can you talk?" I asked, and she nodded. "Good. Your pack mates, your fellow hunters? Hell, *those* fucks…" I gestured to the bodies on the floor and the still sitting werewolf that was utterly incapable of moving without a direct command. "…all wanted to kill me. You don't seem to. Why?"

"Weeee do!" snarled a hulking, black-furred male, stepping forward and growling, until the female backhanded him, staggering him and snarling at his words.

The male bared his teeth before slowly backing up and looking down and away. Once this was done, and the pack hierarchy solidified, the female turned back to me and hesitated, watching me.

"Youuuu know what we arrrre?" she asked.

"Dark legionnaires who failed the Dark Wanker somehow," I said, the spirit of Amon still there inside me, making me feel invincible. Yet, as the seconds passed, His presence faded. Having given me the power and help He had, He was releasing his final grip on me now, His spirit drawing in its missing fragments.

"Yesss and noooo…I wasss changeddd by Thomasss, hisss blood, he ssssaved me…then hee abandoned hissss posssst, leffft usss," she said, clearly having difficulty speaking. I frowned as I worked out what she meant, conversations that I'd had with Thomas running through my mind.

"Belladonna?" I asked, and she nodded her head. "Fuck, you're Belladonna? The woman he's in love with?"

She nodded again, before freezing as I mentioned love. Expression falling, she looked down at her monstrous form and growled in fury, mourning what had been taken from her. I looked to the side, seeing Oracle, who still held the sobbing girl, and I raised one eyebrow in question.

"She needs me," Oracle said calmly. "You can do this."

I snorted, climbing back to my feet and walking forward, looking down at the massive figure as I strode down the steps and through the legionnaires to face her.

Lydia, Grizz, Restun, Augustus, and Lucian all moved around me, prepared and unhappy that I'd put myself at risk like this.

I reached out my right hand, hesitating as I rested it over her heart and began to channel Surgeon's Scalpel into her. I closed my eyes as I worked, finding the paths of her body and the changes that filled it.

There were dozens of different genomes in her, patterns that were in direct competition. They were breaking down by the second. I found some genes that were complimentary, some that were actively working to rebuild her and others that were destroying her. I found entire sections of her body that were failing and others that were frankly magnificent. Her recovery was off the charts. Her strength was far higher than mine was, or should be, if Amon wasn't reinforcing me, anyway.

I searched and searched, before sighing and backing up. I saw the way her shoulder sagged, accepting that she would forever be a monster, and I smiled at her, before casting my communication spell.

Seconds were all that it took, and then I felt the presence of Jenae and the others fill the room to bursting.

"Thank you for responding, Goddess Jenae, Sint, Lagoush," I called out, naming each of the Gods in turn. "Now that we've taken the Command Center, and the final phase of clearing out the Dark Shitstain has begun, I need to ask for some advice." I looked around, seeing the Gods, hazy and indistinct, but clearly listening and waiting.

"There are several of those here who were forcibly changed, followers of Nimon, forced into giving up their lives, transformed, is there anything that can be done for them?" I asked, then felt strange pressures as the Gods used Their powers. A long minute passed before Lagoush answered me, Her voice filling the air like the tinkling of rivers, flowing cool waters that fed the world.

"Much as there was for your brother, there are ways to improve these warriors' lives, ways for them to return to their earlier selves, in part at least. But the process will be long and painful, as well as highly exhausting and intensive in terms of our effort," She said.

"We all have a need for more warriors, and we owe Jax much…" Sint interrupted. *"I have examined the souls of those before us. I will claim one, should he be willing, and make him a paladin-aspirant of Order and Light, though I warn him now, his new path will be hard, and he must earn redemption before he tastes power again.*

"He will serve the lowest of the low, and I will gift him with a healing spell, one that he will use on those society has abandoned. His task will be to give hope to the hopeless and to lead those who have wandered back to the Light. As he guides their redemption, so too shall he find his own." A long minute passed before the one who'd started to challenge Belladonna stepped forward and sank to one knee.

"I willll take thatttt chance…" he growled. Sint smiled, nodding slowly.

"You will earn my mercy ten times over, Edvard, but know this, your soul is strong, and the voice that has tempered you through your years is wiser than you know. The first step is always the hardest, and you will earn your original form back ten times and more."

With that, Sint stepped forward, resting one hand on Edvard's shoulder, and used His divine powers. At first, nothing seemed to happen. Then, as the seconds passed, Edvard screamed and twisted, bones popping as he shrank slightly, his face and form becoming less monstrous and more human.

Then he stopped, still noticeably inhuman, but now resembling a human with longer teeth and ears, thicker hair, yellowed eyes, and larger muscles, rather than a standard human. But he also looked like a hell of a fighter, and for that alone, I nodded.

I recognized him, vaguely, but the other Gods were stepping forward, or a few of them at least. Cruit claimed the one who I'd basically beaten and made my bitch, changing him drastically to suit his new life serving the God of Earth, making changes to allow him to survive in deep places: thicker skin, larger eyes, heavier muscles, but more human as well.

All were claimed, save one: Belladonna. I frowned, turning to look at Jenae, who shook Her head sadly.

"She does not yearn for Knowledge, my Champion. She would find a poor fit in our ranks. She lusts to fight, to kill, and to dominate. She loves her time as a warrior, and has little love for anything save the challenge…"

"Then she sounds like she will fit in with my children," Tamat interrupted. *"Jax, we have had our…differences…in the past."*

I snorted a laugh before nodding and trying to be respectful. "That's true, Goddess Tamat."

"I would offer you a trade," Tamat said, stepping forward, no longer hazy and indistinct but solid, leather-clad, and smiling darkly. She strode up to me and leaned in, putting Her lips close to my ear and whispering in a voice that was half seductive purr and half-drawn blade pressed to my balls-threat.

"I know what you took from me, and I want it back. You hand my blood over, and I'll take your pet as a Shadow Paladin. Refuse, and…"

"I accept." I whispered.

She drew back slightly, staring into my eyes. I reached into my bag and pulled the bloody claw free, holding it in my palm, concealed as I offered my hand to shake. Tamat smiled, then shook my hand, palming the claw and leaning in to whisper in my ear.

"Then the deal is done. Perhaps we can discuss things again later…in private." The last word was purred into my ear in a way that made me well aware I needed to adjust my pants, or possibly pole vault across the room. She moved back, smiling mischievously at me before turning to Belladonna.

"Your heart is dark, full of the murders of those who sought to take advantage of you, my daughter. I have weighed your soul, and I find you to be a fitting addition to my children. I name you a paladin-aspirant and will gift you with skills that suit your own. You will find serving me far more entertaining than my asshole of a brother…as well as more rewarding!"

"Thank you, Tamat."

She laughed, a warm sound that sent shivers up my spine. *"Oh, don't thank me yet, my darling boy. I'm no healer; My gifts lie in other directions. So, while I'll provide the divine 'oomph' to your spells, it will still be you who needs to fix her."*

"Fuck," I muttered, shaking my head, realizing that I'd basically been had.

"I recommend you lay your hand on her heart and start there," Tamat purred. I did as She said, Oracle already working behind the scenes, helping me as I started to cast the spell. Before I released it, I looked in Belladonna's eyes and saw the pain and the hope there.

I muttered to myself. "This one's for you, bro."

Minutes passed as I stood there, my magic sinking into her, and I examined her minutely, gathering up the strands that made her…her.

Once I had them firmly grasped in my mind, I sorted through the others, picking the fragments that I thought were complementary and discarding the ones that weren't. I tried to maintain her old appearance, or as much of it as her genes showed me, including a few of the new advantages, such as denser muscles, stronger bones, and better eyesight.

It felt like seconds became minutes, and elsewhere, I occasionally heard Oracle or Augustus giving orders. I ignored them, knowing Oracle would get me if I was needed.

When I finished, I held the image in my mind, and I breathed out, the power of the spell that had been building all this time, augmented by the divine power of Tamat. It flooded out of my left hand, and I grabbed her shoulder with my right, steadying us both as the magic tore through. It left me feeling weak and unsteady, and her much the same as the myriad changes were wrought.

When I got my head back together, I blinked and shook myself, looking into the stunning beauty of the Elf maiden Thomas had fallen in love with.

She was tall, almost six and a half feet now, regardless of her height before this, but well-muscled and lithe. Her skin was a pale cream, unlike the dead gray of most of the Drow. Her kind tended towards pale cream to light gold, and combined with her statuesque figure and hair so black it seemed almost blue…

"Scion?" she whispered through a throat hoarse from the screams I vaguely remembered from the change.

"Yeah?" I asked her shakily.

"Remove. Your. Hand."

I glanced down. My right hand was still resting on her shoulder, the other…I snatched it back quickly, wincing.

When I'd cast the spell, my hand was directly over her heart and angled to the side. Her chest had been furred and muscled, more beast than anything. After the change, however, she was now very noticeably a female Elf, absolutely stacked, and stark raving naked.

I'd been cupping her right tit without realizing.

"Fuck, sorry," I muttered, wanting to facepalm, but instead satisfying the need to do something by pulling a cloak out of my bag and passing it to her.

She wrapped it around herself quickly and tried to stop the glare she was giving me as she thanked me.

"Naughty boy," Tamat whispered in my ear. I glared at Her, seeing that the others had been moved away and were either kneeling in discussion with their Gods, resting, or gone already.

"You and I are due a little chat about Bane, Tamat, don't think I've forgotten that, You crazy bitch." I sent to Her mentally, getting a grumble in return. I marked that as a conversation to have later, maybe in a day or two when I'd had the chance to calm down a bit more. I turned away from Tamat and looked to Jenae.

"Thank you, Goddess," I said formally. She smiled, Her attention returning.

"Jax, you and your people have succeeded beyond all expectation. We must leave you now, but know that We are proud of you. Your abilities grow, as does your right to rule. You have many notifications to sort through, I know. But before you lose yourself in them, I recommend you make any necessary changes to your troops and get the city in order. Then rest. Thomas and Mal are heading back to the city now, and their ships will bring news."

"And it's not good, I bet," I whispered, before shaking my head. "Okay, thank you Jenae. I'll make sure to get the city chapels and so on purged as well." I got a small smile from Her before She nodded and vanished, the sense of the Gods being close to hand leaving as well, as the others left soon after.

I moved back to the throne, finding a second seat had been set up nearby, the throne itself now alone on the highest dais. The thrones that were intended for the Death God and the one that the arch-priest had occupied had been thrown down.

The second seat was on the next level down from the dais and was more like a low sofa than a formal chair. It was also filled with Oracle, in her full-sized form, and Tirana, the child who'd been raised into the role of the Mistress of the City and forced into what was basically a locked closet. She was curled up after crying herself to sleep in what was clearly the arms of the only person who'd been even remotely kind to her for a long time.

I shared a smile with Oracle before looking to Augustus and, much to my surprise, Jon and several of the remaining legionnaires.

"Jon," I said, smiling. He straightened, cutting off from his conversation with Augustus and stepping forward with a brisk salute.

"It worked," he said without preamble. "The attack of Horkesh and her Wild Riders against the city drove many of the dark legionnaires who were…less than brave…to flee. Then, the sight of the panicked arch-priest and the remains of his guard fleeing the city prompted the remnants of the Dark Legion to join him."

"There are still stragglers out there," Augustus clarified quickly, "but they're either running or dying. The local forces seem to be more than happy to step up and involve themselves in hunting their previous allies. The city's gangs seem to be using the opportunity to even a few scores with the Dark Legion. At least as many are dying from assassination or accidents as from battle."

"Sounds like it's going well," I said, smiling. "How…"

"Denny is on his way," Augustus replied. "Most of the diamonds are either in place or are being moved up now, with the golems doing a lot of the heavy lifting. Our forces managed to kill nearly half of the Dark Dicks when they broke and ran. Denny's crystal bombs and the claymores you taught him about certainly saw to that. Oh, and he's putting the second batch out as well now, just in case he needs them again."

"Thank fuck," I muttered, sitting back with a groan. "I don't know about you guys, but I need a week in a spa."

"What's a spa?" Augustus asked, confused.

"You know that pool that's under the keep in Narkolt?" I asked and he nodded. "It's like that place, but lots of them, places you can get massages and so on as well, and you just chill out for days getting massaged and lying around in the pool."

"Hmm, sounds, well…don't you get bored after a while?" Jon asked, frowning.

"I've no idea," I admitted honestly. "Where I come from, the ladies all love them, and go on about going to these places as a couple and 'recovering from life' and all that shit." I shrugged. "I never went, but damn, I want to go now."

"I'll take your word for it," Augustus said. "Romanus is asleep, but he's getting better as well."

"Oh, thank the Gods!" I muttered sitting forward. "How long…"

"He won't be up to taking over for some time to come, I'm afraid," Jon said firmly. "You're stuck with us pale imitations for several more days, at the least."

"Jon, you've done a great job. I've faith in you." I said, shaking my index finger at him. "Romanus is just…"

"He's the father of the Legion. We all look up to him." Augustus smiled. "But for now, Denny should be here soon."

With that, an elite soldier hurried into the room, slowing and making sure to keep his hands clear of his weapons as every legionnaire reacted. Jon waved him forward, speaking quietly before dismissing him with a sigh.

"The Dark Legion attempted to push Denny and his people back. They fought them off, but he doesn't want to leave his post and asks for reinforcements," Jon said tiredly, making me groan as I clambered to my feet.

"Sounds like it's time to get the soldiers sorted out, then," I muttered, waving Oracle back down as she made to get up. "It's fine. Stay there; I can sort the Oath myself. I just want to meet the Himnel soldiers' leadership. You stay with the girl; you both need to rest."

"I don't like you going without me," she said.

I smiled, stepping in close and kissing her lightly on the forehead.

"I'll be fine, I'll sort this, then I'll be back, and we can get a room somewhere, sleep this shit off, and get ready for the next day."

With that, I strode down from the dais, noting the way the Legion split in half, one side staying and surrounding Oracle wordlessly, while the other half went with me.

"Where are the leaders of the army and so on?" I asked, and Jon pointed to a door down the hall.

"Until they've sworn and we know we can trust them, I ordered them to wait in there," he said.

I sighed, knowing after the wonderful experience with Alistor that it wasn't as secure a method as we'd believed.

"Good choice, Jon," I said firmly, covering the few feet to the door with an easy stride before letting Grizz enter ahead of me. I followed him in, accepting that I'd probably never be the first to enter a room in a situation like this ever again.

I greeted the three men in the room with a smile and accepted their salutes, ignoring the obvious fear and no longer trying to reassure people, as I once had. Amon watched them and subtly hinted at things as he faded, the long sleep slowly taking more and more of him as the men explained their positions, their various spheres of influence, air, external, and internal, commanding the airships and fixed defenses, the army and the guard forces, respectively.

"Thank you all," I said firmly. "Now, my forces are arrayed outside the city, mainly tying down the Dark Legion, so first you'll be taking an Oath, and then what I need you to do is…"

Chapter Sixty-Two

The next morning dawned clear and bright, the sun slowly rising and bringing a brightness to the room that woke me with a groan.

The previous day had degenerated into a blur of meetings and assholes, several of which ended up discovering exactly why I was renowned for having fuck all patience with bullshit. One even managed to get a rise out of Amon, who'd been so silent that I thought he'd already left me.

That particular dick was the reason one of the rooms we were using as a meeting room had to be redecorated now, and we'd had to move to another one.

It had felt a bit less serious, sitting in what was apparently called a smoking room for our meeting. Even more so when Grizz, who'd come with us, ostensibly on guard, found the catch that opened the wall covering.

The rows of expensive brandy, rum and more, and hundreds of cigars that appeared when the covers were withdrawn meant that the rest of the meetings were far more genial and slightly more muddled by the end.

Denny had arrived about an hour into us being in the smoking room, and was clearly pissed at first. His ire melted into elation when he found that he could help himself to whatever he wanted, staggering out of the room three hours later with a bag full of expensive booze and cigars as a reward for his hard work.

The legionnaires were brought in in small groups as the day went on, and I thanked them personally. It wasn't much, considering what they'd done, and what I'd end up asking them to do again very soon, but it was important to me to make sure they knew I did care, after everything they'd been through for me.

By the time it was all done, I'd resorted to healing spells and more to purge myself of the toxin buildup. When Oracle brought in Tirana, she was the last meeting of the day.

She basically abdicated as soon as she rose from the curtsy she gave me, desperate to have it over and done with, and had asked if she could go. I'd looked at Oracle, who subtly shook her head, and I sat up straighter and told her to take a seat.

The next twenty minutes had been painful, but it'd come out that she was a descendant of someone who had come through the portal about seventy-five years ago. Her great-grandfather got her great-grandmother pregnant in a whirlwind romance and had tried to skip out of town, claiming to be a lord.

He'd been lynched by her family, and the resulting daughter was raised in a loving home. The years had been hard but good ones for the family, until the day that the grim-faced priest had come, demanding a blood offering to the Death God.

Her blood had triggered something on the small stone that it was rubbed across, that only the priest could see. When she'd tried to run away, the priest had her father killed. Then, he threatened to do the same with the rest of the family, if she didn't immediately do as he ordered.

She'd boarded the coach and had been brought to the palace. A lot of scary men and women had taken more and more blood and argued over her. Then she'd been made to say and do things she'd not understood, before being forcibly bonded to the wisp.

The poor wisp was a tiny, confused creature, already traumatized by everything it had been through. After it'd tried to protect Tirana, and I'd wrapped it up and cut it off from even her, it'd basically gone catatonic.

Oracle had spent the entire afternoon coaxing it back into responding to the world around it, with both Tirana and Selkie, the name it had chosen, being plain terrified of the world around them.

I'd sensed a maleness to Selkie when I'd faced it, but it apparently chose to be both, and neither, responding to he, she, and they all in the same way. I just shrugged and accepted that the world was weird, that the weirdest people in it were generally the most interesting and accepted it as that.

The rest of Tirana's family, mainly an aunt, uncle, cousins, and a brother, were summoned and she was given a room nearby in the keep. She was under guard, but only because she was so messed up right now and had a bloodline that made her a target for others.

She and Selkie were given food, and Oracle helped them to come to terms with their situation as best they could.

Oracle.

I rolled over and tossed the covers back, grinning at the perfectly rounded ass that greeted me, laid half-diagonally across the bed from me and naked.

We'd ended up getting Barabarattas' rooms cleaned while I was in meetings, and the bed itself stripped and remade with a new mattress and fresh sheets, just in case.

I wasn't particularly interested in the room. I'd have been happy in a room that was one tenth of the size, but it was a formality thing, and as master of the city, I needed to be seen doing it the right way.

That thought had floated up from Amon, as many others had throughout the day. Hints and memories, little nudges, and I'd wondered if this was what it would have been like with a family to guide me.

I shifted on the bed, reaching out to draw a finger down Oracle's bare back, stroking the skin as I admired the view, the bright, spotless white, fluffy blankets piled up on either side of her, and her golden hair strewn across her upper back and the bed next to her.

I gently traced a little pattern on her lower back, and she groaned, waving one hand to get me to keep going when I stopped.

"More?" I asked, and she gave a little grunt of affirmation.

I snorted and shifted around on the bed, laying alongside her and admiring the view, stroking my hand down her back, one fingertip drawing fanciful designs on her skin and making her shiver lightly in pleasure, before turning and rolling onto her back to gaze up at me.

"Morning," she whispered. I leaned in for a long kiss, tasting vanilla and strawberries before pulling back and shaking my head in amazement. She was literally perfect in every way, and as I glanced down the length of her…

Yeah, literally perfect.

"I'm tired," she said, stretching in a way that drew my eyes.

"Is this from the changes?" I asked with a frown. "The ones that made you able to sleep?"

"I think so." She smiled up at me. "I just know I really can't be bothered to get up right now, but I also want some attention, so I think it's my turn to lie here, and your turn to put all the effort in." She lifted up and kissed me again, before shifting around to lift her right ankle over my left shoulder and nodding downward with a naughty smile.

"Get to work," she ordered, lying back as I moved, the last words that she could make out clearly being, "Yes, ma'am."

Several hours later, we left our room at the top of the keep, the view from the asshole's suite being clear and high enough that we could see the Dark Citadel in the distance, and the diamonds that surrounded it.

It was too far to make out much clearly, but it was also clear that there wasn't anyone fighting. I'd made the most of the view, mainly by banging Oracle up against the massive windows at one point.

The day had started magnificently, as far as I was concerned, and continued that way when I discovered that Barabarattas had a stash of the really good coffee I was basically addicted to by now, as well as a chef who knew his stuff.

Ten minutes of explanations and half an hour later, I was eating their version of a full English breakfast, watching the airships as they moved around in their constant dance of replenishment and patrols.

Twice, small ships had attempted to leave the citadel while I slept, ocean-going ones, as they had no airships of their own. Augustus had apparently waited as they left under cover of darkness, making sure they got far enough out that they couldn't just turn back, then had an airship fly in and ask them to surrender.

As they did it, right after firing a barrage from the ripple-fire cannons at the citadel for emphasis, the ships were very well-behaved.

The rest of the day was spent in meetings with military commanders as we made arrangements for the siege, the situation being totally different for the Dark Legion in their citadel than it had been with an actual city. Each day for them brought them one step closer to starvation, while we only grew stronger.

Restun took charge of the next phase of training, planning out camps for the soldiers to be trained in, physical fitness standards, and more, the Armies of Himnel and Narkolt being essentially reconsolidated into simply the Imperial Army and the airships being designated the fleet.

There were hiccups, and good Gods there were bumps, as the crews of airships from Himnel and Narkolt clashed, arguing over doing things, or the other side not doing them. As the Scion, I simply stayed out of it, and left Oren, Decin, and surprisingly Elise to deal with things.

Where Oren held nominal command of the airships and the fleet overall, and Decin was ostensibly his second, the one that all the fleet lived in true terror of was Elise.

As the Chief Engineer for the fleet, and by now, a fast friend of Ame and Riana, the three of them tended to descend on any troublemakers and "discuss" things with them.

People who annoyed Riana tended to find supplies running out, requests for upgrades being lost, and so on. Ame tended to more of the "instill utter terror" way of dealing with anyone who annoyed her. Elise simply beat the living crap out of anyone who crossed her.

It was a good combination, one that resulted, after five hours of their being on site, in a VERY respectful group of sailors.

Especially when they saw the rewards, which were the enormous mark-two ripple-fire cannons.

The mark-two was a far more elegant system. Where the original was a boxy, five-by-five set of tubes held in a wooden frame and pretty much kept together out of hope and spit, the mark-two was a set of twelve of the smaller cannons wrapped around a single, much larger one, attached to a pivoting mount.

I'd explained the vague memories of anti-aircraft guns on the old, decommissioned warships I remembered from growing up. The sights had fascinated Elise especially, and this was the result, along with a complicated system of gears that could be raised and lowered to adjust the cannon's targeting.

The cannons fired in a ripple still, starting at the nine-o-clock point and working all the way around clockwise to eight, before the main cannon fired. The smaller ones were all Magic Missile variants, high-velocity ones, but the main cannon was something that Ame called Dragon's Wrath.

I called it a fucking plasma lance, and I loved it.

It was only active for a few seconds, then it needed to be cooled and checked for damage. The test that they'd Demonstrated to me had the potential to change the realm, as it'd superheated a section of rock to the point it'd started to melt, running like butter by the time she stopped it, and it wasn't a small rock.

I'd ordered her to make more, but the timescales were daunting, as were the ingredients.

I could make a crafter golem for the same requirements, and not a basic one. Under different circumstances, I'd have never considered it, as a crafter golem was so much more useful, but in a war? The first was due to be completed in a week, and the sight of the weapons coming had made the fleet sit up and beg.

Oracle came in and out of the meetings as she felt the need. Selkie and Tirana followed her and were joined at the hip. Selkie assumed a form that was similar in size to Tirana's, if amorphous in many ways.

They appeared to be made of gray smoke, the eyes the only constant, with their figure changing each time they spotted something interesting.

I was also looking forward to Thomas's arrival in a few hours, Tenandra and Mal's ships clear as they limped along in the distance. I was hoping like hell that there was going to be a few more wisps aboard, and they could take their turn with Selkie.

It wasn't that Selkie was difficult, or Tirana. Hell, the pair of them were essentially traumatized kids, and they did anything we asked, happily usually, especially since her surviving family had been gathered in and given quarters with her.

It was the *curiosity*.

At one point, the night before, when Oracle and I were…busy…I'd looked up to see Selkie on the other side of the window, watching with apparently great interest, and shifting their form to mimic Oracle, then me.

It'd put me right off my rhythm, and made Oracle laugh her ass off when she realized. She'd taken a few seconds to explain to Selkie and had sent them away, but for the rest of the evening, I kept catching glimpses of eyes out of the corner of my vision.

I intended to make the most out of being the Scion by getting someone else to help out there…preferably Jian and Tenandra, with Sehran's help.

Sehran had become another issue, one that I wasn't quite sure how to handle. She'd found an orphanage and seemed to have basically adopted the kids there, with Jian helping her to get things in order. I knew it was going to be an issue soon, mainly because the kids were so damn happy, I couldn't imagine that separating the powerful Succubus from them to go adventuring was going to go down well.

I'd been made aware that the rumors had already started, that she was using them for blood sacrifices, that she fed on them, that there was a brothel attached…

The first two rumors were being squashed mercilessly. The third…

After I'd made it very clear that using kids in that way was an offense punishable by death under Imperial Law, it seemed that a lot of the sickest bastards in the city assumed that the rules still didn't apply to them. So, we sat back and let Sehran take care of the problem of those who wanted to abuse her charges personally, along with Lio, who apparently had a soft spot for the kids as well. With Lio's training, she basically set herself up to be bribed by the animals who wanted to get their kicks.

They sought her out, paid their money to her, and were led into a dark room…
Where Sehran waited.

It'd been reported to me cautiously by one of the city guards, clearly unsure if he was going to be punished for reporting something like this to me, but he'd done it anyway. I'd shrugged and said that, as far as I was concerned, sick bastards who tried to do that deserved all they got.

The guardsman had sagged in relief and made to leave, when I'd ordered him to stay. I asked why the hell he was reporting this to me, and where his boss, Ishmael Severin, the Captain of the Guard was.

"Umm, we found out about it because the former Captain of the Guard was one of those who attended the club, Scion," he admitted, shamefaced.

"Fuck's sake," I rubbed the bridge of my nose. "I take it you're the next in line?"

"Umm, yes and no, sir. Robichaud was next, but he went along, too."

"What the hell is wrong with these people?" I muttered into my hand before fixing him with a hard look. "What's your name, Guardsman?"

"Lars, sir!" he barked, standing straight.

"And where do you fall in the chain of command?" I asked.

"I'm fifth in command, sir," he said, trailing off and clearly leaving something not said.

"Are the remaining two likely to attempt to visit the same place?" I asked. He swallowed hard.

"One probably would have, sir. He's a close personal friend of the other two, but he's aware of the situation now."

"And the other?"

"He's a bit busy counting his gold, sir," Lars responded, sighing. "The upper echelons of the guard have quite a few noble sons who have many responsibilities those of us who are…lower born, don't."

"Such as polishing his gold and adding to it?"

He nodded.

"Great. I'm going to make this clear, as you've already sworn to me. I order you to tell me if you have lied to me in the last few minutes," I stated, watching him. He struggled for a few seconds, then sighed and spoke up.

"I did lie, sir. I made it sound as though there was doubt regarding the actions of the third and fourth in line. There isn't. The fourth in line is well known for being available to sort any issue for a fee and does nothing but intercede on behalf of the various criminal gangs that own him. The third is a notorious pederast."

"Then thank you for your honesty and your balls in bringing this to me. Congratulations, Lars, you're the new Captain of the Guard. My brother, Thomas, will be working with you soon. But for now, I imagine you have a good idea of who's corrupt in the guard and who isn't?"

"About half of us," Lars admitted, wincing.

"Well, the army needs shock troops. Draw up a list and pass it to Augustus. He'll help you. Any you need to take action against straight away, deal with now." I waved him away, and I saw the way Augustus left with him, summoning legionnaires to assist.

"Lydia," I called to her, working down the list of jobs again.

"Aye, Jax?" she responded, and I smiled at her.

"How's your job going?"

The answering smile was like the sun coming up. "It's amazing. They be gathered in tha compound outside, every single one Ah could find in tha City…Nearly ten thousand set free already."

"That many?" I asked in amazement.

"Ah think there's more, probably a lot more, but their masters think they can keep 'em hidden."

"Well, as near as I can tell, once you fully claim this section of the continent, removing the Dark Legion, you'll have sufficient landmass under your belt for the next stage," Cai confirmed, tapping his fingers on an ancient gold-bound book.

The cover was faded with age, the red leather and purple stitching as hard as the gold leaf now, but as he opened the book to the appropriate page and started to read, I smiled grimly.

"'And so it came to pass that Sanguis, the Earl of Blood, conquered his ten thousandth mile of land for the Empire. The Imperial Throne recognized his claim as coming of Age and Right to Rule.' There's some more formal phrasing, but the upshot is that ten thousand square miles appears to be the deciding limiter. Once you pass that count…"

"Then I can formally accept my place as a prince of the Empire and hopefully use the damn Ability to free the rest," I growled.

"Sanguis moved from Baron to Earl, according to the records, but yet, his title was Prince of the Empire as well, so…?" Cai shrugged.

"I wonder why the hell he always went by Baron, then?" I asked rhetorically. "He's enough of a prick that he'd have never stopped going on about being a prince, if that was his rank."

"He probably lost it when he took up arms against the Emperor." Lucian suggested. "His rank of Baron was linked to a specific place, while his rank of Prince would have been contingent upon the Emperor's will."

"And, as you've already been acknowledged as Scion, you have the right to take the next step, once you've confirmed your sigil," Cai continued, tapping the book again.

"Seriously?" I asked, shaking my head. "I need a sigil?"

"As much as most of this stuff appears frivolous, some things will be linked to the Rite of Ascension, so I suggest we make sure as many things are in place as possible," Cai said firmly.

"Fine. Do I need to draw it myself or…?"

He shook his head. "I suggest something simple, a symbol that is recognizable as your own, yet different to the ones that were used in the past. I'll have Renna work on several designs with you later today," Cai offered. I always enjoyed talking to Renna. We'd gotten to know each other fairly well over the dozens of hours she'd spent tattooing me so far, and when I'd had the second set added? Well, by now I'd spent about as much time talking to her as I had talking to Nerin about my problems.

I reflected for a minute that, where others used to admit their sins to priests, it was more commonplace for my generation to do it to our tattooists.

We spent some time discussing placements for the various airships that were fitted with ripple-fire cannons for the next week, covered the build schedule for the war golems, and the plans for the Imperial armory and production centers.

Two golem production and storage facilities had been marked on the city interface, both having been claimed by Tirana and handed over to Barabarattas. My claiming of the city had transferred them to my command, and I'd spent a solid minute doing a happy dance when I found that the war golems that were in production were automatically transferred to my command as well.

The Imperial armory was marked with a shield symbol on the main facility, but when Augustus had attended the site, with orders to be very careful about locked doors, disappointment had been waiting for us.

While the golems had ended up under our control, whatever had been stored at the shield site was long gone, and I had to assume that the Dark Dicks had won that round.

Mal and Thomas arrived together a few hours later, their ships landing in the palace compound, the guard having to practically force people to move to give them room to land.

"Hey bro," said Thomas, striding down the gangplank and grinning at me tiredly, while I shook my head in stunned amazement.

Jian and Sehran had been frantic to board Tenandra as soon as her condition became clear, and the sight of the two of them running to her flesh-body and hugging her tight was a good one.

"Man, you look like shit." I told Thomas, pulling him into a bear hug.

"You should see the other guys." He grinned, shrugging. "Well, you can see what's left of their ship," He half turned back and gestured to Tenandra's ship-body.

The former sleek, aged teak and copper-bound hull was vastly different, entire sections of the superstructure were replaced with much lighter oak and iron. Her engines had been added to, nearly doubling in number, and the former sails that had graced her sides to add additional propulsion were gone.

In their place were two larger engines that extended outward from the upper deck, looking more like giant turbines than anything else. The prow of the ship had lengthened, becoming sharper and taller. Entire sections had clearly needed to be rebuilt, and some simply couldn't be done while in flight, judging from the condition of the ship.

She'd been beautiful, but now, halfway through the repairs and modifications that Tenandra was obviously putting into place, she was a Frankenship.

"Seriously man, what happened?" I asked, eyeing Tenandra with the other two, obviously exhausted and practically broken by the journey.

"We got mauled," Thomas answered. "The ship they'd sent was heavily armed, outclassed us in weight and weapons by at least five times. Hell, if we'd not had the ripple-fire, we'd have died. We managed to take her out, but the damage to Tenandra…" He shook his head.

"I can see," I said.

He shook his head harder. "No, bro, seriously, you've no idea. More than half of her internals are gone, entire decks were on fire. We had to reattach engines, hell, the other ship was drifting, and we had to board her and guide her down, with the damn paladin's wisp going mental and trying to feed on everyone."

"You found the wisps?" I asked.

"Yeah, don't expect any help from there. One of them came with us, and it's unhinged as all hell, hates us all, came to try and save the others. It thinks Tenandra is an abomination, so I doubt…oh shit." Thomas broke off as a bright light lifted out of a hole in the side of the ship and flew straight towards Oracle and Selkie, who were walking with Tirana from the keep to join us.

They were too far away to make out words, but after a solid minute of flashing lights and crackling power, Oracle suddenly lifted into the air, exuding a palpable sense of menace that made the people nearby shy away.

"You'll take her over my dead body!" she shouted, and the other wisp was blown backwards, as though a leaf in a hurricane.

"Fuck," I muttered eloquently, hurrying over. "Oracle, what?"

"Slaver! Defiler!" it screamed as a tiny bright light flew at me. The light was red and purple, pulsing dangerously with lighting arcing through it. Before I could react, I was hit by a blast of power, flames tearing over my skin and causing fats to pop and hair to flash away.

The little bastard had charged itself full of flame and slammed into my chest!

The smart tunic I was wearing was utterly useless in a fight. I cried out in pain before grabbing the wisp, feeling it sliding in and out of corporeal form before it was blasted backwards from me, the crowd fleeing the obvious magical confrontation in terror.

"No!" Woodite bellowed, running down the gangplank, his hand extended pleadingly as Oracle struck out, a whip of lightning appearing to flail outward, slamming into the wisp and tearing it from the air with a scream of agony.

The wisp screamed in fury and redoubled its efforts, hurling vile imprecations at me as it tried to get around Oracle, who'd taken up station between us.

She was glowing and furious, literally covered in arcs of lightning that popped and crackled, as I clutched my chest and the hole the little bastard had burned into it.

"Hold still, bro," Thomas looked down and started his healing spell. It hit me like a cooling wave of water washing across my skin. I looked down, seeing the way the spell reacted differently from my own. The flowing, watery nature of his spell made me frown. "There, that's better. Hell, man, I could see bone before," Thomas muttered before catching the look I was giving his spell as it finished. The surviving Legion fell in around us. "I'm Lagoush's champion, remember?"

"Water!" I grunted, nodding in understanding. I tended to fall back on fire-based spells whenever I didn't see a need for one spell in particular. Since becoming Jenae's champion, it became more and more obvious that her blessing had improved my affinity with fire in some way.

Fire-based spells were faster, more powerful, and cost me less than they should, as near as I could tell, and they just seemed to work when I tried things. Thomas's position with Lagoush had clearly come with similar benefits, and he nodded confirmation when I asked him if that was right.

"I did a LOT of healing on this mission. When I got the option to specialize and evolve the spell, well, Waters of Life was an obvious one. It replaces the fluids in a body as well as fixes the physical damage. Believe me, that's a good thing."

He shook his head as Mal jogged over from where he'd landed further around, and he spoke quickly before Mal could hear us. "It means I can wash a hangover away as well, but don't tell Mal!"

I grinned as I rubbed my chest unconsciously before looking over at the wisp that Oracle had now restrained.

"Little Sister," Woodite rumbled grimly. "You cannot hold your brethren prisoner. I will not permit this!"

"Woodite!" Thomas snapped back at the massive grove tender as it strode up. Once again, I was amazed by the sentient offshoot of the trees. "You had to see that crazy fucker attack Jax!"

"I saw Oracle and the one she holds facing each other. I do not support this one's actions, but equally, wisps cannot be held to the standard of other creatures. Long they have been hunted and harvested. They must be permitted to be free…"

"That crazy little fuck attacked me, Woodite," I growled, pointing to the burned patch on my tunic.

"And yet you are hale and strong."

"Because Oracle kicked its ass, and my brother healed me!" I pointed out.

The massive figure let out a sigh. "I accept that the wisp is unstable and was perhaps not the best choice for its brethren to send to search for the others that were taken. But it chose to do this, and it is powerful enough that it stands a chance of success. The younger members did not," Woodite grumbled.

"Not if it keeps this shit up, it doesn't," I said. "Oracle, let the fucker go. Let's see if it's learned any manners yet."

Oracle released it from a crackling whip of lightning that had been wound around it, and the wisp fell to the ground, a small ball of hovering light that dipped and wove unsteadily inches above the ground.

"Now, wisp, you attacked me, and you got beaten for it. How about you try polite conversation instead?" I suggested. After a few seconds, I felt a powerful burst of abuse directed at me.

The wisp lifted from the ground unsteadily, before starting to circle me, sending a barrage of insults that practically split the air as it went.

"Hey, I think this wisp an' me could get along just fine…can I be the one to bond it?" Mal asked, grinning, at just the wrong time.

The comment wasn't serious, everyone that knew Mal understood the dumb fuck was trying to diffuse the tension, but the wisp didn't know him, and took the request to bond it as a threat.

It lashed out with a powerful burst of mana twisted into a sonic attack that sent people in all directions reeling, eardrums burst and bleeding, and it vanished into a drain before Oracle could do anything to stop it.

I couldn't help but shout abuse at Mal, calling him all the names under the sun, even though I couldn't hear myself beyond a faint, distant sound, my head feeling like it'd been gripped by a vise and there was blood running down my ears.

The courtyard cobbles slammed into my ass as I sat down heavily, my balance buggered well and truly as Oracle hit me with a healing spell, one that took several seconds to fix the damage.

"Thank you, Oracle," I whispered a little later, getting to my feet and wiping the blood away, before starting to cast again and again, slowly healing those around me. Legionnaires hurried in to take their turns, and Nerin and her people were there, too, increasing the speed of healing massively over what Oracle and I could have managed.

By the time we got those around the epicenter healed, and I'd managed to calm myself to the point that I wasn't going to lynch Mal for terminal stupidity or hunt the wisp down and staple it to the bottom of the latrines for a month, it was too late.

The wisp was long gone, and even Woodite had to agree that the crazy fucker was unhinged beyond all expectations of mercy now, so we moved to join Tenandra and the others, with Mal and Soween joining us.

"Tenandra, are you all right?" I asked when we reached them. She, Jian and Sehran had all started healing those nearby after the mad wisp fled, and she nodded to me with a faint smile as we reached them.

"I am, thank you, Jax," she said. "While I require significant repairs, my structure is intact, and my surviving crew have made a significant start on the repairs."

"I'm sorry for your loss." I said, noting the three Gnomes I could make out on the deck moved listlessly, and Giint stood amongst them, his head bowed in sadness. "How many survived?" I asked, swallowing hard at the thought of the price the Gnomes had paid for following me out of the Prax.

"Seven of the Gnomes still live, eight counting Giint, and I am truly fortunate they chose to travel with me on this mission. Another four of the rest of my crew, and of the Legion and Thomas's teams, eleven survived of twenty," she recounted sadly. "The cannons of Himnel's Vanquisherwere horrific in close quarters."

"I'm sorry," I replied, not knowing what else to say. I'd sent them on that mission, sent them to help wisps that apparently hated us and were intent on fighting me. I silently cursed myself, before turning to Thomas and speaking to him. "I'm sorry, bro. I saw you were alive, and I just looked to Tenandra…your people…"

"They died to serve the Empire," Thomas said. I froze, looking at him. "Don't look at me like that, you crazy fuck. Seriously, they died for the Empire, they died for the promise of what tomorrow could be, rather than the shit show yesterday was. As long as we make their sacrifice count, then they died well. Don't think of it more than that, not right now, because there's a fuck load of fights coming. When it's all over, and we're sitting drinking rum, we can raise a glass and second guess ourselves to all hell. Until then, if we do anything but keep fighting for the thing they died for, we dishonor their memory."

"When did you get so wise?" I asked him quietly.

"I lost members of my team time and time again since coming here. I led adventuring parties, did I tell you that?" He asked, looking away, unable to meet my gaze. "Total party wipes, bar me, three times over. I was named as cursed. Had to make my teams up from the people nobody else would work with, then I got them all killed, as well. I'd given up, convinced there was nothing in this life for me any more before Edvard made me a dark…what? Why are you looking at me like that?" he asked.

"Yeah, we need to have a talk about Belladonna, Edvard, and your old team, man," I said in a low voice, wincing.

"Why…Wait, before I forget, that Arbuton thingy? The big tree mofo? He took the altar from me for Ashante and basically kicked me out of the grove. Sorry, man."

"Dick," I muttered, before shaking my head as Thomas raised one eyebrow. "Not you, bro, that's fine, I'll deal with that ass later. For now, though, I need to tell you something about Belladonna."

CHAPTER SIXTY-THREE

"That's going to end badly…" Mal said to Soween in a low whisper that could have carried across the Pacific Ocean. I turned back from the rapidly vanishing back of my brother and glared at Mal, who attempted to look innocent.

"Mal…you…" I started, my fingers flexing as I tried to restrain my urge to grab his neck and start squeezing.

"We succeeded," Soween said quickly, stepping between Mal and me, lifting a bag to break our eye contact.

"What happened, and what did you get?" I asked her after a few seconds of effort to not throttle Mal.

"We were attacked by the site's guardians. A hint at least would have been good," Mal snarled.

I turned back to him, glaring as my anger sparked again.

"A hint? Fuck's sake, Mal, you knew what I knew! I told you, Tamat said the site was an old stash of hers for her people, gear and so on was kept there, that's it! That's all I knew!"

"What kinda fool doesn't ask more questions? Just accepting a mission like that, hell boy, it was a meat grinder! Trolls lived in those caves!"

"Oh, I don't know, Mal, maybe the kinda fool that accepted the mission and fucked off without asking for more details?" I shot back.

"We did that on trust! We, *I*, trusted you!"

"I told you what I knew, Mal!"

Soween and Lydia separated us, and Oracle stepped in between both groups, along with Tenandra.

"Jax," Tenandra said calmly. "Mal stayed with me on the way back, assisting us when we needed help and dropped some of his own crew over to help us."

"Yer can't kill 'im, yer know this. 'E's a good man, just got 'is mouth attached te 'is arse rather than 'is brain," Lydia growled.

I paused, taking a deep breath and closing my eyes, before opening them again and speaking through gritted teeth.

"Thank you, Mal," I said carefully. "Thank you for completing the mission and for helping Tenandra and Thomas. I'm sorry for your losses." I sighed, forcing myself to let go of the irritation. "I would have told you any information I had regarding the mission, I promise."

He snorted, about to respond. Then a strange look crossed his face, and he coughed.

"Ah, that's fine, Jax. Don't worry about it. We're good?" he asked, the words sounding half-hopeful and half-begging. When I nodded, Soween stepped away from him, sheathing a dagger unobtrusively, as Mal checked himself and let out a whimper of relief. I glanced at her and got a bland smile in return. Then, just as I turned away, I swear I saw her wink.

"So," I said carefully, trying to keep the smile from my face. "What did you get, then?" I took the bag and pulled up the inventory.

The storage was nearly full, over seventy slots of items, and many of the individual slots were stacks. Grappling hooks and ropes for example, there were seven of each in a stack, throwing stars, there were sixty in a single stack. There were potions for virtually every possibility, from granting underwater breathing to tasteless and odorless poisons that would knock out, kill, or even turn a target to stone.

There were several antidotes, some recipes for various poisons, a collection of weapons, most of which were of average ability, compared to those my people already had, but the armor…

There were five full sets, with everything from boots to cowls, gloves, and codpieces, and they were fantastic. They were all incredibly rare or legendary, and each individual piece gave between two and seven points of increase in the wearer's stealth skill.

Sure, the cuirasses would need a little work, as Bane and the other Mer would have serious issues with them as they were, unless they fancied lopping off a pair of arms. But hell, they were fantastic.

Along with the various armor kits were two cloaks, both black and covered in runic script. The only description I could get was that they were Midnight's Helper, and that they were legendary.

I nodded to myself, pleased.

"Thank you Mal, Soween," I said, meaning it. "I know you, Mal, so I'll ask Soween this, but did you already take your set of armor from the bag?"

"We did, thank you, sir," Soween said, gesturing. For the first time, I actually registered what she was wearing.

In place of the dark gray and brown leather she normally wore, today she was dressed in new black leather with a gentle gray patterning. Looking at it, I remembered an instructor back at the Baron's chateau telling me that solid blacks or any dark color might as well be white for a stealth build. Solid sections or lines draw the eye. That's apparently why ghillie suits worked so well. Our brains were hard-wired to see other humans as threats, so the outline of a human where they shouldn't be stood out with giant red flashing "oh fuck" markers.

Instead, the grays and blacks of Soween's outfit broke up her outline in the dark. I realized that was why there were dozens of different shades, so that some at least would match with the darkness, making arms and legs vanish.

The cloak she wore was a thing of beauty. I paused, knowing damn well that the suit was the deal, but internally shrugging as I moved on, knowing that she was worth it.

"How good is it?" I asked, nodding toward the outfit she wore.

She smiled, saying, "Very."

"Well, I know *Josh* likes it," Mal said. Soween glared at him. He faltered, coughing and clearing his throat. "I mean, uh, good, Jax, it's uh…good."

"Glad to hear it. Uh, sorry about before. The mission, I should have taken the time to…"

He shook his head. "Nah, I should have asked questions as well. As much as it pisses me off at times, I know you've got a lot to do. We went in there expecting a drake or something, from the bones strewn around, tooled up accordingly, then it was a pack of damn trolls. Bastards took out four of my lads."

"Then I'm sorry, mate," I said, and I meant it. "We can arrange to teach a few more of your people magic, if it'll help."

"It'd make a hell of a difference." He nodded, then covered his eyes with one hand. "I can't believe I'm asking this, but he made me swear I would…"

"Go on."

"Jay…he wants to know if you'll teach him the spell to summon a Succubus."

I snorted, the pair of us looking at Sehran, who grinned back at us, before we looked at each other again and said "No" at the same time.

"Just the thought of Jay with that kind of power?" I shuddered.

"Just the thought of what would be happening aboard my ship every time the fucker wasn't needed to hit someone," Mal said at the same time, gagging.

"I could reach out to my sisters," Sehran offered, not understanding. We all shook our heads.

"No."

"Nope."

"Hell no."

"Never gonna happen."

"Nope!"

"So, now that's taken care of," I said to Mal, breaking off as he grinned evilly and spoke to Sehran.

"I don't suppose any of your sisters are in the six-hundred-pound range in weight? Buck-toothed?" he asked.

I paused, considering if the thought of doing that to Jay was actually worth the stress.

"No," Sehran said slowly, and we all heaved a collective sigh of dismay. "But there's an Incubus like that. Remoi, he used to imitate Gluttony. He usually shows himself with an illusion…he won't fit in the Oath Circle, after all."

"Are we really that evil?" I asked, rhetorically, rubbing my chin and looking over at Mal.

"Oh, we are," he said firmly. "We could do it at the Kneeling Lady. Some of the rooms have special mirrors so you can see what's going on." He paused, seeing the looks we were all giving him. "Don't look at me like that! Alyssa told me about them!"

"Are we really talking about summoning an Incubus across space and time to play a prank?" I asked Mal, getting a firm nod in return.

"Okay, just making sure!" I grinned. "Sehran, I know this is a bit evil, and traveling the planes requires a lot of magic."

"He'll be happy to come, if he can get a snack on this side?" she offered.

"Define snack," I ordered, frowning.

"You said you were going to execute anyone in the jails for sexual crimes, right? Well, could I give him one of those?"

I thought about it. A convicted child murderer getting fed to a Demon?

"Hell yes, talk to Thomas after this. Once he's got his head together, he's to check the prisons like he did in Narkolt, anyone who did shit like that? They're all yours. In fact…"

Just over an hour later, I was walking back inside the palace, heading up to the Throne Room to sit and talk to my advisors, Romanus having recovered enough that he could attend, thank the Gods.

The remainder of the day was filled with minor details, arranging supplies to be taken to each of the diamonds, shift changes, some insanely complex math that worked out that each diamond required thirty-seven-point-two people to man them to ensure maximum efficiency.

I glazed over for a lot of it, and the table broke down into arguments between values for the people in the diamond. Was a new archer in the army worth a single slot? If so, what did a highly experienced legionnaire come in at? That was the kind of shit that came out of it, and after an hour, I put my foot down and ordered that the diamonds be made up of the army exclusively.

There was a general acceptance that these kind of decisions were just what lords did, and that there was no need for further input from the army and airship commanders, with Lars for the guard simply bowing his head and being visibly relieved I wasn't arbitrarily ordering *his* people out there.

The airships started the bombardment runs, essentially orbiting the Dark Citadel constantly, swapping in and out as the crews needed rest, and using the ripple-fire cannons to systematically reduce the outer walls of the citadel to rubble. The inner structure's shields moved closer and closer to collapse with each barrage.

"Romanus, Restun," I said, getting their attention. "Are the former slave recruits integrated into the Legion-Aspirants now? How many are we up to?"

"Six hundred and eleven," Restun said.

"Holy shit, that many?"

His smile was equal parts triumphant and terrifying. "You said we could have as many as we wanted. Well, the Legion wants them all," he said. "I've set up three training cohorts, mainly using the older, formerly retired legionnaires as trainers, along with some of the most experienced specialist trainers that Narkolt and now Himnel have to offer.

"We've essentially taken the elite trainers from each and every armed force, the guard, the army, the noble houses, the private trainers. All of them were made an offer they couldn't refuse, as your brother would say. They train the recruits from two hours before daybreak to three hours after sunset, and the Legion-aspirants are coming along fantastically."

I looked at him, surprised, having never thought to hear such a glowing recommendation from Restun for anything before.

"The addition of healers to our ranks and of other healers we can call upon has resulted in a great many wounds, but that's fine. It teaches the aspirants that actions have consequences, gives the healers practice, and while the pain is obviously extreme for some injuries, knowing that, in less than a minute in most cases, they can be up and walking around again? This new core of the Legion is truly fearless, especially after we introduced the rankings."

"Oh?" I asked and he nodded.

"The trainees are, as you ordered before, split into teams of ten, but the teams are now ranked, with the best performing team getting a bonus each day. That might be steak dinners, or additional private training for the members on a one-to-one basis with a favored instructor, or a trip to the Street of Negotiable Affection, depending on the day. The worst-performing team gets to serve the others their dinner, get up even earlier to make the breakfast, do the dishes, clean the cesspits, and gain an extra lap of everything throughout the day."

"I bet you don't have many that lose twice," I said, grinning.

Restun allowed himself another small smile in agreement.

"So, use the Legion in this for now," I continued. "I've not freed them of the diamonds because they're my favorites. I've done it because, if these aspirants are to become legionnaires, they need to understand the Legion, its history, its focus. Use the surviving legionnaires to achieve this." I felt terrible about the losses the Legion had faced so far. There were just over sixty active fighting members now, and that included those who would normally not have been called up, such as Thorn, the Legion armorer.

All legionnaires were legionnaires first, though. In our need, we'd plundered the entire ranks. The retired legionnaires, or those who were frankly too old, too weak through long years of wasting illnesses or in the case of one man, too godsdamn fat to get back into his armor, only a year after he'd retired...These were ideal for trainers, for teachers, and to start to fill the thousands of roles that the training cadre needed.

The overall plan eventually for Restun and Romanus, hell, for all members of the Legion was that the army would be folded into the Legion. Their members would be trained and reborn into the Legion, and one day there would be tens of thousands of legionnaires on Dravith again. But that day was a long time away, and for now, we simply had to survive.

The meeting broke up after another hour, when it was obvious that there wasn't a great deal more to be dealt with. Romanus, who was far from fully recovered, was struggling. But, as the others started to leave the room, Romanus and Restun took a minute to talk on a more sensitive subject...one that they insisted only Lydia remain for, and I asked Bane and Tang to wait outside as well.

"What's up?" I asked, concerned, as Restun and Romanus exchanged a long look.

"Grizz," Romanus started. I covered my eyes and groaned.

"What's the mad bastard done now?" I asked.

"No, you misunderstand, Jax. As part of the healing and augmentation process that the Gods bestowed upon him after the fight with the Valspar..." Romanus sighed, shaking his head.

"I noticed it in the days first following the event. He healed quickly, but still had considerable pain at any movement," Restun recalled, taking over the narrative. "When I checked on him, he denied everything. It took involving Nerin to examine him to find this out, but he is evolving...to what, we cannot be sure, but he is growing in both physical capacity and mental, and as such, we need to watch over him."

"Wait, why do we need...?"

Romanus stepped in. "Not in a negative way, Jax. Grizz has essentially been blessed by several Gods, then improved by them when they were apparently distracted. He is changing, and we, as his superiors, have a responsibility to watch over him, to ensure he is safe and guided in the changes coming in the best possible way."

"Sounds like you want to make these choices for him," I suggested.

"No, no we don't. But he's already improving significantly in all his physical pursuits, as well as paying attention in areas he always dismissed before. To be very clear, Grizz is one of the best legionnaires we have, but I would never have recommended him for a leadership role until now, because he was also the record holder for both the most demerits *and* punishment drills in the last hundred years.

"He's an idiot, and a damn fine man," Romanus said quickly. "What we wanted to do was make you aware he's growing, and not now, but soon, in the months to come perhaps, it may be worth giving him more responsibility."

"Right," I said slowly, feeling conflicted, not wanting to let Grizz leave my team, but also not wanting to hold him back from making the most of the gifts the Gods had given him.

"Just consider it, Jax. That's all this was about. Watch him and possibly think about his future."

As the others left the room, I turned to Lydia, and we sat in silence for a few minutes. Oracle was teaching magic to the trainees, Magic Missile and Complex Healing, and she was teaching Selkie and Tirana to do it, too. Mainly to keep them busy as much as anything else, but it'd become an unspoken rule that no matter where I was, if I was outside of my quarters, I now had a member of the team with me.

Two really, considering that I always had Bane, Tang, Cheena, Lio, or occasionally Flux in full stealth somewhere close, as well.

"Well? There's nothing ta do fer Grizz yet, so…?" she asked after a minute.

I couldn't help but sigh and nod. "Yeah, let's go see what's happening then, I guess." I grumbled, pushing myself to my feet and heading down the hall, passing out of the main floors of the keep and heading down the steps, following the direction the two legionnaires who had been guarding the throne room gave me.

It took twenty minutes, and we'd have missed them, if not for the shouting.

It made it clear where the majority of them were, as we closed in, finally stepping into a long, low room that had been a lower dining hall or some such at one time.

Now it had been converted to a combination of dojo, barracks, and dining room. In the middle of it, Edvard and Thomas were stripped to the waist and fighting each other.

"You betrayed us!" Edvard roared in response to something Thomas had said, a right cross hammering home and staggering the younger, bigger man, before a left uppercut lifted him from his feet.

I paused on entering the room, the two elite guards that stood outside it making motions to join us before I waved them away.

I moved to a table that had been pushed back against the wall to the right of the door and hopped up to sit on it, staying quiet, but pulling a beer each from my bag for Lydia and myself.

Thomas rolled to his feet, spitting blood, before lifting his hand to his split lip and grunting, seeing the blood there and spitting on the floor again.

"I didn't betray you!" Thomas growled. "Your asshole of a God did that!" He dropped back into a fighting stance. Edvard attacked again, punches flying, side kicks snapping out, and blocks blurring the air as the two men fought viciously.

There were three other men sitting or laying on the floor around the mat they fought on. Clearly, Thomas had already fought them, judging from the blood, the injuries, and the general exhaustion, with Edvard facing him now in some ritual I could only guess at.

The room was a long narrow one with the ceiling vaulted and the brickwork exposed, a large fireplace set into the wall on the right, and the lack of any windows making the room swelteringly hot, as the sweat running down both men's bodies attested.

Thomas blocked two punches, slapped a third aside, and twisted, taking a kick on the outside of his thigh, robbing it of a lot of the force Edvard had imbued it with. He moved with it, counterattacking.

He closed the distance as fast as he could, snapping out punches to the stomach, forcing Edvard to lower his arms from protecting his head, lest he have all his ribs broken. Then, as soon as Edvard's hands lowered, a left cross slammed into the older former-dark paladin's face, splitting the skin above the right eye.

Edvard staggered back, lifting his arms again. Thomas landed a heavy blow to the bottom left of Edvard's chest, the audible crack as a rib broke hanging in the air as Edvard grunted in pain.

"You volunteered to fucking hunt me!" Thomas shouted, slamming a left into the ribs on Edvard's right, a second crack echoing, as Thomas started to shift, his muscles bunching, growing in size. "You betrayed ME!" He ducked down as Edvard tried for an uppercut, a blow that Thomas blocked by grabbing Edvard's arms and yanking him in close.

I grimaced, knowing what was coming as Thomas hauled Edvard in and leaned back. He slammed his forehead down on the older man's nose. The crunch of breaking cartilage and bone rang clear as not only was Edvard's nose spread across his face, but his right cheek deformed inward.

Thomas released his former mentor, letting him stagger backwards before clenching his right fist one more time, drawing back and sneering as Edvard staggered drunkenly, dazed.

Before he could land the blow though, Belladonna kicked him from behind, staggering him in turn.

Thomas spun, roaring, and Belladonna matched his massive berserker strength with speed, agility and skill, slapping his blows aside, dodging when he tried to grapple and deliberately falling onto her back as he lunged at her.

Thomas fell down upon her, hands reaching for her throat, and she coiled her legs up under him, planted her feet against his stomach and kicked out before he could get a good grip on her, sending him sailing out of the fighting area.

He slammed into a table, sending old food, plates, and general detritus flying in a crash of broken wood and crap.

Thomas rolled to his feet, kicking the remains of the table aside and rushed her. Edvard sat down to one side to watch with the others, as Belladonna taught Thomas that muscle and might didn't *always* make right.

I winced as she deflected his blows easily, seeming to tap them aside, before delivering stinging slaps to his face, sending him into a greater rage.

I watched in stunned amazement as Thomas changed even more, the massively bulging muscles growing larger and larger, and I wondered how the hell a warrior like this was ever supposed to fight in armor, before remembering Thomas' descriptions of the armor he'd been given after his first berserker session. It'd been fitted with two improvements over the standard stuff. First, several internal sections were made to expand, literally. Sections overlapped with rollers that could move out or in, expanding to accommodate the new size. It was more uncomfortable than the standard stuff, but massively helpful to a berserker. The second option was quick-release latches.

Those meant the crazy fuckers could get out of their armor in a flash.

It was ingenious, but still, fucking insane didn't begin to describe it, when a soldier in battle threw their own armor aside.

I deliberately didn't consider my own past in fights when it came to that.

I folded my legs up under me and relaxed, Lydia climbing onto the table to sit next to me, enthralled by Belladonna's almost supernatural grace as she beat Thomas into a greater and greater rage, while we drank our beers.

Thomas threw back his head and roared, clearly losing his fucking mind. As soon as he did, she acted. The first blow was to the base of his throat, stunning him and cutting the roar off, the second was a flashing knuckle strike to the nerve cluster at the top of his right arm and shoulder, a memory flaring to remind me of its name: the branchial plexus. Then, another hit impacted the other side as he tried to strike back, looking clumsy and slow as she slid aside.

Next it was the legs, the inside and the outside of the thighs, her arms moving like pistons as he staggered. Then a heel strike to the jaw sent him reeling.

She stepped forward, clearly intent on finishing the fight, and he lashed out, instinct driving the kick that slammed into her stomach.

Where Thomas was massive muscle, Belladonna was all lean grace, far faster than he was. But that meant, when a blow landed, it did so to devastating effect.

She stumbled backward, and some part of the years of training Thomas and I had lived through clearly took over as he followed her. This time it was him on the attack, as she flashed out strike after strike, and he shrugged them off like bee stings.

She tried a high kick, and he flashed down, moving inside her center line, and flicking his left arm up and around, catching and trapping her right leg over his shoulder before grabbing her under the ribs on her left side and lifting, spinning her around and slamming her down, hard, on the mat.

The impact sounded like she broke several bones, but it was when he fell atop her, pinning her, that she finally cried out in pain.

He growled as she punched him in the face, then lifted a leg up to wrap around his neck, attempting a sleeper hold. This time, Thomas simply reared back, lifting her off the mat and slammed her down with all his might again.

This time the bones breaking were clearer, and she coughed up blood that coated her lips, before stopped moving fast.

From where we sat, the fight suddenly froze, and I couldn't see why, but as the seconds passed, with Thomas and Belladonna glaring at each other from inches apart, it was clear something had changed. A degree of fear built, wonder at what the hell had just happened, when Edvard coughed out a weak laugh and groaned, before saying the last thing I expected during a fight.

"For the love of the God, just kiss him and get it over with," Edvard wheezed. A low laughter came from those around the mat as Belladonna leaned backward, her hand moving away from Thomas' throat, revealing the hidden knife she'd pulled on him.

He grunted out a laugh and coughed, his hand raising to his throat and rubbing gently as Belladonna unwound her legs from around him. He sagged to the side, lying on the mat next to her.

There was a long minute of silence, as everyone waited, before Thomas struggled to lean up on one elbow, looking down at the Elf maiden, who watched him silently. I grinned to myself as I felt the moment Thomas threw caution to the wind and leaned in, kissing her.

She froze, the knife blurring back to his throat and tapping gently, before she tossed the blade aside, and her other arm lifted to wrap around his neck, pulling him in closer as she returned the kiss.

"Damn…I'm never going to be able to claim the pool, now," Edvard muttered, sounding wistful as he tried to smile through his broken face at his former protégée kissing his most accomplished squad leader.

"Anyone want healing?" I asked from my perch on the table. The entire group jumped, clearly having had no idea we were there.

"Uh, we have potions," Edvard said, clambering to his feet with a stifled groan.

"Yeah," I said, shaking my head. "Seriously, magic is better, and hell, you've got a healing spell now, haven't you?"

"Lord Sint instructed me to use his gift to aid the most in need. We can manage."

"Fuck's sake man, seriously? Look, I get that you've had your head screwed up by a mad God for a while, but there's nothing noble about suffering. Hell, Sint would be more pissed at you if you can't help people because you're crippled than anything else. Seriously, He's a warrior God and a good guy, don't worry about it," I said, casting Surgeon's Scalpel on Edvard and wincing.

"What?" he asked, catching the way I was looking at him suddenly.

"So, uh, first of all, I'd forgotten I cut your arm off. Sorry about that," I said, cocking my head to one side in amazement as I looked over the damage and the shitty healing he'd had done in the past. He was a mass of scars, and not like mine and Thomas' bodies were, with growing up with the Dreams. A lot of our bodies were covered with thin scar lines, ones that had been healed properly, resulting in no more tugging or restrictions where the healing had gone wrong. Now they were essentially patterns on our skin, where they'd not been healed away fully.

Edvard's body, though…it was covered in issues, sections where bones were fused improperly, bits of metal that had been left in, causing infection that needed to be cleansed again and again. Sections remained where he couldn't twist as well as he should, a weak right knee, his left elbow where it gave way if he put too much pressure on it when bent inward.

"Fuck's sake, man, this is going to be a major rebuild." I muttered, getting a grim look from Edvard.

"I'm *fine,* High Lord…"

"Bullshit, lie on the table. Now," I ordered. It was obvious he was afraid of healing, even if he was acting the Big Yan, but he was an utter mess, and he couldn't go on the way he was.

He did as he was ordered, gritting his teeth as I started, figuring that the logical place to start was at the top, and going from the crown of his head all the way down.

I fixed literally dozens of issues, mainly minor, the beginning of a cataract in his left eye, an old fracture in his jaw that had caused an impacted tooth, bones with fragments of who knew what in them and more. It took just under an hour, moving from issue to issue, hearing Lydia using her Complex Healing on the others, as Thomas used his own on Belladonna.

By the time I'd finished, I grinned, the additional flashing of a new notification making me damn well aware of what I'd gained, but I ignored it while I dealt with Edvard.

"Right, there you go, you cheerful fucker," I said, gesturing for him to get off the table.

"What?" he asked, surprised, staring at me.

"You're done. All fixed, full service, fresh oil, and topped off the washers. That'll be a hundred and fifty quid," I joked, grabbing his hand and helping him sit up. I shook my head at the clear confusion in his eyes and tried again. "Edvard, seriously, relax, you're healed. Try walking around." He did so, shifting from side to side, clearly looking for the pain he was sure was waiting.

When it didn't come, he moved more enthusiastically, crouching, bending, and bouncing on one knee. The look of wonder on his face was a sight to behold, and I couldn't help but frown.

"Seriously Edvard, what's wrong here? Why didn't you want healing?" I asked, worried as a thought of some kind of macho culture I'd not considered filled me.

"I've been healed a hundred times or more, High Lord," he said firmly, flexing his fingers and shaking his hands out. "Each and every time the cost of the healing was in pain, pain that the priests would extract for their own enjoyment. The vast majority of the time, there were problems left behind. Now?" He shook his head in amazement.

"Ah, so they're kinky fucks, got it," I said, nodding. "Right, one more reason to kill them all. Anyway, there's one issue left that I didn't want to deal with fully." I saw the way he tensed, and I barreled on, regardless. "Your right side, in your gut, you've got some metal fragments. We need to cut them out, then heal the flesh properly. We can leave them in, but I can see marks of infection, and I'd imagine you get a bad gut a lot?"

He nodded slowly.

"Well, if you want that to stop, we can make sure of it, but it'll be a minor operation. We've got potions that can knock you out." I shrugged. "I know you don't trust me yet, Edvard, and hell, I don't entirely trust you, you fucker. But Sint chose you, and believe me, I trust Him. He says you can atone for whatever you've done and be a paladin of His? That carries a lot of weight with me." I smiled at him, hoping I was reading him right.

"The world is a lot different than you were raised to believe, so just take it slow and maybe ask Thomas questions when you need to," I suggested, getting a nod of agreement from him. "So…" I turned back to Thomas, finding that he and Belladonna were standing side by side, watching the room and saying nothing, despite the ruffled clothes they both had now and the dried blood that was smeared on their faces in opposing patterns.

"Fuck's sake, you two…" I muttered, shaking my head. "Go get a shower and screw each other's brains out. Thomas, you need a new team, or part of one. Maybe it's time to get that sorted out. But either way, get this out of your system, because I know you, bro. You've been pining for her since we reunited, and you're going to be fuck all use 'til you've had some fun time." I waved at them as I started walking towards the door, before pausing and looking back at Thomas.

"Do you trust them?" I asked him bluntly. He glanced around the room.

"Edvard and Bella? Utterly. Coran…well, as long as he's not dicing or drinking. Dashiki and Sip?" He glared at them for several seconds before sighing. "More or less."

"Well, they've sworn the Oath, and they're your responsibility now," I said, grinning at him. "I don't see any need to have them watched any more, do you?"

He paused, then shook his head, the group relaxing as I left, giving the guards their orders to cancel the watch on the small team.

I'd seen them in one of the groups that had been brought to swear to me earlier in the day, and while I'd generally mistrusted them at first, the sense I got from Oracle as she'd watched them was that they'd genuinely sworn the Oaths.

As we walked down the corridor, I pulled up my notifications, having suppressed them for as long as possible. I damn well knew the descriptions of the dead were going to be in there. Frankly, beyond everything else, I was directly responsible for them.

Congratulations!

You have killed the following:
- 2x Elder Vampyr of various levels for a total of 562,884xp

A party under your command killed the following:
- 4x SporeMothers of various levels for a total of 492,964xp
- 67x DarkSpore-Infected Slum Dwellers of various levels for a total of 61,673xp
- 67x DarkSpore of various levels for a total of 5,025xp
- 1x Oathbreaker Legionnaire, level 33 for 58,350xp
- 4x Elder Vampyr of various levels for a total of 963,913xp
- 1x Dark Hunter, level 34 for 59,372xp

Total party experience earned: 1,641,297xp
As party leader, you gain 25% of all experience earned
Progress to level 37 stands at 1,956,910/2,360,000

*

You have completed your divine quest: Cleanse the land of the scourge of the Vampyr!

You were offered a quest by your follower Lucian D'Aquitaine, to find his brother Akanji and all those the renegade has infected. Sint wholeheartedly agreed with this quest and upgraded it from a standard quest to a divine quest!

Elder Vampyr killed: 12/13

Greater Scourge (Akanji) killed: 1/1

Vampyr Fledgling killed: 1/1

Rewards have been upgraded by Sint, Lord of Light to be given to all of your team that took part in the battle against the Vampyr

- 2,500,000xp
- +10 points to Perception
- +5 points to Luck
- +5 points to Constitution

Additional Bonus!
In reward for ridding the realm of the Greater Scourge, Akanji, Lord Sint has granted the ancestral treasure of the House of D'Aquitaine to Lucian and recognizes him as the Head of his House.

NOTE: A single member of the coven escaped, and now flees the area, beware the possibilities now unleashed.

*

Congratulations!

You have killed the following:

- 94x Church of Nimon Slave-Aspirants of various levels for a total of 233,810xp

- 74x Church of Nimon Soldier-Aspirants of various levels for a total of 561,691xp

- 23x Church of Nimon Sanctified and Blessed Soldiers of various levels for a total of 209,783xp

- 11x Church of Nimon Dark Chosen of various levels for a total of 275,979xp

- 31x City Guards of various levels for a total of 171,340xp

- 17x Himnel Mages of various levels for a total of 662,104xp

- 29x Himnel Soldiers of various levels for a total of 217,054xp

- 1x Vampyr Fledgling, level 27 for 73,142xp

- 2x Dark Hunters of various levels for a total of 128,503xp

A party under your command has killed the following:

- 89x Church of Nimon Slave-Aspirants of various levels for a total of 218,762xp
- 106x Church of Nimon Soldier-Aspirants of various levels for a total of 811,922xp
- 73x Church of Nimon Sanctified and Blessed Soldiers of various levels for a total of 672,979xp
- 42x Church of Nimon Dark Chosen of various levels for a total of 1,098,652xp
- 57x City Guards of various levels for a total of 363,657xp
- 3x Himnel Mages of various levels for a total of 118,305xp
- 54x Himnel Soldiers of various levels for a total of 388,411xp
- 5x Elder Vampyr of various levels for a total of 1,147,893xp
- 5x Dark Hunters of various levels for a total of 341,037xp
- 1x Greater Scourge, level 92 for 896,419xp

Total party experience earned: 6,058,037xp
As party leader, you gain 25% of all experience earned
Progress to level 37 stands at 8,504,825/2,360,000

*

Congratulations!

You have reached level 37, 38 & 39

You have 28 unspent Attribute points and 0 Meridian points available.

Progress to level 40 stands at 689,825/3,125,000xp

*

You have exercised your Imperial Authority and claimed 12 Imperial Golems, overriding their previous orders and binding them to you

*

Congratulations!

You have practiced enough to raise your Surgeon's Scalpel spell to its next evolution!

Through constant experimentation and usage, you have deepened your understanding of this spell to a new level. Continue to practice and learn to increase this spell further.

You must now pick a path to follow. Will you choose to improve its efficiency with PRACTICE or will you continue to specialize with FOCUS, or even follow the path of the EXPERIMENTER?

Choose carefully, as this choice cannot be undone.

PRACTICE:

The thousands of individual healing spells you have cast have translated to hundreds of hours of healing, and, as the saying goes, "Practice Makes Perfect." For every ten valid uses of this spell, the cost will drop by 1% and the effect increase by the same.

FOCUS:

Focusing obsessively on this one aspect of your magic offers significant returns, as for every person you heal, you gain a deeper understanding of their form, their biology, and their gifts. Gain the Ability to take a single stat point in payment for your efforts.

Sorcerer Bonus: EXPERIMENTER:

Experimentation in healing is rarely approved of, however, you have begun to make great strides in discovering secrets once thought lost to the world. Perhaps there are methods of healing also lost to time's ravages? Risk it all on the roll of the dice, as your new Ability Infusion takes its toll.

Ability: Infusion permits the addition of a random weave of magic to your healing spell that would traditionally not be included, this could help or hinder, but who would know?

This wasn't any kind of a difficult choice at all. On one hand, I had the chance to learn to help heal people totally for free. Yeah, it'd take a thousand or so uses, but it'd literally become free to use and twice as powerful. Or on the other hand, I could strip those I helped of stat points.

Not gonna lie, there was a tiny part of me that was tempted, the sneaky, underhanded part of me that I hated, but I'd resolved to take this chance to be the best man that I could be.

I didn't even pause at the option for experimenter. Yeah, there probably were secrets out there to find, but risking it all like that? Fuck no. I chose Practice and was surprised when my Surgeon's Scalpel spell simply remained the same. I shrugged and moved onto the next notification in line.

Congratulations!

**Through hard work and perseverance,
you have increased your stats by the following:**

Agility +1
Charisma +2
Constitution +2
Luck +1
Strength+1
Wisdom +1

Continue to train and learn to increase this further.

I quickly pulled up my stats and checked for the most efficient use of the points, muttering to myself as I did what I knew I had to do, considering what was yet to come. My heavily trailing Charisma score was starting to nag at me, as I knew I really needed to address that. It was not so much to help me get laid, as

Oracle was clearly happy with me as-is. But, if I could have negotiated things better, I might not have lost so many good people.

Name: Jax Amon				
Titles: Strategos: 5% boost to damage resistance, Fortifier: 5% boost to defensive structure integrity, Champion of Jenae: One search for hidden knowledge every 24 hours, Kobold Ravager: +25% damage to Kobolds, Valspar's Bane: +25% damage to Valspar, Blitzkrieg Commando (2): +10 to Stealth to nearby forces				
Class: Spellsword > Justicar > Champion of Jenae > Imperial Magekiller > Imperial Justicar > Imperial Overlord > Sorcerer		**Renown:** Imperial Scion, Lord of Dravith, Master of Himnel and Narkolt		
Level: 39		**Progress:** 689,825/3,125,000		
Patron: Jenae, Goddess of Fire and Exploration		**Points to Distribute:** 28 **Meridian Points to Invest:** 0		

Stat	Current points	Description	Effect	Progress to next level
Agility	45	Governs dodge and movement.	+385% maximum movement speed and reflexes, (+10% movement in darkness, -20% movement in daylight, +10% overall)	98/100
Charisma	33 (28)	Governs likely success to charm, seduce, or threaten	+230% success in interactions with other beings	97/100
Constitution	63 (58)	Governs health and health regeneration	1260 health, regen 79 points per 600 seconds, (each point invested now worth 20 health)	73/100
Dexterity	70 (65)	Governs ability with weapons and crafting success	+600% to weapon proficiency, +60% to the chances of crafting success	88/100
Endurance	53 (50)	Governs stamina and stamina regeneration	1590 stamina, regen 42 points per 30 seconds, (each point invested now worth 30 stamina)	89/100
Intelligence	115	Governs base mana and number of spells able to be learned	1150 mana, spell capacity: 59 (57 + 2 from items)	N/A
Luck	56	Governs overall chance of bonuses	+46% chance of a favorable outcome	66/100
Perception	54 (44)	Governs ranged damage and chance to spot traps or hidden items	+440% ranged damage, +44% chance to spot traps or hidden items	94/100
Strength	55 (52)	Governs damage with melee weapons and carrying capacity	+56 damage with melee weapons, +560% maximum carrying capacity (+25% to melee damage and maximum carrying capacity)	22/100
Wisdom	46 (36)	Governs mana regeneration and memory	+540% mana recovery, 6.9 points per minute, 360% more likely to remember things, (+50% increased mana regeneration from essence core)	14/100

There were fights to come, sure. But knowing my low Charisma may have cost my people their lives meant I didn't really have another option. I hated doing it, but I dumped twelve of my free points into Charisma, taking me from thirty-three to forty-five. I could have done more, but I just couldn't bring myself to put so many points into it. I kept the remaining sixteen points for later biting my tongue as the changes took place, stumbling along the corridor.

The changes were ridiculous. From when I'd first come to the UnderVerse, and a few points could lay me low, now dozens caused me to stumble slightly. It said a lot about the rest of my life that I'd learned to deal with pain so well.

The rest of the evening passed in a blur, I called out to the Gods to sanctify the main cathedral in the center of Himnel, then sent the priests that had sworn to the various Gods to do the same in my name in the other chapels and churches.

The altars of the various shithead Gods were gathered together, and I made a big show of smashing them, one at a time, with a massive warhammer. With each blow, the skies overhead grew darker and more oppressive. I accumulated points to spend on the next increase in the Constellation of Secrets, which was due to unlock in less than a week, the way I was going.

The next two days passed quickly, our forces being trained as quickly as possible. Oracle and Selkie spent most of their time teaching magic. Tenandra had dozens of engineers working on her frame, adding more and more sections, removing others, and generally upgrading her to all hell.

Ame spent hour after hour with her, having her run tests on integration of shields and dozens of other runes, seemingly intent on making her an absolute work of art.

The iron was removed, the lighter wood stained to match the rest, and fresh, gleaming copper bands attached. The new model ripple-fire cannons that were ready were installed in four banks, two on either side. Her cabins were worked upon, even as Jian and Sehran spent most of their time aboard Tenandra's ship-body…and judging from the exhaustion on Jian's face, *with* her flesh-body as well.

The dark paladin of Nimon that Thomas had captured died, the combination of the wisp abandoning her and staying with its own kind and the heavy drain it'd done on her again and again left her with serious brain damage that wasn't something that could be healed. So, in the end, I decided it was a kindness that she died.

More of the golems were constructed. The prisons were emptied, when I could get Thomas and Belladonna to leave each other the hell alone and do anything besides bang each other senseless, as the pair were like high school kids.

I totally ignored the comparisons by Bane and the others to the early days with Oracle and me, and I maintained an aloof silence when it was mentioned, ignoring them as I checked the freshly arrived notification.

Quest: Return the Rule of Law, Bring Freedom to the Enslaved, and Peace to the Unquiet Dead IV

Note: This Quest cannot be refused without losing your class as an Imperial Justicar.

Punish Breakers of Imperial Law: 1,726/500

Free Unjustly Imprisoned Citizens: 14,894/500

Grant Uneasy Revenants their Eternal Rest: 1,037/500

Reward: 2,500,000xp, Access to Fifth Tier of Evolving Quest

Quest: Return the Rule of Law, Bring Freedom to the Enslaved, and Peace to the Unquiet Dead V

Note: This Quest cannot be refused without losing your class as an Imperial Justicar.

Punish Breakers of Imperial Law: 1,226/2,500

Free Unjustly Imprisoned Citizens: 14,394/2,500

Grant Uneasy Revenants their Eternal Rest: 537/2,500

Reward: 5,000,000xp, Access to Sixth Tier of Evolving Quest

I pulled the details of my next prompt up, unable to help myself from smiling in a way that was making the others worry, considering the shit they'd been throwing around, when I saw the best notification I could have received.

Congratulations! You have reached level 40!

You have 56 unspent Attribute points and 1 Meridian point available.

Progress to level 41 stands at 64,825/3,415,000xp

I pulled up the stat details, reading over the sheet and trying to decide where the points would be best used. After all, forty more godsdamned points on top of the sixteen I'd had was a game changer!

I loved hitting the multiples of ten in leveling, I reflected, although I had to worry what it'd be like hitting a hundred, and the pain of allocating the hundred points that would come with it.

First, and most obvious, I could actually hit my century if I put thirty straight in Dexterity or thirty-seven into Constitution, which was incredibly tempting, but…

The problem was that I was becoming a sort of a one-trick pony, and I damn well knew it. My Intelligence had gone through the roof recently, and that had made a huge difference, both in real world terms from the way I thought, and even more so in the way I fought.

I *wanted* to put all the points in one place, make myself super-human in another way all over again. After all, I was already leaping through the levels, partially because I was constantly at war or questing, and partially because, despite not saying anything about it, I kept getting hints from Jenae that She was artificially boosting my experience rewards.

It was never anything She said, it was just…a feeling, and the way that sometimes when I got my notifications, they would blur slightly and leap up in number.

She'd never said anything, and I got the feeling She wasn't supposed to be doing it, so I never drew attention to it either, but I was damn thankful either way.

Looking at my details, I saw that, while I was at a hundred and fifteen in Intelligence…I was still below fifty in some of my stats. If I placed all my points into one or two stats, they'd become much more powerful, but ignoring the lower stats much longer would be a mistake.

I'd had conversations with Carmen about stats. Hell, I talked to basically everyone I could about them, whenever I could. One of the things that came out is that the stats weren't stand-alone.

Or, at least we *suspected* they weren't.

Stats like Intelligence weren't affected by Wisdom officially, but it blatantly was, considering the know-it-all assholes with massive Intelligence who got nowhere in life because they couldn't understand that telling everyone how smart they were wouldn't help them.

Perception and Dexterity massively affected the damage done with ranged spells as well as weapons, and Strength and Endurance just went hand-in-hand naturally.

Or the way that Endurance and Constitution seemed to reinforce each other in a fight. When one was markedly lower than the other, people seemed to feel the pain of their wounds more and give up sooner.

I had a nagging feeling that they were all like that. If I boosted the few that were lagging behind up to the same level, it would help out overall.

But I really didn't fucking *want* to.

Considering how much physical fighting I normally did, putting any points into Perception, Charisma, or even Wisdom just seemed like a waste, especially considering how damn close I kept coming to dying. I'd probably regret leaving them behind if I waited much longer though I knew.

I desperately wanted to use the points to hit my century on Dexterity as well, even though that was more geared towards crafting than survivability, but I resolved to use these points to fix some of the outstanding issues, despite how much I hated the thought.

I decided to bring all my trailing stats up to at least fifty, as I had enough points to do that, and once they were at that level, I could justify hitting more centuries without having to worry about the other stats as much.

Looking through my stats, the ones that were below fifty without boosts from my gear were Agility at forty-five, Charisma at forty-five, and Wisdom at forty-six.

Groaning at the thought, but knowing I needed to do it, I quickly allocated five to Agility, five to Charisma and four to Wisdom. That left me with forty-two points, and I paused, thinking over my options, before finally nodding, and going for gold.

I dropped thirty-seven points into Constitution, accepting that for me to bring about the changes I was working towards in the future, I needed to damn well survive that long. That would give me my second century, and this time in an area that would help me survive. The remaining five points, I cast about almost aimlessly with, before giving in and dumping them into Wisdom, accepting the changes before I could change my mind.

I gritted my teeth as pain ripped through my body. Assigning this many points at once would have knocked me flat only a few weeks ago, but after experiencing the amount of pain I had recently I barely managed to stay conscious.

Once I recovered from assigning the points, I pulled up my meridians, knowing that Restun was right, and I damn well needed to continue to build on them to truly unleash my potential.

PRIMARY

Brain: 1/10 Spell Cost Reduction: -5% (Primary Bonus: 1 spell slot per point)
Head: Primary Node: Additional points invested will reduce mana cost by 5% (Note: Air Elemental Core results in increased mana regeneration by 50%, self-control decrease of 5%).

SECONDARY

Eyes: 1/10 Vision Improvement (Secondary Bonus: +10% chance to notice important visual details)
Eyes: Important details will glow to your vision. This will level with the relevant skill.

Ears: 0/10 Hearing Improvement
Ears: Important sounds will become clearer with concentration. High levels will aid in translation.

Mouth: 0/10 Vocal Improvement

Mouth: Your voice will become 10% more likely to have a desired effect on a target, soothing, seducing, persuading as required.

Nose: 0/10 Tracking and Detection Improvement
Nose: Scents will be stronger, aiding in tracking.

Heart: 1/10 Health Increase
Heart: You will gain an additional ten points of health for each point invested in your Constitution.

Lungs: 2/10 Stamina Increase
Lungs: You will gain an additional ten points of stamina for each point invested in your Endurance.

Stomach: 0/10 Sustenance Improvement
Stomach: You will gain the abilities to resist poisons by 5% and to gain sustenance from more sources.

Legs: 1/10 Speed Increase
Legs: You will gain a boost of 10% to your speed, as well as better stability over various terrain.
(Note: SporeMother Core results in a gain of 10% to your speed in darkness. Speed in daylight will be decreased by 20%)

Arms: 1/10 Strength Increase
Arms: You will receive a boost of 25% to your carrying capacity and your damage output with melee weapons.

Hands: 0/10 Dexterity Increase
Hands: You will develop crafting abilities at a 10% increased rate, along with a greater chance to succeed in crafting complicated items.

Looking them over and dismissing the ones I already had points in, I was left with Ears, Mouth, Nose, Stomach, and Hands, none of which really appealed to me, as none of them were really geared toward war, and that was my life these days.

Again, in line with my determination to do things right, though, rather than following my gut, I worked through it logically. Ears were for hearing, obviously. It suggested that I'd be able to translate things better with higher investments there. But so far, most people seemed to speak the same language, and I had Bane for stealth detection, so…hard pass.

Mouth…yeah, I'd come back to that, as that seemed to work with the Charisma investment. Nose was all about tracking by smell, and that was not something I needed right now.

Stomach, that seemed more geared towards survival in the wilds, but possibly it'd help with not being killed by poisoning, so I'd come back to that as well.

Hands directly affected crafting…at first, I went to dismiss that as well, before shaking my head in annoyance. My alchemy was insanely powerful, especially when it came to war, as the discoveries I'd started to make were massive.

I selected that straight away, dismissing the rest with a mental "fuck it."

With that done, I pulled up the notification I knew would be waiting for me, even as I approved the points allocation, nearly biting through my damn tongue as my muscles writhed, trying for all they were worth to tear themselves free.

I grunted out an explanation to the others as the room went silent—clearly, someone had noticed my shaking—and I read the final set.

Congratulations, Eternal!

You have reached level forty and have a Class Choice waiting.

<u>**Class Evolution Recommendations**</u>
Common:

Instructor: You've found, through trial and error, that not only are you a gifted teacher, but by acting as a target, you can help your companions improve their own skills. Choosing this as your latest evolution will grant you a one-off bonus of ten points to Wisdom, a randomly chosen Skill increase of five points, and a five percent chance to increase other's skill levels whenever they spar with you for more than three hours.

Streetfighter: You've found your place in life, and it's between those guys and whoever else you can find! As a Streetfighter, you're known for your lack of patience, your love of fighting, and your ability to take a punch and keep on coming. Choosing this as your latest evolution will grant you a one-off bonus of ten points to Constitution and five points to Strength, along with the Ability, once per day, to fly into a Berserker Rage, doubling the damage you deal and halving the damage you take, for 300 seconds.

Captain: You have begun to truly develop your leadership and small unit tactics, reaching the rank of Captain would enable you to call upon additional skills and scouting abilities for your people. Choosing this as your latest evolution will grant you a one-off bonus of ten points to Perception and five points to Wisdom, along with a once per day ability to see through the eyes of a member of your squad for 60 seconds.

Rare:

Fleshweaver: The Fleshweaver has been injured and healed themselves, or been healed by others so frequently, that they've learned to get by with horrific injuries, simply by pulling together the most pressing wounds and keeping on going. Choosing this as your latest evolution will grant you a one-off bonus of fifteen points to Dexterity, along with the Ability Pain? What Pain? When all seems lost, your pain will suddenly vanish, and through the hidden art of Blood Magic, your injuries will reverse, condensing into a single cast spell that will transfer all of your injuries to your target, stealing their health in turn. This Ability may be used once per 144 hours.

Sorcerer II: Magic is more than you thought. Through improving your bond with your companion, and the hints of knowledge that have been bequeathed to you from others, you have come to see the edge of the pattern. You know that it will take centuries of study to understand it fully, if you ever can, but choosing this as your latest evolution will grant you a one-off bonus of Fifteen points to Wisdom, as well as improving the second manapool in your companion's body by boosting it from holding three hundred mana in addition to your own, to six hundred along with gaining one extra choice in future evolutions of spells.

Necromancer Lord: You have built, rebuilt, and augmented your Bone Minion so many times that it has become fully self-aware, and then you claimed control over the undead in their hundreds through a combination of magical artifacts and sheer determination. Choosing this as your latest evolution will grant you a one-off bonus of five points to Wisdom and five points to Intelligence, and the opportunity to raise five Lesser Bone Minions. These Minions will be bound to you and cost the same as your original Bone Minion.

Unique:

Imperial Overlord II: You have claimed dominance of the continent, but as yet, your claim is still contested. Perhaps a boost is just what you need?

Choosing this as your latest evolution will grant you three additional Titles of your choice to award to your followers.

Please see the Examples below:

Arch-Priest: You are currently the highest ranking member of the Pantheon of Flame. Laying claim to the position of Arch-Priest formally will create the ability to induct others into the priesthood, granting them bonuses depending on their deity of choice.

High Inquisitor: People lie, even the best of them. Perhaps it's time to bring the burning light of truth into the darkest places of the soul? Using heat, pain, and sheer brutality, you shall scour the land of their filth! Granting this title will give access to the repeatable Quest Renounce thy Sins.

I read and reread the options before me, seriously tempted by, well, most of them, actually. The least useful one I could see was captain, and even that had serious possibilities. Although, the thought of what I might see through Grizz or Giint's eyes would possibly render me blind for the rest of my natural life.

Realistically for me, as I was right now, it came down to Fleshweaver, Sorcerer Two, Necromancer Lord, or Imperial Overlord Two.

Fleshweaver just fit with the way my godsdamn fights seemed to go these days, and the ability to take the terrible collection of wounds I sometimes got and to give them to someone else?

Hell, that'd be wonderful at times.

Necromancer Lord sounded seriously wrong, especially as there'd been entire wars with necromancers and the Empire on differing sides…but another five I could augment like Bob? Five others that, over time, I could possibly free like him and give him family just like himself? That was both tempting and awesome.

Imperial Overlord Two was awesome, as it was an Empire-wide improvement, really. That was massive! Hell, granting three more titles to my people would make an insane difference, but…

In the end, though, there was just one choice for me, I knew it as soon as I saw it, despite forcing myself to work over the options.

I selected Sorcerer Two, as along with the massive boost in mana for Oracle, and the fifteen points in Wisdom for me, that in turn massively boosted my mana regeneration. The simple truth was that magic seemed of late to be only half the story, like it was just part of what I was seeing in the world, much like knowing that gravity was there, and that the entire realm created it, yet somehow I could overcome it with a thought and damn well fly.

I knew there was something missing in my understanding, both of gravity, which was quite likely, considering that all I remembered of those classes at school was trying to get Kelly to give me a handjob under the table, and of magic.

Name: Jax Amon				
Titles: Strategos: 5% boost to damage resistance, Fortifier: 5% boost to defensive structure integrity, Champion of Jenae: One search for hidden knowledge every 24 hours, Kobold Ravager: +25% damage to Kobolds, Valspar's Bane: +25% damage to Valspar, Blitzkrieg Commando (2): +10 to Stealth to nearby forces				
Class: Spellsword > Justicar > Champion of Jenae > Imperial Magekiller > Imperial Justicar > Imperial Overlord > Sorcerer			**Renown**: Imperial Scion, Lord of Dravith, Master of Himnel and Narkolt	
Level: 40			**Progress**: 64,825/3,415,000	
Patron: Jenae, Goddess of Fire and Exploration			**Points to Distribute**: 0 **Meridian Points to Invest**: 0	

Stat	Current points	Description	Effect	Progress to next level
Agility	50	Governs dodge and movement.	+440% maximum movement speed and reflexes, (+10% movement in darkness, -20% movement in daylight, +10% overall)	98/100
Charisma	50 (45)	Governs likely success to charm, seduce, or threaten	+400% success in interactions with other beings	97/100
Constitution	100 (95)	Governs health and health regeneration	2000 health, regen 130 points per 600 seconds, (each point invested now worth 20 health)	73/100
Dexterity	70 (65)	Governs ability with weapons and crafting success	+600% to weapon proficiency, +70% to the chances of crafting success	88/100
Endurance	53 (50)	Governs stamina and stamina regeneration	1590 stamina, regen 42 points per 30 seconds, (each point invested now worth 30 stamina)	89/100
Intelligence	115	Governs base mana and number of spells able to be learned	1150 mana, spell capacity: 59 (57 + 2 from items)	N/A
Luck	56	Governs overall chance of bonuses	+46% chance of a favorable outcome	66/100
Perception	54 (44)	Governs ranged damage and chance to spot traps or hidden items	+440% ranged damage, +44% chance to spot traps or hidden items	94/100
Strength	55 (52)	Governs damage with melee weapons and carrying capacity	+56 damage with melee weapons, +560% maximum carrying capacity (+25% to melee damage and maximum carrying capacity)	22/100
Wisdom	70 (60)	Governs mana regeneration and memory	+900% mana recovery, 10.5 points per minute, 400% more likely to remember things, (+50% increased mana regeneration from essence core)	14/100

I had to brace myself against the damn wall as the last of the changes tore through me, being hit over and over again with stat increases was horrific, but…

Congratulations!

You have achieved your second Primary Century in point allocation for Constitution and as such you have gained a single new Ability!

> **'Genetic Storage:'** Genetic Storage is an unusual ability that allows you to store a single burst of enhanced healing in your body, set to respond at will should you encounter horrific, possibly life-ending injuries…

> **Cost**: 100 mana per point of HP

That was…that was awesome, but? At a hundred mana for a single point of HP, and I had two thousand mana? I'd look at it later I guessed, I just didn't have the time to dedicate to it right now. I hissed as a ripple of pain flowed through me as the new changes, presumably needed for the century bonus, took hold as well.

When it was over, the world seemed insanely different. I frowned, feeling, *sensing*…the way that magic flowed around us all, and the way we used it currently was even more strongly highlighted to me as being incomplete again.

I grunted and shook the others off as they tried to help me, explaining what had happened and banished the feeling for now. I was determined that I'd work on it once these things were dealt with, and I could actually spend some time working on it.

Then I forced myself upright, drew in a deep breath, and got on with my day as best I could.

As soon as the prisons were emptied, I gathered the nobles together first, just over two hundred, which seemed ridiculous to me for such a small city, compared to back home. I made sure to include a few of the new, loyal nobles from Narkolt in their number to allay suspicion.

When I got to the point in my speech where I offered leniency for those who were honorable enough to step forward and admit their crimes, some fifteen people, all standing around Bol and his wife, stepped forward.

They were obviously nervous, but they trusted him enough, or were in turn honorable or smart enough to see the direction this was going.

Two others in the room stepped forward, and they were all separated out by Legionnaires who asked a simple set of questions after Lucian, as Chief Justicar, ordered them to speak the truth. All of them had committed crimes, mainly smuggling, two counts of murder, one of maiming a fellow noble, and one who apparently used that spell that let them stare in the windows at people getting changed…A LOT.

They were all given various fines and telling offs, while the rest of the room snickered about the fools admitting things.

Once the various fines were given out and years of service agreed to, the Legion signaled me that they were ready to work, separating the wolves from the sheep in the main crowd.

I stood again, strode to the front of the dais, and nodded to Lucian. He in turn gave the signal to begin, and across the city, hundreds of doors were kicked in simultaneously.

Thomas and his new team, made up of half legionnaires and half former dark legionnaires took the biggest concentration of red dots himself, storming one of the gang's hideouts and personally slaughtering the new head of the Copper Ghost Gang.

While this was being done, I smiled and enjoyed explaining the realities of the throne's capabilities to the nobility of Himnel.

"So, now that you know that I can in fact see the various shit that so many criminal gangs around the city had been pulling, you'll all be very relieved, no doubt, because it means that we know when those amongst us have been meeting with criminals!"

I watched the faces of many of the nobles growing paler and others genuinely applauding this. I watched the innocent and the honorable standing there smiling, mentally marking them out as potential real nobles for the future. The guilty, on the other hand, took little steps to the sides, moving to stand closer to the exits.

Then the doors opened, and the elite guards marched in, supported by the Legion, and they moved in and out, taking people by the arm and dragging them forward to stand before Lucian.

I sat back as he went through the sheaf of records he'd managed to put together already.

"Lord Bailish Terevor…Murder, six counts…I order you to respond with the truth…are you guilty of this?" Lucian asked the first man.

"Yes," he whimpered, trying to pull himself free of the elite guard who held him in one gauntleted fist.

"More than these six?"

"Yes…"

"Very well. Death or Service?" he asked me. I looked at the slob, noting the arms like wet noodles and the overhanging gut that probably weighed the same as Grizz in full armor.

"Death," I said flatly, turning back to the crowd that had gone deathly silent as the now blubbering noble was dragged away, and Lucian moved to the next.

"As you can see, if you have the capacity for military service, you *may* be given the chance to serve instead of a death sentence." I paused, looking out over the forty or so in the group at the front, and counted quickly.

"There are seven in this group who may be offered that chance. This depends on their crimes and on their capacity. If they cannot hold a sword and walk a mile, at least, then they waste their time and ours." I shrugged and sat back, watching the crowd as each and every one of the forty before me were brought through and sentenced.

In the end, two of the seven were given the choice of service, and they sobbed in relief as they were led to the barracks instead.

The other thirty-eight were taken to the cells, and being the kind Lord I am, I ordered them all be kept within sight of each other. The sixteen that were guilty of more minor crimes, smuggling, breaking various non-capital laws, thievery, and failure to pay taxes, were kept in the cells and allowed to watch while Sehran and five of her sisters that she'd struck a bargain with had snacks.

Jay's new "friend" was given a full day with the worst of the prisons and the sickest of the nobility. By the end of it, even the corpulent incubus needed to sleep off the meals, and when it recovered, it happily swore to assist the succubai in their jobs, as well as laughing its ass off when Sehran explained the joke to it.

Jay came to the palace at Mal's invitation, ostensibly to help transport some boxes back to the ships and to make sure the various helpers "didn't sneak off to pester the succubai, who were resting."

The "helpers" were all legionnaires who were in on the joke, and it took less than a minute before Jay ordered them to "do their jobs" while he took care of something important, following one of the prettiest succubai down a corridor out of sight.

He lost track of her for a few seconds but found the door at the end of the corridor and the sign on the door warning, "Extremely horny Demon within, do NOT enter." He, of course, went straight in, slammed the door behind himself and strode into the darkness, undoing his pants and calling out for her to "get ready for a good time."

The scream of horror when the incubus lit the lamp next to himself with a lazy flame, exposing not only that he was in there, but his sodding enormous knob, could be heard at the other end of the palace.

Jay appeared seconds later, tearing along the corridor, pants held in one hand and a trio of claw marks across his arse, screaming as he sprinted past the room we all hid inside of.

After that, we all made a point of dropping hints that the succubai all really looked like that when they dropped their glamor spells, and Jay never again tried to contact the Demonic realm.

He did tend to stare a lot at Sehran and Jian in horror though, especially when Sehran loudly commented on how sore she was after a particularly long session with "her Jian."

I'd had the nobles' storerooms, the city armory, and the keep strongrooms raided as a matter of course. All the magical gear was turned over to Ame and her small team. That had gotten me a barrage of abuse from her, although why, I still didn't know. As near as I could tell, it was because she had access to potentially thousands of runes now, and it meant she'd accomplished her lifetime's aim more than a hundred times over.

So, naturally, this meant I was getting it in the neck.

As many weapons as were appropriate were handed out, as well as entire suits of magical armor, in most cases not to the Legion, despite the grumblings of favoritism. The vast majority of magical weapons were specialized ones, such as great axes, and few of the surviving legionnaires were skilled with them, as opposed to the more traditional ones they carried.

Some did have new gear. Tang and Bane, for example, both had a set of the new armor that had been looted by Mal. Flux, Cheena, and Lio, who also had the armor, were making a game out of stealthing their way across the city in an epic game of capture the flag after Thomas had explained it to them. Bane and Tang, of course, were taking turns staying with me.

Another member of the team finally got magical weapons that were both size and style appropriate, as well as an old Legion shield that Barabarattas had in his personal vault, the cheeky fuck.

Knight's Revenge		Further Description *Yes/No*	
Damage:		**5-500**	
Defense:		**+12-50**	
Details:		This Imperial Legion Shield has been reinforced with banded steel and Orichalcum, then overlaid with a thin patina of Francicanin Scales. **Shieldwall:** Able to take part in a standard Legion Shieldwall, but will add +12 defense to the overall defense instead of the standard +5. **Revenge:** Any attacks blocked by this shield will result in a 10% reflection of the damage defended against being redirected upon the attacker. **Knight:** The Imperial Legion Knights were a specialist team, when a confirmed Knight wields this shield the Defensive properties are doubled.	
Rarity:	**Magical:**	**Durability:**	**Charge:**
Legendary	Yes	98/100	100/100

Romanus's face when he examined not only the shield but also the sword that had been stored with it, was memorable. The brave, selfless man sighed, tears filling his eyes as he commented that he thought all trace had been completely lost.

Flame of the Righteous		Further Description *Yes/No*	
Damage:		**50-500 + 25-250 Fire Damage**	
Details:		This Imperial Legion sword has been constructed from Chromium and Electrum with the hilt wrapped in Francicanin Scales. **Punishment:** The Ability 'Punishment' allows a Confirmed Knight of the Empire to use a charge to deliver a single blow that results in 10x the weapon's maximum damage, but the Knight will be drained of all mana and stamina in the use of this Ability and will be stunned until they recover 10% of their loss. **Last Stand:** A Knight stands alone at times, outnumbered, and without hope. In these dark times they may consume their own health, mana, and stamina at a rate of 3 points per second, to increase the damage they wield by the same, and until one of these pools are depleted, the damage will continue to build. **Bulwark:** The Imperial Legion Knight is a Legionnaire that stands between the innocent and all that would do them harm. For so long as they stand in defense of another, their Constitution gains +10.	
Rarity:	**Magical:**	**Durability:**	**Charge:**
Legendary	Yes	97/100	100/100

He read the details on the sword and shield, looking at them in awe. The shield was similar to the huge shields the Legion bore, but though they were efficient, it was accepted that eventually they'd fail. This one looked like it'd still be in perfect condition at the end of days, while the sword…

The sword was different from the standard Legion gladius design that was commonly used. It was longer, slightly serpentine, and with a thicker back, clearly reinforced to allow it to be used against heavily armored targets.

It was single-edged, and the blade itself was inlaid with a pattern of a red Dragon. The flames that the Dragon breathed onto the steel seemed to move and alter as we watched. When Ame had brought it to me the night before, I'd known who it was destined for immediately.

I'd summoned Lucian and Augustus, then on their advice, Restun as well. We'd discussed the history of the knights of the Legion, a group I'd never even heard referenced before.

Where the praetoria were tasked with the protection of the Emperor and the carrying out of his will, the knights were much like the Speculatores, in that they meted out justice. The primary difference was that where the Speculatores were often alone, or in small teams. Knights were their members who had distinguished themselves through massive deeds. They were the Speculatores who slew gorgons and krakens alone, the men and women who, when all else had been tried, and the Legion were being raised to face a problem, were sent in to be the thin red line between the oncoming devastation and the Empire.

We discussed it, and then I ordered Grizz to present himself in the throne room, formally.

Restun went to him, ordering him to leave the training he was going through with a small team, and virtually dragging the big legionnaire through the city to stand before me.

When he arrived, Yen and the rest of the team were there already, standing at attention and watching him, as were nearly thirty of the remaining legionnaires. All those closest to him stood waiting as he walked into the room.

I sat on the throne, facing him. The hesitation on his face turned to grim determination as he resolved to face whatever he had done full in the face.

He strode down the center of the carpet, coming to a halt at the genuflection line, and clapped a fist to chest in salute of his Scion, holding that salute as I stood, looking down into his eyes.

"Grizz," I said, before smiling. "Relax, man, you're not guilty of anything new, or at least I don't know of anything *yet*." I offered him a wink. He relaxed slightly as I returned the salute, then he stood at the Legion equivalent of parade rest, clearly waiting and wondering.

Ronin began to play an old song, one of the Legion's original battle hymns, and one that every legionnaire knew by heart, as it was played as they were raised from aspirant to full legionnaire.

It was the ceremonial welcome to the next phase of their lives, and I smiled down at my friend as I spoke.

"Centurion Grizz! There was a discovery made recently, a discovery that brought a team of the Legion back into the light long after they'd been forgotten by seemingly most of the realm. I'd never heard of them, but their bravery, their deeds were the stuff of legends. Their members may have been long forgotten, their deeds become myth, but two artifacts of their lives remained, hidden away in Barabarattas' vault."

I turned, and Yen, the woman who Grizz loved with all his heart, stepped forward, carrying the shield, even as Augustus, his Primus, stepped forward carrying the sword.

"These were the weapons of a Legion knight, Centurion Grizz, a knight who embodied the very ideals of the Legion in all they did. Prefect Romanus, Primus Praetoria Restun, Heir Augustus, and Chief Justicar Lucian all agree. If only one legionnaire could be gifted with these weapons and given the chance to resurrect the knights of the Legion, then it should be you."

There was a moment of silence as we watched the look on his face as he realized what I was saying. Then Augustus ordered him, in a gruff, proud and fatherly voice, that was audible to all, "Kneel son, you earned this."

Grizz sank to one knee, looking up at me in awe as I took the sword from Augustus. My heir saluted me and stepped back, smiling down at his protégé with clear pride on his face.

"As Scion, I have the right, as no Emperor sits on the throne, to name Grizz Borrowman, Centurion of the Imperial Legion, to the rank of Knight of the Legion." I gently rested the sword on his right shoulder, tapping it once, as Amon's memories seemed to suggest was appropriate. I lifted it, flipping the blade over, so that the side which had rested facing up on his right shoulder was the same side that came down on his left and I tapped it lightly again.

"Rise, Sir Grizz," I said, offering my hand.

He grinned up at me, tears streaming down his cheeks unashamedly, as I pulled the big man upright. Augustus held the sheath out for me, and I slid the blade into it, then handed it to Grizz, letting Yen give her lover his new shield.

He stood there, awkward as all hell, clearly unsure what to do as the gathered Legion cheered their brother and his ascension.

"I…I don't…" he mumbled, shaking his head, while clinging to the sword and shield with white knuckles.

"You earned this, Grizz," I said firmly. "Others have earned rewards, and they'll come in time. But we've a war to fight, and these are tools that will help you to win it for the Empire, so it seemed appropriate to do this tonight."

Oracle stepped forward and hugged him, joined by the rest of the squad. Close friends stepped up, as formality was discarded and the drink started to flow.

With that, and a thousand other jobs done, I was starting to feel like the world was finally getting sorted.

And that, of course, was when it all went wrong.

CHAPTER SIXTY-FOUR

It started with the mist, wispy at first, but building throughout the night. By morning, it was thick enough that you could practically walk on it. The entire city vanished behind a white, sound-deadening wall, from the perspective of the upper windows of the keep, at least.

I'd risen early, planning on chasing Oracle around the bedroom a few times at least before starting on another day of soul-destroying meetings, but as I left the bathroom, I'd glanced at the windows, curious as to the time.

I drew the heavy velvet curtains back to a thick white wall, and I damn well knew in my heart that something had gone very, very wrong.

I reached out to Jenae, instinct making me want to speak to my oddess, and I got a response or lack thereof that made my balls want to move northward. "Fuck," I muttered, eyes wide as I felt the blockage between us. It was like a wall had been put up between me and the Gods, and the harder I tried to reach out to the Gods, the thicker the wall became.

"Nimon." I cursed, and Oracle, who'd been asleep again, reveling in the change in her form, woke with a start as she felt the emotions racing through me.

"What's wrong?" Oracle sat up on the bed and stared across the dark room, her skin a beautiful golden olive that stood out against the white sheets in the darkness.

"I don't know," I said, swallowing hard. "But I can't reach Jenae, and…" I gestured to the wall of fog outside, and Oracle lifted from the bed, floating to my side and staring out as she cuddled in.

We stood there staring out for long seconds, then something flapped past close enough that it made the fog swirl, and she hissed in horror.

"What is it?" I asked, and she shook her head.

"I don't know, but it felt…" She shook her head again. "We've got to move, Jax, this isn't good!"

I had to agree.

We dressed quickly, which is to say I pulled my underclothes on, then donned my armor next, while Oracle blurred slightly and was fully dressed.

She moved to the door to our sitting room and called out loudly.

"Bane!" she snapped.

In a swirl of dissipating stealth, he appeared by her side, sensing the seriousness of the summons. "Get the others; we need a full Council of War in the throne room, right godsdamn now!"

I grinned to myself at her phrasing. Apparently, my bad habits were rubbing off on her. Forcing my fingers to move nimbly at blistering speed, I assembled my armor.

Ten minutes later, I was stomping down the corridors and towards the throne room, the others appearing as Oracle and I made it in. Romanus huffed his way down the stairs at the end of the hallway, even as others appeared.

I turned to enter the room, then paused, leaning back out and seeing the figure continuing down the stairwell, parting from Romanus with one last kiss as she moved off, presumably to gather her people. I grinned, winking at Romanus as he turned back to me.

He paused, as though embarrassed to be caught, then straightened and continued along to join the rest of us. I let it go, deciding that now wasn't the time, but I'd be sure to remember the kiss between the Legion prefect and the captain of the *Dreadnought* for later use.

It only took a few minutes for the others to assemble, and I looked around the table, the others standing around the throne as I manipulated the city interface to bring up what I damn well knew was going to be out there.

The map of the city appeared, large enough for everyone to see, and it was covered in red dots that flashed in and out, appearing and vanishing. Hundreds of these dots rose from the sea, clustering up around the beaches closest to the Dark Citadel.

"What the hell are they?" Romanus asked, his voice hoarse.

"Not sure." I shook my head. "But they've been summoned by the God of Death, so I'm guessing they're not coming for fucking cake."

"The majority of these appear to be flying undead," Oracle interjected, gesturing to the red. "I don't think the map is accurate, as it appears to maintain the last seen position until it recognizes the new contact as one it already had, but had lost sight of. With that in mind, there are still at least a hundred undead fliers scouting the city, and..." She paused, looking to me.

I nodded, taking over the narrative.

"And the Gods aren't responding," I said. "It seems like there's a barrier between Them and me, but They are still there, I can tell that much."

"Have they been banished again?" Cai asked grimly.

I shook my head, as did the others with a more personal connection to the Gods, such as Lydia and Lucian.

"No, they're still there. I'd guess that it's Nimon playing games...even though He's a God, He's not all-powerful, so He can't keep this up for the long haul. This is just my impression, but I think He's using a lot of His power to block the others from reaching us. We're on our own to deal with whatever is out there, but once it's done, Nimon's probably going to be weaker, and the Gods can kick that fucker's head in."

"What do we know about the creatures out there?" Romanus asked, but there was no hope in the question.

"Absolutely bugger all," I answered frankly. "Oracle thinks the first one, the flying thing that went past our window, was undead. Logically, the God of Death would have access to undead, so..."

"So the ones that are swarming out of the sea are likely to be the dead," Augustus finished for me, before rubbing his chin. "There's a simple way to be sure." He tapped a location to the east of the city, between the citadel and the Tower. "This is a graveyard; the upper levels contain a great many mausoleums. If he's raising the dead..."

"Then they'll be rising there as well, given that it's both between the city and the citadel, and behind the damn diamonds!" I cursed. "Augustus, get a team and a few hundred soldiers, get out there and make sure the dead stay down. If need be, turn that fucking hill to glass."

Augustus saluted, fist to chest, then ran for the door, as I turned to the others. "Oren, can we…"

"We canna fly, laddie," he said mournfully. "We can no' see anythin' oot there, we'd be crashin' in te each other, an' no clue what we'd be firin' at."

"Shit," I muttered, knowing he was right. Our greatest advantage in the fight was effectively nullified by sodding water vapor.

"Ah'm sorry, laddie," Oren said, clearly upset.

I waved him down. "No, Oren, it's not your fault. Get your crews ready, though. As soon as the weather clears, I need you and yours up there. Even that Dark Dick can't keep the sun out forever."

Oren saluted and ran for the door as I turned to Restun and Romanus.

"The trainees, where are they in terms of skill?"

"They all had a military, adventuring, or soldiering background before joining, so they're currently at the level of advanced troops for the army, I would estimate," Restun said, getting a grumble from Asimah, current commander of the Himnel Army.

"You disagree?" I asked him, a note of challenge in my voice.

"High Lord, my army has been ignored most of the time in favor of the Legion. In reality, the Legion could never hold a candle to my forces. You see…" he said, clearly building up to teach us all our places.

I snorted and shook my head. "Asimah, I personally killed over a hundred and fifty of the Dark Legion, their aspirants, and *your* army in storming the city, and the vast majority of the Legion are far, *far* more skilled than me. I'd put money on Grizz against an entire platoon of regular troops, so forget your ego. Are your soldiers more skilled than the Legion?"

"Well, the Legion has better equipment, High Lord."

I shook my head in disgust. "Keep quiet when the adults are speaking, if you've nothing to say." With that, I turned back to the map. "Lars, how many elites do you have?"

"Sixty-seven," Lars, commander of the city guard declared proudly. "The increased signing bounty helped considerably, so thank you, High Lord."

"Good. Get them and the Legion fliers. Gather all our flying forces, in fact. You're in charge of defending the city. Your job is to take those flying fucks down and clear our skies. Once that's done, you can assist us in smashing the citadel." He saluted.

I straightened. "This is it, people. Nimon's throwing it all at us to beat us back. We kill them, and the citadel will be weakened. We cannot afford to wait longer, so as soon as there's a break, we storm the citadel. There has to be a focal point for this magic that's raising the dead. That's either a lich, an artifact, or just that ball-licker of an arch-priest. Either way, when we destroy them, we win this fight."

"I'm ready to assume my position," Romanus said.

"Remind me one day to discuss innuendoes with you," I said dryly before turning to look at the others gathered there. "While normally I'd prefer to plan something like this a little better, with the fog, we can't be sure what we're facing. We can't use the majority of our advantages, so this is going to be a hack and slash job. Romanus, you are in overall command of our forces, me and mine will be in this diamond here." I indicated the diamond at the center of the line between the swelling red horde of markers and the city. "And before you comment on risk, let me be clear, my team are *the best* when it comes to close quarters and magic. Spread the rest of the Legion out as you see fit."

"We're with you," Thomas said, and I turned to look at him and Belladonna, who stood behind him in new armor.

"We could use you elsewhere," I said.

"This is looking like the big one, bro. We're brothers; we stand together," Thomas said with his jaw set.

I paused, noting Romanus's subtle nod out of the corner of my eye, and smiled. Damn, if it wasn't a comfort knowing, after all this time, I had my brother fighting at my side once again.

"Thank you, man," I said, then turned back to Romanus. "We've got nearly fifty war golems in reserve, as we've still not managed to create a high enough ranked golem to lead them, or at least not high enough that we'd trust them in battle alongside our troops."

"I'll keep them in reserve and use them as expendable shock troops." Romanus said. I nodded my agreement, reaching out mentally and gathering up the threads that led to the war golems. I focused on them and impressed my will for their commanders, then I released them.

"They'll follow your orders as well as Augustus, Jon, and Restun's orders," I confirmed to him, before sitting back and watching Romanus.

Where I basically gave orders to people as they fell under my eyes, he was far more disciplined, organizing people into groups: the defenders for the city, the diamonds, and the reserve. He made a point about keeping the undead from the city, as it was essentially a smorgasbord for them as well as a great place for them to get reinforcements. The notion of my people, the Empire's people, becoming snacks and reinforcements for the enemy…I couldn't help wincing at the thought.

In less than fifteen minutes, it was done, the final orders were given, and I was jogging through the keep on my way to the ground floor where carriages awaited us.

There were six of them, enough for my team, Thomas's, and the various others that were heading our way. As we clambered into them, Lydia cursed as she caught a wing on the door jamb, and I grinned at the cushioned seat.

Unlike the ones I'd been subjected to in Narkolt, the Himnel carriages were simple, well-made, and comfortable, and that was a massive relief.

We were just starting to pull out of the courtyard when shouting held us up. Grizz, now even more protective than before, stuck his head out of the window to see what was happening, then ducked back inside with a grin.

"What's up?" I asked.

"We've got reinforcements," he said, waving me over.

I stuck my head back out. The fog was getting even damn thicker, considering the carriage behind us was less than ten meters away, and all I could see were shadows boarding it.

"Who the hell is that?" I asked Bane, looking up towards the roof of the carriage where he crouched.

"Mal and a few of his team," Bane whispered.

I frowned, shaking my head. I had no idea why that crazy bastard was coming with us, nor where the hell he'd been. As he'd not made it into the meeting, I resolved to find out…later.

The ride through the city seemed to take forever, marked by the occasional scream from beyond the veil of the fog. Every so often, the *thwack* of a crossbow being fired from the roof of the carriage resounded as Bane picked off the flying undead.

I grinned as I guessed that we had an unexpected advantage there, as Bane didn't see the way we did. But then I grimaced, as it occurred to me that neither did the undead. After all, most of the time, their eyes had long since rotted away.

Eventually, the bouncing carriage left the cobblestones of the main streets and rocked across the hardened stone of the main gates, out onto the bridge over the moat that surrounded the city.

The change of the wheels from cobbles to stone to hard-packed dirt and mud made Thomas snort, shaking his head.

The carriages were huge affairs, meaning that myself, Oracle, Grizz, Yen, Lydia, Ronin, Thomas, and Belladonna were able to fit inside. But the way everyone sat, giving her a wide berth, showed that nobody was comfortable with her quite yet.

"What's up?" I asked Thomas, as much to break the silence as anything else.

"You remember I was in jail here? Well, the jailor, a complete turd by the name of Boris, sold me and the others in the cells to Edvard." He shrugged, smiling faintly as he remembered it. "I was broken, you know? Months of no sleep, beatings around the clock. The guards rented my body out, and I don't mean in a fun way." He was joking, but his lips were set in a hard line with no mirth in them.

"I was used as a punching bag, chained to the ceiling so that bare-knuckle fighters could get practice in. More than half my bones were broken, hardly any water, piss-soaked bread, the lot. When I overheard that I was being sold as a slave to the Dark Legion? Man, it was like all my Christmases had come at once. I remember the journey. I had a hood over my face, so all I could sense was the bouncing of the cart and the creak of the wheels…seems so weird to be going back this way now. Slight difference in rank and all that."

"Speaking of rank," Belladonna interrupted. "Why is Thomas not the heir?"

There was a long minute of silence as she stared at me, waiting, and I realized slowly that it wasn't a new girl standing up for her man situation, but a genuine question, so I relaxed. I'd told her to treat me as anyone else, unless I gave an order, and she'd clearly taken me at my word.

"Truthfully, because Augustus is a better choice than Thomas or me." I said, sitting back. "Sorry bro, but it's the truth."

"Fuck no, man! He's better at this kinda thing than I ever could be!" Thomas said quickly. "Last thing I want is your job. Hell, all I ever wanted was a hot girl, a cold beer, and someone to fight when I got bored. My life's fucking perfect right now."

"Same," I said grinning. "Seriously though, Bella…am I alright calling you that?" She hesitated for a second, then nodded.

"Thanks. Okay, Bella, so Thomas and I are brawlers, basically. We've got the blood, and the right to rule, but neither of us has the training or the mentality. Augustus has, but his blood is much weaker than ours. Normally, that would mean he could never ascend to the Throne, *but* I can name him as my heir. That alone bypasses the usual requirements, and his blood, while watered down, is still royal at its base, so fuck it." I shrugged, crossing my arms and settling myself back a bit more comfortably, trying to keep myself calm as we traveled to the fight.

"Basically, if you could see our shitbag of a father and compare him to Augustus? You'd be in no doubt who the royal one is. Augustus is a God among men. Noble, good to a fault, and insanely fucking lethal with every weapon in existence. Baron Sanguis…well, if he wasn't the Baron, he'd need documentation in triplicate to prove he was a man and not a cockroach that had learned to walk upright. I don't give two shits what anyone else thinks; blood might matter, but it's not the be-all and end-all."

"Could he not have claimed the throne before you came along, then? Much as this Tirana did?" she asked.

I shook my head. "Tirana managed it despite the low blood concentration because she was divinely acknowledged. The Dark Cockwomble Himself raised her up. Without that, she couldn't have done it. Until I claimed my place, acknowledged by Amon as the Scion, the Imperial Throne was in a sort of limbo. Without Amon's actions, anyone else would have had to travel to the capital and sit atop the throne, declaring themselves as the Imperial-Heir-in-Waiting and keep control of the capital for a full year. Lots tried it, nobody managed it," I said, feeling the knowledge bleeding through.

"He's almost gone, isn't He?" I asked Oracle through our bond, getting a slight smile in return.

"He's trying to hang on, to see you safe, but it won't be long now. Then He'll be gone for good."

I nodded sadly to her before looking out of the window as an unearthly shriek split the darkness.

"What the hell…" I started, and Grizz growled.

"Banshee!" he snapped.

Ronin spoke quickly. "Banshees use a sonic attack to paralyze their victims. The closer you are to their wail, the worse the effect. Beheading them and burning is the only sure way to kill them, uh…oh, and they hate sunlight!" he added, smiling brightly at the chance to use his encyclopedic knowledge of everything wanting to fuck up my day.

"Well that's fucking fantastic. You seen the fog out there?" Thomas interjected.

Ronin winced, immediately going on the defensive. "Okay, fair point, but it's an important detail!"

"Okay, how far are we from the Banshees?" I asked, sticking my head out of the window.

As if his response was answer enough, Ronin started to play, his music discordant and jarring, but somehow removing the feeling of lassitude that had begun to creep up, even at this distance.

"There are three out there," Bane said, before thrumming in pleasure. "And their song has no effect on me!"

"Go have fun!" I told him, feeling the carriage rock as he leapt off the top, vanishing into the fog.

The carriage turned a few minutes later, clearly following a path, one I damn well hoped led to the right place.

Abruptly, one of the horrible wails cut off.

The other two were still going in the distance, but the sudden loss of this one made everyone feel a hell of a lot better. As we pulled alongside the first diamond, turning right and picking up speed, I had to grin, the soldiers inside the diamonds were ready for a fight. Damn, I fancied their chances now, considering the defensive creations were massive.

The ground before the diamonds had been dug into, creating a deep trench that anyone would have to cross to assault the walls, with wooden spears pointing outward, their ends charred lightly to dry them out and toughen them.

Looking at the trench, the thick walls and the armed and ready, grim-faced soldiers inside the fortification, I couldn't help but nod in satisfaction, right up until we passed the third diamond, and the first creature fell from the air.

We were watching the soldiers making preparations, a small group at the back of the diamond getting food ready while the others sat grimly watching the fog rolling back and forth, trying to ignore the sounds that floated out of it.

The creature that slammed into their midst was the size of a large dog, or at least it was when it impacted. The mass of bones, teeth, and red torn flesh slammed into the small group standing around. The thing that had carried it whirled away in the fog, screaming its victory.

The creature that hit the small group killed one of the men outright, his body practically detonating under the sudden impact, while a mass of flesh tore out, wrapping around the others and yanking them inward, adding their frantic, suddenly screaming forms to its own.

I'd seen it as we raced past, and I froze, the unexpected attack rendering me useless for several seconds, until another man was yanked inward, screaming.

"Stop!" I roared up at the driver, kicking the door open and leaping from the fast-moving carriage, tucking my legs up and wrapping my arms around myself as I rolled. The wet muck splattered across my, until now, spotless armor. I growled as I jumped to my feet, slightly shaken, soaked, and ready for a fight.

I raced forward, the carriage skidding to a halt behind me as the driver blew a short series of notes on his whistle to warn those following us. The others piled out, some confused by the reason, while others saw the creature and swore.

"Flesh golem!" Ronin screamed, his fingers accidentally setting a discordant blast of notes free of his lute. "Destroy the core!"

"Weaknesses?" Lydia bellowed, slamming her shield into place on her arm and yanking out her mace, while flexing her wings and shaking them out.

"Fire!" Ronin screamed, ducking down as something screeched and dive-bombed the carriage, leaving a trail of scoured wood across the top of it. "Fuckers!" he shouted, frantically strumming his instrument. "All undead fear fire or light magic; fuck's sake, Lydia haven't you got that yet?!"

"Remind me te kick yer teeth in later!" Lydia snapped, putting her mace back and summoning Magic Missile.

The fog lit up behind me with the glow of multiple castings, but I was already scrambling up the back of the diamond. I jumped back down inside, skidding on the loose earth and muddy puddles as I raced for the creature, the fog rolling back in and cutting the world off.

I yanked my naginata free, feeding it with a massive pulse of fire, and making the fog light up again. This time, the weapon reflected the yellows and reds of cooler flame before it turned blue, then white with heat.

A tentacle flashed out of the obscuring mess to my right, and I twisted my weapon around, lopping it off with barely more than a slight tug before the remaining end was yanked backward with a scream of hatred.

I followed it, the massive bulk becoming fully visible out of the mist over the next few seconds. It was globular now, with multiple segmented arms, made of other limbs stitched together. The body was made up of dozens of screaming soldiers, all compressed inward, clothes systematically ripped away, their skin running like candle wax and melding together with others.

The body grew as another figure was yanked backward, arms flailing through the mist, to be slammed unceremoniously into the bulk. Hands reached out of the mass, grabbing and ripping. They sent cloth and steel flying as the soldier screamed and stabbed, frantically trying to get free, even as flesh reached up hungrily and started to subsume him into the mass.

I winced in disgust, then roared, letting fury overtake me and power me forward.

As the others fell in behind my advance, I slid in a spray of mud and water. With a lunge, I threw myself aside, passing under a multi-jointed arm that lashed out, six-fingered, no longer human hands reaching. I flicked the naginata upward. The blade, blazing with magic and suppressed fury, cut through the limb with ease, sending a spray of thick, coagulating blood into the air, along with a noxious smell. I planted my right foot and kicked up, bringing myself to my feet and lashing the blade around, carving an entire section of the creature free.

A section, over a meter in length and height, fell free, the people stitched into the beast screaming in agony, even as a deep-throated howl of hatred and pain echoed down from overhead. The bulk twisted frantically, bringing a misshapen face into view.

It was wider than it was high, huge jowls resting on the rounded mass of its shoulders. Dozens of eyes fixated on me, many rolling insanely, others focused with laser-like intent.

Then it screeched and lunged at me.

I danced back a dozen steps, weapon blurring as I carved more and more of it free, entire sections collapsing before the missiles flashed overhead, hammering into the middle and detonating, entire sections of flesh being blown free.

It took less than a minute before an evilly glowing skeletal creature appeared in the middle, its skull radiating a sickly green light as multiple arms, like a humanoid spider, reached out, tugging and pulling on the flesh around it. It stretched it like rubber, making the bodies connected to it wail in fear and pain as it tried to bury itself inside the cocoon of soldiers again.

I snarled and lunged, the naginata stabbing and slashing, even as more arms flashed around, aiming for me. I ducked then leaped, my feet barely clearing a low-sweeping arm. Then Grizz was there, his new sword slashing downward. Where my weapon was a giant murderstick, all finesse and grace, or at least people commented that it looked that way at times, Grizz was the definition of power and butchery.

He shield-slammed the arms that tried to grab him aside and hacked his way forward with the sword, carving great chunks of the flesh golem aside. Before it could respond and repair itself, he was there, the blade slamming into the skull and shattering it into hundreds of pieces as he used one of his new sword's abilities.

As soon as the skull was destroyed, the creation collapsed, the animating force ripped free, and we were left with the aftermath…dozens of partially melted, crippled soldiers.

Most of them were thankfully maddened by the experience, but the few who weren't, who begged for help…

Oracle shook her head when I looked at her sadly, and I knew what I had to do. I ordered the others back, and I did it myself, quick blows, surgical in nature. One stab, one kill, hot tears tracking down my cheeks as I whispered my thanks to them for their service, even as I did it.

"I'm sorry, Jax. They couldn't be saved. Magic couldn't heal them; their new form is too complete. It was all they could have been," she whispered in my mind. I nodded that I understood, unable to trust myself to talk.

Screams rose dimly in the distance, and I gritted my teeth, knowing that this was happening again and again in the diamonds on either side.

"Go," I snapped to the others. Thomas and his team broke off left, and the legionnaires who had come with me going right, while I turned to my squad and huffed out a deep, ragged breath.

"They can't have many of those things, or they'd have done it in the city and killed us all," I stated through the gorge that had taken up semi-permanent residence in my throat. "That means they wanted these diamonds cleared for a reason."

"They're coming this way," Lydia said softly.

"They're coming," I agreed, turning and striding toward the front of the diamond, kicking the scattered gear free of where it'd fallen and staring out at the thick fog.

"Oracle, you get the chance to work on reproducing the original Cleansing Fire spell?" I asked. There was a brief silence before she shook her head. "Then do it now, please, my love."

"Of course," she said, before flinching as the fog nearby swirled, and Bane appeared.

"What, no jump?" he asked me jokingly before his vibrations brought back the mass of misshapen flesh behind us, cooling, and the lack of any forces to stand with us. "I see."

"Yeah," I said. "How far are they?"

Bane turned, taking a deep breath and letting loose a long, strong pulse of his worldsense.

I reached out and ordered the golems that had been set aside for the reserve to come to me. Romanus would have to damn well understand, as I was going to need them.

It seemed to hang in the air, the fog shivering with it for several seconds, before he straightened again and turned to me.

"Not far at all," he replied, as the first dark shapes stumbled out of the dimly lit fog.

CHAPTER SIXTY-FIVE

We spread out as far as we could inside the diamond, trying to cover as much ground as possible. But with the small number of us and the massive numbers of the undead, there was no way we could fight them all, so we relied on our magic to even the odds.

At first it was easy. Barrages of Magic Missiles flashed out, slamming into the undead, before Lydia took charge and sorted us into relay teams.

We quickly found that two impacts on average was sufficient to kill a standard shambling undead, one to crack the skull, one to destroy it, then the animated corpse would collapse. Occasionally, a particularly lucky shot or weak skull meant that a single strike was enough. At other times, such as when one of the lumbering shir corpses appeared, it took multiple hits.

We took turns, each of us covering our section, and for the first few minutes it was fine, and we racked up dozens of kills each. Then the crowds got thicker…and thicker.

The handful became dozens, which then became hundreds. Mixed in among the humanoid monsters were others, giant creatures that stumbled forward atop rotting fins, clearly reanimated and thrown out of the ocean.

Worst were the amalgamations, like the flesh golem. They appeared, towering over the smaller ones, scooping them up and pressing the wriggling bodies to themselves, growing as they went. Whenever they appeared, Bane directed our massed fire, the Flames of Wrath and Explosive Compression barrages slamming into them over and over again until we smashed the pilot.

The towering creations would collapse then, the individual undead trying to struggle free to attack us, while we stood inside the diamond.

We took turns on the front, fighting in melee and destroying the undead as fast as we could, while the others battered them with spells. Then we'd swap while we recovered mana and went back to it again.

It seemed like both bare minutes and hours had passed, but all too soon the piles of bodies grew too high, and we knew we'd have to retreat soon.

"Explosive Compression!" I barked at the others. "Ten meters out, layer them to overlap."

While they did this, slowly backing up as everyone cast and the undead scaled the walls, I growled to myself and cast Gravitational Vortex.

It took a hell of a lot of my mana, hell it was almost six hundred points, and it didn't last anywhere near as long as I needed it to. But it'd shatter the bones into fragments, as would the weaker Compression spells. This would create a space for us to hopefully kill those who had made it inside and let us back up without getting overrun.

Flashes of spells preceded distant explosions from either side, deep in the fog. I just had to hope the others were doing better than we were.

The others slammed their spells out in a ragged line. Then the spells detonated, smashing dozens of undead into paste, shattering bones and dragging the fragments into the center, compressing it into a single mass. Finally, I finished my own spell.

It lashed out, cutting through the fog and leaving a line of disturbed air that hung, slowly settling again, until it exploded outward.

The outward expansion alone killed dozens, and the overlapping fields of the spell, combined with the massively higher power gradient, dragged literally hundreds more inward, the shattering of bones filling the air.

The undead screamed in hatred occasionally, but there was no life in most of them, simply risen, mechanically acting bones, but when the Vortex was done, a new sound entered the battle.

The iron horns that declared that the Dark Legion was taking the field.

"That's our cue!" I called to the others, staggering a little as I caught my breath. Bane blurred past me, arms pistoning out and disassembling the undead with ease.

The undead were still coming, and coming in their thousands now, a force we couldn't hold against, thanks to the combination of the mounds of bodies that they could practically walk across to step into the diamonds now and the lack of other defenders to take our place as we fell from exhaustion.

Knowing that somewhere out there, in the distance, the Dark Legion was taking the field as well?

"Fuck, fuck, fuck!" I snarled, furious that all the preparations we'd labored over for so long were…"Denny!" I said, grinning as a memory came to me.

The memory was of that mad bastard setting off the huge detonation of Sun Crystals in the forest and killing hundreds of dark legionnaires.

"Oracle!" I called, and she flew forward, drenched in sweat, grinning at me with a spark of hope and pride in her beautiful eyes.

"Done! I've reworked Cleansing Fire. Check your notifications."

"Fantastic, but no time!" I said. "Get in touch with Tenandra. I know she can sense through the fog to some degree."

"She can, but the fliers will mob her. As she's the only one who can see, she'll be torn apart if she takes off alone."

"Tell her to get the Legion and ALL the marine contingent aboard. Make sure Denny and his priests are on there, too. The Dark Legion is coming, and I want those fuckers torn limb from limb!"

"Right!" Oracle replied, her mind coming to the conclusions I had mere seconds after me, the magical mass of calculations and crap she'd had to do still making her fuzzy.

She hovered there for several seconds as I called out to the others.

"Oracle's working; we need to give her some time!" I roared. Suiting action to words, I lashed out, lopping the outstretching hand from an undead, then taking the head on the backswing.

Less than a minute later, she was back, blinking awake and spinning. She found me near the barrier, killing the undead as they clambered upward in a wave.

"Jax!" she cried, flitting across to me and summoning a barrage of Magic Missiles almost distractedly. They fired out, slamming into the undead as she spoke. "Tenandra is gathering them all. She says it'll take a few minutes to get them, and ten more to reach us. But she needs me here; there's something in the fog that's making it much harder for her to sense the world than it should be."

"Nimon!" I snarled.

"Probably," Oracle agreed. "She needs me here; she needs me as a beacon."

"Then we make our stand, after all!" I roared, sweeping the wall clear again and shouting to the others as I pulled up my notifications.

"Hold this ground!" I ordered, looking for the details on the new spell Oracle had created.

Congratulations!

You have created a new personal spell: Imperial Territory!

Imperial Territory:
This personal spell has been created using the knowledge of former Emperor Amon, Lady Wisp Oracle, and Scion Jax. It builds upon three pillars, primarily: Imperial Land, Might, and Fire.

The first pillar is Imperial Land; this land has been fought for and bled over by the Empire. It is land that has belonged to the Empire for eons and is magically infused from the legacy of that past.

The second pillar is Might; this land is strong with life, blessed by the Goddess of Life Herself when She agreed to aid you. All territory claimed by Jax for the Empire is imbued with an additional spark of Life by Ashante Herself. While this is draining for Her, the rewards both for Herself and all life within these boundaries are significant, including greater health, fecundity, and greater immunity to disease and rot.

The final pillar is Fire; Fire is the element you are most familiar with, one that you use at an almost instinctive level, and after so much work, blessings by the Goddess of Fire and knowledge gifted to you, the flames recognize you as one of their own. No longer will neutral or aligned flames burn you. Now you need fear only the fire of your enemies.

Imperial Territory casts a ritual circle of six meters in all directions, then fills it with Fire! All those who bear you ill will inside the spell's radius will be attacked by the flames, tearing the life from them, and using their mana to fuel the continuation of the spell, while those who revere the Empire, and you personally, will gain +2 points of health, stamina, and mana per second while the Circle is active.

Cost: 500 mana for one minute, followed by 250 mana per minute active, thereafter, should there be no mana for the spell to feed on.

I read it and swore in amazement, before popping the top off a mana potion and downing it in one shot, then lashing out with my naginata again, as I felt Oracle casting the new spell.

"New spell incoming, everyone!" I shouted out. "Don't fear the fire!" That was all I had the time to say as a skeletal horseman leapt out of the mist. I dove aside before the hooves could take me down.

The bastard had raced across the now-filled ditch. The goddamn undead we were exhausting ourselves to destroy had simply been fodder to tire us out. Now, the real challenge was coming to play, as a thunder of hooves followed this fucker.

I growled and rolled to my feet, sweeping my weapon around in a wide circle. The arc caught a second figure as that leaped in as well. This time, the horse collapsed, its spine severed midway down. The skeletal rider crashed to the floor, a pile of broken bones that tried to pull itself back together.

Lydia slammed her mace down hard, smashing the skull into a dozen fragments. At the same instant, Bane leaped atop the back of the first horse, tearing the undead rider's head free. His lower arms scissored his blade inward, lopping the horse's head off as well.

He threw himself clear as the animating force vanished, the beast collapsing into a pile of broken bones, and the rest of us adjusted to meet the new threat.

Laughter echoed out of the darkness as a robed figure slowly shuffled forward, the fog rolling back like a duvet pulled aside to expose the figure as it came to a halt, surrounding our party with heavily armed and armored undead.

Those we'd been fighting had been almost exclusively unarmed, mainly naked, and mostly skeletal. These figures were different, clad entirely in ancient armor, with weapons that shimmered with magic. Nine of them stood in a semi-circle behind the cackling lich. I growled, the shadowy figures of hundreds more appearing behind them, many on horseback or clad in rusting plate armor.

"Did you enjoy your lives?" the lich asked slowly, its head shuddering atop the rotten neck as it shifted, searching the group. Eventually it fixated on me, and it nodded as if reaching a decision. *"You were responsible for the death of my tool,"* it declared.

I grimaced, hitting it with a Greater Examination and cursing as the information showed up. Amused, the lich made an open-handed gesture, making it clear that it knew what I was doing and was permitting it.

Arch-Lich Ghastool

The Arch-Lich Ghastool has rarely been seen in recent years, causing many to believe, in error, that it had finally died. Ghastool was an Elven High Necromancer who sold his soul to Nimon in the years following the Cataclysm, in exchange for the knowledge of Lichdom.

After centuries of brooding, the Lich finally took an apprentice, Veriman, sending it out into the world to secure more subjects for its experiments. This valued tool that Ghastool spent long centuries instructing was destroyed recently by the Empire. Ghastool, when Nimon offered it the chance to return to the continent of Dravith, quickly agreed, determined to punish those who wasted its efforts.

Weaknesses: 50% weakness to Fire, 100% additional damage taken from Light Magic; crushing attacks inflict double damage, due to brittle bones.

Resistances: The undead nature of this creature reduces the effectiveness of slashing and piercing weapons. Death Magic heals this creature, and Dark Magic does 75% less damage.

Level: 74
Health: 38,000/38,000
Stamina: 480/480
Mana: 411,276/620,000

"Fuck me sideways and dip me in ketchup," I mumbled, stunned and unable to look away from the manapool.

"What is it?" Lydia asked, and I spoke without thinking.

"Remember that Lich in the arena? Veriman?"

"Yeah?" she asked, frowning.

"Well, this is his corpse-daddy, and he's *pissed.*"

"Arch-ich Ghastool?" Yen asked. I nodded while the lich bowed elegantly at the recognition. "Oh, great."

"We just have…to hold on…I can direct…Tenandra…" Oracle whispered into my mind, the spell she was building clearly straining her. I nodded in response to her words.

"So, what are you doing here, then, Ghastool?" I asked.

The lich cocked its head to one side as though confused. *"You killed my servant. You know why I have come!"*

"I know you're here, in my *territory,* and about to get your teeth kicked in." I answered, shooting Oracle a hold gesture as she finished the spell.

She frowned, but held it ready.

"You interfered in my work, mortal," the arch-lich declared.

I snorted, holding up one finger. "You just wait right fucking there, pal!" I snapped, passing my naginata to Ronin, who stood nearby, gently strumming his lute. I grabbed the wall, pulling myself upward, clambering onto the top of it so that I could see him better. I leaned down and took my weapon from Ronin, who whispered as I took it.

"He can't go far from the phylactery. Destroy it, and he's done, doesn't matter how much health he has."

I winked at Ronin as I turned back, facing the lich.

"I'm always curious, you know?" I asked him, leaning slightly on my weapon as I played for time. "Is there, like, a handbook you fuckers get? You know, here you go, you've declared for the forces of evil, take one 'fugly' pill, two additional stupidity pills, and make sure to read your evil monologues for dummies book?"

"What?" it asked, clearly confused.

"I mean, honestly, you've got to be what…the fifteenth asshole who's called me 'mortal' now? Seriously, do none of your henchmen talk to each other? Admittedly, it's not like we leave many alive, but you'd think the survivors would need a new evil overlord, and eventually word would get round?"

"What word?"

"Hell, man, that I'm not fucking mortal!" I said, shrugging. "I've been beaten, blown up, stabbed, cut into tiny bits, eaten alive, beheaded, all of it, and still I'm here! In an hour, when I'm wiping what's left of your face off my boots, I'm gonna forget your name, just like all the rest."

"Then perhaps the time has come to burn you alive," the lich suggested, lifting its right hand. The staff it clutched in its left hand sparkled, the crystal held in a knot of twisted branches at its tip flaring with a green and purple light.

"Nope, didn't work," I said, shrugging. "Plus, FYI, I kinda have a thing going with fire. I hear it works well on you, though?"

"And CorpseFire?" he hissed as a ball of flames grew in his hand, the colors alone making me feel sick, reminding me of gangrene and the purple-black of bloody bruises.

"I'll admit, that's a new one," I said slowly. "Care to explain?"

"Fire, like all things, has its opposite. The foolish believe water is the antithesis of fire. But where fire brings new growth, and heat can bring life, its opposite brings only death. CorpseFire is fire that has kindled in the deepest realm of Death, and only HIS chosen have access to it."

The flames flickered and jumped, dancing around the lich's fingers. I growled to myself, knowing already that this was going to fucking suck.

"So…no way I can persuade you to just chalk this all up to a disagreement, and I give you some gold to turn your undead around and feed on the Dark Legion, then?" I asked, not really expecting a positive answer, but figuring it had to be tried.

"My lair is filled with more gold and platinum than your pitiful Empire could imagine."

"Coolio," I said, nodding and looking back at Lydia. "Make a note of that. Once he's toast, we need to find that lair. I've a use for a fuck ton more wealth."

"Your kind would find my lair inhospitable to life, deep beneath the waves," he growled.

"Nice. Lydia, he's just saved us having to waste time searching the land. Make a note that we need to search wherever there's been a fuck ton of sunken ships. There's that island out there somewhere that sank, right? Can't be that far if he walked with all these dickheads, after I pissed Nimon off." I paused and looked back at Ghastool. "Any other hints you want to drop? Maybe draw me a map?"

"Silence, worm!" I shall feed on your…"

"Entrails, yeah, yeah. Seriously, been said before, tried a few times. Want me to give you a few minutes to monologue?" I asked. When he paused, I made a show of sighing and shaking my head. "For the love of the Gods, save me from the uneducated!

"Monologuing is the practice of a great, rambling speech, often given by a villain—that'd be you, by the way—to a noble band of heroes, namely *us.* Tradition dictates that, while you do it, we get ready and pull a few tricks out, then we slaughter you thanks to your own stupidity in giving us time to prepare. So, anything else you want to say?"

"I am not so foolish as to…"

I grinned and pointed my right hand, cocking my finger like a gun. "Boom."

Oracle had been keeping a steady, low-level commentary up in the back of my mind as Tenandra approached. While the fog was obviously controlled at least in part by Ghastool, he either couldn't see far enough or was too distracted to notice the ship as it gently pivoted, half a mile or so behind us.

Using Oracle and her own senses, as well as relying on a dangerous amount of luck, Tenandra opened fire with two full banks of ripple-fire cannons. The whoosh of them unleashing behind me and flashing past to slam into the massed ranks of the undead was frankly fucking *glorious*.

Once the fifty or so tubes had fully unloaded, Tenandra turned, firing the engines on full and lighting the fog as she raced closer. The thirty marines and legionnaires she was able to grab quickly all started to cast, ready for a barrage of Magic Missiles to deal with anything that fucked with the Empire.

I leaped off the wall, sprinting forwards. Triggering both Hyper-Cognition and Mana Overdrive as I went, my feet kicked up clods of dirt as Oracle activated the new Imperial Territory spell. She attached it to me, ensuring I was kept at the center of it.

My mana practically bottomed out, there being less than a hundred points left in the tank, but when it activated, I was crossing the final few meters between the outer circle of the spell and the lich, and the scream of rage when the two met was worth it.

I kept going, the spell flaring brighter and brighter as more and more creatures fell inside the radius. I grinned, leveling my naginata, convinced I was about to gut a centuries-old, massively powerful lich.

So naturally, that was when it all went tits up.

The Lich roared in fury and slammed its staff down hard, once. There was a massive blast of black smoke that flashed outward. I was sent flying through the air, slamming back into the wall of the diamond with my head rattled to buggery. Oracle fell from the sky, clutching her head in pain as our spell was broken, the sharp edges of it flaying our brains as we rolled around. The lich hissed and threw its hand forward.

"Kill them all!" it screamed. The survivors around it broke into a sprint, racing toward the diamond. I lay against the outer wall, stunned, on the wrong side, and facing them coming.

Grizz leaped over the barrier, scooped me up like I weighed nothing, and bodily threw me back over as dozens of arrows slammed into the metal inches from my face.

The big man gritted his teeth as he pulled himself over the top, falling down beside me. The fletching of three arrows protruded from the back of his armor, where they'd pierced straight through, lodging inside him.

"Fuuuuck," Grizz grunted, coughing some blood onto the ground between us.

I groaned, trying to get my potions free, the world spinning as I chewed my tongue, trying to get the words out.

"Well boss, looks like I fucked up," Grizz mumbled, his head slowly sagging forward until his chin rested on the front of his armor. "Sorry, man," he whispered.

I shoved my hand into the bag harder, trying to make the world make sense, but to no avail.

He sagged to one side, and I watched my friend die. Again.

"Grizz!" Yen screamed from somewhere to my right, terrible loss filling her voice as she screamed in rage and threw spells at the onrushing undead.

"Fall in around Jax!" Lydia snarled, slamming her wings down hard and launching herself into the air, glowing with an unearthly light as she triggered a class Ability, the fog suddenly rolling back, forced by the call of the Power of Starlight.

It didn't matter that the sun was high overhead, nor that the lich hissed its hatred of the daystar, gesturing frantically for the fog to return, to shield it, because as soon as Lydia called upon it, the solar radiation responded.

At first, there was a beam like the searchlight, easily twenty meters across. Then it narrowed by half, then half again. Each time it shrank, the radiance grew stronger, until, when it reached the smallest size Lydia could yet manage, just slightly larger than a coffee cup, it punched clean through the blackened armor of an undead death knight as it gathered itself atop its skeletal mount.

The light slammed through it, from left to right from above, an entire section simply vanishing into sooty wisps. Then the beam swept back and forth with terrible speed. Where it touched, it brought the cleansing of the stars, removing the foul presence of the undead by the simple expedient of vaporizing them.

Lydia held the beam for just under six seconds before falling, exhausted, barely conscious and landing like a bird with a broken wing, hard and fast.

But in those five and three-quarter seconds, she'd destroyed over a hundred undead, and she'd devastated the shield Ghastool held over itself, reducing it to a fraction of its power.

The arch-ich screamed, seeing so many of its creations destroyed, even as I forced myself upright, my brain still seemingly full of pummeled mince, and my thoughts difficult to follow through. Jian leaped up at the edge of the diamond, swords dropping to the floor as he lifted both hands, cupping them around a golden disc that had appeared between his fingers.

It was small and weak, compared to Lydia's ability, but the fire-based beam that Jian lashed out with was still powerful enough to kill dozens of the undead before he ran out of mana and collapsed. Sehran frantically sprinted to him, the potions in her hands clattering as she reached for him.

I knew one thing, though.

That fucker had killed my friend.

No, *I'd* killed Grizz. My own stupidity, my arrogance, my damn fool demand to *just do it*, seeing a chance and taking it despite the cost to those around me. I snarled, forcing myself up, managing to pull a healing potion free at last and ramming it half down Grizz's throat, making him drink it, praying it would give him the seconds he needed. I yanked the pouch free, tossing it to Giint, and slurring my words as I ordered him to force feed every single godsdamned potion in there to Grizz if he had to, unable to accept that it was far, far too late for him.

I forced myself up and glared at the undead fuck on the far side of the battlefield, even as I called out to Tenandra.

"Tenandra! Pound that fuck into the ground!" I ordered. No doubt, no request. It was a command from the Scion of the Empire.

She responded instantly, turning the ship sideways, her crew and passengers staggering. None fell, thankfully, as the second battery of ripple-fire cannons flared to life. Mana flooded them as they charged faster than they were intended to. I dragged myself over the top of the wall, snarling my hatred of the undead.

The ground shook, and fifty war golems thundered forward. They broke around the diamond at my back as they rushed towards us.

"HEY, COCKFACE!" I roared. "YOU PICKED THE WRONG DAY TO FUCKING VISIT!" I set off running.

Tenandra opened fire. A full broadside, two sets of cannons, all unleashed hell. The Missiles streaked across the sky first. They impacted the massed undead before the fog could fully roll back to obscure them, followed by Fireballs the size of bulls. Lightning bolts thicker than Augustus's thighs slammed into the undead.

Most that caught a bolt simply exploded.

No dried-out thing, creation of Death Magic or not, could maintain structural integrity under the hellfire of the ripple-fire cannons. Even the lich screamed in pain and disbelief as its shield was hit over and over, flames washing across it as it counterattacked.

"DIE!" it screamed, hurling the CorpseFire through the air at the ship.

Where it hit, it *burned.*

Tenandra's psychic scream echoed in my mind, the pain of the cursed flames burrowing into her hull, spreading, multiplying. I covered the last few meters, even as the war golems arrived.

I felt the change.

My mind was battered, my body frazzled, and pain wracking me. The aftereffects of the broken spell lashed me, and the fifty golems all took a fragment of my mind to control.

The fear that bound me to the others, the agony of losing my friends, the terror of not being one of them anymore, the gut-wrenching guilt that my stupidity killed Grizz…

All of it flashed through me and back, reverberating through my soul. The rage that maintained me through all of this bounced around inside my mind, building in power and ferocity as it searched for a way out. Then the remaining fragments of Amon dissipated as He bequeathed the last of His strength unto me.

I heard His voice.

"You are ready, my heir. My child. My Scion. I see you, and I know you now. You are me, and YOU WILL DO BETTER!"

I felt the final tethers snap as my mortal body flashed forward. And suddenly, I knew.

The thing that had been holding me back all this time wasn't that my body wasn't ready. It was that I'd been afraid.

I was afraid of losing this. Losing my life, my friends. Afraid of stepping across that final line in truth and becoming the prince of the Empire, the final step before Emperor, and being…not me.

I had been terrified of the thing I was becoming, and I'd never even known it.

I wanted to stay in my safe little den, stay a cub, terrified of taking the final step to becoming a lion.

The loss of points every time I overreached—that wasn't because I *shouldn't* reach for that power. It was because I wasn't *ready*, just as the prompts had said.

I could have been alone, unrecognized, and unremarkable as far as the world knew, and I could have used these abilities safely. The problem had been me all along.

I'd created blockages in my mind and in my soul, terrified of the power, of becoming Amon and no longer being me. The damage these blockages caused had cost me my points.

"NO MORE," I hissed through clenched teeth, and I reached *out* and *in*.

The world around me warped as a new master of mana was born. I reached out, sneering at the lich's shield. It snarled at me, confident in its power, right up until my hand passed straight through the shield, and I grabbed it by the throat.

"*Impossible!*" it hissed, not needing air to speak.

I snarled. The shield had burst like a bubble when I touched it, the mana flooding into me. The constant stream the lich had been feeding the shield cut off in a panic as I pulled on that as well. I sneered at the attempt to deny me what belonged to me by right.

I reached into the lich, feeling the mana that flowed in imperfect patterns holding the entire construct of the lich's earthly form together and bound to a large gem that it wore around its neck. I ripped the mana from it, even as its hands, previously filling with CorpseFire, had been lifting to me.

The lich collapsed, the undead half-life that had sustained it for hundreds of years undone in one simple motion: I simply reached out and unfastened the knot with my mind.

I drew in a deep breath, sucking the life-force from the lich, and it collapsed into dust, the chemical energy that had held its individual cells having long since given up.

The mana rushed into me, energizing my body, filling my cells, and I saw the world differently. The connections between all things flooded my vision again. The ones the lich had maintained were corpse-gray, flowing out to the creations it had maintained and back to it. I saw it anew as a mana-leech more than anything else. The ties it had maintained allowed it to pull in more mana through each of its creations, feeding them, sustaining them, and it existed through them.

The strings and chains binding them to the lich failed. As the lich became dust, so too died its army. The golems thundered on, barely slowing as they shifted from fighting to running again.

I remembered Jenae's words, Her references to "that interesting Ability." It became clear, in the way that a picture of a wizened old woman could be a young girl as well, as a trick of expectation and perception *shifted* reality for me.

The "Interesting Ability" wasn't as I'd thought at the time. The spell that Oracle had been using so heavily to repair and upgrade me to a form of genetic perfection wasn't *entirely* that.

It was also the way that I'd somehow reached out and simply controlled the mana of the realm.

I felt the mana around me. I remembered the rage that had filled me, and the way that the storm had responded to me.

I remembered and understood that spell now, the way that the storm clouds had acted as a funnel, drawing more and more mana inward, feeding it into the spell I'd bodged together, and I *UNDERSTOOD* in a moment of transcendent wisdom.

I reached out, knowing somehow that I was seeing an evolutionary step, and I accepted it, opening myself to it and drinking in the capabilities that were there for the taking and the limitations I was constrained by.

I felt the potential in my form as it existed now, the mess that was left in my genes, the misfiring neurons, the genetic crapshoot that was the modern human, a partially evolved ape that was only a few meals away from being feral at the best of times.

While I couldn't fix it all and I couldn't change it all, the actual GODS couldn't enforce utter perfection in their forms, and my genetic code was filled with alterations, including the meridians and the changes they had wrought.

I reached up. I pulled the mana in the local area, and I formed it into a massive charge, funneling it through the spell and down into myself, washing it through in a single full blast, one that took my overall genetic viability towards perfection from a mere twenty-six percent all the way up to forty-two.

Even that seemed pathetic, but as it happened, I breathed in the world around me. The changes were both wonderful…and terrible.

I lifted into the air. A single thought all that it took, as I continued to channel the power of the realm into me. Silvery scales of armor grew outward from my skin, flowing across my usual armor and cladding me in magic as completely as if I were a wisp like Oracle.

I reached out, my mind telling reality what WOULD happen, not trying to make it so, not casting spells, simply willing that it *was*. This place, this center of all that could be, changed willingly.

Grizz gasped, then coughed, sending a spray of healing potions into the air, as I told reality that he'd not died. He was *ALIVE*.

The arrows crumbled to dust, and Giint leaped back, startled. "Giint save Grizz. Giint owed life debt now," he stated, oozing satisfaction, fully convinced his actions had achieved this wonder.

The CorpseFire that was steadily consuming the side of Tenandra's hull winked out, the mana that had made it up instead shifting and blurring into a new form as it began to heal the ship, despite her not being alive, because I told reality that this simply was how it had been, how it was, and how it always would be, and that it had been *reality* that was wrong.

I floated forward, the fog rolling back as I exerted my will, the thousands of years of experience that had been Amon's, the drive to *know*, that even many of the Gods had envied and slightly feared, all of it was mine. With a gesture, the fog between me and the Dark Legion rolled back, exposing their none-too-stealthy approach.

Whatever else they were, they weren't cowards. They opened fire almost as soon as they saw me glowing in the sky. Crossbow bolts, Magic Missiles, Darkbolts, arrows, Lightning, Fireballs, all of them lifted into the air, and all of them failed.

The magic simply…unraveled. It separated out, shifting from the weaves its caster had specified. Instead, they rushed to me, flooding into me, as the clouds high overhead began to turn slowly, caught in the developing eye of the storm I was becoming.

The solid projectiles hung in the air for a second. Then they fell, clattering to the ground, and still the golems raced forward, straight at the gathered army.

Thousands of the Dark Legion remained, nearly four hundred elites, eighteen hundred aspirants, and four and a half thousand fodder had been contained in the Dark Citadel, or had fallen back when the city was lost. These forces had been intended to be a terrible surprise for my own armies. They had marched blithely into the middle of the Sun Crystals that Denny had buried, along with tens of thousands of roughhewn balls that were packed around them.

I reached out and flicked the first with my mind, and death bloomed in their midst.

Those closest to the explosion were simply vaporized. No part of their bodies survived; the farther away from the heart of an individual explosion, the greater the chance of survival, but the overlapping fields of fire from the roughly hewn balls changed the sheer hell of the detonation from simply a colossal release of energy into a terrible shower of death.

Teeth would be later found as far as ten miles away, fragments of armor were embedded in fishing vessels out at sea, and a hundred years from now, people trawling the bay for crustaceans would pull up the remnants of cuirasses, hundreds of holes making it clear how well they'd fared against the weapon.

In reality, less than two thousand were killed instantly, but for any force, no matter how well-disciplined, losing the center of their marching army in a single terrible blast of energy and steel, one that left the remaining two-thirds reeling, with a full third of those bleeding out, all of them deafened, and so much blood being spilled in under a second that it formed an actual mist, well…that left a lasting impression on a force's morale.

What was worse for that morale was that the golems didn't slow. They simply plowed straight through the center, cutting down the few who tried to strike back. I floated serenely above, glowing with crackling power while the survivors began to flee in utter panic.

I glanced at the walls of gray fog that pressed back inward, roiling against the walls that I'd erected. I sneered, sensing Nimon's hand in them. He'd given command over them to His lich, but He'd created the fog, and He was holding it in place.

No person born mortal, no matter how strong, could ever fight a God one-on-one, not one in full possession of Its power, not the way that Nimon was. Especially not as He held the power of Death…each and every death in the field below had given Him a slight bump in power, after all.

No, I couldn't destroy Him, not as I was. Our gulf of power was too much, too huge, but…

I *could* defeat Him.

He didn't simply exist on a throne of power eating fucking peeled grapes all day. Part of the knowledge that Amon had bequeathed to me included the reality of the Gods, or at least as He saw it. They were exceedingly powerful beings, but They weren't, in fact, what I would have thought of as Gods.

They were not the Gods I'd grown up understanding, the omnipotent and all-powerful kind.

These were more like manifestations of power given personality, a mixture of many parts. I understood that Jenae was both the Goddess of Fire and Hidden Knowledge because She'd been the greatest practitioner of fire magic long, LONG ago. When the previous God of Fire had…died? Given up?

When It had ceased to exist, either way, there'd been a void left behind. She, as the most powerful practitioner of that magic, had evolved. She had *become* fire, but when that happened, it didn't mean that She became all-powerful. She still needed to accumulate power to do things. While fire responded to Her at will, it wasn't part of Her entirely, although it did in part shift to become Her, as well. It was complicated as fuck, and I didn't understand all of it. But what I did grasp was that there was a hell of a lot more to Godhood than I expected, and part of that was the limitations.

Much of it was lost on me. Other details weren't entirely known, not by Amon, and not by the Gods Themselves, but They were in part at least an embodiment of those natural forces.

While Jenae was powerful, a portion of Her power was taken up with providing power to the fire that fed Her. A fragment of power ensured that the radioactive materials in the heart of the planet continued to burn, that lava retained its heat, that a kettle boiled. All of those interactions took a portion of the power She wielded. While She was insanely powerful compared to a regular human…a regular human was a God compared to an ant.

It was all about perspective. Nimon was the embodiment of death and all that power fed Him, but it also took from Him. Each soul that sank into slumber, passing through the veil, took a fragment of that power with it.

Every undead out there that radiated its un-life into the void required His dark gift in place of the life that the living enjoyed.

While the God of Death had a huge amount of theoretical power, much of it was tied up in other things at any one time. As He was throwing most of His power into holding back the other Gods right now…

I reached out and focused, adjusting my sight of the realm and finding the weave that flowed across this section of reality, finding a combination of water, air, and fire, and snipping it free with a thought.

The thread holding the water vapor resisted for a split second, then it broke away and began to dissipate, the heat of the sun burning it away. It would take hours normally to dissipate fully, as thick as it had been. But a second twist into the air, and a sudden breeze sent the fog rolling back.

The loss of His fog infuriated Nimon, as I felt His presence even more strongly, His fury beating down on me. I simply ignored Him, floating through the air as the wind picked up more and more.

The clouds high above were churning steadily now, drifting in a circle that was picking up speed. The fog drifted out toward the spinning winds, joining the building storm.

I flew toward the Dark Citadel, the hundreds of impact marks from the cannons over the last few days making the outer wall look decrepit. But the citadel itself was protected by Nimon and shone like polished obsidian as I closed on it.

"You dare! I shall make your death a thing of legend! Generations will quake in fear!" the God of Death rumbled at me.

I ignored Him still. As Jenae had said, and the knowledge that Amon had gifted me hinted, there were reasons Nimon couldn't simply snuff my life out. Even if I didn't understand them, that made them no less real.

I flew across the grass, the early morning sun reflecting up from the dew that the fog had left behind. The mass of devastation that was left from the Dark Legion meeting Denny's presents passed under my hanging feet. I dismissed it as unimportant, leaving the screams of the dying as I followed my golems.

The survivors of the Sun Crystals' detonation, those that were able to run, at least, had broken into two distinct groups. One headed frantically for the citadel, which was bloody stupid, while the other group fled in every direction *but* the citadel, clearly having considered where I'd be going next.

As I closed the distance, I formed the creation I needed. A simple ball of blue-black energy appeared as I held my right hand palm up before me.

The naginata I gripped in my left hand blazed with energy, fit to outshine the sun. The ball in my right hand grew, building upon itself.

There was no spell, no layering of the thousand weaves and more that would be needed for something this complex. I simply told reality that this existed, and it did.

It was a creation of Amon's, or more accurately, of Darioush the Great, one of his court mages. Amon had seen it used, and even He'd been impressed by its lethality.

I held the baseball-sized ball out and ordered it to impact the gatehouse, and it vanished from my palm with a crack as the sound barrier shattered.

The ball was a creation discovered in the attempts to create new metals for the Prax construction, in compressing certain metals, Darioush discovered that there was a massive exothermic reaction as the various atoms that made them up were forcefully melded together. The resulting detonation was, while far smaller than a nuke, similar in power.

The vast majority of the ball wasn't the fuel, it was a containment sphere, one designed to compress, channel, then release the focused energy disruption in a singular direction.

In this case, that direction was the Dark Citadel itself.

The ball impacted the outer wall's gates, passing through two people who had been banging on the gates and pleading to be let back in.

As it impacted, the ball expanded, flaring out to a mere two meters in diameter before beginning to spin, building up speed as the core compressed into a shimmering marble.

It held for less than a second before exploding, the rapidly spinning containment sphere tilting crazily and pointing dead ahead at the bottom of the citadel.

The energy release was contained for three seconds, building until it could no longer be held. Then, it tore out of the small hole the containment sphere's magnetic field released.

The beam shot across the distance between the gate and the wall, slamming into it and carving a chest-height hole a foot in diameter all the way through the building.

The beam erupted out of the far side, moving from right to left, then shut off, expended. The creak that echoed from the structure brought terror to the hearts of its inhabitants as walls and floors shifted.

The loss of a foot in diameter from a structure with a mass in the tens of thousands of metric tons seemed minor, especially as it was essentially in the same place, a laser-beam equivalent of negative mass moving from left to right. But the loss of structural integrity was down to more than just mass.

Sections of walls were bonded together, not simply stacked atop each other. The loss of that was terrifying, especially for a building that suddenly dropped by a foot. The impact when the upper section met the lower sent cracks radiating through the structure, then it began to shift.

Some walls held strong, having landed at just the right point. They simply forgot there had once been a separation between them and sat calmly atop the section now below them.

Other sections, notably corners, doorways, and so on, cracked when they landed on a section below whose gap was wider than it had been before.

Those cracks released a handful of stones, up to the entire doorway or edge of the room collapsing.

This, too, could have been survived in a normal building. A warehouse, for example, would have been a mess, but hardly terminally damaged.

The citadel, however, was hundreds, if not thousands of rooms. The cascade effect of all of those cracks, all the rocks that tumbled, the literal thousands of slabs of marble and onyx that shattered, meant that the weight increased in places the architects had never intended.

Great cracks began to climb the sides of the building. I felt the moment Nimon changed His focus, releasing the Gods. Much as I had done, Nimon frantically tried to change reality to save His citadel.

It was too late, though, as it began to collapse. The God of Death screamed His fury, a wail that made the Banshees' screech earlier seem like a lullaby.

"I will personally tear your life from you for this! I will eat your soul! I will…"

"You are constrained as we all are, Nimon!" Jenae snarled, making the furious God pause before He snarled again.

"Then I invoke the rite of Challenge!" Nimon screamed in fury. The entire realm seemed to hold its breath as the other Gods paused, Their grim determination to slay Their brother sidelined in shock.

"What the hell is…" I asked, and Jenae was there in a millisecond, hovering by my side.

"The Rite of Challenge is as it sounds. When two Gods had a disagreement long ago, rather than allow the devastation that could come from us fighting directly, We would imbue a pair of challengers to face each other." She paused. *"As the challenged party, you can set the terms or permit one of us, as your allies, to do so."*

"Sint," I said firmly. "Sint may set my terms." I turned my head and looked at Jenae, my heart too full of cold rage to manage a smile as I spoke. "It's not that I don't trust you Jenae, I do, but…"

"But Sint is a Warrior God," She finished with a grim nod. *"You chose rightly, Jax."*

"I accept the request to set terms!" Sint cried, appearing to my left as Jenae hovered on my right. *"The terms are simple and clear. Jax Amon, Scion and High Lord of Dravith will meet the champion of Nimon in formal combat, combat to the death. In exchange, Nimon will relinquish His hold on all but those functions relating to His sphere of influence on the Continent of Dravith and one hundred miles outside it in all directions, as will all His Pantheon."*

I looked at Jenae, and She shrugged.

"If you beat His champion, then He's kicked off the continent. Death will still exist, and the power that comes from it will still go to Him. It's better this way, as otherwise, we'll have a thousand liches trying to claim it."

"I accept, and when my champion wins, I will claim the soul of Jax Amon."

"Unacceptable!" Sint roared in fury.

"Nimon wants to destroy your soul and the knowledge you've gained so far," Jenae whispered.

"Fine," I said, cutting Her and Sint off.

"What?" Jenae asked, stunned.

"I said 'fine'!" I repeated. "Nimon! You want me? Fine, I'll face you. I'll fight your Champion and accept your terms, on one condition!"

"Name it!" Nimon screamed.

"You fight me personally, dickbag! You restrict Yourself to equal physical power as me, and we both fight with that alone!"

There was a long minute of silence before the words I'd prayed to hear rolled out across the battlefield like thunder in the distance.

"I accept," hissed the God of Death.

CHAPTER SIXTY-SIX

I landed gently. The grass below my feet was damp and lush, the loam springy as I shifted, rolling my shoulders. Sint and the others appeared, stepping forth from the Realm of the Gods, their presences no longer overpowering to me as I turned, feeling their approach.

The carriages rolled across the fields toward us as I stood surrounded by the Gods, Tenandra shifting and angling herself to land nearby as Cruit stepped forward, raising an octagonal slab of white marble from the churning earth to rest before us, ten meters to a side. It was huge, giving me plenty of room to fight.

I strode forward, my mind still caught between that strange state where the majority of my power awaited. The Imperial Abilities and more remained deep inside, and there were more Abilities waiting there than the ones I'd used so far.

"You are brave, as always, Jax," Sint rumbled, stepping up onto the marble to stand beside me.

"Just don't know when to quit, that's all," I muttered. He smiled gently, shaking His head.

"You were willing to give your life, not so long ago, to earn your people a few more minutes of freedom. Do you remember what you said to us?"

"Not really; it was kinda a blur," I admitted, guessing He meant the fight when I faced Thomas.

"You asked us to make sure your people were okay and to tell them you died a hero, even if it wasn't true."

"And...?"

"And I told you that you were a hero in truth, Jax," Sint said, His voice clearly full of pride. *"A hero is not necessarily someone who spends their entire life standing up against evil, not always. Most of the greatest heroes in the realm were in fact farmers, laborers, and servants. They weren't the great Knights of the Realm, they were the people nobody noticed, not until the day they stood tall and declared 'no more.' When those simple people stood, willing to die, to defend another, they became heroes.*

"You have been a hero for as long as you have been able to stand on your own feet. You think Amon's spell could have pulled you through the veil of worlds without your heart being true? It could not. Your soul is strong, and that is why you and your brother were called upon again and again.

"The Baron and others of his ilk believed that their runes kept them from being summoned. They were wrong. The rune was simply an outward sign to match the internal hatred that filled their souls. The reason you and your brother were brought again, again, and again was because your souls cried out to protect these people.

"This is why Amon anointed you, why He bequeathed His power to you, at the loss of a fragment of His soul. And this is why I, too, shall give you a gift. YOU ARE A HERO, JAX. Believe it or not, I know the truth, and I stand witness."

With that, He reached out His right hand and rested it on my shoulder, infusing His power into me, as each of the Gods stepped up and did the same, one by one, gifting a fragment of Their power to create my armor and stating that They bore witness.

I felt the changes They wrought, and I looked down, seeing the silvery armor that Tuthic'Amon had bound to me. I sensed his presence as he reached out, his soul touching mine gently.

The armor I wore was an amalgamation of pure power, of magical intent, and a gift from the Dragons. It was born of the rage my heart had been filled with, but as the Gods each gave me Their blessing, it shimmered and changed, becoming somehow less ethereal and more…real.

My helm was the first to change. The plume was made of a thousand tiny spines which blurred and ran together. It shifted, no longer two inches wide and three inches high, attached to the crown of the helm. Now it flowed. The gap between the helm proper and the plume vanished as the plume sank into the metal slightly, no longer attached, but instead a part of it. A single, razor-sharp blade jutted forward at an aggressive seventy-five-degree angle from the top of the helm.

The main form of the helm altered as well, shifting to sit more like a motorbike helmet, snug, cushioned, and protective. A narrow Y-shaped slit in the front gave me the best possible vision, while being narrow enough that it was unlikely that a weapon could sink into it.

The cheeks were long, Spartan-style, and it felt and looked frigging awesome. It had Abilities, I knew, but they were the kind that needed to be awakened, not simply bestowed.

The neck was a scaled design that flowed smoothly, feeling like water in the way it moved, but it would turn most blades.

The cuirass was one piece, solid and fitted, molded to my skin. The seams to remove it were so well smithed, I'd have to search for them visually as much as with my fingers. The shoulders were curved, following the line of my muscles.

Seams where the armor hinged open flowed along the side of major muscle groups, making me feel like, instead of being restrained by the armor, I could run faster and fight harder in it than out of it.

The waist was the natural continuation of my abs. Each individual major muscle seemed to have its own section, and hell, there was even a comfortable, fitted pouch holding my crown jewels. The legs were banded metal on the outside, thick and strong, and scale on the inside, flexible and allowing for maximum movement.

I flexed my hands in gauntlets that moved effortlessly, and shifted to test the range of movement.

"Thank you, thank you all," I said slowly, as each of the Gods bowed Their heads in respect. Not as an equal, but still, they were fucking Gods after all, and I had a fair way to go before I attained that lofty pinnacle, if ever.

Oracle landed next to me, reaching out. The Gods stepped back, permitting me a brief moment as I held her, ashamed that I'd left her without a word, but having known that she was better with the others than next to me.

"Oh, my love," she whispered, reaching up and touching the cold perfection of my armor. "What have you done?"

"What I had to," I replied. "Facing Him is our best chance to end this and to give us time to rebuild and to live, without that cocksucker screwing with us every time we turned around."

"But without your powers…"

"Hey, He's without them, too," I pointed out. She shook her head, clearly getting something I didn't.

"Jax, He's a God…specifically, the God of Death!"

"He's a dick, is what He is," I said, as the others stepped up.

Thomas was the first, wrapping his arms around me and Oracle together and holding us tight.

"What kind of an idiot are you, bro?" he whispered, holding onto us. "Picking fights with the Gods? Man, I'm gonna have to knock out the universe to top this one!"

"You know me, bro. Can't do half-measures."

"You kick His ass, you hear me?" Thomas said through gritted teeth. "You kick His ass, because if you don't, I'm challenging Him right after you."

"You can't do that."

"I can, and I fucking will, so win!" Thomas said, before releasing me and stepping back with Oracle as Lydia took his place.

"It's supposed te be us before yer," she said through a lump in her throat. I took her in my arms, our armor clanging gently as we hugged, her massive wings wrapping around me. "I'm yer Valkyrie, so if 'e takes yer soul, Ah'll be comin' after it." She rested her helm against mine with a *ting* that echoed in the air.

"I should have let you fight Him. You'd have won, no bother," I said, smiling. "Lydia…"

"Yeah?"

"I'm proud of you," I said, releasing her as she struggled with the words she kept bottled up in there.

"Boss," Grizz said, stepping up and grabbing me. The man-mountain lifted me off my feet in a massive bear hug before setting me down gently. "You saved me, Jax. I…I was…"

"You saved me first, brother." I gripped his shoulders and stared into his eyes. "I don't know how it's done here, but you've a decision to make. I think it's one that you've been putting off?" I asked, nodding my head to the side where Yen stood.

"Once you kick this God's ass, I'll do it, and you'll stand with me, right?" he asked.

I smiled, tears in my eyes as I knew what he was asking.

"Always brother, always," I said.

He grinned, stepping back.

Yen took his place, holding me tight for a long second before leaning back, staring into my eyes and nodding as she came to a conclusion. "You're a good legionnaire. I'm proud to be in your squad. Thank you for bringing him back to me."

I smiled, Yen's words clearly being all she could bring herself to say, yet meaning the world to me. I hugged her again.

"Thank you, Yen. I'm proud of you, too." I let go. She stepped back, and Ronin stepped up and clung to me, making me laugh as I hugged him back.

"Don't you fucking dare die, Boss, I mean it!" he said with a grim set to his jaw. "I'm a bard watching the Scion of the Empire fight the God of Death, so make sure you make good show of it. I don't want to be singing 'and he got his ass spanked' for the rest of my life! Trying to make a rhyme with that would be murder."

"Well, now I've got a real reason to win, I guess." I grinned at Ronin as he backed up. Bob stepped up next, clearly not understanding the cultural or emotional meaning of the hugs but determined to have one.

"Live," he said, then nodded his head in the direction of the black cloud that was forming a body on the stage. *"Kill."*

"I will, Bob, thank you, man."

He nodded. *"I have quests for you,"* was all he said before stepping back and folding his arms in imitation of others, while Giint stepped up and awkwardly patted my knee.

"Kill God, become God?" he asked, his speech patterns slipping again.

"I don't think it works that way," I said.

He shrugged. "If you become God, make Giint God, too?"

"Fuck no! You're mental."

"Agreed," he said, nodding and stepping back.

Arrin was next, and he clung to me for a long time before speaking. "You made me who I am. I was a slave, and I had no chance. Now I'm a…what was it he said…a 'goddamn sexual tyrannosaurus'," he told me, grinning. "Seriously, boss, you taught me magic, made me free. I get laid like every night, so don't die, okay? I don't want this ride to end."

I grinned at him, recognizing Thomas' favorite line from the movie, and I nodded. But before I could answer, I was practically smothered by an amazing pair of boobs as Sehran jumped onto me, wrapping her arms and legs around me.

"Uh…" I said, shaking my head, unsure if I was glad I was wearing the helm or wishing I wasn't so that I could motorboat them.

"Thank you," she said, leaning back and looking at me seriously. "Thank you for seeing more than just my tits and ass, thank you for letting me be me, for letting me be more, and for giving me the chance to prove that not all Demons are evil."

"You *do* eat peoples' souls," I pointed out.

She frowned. "Well, yeah…but assholes, though."

"Fair point," I agreed. "So, if you're happy to not be seen just as tits and ass, why the face full?"

A grin split her cheeks. "Because you love them, really!" She hopped off me and backed away. "Oh! And my sisters say if you and Oracle want to play before they go back, just to let them know!" I glanced at the three other succubai, along with the incubus who stood off to one side, and they all made kissing motions, waved, or in one case, swung his enormous manhood in a way that was clearly meant to be inviting.

I'd planned for them to be here to use their powers to distract the Dark Legion…but clearly, things had ended up so that they weren't needed.

I turned to Oracle and inclined my head to the group, sending her a silent message.

"Tell me I don't look like that when I helicopter it for you?" I asked.

She shook her head slightly. *"No, it's okay. He's much bigger."*

"Thank fuck, I—wait, what?" I turned back to Jian as he stepped in, grinning. He grabbed my shoulders and stared into my eyes. "You've got this. Kick His ass, and the beers are on me."

"Sounds good to me, man."

Tang stepped up next, discarding his stealth as there were literal Gods in play. He reached out one hand, resting it on my shoulder, and looked into my eyes as he smiled. "Well boss, it's been a hell of a ride so far…make sure you kick His ass quick, okay? I've got a date tonight with Carmen, and you wouldn't want me to be late…right?"

"Hah! No worries, man, I'll make sure this doesn't take long," I said with a wink, before Bane spoke. Typical for the bastard he was, he whispered in my ear from behind.

"You'd better. I've got gold on Carmen trading him in soon."

I turned, seeing the Mer that had become one of my best friends over the last few months.

Bane cocked his head to one side, hesitant, then sighed and reached out, all four arms reaching around me and hugging me close.

"You've got this, Jax. Seriously, if I had to bet on anyone to fight a God and walk away afterwards, it'd be you. So don't let Him beat you, brother."

"Thank you, Bane," I whispered, squeezing him tight, then letting go, my heart full of love from my people.

There were more, dozens more, gathering around, and I could see hundreds more coming. Tenandra had landed, and she was hurrying over, along with the surviving Legion. Belladonna looked like she wanted to say something, as did Edvard, but they simply saluted, unsure how to articulate the words.

Others fell in around the group, dozens becoming hundreds as more and more of my elites, my soldiers and my Legion arrived, but it was time. I turned, squeezed Oracle's hand once more, then climbed the steps.

I let out a long, slow breath as I cleared the top step, the silvery white armor that covered me shifting as I breathed. I grinned slightly, rolling my wrists, flexing unconsciously and checking for anything that would interfere with my movements.

The black cloud across from me condensed as I neared it. The figure that stepped out of it wore the opposite of my armor. Where mine was all flowing grace, rippling scale, and more, his was simply massive slabs of metal.

I frowned, considering the weight that much metal had to have. "Equal physical power," I stated flatly. Nimon, encased in a physical form with hatred glowing in His eyes, spoke with a hiss.

"I agreed."

That was it, seemingly that was all He was going to say, so I glanced at Sint, who nodded.

"He is your physical equal in some ways now, Jax, but remember, your phrasing matters. Your exact words were 'equal physical power' and that equates to your stats as much as anything else. Your physical stats: Agility, Constitution, Dexterity, Endurance, and Strength come to a total of three hundred and twenty-eight points…Nimon has limited himself to a form that has these exact stats, allocated as He has chosen instead."

I frowned, then looked back at Nimon, then to Sint, seeing the faint smile that creased the corners of Sint's mouth. I nodded, understanding filling me.

I'd made sure my build was as even as I could make it, unable to countenance min-maxing when it was my godsdamn life on the line. Nimon had clearly not read the memo and had put a *lot* of His points into Strength.

I nodded, seeing the weapon that Nimon wielded was a counter to my own naginata. Namely, He'd chosen a halberd, the axe head on one side and vicious hook on the other, clearly designed to take me down fast, along with the spear tip on the top that looked like it could split atoms.

I looked Him over, seeing the massive slabs of steel that covered almost all of Him, and I realized why He'd chosen this form.

He was an organic tank!

The massive slabs of steel meant that He could take tremendous punishment, and while I didn't know the rest of His build, I could see that being a problem already.

Sint and the others were backing away as we faced each other, and I frantically wracked my brain, looking for weaknesses. Arms, throat, wrists, elbows, ankles, all of them were well-protected, and I allowed myself a grim chuckle.

All I had to do was win against death.

I could totally fucking do that.

"Begin!" Sint bellowed, and I jumped to the right immediately. The wicked spear tip blurred as it shot out, barely missing me. I slammed my naginata to the left, blocking His weapon as He swung it at me, feeling as He tried to twist it, hooking the shaft of my weapon into place.

I twisted and kicked the shaft of His halberd before He could lock it, sending Him back a foot or so before slamming my blade down atop the shaft and sliding it as fast and hard as I could for His fingers.

He tilted it up, twisting it around mine, trying to send me off my center, while attempting to hook me again.

I shoved my shaft against His again, hard, holding it vertical as I hurried in closer. The halberd was lethal at range, but awkward to use close in, while my own naginata was far more effective, being a long blade...if I could get past His armor.

I jumped, lifting the naginata as He swung under me, and I landed as He swung out of position, the heavy armor making Him slow to respond as I shoulder-checked Him. Off-balance as He was, He staggered backward, and I braced the naginata against His side and shoved, sending Him tumbling to the floor.

I grinned, sensing an early win, and reversed my weapon, sending it stabbing down, aimed at His throat. But He released His own, slapping my blade aside and sending the tip glancing off the marble in a shower of stone fragments.

This time, I was the one off-balance, and the fucker punched me in the side of my right knee, and it buckled, sending me crashing to the floor.

As I fell, He reached back over, grabbing His halberd. He whipped it overhead, slamming it down hard, aimed for my head.

I managed to roll free, feeling the tug of displaced air as it flashed past my face. I snarled, bunching my legs under me and kicking off, driving forward and landing atop His body.

He was still half-turned over, trying to bring the halberd back. I landed on Him, grabbing His right shoulder with my left hand and driving the naginata upward, blade aimed for the underside of His helm. He twisted, bringing His helm down a split second before impact. Instead, I sent a spray of sparks flying as the blade bounced off, carving a line across the metal cheek plate.

He roared, dragging His arms free of where I half-laid across Him, trapping them. I frantically dove free, rolling and coming to my feet as He twisted, trying to get up.

I grinned, backing up a little and waiting as He eyed me, trying to get to His feet.

"So…didn't fancy Agility at all, then, eh?" I asked as He tried to get up, His massive muscles clearly making it impossible for Him to do so much as scratch his own arse.

"I'm betting Strength, Endurance, and Constitution, considering the size of you," I muttered, mostly to myself as the Legion bayed for His blood.

I moved backward and forward, side to side, watching the way He moved. My mind was fully focused on the fight, teeth exposed as my lips curled back, and I growled low in my throat.

I let Him get to his feet, and He reached down, watching me carefully as He tried to pick up the halberd. I struck, sprinting forward, slamming my naginata down on the shaft of His weapon and running along it, giving Him the option of releasing it or losing His fingers.

Regardless of how thick His gauntlets might be, the blade would take at least some of them before He could stop it. He clearly knew it, too, dropping the weapon with a hiss and backing up.

I grinned, moving closer, making Him back up, stabbing outward until I could kick His weapon aside, moving it well out of His reach.

He glared at me, then started to laugh.

"Something funny, dickhead?" I asked Him.

"Very. You think I need a weapon to defeat you?" He asked before kicking off and barreling forward, picking up speed with each step.

"I think you're clumsy as fuck!" I sprinted to the left and made Him turn to chase me.

"Come here, little fly," Nimon called, lumbering after me.

I jogged slightly ahead of Him, half-turned to face Him and still easily able to stay out of reach. I scanned His body, looking for weaknesses before gritting my teeth and doing what I knew I had to.

I sprinted in, aiming for the throat. Then, when His hands came up to deflect, I twisted, rolling my shoulders and stabbing low before He could adjust.

I slammed the blade into the overlapping scales that covered the inside of His left knee, then I pirouetted aside, out of reach, as He grunted.

I backed up, then flashed in again, doing the same but to His right knee, then His left ankle. Each blow made Him grunt in pain, but unable to pass through the scales protecting those areas.

They were bent, twisted, and missing in places, but the actual damaged areas were small, barely bigger than a large coin. Even though I had good stamina, I couldn't keep this up all day, especially not the way He was moving. I had to get lucky a dozen times.

He had to get lucky once.

I changed direction. The next blow came in the same pattern as the others had. He moved to block, His hands reaching down low, thinking I was as dumb as He fucking was, when instead I flipped the naginata around and slung the weighted end at His head, swinging like I was a godsdamn golfing legend.

It connected!

He staggered, stunned, the side of His helm dented inward and blocking His sight on that side as I dropped the naginata from numbed fingers, cursing. I lifted my hands, barely able to feel them and knowing damn well that I had at least a few broken fingers.

I looked at Him in shock, knowing that for me to have broken my fingers and Him to still be alive, He had to have insane Constitution.

I growled, the world narrowing even further. I sprinted to the right, throwing myself down and skidding, sweeping up His halberd and popping back upright, twisting around and running at Him. He was twisting this way and that, trying to see me, and I sprinted to my left, deliberately keeping out of His line of sight, racing inward.

I leveled the halberd and put my weight behind it, slamming it into the back of His left knee, feeling the spear tip slam through the thin scales and tear out of the front, hitting the inside of His armor before stopping dead, wedged.

I roared in triumph, racing in toward Him, leaving the weapon wedged there. When He spun around to face me, the leg gave out beneath Him, but not enough to let me fully avoid the punch that felt like I'd run face-first into a girder.

My legs went out from under me, my body rising as He essentially clotheslined me, the wonder being that my neck didn't snap on impact. The world spun in silence, my dazed brain unable to process the garbled input for seemingly weeks, then I slammed into the floor with all the grace of a chimney collapse.

I tried to make sense of the world. Nothing seemed to work properly as I flailed my arms around. Then I was lifted as a massive, gauntleted hand slid under my chin, closing around my throat and lifting me into the air.

"Pathetic!" Nimon bellowed. "What, worm? You think that a God cares about a mortal form's injuries?" He asked, sneering.

I looked into His eye, the right one still visible, the left clearly crushed beneath the dented helm. Desperately, I slapped at His forearm ineffectually with both hands, before letting my left hang loose, slapping at the air as He shook me. The fingers of my right hand scrabbled for purchase on His armor. He laughed, turning to look at the other Gods.

"You see this, you fools! Your Champion! Pathetic!" He bellowed, opening His mouth to say something more, before gasping as something thin, yet oh so strong settled around the back of His neck.

He turned, looking down at His chest in confusion, trying to see what He clearly couldn't at that angle. A chain led along His outstretched arm to my left hand. A second end, similar in every way, led to my right.

He paused, head flashing up to lock His one eye on mine, as I grinned and yanked, first one way, then the other, His massive armor meaningless to the small chain that had slid easily beneath it. His huge, overdeveloped trapezius muscles shredded as my trusty razor wire, a weapon He'd totally overlooked, sliced effortlessly through them.

There was a slight snag as it caught on the spine. He flinched as He tried to shrug it away, but that opened the gap just enough for me. I sawed in deeper, severing the nerve column and ceasing the message His frantic brain was sending to crush my throat once and for all.

His body collapsed, the ground slamming into my boots hard enough that I nearly fell over, barely catching my balance as I stared down at the one eye that watched me in horror, His body slamming into the stone, black blood spreading out as He stared up at me in disbelief.

"Yeah, that's right, bitch," I whispered, knowing He could hear me. "You missed this, and now I'm going to make a fucking cup out of your avatar's skull!"

I stepped over Him, planting my left foot on the forehead of the helm and pushed back, exposing the neck as I gathered up the toggles at either end again, having dropped them as I fell. I stared down before starting to saw.

I yanked in smooth motions, left then right. The alternating teeth chewed through His thick neck easily, sending blood and bits of flesh flying. Finally, I let go, grabbing the head as it rolled free of the helm and lifted it as it fell free.

I raised it up to stare into its one eye as life faded from it, and I brought up a thick wad, snorting disgustingly, and spat it directly into the eye of the God of Death.

"Thanks for the experience points, dickhead!" I sneered at Him, then I tossed the fucking thing into the air. It rose, then fell right into my rising foot as I punted it free of the marble. Then, I strode back across the marble toward the love of my life, the madly cheering crowd, and the Gods standing proud. Each bent Their necks, bowing Their heads in respect to Jax, Scion of the Empire…*Godslayer*.

I reached out to Oracle, pulling her in tight and clutching her to me, feeling her arms holding tight to me. With a portion of my mind, I idly wondered how hard it'd be to get the eye sockets filled in, in Nimon's skull.

It was going to make an awesome goblet.

The rest of my mind was filled with the scent of Oracle's hair, of the cheering and love of the people who I in turn loved, and the pride I felt emanating from the Pantheon of Gods.

Today was a good fucking day, after all, I decided, as Grizz pulled Yen in for a tender kiss. I saw Jian, Sehran and Tenandra, the insane coup…*thruple* that they were, and the others around me.

I saw Bob, standing stoically, while Giint leaped up and down crazily, before sidling across to Lydia, who was already holding a stick of his catnip out, while trying to pretend she wasn't.

EPILOGUE

The party that night was insane, the cloud of war having been lifted from the twin cities, the majority of the noble houses basically disbanded, arrested for their crimes or swearing utter loyalty to a man who absolutely embodied terror for them.

Through it all, I smiled, I hugged, and I celebrated, but I felt a leaden weight inside me growing.

Hours later, sitting on our balcony, staring out over the city, with the sounds of cheering and parties still echoing from below as people came to understand that no matter what else had happened, the Dark Legion was never going to place its boot atop their throat again, Oracle sat next to me, reaching out and holding my hand.

"What's wrong, my love?" she asked.

I sighed, not really sure myself. "I still feel it," I admitted after a few long minutes of introspection.

"Feel what?"

"The power, the coldness, the Imperial Right…all of it," I said, finding that, after killing the God, the power hadn't left me, as I'd half expected it to. Instead, it had grown massively, as some part of me absorbed some of death's power, regardless of the deal that had been struck.

"What did you expect, Godslayer?"

I didn't know. I just knew that I had expected something different, and I didn't know why. It felt like the universe, no, the *UnderVerse*, was holding its breath, waiting for the other shoe to drop, and I just didn't know why.

"Have you read your notifications?" Oracle asked, knowing damn well that I hadn't. I shook my head numbly. "Well, you need to. Once you've done that, I have a present for you. So go on." She moved around and straddled me, sitting and facing me as I pulled them up.

I dismissed the usual suspects: killed this, injured that. I'd gained nearly a dozen points in my stats.

Congratulations!

**Through hard work and perseverance,
you have gained points to the following stats:**

**Agility +3
Constitution +2
Dexterity +1
Luck +4
Perception +1
Wisdom +1**

Continue to train and learn to raise this further…

That was nice; clearly going one-on-one with a God was good for leveling at least. I dismissed the accumulated experience popup before it could fully form, the number that started to appear, making me damn well sure I'd hit a few levels at least, dismissing them all, until I came to it, knowing that this was one of the ones she meant.

Congratulations and Salutations, Scion.

You have earned your first Fragment of a Divine Soul in battle, and as such you have taken the first step upon the road to Godhood.

Are you ready?

I read it again and again. The phrasing was weird, more personal than they usually were, and I shrugged. But before I could respond to it, it changed, clearly aware of my acceptance.

Good.

*

Let all be aware!

Jax Amon, former son of the disgraced House of Sanguis, has beaten Nimon, the God of Death, in formal combat.

In claiming a fragment of the divine, he has claimed rulership and dominion over more than a quarter of a million souls and taken control of the entirety of the Imperial Territory of Dravith.

While the continent is only partially secured, the entirety of the Imperial foothold of old has been regained.

The Eternal Emperor Amon is proud to declare Jax Amon His descendant, His Heir, Scion of the Empire, and PRINCE OF DRAVITH!

The Imperial Succession has begun!

All those who wish to contest the rise of Jax have one year to state their grievance and face him.

If he still stands in control of a Greater Territory and as a Prince of the Empire, then and only then may he ascend the Crystal Steps and be proclaimed Emperor!

All Hail Jax Amon! All Hail the Prince of the Empire!

"Oh shit," I muttered, looking up as the gold and red proclamation dissipated. The silence from below was shattered as thousands of voices rose in roaring celebration.

As soon as I'd dismissed it, the final prompt waited.

Congratulations!

You have made progress in your Quest: The Deeper Secret

In rage and fear, love and hatred, you have discovered a terrible secret about yourself. While you are unsure of its meaning, you have made progress in your quest.

You have faced the God of Death, Nimon, both in magic and physically, and found that while He is powerful and terrible, the gulf of power between you is not all you had imagined. In doing so, you have discovered a new form of magic, your first in the new aspect, yet what is it?

How do you use it and why does reality itself bend to your will when you wield it? Last of all, what are the consequences of such an action? For understand this, all power has consequences, and power summoned must come from somewhere.

Forms of Magic Discovered: 6/10

Reward: New forms of magic, 10,000,000xp, Unknown

"Exactly…well, umm…are you ready for my surprise?" Oracle asked me nervously. I nodded, absently, wondering what the hell she thought would top the fact that open season had just been declared on us, rather than us gaining the time we needed to prepare, and just fucking live, and that I'd somehow found a hint of what might very well be the underlying fabric of all of reality.

"Umm…well…congratulations, my love…I…I'm pregnant!" she declared, her cheeks red with embarrassment and clearly terrified about how I was about to take it.

The screens all vanished instantly as I stared at her in shock.

My lips flapped as sounds with no meaning behind them tried to escape. I ran her words through my mind, over and over again, making sure that what I'd heard was what I thought I'd heard.

I stared into her eyes, seeing the nervous excitement, the fear of rejection, and the desperate longing there. All my confusion and shock vanished.

Tears welled up in my eyes, surprise giving way as I leaned forward and wrapped her in my arms, lifting her into the air and kissing her soundly. I turned, setting her down gently and facing the realm, and bellowed outward, telling the UnderVerse, the living, the dead, divine, and mortal alike.

"I'M GOING TO BE A FATHER!" I roared, filled with joy. An instant later, utter terror filled me, and I sat backward, my ass hitting the chair with a thump. "Oh, fuck! I don't know how to be a dad!"

SANGUIS

"HOW *DARE* HE!" Baron Sanguis screamed, his face mottled red and white. The elegantly appointed room he'd been meeting Daphne in was now a scene of utter wreckage. He screamed and raged, frothing and foaming at the mouth as he took out his fury on anything and everything within reach.

His servants cowered and tried desperately not to attract his ire, while he lifted an antique desk, one that had once belonged to a Leonardo Da Vinci, a local human of some repute, then he smashed it into kindling.

The incandescent temper tantrum lasted four hours, give or take. By the end of it, the entire wing of his summer palace was devastated beyond repair.

Hundreds of priceless artifacts were ruined, and the sight of one of his favorite Fabergé eggs, long considered lost by the wider world, glittering in a thousand pieces filled him with a smoldering rage as he whispered commands to his people.

"You gather them all, you hear me? The entire force! Every single mercenary that owes me their allegiance. Get them all to the citadel, *every single wastrel one of them*. Open the armories! We open the portal in three days, regardless of the risk! We return home!"

LYDIA

THE END OF BOOK SIX

In Memoriam

Rest in Peace to my father-in-law, Alan Cormack, 14/09/1947 – 03/05/2021, a better man than I knew and a far better father than I deserved.

UNDERVERSE 7

6th December 2022

The War of the Gods has stalled while both sides recover, borders have been established, and a form of uneasy peace descends on the Imperial Territory of Dravith…

It should be a time of consolidation, of rest and giving the survivors the chance to rearm and train.

But life rarely goes as Jax expects.

New and old enemies are on the horizon, the land itself is disturbed, and worst of all, the Gods may not be all he believed they were…

The Dark Tide Rises…

REVIEWS

Hey! Well, I hope you enjoyed the book? If so, please, please remember to leave a review, its massively important, as not only does it let others know about the book, it also tells Amazon that the book is worth promoting, and makes it more likely that more people will see it.

That in turn will hopefully keep me able to keep writing full time, while listening to crazy German bands screaming in my ears, and frankly, I kinda really like that!

If you want to spread the good word, that'd be amazing, and if you know of anyone that might be interested in stocking my books, I'm happy to reach out and send them samples, but honestly, if you enjoy my madness, that's massive for me.
Thank you.

FACEBOOK AND SOCIAL MEDIA

If you want to reach out, chat or shoot the shit, you can always find me on either my author page here:

www.facebook.com/JezCajiaoAuthor

_**OR**_

We've recently set up a new Facebook group to spread the word about cool LitRPG books. It's dedicated to two very simple rules, 1; lets spread the word about new and old brilliant LitRPG books, and 2: Don't be a Dick!
They sound like really simple rules, but you'd be amazed…
Come join us!

https://www.facebook.com/groups/litrpglegion

I'm also on Discord here: **https://discord.gg/u5JYHscCEH**

Or I'm reaching out on other forms of social media atm, I'm just spread a little thin that's all!

You're most likely to find me on Discord, but please, don't be offended when I don't approve friend requests on my personal Facebook pages. I did originally, and several people abused that, sending messages to my family and being generally unpleasant, hence, the author page:

https://www.facebook.com/JezCajiaoAuthor

I hope you understand.

PATREON!

Okay then, now for those of you that don't know about Patreon, its essentially a way to support your favorite nutcases, you can sign up for a day or a month or a year, and you get various benefits for it, ranging from my heartfelt thanks, to advance access to the books, to signed books, naming characters and more.

At the time of me writing this, the advanced Patreon readers are getting a sneak peek at Age of Steel, and are voting on the next batch of Character Art as well, so yeah, you get plenty for the support!

There's three wonderful supporters out there that I have to thank personally as well; ASeaInStorm, Leighton, and Nicholas Kauffman, you utter legends you. Thank you all and as promised, the characters are in the works.

www.patreon.com/Jezcajiao

RECOMMENDATIONS

I'm often asked for personal recommendations, so if this book has whetted your appetite for more LitRPG, please have a look at the following, these are brilliant series by brilliant authors!

Ascend Online by Luke Chmilenko

The Land by Aleron Kong

Challengers Call by Nathan A Thompson

SoulShip also by Nathan

Endless Online by M H Johnson

Silver Fox and the Western Hero, also by M H Johnson

The Good Guys/Bad Guys by Eric Ugland

Condition: Evolution by Kevin Sinclair

Space Seasons by Dawn Chapman

The Wayward Bard by Lars M

LITRPG!

To learn more about LitRPG, talk to other authors including myself, and to just have an awesome time, please join the LitRPG Group

www.facebook.com/groups/LitRPGGroup

FACEBOOK

There's also a few really active Facebook groups I'd recommend you join, as you'll get to hear about great new books, new releases and interact with all your (new) favorite authors! (I may also be there, skulking at the back and enjoying the memes…)

www.facebook.com/groups/LitRPGsociety/

www.facebook.com/groups/LitRPG.books/

www.facebook.com/groups/LitRPGforum/

www.facebook.com/groups/gamelitsociety/